THE YEAR OF THE
DEATH OF
RICARDO REIS

THE GOSPEL ACCORDING
TO JESUS CHRIST

BLINDNESS

THE YEAR OF THE DEATH OF RICARDO REIS

THE GOSPEL ACCORDING TO JESUS CHRIST

BLINDNESS

JOSÉ SARAMAGO

Translated from the Portuguese by Giovanni Pontiero

Quality Paperback Book Club
New York

CONTENTS

THE YEAR OF THE
DEATH OF
RICARDO REIS

Wise is the man who contents himself with the spectacle of the world.

——RICARDO REIS

To choose ways of not acting was ever the concern and scruple of my life.

——BERNARDO SOARES

If they were to tell me that it is absurd to speak thus of someone who never existed, I should reply that I have no proof that Lisbon ever existed, or I who am writing, or any other thing wherever it might be.

——FERNANDO PESSOA

Here the sea ends and the earth begins. It is raining over the colorless city. The waters of the river are polluted with mud, the riverbanks flooded. A dark vessel, the *Highland Brigade*, ascends the somber river and is about to anchor at the quay of Alcântara. The steamer is English and belongs to the Royal Mail Line. She crosses the Atlantic between London and Buenos Aires like a weaving shuttle on the highways of the sea, backward and forward, always calling at the same ports, La Plata, Montevideo, Santos, Rio de Janeiro, Pernambuco, Las Palmas, in this order or vice versa, and unless she is shipwrecked, the steamer will also call at Vigo and Boulogne-sur-Mer before finally entering the Thames just as she is now entering the Tagus, and one does not ask which is the greater river, which the greater town. She is not a large vessel, fourteen thousand tons, but quite seaworthy, as was demonstrated during this crossing when, despite constant rough weather, only those unaccustomed to ocean voyages were seasick, or those accustomed but who suffer from an incurably delicate stomach. On account of the homey atmosphere and comforts on board, the ship has come to be affectionately known, like her twin the *Highland Monarch*, as the family steamer. Both vessels are equipped with spacious decks for games and sunbathing, even cricket, a field sport, can be played on deck, which shows that for the British Empire nothing is impossible. When the weather is fine, the *Highland Brigade* becomes a garden for children and a paradise for the elderly, but not today, because it is raining and this is our last afternoon on board. Behind windowpanes ingrained with salt the children peer out at the gray city, which lies flat above the hills as if built entirely of one-story houses. Yonder, perhaps, you catch a glimpse of a high dome, some thrusting gable, an outline suggesting a castle ruin, unless this is simply an illusion, a chimera, a mirage created by the shifting curtain of the waters that descend from the leaden sky. The foreign children, whom nature has endowed more generously with the virtue of inquisitiveness, are curious to know the name of the port. Their parents tell them or it is spelled out by their nurses, *amas*, *bonnes*, *Fräuleins*, or perhaps by a passing sailor on his way to some maneuver. Lisboa, Lisbon, Lisbonne, Lissabon, there are four different ways of saying it, leaving aside the variants and mistaken forms. And so the children come to know what they did not know before, and that is what they knew already, nothing, merely a name, causing even greater confusion in their childish minds, a name pronounced with the accent peculiar to the Argentinians, if that is what they happen to be, or to the Uruguayans, the Brazilians, the Spaniards. The latter, writing Lisbon correctly in their respective versions of Castilian or Portuguese, then pronounce it in their own way, a way beyond the reach of ordinary hearing or any representation in writing. When the *Highland Brigade* sails up the straits early tomorrow morning, let us hope there will be a little sunshine and a clear sky, so that the gray mist does not completely obscure, even within sight of land, the already fading memory of those voyagers who passed here for the first time, those children who repeated the word Lisbon, transforming it into some other name, those adults who knitted their eyebrows and shivered with the general dampness which penetrates the wood and metal, as if the *Highland Brigade* had emerged dripping from the bottom of the sea, a ship twice transformed into a phantom. No one by choice or inclination would remain in this port.

A few passengers are about to disembark. The steamer has docked, the gangplank has been lowered and secured, unhurried baggage handlers and stevedores appear below, guards emerge from the shelter of their huts and sheds, and the customs officers begin to arrive. The rain has eased off and almost stopped. The passengers gather at the top of the gangplank, hesitant, as if in some doubt as to whether permission has been granted to disembark, or whether there could be a quarantine, or perhaps they are apprehensive about those slippery steps. But it is the silent city that frightens them, perhaps all its inhabitants have perished and the rain is only falling to dissolve into mud what has remained standing. Along the quay-side grimy portholes glow dimly, the spars are branches lopped from trees, the hoists are still. It is Sunday. Beyond the docksheds lies the somber city, enclosed by façades and walls, as yet protected from the rain, perhaps drawing back a heavy, embroidered curtain, looking out with vacant eyes, listening to the water gurgling on the rooftops, down the drainpipes to the gutters below, and onto the gleaming limestone of the pavement to the brimming drains, some of their covers raised where they have flooded.

The first passengers disembark. Their shoulders bent under the monotonous rain, they carry sacks and suitcases and have the lost expression of those who have endured the voyage as if in a dream of flowing images, between sea and sky, the prow going up and down like a metronome, the waves rising and falling, the hyp-notic horizon. Someone is carrying a child in his arms, a child so silent it must be Portuguese. It does not ask where they are, or else it was promised that if it went to sleep at once in that stuffy berth, it would wake up in a beautiful city where it would live happily ever after. Another fairy tale, for these people have been unable to endure the hardships of emigration. An elderly woman who insists on opening her umbrella has dropped the green tin box shaped like a little trunk that she was carrying under her arm. The box has crashed onto the pebbles on the quayside, breaking open, its bottom falling out. It contained nothing of value, a few souvenirs, some bits of colored cloth, letters and photographs scattered by the wind, some glass beads shattered into smithereens, balls of white yarn now badly stained, one of them disappearing between the quayside and the side of the ship. The woman is a third-class passenger.

As they set foot on land, the passengers run to take shelter. The foreigners mutter about the storm as if we were responsible for the bad weather, they appear to forget that in their beloved

France or England the weather is usually a great deal worse. In short, they use the slightest pretext, even nature's rain, to express their contempt for poorer nations. We have more serious reasons for complaint, but we remain silent. This is a foul winter, with whatever crops there were uprooted from the fertile soil, and how we miss them, being such a small country. The baggage is already being unloaded. Under their glossy capes the sailors resemble hooded wizards, while, down below, the Portuguese porters move swiftly in their peaked caps and short jackets weatherproofed and lined, so indifferent to the deluge that they astonish all who watch. Perhaps this disdain for personal comfort will move the purses of the passengers, or wallets as one says nowadays, to take pity on them, and that pity will be converted into tips. A backward clan, with outstretched hand, each man sells what he possesses in good measure, resignation, humility, patience, may we continue to find people who trade in this world with such wares. The passengers go through customs, few in number, but it will take them some time to get out, for there are many forms to be filled in and the handwriting of the customs officers on duty is painstaking. It is just possible that the quickest of them will get some rest this Sunday. It is growing dark although it is only four o'clock, a few more shadows and it will be night, but in here it is always night, the dim lamps lit all day long and some burned out. That lamp there has been out for a week and still hasn't been replaced. The windows, covered with grime, allow a watery light to penetrate. The heavy air smells of damp clothing, rancid baggage, the cheap material of uniforms, and there is not a trace of happiness in this homecoming. The customs shed is an antechamber, a limbo, before one passes on to what awaits outside.

A grizzled fellow, skin and bones, signs the last of the forms. Receiving copies, the passenger can go, depart, resume his existence on terra firma. He is accompanied by a porter whose physical appearance need not be described in detail, otherwise we should have to continue this examination forever. To avoid confusing anyone who might need to distinguish this porter from another, we will say only that he is skin and bones, grizzled, and as dark and clean-shaven as the man he is accompanying. Yet they are both quite different, one a passenger, one a porter. The latter pulls a huge suitcase on a metal cart, while the other two suitcases, small by comparison, are suspended from his neck with a strap that goes around the nape like a yoke or the collar of a religious habit. Once outside, under the protection of the jutting roof, he puts the luggage on the ground and goes in search of a taxi, they are usually here waiting when a ship arrives. The passenger looks at the low clouds, the puddles on the rough ground, the water by the quayside contaminated with oil, peelings, refuse of every kind, then he notices several unobtrusive warships. He did not expect to find them here, the proper place for these vessels is at sea, or, when not engaged in war or military maneuvers, in the estuary, which is more than wide enough to give anchorage to all the fleets in the world, as one used to say and perhaps still says, without bothering to see what fleets they might be. Other passengers emerged from customs, accompanied by their porters, then the taxi appeared, splashing water beneath its wheels. The waiting passengers waved their arms frantically, but the porter leaped onto the running board and made a broad gesture, It's for this gentleman, thus showing how even a humble employee in the port of Lisbon, when rain and circumstances permit, may hold happiness in his meager hands, which he can bestow or withhold at a moment's notice, a power attributed to God when we talk of life. While the taxi driver loaded his luggage into the trunk, the passenger, betraying for the first time a slight Brazilian accent, asked, Why are warships moored here. Panting for breath as he helped the taxi driver lift the heavy suitcase, the porter replied, Ah, it's the naval dock, because of the weather these ships were towed in the day before yesterday, otherwise they would have drifted off and run ashore at Algés. Other taxis began to arrive. Either they had been delayed or else the steamer docked an hour earlier than expected. Now there was an open-air market in the square, plenty of taxis for everyone. How much do I owe you, the passenger asked. Whatever you care to give on top of the fixed fare, the porter replied, but he did not say what the fixed fare was or put an actual price on his services, trusting to the good fortune that protects the courageous, even when the courageous are only baggage handlers. I have only English money, Oh, that's fine, and he saw ten shillings placed into his right hand, coins that shone more brightly than the sun itself. At long last the celestial sphere has banished the clouds that hovered oppressively over Lisbon. Because of such heavy burdens and deep emotions, the first condition for the survival and prosperity of any porter is to have a stout heart, a heart made of bronze, otherwise he will soon collapse, undone. Anxious to repay the passenger's excessive generosity, or at least not to be indebted in terms of words, he offers additional information that no one wants, and expressions of gratitude that no one heeds. They are torpedo boats, they are ours, Portuguese, this is the *Tejo*, the *Dão*, the *Lima*, the *Vouga*, the *Tâmega*, the *Dão* is that one nearest you. No one could have told the difference, one could even have changed their names around, they all looked alike, identical, painted a drab gray, awash with rain, without a sign of life on the decks, their flags soaked like rags. But no disrespect is intended, we know that this destroyer is the *Dão*. Perhaps we shall have news of her later.

The porter raises his cap and thanks him. The taxi drives off, Where to. This question, so simple, so natural, so fitting for the place and circumstances, takes the passenger unawares, as if a ticket purchased in Rio de Janeiro should provide the answer to all such questions, even those posed in the past, which at the time met with nothing but silence. Now, barely disembarked, the passenger sees at once that this is not so, perhaps because he has been asked one of the two fatal questions, Where to. The other question, and much worse, is Why. The taxi driver looked into his rearview mirror, thinking the passenger had not heard him. He was opening his mouth to repeat, Where to, but the reply came first, still indecisive, hesitant, To a hotel. Which hotel, I don't know, and having said, I don't know, the passenger knew precisely what he wanted, knew it with the utmost conviction, as if he had spent the entire voyage making up his mind, A hotel near the river, down in this part of the city. The only hotel near the river is the Bragança, at the beginning of the Rua do Alecrim. I don't remember the hotel, but I know where the street is, I used to live in Lisbon, I'm Portuguese. Ah, you're Portuguese, from your accent I thought you might be Brazilian. Is it so very noticeable. Well, just a little, enough to tell the difference. I haven't been back in Portugal for sixteen years. Sixteen years is a long time, you will find that things have changed a lot around here. With these words the taxi driver suddenly fell silent.

His passenger did not get the impression that there were many changes. The avenue they followed was much as he remembered it, only the trees looked taller, and no wonder, for they had had sixteen years in which to grow. Even so, because in his mind's eye he could still see green foliage, and because the wintry nakedness of the branches diminished the height of the rows, one image balanced out the other. The rain had died away, only a few scattered drops continued to fall, but in the sky there was not a trace of blue, the clouds had not dispersed and they formed one vast roof the color of lead. Has there been much rain, the passenger inquired. For the last two months it has been bucketing down like the great flood, the driver replied as he switched off his windshield wipers. Few cars were passing and even fewer trams, the occasional pedestrian warily closed his umbrella, along the sidewalks stood great pools of muddy water caused by blocked drains. Several bars were open, side by side, murky, their viscous lights encircled by shadows, the silent image of a dirty wineglass on a zinc counter. These façades are the great wall that screens the city, and the taxi skirts them without haste, as if searching for some break or opening, a Judas gate, or the entrance to a labyrinth. The train from Cascais passes slowly, chugging along at a sluggish pace yet still with enough speed to overtake the taxi, but then it falls behind and enters the station just as the taxi turns into the square. The driver informs him, The hotel is that one as you enter the street. He halted in front of a café and added, You'd better ask first if they have any rooms, I can't park outside the door because of the trams. The passenger got out, glanced fleetingly at the café, which was named Royal, a commercial example of monarchical nostalgia in a republican era, or of reminiscences of the last reign, here disguised in English or French. A curious situation, one looks at the word without knowing whether it should be pronounced *rôial* or *ruaiale*. He had time to consider the problem because it was no longer raining and the road went uphill. Then he imagined himself walking back from the hotel, with or without a room, and no sign of the taxi, it has vanished with all his luggage and clothes, his papers, and he wondered how he could exist deprived of these things and all his other worldly goods. Climbing the front steps of the hotel, he realized from these musings that he was exhausted, that he was suffering from an overwhelming fatigue, an infinite weariness, a sense of despair, if we really know what despair means when we say that word.

As he pushed open the door of the hotel, an electric buzzer sounded. At one time it would have been a little bell, ting-a-ling-a-ling, but one must always count on progress and its improvements. There was a steep flight of stairs and on the post at the bottom stood a figurine in cast iron holding aloft, in its right hand, a glass ball. The figurine represented a page in court dress, if the expression isn't redundant, for who ever saw a page not in court dress. It would be clearer to say a page dressed as a page, and judging from the cut of his costume, he was of the Italian Renaissance. The traveler went up endless steps. It seemed incredible that one should have to climb so far to reach the first floor, it was like scaling Mount Everest, a feat which continues to be the dream and utopia of every mountaineer. To his relief, a man with a mustache appeared at the top of the stairs offering words of encouragement, Up you come then. The man did not say these words but that was how one might have interpreted the look on his face as he leaned over the landing to investigate what fair winds and evil times had brought this guest. Good evening, sir. Good evening, he has no breath left for more. The man with the mustache smiles patiently, You need a room, the smile becomes that of someone apologizing, There are no rooms on this floor, this is the reception desk, dining room, lounge, and through here is the kitchen and pantry, the rooms are upstairs, and to inspect them we must go up to the second floor. This room is no good, it is small and gloomy, nor this, it looks onto the back, and these are already occupied. What I wanted was a room with a view of the river. Ah, in that case you will like room two hundred and one, it was vacated only this morning, I'll show it to you right away. The door at the end of the hallway had a little enameled plate, black numerals on a white background. If this were not a humble hotel room without any luxuries, and the room number were two hundred and two, and if the guest were called Jacinto and like Eça de Queirós's hero owned an estate in Tormes, then this episode would be set not in the Rua do Alecrim but on the Champs Elysées, on the right as one goes up, just like the Hotel Bragança, but that is the only detail they have in common.

The traveler approved of the room, or rooms to be precise, for there were two of them connected by a broad archway, on that side the bedroom, which once upon a time would have been described as an alcove, and on this side the sitting room, living quarters as satisfactory as in any apartment, with dark furniture in polished mahogany, drapes over the windows, and lampshades. The traveler heard the harsh screeching of a tram going up the street. The taxi driver was right. It seemed ages since the traveler had left the taxi waiting, and he smiled inwardly at his fear of being robbed. Do you like the room, the manager asked with the voice and authority of his profession but ever courteous, as befits someone negotiating a rental. It's fine, I'll take it, How long are you staying, I can't tell you, much depends on the time it takes to settle my affairs. It is the usual dialogue, the exchange one expects in such situations, but on this occasion there is an element of falsehood, because the traveler has no affairs to settle in Lisbon, no affairs worthy of the name, he has told a lie, he who once declared that he despised inaccuracy.

They descended to the first floor and the manager summoned an employee, a messenger and luggage porter, whom he sent to fetch the gentleman's suitcases. The taxi was waiting in front of the café and the traveler went down with him to pay the fare, an expression that harks back to the days of the horse-drawn cab, and also to check that there was nothing missing, but his mistrust is misguided, undeserved, the driver is an honest fellow and wishes only to be paid what is on the meter plus the customary tip. He will not share the good fortune of the baggage handler at the docks, there will be no further distribution of silver coins, for the traveler by now has changed some of his money at the reception desk, not that we disapprove of generosity, but enough is enough, too much ostentation is an insult to the poor. The suitcase weighs a great deal more than money, and when it reaches the landing, the manager is waiting to supervise its transportation. He moves forward to help by placing his hand underneath, a symbolic action, like someone laying the first stone, for the load is carried up on the errand boy's shoulders. A boy by profession rather than age, and he is beginning to feel his years as he carries up the heavy suitcase, supported on either side by futile gestures of assistance, for those made by the guest are not much help as he looks on in distress at the man's exertions, One more flight to go and you are there. It is room two hundred and one, Pimenta. This time Pimenta is in luck, he does not have to climb to the upper floors.

Meanwhile the guest returns to the reception desk, somewhat out of breath after all that effort. He takes the pen and enters the essential details about himself in the register of arrivals, so that it might be known who he claims to be, in the appropriate box on the lined page. Name, Ricardo Reis, age, forty-eight, place of birth, Oporto, marital status, bachelor, profession, doctor, last place of residence, Rio de Janeiro, Brazil, whence he has arrived aboard the *Highland Brigade*. It reads like the beginning of a confession, an intimate autobiography, all that is hidden is contained in these handwritten lines, the only problem is to interpret them. And the manager, who has been craning his neck to follow the linking of words and decipher their meaning at the same time, thinks he knows more or less everything. He introduces himself, beginning, Doctor. This is not intended as flattery but rather as a sign of respect, the acknowledgment of a right, a merit, a quality, which warrants immediate recognition even when not made known in writing. My name is Salvador, I am in charge of this hotel, should you require anything, Doctor, you need only tell me. At what time is dinner served. Dinner is at eight, Doctor, I hope you will find our cuisine satisfactory, we also serve French dishes. Doctor Ricardo Reis concedes with a nod that he shares that hope, retrieves his raincoat and hat from a chair, and withdraws.

The porter was waiting for him in the open doorway of his room. Ricardo Reis saw him there as he entered the corridor and knew that the man would hold out a hand, servile yet nonetheless imperious, demanding according to the weight of the luggage. As he proceeded, he noticed something he had failed to observe before, there were doors only on one side of the corridor, on the other side was the wall that formed the well of the staircase. He thought about this as if it were an important matter that must be borne in mind, really feeling very tired. The man hefted the tip rather than look at it, from long experience, and was satisfied, so much so that he said, Many thanks, Doctor. We cannot explain how he knew, for he had not seen the register of arrivals. The fact is that the lower orders are every bit as shrewd and perceptive as those who have been educated and lead a privileged existence. All that bothered Pimenta was the wing of his shoulder blade, for one of the straps reinforcing the suitcase had not been adjusted right. One would think that he did not know how to carry luggage.

Ricardo Reis sat on a chair and looked around him. This is where he will live who knows for how many days, perhaps he will rent a house and open consulting rooms, or he might decide to return to Brazil. But for the moment the hotel will do nicely, a neutral place requiring no commitment. He is in transit, his life is suspended. Beyond the smooth drapes the windows have suddenly become luminous, an effect created by the street lamps. Already so late, this day has ended, what remains hovers in the remote distance over the sea and is fast escaping. Yet only a few hours ago, Ricardo Reis was still sailing those waters. Now the horizon is within arm's reach, embodied by walls, pieces of furniture that reflect the light as a black mirror, and instead of the deep vibration of the steamer's engines he can hear the whispering, the murmuring of the city, six hundred thousand people sighing, calling in the distance. Then cautious footsteps in the corridor, a woman's voice saying, I'm coming at once. These words, this voice, it must be the maid. He opened one of the windows and looked outside. The rain had stopped. The fresh air, damp with the wind that was sweeping over the river, pervaded the room and cleared away the musty smell, the smell of dirty linen forgotten in some drawer. He reminded himself that a hotel is not a home, smells of one kind or another linger, the perspiration of insomnia or of a night of love, a drenched overcoat, mud brushed from shoes at the hour of departure, the maids who enter to change the beds and sweep the rooms, the odor peculiar to women, unavoidable smells, the signs of our humanity.

He left the window open and went to open another. In his shirt sleeves, refreshed, his vigor suddenly restored, he began to unpack his suitcases. Within half an hour he had emptied them and transferred his clothes to the chest of drawers, his shoes to the shoe rack, his suits to the hangers in the closet, his black suitcase with the medical instruments to a dark recess of a cupboard. The few books he had brought with him were placed on a shelf, some Latin classics which he had got out of the habit of reading, some well-thumbed editions of his favorite English poets, three or four Brazilian authors, less than a dozen Portuguese authors. Among them he found one from the library of the *Highland Brigade*, a book he had forgotten to return. If the Irish librarian notices the book is missing, grave and grievous accusations will be made against the Lusitanian nation, a land of slaves and brigands, as Byron once quipped, and O'Brien will concur. Insignificant local transgressions often give rise to resounding and universal consequences. But I am innocent, I swear it was merely forgetfulness on my part and nothing more. He placed the book on his bedside table, intending to finish it one of these days, *The God of the Labyrinth* by Herbert Quain, also Irish, by no unusual coincidence. But the name itself is certainly most unusual, for without any great variation in the pronunciation one might read Quain as the Portuguese for Who. Take note, Quain, *Quem*, a writer who is no longer unknown because someone discovered him on the *Highland Brigade*. And if that was the only copy, and even it is now missing, all the more reason for asking ourselves Who. The tedium of the voyage and the book's evocative title had attracted him. A labyrinth with a god, what god might that be, which labyrinth, what labyrinthine god. In the end it turned out to be a simple detective story, an ordinary tale of death and investigation, the murderer, the victim, and finally the detective, all three accomplices to the crime. In my honest opinion, the reader of a mystery is the only real survivor of the story he is reading, unless it is as the one real survivor that every reader reads every story.

There are also documents to be stored away, handwritten sheets of verse, the oldest of them dated the twelfth of June, nineteen fourteen. War was about to break out, the Great War, as they were later to call it, until they experienced one even greater. *Maestro, placid are the hours we lose, if in losing them, as in a vase, we place flowers.* And then it finished, *Tranquil, we depart this life, feeling no remorse at having lived.* The most recent sheet of all is dated the thirteenth of November, nineteen thirty-five, six weeks have passed since he wrote it. Still fresh, the lines read, *Innumerable people live within us. If I think and feel, I know not who is thinking and feeling, I am only the place where there is thinking and feeling,* and, though they do not end here, it is as if everything ends, for beyond thinking and feeling there is nothing. If I am this, muses Ricardo Reis as he stops reading, who will be thinking at this moment what I am thinking, or think that I am thinking in the place where I am, because of thinking. Who will be feeling what I am feeling, or feel that I am feeling in the place where I am, because of feeling. Who is using me in order to think and feel, and among the innumerable people who live within me, who I am, Who, *Quem,* Quain, what thoughts and feelings are the ones I do not share because they are mine alone. Who am I that others are not nor have been nor will come to be. He gathered together the sheets of paper and put them into a drawer of the little writing desk, closed the windows, and went to run the hot water for a bath. It was after seven.

As the last stroke of eight echoed on the pendulum clock that adorned the wall above the reception desk, Ricardo Reis descended punctually to the dining room. The manager, Salvador, smiled, raising his mustache above his teeth, which looked none too clean, as he hurried forward to open the double doors. Their glass panels, engraved with the initials H and B, the B entwined with curves and countercurves, with appendages and floral elongations, stylized acanthuses, palm fronds, and spiraling foliage, bestowed dignity on this otherwise modest hotel. The maître d' led the way. There were no other guests in the dining room, only two waiters who had finished setting the tables. Noises could be heard coming from behind the pantry door, which bore the same monogram. From that door soup tureens, covered dishes, and platters would soon make their entrance. The furnishings were what you might expect, anyone who has seen one of these dining rooms has seen them all, a few dim lights on the ceilings and walls, immaculate white cloths on the tables, the pride of the establishment, freshened up with bleach in the laundry, if not in the Caneças, which only uses soap and sunshine, but with so much rain for days on end, it must be well behind with its work. Ricardo Reis is now seated. The maître d' tells him what is on the menu, soup, fish, meat, unless the doctor prefers something lighter, that is, another kind of meat, fish, soup. I should advise the latter until you get used to your new diet, since you have just come back from the tropics after an absence of sixteen years. So even in the dining room and kitchen they know all about him. The door leading from the reception desk was pushed open in the meantime and a couple entered with two young children, a boy and a girl, both of them the color of wax though their parents were florid, but both legitimate, to judge from appearances, the head of the family in front, guiding his tribe, the mother pushing her children forward from behind. Then a man appeared, fat and heavy, with a gold chain crossing his stomach from one little waistcoat pocket to another, and almost immediately after him came another man, very thin, with a black tie and a mourning band on his arm. No one else arrived for the next quarter of an hour. The noise of cutlery could be heard against the plates. The father of the children, authoritative, struck the knife against his wineglass to summon the waiter. The thin man, his mourning disturbed and good breeding offended, gave him a severe look, but the fat man calmly went on chewing. Ricardo Reis contemplated the blobs of grease that floated on his chicken broth. He had chosen the lighter meal, following the maître d's suggestion out of indifference rather than conviction, for he could see no real advantage to it. A ruffling sound against the windowpanes told him that it had started raining again. These windows do not face onto the Rua do Alecrim, what street could it be, he cannot remember, if he ever knew, but the waiter who comes to change his plate informs him, This is the Rua Nova do Carvalho, Doctor, before asking, Did you enjoy your soup. From the waiter's pronunciation, which is good, one can tell that he is Galician.

Through the door now entered a middle-aged man, tall and distinguished in appearance, with a long, lined face, along with a girl in her twenties, if that, and thin, although it would be more correct to describe her as slender. They made their way to the table facing Ricardo Reis and it suddenly became clear that the table had been awaiting them, just as an object awaits the hand that frequently reaches out and takes possession. They must be regular clients, perhaps the owners of the hotel. It is interesting how we forget that hotels have an owner. These two, whether the owners or not, crossed the room at their leisure as if in their own home. Such details you notice when you pay attention. The girl sat in profile, the man with his back to Ricardo Reis, and they conversed in a whisper, but she raised her voice as she reassured him, No, Father, I'm fine. So they are father and daughter, an unusual pairing in any hotel nowadays. The waiter came to serve them, solemn but friendly in his manner, then went away. The room was silent again, not even the children raised their voices. How strange that Ricardo Reis cannot remember having heard the children speak, perhaps they are mute or have their lips stapled together with invisible clips, an absurd thought, since they are both eating. The slender girl, finishing her soup, puts down the spoon, and her right hand starts to caress her left hand as if it were a little lapdog resting on her knees. Surprised by this, Ricardo Reis realizes that her left hand has never moved, he remembers that she used only her right hand to fold her napkin, and now she is holding the left and is about to rest it on the table, very gently, like the most fragile crystal. There she leaves it, beside her plate, a silent presence at the meal, the long fingers extended, pale, inert. Ricardo Reis feels a shiver, no one is feeling it for him, his skin shivers within and without, as in utter fascination he watches that hand, paralyzed and insensible, ignorant of where it should go unless taken, resting to catch the sun or listen to the conversation or be seen by the doctor who has just arrived from Brazil. A tiny hand which is left on two counts, left because it is lying on the left side and left because it is a gauche, disabled, lifeless, and withered thing that will never knock on any door. Ricardo Reis observes that the plates for the girl come from the pantry already prepared, the fishbones removed, the meat diced, the fruit peeled and cut into segments. It is clear that the daughter and father are well known to the hotel staff, they may even live in the hotel. He finished his meal but lingered a while, to allow time, but what time and for what. At last he got up, drew back his chair, and the noise he made, too loud perhaps, caused the girl to turn around. Seen from the front, she looks older than twenty, but in profile her youth is immediately restored, her neck long and fragile, her chin finely molded, the entire restless line of her body insecure, unfinished. Ricardo Reis got up from the table, headed for the glass-paneled door with the monograms, where he was obliged to exchange courtesies with the fat man who was also leaving. After you, sir, Please, after you. The fat man went out, Thank you, kind sir, a somewhat obsequious use of the word *sir*, for if we are to take all words literally, Ricardo Reis would have passed first, for he is innumerable men, according to his own understanding of himself.

The manager Salvador is already holding out the key of room two hundred and one. He makes a solicitous gesture, as if about to hand it over but then slyly drawing back. Perhaps the guest wishes to slip out quietly in search of Lisbon by night and its secret pleasures, after so many years in Brazil and so many days crossing the ocean, although the wintry night makes the cozy atmosphere of the lounge seem more enticing, here at hand, the deep high-backed armchairs in leather, the chandelier in the center of the room so rich in crystal pendants, and that big mirror that encompasses the entire room and duplicates it in another dimension. This is no simple reflection of the common and familiar proportions the mirror is confronted with, length, width, height, they are not reproduced in it one by one and readily identifiable. Instead they are fused into a single intangible apparition on a plane that is at once remote and near, unless there is some paradox in this explanation which the mind avoids out of laziness. Here is Ricardo Reis contemplating himself in the depths of the mirror, one of the countless persons that he is, all of them weary. I am going up to my room, I'm exhausted after my journey, two whole weeks of the most awful weather, have you by any chance some newspapers, I'd like to catch up on the national news until I'm ready to fall asleep. There you are, Doctor, help yourself. Just at this moment the girl with the paralyzed hand and her father passed into the lounge, he in front, she behind, one pace apart. Ricardo Reis had already picked up his key and the newspapers, the color of ashes, the print blurred. A gust of wind caused the front door to bang downstairs, the buzzer sounded. There is no one there, only the storm which is gathering. This night will bring nothing more of interest, only rain, tempest over land and sea, solitude.

The sofa in his room is comfortable, the springs on which so many bodies have reclined form a human hollow, and the light from the lamp which stands on the writing desk illuminates the newspaper at the correct angle. This is like being at home, in the bosom of one's family, by the fireside I do not possess and perhaps never will. These are the newspapers of my native Portugal, they inform me that the Head of State has inaugurated an exhibition in honor of Mousinho de Albuquerque at the Colonial Office, one is not spared imperial commemorations or allowed to forget imperial personages. There is cause for anxiety in Golegã, I can't even remember where it is, ah yes, in the province of Ribatejo, that the floods may burst the dike known as Vinte, a most curious name, where could it have come from, we shall see a repetition of the disaster of eighteen ninety-five. In ninety-five I was eight years old, naturally I don't remember. The tallest woman in the world is Elsa Droyon, two and a half meters tall, the water won't rise that much. And that girl, I wonder what her name is, that paralyzed hand, so limp, it might have been an illness or perhaps some accident. The fifth national contest for beautiful babies, half a page of photographs of infants, stark naked, their rolls of puppy fat bulging, nourished on powdered milk. Some of these babies will grow up to become criminals, vagabonds, and prostitutes, after being photographed like this, at such a tender age, before the lewd eyes of those who have no respect for innocence. The military operations in Ethiopia continue. What news from Brazil, nothing new, everything destroyed. General advance of the Italian troops. There is no human force capable of stopping the Italian soldier in his heroic onslaught, what can the Abyssinian rifle achieve against him, the inferior lance, the wretched cutlass. The lawyer of a famous woman athlete has announced that his client has undergone a major operation in order to change her sex, within a few days she will be a man, as if from birth, do not forget to change her name too, what name, Bocage, before the Tribunal of the Holy Office. A painting by the artist Fernando Santos, the fine arts are cultivated in this country. At the Coliseu they are showing *The Last Wonder* with Vanise Meireles, a statuesque figure clad in silver, a Brazilian celebrity. Funny, I must have missed her in Brazil, my fault. Here in Lisbon one can get a seat in the gallery for three escudos, a seat in the stalls costs five escudos and up, there are two performances daily and matinées on Sundays. The Politeama is showing *The Crusades*, a spectacular epic. Numerous contingents of English troops have landed at Port Said, every era has its crusades, these are the crusades of modern times, it is rumored that they are making for the borders of Italian-occupied Libya. A list of the Portuguese who have died in Brazil during the first half of December. These names are unknown to me, I don't need to express my sympathy or go into mourning, but clearly lots of Portuguese immigrants die down there. Charity fêtes with free dinners for the poor throughout the country, the quality of food has been improved in the hospices for the poor, the elderly are so well treated in Portugal, not to mention abandoned children, little flowers left on the streets. Then this item of news, the president of the city council in Oporto sent a telegram to the Minister of the Interior, At today's session the council over which I preside resolved, after discussion of the decree which will provide assistance for the poor throughout the winter, to congratulate Your Excellency on this admirable enterprise. Other news, polluted drinking troughs full of cattle dung, smallpox is spreading in Lebução and Fatela, an outbreak of flu in Portalegre and typhoid fever in Valbom, a sixteen-year-old girl has died of smallpox, a pastoral flower of bucolic innocence, a lily cruelly severed from its stem and so prematurely. I have a foxhound bitch, not a purebred, who has already had two litters and on both occasions she was found eating her young, not one escaped, tell me, dear editor, what should I do. In reply to your question, dear reader, the cannibalism of bitches is generally due to malnutrition during the period of gestation. The dog must be well fed with meat as her staple diet and supplemented with milk, bread, and vegetables, in brief, a well-balanced diet. If this does not change her habits, there's no remedy, either destroy the dog or do not allow her to mate, let her put up with being in heat or you can have her spayed. Now let us try to imagine what would happen if women suffering from malnutrition during pregnancy, starved of meat, bread, and green vegetables, which is fairly common, were also to begin eating their infants. After trying to imagine it and having confirmed that such crimes do not occur, it becomes easy to see the difference between people and animals. The editor did not add these comments, nor did Ricardo Reis, who is thinking about something else, a suitable name for the bitch. He will not call her Diana or Lembrada, but a name to throw light on her crime or motives, and will the wicked creature die from eating poisoned food or from a rifle shot fired by her own master. Ricardo Reis persists and finally finds the right name, one which comes from Ugolino della Gherardesca, that most savage, lusty nobleman who ate his children and grandchildren, there are testimonies to this in the *History of the Guelphs and Ghibellines*, also in the *Divine Comedy*, chapter thirty-three of the *Inferno*. Therefore let the bitch who eats her young be called Ugolina, so unnatural that her heart suffers no compassion as she tears the warm and tender skin of her defenseless brood with her jaws, slaughtering them, causing their delicate bones to snap, and the poor little pups, whining, perish without realizing who is devouring them, the mother who gave them birth. Ugolina, do not kill me, I am your offspring.

The page which calmly narrates these horrors falls onto the lap of Ricardo Reis. He is fast asleep. A sudden gust of wind rattles the windowpanes, the rain pours down like a deluge. Through the deserted streets of Lisbon prowls the bitch Ugolina slavering blood, sniffing in doorways, howling in squares and parks, furiously biting at her own womb, where the next litter is about to be conceived.

After a night of severe winter, of violent storm, the latter two words, violent storm, have been linked together since their inception, the first pair not quite as much, but both phrases are so pertinent to the circumstance that they spare one the effort of having to invent new words, the morning might well have dawned with bright sunshine, blue skies, and joyful flutterings of pigeons in flight. But there was no change in the elements. The swallows continue to fly over the city, the river is not to be trusted, the pigeons scarcely venture there. It is raining, but tolerably for anyone going out with a raincoat and umbrella, and in comparison with the gales earlier this morning, the wind is a mere caress on one's cheek. Ricardo Reis left the hotel early, he went to the Banco Comercial to change some of his English money into escudos, and for every pound sterling he received one hundred and ten thousand reis. A pity those pounds were not gold, otherwise he could have changed them for almost double that amount. Even so, the returning traveler has no real cause for complaint, seeing as he leaves the bank with five thousand escudos in his wallet, a small fortune in Portugal. From the Rua do Comércio, where he finds himself, the Terreiro do Paço is only a few meters away, but Ricardo Reis will not risk crossing the square. He looks into the distance under the protection of the colonnades, the river dark and choppy, the tide high. When the waves rise offshore, one imagines they are about to inundate and submerge the square, but that is an optical illusion, they disperse against the wall, their impact broken by the sloping steps of the wharf. He recalls having sat there in days gone by, days so remote he doubts whether he really experienced them. It may have been someone on my behalf, perhaps with the same face and name, but some other person. His feet are cold and wet, he also feels a shadow of gloom pass over his body, not over his soul, I repeat, not over his soul. The impression is physical, he could touch it with his hands were they not both gripping the handle of his umbrella, which is needlessly open. This is how a man alienates himself from the world, how he exposes himself to the jesting of some passerby who quips, Hey mister, it's not raining under there. But the man's smile is spontaneous, without a hint of malice, and Ricardo Reis smiles at his own distraction. Without knowing why, he murmurs two lines from a poem by João de Deus, well known to every child in nursery school. Under this colonnade one could comfortably spend the night.

He came here because the square was so near and in order to verify in passing if his memory of the place, clear as an engraving, bore any resemblance to the reality. A quadrangle surrounded by buildings on three sides, a regal equestrian statue in the middle, a triumphal arch which he cannot see from where he is standing. But everything is diffuse and hazy, the architecture nothing but blurred lines. It must be the weather, the hour of day, his failing eyesight. Only the eyes of remembrance remain, as sharp as those of a hawk. It is almost eleven o'clock, and there is much activity under the colonnades, but activity is not the same thing as haste. This dignified lot move at a steady pace, all the men in soft hats, their umbrellas dripping, few women are in sight at this hour, the civil servants are arriving at their offices. Ricardo Reis walks on in the direction of the Rua do Crucifixo, resisting the insistent pleas of a lottery-ticket vendor who tries to sell him a ticket for the next draw. It is number one thousand three hundred and forty-nine, the wheel will spin tomorrow. That is not the number and the wheel will not be spinning tomorrow, but this is how the soothsayer's chant goes, a licensed prophet with a badge on his cap. Do buy a ticket, sir, if you refuse to buy, you will live to regret it, believe me, it's a winner. There is menace in this imposition. Ricardo Reis enters the

Rua Garrett, goes up the Chiado, where four porters lean against the plinth of the statue, paying no heed to the drizzle. This is the island of the Galicians. Farther ahead it has actually stopped raining. There is a white patch of light behind Luís de Camões, a nimbus. That is the trouble with words, *nimbus* signifies rain as well as cloud as well as halo, and since the poet is neither God nor saint, the rain stopping was merely the clouds thinning out as they passed. Let us not imagine that these are miracles like the ones at Ourique or Fátima, not even the simple miracle of the sky turning blue.

Ricardo Reis goes to the newspaper archives. Yesterday he made a note of the directions before going to bed. There is no reason to believe he slept badly, that he found the bed or country strange. When one awaits sleep in the silence of a room that is still unfamiliar, listening to the rain outside, things assume their real dimension, they all become great, solemn, heavy. What is deceptive is the light of day, transforming life into a shadow that is barely perceptible. Night alone is lucid, sleep, however, overcomes it, perhaps for our tranquillity and repose, the peace of our souls. Ricardo Reis goes to the newspaper archives, where everyone must go who wishes to know what has taken place, for here in the Bairro Alto the entire world passes, leaving footprints, broken twigs, trampled leaves, spoken words. What remains is this necessary invention, so that of the aforesaid world a face may be preserved, a look, a smile, a mortal agony. The unexpected death of Fernando Pessoa caused much sadness in intellectual circles. The poet of *Orfeu*, an admirable spirit who not only composed poetry in original forms but also wrote cogent critical essays, died the day before yesterday, in silence, just as he had always lived. Since no one can earn a living in Portugal by writing literature, Fernando Pessoa found employment as a clerk in a commercial firm. Some lines further on, his friends left wreaths of remembrance beside his tomb. This newspaper gives no more information. Another reports the same facts with different words, Fernando Pessoa, the extraordinary poet of *Mensagem*, an ode of patriotic fervor and one of the most beautiful ever written, was buried yesterday, taken unawares by death in a Christian bed at the Hospital of São Luís during the late hours of Saturday night. In his poetry he was not only Fernando Pessoa but also Alvaro de Campos, Alberto Caeiro, and Ricardo Reis. There you are, an error caused by not paying attention, by writing what one misheard, because we know very well that Ricardo Reis is this man who is reading the newspaper with his own open and living eyes, a doctor forty-eight years of age, one year older than Fernando Pessoa when his eyes were closed, eyes that were dead beyond a shadow of doubt. No other proofs or testimonies are needed to verify that we are not dealing with the same person, and if there is anyone who is still in doubt, let him go to the Hotel Bragança and speak to the manager Senhor Salvador, ask him if there is not a gentleman in residence there called Ricardo Reis, a doctor, newly arrived from Brazil. He will say Yes, the doctor said he would not be back for lunch but would almost certainly be dining here this evening, if you would care to leave a message, I shall see that he receives it. Now who will dare impugn the word of a hotel manager, an excellent physiognomist and well practiced in establishing identities. But rather than satisfy ourselves with the word of a man whom we cannot claim to know intimately, here is another paper which has reported the news on the page under obituaries. It outlines his career in detail, Yesterday there took place the funeral of Fernando António Nogueira Pessoa, bachelor, forty-seven years of age, forty-seven, take note, born in Lisbon, studied literature at an English university, became established as a writer and poet in literary circles, on his coffin were placed sprays of wild flowers, worse luck for them, as they wither so quickly. While he is waiting for the tram that will take him to Prazeres, Doctor Ricardo Reis reads the funeral oration delivered at the graveside, he reads it near the place where a man was hanged, as everyone knows, almost two hundred and twenty-three years ago, during the reign of Dom João V, who is not mentioned in the *Mensagem*. They hanged a Genoese swindler who for the sake of a piece of cloth killed one of our countrymen, stabbing him in the throat with a knife, then doing the same to the dead man's mistress, who died on the spot. He then inflicted two wounds on their servant, which were not fatal, and put out another's eye as if he were a rabbit. The murderer was arrested, and sentenced to death here, since it was near the house where he committed the crimes, in the presence of the crowd that had gathered to watch. Scarcely comparable with this morning in nineteen thirty-five, the month of December, the thirtieth to be precise, the sky overcast, and only those who cannot avoid it out walking in the streets, even though it is not raining now as Ricardo Reis, leaning against a lamppost at the top of the Calçada do Combro, reads the funeral oration. Not for the Genoese swindler, who did not receive one, unless you count the insults of the rabble, but for Fernando Pessoa, poet and innocent of any murders. Two words about the poet's earthly passage. For him two words suffice, or none. Indeed silence would be preferable, the silence that already enshrouds both him and us and which is in keeping with his temperament, for what is close to God is close to him. Yet those who were his peers in extolling beauty should not, could not have allowed him to descend into the earth, or rather ascend to the final horizons of Eternity without voicing their protest, calm yet aggrieved at this departure, the companions of Orpheus, more brothers than companions, who pursued the same ideal of beauty, they could not, I repeat, abandon him in this final resting place without having showered his gentle death with the white lilies of silence and suffering. We mourn the man whom death takes from us, and the loss of his miraculous talent and the grace of his human presence, but only the man do we mourn, for destiny endowed his spirit and creative powers with a mysterious beauty that cannot perish. The rest belongs to the genius of Fernando Pessoa. Come now, come now, exceptions can fortunately still be found to the normal rules of life. Since the time of Hamlet we have been going around saying, The rest is silence, in the end it's genius that takes care of the rest, and if this genius can do it, perhaps another genius can too.

The tram has come and gone, Ricardo Reis has found a seat all to himself. The ticket cost seventy-five centavos, in time he will learn to say, One at seven and a half. He resumes his reading of the funeral oration, unable to convince himself that it is dedicated to Fernando Pessoa, who must be dead if we look at the press reports, because the poet would not have tolerated such grammatical and lexical bombast. How little they must have known him, to address him and speak of him in this way. They take advantage of his death, his feet and hands are bound. They call him a despoiled lily, a lily like a girl stricken by typhoid fever, and use the adjective *gentle*. Such banality, dear God. Since gentle means noble, chivalrous, gallant, elegant, pleasing, and urbane, which of these would the poet have chosen as he lay in his Christian bed in the Hospital of São Luís. May the gods grant that it be pleasing, for with death one should lose only life.

When Ricardo Reis reached the cemetery, the bell at the gate was ringing, its peals filled the air with the sound of cracked bronze like the bell of some rustic villa ringing out in the drowsy heat of the siesta. About to disappear, a bier was carried by hand, its funeral valances swaying, the women's faces covered with black shawls, the men attired in their Sunday best, purplish chrysanthemums in their arms, more chrysanthemums on the upper ledges of the coffin, not even flowers enjoy a common destiny. The bier disappeared into the depths and Ricardo Reis went to the registry office to inquire where he might find the grave of Fernando António Nogueira Pessoa who died on the thirtieth day of last month, buried on the second of this month, laid to rest in this cemetery until the end of time, when God will command poets to awaken from their temporary death. Realizing that he is in the presence of an educated man of some standing, the clerk carefully informs him about the road and the number, for this is just like any city, sir. In order to make quite certain that his instructions are clear, he comes around the counter, accompanies him outside, and points, Go straight down the avenue, turn right at the bottom, then straight ahead, it's on the right-hand side about two-thirds down the path, look carefully, the tomb is small and you could easily miss it. Ricardo Reis thanks him for his assistance. The winds that come from afar over sea and river, he does not hear them wailing as one might expect in a cemetery, there are only these gray skies, these damp marble stones glistening after the recent rain, the dark-green cypresses darker than ever. As instructed, he starts to descend the road lined with poplars, in search of the grave numbered four thousand three hundred and seventy-one, a number which was drawn in the lottery yesterday and will be drawn no more, drawn by destiny rather than fortune. The road slopes gently downward, one is almost strolling. At least those remaining few steps were not difficult, that final walk of the funeral procession, for nevermore will Fernando Pessoa be accompanied, if during his lifetime he was truly accompanied by those who brought him here. Here is the corner we must take. We ask ourselves why we came, what tears remain to be shed, and why, if we did not shed them before. Perhaps we were more shocked than grieved, the sorrow came later, dull, as if our entire body were a single muscle being crushed internally, no black stain visibly locating our grief. On either side, the chapels of the family tombs are locked, the windows are covered with curtains made of lace, the finest linen like that of handkerchiefs, the most delicate flowers embroidered between two plants, or in heavy crochet made with needles like naked swords, or saying *richelieu* or *ajour*, Gallicisms pronounced God alone knows how. It reminds me of those children on the *Highland Brigade*, now far, far away, sailing northward over seas where the salt of Lusitanian tears is that of fishermen amid the waves that claim their lives and of their families crying on the shore. The threads of this embroidery were made by the Coats and Clark Company, Anchor Brand, so as not to stray from the disasters of maritime history. Ricardo Reis has already proceeded halfway along the path, constantly looking to the right. Eternal regret, Sad remembrance, Here lies in loving memory of, we would see the same inscriptions if we looked on the other side, angels with drooping wings, lachrymose statues, fingers entwined, folds carefully arranged, drapes neatly gathered, broken columns. Perhaps the stonemasons cut them like that, or delivered them in perfect condition so the relatives of the deceased could break them as a token of their grief, like those warriors who marked the death of their leader by solemnly smashing their shields. Skulls at the foot of the crosses. The evidence of death is the veil with which death masks itself. Ricardo Reis has gone past the tomb he was looking for. No voice called out, Hello, it's here, yet there are still those who insist that the dead can speak. What would become of the dead if there were no means of identifying them, no name engraved on a tombstone, no number as on the doors of the living. A good thing they taught us how to read, for you can imagine some illiterate needing to be led by the hand and told, The tomb is here. He will look at us suspiciously, because should we mislead him, either out of error or malice, he would find himself praying to Capuletto instead of Montecchio, to Gonçalves instead of Mendes.

These are titles of property and occupation, the tomb of Dona Dionísia de Seabra Pessoa inscribed on the front, under the overhanging eaves of this sentry box where the sentinel, a romantic touch, is sleeping. Below, at the height of the door's lower hinge, another name and nothing more, that of Fernando Pessoa, with the dates of his birth and death, and the gilded outline of a funeral urn that says, I am here. Ricardo Reis repeats the words aloud, He is here. At that moment it starts raining again. He has traveled so far, all the way from Rio de Janeiro, days and nights on the high seas, the voyage seems so recent and yet so remote, now what is he to do, alone in this road, among graves, his umbrella open. Time to be thinking about lunch. In the distance he could hear the hollow sound of a bell tolling, the sound he had expected to hear upon arrival, when he touched these railings, his soul gripped by panic, a deep laceration, an inner turmoil, like great cities collapsing in silence because we are not there, porticoes and white towers toppling. In the end nothing but a gentle sensation of burning in one's eyes, no sooner felt than gone, not even time to think about it or be troubled by the thought. There is nothing more to be done in this place, what he has done is nothing. Inside the tomb is a mad old woman who cannot be left to roam at will. Under her watchful eye is also the decomposing body of a composer of verses who left his share of madness in the world. The great difference between poets and madmen is the destiny of the madness that possesses them. He felt afraid, thinking about grandmother Dionísia lying in there, and about her afflicted grandson Fernando, she keeping vigil with eyes wide open, he with eyes averted, looking for a gap, a breath of air, a glimmer of light, his uneasiness turned to nausea as if he were being assailed and suffocated by a great sea wave, he who throughout the fourteen days of the voyage had not once been seasick. Then he thought, It must be my empty stomach, and he was probably right, for he had eaten nothing all morning. The rain came pouring down, arriving just in time. Now Ricardo Reis will have his answer ready if anyone questions him, No, I didn't spend much time there, it was raining so heavily. As he started to climb

32

the road, walking slowly, he felt the nausea pass. All that remained was a slight headache, perhaps an emptiness in his head, like an absence, a piece of brain missing, the piece relinquished by Pessoa. He found his informant standing in the doorway of the registry, and it was obvious from the grease on the man's lips that he had just finished eating lunch. Where, right here, a napkin spread out on his desk, the food he brought from home, still warm because wrapped in newspapers, or perhaps reheated on a gas flame, there at the far end of the filing cabinets, interrupting his chewing three times to file. So I must have spent more time there than I thought. Then you found the tomb you were looking for. I found it, Ricardo Reis replied, and as he went through the gate he repeated, Yes, I found it.

Famished and in a hurry, he gestured toward the row of taxis. Who knows if he can still find a restaurant or eating house prepared to serve him lunch at this late hour. The driver was methodically chewing a toothpick, passing it from one corner of his mouth to the other with his tongue. It must have been with his tongue, since his hands were occupied with the steering wheel. From time to time he noisily sucked the saliva between his teeth. The sucking sound, the intermittent warbling of digestion, made two simultaneous notes like birdsong, Ricardo Reis thought to himself and smiled, but at the same moment his eyes filled with tears. Strange that such a sound should have such an effect. Or it might have been the sight of a little angel being carried to its grave on a white bier, some Fernando who did not live long enough to become a poet, some Ricardo who could not become a doctor or poet. Perhaps the reason for this outburst of weeping is simply that the moment had come for the release of pent-up emotions. These physiological matters are complicated, let us leave them to those who understand them, particularly if it should prove necessary to follow the path of sentiment into the tear glands themselves, to determine, for example, the chemical difference between tears of sadness and tears of joy, almost certainly the former are more salty, which explains why one's eyes smart so much. In front, the driver pushed the toothpick between his canine teeth on the right. Silently he moved the toothpick up and down, respecting the passenger's sorrow, something he is used to doing when he picks up people at the cemetery. The taxi descended the Calçada da Estrela, turned at the Cortes, heading toward the river, and then, reaching the Baixa, went up the Rua Augusta. As it entered the Rossio, Ricardo Reis suddenly remembered, Stop at the Irmãos Unidos, the restaurant just ahead, draw up on the right, there is an entrance at the back, in the Rua dos Correeiros. One can be sure of a good meal here, the food is excellent, the atmosphere traditional, because the restaurant is situated on the very spot where the Hospital de Todos os Santos once stood many years ago. You would think we were narrating the history of another nation. An earthquake comes along, and behold the result, but whether we change for better or for worse depends on how alive we are and hopeful.

Ricardo Reis lunched without worrying about his diet. Yesterday had been an act of weakness on his part. When a man comes ashore after an ocean voyage he is like a child, sometimes seeking a woman's shoulder on which to rest his head, at other times ordering one glass of wine after another in some tavern until he finds happiness, provided happiness has been poured in that bottle beforehand. At other times it is as if he has no will of his own. Any Galician waiter can decide what he should eat, I'd suggest a little chicken if you are feeling queasy, sir. Here no one wishes to know whether he disembarked yesterday, whether tropical dishes have ruined his digestion, what special food will cure his nostalgia for his native land, if that is what he suffers from. If not, why did he come back. From the table where he is sitting, between the gaps in the curtains he can see the trams pass outside, he can hear them creaking on the turns, the tinkling of their little bells, a liquid sound in the rain, like the bells of a submerged cathedral or the strains of a harpsichord echoing ad infinitum within a well. The waiters hover patiently, waiting for this last customer to finish his lunch. He arrived late and pleaded with them to serve him, and his request was granted, although the kitchen staff was already clearing away the pots and pans. Now he's done, he thanks the waiters, politely wishing them a pleasant afternoon as he leaves by the door to the Rua dos Correeiros, which opens onto that Babylon of iron and glass, the Praça da Figueira. Still bustling with activity, the market is calm by comparison with the morning hours, when the noisy cries of the tradesmen grow louder and louder. One inhales a thousand pungent odors, kale trampled and wilting, the excrement of rabbits, the feathers of scalded chickens, blood, bits of flayed skin. They are washing the benches and the alleyways with buckets, hoses, and brooms with tough bristles. From time to time you can hear the scraping of metal, then a sudden boom as a shutter is rolled down. Ricardo Reis went around the square from the southern side and turned into the Rua dos Douradores. The rain almost over, he could now close his umbrella and look up at the tall, grimy façades. Rows of windows at the same height, some with sills, others with balconies, the monotonous stone slabs extending all along the road until they merge into thin vertical strips which narrow more and more but never entirely disappear. Down in the Rua da Conceição, appearing to block the road, rises a building of similar color with windows and grilles of the same design or only slightly modified. All exude gloom and humidity, releasing into the courtyards the stench of cracked sewers, with scattered whiffs of gas. Little wonder that the shopkeepers standing in their doorways have an unhealthy pallor. Dressed in their smocks or aprons of gray cotton, their pens stuck behind one ear, they look disgruntled, because this is Monday and Sunday was disappointing. The road is paved with rough irregular stones, the gravel almost black where the metal wheels of the carts have bounced as they passed. It used to be that in the dry season, which this is not, the iron shoes of the mules gave off sparks when the loads they hauled exceeded the strength of man and beast. Today only lighter freight is carried, such as those sacks of beans which appear to weigh about sixty kilos and are now being unloaded by two men, or should one say liters when referring to beans and seeds. Since the bean by its nature is light, every liter of beans weighs approximately seven hundred and fifty grams, so let us hope that those who filled the sacks took this into account and reduced the load accordingly.

Ricardo Reis started walking back to his hotel and suddenly remembered the room where he had spent his first night like a prodigal son under a paternal roof. He remembered it as if it were his home, not the one in Rio de Janeiro, nor in Oporto, where we know he was born, nor here in Lisbon, where he lived before sailing off to exile in Brazil, none of these, even though they had all been homes to him. A strange sign, and of what, a man thinking of his hotel room as if it were his own home. Disquieted, uneasy at being out for so long, since early morning, he murmured, I'll go back at once. He fought down the urge to hail a taxi, allowed a tram to pass that would have dropped him almost at the hotel door, managed in the end to quell this absurd anxiety, to force himself to be simply someone going back to his hotel, unhurried yet without any needless delay. He may see the girl with the paralyzed arm in the dining room this evening, it is a possibility, like that of seeing the fat man, the thin man in mourning, the pale children and their ruddy parents, who knows what other guests, mysterious arrivals from an unknown place enshrouded in mist. Thinking about them, he felt a consoling warmth in his heart, a deep sense of reassurance, Love one another were the words once spoken, and it was time to begin. The wind blew with force, channeled into the Rua do Arsenal, but it was not raining, all that fell on the pavements were some heavy drops shaken from eaves. Perhaps the weather will change for the better, this winter cannot last forever. For the last two months there has been nothing but heavy showers, the taxi driver told him yesterday, in the tone of one who no longer believes that things will improve.

A sharp buzz as he opened the door, and it was as if he were being welcomed by the statue of the Italian page. Pimenta looked down the steep flight of stairs from the landing above, waiting to greet him, deferential and punctilious, his back slightly stooped, perhaps the result of those loads he is constantly carrying. Good afternoon, Doctor. The manager Salvador also appeared on the landing, saying the same words but in a more refined tone. Ricardo Reis returned their greetings. No longer manager, hotel porter, and doctor, they became simply three men smiling, pleased to be seeing one another again after such a long time, not since early that morning, just imagine, and such nostalgia, dear God. When Ricardo Reis entered his room and observed how carefully it had been cleaned, the bedspread neatly arranged, the washbasin shining, the mirror spotless despite the dents it had collected over the years, he sighed with satisfaction. Changing his clothes and getting into slippers, he pulled open one of the bedroom windows, the gesture of someone who is glad to be home, then settled in the armchair. It was as if he had fallen into himself, a sudden violent fall inside. And now, he asked, And now, Ricardo Reis or whoever you are, as others might say. In an instant he understood that the real conclusion of his voyage was this precise moment, that the time which had elapsed since he set foot on the quay at Alcântara had been spent, so to speak, in the maneuvers of berthing and dropping anchor, probing the tide, throwing the cables, because this was what he'd been doing when he looked for a hotel, read those first newspapers, then visited the cemetery, lunched in the Baixa, strolled down to the Rua dos Douradores. That sudden longing for his room, the impulse of indiscriminate, universal affection, the welcome extended by Salvador and Pimenta, the immaculate bedspread, and finally the wide-open window, its net curtains fluttering like wings. And what now. The rain has started up again, making a noise on the rooftops like sand being sieved, numbing, hypnotic. Perhaps during the great flood God in His mercy put men to sleep in this way so death might be gentle, the water quietly penetrating their nostrils and mouths without suffocating them, rivulets gradually filling, cell after cell, the entire cavity of their bodies. After forty days and forty nights of sleep and rain, their bodies sank slowly to the bottom, at last heavier than water itself. Ophelia, too, allows herself to be swept away by the current, singing, but she will inevitably die before the end of act four. Each human being has his own way of sleeping and dying, but the flood continues, time rains on us, drowns us. On the waxed surface of the floor raindrops collected and spread, having entered through the open window or spluttered from the sill. Some careless guests give no thought to humble labor, perhaps believing that the bees not only make the wax but also spread it on the floorboards and rub it and buff it until it shines, but it is maids, not insects, who do this work, and without them these shining floors would be drab and grimy. The manager will soon rebuke and punish them, because that is a manager's job, and we are in this hotel for the greater honor and glory of God, whose deputy is Salvador. Ricardo Reis rushed to close the window, with the newspapers mopped up most of the water, and having no other means to finish the job properly he rang the bell. That's the first time I've used it, he thought, like someone begging his own pardon.

He heard steps in the corridor, knuckles tapped discreetly on the door. Come in, words of entreaty rather than command. When the maid opened the door, he said, scarcely bothering to look at her, The window was open, the rain came in, there was water all over the floor. Then he fell silent, realizing that he had produced doggerel, he, Ricardo Reis, the author of Sapphic and Alcaic odes. He almost continued in stupid anapests, Could you do me a favor and clean up this mess. But the maid, without verses, understood what had to be done. She went out and returned with a mop and bucket, and down on her knees, her body wriggling, did her vigorous best to remove the offending moisture. Tomorrow she will give the floor another coat of wax. Can I do anything else for you, Doctor. No, much obliged. They looked straight into each other's eyes. Beating heavily on the windowpanes, the rain's rhythm accelerated, ruffling like a great drum, causing those who were asleep to wake up in alarm. What is your name. Lydia, sir, she replied, then added, At your service, Doctor. She could have expressed it more formally, saying, for example, in a louder voice, I was instructed to do my utmost to please the doctor, for the manager said, Look here, Lydia, take good care of the guest in room two hundred and one, Doctor Reis. The doctor made no reply, he appeared to be whispering the name Lydia in case he should need to call her again. There are people who repeat the words they hear, because we are all like parrots repeating one another, nor is there any other way of learning. This reflection is inappropriate, perhaps, since it was not made by Lydia, who is the other interlocutor and already has a name, so let us allow her to leave, taking her mop and bucket with her. Ricardo Reis remains there smiling ironically, moving his lips in a way that deceives no one. Lydia, he repeats, and smiles, and smiling goes to the drawer to look for his poems, his Sapphic odes, and reads the verses which catch his eye as he turns the pages. *And so, Lydia, sitting by the hearth, Lydia, let the image be thus, Let us show no desire, Lydia, at this hour, When our autumn comes, Lydia, Come sit with me, Lydia, on the riverbank, Lydia, the most abject existence is preferable to death.* There is no longer any trace of irony in his smile, if the word *smile* is an apt description for those parted lips exposing his teeth, the facial muscles fixed into a sneer or pained expression, with which one might say, This, too, shall pass. Like his face reflected in a tremulous mirror of water, Ricardo Reis leans over the page and recomposes old verses. Soon he will be able to recognize himself, It is I, without irony, without sorrow, content to feel not even contentment, as a man who desires nothing more or knows that he can possess nothing more. The shadows in the room thicken, some black nimbus must be passing in the sky, a cloud black as lead, like those summoned for the deluge. The furniture suddenly falls asleep. Ricardo Reis makes a gesture with his hands, groping the colorless air, then, barely able to distinguish the words he traces on the paper, writes, *All I ask of the gods is that I should ask nothing of them.* Having written this, he does not know how to continue. There are such moments. We believe in the importance of what we have just said or written, if for no other reason than that it is impossible to take back the sounds or erase the marks, but the temptation to be silent pervades our body, the fascination of silence, to be silent and immobile like the gods, watching and nothing more. He moves over to the sofa, leans back, closes his eyes, feels that he could sleep, is already half asleep. From the closet he takes a blanket, wraps himself in it, now he will sleep, and dream that it is a sunny morning and he is strolling along the Rua do Ouvidor in Rio de Janeiro, not exerting himself, for it is very hot. In the distance he hears shooting, bombs, but does not awaken. This is not the first time that he has had this dream, nor does he hear the knocking at the door and a voice, a woman's voice asking, Did you call, Doctor.

Let us say that it was because he slept so little the previous night that he slept so soundly now. Let us say that they are fallacies of doubtful depth, these interchanging moments of enchantment and temptation, of immobility and silence. Let us say that this is no story about deities and that we might have confidentially told Ricardo Reis, before he dozed off like any ordinary human being, What you are suffering from is a lack of sleep. There is, however, a sheet of paper on the table and on it is written, *All I ask of the gods is that I should ask nothing of them*. This page exists, the words occur twice, each word by itself and then together, and when they are read together they convey a meaning, no matter whether there are gods or not, or whether the person who wrote them has fallen asleep or not. Perhaps things are not as simple as we were inclined to show them at first. When Ricardo Reis awakens, the room is plunged in darkness, the last glimmer dispersed on the clouded windowpanes, in the mesh of the curtains. An enclosing heavy drape blocks one of the windows. There is not a sound to be heard in the hotel, now transformed into the palace of the Sleeping Beauty, where Beauty has withdrawn or never was. Everyone is asleep, Salvador, Pimenta, the Galician waiters, the guests, the Renaissance page, even the clock on the landing has stopped. Suddenly the distant sound of the buzzer at the entrance can be heard, no doubt the prince is coming to wake Beauty with a kiss, he is late, poor fellow, *I came feeling so merry and left in despair, the lady gave me her promise then sent me away*, it's a nursery rhyme rescued from the depths of memory. Children shrouded in mist are playing at the bottom of a wintry garden, singing with high, sad voices, they move forward and backward at a solemn pace, unknowingly rehearsing the pavane for the dead infants they will join upon growing up. Ricardo Reis pushes away the blanket, scolds himself for having fallen asleep without first undressing. He has always observed the code of civilized behavior, the discipline it requires, not even sixteen years in the languors of the Tropic of Capricorn succeeded in blunting the sharp edge of his dress and his verse, so that he can claim in all honesty that he has always tried to conduct himself as if he were being observed by the gods themselves. Getting up from the armchair, he goes to switch on the light, and, as if it were morning and he were awakening from some nocturnal dream, he looks at himself in the mirror and strokes his face. He should shave before dinner, at least change his clothes, he must not go to dinner with his clothes all crumpled. He needn't bother. He has not noticed how carelessly the other residents are dressed, their jackets like sacks, trousers bulging at the knees, ties with a permanent knot which are slipped on and off over the head, shirts badly cut, wrinkles, creases, the signs of age. And long, pointed shoes so that one has room to wiggle one's toes, although the result is otherwise, for in no other city in the world do calluses, corns, bunions, and growths, not to mention ingrown toenails, flourish in such abundance, an enigma for any podiatrist and one that requires closer study, which we leave to you. He decides not to shave after all, but puts on a clean shirt, chooses a tie to match his suit, combs his hair in the mirror, and parts it carefully. Although it is not yet time for dinner, he decides to go down, but before leaving, and without touching the sheet of paper, takes another look at what he wrote, looks with a certain impatience, as if finding a message left by one whom he dislikes or who once annoyed him beyond the bounds of tolerance and forgiveness. This Ricardo Reis is not the poet, but simply a hotel guest who, ready to leave his room, discovers a sheet of paper with one and a half stanzas written on it. Who could have left it here. Surely not the maid, not Lydia, this Lydia or any other, how aggravating. It never occurs to people that the one who finishes something is never the one who started it, even if both have the same name, for the name is the only thing that remains constant.

The manager Salvador was at his post, stationary, beaming his perennial smile. Ricardo Reis greeted him and walked on, but Salvador pursued him, wanting to know if the doctor would like to have a drink before dinner, an apéritif. No, thank you, this was another habit Ricardo Reis had not acquired, perhaps in years to come, first the taste, then the need, but not just yet. Salvador lingered for a moment in the doorway to see if the guest might change his mind or make some other request, but Ricardo Reis had already opened one of the newspapers. That entire day he had spent in ignorance of what was happening in the world. Not that he was an assiduous reader by nature, on the contrary, he found those large pages and verbose articles tiresome, but here, having nothing better to do and in order to avoid being fussed over by Salvador, he made the paper with all its news from abroad serve as a shield against this more immediate and encroaching world. The news of the distant world can be read as insignificant dispatches whose use and destination are questionable. The Spanish Government has resigned, the dissolution of Parliament has been decreed, says one headline. The Negus, in a telegram to the League of Nations, claims that the Italians are using asphyxiating gases. How typical of newspapers, all they can talk about is what has already happened and nearly always when it is much too late to rectify mistakes, prevent shortages, or avert disasters. A worthwhile paper should tell you, on the first day of January in the year nineteen fourteen, that war will break out on the twenty-fourth of July, then we would have almost seven months at our disposal to ward off the threat. Perhaps that would be enough time. Better still if a list were published of those about to die. The millions of men and women who, as they drink their morning coffee, come upon the announcement of their own deaths, their destinies sealed and shortly to be fulfilled, the day, hour, and place, their names printed in full. What would they have done, what would Fernando Pessoa have done if he had read two months beforehand, The author of *Mensagem* will die on the thirtieth of next November from hepatitis. Perhaps he would have consulted a doctor and stopped drinking, or else he would have started drinking twice as much in order to die sooner. Ricardo Reis lowers the newspaper to look at himself in the mirror, a reflection that is twice deceiving because it shows a deep space then shows that the space is a mere surface where nothing actually happens, only the illusion, external and silent, of persons and things, a tree overhanging a lake, a face seeking itself, a face undisturbed, unaltered, not even touched, by the images of tree and lake and face. The mirror, this one and all others, is independent of man. Before it we are like a conscript departing for the nineteen-fourteen war. Admiring his uniform in the mirror, he sees something more than himself, not knowing that he will never see himself again in this mirror. We are vanity and cannot endure, but the mirror endures, the same, because it rejects us. Ricardo Reis averts his eyes, changes position, leaves, he the one rejecting, turning his back on the mirror. Perhaps, then, he too is a mirror.

The clock on the landing struck eight, and the last echo had scarcely died away when an invisible gong rang out in muted tones. It can only be heard in the immediate vicinity, the guests on the upper floors certainly cannot hear it. But one must bear in mind the weight of tradition, it is not just a matter of pretending that wine bottles are encased in wickerwork when wicker is no longer available. Ricardo Reis folds the newspaper, goes to his room to wash his hands and tidy up. Returning immediately, he sits at the table where he has eaten from his very first day here and waits. Anyone watching him, following those rapid footsteps, would think that he must be either famished or in a great hurry, had an early lunch and eaten little or else bought a ticket for the theater. But we know otherwise, he didn't have an early lunch, we also know that he is not going to the theater or the cinema, and in weather such as this, becoming steadily worse, only a fool or an eccentric would dream of going for a walk. Why, then, the sudden haste, if people are only just arriving for dinner, the thin man in mourning, the placid fat man with the excellent digestion, those others whom I did not see last night. The mute children and their parents are missing, perhaps they were only passing through. As of tomorrow I shall not enter the dining room before half past eight. Here I am as ridiculous as any bumpkin newly arrived in the city and staying for the first time in a hotel. He ate his soup slowly, idly playing with his spoon, then toyed with the fish on his plate, pecked at it, not feeling the least bit hungry. As the waiter was serving the main course, the maître d' guided three men to the table where, the evening before, the girl with the paralyzed hand and her father had dined. So she won't be coming, they've left, he thought, or are dining out. Only then did he admit what he already knew but had pretended not to, that he had really come down early to see the girl whose left hand is paralyzed and who strokes it as if it were a little lap dog, even though it does nothing for her, or perhaps for that reason. Why. The question is a pretense, in the first place because certain questions are posed simply to call attention to the absence of any reply, in the second place because there is something both true and false about the possibility that his interest does not require any deeper explanation. He cut short his dinner and ordered coffee and a brandy. He would wait in the lounge, one way of killing time until he could ask the manager Salvador who those people were. That father and daughter, you know I believe I've seen them before, elsewhere, perhaps in Rio de Janeiro, certainly not in Portugal, that is obvious because sixteen years ago the girl would have been a mere child. Ricardo Reis spins and weaves this web of overtures, so much inquiring to discover so little. Meanwhile Salvador is attending to other guests, one who is leaving early tomorrow morning and wishes to settle his bill, another who complains that he cannot sleep when the window shade starts banging. Salvador attends to all the guests with tact and solicitude, with his discolored teeth and smooth mustache. The thin man dressed in mourning came into the lounge to consult a newspaper and left almost immediately. The fat man appeared at the door biting a toothpick, hesitated when confronted with a blank stare from Ricardo Reis, then quickly withdrew, his shoulders drooping from lack of courage. Some retreats are like this, moments of extreme moral weakness which are difficult to explain, especially to oneself.

Half an hour later the affable Salvador is able to inform him, No, you must have mistaken them for someone else, as far as I know they have never visited Brazil, they've been coming here for the last three years, we have often chatted and they would almost certainly have told me about such a voyage. Ah, so I was mistaken, but you say they have been coming here for the last three years. That's right, they are from Coimbra, they live there, the father is Doctor Sampaio, a lawyer. And the girl. She has an unusual name, she is called Marcenda, would you believe it, but they belong to an aristocratic family, the mother died some years ago. What is wrong with her hand. I believe her whole arm is paralyzed, that's why they come to stay here in the hotel for three days every month, so that she can be examined by a specialist. Ah, every month for three days. Yes, three days every month, Doctor Sampaio always warns me in advance so that I can keep the same two rooms free. Has there been any improvement during the last three years. If you want my frank opinion, Doctor, I don't think so. What a pity, the girl is so young. That's true, Doctor, perhaps you could offer them some advice next time, if you are still here. It's most likely I shall be here, but in any event I am not specialized in that field, I practice general medicine, I did some research into tropical diseases but nothing that would be helpful in a case like hers. Never mind, but it's very true that money doesn't bring happiness, the father so rich and the daughter a cripple, no one has ever seen her smile. You say she's called Marcenda. Yes, sir. A strange name, I've never come across it before. Nor I. Until tomorrow, Senhor Salvador, Until tomorrow, Doctor.

Upon entering his room, Ricardo Reis sees that the bed has been prepared, the bedspread and sheet neatly tucked back at an angle, discreetly, not that unsightly clutter of bedclothes tossed aside every which way. Here there is merely a suggestion, should he wish to lie down, his bed is ready. Not just yet, first he must read the one and a half stanzas he left on the sheet of paper, examine them critically, look for the door that this key, if key it is, can open, and imagine other doors beyond, doors locked and without a key. In the end, after much persistence he found something, it had been left there out of weariness, his or someone else's, but whose, and so the poem ended, *Neither tranquil nor troubled, I wish to lift my being high above this place where men know pleasure and pain*, the pause in the middle, the spondee, should be changed. Good fortune is a burden that oppresses the happy man, because it is no more than a particular state of mind. He then went to bed and fell asleep at once.

Ricardo Reis had told the manager, I would like breakfast brought up to my room at nine-thirty. Not that he intended to sleep so late, but he wished to avoid having to jump out of bed half-awake, struggling to slip his arms into the sleeves of his dressing gown, groping for his slippers, and feeling panic that he wasn't moving quickly enough to satisfy whoever was standing outside his door, arms laden with a huge tray bearing coffee and milk, toast, a sugar bowl, perhaps some cherry preserve or marmalade, a slice of dark grainy quince paste, a sponge cake, brioches with a fine crust, crunchy biscuits, or slices of French toast, those scrumptious luxuries served in hotels. We shall soon learn if the Bragança goes in for such extravagance, because Ricardo Reis is about to sample his first breakfast. It would be nine-thirty on the dot, Salvador promised him, and did not promise in vain, for here at nine-thirty on the dot Lydia is knocking on the door. The observant reader will say that this is impossible, she has both her arms occupied, but we would be in a sorry state if we had to hire only servants who possess three arms or more. This maid, without spilling a drop of milk, manages to knock gently with her knuckles, while the hand belonging to those knuckles continues to support the tray. One must see this to believe it, as she calls out, Your breakfast, Doctor, which is what she was instructed to say, and although a woman of humble origins, she has not forgotten her instructions. If Lydia were not a maid, there is every indication that she would make an excellent tightrope walker, juggler, or magician, for she has talent enough for any of those professions. What is incongruous about her is that, being a maid, she should be called Lydia and not Maria. Ricardo Reis is already dressed and presentable, he has shaved and his dressing gown is tied at the waist. He even left the window ajar to air the room, for he detests nocturnal odors, those exhalations of the body from which not even poets are exempt. The maid finally entered, Good morning, Doctor, and proceeded to put down the tray, less lavish in its offerings than he had imagined. Nevertheless, the Bragança deserves an honorable mention, and it is no wonder that some of its guests would never dream of staying at any other hotel when they visit Lisbon. Ricardo Reis returns the greeting, then dismisses her, No, many thanks, that will be all, the standard reply to the question every good maid asks, Can I get you anything else, sir. If the answer is no, she must withdraw politely, backing away if at all possible, for to turn your back would be to show disrespect to one who pays your wages and gives you a living. But Lydia, who has been instructed to be especially attentive to the doctor's needs, goes on to say, I don't know if you have noticed, Doctor, but the Cais do Sodré is under water. Trust a man not to notice, the water could be forcing its way under his door and he wouldn't see it, having slept soundly all night. He woke up as if he had only been dreaming about the rain. And even in a dream he would not dream that there has been so much rain that the Cais do Sodré is flooded. The water comes up to the knees of a man who finds himself obliged to cross from one side to the other, barefoot, his clothes hitched up, carrying an elderly woman on his back through the flood, she much lighter than the sack of beans carried from the cart to the warehouse. Here at the bottom of the Rua do Alecrim the old woman opens her purse and finds a coin, with which she pays Saint Christopher, who has already gone paddling back into the water, for on the other side there is already someone else making frantic gestures. The second person is young and sturdy enough to cross on his own, but, being smartly dressed, he has no desire to get his clothes dirty, for this water is more like mud than water. If only he could see how silly he looks riding piggyback with his clothes all crumpled, his shins exposed, revealing green garters over white long underwear. Some are laughing now at the spectacle, in the Hotel Bragança, on the second floor, a middle-aged guest is grinning, and behind him, unless our eyes are deceiving us, stands a woman also grinning, yes, a woman, without a shadow of doubt, but our eyes do not always see right, because this one appears to be a maid. It is hard to believe that that is really her station, unless there has been some dangerous subversion of social class and ranking, a thing greatly to be feared, we hasten to add, yet there are occasions, and if it is true that occasion can turn a man into a thief, it can also cause a revolution such as the one we are witnessing. Lydia, daring to look out of the window, stands behind Ricardo Reis and laughs, as if she were his equal, at a scene they both find amusing. These are fleeting moments of a golden age, born suddenly and dying at once, which explains why happiness soon grows weary. The moment has already passed, Ricardo Reis has closed the window, Lydia, once more simply a maid, backs toward the door. Everything must now be done in haste because the slices of toast are getting cold and no longer look quite so appetizing. I shall ring for you to come and remove the tray, Ricardo Reis tells her, and this happens about half an hour later. Lydia quietly enters and quietly withdraws, her burden not as heavy, while Ricardo Reis pretends to be absorbed as he sits in his room leafing through the pages of *The God of the Labyrinth* without actually reading.

Today is the last day of the year. Throughout the world where this calendar is observed, people amuse themselves by weighing the resolutions they intend to put into practice during the incoming year. They swear that they will be honest, just, and forbearing, that their reformed lips will utter no more words of abuse, deceit, or malice, however much their enemies may deserve them. Clearly we are speaking about the common people. The others, uncommon and superior, have their own good reasons for being and doing quite the opposite whenever it suits or profits them, they do not allow themselves to be deceived, and laugh at us and our so-called good intentions. In the end we learn from experience, no sooner is January upon us than we forget half of what we promised, and then there is little point in trying to carry out the rest. It is rather like a castle made of cards, better for the upper part to be missing than have the whole thing collapse and the four suits mixed up. This is why it is questionable whether Christ departed from life with the words we find in the Holy Scriptures, those of Matthew and Mark, My God, my God, why hast Thou forsaken me, or those of Luke, Father, into Thine hand I commit my spirit, or those of John, It is fulfilled. What Christ really said, word of honor, as any man on the street will tell you, was, Good-bye, world, you're going from bad to worse. But the gods of Ricardo Reis are silent entities who look upon us with indifference and for whom good and evil are less than words, because they never utter them, and why should they, if they cannot even tell them apart. They journey like us in the river of things, differing from us only because we call them gods and sometimes believe in them. We were taught this lesson lest we wear ourselves out making new and better resolutions for the incoming year. Nor do the gods judge, knowing everything, but this may be false. The ultimate truth, perhaps, is that they know nothing, their only task being precisely to forget at each moment the good as well as the evil. So let us not say, Tomorrow I shall do it, for it is almost certain that tomorrow we will feel tired. Let us say instead, The day after tomorrow, then we will always have a day in reserve to change our mind and make new resolutions. It would be even more prudent, however, to say, One day, when the day comes to say the day after tomorrow, I shall say it, but even that might not prove necessary, if definitive death comes first and releases me from the obligation, for obligation is the worst thing in the world, the freedom we deny ourselves.

It has stopped raining, the sky has cleared, and Ricardo Reis can take a stroll before lunch without any risk of getting soaked. He decides to avoid the lower part of the city because the flood has still not subsided completely in the Cais do Sodré, its paving stones covered with fetid mud which the current of the river has lifted from deep and viscous layers of silt. If this weather persists, the men from the cleaning department will come out with their hoses. The water has polluted, the water will clean, blessed be the water. Ricardo Reis walks up the Rua do Alecrim, and no sooner has he left the hotel than he is stopped in his tracks by a relic of another age, perhaps a Corinthian capital, a votive altar, or funereal headstone, what an idea. Such things, if they still exist in Lisbon, are hidden under the soil that was moved when the ground was leveled, or by other natural causes. This is only a rectangular slab of stone embedded in a low wall facing the Rua Nova do Carvalho and bearing the following inscription in ornamental lettering, *Eye Clinic and Surgery*, and somewhat more austerely, *Founded by A. Mascaró in 1870*. Stones have a long life. We do not witness their birth, nor will we see their death. So many years have passed over this stone, so many more have yet to pass, Mascaró died and his clinic was closed down, perhaps descendants of the founder can still be traced, they pursuing other professions, ignoring or unaware that their family emblem is on display in this public place. If only families were not so fickle, then this one would gather here to honor the memory of their ancestor, the healer of eyes and other disorders. Truly it is not enough to engrave a name on a stone. The stone remains, gentlemen, safe and sound, but the name, unless people come to read it every day, fades, is forgotten, ceases to exist. These contradictions walk through the mind of Ricardo Reis as he walks up the Rua do Alecrim, where tiny rivulets of water still course along the tram tracks. The world cannot be still, the wind is blowing, the clouds soaring, don't let us talk about the rain, there has been so much of it. Ricardo Reis stops before a statue of Eça de Queirós, or Queiroz, out of respect for the orthography used by the owner of that name, so many different styles of writing, and the name is the least of it, what is surprising is that these two, one called Reis, the other Eça, should speak the same language. Perhaps it is the language that chooses the writers it needs, making use of them so that each might express a tiny part of what it is. Once language has said all it has to say and falls silent, I wonder how we will go on living. Problems already begin to appear, perhaps they are not problems as yet, rather different layers of meaning, displaced sediments, new questioning formulations, take for example the phrase, *Over the great nakedness of truth, the diaphanous cloak of imagination*. It seems clear, compact, and conclusive, a child would be able to understand and repeat it in an examination without making any mistakes, but the same child might recite with equal conviction a different phrase, *Over the great nakedness of imagination, the diaphanous cloak of truth*, which certainly gives one more to ponder, more to visualize with pleasure, the imagination solid and naked, the truth a gauzy covering. If our maxims are reversed and become laws, what world will be created by them. It is a miracle that men do not lose their sanity each time they open their mouths to speak. The stroll is instructive, a moment ago we were contemplating Eça, now we can observe Camões. They forgot to put any verses on his pedestal. Had they done so, what would they have put, *Here with deep sorrow, with mournful song.* Better to leave the poor, tormented creature and climb what remains of the street, the Rua da Misericórdia formerly the Rua do Mundo, unfortunately one cannot have it both ways, it has to be either Mundo or Misericórdia. Here is the old Largo de São Roque, and the church dedicated to that saint, whose festering wounds caused by plague were licked by a dog. The plague was almost certainly bubonic, the animal hardly of the same breed as the bitch Ugolina that knows only how to tear and devour. Inside this famous church you will find the chapel of São João Baptista, its decorations entrusted to Italian artists by Dom João V, king, mason, and architect par excellence, who won such renown during his reign. Take a look at the convent of Mafra and also the aqueduct of Águas Livres, of which the full history has yet to be written. Here too, on the diagonal of the two kiosks that sell tobacco, lottery tickets, and spirits, stands the monument in marble erected by the Italian colony to commemorate the marriage of King Dom Luís, the translator of Shakespeare, and Dona Maria Pia di Savōia, the daughter of Verdi, that is to say, of Vittorio Emmanuele, King of Italy, the only monument in the entire city of Lisbon which resembles a chastising rod or carpet beater with its five eyelets. At least that is what it suggests to the little girls from the orphanages, with their startled eyes, or if blind, they are so informed by their seeing companions, who from time to time pass this way dressed in little smocks and walking in formation, getting rid of the stench of the dormitory, their hands still smarting from the latest caning. This is a traditional neighborhood, exalted in name and location, but low in its way of life, for the laurel branches on the doors of the taverns alternate with women of easy virtue, although, because it is still morning and the roads have been washed by the recent rain, you can sense a freshness, an innocence in the air, an almost virginal breeze. Who would have thought this possible in such a disreputable place, but the canaries affirm it with their song, their cages hanging out on the balconies or at the entrances to the taverns, they warble as if demented. One has to take advantage of the fine weather, especially when it is not expected to last, for once the rain starts up again their singing will die away, their feathers will ruffle. One little bird, more prescient than the others, buries its head under its wing and pretends to be asleep, its mistress is coming to fetch it indoors, and now only rain can be heard, also the strumming of a guitar nearby, where it is coming from Ricardo Reis cannot tell. He has taken shelter in this doorway at the beginning of the Travessa da Água da Flor. It's often said that the sun is here then gone again, the clouds that let it through cover it quickly, but showers, too, come and go, the rain pours down, passes, the eaves and verandahs trickle water, the wash on the clotheslines is dripping, then a cloudburst so sudden there is no time for the women to do anything, to shout, as is their wont, It's raiiiiining, passing the word from one to another like soldiers in their sentry boxes at night. But the canary's mistress is on the alert and manages, in the nick of time, to retrieve it. Just as well that its frail little body has been protected, see how its heart is beating, Jesus, such violence, such speed. Was it the fright, no, it is always like this, a heart that lives for a short time beats fast, in compensation. Ricardo Reis crosses the park to take a look at the city, the castle with its walls in ruins, the terraced houses collapsing along the slopes, the whitish sun beating on the wet rooftops. Silence descends on the city, every sound is muffled, Lisbon seems made of absorbent cotton, soaked, dripping. Below, on a platform, are several busts of gallant patriots, some box shrubs, a few Roman heads out of place, so remote from the skies of Latium, as if one of Rafael Bordalo Pinheiro's native rustics had been set up to make a rude gesture to the Apollo Belvedere. The entire terrace is a belvedere as we contemplate Apollo, then a voice joins the guitar and they sing a fado. The rain appears to have finally disappeared.

When one idea is drawn from another, we say that there has

been an association. Some are even of the opinion that the whole human mental process derives from this succession of stimuli, sometimes unconscious, sometimes only pretending to be unconscious, which achieves original combinations, new relationships of thoughts interlinked by the species and together forming what might be called a commerce, an industry of ideas, because man, apart from all the other things he is, has been, or will be, performs an industrial and commercial function, first as producer, then as retailer, and finally as consumer, but even this order can be shuffled and rearranged. I am speaking only of ideas and nothing else. So, then, we can consider ideas as corporate entities, independent or in partnership, perhaps publicly held, but never with limited liability, never anonymous, for a name is something we all possess. The logical connection between this economic theory and the stroll Ricardo Reis is taking, which we already know to be instructive, will become apparent when he arrives at the entrance of the former convent of São Pedro de Alcântara, nowadays a refuge for little girls pedagogically chastised with the rod. In the vestibule he comes face to face with the tiled mural depicting Saint Francis of Assisi, *il poverello*, freely translated as poor devil, kneeling in ecstasy and receiving the stigmata, which in this symbolic representation reach him by means of five cords of blood that descend from on high, from Christ crucified, who hovers in the heavens like a star, or like a kite launched by urchins in the open countryside where there is no lack of space and where people still remember a time when men could be seen flying. With his hands and feet bleeding, his side a gaping wound, Saint Francis holds on to Christ's cross to prevent Him from disappearing into the cloistered heights. There the Father calls to His Son, Come, come, your time for being a man is at an end. That is why we see Saint Francis twitching in saintly fashion as he struggles to hold on, as he murmurs what some believe to be a prayer, I won't let you go, I won't let you go. From these events, which are only now being revealed, you can see just how urgent it is to dismiss orthodox theology and forge a new theology totally opposed to traditional beliefs. Here is an association of ideas for you, then, to illustrate, because first there were Roman heads on the terrace, which was a belvedere, then Ricardo Reis remembered the obscene gesture of the Portuguese rustic, and now, at the entrance to an old convent in Lisbon, not in Wittenberg, he discovers how and why the common people call that gesture the heraldic arms of Saint Francis, for it is the gesture the desperate saint makes to God when He tries to take away his star. There will be no lack of skeptics and conservatives who reject this hypothesis, but that need not surprise us, it is, after all, what always happens to new ideas, ideas born by association.

Ricardo Reis searches his memory for fragments of poems composed some twenty years ago, how time flies, *Unhappy God, essential to all, perhaps because He is unique. It is not you, Christ, whom I despise, but do not usurp what belongs to others. Through the gods we men stand united.* These are the words he mutters to himself as he walks along the Rua de Dom Pedro V as if looking for fossils or the ruins of an ancient civilization, and for a moment he wonders whether there is any meaning left in the odes from which he has taken these random lines, lines still coherent but weakened by the absence of what comes before and what follows, paradoxically assuming, by that absence, another meaning, one obscure and authoritative, like that of an epigraph to a book. He asks himself if it is possible to define a unity that joins, like a fastener or clip, two things opposed, divergent, such as that saint who went healthy to the mountain and returned oozing blood from five wounds. If only he had succeeded, at the end of the day, in winding up those cords and returning home, weary as any laborer after his toil, carrying under his arm the kite he was able to retrieve only by the skin of his teeth. It would rest by his pillow while he slept. Today he has won, but who can tell if he will win tomorrow. Trying to join these opposites is probably as absurd as trying to empty the sea with a bucket, not because that is so enormous a task, even if one has the time and energy, but because one would first have to find somewhere on land another great cavity for the sea, and this is impossible. There is so much sea, so little land.

Ricardo Reis is also absorbed by the question he posed himself upon arriving at the Praça do Rio de Janeiro, once known as the Praça do Príncipe Real and which one day may go back to that name, should anyone live to see it. When the weather becomes hot, one longs for the shade of these silver maples, elms, the Roman pine which looks like a refreshing pergola. Not that this poet and doctor is so well versed in botany, but someone must make up for the ignorance and lapses of memory of a man who for the last sixteen years has grown accustomed to the vastly different and more baroque flora and fauna of the tropics. This is not, however, the season for summer pursuits, for the delights of beach and spa, today's temperature must be around ten degrees Centigrade and the park benches are wet. Ricardo Reis pulls his raincoat snugly around his body, shivering, he goes back by other avenues, now descending the Rua do Século, unable to say what made him decide on this route, this street so deserted and melancholy. A few grand residences remain alongside the squat, narrow houses built for the poorer classes, at least the nobility in former days were not all that discriminating, they lived side by side with the common folk. God help us, the way things are going we will see the return of exclusive neighborhoods, nothing but private residences for the barons of industry and commerce, who very soon will swallow up whatever is left of the aristocracy, residences with private garages, gardens in proportion to the size of the property, dogs that bark ferociously. Even among the dogs one notices the difference. In the distant past they attacked both rich and poor.

Showing no haste, Ricardo Reis proceeds down the street, his umbrella serving as a walking stick. He taps the paving stones as he goes, beating time with every other step, the sound precise, distinct, sharp. There is no echo, yet the impact is almost liquid, if the term is not absurd, let us say that it is liquid, for so it seems as the tip of the umbrella strikes the limestone. He is absorbed by these puerile thoughts when suddenly he becomes aware of his own footsteps, almost as if, since leaving the hotel, he has not met a living soul. He would swear to that if called upon to testify, I saw no one on my walk. How is that possible, my good man, in a city one could scarcely regard as being small, where did all the people disappear to. He knows, of course, because common sense, the only repository of knowledge which common sense itself assures us is irrefutable, tells him so, that this cannot be true, he must have passed a number of people along the route, and now in this street, for all its tranquillity, there are groups of people, all walking downhill. They are poor people, some almost beggars, entire families with the elderly walking behind, dragging their feet, with sunken hearts, and the children are tugged along by their mothers, who shout, Hurry up, or everything will be gone. What has gone is peace and quiet, the street is no longer the same. As for the men, they try to adopt the severe expression one expects of the head of a family, they walk at their own pace, like someone who has another goal in sight. Together the families disappear. On the next street corner is a stately residence with palm trees in the courtyard, reminding one of *Arabia Felix*. Its medieval features have lost none of their charm, concealing surprises on the other side, not like these modern urban arteries designed in straight lines with everything in sight, as if sight can be so easily satisfied. Ricardo Reis is confronted by a dense multitude crowding the entire width of the road, patient and restless at the same time, heads bobbing like the playing of waves, like a cornfield ruffled by the breeze. Ricardo Reis draws close, asks to be allowed to pass. The person in front of him makes a gesture of refusal, turns to him and is on the point of saying, If you're in a hurry, you should have got here sooner, but comes face to face with a smart gentleman wearing neither beret nor cap, dressed in a light raincoat, white shirt and tie. That is all that is needed to persuade the man to step aside and, as if this were not enough, to tap the shoulder of the man in front, Let this gentleman pass. The other follows suit, which is why we can see the gray hat worn by Ricardo Reis advancing as smoothly amid this human mass as the swan of Lohengrin over the becalmed waters of the Black Sea. His crossing, however, takes time, for the crowd is vast. Besides, as one draws nearer the center, it becomes increasingly difficult to persuade people to let one through, not because of any sudden ill will but simply because no one can move in the crush. What is going on, Ricardo Reis asks himself, but does not dare ask the question aloud, reasoning that where so many have gathered for a purpose known to all, it would be wrong, improper, indelicate, to show one's ignorance. People might take offense, for how can we be certain of the feelings of others when we are often surprised by our own. Ricardo Reis is halfway down the street, standing before the entrance of the large building occupied by *O Século*, the country's leading newspaper. The crowd is less dense in the crescent fronting the building, and only now does Ricardo Reis become aware that he has been holding his breath to avoid the stench of overcooked onion, garlic, of sweat, of clothes that are scarcely ever changed, of bodies that are never washed unless they are going to be examined by a doctor. Olfactory organs in any way squeamish would find this journey a tribulation. Two policemen are posted at the entrance, close by are another two. Ricardo Reis is about to ask one of them, What is this gathering, officer, when the representative of law and order informs him respectfully, for one can tell at a glance that the gentleman making the inquiry is here by accident, It's the charity day organized by *O Século*. But there is such a crowd. Yes sir, they reckon that there are over a thousand here. Are all of them poor. All of them, sir, poor people from the back streets and slums. So many. Yes sir, and they are not all here. Of course, but all these people gathered to receive charity, it is a disturbing sight. It doesn't disturb me, sir, I'm used to it. And what are they given. Each pauper gets ten escudos. Ten escudos. That's right, ten escudos, and the children are given clothing, toys, and books. To help educate them. Yes sir, to help educate them. Ten escudos won't go very far. It's better than nothing, sir. Too true. Some of them spend the whole year just waiting for this distribution of charity, for this one and others, and there are even some who spend all their time running from charity event to charity event, grabbing what they can get, the trouble starts when they turn up in places where they are unknown, in other districts, other parishes, the poor who belong there chase them out, each pauper keeps a sharp eye on the other paupers. A sad business. It may be sad, sir, but otherwise there would be no controlling them. Thank you for the information, officer. At your service, sir, pass this way, sir. With these words the policeman took three steps forward, his arms outspread like someone shooing chickens toward the coop, All right now, move on quietly, unless you want to see me wielding my saber. With these persuasive remarks the crowd moves on, the women protesting as usual, the men acting as if they have heard nothing, the children thinking about the toys they will receive, perhaps a little car, perhaps a cycle, perhaps a celluloid doll, for these they would gladly exchange their sweaters and readers. Ricardo Reis climbed the slope of the Calçada dos Caetanos, from where he had a bird's-eye view and could estimate the size of the crowd. More than a thousand, the policeman was right, a country well endowed with paupers. Let us pray that charity will never dry up for this mob in shawls, kerchiefs, patched shirts, cheap cotton pants with the seats mended in a different material, some people in sandals, many barefoot. Despite the various colors, they form, massed together, a dark smudge, a black, fetid mud like that in the Cais do Sodré. They wait, and will continue to wait until their turn comes, hours and hours on their feet, some since dawn, mothers holding children in their arms, breast-feeding newborn infants, fathers conversing among themselves on topics that interest men, the aged taciturn and glum, shaky on their legs, drooling at the mouth. The day on which alms are distributed is the only day their families do not wish them dead, for that would mean fewer escudos. And there are plenty of people with fever, coughing their heads off, passing a few small bottles of liquor to help pass the time and ward off the cold. If the rain starts up again, they will get soaked, because there is no shelter here.

Ricardo Reis crossed the Bairro Alto, descending by the Rua do Norte, and when he reached the Rua de Camões he felt as if he were trapped in a labyrinth that always led him back to the same spot, to this bronze statue ennobled and armed with a sword, another D'Artagnan. Decorated with a crown of laurels for having rescued the queen's diamonds at the eleventh hour from the machinations of the cardinal, whom, however, with a change of times and politics he will end up serving, this musketeer standing here, who is dead and cannot reenlist, ought to be told that he is used, in turn or at random, by heads of state and even by cardinals, when it serves their interests. The hours have passed quickly during these explorations on foot, and it is time for lunch. This man appears to have nothing else to do, he sleeps, eats, strolls, and composes poetry line by line with much effort, agonizing over rhyme and meter. It is nothing compared to the endless dueling of the musketeer D'Artagnan, and the Lusiads run to more than eight thousand lines, yet

Ricardo Reis too is a poet, not that he boasts of that on the hotel register, but one day people will remember him not as a doctor, just as they do not think of Álvaro de Campos as a naval engineer, or of Fernando Pessoa as a foreign correspondent. Our profession may earn us our living but not fame, which is more likely to come from having once written *Nel mezzo del cammin di nostra vita* or *Menina e moça me levaram da casa de meus pais* or *En un lugar de la Mancha*, of which I do not wish to remember the name, so as not to fall once again into the temptation of saying, however appropriately, *As armas e os barões assinalados*, may we be forgiven these borrowings, *Arma virumque cano*. Man must always make an effort, so that he may deserve to be called man, but he is much less master of his own person and destiny than he imagines. Time, not his time, will make him prosper or decline, sometimes for different merits, or because they are judged differently. What will you be when you discover it is night and you find yourself at the end of the road.

It was almost nightfall before the Rua do Século was clear of paupers. Ricardo Reis had lunched in the meantime, browsed in two bookshops, lingered at the door of the Tivoli debating whether or not he wanted to see the film *I Love All Women* starring Jan Kiepura. In the end, he decided to see the film some other time and return to the hotel by taxi, because his legs were giving him trouble after all that walking. When it started raining, he retreated to a nearby café, read the evening newspapers, agreed to have his shoes shined, clearly a waste of polish on streets like these, where a shower can cause a flood without any warning, but the bootblack insisted that an ounce of prevention was better than a pound of cure, A shoe when it's polished keeps out the rain, sir, and the man was right, because when Ricardo Reis removed his shoes once back in his room, his feet were warm and dry. Just what one needs to keep healthy, warm feet and a cool head. Universities may not recognize this wisdom based on experience, but one has nothing to lose by observing the precept. The hotel is so peaceful, no banging doors, no sounds of voices, the buzzer silent. Salvador is not at the reception desk, most unusual, and Pimenta, who went to look for the key, moves as swiftly and ethereally as a sprite. Obviously he has not had to carry any luggage since early that morning, lucky for him. When Ricardo Reis went down to dinner, it was almost nine o'clock, the dining room, just as he had intended, was empty, the waiters chatting in a corner, but when Salvador appeared, the staff busied themselves, for that is what we must always do when our immediate superior suddenly enters. It is enough, for example, to shift our weight to the right leg if before it was resting on the left, that's all that's required, sometimes even less. Are you serving dinner, the guest asked hesitantly. But of course, that was what they were there for. Salvador told the good doctor that on New Year's Eve they generally had few customers, and the few they had generally dined out, the traditional *réveillon* or *révelion*, what was the word. Once, they used to celebrate the festivities in the hotel, but the owners found it a costly business, the practice was discontinued, such a lot of work involved, not to mention the damage caused by the boisterousness of the guests, you know how things happen, one drink follows another, people start quarreling, and then all the noise, bedlam, and the complaints of those in no mood for merrymaking, because there are always such people. We finally stopped having the *révelion*, but I must confess I'm sorry, it was such a jolly occasion and the hotel enjoyed the reputation of having class and moving with the times. Now, as you can see, it's completely deserted. Well, at least you can get to bed early, Ricardo Reis consoled him, but Salvador assured him that he always waited up to hear the bells ring in the New Year at midnight, a family tradition. They always ate twelve raisins, one for each chime, to bring luck during the next year, a popular custom widely observed abroad. You're talking about rich countries, but do you really believe such a custom will bring you good fortune. I do not know, but perhaps my year would have been even worse had I not eaten those raisins. It is with such arguments that the man who has no God seeks gods, while he who has abandoned his gods invents God. One day we shall rid ourselves of both God and gods.

Ricardo Reis dined with a single waiter in attendance, the maître d' decorously positioned at the end of the dining room, and Salvador installed himself behind the reception desk to while away the hours until it was time for his *révelion intime*. Nothing is known of Pimenta's whereabouts, and as for the chambermaids, either they have disappeared upstairs into the attics, if there are attics, where they will toast one another's health on the stroke of midnight with intoxicating homemade liquors served with biscuits, or else they have gone home, leaving an emergency staff, as in hospitals. The kitchen already looks like an abandoned fortress. But this is mere speculation, guests are generally not interested in knowing how a hotel functions behind the scenes, all they want is a comfortable room and meals at regular intervals. For dessert Ricardo Reis did not expect to be served a large slice of cake specially baked for the festivities of Epiphany or Dia de Reis. These are thoughtful little courtesies which make a friend of every customer. The waiter smiled and quipped, Dia de Reis, you pay, Doctor. Agreed, Ramón, for that was the waiter's name, I'll pay on the Dia dos Reis, but the pun was lost on Ramón. It is still not ten o'clock, time is dragging, the old year lingers on. Ricardo Reis looks at the table where two days before he watched Doctor Sampaio and his daughter Marcenda and felt himself being enshrouded by a gray cloud. If they were present now, they might converse together, the only guests on this night which marks an ending and a new beginning, what could be more appropriate. He visualizes again the girl's pitiful gesture as she took hold of her lifeless hand and placed it on the table, that tiny hand she so dearly cherished while the other, strong and healthy, helped its sister but had its own, independent existence. It could not always assist. For example, shaking the hand of others when formally introduced, Marcenda Sampaio, Ricardo Reis, the doctor's hand would grip that of the girl from Coimbra, right hand with right hand, but while his left hand, should it so desire, could hover close to witness the encounter, hers, dangling at her side, might just as well not be present. Ricardo Reis feels the tears come to his eyes. There are still some people who speak ill of doctors, convinced that because doctors are accustomed to illness and mis-fortune they have hearts of stone, but look at this doctor, he belies any such criticism, perhaps because he is also a poet, though some-what skeptical in outlook, as we have seen. Ricardo Reis is en-grossed in these thoughts, some of them perhaps too difficult to unravel for anyone who like ourselves is on the outside, but Ramón, who sees much, inquires, Do you wish anything else, Doctor, a tactful way of saying, though expecting the negative, that the doctor does. We are so apt at understanding that sometimes half a word suffices. Ricardo Reis rises to his feet, says Good-night to Ramón, wishes him a Happy New Year, and as he passes the reception desk slowly repeats the greeting and the wish to Salvador. The sentiment is the same, its expression more deliberate, after all Salvador is the manager. As Ricardo Reis goes slowly upstairs, he looks worn-out, like one of those caricatures or cartoons in a magazine of the period, the Old Year covered with white hair and wrinkles, his hourglass emptied, disappearing into the deep shadows of the past, while the New Year advances in a ray of light, as chubby as those infants nourished on powdered milk, reciting a nursery rhyme that invites us to the dance of the hours, I am the year nineteen thirty-six, come rejoice with me. Ricardo Reis enters his room and sits down. The bed has been prepared, fresh water stands in the carafe should he feel thirsty during the night, his slippers wait on the bedside mat. Someone is watching over me, a guardian angel, my heartfelt thanks. On the street there is the clatter of tin cans as revelers pass. Eleven o'clock has struck already, and at that moment Ricardo Reis jumps to his feet, almost in anger, What am I doing here, everyone else is out celebrating, having a good time with their families on the streets, in dance halls, theaters, cinemas, nightclubs, I should at least go to the Rossio to see the clock at Central Station, the eye of time, those Cyclopes who hurl not thunderbolts but minutes and seconds, every bit as cruel as thunderbolts and which we must all endure, until finally they shatter me along with the planks of the ship, but not like this, sitting here watching the clock, crouched in a chair. Having finished this soliloquy, he put on his raincoat and hat, grabbed his umbrella, suddenly eager, a man transformed by having made up his mind. Salvador had gone home to his family, so it was Pimenta who asked, You're going out, Doctor. Yes, I will take a little stroll, and he started downstairs. Pimenta pursued him to the landing, When you come back, Doctor, ring the bell twice, one short ring followed by a longer one, then I'll know it's you. Will you still be up. I'll turn in after midnight, but don't worry about me, sir, you come back

whenever you like. Happy New Year, Pimenta. A very prosperous
New Year, Doctor, the phrases one reads on greeting cards. They
said nothing more, but when Ricardo Reis reached the bottom of
the stairs he remembered that one normally tips the hotel staff at
this time of the year, they rely on such tips. Forget it, I have been
here only three days. The Italian page is asleep, his lamp extinguished.

The pavement was wet, slippery, the tram lines gleamed all
the way up the Rua do Alecrim to the right. Who knows what star
or kite holds them at that point, where, as the textbook informs us,
parallel lines meet at infinity, an infinity that must be truly vast to
accommodate so many things, dimensions, lines straight and curved
and intersecting, the trams that go up these tracks and the passengers inside the trams, the light in the eyes of every passenger, the
echo of words, the inaudible friction of thoughts. A whistling up
at a window as if giving a signal, Well then, are you coming down
or not. It's still early, a voice replies, whether of a man or woman
it does not matter, we shall encounter it again at infinity. Ricardo
Reis descended the Chiado and the Rua do Carmo, a huge crowd
going with him, some in groups, entire families, although for the
most part they were solitary men with no one waiting for them at
home or who preferred to be outdoors to watch the passing of the
old year. Perhaps it will truly pass, perhaps over their heads and
ours will soar a line of light, a frontier, then we shall say that time
and space are one and the same thing. There were also women
who for an hour were interrupting their wretched prowling, calling
a halt, wanting to be present should there be any proclamation of
a new life, anxious to know what their share will be, whether it
will be really new or the same as before. Around the Teatro Nacional the Rossio was crowded, there was a sudden downpour,
umbrellas opened like the gleaming carapaces of insects or as if
this were an army advancing under the protection of shields, about
to assault an impassive citadel. Ricardo Reis mingled with the
crowd, less dense than it had appeared from a distance, and pushed
his way through. Meanwhile the shower has passed, the umbrellas
close like a flock of birds shaking their wings as they settle down
for the night. Everyone has his nose in the air, his eyes fixed on

the yellow dial of the clock. From the Rua do Primeiro de Dezembro a group of boys come running, beating on the lids of pots and pans, tang, tang, while others keep up a shrill whistling. They march around the square in front of the station before settling under the portico of the theater, blowing their whistles all the while and banging on their tin lids, and this uproar combines with that of the wooden rattles resounding throughout the square, ra-ra-ra-ra, four minutes to go before midnight. Ah, the fickleness of mankind, so niggardly with the little time they have to live, always complaining that their lives are short, leaving behind only the hushed hiss of effervescence, yet they are impatient for these minutes to pass, such is the strength of hope. Already there are cries of anticipation, and the din reaches a crescendo as the deep voice of anchored ships can be heard from the direction of the river, dinosaurs bellowing with that prehistoric rumble that makes one's stomach churn. Sirens rend the air with piercing screams like those of animals being slaughtered, the frantic hooting of cars nearby is deafening, the little bells of the trams tinkle for all they are worth, which is not much, until finally the minute hand covers the hour hand, it is midnight, the happiness of freedom. For one brief moment time has released mankind, has allowed them to live their own lives, time stands aside and looks on, ironic, benevolent, as people embrace one another, friends and strangers, men and women kissing at random. These are the best kisses of all, kisses without any future. The clamor of the sirens now fills the air, the pigeons stir nervously on the pediment of the theater, some flutter in a daze, but in less than a minute the noise abates, a few last gasps, the ships on the river seem to be disappearing into the mist, out to sea. Speaking of this, there is Dom Sebastião in his niche on the façade, a little boy masked for some future carnival. Since he has not been placed elsewhere, but here, we shall have to reconsider the importance and paths of Sebastianism, with or without mist. It is clear that the Awaited One will arrive by train, subject to delays. There are still groups in the Rossio, but the excitement is over, people are clearing the pavements, they know what will happen next. From the upper stories rubbish comes hurtling down, it is the custom, not so noticeable here because few people inhabit these buildings, which are mainly offices. All the way down the Rua do Ouro the ground is strewn with litter. From windows people are still chucking out rags, empty boxes, cans, leftovers, fish bones wrapped in newspapers, it all scatters on the pavement. A chamberpot full of live embers bursts into sparks in every direction, and pedestrians seek protection under balconies, pressing themselves against the buildings and shouting up at the windows. But their protests are not taken seriously, the custom is widely observed, so let each man protect himself as best he can, for this is a night for celebrating and for whatever amusements one can devise. All the junk, things no longer in use and not worth selling, is thrown out, having been stored for the occasion, these are amulets to ensure prosperity throughout the New Year. At least now there will be some empty space to receive any good that may come our way, so let us hope that we are not forgotten. A voice called from an upper story, Look out, something's coming, considerate of them to warn us, a large bundle came hurtling through the air, describing a curve, almost hitting the tram cables, how careless, it could have caused a serious accident. It was a tailor's dummy, the kind set on three legs and suitable for either a man's jacket or a woman's dress, the black padding ripped open, the frame worm-eaten. Lying there crushed by the impact, it no longer resembled a human body with the head missing and no legs. A passing youth pushed it into the gutter with his foot. Tomorrow the garbage truck will come and clear all this away, the scraps and peelings, the dirty rags, the pots of no use either to the tinker or the metal scavenger, a roasting pan without its bottom, a broken picture frame, felt flowers reduced to tatters. Soon the tramps will be rummaging through the debris and surely find something they can put to use. What has lost its value for one can profit another.

Ricardo Reis returns to the hotel. In many parts of the city the festivities go on, with fireworks, sparkling wine or genuine champagne, and wild abandon, as the newspapers never forget to say. Women of easy or not-so-easy virtue are also available, some quite open and direct, others observing certain rituals in the making of their advances. This man, however, is not adventuresome, he knows about such exploits only from the lips of others, and any experience he has had was a matter of walking in one door and out the other. A group of passing revelers call out in discordant chorus, Happy New Year old man, and he replies with a gesture, a raised hand. Why say anything, they are so much younger than I. He tramples through the rubbish on the street, avoiding the boxes. Broken glass crunches under his feet. They might as well have tossed out their old parents with the tailor's dummy, there is little difference, for after a certain age the head no longer governs the body and the legs do not know where they are taking us. In the end we are like small children, orphaned, because we cannot return to our dead mother, to the beginning, to the nothingness that was before the beginning. It is before death and not after that we enter nothingness, for from nothingness we came, emerging, and when dead we shall disperse, without consciousness yet still existing. All of us once possessed a father and mother, but we are the children of fortune and necessity, whatever that means. It is Ricardo Reis's thought, let him do the explaining.

Although it was already after twelve-thirty, Pimenta had still not gone to bed. He came downstairs to open the door and was surprised, So you came back early after all, you didn't do much celebrating. I was feeling tired, sleepy, and you know, this business of seeing in the New Year is no longer the same. That's true, the festivities are much livelier in Brazil. They made these polite exchanges as they went upstairs. On the landing Ricardo Reis wished him good-night, Until tomorrow, then tackled the second flight of stairs. In reply Pimenta said good-night, then switched off the lights on the landing, then the lights on all the other floors before finally turning in, confident of undisturbed sleep, because no new guests were likely to arrive at this hour. He could hear the footsteps of Ricardo Reis in the corridor. The place is so quiet, no lights from any of the bedrooms, either the occupants are asleep or the rooms are empty. At the end of the corridor the number plate two hundred and one glows dimly, and Ricardo Reis notices a ray of light coming from under the door. He must have forgotten to turn off the light, well, these things do happen. He inserted the key in the lock and opened the door, and there was a man sitting on the sofa. He recognized him at once, though they had not seen each other for many years. Nor did he think it strange that Fernando Pessoa should be sitting there waiting for him. He said Hello, not expecting a reply, absurdity does not always obey logic, but Pessoa did in fact reply, saying, Hello, and stretched out his hand, then they embraced. Well, how have you been, one of them asked, or both, not that it matters, the question is so meaningless. Ricardo Reis removed his raincoat, put down his hat, carefully rested his umbrella on the linoleum floor in the bathroom, taking the precaution of checking the damp silk, no longer really wet, because during the walk back to the hotel there had been no rain. He pulled up a chair, sat in front of his visitor, saw that Fernando Pessoa was casually dressed, which is the Portuguese way of saying that he was wearing neither overcoat nor raincoat nor any other form of protection against the inclement weather, not even a hat, all he wore was a black suit comprising a double-breasted jacket, vest, and trousers, a white shirt with black tie, and black shoes and socks, like someone attending a funeral, or an undertaker. They look at each other with affection, obviously happy to be reunited after years of separation, and it is Fernando Pessoa who speaks first, I believe you came to visit me, I wasn't there, but they told me when I got back. Ricardo Reis replied, I was sure I'd find you there, never imagining you could leave that place. Fernando Pessoa said, For the time being it's allowed, I have about eight months in which to wander around as I please. Why eight months, Ricardo Reis asked, and Fernando Pessoa explained, The usual period is nine months, the same length of time we spend in our mother's womb, I believe it's a question of symmetry, before we are born no one can see us yet they think about us every day, after we are dead they cannot see us any longer and every day they go on forgetting us a little more, and apart from exceptional cases it takes nine months to achieve total oblivion, now tell me, what brings you to Portugal. Ricardo Reis removed his wallet from his inside pocket and took out a folded piece of paper, which he offered to Fernando Pessoa, but the latter made a gesture of refusal, I can no longer read, you read it. Ricardo Reis obeyed, Fernando Pessoa has died Stop I am leaving for Glasgow Stop Álvaro de Campos. When I received this telegram, I decided to return, I felt it was almost an obligation. The tone of the communication is very interesting, unmistakably from Álvaro de Campos, even in those few words one detects a note of malign satisfaction, even amusement, Álvaro is like that. There was another reason, this one a matter of self-interest, in November a revolution erupted in Brazil, many died, many were arrested, and I feared that the situation might get worse, I couldn't make up my mind whether to leave or stay until this telegram arrived, that decided it. Reis, you seem destined to flee revolutions, in nineteen nineteen you went to Brazil because of a revolution that failed, now you are fleeing Brazil because of another that has probably failed as well. Strictly speaking, I did not flee Brazil, and perhaps I would be there still had you not died. I remember reading something about this revolution a few days before my death, I believe it was instigated by the Bolshevists. Yes, the Bolsheviks were responsible, a number of officers, some soldiers, those who weren't killed were arrested, and the whole thing blew over within two or three days. Were people frightened, They most certainly were, Here in Portugal, too, there have been several revolutions, I know, the news reached me in Brazil, Do you still believe in monarchism, I do, Without a king, One can be a monarchist without clamoring for a king, Is that how you feel, It is, A nice contradiction, No worse than some, To advocate by desire what you know you cannot advocate by reason, Exactly, you see I still remember you, Of course.

Fernando Pessoa rose from the sofa, paced a little, then paused in front of the bedroom mirror before returning to the sitting room. It gives me an odd feeling to look in the mirror and not see myself there, Don't you see yourself, No, I know that I am looking at myself, but I see nothing, Yet you cast a shadow, It's all I possess. He sat down again and crossed his legs, Will you now settle for good in Portugal or will you go back to Brazil. I still haven't made up my mind, I brought only the bare necessities, perhaps I'll stay, open an office, build up a clientele, I might also go back to Rio, I don't know, for the moment I'm staying, but the more I think about it, I believe I came back here only because you died, it's as if I alone can fill the void you left behind. No living person can substitute for a dead one. None of us is truly alive or truly dead. Well said, an aphorism suitable for one of your odes. They both smiled.

Ricardo Reis asked, Tell me, how did you know that I was staying at this hotel. When you are dead, replied Fernando Pessoa, you know everything, that's one of the advantages. And how did you get into my room, Just as anyone else gets in, Didn't you come through the air, didn't you pass through the walls, What a ridiculous idea, my good fellow, such things happen only in ghost stories, no, I came from the cemetery at Prazeres, and like any other mortal walked upstairs, opened that door, and sat on this sofa to await your arrival. And did no one express surprise upon seeing a stranger walk in, That is another privilege the dead enjoy, no one can see us unless we so desire, But I see you, Because I want you to see me, besides, if you think about it, who are you. The question was clearly rhetorical, expected no answer, and Ricardo Reis said nothing, had not even heard it. There was a long-drawn-out silence, opaque. The clock on the landing could be heard striking two, as if coming from another world. Pessoa rose to his feet, I must be getting back. So soon. My time is my own, I am free to come and go as I please, it's true that my grandmother is there but she no longer bothers me. Stay a little longer, No, it's getting late and you should rest, When will I see you again, Do you wish me to return, Very much, we could converse, renew our friendship, don't forget that after sixteen years I feel like a stranger here. Remember that we can be together only for eight months, then my time runs out, Eight months, at the beginning, seems a lifetime, Whenever possible, I will come to see you, Wouldn't you like to fix a day, an hour, a place, Impossible, Very well, see you soon, Fernando, it was good seeing you again, And you, Ricardo, Should I wish you a Happy New Year, Go ahead, go ahead, it can't do me any harm, they're only words, as you well know. Happy New Year, Fernando, Happy New Year, Ricardo.

Fernando Pessoa opened the bedroom door and went out into the corridor, his footsteps inaudible. Two minutes later, the time it took to descend that steep flight of stairs, the front door banged, the buzzer having droned briefly. Ricardo Reis went to the window. Fernando Pessoa was already disappearing down the Rua do Alecrim. The tram rails shone, still running parallel.

Whether because they themselves believe it or because someone took them in hand after they failed to respond to suggestions and hints, the newspapers inform us, as if it were a great prophecy, that over the ruins of the mighty states ours, the Portuguese state, will demonstrate its remarkable strength and the prudence and intelligence of the men who govern it. For fall those states shall, and their crash will be resounding. The proud nations who boast of their present supremacy are much deceived, because the day is fast approaching, the happiest day of all in the annals of this nation among nations, when the leaders of other states come to these Lusitanian shores to seek advice, assistance, wisdom, benevolence, oil for their lamp from our great Portuguese statesmen. Who are these rulers, starting with the next cabinet, which is already being formed. In supreme command is Oliveira Salazar, President of the Council and Minister of Finance, then, at a respectful distance and in the order in which the newspapers publish their photographs, Monteiro of Foreign Affairs, Pereira of Commerce, Machado of Colonies, Abranches of Public Works, Bettencourt of the Navy, Pacheco of Education, Rodrigues of Justice, Sousa of War, Sousa of the Interior, the former is Passos de Sousa and the latter Paes de Sousa, write their names out in full so that petitions will reach them without delay. And we must not forget to mention Duque of Agriculture, without whose opinion not a grain of wheat would be produced in Europe or elsewhere. For the posts that remain, In

Parentheses Lumbrales of Finance and Andrade of Corporations, because this new state of ours, although in its infancy, is corporate, which explains why an undersecretary is quite sufficient. The newspapers here also say that most of the country has reaped the abundant fruits of an exemplary administration keen on maintaining public order, and if such a statement smacks of self-praise, read that paper from Geneva, Switzerland, which at length and with greater authority, because it is in French, describes the abovementioned dictator of Portugal, calling us most fortunate to be led by this wise leader, and the author of the article is absolutely right, and we thank him with all our hearts. But please bear in mind that Pacheco is no less wise if tomorrow he should say, as say he will, that elementary education must be given its due and no more, because knowledge, if imparted too soon, serves no real purpose, and also that an education based on materialism and paganism, which stifle noble impulses, is much worse than the darkness of illiteracy, therefore Pacheco concludes that Salazar is the greatest educator of our century, if that is not too bold an assertion when we are only one-third of the way through it.

Do not think that these items all appeared on the same page of the same newspaper, for then they would be seen as linked, they would be given the mutually complementary and consequential meaning they appear to have. These are the reports, rather, of the last few weeks, juxtaposed here like dominoes, each half set against its equal unless it happens to be double, in which case it is placed crosswise. These are current events seen from a distance. Ricardo Reis reads the morning newspapers as he savors his coffee with milk and eats the delicious toast served at the Bragança Hotel, greasy and crisp, clearly a contradiction, the pleasure of an age long forgotten, which explains why combining the two adjectives might strike you as inappropriate. We already know the maid who brings in his breakfast, it is Lydia, who also makes the bed and cleans and tidies up the room. When speaking to Ricardo Reis, she addresses him always as doctor, whereas he calls her simply Lydia, nothing else, but being an educated man he never uses the familiar form when he requests of her, Do this, Bring me that. Unaccustomed to such politeness, she is flattered, because as a rule the guests treat her with the familiarity shown servants, believing that money bestows every right, although to be fair, there is another guest who treats her with the same consideration, that is Senhorita Marcenda, the daughter of Doctor Sampaio. Lydia must be about thirty years of age, a mature and well-developed young woman, dark-haired and unmistakably Portuguese, short rather than tall, if there is any point in mentioning the physical traits of an ordinary maid who so far has done nothing but scrub floors, serve breakfast, and on one occasion laugh as she watched a man on another man's back while this guest stood there smiling. Such a nice person, yet sad, he cannot be happy, although there are moments when his face lights up just like this gloomy room when the clouds allow the sun to come through. It is more moonlight than the light of day, a shadow of light. Because it caught Lydia's head at a favorable angle, Ricardo Reis noticed the birthmark at the side of one nostril. It becomes her, he thought, although later he could not say if he was referring to the birthmark or to her white apron, or to the starched cap on her head, or to the embroidered collar she wore around her neck. Yes, you may remove the tray.

Three days went by and Fernando Pessoa did not reappear. Ricardo Reis did not ask himself the obvious question, Could it have been a dream, he knew that Fernando Pessoa, with enough flesh and bone to embrace and be embraced, had been in this very room on New Year's Eve and had promised to return. He believed him, but was beginning to lose patience at the delay. His life now seemed suspended, expectant, problematic. Meticulously he scanned the newspapers for signs, threads, outlines of a whole, the features of a Portuguese face, not simply to evoke an image of the country but to clothe his own portrait with a new substance, to be able to raise his hands to his face and recognize himself, to be able to place one hand upon another and clasp them together, It is I and I am here. On the last page he came across a large advertisement, two columns wide. In the top right-hand corner was depicted Freire the Engraver, in monocle and cravat, an old-fashioned sketch. Underneath, down to the bottom of the page, a cascade of other drawings advertised his workshops, the only ones that could justly claim to offer a comprehensive range of goods, with explanatory and superfluous captions, as if proving that a picture is as good or better than any description in words, except that no picture can show the excellent quality of the products of a firm established fifty-two years ago by a master engraver, a man of unblemished character and reputation, who studied in the major capitals of Europe and whose children after him have learned the skills and techniques of his trade. Unique in Portugal, he has been awarded three gold medals, has installed in his factory sixteen machines worked by electricity, one worth sixty contos, and these machines can do almost everything except speak, good Lord. A whole world is portrayed here, and since we were not born in time to see the fields of Troy or the shield of Achilles that reflected all heaven and earth, let us admire this Portuguese shield here in Lisbon, depicting the nation's latest wonders, number plates for buildings and hotels, for rooms, cupboards, and umbrella stands, strops for razor blades, whetstones for knives, scissors, pens with gold nibs, presses and scales, glass plates with chains in polished brass, machines for punching checks, seals made of metal and rubber, enameled letters, stamps for labeling clothing, sealing wax, numbered disks for lines at banks, business firms, and cafés, irons with which to brand cattle and wooden boxes, penknives, municipal registration plates for automobiles and bicycles, rings, medals for every type of sport, badges for the caps worn by the employees in milk bars, cafés, and casinos. Look at this one for the Leitaria Nívea, not for the Leitaria Alentejana, since the employees of the latter do not wear caps with badges. And lockers, and those pennants in enameled metal that are placed above the doors of institutes and foundations, and soldering irons, electric lanterns, knives with four blades as well as other types, emblems, puncheons, printing frames, molds for biscuits, toilet soaps, rubber soles, monograms and coats of arms in gold, metal for every imaginable purpose, cigarette lighters, rollers for inking type, stone and ink for taking fingerprints, escutcheons for Portuguese and foreign consulates, yet more plaques for doctors, for lawyers, for registry offices where births and deaths are recorded for the parish council, Midwife, Notary Public, those that say No Entry, and rings for pigeons, and padlocks, etc., etc., etc., and another three etc.'s, to abridge and treat the rest as having been said. Let us not forget

74

that these are the only workshops offering a comprehensive inventory, you can even have made to order ornamental iron gates for family tombs, but enough, period. Compared with this, what are the achievements of the divine blacksmith Hephaestus, he who chiseled and embossed the entire universe on the shield of Achilles but forgot to save a little space on which to engrave the heel of the illustrious warrior pierced by the quivering arrow of Paris. Even the gods forget about death, but no wonder, if they are immortal. Or was this an act of charity on the part of Hephaestus, a cloud cast over the transitory eyes of men, for whom it is enough, in order to be happy, to know neither where nor when nor how. Freire, however, is the more rigorous god and engraver, specifying everything, his advertisement is a labyrinth, a skein, a web. Studying it, Ricardo Reis allowed his coffee with milk to get cold, the butter to congeal on his toast. Please note, esteemed clients, our establishment has no branches anywhere, beware of those who call themselves agents and representatives, they are out to deceive the public with counterfeit tags for marking barrels and counterfeit branding irons for cattle. When Lydia arrived to collect the tray, she was worried, You haven't eaten anything, Doctor, didn't you like it. He protested that he had, but reading the newspaper he became distracted. Should I order some fresh toast, reheat your coffee. There's no need, I'm fine, besides he did not feel hungry, and saying this he got to his feet and placed a reassuring hand on her arm. He could feel the silky texture of her sleeve, the warmth of her skin. Lydia lowered her eyes, moved sideways, but his hand accompanied her and they remained like this for a few seconds. Finally Ricardo Reis released her arm and she gathered up the tray. The crockery shook as if the epicenter of an earthquake were located in room two hundred and one or, to be more precise, in the heart of this maid. Now she departs, she will not regain her composure in a hurry, she will go into the pantry and deposit the tray, her hand resting where that other hand rested, a delicate gesture unlikely in someone of so lowly a profession. That is what those who allow themselves to be guided by preconceived ideas must be thinking, perhaps even Ricardo Reis, who at this moment is bitterly upbraiding himself for having given in to foolish weakness, What an incredible thing I've done, and with a maid. It is his good fortune that he does not have to carry a tray laden with crockery, otherwise he would learn that even the hands of a hotel guest can tremble. Labyrinths are like this, streets, crossroads, and blind alleys. There are those who claim that the surest way of getting out of them is always to make the same turn, but that, as we know, is contrary to human nature.

Ricardo Reis invariably sets out from this street, the Rua do Alecrim, then takes any other, up, down, left, right, Ferragial, Remolares, Arsenal, Vinte e Quatro de Julho. These are the first unwindings of the skein, of the web, Boavista, Crucifixo. After a while his legs begin to tire, a man cannot wander about forever. It is not only the blind who need a walking stick to probe one step ahead or a dog to sniff out danger, even a man with the sight of two eyes needs a light he can follow, one in which he believes or hopes to believe, his very doubts serving in the absence of anything better. Now Ricardo Reis is watching the spectacle of the world, a wise man if one can call this wisdom, aloof, indifferent by upbringing and temperament, but quaking because a simple cloud has passed. One can easily understand the Greeks' and Romans' belief that they moved among gods, under the gaze of the gods at all times and in all places, whether in the shade of a tree, beside a fountain, in the dense, resounding depths of a forest, on the seashore, or on the waves, even in bed with one's beloved, be she woman or goddess, if she agrees. What Ricardo Reis requires is a guide dog, a walking stick, a light before him, because this world, and Lisbon too, is a dark mist in which north, south, east, and west all merge, and where the only open road slopes downward. If a man isn't careful, he will fall headlong to the bottom, a tailor's dummy without legs or head. It isn't true that Ricardo Reis returned from Rio de Janeiro out of cowardice or, to phrase it better, out of fear, it isn't true that he returned because Fernando Pessoa died, because one cannot put a thing back in the space and time from which it was removed, whether it be Fernando or Alberto. Each of us is unique and irreplaceable, which is the greatest of platitudes and may not be entirely true. Even if he appears before me at this very moment, as I make my way down the Avenida da Liberdade,

Fernando Pessoa is no longer Fernando Pessoa, and not only because he is dead. The important and decisive thing is that he is no longer able to add to what he was and what he achieved, to what he experienced and what he wrote. He can no longer even read, poor fellow. It will be up to Ricardo Reis to read him this other article published in a magazine with the poet's portrait in an oval frame. A few days ago death robbed us of Fernando Pessoa, the distinguished poet who spent his short life virtually ignored by the masses, one could say that because he knew the value of his work, he jealously hoarded it like a miser lest it be taken from him, some day full justice will be rendered to his dazzling talent, as has been rendered to other great geniuses in the past, dot dot dot. The bastards. The worst thing about journalists is that they believe they are authorized to put into the readily accepting heads of others ideas such as this one, that Fernando Pessoa hoarded his poems in the fear that others might steal them. How can they print such rubbish. Ricardo Reis impatiently tapped the pavement with the tip of his umbrella, which he could use as a walking stick but only so long as it didn't rain. A man can go astray even when he follows a straight line. He entered the Rossio and might just as well have been at a crossroads formed by four or eight choices which, if taken and retraced, would all end, as everyone knows, at the same point in infinity. There is little to be gained, therefore, in taking any of them. When the time comes, we will leave this matter to chance, which does not choose but simply drives and is driven in turn by forces about which we know nothing, and even if we knew, what would we know. Much better to rely on these nameplates probably manufactured in the fully equipped workshops of Freire the Engraver, which bear the names of doctors, lawyers, notaries, people to whom we have recourse in time of need and who have learned how to use a compass. Their compasses may not coincide, but this matters little, it is enough for the city to know that directions exist. You are not obliged to leave, because this is not the place where streets branch out, nor is it that magnificent point where they converge, rather, it is here that they change their sense, north becoming south, and south north. The sun has stopped between east and west, the city is a scar that has been burned, beset by earthquake, a teardrop that will not dry and has no finger to remove it. I must open an office, don a white coat, receive patients, even if only to allow them to die, Ricardo Reis muses. At least they will keep me company while they are alive, their last good deed being to play the ailing doctor of the ailing doctor. We are not saying that these are the thoughts of all doctors, but of this one certainly, for reasons of his own, reasons as yet barely glimpsed. What kind of practice shall I set up, where, and for whom. If you think that such questions require nothing but answers, you are deceived. We reply with actions, just as with actions we ask questions.

Ricardo Reis is about to descend the Rua dos Sapateiros when he sees Fernando Pessoa standing on the corner of the Rua de Santa Justa. Fernando Pessoa looks as if he has been kept waiting yet shows no sign of impatience, he wears the same black suit, his head uncovered, and, a detail previously unobserved by Ricardo Reis, he is without spectacles. Ricardo Reis thinks he knows why, it would be absurd and in thoroughly bad taste to bury a man in his spectacles, but that is not the reason, they had simply failed to hand them to him in time as he was dying. Give me my spectacles, he had asked, and was left lying there unable to see, for we are not always in time to satisfy the last wishes of the dying. Fernando Pessoa smiles and wishes him good afternoon, Ricardo Reis returns the greeting, and they walk together in the direction of the Terreiro do Paço. A little farther the rain starts up again. One umbrella shelters both of them, and although Fernando Pessoa has nothing to fear from this water, his huddling gesture was that of one who has still not completely forgotten life. Or it could have been the comforting thought of sharing the same roof and so close, Get underneath, there is room for two. No one will turn down such an offer by replying, There's no need, I don't mind the rain. Ricardo Reis is curious, If someone is watching us, whom does he see, you or me. He sees you, or rather he sees a shadowy form that is neither you nor I. The sum of both of us divided by two. No, I would say it is the result of multiplying the one by the other. Does this arithmetic exist. Two, whatever they may be, are not added up, they multiply. Be fruitful and multiply, says the commandment. Not in that restricted biological sense, dear fellow, take me, for example, I've left no children behind. I'm fairly certain that I, too, shall leave no children behind, nevertheless we are multiple, I wrote an ode in which I say that innumerable people exist within us. I don't recall it. Because I wrote it about two months ago. As you can see, each of us says the same thing. Then there was no point in our multiplying. If we had not multiplied, multiplying would not have been possible. Such a precious conversation, with its Paulist and intersectionist theories, as they walk along the Rua dos Sapateiros down as far as the Rua da Conceição, where they turn left into the Rua Augusta, then straight once more. Stopping, Ricardo Reis suggested, Let's go into the Café Martinho, and Fernando Pessoa replied brusquely, That would be unwise, the walls have ears and a good memory, we can go another day when there is no danger of anyone recognizing me, it's a question of time. As they lingered there under the arcade, Ricardo Reis closed his umbrella and said, apropos of nothing, I am thinking of settling here, of establishing a practice, So you have no intention of ever going back to Brazil, why, It's difficult to explain, I'm not even sure that I could give an explanation, let's say that I'm like the insomniac who finally finds a comfortable position on the pillow and can get some sleep. If it's sleep you're after, you've come to the right country. If I accept sleep, it's to be able to dream, To dream is to be absent, to be on the other side, But life has two sides, Pessoa, at least two, we can only reach the other side through dreams, you say this to a dead man, who can tell you from his own experience that on the other side of life there is only death. Well I don't know what death is, but I am not convinced that it is this other side of life we are discussing, because death, in my opinion, limits itself to being. Death is, it does not exist, it is. Are being and existing not the same thing then, No, my dear Reis, being and existing are not the same thing, and not simply because we have these two different words at our disposal, on the contrary it is because they are not the same thing that we have these two words and make use of them. They stood there arguing under the arcade while the rain formed tiny lakes in the square which gathered into larger lakes which became muddy seas. Not even on this occasion would Ricardo Reis go as far as the wharf to see the waves breaking. He was about to say this, to recall that he had been here before, when looking around he saw that Fernando Pessoa was walking away. Only now did he notice that the poet's trousers were too short, making him look as if he were walking on stilts. At last he heard his voice, nearby although Fernando Pessoa was already some distance away, We will continue this conversation another time, I must go now, over there. In the rain he waved his hand but did not say good-bye or I shall return.

The year has started in such a way that deaths are becoming an everyday occurrence. True, every age sweeps away what it can, sometimes with greater ease, when there are wars and epidemics, sometimes at a steady pace, one death after another, but it is most unusual to find so many famous people dying, both at home and abroad, within such a short space of time. We are not referring to Fernando Pessoa, who departed this world a while ago, no one is to know that he comes back from time to time, but to Leonardo Coimbra, who invented creationism, to Valle-Inclán, the author of *Romance de Lobos*, to John Gilbert, who starred in *The Big Parade*, to Rudyard Kipling, the poet who wrote If, and last but not least to the King of England, George V, the only monarch with his succession guaranteed. There have certainly been other misfortunes although much less important, such as the poor old man who was buried by a mud slide or those twenty-three people who came from Alentejo and were attacked by a cat with rabies. They disembarked, as black as a flock of ravens with lacerated wings, old folk, women, children being photographed for the first time in their lives, not knowing where they were supposed to look, their eyes gazing up at the sky, flustered and desperate, poor people, but that isn't all. What you don't know, Doctor, is that last November in the main towns of the region two thousand four hundred and ninety-two individuals died, one of them being Senhor Fernando Pessoa. It is not a large or small number, it is what has to be, but the saddest thing is that seven hundred and thirty-four were children under the age of five. If this is the situation in the main towns, thirty percent, imagine what it must be like in the villages, where even the cats have rabies. But we can always console ourselves with the thought that the majority of the little angels in heaven are Portuguese.

Furthermore, words can be most effective. When a government takes office, people go in droves to pay their respects to the honorable minister, everyone goes, teachers, civil servants, representatives of the three armed forces, leaders and members of the National Alliance, unions, guilds, farmers, judges, policemen, republican guards, excise men, and members of the general public. The minister thanks each of them with a little speech couched in the patriotism of the school primer and adapted to the ears of his audience. Those who are present arrange themselves so that they can all get into the photograph, the ones in the back rows craning their necks and standing on tiptoe to peek over the shoulder of their taller neighbors, That's me there, they will proudly tell their dear wife when they get home. The ones in front are puffed up with conceit, they have not been bitten by the cat with rabies but they have the same foolish expression, startled by the flashbulb. In the confusion some words were lost but can be deduced from the tone set by the Minister of the Interior at Montemor-o-Velho when he inaugurated the installation of electricity, a great improvement, I shall tell them in Lisbon that the leading citizens of Montemor know how to be loyal to Salazar. We can easily visualize the scene, Paes de Sousa explaining to the wise dictator the name he was given by the *Tribune des Nations* and that the good people from the land of Fernão Mendes Pinto are all loyal to your Excellency. With such a medieval regime, it's well known that peasants and laborers are often excluded from that goodness, people who have not inherited possessions, therefore they are not good men, perhaps neither good nor men but creatures no different from these insects that bite or gnaw or infest. You must have had occasion to observe what kind of people inhabit this country, Doctor, bearing in mind that this is the capital of the empire, when you passed the entrance to *O Século* the other day and saw the mob waiting for alms. If you wish to see real poverty, go into those districts, parishes, neighborhoods, and see for yourself the soup kitchens, the campaign for helping the poor during the winter months, an admirable enterprise, as the President of the Municipal Council of Oporto said in a telegram, God bless his soul. Don't you think it would have been better to let them die, then we would have spared ourselves the shameful spectacle of life in Portugal, beggars sitting on the curb eating a crust of bread and scraping the bottom of their bowls. They don't even deserve electric lights, all they need to know is the road from their plate to their mouth and that can be found in the dark.

Inside the body, too, there is profound darkness, yet the blood reaches the heart, the brain is sightless yet can see, it is deaf yet hears, it has no hands yet reaches out. Clearly man is trapped in his own labyrinth. The next two mornings, Ricardo Reis went downstairs to the dining room to have breakfast, a man frightened, alarmed at the possible consequences of a gesture as simple as that of placing his hand on Lydia's arm. He was not afraid that she had complained, after all it was just a gesture, nevertheless he felt some anxiety when he spoke for the first time after the incident with the manager Salvador. Needless anxiety, because the man could scarcely have been more respectful, affable. On the third day, Ricardo Reis decided that he was being foolish and did not go down to breakfast, he pretended to have forgotten breakfast and hoped they would do the same. He did not know Salvador. At the last minute there was a knock, Lydia entered carrying a tray, laid it down on the table and said, Good morning, Doctor, her natural self. It is nearly always like this, a man torments himself, frets, thinks the worst, believes that the world is about to demand a full explanation, when in fact the world has moved on, thinking about other things. It is not certain, however, that upon returning to his room to collect the tray, Lydia is still part of this world moved on, she seems to be waiting behind with an air of uncertainty. She goes through the usual motions, is about to lift the tray, has already gripped it, holds it level, hoists it into the air in a semicircle, and heads for the door. Oh my God, will he speak, not speak, perhaps he won't say anything, perhaps simply touch me on the arm like the other day, and if he does, what shall I do, it won't be the first time a guest has taken liberties, twice I gave into them, why, because this life is so sad. Lydia, Ricardo Reis spoke her name. She put down the tray, raised her eyes filled with terror, tried to say Doctor, but her voice stuck in her throat. He did not have the courage, repeated, Lydia, then said almost in a whisper, horribly banal, the ridiculous seducer,

I find you very pretty. He stood there staring at her for a second, he couldn't bear it for more than a second, and turned away. There are moments when it would be preferable to die, I who have made a fool of myself with hotel maids, you too, Álvaro de Campos, all of us. The door closed slowly, and only later could Lydia's footsteps be heard retreating.

Ricardo Reis spent the whole day out of doors brooding over his shame, all the more so because he had been unmanned not by an adversary but by his own fear. He decided that the following day he would change his hotel or rent part of a house, or return to Brazil on the first available ship. These may seem dramatic effects for such a tiny cause, but each person knows how much it hurts and where. Ridicule is like heartburn, an acidity continuously revived by memory, an incurable wound. He returned to the hotel, dined, and went out again, to see a film at the Politeama, *The Crusades*. Such faith, such ardent battles, such saints and heroes and splendid white horses. The film ended and an aura of religious fervor pervaded the Rua de Eugénio dos Santos, each spectator appearing to have a halo over his head, and yet there are people who remain unconvinced that art can improve mankind. Over and done with, the morning's episode assumed the right proportions, How foolish of me to get into such a state. Pimenta opened the door for him, the building was incredibly peaceful, obviously the hotel staff did not live in. He entered his room and immediately, almost by instinct, looked at the bed. The covers had not been folded back at an angle, as usual, but both sheet and eiderdown had been turned down straight from side to side, and instead of one pillow there were two, the message could not have been clearer. It remained to be seen how it would become explicit, unless it was not Lydia who made the bed but another maid, who thought the room was occupied by a couple. Yes, let us assume that the maids change floors every so often, perhaps so that they have equal opportunities for receiving tips, or to discourage them from becoming too set in their ways, or, and here Ricardo Reis smiled, to prevent them from becoming too friendly with the guests. Well, tomorrow we shall see. If Lydia appears with breakfast, then she must have prepared the bed. And then what. He lay down, switched off the light without bothering to remove the second pillow, closed his eyes firmly. Come, sleep, come, but sleep did not obey. A tram passed in the street, perhaps the last one. Who is that in me who doesn't wish to sleep, whose restless body possesses mine, or is it some intangible force that grows restless in all of me, or at least in this part of me that grows. Good Lord, the things that can happen to a man. He got up angrily and fumbling his way by the pale light that filtered through the windows went to release the latch on the door, then left the door slightly ajar, one only had to push it ever so gently. He returned to his bed. This is childish, if a man wants something, he does not leave it to chance but sets out to achieve it, consider what the Crusaders achieved in their time, swords against scimitars, prepared to die if necessary, and those castles and coats of armor. No longer knowing whether he is awake or finally asleep, he thinks about medieval chastity belts, the keys carried off by the knights, poor deluded creatures. The door of his room opens in silence, now it is closed, a shadowy figure crosses the room, groping toward the edge of the bed. The hand of Ricardo Reis reaches out and meets a frozen hand, draws it to him, Lydia trembles, all she can say is, I am cold. He remains silent, debating whether he should kiss her on the lips, such a depressing thought.

Doctor Sampaio and his daughter are due to arrive today, Salvador announced, as euphoric as if the good news would bring a reward. The lookout from the reception desk sees the train from Coimbra advancing from a distance through the afternoon haze, chug-chug, chug-chug. Quite paradoxical, because the ship that is anchored in port and gathering slime by the quay is the Hotel Bragança and it is the land that is coming here, sending smoke up the funnel. When the train arrives at Campolide, it goes underground before emerging from a black tunnel as it belches steam. There is still time to call Lydia and say, Go and make sure that everything is in order. The rooms of Doctor Sampaio and Senhorita Marcenda, as she is aware, are two hundred and four and two hundred and five. Lydia appeared not to notice that Doctor Ricardo Reis was standing there as she went bustling up to the second floor. How long are they staying, the doctor inquired. They usually stay for three days, tomorrow evening they will go to the theater, I have already reserved their seats. To the theater, which one. The Teatro Dona Maria. Ah. This interjection is not one of surprise, it has been inserted here to terminate a dialogue which we are unable or unwilling to continue. In fact, most people from the provinces, when they visit Lisbon, may Coimbra forgive me for putting it in the provinces, take the opportunity of going to the theater, perhaps a revue at the Parque Mayer or a film at the Apolo or the Avenida, while those with more refined tastes invariably go to the Teatro Dona Maria, also known as the Teatro Nacional. Ricardo Reis moved into the lounge, leafed through a newspaper, looked up the entertainment page, the theater guide, and saw advertised *Mar* by Alfredo Cortez. He decided then and there that he too would go to the theater. As a good Portuguese citizen he should support Portuguese artists. He almost asked Salvador to reserve him a seat by telephone, but changed his mind, deciding to tend to the matter himself next day.

There are still two hours to go before dinner. In the meantime the guests from Coimbra will arrive, unless their train is delayed. But why should I be interested, Ricardo Reis asks himself as he goes upstairs to his room. He tells himself that it is always agreeable to meet people from other parts, civilized people, besides there is the interesting clinical case presented by Marcenda. An unusual name, a name unknown to him, it resembles a murmuring, an echo, the bowing of a cello, *les sanglots longs de l'automne*, alabasters, balustrades, this morbid twilight poetry exasperates him, the things a name can provoke, Marcenda. He passes room two hundred and four, the door is open and inside Lydia is running a feather duster over the furniture. They look furtively at each other, she smiles, he does not. Shortly afterward he is back in his room and hears a gentle knocking on the door, it is Lydia, who steals in quietly and asks him, Are you annoyed with me. He barely replies, tight-lipped. Here in the light of day he does not know how to behave. She is only a chambermaid and he could lecherously stroke her hips now, but he feels much too awkward to make such a gesture. Earlier perhaps, but not after they have already been together, have lain in the same bed, a kind of consecration, mine, ours. If I can, I'll join you tonight, Lydia said, and he made no reply. That she should warn him beforehand seemed inopportune, with the girl with the paralyzed hand so near, sleeping and unaware of the nocturnal secrets of this corridor and of the room at the far end. But he was incapable of saying, Don't come. Lydia left, and he stretched out on the sofa to rest. Three nights of sexual activity after a long period of abstinence, and at his age, no wonder he can scarcely keep his eyes open. He knits his brow, asks himself, without finding the answer, whether he should pay Lydia, give her some little present, a pair of stockings, a cheap ring, something suitable for someone of her class. He must resolve this uncertainty, weighing the motives and reasons for and against. This is not like that business of whether or not to kiss her on the lips, circumstances made that decision for him, the so-called flame of passion, he himself did not know how it had happened, his kissing her as if she were the most beautiful woman in the world. Perhaps this will turn out to be just as easy, as they lie in each other's arms he will say, I'd like to give you a little memento, and she will find it quite natural. She is probably wondering even now why it has taken him so long.

Voices, footsteps can be heard in the corridor, Pimenta saying, Many thanks, sir, then two doors being closed. The travelers have arrived. He was almost asleep, now he stares up at the ceiling, examining the cracks in the plaster meticulously, as if tracing them with his fingertips. He imagines that he has the palm of God's hand overhead and is reading there the lines of life, of a life that narrows, is interrupted and revived, becomes more and more tenuous, a besieged heart solitary behind those walls. The right hand of Ricardo Reis, resting on the sofa, opens upward and reveals its own lines. Those two spots on the ceiling are like eyes. Who can tell who is reading us as we sit reading, oblivious of ourselves. Day turned to night some time ago, perhaps it is already time for dinner, but Ricardo Reis does not wish to be the first to go down. If I didn't hear them leaving their rooms, he thinks to himself, perhaps I slept without knowing it, and woke without realizing that I slept, I thought I was only dozing and I slept for a century. He sits up, uneasy, looks at his watch, it is already after eight-thirty, and at this very moment a man's voice can be heard in the corridor saying, Marcenda, I'm waiting for you. A door opens and there are vague sounds, footsteps moving away, then silence. Ricardo Reis rises, goes to the washbasin to freshen up, to comb his hair. The hair at his temples looks even whiter today, he ought to use one of those lotions or dyes that progressively restore the natural color to one's hair, Nhympha do Mondego, for example, a popular and reliable preparation that can be used to achieve the original tone without going any further, or it may be applied until the hair becomes as black as a raven's wing, if so desired. He is discouraged, however, by the idea of having to examine his hair each day, to check whether it is time to apply more lotion, mix more dye in a bowl, *Crown me with roses, I ask no more.* He changes his trousers and jacket, he must remember to tell Lydia they need pressing, and leaves his room with the incongruous and disagreeable presentiment that he will give this order without the neutrality of tone that an order should have when it is given by someone who naturally commands to someone who must naturally obey, if obeying and commanding are indeed natural. To put it more clearly, what Lydia will she be now, the one who heats the iron, folding the trousers on the ironing board to get a crease, inserting her left hand into the sleeve of the jacket near the shoulder so as to follow the line with the hot iron and restore its shape, no doubt remembering the body that wears these garments. If I can, I'll join you tonight, she said, and now brings down the iron nervously, alone in the laundry room. This is the suit Doctor Ricardo Reis will wear to the theater, if only I could accompany him. What a ninny, what's got into you, she dries two tears that will inevitably appear, they are tomorrow's tears. Ricardo Reis is still here, making his way down to the dining room, he has not told Lydia yet that he needs the suit she has just pressed, and she still does not know that she will weep.

Nearly all the tables are occupied. Ricardo Reis pauses at the entrance. The maître d' comes to guide him to his table, there's really no need, it's where he always sits, but what would life be like without these and other rituals, kneel when you pray, uncover your head when the flag is carried past, sit down, unfold your napkin on your knees, if you look around to see who is sitting near you, do it discreetly, nod to anyone you know. Which Ricardo Reis does. That couple, this guest sitting on his own, these people here. He also knows Doctor Sampaio and his daughter Marcenda, but they do not recognize him, the lawyer looks at him with a vacant expression, perhaps he is searching his memory, but he does not lean toward his daughter and whisper in her ear, Aren't you going to greet Doctor Ricardo Reis who has just arrived. It is she who glances at him a little later, looking over the waiter's sleeve as he serves her, the faintest tremor on her pale face, the faintest blush, an indication of recognition. She remembers, Ricardo Reis thought to himself, and in an excessively loud voice asked Ramón what there was for dinner. This might explain why Doctor Sampaio looked at him, but no, two seconds earlier Marcenda said to her father, That gentleman over there, he was staying in the hotel the last time we were here. As they rose from the table, Doctor Sampaio gave him a little nod, and Marcenda at her father's side not even that, restrained and discreet as befits a dutiful daughter. Ricardo Reis rose ever so slightly from his chair in acknowledgment, one has to be endowed with a sixth sense to measure these subtle gestures and greetings, and their reciprocation must be carefully balanced. Everything has been so perfect on this occasion that it augurs well for a blossoming friendship. Father and daughter have already withdrawn, no doubt they are making their way into the lounge, but no, they retire to their rooms. Later Doctor Sampaio will probably take a stroll despite the rainy weather, because Marcenda goes to bed early, she finds these train journeys exhausting. When Ricardo Reis enters the lounge, all he will see are a few taciturn guests, some reading newspapers, others yawning, while the radio quietly grinds out Portuguese songs from popular revues, strident and grating even though barely audible. In this light, or because of these somber faces, the mirror resembles an aquarium, and when Ricardo Reis crosses the lounge on the far side and comes back by the same route in order not to turn around and make a beeline for the doorway, he sees himself in the greenish abyss as if he were walking on the ocean floor amid wreckage and drowned corpses. He must leave this place at once, reach the surface, breathe again. He goes up to his chilly room. Why should these minor irritations depress him so, if that is what is troubling him, after all they are simply two people who live in Coimbra and come to Lisbon once a month. This doctor is not looking for patients, this poet has plenty of muses to inspire him, this man is not seeking a wife, he did not return to Portugal with that intention, and consider the difference in their ages. It is not Ricardo Reis who thinks these thoughts, nor one of those innumerable beings who exist within him, it is perhaps thought thinking itself while he looks on in amazement as a thread unwinds, leading him down unknown paths and corridors, at the end of which there waits a girl dressed in white, who cannot even hold a bouquet of flowers, because her right arm will be in his as they return from the altar treading the solemn red carpet to the strains of the wedding march. Ricardo Reis, as you can see, has already taken up the reins of thought, already controls and guides it, makes use of it to mock himself. The orchestra and red carpet are flights of fancy, and now, so that this poet's tale may have a happy ending, he accomplishes the clinical miracle of placing a bouquet of flowers in Marcenda's left arm and having it remain there without any assistance. The altar and priest can now disappear, the music cease, the wedding guests vanish in smoke and dust. The bridegroom withdraws, his services no longer required, the doctor has cured the patient, the rest must have been the work of the poet. These romantic episodes cannot be fitted into an Alcaic ode, which goes to prove, if any proof is needed, that what is written is often confused with what, having been experienced, gave birth to it, therefore one does not ask the poet what he thought or felt. It is precisely to avoid having to reveal these things that he composes verses.

The night passed and Lydia did not descend from the attic, Doctor Sampaio came back late, Fernando Pessoa is God knows where, then it was day, Lydia took away the suit for pressing, and Marcenda left with her father to keep their appointment with the specialist. She's gone for physiotherapy, says Salvador, who like most people cannot pronounce the word properly. For the first time Ricardo Reis finds it odd that a disabled girl should come to Lisbon when she lives in Coimbra, a city with such a wide range of specialists, for a course of treatment that can be administered just as easily there as here. Ultraviolet rays for example, unless applied with a certain frequency, provide little benefit. Ricardo Reis turns these doubts over in his mind as he goes down the Chiado on his way to the box office at the Teatro Nacional, but he was distracted at the sight of so many people wearing signs of mourning, a number of women in veils and the men even more conspicuous in their black suits and grave expressions, some even with mourning bands on their hats. George V of England, our oldest ally, was being buried. Despite the official mourning, there is a performance this evening, no disrespect intended, life must go on. The man in the box office sold him a seat in the stalls, and informed him, The fishermen will be in the audience tonight. What fishermen, asked Ricardo Reis before realizing that he had committed an unforgivable blunder. The box-office attendant frowned and altered his tone of voice, snapped, The fishermen from Nazaré, obviously. What others did he expect, there would be little sense in bringing fishermen from Caparica or from Póvoa. The journey and lodgings of the fishermen from Nazaré had been paid so that they might participate in this cultural event. Because they had inspired the play, it was only right that they should be represented, both the men and the women. Let's go to Lisbon, let's go and see the sea there, what gimmicks will be used to produce waves breaking over the stage, and what will Dona Palmira Bastos be like in the role of Ti Gertrudes, and Dona Amélia as Maria Bem, and Dona Lalande as Rosa, and Amarante in the role of Lavagante, how well will they imitate our lives. And since we are going, let's take this opportunity to ask the government, for the sake of the suffering souls in Purgatory, to build us the little port of refuge we have been in such need of since the first boat was launched from our shore, whenever that was. Ricardo Reis whiled away the afternoon in cafés, went to inspect the work being carried out on the Teatro Eden. Any day now they will remove the hoardings, the Chave de Ouro is almost ready to be inaugurated, and both natives and foreigners can see that Lisbon is progressing so rapidly that it will soon be able to compete with the great cities of Europe, and rightly so as the capital of a great empire. He did not dine in the hotel, only went back to change his clothes. His jacket, trousers, waistcoat too had been put neatly on a hanger, beautifully pressed, the work of loving hands, pardon the hyperbole, for how can there be love in the nocturnal coupling of a hotel guest and a chambermaid, he a poet, she by chance named Lydia, a different Lydia, although still fortunate, because the Lydia in his poems never heard his moans and sighs, she only sat on a riverbank listening to someone confide, *I suffer, Lydia, from the fear of destiny*. He ate a steak at the Restaurante Martinho, the one in the Rossio, and watched a keenly contested game of billiards, the chipped ball of Indian ivory rolling smoothly over the green baize. Since it was almost time for the performance to begin, he left, making a discreet approach and entering the theater, flanked by two large family groups. He had no wish to be seen until he himself chose the moment, heaven knows what emotional strategy he was pursuing, and crossed the foyer without pausing, one day it will be called a hallway or vestibule, unless some other term is borrowed from some other foreign language to say the same thing. At the entrance to the auditorium he was met by an usher, who led him down the left-hand aisle to the seventh row, It's that seat there, beside the lady. Don't let your imagination run riot, the man said lady, not girl, an usher in the Teatro Nacional can be relied upon to speak with decorum and the utmost clarity, his masters are the great dramatists of the classical and modern repertoire. Marcenda is sitting three rows ahead and to the right, too far to be near, and not even aware of my presence, she is sitting on her father's right, and just as well, for when she speaks to him and turns her head a little, Ricardo Reis can see her in profile. Is it because she is wearing her hair down that her face seems longer. She raises her right hand to the level of her chin, to clarify some word she has uttered or is about to utter, perhaps she is discussing the specialist who is treating her, perhaps the play they are about to see. Who is this Alfredo Cortez, her father cannot tell her much, he saw *The Gladiators* on his own two years ago and was not impressed, but this play caught his attention because of its traditional theme. It won't be long now before we discover what the play is like. This conversation, assuming it ever took place, was interrupted by the dragging of chairs overhead, by a loud whispering that made all the heads turn around and look upward. The fishermen from Nazaré have arrived and are getting into their seats in the boxes on the upper tier. They sit tall in order to see and be seen, both the men and the women are dressed in their own fashion, they are probably barefoot, one cannot see from down here. Some people in the audience applaud, others condescendingly join in. Irritated, Ricardo Reis clenches his fists, snobbish affectation in one who does not have blue blood, we might say, but this is not the case, it is simply a question of decorum, Ricardo Reis finds the outburst of applause vulgar, to say the very least.

The lights dim, the auditorium is in darkness, the loud knocks ascribed to Molière can be heard onstage, what terror they must strike in the hearts of the fishermen and their wives, perhaps they imagine them to be the last-minute hammerings of carpenters on the set. The curtain opens, a woman is lighting a fire, it is still night, from behind the scenery a man's voice can be heard, calling Mané Zé, Ah, Mané Zé, the play has started. The audience sighs, wavers, sometimes smiles, becomes excited as the first act ends with that great stampede of women, and when the lights go up, faces are animated, a good sign. There is shouting overhead, people calling from box to box, one could mistake those fishermen for the actors themselves, their way of speaking almost the same, whether better or worse depending on the measure of comparison. Reflecting on this, Ricardo Reis decides that the purpose of art is not imitation, that the author has made a serious error of judgment by writing the play in the dialect of Nazaré, or in what he supposed was the dialect of Nazaré, because reality does not tolerate its reflection, rather, it rejects it. Only a different reality, whatever it is, may be substituted for the reality one wishes to convey. The difference between them mutually demonstrates, explains, and measures them, reality as the invention it was, invention as the reality it will be. Ricardo Reis thinks these things with even greater confusion, it is difficult, after all, to think and clap one's hands at the same time. The audience applauds, and he joins in out of sympathy, for despite the use of dialect, grotesque as spoken by the actors, he is enjoying the play. Marcenda is not clapping, she cannot, but she is smiling. Most of the women remain seated, it's the men who need to stretch and exercise their legs, to pay a visit to the gents', to smoke a cigarette or cigar, exchange views with their friends, greet acquaintances, to see and be seen in the foyer. If they remain in their seats, it is generally for reasons of love and courtship. As they stand up, their eyes rove like those of hawks, they are the protagonists of their own drama, actors who perform during the intermission while the real actors back in their dressing rooms discard roles they will shortly resume. As he gets up, Ricardo Reis looks between the heads and sees that Doctor Sampaio is also getting up. Refusing with a nod, Marcenda remains seated. Her father, already on his feet, places his hand affectionately on her shoulder, then moves toward the aisle. Hurrying, Ricardo Reis reaches the foyer first. Shortly they will meet face to face, amid all these people who are walking up and down and conversing in an atmosphere soon thick with tobacco smoke. There are voices and commentaries, Palmira is splendid, In my opinion they've put far too many fishing nets on the stage, What a bunch of harpies, grappling with each other, you'd think they were in earnest, That's because you've never seen them, dear fellow, as I've seen them in Nazaré, there they fight like the Furies, At times it is difficult to make out what they're saying, Well that's how they talk there. Ricardo Reis moved among the groups, as attentive to their words as if he himself were the author of the play, while watching the movements of Doctor Sampaio from a distance, anxious that they should bump into each other as if by chance. Then he realized that Doctor Sampaio had spotted him, was heading his way, and was the first to speak, Good evening, how are you enjoying the play then. Ricardo Reis felt no need to say, What a surprise, what a coincidence, he immediately reciprocated the greeting, assured him that he was enjoying the play, and added, We are staying at the same hotel. Even so he ought to introduce himself, My name is Ricardo Reis. He hesitated, wondering whether he should add, I'm a doctor of medicine, I was living in Rio de Janeiro, I've been back in Lisbon less than a month. Doctor Sampaio barely listened, smiling, as if to say, If you knew Salvador as long as I have, you would realize that he has told me everything about you, and knowing him as well as I do, I guess he has told you about me and my daughter. Doctor Sampaio is undoubtedly shrewd, many years of experience as a notary bring certain advantages, We need hardly introduce ourselves, said Ricardo Reis. That's right. They went on almost immediately to discuss the play and the actors, treating each other with the utmost respect, Doctor Reis, Doctor Sampaio. A pleasant sense of equality is conferred upon them by their titles, and so they remained until the warning bell rang, when they returned to the auditorium together, and said, See you soon. Each went to his seat, Ricardo Reis, the first to sit down, kept watching, saw him speak to his daughter. She looked back, gave him a smile, he returned her smile, the second act was about to begin.

All three of them met during the next intermission. Even

though they knew all about each other, they still had to be introduced, Ricardo Reis, Marcenda Sampaio. It was inevitable, the moment they both awaited, they shook hands, right hand with right hand, her left hand hanging limp, trying to fade from sight, shy, as if nonexistent. Marcenda's eyes shone brightly, she was clearly moved by the sufferings of Maria Bem, perhaps there was a deep reason in her personal life for accompanying, word for word, that final speech made by the wife of Lavagante, If there is a hell, it can be no worse than this, Virgin Mother of the Seven Sorrows. Marcenda would have made this speech in the dialect of Coimbra, but speaking in a different dialect in no way changes these feelings which cannot be explained in words, I fully understand why you do not touch this arm, you who share the same hotel corridor, man of my curiosity, I am she who hailed you with a lifeless hand, don't ask me why, I haven't even asked myself that question, I simply hailed you, one day I will learn what prompted that gesture, or perhaps not, now you will withdraw rather than give me the impression that you are being indiscreet, inquisitive, taking advantage, as one would say, go, I will know where to find you, or you me, for you have not come here by chance. Ricardo Reis did not remain in the foyer but wandered in the aisles behind the boxes on the grand tier and peered up at the boxes overhead to get a closer look at the fishermen. But the warning bell started ringing, this second intermission was shorter, and when he reached the auditorium the lights were already beginning to dim. During the whole of the third act he divided his attention between the stage and Marcenda, who never once looked behind her. But she had slightly altered the position of her body so that he could see a little more of her face, a mere glimpse, and from time to time she drew back her hair on the left side with her right hand, very slowly, as if on purpose. What does this girl want, who is she, because people are not always what they seem. He saw her dry her cheeks as Lianor confesses that she stole the key of the life jacket so that Lavagante would die, and again when Maria Bem and Rosa, the one beginning, the other concluding, declare that this was an act of love and that love, being a noble sentiment, turns to torment when it is frustrated, and finally in the brief closing scene when Lavagante and Maria Bem are about to be united in the flesh. Suddenly the lights went up, the curtain fell to wild applause, and Marcenda was still drying her tears, now with a handkerchief. She was not alone, weeping women could be seen everywhere in the auditorium. Nervously smiling, the actors, such sensitive souls, acknowledged the ovation, made gestures as if returning it to the upper boxes occupied by the real heroes of these tales of love and adventure at sea. All inhibitions forgotten, the audience looked up in their direction, this is the communion of art, and applauded the intrepid fishermen and their courageous womenfolk. Even Ricardo Reis is clapping. Here in this theater one sees how easily understanding can be created between different classes and professions, between the rich, the poor, and those in-between, let us savor this rare spectacle of fraternity. The fishermen are now being coaxed to join the actors on the stage, the dragging of chairs can be heard once more. The performance is not over yet, the audience sits down. Now comes the climax, such merriment, such animation, such rejoicing, as the fishing community of Nazaré comes down the center aisle and climbs onto the stage. There they dance and sing the traditional airs of their region along with the actors, a night to be recorded forever in the annals of the Casa de Garrett. The leader of the group embraces the actor Robles Monteiro, the oldest of the fishwives receives a kiss from the actress Palmira Bastos, they all talk at once, utter bedlam, each speaking in his own dialect but managing to understand the others nonetheless, then there is more singing and dancing. The younger actresses demonstrate the traditional folk dance of Minho until the ushers finally start pushing us gently toward the exits. A dinner is to be served on stage, a communal love festival for the actors and their muses, corks will pop from the bottles of that sparkling wine which stings one's nostrils, the good women of Nazaré will be in fits of laughter once their heads start spinning, unaccustomed as they are to sparkling wine. Tomorrow, when the bus departs in the presence of journalists, photographers, and leaders of the corporations, the fishermen will give loud cheers for the New State and the Fatherland. One cannot be certain if they were paid to do so, but let us assume it is a spontaneous expression of gratitude at having been promised that port they so earnestly desire. If Paris was worth a mass, perhaps a few cheers will gain them salvation.

Ricardo Reis made no attempt to avert a second meeting as he left the theater. On the sidewalk he asked Marcenda if she had enjoyed the play. She confided that the third act had moved her deeply and brought tears to her eyes. Yes, I saw you weeping, he told her, and there the conversation ended. Having hailed a taxi, Doctor Sampaio suggested that Ricardo Reis might care to join them if he intended going straight back to the hotel. Thanking them, he declined. Until tomorrow then, Good-night, Pleased to meet you. The taxi drove off. He would have liked to accompany them, but realized it would be awkward, they would all feel ill at ease, be silent, finding another topic of conversation would not be easy, not to mention the delicate question of the seating arrangement, since there would not be room enough for three on the back seat, and Doctor Sampaio would not wish to travel in front leaving his daughter alone with a stranger. Yes, a stranger, and in propitious darkness, for even if there was not the slightest physical contact between them, the darkness would draw them together with hands of velvet, and they would be drawn together even more closely by their thoughts, which gradually would become secrets difficult to conceal. Nor would it be right to have Ricardo Reis sit beside the driver, you cannot offer someone a lift and then ask him to sit in front, facing the meter. Also, at the end of the ride it is inevitable that the person beside the driver will feel obliged to pay. The host, sitting in the back, cannot find his wallet but insists he will pay, saying, Leave this to me, telling the driver not to accept any money from the man in front, I'm paying the fare. The taxi driver patiently waits for them to make up their mind, this is an argument he has heard a thousand times, taxi drivers have to put up with such absurdities. With no other pleasures or obligations in store, Ricardo Reis walks back to his hotel. The night is cold and damp, but it is not raining. Now he feels like going for a stroll, he descends the entire Rua Augusta, crosses the Terreiro do Paço to take those steps leading down to the quayside where the dark polluted waters turn to spray only to fall back into the river from whence they came. There is no one else at the quayside, yet other men are watching the night, the flickering lights on the opposite embankment, the mooring lamps of the anchored ships. This one man, physically present, is watching today, but there are in addition the innumerable beings he claims to be, the others he has been each time he came here and who remember having been here, even though he does not remember. Eyes accustomed to the dark see much farther. In the distance are gray outlines of ships belonging to the squadron which has left the safety of the harbor. Although still rough, the weather is no longer too rough for the ships, a sailor's life is one of sacrifice. Seen from this distance, a number of ships appear to have the same dimensions, these must be the torpedo boats named after rivers. Ricardo Reis does not recall all of the luggage porter's litany, there was the *Tagus*, now sailing the Tagus, and the *Vouga*, and the *Dão*, which is nearest of all, as the man told him. Here then is the Tagus, here are the rivers that flow through my village, all flowing to the sea which receives water from all the rivers and then restores it. If only this regression were eternal, but alas, it will last only as long as the sun, mortal like all of us. Glorious is the death of those men who died with the setting sun, they did not see the first day but they will see the last.

This cold weather is not good for philosophical musings. His feet are freezing. A policeman paused warily to keep an eye on him. The man contemplating the water didn't strike him as a scoundrel or tramp but might be thinking of throwing himself into the river. At the thought of all the trouble this would cause, having to raise the alarm, fishing out the corpse, writing up a formal report of the incident, the policeman decided to approach him, not quite knowing what to say but hoping that his presence would be sufficient to discourage the would-be suicide, to persuade him to postpone this act of madness. Ricardo Reis heard footsteps, felt the coldness of the flagstones penetrate his feet. He must buy boots with thick soles. It was time to get back to the hotel before he caught a chill. He said, Good evening, officer. The policeman, reassured, asked, Is there anything wrong. No, nothing, it is the most natural thing in the world for a man to stroll along the quay, even at night, to watch the river and the ships. This is the Tagus which does not flow through my village, because the Tagus that flows through my village is called the Douro, but the fact that it does not have the same name does not mean that the river that flows through my village is any less beautiful. The policeman went off in the direction of the Rua da Alfândega, reflecting on the madness of certain people who appeared in the middle of the night. Whatever possessed this man to think he could enjoy a view of the river in such weather, if he were obliged like me to patrol the docks night after night he would soon find it tiresome. Ricardo Reis continued along the Rua do Arsenal and within ten minutes arrived at the hotel. Pimenta appeared on the landing with a bunch of keys, looked down, and withdrew, not waiting, as he usually did, for the guest to come upstairs, why should this be. Asking himself this natural question, Ricardo Reis began to worry. Perhaps he already knows about Lydia, he is bound to find out sooner or later, a hotel is like a glass house. Pimenta, who never leaves the place and knows every nook and cranny, must suspect something. Good evening, Pimenta, he said with exaggerated warmth, and the other replied with no apparent reserve, no trace of hostility. Perhaps I'm mistaken, Ricardo Reis thought, and when Pimenta handed him his key, he was about to continue on but turned back and opened his wallet, This is for you, Pimenta, and handed him a twenty-escudo note. He gave no explanation and Pimenta asked no questions.

No light came from any of the rooms. Ricardo Reis went quietly down the corridor for fear of disturbing the sleeping guests. For three seconds he paused outside the door of Marcenda's room. In his room the air was cold and damp, not much better than out by the river. He shivered, as if still gazing at those livid ships and listening to the policeman's footsteps. What would have happened had he replied, Yes, there is something wrong, although he would not have been able to elaborate. Approaching the bed, he noticed a bulge in the eiderdown, something had been placed between the sheets, a hot-water bottle, he was sure, but to make certain he put his hand on top. It was warm. She was a good sort, Lydia, just like her to remember to warm his bed, these were little comforts for the chosen few. She probably won't come tonight. He lay down, opened the book at his bedside, the one about Herbert Quain, glanced at a couple of pages without taking in the sense. Three motives had been suggested for the crime, each in itself sufficient to incriminate the suspect, on whom all three converged, but the aforesaid suspect, availing himself of the law, argued that the real motive, were it to be proven that he was in fact the criminal, might be a fourth or fifth or sixth motive, each motive equally feasible, and so the full explanation of the crime could be reached only in the interrelation between all these motives, in the effect of each on each in every combination until finally the effects all canceled out, the result being death. Moreover, one had to consider to what extent the victim himself was responsible, which possibility could provide, both morally and legally, a seventh and even definitive motive. Ricardo Reis felt restored, the hot-water bottle was warming his feet, his brain worked without any interference from the outside world, the tediousness of the book made his eyelids heavy. He shut his eyes for a moment, and when he opened them, Fernando Pessoa was sitting at the foot of the bed as if he had come to visit the sick. That same estranged look had been captured for posterity in several portraits, the hands crossed over the right thigh, the head slightly forward, deathly pale. Ricardo Reis put his book aside between the two pillows. I didn't expect you at this late hour, he said, and smiled amiably lest his visitor catch the note of impatience in his voice, the ambiguity of his words which amounted to saying, I could have done without your visit today. And he had good reason, two to be precise, the first being that he felt like talking, but not to Fernando Pessoa, about his evening at the theater, the second being that Lydia might enter the room at any moment. Not that there was any danger of her crying out, Help, a ghost, but Fernando Pessoa, though it was not in his nature, might wish to stay and witness these intimacies of flesh and spirit, the possibility could not be ruled out. God, who is God, frequently does this, nor can He avoid it, since He is everywhere, but that is something we accept. Ricardo Reis appealed to masculine complicity, We cannot chat for long, I am expecting a visitor, you must agree that it could be embarrassing. You don't waste time, you've been here less than three weeks and already you're involved in amorous intrigues, at least I presume they are amorous. It depends what you mean by amorous, she's a chambermaid in the hotel. My dear Reis, you, an aesthete, intimate with all the goddesses of Olympus, sharing your bed with a chambermaid, with a servant, and I used to listen to you speak incessantly and with the utmost constancy of your Lydia, Neaera, and Chloe, and now you tell me you are infatuated with a chambermaid, you deeply disappoint me. The chambermaid's name is Lydia and I am not infatuated, I am not one for infatuation. Ah, so this much-praised poetic justice exists after all, what an amusing situation, you clamored for Lydia at such length that Lydia finally came, you have been more fortunate than Camões who, in order to win his Natércia, was obliged to invent the name but got no further, so the name Lydia came but not the woman, don't be ungrateful, how do you know what the Lydia of your odes is like, supposing such a phenomenon exists, an intolerable embodiment of passivity, thoughtful silence, and pure spirit, indeed, it is doubtful, as doubtful in fact as the existence of the poet who wrote your odes. But I did write them. Allow me to be skeptical, my dear Reis, I see you there reading a detective story with a hot-water bottle at your feet and waiting for a chambermaid to come and warm the rest of you, if you'll pardon the expression, and you expect me to believe that you are the same man who wrote, *Serene and watching life from a distance*, I must ask you where you were when you watched life from a distance. You yourself wrote that a poet is someone who pretends. We utter such intuitions without knowing how we arrive at them, unfortunately I died without discovering whether it is the poet who pretends to be a man or the man who pretends to be a poet. To pretend and to deceive oneself are not the same thing. Is that a statement or a question. It is a question. Of course they're not the same, I only invented, but you invented yourself, if you want to see the difference, read my poems and go back and read your own. This conversation is certain to keep me up all night. Perhaps your Lydia will come and cradle you in her arms, from what they tell me chambermaids who worship their masters can be extremely affectionate. You sound vexed. Perhaps I am. Tell me something, is my pretense that of a poet or a man. Your situation, Reis my friend, is hopeless, you have invented yourself, you are your own invention, and this has nothing to do with either man or poet. Hopeless. Is that another question, It is, Yes, hopeless, first of all because you do not know who you are, And what about you, did you ever discover who you were, I no longer count, I'm dead, but don't worry, there will be lots of people ready to explain everything about me. Perhaps I came back to Portugal to learn who I am. Nonsense, my dear fellow, childish nonsense, revelations of this kind are only to be found in works of mysticism and on roads leading to Damascus, don't forget that we're in Lisbon and no roads lead from here. I can scarcely keep my eyes open. I'll leave you now to get some sleep, sleep is really the only thing I envy you, only fools believe that sleep is the cousin of death, cousin or brother, I can't remember, I think it's cousin, after so few words of sympathy, do you really want me to return. Please do, I don't have many people to confide in. That is certainly a valid reason. Listen, do me a favor, leave the door ajar, it will save me getting out of bed and catching cold. Are you still expecting company. One never knows, Fernando, one never knows.

Half an hour later, the door was pushed open. Lydia, shivering after a lengthy crossing of stairs and corridors, slipped into his bed, curled up beside him, and asked, Was the theater nice, and he told her the truth, Yes, very nice.

Marcenda and her father did not appear for lunch. To discover why did not require any great tactical subtlety on the part of Ricardo Reis, or any of the dialectical cunning of a detective carrying out an investigation, he simply gave Salvador and himself a little time, chatting idly, his elbows resting on the reception desk with the self-assured air of a friendly guest, and in passing, as a parenthesis or fleeting rhetorical digression, a melody that unexpectedly surfaces during the development of another, he informed Salvador that he had met and made the acquaintance of Doctor Sampaio and his daughter, the most agreeable and refined of people. The smile on Salvador's face became slightly contorted, after all he had spoken to the two guests when they left and they had not mentioned the encounter with Doctor Reis in the theater. Now he knew, true, but not until almost two in the afternoon. How could such a thing happen. Of course he did not expect a written note upon their return telling him, We came across Doctor Reis, I met Doctor Sampaio and his daughter, nevertheless he felt it was a great injustice to have kept him in the dark for so many hours. A hotel manager who is on such friendly terms with the guests should not be treated in this way, what an ungrateful world. For a smile to become contorted, since we are on the subject, only a moment is needed, and it may last only a moment, but to explain the contortion may require a little longer. The fact is that the human mind has such deep recesses that if we venture therein with the intention of examining everything, there is a good chance that we will not emerge quickly. Not that Ricardo Reis made any close examination, all he perceived was that a sudden thought had troubled Salvador, and so it had. Yet even had he tried to figure out what that thought was, he never would have succeeded, which goes to show how little we know each other and how soon our patience runs out when from time to time, though not frequently, we try to find motives, to explain impulses, unless we are dealing with a genuine criminal investigation as in *The God of the Labyrinth*. Salvador overcame his annoyance before one could count to ten, as the saying goes, and allowing himself to be guided solely by his good nature he expressed his delight, praising Doctor Sampaio and his daughter, he a thorough gentleman, she a most refined young lady so carefully brought up, what a pity her life was so sad, with that disability or illness. Between ourselves, Doctor Reis, I don't believe there is a cure. Ricardo Reis had not started the conversation to become involved in a medical debate for which he had already declared himself unqualified, therefore he turned the discussion to what mattered, or mattered to him, without knowing to what extent it mattered, the fact that Doctor Sampaio and Marcenda had not come down for lunch. Suddenly aware of the possibility, he asked, Have they already gone back to Coimbra. Salvador, who could at least claim to know everything in this regard, replied, No, not until tomorrow, today they lunch in the Baixa because Senhorita Marcenda has an appointment with the specialist and then they will take a look around and purchase a few items they need. But will they be dining here this evening. Most certainly. Ricardo Reis moved away from the reception desk, took two paces, changed his mind, and announced, I think I'll take a stroll, the weather looks settled. Salvador, with the tone of one who is merely passing on useless information, said, Senhorita Marcenda said she intended to return to the hotel after lunch and that she would not be accompanying her father on some business matters. Now Ricardo Reis went into the lounge, looked out the window with a weather eye, and returned to the reception desk. On second thought, I'll stay here and read the papers, it isn't raining but it must be cold. Salvador, wholeheartedly endorsing this new proposal, said, I'll have a paraffin heater put in the lounge right away. He rang the hand bell twice. A chambermaid appeared, but it wasn't Lydia. Ah, Carlota, light a heater and put it in the lounge. Whether such details are indispensable or not for a clear understanding of this narrative is something each of us must judge for himself, and the judgment will vary according to our attention, mood, and temperament. There are those who value broad ideas above all, who prefer panoramas and historical frescoes, whereas others appreciate the affinities and contrasts between small brush strokes. We are well aware that it is impossible to please everyone, but here it was simply a question of allowing enough time for the feelings, whatever they might be, to develop between and within the protagonists while Carlota goes back and forth, while Salvador struggles with some difficult calculations, while Ricardo Reis asks himself if he has aroused suspicions by suddenly changing his mind.

Two o'clock came, then two-thirty, the Lisbon newspapers with their faint print were read and reread, the headlines on the front page. Edward VIII to be crowned King of England, the Minister of the Interior congratulated by historian Costa Brochado, wolves are prowling urban areas, the Anschluss plan, which, for those who may not know, proposes the annexation of Austria to Germany, has been repudiated by the Austrian Patriotic Front. The French government has tendered its resignation, and the rift between Gil Robles and Calvo Sotelo could endanger the electoral bloc of the Spanish right-wing parties. Then the advertisements. Pargil is the best elixir for oral hygiene, tomorrow evening the famous ballerina Marujita Fontan will make her debut at the Arcádia, we present the latest automobiles manufactured by Studebaker, the President, the Dictator, if the advertisement of Freire the Engraver offered the universe, this one epitomizes the world in which we live today, an automobile called the Dictator, a clear sign of the times and of contemporary taste. From time to time the buzzer sounds, people leaving, people arriving, a guest checking in, a sharp ping on the bell from Salvador, Pimenta carrying up the luggage, then silence, prolonged and oppressive. The afternoon turns gloomy, it is after three-thirty. Ricardo Reis gets up from the sofa, drags himself to the reception desk, Salvador looks at him with sympathy, even compassion, So you've finished reading all the newspapers. Everything now happens so quickly that Ricardo Reis is given no time to reply. The sound of the buzzer, a voice at the bottom of the stairs, I say Pimenta, could I ask you to help me carry these parcels upstairs. Pimenta goes down, comes up again, Marcenda with him, and Ricardo Reis does not know what to do, should he remain where he is, go back and sit down and pretend that he is reading or dozing in the gentle warmth. If he does so, what will that cunning spy Salvador think. He is undecided between these two courses of action as Marcenda arrives at the desk and says, Good afternoon, and is taken by surprise, Why it's you, Doctor. I was reading the papers, he replies, but hastens to add, I've just this minute finished. These are disastrous sentences, much too peremptory, if I'm reading the papers I'm not interested in conversation, and if I've just finished reading them then I'm on my way out. Feeling utterly ridiculous, he goes on to say, It's quite warm in here. Appalled at the banality of this statement, he still cannot make up his mind, he cannot go back and sit down again, not just yet, if he does she will think he wishes to be alone, and if he waits until she goes up to her room she will think that he is going out. Any move on his part must be carefully timed so that she will think that he has been waiting for her. All of which proved unnecessary, because Marcenda simply said, I am going up to put these things in my room and will come right down for a little chat, if you have the patience to bear with me and don't have more important things to do. We should not be surprised that Salvador is smiling, he likes to see his clients strike up friendships, it is good for the hotel's image, creates a pleasant atmosphere, and even if we were surprised, it does not help the story to speak at length of a thing that no sooner does it surface than it disappears. Ricardo Reis also smiled, and speaking slowly, assured her, I would be delighted, or words to that effect, for there are many other expressions equally commonplace, although to our shame we never stop to analyze them. We should remember them, empty and colorless as they are, as they were spoken and heard for the first time, It will be a pleasure, I am entirely at your service, little declarations of such daring that they cause the person making them to hesitate, and cause the person to whom they are addressed to tremble, because that was a time when words were pristine and feelings came to life.

Marcenda lost no time in coming down. She had tidied her hair, freshened her lipstick, some consider such things automatic, responses in the mirror, while others believe that a woman is conscious of her appearance in all circumstances, and of her moods and the least flirtatious gesture. Ricardo Reis rose to greet her and led her to the sofa which stood at a right angle to his own, reluctant to suggest that they should move to another, more spacious sofa where they might sit side by side. Marcenda sat down, resting her left hand on her lap, and smiled in a strange remote way, as if to say, Take a good look, my hand is quite helpless. Ricardo Reis was about to ask, Are you tired, when Salvador appeared and asked if he could bring them anything, some coffee or tea. They accepted, a coffee would be most welcome in this cold weather. But first Salvador checked the heater, which filled the room with a smell of paraffin that made one feel slightly giddy, while the flame, subdivided into a thousand tiny blue tongues, whispered incessantly. Marcenda asked Ricardo Reis if he enjoyed the play. He said he did, although he found the naturalism of the performance somewhat artificial. He tried to explain more clearly, In my opinion, a stage performance should never be natural, what is presented on stage is theater, not life, life cannot be reproduced, even the most faithful of reflections, that of a mirror, transforms right into left and left into right. But did you enjoy it or not, Marcenda insisted. Yes, he said, and after all one word sufficed. At this moment Lydia entered, put the coffee tray down on the table, asked if they wished anything else. Marcenda said, No, many thanks, but Lydia was looking at Ricardo Reis, who had not raised his eyes and who was carefully taking his cup and asking Marcenda, How many spoons. Two, she replied. Lydia's presence was clearly no longer required, so she withdrew, much too hastily to Salvador's mind, and he reprimanded her from his throne, Be careful with that door.

Putting her cup down on the tray, Marcenda placed her right hand over her left. Both were cold, yet between the two was the difference between the quick and the dead, between what can still be salvaged and what is forever lost. My father would not be pleased if he knew that I am about to take advantage of our acquaintance by asking your medical opinion. Do you want my opinion about your infirmity. Yes, about this arm which cannot move, this wretched hand of mine. I hope you will understand my reluctance to offer any advice, first because I am not a specialist, second because I know nothing of your clinical history, third because professional etiquette forbids my interfering in a case being handled by a colleague. I know all that, but no one can prevent an invalid from having a doctor as a friend and consulting him about her personal problems. Of course not. Then answer my question as a friend. I am happy to be your friend, to use your own words, after all we have known each other for a month. Then you will give me your opinion. I will try, but first must ask you one or two questions. Ask me anything you like, this is another of those phrases we could add to the long list of expressions that meant a great deal once, when words were still in their infancy, At your service, Happy to oblige, It will give me great pleasure, Whatever you wish. Lydia came back into the lounge and saw at a glance that Marcenda was blushing, saw the tears in her eyes, saw Ricardo Reis resting his left cheek on his clenched fist. Both were silent, as if they had come to the end of an important conversation or were preparing for one, what could it have been, what will it be. Lydia took the tray. We all know how coffee cups shake if not placed firmly on their respective saucers, something we must always check when we are not altogether certain that our hands are steady and if we do not want to hear Salvador warn, Careful with that crockery.

Ricardo Reis seemed to reflect. Then, leaning forward, he extended his hands to Marcenda and asked, May I. She also leaned forward slightly, and with her right hand put her left into his hands as if it were an injured bird, its wing broken, a lead pellet embedded in its breast. Slowly, gently but firmly applying pressure, he ran his fingers over the hand, up to the wrist, for the first time in his life knowing what is meant by total surrender, the absence of any reaction, be it voluntary or instinctive, of any resistance, worse, it seemed an alien body, not of this world. Marcenda stared fixedly at her hand, that paralyzed mechanism. Other doctors have probed those lifeless muscles, those useless nerves, those bones that protect nothing, now they are being touched by this man to whom she has entrusted them, if Doctor Sampaio were to walk in this moment, he would not believe his eyes. But no one came into the lounge, usually the scene of so much traffic. Today it is a place for quiet intimacy. Slowly withdrawing his hand, Ricardo Reis looked at his own fingers without knowing why, then asked, How long has it been like this. Four years last December, Did it come about gradually or all of a sudden, Would you call a month gradually or all of a sudden, Are you telling me that within a month you completely lost the power in your arm, I am. Was there any prior sign that something might be wrong, No, No injury, heavy fall or blow, None, What did the doctor say, That it is the consequence of my heart disease, You didn't tell me that you suffer from heart disease, I thought you were interested only in my arm, What else did the doctor say, In Coimbra they told me there is no cure, here, the same thing, but the latest specialist, who has been treating me for almost two years now, says that I can get better. What treatment is he giving you, Massage, sunlamp treatment, electric shock, With what results, None, Your arm does not respond to electric shock, It responds, it jumps, trembles, then is still again. Ricardo Reis fell silent, perceiving a sudden note of hostility and resentment, as if Marcenda were telling him to stop asking so many questions, or to ask her other, different ones, this question for example, Can you remember if something important happened at that time, or, more to the point, have you experienced some misfortune. Marcenda's face showed that she was close to tears. Apart from this problem with your hand, are you troubled by some unhappiness, Ricardo Reis asked her. She nodded, began to gesture but could not finish, convulsed by a deep sob as if her heart had been wrenched, and tears ran uncontrollably down her cheeks. Alarmed, Salvador appeared in the doorway, but Ricardo Reis dismissed him brusquely. Salvador withdrew, lingering just outside the door. Marcenda pulled herself together, only her tears continued to flow, but quietly, and when she spoke, the note of hostility, if that was what it had been, was gone from her voice. After my mother died I found I could no longer use my arm. But you told me only a moment ago that the doctors said the paralysis was the result of heart disease. That is what they said, And do you believe them, I do, Then why do you think that there is a connection between your mother's death and the paralysis in your arm, I am certain of it, but cannot explain it. She paused, summoned what remained of her animosity, and snapped, I am not looking for a healer of souls. Nor am I a healer of souls, just an ordinary doctor in general practice. It was now Ricardo Reis who was irritated. Marcenda raised her hand to her eyes and said, Forgive me, I am annoying you. You are not annoying me, I would gladly help you in whatever way I can. Probably no one can, I had to confide in someone, that was all. So you are truly convinced that this connection exists, As truly as we're sitting here together, And are you not able to move your arm just by knowing that the paralysis came about only because your mother died. Is that all it is, Yes, that's all, which is saying a great deal, because for you, given your deep conviction, there was no other cause, the time has come to ask yourself a straightforward question, is your arm immobile because you cannot move it or because you do not wish to. These words were uttered in a whisper, sensed rather than heard, and Marcenda would not have sensed them had she not been expecting them. Salvador strained to hear, but Pimenta's footsteps could be heard on the landing, he came to ask if there were any documents to be taken to the police. This question, too, was asked in a low voice, and for the same reason, so that the reply would not be heard. Sometimes a reply is not even spoken, trapped between one's teeth, one's lips, and if spoken, it remains inaudible, a tenuous yes or no that dissolves in the shadows of a hotel lounge like a drop of blood in a transparent sea, present but invisible. Marcenda did not say, Because I cannot, she did not say, Because I do not wish to, instead she looked at Ricardo Reis and asked, Have you any advice to offer, something that might lead to a cure, some treatment. I already told you that I'm not a specialist, but as far as I can judge, Marcenda, if you are suffering from heart disease, you are also suffering from yourself. That's the first time anyone ever told me that. We are all ill, with one malaise or another, a deep-rooted malaise that is inseparable from what we are and that somehow makes us what we are, you might even say that each one of us is his own illness, we are so little because of it, and yet we succeed in being so much because of it. But my arm doesn't move, my hand is completely useless. Perhaps it does not move because it does not choose to. This conversation, forgive me, has got us nowhere. You said you feel no improvement, I do not, Then why do you keep coming to Lisbon, It is not my doing, my father insists, and he has his own reasons, What reasons, I am twenty-three years of age, unmarried, brought up never to discuss certain things even though I might think them, for thinking is something one cannot avoid. Can't you be more explicit, Is that necessary. *Lisbon, despite being Lisbon and having ships at sea*, What's that, A line of verse, I don't remember who wrote it, Now it's my turn not to understand. Although Lisbon has so much, it doesn't have every-thing, yet there are some who think that here they will find their heart's desire. If in this roundabout way you are asking me whether my father has a mistress in Lisbon, the answer is yes. Surely your father doesn't need to justify his visits to Lisbon when he has a daughter in need of medical advice, besides he is still a young man, widowed, and therefore free. As I said before, I was brought up not to mention certain things, yet I go on mentioning them slyly, I am like my father, given the position he holds and the kind of education he received, I believe that the more secretive the better. A good thing I didn't have children. Why. There is no mercy in the eyes of one's children. I love my father. I believe you, but love is not enough. Obliged to remain behind the desk, Salvador has no idea what he is missing, revelations, confidences freely exchanged between two people who barely know each other, but to hear he would have to be seated here, on this third sofa, leaning forward, reading on their lips the words they scarcely utter. It would almost be easier to understand the murmuring of the paraffin heater than these subdued voices, they come as if from the confessional, may we be forgiven all our sins.

Marcenda placed her left hand in the palm of her right. Untrue, she did not, the sentence suggests that her left hand was capable of obeying such a command transmitted by the brain. One would need to be present to see how this was done. First the right hand slipped underneath the left, then held the wrist with the little finger and fourth finger, and now both came toward Ricardo Reis, each hand offering the other, or pleading for help, or simply resigned to the inevitable. Tell me, do you think I will ever be cured. I cannot say, you have been like this for four years without any improvement, your own doctor has all the details of your medical history, which I don't, besides, as I've already explained, I have no competence in this field. Should I stop coming to Lisbon, tell my father that I accept the situation, that he shouldn't waste any more money trying to find a cure. Your father has two reasons for coming to Lisbon, if you take away one of them he may or may not find the courage to continue coming on his own, but he will have lost the alibi your illness provided, at present he sees himself only as the father who wishes his daughter cured. What should I do then. We two scarcely know each other, I have no right to give you advice, Please, I am asking it, Don't give up, keep coming to Lisbon for your father's sake, even if you no longer believe there is a cure, I have almost stopped believing in a cure, Cling to whatever belief you have left, believing will be your alibi, Alibi for what, To hope, Hope in what, Hope, just hope, one reaches a point where there is nothing but hope, and that is when we discover that hope is everything. Marcenda leaned back on the sofa, slowly stroking her left hand, her back to the window, her face scarcely visible. Normally Salvador would appear now to turn on the chandelier, the pride and joy of the Hotel Bragança, but on this occasion he does not, as if to show his displeasure at being excluded from a conversation which he, after all, made possible. This is how they repay him, sitting there rapt in conversation, whispering almost in darkness. No sooner did he think this than the chandelier went on, Ricardo Reis had taken the initiative, because anyone walking into the lounge would have been suspicious to find a man and a woman together in the shadows, even if the man was a doctor and the woman a cripple. Much worse, this, than the backseat of a taxi. As was to be expected, Salvador appeared, I was coming this very moment to switch on the light, Doctor. He smiled, and they smiled too, gestures and postures according to the rules of civilized behavior, part hypocrisy, part necessity, to disguise our anguish. After Salvador withdrew, there was a long silence, it seemed less easy to speak with all this light, then Marcenda said, Without wishing to pry into your affairs, can I ask you why you have been living for a whole month in this hotel. I still haven't decided whether or not to look for a place, I may return to Rio de Janeiro. Salvador tells me that you lived there for sixteen years, what made you decide to come back. I felt homesick. You've got over it quickly, if already you're talking about leaving. It isn't exactly that, when I embarked for Lisbon, I felt I could put it off no longer, there were important matters to be dealt with here. And now. And now, he broke off, staring into the mirror ahead, now I am like an elephant that senses its approaching end and begins heading for the place where it must die. If you return to Brazil for good, then that will be the place where the elephant goes to die. When a man emigrates, he thinks of the country where he might die as the country where he will spend the rest of his life, and that is the difference. Perhaps, when I return to Lisbon next month, you will no longer be here. By then I might have found a place to live, opened a practice, settled into a routine. Or you might have returned to Rio de Janeiro. You will be informed, our friend Salvador will pass on all the news. I will come in order not to lose hope, And I will be here, if I have not lost hope.

Marcenda is twenty-three. We don't know for certain what kind of education she has received, but being the daughter of a notary, and from Coimbra no less, she almost certainly attended grammar school. Had it not been for her illness, no doubt she would have enrolled in some faculty, perhaps law or arts, preferably arts, because apart from the fact that we already have a lawyer in the family, the tedious study of codes and regulations is not suitable for women. If only she had been born a boy, to continue the Sampaio dynasty and legal practice. But this isn't the problem, the problem here is to find a young woman at this time in Portugal capable of sustaining such a lengthy and elevated conversation, we mean elevated when compared with the standards of the day. She did not make a single frivolous remark, showed no pretentiousness, did not affect wisdom or try to compete with the male, if you'll pardon the expression, she spoke naturally, was obviously intelligent, perhaps in compensation for her disability, something which can happen with women as well as with men. She rises from the sofa, holds her left hand up to her breast and smiles, I am deeply grateful for the patience you have shown me. No need to thank me, I enjoyed our conversation. Are you dining here this evening, Yes, I am, Then we shall see each other soon, good-bye for now. Ricardo Reis watched her leave, she was not as tall as he remembered her, but slender, that was why his memory had deceived him. He heard her say to Salvador, Tell Lydia to come to my room as soon as she is free. Ricardo Reis alone will find this request startling, because certain shameful acts of promiscuity between social classes are weighing on his conscience. What could be more natural than a maid's being summoned to a guest's bedroom, especially if the guest in question needs help to change her dress, for example, because her arm is paralyzed. Ricardo Reis stays a little longer, switches on the radio just as they are broadcasting the music from *The Sleeping Beauty*, one of those coincidences which only a novelist would exploit to draw parallels between a silent lake and a young virgin. Although this has not been mentioned and she herself does not declare it, Marcenda is a virgin, a wholly private matter, even a fiancé, should she ever have one, will not dare to ask, Are you a virgin. For the time being and in this social ambiance one assumes that she is. Later, at the opportune moment, we may discover with some indignation that she wasn't after all. The music came to an end, was followed by a Neapolitan song, a serenata or something of the kind, *amore mio, cuore ingrato, con te, la vita insieme, per sempre*, the tenor was singing these heartfelt protestations when into the lounge came two guests sporting diamond tiepins in their cravats, their double chins concealing the knots. They sat down, lit their cigars, were about to discuss a business deal involving cork or canned fish, we would know for certain except that Ricardo Reis is now leaving, so engrossed that he even forgets to greet Salvador. Something strange is going on in this hotel.

Later that evening Doctor Sampaio arrives. Ricardo Reis and Marcenda have not left their rooms. Lydia has been seen from time to time on the stairs or in the halls, but only where she has been summoned. She was rude to Pimenta, and he gave her as good as he got, the incident occurring out of everyone's hearing, and just as well, because Salvador would certainly have demanded an explanation from Pimenta, who was muttering insinuations about certain people who walked in their sleep and could be found wandering down corridors in the middle of the night. It was eight o'clock when Doctor Sampaio knocked on the door. He would not bother coming in, thank you all the same, he had only called to invite Ricardo Reis to join them for dinner, Marcenda had told him about their little chat, I am greatly indebted to you, Doctor. Ricardo Reis insisted that he come in and sit down for a moment. I didn't do anything, simply listened and gave the only advice that could be given by someone without any special knowledge of the case, to persevere with the treatment, not to become disheartened. That's what I'm always telling her, but she no longer pays attention, you know what children are, yes Papa, but she comes to Lisbon without any real interest, and yet she must come so that the specialist can follow the progression of her illness, though of course the treatment itself is administered in Coimbra. But surely there are specialists in Coimbra. Very few, and those we consulted, without wishing to give offense, did not inspire much confidence, whereas the specialist in Lisbon is a man of considerable skill and experience. These absences from Coimbra must interfere with your work. Sometimes, but no father worthy of the name would refuse to sacrifice some time for his children. In this vein they exchanged a few more phrases matched in subtlety of intent, concealing as much as they revealed, as tends to happen in conversations in general and in this one in particular, for the reasons known to us, until Doctor Sampaio finally decided it was time to withdraw. Well then, we will knock on your door at nine, No, I will come by, I don't see why you should go to any trouble. And so at the appointed hour Ricardo Reis knocked on the door of room two hundred and five. It would have been most indelicate to have knocked on Marcenda's door first, another of those subtle formalities.

Their entrance into the dining room was unanimously greeted with smiles and little deferential nods. Salvador, his annoyance forgotten or diplomatically suppressed, threw open the glass-paneled doors, and Ricardo Reis and Marcenda walked in front as etiquette demanded, he is their guest. From where we are standing we can scarcely hear the radio, there would be much food for thought if it should happen to be the wedding march from *Lohengrin* or the one by Mendelssohn or, less well known, perhaps because it is played as the prelude to disaster, the one in *Lucia di Lammermoor* by Donizetti. Needless to say, the table where they will sit is that of Doctor Sampaio, which is invariably waited upon by Felipe, but Ramón does not abdicate his prerogative, he will assist his colleague and compatriot. Both of them were born in Villagarcia de Arosa, it is the destiny of humans to follow their own distinct paths in life. Some have followed theirs from Galicia to Lisbon, while this man Reis was born in Oporto, for a time lived in the capital, then emigrated to Brazil, and the two people with him have been shuttling back and forth between Coimbra and Lisbon for the last three years. Each is searching, for a cure, for money, for peace of mind, for pleasure, each has his own goal, which explains why it is so difficult to satisfy all who are in need. The dinner passes tranquilly. Marcenda is seated on her father's right, her left hand reclining as usual at the side of her plate, but curiously enough it is not hiding, on the contrary, it almost appears to glory in being seen, and if you think that word excessive, then you certainly haven't heard how ordinary people speak. Let us not forget, either, that this hand has rested in the hands of Ricardo Reis, and how should it feel if not glorious. Marcenda's disability is not discussed, the noose has been mentioned far too often already in the house of this woman condemned to the gallows. Doctor Sampaio is speaking of the wonders of the Athens of Portugal, There I was born into the world, there I was reared, there I graduated, there I exercise my profession, I swear the city is incomparable. His style is vigorous, but there is no danger of entering into an argument at the table about the merits of Coimbra compared with other cities, whether Oporto or Villagarcia de Arosa. Ricardo Reis does not care where one was born, and Felipe and Ramón would never dare to join in the conversation. They know their place, which is not the place of their birth. It was inevitable that Doctor Sampaio should learn that Ricardo Reis had gone to Brazil for political reasons, although it is hard to say how he learned it. Salvador did not tell him, because he does not know either, nor did Ricardo Reis confide it, but certain things are gleaned from broken words, moments of silence, a glance. He only had to say, I left for Brazil in nineteen nineteen, the year in which the monarchy was restored in the north, he only had to use a certain tone of voice, and the notary's sharp ear, accustomed to listening to falsehoods, oaths, confessions, was not deceived. It was inevitable, then, that the conversation should turn to politics. By indirect routes, testing the ground, trying to detect hidden mines or snares, but feeling incapable of changing the topic, Ricardo Reis allowed himself to be carried along, and before the dessert he had already stated that he had no faith in democracies and heartily despised socialism. You're among friends, Doctor Sampaio assured him with a smile. Marcenda showed little interest in their conversation, for some reason she placed her left hand on her lap. If there had been glorying, it was now burned out. What we need, my dear Reis, in this corner of Europe, is a man of vision and firm resolve to head our government and run the country. These were the words spoken by Doctor Sampaio, who continued, There is no possible comparison between the Portugal you knew when you left for Rio de Janeiro and the Portugal you have come back to find, I know that you have only recently returned, but if you have been around and kept your eyes open, you must have noticed enormous changes, greater prosperity, public order, a coherent plan to encourage patriotism, the respect of other nations for the achievements of our fatherland, for its secular history and empire. I haven't seen much, Ricardo Reis confessed, but I'm up to date on what is reported in the newspapers. The newspapers must be read, of course, but that is not enough, you must see with your own eyes the roads, the ports, the schools, the public works everywhere, and the atmosphere of discipline, my dear fellow, the calm on the streets and in people's hearts, an entire nation dedicated to honest labor under the leadership of a great statesman, truly an iron hand in a velvet glove, precisely what we needed. A splendid metaphor, that. Yes, I'm sorry not to have invented it myself, it stuck in my mind, how true it is that a single image can be worth a hundred speeches, it appeared two or three years ago on the front page of *Sempre Fixe*, or was it *Os Ridículos*, an iron hand in a velvet glove, and the drawing was so excellent that both the velvet and the iron were conveyed. In a satirical magazine. Truth, dear Doctor Reis, does not always choose the place. It remains to be seen if the place always chooses the truth. Doctor Sampaio frowned a little, the contradiction disturbing him somewhat, but he treated the remark as if it were too profound to be discussed then and there among the wines from Colares and the cheeses. Self-absorbed, Marcenda nibbled little bits of rind, she raised her voice to say that she did not want any dessert or coffee, then began a sentence which might have diverted the conversation to *Tá Mar*, but her father went on, It's not a literary masterpiece but it's certainly a useful book, easy to read, and should open many people's eyes. What is the book. The title is *Conspiracy*, written by a patriotic journalist, a nationalist, a certain Tomé Vieira, I don't know whether you've heard of him. No, I haven't, living so far away. The book was published only a few days ago, you really must read it and give me your opinion. I'll certainly read it if you recommend it with such enthusiasm. Ricardo Reis was beginning to regret that he had declared himself anti-socialist, anti-democratic, and also anti-Bolshevik, not because he was not all these things but because he was growing tired of such unrelieved nationalism, perhaps even more tired at not having been able to speak to Marcenda. As it so often happens, the thing left undone tires you most of all, you only feel rested when it has been accomplished.

The dinner at an end, Ricardo Reis drew back Marcenda's chair and allowed her to walk ahead with her father. Once' outside, all three hesitated, wondering whether they should pass into the lounge, but Marcenda finally decided to retire to her room, complaining of a headache. Tomorrow we probably will not see each other, we are leaving early, she told him. Ricardo Reis wished them a good journey, Perhaps I will still be here when you return next month. Should you be gone, do leave us your new address, Doctor Sampaio urged him. Now there is nothing more to be said, Marcenda will go to her room, she has or claims to have a headache, Ricardo Reis does not know what he wants to do, Doctor Sampaio will be going out again later this evening.

Ricardo Reis also went out. He wandered, went into various cinemas to look at the posters, watched a game of chess, white won, and it was raining when he left the café, so he took a taxi back to the hotel. Entering his room, he noticed that the covers had not been turned back and that the second pillow had not been removed from the closet. *Vague, foolish sorrow stops at the door of my soul, stares at me awhile, and moves on*, he murmured, smiling to himself.

A man must read widely, a little of everything or whatever he can, but given the shortness of life and the verbosity of the world, not too much should be demanded of him. Let him begin with those titles no one should omit, commonly referred to as books for learning, as if not all books were for learning, and this list will vary according to the fount of knowledge one drinks from and the authority that monitors its flow. In the case of Ricardo Reis, educated by Jesuits, we can form some idea despite the considerable difference between the teachers of yesterday and those of today. Then come the inclinations of youth, those favorite authors, those passing infatuations, those readings of Werther spurring one to suicide or self-preservation, then on to the serious reading of adulthood. Once we reach a certain stage in life we all read the same things more or less, although the starting point always makes a difference, and the living have the distinct advantage of being able to read what others, because they are dead, will never know. To give but one example, here is Alberto Caeiro, who, having died in nineteen fifteen, poor fellow, did not read *Nome de Guerra*, he has no idea what he missed, and Fernando Pessoa, and Ricardo Reis too, will depart this world before Almada Negreiros publishes his novel. This is almost a repetition of the amusing tale about the gentleman from La Palice, who a quarter of an hour before dying was still alive and kicking, as those wits would say. Not for a moment did he contemplate the sorrow of no longer being alive and kicking a quarter of an hour hence. Let us move on. A man, then, will sample everything, even *Conspiracy*, and it will do him no harm whatsoever to come down every now and then from the clouds where he is in the habit of taking refuge, in order to see how commonplace thoughts are forged, because it is these that help people exist from day to day, not those of Cicero or Spinoza. All the more so, when the recommendation, a nagging exhortation, comes from Coimbra, Read *Conspiracy*, my friend, there you will find some sound opinions, any weaknesses of form or plot are compensated for by the worthiness of the message. Coimbra, most learned of cities, teeming with scholars, knows what it is talking about. The very next day Ricardo Reis went out and bought the slim volume, took it up to his room, unwrapped it furtively, for not all acts carried out behind closed doors are what they appear, sometimes they are nothing other than a person's shame at his own private habits, secret pleasures, picking his nose, scratching his scalp. Perhaps this cover, which shows a woman in a raincoat and cap walking down a street by a prison, the barred window and sentry box eliminating any doubt about the fate of conspirators, is no less embarrassing. Ricardo Reis, then, is in his room, comfortably settled on the sofa. It is raining wherever one looks, as if the sky were a suspended sea draining interminably through countless leaks. Everywhere there is flood and famine, but this little book will tell how a woman's soul launched itself into the noble crusade of restoring to reason and to the nationalist spirit a man whose mind became confused by dangerous ideas. Women are extremely able in such matters, perhaps to atone for those wiles more akin to their nature, by which they have perturbed and brought about the downfall of men since Adam. Ricardo Reis has now read the first seven chapters, namely, On the eve of the election, A bloodless coup, The fable of love, The feast of the Holy Queen, A university strike, Conspiracy, and The senator's daughter. The plot is as follows, a university student, a farmer's son, gets into some mischief, is arrested, locked up in the prison of Aljube, and it is the daughter of the aforementioned senator who with patriotic fervor and missionary zeal will move heaven and earth to secure his release, which is not all that difficult in the end, because to the astonishment of the man who brought her into the world, this senator who belonged to the democratic party but is now an unmasked conspirator, she is much esteemed in the upper spheres of government, a father can never tell how his own daughter will turn out. Though there are of course certain differences, she speaks like Joan of Arc. Papa was on the point of being arrested several days ago, I gave my word of honor that Papa would not evade his responsibilities, I also guaranteed that Papa would stop his plotting. Such filial devotion, so touching, Papa invoked three times in one sentence, the bonds of affection reach such extremes in life. The devoted girl continues, You may attend your meeting arranged for tomorrow, nothing will happen to you, I promise, because I know and the police also know that the conspirators are meeting again, but they have decided to turn a blind eye, such a benevolent, kind-hearted police force here in Portugal, and little wonder, since they have an informer in the enemy camp, none other, would you believe it, than the daughter of a former senator and opponent of this regime. Family traditions have been betrayed, but all will end happily for the parties in question if we take the author of the work seriously. Let us now hear what he has to say, The situation in our country has been discussed with enthusiasm in the foreign press, our economic strategy has been upheld as a model, there are constant admiring references to our monetary policies, throughout the land industrial projects continue to provide employment for thousands of workers, every day the newspapers outline governmental steps to overcome the crisis which, on account of world events, has also affected us, but when compared with that of other countries the state of our economy is most encouraging, the Portuguese nation and the statesmen who guide her are quoted worldwide, the political doctrine we pursue here is being studied abroad, and one can confidently say that other nations regard us with envy and respect, the world's leading newspapers send their most experienced journalists to discover the secret of our success, the head of our government is finally coaxed out of his persistent humility, out of his stubborn aversion to publicity, and is featured in newspaper columns throughout the world, his image is given maximum exposure and his political pronouncements are transformed into an evangelical mission. In the face of all this, which is only a pale shadow of what could be said, you must agree, Carlos, that it was utter madness to become involved in university strikes which have never achieved anything worthwhile, are you even aware of the trouble I'm going through to get you out of here. You are right, Marília, but the police have no proof that I did anything wrong, all they know for certain is that it was I who waved the red flag, which wasn't a flag at all or anything remotely like a flag, it was only a handkerchief that cost twenty-five cents, a prank. This conversation takes place in the prison, in the visitors' room, but in a village, also as it happens in the district of Coimbra, another farmer, the father of the sweet girl whom this Carlos will marry toward the end of the story, explains to a gathering of subordinates that there is nothing worse than being a Communist, the Communists want neither bosses nor workers, they don't accept laws or religion, they don't believe anyone should be baptized or get married, for them love does not exist, woman is a fickle creature, all men are entitled to use her, children are not answerable to their parents, and everyone is free to behave as he likes. In another four chapters and in the epilogue, the gentle but Valkyrian Marília rescues the student from prison and the political scourge, rehabilitates her father who abandons his subversive activities once and for all, and declares that within the new corporative plan the problem is being resolved without hypocrisy, conflict, or insurrection. The class struggle is over and has been replaced with a system of good values, capital, and labor. To conclude, the nation must be run like a family with lots of children, where the father imposes order to safeguard their education, because unless children are taught to respect their father everything falls apart and the household is doomed. Bearing these irrefutable facts in mind, the two landowners, the fathers of the bride and groom, after settling some minor disagreements, even help to resolve certain little conflicts between the workers, God need not have bothered expelling us from His paradise, seeing as we have succeeded in regaining it so soon. Ricardo Reis closed the book, it hadn't taken him long to read it. These are the best lessons of all, concise, brief, almost instantaneous, Such stupidity, with this outburst he repays the absent Doctor Sampaio and for a moment loathes the entire world, the incessant rain, the hotel, the book tossed on the ground, Marcenda. But then he decides, without quite knowing why, to exempt Marcenda, perhaps simply for the pleasure of saving something, just as we pick up a piece of wood or stone from a pile of rubble. The shape caught our eye, and without the courage to throw it away we end up putting it in our pocket, for no good reason.

As for us, we are doing fine, as fine as those wonders described above. In the land of *nuestros hermanos*, on the other hand, things are going from bad to worse, the family is sadly divided, Gil Robles may win the election, or Largo Caballero, and the Falange has made it clear that it will confront the Red dictatorship on the streets. In our oasis of peace we watch with regret the spectacle of a chaotic and quarrelsome Europe locked in endless debates, in political squabbles which according to Marília never achieved anything worthwhile. In France, Sarraut has now formed a Coalition Republican government and the right-wing parties have lost no time in pouncing on him, launching a hail of criticisms, accusations, and insults couched in the foul language one associates more with rowdy hooligans than with the citizens of a country that is a model of propriety and the beacon of Western culture. Thank heaven there are still voices in this continent, and powerful voices at that, who are prepared to speak out in the name of peace and harmony, we are referring to Hitler, the proclamation he made in the presence of the Brownshirts, all that Germany wants is to work in a climate of peace, let us banish once and for all mistrust and skepticism, and he dared to go further, Let the world know that Germany will pursue and cherish peace as no other nation has ever cherished it before. Indeed, two hundred and fifty thousand German soldiers are ready to occupy the Rhineland, and within the last few days a German military force invaded Czechoslovakian territory. If it is true that Juno sometimes appears in the form of a cloud, then all clouds are Juno. The life of nations, after all, consists of much barking and little biting, and you will see, God permitting, that all will end in perfect harmony. What we cannot accept is that Lloyd George should assert that Portugal has far too many colonies in comparison with Germany and Italy, when only the other day we observed public mourning to mark the death of their King George V, men in black ties and bands, women in crepe. How dare he complain that we have too many colonies, when in fact we have too few, take a look at the Pink Map of the Portuguese territories in Africa. Had that outrage been avenged as justice demanded, no one would be competing with us now, from Angola to Mozambique there would be no obstacle in our way and everything would be under the Portuguese flag, but the English, true to character, stalked us, the perfidious Albion, one doubts whether they are even capable of behaving otherwise, it is a national vice, and there is not a single nation that does not have reason to complain of them. When Fernando Pessoa turns up, Ricardo Reis must not forget to raise the interesting question as to whether colonies are a good or bad thing, not from the point of view of Lloyd George, whose sole concern is to appease Germany by handing over what other nations have acquired with considerable effort, but from his own point of view, the view of Pessoa, who revived Padre Vieira's dream by prophesying the advent of the Fifth Empire. He must also ask him, on the one hand, how he would resolve the contradiction of his own making, that Portugal has no need of colonies in order to fulfill her imperial destiny yet without them is diminished at home and abroad in material and moral terms, and, on the other hand, what he thinks of the prospect of our colonies being handed over to Germany and Italy, as Lloyd George is about to propose. What Fifth Empire will that be, when we are despoiled and betrayed, stripped like Christ on His way to Calvary, a people condemned to suffering, hands outstretched, the bonds loosely tied, for real imprisonment is the acceptance of imprisonment, hands humbly reaching to receive the alms distributed by *O Século*. Perhaps Fernando Pessoa will reply, as he has on other occasions, As you well know, I have no strong principles, today I argue for one thing, tomorrow for another, I may not believe in what I defend today or have any real faith in what I defend tomorrow. He might even add, by way of justification, For me there is no longer any today or tomorrow, how can I be expected to go on believing or expect it of others, and even if they believe, do they really know what they believe in. My vision of a Fifth Empire was vague and fanciful, why should it become a reality

126

for you, people were too quick to believe in what I said, yet I never attempted to conceal my doubt, I would have done better to remain silent, simply looking on. As I myself have always done, Ricardo Reis will reply, and Fernando Pessoa will tell him, Only when we are dead do we become spectators, nor can we even be sure of that. I am dead and wander about, I pause on street corners, if there are people capable of seeing me, and they are rare, they will think that all I am doing is watching others pass, they do not know that if anyone falls I cannot pick him up, and yet I do not feel that I am simply looking on, all my actions, all my words continue to live, they advance beyond the street corner where I am resting, I watch them go and can do nothing to amend them, even when they are the result of an error. I cannot explain or sum up myself in a single action or word, even if only to replace doubt with negation, shadows with darkness, a yes with a no, both having the same meaning, but worse than that, perhaps they are not even the words I spoke or the actions I performed, worse because irremediable, perhaps they are the things I never did, the words I never uttered, the one word or gesture which would have given meaning to what I was. If a dead man can get so upset, death clearly does not bring peace. The only difference between life and death is that the living still have time, but the time to say that one word, to make that one gesture, is running out for them. What gesture, what word, I don't know, a man dies from not having said it, from not having made it, that is what he dies of, not from sickness, and that is why, when dead, he finds it so difficult to accept death. My dear Fernando Pessoa, you're reading things upside down. My dear Ricardo Reis, I can no longer read. Improbable on two counts, this conversation is reported as if it actually took place. There was no other way of making it sound plausible.

Since Ricardo Reis had given her no cause for jealousy other than to have conversed in public with Marcenda, albeit in a low voice, Lydia's anger could not be expected to last. First they had told her clearly that they wished nothing more, then they had waited in silence while she removed the coffee cups. This was enough to make her hands tremble. For four nights she wept into her pillow before falling asleep, not so much at the humiliation of being ignored, after all what right had she to indulge in such tantrums, but because the doctor stopped having his breakfast in his room, he was punishing her, Why, upon my soul, when I have done nothing wrong. But on the fifth morning Ricardo Reis did not come down to breakfast, and Salvador said, Ah Lydia, take some coffee up to two hundred and one, and when she entered the room, she shook with nerves, poor girl, she could not help it. He looked at her soberly, placed his hand on her arm, and asked, Are you angry with me. She replied, No, Doctor. But you haven't been back. Lydia did not know what to say, she shrugged her shoulders, wretched, and he drew her toward him. That same night she descended to his room, but neither mentioned the reason for their separation, unthinkable that she should dare, I was jealous, or that he should condescend, My darling, what on earth possessed you, no, it could never be a conversation between equals, everybody knows that there is nothing more difficult to achieve in this world.

Nations struggle against each other on behalf of interests that are not those of Jack or Pierre or Hans or Manolo or Giuseppe, all masculine names to simplify matters, yet these and other men innocently consider those interests to be theirs, or which will be theirs at considerable cost, when the moment arrives to settle accounts. The rule is that some eat figs while others watch. People struggle for what they believe to be their values but what may be merely emotions momentarily aroused. Such is the case of Lydia, our chambermaid, and Ricardo Reis, known to everyone as a doctor of medicine, should he finally resume his practice, and to some as a poet, should he ever allow anyone to read what he painstakingly composes. But people also struggle for other reasons, for the same reasons, power, prestige, hatred, love, envy, jealousy, sheer malice, hunting grounds marked out and trespassed on, competition and rivalry, even loot, as occurred recently in the neighborhood of Mouraria. Ricardo Reis had not seen it reported, but Salvador was devouring the details avidly, his elbows resting on the opened newspaper, the pages carefully smoothed out, A dreadful business, Doctor, they're a violent lot, those people in Mouraria, they've no respect for human life, the slightest excuse and they're ready to stab each other without compassion or pity, even the police are frightened, they go in there only when it's all over, to pick up the pieces, listen to this, it says here that a certain José Reis, nicknamed José Rola, fired five shots at the head of one António Mesquita, known as O Mouraria, and killed him, needless to say, no, it had nothing to do with women, the newspaper says it was a case of a quarrel over stolen goods, the one cheated the other, it happens all the time. Five shots, Ricardo Reis repeated, not to appear unconcerned, and grew pensive. He could visualize the scene, the gun firing five shots at the same target, the head receiving the first bullet while still erect, then the body on the ground spurting blood, rapidly growing weaker, and the other four bullets, superfluous yet somehow necessary, two, three, four, five, a whole barrelful of hatred in every shot, the head jerking on the pavement each time, terror and dismay on all sides, then uproar, women screaming out of the windows. It's doubtful that anyone would have had the courage to grab José Rola by the arm, most likely the bullets in the magazine were used up, or his finger suddenly froze on the trigger, or his hatred was satisfied. The assassin will escape, but he will not get far, for no one gets away with anything in Mouraria. The funeral is tomorrow, Salvador informs him, were I not on duty I would be there. Do you like funerals, Ricardo Reis asks him. It's not exactly a question of liking them, but a funeral such as this one is worth seeing, especially when there has been a crime. Ramón lives in the Rua dos Cavaleiros and he has heard rumors which he passes on to Ricardo Reis at dinnertime. The whole neighborhood is expected to turn up, Doctor, and it is even said that the cronies of José Rola are threatening to smash open the coffin, if they carry out their threat there will be merry hell, I swear by Jesus. But if O Mouraria is dead, what more can they do to him, a man like that is not likely to come back from the other world to finish what he began in this one. With people of that sort you can never tell, deep hatred doesn't end with death. I'm almost tempted to attend this funeral myself. Go, then, but don't get too close, and if there is trouble, take shelter under a staircase and let them fight it out among themselves.

Things did not come to that pass, perhaps because the threat had been nothing but bravado, perhaps because two armed policemen were patrolling the neighborhood, a symbol of protection which would have proved ineffectual if the troublemakers had gone ahead with their gruesome plan, but when all is said and done, the presence of the law commands some respect. Ricardo Reis appeared discreetly before the funeral cortege was due to set off, he watched from a distance as he had been advised, having no desire to find himself in the midst of a sudden riot, and was amazed at the hundreds of people cramming into the street in front of the morgue, just like the charity day organized by *O Século*, were it not for all those women dressed in garish red, their skirts, blouses, shawls, and their youths in suits of the same color, a most unusual expression of mourning if these are friends of the deceased, and a blatant provocation if they are his enemies. This looks more like a carnival parade. Now the bier comes into sight, drapes flapping as it heads for the cemetery, drawn by two mares with plumes and trappings, and two policemen march, one on either side of the coffin, a guard of honor for O Mouraria, these are the ironies of fate, who would have imagined it. There go the military policemen with their swords knocking against their legs and their holsters unbuttoned, and the mourners wail and sob, those dressed in red making as much noise as those in black, the latter for the dead man being carried to his grave, the former for his assassin locked up in jail. Lots of people barefoot and covered with rags. Some women, dressed in all their finery and wearing gold bracelets, walk arm in arm with their menfolk, the latter have black sideburns and clean-shaven faces still blue from the razor, they look around them with suspicion, other women shout insults, their bodies sway at the hips, but however sincere or false their sentiments all the people show a kind of ferocious gaiety which has brought friends and enemies together. This tribe of criminals, pimps, whores, pickpockets, and burglars fences the black horde that marches across the city. Windows open to watch them file past. The courtyard of the miracles, reminiscent of Victor Hugo's *Notre Dame de Paris*, has emptied, and the residents tremble with fear, because the thief who will enter their house tomorrow might be out there. Look, Mummy, the children shout, but for children everything is one big celebration. Ricardo Reis accompanied the funeral cortege as far as the Paço da Rainha. Women began to cast furtive glances at the well-dressed gentleman,

Who can he be, this is feminine curiosity, natural in those who spend their life sizing up men. The cortege disappeared around a corner, almost certainly heading toward the Alto de São João, unless it took another turn farther on, to the left, in the direction of Benfica, it was definitely not heading toward the Cemetery of Prazeres, and what a pity, for we are losing an edifying example of the equality bestowed by death, O Mouraria lying side by side with Fernando Pessoa. What conversations would those two have under the shade of the cypress trees as they watched the ships enter the harbor on sultry afternoons, the one explaining to the other how words must be juggled in order to pull off a confidence game or pull off a poem. That same evening, as he served the soup, Ramón explained to Doctor Ricardo Reis that the red garments indicated neither mourning nor disrespect, rather it was a custom peculiar to the neighborhood, whose inhabitants donned red for all special occasions. The tradition existed before he arrived from Galicia, and he learned about it from others. Did you catch sight of a very striking woman at the funeral, tall, dark eyes, dressed in fine clothes, wearing a stole made of soft merino wool. My dear fellow, there were so many women in the crowd, hundreds of them, who was she. The lover of O Mouraria, a singer. No, I didn't notice her. Such a beauty and what a voice, it will be interesting to see who grabs her now. It's not likely to be me, Ramón, and I don't think it will be you either. That I should be so lucky, Doctor, that I should be so lucky, but that kind of woman costs money. This is just talk, wishful thinking, a fellow has to say something, does he not, but as for the red garments, I believe the custom goes back to the time of the Moors, the devil's weeds, nothing to do with Christianity. When Ramón came back later to remove his plate, he asked Ricardo Reis what he thought about the news arriving from Spain as the elections drew near, and who in his opinion would win, The outcome won't affect me, I am doing all right here, but I'm thinking about my father back in Galicia, where I still have some relatives, although most of them have emigrated. To Portugal. All over the world, in a manner of speaking, between brothers, nephews, and cousins my family is scattered throughout Cuba, Brazil, and Argentina, I even have a godson in Chile. Ricardo Reis told him what he knew from press reports, the right-wing parties were expected to win, and Gil Robles had said, You know who Gil Robles is, I've heard the name, Well, he said that when he comes to power he will abolish Marxism and the class struggle and establish social justice. Do you know what Marxism is, Ramón, No I don't, Doctor, And the class struggle, No, And social justice, I've never had any dealings with the law, thanks be to God. Well, within the next few days we will know who has won, probably nothing will change, Better the devil you know, as my grandfather used to say, Your grandfather was right, Ramón, your grandfather was a clever man.

Whether he was or not, the left won. The following morning the newspapers reported that at first it looked as if the right had won in seventeen provinces, but when all the votes were counted, it became apparent that the left had elected more deputies than the center and right put together. Rumors were already circulating that a military coup was being planned with the connivance of Generals Goded and Franco, but these were being denied. President Alcalá Zamora entrusted Azaña with the task of forming a government. Let's see what this will bring, Ramón, whether it will be good or bad for Galicia. Here, walking in these streets, one sees grim faces, but a few dissimulate, if that gleam in their eye is not one of satisfaction, you could have fooled me. *Here* in the last sentence does not mean all of Lisbon let alone all Portugal, who knows what is happening in the rest of the country, *Here* means only the thirty streets located between the Cais do Sodré and São Pedro de Alcântara and between the Rossio and Calhariz, like an inner city surrounded by invisible walls that protect it from an invisible siege. The besieged and besiegers coexist, each side refers to the other as They, because the two are different, mutually foreign, they eye each other with suspicion, one side craves more power, the other side finds its strength insufficient. The wind blowing from Spain, what will it bring us, what nuptials. Fernando Pessoa replied, Communism, it won't be long in coming. Ironically he added, Hard luck, my dear Reis, you fled from Brazil in order to live the rest of your days in peace, and the next thing you know our neighbor, Spain, is in turmoil, soon they will invade us. How often do I have to tell you that if I came back, it was because of you. You still haven't convinced me. I'm not trying to convince you, all I ask is that you spare me your views on this matter. Don't be angry with me. I lived in Brazil, now I'm here in Portugal, I have to live somewhere, when you were alive you were sufficiently intelligent to understand this and more. This is the drama, my dear Reis, one has to live somewhere, for there is nowhere that is not somewhere and life cannot be other than life, at long last I am becoming aware of this, the greatest evil of all is that a man can never reach the horizon before his eyes, and the ship in which we do not sail, we would have that be the ship of our voyage, *Ah, the entire quay, a memory carved in stone.* And now that we have yielded to sentiment and started quoting verses, here is a line by Álvaro de Campos, who someday will achieve the recognition he deserves, *Console yourself in the arms of Lydia, if your love endures,* and remember that that too was denied me. Good-night, Fernando, Good-night, Ricardo. Carnival will soon be here, enjoy yourself but don't expect to see me for the next few days. They had met in a local café, half a dozen tables, no one there knew them. Fernando Pessoa came back and sat down again, I've just had an idea, why don't you dress up as a horse trainer, high boots and riding breeches, a red jacket with braiding, Red, Yes, red is just the color, and I will dress as death, in black mesh with bones painted on it, you cracking your whip and I scaring the old women, I'll carry you off, I'll carry you off, and fondling the young girls as we go, at a masked ball we would easily win first prize. I've never been one for dancing, There's no need, the crowd would only have ears for your whip and eyes for my bones, Don't you think we're both a little old for such games, Speak for yourself, I've stopped being any age. With these words Fernando Pessoa got to his feet and departed. It was raining outside and the waiter behind the bar said, Without a raincoat or umbrella that friend of yours is going to get a soaking. He doesn't mind, he's accustomed to it.

When Ricardo Reis returned to the hotel, he felt something stirring in the air, a restless buzz, as if all the bees in a hive had suddenly gone crazy. The weight on his conscience, of which we are well aware, made him immediately think, They've discovered everything. A romantic, he is convinced that the day his little adventure with Lydia comes to light the Bragança will crumble under the scandal, he lives with the constant fear or perhaps the morbid desire that this should happen, an unexpected paradox in a man who claims to be so detached from the world yet who after all wants the world to trample on him. Little does he suspect that the story is already circulating, whispered amid furtive smiles. This was the work of Pimenta, not the type of person to mince words. The guilty walk in innocence, but Salvador has not yet been informed, what verdict will he deliver when at last some envious informant, man or woman, says to him, Senhor Salvador, this affair between Lydia and Doctor Reis is scandalous. He would do well to repeat nobly the words of the Bible, *He that is without sin among you, let him cast the first stone.* Ricardo Reis walked up to the reception desk feeling apprehensive. Salvador was on the telephone, speaking in a loud voice, there was a bad connection, Your voice sounds as if it were coming from the other side of the world, hello, can you hear me, yes, Doctor Sampaio, I must know when you are coming, hello, hello, yes now I can hear you, the problem is that I have scarcely any rooms left, why, because of all the Spaniards, yes, from Spain, they arrived today, on the twenty-sixth then, after Carnival, very well, the two rooms are reserved, no, Doctor, not at all, our special guests come first, three years are not three days, my regards to Senhorita Marcenda, by the way, sir, Doctor Reis is standing right beside me and sends his regards. It was true, Ricardo Reis, by means of signs and mouthed words, was sending his greetings, for two reasons. First, to feel himself close to Marcenda, even through a third party, and second, to become friendly with Salvador, thus removing the man's authority over him, which may seem a blatant contradiction but is not. Relations between two people cannot be explained simply by adding and subtracting arithmetically. How often we think we are adding, only to end up with a remainder, and how often, on the other hand, we think we are subtracting, and it turns out to be not even the straightforward opposite, addition, but multiplication. Salvador put down the receiver, triumphant, having succeeded in a coherent and conclusive telephone conversation with the city of Coimbra, and now he was answering Ricardo Reis, who had asked how things were going. I've just signed in three Spanish families who turned up without any warning, two from Madrid and one from Cáceres, refugees. Refugees. Yes, because the Communists have won the election. It wasn't the Communists, it was the left-wing parties. It comes to the same thing. But are they really refugees. Even the newspapers are carrying the story. I missed that. Well, from now on he would no longer be able to say so, he could hear Spanish being spoken on the other side of the doors, not that he was listening, but the sonorous language of Cervantes penetrates everywhere. There was even a time when it was spoken throughout the universe, we Portuguese never achieved as much. That these were wealthy Spaniards became apparent at dinner, judging from their clothes, their jewels, both the men and women bedecked with rings, cuff links, tiepins, clasps, bangles, bracelets, chains, earrings, necklaces, strands, cords, chokers of gold studded with diamonds and an occasional ruby, emerald, sapphire, or turquoise. They spoke in high-pitched voices from table to table, flaunting their triumph in misfortune, if one may be permitted this contradiction in terms. Ricardo Reis could find no other expression which reconciled their imperious tone with their bitter lamentations. When they spoke of the Reds, they twisted their lips with contempt. The dining room in the hotel Bragança is transformed into a stage set, Calderón's droll *gracioso*. Clarín is likely to appear at any minute and tell us, *Here concealed, I watch the festivities*, that is to say, the Spanish festivities as seen from Portugal, *for death will not find me now, I don't give a damn for death*. The waiters Felipe and Ramón, and there is a third waiter, but he is a Portuguese from Guarda, are rushed off their feet and irritable. This is not the first time they have waited on their countrymen, but never so many at a time and in circumstances such as these. They who have seen so much of life are unaware or have not yet had time to notice that these families from Cáceres and Madrid do not address them as fond compatriots whom misfortune has reunited. Anyone standing on the side can hear the tone of voice, it is the same when they address the Galicians as when they refer to the Reds, substituting scorn for hatred, but now Ramón is seething with resentment, offended by their surly looks and haughty language, and when he comes over to serve Ricardo Reis he can contain himself no longer,

They needn't have troubled coming in here decked up in all that jewelry, nobody will steal it from their rooms, this is a respectable hotel. A good thing that Ramón says so, it will obviously take more than Lydia's visits to a guest's room to make him change his mind. Moral attitudes vary, as do other attitudes, sometimes for the slightest thing, more often than not because of knocks to one's self-esteem, now it is Ramón's that is bruised, hence his need to unburden himself to Ricardo Reis. Let's be fair, however, at least as fair as possible, these people here in the dining room have been driven to Portugal by fear, they have brought their jewels, their money, in the circumstances of their hasty flight what else could they have brought to live on. It is doubtful that Ramón will give or lend them a cent, and why should he, charity is not one of God's commandments, and if the second commandment, *Love thy neighbor as thyself,* has any validity, it would still take another two thousand years, more, before these neighbors from Madrid and Cáceres would come to love Ramón. But the author of *Conspiracy* says we are on the right road, thanks be to God, capital, and labor, and it is probably in order to decide who will pave that road that our procurators and deputies have assembled for a confraternity dinner at the spa of Estoril.

Because of this wretched weather, day and night, which shows no sign of clearing and gives no respite to farmers and agriculturists, with flooding that is reckoned to be the worst in the last forty years, a fact confirmed by the records and testimonies of the elderly, Carnival will be memorable this year, memorable in itself but especially with these dreadful floods that have nothing to do with it but will be talked about for years to come. As we have already stated, Spanish refugees are pouring into Portugal. If they can raise their spirits, they will find plenty of diversions here which are sadly lacking in their own country, now more than ever before. Here we have every reason to feel self-satisfied. Consider the government's decision to go ahead with the plan to build a bridge over the Tagus, or the decree that will limit the use of state automobiles to official functions and services, or the aid given to the workers in the Douro with the distribution of five kilos of rice, five kilos of dried cod, and ten escudos per worker, and no one need be surprised at such lavish generosity, because cod is the cheapest commodity available. And within the next few days a government minister will make a speech announcing the establishment of a soup kitchen for the poor in each parish, and the same minister, returning from Beja, will assure journalists as follows, I have witnessed in Alentejo the importance of organizing private charities in order to combat the labor crisis, which translated into everyday Portuguese reads, Some alms, kind sir, for the sake of your dear ones in Purgatory. Best of all, however, because it emanated from a supreme authority subordinate only to that of Almighty God, was the speech by Cardinal Pacelli in which he praised Mussolini as the mighty defender of Rome's cultural heritage. Clearly this cardinal, so wise and likely to become even wiser, deserves to be Pope, may the Holy Spirit and the conclave not forget him when that blissful day comes. Even now, the Italian troops are on their way to bombard Ethiopia, and God's humble servant is already prophesying empire and emperor, Hail Caesar, Hail Mary.

But how different Carnival is here in Portugal. Yonder, in that land across the ocean discovered by Cabral, where the thrush sings and the Southern Cross shines, beneath that glorious sky, and where even when the sky is overcast there is plenty of heat, at Carnival schools parade, dancing sambas down the city's main boulevard, bedecked with glass beads that look like diamonds, sequins that glitter like precious stones, clothes that may not be made from silk or satin but cover bodies as if they were plumes and feathers, with parrots, birds of paradise, and peacocks swaying on their heads, and the samba, the samba, that tremor in one's soul. Even Ricardo Reis, serious by nature, often felt a repressed Dionysian turmoil stirring within. Only the fear of his own body prevented him from throwing himself into that wild frenzy, we never know how such things will end. In Lisbon there are no such risks, the sky remains as before, drizzling, but cheer up, not so wet as to spoil the parade which is about to descend the Avenida da Liberdade, flanked on either side by the familiar hordes of poor families from the nearby neighborhoods. True, chairs can be rented by those who can afford them, but there will be few customers. Daubed with multicolored figures, the floats creak, sway above people laughing and making faces. Masqueraders both ugly and pretty throw streamers into the crowd, and little bags of corn and beans, which can maim when they hit their target, and the crowd retaliates with diminished enthusiasm. Some open carriages go past, carrying a supply of umbrellas. Young ladies and their beaux wave from their carriages and throw confetti at each other. Merry pranks such as these are also played among the spectators, for example take this girl watching the procession and this youth creeping up behind her with a handful of confetti. He presses it to her lips, rubs vigorously, then takes advantage of her surprise to fondle her as best he can, the poor girl coughs and sputters while he goes off laughing, these are flirtations in the Portuguese tradition, some marriages even begin like this and turn out to be happy. Atomizers are used to squirt water at people's necks or in their faces. They are still called perfume sprayers, the name remaining from the days when one used them to inflict gentle violence in drawing rooms, later they descended to the streets, and you are fortunate if the water is not from some sewer, as has been known to happen. Though soon bored with this tawdry procession, Ricardo Reis stayed, he had nothing more important to do. Twice there was a drizzle and once a downpour, yet there are those who continue to sing the praises of the Portuguese climate, I'm not saying the climate isn't good, but it's not good for carnival parades. By late afternoon, the procession over, the sky cleared, but too late. The floats and carriages went on to their destination, there they will remain to dry out until Tuesday, their faded paint will be touched up, their festoons hung to dry, but the masqueraders, although drenched from head to foot, continue their merrymaking in the streets and squares, alleyways and crossroads. What cannot be committed out in the open they pursue under some staircase, where things can be done more quickly and cheaply. The flesh is weak, the wine helps, the day of ashes and oblivion doesn't come till Wednesday. Ricardo Reis feels slightly feverish, perhaps he has caught a cold watching the procession go past, perhaps melancholy can bring on a fever, nausea, delirium, but he is not that far gone yet. A hopelessly drunk old man in a mask came up to him, armed with a large wooden cutlass and club, striking the one against the other, making an uproar and ambiguously pleading,

Punch me in the belly. He hurled himself on the poet, his bulging stomach padded with a cushion or a roll of cloth, and the crowd hooted with laughter at the sight of the gentleman in a hat and raincoat dodging an old clown dressed in a two-cornered hat, a silk jacket, breeches, and hose, Punch me in the belly. What the man really wanted was money for wine. When Ricardo Reis gave him some coins, the old drunk broke into a grotesque little dance, striking his cutlass against his club, before reeling off, followed by a trail of urchins, the acolytes of this expedition. In a little carriage resembling a pram sat an enormous man with his legs sticking out, his face painted, a baby's bonnet stuck on his head, a bib around his neck. He pretended to sob, or else was genuinely sobbing, until the ugly brute who was playing nanny pushed a feeding bottle filled with red wine into his mouth. This he sucked avidly, to the amusement and delight of the assembled crowd, from which a youth suddenly came running, quick as a flash, fondled the nanny's enormous false breasts, then scampered off, while the nanny yelled after him in a hoarse voice, unmistakably male, Come back here you son of a bitch, come and fondle this, and as he shouted he exposed something that caused all the women to avert their eyes once they had taken a good look. At what, Well, nothing too obscene, the nanny was wearing a dress that came down below the knee, and what protruded from under the dress he grabbed with both hands. Innocent horseplay, this is Carnival in Portugal. A man walks past in an overcoat. Unknown to him he has a sign stuck to his back, a paper dangling from a safety pin, Beast of burden for sale, no one has asked the price so far, even though they taunt him as they pass, Are you such a beast that you don't feel your burden. They amuse themselves teasing. Finally suspicious, he puts his hand behind his back, pulls away the sign, and tears it up in a rage. These same pranks are played on us year after year, and we always react as if it were something new. Ricardo Reis feels safe, knowing how difficult it is to stick a pin into a raincoat, but threats come from all sides. A broom attached to a cord suddenly descends from an upper story, knocking his hat to the ground, and he can hear the two girls who live above shrieking with laughter, Carnival time is fun time, they cry in unison, and the argument is so overwhelming that Ricardo Reis simply retrieves his hat, now covered with mud, and goes silently on his way. It is time he was getting back to the hotel. Fortunately there are the children, they walk about holding on to their mother, aunt, or grandmother, they show off their masks, enjoy being admired, for them there is no greater happiness than going around in disguise. They attend the matinées, fill the parquets and galleries of a bizarre world, utter bedlam, they trip in their long balloon-shaped skirts, their feet hurt, they twist their mouths and milk teeth to grip their pipe, their mustache and sideburns smear, there is surely nothing nicer in this world than children. There they go, the little innocents, carrying their gauze satchels filled with paper streamers, their cheeks painted red or white, wearing pirate eye patches, we do not know if they are dressed as they wish or are simply playing a role devised by the adults who selected and paid for these rented costumes, these Dutch boys, rustics, washer-women, mariners, fado singers, grand dames, serving maids, sol-diers, fairies, army officers, flamenco dancers, poultry vendors, pierrots, train engineers, girls from Ovar in traditional costume, pages, scholars in cap and gown, peasant girls from Aveiro, po-licemen, harlequins, carpenters, pirates, cowboys, lion tamers, Cos-sack riders, florists, bears, Gypsies, sailors, shepherds, nurses, later they will be photographed and appear in tomorrow's newspapers. Some of the little masqueraders who visited the newspaper office obliged the photographer by removing the domino they wore over their costume, even the mysterious domino of Columbine, to show their faces so that their grandmothers might boast with ecstasy, That's my little granddaughter. With a pair of scissors she will lovingly cut out the photograph, it will go into her box of souvenirs, that green one there in the shape of a little trunk, which will break open when it falls onto the pebbles on the quayside. Today we laugh, but the time will come when we will want to weep. It is almost night, Ricardo Reis is dragging his feet, it could be weariness, melancholy, that fever he suspected. Feeling a sudden chill in his back, he is tempted to hail a taxi, but the hotel is now near, In ten minutes I'll be tucked in bed, I'll skip dinner, he murmured to himself, and at this very moment there appeared a group of pretend-mourners approaching from the Rua do Carmo, the men all dressed as women, with the exception of the four pallbearers, who bore on their shoulders the coffin, on top of which lay a man representing a corpse, jaw bound and hands clasped. Now that the rain had stopped, they were venturing out into the street with their mummery. Ah my beloved husband whom I shall see no more, one of the louts, swathed in crepe, cried out in falsetto. Several others played the part of little orphans, Ah dear Papa whom we so greatly miss. Their cronies circled them begging alms from the bystanders for the funeral expenses, The poor man died three days ago and the corpse is beginning to smell something awful. Which was true, someone must have cracked open a bottle of hydrogen sulfide, corpses do not normally smell like rotten eggs but this was the nearest thing they could find. Ricardo Reis gave them a few coins, just as well he was carrying small change, and was about to proceed up the Chiado when he was struck by a strange figure in the procession, despite its being the most logical of all, namely Death, for this was a funeral even if only a mock one. The man was clad in close-fitting black fabric, probably tricot, and over this material were traced out all his bones from head to foot. The craze for fancy costumes often reaches extremes. Ricardo Reis began to shiver again, but this time he knew why, Could it be Fernando Pessoa, that's absurd, he murmured, he would never do such a thing, and even if he were so inclined, he would never keep company with such rabble. Before a mirror, yes, he might stand, that is certainly possible, and dressed thus he might be able to see himself. Muttering this or merely thinking it, Ricardo Reis approached the man to take a closer look, he had the height, the build of Fernando Pessoa, and although he looked slimmer, it might have been because of the close-fitting costume he was wearing. The fellow gave him a quick glance and moved to the back of the procession. Ricardo Reis pursued him, saw him ascend the Calçada do Sacramento, a terrifying sight, nothing but bones in the fading light, as if the man had painted himself with phosphorescent paint, and as he rushed away he appeared to leave a luminous trail. He crossed the Largo do Carmo, turned and ran past the gloomy and deserted Rua da Oliveira, but Ricardo Reis could see him distinctly, neither near nor far, a walking skeleton, a skeleton like the one he had studied in the Faculty of Medicine, the heel bone, the tibia and fibula, femur, ilium, spinal column, rib cage, the shoulder blades like wings incapable of growing, the cervicals supporting the cranium, pallid and lunar. Those who encountered him called out, Hey, Death, hey scarecrow, but the masquerader neither replied nor looked back, he rushed straight on, at a rapid pace, climbed the Escadinhas do Duque two steps at a time, an agile fellow, surely not Fernando Pessoa, who despite his British upbringing was never one for physical exertion. Nor is Ricardo Reis, who could be excused as a product of Jesuit teaching. But the skeleton halted at the top of the stairs, looked down as if to give him time to catch up, then crossed the square to enter the Travessa da Queimada. Where is wretched Death leading me, and I, why am I following him. Then, for the first time, he wondered if the masquerader was in fact a man. It could be a woman, or neither woman nor man, simply Death. It's a man, he thought, on seeing the figure enter a tavern to be greeted with cheers and applause, Look at the masquerade, look at Death. Watching carefully, he saw the skeleton drinking a glass of wine at the bar, head thrown back. Its chest was flat, this was no woman. The masquerader came toward him, and Ricardo Reis had no time to retreat, he broke into a run but the other caught up with him on the corner. The teeth were real, the gums moist with saliva, but the voice was not that of a man, it was that of a woman, or something in between, Tell me, you gawping idiot, who do you think you're following, are you a queer by any chance, or just in a hurry to die. No sir, from a distance I thought I recognized you as a friend of mine, but from your voice I can see I'm mistaken. How do you know I'm not shamming, and the voice now sounded quite different. Please excuse me, said Ricardo Reis, and the masquerader replied in a voice now resembling that of Fernando Pessoa, Go to hell you shit, and he turned away and disappeared into the gathering night. As the little girls with the broom said, Carnival time is fun time. It was raining again.

He spent the night in a fever, slept badly. Before stretching out on the bed, exhausted, he took two aspirins and put the thermometer under his armpit. His temperature was over a hundred, it was to be expected, influenza, he thought to himself. He fell asleep, woke up, dreamed of vast plains bathed in sunlight, flowing rivers meandering among trees, ships that solemnly drifted with the current, remote, alien, himself sailing in all of them, multiplied, divided, waving to himself like someone saying farewell or eager for an encounter. The ships entered a lagoon or estuary, tranquil, still water, they did not stir, there could have been ten of them, or twenty, or more, without sail or oar, within calling distance, but the sailors were all speaking at the same time. Since they were saying the same words they could not hear one another, and finally the ships began to sink, the chorus of voices died away. Dreaming, Ricardo Reis tried to capture those final words, thought that he had succeeded, but as the last ship went to the bottom, the syllables, disconnected, gurgling in the water, came to the surface. Sonorous yet meaningless, the drowned words carried no farewell, pledge, or testament, and even if they had, there was no longer anyone to hear them. Asleep or awake, he debated, had the masquerader really been Fernando Pessoa. First he decided yes, then rejected what was obvious for the sake of what was profound. The next time they met, he would ask. But would he receive a truthful answer. Reis, surely you cannot be serious, can you imagine me going around disguised as Death the way they did in medieval times, a dead man does not cut capers, he is sober, prudent, aware of his condition, discreet, he loathes the absolute nakedness to which he is reduced as a skeleton, therefore when he appears, either he appears as I do now, wearing the smart suit he was dressed in for burial, or, when he wants to give someone a fright, he wraps himself in his shroud, which is a thing that I as a man of some breeding and refinement would never do, I trust you will agree. I needn't have bothered asking him, Ricardo Reis muttered. He switched on the light, opened *The God of the Labyrinth*, read a page and a half, saw that it dealt with two men playing chess but could not tell whether they were playing or conversing. The letters became blurred and he laid the book aside. He was back in his apartment in Rio de Janeiro, from his window he could see planes in the distance dropping bombs over Urca and Praia Vermelha, smoke rising in great black coils, but no sound could be heard, perhaps he had grown deaf or had never possessed any sense of hearing and was therefore unable to imagine, even with the aid of sight, the roar of grenades, the discordant chatter of gunfire, the cries of the wounded. He woke up bathed in sweat. The hotel was submerged in the deep silence of night, the guests all fast asleep, even the Spanish refugees, should anyone suddenly rouse them and ask, Where are you, they would reply, I'm in Madrid, I'm in Cáceres, deceived by the comfort of their beds. At the top of the building Lydia is probably asleep. Some nights she descends, others she does not, their meetings are now arranged beforehand, it is with the utmost circumspection that she comes to his room in the middle of the night. The excitement of the first weeks has waned, as is only natural, nothing fades more rapidly than passion, yes passion, even in these ill-matched liaisons passion has some role. It is wise to allay suspicions, if there are any, to stop harmful gossip, if any is circulating, to avoid public scandal at all costs, let us hope Pimenta went no further than malicious insinuations. True, there could be other reasons for the waning, biological for instance, such as Lydia menstruating, or as the English put it having her period, or to quote a popular saying, The Redcoats have reached the straits, that irrigation canal of the female body, its crimson discharge. He woke, then woke a second time. The light, ashen, cold, dull, as yet more night than day, filtered through the lowered blinds, the windowpanes, the curtains, it traced out the heavy drapes not properly closed, it covered the polished surfaces of the furniture with the most subtle opalescence. The frozen room dawned like a gray landscape, and the hibernating animals, cautious Sybarites, were pleased, for there has been no news of any having died in their sleep. Ricardo Reis took his temperature once more. Still feverish, he started coughing, I've caught a bad flu this time and no doubt about it. The day, so slow in coming, suddenly arrived like a door thrown open, the murmur of the hotel merging with that of the city. This was Monday, Carnival, another day, in what room or grave will the skeleton of Bairro Alto be waking up or still be sleeping, perhaps he has not even undressed but went to bed in his costume, he too sleeps alone, poor fellow. Any living woman would run screaming in terror if such a bony arm were to embrace her under the sheets, even if it were her lover's, *We count for nothing, we are less than futile.* As these lines came to mind, Ricardo Reis recited them in a murmur, then thought to himself, I must get up, a cold or flu only requires precaution, little if any medication. But he continued to doze. Opening his eyes, he repeated, I must get up. He had to wash, shave, he detested the white hairs on his face, but it was much later than he imagined, he had not looked at the clock. Someone was knocking at his door, it was Lydia bringing his breakfast. Pulling his dressing gown around his shoulders, his slippers coming off, still half asleep, he went to open the door. Seeing that he still hadn't washed, hadn't combed his hair, Lydia thought at first that he must have turned in late, perhaps he went to a dance hall chasing after women. Would you like me to come back later, she asked. As he staggered back to bed, seized by a sudden longing to be treated and nursed like a child, he replied, I am ill, which was not what she had asked. She put the tray on the table and approached the bed, and quite spontaneously put her hand on his forehead, You have a fever. Not a doctor for nothing, Ricardo Reis did not need to be told this, but hearing her say it made him feel sorry for himself. He placed a hand over Lydia's and closed his eyes, If there are only these two tears, I will be able to keep them back, he thought, holding Lydia's work-roughened, almost coarse hand, so different from the hands of Chloe, Neaera, and that other Lydia, and from the tapered fingers, manicured nails, and soft palms of Marcenda. From Marcenda's one living hand, I should say, because her left hand is anticipated death. It must be influenza, but I'm getting up, Oh no, you mustn't, you will end up with pneumonia, I'm the doctor here, Lydia, I know what I have to do, there is no need for me to stay in bed playing the invalid when all I need is someone who will go to the pharmacist to fetch two or three medicines. Don't you worry, I'll go, or send Pimenta, but you mustn't get out of bed, eat your breakfast before it gets cold, then I can tidy up and air your room. With these words she eased Ricardo Reis into a sitting position, adjusted his pillow, brought the tray, poured some milk into his coffee, added sugar, cut the slices of toast in half, handed him the marmalade, blushing with happiness, a woman can feel happy just watching the man she loves prostrate on a bed of suffering. She looks at him with such a gleam in her eyes, or could it be worry and concern, that she herself appears to be feverish, one more example of the common phenomenon whereby different causes can produce the same effect. Ricardo Reis allowed himself to be tucked in, pampered, stroked gently by Lydia's fingers as if she were anointing him, whether the first anointing or the last it is difficult to say. Finishing his coffee, he felt deliciously languid. Open the closet for me, there is a black suitcase at the back on the right, bring it here, many thanks. From the suitcase he extracted a prescription pad with a printed heading, Ricardo Reis, general practitioner, Rua do Ouvidor, Rio de Janeiro. When he first bought this pad, he could not have imagined that he would be using it so far away, such is life, without any stability, or with the kind of stability that always has some surprise in store. He scribbled a few lines and instructed, You mustn't go to the pharmacy unless you are asked, give this prescription to Senhor Salvador, any orders should come from him. Bearing the prescription and the tray, she left, but not before kissing him on the forehead, such impudence, a mere servant, a hotel chambermaid, would you believe it, but perhaps she has the natural right, although no other, which he won't deny her, because this is a situation *in extremis*. Ricardo Reis smiled, made a vague gesture, and turned to the wall.

He fell asleep at once, unconcerned about his gray scraggly hair, his sprouting beard, his skin damp and sallow after a night of fever. A man can be more ill than this and still enjoy his moment of happiness, whatever it may be, even just to imagine that he is a desert island over which a migrating bird now flies, brought and carried by the inconstant wind.

All that day and the following, Ricardo Reis did not leave his room. Salvador, who had been informed by Pimenta, paid him a visit, The entire staff wishes you a speedy recovery, Doctor. As if by some tacit agreement rather than following formal instructions, Lydia assumed all the functions of a nurse in attendance, with no qualifications other than those with which women have always been endowed, changing the bedclothes, folding the sheets back with extreme care, bringing cups of lemon tea, giving the patient his pill or a spoonful of cough syrup at the appointed hour, and the disturbing intimacies concealed from others, a back rub, mustard poultices on the patient's calves to draw the humors oppressing his head and chest to the lower extremities, and if this medication did not help, it nevertheless served an important purpose. No one was surprised that Lydia, entrusted with these duties, should spend all her time in room two hundred and one. Any inquiry as to her whereabouts received the reply, She is with the doctor. Malice did not bare its fangs, it reserved its sharpened claws for the right moment, yet there could have been nothing more innocent than Ricardo Reis reclining on the pillow, Lydia insisting he take one more spoonful of chicken broth, but he refuses, he has no appetite, he also wants to hear her plead with him, a game which would seem absurd to anyone in a blissful state of perfect health. To tell the truth, Ricardo Reis is not so ill that he is unable to feed himself, but that is not our affair. If by chance a closer form of contact occurs between them, such as his placing his hand on her bosom, they go no further, perhaps because there is a certain dignity in illness, something almost sacred, although in this religion heresies are not uncommon, outrages against dogma, excessive liberties, such as the one taken by him but denied by her, It could do you harm. Let us praise the nurse's scruples, the lover's restraint. These are details we could dispense with, but there are others of greater relevance, such as the rains and storms which have intensified during the last two days, wreaking havoc on the ragged Shrove Tuesday procession, but to speak of them is as tiring for the narrator as for the reader. And then there are all those outside episodes that have no bearing on our story, such as that of the man who was reported missing last December and whose corpse has been found in Sintra, identified as Luís Uceda Ureña, a mystery in the criminal files which so far remains unsolved, and it looks as if we shall have to wait for the Day of Judgment, because no witness came forward at the time, so we are left with these two, guest and maid, at least until he gets over his flu or cold. Then Ricardo Reis will return to the world, Lydia to her chores, and both to those nocturnal embraces, which are brief or prolonged according to their need and the necessity for discretion. Tomorrow, Wednesday, Marcenda arrives. Ricardo Reis has not forgotten, but he discovers, and if the discovery surprises him it is in the same distracted manner, that illness has dulled his imagination. After all, life is little more than lying in bed convalescing from an illness that is incurable and recurring, with moments of respite we call health, we have to call it something in order to distinguish between the two states. Her hand dangling by her side, Marcenda will come in search of an impossible cure, with her father, the notary Sampaio, who is more hopeful of finding a mistress than a cure for his daughter. Perhaps it is because he has lost hope in a cure that he comes to unburden himself on a bosom not all that different from this bosom Ricardo Reis has just embraced, and Lydia is less reluctant now, even she, who knows nothing about medicine, can see that the doctor is feeling better.

On Wednesday morning Ricardo Reis is served a writ. Given the significance of the document, it is delivered by none other than Salvador in his capacity as manager. It comes from the Police Department for State Security and Defense, an entity whose full name was not mentioned until now because there was no opportunity, but not speaking about certain things does not mean that they do not exist, and here we have a good example. On the eve of Marcenda's arrival there appeared to be nothing more important in this world than the fact that Ricardo Reis was ill and Lydia was nursing him, meanwhile, unsuspected, a clerk was preparing the writ, that's life, old man, no one knows what tomorrow brings. Salvador shows reserve, he is not exactly frowning, his expression is one of puzzlement, that of a man who upon checking his monthly balance finds the total to be much less than what he calculated in his head. This writ has been delivered, he declares, his eyes fixed on the object of the writ as if suspiciously examining a column of figures, Where is the error, twenty-seven and five come to thirty-one when we know that they should add up to thirty-two. A writ addressed to me. Ricardo Reis has every reason to be alarmed, his only crime, and one not usually punishable by the law, if indeed it is a crime, is having received a woman into his bed in the dead of night. He is less disturbed by the document, which he still has not taken into his hand, than by Salvador's face and the hand that is almost trembling. Where does this come from. Salvador makes no reply, certain words must not be said aloud, only whispered or conveyed by signs or read in silence as Ricardo Reis now does, Police Department for State Security and Defense. What am I supposed to do with this, he asks airily with a note of contempt, then adds appeasingly, There must be some mistake. He says this to allay Salvador's suspicions. I'll just sign here on this line acknowledging safe receipt, confirming that I will present myself on the second of March at ten o'clock in the morning, Rua António Maria Cardoso. It is not far from here, first you go up to the Rua do Alecrim as far as the church on the corner, then you turn right, then right again until you come to a cinema, the Chiado Terrasse, opposite the Teatro São Luís, named after the King of France, ideal places for enjoying the arts of stage and screen, and the police headquarters is just a little farther on, you cannot go astray. But perhaps it is because he has gone astray so often in the past that he has been summoned. Salvador solemnly withdraws, to hand over to the police envoy the formal guarantee that the writ has been served, while Ricardo Reis, already out of bed and reclining on the sofa, reads the instructions over and over again, You are summoned to appear for questioning. But why, ye gods, if I have committed no crime, I neither borrow nor steal, I do not conspire, more opposed than ever to any such thing after reading *Conspiracy*, a work recommended by Coimbra, I can hear the words of Marília, dear Papa may be arrested, and if that can happen to a father, what will happen to those who have no children. The entire hotel staff already knows that the guest in room two hundred and one, Doctor Reis, the gentleman who arrived from Brazil two months ago, has been summoned to appear at police headquarters. He must have been up to something in Brazil, or here, I shouldn't like to be in his shoes, It will be interesting to see if they release him, although if this were a case of imprisonment, the police would simply have showed up and arrested him. That same evening Ricardo Reis feels steady enough to go down early to dinner, he will see how the staff eyes him, but Lydia does not behave in this cold, distrusting manner. Salvador no sooner descends to the first floor than she bursts into the room, They tell me you've been summoned by the International Police. The poor girl is terrified. It's true, the writ is right here, but there is no need to panic, it must be something regarding my papers. I hope you're right, from what I hear you can expect nothing but trouble from that lot, my brother has told me things. I didn't know you had a brother. There was no reason to tell you, I never talk much about other people. You've never told me about yourself, You never asked, That's true, all I know about you is that you live here in the hotel, that you go out on your days off, that you are single and unattached as far as one can see, What could be better, Lydia retorted, and with these four words she wrung the heart of Ricardo Reis. It is banal to say so, but that is precisely how they affected him, they wrung his heart. She probably wasn't even aware of what she said, was only expressing her resentment, why resentment, well perhaps resentment's too strong a word, perhaps she simply wanted to state a fact, as if announcing, Oh look it's raining, but instead voiced that bitter irony found in novels, Sir, I am a simple chambermaid scarcely able to read and write, therefore if I have a life of my own, how could it possibly interest you. We could go on in this manner multiplying words, adding them to the four already spoken, What could be better. If this were a duel with swords, Ricardo Reis would already be losing blood. Lydia is about to leave, a clear indication of not having spoken at random. Certain phrases may seem spontaneous, a thing of the moment, but God alone knows what millstone ground them, what invisible sieve filtered them, so that when pronounced they ring like the judgments of Solomon. The best one could hope for now is silence, or that one of the two interlocutors should depart, but people usually go on talking and talking, until what was for a moment definitive and irrefutable is completely lost. What did your brother tell you and what does he do, Ricardo Reis asked. Lydia turned back and began to explain, her outburst forgotten, My brother is in the navy. Which navy, He's on a warship, the Afonso de Albuquerque, Is he older or younger than you, He is just twenty-three, his name is Daniel, I don't even know your last name, My family name is Martins, On your father's side or your mother's, On my mother's side, I don't know my father's name, I never knew him, But your brother, He's my half-brother, his father died, I see. Daniel is opposed to the regime, he's told me so, Say no more unless you're sure you can trust me, Doctor, why shouldn't I trust you. Here there are two possibilities, either Ricardo Reis is an inept fencer who leaves himself exposed, or this Lydia is an Amazon with bow and arrow and broadsword. Unless we wish to consider a third possibility, that heedless of their relative strengths and weaknesses the two of them are finally speaking frankly, he seated, so entitled because convalescent, she standing though his social inferior, both of them probably surprised at how much they have to say to each other, because this is a lengthy conversation when compared with the brevity of their dialogues in the night, which are little more than the simple, primitive murmuring of bodies. Ricardo Reis has discovered that the police headquarters where he is to present himself on Monday is a place of ill repute and that its operations are even worse than its reputation, God help anyone who falls into their clutches, that place means torture, interrogation at any hour of day or night. Not that Daniel has experienced it himself, he is only repeating what others have told him, but if one believes in the proverbs, Tomorrow is another day, There are more tides than sailors, No one knows what the future will bring, then God does not reveal His intentions lest we take precautions. Besides, He manages His own affairs badly, seeing as He wasn't even able to escape His own fate. So even in the navy there are some who are dissatisfied with the regime, Ricardo Reis concluded. Lydia merely shrugged. These subversive opinions were not hers but those of Daniel, sailor, younger brother, man, for such bold statements are generally made by men. When women come to learn something, it's because they have been told, Careful what you say now, don't go blabbing, too late, but she meant well.

Ricardo Reis went down to dinner before the clock struck the hour, not particularly hungry but suddenly curious as to whether any more Spaniards had checked in or if Marcenda and her father had arrived. He spoke Marcenda's name in a low voice, and observed himself carefully, like a chemist who has mixed an acid with a base and is shaking the test tube. There is not much to see without the help of one's imagination, the salt produced was as expected, for so many thousands of years have we been mixing sentiments, acids and bases, men and women. He recalled the youthful infatuation with which he had first looked upon her, then persuaded himself that he had been moved by pity, compassion for that embittering infirmity, the limp hand, the pale, sad face. Then followed a long dialogue before the mirror, the tree of knowledge of good and evil, no knowledge is needed, it is enough to look. What extraordinary words could these reflections exchange. But there is nothing but a repeated image, a repeated movement of lips. Perhaps a different language is spoken in the mirror, different words uttered behind this crystal surface, different meanings expressed, perhaps gestures only appear to repeat themselves like shadows in that inaccessible dimension, until finally what was spoken on this side also becomes inaccessible, lost, only a few fragments of it preserved by memory, which explains why yesterday's ideas are not today's, they were abandoned en route, in the broken mirror of memory. As he goes downstairs, Ricardo Reis feels a slight trembling in his legs. Little wonder, as influenza tends to have this effect, and we would show great ignorance of the subject if we were to suppose that such trembling could be provoked by his laborious thoughts. It is not easy to think when you are walking downstairs, try it yourself, but watch that fourth step.

At the reception desk Salvador was answering the telephone, taking notes with a pencil and saying, Very well, sir, at your service. He flashed a cold and mechanical smile, which was meant to look like preoccupation, or was the coldness instead in his unflinching stare, like that of Pimenta, who had already forgotten the generous, sometimes even excessive tips. So, you are feeling a little better, Doctor, but his gaze said, I rather fancied there was something shady in your life. Those eyes will go on saying this until Ricardo Reis has been to the police and comes back, if he ever does. Now the suspect has passed into the lounge, the conversations in Spanish are noisier than usual, it is like a hotel on Madrid's Gran Via. Any whispering to make itself heard during a pause is some modest conversation between Lusitanians, the voice of our small nation timid even on its own soil, rising to a falsetto in order to affirm timidly some familiarity, real or assumed, with the language across the border, *Usted, Entonces, Muchas gracias, Pero, Vaya, Desta suerte,* no one can claim to be truly Portuguese unless he speaks another language better than his own. Marcenda was not in the lounge, but Doctor Sampaio was present, engaged in conversation with two Spaniards who were explaining current political events in Spain with a graphic description of their odyssey after fleeing their homes, *Gracias a Dios que vivo a tus pies llego.* Joining them, Ricardo Reis sat down at one end of the larger sofa, some distance away from Doctor Sampaio. Just as well, he had no wish to enter into this Spanish cum Portuguese discussion, wanting only to know if Marcenda had arrived or had remained in Coimbra. Doctor Sampaio, showing no sign of having noticed his presence, nodded gravely as he listened to Don Alonso, redoubled his attention when Don Lorenzo came up with some forgotten detail, and never once looked over, even when Ricardo Reis, still suffering the aftereffects of influenza, had a violent fit of coughing that left him breathless and with eyes watering. Ricardo Reis then opened a newspaper and read that in Japan there had been an insurrection of army officers who were demanding that war be declared on Russia. He had first heard the news this morning, but now appraised it in greater depth. If she is here, Marcenda will be down shortly, and you will be obliged to speak to me, Doctor Sampaio, whether you wish to or not, I am anxious to see whether your eyes are as unfriendly as those of Pimenta, for no doubt Salvador has already informed you that the police wish to question me.

The clock struck eight, the superfluous gong sounded, several guests got up and left. The conversation subsided, the two Spaniards uncrossing their legs impatiently, but Doctor Sampaio detained them with the reassurance that they would be able to live tranquilly in Portugal for as long as they wished. Portugal is an oasis of peace, here politics is no pursuit for the lower orders, that makes for a peaceful existence, the calm you witness on the streets is the calm in the souls of our people. But this was not the first time the Spaniards had listened to words of welcome and goodwill, and an empty stomach cannot be nourished on words, so they took their leave, See you soon, their families were waiting to be summoned from their rooms. Doctor Sampaio, coming face to face with Ricardo Reis, exclaimed, You've been here all this time, I didn't see you, how are things, but Ricardo Reis was fully aware that he was being watched by Pimenta, or was it Salvador, one could scarcely tell the difference between manager, notary, and porter, all three suspicious. I saw you but didn't want to intrude, I hope you had a good journey, how is your daughter. No better and no worse, that is the cross we share. One of these days you will see your perseverance rewarded, these cures take time. After this brief exchange they both fell silent, Doctor Sampaio feeling ill at ease, Ricardo Reis being ironic. The latter benevolently tossed a piece of wood onto the dying embers. By the way, I've read the book you recommended, Which book, The one about conspiracy, don't you remember, Ah yes, I suspect it made little impression. On the contrary, I found much to admire in its endorsement of nationalism, its command of idiom, the strength of its arguments, the finesse and penetration of its psychology, but above all the tribute it pays to the generous nature of womanhood, one comes away from the book purified, I truly believe that for many people in Portugal *Conspiracy* will be like a second baptism, a new Jordan. Ricardo Reis completed this encomium by assuming the expression of someone inwardly transfigured, which left Doctor Sampaio disconcerted by the contradiction between these words and the writ Salvador had mentioned in confidence. Oh, was as much as he could say, resisting an impulse to revive their friendship. He decided to remain aloof, to sever relations at least until this business with the police was resolved, I must go and see if my daughter is ready to come down to dinner, and he departed in haste. Ricardo Reis smiled and returned to his newspaper, determined to be the last guest to enter the dining room. Presently he heard the voice of Marcenda, Are we dining with Doctor Reis, whereupon her father said, We made no arrangement. The rest of the conversation, if any took place on the other side of the glass doors, might have gone something like this, As you can see, he is not even here, besides certain matters have been brought to my attention, it's better that we should not be seen together in public. What matters, Father. He has been summoned by the Police Department for State Security and Defense, can you imagine, between ourselves this comes as no great surprise, I had a feeling there was something there not right. By the police, Yes, the police. She retorted, But he is a doctor who only recently arrived from Brazil. All we know is that he claims to be a doctor, but he could be on the run, Really, Father, You are young, you have no experience of life, look, let's sit over there beside that Spanish couple, they seem personable, I'd prefer to be alone with you, Father, All the tables are occupied, we must either join someone or wait, and I'd rather sit down now and hear the latest news from Spain, Very well, Father. Ricardo Reis changed his mind, decided to return to his room, requesting that dinner be sent up. I still feel a little weak, he explained, and Salvador assented with a mere nod, anxious to discourage any further intimacy. That same night, after dinner, Ricardo Reis wrote some verses, *Like the stones that border flowerbeds we are placed by fate, and there we remain, nothing more than stones.* Later he would see if he could expand this fragment into an ode, to continue giving that name to a form that no one knew how to sing, if it indeed was singable, and with what music, what must the Greek odes have sounded like in their time. Half an hour later, he added, *Let us accomplish what we are, we possess nothing more than that,* and put the sheet of paper aside, muttering, How many times have I written this with different words. He was sitting on the sofa, facing the door, silence weighing upon his shoulders like a wicked goblin, when he heard the soft shuffling of feet in the hall. It sounds like Lydia, so soon, but it was not Lydia. From under the door appeared a folded white note, advancing slowly, then brusquely pushed. Ricardo Reis realized that to attempt to open the door would be a mistake. He knew with such conviction who had written the note that he was in no hurry to get up, he sat there staring at it, already half open. It had been badly folded, doubled in haste, written with a nervous, edgy handwriting now seen for the first time. How does she manage to write, perhaps by resting a heavy object on the upper part of the sheet to keep it steady, or by using her left hand as a paperweight, both equally inert, or with the help of one of those springed clamps used in a notary's office to keep documents together. I was sorry not to see you, the note reads, but it was better so. My father is only interested in being with the Spaniards. When they informed him, the moment we arrived, about your trouble with the police, he decided to avoid being seen in your company. I am anxious to talk to you and I will never forget your help. Tomorrow between three and three-thirty I will take a stroll through the Alto de Santa Catarina, and if you wish we could meet and converse a little. A young woman from Coimbra in a furtive note agrees to meet a middle-aged doctor who has arrived from Brazil, he perhaps on the run and certainly suspect, what a tragic love affair is about to be enacted here.

The following day, Ricardo Reis lunched in the Baixa. For no particular reason he returned to the Irmãos Unidos, perhaps attracted by the name of the restaurant. He who has never had any brothers or sisters and finds himself with no friends is assailed by such longings, especially when he is feeling weak, it is not only his legs that tremble in the aftermath of influenza but also his soul, as we pointed out on another occasion. The day is overcast, a trifle chilly, Ricardo Reis slowly ascends the Rua do Carmo, gazing at the shopwindows, still too early for his meeting. He tries to remember if he was ever before in such a situation, a woman actually taking the initiative to arrange a meeting, Be in such a place at such a time, he cannot remember a similar experience, life is full of surprises. But the greatest surprise of all is that he does not feel the least bit nervous, though given all this circumspection and secrecy it would be only natural. He has the impression of being trapped in a cloud, of not being able to focus his thoughts, perhaps he does not really believe that Marcenda will show up. He entered the Café Brasileira to rest his legs, he drank a coffee, listened to a conversation of a group of men, obviously men of letters, they were heaping abuse on some man or beast, Such an idiot, and another, authoritative voice intervened to explain, I received it directly from Paris, No one is arguing with you, someone said. Ricardo Reis could not tell who the remark was addressed to or its meaning, or whether the person was an idiot or not. He left, it was a quarter to three, time to be getting on his way, he crossed the square past a statue of the poet, all roads in Portugal lead to Camões, everchanging Camões according to the beholder, in life his arms prepared for battle and his mind fixed on the muses, his sword is now in its scabbard, his book is closed, and his eyes blind, both of them, wounded by the pigeons and the indifferent stares of passersby. It is not yet three when Ricardo Reis arrives at the Alto de Santa Catarina. The palm trees look as if they have been pierced by the breeze coming from the sea, yet their rigid blades barely stir. He simply cannot remember if these trees were here sixteen years ago when he left for Brazil. What most certainly was not here is this huge, roughly hewn block of stone, it looks like an outcrop but is really a monument. If the furious Adamastor is here, then the Cape of Good Hope cannot be far away. Below are frigates navigating the river, a tugboat with two barges in tow, warships moored to the buoys, their prows facing the channel, a clear sign that the tide is rising. Ricardo Reis tramples the damp gravel of the narrow pathways, soft mud underfoot, there is no one here in this belvedere except for two silent old men seated on the same bench. They have probably known each other so long that they no longer have anything to say, perhaps they are waiting to see who will die first. Feeling chilly, Ricardo Reis turns up the collar of his raincoat and approaches the railing that surrounds the first slope of the hill. To think that they set sail from this river, what ship, what armada, what fleet can find the route, which route and leading where, I ask myself. I say, Reis, are you waiting for someone. The voice, biting and sardonic, is that of Fernando Pessoa. Ricardo Reis turned to the man dressed in black standing beside him and gripping the railing with his white hands. This was not what I expected when I sailed back here over the ocean waves, but yes, I am waiting for someone. You don't look at all well. I've had a bout of the flu, it was bad but soon passed. This is not the best place for someone recovering from influenza, up here you're exposed to the wind from the open sea. It's only a breeze blowing from the river, it doesn't bother me. Are you expecting some woman. Yes, a woman. Bravo, you've obviously given up those spiritual abstractions of the ideal woman, exchanged your ethereal Lydia for a Lydia one can hold in one's arms, as I saw with my own eyes back in the hotel, and now here you are waiting for another woman, playing Don Juan at your age, two women in such a short time, congratulations, at this rate you'll soon arrive at one thousand and three. Many thanks, I'm beginning to realize that the dead are worse than the elderly, once they start talking they don't know when to stop. You're right, perhaps they regret everything left unsaid when there was still time. I stand warned. However much one speaks, however much we all speak, there's no advantage in being warned, there will always be some little word we leave out. I won't ask you what it is. Very wise, by refraining from questions we can go on deluding ourselves that one day we may know the answers. Look, Fernando, I'd rather you didn't see the person I'm waiting for. Don't fret, the worst that can happen is that she will see you from a distance talking to yourself, and who cares, everyone in love behaves like this. I am not in love. Well, I'm sorry to hear it, let me tell you that Don Juan was at least sincere, capricious but sincere, but you are like the desert, you don't even cast a shadow. It is you who cast no shadow. I beg your pardon, I can most certainly cast a shadow when I please, what I cannot do is look at myself in the mirror. Which reminds me, was that you masquerading as Death in the Carnival procession, Really, Reis, can you imagine me going around disguised as Death, like an allegory in the Middle Ages, a dead man does not cut capers, he abhors the absolute nakedness of his skeletal form, therefore when he appears, either he does as I do, putting on his best suit, the one in which he was buried, or he wraps himself up in his shroud if he's out to give someone a good fright, but as a man with a sense of decorum and who values his reputation I would never indulge in such low pranks, that much you must concede. I had a feeling that that would be your answer, and now I must ask you to leave, the person I've been waiting for is approaching. That girl there, Yes, She's quite attractive, a little too thin for my taste, This is the first time I've ever heard you pass a comment on a woman, *Thou furtive satyr, Thou cunning knave.* Goodbye, dear Reis, until we meet again, I leave you to woo your maiden, you've turned out to be a disappointment, seducing chambermaids, chasing after virgins, I thought rather better of you when you viewed life from a distance. Life, Fernando, is always at hand. Well, you're welcome to it if this is life. Marcenda came down between the flowerbeds bereft of flowers, and Ricardo Reis walked up to meet her. Were you talking to yourself, she asked. Yes, after a fashion, I was reciting some poetry written by a friend of mine who died a few months ago, perhaps you've heard of him. What was his name. Fernando Pessoa. The name sounds familiar but I don't remember having read his poetry. *Between what I live and life, between what I appear to be and am, I slumber on a slope, a slope I will not leave.* Was that what you were reciting, It was, It could have been written for me, if I've understood it properly, it is so simple. Yet it needed this man to write it, it's like all things, both good and bad, someone has to do them, take the *Lusíadas* for instance, do you realize that we'd never have had the *Lusíadas* were it not for Camões, have you thought what our Portugal would be without them. It sounds like a word game, a riddle. Nothing could be more serious if we take it seriously, but let's talk about you, how have you been, is your hand improving. No better, I have it here in my pocket like a dead bird. You mustn't lose hope. I feel I've given up, one of these days I may make a pilgrimage to Fátima to see if an act of faith will save me. You have faith, I'm a Catholic, Practicing, Yes, I attend Mass, and I go to confession, and I take Communion, I do everything good Catholics are supposed to do. You don't sound terribly devoted, Pay no heed to what I'm saying. Ricardo Reis made no attempt to reply. Words, once uttered, remain open like doors, we nearly always enter, but sometimes we wait outside, expecting some other door to open, some other words to be uttered, these for example are as good as any, I must ask you to excuse my father's behavior, the outcome of the elections in Spain has unsettled him, he spent all of yesterday conversing with the refugees. And to make matters worse, Salvador had to go and tell him that Doctor Reis had been served a writ by the police. We hardly know each other, your father has done nothing to require my forgiveness, I suspect it is some trifling matter, and on Monday I shall find out and answer any questions put to me, and that will be the end of it. I'm glad you're not letting it worry you. There is no reason, I have nothing to do with politics, I lived all those years in Brazil without anyone hounding me and there is even less cause for anyone to hound me here, to tell you the truth I no longer even think of myself as being Portuguese. God willing, everything will be all right. We say, God willing, but it is meaningless, because no one can read God's mind or guess His will, you must forgive my petulant mood, who am I to say such things, it's just that we are born into this world, we watch others live, then we start living too, imitating others, repeating set phrases like God willing without knowing why or to what purpose. What you say makes me feel very sad. Forgive me, I'm not being very helpful today, I've forgotten my obligations as a doctor, I should be thanking you for coming here to apologize for your father's behavior. I came because I wanted to see you and speak to you, tomorrow we go back to Coimbra, and I was afraid there might not be another opportunity. The wind has started to blow more fiercely, wrap up well. Don't worry about me, I'm afraid I chose the wrong spot for our meeting, I should have remembered that you are still convalescing. It was simply a bout of influenza, perhaps not even that, a mere chill. It will be another month before I come back to Lisbon, there will be no way of finding out what happens on Monday. I've already told you it's not important. Even so, I'd like to know, That will be difficult, Why don't you write to me, I'll leave you my address, no, better still, address your letter poste restante, my father might be at home when the mail is delivered. Is it worth the bother, mysterious letters posted from Lisbon under a cloak of secrecy. Don't make fun of me, I should find it very distressing to wait a whole month for any news, a word is all I ask. Agreed, if you receive no letter it will mean that I've been condemned to some dark dungeon or locked up in the highest tower in the realm, from which you must rescue me. God forbid, but now I must leave you, my father and I have an appointment to see the specialist. Using her right hand, Marcenda maneuvered her left hand out of her pocket, then stretched out both, for no good reason, the right one was all she needed to shake his hand, now both her hands are nestled in those of Ricardo Reis. The old men look on and fail to understand. I'll be in the dining room this evening, but I will only nod to your father from a distance rather than embarrass him in front of his newfound friends from Spain. I was just about to ask you this favor, That I shouldn't approach him, That you should dine downstairs, so I can see you, Marcenda, why do you want to see me, Why, I don't know. She moved off, walked up the slope, paused at the top of the hill to rest her left hand more comfortably in her pocket, then continued on her way without turning around. Ricardo Reis noticed a large steamer about to enter the channel, it was not *The Highland Brigade*, one ship he'd had time to get to know extremely well. The two old men were chatting. He could be her father, one of them said, They are definitely having an affair, the other replied, what I don't understand is why that fellow in black has been hanging around all this time, What fellow, That one leaning against the railing, I can't see anyone, You need glasses, And you're drunk. It was always the same with these two old men, they would start chatting, then argue, then move to separate benches, then forget their quarrel and sit together once more. Ricardo Reis moved away from the railing, skirted the flowerbeds, followed the same route by which he had come. Looking to the left, he happened to spot a house with inscriptions on the upper story. A gust of wind shook the palm trees. The old men got to their feet. Then there was no one left on the Alto de Santa Catarina.

Anyone who says that nature is indifferent to the cares and sufferings of mankind knows little about mankind or nature. A regret, however fleeting, a headache, however mild, immediately disrupts the orbit of the stars, alters the ebb and flow of the tides, interferes with the moon's ascent, and troubles the currents in the atmosphere and the undulating clouds. Let one cent be missing from the sum collected at the last minute to settle a bill, and the winds grow violent, the sky becomes heavy, all nature commiserates with the anguished debtor. Skeptics, who make it their business to disbelieve everything, with or without proof, will say that this theory is unfounded, that it is nonsense, but what other explanation could there be for the continuous bad weather that has lasted months, perhaps years, because there have always been gales here, storms, floods, and enough has been said about the people of our nation for us to find in their misfortune sufficient reason for these unruly elements. Need we remind you of the wrath of the inhabitants of Alentejo, the outbreak of smallpox in Lebução and Fatela, or typhoid in Valbom. And what about the two hundred people who live on three floors of a building at Miragaia in Oporto, without electricity, in primitive conditions, waking each morning to shouting and screaming, the women lining up to empty their chamber pots, the rest we leave to your imagination, which ought to be put to some use. Little wonder, then, that the weather has unleashed this hurricane, with trees uprooted, roofs blown off, and telegraph poles knocked to the ground. Ricardo Reis is on his way to police headquarters, filled with anxiety, holding on to his hat lest it be carried away. If the rain should start falling in proportion to the wind that is blowing, God help us. The wind is coming from the south and at our back as we ascend the Rua do Alecrim, a blessing preferable to that bestowed by the saints, who assist only during one's descent. We have the itinerary more or less worked out, turn here at the Igreja da Encarnação, sixty paces to the next corner, you cannot go wrong. More wind, a head wind this time, which could be why he slows down, unless it is his feet refusing to walk that road. But he has an appointment and this man is punctuality personified, it is not yet ten o'clock and already he is at the door. He shows the paper they sent him, You are asked to appear, and he has appeared, hat in hand, relieved, absurd as it may seem, to be out of the wind. They send him up to the second floor, and up he goes, holding the writ like a lamp before him, without it he would not know where to put his feet. This document is a sentence that cannot be read, and he is an illiterate sent to the executioner bearing the message, Chop off my head. The illiterate may go singing, because the day has dawned in glory. Nature, too, is unable to read. When the ax separates the head from his trunk the stars will fall, too late. Told to wait, Ricardo Reis sits on a long bench, bereft, because they have taken the writ from him. He sits with other people waiting. If this were a doctor's office, they would be chatting among themselves as they waited, Something's wrong with my lungs, My trouble is my liver or maybe it's my kidneys, but no one knows what is ailing these people, who sit in silence. Were they to speak, they would say, I suddenly feel much better, may I go now. A foolish question, for as we know the best remedy for a toothache is to walk through the door when the dentist calls. Half an hour passed, and Ricardo Reis was still waiting to be called. Doors opened and closed, telephones could be heard ringing, two men paused nearby, one of them gave a loud laugh, He doesn't know what's in store for him, he said, then they disappeared behind a curtain. Are they referring to me, Ricardo Reis asked himself with a tightening in his stomach. At least we shall find out what the charges are. He raised his hand to his waistcoat pocket to take out his watch, to see how long he had been waiting, but stopped himself halfway, he must not betray any impatience. At last a man drew back a curtain ever so slightly, beckoned him with a nod, and Ricardo Reis rushed forward, then stopped himself, held back out of an instinctive sense of dignity, if dignity has anything to do with instinct. Not rushing was the only form of refusal open to him, albeit only a pretense of refusal. He followed the man, who reeked of onion, through a long corridor with doors on either side, all firmly shut. Upon reaching the far end, his guide knocked gently on one of the doors and opened it. A man seated at a desk told the guide, Wait here, you might be needed, and turning to Ricardo Reis he pointed at a chair, Sit down. Ricardo Reis obeyed, now feeling irritated, extremely frustrated, They are doing this just to intimidate me, he thought to himself. The man behind the desk took the writ, read it slowly, as if he had never seen such a document before, then put it down carefully on the green blotting paper and looked hard at him, the look of someone making a final check to avoid any mistake. Your identification if you please, were his opening words, and those three words, If you please, made Ricardo Reis feel less nervous. It is certainly true that one can achieve a great deal simply by being polite. Ricardo Reis took his identity card from his wallet and raised himself slightly in his chair to hand it over, causing his hat to fall on the floor, which made him feel ridiculous, nervous again. The man read the card line by line, compared the photograph with the face of the man before him, took some notes, then placed the card, with the same scrupulous care, in the folder beside the writ. Maniac, thought Ricardo Reis, but said, I'm a doctor, I arrived here from Rio de Janeiro two months ago. You have been staying at the Hotel Bragança all this time, asked the man. Yes sir. On which ship did you travel. The *Highland Brigade*, which belongs to the Royal Mail Line, I disembarked in Lisbon on the twenty-ninth of December. Did you travel alone or accompanied, Alone, Are you married, No sir, I am not married, and I should like to know why I have been summoned here, why the police want to question me, this is the last thing I ever expected. How many years did you reside in Brazil. I went there in nineteen nineteen, why do you ask. Just answer my questions and leave the rest to me, that way we will get along fine. Very well sir. Was there some special reason for your emigrating to Brazil, I decided to emigrate, that's all, Doctors don't usually emigrate, I did, Why, couldn't you find patients here, I had any number of patients, but I wanted to see Brazil, to work there, that's all. And now you've come back, Yes, I've come back. To do what, if you haven't come back to practice medicine. How do you know I'm not practicing medicine. I know. For the moment I'm not practicing, but I'm thinking of opening an office, of putting down roots once more, after all, this is my native land. In other words, after being away for sixteen years, you suddenly felt homesick for your native land. That is so, but really I fail to see the purpose of this interrogation. It is not an interrogation, your statements, as you can see, are not even being recorded. Then why am I here. I was curious to meet this Portuguese doctor who was earning a good living in Brazil, who returned after sixteen years, who has been living in a hotel for two months and does not work. I told you I intend to resume my practice, Where, I haven't yet started to look for a location, it is an important decision. Tell me something else, did you get to know many people in Rio de Janeiro or elsewhere in Brazil. I didn't travel much, my friends all lived in Rio, What friends, My private life is my own affair, I am under no obligation to answer such questions, otherwise I must insist upon my lawyer being present. You have a lawyer, No, but there is nothing to prevent me from hiring one. Lawyers are not permitted to enter these premises, besides, Doctor, you haven't been charged with any crime, we are simply having a little chat. But not of my choosing, and the drift of the questions being put to me suggests that this is more than a friendly chat. To return to my question, who were these friends of yours. I refuse to answer. Doctor Reis, if I were in your position, I would be more cooperative, it's in your best interest to answer, so as to avoid unnecessary complications. Portuguese, Brazilians, people who came to consult me professionally and subsequently became my friends, there's no point in my naming people you do not know. That is where you are wrong, I know a great many names, I am giving no names, Very well then, I have other means of finding out, should it prove necessary, Suit yourself. Were there any military personnel or politicians among those friends of yours. I didn't move in such circles. No one attached to the armed forces or engaged in politics. I cannot guarantee that such people might not have consulted me in my capacity as a doctor. But you did not become friendly with any of them. As it happens, no, With none of them, That's right. You were living in Rio de Janeiro when the last revolution took place, I was. Don't you find it something of a coincidence that you should return to Portugal so soon after a revolutionary conspiracy was discovered. No more than to discover that the hotel where I am staying is full of Spanish refugees after the recent elections held in Spain. Ah, so you are telling me that you fled from Brazil, That was not what I said, You compared your own situation with that of the Spaniards who have arrived in Portugal, Only to make the point that coincidences mean nothing, as I've already told you, I longed to see my native land once more. You did not return because you were afraid. Afraid of what. Of being hounded by the authorities there, for example. No one hounded me either before or after the revolution. These things sometimes take time, we didn't summon you until two months after your arrival. I'd still like to know why. Tell me something else, if the rebels had succeeded, would you have remained in Brazil. I've already told you that the reason for my return had nothing to do with either politics or revolutions, besides this was not the only revolution in Brazil during my stay there. A shrewd reply, but there are revolutions and revolutions and not all for the same cause. I am a doctor, I neither know nor wish to know anything about revolutions, I am interested only in caring for the sick. Apparently not all that interested these days. I will soon be practicing medicine once more. While living in Brazil, were you in trouble with the authorities, I am a peaceful man. And here in Portugal, have you renewed any friendships since your return, Sixteen years is long enough to forget and be forgotten. You haven't answered my question, I have no friends here. Did you ever consider becoming a Brazilian citizen, Never. Do you find Portugal much changed since you left for Brazil, I cannot answer that, I haven't been outside Lisbon. What about Lisbon itself, do you find much difference, Sixteen years have brought many changes. Don't you find more calm on the streets, Yes, I've noticed. The National Dictatorship has set the country to work, I don't doubt it, There is patriotism, a willingness to strive for the common good, no sacrifice is too great in the national interest. The Portuguese are fortunate. You are fortunate, since you are one of us. I will not refuse what is due me when these benefits are made available, soup kitchens, I understand, are to be organized for the poor. You are surely not poor, Doctor, I may be one day, God forbid, Thank you for your concern, but when that happens, I'll go back to Brazil. Here in Portugal there is little likelihood of revolution, the last one occurred two years ago and ended disastrously for those involved. I don't know what you're talking about and have nothing to add to what I've told you already. I have no more questions. May I go now, You may, here is your identity card, oh, Victor, will you show the doctor to the door. Victor approached, said, Follow me, his breath reeking of onion. Incredible, Ricardo Reis thought to himself, so early in the day and this awful stink, the man must eat onions for breakfast. Once in the corridor, Victor told him, I could see you were out to provoke our deputy chief, just as well you found him in a good mood, Provoke him, what do you mean, You refused to answer his questions, you beat around the bush, a grave mistake, luckily our deputy chief has some respect for the medical profession. I still don't know why I was asked to come here. No need, just raise your hands to heaven and thank God it's over. Let's hope so, once and for all. That's something one never knows, but here we are, hey Antunes, the good doctor here has permission to leave the building, good-bye, Doctor, if you need anything, you know where to find me, the name is Victor. Ricardo Reis touched the guide's extended hand with the tips of his fingers, afraid that he himself would start smelling of onions, that he would be sick. But no, the wind hit him in the face, jolted him, dispelled the nausea, he found himself in the street, not sure how he got there, the door behind him closed. Before Ricardo Reis reaches the corner of the Rua da Encarnação there will be a mighty downpour. Tomorrow's newspapers will report heavy showers, an understatement for torrential and persistent rain. The pedestrians all take shelter in doorways, shaking themselves like drenched dogs. There is only one man on the sidewalk by the Teatro São Luís, obviously late for an appointment, he looks as worried as Ricardo Reis had been, which explains all this rain overhead. Nature might have shown her solidarity in some other fashion, for example by sending an earthquake capable of burying Victor and the deputy chief in rubble. Let them rot until the stink of onion evaporates, until they are reduced to clean bones.

When Ricardo Reis entered the hotel, water was dripping from his hat as from a gutter, his raincoat was soaking wet, he looked like a gargoyle, a grotesque figure without any of the dignity one expects in a doctor, and his dignity as a poet was lost on Salvador and Pimenta, because when the rain falls, heavenly justice, it falls on everyone. He went up to the reception desk to retrieve his key. Why, Doctor, you're drenched to the skin, the manager exclaimed, but his dubious tone betrayed his thoughts, What condition are you really in, how did the police deal with you. Or, more dramatically, I didn't expect to see you back so soon. If we address God with the familiar you, even if it is in capital letters, what is to prevent us from taking such a liberty with a hotel guest suspected of subversive activities, both past and future. Ricardo Reis simply muttered, What a deluge, and rushed upstairs, dripping water all over the stair carpet. Lydia will be able to follow his trail, footprint by footprint, a broken twig, trampled grass, but we are daydreaming, talking as if we were in some forest, when this is only a hotel corridor leading to room two hundred and one. So, how was it, she will ask, did they treat you badly. Certainly not, Ricardo Reis will reply, what an idea, there was no problem, the police are very civilized, very polite, they invite you to have a seat. But why did they make you go there. It is apparently the normal procedure when people return after a number of years abroad, a routine check, that's all, to make sure everything is in order, to see if a person needs any assistance. You're joking, that's not what my brother told me. Yes, I'm joking, but don't worry, there was no problem, they only wanted to know why I've returned from Brazil, what I was doing there, what I plan to do here. Have they the right to ask these things. My impression is that they can ask anything they like, now be off with you, I must change before lunch. In the dining room the maître d', Afonso, for Afonso is his name, showed him to his table, keeping a distance of half a pace more than custom or etiquette required, but Ramón, who in recent days had also kept his distance and hurried off to attend to less contagious guests, took his time ladling out the soup, The smell is so appetizing, Doctor, it could awaken the dead. And he was right, after that stink of onions everything smelled good. There should be a study, Ricardo Reis reflected, about what smell we give off at any given moment and for whom, Salvador finds my smell unpleasant, Ramón now finds it tolerable, as for Lydia, her poor sense of smell deludes her into thinking I'm anointed with roses. Entering the dining room, he exchanged greetings with Don Lorenzo and Don Alonso, and also with Don Camilo, who had arrived only three days ago, but Don Camilo remained politely aloof. Whatever Ricardo Reis learns about the situation in Spain he overhears as guests converse over dinner, or he reads in the newspapers. Hotbeds of dissent, the wave of propaganda launched by Communists, anarchists, and trade unionists, which is infiltrating the working classes and has even influenced members of the army and navy. We can now understand why Ricardo Reis was summoned by the Police Department for State Security and Defense. He tries to recall the features of the deputy chief who interrogated him, but all he can see is a ring with a black stone worn on the little finger of the left hand, and the vague image of a round, pale face, like a bun that was not properly baked in the oven. He cannot make out the eyes, perhaps the man had none, perhaps he had been speaking to a blind man. Salvador appears unobtrusively in the doorway, to make sure that all is in order, especially now that the hotel has become international, and during this rapid inspection his eyes meet those of Ricardo Reis. He smiles from afar, a diplomatic gesture, what he wants to know is what happened at the police station. Don Lorenzo reads aloud for Don Alonso from *Le Jour*, a French newspaper published in Paris, he reads an article in which Oliveira Salazar, the Head of the Portuguese Government, is described as an energetic and unassuming man whose vision and judgment have brought prosperity and a sense of national pride to his country. That's what we need in Spain, remarks Don Camilo, and raising his glass of red wine he nods in the direction of Ricardo Reis, who conveys his gratitude with a similar nod but restrained, mindful of the famous battle of Aljubarrota, when Portugal's tiny army routed the Spanish forces. Satisfied, his mind at rest, Salvador withdraws, later or perhaps tomorrow Doctor Ricardo Reis will tell him what happened in the Rua António Maria Cardoso, and should he refuse or give the impression of withholding certain facts, Salvador has other means of finding out, an acquaintance of his works there, a man called Victor. If the news is reassuring, if Ricardo Reis is above suspicion, happiness will be restored, Salvador will simply have to caution him, with tact and diplomacy, to apply the utmost discretion in his dealings with Lydia, For the sake of the hotel's reputation, Doctor, at least to protect our good name, that is what he will tell him. We would take an even more favorable view of Salvador's magnanimity if we considered how much more advantageous it would be to have room two hundred and one vacated, because it is large enough to accommodate an entire family from Seville, a Spanish nobleman, for example, the Duke of Alba, the very thought makes me tremble with excitement. Finishing his lunch, Ricardo Reis nodded to the immigrants still savoring cheeses from the Serra, waved to Salvador, leaving him racked with expectation, with the moist eye of a dog begging for a bone, and went up to his room. He was anxious to write a quick note to Marcenda, poste restante, Coimbra.

It is raining out there with such a deafening noise that it seems that the rain is falling throughout the world, that as the globe turns, its waters hum in space as if on a spinning top. *The dense roar of the rain fills my mind, my soul is an invisible curve drawn by the sound of the wind that blows relentless, an unbridled horse rejoicing in its freedom, hooves clattering through these doors and windows while the voile curtains, inside, sway ever so gently.* A man surrounded by tall pieces of furniture is writing a letter, composing his text so that the absurd appears logical and the incoherent clear, so that weakness becomes strength, mortification dignity, and fear boldness, because what we would like to have been is as valuable as what we have been. Ah if only we had shown courage when called to account. To know this is to be halfway there, knowing this we will find the courage at the right moment to travel the other half. Ricardo Reis vacillated, debated which form of address to use. A letter is a most hazardous business, the written word allows no indecision, either distance or familiarity will emphasize the tone the letter establishes, and you end up with a relationship that is a fiction. Many an ill-fated attachment has started precisely in this way. Ricardo Reis did not even consider the possibility of addressing Marcenda as Most excellent Lady or Esteemed Madam, his concern about propriety did not go that far, but once he ruled out these conventional and therefore impersonal forms of address, he was left with a vocabulary that verged on the intimate. My dear Marcenda, for example. Why his, why dear. True, he could write Senhorita Marcenda, but Senhorita was ridiculous. After tearing up several sheets of paper, he found himself addressing her simply by her name, the way we should address everyone, that is why we were given names. Marcenda, I am writing as promised to give you my news. He stopped to think, then continued, composing the phrases, drawing them together, filling in gaps, if he did not tell the truth, or not all of it, he told one truth, the important thing is that the letter make the writer and the one who receives it happy, that both discover in it an ideal image of themselves. There had been no formal interrogation at police headquarters, nothing that could be used against him in the courts, he had simply been summoned for a little chat, as the deputy chief had been kind enough to point out. It is true that Victor witnessed everything, but he no longer remembers the details and tomorrow will remember even less, Victor has other, more important, matters on his mind. And there are no other witnesses, there is only the letter written by Ricardo Reis, and it may soon go astray, that is altogether likely, because certain documents should not be kept. Other sources may come to light, but they will be suspect, apocryphal if feasible, and in the absence of any firm evidence we will find ourselves obliged to invent a truth, a dialogue, a Victor, a deputy chief, a wet, windy morning, a nature that sympathizes, all false and at the same time all true. Ricardo Reis finished his letter with respectful greetings, wished her good health, a forgivable commonplace, and after some hesitation told her, in a postscript, that she might not find him here on her next visit to Lisbon, because he was beginning to find life in the hotel irksome, monotonous. He must find a place of his own, open an office, The time has come to see how deep these new roots of mine can go, all of them. He was about to underline the last three words but decided to leave them as they stood, their ambiguity transparent. When I finally get around to leaving the hotel, I shall write to you at this same address in Coimbra. He reread the letter, folded the sheet of paper, sealed the envelope, then concealed it among his books. Tomorrow he will post it, today, blessed are those, with this storm, who have a roof over their heads, even if it is only that of the Hotel Bragança. Ricardo Reis went up to the window and drew back the curtains, but the rain was pouring down in one vast sheet of water and he could see little, then not even that, his breath clouded the window-pane. Under the protection of the shutters he opened the window. The Cais do Sodré was already flooding, the kiosk that sold tobacco and spirits was transformed into an island, the world had broken free of its wharf, had drifted away. Sheltered in the doorway of a tavern on the other side of the street, two men stood smoking. They had been drinking and now were rolling their cigarettes slowly, deliberately, while they discussed some metaphysical problem or other, perhaps even the rain that was keeping them from getting on with their lives. They soon disappeared into the darkness of the tavern, if they had to wait, they might as well use the opportunity and have another drink. A man dressed in black and bareheaded came to the door to contemplate the sky, then disappeared as well. Closing the window, Ricardo Reis switched off the light, stretched out wearily on the sofa, and spread a blanket over his knees. Like a silkworm in its cocoon he listened to the mournful noise of the rain. Unable to sleep, he lay with his eyes wide open, *You are alone, no one knows you, be silent and pretend,* he murmured, words written in other times, despising them because they did not express loneliness, merely voiced it. And silence and pretense, these words too were not what they spoke, to be alone, my friend, is much more than a word or a voice saying it.

Later that afternoon he went down to the first floor, to give Salvador the opportunity he so craved, sooner or later he would be forced to broach the subject, so better that he choose the time and place, No, Senhor Salvador, it went extremely well, they were most courteous. The question, when it came, was phrased with great delicacy, Now then, Doctor, tell me, how did you get on this morning, did they give you a difficult time. No, Senhor Salvador, it went extremely well, they were most courteous, all they wanted was some information regarding the Portuguese Consulate in Rio de Janeiro, where I should have been given a signed document, pure bureaucracy and nothing more. Salvador appeared to be satisfied, but he remained suspicious, as one might expect of a man who has seen so much of life, especially working in a hotel. Tomorrow he will get to the bottom of this matter, ask his acquaintance, Victor, I should know the people I have staying in my hotel, and Victor will warn him, Salvador, my friend, keep an eye on that fellow, right after the interrogation the deputy chief said, This Doctor Reis is not what he appears to be, he must be watched, no, we have no definite suspicions for the moment, only an impression, keep an eye on him, tell us if he receives any mail, So far, not a single letter, That too is strange, we must pay a visit to the post office, to see if anything is being held for him, and contacts, does he have any, Here in the hotel, none whatsoever, Well, if you see anything suspicious, just let me know. After this private conversation, the atmosphere in the hotel will once again grow tense, every member of the staff will adjust his or her sights to conform to the aim of Salvador's rifle, a constant vigilance that might well be called surveillance. Even the good-natured Ramón has become cool, Felipe mutters, there is of course one exception, as everybody knows, Lydia, poor thing. She goes around looking worried, and with good reason, today Pimenta burst out laughing, malicious fellow that he is, We haven't seen the end of this story yet. Tell me what is going on, please, she said, I won't breathe a word to a soul. There is nothing going on, Ricardo Reis told her, it is just a pile of nonsense invented by people who have nothing better to do than meddle in the affairs of others. It might be a pile of nonsense, but it can turn a person's life into a nightmare. Don't you worry, once I leave the hotel, the talk will stop. Are you going away, you didn't tell me. Sooner or later I will go, I never intended to spend the rest of my life here. Then I will never see you again, and Lydia, who was resting her head on his shoulder, shed a tear, which he felt. Now then, you mustn't cry, that's life, people meet, they part, one of these days you will marry. Bah, marry, I'm already too old, but what about you, where will you go. I will look for a place, I will find something suitable. If you want, If I want what, I could come and spend my days off with you, I have nothing else in life. Lydia, why do you like me. I don't know, perhaps because of what I said, that I have nothing else in life. You have your mother, your brother, you must have had affairs with men before this, and no doubt there will be others, you are pretty, you'll marry one day, start a family. Perhaps, but for now you are all I have. You are a likable girl, You haven't answered my question, What was that, Do you want me to come and spend my days with you when you have a place of your own, Would you like that, Of course I would, Then you must come until such time as. Until you find someone of your own station. That was not what I was going to say. When that happens, you need only say to me, Lydia, I don't want you to come anymore. Sometimes I feel I don't really know you. I'm a hotel chambermaid. But your name is Lydia, and you have a curious way of saying things. When people start talking their hearts, as I'm doing now with my head on your shoulder, the words aren't the same. I hope you find yourself a good husband someday. It would be nice, but when I listen to other women, those who say they have good husbands, it makes me wonder. You think they're not good husbands, Not for me, What is a good husband, in your opinion, I don't know, You're hard to please. Not really, lying here without any future, I'm happy with what I have now. I will always be your friend. We don't know what tomorrow brings. And you will always be my friend. Who, me, that's something else. Explain yourself, I can't, if I could, I would be able to explain everything, You explain more than you imagine, Don't be silly, I'm not educated, You can read and write, Not very well, I can barely read and can't write without making mistakes. Ricardo Reis drew her to him and she embraced him, the conversation had gradually brought them to an inexplicable emotion akin to pain, so that what they did next was done with extreme delicacy, and we all know what that was.

During the days that followed, Ricardo Reis set about looking for lodgings. He left early each morning and returned at night, having lunched and dined out. The classified section in the *Diário de Notícias* served as his vade mecum, but he did not travel far, residential areas on the outskirts suited neither his needs nor inclinations. He would have hated to live, for example, near the Rua dos Heróis de Quionga in Moraes Soares, where apartments had been built with five or six rooms and the rent was incredibly cheap, from a hundred and sixty-five to two hundred and forty escudos a month, but they were so remote from the Baixa and had no view of the river. He was looking for furnished quarters, otherwise he would need to select furniture, linen, dishes, and without a woman at his side to advise him, because no one could possibly imagine Lydia, poor girl, going in and out of department stores with Doctor Ricardo Reis, telling him what to buy. And as for Marcenda, even if she were here and her father permitted it, what would she know about such practical matters, the only house she had ever known was her own, and it wasn't really hers at all, because strictly speaking the word mine means something made by me and for me. And these are the only two women Ricardo Reis knows, there are no others. Fernando Pessoa was exaggerating when he dubbed him Don Juan. It is not so easy, after all, to leave the hotel. Each life creates its own ties, each its own inertia, incomprehensible to any external observer and no less incomprehensible to the person observed. In a word, let us content ourselves with the little we understand of others, they will be grateful and perhaps even thank us. But Salvador does not content himself. The prolonged absences of this hotel guest, so different from the regime he previously kept, make him nervous. Salvador even considered having a word with Victor, but a qualm made him change his mind at the last moment, what if he became involved in some situation which, if badly handled, might implicate him too, or worse. He grew exceedingly attentive to Ricardo Reis, an attitude which altogether disconcerted the hotel staff, no longer sure how they were expected to behave. Forgive these prosaic details, but they also have their importance.

Such are the contradictions of life. Just recently it was reported that Luís Carlos Prestes was arrested. Let us hope the police do not arrive to ask Ricardo Reis if he knew Prestes in Brazil or if Prestes had been one of his patients. Just recently, Germany denounced the Locarno Pact and after endless threats finally occupied the Rhineland. Just recently, a spring was inaugurated in Santa Clara amid wild excitement on the part of the inhabitants, who formerly had to get their water supply via fire pumps, and it was a lovely ceremony, two little innocents, a boy and a girl, filled two pitchers of water to much applause and cheering. Just recently, there appeared in Lisbon a famous Romanian called Manoilescu, who upon his arrival declared, The new doctrine currently spreading throughout Portugal lured me across these frontiers, I come as a respectful disciple, as a jubilant believer. Just recently, Churchill made a speech in which he said that Germany is the only nation in Europe today that does not fear war. Just recently, the Fascist party in Spain, the Falange, was banned, and its leader, José Antonio Primo de Rivera, imprisoned. Just recently, Kierkegaard's *Human Despair* was published. Just recently, at the Tivoli, the film *Bozambo* opened, it portrays the noble efforts of the whites to extinguish the fierce warring spirit of the primitive races. And Ricardo Reis has done nothing except look for lodgings, day after day. He is disheartened, near despair, as he leafs through the newspapers, which inform him about everything except what he wants to know, they tell him that Venizelos is dead, that Ortins de Bettencourt has said an internationalist cannot be a soldier much less a Portuguese, that it was raining yesterday, that the Reds are on the increase in Spain, that for seven and a half escudos he can buy *The Letters of a Portuguese Nun,* what they do not tell him is where he can find the accommodations he needs so badly. Notwithstanding Salvador's great solicitude, he is anxious to escape the stifling atmosphere of the Hotel Bragança, particularly now that he knows he will not lose Lydia by leaving. She has given her promise, has guaranteed the gratification of those desires with which we are all familiar. Ricardo Reis seems to have forgotten Fernando Pessoa, the poet's image has faded, like a photograph exposed to sunlight or a plastic funeral wreath that has lost its color. The poet himself warned him, Nine months, perhaps not even that, and he has not reappeared, perhaps he is in a bad mood or angry, or perhaps, being dead, he cannot escape the obligations of his condition. We can only speculate, we know nothing, after all, of life beyond the grave, and Ricardo Reis forgot to ask him when he had the opportunity, the living are so selfish and unfeeling. The days pass, monotonous, gray. There is news of more storms in Ribatejo, cattle swept away by floods, houses collapsing, sinking into the mud, cornfields submerged. All that is visible, on the surface of the vast lake covering the marshes by the river, are the rounded crests of weeping willows, the battered spurs of ash trees and poplars, their highest branches entwined with floating brushwood and vernal grass that was torn from its roots. When finally the waters subside, people will say, Look, the water came up to here, and no one will believe it. Ricardo Reis neither suffers nor witnesses these disasters, he reads the newspaper reports and studies the photographs. Scenes of tragedy, says the headline, and he muses on the persistent cruelty of fate, which can remove us from this world in so many ways yet takes perverse pleasure in choosing iron and fire and this endless deluge. We find Ricardo Reis reclining on a sofa in the hotel lounge, enjoying the warmth of the paraffin heater and the cozy atmosphere. Were we not endowed with the gift of reading the human heart, we would never know the sad thoughts that assail him, the misery of his neighbor some fifty, eighty kilometers away. Here I am, meditating on the cruelty of fate and the indifference of the gods, for they are the same thing, as I hear Salvador telling Pimenta to go to the kiosk to buy a Spanish newspaper, and the unmistakable footsteps of Lydia climbing the stairs to the second floor. Distracted, I pick up the classifieds again, my current obsession, rooms to rent, carefully I go down the list with my forefinger, nervous, not wanting Salvador to catch me. Suddenly I come to a halt, Furnished rooms to let, Rua de Santa Catarina, deposit required. I can see the building as clearly as the photographs of the flood, its upper story decorated with inscriptions, it's the one I noticed that afternoon when I met Marcenda, how could I have forgotten it, I'll go there right now, but I must be calm, betray no excitement, behave naturally. Done reading the *Diário de Notícias*, I now fold it carefully, leave it just as I found it, not like some people who scatter the pages everywhere. I get up, say to Salvador, I'm going for a stroll, the rain has stopped, what further explanation should I give if pressed. Ricardo Reis suddenly realizes that his relationship with the hotel, or with Salvador, is that of a dependent. He looks at himself in the mirror and once more sees a pupil of the Jesuits, a rebel against the code of discipline simply because it is a code of discipline. But this is worse, because he cannot even muster the courage to say, Salvador, I'm off to look at an apartment, and if I find it suitable, I will be leaving the hotel, I'm fed up with you and Pimenta, with all of you, except Lydia, of course, who deserves something better than this place. He does not say any of this, but only, See you in a while, almost as if he were asking to be excused. Cowardice is shown not only on the battlefield or when one is confronted with a knife pointed at one's entrails. There are people whose courage wobbles like jelly, but it's not their fault, that's how they were born.

Within a few minutes Ricardo Reis had reached the Alto de Santa Catarina. Seated on the same bench were the same two old men gazing at the river. They turned around when they heard footsteps, and one remarked to the other, That's the fellow who was here three weeks ago. You mean, the other said, the one with the girl, because although many other men and women had come here, strolling past or stopping to take in the view, the old men knew perfectly well which man. It is a mistake to think that one loses one's memory with old age, that the elderly preserve only remote memories which gradually surface like submerged foliage as the swollen waters recede. There is a dreadful memory that comes with old age, the memory of the final days, the final image of the world, of life, That was how I left it, who can tell if it will remain like that, they say when they reach the other side, and these two old men will say the same, but today's image is not their last. On the front door of the building Ricardo Reis found a pinned notice. It read, Prospective viewers should apply to the agent. The address given was in the Baixa, there was still time. He ran all the way to the Rua do Calhariz, hailed a taxi, and came back accompanied by a stout gentleman, Yes sir, I am the agent, he had brought the keys. They went up, here is the apartment, spacious, adequate for a large family, furniture made of dark mahogany, an enormous bed, a tall closet, a fully furnished dining room, a sideboard, a credenza for silver or china according to one's means, an extending table, and the study paneled with maple, the desk covered with green baize like a billiard table, threadbare in one corner, and a kitchen, and a bathroom rudimentary but adequate. Every item of furniture was bare, empty, not a single utensil, dish, or ornament, no sheets or towels, The last tenant was an old woman, a widow, who has gone to live with her children and taken all her belongings, the place is to be let with only the furniture you see here. Ricardo Reis went to one of the windows, there were no curtains, and he could see the palm trees in the square, the statue of Adamastor, the old men seated on the bench, and beyond, on the mud-polluted river, the warships with their prows turned landward. One cannot tell, watching them, if the tide is about to rise or fall. If we linger here a little longer, we will see. How much is the rent, what kind of deposit do you expect for the furniture, and within half an hour, if that, of discreet bargaining they reached an agreement. The agent was reassured that he was dealing with a gentleman of some distinction, Tomorrow, sir, if you would care to call at my office we can sign the contract, here is your key, Doctor, the apartment is yours. Ricardo Reis thanked him, insisted on leaving a deposit in excess of the usual percent. The agent wrote out a receipt then and there, he sat at the desk and took out a fountain pen overlaid with a filigree of stylized leaves and branches. In the silence of the apartment all that could be heard was the scraping of the nib on the paper and the agent breathing, wheezing a little, clearly asthmatic, Done, there you are, no, please don't disturb yourself, I can take a taxi, I assume you'll want to stay a while to get the feel of your new home, I fully understand, people become attached to their homes, the woman who lived here, poor old girl, how she wept the day she left, inconsolable, but we are often forced by circumstances, illness, widowhood, what must be, must be, we are powerless, well then, I'll expect you at my office tomorrow. Now alone, holding the key in his hand, Ricardo Reis went through the rooms again, thinking of nothing, merely looking, then went to the window. The prows of the ships pointed upstream, a sign that the tide was going out. The old men remained seated on the bench.

That same night Ricardo Reis told Lydia that he had rented an apartment. She wept a little, complained that she would no longer be able to look at him at every moment, an exaggeration on her part, words spoken in passion, because she could not look at him at every moment when they spent the night together with the light off in case anyone was spying, and during the day Lydia avoided him or addressed him with the utmost formality, a scene relished by malicious witnesses who were waiting for an opportunity to take their revenge. He comforted her, Don't cry, we will see each other on your days off, undisturbed by anyone, that's if you want to come, a question that required no answer. Of course I want to come, I already told you so, when are you thinking of moving to your apartment. The moment it's ready, there is some furniture, but no linen, no kitchen things, I don't need much to start, a few towels, sheets, blankets, then little by little I will get the rest. If the place has been closed up for some time, it will need cleaning, so I'll do it. What an idea, I can employ some woman in the neighborhood. I won't have it, you can rely on me, why go looking for someone else. You are a good girl, Pooh, I am who I am. This is one of those statements that brooks no reply. Each of us should know who he is, there has certainly been no lack of advice on that score since the time of the Greeks and Romans, Know thyself, hence our admiration for this Lydia, who does not appear to have the slightest doubt.

Next day, Ricardo Reis went out and bought two complete sets of bed linen and towels in various sizes. Fortunately the water, gas, and electricity had not been cut off by the respective companies and the accounts could remain in the name of the previous tenant, or so the agent suggested, and he agreed. He also bought some pots and pans, enamel and aluminum, a coffee pot, cups and saucers, napkins, coffee, tea, and sugar, all the things he would be likely to need for breakfast. Lunch and dinner he would have out. He enjoyed this little shopping expedition, it reminded him of his first days in Rio de Janeiro, where without any assistance he had done the same thing. Between trips to and from the shops, he wrote a short letter to Marcenda, communicating his new address, by extraordinary coincidence very near the spot where they had had their meeting. How typical of this vast world, where men, like animals, have their own territory, each his own yard or coop, his own spider's web, which is the best comparison of all. One spider spins a web as far as Oporto, another as far as Rio, but these are only supports, points of reference, mooring posts, it is in the center of the web that the spider and the fly play out their destiny. In the late afternoon Ricardo Reis took a taxi from shop to shop collecting his purchases, then bought a few pastries, some crystallized fruit, and a selection of biscuits, tea, digestive, and arrowroot. He returned to the Rua de Santa Catarina, arrived just as the two old men were descending to their homes somewhere in the neighborhood. While Ricardo Reis lifted his parcels from the taxi and carried them up, making three trips, the old men stopped and watched, and seeing the lights go on in the apartment on the third floor, they said, Look, someone is living in the apartment Dona Luísa used to occupy. They only moved away when the new tenant appeared at the window and saw them. They went off in a state of nervous excitement, which sometimes happens, and just as well, a welcome break in the monotony of existence. We think we have arrived at the end of the road, but it is only a bend opening onto a new horizon and new wonders. From his windows bare of drapes Ricardo Reis watched the river's expanse. To get a better view he switched off the light. Gray light fell like pollen from the skies, becoming darker as it settled. Ferry boats to and from Cacilhas, their lamps already lit, plied the dingy waters alongside the warships and anchored barges. One last frigate, almost concealed behind the outline of the rooftops, is about to dock. The scene reminds you of a child's drawing. The evening is so sad that a desire to weep surges from the depths of the soul. His head resting against the windowpane, shut off from the world by a cloud of condensation as he breathes on the smooth, cold surface, he watches the contorted, defiant figure of Adamastor gradually dissolve. It was already dark when Ricardo Reis went out. He dined in a restaurant in the Rua dos Correeiros, on a mezzanine floor with a low ceiling, solitary among solitary men. Who were they, what kind of existence did they lead, what brought them to this place, chewing cod, baked hake, steak and potatoes, nearly everyone drinking red wine. More formal in their appearance than in their table manners, they rap on their glasses with their knives to summon the waiter, they pick their teeth, tooth by tooth, with fierce satisfaction, extracting some stubborn fiber with thumb and forefinger used like pliers. They belch, loosen their belts, unbutton their vests, unshoulder their suspenders. Ricardo Reis thought to himself, This is what all my meals will be like from now on, this clatter of cutlery, the voices of the waiters shouting into the kitchen, One soup, the muffled sounds of those eating, the dismal light, the grease congealed on the cold plates, the adjacent table still not cleared, wine stains on the tablecloth, bread crumbs, a cigarette butt still burning. Ah how different life is in the Hotel Bragança, even if it is not first class. Ricardo Reis suddenly feels bereft of Ramón's presence, even though he will see him again tomorrow, today is only Thursday, he is leaving the hotel on Saturday. Yet he knows that such moments of nostalgia tend to be short-lived, it is all a question of habit, you lose one habit and gain another. He has been in Lisbon less than three months and already Rio de Janeiro is like a distant memory, perhaps of some other life, not his, one of those innumerable lives. Yes, at this very moment another Ricardo Reis may be dining in Oporto or lunching in Rio de Janeiro, if not farther afield. It has not rained all day and he has been able to do his shopping with the utmost tranquillity. He is now making his way back to the hotel, there he will inform Salvador that he is leaving

Saturday, just like that, I am leaving Saturday, but he feels like the adolescent who, having been refused a key to the house by his father, dares to take it without permission, trusting in the power of deeds once they have been carried out.

Salvador is still behind the reception desk but has told Pimenta that as soon as the last guest leaves the dining room he will go home, his wife is laid up with the flu. A seasonal fruit, Pimenta quips in a familiar tone, as they have known each other for many years. Salvador growls in reply, No chance of my being ill, a sibylline statement open to several interpretations. It could be the complaint of one who enjoys robust health or a warning to the powers of evil that it would be a great loss to this hotel if the manager were to fall ill. Ricardo Reis enters, wishes everyone a good evening, wonders for a second whether he should call Salvador to one side, then decides that such secrecy would be ridiculous, to murmur, for example, Look, Senhor Salvador, it wasn't really my intention, but you know how these things are, one's circumstances change, life goes on, the point is that I've decided to leave your admirable hotel, I've found a place of my own, please don't take offense, I hope we can go on being friends. Suddenly he finds himself sweating, as if he were once more a pupil of the Jesuits kneeling at the confessional, I lied, I was envious, I had impure thoughts, I played with myself. Salvador, at the reception desk, has reciprocated his greeting and turned away to take the key from the hook. Ricardo Reis must utter these liberating words at once, before Salvador can catch him off balance or trip him up. Senhor Salvador, could I ask you to prepare my bill, I will be checking out on Saturday. No sooner did he speak in this dry manner than he felt remorseful, because Salvador, standing there with the key in his hand, was the very image of wounded surprise, the victim of an act of betrayal. This is no way to treat a hotel manager who has shown himself to be such a staunch friend. What we should have done was call him to one side and say, Look Salvador, It wasn't really my intention, but no, guests can be so ungrateful and this guest is the most ungrateful of all, he came here for sanctuary, was well treated despite his affair with one of the chambermaids, any other manager would have sent both of them packing or complained to the police. I should have heeded Victor's warning but I let my heart rule my head, everyone takes advantage of my good nature, but I swear it's the last time. If all the seconds and minutes were exactly the same, as marked on the clock, we would not always have time to explain what takes place in them, the substance they contain, but fortunately for us the episodes of greatest significance tend to occur in seconds of long duration and minutes that are spun out, which makes it possible to discuss at length and in some detail without any serious violation of the most subtle of the three dramatic unities, which is time itself. With a halting gesture Salvador handed him the key, assumed a dignified expression, addressed him in a grave, paternal tone, I hope we have given every satisfaction during your stay here, Doctor. These modest words, so professionally phrased, with their underlying acerbic note of irony, could be misunderstood as alluding to Lydia, but no, for the moment Salvador is only trying to convey his disappointment and wounded feelings. Every possible satisfaction, Senhor Salvador, Ricardo Reis assured him warmly, it is simply that I've found an apartment, I have decided to settle in Lisbon once and for all, and a man needs a place he can call his own. Ah, well, perhaps I could ask Pimenta to help you transport your luggage, if the apartment is here in Lisbon, obviously. Yes, it's in Lisbon, but I can manage, thanks just the same, I'll hire a porter. Pimenta, prompted by the manager's generous offer of his services, curious as to where Doctor Reis was moving, and aware of his employer's interest, took it upon himself to insist, Why hire a porter, Doctor, when I can carry your suitcases. Thanks for offering, Pimenta, but I can easily get a porter, and to avoid any further insistence Ricardo Reis made his little farewell speech in advance, I can assure you, Senhor Salvador, that I shall take away the happiest memories of your hotel, where I have found the service excellent, where I felt completely at home and was treated with the utmost care and solicitude, I should like to express my deep gratitude to the entire staff, without exception, for the cordiality and affection they have shown me upon my return to my native Portugal, where I now intend to remain, to all of you my heartfelt thanks. Not all the staff were present, but that did not matter. Feeling very self-conscious, Ricardo Reis, as he spoke, found himself using words that were sure to spark sarcastic thoughts in those of his listeners who would think of Lydia at the mention of solicitude and affection. Why is it that words often make use of us, we see them approach menacingly, like an irresistible abyss, yet are unable to ward them off and end up saying precisely what we did not wish to say. Salvador replied with a few words, not that it was necessary, all he needed to say was how honored they had been to have Doctor Ricardo Reis as their guest, We were only doing our duty, and I speak for the entire staff when I say that we will miss you, Doctor, is that not so Pimenta. With this unexpected question the solemnity of the moment was dissolved, he appeared to be asking for his sentiment to be seconded, but the effect was quite the opposite, a wink, a glint of malice, If you understand what I mean, and Ricardo Reis understood, he wished them good-night and went up to his room, certain that they were discussing him behind his back, already uttering Lydia's name. What he did not suspect was that the conversation continued like this, You must find out the name of the porter he hires, I want to know where he's moving to.

The clock has certain hours which are so empty of significance, the hands appear to crawl toward infinity, the morning drags, the afternoon is neverending, the night seems eternal. This was how Ricardo Reis spent his last day in the hotel. Moved by some unconscious scruple, he decided that he should be visible all the time. Perhaps he did not want to appear ungrateful or indifferent. His departure was acknowledged by Ramón as he ladled the soup into his plate, So you are leaving us, Doctor, words which convey deep sadness when uttered as only humble servants know how to utter them. And Lydia's name was never off Salvador's lips, he summoned her for everything and for nothing, ordered her to do one thing then the opposite, he watched her every movement, expression, her eyes, seeking signs of unhappiness, tears, only natural in a woman who is about to be abandoned and knows it. Yet he had never seen her look so peaceful and composed, one would think she had no sins on her conscience, no weakness of the flesh or willful prostitution. Salvador reproached himself for not having punished such immoral conduct the moment he suspected it, or when it became public knowledge, starting with rumors in the kitchen and the storeroom. It is too late now, the guest is leaving, no point in raking up mud, especially when his conscience tells him that he himself is not entirely without blame, he knew what was going on and said nothing, he was an accomplice. I simply felt sorry for him, he arrived from Brazil, from the wilderness, without any family to receive him, so I treated him as if he were a relative. Three or four times Salvador consoled himself with this thought, then spoke aloud, When room two hundred and one is vacated, I want it cleaned from top to bottom, it has been reserved for a distinguished family from Granada. As Lydia walked away, having received these instructions, he stared at the curve of her hips. Until today he has been an exemplary manager, upright, never mixing business with pleasure, but now he has a score to settle, Either she consents or she'll be out on the street. We feel certain that this anger will go no further, most men lose their courage at the last moment.

After lunch on Saturday, Ricardo Reis went to the Chiado, where he contracted the services of two young porters, and in order not to have them trailing after him down the Rua do Alecrim like a guard of honor, he told them what time they should come to the hotel. He waited in his room with the same sense of veering off course he experienced when he saw the mooring cables drop from *The Highland Brigade* to the quay in Rio de Janeiro. He is alone, seated on the sofa, Lydia will not appear, that was what they have agreed. A clatter of heavy footsteps in the corridor announces the arrival of the porters, Pimenta with them. This time Pimenta does not have to exert himself, at most he will make the same gesture Ricardo Reis and Salvador made when he first carried up the large suitcase, a helping hand underneath, a note of caution on the stairs, a word of advice, unnecessary for those who have mastered all there is to know about lifting luggage. Ricardo Reis goes to say good-bye to Salvador and leaves a generous tip for the staff, Share it among yourselves as you see fit. The manager thanks him. Some guests who happen to be present smile approvingly on the nice friendships formed in this hotel, and the Spaniards are deeply moved at the sight of such goodwill. Little wonder that their own divided land comes to mind, these are peninsular contradictions. Below, on the street, Pimenta has already asked the porters where they are taking the luggage, but the gentleman has said nothing, one of them thinks it cannot be far away, the other is not so sure. But there is no need for concern, Pimenta knows the two men, one of them even worked for the hotel, and they can always be found hanging around the Chiado. When he wants to get to the bottom of the mystery, he will not have far to go. Ricardo Reis tells him, I've left you a little token of gratitude, and Pimenta replies, Many thanks, Doctor, whenever you need any help, you can rely on me. Empty words, hypocritical words, the Frenchman who said that man has been endowed with words to hide his thoughts spoke true, still we should not make hasty judgments, what is certain is that words are the best tools we can hope for in our attempt, always frustrated, to express what we call thought. The two porters now learn where they must take the suitcases, Ricardo Reis tells them as soon as Pimenta has withdrawn, and off they go, up the street. They use the sidewalk, which is less broken. This is not a heavy load for men accustomed to moving pianos and other monstrosities with levers and ropes. Ricardo Reis walks in front, far enough ahead to avoid giving the impression that he is leading this expedition but not so far ahead as to make the porters feel they are unaccompanied. Nothing could be more delicate than these contacts between different classes. Social harmony is a question of tact, finesse, and psychology, and whether these three qualities strictly coincide with one's feelings is a problem we have given up trying to solve. Halfway up the street the porters are obliged to move to one side, and they take this opportunity to rest their load and get their breath back, because a procession of trams crammed with people with blond hair and pink complexions is coming down the road, German tourists, workers belonging to the German Labor Front. Nearly all of them are in Bavarian costume, knee breeches, shirt and shoulder straps, little hats with narrow brims. Some of the trams are open, like wheeled cages into which the rain can fall at will, the striped canvas awning giving little protection. What must these Aryan workers be saying about our Portuguese civilization, what do these sons of so privileged a race think of the rustics who pause now to watch them pass. Look at that dark-haired gentleman in the light raincoat, and those two unshaven types dressed like tramps, hoisting the load back onto their shoulders and resuming their climb. The last of the trams go by, there were twenty-three trams altogether, if anyone had the patience to count them, heading for the Torre de Belém, the Mosteiro dos Jerónimos, and the other landmarks of Lisbon, such as Algés, Dafundo and Cruz Quebrada.

With lowered heads, because of their burden no doubt, the porters crossed the square where the statue of the epic poet stands. Ricardo Reis now followed, embarrassed at traveling so light, his hands in his pockets. He had not even brought a yellow parrot from Brazil, and perhaps just as well, for he would not have had the courage to go through these streets carrying the stupid creature on a perch, with people teasing it, Give me your claw, yellow parrot, perhaps referring, with typical Portuguese wit, to those blond Germans going past in trams. At the bottom of this road you can see the palms of the Alto de Santa Catarina between the mountains on the opposite coast. Heavy clouds appear like buxom women at their windows, a metaphor that would make Ricardo Reis, a poet for whom clouds barely exist, shrug with scorn. Fleecy clouds, racing clouds, so white and hackneyed, and if it is raining, that means Apollo has hidden his face. This is the entrance to my apartment, here is the key and there is the staircase, second landing, number two, this is where I will live. No windows opened when we arrived, no doors were ajar, it would appear that the least inquisitive inhabitants of Lisbon all live in this building, or else they are spying through peepholes, the pupils of their eyes flashing. Now in we go, the two small suitcases, the larger one, the money agreed upon is paid, the expected tip. There is a pungent odor of sweat. Whenever you need any help, boss, we're always available. They said always so earnestly that Ricardo Reis believed them, but he did not reply. A man, if he has studied, learns to be skeptical, especially since the gods are so inconstant. The only certainty, theirs from knowledge, ours from experience, is that everything comes to an end, and always soonest. As the porters left, Ricardo Reis closed the door to the landing. Then, without switching on the lights, he went through the entire apartment, his footsteps echoing on the bare floorboards. Furniture empty and smelling of old mothballs, frayed sheets of tissue paper still lining some of the drawers, fluff accumulating in corners, and near the kitchen and bathroom a strong smell from the drains, because the water was low in the cistern. Ricardo Reis opened the spigots and flushed the toilet several times. The apartment filled with noises, the running of water, the vibration of pipes, a tapping sound from the meter, then gradually silence was restored. At the rear of the building was a yard with washing hanging up to dry, small vegetable patches the color of ashes, troughs, vats made of cement, a dog kennel, rabbit hutches, and chicken coops. Looking at them, Ricardo Reis reflected on the linguistic conundrum whereby rabbits had hutches and chicken had coops, and not the other way around. He returned to the front of the apartment to look out the grimy bedroom window at the deserted street. There stood Adamastor, livid against the dull clouds, a giant raging in silence. Some people are watching the ships, they look up from time to time as if expecting rain, and seated on the same bench, the two old men lost in conversation. Ricardo Reis smiled, Well done, they are so absorbed they did not even notice the arrival of the suitcases. He had never been one for jokes but was amused, as if he had just played a harmless trick on both of them, a friendly game. Still wearing his raincoat, as if having just dropped by for a second, a doctor's visit, as the adage cynically puts it, to make a quick inspection of the place where he might take up residence someday, he finally said aloud, like a message he must not forget, I live here, this is where I live, this is my home, this, I have no other, and suddenly he felt fear, the terror of a man who finds himself in a deep cave and pushes open a door that leads into the darkness of an even deeper cave, or to a void, an absence, nothingness, the passage to nonbeing. Removing his raincoat and jacket, he realized the apartment was cold. As if going through motions already made in another life, he unpacked methodically, his clothes, shoes, papers, books, and all those small objects, essential or nonessential, we take with us from one abode to another, the crossed threads of a cocoon. He found his dressing gown, put it on. Now he is a man settled in his own home. He turned on the lamp that hung from the ceiling, it needed a shade, tulip-shaped, spherical, conical, any of these will do so long as they eliminate the glare which is hurting his eyes. Engrossed in putting away his things, he did not notice at first that it had started to rain, but a sharp gust of wind sent the water drumming against the panes. Such weather. He went to the window. The old men, like somber insects attracted by the light, were standing on the sidewalk opposite, one tall, the other short, each armed with an umbrella, their heads upturned like praying mantises. This time they were not intimidated by the face that appeared. Only when the rain became much heavier did they proceed down the street. When they get home their wives, if they have wives, will scold them, Soaked to the skin, just look at you, you could catch pneumonia, then I'll have all the trouble of nursing you, and the old men will tell them, Someone has moved into Dona Luísa's apartment, a man who seems to be by himself, not another living soul to be seen, Imagine, a big place like that for a bachelor, what a waste of good space. You might well ask how these good women know the apartment is large. Who can tell, perhaps in the time of Dona Luísa they did some charring there. Women of that class will turn their hand to anything that comes their way if their husbands earn low wages or pocket some of it to spend on booze and whores. The unfortunate wives are forced to scrub stairs and take in washing, some even specialize, doing nothing except scrubbing stairs or laundry, and so become mistresses of their craft. They have their own little ways, taking pride in the whiteness of their sheets, the cleanliness of their stairs scrubbed with carbolic soap, and their sheets could pass for altar cloths, you could eat spilled marmalade from their doorstep without any qualms. But where is this digression leading us. Now the sky is overcast and night will soon be here. When the old men were standing on the sidewalk looking up, they appeared to bask in the full light of day, but this was simply the effect of their white beards after eight days without shaving. Not even today, Sunday, did they sit in the barber's chair or use their own razor, but tomorrow, if the weather clears up, they will be cleanshaven, their skin lined with wrinkles and alum. When we say their hair is white, we mean only lower down, because on top they have nothing but a few sad wisps over their ears. But to return to where we left off. When they were standing there on the sidewalk, there was still daylight, although it was fast waning, so after watching the tenant on the third floor while the rain became heavier, they started walking downhill, walked on as it grew steadily darker, and by the time they reached the corner it was night. A good thing the street lamps were lit, casting pearls on the windowpanes. It must be said that these street lamps are nothing like those of the future, when the fairy Electricity with her magic wand will reach the Alto de Santa Catarina and environs and all the lamps will light up in glory at the same time. Today we have to wait until someone comes to light them, one by one. With the tip of his spill the lamplighter opens the door of the lantern, with the hook he turns the gas valve, then this son of Saint Elmo moves on, leaving signs of his passing throughout the city streets. A man bearing light, he is Halley's comet with a star-spangled trail, this is how the gods must have seen Prometheus when they looked down from on high. This particular firefly, however, is named António. Ricardo Reis feels a chill across his forehead, which was pressed against the windowpane as he watched the falling rain. The lamplighter appears, then each lamp is left with its glow and aura. A pale light covers the shoulders of Adamastor, the Herculean muscles of his back glisten, perhaps from the water descending from the sky, or perhaps it is the sweat of his agony as Thetis smiles derisively and mocks him, What nymph could offer enough love to satisfy the love of a giant. Now he knows what those promises of riches were worth. Lisbon is a great murmuring silence, nothing more.

Ricardo Reis returned to his domestic chores, put away his suits, shirts, handkerchiefs, socks, item by item, as if composing a Sapphic ode, laboriously working with an awkward rhyme scheme. The color of the tie he has just hung up requires a matching suit, which he must buy. Over the mattress that belonged to Dona Luísa, certainly not the one on which she lost her virginity many years ago but the mattress where she bled giving birth to her last child, and where her dear husband, a high court judge, suffered and died, over this mattress Ricardo Reis spread sheets still smelling of newness, two fleecy blankets, a pale bedspread. He slipped the pillow and woolen bolster into their cases, doing the best he could, clumsy as any male. Eventually Lydia will appear, perhaps tomorrow, with those magical hands of hers, magical because they are the hands of a woman, to tidy up this chaos, this resigned sorrow of things badly arranged. Ricardo Reis carried the suitcases into the kitchen, hung up the towels in the ice-cold bathroom, stored his toiletries in the little wall cabinet, which had a definite mildew smell. As we have already seen, he is a man fastidious about his appearance, it is a question of personal pride. All that remains to be done now is arrange his books on those warped black bookshelves in the study and put his papers in the drawers of the wobbly black bureau. Now he feels at home, he has found his bearings, the compass rose, north, south, east, west, unless some magnetic storm comes to send this compass into a frenzy.

At half past seven the rain has not stopped. Ricardo Reis sits on the edge of the high bed and examines the cheerless room. The window is bare of any curtains or netting. It occurs to him that the neighbors across the way might be spying, whispering among themselves, You can see everything that's going on in there. Eagerly they look forward to sights even more provocative than this one of a man sitting alone on the edge of an old-fashioned bed, his face hidden in a cloud. Ricardo Reis gets up and closes the inner shutters. Now the room is a cell, four blind walls, the door, should he open it, would lead to another door, or to a dark yawning cave, we have already used that image, it does not bear repeating. Shortly, in the Hotel Bragança, the maître d', Afonso, will strike the three blows of Vatel on that ludicrous gong, and the Portuguese and Spanish guests, *nuestros hermanos, los hermanos suyos*, will descend to the dining room. Salvador will smile at each in turn, Senhor Fonseca, Doctor Pascal, Madame, Don Camilo, Don Lorenzo, and the new arrival in room two hundred and one, surely the Duke of Alba or of Medinaceli, dragging his mighty sword, pressing a ducat into Lydia's outstretched hand. She curtsies, as befits a servant, and smilingly accepts a pinch in the flesh of her arm. Ramón will be bringing in the soup, today there is something special and he is not joking, from the deep tureen comes the fragrant smell of chicken, from the platters intoxicating aromas. We need not be surprised that Ricardo Reis feels his stomach rumble, it is, indeed, time for dinner. But even with the shutters closed you can hear the water from the eaves spattering on the sidewalk. Who would be so bold as to venture forth in weather like this, except for some pressing obligation, to save one's father from the gallows, for example, if one's father is still alive. The dining room of the Hotel Bragança is a lost paradise, and like any lost paradise it is sorely missed by Ricardo Reis, who would like to return but not to remain. He goes to get his parcels, the pastries and crystallized fruit, to satisfy his hunger. For drinking there is only tap water, which tastes of carbolic acid. Adam and Eve must have felt just as deprived that first night after their expulsion from the Garden of Eden, clearly it was raining buckets then too. As they stood in the doorway and Eve asked Adam, Would you like a biscuit, having only one, she broke it in half and gave him the larger piece. Adam munched slowly, watching Eve peck at her tiny portion, tilting her head like an inquisitive little bird. On the other side of the door now closed to them forever, without any evil intent or any prompting on the part of the serpent, she had offered him an apple. It is said that Adam only became aware of her nakedness when he bit into the apple, and that Eve, who did not have time to get dressed, remained like the lilies of the field who neither spin nor weave. Not far from the threshold of Eden they both spent the night comfortably, having eaten a biscuit for their supper, while on the other side God listened and felt sad, barred from a feast He had neither provided for nor foreseen. One day another maxim will be invented, Where man and woman join, God is, because paradise is not at all where it was said to be, it is here on earth and God will be obliged to come every time He wishes to enjoy it. But certainly not in this house. Ricardo Reis is alone. The cloying sweetness of a crystallized pear has made him feel sick, a pear, not an apple, it is indeed true that temptations are no longer what they were. He went into the bathroom to clean his sticky hands, his mouth, his teeth, he cannot bear this *dolceza*, a word that is neither Portuguese nor Spanish but an adaptation of the Italian, it is the only word that seems appropriate at the moment. Solitude weighs on him like night, and the night devours him like bait. Through the long narrow corridor under the greenish light that descends from the ceiling he is a marine animal with sluggish movements, a defenseless tortoise without its shell.

He rummages at the desk, through the manuscripts of his poems, he called them odes and so they have remained, because everything must have a name. He reads at random and asks himself if he is their author, for he does not recognize himself in what is written, in this detached, calm, resigned person, almost godlike, for that is how gods are, composed as they assist the dead. Vaguely he muses, he must organize his life, his time, decide how he will spend his mornings, afternoons, and evenings, get to bed early and rise early, find one or two restaurants that serve simple, wholesome meals, and he must reread and revise his poems for the anthology he plans to publish at some future date, and he must find suitable premises for his practice, get to know people, travel to other parts of the country, visit Oporto, Coimbra, call on Doctor Sampaio, run into Marcenda unexpectedly in the city's Poplar Grove. He no longer thinks about his plans and objectives, he feels compassion for the invalid, then for himself, and his compassion turns to self-pity. As he sits there, he begins a poem, then suddenly remembers that he once wrote, *I stand firmly upon the foundation of the poems I fashioned.* Anyone who has drawn up a testament such as this cannot now say the opposite.

It is not yet ten o'clock when Ricardo Reis goes to bed. The rain is still falling. He has brought a book to bed, he chose two but then decided against *The God of the Labyrinth.* After ten pages of the Sermon for the first Sunday in Lent his ungloved hands were freezing, those ardent words were not enough to warm them, *Search your house, look for the most worthless thing therein, and you will find that it is your own soul.* He put the book on the bedside table, huddled up with a sudden shiver, pulled the fold of the sheet up to his mouth, and closed his eyes. He knew he ought to switch off the light, but if he did that, he would feel obliged to fall asleep and he was not ready just yet. On cold nights like this Lydia would put a hot-water bottle between the sheets, will she be doing that now for the Duke of Medinaceli, calm yourself, jealous heart, the duke was accompanied by the duchess, the nobleman who pinched Lydia's arm in passing was the other duke, the Duke of Alba. The Duke of Medinaceli is old, sick, and impotent, he carries a tin sword, swears it is the mighty Colada that belonged to Cid Campeador and was passed from father to son in the Alba dynasty. Even a Spanish grandee is capable of telling lies. Ricardo Reis had fallen asleep, he realized it when he awoke, startled, to the sound of knocking at the door. Could it be Lydia, who has cunningly slipped out of the hotel and come in all this rain to spend the night with me, foolish girl. Then he thought, I've been dreaming. And so it appeared, for he heard nothing more in the seconds that followed, Perhaps there are ghosts in this apartment, perhaps that is why they couldn't rent it, so central, so spacious. But the knocking started up again, rat-tat-tat, discreetly, so as not to disturb the neighbors. Ricardo Reis got out of bed, pulled on his slippers, wrapped his dressing gown around him, shuffled across the room into the hall-way, shivering all the while, and looked at the door as if it were threatening him, Who is there. His voice sounded hoarse and fal-tering. Clearing his throat, he repeated the question. The reply came in a murmur, It's me. It was no ghost, it was Fernando Pessoa, trust him to choose an awkward moment. Ricardo Reis opened the door, and it was he all right, wearing his black suit, with neither coat nor hat, yet though he was coming in off the street there was not a drop of water on him. May I come in, he asked. You've never asked my permission before, why the sudden scruple. Things have changed, you're in your own home now and, to use an English expression which I learned as a schoolboy, a man's home is his castle. Come in, I was in bed, Were you asleep, I believe I dozed off, No need to stand on ceremony with me, get back into bed, I'm only dropping by for a few minutes. Ricardo Reis slipped nimbly between the sheets, his teeth chattering with cold but also from a residue of fear. He did not take off his dressing gown. Fernando Pessoa sat in a chair, crossed his legs, clasped his hands on his knee, and looked around with a critical eye, So, this is where you've taken up residence. It would seem. I find it rather dreary. Places that have been empty for some time always give that impression. Do you mean to live here on your own. Evidently not, I only moved in today and already have a visitor. I don't count, I'm scarcely company for anyone. You counted enough for me to have to get out of bed in this cold to open the door, soon I will be giving you a key. I wouldn't know what to do with it, if I could pass through walls I would spare you the trouble. Don't give it another thought, you mustn't take my words amiss, to be frank, I'm delighted to see you, this first night is not easy. Are you frightened. I felt a little nervous when I heard knocking, I forgot that it might be you, but it wasn't fear, only loneliness. Come now, you have a long way to go before you know what loneliness is. I've always lived alone. I too, but loneliness is not living alone, loneliness is the inability to keep someone or something within us company, it is not a tree that stands alone in the middle of a plain but the distance between the deep sap and the bark, between the leaves and the roots. You're talking nonsense, the things you mention are connected, there is no loneliness there. Let us forget the tree, look inside yourself. As that other poet said, *To walk alone among men*. It is even worse to be alone where we ourselves are not. You are in low spirits today. I have my days, but I was speaking not of this loneliness but of another, the one that travels with us, a bearable loneliness that keeps us company, Even that loneliness, you must agree, is sometimes unbearable, we long for a presence, a voice. Sometimes that presence and that voice only serve to render it intolerable. Is this possible. It most certainly is, the other day when we met at the belvedere, do you remember, you were waiting for your mistress. I've already told you that she is not my mistress. All right then, no need to lose your temper, but she might become your mistress, you don't know what tomorrow has in store for you. I am old enough to be her father. So what. Let us change the subject, finish what you were telling me. It was apropos of your having had the flu, it reminded me of a little episode during my own illness, this recent, terminal illness. How repetitive, your sense of style has sadly deteriorated. Death too is repetitive, it is in fact the most repetitive thing of all. Go on. A doctor came to the house, I was lying in the bedroom when my sister opened the door. You mean your half-sister, life is full of half-brothers and half-sisters. What are you trying to suggest. Nothing in particular, go on. She said, Do come in Doctor, the faker is in here, the faker in question was I, as you can see, loneliness has no bounds, it is everywhere. Have you ever felt yourself to be truly useless. Difficult to say, I don't recall ever having felt myself to be truly useful. I believe that this is the first loneliness, to feel that we are useless. Fernando Pessoa got up, half-opened the shutters, and looked out. An unpardonable oversight, he said, not to have included Adamastor in my *Mensagem*, such a popular giant, whose symbolic meaning is clear. Can you see him from there. Yes, poor creature, Camões used him for declarations of love which were probably in his own soul, and for prophecies that were less than clear. To forecast shipwreck to those who sail the high seas no special gifts of divination are needed. Prophesying disaster was ever a sign of loneliness, had Thetis reciprocated the giant's love, his discourse would have been quite different. Fernando Pessoa was sitting once more, in exactly the same position. Do you intend staying long, Ricardo Reis asked him. Why. I am tired. Don't worry about me, sleep to your heart's content, unless you find my presence disturbing. What disturbs me is to see you sitting here in the cold. The cold doesn't bother me, I could sit here in my shirt sleeves, but you shouldn't be lying in bed wearing your dressing gown, I'll take it off now. Fernando Pessoa spread the dressing gown over the top cover, pulled up the blankets, straightened the fold of the sheet maternally, Now sleep. I say Fernando, do me a favor, switch off the light, I'm sure you don't mind sitting in the dark. When Fernando Pessoa found the switch, the room was plunged into darkness. Then, very slowly, the light from the street lamps insinuated itself through the chinks of the shutters, a luminous band, a tenuous, uncertain pollen gathered on the walls. Ricardo Reis closed his eyes, murmured, Goodnight Fernando, and it seemed to him that a long time passed before he heard him reply, Good-night Ricardo. When he thought he had counted up to a hundred, he opened his eyes with difficulty. Fernando Pessoa was sitting in the same chair, hands clasped on one knee, the image of ultimate loneliness. Perhaps because he is without his glasses, Ricardo Reis thought, and this struck him, in his confused state, as being the most terrible of misfortunes. He awoke in the middle of the night. The rain had stopped, the world was traveling through silent space. Fernando Pessoa had not altered his position, he looked in the direction of the bed, his face expressionless, like a statue with vacant eyes. Much later, Ricardo Reis awoke again as a door banged. Fernando Pessoa was no longer there, he had left with the first light of morning.

As one has already seen in other times and other places, life has its vexations. When Ricardo Reis awoke late next morning, he sensed a presence in the room. Perhaps not quite loneliness, but silence, its half-brother. For several minutes he watched his courage desert him, it was like watching sand run through an hourglass, an overworked metaphor which nevertheless keeps recurring. One day, when we live two hundred years and ourselves become the hourglass observing the sand inside it, we will not need the metaphor, but life is too short to indulge in such thoughts, we were speaking of vexations. When Ricardo Reis went into the kitchen to light the heater and the range, he found that he had forgotten to buy matches, and since one lapse of memory tends to accompany another, he realized that he also was without a coffee strainer. It is indeed true that a man on his own is useless. The easiest and most immediate solution would be to knock on a neighbor's door, Please excuse me, senhora, I am the new tenant on the third floor, I only moved in yesterday, I was hoping to make myself some coffee, have a wash, shave, and I find I have no matches, I also am without a coffee strainer, but that is not important, I have tea, that at least I remembered, the main problem is hot water for a bath, if you could lend me a match, I'd be most grateful, forgive me for disturbing you. Since all men are brothers, or half-brothers, nothing could be more natural, he should not even have to go out into the cold stairway, they should come and ask him, Do you need anything, I saw you moving in yesterday, everybody knows that moving is like this, if it is not the matches that are missing, the salt has been forgotten, if the soap turns up, the scrubbing brush has been lost, what are neighbors for. But Ricardo Reis did not go to seek help, and no one came to ask if he needed anything. He had no choice but to dress, put on his shoes, wrap a scarf around his neck to conceal the fact that he had not shaved, and pull his hat down over his eyes. He was irritated at his forgetfulness and even more so at having to go out in this sorry state looking for matches. First he went to the window to see what the weather was like. The sky was overcast, no sign of rain. Adamastor stands alone, it is still too early for the old men to come and watch the ships, at this hour they will be at home shaving with cold water, or perhaps their careworn wives are heating mugs of water, but only tepid, not hot, because the Portuguese male, second to none in virility, cannot bear to be pampered. Let us not forget that we are the direct descendants of those Lusitanian heroes who bathed in the frozen lakes of the Serra da Estrela, no sooner emerging than they were off to impregnate some Lusitanian maiden. From a coal merchant who runs a tavern in the lower part of the neighborhood Ricardo Reis bought matches, a half-dozen boxes lest the man find this early morning sale insufficient. In fact the coal merchant could not remember ever having made such a sale at one go, here it is still customary for people to ask their neighbors for a light. Invigorated by the cold air, comforted by his scarf and the absence of people on the street, Ricardo Reis walked up to get a view of the river and the mountains on the other side. From here the mountains looked squat, and the sun's reflection on the water appeared and disappeared as low clouds passed. He walked around the statue, trying to find the name of the sculptor. The date is engraved there, nineteen twenty-seven. Ricardo Reis has the kind of mind which is always searching for patterns of symmetry in the chaos, Eight years after my departure into exile, the statue of Adamastor was erected on this spot, and Adamastor had been standing here for eight years when I returned to the land of my ancestors, O fatherland, it was the voices of your illustrious past that summoned me. The old men appear on the sidewalk, their cleanshaven faces marked with wrinkles and alum, an umbrella over one arm. They have left their capes unbuttoned and wear no tie, but their shirts are buttoned to the neck, not because it is Sunday, a day of respect, but out of a sense of what is fitting and dignified, however shabby their attire. Suspicious of this loitering at the statue, the old men come face to face with Ricardo Reis, they are convinced that there is something odd about the fellow, Who is he, what is he doing, how does he earn his living. Before sitting down, they place a length of folded sackcloth on the damp bench, then with the measured gestures of those who refuse to be hurried they make themselves comfortable, clear their throats loudly. The fat one produces a newspaper from the inside pocket of his cape, *O Século*, the newspaper that organizes charity events. They always buy it on Sunday, the fat man one week, the thin man the next. Ricardo Reis circles the statue of Adamastor a second time, a third. The old men, he sees, are becoming impatient, his restless presence makes it difficult for them to digest the news, which the fat one reads aloud to assist his own understanding and for the benefit of the thin one, who can neither read nor write. He pauses over the difficult words, but there are not too many of them, because the journalists never forget that they are writing for the masses. Ricardo Reis went over to the railing, where he pretended to ignore the old men absorbed in their paper, their murmuring, the one reading, the other listening and commenting, In Luís Uceda's wallet there was found a colored portrait of Salazar. This country is plagued with unsolved crime. A man is found dead on the road to Sintra, they say he was strangled after being put to sleep with ether, that he had been abducted, kept without food, that the crime was vile, a word that immediately shows our disapproval of crime, and now we learn that the murdered man was carrying a portrait of the wise, all-paternal dictator, to quote that French writer, whose name, recorded for posterity, is Charles Oulmont. Later on the investigation will confirm that Luís Uceda was indeed a great admirer of the eminent statesman, and it will be revealed that embossed on the leather of the aforesaid wallet was further proof of Uceda's patriotism, namely the emblem of the Republic, the armillary sphere with its castles and heraldic shields and the following inscription, Buy Portuguese Products.

Ricardo Reis discreetly withdraws, leaving the old men in peace. They were so absorbed in the mystery that they did not even notice his departure.

Nothing of consequence occurred that morning. There was a little trouble with an awkward heater that had not been used for weeks, he wasted match after match before getting the flame to stay on. Nor need we dwell on his melancholy repast, a cup of tea and three small sponge cakes left over from the previous evening's supper. Nor his bath amid a cloud of steam in the deep tub which was somewhat stained. He meticulously shaved, once, twice, as if in preparation for a secret rendezvous with some woman, her identity concealed by a high collar and a veil. How he would love to inhale the scent of her soap, of her lingering eau de Cologne, until that fused with more pungent and natural smells, the compelling smell of human flesh, which quivering nostrils take in and which leaves the breast panting, as if after a vigorous chase. The minds of poets, too, rove in this earthly fashion, stroking the bodies of women, even distant women, what is written here is a thing of the moment and of the imagination only, that mistress of great power and generosity. Ricardo Reis is ready to leave. He has no one waiting for him, and he is not going to eleven o'clock Mass to offer holy water to the Eternal Incognita. The sensible thing would be to stay at home until lunchtime. He has papers to arrange, books waiting to be read, and decisions to make, what kind of future does he want, what kind of job, where can he find the motivation to live and work, the reason. He had not intended to go out this morning, but now he must, it would be absurd to get undressed again, to admit that he got dressed to go out without being aware of what he was doing. This often happens, we take the first two steps because we are daydreaming or distracted and then have no choice but to take the third step, even when we know that it is wrong or ridiculous. Man, in the final analysis, is an irrational creature. Ricardo Reis returned to his room, thought perhaps he should make the bed before going out, he must not allow himself to become lax in his habits, but it was hardly worth the effort, he was not expecting visitors, so he settled in the chair where Fernando Pessoa had spent the night, crossed his legs as he had seen him do, clasped his hands on his knee, and tried to imagine himself dead, to contemplate the empty bed with the lifeless eyes of a statue. But there was a vein throbbing in his left temple, and the left eyelid twitched. I am alive, he murmured, then in a loud, sonorous voice he repeated, I am alive, and since there was no one there to contradict him, he was convinced. He put on his hat and went out. The old men had been joined by children playing hopscotch, jumping from chalked square to chalked square, each with its own number. This game has been given so many names, some call it monkey, others airplane, heaven and hell, roulette, also glory, but the most apt name of all would be the game of man, because that is what it looks like, the straight body, the extended arms, the upper circle forming the head or brain. The man lies on the paving stones looking up at the clouds while the children hop over him unaware of their cruelty, they will learn what it means when their time comes. Also present are some soldiers, who have arrived too early, because it is in the midafternoon that the housemaids take a stroll here if the weather is fair, otherwise their mistresses will say, Look, Maria, it is raining cats and dogs, you'd better stay in today, do a little ironing, I'll give you an extra hour on your day off, which is a whole two weeks away, a detail worth adding for those who never experienced such privileges firsthand or know nothing about the past and its customs. Ricardo Reis leaned over the upper railing. The sky had cleared a little, toward the straits there was a great strip of blue. If any steamships are due today from Rio de Janeiro, they will enter port in ideal conditions. Trusting in the signs of better weather, he started walking along the Calhariz, and descended as far as Camões, where he felt a sudden longing to visit the Hotel Bragança, like those timid students who have graduated and are no longer obliged to attend a school which they detested on so many occasions but who continue paying visits to their former teachers and classmates, until everyone grows weary of this pilgrimage, as useless as all pilgrimages, and the institution itself begins to ignore them. What would he do at the hotel, greet Salvador and Pimenta, So you haven't forgotten us, Doctor, Have a word with Lydia. Poor girl, so nervous, deliberately summoned to the reception desk out of malice, Come here, Doctor Reis wants to have a word with you. There was no particular reason for paying you a visit, I simply wished to thank you all for treating me so well and for giving me such excellent instruction on both the primary and secondary levels, if I failed to learn more, only my stupidity is to blame. On the sidewalk in front of the Igreja dos Mártires Ricardo Reis can smell balsam in the air, the precious exhalation of the devout women praying within. The Mass has just begun for those chosen souls who belong to a superior world. Here you can recognize, if you have a good nose, souls of worth and distinction. From the pleasant aroma one knows that the canopy over the altars is decked with pompons and tassels covered with talcum powder and that the chandler has added to the lavish candles a generous amount of patchouli. Once heated, fused, and fired with the quantum satis of incense, this ingredient inebriates the soul beyond resistance, it enraptures the senses, then the body grows weak, the face blank, ecstasy at last, Ricardo Reis doesn't know what he's missing, believing, as he does, only in dead religions, the religions of ancient Greece and Rome, for he invokes both in his poems, asking that there be gods rather than one God. He descends to the heart of the city, a familiar itinerary, the place as tranquil as a Sunday in the provinces. Not until later, after lunch, will the people of the surrounding neighborhoods come to gaze in the shop windows. They go through the week waiting for this day, entire families, the children carried in arms or led by the hand, exhausted by evening, their heels blistered because of a tight shoe, then they ask for a rice cake, and if their father is in a good mood and wishes to make a public show of his prosperity, the whole family ends up at a milk bar, large drinks all around so they can economize on the dinner. The man who goes hungry on a full belly will come to no great harm, besides he can always eat tomorrow. When it is time, Ricardo Reis goes to lunch, on this occasion to the Chave de Ouro, for a steak, to get rid of the sickening taste of all that sugar, and with so many hours to go before nightfall he buys a ticket for a movie, he will see *The Volga Boatmen*, a French film with Pierre Blanchard, what Volga can they possibly have invented in France. Films, like poetry, are the art of illusion, by adjusting a mirror you can transform a bog into the ocean. As he left the theater, it looked like rain, so he decided to take a taxi, and a good thing, because no sooner did he enter the apartment and hang up his hat and coat than he heard two raps coming from the iron knocker on the front door. Strange, for Fernando Pessoa to appear in daytime making such a din, a neighbor might come to her window and ask, Who's there, then start screaming her head off, Help, a spirit from the other world. If she can identify them so readily, then she must be familiar with them. He opened the window and looked out. It was Lydia, on the point of opening her umbrella as the first drops fell, what brought her here. A moment earlier he had been thinking that there was nothing more wretched than a solitary life, and now he felt annoyed that this woman was disturbing him, even though he could, if he wished, take advantage of the situation, a little erotic combat might steady his nerves and calm his thoughts. Going to the staircase to pull the wire cord, he saw that Lydia was already coming up, eager and on her guard. If there is a contradiction between these two states of mind, she had resolved it. He drew back into the doorway, cool, reserved, to the degree that being taken unawares could justify. I wasn't expecting you, how are things, these were his words as she entered, the door closing behind her. It is amazing, to have such neighbors, now we know neither their name nor what they look like. Lydia stepped forward to receive his embrace, and he obliged, meaning only to oblige her, but the next moment he was pressing her to him, kissing her neck. He still finds it awkward to kiss her on the lips, as if she were his equal, unless they are in bed together, the supreme moment approaching and he forgets everything, but she does not as much as dare, she allows him to kiss her to his heart's content, and the rest. But not today. I only came to see if you have settled in, an expression she has picked up in the hotel trade, I only hope no one notices that I've slipped out, besides I wanted to see what the apartment looks like. He tried to lead her into the bedroom, but she broke free, I mustn't, I mustn't, her voice faltered, but her mind was made up. In other words she would have liked nothing better than to lie on that bed and receive this man, to feel his head on her shoulders, to stroke the hair on his head, but behind the reception desk at the Hotel Bragança Salvador is asking, Where the devil is Lydia. She hurries through the entire apartment as if she can hear his voice, her experienced eye sees what is needed, there are no scrubbing brushes, buckets, mops or dusters, no marbled soap, no household soap, bleach, pumice stones, no brooms or hard brushes, no toilet paper. Men are as careless as children, they sail across the world in search of a route to India, and then find they do not have, so help me, the most basic thing, what could that be, I don't know, perhaps the color of life itself. Here, all one sees is dust, fluff, threads, sometimes gray hairs, which generations go on shedding. As their sight fails, the old no longer notice. Even spiderwebs age, weighed down by dust. One day the spider dies, suspended in its aerial tomb, its body dries up, its claws shrivel, and the remains of the flies are reduced almost to nothing. No creature escapes its destiny, no creature endures to give seed, this is the solemn truth. Lydia tells him she will come to do some cleaning on Friday, she will bring what is needed, Friday is her free day. But won't you be visiting your mother. I'll send her a message, then see what can be done, I'll telephone a store nearby. You will need money to buy things. I'll use my own money and you can pay me back. What an idea, take this, it should be enough. Holy Jesus, a hundred escudos is a small fortune. I'll expect you on Friday, then, but I feel bad that you're coming to do the cleaning. You can't live in this place the way it is now. Later, I'll give you a little present, I don't want any presents, just treat me as if I were the charwoman. Everyone should be paid a fair wage, My wage is to be treated kindly. These words certainly deserve a kiss, and Ricardo Reis gives her one, this time on the lips. His hand is already on the doorknob, there appears to be nothing more to say, the contract has been signed and sealed, but without any warning Lydia blurts out, as if unable to contain herself, Senhorita Marcenda arrives tomorrow, they telephoned from Coimbra, would you like me to give her your new address. With equal haste Ricardo Reis replies, almost as if he has rehearsed this, No, please don't, pretend you don't know where I am living. Happy to be the only person entrusted with his secret, Lydia leaves, completely deceived. Descending the stairs quickly and noticing that a door on the second floor has been left ajar, because sooner or later the other tenants in the building will have to have their curiosity satisfied, she calls up for all to hear, See you on Friday,

Doctor, when I come to do the cleaning, as if saying to the neighbor, Listen carefully, dear, I'm the new tenant's charwoman, so don't you go imagining things, and she greets the woman most politely, Good evening, senhora. But the woman barely replies, gives her a mistrusting look. Charwomen are not usually so bright and breezy, they tend to be surly, dragging their leg, which has stiffened up with rheumatism or varicose veins. The neighbor watches Lydia with a sour, hostile expression, Who is this little madam, while on the landing above, Ricardo Reis has already closed the door, conscious of his duplicity and turning it over in his mind. Had he been a faithful and honest man, he would have said to Lydia, I already gave Marcenda my address in a letter I sent her poste restante lest her father become suspicious. And he would have added, baring his heart, From now on I will be staying indoors, leaving the apartment only to have my meals and then coming straight back, and I will watch the clock at all hours, for as long as Marcenda remains in Lisbon. Tomorrow, Monday, she will certainly not come, the train gets in too late, but she might come on Tuesday, Wednesday, Thursday, or Friday. Not Friday, Lydia will be here doing the cleaning. Well, but what does that matter, the chambermaid and the girl from a good family, each in her own place, there is no danger of getting them mixed up, besides Marcenda never stays long in Lisbon, she only comes to consult the specialist, of course there is also that business of her father. Fine, but what do you expect will happen if she comes to your apartment. I don't expect anything, I only wish that she would. Do you really believe that a young woman like Marcenda, with her strict upbringing and the rigorous moral code upheld by her father, a man of the legal profession, would visit a bachelor in his own home, unaccompanied, do you think such things happen in real life. One day I asked her why she wanted to see me, and she replied that she didn't know, I find that the most hopeful reply of all. The one doesn't know, the other pleads ignorance. So it would appear, it's like Adam and Eve in the garden of Eden, not that she is Eve or I Adam. As you know, Adam was only a little older than Eve, a difference of several hours or days, I don't remember precisely. Adam is all men, Eve is all women, equal, different, and essential, and each one of us is the first man and the first woman. Fortunately, though, if I am not mistaken, woman continues to be more Eve than man Adam. Do you base this on your own experience. No, I say this because for all of us it should be so. What you would have liked, Fernando, is to go back to the beginning. My name is not Fernando. Ah.

Ricardo Reis did not go out to dine. He had some tea and cakes on the large table in the living room surrounded by seven empty chairs. Under a chandelier with seven branches and two bulbs he ate three small sponge cakes, leaving one on his plate. He counted again and saw that the numbers four and six were missing. He soon found the four, the corners of the rectangular room, but for six he had to get up and look around, which resulted in eight, the empty chairs. Finally he decided that he himself would be six, he could be any number if he was truly innumerable. With a smile that expressed both irony and sorrow he shook his head and went into the bedroom muttering to himself, I believe I'm going mad. From the street below came the incessant murmur of rain running down the gutters to the low-lying neighborhoods of Boavista and Conde Barão. Searching among the pile of books that were waiting to be sorted, he fished out *The God of the Labyrinth*, sat in the chair where Fernando Pessoa had sat, took one of the blankets from the bed to cover his knees, and started afresh on the opening page. The body discovered by the first chess player occupied the squares of the King and Queen and their two followers, its arms outstretched in the direction of the enemy camp. He continued to read, but even before reaching the place where he had left off last time, he began to feel drowsy. He lay down, read two more pages with effort, fell asleep between the thirty-seventh and thirty-eighth move, just as the second chess player was pondering the fate of the Bishop. He didn't remember turning off the light, but it was off when he awoke in the middle of the night, he must have got up and turned it off after all. These are things we do automatically, our body, acting on its own, avoids inconvenience whenever possible, that is why we sleep on the eve of battle or execution, and why ultimately we die when we can no longer bear the harsh light of existence.

Since he had forgotten to close the shutters, the gray light of an overcast morning filled the room. He had a long day before him, a long week, more than anything he wanted to stay in bed, under these warm blankets, let his beard grow, turn into moss, until someone came and knocked at the door, Who's there, It's Marcenda, One moment, he would cry out in excitement, within seconds make himself presentable, shaved, his hair combed, fresh from his bath, smartly dressed in clean clothes, ready to receive the expected visitor, Do come in, what a pleasant surprise. Not once but twice they came to knock at his door, first the milkman, to find out if the gentleman wished milk to be delivered every morning, then the baker, to find out if he required bread every day. Yes, he replied to both of them. In that case, sir, put the milk jug out on the doormat each evening, In that case, sir, hang the bread bag from the doorknob the night before. But who told you I had moved in here, The woman on the second floor, I see, and how would you like to be paid, Either weekly or monthly, Shall we say weekly then, That will be fine, Doctor. Ricardo Reis did not ask how they knew he was a doctor, there was no point in asking, but we heard Lydia address him as doctor when she left, and the woman downstairs was there and heard it. Provided with milk, tea, and fresh bread, Ricardo Reis enjoyed a wholesome breakfast. He had no butter or marmalade, but such bread is best savored on its own. Had Queen Marie Antoinette been served bread like this, she would not have needed to subsist on brioches. Now all that's wanting is a newspaper, but even that will soon be delivered. In his bedroom Ricardo Reis hears the cry of the newsvendor, *O Século, O Notícias.* He rushes to open the window, and the newspaper comes flying through the air, folded like a secret missive, moist from the ink which the weather has not allowed to dry. Greasy black smudges stain his fingers. Now each morning this carrier pigeon will tap on the windowpanes until they are opened from within. The newsvendor's cry can be heard from the far end of the street, and if the window is slow in opening, which nearly always happens, the paper is thrown up into the air, revolving like a discus, it strikes once, comes back, is thrown a second time. Ricardo Reis has already opened the window wide and received into his arms this winged messenger that brings him the world's news. He leans over the sill to say, Many thanks, Senhor Manuel, and the newsvendor replies,

Until tomorrow, Doctor. But this comes later, when an arrangement is reached, the payment this time will be monthly, as usual when dealing with reliable customers, it saves a person the effort of collecting three cents every day, a paltry sum.

Now, it is a question of waiting. On this first day, he can pass the time reading the newspapers, the evening editions too, he can reread, analyze, ponder, then work on his odes, or resume his reading of the labyrinth and its god, contemplate the sky from his window, and listen to the woman who lives on the second floor gossiping on the stairs with the woman from the fourth floor. He realizes that he will be hearing those shrill voices a great deal. And he will sleep, dozing and waking up, and leave the apartment only to have lunch, a hasty lunch at a nearby eating house on the Rua do Calhariz, then return to the newspapers he has already read, to his lukewarm odes, to the six hypotheses about the outcome of the forty-ninth move, and pass before the mirror, turning back to see if the person who passed is still there. He will decide that this silence is unbearable without a note of music, that one of these days he must buy a gramophone. To see which model will suit him best he looks through the advertisements for specific makes, Belmont, Philips, RCA, Philco, Pilot, Stewart-Warner. He takes notes, writes superheterodyne, understanding only the super in it and not even that with any certainty. Poor solitary creature, he is flabbergasted when confronted with an advertisement that promises women the perfect bosom within three to five weeks using the Parisian method, Exuber, which combines those three fundamental desiderata, Bust Raffermer, Bust Developer, and Bust Reducer. This Franglais is translated into concrete results under the supervision of Madame Hélène Duroy of the Rue de Miromesnil, which is in Paris, of course, where ravishing women firm up, develop, and reduce their busts, successively or all at the same time. Ricardo Reis examines other startling advertisements, for the restorative tonic Banacao, a wine with nutritional ingredients, for the Jowett automobile, for Pargil mouthwash, for a soap called Silver Night, for Evel wine, for the works of Mercedes Blasco, for Selva, for Saltratos Rodel, for those everpresent *Letters of a Portuguese Nun*, for the books of Blasco Ibañez, for Tek toothbrushes, for the painkiller Veramon, for Noiva hair dye, for Desodorol, which is rubbed into the armpits, then he returns with a sigh to the news items he has already digested, Alexander Glazunov, the composer of *Stenka Razin*, has died, Salazar, the all-paternal dictator, has installed canteens in the National Foundation to keep the workers happy, Germany swears that she will not withdraw her troops from the Rhineland, recent storms caused havoc in the Ribatejo, a state of war has been declared in Brazil and hundreds of people have been arrested, a quote from Hitler, Either we triumph over our destiny or we perish, and military forces were dispatched to the province of Badajoz, where thousands of workers have invaded rural estates. In the House of Commons several speakers declare that the Reich must be granted equal rights, there are new and interesting developments in the Uceda case, they have started filming *The May Revolution*, which tells the story of a refugee who arrives in Portugal to foment revolt, not this one, another one, and he is won over to the Nationalist cause by the daughter of the landlady at the boardinghouse where he is staying incognito. This last item Ricardo Reis read once, twice, three times, in an effort to rid himself of a faint echo buzzing deep inside his memory, but all three times his memory failed him, and it was only when he moved on to another news story, the general strike in La Coruña, that this tenuous thought became clear and defined. It was nothing distant, it was *Conspiracy*, that book, that Marília, that story of another conversion to Nationalism and its ideals, apparently the tale has its most effective propagandists among the women, with such magnificent results that literature and the seventh art pay tribute to these angels of chastity and self-sacrifice who seek out the wayward if not lost souls of men. No one can resist them when they place a hand upon a shoulder or cast a chaste glance beneath a suspended tear. They don't need to issue writs, interrogate, become inscrutable like the deputy chief of police, or hover vigilantly like Victor. This feminine influence surpasses the abovementioned techniques of making firm, developing, and reducing, although it might be more correct to say that this influence initially derives from these three, as much in the literary sense as in the biological, for it includes impassioned outbursts, exaggerated metaphors, and wild associations of ideas. Holy women, angels of mercy, Portuguese nuns, daughters of Mary and pious sisters, be they in convents or in brothels, in palaces or in hovels, the daughters of some boardinghouse landlady or of a senator, what astral and telepathic messages must they exchange among themselves, so that from such varied circumstances and conditions there should result so concerted an effect, which is nothing more or less than the redemption of a man in danger of losing his soul. As the supreme reward, these women offer him sisterly friendship, or sometimes their love, even their bodies and all the other advantages a beloved spouse can provide, and this sustains a man's hope in the happiness that will come, if it comes at all, in the wake of the good angel descended from the altars on high, for ultimately, let us confess it, this is nothing other than a secondary manifestation of the Marian cult. Marília and the daughter of the landlady, both incarnations of the Most Holy Virgin, cast pitying glances and place their healing hands on physical and moral sores, working the miracle of health and political conversion. Humanity will take a great step forward when such women begin to rule. Ricardo Reis smiled as he thought these sad irreverences. There is something disagreeable about watching a man smile to himself, particularly if he is smiling into his mirror, a good thing there is a closed door between him and the rest of the world. Then he asked himself, And Marcenda, what kind of woman is Marcenda. The question is beside the point, a mere mental game for one who has no one to talk to. First he must see if she has the courage to visit him in his apartment, then she will have to explain, however reluctant, however inarticulate, why she came to this enclosed and lonely place like an enormous spiderweb at the center of which lurks a wounded tarantula.

Today is the last day of the fixed term no one has agreed upon. Ricardo Reis looks at the clock, it's just after four. The window is closed, the few clouds in the sky are high. If Marcenda fails to come, she will not have the simple excuse so common of late, I dearly wanted to come but the rain was so heavy, and although my father was out, no doubt on one of his amorous pursuits, the manager Salvador would almost certainly have asked me, Surely you are not going out, Senhorita Marcenda, in this weather. Ricardo Reis looks at his watch, it is half past four. Marcenda has not come and will not come. The light indoors is fast disappearing, the furniture hides behind quivering shadows, one can now understand the suffering of Adamastor. The suspense grows almost unbearable, when suddenly there are two raps from the front door knocker. The building seems to tremble from top to bottom as if an earthquake were rocking the foundations. Ricardo Reis does not rush to the window, so he has no idea who will appear when he goes out onto the landing to pull the wire cord. He hears the woman upstairs open her door and say, Oh, I'm sorry, I thought it was for me, a familiar phrase handed down through generations of nosy women. It is Marcenda. Leaning over the banister, Ricardo Reis sees her. Halfway up the first flight of stairs, she looks up, anxious to make sure that the person she seeks really lives here, and she is smiling, it is a smile that has a future, unlike those reflected in a mirror, that is the difference. Ricardo Reis backs toward the door, Marcenda is climbing the last flight of stairs, only now does he notice that the light in the stairwell is off, that he is about to receive her almost in darkness, and while he vacillates, on another level of thought he wonders with surprise, How is it possible for her smile to be so radiant. When she stands before me, what should I say, I cannot ask, How have you been, nor exclaim in an even more plebeian fashion, Fancy seeing you here, nor sigh romantically, I had almost given up hope, I felt so desperate, why did you take so long. She walks in, I close the door, neither of us has said a word. Ricardo Reis takes her right hand, only to guide her into the domestic labyrinth. Into his bedroom would be improper, into the dining room would be absurd, in which of the chairs around that long table would they sit, side by side or facing, and how many would be seated there, he being innumerable, and she is certainly more than one, so let it be the study, Marcenda on one sofa, I on another. They have entered now, the ceiling light is on, also the lamp on the desk. Marcenda looks around at the heavy furniture, the two bookcases with their handful of books, the green blotting paper, then Ricardo Reis tells her, I am going to kiss you. She is silent. Slowly she supports her left elbow with her right hand, is it a protest, a plea for mercy, a surrender. She places her arm across her body like a barrier. Ricardo Reis takes a step forward, but she does not move. When he is almost touching, Marcenda releases her elbow, allows her right hand to drop, it hangs as dead as her other hand, whatever life is within her is divided between her throbbing heart and her trembling knees as she watches this man draw near. She feels a sob forming in her throat, their lips touch, Is this a kiss, she wonders. But it is only the beginning of a kiss. His mouth presses against hers, his lips open hers, this is the body's destiny, to be opened. The arms of Ricardo Reis now are around her waist and shoulders, and for the first time her bosom is in contact with a man's chest. The kiss, she realizes, is not over yet, it is inconceivable that it could ever end and the world return to its primeval innocence, she also realizes that she must do something other than stand there with her arms down. Her right hand moves up to the shoulders of Ricardo Reis, her left hand, dead or asleep, dreams, recalls the movements it once made, fingers entwining fingers, crossing behind the man's neck. She repays Ricardo Reis kiss for kiss, her hands in his hands, I knew it when I decided to come, I knew it when I left the hotel, I knew it when I climbed those stairs and saw him leaning over the banister, I knew that he would kiss me. Her right hand leaves his shoulder, slips down, weary, her left hand was never there. This is the moment when the body recoils, almost staggers, when the kiss has reached the point where it is no longer enough. Let us separate them before the rising force compels us to proceed to the next stage, a renewed explosion of kisses, precipitate, short-lived, eager, lips no longer satisfied with lips yet constantly returning to them. Anyone with any experience knows this sequence, but not Marcenda, who is being kissed and embraced by a man for the first time in her life and suddenly finds that the longer a kiss lasts, the greater the need to repeat it, a crescendo of need that seems to have no end. Her escape lies elsewhere, in this sob in the throat, which neither swells nor finds release, a faint voice that pleads, Let me go, then adds, moved by who knows what scruples, as if afraid of having given offense, Let me sit down. Ricardo Reis leads her to the sofa, does not know what to do next, what to say, whether he should make a declaration of love or simply ask her forgiveness, whether he should kneel at her feet or remain silent, waiting for her to speak.

All this strikes him as false, the only true thing was when he said, I'm going to kiss you, and did. Marcenda is seated, her left hand resting in her lap in full view, like a witness. Ricardo Reis is also seated, and they look at each other, conscious of their bodies, as if each were a great whispering shell. Marcenda tells him, Perhaps I shouldn't say this, but I knew you would kiss me. Ricardo Reis leans forward, raises her right hand to his lips, and finally speaks, I don't know whether I kissed you out of love or despair. She replies, No one has ever kissed me before, therefore I cannot tell the difference between love and despair. But at least you must know what you felt. I felt your kiss as the sea feels the wave, if these words have any meaning. I have been waiting for you all these days, asking myself what would happen if you came, I never thought that things would turn out like this, but when you walked in here, I realized that to kiss you was the only thing I could do, when I said a moment ago that I could not tell whether I had kissed you out of love or despair, if I knew then what I meant, I no longer do. So you feel no despair after all, and no love for me. Every man feels love for the woman he kisses, even if the kiss is one of despair. What reasons do you have for despair. Only one, this sense of emptiness. How can a man who has the use of both hands complain. I am not complaining, I am simply saying that a man has to experience despair before saying to a woman, as I've just said to you, I am going to kiss you. You might have said it out of love. Had it been love, I'd have kissed you without telling you beforehand. So you do not love me. I'm extremely fond of you. But that is not why we kissed each other, Well, no. What are we going to do now, after what has happened, here I am in the apartment of a man with whom I've conversed three times in my whole life, I came here to see you, to speak with you and be kissed, I don't want to think about the rest. Someday we may have to think about it, Someday perhaps, but not today. I'll get you a cup of tea, I have some cakes. Let me help you, but then I must go, my father might return to the hotel and ask where I am. Make yourself comfortable, why don't you take off your jacket. I'm fine like this.

After they drank their tea in the kitchen, Ricardo Reis showed her around the apartment, they took only a glimpse at the bedroom, then returned to the study, where Marcenda asked him, Have you started seeing patients. Not yet, I might try setting up a practice, even if only for a few hours a day, it's a question of readjusting myself. It will be a start. That's what we all need, a start. Have the police given you any more trouble, No, and now they do not even know where I am living, If they want to, they can find out. And what about your arm. You need only look at it, I no longer hope for a cure, my father, Your father, My father thinks I should go to Fátima, he says that if I have faith, there might be a miracle, as there have been for others. When one starts to believe in miracles, there is no longer hope. I suspect that his amorous pursuits are coming to an end, they've been going on for some time. Tell me, Marcenda, what do you believe in, At this very moment, Yes, At this very moment I believe only in the kiss you gave me. We could have another, No, Why not, Because I'm not sure that I would feel the same thing, and now I must be off, we leave early tomorrow morning. At the door, she stretched out her hand, Write to me and I'll write to you, Until next month, If my father still wishes to return, If you don't come, I'll go to Coimbra. Let me go, Ricardo, before I start asking you for another kiss. Marcenda, please stay, No. She descended the stairs rapidly without once looking up. The front door slammed. When Ricardo Reis went into the bedroom, he heard footsteps above him, then a window open. It is the neighbor on the fourth floor, she wants to see for herself what sort of woman has been visiting the new tenant, wants to see if she sways her hips, either I'm much mistaken or there is something fishy going on, and to think that this building was so peaceful and respectable.

Dialogue and passing judgment. Yesterday one came, today another one, comments the neighbor on the fourth floor. I didn't see the one yesterday, but the one who was here today is coming to clean his apartment, reports the neighbor from the second floor. She doesn't look like a charwoman to me, You're right there, I'd have taken her for a housemaid from some well-to-do family had she not come laden with packages, and carrying household soap too, I could tell by the smell, and brushes, I was here on the stair shaking my doormat when she arrived. The one who came yesterday was a youngish girl with one of those fetching hats that are all the fashion these days, but she didn't stay long. What do you make of it, Frankly, I don't know what to say, he moved in only a week ago and two women have been here already. This one came to do the cleaning, it's only natural, a man on his own needs someone to keep the place tidy. The other one could be a relative, he must have relatives. But I find it very odd, did you notice that all this week he never left the apartment except at lunchtime. Did you know he's a doctor, I knew that right away, the charwoman addressed him as doctor when she was here Sunday, Do you think he's a doctor of medicine or a lawyer, I couldn't tell you, but don't worry, when I go pay the rent, I'll ask, the agent is bound to know. It's always good to have a medical doctor in the building, you never know when we might need him. So long as he's reliable. I must see if I can catch this charwoman of his, to remind her to wash her flight of stairs once a week, these stairs have always been kept spotless, Yes, do tell her, don't let her think she can treat us like a couple of dogs. She'd better know who she's dealing with, said the neighbor from the fourth floor, thus concluding the judgment and the dialogue. The only thing left to mention is the silent scene of her slowly climbing back upstairs to her apartment, treading softly in her woven slippers. At the door of Ricardo Reis she listens carefully, putting her ear to the keyhole. She can hear the noise of running water, and the charwoman singing in a low voice.

It was a very busy day for Lydia. She put on the smock she had brought with her, tied up her hair and covered it with a kerchief, rolled up her sleeves, and set to work with enthusiasm, nimbly avoiding the playful teasing that Ricardo Reis felt was expected of him when their paths crossed, an error on his part, from a lack of experience and psychological insight, because this woman at the moment seeks no pleasure other than that of dusting, washing, and sweeping. She is so accustomed to these chores that there is really no effort involved, and so she sings, but softly lest the neighbors think that the charwoman is taking liberties on this her first day working for the doctor. When it was time for lunch, Ricardo Reis, who during the morning had been driven from the bedroom to the study, from the study to the dining room, from the dining room to the kitchen, from the kitchen to the bathroom, emerging from the bathroom only to begin all over again in reverse order, with brief respites in the two empty rooms, saw that Lydia was showing no signs of interrupting her work, so he said, with embarrassment, As you know, I have no food in the house. An awkward rendering of his thoughts. Without disguise the sentence would sound like this, I'm going out for lunch, but I can't take you with me to the restaurant, it wouldn't look right, what will you do. She would reply with exactly the same words she uses now, Lydia, at least, cannot be accused of being two-faced, Go and have your lunch, I brought a small bowl of soup from the hotel and some stewed meat, I'll heat them up and that'll do me fine, and take your time, too, then we won't be tripping over each other's feet. She laughed as she spoke, wiped the perspiration from her face with the back of her left hand while with the other she adjusted the kerchief, which was slipping down. Ricardo Reis touched her on the shoulder, said, Well, good-bye for now, and left. He was halfway down the stairs when he heard doors open on the second and fourth floors, these were the neighbors coming to warn Lydia in chorus, Now then, dear, don't forget to wash your master's stairs, but on seeing the doctor they scurried back inside. The moment Ricardo Reis steps onto the pavement, the woman on the fourth floor will go down to the woman on the second floor and the two of them will whisper, I got such a fright, Have you ever known a tenant to go out and leave the charwoman in the apartment on her own, Very trusting, I must say, perhaps she cleaned for him at his previous place, Perhaps, senhora, perhaps, I don't deny it, but they could also be having an affair, men are such rogues, they never miss an opportunity. Away with you, he is a doctor of medicine, A doctor could still be a rogue, men are a bad lot, Mine isn't so bad, Nor mine. Until later, senhora, and don't let that hussy give us the slip, Don't you worry, she won't get past my door without being given her orders. It proved unnecessary. In the middle of the afternoon Lydia went out onto the landing armed with a brush, mop, and bucket. The woman on the fourth floor quietly watched from above as the wooden steps resounded to the blows of the heavy brush. The dirty water was mopped up and squeezed into the bucket, the bucket water was emptied three times, and the entire building filled with the clean smell of strong soap. There's no denying it, this charwoman knows her job, the neighbor on the second floor can tell at once, and she goes out of her way to speak to her on the pretext of taking in her doormat just as Lydia reaches her landing, My word, girl, you've done a splendid job on those stairs, it's nice to know we have such a reliable tenant on the third floor. The doctor insists that everything be clean and tidy, he likes to see things done properly, it makes a pleasant sight. It most certainly does. These words were spoken not by Lydia but by the neighbor on the fourth floor, who was leaning over the banister. There is something voluptuous in the contemplation of newly washed stairs, in the smell of scrubbed wood, this is a fraternity of women who take pride in their domestic chores, it is a kind of mutual absolution, even if more fleeting than the rose. Lydia wished them a good afternoon, climbed back upstairs carrying her bucket and brush, her cloth and soap, shut the door firmly behind her, and muttered, Snooty old bitches, who do they think they're bossing around. She has finished, everything is spick-and-span, Ricardo Reis can now return, pass his finger over the surfaces of the furniture like those housewives always trying to find fault, inspect every nook and cranny. Suddenly Lydia is overcome by a great sadness, a sense of desolation, not because she is tired but because she realizes, though unable to express it in words, that she has served her purpose, all that remains to be done now is await her master's arrival, he will thank her, will wish to offer compensation for her industry and diligence, she will listen with an impassive smile, receive or not receive payment, and return to the hotel. Today she did not even visit her mother in order to find out if there was any news from her brother, not that she feels remorse, but it is as if she possesses nothing of her own. Now she changes back into her blouse and skirt, and as the perspiration cools on her body she sits on a bench in the kitchen, hands folded in her lap, waiting. She hears footsteps on the stairs, the key inserted into the lock, it is Ricardo Reis, he is in the passageway saying jocularly, This is like entering the abode of angels. Lydia gets to her feet, smiles at such flattery, suddenly feels contented, then deeply moved as he approaches with hands outstretched and open arms, Oh, don't touch me, I'm covered with sweat, I was just about to leave. Don't go yet, it's early, have a cup of coffee, I bought some cream cakes, why don't you have a bath first to freshen up. What an idea, me have a bath in your apartment, who ever heard of such a thing. It has never been heard of, but there is always a first time, do as I say. She objected no more, could not object, even if social convention decreed otherwise, because this was one of the happiest moments in her life, running the hot water, taking off her clothes, lowering herself slowly into the tub, feeling her weary limbs relax in the sensuous warmth of the water, using soap and sponge to lather her body, her legs, her thighs, her arms, her belly, her breasts, knowing that on the other side of the door a man is waiting for her. I can imagine what he is doing, what he is thinking, but if he should come in here, if he should see me, watch me sitting here naked, how shameful. Can it be shame that causes her heart to beat so fast, or is it fear. She steps from the bath. The human body always looks beautiful when it emerges glistening from water, Ricardo Reis thinks as he opens the door. Lydia, stark naked, covers her breasts and crotch with her hands, begs, Don't look at me. It is the first time she has faced him like this. Please go away, let me get dressed, she says in a low voice of embarrassment, but he smiles a smile of tenderness, desire, even mischief, and tells her, Don't put your clothes on, just dry yourself. He holds out a large towel, wraps it around her, then goes into the bedroom and removes his own clothes. The bed has just been made, the sheets smell new. Lydia enters, holding the towel tightly to conceal her body, she does not hold it like a transparent veil, but as she approaches the bed she drops it, finally courageous. This is no day for feeling cold, her body is burning inside and out, and now it is Ricardo Reis who is trembling, reaching out to her like a child. For the first time they are both naked, after waiting for so long. Spring was slow in coming but better late than never. On the floor below, perched on two high kitchen stools, one atop the other, at the risk of falling and dislocating her shoulder, the downstairs neighbor is trying to decipher the meaning of the sounds that now penetrate the ceiling. Her face is crimson with curiosity and excitement, her eyes shine with repressed depravity, this is how these women live and die, Would you believe what the doctor and that minx are up to. But who knows, perhaps they are only engaged in the honorable task of turning and beating the mattresses, though that takes some believing. When Lydia departed half an hour later, the neighbor on the second floor did not dare open her door, even daring has its limits, but contented herself with looking through the peephole with the eye of a hawk at an agile figure that swiftly passed, swathed in the odor of man as if it were armor. Ricardo Reis, in bed, closes his eyes. Now that his flesh has been gratified, he can begin to add the delicate and elusive pleasure of loneliness. He rolls over into the spot that Lydia occupied. Such a strange smell, the smell of a strange animal, but mutual, not of the one nor the other but of both. Enough, let us be silent, we do not belong here.

Day starts with morning, the week with Monday. At first light,

Ricardo Reis began a long letter to Marcenda, laboriously pondering. What do we write to a woman whom we have kissed without declaring our love. To ask her forgiveness would be offensive, especially since she returned the kiss with passion. If on the other hand we did not say, upon kissing her, I love you, why should we invent the words now, at the risk of not being believed. The Romans assure us in the Latin tongue that actions speak louder than words, let us therefore consider the actions as done and the words superfluous, words are the first layer of a cocoon, frayed, tenuous, delicate. We should use words that make no promise, that seek nothing, that do not even suggest, let them protect our rear as our cowardice retreats, just like these fragmented phrases, general, noncommittal, let us savor the moment, the fleeting joy, the green restored to the budding leaves. I feel that who I am and who I was are different dreams, the years are short, life is all too brief, better that it should be so if all we possess is memory, better to remember little than much, let us fulfill what we are, we have been given nothing else. This is how the letter ends. We thought it would be so difficult to write yet out it flowed, the essential thing is not to feel too deeply what one is saying and not to think too much about what one is writing, the rest depends upon the reply. In the afternoon, as he had promised, Ricardo Reis went in search of employment as a locum tenens, two hours a day three days a week, or even once a week, to keep his hand in, even if it meant working in an office with a window looking onto a backyard. Any small consulting room would do, with old-fashioned furniture, a simple couch behind a screen for routine examinations, an adjustable desk lamp to examine a patient's coloring more closely, a spittoon for those suffering from bronchitis, a couple of prints on the wall, a frame for his diploma, a calendar that tells us how many days we still have to live. He began his search some distance away, Alcântara, Pampulha, perhaps because he had passed through those parts when he entered the straits. He inquired if there were any vacancies, he spoke to doctors he did not know and who did not know him, feeling ridiculous when he addressed them as Dear Colleague and when they spoke to him in the same way, We have a vacancy here but it is temporary, a colleague who is on leave, we expect him back next week. He tried the neighborhood around Conde Barão, then the Rossio, but all the vacancies had been filled. A good thing, too, that there is no shortage of doctors, because in Portugal we have more than six hundred thousand cases of syphilis, and the infant mortality rate is even more alarming. For every thousand infants born a hundred and fifty die. Imagine, then, what a catastrophe it would be if we did not have such excellent medical practitioners at our disposal. It must have been the hand of fate, because after searching so hard and so far afield, Ricardo Reis finally discovered, on Wednesday, a haven virtually on his own doorstep, in the Praça Camões, and such was his good fortune that he found himself installed in an office with a window overlooking the square. True, he had only a rear view of D'Artagnan, but communication was ensured, the receipt of messages guaranteed, as became apparent when a pigeon flew from the balcony onto the poet's head. It probably whispered in his ear, with columbine malice, that he had a rival behind him, a spirit akin to his and devoted to the muses but whose hand was skilled only in the use of syringes. Ricardo Reis could have sworn he saw Camões shrug. The post is a temporary replacement for a colleague who specializes in diseases of the heart and lungs and whose own heart has let him down. The prognosis is not serious, but his convalescence could take three months. Ricardo Reis was no luminary in this field, we may recall that he said he was not qualified to voice any opinion about Marcenda's heart condition, but fate not only sets things in motion, it is capable of irony, and so our doctor found himself obliged to scour the bookshops in search of medical texts that might refresh his memory and bring him up to date with the latest techniques in therapeutic and preventive medicine. He called on the colleague who was convalescing, assured him that he would do everything in his power to uphold the standards of a man who was and would continue to be, for many years to come, the foremost specialist in that venerable field, and whom I shall unfailingly consult, taking advantage of your great knowledge and experience. The colleague did not find these eulogies in the least exaggerated and promised his full cooperation. They then proceeded to discuss the terms of this Aesculapian sublease, what percentage toward the administration of the clinic, the salary of the nurse under contract, the equipment and running costs, and a fixed sum for the convalescing heart specialist, whether he be ill or return to health. The remaining income is not likely to make Ricardo Reis a rich man, but he still has a fair amount of Brazilian currency in reserve. In the city there is now one more doctor practicing medicine, and since he has nothing better to do, he goes to the office on Mondays, Wednesdays, and Fridays, invariably punctual. First he waits for patients who do not appear, then, when they do appear, makes sure they do not escape, then the novelty loses its excitement and he settles into the routine of examining collapsed lungs and necrotic hearts, searching the textbooks for cures for the incurable. He scarcely ever telephones his colleague, despite his promise to visit regularly and consult with him. We all make the best of our life and prepare for death, and what a lot of work this gives us. Besides, how awkward it would be to ask, What is your opinion, colleague, I myself have the impression that the patient's heart is hanging by a thread, can you see any way out, colleague, apart from the obvious one that leads into the next world. It would be like mentioning rope in the house of a man condemned to be hanged.

No reply, so far, from Marcenda. Ricardo Reis has sent her another letter, telling her of his new life, that he is practicing medicine once more, under the borrowed credentials of a well-known specialist, I receive my patients in consulting rooms on the Praça de Luís de Camões, within a stone's throw of my apartment and close to your hotel. With its multicolored houses Lisbon is a very small city. Ricardo Reis feels as if he is writing to someone he has never seen, to someone who lives, if she exists at all, in an unknown place, and when he reflects that this place has a name, Coimbra, which is a city he once saw with his own eyes, the thought seems as absurd as the sun rising in the west, because no matter how hard we look in that direction, we shall see the sun only dying there. The person he kissed, the memory he still preserves of that kiss gradually fades behind the mist of time. In the bookshops he can find no text capable of refreshing his memory. He finds, instead, information on cardiac and pulmonary lesions, and even so, it is often said that there are no diseases, only persons diseased. Does this mean that there are no kisses, only persons kissed. It is true that Lydia nearly always comes when she has a free day, and judging from the external and internal evidence Lydia is a person, but enough has been said about the aversions and prejudices of Ricardo Reis. Lydia may be a person, but she is not that person.

The weather improves, the world, however, is getting worse. According to the calendar it is already spring, and new buds and leaves can be seen sprouting on the branches of the trees, but from time to time winter invades these parts. Torrential rains are unleashed, leaves and buds are swept away in the flood, until eventually the sun reappears, its presence helping us forget the misfortunes of the last harvest, the drowned ox that comes floating downstream, swollen and decaying, the shack whose walls caved in, the sudden inundation that pulls the corpses of two men into the murky sewers of the city among excrement and vermin. Death should be a simple act of withdrawal, like a supporting actor who makes a discreet exit. He is denied the privilege of a final speech when his presence is no longer required. But the world, being so vast, contains events more dramatic, it ignores these complaints we mutter with clenched teeth about the shortage of meat in Lisbon. This is not news one should broadcast or leak abroad, leave that to other nations who lack our Lusitanian sense of privacy. Consider the recent elections in Germany, at Brunswick, where the mobilized National-Socialist corps paraded through the streets with an ox carrying a placard that read, This ox casts no vote. Had this been in Portugal, we would have taken the ox to vote, then would have eaten it, fillet, loin, and belly, and used the tail to make soup. The German race is obviously very different from ours. Here, the masses clap their hands, rush to watch parades, salute in Roman style, dream of uniforms for civilians, yet they play a most humble role on the great stage of the world. All we can hope for is to be hired as extras. This explains why we never know where to put our feet or what to do with our hands when we line the streets to honor the youths that march past. An innocent babe in its mother's arms doesn't take our patriotic fervor seriously, pulling at our middle finger which is within reach. With a nation like ours it is impossible to be smug and solemn or to offer one's life on the altar of the fatherland, we should take lessons, watch how the abovementioned Germans acclaim Hitler in the Wilhelmsplatz, hear how they fervently plead, We want the Führer, we beseech you Führer, we want to see you Führer, shouting until they become hoarse, faces covered with sweat, little old women with white hair weeping tender tears, pregnant women throbbing with swollen wombs and heaving breasts, men endowed with strong muscles and wills, all shouting and applauding until the Führer comes to the window, then their hysteria knows no bounds, the multitude cries out with one voice, Heil. That's more like it. If only I had been born a German. But one need not be quite so ambitious. Without comparing them with the Germans, consider the Italians, who are already winning their war. Only a few days ago their planes flew all the way to the city of Harar and reduced everything to ashes. If a nation like Italy, known for its tarantellas and serenatas, can take such risks, why should we be hindered by the fado and the vira. Our misfortune is the lack of opportunities. We have an empire, one of the greatest, which could cover the whole of Europe and still have land left over, yet we are unable to conquer our immediate neighbors, we cannot even win back Olivença. But where would such a bold initiative lead us. Let us wait and see how things turn out over the border, and in the meantime let us continue to receive into our homes and hotels those affluent Spaniards who have escaped the turmoil, this is traditional Portuguese hospitality, and if someday they are declared Spain's enemies, we will hand them over to the authorities, who will deal with them as they see fit, the law was made to be enforced. Among the Portuguese there is a strong desire for martyrdom, an eagerness for sacrifice and self-denial, only the other day one of our leaders said, No mother who has ever begotten a son could guide him to a loftier and nobler destiny than that of giving his life in defense of the fatherland. The bastard. We can just see him visiting maternity wards, probing the bellies of pregnant women, asking when they expect to give birth, telling them that soldiers are needed in the trenches, which trenches, never mind, there will be trenches. As we can see from these omens, the world promises no great happiness. Now Alcalá Zamora has been removed from the presidency of the Republic and the rumor is spreading that there will be a military coup in Spain. If that happens, sad times lie ahead for many people. But this is not the reason people emigrate. The Portuguese do not care whether they live in the fatherland or the outside world, the important thing is to find a place where we can eat and save a little money, whether it be Brazil, to which six hundred and six Portuguese emigrated in March, or the United States of North America, to which fifty-nine emigrated, or Argentina, to which more than sixty-five emigrated, but to all the other countries put together only two went. France is no place for Portuguese bumpkins, there one finds another kind of civilization.

Now that Easter has arrived, the government is distributing alms and provisions throughout the land, thus uniting the Roman Catholic commemoration of the sufferings and triumphs of Our Lord Jesus Christ with the temporary appeasement of protesting stomachs. The poor, not always orderly, form lines at the doors of the parish councils and almshouses, and there are already rumors that at the end of May a splendid banquet will be held on the grounds of the Jockey Club for the benefit of those left homeless by the floods in Ribatejo, unfortunates who have been going around with the seat of their pants soaking wet for many months. The organizing committee has already enlisted some of the most prominent names in Portuguese high society, one more distinguished than the next in terms of both moral and material wealth, Mayer Ulrich, Perestrello, Lavradio, Estarreja, Daun e Lorena, Infante da Câmara, Alto Mearim, Mousinho de Albuquerque, Roque de Pinho, Costa Macedo, Pina, Pombal, Seabra e Cunha, the inhabitants of Ribatejo are extremely fortunate, provided they can put up with their hunger until May. In the meantime, governments, even if they are as supreme as ours, which is perfect in every respect, are showing symptoms of failing eyesight, perhaps because of too much bookwork or strain. The fact is that, situated as they are on high, they can see things clearly only at a distance, not noticing that salvation is often to be found, as it were, under one's nose, or in this case in a newspaper advertisement. There is no excuse for missing this one, because it even has a sketch of a recumbent lady in a nightgown that allows a glimpse of a magnificent bosom that probably owes something to the treatment provided by Madame Hélène Duroy. Yet the delicious creature looks a trifle pale, not so pale as to suggest that her illness might prove fatal, we have every confidence in the doctor who is seated at her bedside, bald-headed with mustache and goatee, saying to her in tones of mild reproach, If you had taken It, you would not be so pale. He is offering her salvation in the form of a jar of Bovril. If the government paid more attention to those newspapers it scrupulously censors morning, noon, and night, sifting proposals and opinions, it would discover how simple is the solution to the problem of famine. The solution is here, it is Bovril, a jar to every Portuguese citizen, for large families a five-liter flagon, a national diet, a universal nutrient, an all-purpose remedy. If we had drunk Bovril from the outset, Dona Clotilde, we would not now be skin and bones.

Ricardo Reis gathers information, takes note of these useful remedies. He is not like the government, which insists on ruining its eyes by reading between the lines, overlooking the facts to dwell on the theories. If it is a fine morning, he goes out, a little gloomy despite Lydia's solicitude and attentiveness, to read his newspapers sitting in the sun under the protective gaze of Adamastor. As we have already seen, Luís de Camões greatly exaggerated the scowl, the tangled beard, the sunken eyes. The giant's attitude is neither menacing nor evil, it is only the suffering of unrequited love, Adamastor could not care less whether the Portuguese ships succeed in rounding the Cape. Contemplating the luminous river, Ricardo Reis recalls two lines from an old ballad, *From the window of my room I watch the mullet leap.* All those glints in the waves are fish leaping, restless, inebriated by the light. How true, that all bodies are beautiful as they emerge, quickly or slowly, from the water, like Lydia the other day, dripping, within arm's reach, or these fish too far away for the eye to distinguish. Seated on another bench, the two old men converse, waiting for Ricardo Reis to finish his newspaper, because he usually leaves it on the bench. The old men come here every day in the hope that the gentleman will appear in the park. Life is an inexhaustible mine of surprises, we reach an age where we have nothing else to do but watch the ships below from the Alto de Santa Catarina and suddenly we are rewarded with a newspaper, sometimes for two days in succession, depending on the weather. Once Ricardo Reis actually saw one of the old men break into a nervous trot and hobble toward the bench where he had been sitting, so he did the charitable thing, offering it with his own hand and saying, The newspaper. They accepted, of course, but are resentful now that they owe him a favor. Reclining comfortably on the bench with his legs crossed, feeling the gentle warmth of the sun on his half-closed eyelids, Ricardo Reis receives news of the vast world. He learns that Mussolini has promised the imminent annihilation of the Ethiopian military forces, that Russian weapons have been sent to the Portuguese refugees in Spain, besides other funds and resources intended to establish a Union of Independent Ibero–Soviet Republics, that in the words of Lumbrales, Portugal is God's creation throughout successive generations of saints and heroes, that some four thousand five hundred workers are expected to take part in a parade organized by the Corporative Movement in northern Portugal, in their number are two thousand stevedores, one thousand six hundred and fifty coopers, two hundred bottlers, four hundred miners from São Pedro da Cova, four hundred work- ers from the canning factories at Matosinhos, and five hundred associate members from the union organizations in Lisbon, and he learns that the *Afonso de Albuquerque*, a luxury steamboat, will depart for Leixões in order to attend the workers' celebration to be held there, that the clocks will be set forward by one hour, that there is a general strike in Madrid, that the newspaper *O Crime* is on sale today, that there has been another sighting of the Loch Ness Mon- ster, that members of the government presided over the distribution of food to three thousand two hundred paupers in Oporto, that Ottorino Respighi, composer of *The Fountains of Rome*, has died. Fortunately the world has something for everyone. Ricardo Reis does not relish everything he reads, but he cannot choose the news and must accept it, whatever it is. His situation is entirely different from that of a certain old American who each morning receives a copy of *The New York Times*, his favorite newspaper. It is a special edition, which guards the precarious health of this senile reader who has reached the ripe age of ninety-seven, because each day it is doctored from start to finish, with nothing but good news and articles brimming with optimism, so that the poor old man will not be troubled by the world's disasters, which are likely to grow more disastrous. His private copy of the newspaper explains and proves that the economic crisis is fast disappearing, that there is no more unemployment, and that Communism in Russia is tending toward Americanism, as the Bolshevists have been forced to recognize the virtues of the American way of life. Fair tidings, these, that are read out to John D. Rockefeller over breakfast, and after he has dismissed his secretary he will peruse with his own weary, myopic eyes the paragraphs that reassure and delight him. At long last there is peace on earth, war only when it is advantageous, dividends are stable, interest rates guaranteed. He does not have much time left to live, but when the hour comes, he will die happy, the sole inhabitant of a world privileged with a strictly individual and non-transferable happiness. The rest of mankind has to be satisfied with whatever remains. Fascinated by what he has just learned, Ricardo Reis rests this Portuguese newspaper on his lap and tries to picture old John D. opening the magic pages of printed happiness with tremulous, scrawny hands, unaware that they are telling him lies. Everyone else knows it, because the deception has been telegraphed by news agencies from continent to continent, that in the editorial offices of *The New York Times* orders have been issued to suppress all bad news in the special copy for John D., the household cuckold who won't even be the last to know. Such a wealthy and powerful man allowing himself to be fooled in this way. The two old men pretend to be lost in conversation, arguing at their leisure, but keep looking out of the corner of one eye, waiting for their version of *The New York Times*. Breakfast used to be only a crust of bread and a cup of barley coffee, but our bad news is assured now that we have a neighbor who is so rich that he can afford to leave newspapers on park benches. Ricardo Reis rises to his feet, gestures to the old men, who exclaim, Oh, thank you so much, kind sir. The fat one advances, smiling, lifts the folded paper as if from a silver tray, good as new, this is the advantage of having the skilled hands of a medical practitioner, hands as soft as those of any lady, and he returns to his bench, settling once more beside the thin man. Their reading does not begin on the first page, first we must check to see if there are reports concerning riots or outbreaks of violence, disasters, deaths, crimes, especially, oh, how it makes one shudder, the mysterious death of Luís Uceda, still unsolved, and that dreadful business about the martyred child in the Rua Escadinhas das Olarias, number eight, ground floor.

When Ricardo Reis returns to his apartment, he discovers an envelope on the doormat, pale violet in color, bearing no indication of the sender, nor is that necessary. With some effort the smudged postmark can be deciphered as Coimbra, but even if for some inexplicable reason the name stamped there were Viseu or Castelo Branco it would make no difference, the city whence this letter really comes is called Marcenda. Soon a month will have passed since she was here in his apartment, where, if we are to believe what she said, she was kissed for the first time in her life. Yet once she returned home, not even this shock, which must have been profound, which must have shaken her to her very roots, was enough to prompt her to write a few lines, cautiously disguising her feelings, betraying them perhaps in two words brought together when her trembling hand was incapable of keeping them apart. Now she has written, to say what. Ricardo Reis holds the unopened letter in his hand, places it on the bedside table, on top of *The God of the Labyrinth*, illuminated by the soft light of the lamp. He would love to leave it there, perhaps because he has just come back, exhausted after hours of listening to the rattling of broken bellows, the tubercular lungs of the Portuguese, weary, too, of trudging through the circumscribed area of the city he constantly travels like a blindfolded mule turning a waterwheel, feeling at certain moments the menacing vertigo of time, the stickiness of the ground, the softness of the gravel. But if he doesn't open the letter now, he will never open it, he will say, if anyone should ask him, that it must have gone astray in the long journey between Coimbra and Lisbon, perhaps it dropped out of the courier's satchel as he was crossing a windy plain on horseback, sounding his bugle. It was in a violet envelope, Marcenda will tell him, envelopes of that color are not common. Then perhaps it fell among the flowers and merged with them. But someone may discover the letter and send it on, you can still find honest people who are incapable of keeping what does not belong to them. Unless someone opened and read it even though it was not addressed to him. Perhaps the words written there said exactly what he longed to hear, perhaps that person carries the letter in his pocket wherever he goes and reads it from time to time for consolation. I should find that very surprising, Marcenda replies, because the letter does not touch on such matters. I thought as much, that is why I have taken so long to open it, says Ricardo Reis. He sat on the edge of the bed and began to read. Dear friend, I received your letters with great pleasure, especially the second one in which you tell me that you have started seeing patients again, I enjoyed your first letter too, but didn't quite understand everything you wrote, or perhaps I am a little afraid of understanding, believe me, I do not wish to sound ungrateful, for you have always treated me with respect and consideration, but I cannot help asking myself what is this, what future is there, I don't mean for us but for me, I know neither what you want nor what I want, if only one's whole life could consist of certain moments, not that I've had much experience, but now I've had this one, the experience of a moment, and how I wish it were my life, but my life is my left arm which is dead and will remain dead, my life is also the years that separate us, one of us born too late, the other much too soon, you needn't have bothered traveling all those kilometers from Brazil, the distance makes no difference, it is time that keeps us apart, but I do not want to lose your friendship, that in itself will be something to treasure, and besides there is little point in my asking for more. Ricardo Reis passed a hand across his eyes, then read on. One of these days I will come to Lisbon as usual, I will visit your office, where we can have a chat, I promise not to take up too much of your time, it is also possible that I won't come, my father has grown disheartened, he admits that there probably is no cure for me, and I believe he is telling the truth, after all, he doesn't need this excuse to visit Lisbon whenever he pleases, his latest suggestion is that we go on a pilgrimage to Fátima in May, he is the one who has faith, not I, but perhaps his faith will suffice in the eyes of God. The letter ended with words of friendship, Until we meet, dear friend, I will call you the moment I arrive. If the letter were lost among fields of flowers, if it were being blown by the wind like a huge violet petal, Ricardo Reis would now be free to rest his head on the pillow and let his imagination run, What does it say, what doesn't it say, he could imagine the nicest things possible, which is what people do when they feel the need. He closed his eyes, thought to himself, I want to sleep, insisted in a low voice, Sleep, as if hypnotizing himself, Come now, sleep, sleep, sleep, but he still held the letter with limp fingers. To give greater conviction to his pretended scorn he let it drop. Now he sleeps gently, a twitch wrinkles his forehead, a sign that he is not sleeping after all, his eyelids tremble, he is wasting his time, none of this is true. He retrieved the letter from the floor, put it in its envelope, concealed it between two books. But he must not forget to find a safer hiding place, one of these days Lydia will come to clean and discover the letter, and then what. Not that she has any rights, she has none whatsoever, if she comes here it is because she wants to, not because I ask her, but let's hope she does not stop coming. What more does Ricardo Reis want, the ungrateful man, a woman goes to bed with him willingly so he does not need to prowl abroad and risk catching a venereal disease. Some men are extremely fortunate, yet this one is still dissatisfied, because he has not received a love letter from Marcenda. All love letters are ridiculous, ridiculous to write one when death is already climbing the stairs, even more ridiculous, it suddenly becomes clear, never to have received one. Standing before the full-length closet mirror, Ricardo Reis says, You are right, I never received a love letter, a letter that spoke only of love, nor did I ever write one, these innumerable beings that exist in me watch me as I write, then my hand falls, inert, and in the end I give up writing. He took his black suitcase, the one with the medical instruments, and went to the desk, and for the next half hour wrote up the clinical histories of several new patients, then went to wash his hands. Studying himself in the mirror, he dried his hands slowly, as if he had just finished carrying out an examination, checking samples of phlegm. I look tired, he thought, and went back into the bedroom and half-opened the wooden shutters. Lydia said she would bring the curtains on her next visit, they are badly needed, the bedroom is so exposed. Darkness was closing in. A few minutes later, Ricardo Reis went out to dinner.

One day, some curious person may inquire how Ricardo Reis

conducted himself at the table, whether he slurped as he drank his soup, whether he changed hands when using knife and fork, whether he wiped his mouth before drinking or left smears on his glass, whether he made excessive use of toothpicks, whether he unbuttoned his vest at the end of a meal, and whether he checked the bill item by item. These Galician-Portuguese waiters will probably say that they never paid much attention. As you are well aware, sir, one meets all sorts, after a while we don't notice anymore, a man eats as he's been taught, but the impression made by the doctor was that of someone refined, he would come in, wish everyone good afternoon or good evening, would order immediately what he wanted, and then it was almost as if he wasn't there. Did he always eat alone, Always, but he did have one curious habit, What was that, Whenever we began to remove the setting at the opposite side of the table, he always asked us to leave it there, he said the table looked more attractive set for two, and on one occasion when I was serving him there was a strange little incident. What incident. When I poured his wine, I made the mistake of filling both glasses, his and that of the missing guest, if you see what I mean. Yes, I see, and then what happened. He said that was perfect, and from then on he always insisted that the other glass should be filled, and at the end of the meal he would drink it in one go, keeping his eyes closed as he drank. How odd. As you probably know, sir, we waiters see some curious sights. Did he do this in all the other restaurants he frequented, Ah, that I couldn't tell you, you would have to ask around. Can you recall if he ever met a friend or acquaintance, even if they did not sit at the same table. Never, he always gave the impression of someone who had just arrived from abroad, just like me when I first came here from Xunqueira de Ambia, if you get my meaning. I know exactly what you mean, we have all had that experience. Do you require anything more, sir, I must go and serve the customer over in the corner, By all means, carry on, and many thanks for the information. Ricardo Reis finished drinking the coffee he had allowed to go cold and asked for his bill. While waiting, he held the second glass, still almost full, between his two hands, raised it as if he were toasting someone sitting across from him, then, slowly, half-closing his eyes, he drank the wine. Without checking the bill, he paid, left a tip neither miserly nor excessive, the tip one might expect from a regular client, wished everyone good-evening and left. Did you see that, sir, that's how he behaves. Pausing at the edge of the sidewalk, Ricardo Reis seems undecided. The sky is overcast, the air humid, but the clouds, although lying quite low, do not appear to augur rain. There is that inevitable moment when he is assailed by memories of the Hotel Bragança. He has just finished eating his dinner, has said, Until tomorrow, Ramón, and has gone off to sit on a sofa in the lounge, his back to the mirror. Presently Salvador will come to ask if he would like more coffee, A brandy perhaps, or a liqueur, Doctor, the specialty of the hotel, and he will say no, he rarely drinks spirits. The buzzer at the bottom of the stairs has sounded, the page raises his lamp to see who is entering, it must be Marcenda, today the train from the north was very late in arriving. A tram approaches, on its illuminated destination panel it has Estrela written, and the stop, as it happens, is right here, the driver sees the gentleman standing at the edge of the sidewalk. True, the gentleman made no sign requesting the tram to stop, but an experienced driver can tell that he has been waiting. Ricardo Reis gets on. At this hour the tram is practically empty, ping-ping, the conductor rings the bell. The journey takes some time, the tram goes up the Avenida da Liberdade, along the Rua de Alexandre Herculano, across the Praça do Brasil, and up the Rua das Amoreiras. Once at the top, it goes along the Rua de Silva Carvalho, through the Campo de Ourique to the Rua de Ferreira Borges, and there at the intersection with the Rua de Domingos Sequeira, Ricardo Reis gets out. As it is already after ten, there are not many people around and few lights are to be seen in the tall façades of the buildings. This is to be expected, the residents tend to spend most of their time in the rear of the building, the women in the kitchen washing up the last of the dishes, the children already in bed, the men yawning in front of their newspaper or trying, despite the bad reception due to atmospheric disturbances, to tune in Radio Seville, for no particular reason, perhaps simply because they never had the opportunity of going there. Ricardo Reis proceeds along the Rua de Saraiva de Carvalho in the direction of the cemetery. As he gets closer, he meets fewer and fewer people, and with some way to go, the road is already deserted. He disappears into the dark stretch between two lampposts, emerges once more into the amber light. Ahead in the shadows he can hear the sound of the keys of the local night watchman, who is starting his rounds. Ricardo Reis crosses the square toward the main gate, which is locked. The watchman looks at him from afar, then continues walking, Someone, he thinks, about to unburden his sorrow by weeping in the night, perhaps he has lost a wife or child, poor man, or his mother, probably his mother, mothers are always dying, a frail little woman and exceedingly old, who closed her eyes without seeing her son, I wonder where he is, she mused, then passed away, that is how people part. Perhaps it is because he is responsible for the tranquillity of these streets that the night watchman is given to such tender thoughts. He has no memories of his own mother. How often this happens, that we feel sorry for others, never for ourselves. Ricardo Reis goes up to the grating, touches the bars with his hands. From within, almost inaudible, comes a whispering, the breeze circling the branches of the cypress trees, poor trees, stripped bare of leaves. But the senses are deceived, the noise we hear is only the snoring of those who are asleep in those tall buildings, and in those low houses beyond the walls, strains of music, the hum of words, the woman who murmurs, I feel so tired, I'm going to lie down. That is what Ricardo Reis is saying to himself, I feel so tired. He puts his hand through the grating, but no other hand comes to shake his. Reduced to corpses, these people cannot even lift an arm.

Fernando Pessoa appeared two nights later. Ricardo Reis was returning after dining on soup, a plate of fish, bread, fruit, coffee. There are two glasses on the table. He finishes every meal, as we know, with a glass of wine, yet there is not a single waiter who can say of this customer, He was in the habit of drinking too much, he would rise from the table, almost fall over. Language owes its fascination to contradictions such as these, no one can rise and fall at the same time, yet we have seen it happen often or possibly even experienced it ourselves. But whenever Fernando Pessoa has appeared, Ricardo Reis has always been clearheaded, and he is clearheaded now as he watches the poet, whose back is turned to him, seated on the bench closest to Adamastor. That long, slender neck is unmistakable, and the sparse hair on the crown of the head. Besides, there are not many people who go around without a hat or raincoat. The weather has certainly been milder, but it still turns chilly at night. Ricardo Reis sat down beside Fernando Pessoa. In the darkness the pallor of the poet's skin, the whiteness of his shirt, is accentuated, the rest is dim, his black suit barely distinguishable from the shadow thrown by the statue. There is no one else in the park. Over on the other bank of the river, a row of flickering lights can be seen on the water, but they look like stars, they sparkle, quiver as if about to go out, but persist. I thought you would never come back, said Ricardo Reis. I came a few days ago to visit you, but at your door I saw that you were occupied with Lydia, so I left, I was never fond of tableaux vivants, Fernando Pessoa replied, and one could make out his wan smile. His hands were clasped on his knee, his expression that of someone patiently awaiting his turn to be summoned or dismissed and who speaks in the meantime because silence would be more insufferable. I never expected that you would show such enterprise as a lover, that the fickle poet who sang the praises of the three muses, Neaera, Chloe, and Lydia, should settle for one of the three in the flesh is quite an achievement, tell me, have the other two never appeared. No, nor is that surprising, they are names one rarely hears nowadays. And what about that attractive girl, so refined, the one with the paralyzed arm, did you ever get around to telling me her name. Her name is Marcenda. A pretty name, tell me, have you seen her lately. I saw her the last time she was in Lisbon, about a month ago. Are you in love with her, I don't know, And what about Lydia, do you love her, That's different, But do you love her or not. She does not deny me her body. And what does that prove. Nothing, at least not as far as love is concerned, but do stop questioning me about my private affairs, I am much more interested in knowing why you didn't come back. To put it bluntly, because I was annoyed, With me, Yes, with you as well, not because you are what you are but because you are on that side, What side, The side of the living, it is difficult for one who is alive to understand the dead. I suspect that it is just as difficult for a dead man to understand the living. The dead man has the advantage of having been alive, he is familiar with the things of this world and of the other world, too, whereas the living are incapable of learning the one fundamental truth and profiting from it. What truth is that, That one must die. Those of us who are alive know that we will die. You don't know it, no one knows it, just as I didn't when I was alive, what we do know without a shadow of a doubt is that others die. As a philosophy, that strikes me as rather trivial. Of course it's trivial, you have no idea just how trivial everything becomes when seen from this side of death. But I am on the side of life. Then you ought to know what things on that side are significant, To be alive is significant. My dear Reis, choose your words carefully, your Lydia is alive, your Marcenda is alive, yet you know nothing about them, nor could you learn, even if they attempted to tell you, the wall that separates the living from one another is no less opaque than the wall that separates the living from the dead. For anyone who believes this, death must be a consolation after all. Not really, because death is a kind of conscience, a judge who passes judgment on everything, on both himself and life. My dear Fernando, choose your words carefully, you put yourself at great risk of being absurd. If we do not say all words, however absurd, we will never say the essential words. And you, do you now know them. I have only started to become absurd. Yet once you wrote, *Neophyte, there is no death*, I was mistaken, Are you saying that now because you are dead, No, I am saying it because I was once alive, but I am saying it, above all, because I will never be alive again, if you can imagine what that means, never to be alive again. It sounds like something Pero Grulho would say. We've never had a better philosopher.

Ricardo Reis looked across the river. Some lights had gone out, others, barely visible, grew even dimmer as a soft mist began to gather over the water. You said the reason you didn't come back was that you were annoyed, It's true, Annoyed with me, Not so much with you, what has annoyed me and left me feeling weary is all this going back and forth, this tug of war between memory that pulls and oblivion that pushes, a useless contest, for oblivion and forgetting always win in the end. I haven't forgotten you. Let me tell you something, on this scale you do not weigh much. Then what is this memory that continues to summon you, The memory I retain of the world, I thought you were summoned by the memory the world retains of you, What a foolish idea, my dear Reis, the world forgets, as I've already told you, the world forgets everything. Do you think you've been forgotten. The world is so forgetful that it even fails to notice the absence of what has been forgotten. There is much vanity in these words. Of course, no poet is vainer than a minor one. In that case, I must be vainer than you. Allow me to say, without wishing to flatter you, that you are not a bad poet, But not as good as you, I believe you are. After we are both dead, if by then we are still remembered, or for as long as we are still remembered, it will be interesting to see on whose side the pointer of the scale leans. We will not care in the least about weights and weighers then. Neophyte, does death exist, It does. Ricardo Reis drew his raincoat tightly around him, It's getting chilly, if you wish to accompany me home, we can converse a while longer. Aren't you expecting any visitors today. No, and you are welcome to stay, as you did the last time. Are you feeling lonely tonight. Not to the extent of being desperate for company, but only because it occurs to me that a dead man might occasionally like to sit on a chair, under a roof, in comfort. I don't remember your being so facetious, Ricardo. I'm not trying to be facetious. He got to his feet and asked, Well, are you coming. Fernando Pessoa followed him, caught up with him at the first lamppost. At the entrance they encountered a man with his nose in the air. From the way he tilted his body, as if he were about to lose his balance, he appeared to be examining the windows, he looked as if he had paused for a moment after a hard climb up that steep road. Anyone seeing him would have said to himself, Here is one of the many night birds you come across in this city of Lisbon, not everyone goes to bed with the lamb. But when Ricardo Reis drew closer, he was overcome by a strong whiff of onion. He recognized the police informer immediately. There are smells, each worth a hundred words, smells both good and bad, smells as revealing as full-length portraits, what brings this fellow prowling here. Perhaps because he did not wish to disgrace himself in the presence of Fernando Pessoa, he took the initiative and spoke first, What brings you here at this hour of night, Senhor Victor. The other replied as best he could, having no explanation prepared at this early stage of the surveillance, A coincidence, dear Doctor, a pure coincidence, I have just been visiting a relative who lives in the Rua do Conde Barão, poor woman, she has caught pneumonia. Victor did not entirely lose face, And so, Doctor, you are no longer staying at the hotel, with this clumsy question he showed his hand. After all, one can be a guest at the Hotel Bragança and take a stroll at night on the Alto de Santa Catarina. Ricardo Reis pretended not to notice, or he really did not notice, No, I am now living here, on the third floor. Oh. This cry of regret, although brief, polluted the atmosphere with an overpowering stench, a good thing that Ricardo Reis had the wind at his back, these are mercies granted by heaven. Victor said good-bye, releasing another whiff of foul breath, I wish you good luck, Doctor, should you need anything, remember, come and speak to Victor, only the other day our deputy chief remarked that if everybody was like Doctor Reis, so honest and polite, our job would be almost a pleasure, he will be delighted when I tell him we bumped into each other. Good-night, Senhor Victor, common courtesy demanded that he say something in reply, besides, he had his reputation to consider. As Ricardo Reis crossed the street followed by Fernando Pessoa, the police informer had the impression there were two shadows on the ground. These are the effects of reflected light, an illusion, after a certain age the eyes are not capable of distinguishing between the visible and the invisible. Victor continued to loiter on the sidewalk, waiting for the light to go on on the third floor, a routine, simple confirmation, he now knew that Ricardo Reis lived there. Not much walking or interrogating had been necessary, with the help of Salvador he had tracked down the porters and with the help of the porters had located the building, people are right when they say that anyone with a tongue in his head can travel to Rome, and from the Eternal City to the Alto de Santa Catarina the distance is not great.

Comfortably settled on the sofa in the study, Fernando Pessoa asked as he crossed his legs, Who was that friend of yours. He is not a friend. Thank goodness, he stank to high heaven, I've been wearing the same suit and shirt for the last five months, I haven't even changed my underwear, and I don't smell like that, but if he's not your friend, who is he then, and that deputy chief who seems to think so highly of you. They're both members of the police force, not long ago I was called in for questioning. I thought you were a law-abiding man, incapable of upsetting the authorities, I am a law-abiding man, You must have done something to be called in for questioning, I arrived here from Brazil, that is all. I'll bet Lydia was a virgin and she went, anguished and dishonored, to lodge a formal complaint. Even if Lydia had been a virgin and I had dishonored her, it would not be to the Department for State Security and Defense that she would have taken her complaint. Is that the department that called you in, Yes, And here I was thinking it was an offense against public morality, There is nothing wrong with my morals, they are certainly no worse than those I see around

241

me. You never mentioned this brush with the police, There was no opportunity, you stopped coming to see me. Did they do you any harm, arrest you, charge you, No, I was only asked a few questions, who were my friends in Brazil, why did I come back here, what contacts I made in Portugal since my return. What a joke if you had told them about me. I can imagine the look on their faces if I told them that from time to time I met with the ghost of Fernando Pessoa. Excuse me, my dear Reis, but I am no ghost. What are you then, I can't tell you, a ghost comes from the other world, I simply come from the cemetery at Prazeres. Then is the dead Fernando Pessoa the same as the Fernando Pessoa who was once alive. In one sense, yes. Anyhow, it would be extremely difficult to explain these meetings of ours to the police. Did you know that I once wrote some verses attacking Salazar, Did he realize that he was the object of the satire, I don't believe he did, Tell me, Fernando, who is or what is this Salazar that fate has wished upon us. He is Portugal's dictator, protector, paternal guide, professor, gentle potentate, one quarter sacristan, one quarter seer, one quarter Sebastião, one quarter Sidónio, the best of all possible leaders, given our character and temperament. Many p's and s's. A coincidence, I was not trying for alliteration. There are certain people who have that mania, they go into rapture over repetitions, actually believing that this device brings order to the world's chaos. We must not laugh at them, they are fastidious people, like the fanatics of symmetry. The love of symmetry, my dear Fernando, comes from a vital need for balance, it keeps us from falling, Like the pole used by tightrope walkers, Precisely, but to get back to Salazar, he is much praised in the foreign press. Bah, those are articles commissioned and paid for by the contributors themselves, as I've heard people say, But the press here also waxes lyrical in singing his praises, you only need to pick up a newspaper in order to learn that our Portugal is the most prosperous and contented nation on earth, or will be very soon, and that if other nations follow our example they will prosper. That's the way the wind is blowing. I can see you don't have much faith in newspapers, I used to read them, You say that in a tone that suggests resignation, Exhaustion, rather, you know what I mean, after one makes a strenuous physical effort the muscles become slack, one feels like closing his eyes and sleeping. You are sleepy. I still feel the exhaustion I experienced in life. Death is a strange thing, Stranger still when you see it from the shore where I am standing and suddenly realize that no two deaths are alike, to be dead is not the same for everyone, in some cases a man takes with him all life's burdens. Fernando Pessoa closed his eyes and lay back on the sofa. Ricardo Reis thought he saw tears between his eyelashes, but they might have been like the two shadows seen by Victor, the effects of reflected light, for as everyone knows, the dead do not weep. That exposed face without glasses, and with a thin mustache, because the hair on one's face and body lives longer, expressed a deep sorrow, a sorrow without redress, like the hurts of childhood. Then Fernando Pessoa opened his eyes, smiled, I dreamed I was alive. An interesting illusion. What is interesting is not that a dead man should dream he is alive, after all he has known life, he has something to dream about, but rather that a man who is alive should dream that he is dead, because he has never known death. Soon you will be telling me that life and death are the same. Precisely, my dear Reis. In the space of one day you have stated three quite different things, that there is no death, that there is death, and now that life and death are the same. There was no other way of resolving the contradiction of the first two statements. And, as he said this, Fernando Pessoa gave a knowing smile.

Ricardo Reis got to his feet, I'm going to heat some coffee, I'll be right back. Listen Ricardo, since we've been discussing the press, I'd like to hear the latest news, it's one way of rounding off our evening. For the last five months you have not been in touch with the world, there are lots of things you will find difficult to understand. You, too, must have been puzzled by certain changes when you disembarked here after an absence of sixteen years, no doubt you had to connect the threads across time, finding certain threads without knots and certain knots without threads. The newspapers are in my bedroom, I'll go and fetch them, said Ricardo Reis. He went to the kitchen, returned with a small white-enamel coffeepot, a coffee cup, spoon, and sugar bowl, which he placed on the low table between the sofas, went out again, returned with the newspapers, poured the coffee into the cup, stirred in some sugar. Obviously you are no longer able to drink, If I had an hour of existence left, I would probably exchange it this very minute for a hot cup of coffee, You give more than England's King Henry, who exchanged only his kingdom for a horse, In order not to lose his kingdom, but forget the history of England and tell me what is happening in the world of the living. Ricardo Reis drank half a cup of coffee, then opened one of the newspapers and asked, Did you know it was Hitler's birthday, he is forty-seven. I don't consider that an important item of news. That's because you aren't German, if you were, you'd be less contemptuous. What else is there of interest. It says here that Hitler reviewed a parade of thirty-three thousand soldiers in an atmosphere of veneration that was almost sacred, the very words used here, and just to give you an idea, listen to this extract from the speech made by Goebbels to mark the occasion. Read it to me. When Hitler speaks, it is as if the vault of a temple were raised over the heads of the German people, How poetic, But that is nothing compared with the words of Baldur von Schirach. Who is this von Schirach, I don't recall the name, He is the leader of the Reich's Youth Movement, And what did he have to say. Hitler is God's gift to Germany, worship for our Führer transcends all differences of creed and allegiance. Satan himself couldn't have thought up that one, worship for a man uniting what worship for God has divided. And von Schirach goes further, he declares that if German youth pledges its love for Hitler, who is its god, if German youth strives to serve him loyally, it will be obeying the commandment received from the Eternal Father. Magnificent logic, here we have a god acting on behalf of another god for his own ends, the Son as arbiter and judge of the authority of the Father, which makes National Socialism a most holy enterprise. And here in Portugal we are not doing that badly when it comes to confusing the divine with the human, it looks almost as if we are turning back to the gods of antiquity. To those of your choice. I only borrowed the names. Go on. Well, according to a solemn declaration made by the Archbishop of Mitilene, Portugal is Christ and Christ is Portugal. Is that written there, Word for word, That Portugal is Christ and Christ is Portugal, Exactly. Fernando Pessoa reflected for a moment, then laughed, a dry chuckle like a cough, really rather unpleasant, Pity this land, pity this people. Pity this land, he repeated with real tears in his eyes, still chuckling, I thought I had gone too far when I called Portugal holy in *Mensagem*, it is written there, São Portugal, and here a prince of the Church comes and proclaims that Portugal is Christ. And that Christ is Portugal, don't forget. If that is the case, we had better find out, and soon, what virgin gave birth to us, what devil tempted us, what Judas betrayed us, what nails crucified us, what grave we lie in, what resurrection awaits us. You forgot the miracles. What greater miracle could you wish for than the simple truth that we exist, that we continue to exist, I'm not speaking about myself, obviously. The way we're going, I don't know how long we will continue to exist. But you have to admit that we are well ahead of Germany, here it is the Church itself that establishes our divinity, we could even do without this God-sent Salazar since we are Christ Himself. A pity that you died so young, my dear Fernando, because Portugal is now about to fulfill her destiny. Then let us and the world believe the words of the archbishop. No one can deny that we are doing our utmost to achieve happiness, would you now like to hear what Cardinal Cerejeira said to the seminarians. I'm not sure whether I could stand the shock. You are not a seminarian. All the more reason, but who am I to question the will of God, go ahead, read it to me. Be angelically pure, eucharistically fervent, and ardently patriotic. He said that, He did, It only remains for me to die, But you are already dead, Poor me, not even that is left. Ricardo Reis poured himself another cup of coffee. If you drink one coffee after another, you won't sleep, Fernando Pessoa warned him. Never mind, a sleepless night never did anyone harm, and sometimes it can be a help. Read me some more news. In a minute, first tell me, don't you find this latest novelty in Portugal and Germany disturbing, the political use of God. It may be disturbing but it is hardly a novelty, ever since the Hebrews promoted God to the rank of general others have followed suit, the Arabs invaded Europe to the cries of God wills it, the English enlisted God to guard their king, and the French swear that God is French. Our Gil Vicente swore that God is Portuguese. He must be right, if Christ is Portugal, but read me some more news before I take my leave. Aren't you staying, There are certain rules I must observe, last time I broke three in a row. Do the same tonight. No. Then listen carefully, I will now read without interruption, and if you have any comments to make, save them till the end, Pope Pius I condemns the immorality of certain films, Maximino Correia has declared that Angola is more Portuguese than Portugal, because since the time of Diogo Cão the only sovereignty Angola has recognized is that of the Portuguese, in Olhão bread has been distributed to the poor in the barracks square of the National Republican Guard, there are rumors that a secret faction has been formed by the military in Spain, at a reception held at the Geographical Society to celebrate Colonial Week women prominent in high society sat cheek by jowl with the lower orders, according to the newspaper *Pueblo Gallego* fifty thousand Spaniards have taken refuge in Portugal, in Tavares salmon is selling at thirty-six escudos per kilo, That's much too expensive, Do you like salmon, I used to loathe it. That's all, unless you want to hear about outbreaks of disorder and violence. What time is it, Almost midnight, How time passes, Are you going, I am, Would you like me to accompany you, For you it is still too early, Precisely, You misunderstand, what I meant is that it is too early for you to accompany me where I am going. I am only one year older than you, by the natural order of things. What is the natural order of things. That is how one usually expresses it, by the natural order of things I should have died first. As you can see, things have no natural order. Fernando Pessoa rose from the sofa, buttoned his jacket, and adjusted the knot in his tie, going by the natural order of things he would have done just the opposite, Well, I'm off now, I'll see you one of these days, and thanks for being so patient, the world is in even worse shape than when I left it, and Spain is almost certainly heading for civil war. Do you think so. If the best prophets are those who are already dead, then at least I have that advantage. Try not to make any noise when you go downstairs, on account of the neighbors. I shall descend like a feather. And don't bang the front door, Don't worry, the lid of the tomb makes no echo. Good night, Fernando, Sleep well, Ricardo.

Whether it was the effect of this somber conversation or because he had drunk too much coffee, Ricardo Reis did not sleep well. He woke up several times, and in his sleep imagined he could hear his own heart beating inside his pillow. When he awoke, he lay on his back to stop the noise, then he began to hear it again inside his chest, his rib cage, he remembered the autopsies he had witnessed and could see his living heart throbbing in anguish as if each contraction were its last. Difficult sleep returned, and finally settled into deep sleep as dawn began to break. When the paper boy arrived and threw the newspaper at his window, he made no attempt to get up. In such cases the boy climbs the stairs and leaves the paper on the doormat, the new one on top, because the others, delivered on previous days, are now used to clean the dirt off one's shoes, *Sic transit notitia mundi*, blessed be he who invented Latin. Standing in one corner of the doorway is the pitcher with the daily quart of milk, hanging from the doorknob is the bag of bread. Lydia will bring these things inside when she arrives after eleven o'clock, because this is her day off. She could not get away any earlier, at the last minute Salvador, as demanding and unreasonable as ever, ordered her to clean and prepare another three rooms. Nor can she stay long, she must go and visit her mother, who is all on her own, to find out if there is any news from her brother, who sailed to Oporto aboard the *Afonso de Albuquerque* and has returned. Hearing her come in, Ricardo Reis called out in a sleepy voice. She appeared in the doorway, still holding the key, the bread, the milk, and the newspaper in her arms, and said, Good morning, Doctor. He replied, Good morning, Lydia. This is how they greeted each other the first day they met and this is how they will go on greeting each other, she will never summon the courage to say, Good morning, Ricardo, even if he asks her to, which is not likely, he is being much too familiar as it is, receiving her in this state, unshaven, unwashed, hair uncombed, breath bad. Going to the kitchen to deposit the milk and bread, Lydia returned with the newspaper, then went off to prepare breakfast, while Ricardo Reis unfolded and opened the pages, holding them carefully by the margins so as not to dirty his fingers, lifting the paper high so as not to dirty the top fold of his sheet. These are the fussy little gestures, consciously cultivated, of a man who surrounds himself with boundaries. Opening the paper, he remembered doing the exact same thing several hours earlier, and once more felt that Fernando Pessoa had been there a very long time ago, as if a memory so recent were really a memory from the days when Fernando Pessoa, having broken his glasses, had asked him, I say, Reis, read me the news, the more important items. The reports on the war, No, they're not worth bothering with, I'll read them tomorrow, besides they never vary. This was in June in the year nineteen sixteen, and only a few days before that Ricardo Reis had written the most ambitious of his odes, the one that begins, *I have heard it said that in times gone by, when Persia*. From the kitchen comes the appetizing smell of toasted bread, the muffled sounds of crockery, then Lydia's footsteps in the hallway. Quite composed this time, she carries in the tray, goes through the same professional routine, except there is no need to knock, the door is open. Without fear of appearing to take liberties she can ask this long-standing guest, So you're still in bed this morning. I didn't have a very good night, it took me forever to get to sleep, Did you stay out late, I wish I had, as it happened I was in bed before midnight, I didn't even leave the apartment. Whether Lydia believes him or not, we know that he is telling the truth. The tray rests on the guest's lap in room two hundred and one, the maid pours his coffee and milk, arranges the toast and marmalade within his reach, adjusts the position of the napkin, then informs him, I can't stay today, I'll give the place a quick tidy-up and then I'm off, I want to visit my mother, she is starting to complain that she hardly ever sees me these days, I rush in and out, she even asked me if I found myself a man and was thinking of getting married. Ricardo Reis smiles, disconcerted, not knowing how to react. We certainly do not expect him to say, You already have a man, and as for marriage, it is just as well that you brought up the subject, it is time we discussed our future. No, he simply smiles, looks at her with an expression that has suddenly become paternal. Lydia retired to the kitchen, took with her no reply, if she ever expected one. She blurted out these words unintentionally, her mother has never once mentioned either men or marriage. Ricardo Reis finished eating, pushed the tray to the foot of the bed, leaned back to read the newspaper. The grand parade organized by the corporative organizations has shown that it is not impossible to reach a fair and reasonable agreement between employers and workers. He went on reading quietly, paying little attention to the argument, in his heart of hearts he could not decide whether he agreed or disagreed. Corporatism, the adjustment of each social class to the ambiance and setting best suited to it, provides the best way of transforming modern society. With this new prescription for a heaven on earth he concluded his reading of the lead article, then turned to the foreign news, In France the first ballot in the legislative elections will be held tomorrow, the troops under the command of Badoglio are preparing to resume their advance on Addis Ababa. At this moment Lydia appeared at the door of the bedroom with her sleeves rolled up, anxious to know, Did you see the airship yesterday, What airship, The Zeppelin, it passed right over the hotel, I didn't. But he was seeing it this very minute, on the open page of the newspaper, the gigantic, Adamastorlike dirigible bearing the name and title of the man who built her, Graf Zeppelin, German count, general, and aeronaut. There it goes flying over the city of Lisbon, over the river and the houses. People stop on the sidewalk, emerge from the shops, lean out of tram windows, appear on their balconies, they cry out to one another in order to share this wondrous sight, and a wit makes the inevitable quip, Look at the flying sausage. There's a picture here, Ricardo Reis said, and Lydia approached the bed, came so close that it seemed a shame not to embrace her hips with his free arm. She laughed, Behave, then said, It's huge, in the paper it looks even bigger than the real thing, and what about that cross stuck there at the back. They call it the gammadion or swastika. It's ugly. I can assure you there are many people who think it is the nicest cross of all, It reminds me of a spider, There were once religions in the Orient for which this cross represented happiness and salvation, Really, Yes, I'm not joking. Then why put the swastika on the tail of the Zeppelin. Because the airship is German and the swastika has now become the emblem of Germany, Of the Nazis, What do you know about the Nazis, Only what my brother has told me, Your brother who is in the Navy, Yes, Daniel, the only brother I have. Has he come back from Oporto, I haven't seen him yet, but he has, How do you know, His ship is anchored in front of the Terreiro do Paço, I would recognize it anywhere. Don't you want to come to bed, I promised my mother I would be there in time for lunch, Just for a little while, then you can go. Ricardo Reis lowered his hand to stroke the curve of her leg, lifted her skirt, reached above her garter, touched her bare skin. Lydia said, No, no, but started to weaken, her knees trembling. That was when Ricardo Reis found that his penis, for the first time in his life, was not reacting. In panic he withdrew his hand and muttered, Run the water for me, I want to take a bath. She did not understand, had started to unfasten the waistband of her skirt, to unbutton her blouse, when he repeated in a voice suddenly shrill, I must have a bath, run the water for me. He tossed the newspaper to the floor, brusquely slipped under the sheets and turned his face to the wall, almost overturning the breakfast tray. Lydia watched him in bewilderment, What have I done, she wondered. His hands, unseen by her, were trying to rouse his limp penis, they struggled in vain, one moment with violent rage, the next with despair. Sadly, Lydia withdrew, taking the tray with her, she went to wash the dishes until they sparkled like the morning sun, but first she lit the heater, started running water into the bathtub, checked the temperature as it poured from the spigot, passed wet fingers over her wet eyes. What could I have done to upset him when I was ready to get into bed with him. Misunderstandings of this nature are impossible to avoid, if only he had said to her, I cannot, I'm not in the mood, she would not have minded. Even if there was no question of coupling she would have joined him, she would have lain down beside him in silence, and comforted him until he overcame that moment of panic, perhaps she would have placed her hand on his penis, gently, without any design, simply to reassure him, Stop worrying, it's not the end of the world. They would both sleep peacefully, she having forgotten that her mother was expecting her with the lunch on the table, the mother finally saying to her sailor son, Let's have our lunch, you can no longer rely on your sister, she doesn't seem to be the same girl these days. Such are life's contradictions and injustices.

Lydia appeared at the door of the bedroom. I'll see you in a week, she said, and departed, miserable, leaving him no less miserable, she not knowing what evil she has done, he knowing full well what evil has befallen him. The sound of running water, the smell of steam pervades the apartment. Ricardo Reis remains in bed a few more minutes, he knows that the bathtub is immense, a Mediterranean sea when full, finally he gets up, throws his dressing gown over his shoulders, and shuffles on slippered feet to the bathroom. Fortunately he cannot see himself in the mirror clouded by steam, this must be the compassion shown by mirrors at certain critical moments. Then he thinks, It's not the end of the world, this can happen to anyone, my turn had to come sooner or later. What do you think, Doctor. Don't worry, I'll give you a prescription for some new pills that ought to remedy this little problem, the important thing is not to worry, to get out and distract yourself, go see a movie, if this is truly the first time it has happened, then you can consider yourself a lucky man. Removing his clothes, Ricardo Reis ran a little cold water into that great scalding lake and immersed himself little by little, as if he were abandoning the world of air. Relaxed, his limbs were pushed to the surface, to float between two bodies of water, even his withered penis stirred, caught like uprooted seaweed on the tide, beckoning. Ricardo Reis gloomily watched, as if the thing did not belong to him, Is it mine or do I belong to it, he sought no answer, the question alone causing as much anguish as he could bear.

Three days later, Marcenda appeared at the office. She told the receptionist that she wished to be seen last, that she was not there as a patient. Tell the doctor, when all the other patients have gone, that Marcenda Sampaio is here, and she slipped a twenty-escudo note into the receptionist's pocket. The message was delivered at the opportune moment, when Ricardo Reis had already removed his white coat, almost like a cassock and barely three-quarter length, which explains why he was not and never would be a high priest of this hygienic cult, but only the sacristan responsible for emptying and washing the altar cruets, for lighting and putting out the candles, for inscribing the certificates, needless to say, of death. At times he experienced the vague regret that he had not specialized in obstetrics, not because this dealt with women's most private and precious organs but because it meant bringing children into the world, other people's children, who serve as consolation when we have no children of our own, at least none we are aware of. As an obstetrician he would feel new hearts beating as they came into the world, on occasion hold in his own hands those skinny, sticky little creatures covered with blood and mucus, tears and sweat, and hear that first cry which has no meaning or a meaning beyond our understanding. He slipped back into his dressing gown, struggled to find the sleeves, which were suddenly twisted, and tried to decide whether he should receive Marcenda at the door or wait for her behind his desk with one hand placed professionally on his vade mecum, the font of all medical knowledge, the bible of sorrows. Approaching the window that looked onto the square, the elms, the linden trees in flower, the statue of the musketeer, he chose the square as the place to receive Marcenda, if he could say to her without sounding absurd, It is spring, look how delightful, that pigeon perched on the head of Camões, others perched on his shoulders. The only real justification for statues is to provide perches for pigeons. But social convention prevailed, Marcenda appeared at his door, Do go in, the receptionist was saying obsequiously, a woman of subtle perception, experienced in the art of discriminating between the different social classes. Ricardo Reis forgot the elms, the linden trees, and the pigeons took flight, something must have startled them. In the Praça de Luís de Camões shooting is prohibited throughout the year. If this woman were a pigeon, she would be unable to fly with that injured wing. How have you been, Marcenda, I'm delighted to see you, and your father, is he well. He's fine, thank you, Doctor, he was unable to come but sends his greetings. Obeying her instructions, the receptionist withdrew, closed the door behind her. Ricardo Reis continued to hold Marcenda's hand, and they remained thus, in silence, until he pointed to a chair. She sat, left hand still in her pocket. Even the receptionist, who misses nothing, would swear that the girl now in the consulting room shows no signs of any physical infirmity, in fact she is really quite attractive, a little on the thin side, perhaps, but she is so young, thinness suits her. Now then, how is your health these days, Ricardo Reis inquired. Marcenda replied, Much the same, I doubt that I will be going back to the specialist, at least not the one here in Lisbon. There are no signs of improvement, no indication of movement or that you are getting back some feeling. Nothing that encourages me. And what about your heart, That is functioning perfectly, do you wish to check it, I am not your doctor. But now that you are a heart specialist, you must have gained some knowledge, which means I can consult you. Sarcasm doesn't become you, I do my best, and that is precious little, I'm merely standing in for a colleague temporarily, as I explained in my letter. In one of your letters. Pretend you never received the other letter, that it went astray. Do you regret having written it. There is nothing more pointless in this world than regret, people who express it merely want to be forgiven, then they fall back into their weakness, for each of us, deep down, continues to take pride in his weakness. I did not regret that I went to your apartment, I do not regret it even now, and if it is a mistake to have allowed you to kiss me, to have kissed you, I still take pride in this mistake. Between us there was only a kiss, not a mortal sin. It was my first kiss, perhaps that is why I feel no remorse. No one ever kissed you before, That was my first kiss. It will soon be time to close the office, would you like to come back to the apartment, where we can talk in greater privacy. I'd rather not. We could enter the building separately, letting some time elapse in between, I won't expose you to shame. No, I'd prefer to stay here a little longer, if you can spare the time. Believe me, I wouldn't harm you, I'm really quite harmless. What does that smile mean. Nothing, only that I'm a gentle soul by nature, if you want me to spell it out, I would say that at this moment I'm at peace with the world, the waters are tranquil, that was all my smile was saying. I'd rather not go to your apartment, let's stay here and talk, pretend I am one of your patients. What's the problem, then. This smile is much better than the other one. Marcenda took her left hand from her pocket, settled it on her lap, covered it with the other hand, seemed about to say, as one confiding an ailment, Can you believe it, Doctor, fate saddled me with this arm after saddling me already with an errant heart, but instead she said, We live so far apart, there is such a difference in our ages, in our destinies. You repeat what you wrote in your letter. The truth is that I like you, Ricardo, only I cannot say to what extent. A man, when he reaches my age, looks foolish when he starts making declarations of love. But I enjoyed reading them, and now hearing them. I am making no declaration of love, But you are. We are exchanging greetings, sprigs of flowers, it is true that they are pretty, I mean the flowers, but they are cut, they will soon wilt, they are unaware of this and we pretend not to notice. My flowers I place in water, and will watch them until the colors fade. Then you will not watch them long. Now I am watching you. I am no flower. You are a man, I am capable of knowing the difference. A tranquil man, who sits on a riverbank watching what the current carries past, perhaps waiting for himself to be swept away. At this moment it is me that you are watching, your eyes tell me so, It is true, I see you being swept away like a branch in flower, a branch on which a bird sits warbling, Don't make me cry. Ricardo Reis went to the window, drew back the curtain. There were no pigeons perched on the statue, instead they were flying in rapid circles above the square, a swirling vortex. Marcenda approached him, On my way here I saw a pigeon perched on the statue's arm, close to its heart. That's quite common, they prefer a sheltered spot, You cannot see the statue from here, it faces the other way. The curtain was closed once more. They moved away from the window, and Marcenda said, I must go. Ricardo Reis held her left hand, brought it to his lips, then stroked it slowly, as if he were reviving a bird numb with cold. The next moment he was kissing Marcenda on the lips and she him, a second kiss, then Ricardo Reis can feel his blood descending, thundering like a mighty cascade, into deep caverns, a metaphorical allusion to the corpora cavernosa, in other words his penis stiffens, So it wasn't dead after all, he didn't believe me when I told him not to worry. Marcenda feels it and pulls away, then embraces him again to feel it. If questioned, she would swear that was not true, foolish virgin, but their lips have not separated. At last she moaned, I must go. Her strength drained, she broke free and collapsed into a chair. Marcenda, marry me, Ricardo Reis pleaded. She looked at him, pale, and said, No, said it very slowly, who would have believed that anyone could take so long to utter so short a word, it did not take her as long to say what followed, We would not be happy. For several minutes they remained silent. For the third time Marcenda said, I must go, but this time she got up and made for the door. He followed her, tried to detain her, but she was already in the hall, the receptionist appeared at the far end, whereupon Ricardo Reis said in a loud voice, I'll see you out, which he did. They said good-bye and shook hands. He said, Give my regards to your father. She began, One day, but did not finish, someone else will finish it, who knows when and for what reason, but for now there is only this, One day. The door is closed, the receptionist asks, Do you need me, Doctor. No. Well, if you will excuse me, I'll be off, everyone has gone now, the other doctors too. I'll stay a few more minutes, I must sort out some papers. Good evening, Doctor, Good evening, Carlota, because that was her name.

Ricardo Reis returned to his office, drew back the curtain. Marcenda still had not reached the bottom of the stairs. The shadows of twilight enshrouded the square. The pigeons were nestling on the uppermost branches of the elm trees, as silent as phantoms, or else it was the shadows of the pigeons that had perched on those very branches in years gone by, or perched on the ruins that once stood here, before the ground was leveled in order to build the square and erect the statue. Now, crossing the square in the direction of the Rua do Alecrim, Marcenda turns around to see if the pigeon is still perched on the arm of Camões, and between the flowering branches of the linden trees she catches a glimpse of a white face behind a windowpane. If anyone witnessed these movements he would not have understood their meaning, not even Carlota, who had concealed herself under the stairs to spy, suspecting that the visitor would return to the office to converse to her heart's content with the doctor. Not at all a bad idea, but it never even occurred to Marcenda, and Ricardo Reis never got around to asking himself if that was the reason he stayed behind.

A few days later a letter arrived, the same pale violet color, the same black postmark, the unmistakable handwriting, angular because the sheet of paper is not held in place by the other hand. There is the same long hesitation before Ricardo Reis finally opens the envelope, the same jaded face, and the same words, What a fool I was to visit you, it won't happen again, we will not see each other anymore, but believe me, I will never forget you as long as I live, if things had been different, if I had been older, if this incurable arm, yes, the specialist finally admitted that there is no cure, that the sun-lamp treatment, the electric shocks, and massage were a waste of time, I suspected as much, I did not even weep, it is not myself I pity but my arm, I nurse it as if it were a child that will never leave the cradle, I stroke it as if it were a small stray animal found abandoned on the street, my poor arm, what would become of it without me, and so farewell, dear friend, my father continues to insist that I go to Fátima and I have decided to go, just to please him, if this is what he needs to ease his conscience and convince him that it is the will of God, for we can do nothing contrary to the will of God and should not try, I am not asking you to forget me, my friend, on the contrary, I hope you will think of me every day, but do not write, I will make no more visits to the poste restante, now I must close, I have said all I had to say. Marcenda does not write in this manner, she observes all the rules of syntax and punctuation, it is Ricardo Reis who jumps from line to line in search of the essential, ignoring the texture of her phrasing. The exclamation marks are his, the sudden breaks that make for eloquence, but though he read the letter a second and third time, he learned no more, because he had read everything, just as Marcenda had said everything. A man receives a sealed letter as his ship leaves port, and opens it in midocean. There is nothing except sea and sky and the deck on which he is standing, and the letter says that from now on there will be no more ports of refuge for him, no more uncharted lands to discover, no destination, nothing left for him but to navigate like the Flying Dutchman, hoist and furl the sails, man the pump, mend and sew, scrape away the rust, and wait. Still holding the letter, he goes to the window and sees Adamastor, the two old men seated in the giant's shadow, and he asks himself if his disappointment is genuine, not playacting, if he truly believed he was in love with Marcenda, if in his heart of hearts he ever really wanted to marry her, or whether all this might not be the banal effect of loneliness, the simple need to believe that there are some good things in life, love, for example, that happiness which unhappy people are continually talking about, if happiness and love are possible for our Ricardo Reis, or for Fernando Pessoa, if he were not dead. There is no doubt that Marcenda exists, this letter was clearly written by her, but Marcenda, who is she, what is there in common between the girl seen for the first time in the dining room of the Hotel Bragança, when she was a stranger to him, and this Marcenda whose name and person now fill the thoughts and feelings and words of Ricardo Reis. Marcenda is a place of anchorage. What was she then, what is she now, a wake on the surface of the sea that disappears once the ship has passed, there is still some spray, the churning of the rudder, I have passed through the spray, what thing has passed through me. Ricardo Reis reads the letter one more time, the closing paragraph, where she writes, Do not write to me, and tells himself that of course he will write, to say who knows what, he will decide later, and if she keeps her promise, then let the letter sit at the poste restante, the important thing is to write. But then he remembers that Doctor Sampaio is well known in Coimbra, a notary is always a prominent figure in society, and post offices are staffed, as everyone knows, by many conscientious and loyal employees, so it is not at all impossible that the secret letter will find its way to his residence, or worse still, to his office, provoking outrage. He will not write. In this letter he would have put all the things he never got around to saying, not in the hope of changing the course of events but in order to make it clear that those events are so numerous that even saying everything about them will not change their course. Yet he would have liked at least to let Marcenda know that Doctor Reis, the man who kissed her and asked her to marry him, is a poet and not just an ordinary general practitioner acting as locum tenens for an indisposed specialist in diseases of the heart and lungs, and not a bad locum tenens either, despite his lack of scientific training, for there is no evidence that the mortality rate has risen since he came into the practice. Imagine Marcenda's surprise if he had said to her at the outset, Did you know, Marcenda, that I am a poet, in the casual tone of one who does not attach any great importance to his talent. Naturally she would realize that he was being modest, she would be flattered that he took her into his confidence, would look at him with romantic tenderness, How wonderful, how fortunate I am, I can now see what a difference it makes to be loved by a poet, I must ask him to read me his poems, I feel certain he will dedicate some to me, a common habit among poets, who are much given to dedications. Ricardo Reis, to avoid any eventual outbursts of jealousy, will explain that the women Marcenda finds mentioned in his poems are not real women, only lyrical abstractions, fictions, imaginary interlocutresses, if one can give the name of interlocutress to one who has no voice. A poet does not ask that his muses speak, only that they exist, Neaera, Lydia, Chloe. There's a coincidence for you, that after writing poems for so many years to an anonymous, ethereal Lydia I should come across a chambermaid with this name, only the name, in all other respects there is no resemblance whatsoever. Ricardo Reis explains, and then explains a second time, not because the matter is so very complicated but because he is apprehensive about the next step, which poem will he choose, what will Marcenda say when she hears it, what will be the expression on her face, she might ask to see with her own eyes what she has heard him read, then read the poem herself in a low voice, *In a changing, uncertain confluence, as the river is formed by its waves, so contemplate your days, and if you see yourself pass as another, be silent.* He reads it, reads it a second time, he sees from her face that she understands, perhaps some memory has helped her, the memory of those words he spoke in the consulting room the last time we were together, about a man who sits on a riverbank watching what the water carries past, waiting to see himself going past with the current. Clearly there is a difference between prose and poetry, that is why I understood it so well the first time and now find myself struggling to understand it. Ricardo Reis asks her, Do you like it, and she says, Oh, very much. There could scarcely be a more gratifying response, but poets are eternally dissatisfied, this one has been told everything a poet could wish to hear, God Himself would be delighted to hear such praise for the world He created, Ricardo Reis, however, looks gloomy and sad, an Adamastor who cannot wrench himself free of the marble in which he has been trapped by fraud and deception, his flesh and bones transformed into stone, his tongue likewise. Why have you become so quiet, Marcenda asks, but he does not answer.

If these are private sorrows, Portugal, taken as a whole, is not without its joys. Two anniversaries have just been celebrated, the first was Professor António de Oliveira Salazar's entrance into public life eight years ago, it seems like yesterday, how time flies, to save his country and ours from the abyss, to restore its fortunes, to provide a new political doctrine, to instill faith, enthusiasm, and confidence in the future, as the newspaper says. The other anniversary also concerns the esteemed professor, albeit the event is one of more personal joy, his and ours, namely his forty-seventh birthday, he was born the same year Hitler came into the world, only a few days separate them, there is a coincidence for you. And we are about to celebrate National Labor Day with a parade of thousands of workers in Barcelos all with their arms outstretched in Roman style, the gesture has survived from the time Braga was called Bracara Augusta, and a hundred decorated floats will depict scenes of country life, one representing the wine harvest, another the pressing of grapes, then hoeing, husking, threshing, then the kiln where they make clay cocks and fifes, then the embroideress with her lace bobbins, the fisherman with his net and oar, the miller with his donkey and sack of flour, the spinstress with her spindle and distaff, that makes ten floats and there are ninety more. Ah how the people of Portugal strive to be good and industrious, and as a reward they are well provided with entertainments, concerts given by their philharmonic band, light shows, dance exhibitions, fireworks, battles with flowers, banquets, one long continuous festival. Now, in the face of such high-spirited merrymaking we might remark, indeed it is our duty to do so, that May Day everywhere has lost its traditional meaning, if in the streets of Madrid they sing the *Internationale* and applaud the Revolution. It is not our fault, such excesses are not tolerated in our country. Thanks be to God, cry in chorus the fifty thousand Spaniards who have taken refuge in this oasis of peace. And now that the Left has won the elections in France and the Socialist leader Blum has declared himself ready to form a Popular Front government, we can expect another horde of refugees. Over the august forehead of Europe storm clouds gather, they are not content with riding on the haunches of the raging Spanish bull, Chanticleer now triumphs with his ardent crowing, but when all is said and done, the first corn may go to the sparrows but the pick of the harvest goes to the deserving. Let us listen attentively to Marshal Pétain who despite his eighty venerable winters does not mince words. In my experience, the old man says, everything that is international is pernicious, everything that is national is beneficial and productive. One who speaks in this vein will not die without leaving his mark.

And the war in Ethiopia has ended. Mussolini made the announcement from the palace balcony, I hereby declare to the Italian people and the world that the war has ended, and in response to this powerful voice the multitudes of Rome, Milan, Naples, and all Italy acclaimed him il Duce, farmers abandoned their fields, workers left their factories, dancing and singing through the streets with patriotic fervor. Benito was telling the truth when he said that Italy had an imperial soul. From historic tombs arose the majestic shadows of Augustus, Tiberius, Caligula, Nero, Vespasian, Nerva, Septimius Severus, Domitian, Caracalla, and *tutti quanti*, restored to their former glory after years of waiting and hoping, there they stand lined up, forming a guard of honor for the new heir, for the imposing presence of Victor Emmanuel III, proclaimed in every tongue Emperor of Italian East Africa, while Winston Churchill gives his blessing, In the present world situation, the maintenance or escalation of sanctions against Italy could result in a shameful war without bringing the slightest benefit to the Ethiopian people. So let us remain calm. Should it come, war will be war, since that is its name, but it will not be shameful, just as the war against the Abyssinians was not shameful.

Addis Ababa, such a poetic name, such a handsome race, it means New Flower. Addis Ababa is in flames, her streets covered with dead bodies, marauders are destroying homes, committing rape, looting and beheading women and children as Badoglio's troops approach. The Negus has fled to French Somalia, from where he will sail to Palestine aboard a British cruiser, and later, toward the end of the month, before a solemn gathering of the League of Nations in Geneva he will ask, What reply should I take back to my people. But after he speaks, no one replies, and before he got up to speak, he was jeered by the Italian journalists. Let us show tolerance, it is well known that nationalist fanaticism can easily dim one's intelligence, so he that is without sin, let him cast the first stone. Addis Ababa is in flames, her streets are covered with dead bodies, marauders are destroying homes, committing rape, looting and beheading women and children, as Badoglio's troops approach. Mussolini declared, This remarkable achievement has sealed the fate of Ethiopia, and the wise Marconi warned, Those who would seek to offer resistance to Italy are committing the most dangerous of follies, and Anthony Eden argued, Circumstances advise the lifting of sanctions, and *The Manchester Guardian*, speaking for the British Government, said, There are many reasons why colonies should be handed over to Germany, and Goebbels said, The League of Nations is a good thing but flying squadrons are better. Addis Ababa is in flames, her streets are covered with dead bodies, marauders are destroying homes, committing rape, looting, beheading women and children, as Badoglio's troops approach, Addis Ababa was in flames, homes burned, castles were sacked, bishops stripped, women raped by knights, their children pawns skewered with swords, and blood flowed in the streets. A shadow crosses the mind of Ricardo Reis. What is this, where do these words come from, the newspaper says only that Addis Ababa is in flames, that marauders are looting, committing rape, and beheading women and children as Badoglio's troops approach, the *Diário de Notícias* makes no mention of knights, bishops, and pawns, there is no reason to think that in Addis Ababa chess players were playing a game of chess. Ricardo Reis consulted *The God of the Labyrinth* on his bedside table. Here it is, on the opening page, The body discovered by the first chess player, its arms outstretched, occupies the squares of the King and Queen and their two pawns, its head is toward the enemy camp, its left hand in a white square, its right hand in a black square. In all the pages he has read there is only this one corpse, so it clearly was not along this route that the troops of Badoglio advanced. Ricardo Reis puts *The God of the Labyrinth* back in its place, he now knows what he is looking for. He opens a drawer of the desk that once belonged to an Appeals Court judge, in years gone by handwritten notes relating to the Civil Code were kept in it, he takes out a folder tied with a ribbon, it contains his odes, the secret poems he never discussed with Marcenda, and manuscript pages, all first drafts, jottings, Lydia will come across them one day, at a time of irreparable loneliness. *Master, placid are*, the first sheet reads, and other sheets read, *The gods are in exile, Crown me with roses while yet others tell, The god Pan is not dead, Apollo in his chariot has driven past, Once more, Lydia, come sit beside me on the riverbank, this is the ardent month of June, War comes, In the distance the mountains are covered with snow and sunlight, Nothing but flowers as far as the eye can see, The day's pallor is tinged with gold, Walk empty-handed, for wise is the man who contents himself with the spectacle of the world.* More and more sheets of paper pass, just as the days have passed, the sea stretches level, the winds wail in secret, each thing has its season, so let there be days for renewal, let us keep this moist finger on the page, here it is, *I heard how once upon a time when Persia*, this is the poem, no other, this the chessboard and we the players, I Ricardo Reis, you, my reader. They are burning homes, castles have been sacked and bishops stripped, but when the ivory King is in peril who cares about the flesh and bones of sisters and mothers and children, if my flesh and bones have been turned to stone, transformed into a player playing chess. Addis Ababa means New Flower, all the rest has been said. Ricardo Reis puts away his poems, locks the drawer. Cities have fallen and people are suffering, freedom and life are ending, but you and I, let us imitate the Persians of this tale. If we jeered at the Negus like good Italians in the League of Nations, let us now croon like good Portuguese to the gentle breeze as we leave our homes. The doctor is in good spirits, the neighbor on the fourth floor remarks. Are you surprised, the one thing there is never any shortage of is patients, the neighbor from the second floor retorts. Two opinions, as the doctor from the third floor leaves the building talking to himself.

Ricardo Reis is in bed, Lydia's head resting on his right arm, their perspiring bodies covered only by a sheet. He is naked, and her chemise is above her waist. Both have forgotten, or put from their minds, the morning he was impotent and she did not know what she had done to be rejected. The neighbors, on their balconies at the rear of the building, exchange words with broad hints, emphatic gestures, much nodding and winking. They're at it again, The world is depraved, Who would believe it, They've lost all shame. These sour and envious women are unable to recapture their youth, when as little girls in short dresses they danced and sang Ring-a-ring-o' roses in the garden, ah how pretty they were in those days. Lydia is happy. A woman who goes to bed so willingly with a man is deaf to gossip, let voices slander her in hallways and courtyards, they cannot harm her, nor can hostile eyes when she bumps into those virtuous hypocrites on the stairs. Soon she will have to get out of bed and wash the dirty dishes which have accumulated, and iron the bedsheets, the shirts worn by this man who is lying beside her. Who could have told me that I would be, how shall I describe myself, his mistress. Not mistress, for no one will say of this Lydia, Did you know that she is having an affair with Ricardo Reis, or, Do you know Lydia, that woman who is the mistress of Ricardo Reis. If anyone ever mentions her, he will say, Ricardo Reis has a really good maid, she does everything, he got a bargain there. Lydia stretches her legs, draws close to him, one last gesture of tranquil pleasure. It's hot, Ricardo Reis says, and she moves away a little, frees his arm, then sits up in bed and looks for her skirt, it is time to start doing some work. At that moment he tells her, Tomorrow I'm going to Fátima. She thought she had misunderstood, You're going where. To Fátima. I thought you didn't approve of such things. I'm going out of curiosity. I've never been there myself, my family doesn't go in much for religion. You surprise me. What Ricardo Reis meant was that it is usually people from the lower classes who believe in these devotions, but Lydia did not reply. Dressing in haste, she barely heard Ricardo Reis add, The trip will do me good, I've been cooped up here for so long, because she had other things on her mind now. Will you be away long, she asked, No, there and back, And where will you sleep, the place is so crowded, people have to sleep out in the open. I'll see when I get there, no one ever died from spending a night out of doors. Perhaps you'll bump into Senhorita Marcenda, Who, Senhorita Marcenda, she told me that she was hoping to go to Fátima sometime this month. Oh. She also said that she no longer visits the specialist in Lisbon, they've told her there is no cure, poor girl. You seem to know a great deal about Senhorita Marcenda. Very little, only that she is going to Fátima and that she won't be coming back to Lisbon anymore. Are you sorry. She was always very kind to me. I shouldn't think it likely that I will meet her among that multitude. Sometimes these things happen, look at me here in your apartment, who would ever have believed it, when you arrived from Brazil, after all, you might have gone to another hotel. Such are life's coincidences. It is fate. Do you believe in fate, There is nothing more certain than fate, Death is more certain, Death, too, is part of fate, but now I must iron your shirts and wash the dishes, and if there is still time I'll go and visit my mother, she's always complaining that she doesn't see much of me these days.

Lying back on the pillows, Ricardo Reis opened a book, not the one about Herbert Quain, which he had begun to wonder if he would ever finish, this was *O Desaparecido* by Carlos Queirós, a poet who might have been the nephew of Fernando Pessoa, had fate so ordained. A minute later he became aware that he was not reading, his eyes, rather, were fixed on the page, on a line whose meaning had suddenly become obscure. An extraordinary girl this Lydia, she says the simplest things, as if she were merely skimming the surface of more profound words which she cannot or will not utter. If I had not told her that I was going to Fátima, who knows whether she would have mentioned Marcenda, concealing her knowledge out of resentment and jealousy, emotions she betrayed back in the hotel. And these two women, the guest and the chambermaid, the rich girl and the poor servant, what did they have to discuss with each other. What if they should discuss me, neither suspecting the other, or just the reverse, playing Eve against Eve with much probing, scheming, parrying, subtle insinuations, clever silences. It is not inconceivable, on the other hand, that Marcenda simply said one day, Doctor Reis gave me a kiss, but we didn't go any further, and that Lydia simply replied, I sleep with him and I slept with him before he ever kissed me, that they then proceeded to discuss the significance of these differences. He only kisses me when we are in bed together before and during you-know-what, never afterward. To me he said, I'm going to kiss you, but as for you-know-what, what men do to women, I am ignorant of it, because they've never done it to me. Do not worry, Senhorita Marcenda, one day you'll get married and then you'll find out what it's all about. You've experienced it, tell me, is it good. When you like the other person, And do you like him, I do. So do I, but I shall never see him again. You could marry him. If we married, perhaps I wouldn't like him anymore. As for me, I think I will always like him. The conversation did not end there, but their voices lowered to a whisper, perhaps they are confiding their intimate feelings, the weakness of women, now the talk is truly between Eve and Eve. Begone, Adam, you are not wanted here. Ricardo Reis, reading, not reading, came across a fishwife on the page, capitalized, *O Fishwife, pass, I beseech you pass, flower of the race. Lord do not forgive them, for they know exactly what they are doing.* The poetic discussion between this uncle and nephew would be intense. You're incorrigible, Pessoa, and you too Queirós, I'm content with what the gods in their wisdom have given me, a lucid and solemn awareness of things and human beings. He got up, put on his dressing gown, and in his slippers went to look for Lydia. In the kitchen ironing, she had removed her blouse in order to feel a little cooler. Seeing her like this, her white skin flushed with exertion, Ricardo Reis thought he owed her a kiss. He gripped her gently by her bare shoulders, drew her toward him, and without any further thought kissed her slowly, giving time to time and space to their lips, their tongues, their teeth. Lydia was breathless, he had never kissed her like this before, now she will be able to tell Marcenda if she ever sees her again, He didn't say, I'm going to kiss you, he just kissed me.

Early next morning, so early that he thought it prudent to set his alarm clock, Ricardo Reis departed for Fátima. The train pulled out of the Rossio station at five-fifty-five, but half an hour before it even arrived, the platform was crammed with passengers, people of all ages carrying baskets, sacks, blankets, demijohns, all chatting in loud voices and calling out to each other. Ricardo Reis had taken the precaution of buying a first-class ticket, with a reserved seat, the guard obsequious with cap in hand. He had scarcely any luggage, a simple suitcase, ignoring Lydia's warning that in Fátima people slept out in the open, he would see when he arrived, there was bound to be accommodation for tourists and pilgrims of some social position. Seated comfortably by the window, Ricardo Reis contemplated the landscape, the mighty Tagus, the marshlands still flooded here and there, bulls grazing at random, frigates sailing upriver over resplendent water. After an absence of sixteen years, he had forgotten this view, and now fresh images imprinted themselves beside those restored by memory, as if it were only yesterday that he had made this journey. At the stations and signal stops en route, more and more people got on. The train is a real cattle train, there cannot have been a single empty seat in third class since it left the Rossio, and passengers are crammed into the gangways. No doubt second class has already been invaded, and soon they will start invading here, but there's no use complaining, anyone who wants peace and quiet should travel by car. After Santarém, on the long climb up to the Vale de Figueira, the train puffs along, sends up sudden gusts of steam, wheezes under its heavy load, and goes so slowly that one could easily step off, pick some flowers on the embankment, and with three strides jump back onto the running board. Listening, Ricardo Reis learns that among the passengers traveling in this compartment only two will not alight in Fátima. The pilgrims talk of their vows, debate who has made the greatest number of pilgrimages. One claims, perhaps truthfully, perhaps lying, that in the last five years he has not missed a single pilgrimage, another says that counting this one he has made eight. So far no one has boasted that he knows Sister Lúcia personally. Hearing these exchanges, Ricardo Reis is reminded of the talk in his waiting room, those depressing confidences about the orifices of the human body, where every pleasure is experienced and every misfortune can strike. At the station of Mato de Miranda, despite the fact that no passengers boarded the train, they were delayed. The noise of the engine could be heard in the distance, but here, on the bend, among the olive groves, reigned the most perfect calm. Ricardo Reis lowered his window to look outside. An elderly woman, barefoot and in dark clothes, was embracing a skinny little boy about thirteen years old and saying, My dear. Both were waiting for the train to move so they could cross the track. These two were not traveling to Fátima, the old woman had come to meet her grandson who lived in Lisbon. At last the station master blew his whistle, the locomotive hissed, went puff, puff, and slowly began to accelerate. Now the route is straight, and one could almost believe that this is a fast train. The morning air gives Ricardo Reis an appetite, and although it is much too early for lunch, people are starting to untie bundles of food. Eyes closed, he dozes, rocked by the swaying carriage, as if in a cradle. He has vivid dreams, yet when he awakes he cannot remember them. He remembers that he had no opportunity to tell Fernando Pessoa that he was going to Fátima. What will he think if he comes to the apartment and doesn't find me there, he may think I've gone back to Brazil without a word of farewell, my last farewell. Then he imagines a scene with Marcenda as the central figure, he sees her kneeling, the fingers of her right hand folded with those of her left, supporting in the air the dead weight of her withered arm. The effigy of Our Blessed Lady passes but no miracle takes place, not surprising, given Marcenda's lack of faith. She gets to her feet, resigned. Ricardo Reis sees himself approach, touch her, his middle and index finger together, on the breast, near her heart, no more is needed. Miracle, miracle, the pilgrims cry, their own woes suddenly forgotten, another's miracle is all they ask. Now they come flocking, swept along by the crowd or dragging themselves, the crippled, paralytic, consumptive, diseased, demented, blind, a multitude surrounds Ricardo Reis, beseeching another act of mercy. Behind this forest of wailing pilgrims Marcenda waves, both arms upraised, then disappears from sight. Ungrateful creature, she was healed and departed. Ricardo Reis opened his eyes, uncertain as to whether he had slept or not, and asked the passenger beside him, How much longer. We're almost there. So he had slept, and for a considerable time.

At the station in Fátima, the train emptied. Stirred by the odor of sanctity in the air, pilgrims jostled each other, there was alarm and confusion as families suddenly found themselves divided. The broad open space resembled a military encampment preparing for a battle. Most of the pilgrims will make the twenty-kilometer journey on foot to the Cova da Iria, but some rush to join the lines for buses, these are the pilgrims with weak legs and little stamina, who tire at the slightest exertion. The sky was clear, the sun bright and warm. Ricardo Reis went off in search of a place to eat. There were plenty of street vendors selling pancakes, cheesecakes, biscuits from Caldas, dried figs, pitchers of water, fruits in season, garlands of pine kernels, peanuts, and pips and lupine seeds, but not a single restaurant worthy of the name. The few eating houses were full, the taverns were packed to the door, he will need a lot of patience before he finds himself seated in front of a knife and fork and a plate of food. Yet he benefited from the Christian spirit that permeated this place, for when they saw him so smartly turned out in his city clothes, a number of customers in the line, like good provincials, allowed him to go before them, thus Ricardo Reis was able to have his lunch sooner than he had hoped, a little fried fish with boiled potatoes dressed with oil and vinegar, then a couple of scrambled eggs. He drank wine that tasted like altar wine, ate good country bread, moist and heavy, and having thanked his hosts he went to look for transportation. The square was less crowded, ready for another trainload from the south or north, but pilgrims steadily continued to arrive on foot from remote parts. A bus gave a raucous honk, touting for passengers to fill the few remaining empty seats. Ricardo Reis, breaking into a trot, stepping over baskets and bundles of mats and blankets, managed to obtain a seat, a major struggle for a man who is trying to digest his food and is exhausted by the heat. Rattling loudly, the bus pulled away, sending up clouds of dust from the poorly paved road, and the filthy windows barely allowed one to catch a glimpse of the rolling, arid land. The driver honked without respite, sending groups of pilgrims scattering into the ditches at the side of the road, steered sharply to avoid potholes, and every few minutes spat noisily out an open window. The road swarmed with an endless column of pilgrims on foot, but there were also wagons and ox-driven carts, each advancing at its own pace. From time to time an expensive limousine with a chauffeur in livery would pass, sounding its horn, carrying elderly women dressed in black or gray or midnight blue, and corpulent gentlemen in dark suits with the circumspect air of those who have just finished counting their money only to find that it has multiplied. The occupants could be seen when the limousine was forced to slow down because of some large procession of pilgrims led by their parish priest, the priest acts as both spiritual and tour guide, and deserves our praise for making the same sacrifices as his flock, on foot like them with his hooves in the dirt. The majority of the faithful walk barefoot. Some carry open umbrellas to protect themselves from the sun, these are people with delicate heads, not of the lower orders, and prone to fits of fainting and vertigo. The hymns they sing out of tune. The shrill voices of the women sound like an endless lamentation, a weeping as yet without tears, and the men, who nearly always forget the words, sing only the rhyming syllables by way of accompaniment, in a sort of basso continuo, no more is asked of them, only that they keep up the pretense. From time to time people can be seen sitting along hedgerows under the shade of trees, gathering strength for the final stretch of the journey, taking advantage of this pause to nibble a chunk of bread and sausage, a cod fritter, a sardine fried three days ago back in their obscure village. Then they get back on the road, feeling restored. Women carry baskets of food on their heads, some even suckle infants as they walk, and the dust descends on them all in clouds as yet another bus goes past, but they feel nothing, pay no attention, it shows what habit can do. Sweat trickles down the foreheads of monk and pilgrim, forms tiny channels in the dust, they wipe their faces with the back of their hands, worse than they thought, this is not just dirt but mud. The heat blackens their faces, yet the women do not remove the kerchiefs from their heads and the men keep on their jackets, they neither undo their shirts nor loosen their collars. This race preserves unawares the custom of the desert, which says that what protects from the cold protects also from the heat, therefore they wrap up as if to conceal themselves.

At a bend in the road a crowd has gathered under a tree, people are shouting, women are tearing their hair, and the body of a man is stretched out on the ground. The bus slows to allow the passengers to watch this spectacle, but Ricardo Reis says, or rather shouts to the driver, Stop here, let me see what has happened, I'm a doctor. Murmurs of protest can be heard, the passengers are in a hurry to reach the land of miracles, but they soon quiet down, anxious not to appear hard-hearted. Ricardo Reis got off, pushed his way through the crowd, knelt in the dust at the old man's side, and felt the artery in his neck. He is dead, he said. He need not have bothered interrupting his journey just to make this announcement. The news provoked a renewed outburst of tears, the dead man had numerous relatives, but his widow, a woman even older than the dead man, who now was no age, looked at the corpse with dry eyes, only her lips trembled as she stood there twining the fringes of her shawl. Two of the men in the crowd got on the bus, to report the death to the authorities in Fátima, who will make arrangements for the corpse to be taken away and buried in the nearest cemetery. Ricardo Reis has returned to his seat on the bus, now the object of everyone's curiosity, Fancy that, we have a doctor in our midst, who could ask for more reassuring company, even though he did nothing on this occasion but confirm a death. The two men inform those around them, He was already very sick when he got here, he should have stayed home, but he insisted on coming, he said he would hang himself from the rafters of the house if we left him behind, in the end he died far from home, no one escapes his destiny. Ricardo Reis nodded in agreement, not knowing that his head was moving. Yes sir, that's destiny, let's hope someone sticks a cross under that tree so future travelers can say a paternoster for the soul of one who died unconfessed and without receiving the last rites of the Church though he was already heading for heaven the moment he left his house. If this old man were called Lazarus and Jesus Christ appeared at the bend in the road on His way to the Cova da Iria to witness the miracles, He would understand at once what had happened, having experience in such things, and would elbow His way through all those gaping onlookers, and if anyone tried to stop Him, Jesus Christ would rebuke him, saying, Don't you know who you're talking to. Going up to the old woman who finds herself unable to weep, He would say, Leave this to me, and take two steps forward, make the sign of the Cross, remarkable prescience on His part, since we know that He has not been crucified yet, and He would cry out, Lazarus, arise and walk, whereupon Lazarus would get to his feet, another miracle. Lazarus would embrace his wife, who could now weep at last, and everything would be as before, and when the wagon came with the stretcher bearers and the authority to take away the body, someone would be sure to ask, Why are you looking for a dead man among the living, he is not here, he has been brought back to life. But in the Cova da Iria no such miracle, hard as people tried, was ever achieved.

This is the place. The bus comes to a halt with several final blasts of exhaust, its radiator is boiling like one of hell's cauldrons, and as the passengers step out, the driver goes to unscrew the cap, protecting his hands with old rags. Clouds of steam, the sweet-smelling incense of mechanics, rise into the air in this scorching heat, little wonder that we feel delirious. Ricardo Reis joins the stream of pilgrims. He tries to imagine what the spectacle must look like seen from heaven, a swarm of ants converging from every cardinal and collateral point like a huge star. This thought, or was it the noise of an engine, made him raise his eyes to lofty heights and ethereal visions. Overhead, tracing out an enormous circle, an airplane was dropping leaflets, perhaps prayers for intoning in unison, perhaps maps showing the way to the gates of paradise, or could they be messages from our Lord God, an apology for not being with us today, in His place He has sent His Divine Son, who already worked a miracle at the bend in the road, and a good miracle it was too. The leaflets descend slowly, there is not a breath of wind. Noses in the air, the pilgrims reach out eagerly to catch them, white, yellow, green, blue. Many who cannot read, and they form the majority in this spiritual gathering, hold the leaflets, not knowing what to do with them. A man dressed in peasant attire, after deciding that Ricardo Reis looks like someone who can read, asks, What is written here, sir. Ricardo Reis tells him, It's an advertisement for Bovril. The man looks at him suspiciously, debates whether to ask him to explain what Bovril is, then folds the paper in four and puts it into his jerkin pocket. Always hold on to what is useless, you will always find a use for it.

A sea of people. Around the great concave esplanade are pitched hundreds of canvas tents under which thousands are camping, there are frying pans on open fires, dogs guarding provisions, children crying, flies getting into everything. Ricardo Reis strolls between the tents, intrigued by this courtyard of miracles, it is as large as any city. This is a Gypsy encampment, complete with wagons and mules, and the donkeys, to the delight of the horseflies, are covered with sores. Carrying his suitcase, he does not know where he is heading, he has no shelter awaiting him, not so much as a tent, and has now satisfied himself that there are no lodging houses in the vicinity, let alone hotels. And if there should be, hidden somewhere, a hospice for pilgrims, it is unlikely that it will have any spare pallets left, they will have been reserved God knows how long in advance. May the will of God Himself be done. The sun is scorching, night is still a long way off, and there are no indications that it will become any cooler. When Ricardo Reis betook himself to Fátima it was not with physical comfort in mind, he came in the hope of seeing Marcenda. His suitcase is light, containing only his razor, soap, shaving brush, a change of underwear, socks, and a pair of sturdy shoes with reinforced soles which he must change into or he'll ruin the patent shoes he is wearing. If Marcenda is here, she will not be sitting in a tent, a notary's daughter from Coimbra deserves something better, but where will she find it. Ricardo Reis went to the hospital, a good place to start. Using his credentials as a doctor, he was allowed in, and forced his way through the rabble. Everywhere he looked, in complete confusion throughout the wards and corridors, the sick lay on stretchers and mattresses on the ground, but their relatives made far more noise than they did, keeping up an endless drone as they prayed, a drone interrupted from time to time by deep sighs, piercing cries, and pleas to the Virgin. In the infirmary there were not more than thirty beds and the sick numbered around three hundred. People lay wherever space could be found, one had to step over them, a good thing we no longer believe in the evil eye, You bewitched me, now break the spell, and the custom is to repeat the movement in reverse, if only all misfortunes could be made to disappear so easily. Marcenda is not here, nor is Ricardo Reis surprised, after all she is perfectly capable of walking on her own two feet, only her arm is crippled, and so long as she refrains from taking her hand out of her pocket, no one even notices. Outside, the heat is worse, but the sun, to his relief, does not give off a bad smell.

If such a thing is possible, the crowd is growing, as if reproducing itself by fission. Like a great black swarm of bees in pursuit of divine honey it buzzes, drones, crackles, moves in slow waves, lulled by its own size. Impossible to find anyone in this cauldron, which is not the cauldron of Pêro Botelho but burns all the same. Ricardo Reis is resigned, whether he finds or doesn't find Marcenda seems of no great importance now. If fate decrees that we meet, then we will meet, even if we attempt to hide from each other. How foolish he was, to express his thoughts with these words, Marcenda, if she is here, does not know that I am here so she will not attempt to hide, therefore the chance is greater that we will meet. The airplane continues to circle overhead, the colored leaflets dance through the air, but no one pays attention now, only the new arrivals seeing them for the first time. What a pity these leaflets do not carry the much more persuasive illustration from the newspaper advertisement, the one depicting the doctor with the goatee and the ailing damsel in the negligee, If only she had taken Bovril, she would not be in this condition. Here in Fátima there are many people in much worse condition, they would surely find that miraculous jar a godsend. His face flushed, Ricardo Reis has removed his jacket and rolled up his sleeves, and fans himself with his hat.

His legs suddenly heavy with exhaustion, he goes in search of shade. Some of his fellow pilgrims are having their siesta, worn out by the long journey and all those prayers en route, they are recovering their strength before the statue of the Virgin is brought out, before the procession of candles begins, and the long nocturnal vigil by the light of bonfires and oil lamps. He, too, dozed a little, his back against the trunk of an olive tree, the nape of his neck on soft moss. Opening his eyes, he saw patches of blue sky amid the branches and remembered the skinny boy at the train station, whose grandmother, she must have been his grandmother, called him My dear. What is the child doing at this very minute, almost certainly he has taken off his shoes, that is the first thing he does when he arrives at the village, the second is to go down to the river. His grandmother is probably cautioning him, Don't go yet, the sun is too hot, but he does not listen and she does not expect to be heard. Boys of his age want to be free, not clinging to their mother's skirts, they throw stones at the frogs and do not think they are causing any harm, but one day they will feel remorse. Too late, because for frogs and other tiny creatures there is no resurrection. Ricardo Reis finds this all absurd, the idea that he has traveled from Lisbon like someone pursuing a mirage, knowing all the while that it was a mirage and nothing more, his sitting in the shade of an olive tree among people he does not know, waiting for nothing whatsoever, and these thoughts about a boy whom he saw for only a moment in a remote provincial train station, this sudden desire to be like him, to wipe his nose with his right arm, play in puddles, pick flowers, admiring them and forgetting them, steal fruit from the orchards, scamper away weeping when pursued by dogs, or chase girls and lift up their skirts because they don't like it or do like it but pretend they don't, and because it gives him secret pleasure. Have I ever really experienced life, Ricardo Reis murmured to himself. The pilgrim lying beside him thought the murmur was some new prayer, a prayer yet to be put to the test.

The sun goes down but the heat does not abate. In the immense square there does not appear to be room for a pin, yet the crowd continues to mill around the periphery, there is a steady, constant stream of people, on this side they are still trying to get better vantage points, they must be doing the same over there. Ricardo Reis, strolling in the immediate vicinity, suddenly becomes aware of another pilgrimage, that of beggars. He sees true beggars and false beggars, and the difference is important, a true beggar is simply a poor man who begs, while your false beggar has turned begging into a profession, it is not unknown for people to become rich this way. Both use the same techniques, the whimpering, the pleading with outstretched hand, or sometimes two hands, a theatrical tour de force which is difficult to resist, Alms for the sake of the souls of your dear departed, God will reward you, Have pity on a poor blind man, have pity on a poor blind man, and some display an ulcerated leg, an amputated arm, but not what we are searching for. It is as if the gates of hell have been opened, for only from hell could such horrors have come. And now it is the turn of those selling lottery tickets, they make such an uproar as they call out winning numbers that prayers are arrested in midflight to heaven. A man interrupts his paternoster because he has a sudden hunch about the number three thousand six hundred and ninety-four. Clutching his rosary in a distracted hand, he fondles the ticket as if weighing its potential, then shakes from his handkerchief the necessary number of escudos and resumes his prayer where he broke off, *Give us this day our daily bread*, words now recited with greater hope. An attack is now launched by vendors of blankets, ties, handkerchiefs, and baskets, and by the unemployed, who wear armbands and sell holy pictures. They are not really selling, first they receive alms, then they hand over the picture, it is one way of maintaining their dignity. This poor wretch is neither a true beggar nor a false beggar, he asks for alms only because he is out of work. Now here is an excellent idea, let all the unemployed wear armbands, strips of black cloth bearing bold white letters for all the world to see, Unemployed, it would make the counting of them easier and ensure that we do not forget them. But worst of all, because they upset our spiritual peace and disturb the tranquillity of this holy place, are the hordes of hawkers. Let Ricardo Reis steer clear, otherwise they will pounce on him at once with that infernal shouting, Look, it's a bargain, Look, this has been blessed, the image of Our Blessed Lady painted on trays and statues, bunches of rosaries, crucifixes by the dozen, tiny medals, Sacred Hearts of Jesus and Ardent Hearts of Mary and three little shepherds with their hands joined in prayer and kneeling on the ground. One shepherd is a boy, but there is no evidence in either the hagiographical reports or the process of beatification that he ever lifted the skirts of little girls. The entire merchant confraternity cries out as if possessed, Woe to the trading Judas who tries with sly blandishments to steal a fellow trader's customer, whereupon the veil of the temple is torn and curses and insults rain down on the head of the treacherous rogue. Not even in Brazil can Ricardo Reis recall ever having heard such fiery rhetoric, clearly this branch of oratory has made considerable progress.

The precious gem of Catholicism sparkles with many facets, the facet of suffering for which there remains no hope other than that of returning each year, the facet of faith which in this holy place is sublime and fertile, the facet of common charity, the facet of Bovril, the facet of trading in scapulars and the like, the facet of trinkets and baubles, of printing and weaving, of eating and drinking, of lost and found, searching and finding. Ricardo Reis continues searching, but will he find. He has been to the hospital, he has explored the tents, he has gone through the open-air market in every direction, now he descends into the bustling esplanade, plunges into the dense multitude, sees their spiritual exercises, their acts of faith, their pitiful prayers, the vows they fulfill by crawling on all fours with bleeding knees, sees hands supporting a penitent woman under the armpits before she faints from pain and unbearable ecstasy, and the sick who have been brought from the hospital, their stretchers set out in rows. Between those rows the statue of Our Blessed Lady the Holy Virgin will be carried on a litter adorned with white flowers. Ricardo Reis lets his eyes wander from face to face, they search but do not find, as if he were in a dream that has no meaning, like the dream of a road that goes nowhere, of a shadow cast by no object, of a word which the air has uttered and then denied. The hymns are primitive, sol and do, sol and do, the choir is one of quavering shrill voices that constantly break off and start again. On the thirteenth of May in the Cova da Iria there is suddenly a great silence, the statue is about to make its exit from the Chapel of the Apparitions. A shudder goes through the crowd, the supernatural has come and blown over two hundred thousand heads, something is bound to happen. Gripped by mystical fervor, the sick hold out handkerchiefs, rosaries, medals, the priests take them, touch the statue with them, and return them to the supplicants, while the poor wretches implore, Our Lady of Fátima give me life, Our Lady of Fátima grant me the miracle of walking, Our Lady of Fátima help me to see, Our Lady of Fátima help me to hear, Our Lady of Fátima give me back my health, Our Lady of Fátima, Our Lady of Fátima, Our Lady of Fátima. The dumb do not plead, they simply look on, if they still have eyes to see with. However hard Ricardo Reis strains, he does not hear, Our Lady of Fátima look upon this left arm of mine and cure me if you can. Thou shalt not tempt the Lord Thy God or His Holy Mother, and if you think it over carefully you will realize that one should not ask for anything, instead one should resign oneself, that is what humility demands, because only God knows what is good for us.

The statue was brought out, carried around in procession, then it disappeared. The blind still could not see, the dumb still could not speak, the paralyzed still were paralyzed, missing limbs did not grow back, and the pains of the afflicted were not diminished. Weeping bitter tears, they accused and blamed themselves, My faith was lacking, *mea culpa, mea culpa, mea maxima culpa*. Prepared to concede a few miracles, the Virgin had left her chapel, but she found the faithful wavering, No burning bushes here, no everlasting oil lamps, this will not do, let them come back next year. The evening shadows lengthen as twilight approaches, it too at a processional pace. Little by little the sky loses the vivid blue of day, turns pearl, but over there the sun, hidden behind the trees on distant hills, explodes into crimson, orange, red, more volcano than sun, it seems incredible that this should happen in silence. Soon night will fall, campfires are lit, the vendors have stopped shouting, the beggars are counting their coins, beneath trees bodies are being nourished, knapsacks are opened, people munch stale bread, raise the cask or wineskin to their parched lips, all eat, but the food varies according to their means.

Ricardo Reis found shelter with a group of pilgrims sharing a tent. There was no discussion, they saw him standing there with a lost look on his face, a suitcase in his hand, a blanket he had bought rolled up under his arm. He in turn saw that the tent would do him nicely as long as the night did not become too cold. They told him, Make yourself comfortable. He started to say, No, thanks just the same, but they insisted, Look, our offer comes from the heart, and it was true, he realized, and joined the large group from Abrantes. This snuffling, which can be heard throughout the Cova da Iria, comes as much from chewing as from praying, because while some seek solace for their tormented souls, others satisfy the pangs of hunger, or alternate between the two. By the dying light of the campfires Ricardo Reis does not find Marcenda, nor will he see her later on during the procession of candles, nor in his sleep, when he is overcome with exhaustion, frustration, the desire to disappear from the face of the earth. He sees himself as two people, the dignified Ricardo Reis who each day washes and shaves, and this other Ricardo Reis, a vagrant with a stubble, crumpled clothes, creased shirt, hat stained with sweat, shoes covered with dust. The first asks the second to explain, please, why he has come to Fátima without any faith, with only a wild dream, And if you do see Marcenda, what will you say to her, can you imagine how absurd you would look if she appeared before you now at her father's side, or, worse still, alone, take a good look at yourself, do you really believe that a girl, even one with only one arm, would fall madly in love with a ridiculous middle-aged doctor. Ricardo Reis humbly accepts this criticism and, deeply ashamed that he is in such shabby and filthy condition, pulls the blanket over his head and goes back to sleep. Nearby, someone is snoring without a care in the world, and behind that sturdy olive tree there is murmuring that cannot be mistaken for prayers, chuckling that scarcely suggests a choir of angels, sighs that are not provoked by spiritual ecstasy. Dawn is breaking, some early risers stretch their arms and get up to poke the fire, a new day is beginning, posing fresh trials to those who seek the fruits of paradise.

Ricardo Reis decides to leave before noon, he does not wait for the farewell ceremony in honor of the Virgin, he has said his good-byes. The airplane passed over twice, meanwhile, and dropped more leaflets advertising Bovril. The bus back has few passengers, as expected, the great exodus will come later. At the bend in the road a wooden cross has been stuck into the ground. There was no miracle after all.

Trusting in God and Our Blessed Lady from the time of Afonso Henriques to the Great War. This is the phrase that has haunted Ricardo Reis since his return from Fátima. He cannot recall whether he read it in a newspaper or book, or whether he heard it in a sermon or speech, it may even have been in the advertisement for Bovril. The words fascinate him, the expression is eloquent and calculated to rouse passions and kindle hearts, for it proves that we are a chosen people. There have been other peoples in the past and there will be other peoples in the future, but there are none that have endured as long, eight hundred years of steadfast loyalty, of constant intimacy with the heavenly powers. It is true that we were slow in creating the fifth empire, that Mussolini forged ahead of us, but the sixth empire will not elude us, nor the seventh, all we need is patience, and patience is in our nature. We are already on the right road, according to a public statement made by His Excellency the President of the Republic, General António Oscar de Fragoso Carmona, in a speech that should serve as a model for all the supreme magistrates of the nation to come. In his words, Portugal is now respected throughout the world, and we should be proud to be Portuguese, a sentiment no less noble than the one that precedes it, both of them eminently quotable. We can take pride in this worldwide respect, we who navigated the high seas, even if it is only in the capacity of most loyal ally, it does not matter of whom, what matters is loyalty, without it how could we live. Ricardo Reis, who returned from Fátima tired and sunburnt, without seeing either a miracle or Marcenda, and who for three days after that did not leave his apartment, reentered the outside world through the great door of this patriotic speech by the Honorable President. Taking his newspaper with him, he went to sit in the shadow of Adamastor. The old men were there, watching and perplexed by the arrival of the ships that had come to visit this promised land so avidly discussed by other nations, numerous ships bedecked with flags, sounding their festive sirens, their crews lined up on deck saluting. Light finally dawned in the heads of these two sentinels when Ricardo Reis gave them the newspaper he had by now digested and practically memorized, Yes, it was worth waiting eight centuries to feel proud of being Portuguese. From the Alto de Santa Catarina eight centuries salute you, O mighty sea. The old men, the thin one and the fat one, wipe away a furtive tear, sorry that they cannot remain for all eternity on this belvedere to watch the ships arriving, such bliss is harder to bear than the shortness of their lives. From the bench where he is seated Ricardo Reis witnesses love play between a soldier and a housemaid, the soldier takes liberties, the housemaid wards him off with provocative little slaps. This is a day for singing alleluias, which are the evoes of those who are not Greek, the flower beds are in full bloom, all a man needs to be happy unless he is eaten by insatiable ambitions. Ricardo Reis takes stock of his own ambitions and concludes that he craves nothing, that he is content to watch the river and the passing ships, the mountains and the peace that reigns there, yet he feels no happiness inside him, only this dull insect-gnawing that never stops. It's the weather, he murmurs, then asks himself how he would be feeling now if he had met Marcenda in Fátima, if, as people often say, they had fallen into each other's arms, We shall nevermore be parted, only when I thought I had lost you did I realize just how much I love you. She would use similar words, and then they would not know what else to say, even if they were free to run behind an olive tree and repeat for themselves the whispers, laughter, and sighs of others. Once more Ricardo Reis doubts, once more he feels the insect-gnawing in his bones. One cannot resist time, we are within it and accompany it, nothing more.

Finished with the newspaper, the old men toss a coin to see who will take it home, even the one who cannot read covets this prize, as there is nothing better than newspaper for lining drawers.

When he arrived at his office that afternoon, the receptionist Carlota informed him, A letter has come for you, Doctor, I left it on your desk. Ricardo Reis felt as if a blow had been delivered to his heart or stomach. At such moments we lose all our self-possession, nor can we locate the blow, because the distance that separates the heart from the stomach is so small and there is also a diaphragm in the middle which is as much affected by the palpitations of the former as by the contractions of the latter. If God, who has learned so much over the years, were to create the human body today, He would make it much less complicated. The letter is from Marcenda, it must be, she has written to tell him that she could not travel to Fátima after all, or that she did go and saw him in the distance, even waved with her good arm, and felt despair, first because he did not see her and second because the Virgin did not heal her, Now, my love, I await you in the Quinta das Lágrimas, if you still love me. Obviously a letter from Marcenda, there it lies in the middle of the rectangular sheet of green blotting paper, the envelope pale violet. No, seen from the door it is white, an optical illusion, we are taught in school that blue and yellow make green, green and violet make white, and white and anxiety make us pale. The envelope is not violet, nor does it come from Coimbra. Ricardo Reis opened it carefully and found a small sheet of paper, on which was written, in the awful scrawl one expects from a doctor, Dear colleague, this is to let you know that I have made a good recovery and hope to resume my practice as of the beginning of next month, I wish to take this opportunity to express my deep gratitude for your willingness to stand in for me during my illness, I also wish you every success in soon finding a new appointment that will permit you to put your considerable skill and experience to good use. The letter continued for several more lines, the usual formalities observed by nearly everyone when he writes letters. Ricardo Reis, rereading these clichéd phrases, appreciated his colleague's finesse, which transformed the favor he had done for Ricardo Reis into the favor Ricardo Reis had done for him, thus allowing Ricardo Reis to leave with his head held high. And he would have a reference now to show when he went to look for work, not simply a letter of recommendation but written evidence of good and loyal service, just like the one the Hotel Bragança will give to Lydia if she ever decides to leave for another job or to marry. He put on his white coat and called in the first patient. In the waiting room there are five more patients to be examined, he will not have time now to cure them, happily their conditions are not so serious that they will die on his hands in the next twelve days, before the month expires, just as well.

No sign of Lydia. This is not her day off, true, but knowing that his trip to Fátima was simply a matter of going and coming straight back, and knowing that he could have met Marcenda there, she might at least have come to see if there was any news of her friend and confidante, to find out if Marcenda was well, if her arm had been cured. In half an hour Lydia could come to the Alto de Santa Catarina and go back, or she could call at his office, which is even closer and quicker. But she has not come, she has not asked. It was a mistake for him to have kissed her without taking her to bed, perhaps she thought that he was buying her with that kiss, if such thoughts occur to people of humble background. Alone in his apartment, Ricardo Reis leaves only to work and to dine, from his window he watches the river and the distant slopes of Montijo, the rock of Adamastor, the punctual old men, the palm trees. Occasionally he goes down to the park and reads a few pages of some book. He retires early, thinks about Fernando Pessoa, who is dead now, and about Alberto Caeiro, who disappeared in his prime and for whom there had been such high hopes, and about Álvaro de Campos, who went to Glasgow, at least that is what he said in his telegram, he will probably settle there, building ships to the end of his days or until he is pensioned off. Occasionally Ricardo Reis goes to the movies and sees *Our Daily Bread* directed by King Vidor, or *The Thirty-Nine Steps* with Robert Donat and Madeleine Carroll, and he could not resist going to the São Luís to see *Audioscopes*, a 3-D film. As a souvenir he brought home the celluloid spectacles one has to wear, green on one side, red on the other, these spectacles are a poetic instrument to see things for which normal vision is not enough.

They say time stops for no man, that time marches on, commonplaces that are still repeated, yet there are people who chafe at the slowness with which it passes. Twenty-four hours to make a day, and at the end of the day you discover that it was not worthwhile, and the following day is the same all over again, if only we could leap over all the futile weeks in order to live one hour of fulfillment, one moment of splendor, if splendor can last that long. Ricardo Reis starts toying with the idea of returning to Brazil. The death of Fernando Pessoa, apparently, was a valid reason for crossing the Atlantic after an absence of sixteen years, for staying in Portugal, resuming his practice, writing a poem now and then, growing old, taking the place, after a fashion, of the poet who died, even if no one noticed the substitution. But now he wonders. This is not his country, if, in fact, it is anyone's. Portugal belongs only to God and Our Blessed Lady, it is a dreary, two-dimensional sketch with no relief in sight, not even with the special spectacles of *Audioscopes*. Fernando Pessoa, whether shadow or ghost, appears from time to time in order to make some ironic comment, to smile benevolently, then disappear. Ricardo Reis need not have bothered returning because of him. And Marcenda has ceased to exist, she lives in Coimbra on an unknown street, her days pass, one by one, without a cure. She may have hidden his letters in some corner of the attic, in the padding of a chair, or in a secret drawer used by her mother before her, or, even more cleverly, in the trunk of a housemaid who cannot read and is trustworthy, perhaps Marcenda reads them over and over, like one who recites a dream lest he forgets it, in vain, because in the end our dreams and what we remember of them have nothing in common. Lydia will come tomorrow because she always comes on her day off, but Lydia is the nursemaid of Anna Karenina, she is useful for keeping the house clean and for certain other needs, she cannot fill, with the little she has to offer, the emptiness of Ricardo Reis, not even the universe would suffice, if we accept his image of himself. As of the first of June he will be unemployed, he will have to go forth once more in search of a vacancy, a locum tenens position to make the days pass more quickly. Fortunately he still has a large wad of English pound notes he has not touched, and there is the money still deposited in a Brazilian bank, these various sums would be more than enough to rent an office and build a general-medicine practice of his own, for general medicine is all most patients require. No need to dabble in diseases of the heart and lungs. He might even employ Lydia to attend the patients, intelligent and easygoing Lydia would soon learn how, with a little guidance she could improve her spelling and escape the drudgery of life as a chambermaid. But this is only the daydream of one who is passing the time in idle thought. Ricardo Reis will not seek work, no, the best thing for him to do is take *The Highland Brigade* back to Brazil when she makes her next voyage. He will discreetly return *The God of the Labyrinth* to its owner, and O'Brien will never discover how the missing book suddenly reappeared.

Lydia arrived, said good afternoon, but seemed a little cold, withdrawn, she asked no questions and he was forced to speak first, I went to Fátima. She asked, Oh, how did you like it. How should Ricardo Reis reply, as a nonbeliever he is not likely to have experienced spiritual ecstasy, on the other hand he did not go purely out of curiosity, therefore he confines himself to generalities, Lots of people, dust everywhere, I had to sleep in the open, as you warned me, fortunately the night was warm. Doctor, you are not the sort of person to be roughing it on pilgrimages. I went to see what it was like. Lydia stays in the kitchen, is now running the hot water to wash the dishes, without saying much she has made it clear that there will be no carnal pleasures today. Could the reason for this embargo be the familiar problem of menstruation, or is it some lingering resentment, or the combination of both blood and tears, two insurmountable rivers making an impassable, murky sea. He sat on a bench in the kitchen watching her as she worked, not something he was in the habit of doing, it was a gesture of goodwill, a white flag waving over the fortifications to test the mood of the enemy general. I didn't come across Doctor Sampaio and his daughter after all, which was only to be expected with such a crowd, these words are spoken casually, they hover in midair, waiting for someone to pay attention. But what kind of attention, he could be telling the truth, he could be telling a lie, such is the inadequacy, the built-in duplicity of words. A word lies, with the same word one can speak the truth, we are not what we say, we are true only if others believe us. Lydia's belief is unknown, for she simply asks, Were there any miracles. If there were, I didn't see them, and no miracles were reported in the newspapers. Poor Senhorita Marcenda, if she went there in the hope of being cured, how disappointed she must have been. She had little hope, How do you know. Lydia fixed her gaze on Ricardo Reis as quick as a startled bird. Trying to catch me, he thought to himself as he replied, When I was still staying at the hotel, Marcenda and her father were already planning a visit to Fátima. Oh, really. These are the little duels with which people wear themselves out and grow old. Better to change the subject, and this is where newspapers become useful, they store facts in one's memory and help keep conversations going, both for the old men on the Alto de Santa Catarina and for Ricardo Reis and Lydia, because some silences are not preferable to words. What news about your brother, this is just an opening. My brother is fine, why do you ask. I was reminded of him because of something I read in the paper, a speech by a certain engineer named Nobre Guedes, I still have the paper here. I've never heard of the gentleman. Given what he has to say about sailors, I doubt that your brother would call him a gentleman. What does he say. Wait, I'll get the paper. Ricardo Reis left the kitchen, went into the study, returned with *O Século*, the text of the speech took up almost an entire page, This is the speech Nobre Guedes made on the National Radio condemning Communism, and at one point he refers to sailors. Does he say anything about my brother. He doesn't mention your brother by name, but to give you an example, he had this to say, There is in circulation an execrable leaflet known as *The Red Sailor*. What does execrable mean. Execrable means that something is evil, wretched, very bad. It means you want to curse it. Exactly, to execrate is to curse. I've seen *The Red Sailor* and it didn't make me feel like cursing. Did your brother show it to you. Yes, it was Daniel. Then your brother is a Communist. I'm not sure about that, but he's certainly in favor of Communism. What's the difference. To me he doesn't look different from other people. Do you think that if he were a Communist he would look different. I don't know, I can't explain. Well, this engineer Guedes also says that the sailors of Portugal are not red or white or blue, they are Portuguese. What, he thinks Portuguese is a color. That's very witty, anyone looking at you would say you couldn't break a plate, yet every so often you pull down a whole cupboard of plates. My hand is steady, I'm not in the habit of breaking plates, take a look, here I am washing your dishes and nothing slips from my hands. You're an extraordinary girl. This extraordinary girl is only a hotel chambermaid, but tell me, did this fellow Guedes have anything else to say about the sailors. About the sailors, no. I now remember that Daniel did mention a sailor, also Guedes, but his first name was Manuel, Manuel Guedes, and he is waiting to be sentenced, there are forty men altogether who are facing trial. Many have the name Guedes. Well, this one is Manuel. The dishes are washed and left to drain, Lydia has other chores to do, she must change the sheets, make the bed, open the window to air the room, clean the bathroom, put out fresh towels. This done, she returns to the kitchen and is drying the dishes when suddenly Ricardo Reis steals up from behind and puts his arm around her waist. She tries to avoid him, but he kisses her on the neck, causing the plate to slip from her hands, and it breaks into pieces on the floor. So you've finally broken a plate, it had to happen sooner or later, no one escapes his fate, he laughed, turning her toward him and kissing her full on the lips. She no longer resisted, but simply said, We cannot today. Now we know that the problem is physiological, the other obstacles have been overcome. It doesn't matter, he replied, it can keep until next time, and went on kissing her. Later she will have to sweep up the bits of crockery that are scattered all over the kitchen floor.

Then it was Fernando Pessoa who visited Ricardo Reis. Several days later, he appeared just before midnight, when all the neighbors were in bed. He came upstairs on tiptoe, taking this precaution because he was never sure that he would be invisible. Sometimes people looked right through him, he could tell from their lack of expression, but on rare occasions they stared, as if there was something strange about him but they could not put their finger on it. If anyone were to tell them that this man dressed in black was a ghost, they would not believe it, we are so familiar with white sheets and tenuous ectoplasms, but a ghost, if he is not careful, can be the most solid thing in the world. So Fernando Pessoa climbed the stairs slowly and rapped on the door with the agreed signal, anxious not to cause a scene, the clatter of someone stumbling upstairs could bring a bleary-eyed neighbor out on the landing, and she would scream at the top of her voice, Help, a thief. Poor Fernando Pessoa a thief, he who has been robbed of everything, even life. In his study, trying to compose a poem, Ricardo Reis had just finished writing, *Not seeing the Fates that destroy us, we forget their existence*, when the silence that filled the building was broken by a gentle tap-tap. He knew immediately who it was and hastened to open the door, What a pleasant surprise, where on earth have you been. Words can be tricky, these used by Ricardo Reis suggest a note of black humor in the worst possible taste, when he knows as well as we do that Fernando Pessoa has come from in the earth and not on it, from the rustic graveyard at Prazeres, where he does not even rest in peace, because his ferocious grandmother Dionísia, also buried there, demands a detailed account of his comings and goings. I've been for a stroll, her grandson replies sourly, just as he is now replying to Ricardo Reis, but without the same irritation. The best words are those that reveal nothing. Fernando Pessoa sank to the sofa with a gesture of infinite weariness, raised his hand to his forehead as if trying to assuage a pain or drive away some cloud, then he ran his fingers down his face, uncertainly over his eyes, pressing the corners of his mouth, smoothing his mustache, stroking his pointed chin. The fingers seemed to want to remodel his features, to restore them to their original design, but the artist has picked up an eraser instead of a pencil, and it obliterates as it passes, one whole side of the face loses its outline, which is only to be expected, because almost six months have passed since Fernando Pessoa's death. I see less and less of you these days, Ricardo Reis complained. I warned you on the first day, I become more forgetful as time passes, even now, there on the Rua do Calhariz, I had to rack my brains to remember the way to your apartment. You only had to locate the statue of Adamastor. If I had thought of Adamastor I would have been even more confused, I would have started to believe myself back in Durban, eight years old again, and then I would have been twice lost, in time as well as space. Try coming here more often, that will be one way of refreshing your memory. Today I was guided by a lingering smell of onion, A smell of onion, That's right, onion, your friend, it would appear, has not given up spying on you. That is ridiculous, the police must have precious little to occupy them when they can afford to waste time with someone who is innocent of any crime and has no intention of committing one. You can never tell what is going on in the mind of a policeman, perhaps you made a good impression, perhaps Victor would like to win your friendship but realizes that you live in the world of the chosen, he in the world of the damned, and that is why he whiles away the night gazing up at your window, watching to see if there is any light, like a man madly in love. Go ahead, have your little joke at my expense. You cannot imagine how sad one has to be to joke like this. But this constant spying is totally unjustified. I wouldn't say totally unjustified, after all is it normal for someone to be visited by a person who comes from the beyond. But no one can see you. That depends, my dear Reis, that depends, sometimes a dead man does not have the patience to be invisible, or sometimes he lacks the energy, and this does not take into account the fact that certain people among the living have eyes that can see the invisible. Surely that isn't true of Victor. Perhaps, although you must agree that one could hardly imagine a more useful ability in a policeman, by comparison Argos of the thousand eyes would be a nearsighted wretch. Ricardo Reis lifted the sheet of paper on which he had been writing, I have some lines here, I don't know how they will turn out. Read them to me. They are just a beginning, and they might even begin in a different way. Read them. *Not seeing the Fates that destroy us, we forget that they exist.* I like it, but as I recall, you wrote much the same thing, a thousand times and in a thousand different ways, before you left for Brazil, the tropics don't appear to have enriched your poetic genius. I have nothing more to say, I'm not like you. You will become like me, don't worry. My inspiration is what one might call internal. Inspiration is only a word. I am an Argos with nine hundred and ninety-nine eyes and all blind. A nice metaphor, which also implies that you would not be much good as a policeman. By the way, Fernando, did you ever come across a certain António Ferro, Secretary for National Propaganda. Yes, we were friends, I owe it to him that I was awarded a prize of five thousand reis for *Mensagem*, why do you ask. You will see in a moment, I have a piece of news here, did you know that the literary prizes administered by that department were awarded several days ago. How could I have known. Forgive me, I keep forgetting that you can no longer read. Who won the prize this year, Carlos Queirós, Ah, Carlos, Did you know him, Carlos Queirós was the nephew of a woman named Ophelinha, spelled with a *ph* instead of an *f*, whom I loved for a time, we worked in the same office. I cannot imagine you falling in love. We all fall in love at least once in our lifetime, and that is what happened to me. I'm curious to know what kind of love letters you wrote. I remember them as being rather less banal than most love letters. When was this, The affair began as soon as you left for Brazil, And did it last long, Long enough for me to be able to say, like Cardinal Gonzaga, I, too, have known love. I find this hard to believe, Do you think I'm lying, Certainly not, how could you say such a thing, we have never lied to each other, when the need arose, we confined ourselves to using words that lied. What do you find so hard to believe, then. That you should have fallen in love, the fact is that as I see and know you, you are precisely the kind of person who is incapable of loving. Like Don Juan, Yes, like Don Juan, but for a different reason, Explain, In Don Juan there was an excess of lust, which had to be dispersed among the women of his desire, while your situation, as far as I can recall, was pretty much the opposite. And what about you. I am somewhere in the middle, I am ordinary, average, neither too much nor too little. In other words, the well-balanced lover, Not well balanced, it is not a question of geometry or mechanics. Are you telling me that your love life, too, is less than perfect, Love is complicated, my dear Fernando, You can't complain, you have your Lydia, Lydia is a chambermaid, And Ofélia was a typist. Instead of discussing women, we seem to be discussing their professions. And there is also that girl you met in the park, what was her name, Marcenda, That's it, Marcenda is nothing to me. You dismiss her so roughly, it sounds like resentment. My limited experience tells me that resentment is the common attitude of men toward women. My dear Ricardo, we should have spent more time together. The empire decreed otherwise.

Fernando Pessoa got to his feet, paced awhile up and down

the study, lifted the sheet of paper on which Ricardo Reis had written the lines he had read, How did you express it, *Not seeing the Fates who destroy us, we forget that they exist*, one would have to be blind indeed not to see how the fates destroy us day by day, as the proverb says, *There are none so blind as those who will not see.* Fernando Pessoa put down the sheet of paper, You were telling me about Ferro, let's get back to where we were. During the awards ceremony, António Ferro observed that writers who grumble under repressive regimes, even when the repression is purely intellectual, such as that which emanates from Salazar, forget that creative output has always increased during reigns of law and order. This idea of the benefit of intellectual repression, that the Portuguese have become more creative under the surveillance of Victor, is absurd. Then you don't agree. History itself disproves what Ferro claims, you need only think of your own youth, of *Orfeu*, tell me if that was a reign of law and order, although your odes, my dear Reis, if one looks at them closely, might be considered a paean to law and order. I never thought of them like that. But that is what they are, human unrest is futile, the gods are wise and indifferent, and above them is fate, the supreme order to which even gods are subject. And what of men, what is their function. To challenge order, to change fate. For the better. For better or for worse, it makes no difference, the point is to keep fate from being fate. You sound like Lydia, she is always talking about fate. Fortunately when it comes to fate, one can say whatever he likes. We were speaking of Ferro. Ferro is a fool, believing that Salazar is Portugal's fate. The Messiah. Rather the parish priest who baptizes, christens, and marries us, and commends our souls to God when we die. In the name of order. Exactly, in the name of order. As I recall, when you were alive you were much less subversive. When one dies, one sees things differently, and with this irrefutable sentence I take my leave, irrefutable because you, being alive, cannot possibly dispute it. Why are you reluctant to spend the night here. The dead should not fall into the habit of living with the living, just as the living should not keep the dead with them. Humanity consists of both the living and the dead. That is true, but not altogether true, otherwise you would not only have me here, you would have the Court of Appeals judge too and all the other deceased members of his family. How do you know a Court of Appeals judge lived here, I don't remember ever having told you. It was Victor. Which Victor, mine. No, a Victor who is dead but who also has a tendency to stick his nose into the affairs of others, not even death has cured him of this obsession. Does he stink of onion. He does, but it's bearable, the smell is gradually disappearing as time passes. Farewell, Fernando. Farewell, Ricardo.

There are signs that Salazar's intellectual repression is not spreading as effectively as intended by its prime mover. A recent episode right here on the banks of the Tagus showed its weakening influence, when the second-class dispatch boat *João de Lisboa* was launched with all due ceremony in the presence of our venerable Head of State. The boat is on the slipway, festooned, everything spick-and-span, the tracks greased, the wedges adjusted, the crew lined up on the quarterdeck, and His Excellency the President of the Republic, General António Oscar de Fragoso Carmona, the very same who declared that Portugal is now respected throughout the world and that we should be proud to be Portuguese, arrives with his entourage, civilian and military, the latter in dress uniform, the former in tails, top hat, and striped trousers. The President, proudly stroking his handsome white mustache, proceeds with caution, perhaps on his guard not to repeat on this occasion the phrase he always uses when he is invited to open an exhibition of paintings, Very chic, very chic, most enjoyable. They are now mounting the steps to the platform, the highest dignitaries in the land, without whose presence not a single vessel can be launched, there is also a representative from the Church, the Catholic Church of course, from which advantageous blessings are expected, may it please Almighty God that this ship kill many and lose few. All present are proud to be part of this splendid occasion with its gathering of notables, curious bystanders, shipyard workers, and photographers and reporters. The bottle of sparkling wine from Bairrada awaits its moment of explosive glory, when lo and behold, the *João de Lisboa* begins to slip down the slipway though no one has as much as touched it. There is confusion, the President's white mustache quivers, puzzled top hats wave, and there goes the ship. As she enters the water, the crew shout hip hip hurrah according to custom, the seagulls soar, startled by the sirens of the other ships and also by the loud guffaws that echo now throughout the Ribeira de Lisboa. The shipyard workers, a particularly nasty lot, are clearly responsible for this insult, and Victor is already investigating the incident. The tide recedes, the hatchways even now give off the toxic stench of onion, the President withdraws in a rage as his entourage disperses in shame and indignation, he demands to know im-me-diately the names of those responsible for this unpardonable outrage against the dignity of our sailors not to mention the Fatherland in the person of its highest magistrate. Yes, Mr. President of the Council, says Captain Agostinho Lourenço, Victor's boss. But they cannot shake off the public ridicule, such fun, the whole of Lisbon is talking about it, even the Spaniards at the Hotel Bragança, although somewhat nervously, *Cuídense ustedes, eso son artes del diablo rojo*, but since these are matters concerning Lusitanian politics, they make no further comment. The dukes of Alba and Medinaceli arrange a visit to the Coliseu, an outing for the men only, to watch the terrifying, amazing wrestling contests featuring their compatriot José Pons, Count Karol Nowina a Polish nobleman, the Jewish wrestler Ab-Kaplan, the White Russian Zikoff, the Czech Stresnack, the Italian Nerone, the Belgian De Ferm, the Fleming Rick de Groot, the Englishman Rex Gable, and a certain Strouck whose nationality remains obscure, all champions *extraordinaires* of this other human spectacle, who have mastered the graceful art of slams and kicks, head butts and scissor holds, full nelsons and bridges. If Goebbels had to enter this ring, he would play safe and send the *Luftwaffe* on ahead.

It is precisely about planes and aviation that discussions are taking place in the capital now. As for the serious breach of discipline committed by certain members of the navy, we should mention in passing, since we shall not touch on the subject again, that despite Victor's investigations the culprits were not found, for no one believed that the incident of the *João de Lisboa* could possibly have been the work of a simple caulker or riveter. Since it is evident to everyone that the clouds of war are gathering over the skies of Europe, the Portuguese government has decided, by way of example, which is the best lesson of all, to show its citizens what they must do to protect themselves in the event of an air raid. The name of the enemy is not mentioned, but everyone assumes that it is the traditional enemy, that is, Castilian, which is now Red. The range of modern planes is still very limited, so we are not likely to be attacked by the French, and even less by the English, who in addition happen to be our allies. As for the Italians and Germans, they have given so many proofs of friendship, our nations linked by a common ideal, that we are confident they will help us one day rather than attempt to exterminate us. Therefore the government has announced in the newspapers and over the radio that on the twenty-seventh of this month, the eve of the tenth anniversary of the National Revolution, Lisbon will witness a spectacle without precedent, namely a mock air raid somewhere in the Baixa, more technically it will be a demonstration of an attack by air with the purpose of destroying the Rossio railroad station and blocking all points of access to the aforementioned station by filling the area with tear gas. First a reconnaissance plane flies over the Rossio and marks the target with a smoke signal. Certain critics say that the attack would be far more effective if the planes dropped their bombs without giving any warning, what perverted disregard for the laws of chivalry. The moment the smoke rises in the air, the defense artillery fires a shot and the appropriate sirens sound, an alarm that no one could possibly fail to hear. The police, the National Republican Guard, the Red Cross, and the fire brigade go into action immediately, the population is evacuated from those streets at greatest risk, while emergency squads rush to offer assistance and fire engines, their hoses at the ready, head for the areas where fire is most likely to break out. Meanwhile the rescue teams have been assembled, and among them is the well-known actor of stage and screen, António Silva, who leads a group of volunteer firemen from Ajuda. The squadron of enemy bombers, a fleet of biplanes, can now finally advance, they are obliged to fly low because their open cockpits are exposed to the rain and wind, and then the defending machine guns and antiaircraft artillery go into action, but since this is only a mock air raid, no planes are shot down, they swoop and attack without fear of reprisal, they do not even have to make the pretense of dropping bombs, the bombs explode by themselves down here in the Praça dos Restauradores, whose patriotic name could not save it if this were a real air raid. Nor was there any salvation for an infantry division that was heading for the Rossio, it was wiped out to the last man, we cannot imagine what they hoped to accomplish at a location which the enemy had humanely warned us was to be heavily bombed. Let us hope that this lamentable episode, a shameful blot on our army's reputation, will not be hushed up and that the General Staff will be brought before the Council of War for collective and summary execution by firing squad. The emergency services are beginning to feel the strain, stretcher bearers, nurses, and doctors selflessly struggle in the line of fire, collecting corpses, saving the wounded, the latter daubed with Mercurochrome and tincture of iodine, swathed in bandages that later will be washed and reused when there are real wounds to deal with, even if it means waiting another thirty years. Despite this heroic defense, the enemy planes launch a fresh attack, incendiary bombs land on Rossio Station, which is now devoured by flames and reduced to a pile of rubble, but our hopes of a final victory have not been entirely dashed, because there on his pedestal, bareheaded, miraculously unharmed, the statue of the king, Dom Sebastião, remains standing. Elsewhere the bombardment has caused havoc, fresh ruins now cover the old ruins of the Convento do Carmo, columns of smoke emerge from the Teatro Nacional, the casualties increase, on all sides are houses in flame, mothers scream for their little ones, children cry for their mothers, and husbands and fathers are forgotten, war is hell. In the sky overhead, the pilots, satanic, drink to the success of their mission with glasses of Fundador brandy, which also restores warmth to their frozen limbs now that the heat of the battle is waning. They make notes, draw sketches, take photographs for their dispatches, then, dipping their wings in derision, off they fly in the direction of Badajoz. We were right when we surmised that they had come from across the river Caia. The city has been transformed into a sea of flame, thousands have lost their lives, another earthquake has befallen us. Then the antiaircraft artillery fires a final shot, the sirens sound once more, and the exercise is over. The people leave their shelters and return to their homes, there are no dead or wounded, the buildings are still standing, it was all one huge joke. This, at any rate, is the program for today's spectacle.

Ricardo Reis has seen the bombardment of Urca and Praia Vermelha, but at such a distance that they might well have been mistaken for training maneuvers similar to this one, except that the next day the newspapers reported real deaths. He decides to go and take a look at the scene and the actors from the Santa Justa footbridge, keeping far enough from the center of operations to preserve the illusion of reality. But others had thought of it before him, and when Ricardo Reis arrived, there was no room on the bridge, so he started to walk down the Calçada do Carmo and found himself taking part in a pilgrimage. Had the pavement been broken and dusty, he would have thought himself on the road to Fátima, for these are all things of the spirit, airplanes, airships, and visions. He was reminded, for some reason, of the flying machine, the giant bird of Padre Bartolomeu de Gusmão, perhaps by some association of ideas, going from today's mock exercise to the air raids on Praia Vermelha and Urca, and from them, since that was Brazil, to the flying priest and the Passarola that immortalized his name, even though Padre Bartolomeu himself never flew it, whatever people may have said or will say to the contrary. At the top of the steps that descend in two flights to the Rua do Primeiro de Dezembro, Ricardo Reis sees that a crowd has gathered in the Rossio. Surprised that the public is allowed to get so close to the bombs, he nevertheless allows himself to be swept along with the stream of avid spectators who press toward the theater of war. Entering the square, he finds that the crowd is much larger than it seemed before, and too packed for anyone to pass. But he has had time to master the wiles practiced in these parts, and says as he goes, Excuse me, please, I'm a doctor. Thanks to this strategy, a lie though it is the truth, he succeeds in reaching the front lines, where he can see everything. So far no airplanes have been sighted, but the police are nervous, in the cleared areas in front of the theater and the railroad station the commanding officers issue orders, an official State automobile passes, inside are the Minister of the Interior and members of his family, including women. Other members of the entourage follow in the car behind. They will watch the exercise from the windows of the Hotel Avenida Palace. Suddenly the warning shot is fired, the anguished sirens wail, the pigeons in the Rossio soar in a flock, flapping. Something has gone wrong with the plan, excessive haste, perhaps, on the part of novices, the enemy plane was supposed to drop a smoke signal first, then the sirens were to begin their mournful chorus and the antiaircraft guns their firing. What does it matter, the day will come when bombs fall ten thousand kilometers away and we know exactly what the future holds for us. Finally the plane appears, the multitude sways, they raise their arms, There she is, there she is. A cavernous roar, an explosion, and a dense cloud of smoke rises into the sky, there is great excitement, anxiety makes people's voices hoarse, the doctors put their stethoscopes to their ears, the nurses prepare their syringes, the stretcher bearers, in their impatience, drag the stretchers on the ground. In the distance now you can hear the hum of the engines of the flying fortresses. As the moment approaches, the more timid of the spectators begin to wonder if this is not in earnest after all, some hurriedly retreat and huddle in doorways to avoid being hit by shrapnel, but the majority stay put, and once it has been confirmed that the bombs are harmless, the crowd doubles. Shells explode, the soldiers slip on their gas masks, there are not enough masks for everyone, but the important thing is to give an impression of real warfare, we know immediately who will die and who will be saved from this attack with chemical weapons, because the time has not yet come for all to perish. There is smoke everywhere, the spectators cough and sneeze, behind the Teatro Nacional erupts a turbulent black volcano, the theater itself seems to be on fire. But it is difficult to take any of this seriously. The police drive back the people in front, they are in the way of the rescue teams, while the wounded, on stretchers, forget the dramatic role assigned them and giggle like idiots, perhaps the gas they inhaled was laughing gas. Even the stretcher bearers have to stop to wipe away tears of laughter. To cap it all, just as the imaginary peril reaches its climax, a municipal road sweeper arrives on the scene with his pushcart and broom and starts sweeping up the bits of paper strewn along the gutter. He lifts the litter with his shovel, empties it into his trash can, and moves on. Oblivious of the uproar, of the people running in every direction, he enters clouds of smoke and reemerges unscathed, he does not even look up to see the Spanish planes. Once is usually enough, twice is often too much, but history is indifferent to the fine points of literary composition, which explains why she now causes a postman to appear with his bag of mail, tranquilly crossing the square. How many people must be anxiously awaiting his arrival, a letter from Coimbra may come today, a message saying, Tomorrow I shall be in your arms. This postman, aware of his responsibilities, is not one to waste time on spectacles in the street. Ricardo Reis is the only man of learning in the crowd, the only one who can see a Lisbon road sweeper and a postman and think of that famous youth in Paris who sold his cakes in the street while the enraged mob stormed the Bastille. There is really no difference between us Portuguese and the civilized world, we too have our alienated heroes, self-absorbed poets, road sweepers who tirelessly sweep, and postmen who cross the square without remembering that the letter from Coimbra should be delivered to that gentleman over there. But there's no letter from Coimbra, he says as the road sweeper sweeps and the pastry seller cries out, Cheesecakes from Sintra.

A few days later, Ricardo Reis narrated what he had seen, described the airplanes, the smoke, the deafening noise of the anti-aircraft artillery, the volleys of the machine guns, and Lydia listened attentively, sorry to have missed the fun. She laughed, Oh how funny, the business with the road sweeper, when suddenly she remembered that she also had something to tell, Do you know who escaped. She did not wait for Ricardo Reis to answer but went on, Manuel Guedes, the sailor I mentioned the other day, do you remember. Yes, I remember, but where did he escape. As he was being taken before the tribunal, and Lydia laughed with gusto. Ricardo Reis simply smiled. This country is going to the dogs, ships that launch themselves prematurely, prisoners who escape, and road sweepers, but what can one expect from a road sweeper. But Lydia was very pleased that Manuel Guedes had managed to escape.

Invisible, the cicadas sing in the palm trees on the Alto de Santa Catarina. Adamastor is deafened by their strident chorus, which scarcely merits the sweet name of music, but the question of music depends a great deal on who is listening. The enamored giant would not have heard them as he paced the shore waiting for the procuress Dóris to arrive and arrange the much desired encounter, for the sea was singing then and the beloved voice of Thetis hovered over the waters, as is usually said of the spirit of God. But it is the male cicada that sings, rubbing his wings furiously to produce this obsessive, relentless sound, like a marble cutter's screech upon striking some harder vein inside the stone. It is stifling hot. In Fátima the sun had been a burning ember, but then for days the sky was overcast, it even drizzled. In the lowlands, the flood has finally subsided, all that remains of that vast inland sea are small pools of scummy water which the sun is gradually drying up. In the morning, when the air is still fresh, the old men bring their umbrellas, but the heat now has grown oppressive, so the umbrellas serve as parasols, which leads us to conclude that the usefulness of an object is more important than the names we give it, yet in the final analysis, like it or not, we always come back to words. The ships enter and leave with their flags, smokestacks, antlike sailors, deafening sirens. A sailor, after hearing that din so often during storms at sea, ends up learning to speak on equal terms with the deity of the deep. These two old men have never been to sea, but their blood does not chill when they hear that mighty roar, mighty though muffled by distance, it is deeper down that they quake, as if there were ships sailing through the channels of their veins, ships lost in the darkness of their bodies, amid the gigantic bones of the world. As the heat becomes sultry, the old men retrace their steps, it is time for lunch and those time-honored hours of siesta in the shade of their own homes. When the heat abates, they will return to the Alto to sit on the same bench, but with their umbrellas open, because the protection of the trees, as we know, is unreliable, the sun only has to descend a little and the shade of the palm trees is gone. These old men will die without learning that palm trees are not trees, incredible, that people can be so ignorant. But, as in the case of umbrella and parasol, it is of no importance that a palm tree is not a tree, what matters is the shade it gives, and if we were to ask that gentleman, the doctor who comes here every afternoon, whether a palm tree is a tree or not, he would have to go home to consult his encyclopedia of botany, unless he left it behind in Brazil. Most likely all he knows about the vegetable world is the skimp imagery with which he adorns his poems, flowers in general, a few laurels because they date from mythological times, some trees bearing no name but tree, vines and sunflowers, the rushes that tremble in the current, the ivy of oblivion, the lilies, and the roses, the roses. The old men converse freely with Ricardo Reis, but when he leaves his apartment it does not cross his mind to ask them, Did you know that a palm tree is not a tree. And because they are so sure of what they think they know, it will never occur to them to ask him, Doctor, is the palm tree a tree. One day they will go their separate ways and the fundamental question of whether the palm tree is a tree because it resembles a tree, or whether this passing shadow we cast on the ground is life because it resembles life, will remain unanswered.

Ricardo Reis has got into the habit of rising late. He has learned to suppress any desire to eat in the morning. The opulent trays Lydia used to bring to his room at the Hotel Bragança now seem to belong to someone else's past. He sleeps late, wakes up and goes back to sleep again, he studies his own sleeping, and after numerous attempts has succeeded in fixing his mind on a single dream, always the same dream, about one who dreams that he does not wish to conceal one dream with another, like erasing telltale footprints, It is simple, all you have to do is drag the branch of a tree behind you, leaving only scattered leaves and pieces of twig, which soon wither and merge with the dust. When he gets up, it is time for lunch. Washing, shaving, dressing are mechanical acts in which the mind barely participates. This face covered with lather is a mask that could fit any man's face, and when the razor little by little reveals what is underneath, Ricardo Reis is intrigued by what he sees, and disturbed, as if afraid that some evil might emerge. He examines himself carefully in the mirror, comparing this face with the different, unknown face he once had. He tells himself that as long as he shaves every day, sees every day these eyes, this mouth, this nose, this chin, these pale cheeks, these crumpled, absurd appendages called ears, that such a change is impossible, and yet he feels certain he spent years in some place without mirrors, because today he looks and does not recognize himself. Often, going out to lunch, he encounters the old men coming down the street, they greet him, Good afternoon, Doctor, and he replies, Good afternoon, though he does not know their names, they might as well be trees or palms. When he feels inclined, he goes to a movie, but usually he returns to his apartment after lunch. The park is deserted in the fierce glare of the sun, the river's shimmering gleam dazzles the eyes, and Adamastor, embedded in rock, is about to send forth a mighty cry, enraged at the face the sculptor gave him, aggrieved for reasons we have known ever since Camões's epic. Like the old men, Ricardo Reis takes refuge in the shade of his dwelling, where little by little the former mustiness has returned. Lydia opens all the windows when she comes, but it doesn't help, the smell seems to emanate from the furniture, from the very walls, the contest is definitely unequal, and Lydia comes less frequently these days. Toward evening, with the first breeze, Ricardo Reis goes and sits on a bench in the park, neither too close nor too far from the old men. Giving them his morning newspaper when he is done with it is his only act of charity. He does not offer them food, they have not asked for any, although they have not asked for these printed sheets of news either, you can decide which act of generosity would be the greater if both were made. If we asked Ricardo Reis what he does at home, alone all that time, he would simply shrug, perhaps he has forgotten that he did some reading, wrote a little poetry, wandered down corridors, spent some time at the rear of the building looking into the courtyard below, the clotheslines, white sheets, towels, and the hen coops, and the cats sleeping on the walls in the shade. There are no dogs, but, then, there are no possessions that need guarding. Then he went back to his reading, to his poetry, writing, rewriting, or tearing up when the poem was not worth keeping. Then he waited for the heat to abate, for the first breeze of the evening. As he was going downstairs, the neighbor on the second floor appeared on the landing. Time had softened the malicious gossip, there was no longer the same interest, the entire building had been restored to harmony and amiable coexistence. Well now, is your husband feeling better, he inquired, and the neighbor replied, Thanks to you, Doctor, your help was an act of providence, a miracle. That is what we are all seeking, acts of providence and miracles, and is it not a miracle to have a doctor living next door who can come to our assistance when we have a pain in the tummy. Has he emptied his bowels. He got rid of the whole load, thanks be to God, Doctor. Such is life, the hand that writes the prescription for the laxative also writes the sublime or at least acceptable line, *You have sun if there is sun, flowers if there are flowers, and good fortune if fortune smiles.*

The old men read the newspaper. We already know that one of them is illiterate, he is therefore more generous when it comes to making comments, his opinions are a way of balancing the scale. If one man knows, the other explains. I say, this story about Loon Six Hundred is really very funny, I've known him for years, I knew him when he drove a tram, he was always crashing into carts and wagons, he loved it, they put him in jail thirty-eight times and finally sacked him, he was incorrigible, but the cart drivers were partly to blame, they go at a snail's pace, never hurry, and there was Loon Six Hundred stamping on the bell with the heel of his boot, foaming at the mouth until he could stand it no longer, so he rammed them, bang, and there was a fight, and the police came and marched everybody off to jail, but now Loon Six Hundred drives a cart too and fights with the tram drivers, his former colleagues, because they treat him the way he used to treat the cart drivers, as the old saying goes, As ye sow. Thus concluded the old man who could not read, with an aphorism, which had a medicinal, binding effect on his speech. Ricardo Reis was seated on the same bench, a rare occurrence, but today all the others were occupied. Aware that the old man's monologue was for his benefit, he asked, This nickname Loon Six Hundred, how did he get it. Whereupon the illiterate replied, Six hundred was his number when he worked for the tram company and people called him Loon because of his behavior. I see. When the old men went back to their reading, Ricardo Reis allowed his thoughts to wander, What nickname would suit me, perhaps Doctor Bard, Back-from-Brazil, the Spiritualist, Jack the Ode Maker, Chess Player, Casanova of Chambermaids. Suddenly the old man who was reading said, Orphan of Fortune, the nickname of a petty thief, a pickpocket caught in the act. Why not Orphan of Fortune for Ricardo Reis and Ricardo Reis for the pickpocket, a criminal could have his name, names do not choose destinies. The old men love to read about the colorful dramas of everyday life, the cases of fraud, disorderly conduct, acts of violence or despair, dark deeds in the night, crimes of passion, an abandoned fetus, a car crash, a calf born with two heads, a bitch that suckles cats, at least this bitch is not like Ugolina who ate her young. Their conversation now turns to Micas Saloia whose real name is Maria Conceição and who has received one hundred and sixty prison sentences for theft besides being exiled to Africa several times. Then there was Judite Meleças the bogus countess from Castelo Melhor who cheated a lieutenant of the National Republican Guard out of two contos and fifty reis, a sum of money that will seem rather paltry fifty years from now but in these lean times it is almost a fortune, as the women of Benavente, who work from dawn to dusk for ten thousand reis, can testify. The rest is less interesting. As announced, a gala day was held at the Jockey Club with thousands of guests, we need not be surprised that so many attended, we know how the Portuguese love celebrations, particularly celebrations organized on behalf of the flood victims of Ribatejo, among whom is Micas da Borda d'Agua from Benavente, who will receive her share of the forty-five thousand seven hundred and fifty-three escudos and five and a half centavos collected, although some accounting still has to be done, because there are a few not inconsiderable invoices outstanding, and tax bills. But the high standard and elegant presentation of the events on the program made it all worthwhile, the band of the National Republican Guard gave a concert, two troops of horsemen from the same guard staged a carousel and charge, patrols from the Cavalry School of Torres Novas demonstrated various maneuvers, there was a display of cowboy skills, the rounding up and throwing of steers from Ribatejo, and *nuestros hermanos* were represented, cattle drovers from Seville and Badajoz come expressly to take part in the festivities. In order to have a chat with them and hear the latest from Spain, the dukes of Alba and Medinaceli, guests at the Hotel Bragança, descended into the arena, a fine example of peninsular solidarity on their part, there is nothing like being a Spanish grandee in Portugal.

News from the rest of the world has not changed a great deal, the strikes continue in France, where there are now about five hundred thousand workers on strike, the government headed by Albert Sarraut is expected to resign and be succeeded by a new ministry which Léon Blum will organize, and the impression will be created, at least temporarily, that the demonstrators are satisfied. As for Spain, the drovers from Seville and Badajoz converse with the dukes, Here we are respected more than grandees of Portugal, Then remain here with us and we shall drive cattle together. In Spain, as we were saying, the strikers are sprouting up like mushrooms and Largo Caballero warns that until the working classes are protected by the law, outbreaks of violence can be expected, and if he says that, a man who supports the working classes, it must be true, therefore we must prepare ourselves for the worst. Better late than never, on the other hand there's no point closing the stable door after the horse has bolted, look at the British, they abandoned the Ethiopians to their fate and now applaud their Emperor, if you ask me, my dear fellow, this is nothing but one great swindle. The old men on the Alto de Santa Catarina chat pleasantly on, though the doctor has returned to his apartment, they talk about animals, about the white wolf that appeared in Riodades, near São João da Pesqueira, and that the local inhabitants call Pombo, and about the lioness Nádia that mauled the fakir Blacaman's leg in the Teatro Coliseu in full view of the audience, thus proving that circus artists really do put their lives at risk. If Ricardo Reis had not left so soon he could have taken this opportunity to tell them the story of the bitch Ugolina, completing the triumvirate of wild beasts, the wolf still at large, the lioness whose dose of drugs will have to be increased, the bitch, who eats her children, Pombo, Nádia, Ugolina, animals have nicknames as well as men.

Early one morning, as Ricardo Reis lies dozing, very early indeed considering his indolence of late, he hears the warships on the Tagus firing salvos, twenty-one solemn booms at regular intervals, making the windowpanes rattle. He thought another war had broken out, then remembered what he had read the previous day, this is the tenth of June, Portugal's National Holiday commemorating our forefathers and affirming our dedication to the achievements of the future. Half-asleep, he wondered whether he had the energy to jump out of these grubby sheets and throw the windows wide open to let the heroically echoing salutes enter unimpeded and disperse the shadows from his apartment, the mildew, the insidious smell of must. But while he was turning this over in his mind and debating with himself, the last vibrations fell away. Once more a great silence descended upon the Alto de Santa Catarina, but Ricardo Reis did not notice, he had closed his eyes and gone back to sleep. Such is a life badly managed, we sleep when we should be on our guard, we depart when we should be arriving, we close the window when we should leave it open. In the afternoon, returning from lunch, he saw bunches of flowers at the foot of the statue of Camões, homage from the Federation of Patriots to the epic poet, the great bard of the nation's valor, that all may know that we have shaken off the enfeebling and degrading melancholy we suffered in the sixteenth century. Today, believe me, we are a very happy people. As soon as darkness falls we will switch on floodlights here in the square and Senhor Camões will be lit up, what am I saying, he will be completely transformed by the dazzling splendor. True, he is blind in the right eye, but he can still see with his left, and if he finds the light too strong let him speak up, we can easily dim the intensity to twilight, to the original gloom that we have by now grown so accustomed to. Had Ricardo Reis gone out this evening, he would have met Fernando Pessoa in the Praça de Luís de Camões, seated on one of those benches as if enjoying the breeze. Both families and solitary souls have come in search of the same refreshment, and there is so much light, it is almost like day, faces glow as if touched by ecstasy, one can understand why this day is called the Feast of the Nation. To mark the occasion, Fernando Pessoa tries to recite, in his mind, the poem from *Mensagem* that is dedicated to Camões, and it takes him some time to realize that there is no such poem. Can this be possible. Only by looking it up can he be certain. From Ulysses to Dom Sebastião not a single hero escaped him, not even the prophets Bandarra and Vieira, yet apparently he failed even to mention the One-Eyed Bard. This omission causes Fernando Pessoa's hands to tremble, his conscious asks, Why, his unconscious can provide no explanation, then Luís de Camões smiles, his bronzed mouth has the knowing expression of one who died long ago, It was envy, my dear Pessoa, but forget it, don't torment yourself so, here nothing has importance, the day will come when they disown you a hundred times, another day will come when you wish to be disowned a hundred times. At this very moment, in his third-floor apartment on the Rua de Santa Catarina, Ricardo Reis is trying to write a poem to Marcenda so that posterity will not say she passed in vain, *Already impatient for the summer, I also weep for its flowers, knowing they must fade.* This will be the first part of the ode, so far no one would guess that he speaks of Marcenda, but poets often begin at the horizon, for that is the shortest path to the heart. Half an hour later, or an hour later, or more, because when it comes to writing poetry time either drags or races, the middle part has taken form, it is not the lament it first seemed, rather the acceptance of that which has no remedy, *Having crossed the inevitable threshold of each year, I begin to see before me the flowerless valley, the rumbling abyss.* It is dawn, the entire city sleeps, and the floodlights on the statue of Camões, because with no onlookers they now serve no purpose, have gone out. Fernando Pessoa returns home, says, I'm back,

Grandmother, and at that precise moment the poem completes itself, with difficulty, a semicolon was reluctantly inserted, Ricardo Reis long resisted it, did not want it, but it won, *And I pick the rose because fortune picks Marcenda, and cherish it, let it wither on my breast and not on the vast diurnal curving bosom of the globe.* Ricardo Reis lay fully dressed on the bed, his left hand resting on the sheet of paper, if he should pass now from sleep to death, people will mistake it for his will, a letter of farewell, they will not know what to make of it even after they read it, for whoever heard of a woman called Marcenda. Such a name comes from another planet, Blimunda too is an example, a mysterious name waiting to be used by an unknown woman. At least a woman named Marcenda has been found, but she lives far away.

Here beside him on this same bed was Lydia, when they felt the earth move. The tremor was brief but shook the building from top to bottom before it passed, sending the neighbors onto the stairs in hysterics and causing the chandelier to swing like a pendulum. Gripped by terror, those voices sounded obscene. The entire city, perhaps with the terrible memory of other earthquakes still embedded in its stones, waited in suspense, in the unbearable silence that follows the tremor, when one cannot think but asks himself, Will the tremor return, Will I die. Ricardo Reis and Lydia stayed in bed. They were naked, lying on their backs like statues without even a sheet covering them. Death, had it come, would have found them submissive, satisfied, still breathing heavily, wet with sweat and intimate secretions, their hearts pounding, because their bodies had separated only a few minutes ago, as full of life as possible. Suddenly the bed shudders, the furniture rocks, the floor and ceiling creak, this is not the vertiginous final moment of orgasm, it is the earth roaring from its depths. We are going to die, Lydia said, yet she did not clutch the man beside her as one might have expected. Women as a rule are like this, it is the men who say in terror, It's nothing, stay calm, it has passed, words spoken to reassure themselves, not others. Trembling with fear, Ricardo Reis said this too, and he was right, the tremor passed, the neighbors shouting on the stairs gradually calmed, but the discussion continued, one of them went down to the street, another went to her window, both watching the general uproar. As peace is gradually restored, Lydia turns to Ricardo Reis and he to her, the arm of each over the body of each, and he repeats, It was nothing, and she smiles, but her smile has a different meaning, she is clearly not thinking about the tremor. They lie looking at each other yet so distant from each other, so apart in their thoughts, as we now see when suddenly she confides, I think I'm pregnant, I'm ten days late. The student of medicine has been taught the mysteries of the human body, he knows therefore how the spermatozoa swim upstream inside the woman until they reach the source of life, from books he learns these things and sees them confirmed in practice, yet look how stunned he is, as stunned as an ignorant Adam who cannot fathom how this could have happened however much Eve explains. He tries to gain time, What did you say. I'm ten days late, I think I'm pregnant. Once again, of the two she is the more composed. For the past week, every day, every second, she has thought of nothing else, perhaps she thought of this even a moment ago when she said, We are going to die. One wonders whether Ricardo Reis was included in that plural. He expects her to ask a question, for example, What should I do, but she remains silent, concealing her pubis with a slight bending of the knees. There is no visible sign of pregnancy, unless we can decipher what her eyes are saying, fixed on some personal horizon, if eyes possess such a thing. Ricardo Reis searches for the right words but all he finds within himself is indifference, as if, though aware that he is obliged to help solve the problem, he does not feel implicated in its cause. Rather, he sees himself in the role of the doctor to whom a patient has blurted out her guilty secret, Ah, Doctor, what is to become of me, I am pregnant and this could not have happened at a worse moment. The doctor does not tell her, Have an abortion, don't be a fool. On the contrary, he puts on a grave air, If you and your husband have taken no precautions, in all probability you are pregnant, but let's wait a few more days, you could simply be late, sometimes that happens. But Ricardo Reis cannot speak with such neutrality, he is the father, for there is no evidence that in the last few months Lydia has slept with any man but him, still the father is at a loss for words. Finally, feeling his way with the utmost caution, weighing every phrase, he distributes the blame, We were careless, this had to happen sooner or later. But Lydia does not ask, What care should I have taken. He never withdrew at the critical moment, never used those rubber caps, but this does not worry her, she simply says, I'm pregnant. After all, it happens to nearly every woman, becoming pregnant is no earthquake. Ricardo Reis makes a decision, he must know her intentions, there is no point in evading the issue any longer, Are you thinking of having the child. Just as well that there is no one eavesdropping, otherwise Ricardo Reis would find himself accused of suggesting an abortion, but before the witnesses have been heard and the judge passes sentence, Lydia steps forward and declares, I am going to have the baby. For the first time, Ricardo Reis feels a finger touch his heart. It is not pain he experiences, or a twitch or chill, but a sensation like no other, like the first hand-shake of men from two different planets, both human beings yet completely alien to each other. What is an embryo of ten days, Ricardo Reis asks himself, and can find no answer. In his years as a doctor he has seen cells multiply through a microscope, he has seen detailed illustrations in books, but now he sees nothing but this silent, somber, unmarried woman, a hotel chambermaid by profession, Lydia, her breasts and belly exposed, only her pubis shyly hidden as if keeping a secret. He pulled her to him, and she yielded like someone finally taking refuge from the world, suddenly blushing and overjoyed and pleading like a timid bride, You aren't angry with me. What an idea, why should I be angry. These words are not sincere, because a great anger now surges inside Ricardo Reis, I've got myself into a fine mess, he is thinking, if she doesn't have an abortion, I'll end up with a child on my hands, I'll have to acknowledge it as mine, I am morally obliged, what a mess, I never thought anything like this would happen to me. Snuggling up closer, Lydia wanted him to hold her tight, because it felt good, and casually she uttered these incredible words, If you don't want to acknowledge the child, I don't mind, the child can be illegitimate, like me. Ricardo Reis felt his eyes fill with tears, some tears of shame, some of pity, if anyone can tell the difference, and in a sudden impulse, sincere at last, he embraced and kissed her. Imagine, he kissed her long and on the lips, relieved of this tremendous burden. There are such moments in life, we think we are experiencing passion and it is merely a rush of gratitude. But sensuality pays little attention to these subtleties, within seconds Lydia and Ricardo Reis are copulating, moaning and sighing, they need not worry now, the child has already been conceived.

These are days of bliss. On vacation from her job at the hotel, Lydia spends nearly all her time with Ricardo Reis and goes home only to sleep at her mother's house, out of propriety, to avoid gossip among the neighbors, who notwithstanding the good relations established ever since the doctor offered some medical advice, continue to comment slyly on these disgraceful associations between master and servant, all too common in this Lisbon of ours no matter how carefully disguised. Someone of greater moral fastidiousness might insinuate that people can also do during the day what they normally do at night, but another could reply that during the day there is no time, because of the great spring cleaning done in houses every Easter after the long winter, which explains why the doctor's charwoman comes early each morning and leaves almost at dusk, and work she does, for all to see and hear, with feather duster and cloth, scrub brush and broom. Sometimes the windows are closed and there is a sudden silence, but is it not natural for a person to rest between one chore and another, to untie the kerchief on her head, to loosen her clothes, to groan from a new and sweet exertion. The apartment is celebrating Resurrection Saturday and Easter Sunday by the grace and labor of this humble servant who passes her hands over things and leaves them spotless and gleaming, not even in the days of Dona Luísa and the Appeals Court Judge, with a regiment of maids to do the shopping and the cooking, did these walls and furniture shine with such luster, blessed be Lydia among women. Marcenda, were she living here as the legitimate mistress of the household, could not compete, not even with two good hands. A few days ago the place smelled of mildew, dust, must, blocked drains, and now light penetrates the most remote corners, makes all the glass look like crystal, polishes every surface, the ceiling itself becomes starlit with reflections when the sun enters the windows, a celestial abode, a diamond within a diamond, and it was through menial housework that this sublime transformation was achieved. Perhaps also the abode is celestial because of the frequency with which Lydia and Ricardo Reis make love, such is their pleasure in giving and taking, I cannot think what has come over these two that they are suddenly so demanding and so generous with their favors. Could it be the summer that is heating their blood, could it be the presence of that tiny ferment in her womb, the ferment is nothing in this world as yet, yet already it has some influence in governing it.

But now Lydia's vacation is over and everything returns to normal, she will come, as before, once a week on her day off. Now, even when the sun finds an open window, the light is different, weaker, and the sieve of time has started once more to sift the impalpable dust that makes outlines fade and blurs features. When Ricardo Reis turns down the bedcover at night, he barely sees the pillow where he will rest his head, and in the morning he cannot rise without first identifying himself with his own hands, line by line, what he can still find of himself, like a fingerprint partially obliterated by a large scar. One night Fernando Pessoa, who does not always appear when he is needed, knocked on his door. I was beginning to think I'd never see you again, Ricardo Reis told him. I haven't been out much of late, I get lost so easily, like a forgetful old woman, the only thing that saves me is the mental picture I still have of the statue of Camões, working from there, I can usually get my bearings. Let's hope they don't remove him, given this latest mania of removing things, you should see what's happening on the Avenida da Liberdade, they have stripped it bare. I haven't been back there, I know nothing about it. They have removed or are about to remove the statue of Pinheiro Chagas, and that of a certain José Luís Monteiro, whom I've never heard of. Nor I, but as for Pinheiro Chagas, they have done the right thing. Be quiet, you don't know what awaits you. They will never erect a statue to commemorate me, only if they have no shame, I'm not one for statues. I couldn't agree more, there can be nothing more depressing than having a statue as part of one's destiny, let them raise statues to military leaders and politicians, who like that sort of thing, we are men of words only and words cannot be set in bronze and stone, they are words, nothing more, look at Camões, where are his words. That is why they made him a fop at court. A D'Artagnan. With a sword at his side, any puppet looks good, I'm sure I would cut a ridiculous figure. Don't upset yourself, you might escape this curse, and if you don't, like Rigoletto, you can always hope that they will pull your statue down one day, as in the case of Pinheiro Chagas, and transfer it to a quiet spot or store it in some warehouse, it is happening all the time, some people are even demanding that the statue of Chiado be removed. Chiado too, what do they have against Chiado. They say he was a scurrilous buffoon and is not fit for the elegant site where his statue stands. On the contrary, Chiado could not stand in a better place, one cannot imagine Camões without Chiado, besides they lived in the same century, if there is anything that needs changing it is the position in which they put the friar, he should be turned to face the epic poet with hand outstretched, not a begging hand but an offering, giving hand. Camões needs nothing from Chiado. Camões is no longer alive, therefore we have no idea what he needs or doesn't need. Ricardo Reis went to the kitchen to get some coffee, returned to the study, sat opposite Fernando Pessoa, and said, It always feels strange not being able to offer you a cup of coffee. Pour another cup and put it in front of me, I'll keep you company while you drink. I cannot get used to the idea that you do not exist. Seven months have passed already, enough time to engender a life, but you know more about that than I do, you are a doctor. Is there some veiled hint in that last remark. What veiled hint should I make. I'm not sure. You are touchy today. Perhaps it's this business of removing statues, this proof of how fickle human loyalties can be, the Discus Thrower is another example. What discus thrower, The one on the Avenida, Now I remember, that naked youth pretending to be Greek, Well, he too has been removed. But why. They said he looked effeminate, they spoke of moral health and protecting the eyes of the city's inhabitants from shameful displays of nudity. If the youth was not exaggerated in any of his physical proportions, what harm was he doing. Those so-called proportions, although neither exaggerated nor excessive, were more than sufficient to illustrate certain details of the male anatomy. But I thought they said the youth looked effeminate, is that not what they said. Yes. Then surely he offended because he was found wanting, not because there was too much of him. I am only repeating as best I can the rumors circulating in the city. My dear Reis, are the Portuguese gradually taking leave of their senses. If you who lived here ask this question, how can a man who lived abroad for so many years be expected to answer it.

Ricardo Reis, finishing his coffee, now debated whether or not to read the poem he had dedicated to Marcenda, the one beginning, *Already impatient for the summer*. When finally he made up his mind and began to rise from the sofa, Fernando Pessoa pleaded with him with a sadly vacant smile, pleaded, Distract me, you must have other scandals to confide. Whereupon Ricardo Reis, without needing to pause for thought, announced in seven words the biggest scandal of all, I am about to become a father. Fernando Pessoa looked at him in astonishment, then burst out laughing, he could not believe it, You're joking. Ricardo Reis said somewhat stiffly, I am not joking, besides I fail to understand your surprise, if a man regularly sleeps with a woman, in all likelihood she will conceive, that is what happened in my case. Who is the mother, your Lydia or your Marcenda, or is there a third woman, with you one never knows. There is no third woman, and I did not marry Marcenda. Ah, so you would have a child with Marcenda only if you were married to her. Well, obviously, you know the strict morality observed in traditional families. And chambermaids have no such scruples. Sometimes they do. True, remember when Álvaro de Campos told us how he was mocked by a hotel chambermaid. Not in that sense. In what sense, then. A hotel chambermaid is also a woman. The things one learns after one is dead. You don't know Lydia. My dear Reis, I shall always treat the matter of your child with the greatest respect, nay, veneration, but having never been a father myself, I know not how to translate these metaphysical feelings into the tedious reality of everyday life. Stop being ironic. Your sudden paternity must have dulled your senses, otherwise you would perceive that there is nothing ironic in what I am saying. Irony there most certainly is, though it may go under the guise of something else. Irony, rather, is the disguise. A disguise for what. Perhaps for grief. Don't tell me that it grieves you never to have had a child. Who knows. Have you regrets. I am the most regretting

315

of persons and today do not even have the heart to deny it. You regret that you regret. That habit I had to give up when I died, there are certain things on this side that are not permitted. Fernando Pessoa stroked his mustache and asked, Are you still thinking of going back to Brazil. There are days when I seem to be back there already, and there are days when I have the impression that I was never there at all. You are floating, in other words, in midocean, neither here nor there. Like the rest of the Portuguese. But this gives you an excellent opportunity to make a new life for yourself, with a wife and child. I have no intention of marrying Lydia, and I still haven't decided whether I will acknowledge the child as mine. If you will allow me to express an opinion, my dear Reis, you are a cad. Perhaps, but Álvaro de Campos took loans he never repaid, He was a cad too, You never really got along with him, I never really got along with you, We never really understood each other, That was inevitable, since each of us was a multitude of different people. What I do not understand is this high moral tone of yours, this conservatism. A dead man by definition is a conservative, he cannot bear any tampering with order. You once fulminated against order. Now I fulminate on its behalf. If you were alive and found yourself in my shoes, with an unwanted child, its mother from a lower class, you would have the doubts I have. The very same. The doubts of a cad. That's right, dear Reis, of a cad. I may be a cad, but I have no intention of abandoning Lydia. Perhaps because she is making things easy for you. True enough, she told me there was no need for me to acknowledge the child as mine. Why are women like this, Not all of them, Agreed, but only women can be like this. Anyone listening to you would think you had a great deal of experience with women. The only experience I have is that of a spectator, an observer. No, one has to sleep with them, make them pregnant, even if it ends in abortion, one has to see them when they are sad and happy, laughing and weeping, silent and talkative, one has to watch them when they do not know that they are being watched. And what does an experienced man see at such moments? An enigma, a labyrinth, a charade. I was always good at charades, But a disaster when it came to women, My dear Reis, that is not kind, Forgive me, my nerves are humming like a telephone wire in a strong wind. You are forgiven. I have no job and no interest in looking for one, I spend my days sitting here in my apartment, sitting in some restaurant, or on a bench in the park, as if I had nothing to do but sit and wait for death. Let the child be born. It isn't up to me, and a child wouldn't solve anything, I feel that it does not belong to me. You think someone else might be the father. No, I'm certain I'm the father, that's not the problem, the problem is that only the mother truly exists, the father is an accident. A necessary accident. Undoubtedly, but dispensable once the necessity has been provided, so dispensable that he could die at once, like a praying mantis. You are as frightened of women as I was, Perhaps even more. Did you ever hear from Marcenda again, Not a word, but I wrote a poem to her several days ago, Are you serious, Well, to be frank, it's only a poem in which her name appears, would you like me to read it to you. No. Why not. I know your poetry by heart, both the poems you have written and the poems you will write, the only novelty would be the name Marcenda. Now it is your turn to be unkind. Nor can I ask to be forgiven on the grounds that my nerves are bad, go ahead, then, and read me the poem. *Already impatient for the summer.* And the second line could be, *I also weep for its flowers.* That's right. As you can see, we know everything about each other, or at least I about you, Is there anything that belongs only to me, Probably not. After Fernando Pessoa left, Ricardo Reis drank what remained of the coffee in his cup, it was cold but tasted good.

A few days later the newspapers reported that twenty-five Hitler Youth students from Hamburg, visiting our country in order to study and promote National-Socialist ideals, were guests of honor at the Teacher Training College. After an extensive tour of the Exhibition to Mark the Tenth Anniversary of the National Revolution, they wrote the following in the Roll of Honor, We are nobody. This meant, as the clerk on duty hastened to explain, that the people are indeed nobody if not guided by the elite, the cream, the flower, the chosen few of our society. Note that the word *chosen* derives from *choice* which implies *election*, for we would have our people guided by the chosen few if they can choose them, whereas to be guided by a flower or by a cream is ridiculous, at least in the

Portuguese language, so let us use the French word *élite* until such time as we find something better in German. Perhaps with this in mind the creation of the Portuguese Youth Movement has been decreed, in October its activities will start in earnest, the Movement will have a membership of two hundred thousand youths, the flower or cream of our youth, from which, hopefully, the elite will emerge, destined to govern us when the present regime comes to an end. If Lydia's child is born and survives, in a few years' time he will be able to take part in parades, enroll in the junior ranks of the Portuguese Youth Movement, don the green and khaki uniform, display on his belt the letter S, which stands for Serve and Salazar, or Serve Salazar, therefore a double S, SS, extending his right arm in Roman-style salute. And Marcenda, with her aristocratic background, will enroll in the Women's Organization for National Education, she too will raise her right arm, since it is only the left that is paralyzed. To show how our patriotic youth is shaping up, representatives of the Portuguese Youth Movement will travel to Berlin in uniform, let us hope they will have an opportunity to repeat that celebrated phrase, We are nobody. They will also attend the Olympic Games, where, needless to say, they will make a splendid impression, these proud and comely youths, the glory of the Lusitanian race, the mirror of our future, a blossoming tree that extends its branches in Roman salute. My son, Lydia tells Ricardo Reis, will have nothing to do with such a farce, and with these words we could start an argument that would last ten years, if we live that long.

Victor is nervous. This mission is one of enormous responsibility, not to be compared with the routine job of tailing suspects, bribing hotel managers, interrogating porters who spill the beans immediately. He puts his right hand to his hip to feel the reassuring presence of his pistol, then takes from the inside pocket of his jacket, very slowly, with the tip of his fingers, a peppermint lozenge. He unwraps it with infinite care, because in the silence of the night the sound of rustling paper can be heard ten paces away, this is unwise of him, an infringement of security regulations, but the smell of onion, perhaps because of his nervousness, has become intense and there is the danger that at the critical moment his prey might flee, being downwind of him. Hidden behind tree trunks, concealed in doorways, Victor's henchmen are waiting for the signal, they gaze steadily at the window from which filters an almost invisible thread of light, the fact that the inside shutters are closed in this heat is itself an indication of conspiracy. One of Victor's henchmen hefts the crowbar with which he will prize open the door, another slips the fingers of his left hand into an iron knuckle-duster, both men, much experienced, will leave a trail of shattered hinges and broken jaws. On the sidewalk opposite stands another policeman, behaving like an innocent passerby or rather a law-abiding citizen returning home to this building, but he does not rap with the knocker for his wife to come and open up, What kept you so late. In less than fifteen seconds the door is opened just as effectively by crowbar, the first obstacle overcome. The policeman waits on the staircase, his job is to listen carefully, to give warning if he hears anything, to let Victor know, for Victor is the brains behind this operation. In the doorway the shadowy form of the policeman appears, he lights a cigarette, which means that all is well, no suspicions have been aroused on the floor they have surrounded. Victor spits out the peppermint, he is afraid of choking at the height of the action, should there be hand-to-hand combat, he breathes through his mouth, relishes the freshness of the peppermint, he no longer seems the same Victor. But he has barely taken three steps before that telltale effluvium again rises from his stomach, its one advantage, considerable, is that the henchmen, following their leader, will not lose him. Only two remain behind, watching the window for any attempt to escape, in which case they have been given orders to shoot without first calling out. The squad of six men ascends Indian file, like a procession of ants, in the total silence, and the air grows close and electric with tension. The men have all become so nervous, they do not even notice their chief's stench, you could almost say that everything now smells the same. Having reached the landing, they begin to wonder if there is really anyone in the building, the silence is so deep that the entire world appears to be asleep. If Victor's information were not so reliable, he would give everyone orders to return to the usual snooping, shadowing of suspects, asking questions, paying for answers. Inside the apartment someone coughs. The tip-off has been confirmed. Victor aims his flashlight at the door, like a wise cobra the cleft crowbar advances, introduces its fangs between the jamb and the door, and waits. Now it is Victor's turn, with his knuckle-duster he strikes the door with the four blows of destiny, yells, Police, the crowbar gives the first wrench, the jamb splinters, the lock grates, inside there is uproar, chairs overturned, the sound of rapid footsteps, voices. No one move, Victor shouts in a commanding voice, his nervousness gone, and suddenly the lights go on on all the landings. The neighbors, wanting to join the fun, dare not enter the stage but have illuminated it. Someone must have opened a window, because three shots can be heard from the street. Changing position, the crowbar tries the crack at the lower hinge, the door splits from top to bottom, gapes open, and with two mighty kicks the henchmen bring it to the ground. The door first crashes against the facing wall of the corridor, then collapses sideways, making a large gash in the plaster. A great silence has descended on the apartment, there is no escaping now. Victor advances with pistol in hand, Nobody move. Flanked by two henchmen, he enters the room, which looks onto the street, the window is open and outside, below, the men are keeping watch, while here in the room are four men on their feet, their hands in the air, their heads lowered, defeated. Victor smiles with satisfaction, You are all under arrest, you are all under arrest. He gathers up some papers, which lie scattered on the table, orders the search to begin, calls the policeman over, the one with the knuckle-duster who is looking very sorry for himself because there was no resistance and thus no chance to land a single blow, and tells him to go to the back and see if anyone escaped. They hear him call out from the kitchen hatch, then from the fire escape, to his colleagues who were covering the other exits, Did you see anyone escape. They replied that one escaped, in the report to-morrow it will be written that a man was seen climbing over the walls of the courtyard or jumping from rooftop to rooftop, the versions will vary. The policeman with the knuckle-duster returns, looking very sour, Victor does not need to be told, he starts bellowing, livid with rage, the last trace of peppermint gone, What a bunch of idiots. And when he sees that the arrested men cannot suppress a smile of triumph, however wan, he realizes that it was none other than the ringleader who gave them the slip, now he is foaming at the mouth, uttering dire threats, demanding to know the fugitive's name, his destination, Speak or you all die. His henchmen aim their pistols, the one with the knuckle-duster raises his arm, fist clenched, then the director says, Cut. Still beside himself with rage, Victor cannot calm down, for him this is no laughing matter, ten men needed to capture five, and they allowed the ring-leader, the brains behind the conspiracy, to give them the slip, but the producer intervenes good-naturedly, the filming has gone so well that there is no need for a retake, Forget it, don't let it upset you, if we had caught him, that would have been the end of the film. But dear Senhor Lopes Ribeiro, the police are made to look such fools, the corps is brought into disrepute, seven men sent to kill a spider and the spider escapes in the end, that is to say the fly, because we are the spider. Let it escape, there is no lack of spiders' webs in the world, from some you escape, in others you die. The fugitive will find shelter in a boardinghouse under an assumed name, thinking he is safe, he has no idea that his spider will be the daughter of the landlady, according to the script a very serious young woman, a dedicated nationalist who will regenerate his heart and mind. Women are a powerful force, real saints, and the producer is clearly an intelligent man. They are engaged in this conversation when the cameraman, a German newly arrived from Germany, approaches, and the producer understands him, for the man practically speaks Portuguese, A *gross* plan of the *Polizei*. Victor too understands, gets into position, the cameraman's assistant claps the boards, bang, May Revolution second take, or some other phrase in a similar jargon, and Victor, brandishing his pistol, reappears at the door with a menacing and derisive smirk, You're all under arrest, you're all under arrest. If he now shouts it with less force, it's to avoid choking on the peppermint lozenge he has just popped into his mouth in order to purify the air. The cameraman declares himself satisfied, *Auf Wiedersehen, ich habe keine Zeit zu verlieren, es ist schon ziemlich spät*, Good-bye, I've no time to waste, it's getting late. Turning to the producer, *Es ist Punkt Mitternacht*, It is midnight on the dot, to which Lopes Ribeiro replies, *Machen Sie bitte das Licht aus*, Turn off the light. The translation is supplied because our German is still rudimentary. Victor has already descended with his squad, who lead their captives away handcuffed, so conscious of their duty as policemen that they take even this masquerade seriously, an arrest is an arrest even if it is only make-believe.

Other raids are being planned. Meanwhile Portugal prays and sings, because this is a time of festivities and pilgrimages, for much chanting of mystical psalms, for fireworks and wine, folk dances from Minho and open-air concerts, processions of angels with snow-white wings and floats carrying religious figures. All this under a blazing sky, heaven's reply to those long days of miserable winter, but heaven will continue to send us scattered showers and thunderstorms, because they too are the fruits of the season. And at the

Teatro de São Luís, Tomás Alcaide is singing in *Rigoletto, Manon,* and *Tosca,* and the League of Nations has decided once and for all to lift the sanctions against Italy, and the English are objecting to the flight of the zeppelin Hindenburg over factories and other strategic locations in Britain, and people are still saying that the German annexation of the Free City of Danzig is imminent, but that need not concern us, because only a sharp eye and the finger of an experienced cartographer would be able to find that tiny dot and barbaric word on the map, and the world will certainly not come to an end on that account. When all is said and done, the peace and quiet of our own hearth and home is not helped by interfering in the affairs of our neighbors. They make their own lives, let them unmake them. A rumor has been circulating, for example, that General Sanjurjo plans to enter Spain covertly to head a monarchist movement, though he tells the press that he has no intention of leaving Portugal, he and his entire family live in Monte Estoril in the villa Santa Leocádia, with a view of the sea and his conscience at rest. Some of us might say to him, Go, save your country, while others might say, Leave well enough alone, don't get involved in these problems. Because are we not all obliged to be good hosts, as we were with the dukes of Alba and Medinaceli, who not a moment too soon found refuge at the Hotel Bragança, where they say they intend to remain for some time. Unless all this is nothing more than another police raid with the script already written, the cameraman at the ready, and everyone waiting for the director to say, Action.

Ricardo Reis reads the newspapers. He remains unperturbed by the world news that reaches him, perhaps because of his temperament, or perhaps because he believes in the popular superstition which says that the more one cries doom, the less doom occurs. If this is true, then man should embrace pessimism as the surest road to happiness, and perhaps by persevering in his fear of death he may attain immortality. Ricardo Reis is not John D. Rockefeller, the newspaper he buys is the same as all the other newspapers the boy carries in his satchel or displays on the sidewalk. The world's threats are universal, like the sun, but Ricardo Reis takes shelter under his own shadow, What I do not wish to know does not exist, the only real problem is how to play the queen's knight. But reading the newspapers, he forces himself to worry a little, Europe is seething and perhaps will boil over, and there is no place for a poet to rest his head. The two old men, on the other hand, are very excited, so much so that they have decided to make the great sacrifice of buying a newspaper every day, one will buy it one day, the other the next, they can no longer wait until late afternoon. When Ricardo Reis appeared in the park to perform his customary act of charity, they were able to respond with the arrogance of the pauper who is ungrateful at heart, We already have a newspaper. They unfolded the large pages with noisy ostentation, proving yet again that one cannot trust people.

Having reverted, after Lydia's vacation, to his habit of sleeping practically until lunchtime, Ricardo Reis must have been the last person in Lisbon to learn of the military coup in Spain. Bleary-eyed, he went to pick the morning newspaper off his doormat and returned to his bedroom yawning. Ah, the pretense of calling the tedium of life serenity. When his eyes met the headline, Military coup on Spanish mainland, he was overcome by vertigo, a feeling of hurtling through the air. He should have foreseen this. The Spanish army, the guardian of the nation's virtues and traditions, was about to speak with the voice of military force, the merchants would be expelled from the temple, the altar of the Fatherland would be rebuilt, and the immortal glory of Spain, which a few of her degenerate sons had brought into decline, would be restored. On an inside page Ricardo Reis came across the text of a telegram which had been intercepted, In Madrid there are fears of a Fascist revolution. The adjective bothered him. Granted, the telegram comes from the Spanish capital where the left-wing government is installed, and one expects them to use such language, but it would be much clearer if they said, for example, that the monarchists have struck a blow against the republicans. That way, Ricardo Reis would know where the line is drawn, for he himself is a monarchist, as we may recall or should remind ourselves. But General Sanjurjo has issued a formal denial of that rumor circulating in Lisbon that he was planning to head a monarchist movement in Spain, so Ricardo Reis need not take sides, this battle, if it should become a battle, is not his, the disagreement is between republicans and republicans. Today the newspaper has printed all the news at its disposal, tomorrow it may tell us that the revolution has failed, that the rebels have been vanquished, that peace reigns throughout Spain. Ricardo Reis does not know whether this would cause him relief or distress. When he goes out for lunch, he pays close attention to people's faces, to what they are saying, there is tension in the air but the tension is kept under control, perhaps because there is still little news, or perhaps because people are keeping their feelings to themselves. Between his apartment and the restaurant he sees some expressions of triumph, a few of gloom, and realizes that it is not a question of a skirmish between republicans and monarchists.

We now have a fuller picture of what happened. The insurrection began in Spanish Morocco and its leader appears to be General Franco. Here in Lisbon, General Sanjurjo has declared that he is on the side of his comrades in arms but repeats that he does not wish to play an active role. Any child can see that the situation in Spain is serious. Within forty-eight hours the government headed by Casares Quiroga fell, Martinez Barrio was entrusted with forming a government, Martinez Barrio resigned, and now we have a cabinet formed by Giral, we'll see how long that lasts. The military boasts that the revolution has triumphed, if things progress in this way the days of Red domination in Spain are numbered. Even if the abovementioned child does not read, he will know the truth of this statement just by looking at the size of the headlines and at the bold exuberance of typefaces, which will spill over into the small lettering of the editorials within the next few days. Then tragedy struck. General Sanjurjo, en route to take his seat on the military directorate of the revolution, met a horrible death. His airplane, either because it was carrying too many passengers or because there was insufficient power in the engine, if that does not amount to the same thing, was unable to climb and collided with a few trees and then a wall, in full view of the Spaniards who had come to watch the takeoff. Under an implacable sun both plane and general burned in one great bonfire. The lucky pilot, Ansaldo by name, got away with nothing more serious than minor bruises and burns. The general had sworn he had no intention of leaving

Portugal, but we must understand that deception is the very substance of politics, though God may not approve of it. Perhaps this was divine punishment, because everyone knows that God does not castigate with sticks and stones but tends to favor fire. Now, while General Queipo de Llano is proclaiming military dictatorship throughout Spain, vigil is being kept over the corpse of General Sanjurjo, also known as the Marquês de Riff, in the Igreja de Santo António do Estoril. When we say the corpse, we mean what is left of it, a charred stump, a man so corpulent in life now reduced in death to sad ashes, his tiny coffin could be that of an infant. How true it is that we are nothing in this world, yet no matter how often we repeat these words and though we see them confirmed every day, they are always hard to accept. Members of the Spanish Falange form a guard of honor for the great warlord, wearing their full uniform of blue shirt, black trousers, a dagger in a leather belt. Where did these people come from, I ask myself, because they were certainly not dispatched in haste from Morocco to attend the solemn funeral rites. But the abovementioned illiterate child could tell us, and the *Pueblo Gallego* reports, that there are fifty thousand Spaniards in Portugal. Obviously besides a change of underwear they packed their black trousers and blue shirts and daggers, little dreaming that they would wear their uniforms in public and in such sad circumstances. But on these faces marked by a virile grief there is also a gleam of triumph, for death is the eternal bride whose arms welcome the man of valor, death is an unblemished virgin and she prefers Spaniards among all men, especially if they are soldiers. Tomorrow, when the mortal remains of General Sanjurjo are transported on a horse-drawn gun carriage, the news will hover overhead, like angels bringing fair tidings, that motorized columns are advancing on Madrid, that the siege has been consummated, that the final assault will be made in a matter of hours. People are saying that there is no longer any government in the capital, they also say, contradicting themselves, that the government in the capital has authorized members of the Popular Front to take whatever arms and ammunition they need. But this is only the death rattle of the demon, the day is at hand when the Virgin of Pilar will crush the serpent beneath her immaculate feet and the crescent moon will soar above the graveyards of iniquity. Thousands of Moroccan troops have already landed in southern Spain, and with their help we shall restore the empire of the cross and rosary over the odious symbol of the hammer and sickle. The regeneration of Europe is making giant strides, first there was Italy, then Portugal, then Germany, and now Spain, this is the good land, this the best seed, tomorrow we reap the harvest. As the German students wrote, We are nobody, and those same words were muttered by the slaves to each other as they built the pyramids, We are nobody, the masons and drovers of Mafra, We are nobody, the inhabitants of Alentejo bitten by the cat infected by rabies, We are nobody, the recipients of the alms distributed by charitable organizations and relief agencies, We are nobody, those flood victims of Ribatejo for whose benefit a gala day was held at the Jockey Club, We are nobody, the national unions which paraded in May with their arms outstretched, We are nobody. Perhaps the day will come when we will all be somebody, this is not a quote, it is merely a feeling.

To Lydia, who is also nobody, Ricardo Reis speaks of the events in the neighboring nation. She tells him that the Spaniards in the hotel celebrated the latest news with a great party, not even the general's tragic death dampened their spirits, and now not an evening passes without bottles of French champagne, Salvador is as happy as a clam, Pimenta talks in Castilian to the manner born, and Ramón and Felipe could not contain their joy upon learning that General Franco is Galician, a native of El Ferrol. Only the other day someone had the idea of hoisting a Spanish flag on the hotel verandah to mark the Hispano-Portuguese alliance. And you, Ricardo Reis asked, what do you think of Spain, of what is happening there. I am not educated, you are the one who ought to know, Doctor, with all the books you've read to get where you are today, the higher one goes, the farther one can see. Therefore the moon shines on every lake. Doctor, you say the prettiest things. The situation in Spain had been going from bad to worse to utter chaos, it was about time someone came along to put an end to all the squabbling, the only hope was for the army to step in, just as happened here, it's the same everywhere. I know nothing about these things, but my brother says. I already know what your brother says. How can you know, Doctor, you and my brother are such different people. What does he say then. He says that the military will not win because all the people will be against it. Let me assure you, Lydia, that the people are never all on one side, but I'm curious to know what you mean when you say the people. The people are like me, a hotel chambermaid who has a revolutionary brother and sleeps with a doctor who is against revolutions. Who taught you to say these things. When I open my mouth to speak, the words are already there, it's just a matter of letting them come out. Generally, one thinks before he speaks. Well perhaps in my case it is like having a baby, which grows without our noticing it and is born when the time comes. How have you been feeling lately. If it weren't for missing my periods, I wouldn't believe I was pregnant. You are still determined, then, to have the child, My baby boy, Your baby boy, Yes, and I am not likely to change my mind, Think about it carefully, But I don't think. With these words Lydia gave a contented laugh, and Ricardo Reis was left without a reply. He drew her to him, kissed her on the forehead, then on the corner of her mouth, then on her neck, the bed was not far and soon both serving maid and doctor were on it. No more was said about her sailor brother. Spain is at the other end of the world.

Les beaux esprits se rencontrent, as the French say, a remarkably subtle race. Ricardo Reis speaks of the need to preserve order, and in an interview given to the Portuguese newspaper *O Século* General Francisco Franco has just declared, We desire order in our nation. This prompted the newspaper to print in bold letters, The Spanish Army's Task of Redemption, thus showing how numerous those *beaux esprits* are, if not indeed innumerable. A few days later, the newspaper raises the question, When will a First International of Order be organized against the Third International of Disorder. The *beaux esprits* are already giving their reply, the initiative is under way, Moroccan soldiers continue to land, a governing junta has been set up in Burgos, and there is a rumor that within a matter of hours the final confrontation will take place between the army and the forces of Madrid. As for the fact that the population of Badajoz has taken up arms to resist the military advance, we should not attribute any special importance to that, it provides only an interesting footnote to our discussion about what the people are or are not. Men, women, and children armed themselves with rifles, swords, cudgels, scythes, revolvers, daggers, and hatchets, whatever came to hand, perhaps this is the way the people arm themselves, but the philosophical question of what the people are, if you will forgive my presumption, remains a moot point.

The wave swells and gathers. In Portugal, volunteers are flocking to enroll in the Portuguese Youth Movement, these are patriotic youths who decided not to wait for the inevitable conscription. With a hopeful hand and neat lettering, under the benevolent gaze of their fathers, they sign the letter and vigorously march to the post office, or, trembling with civic pride, they deliver the letter personally to the doorman at the Ministry of National Education. Only their respect for religion prevents them from declaring, Here is my body, here is my blood, but it is clear for all to see that they long for martyrdom. Ricardo Reis runs his eye down the lists, trying to visualize faces, postures, ways of walking that might give substance, meaning to the abstraction of these proper nouns, which are the emptiest words of all unless we put human beings inside them. In years to come, twenty, thirty, fifty years, what will these grownup men or old men, if they live that long, think of their ardent youth, when they heard or read the clarion words of the German youths who said, We are nobody, and rallied like heroes repeating, We, too, we, too, are nobody. They will use such phrases as, The foolishness of youth, A mistake made in my innocence, I had no one to turn to for advice, I have repented at leisure, My father ordered me to sign up, I sincerely believed in the movement, The uniform was so impressive, I would do it all over again, It was one way of getting on with my life, The first to enlist were much admired, A young man is so easily persuaded, so easily deceived. These and similar excuses are offered, but now one man gets to his feet, raises his hand, requesting to be heard. Ricardo Reis nods, anxious to hear a person speak of one of the other people he once was, to hear age describing youth, and this is the speech the man made. You have to consider the individual motives, whether the step we took was taken out of ignorance or malice, whether of our own free will or because we were compelled. The judgment, of course, will vary, depending on the times and on the judge. But whether we are pardoned or condemned, our life must be weighed on the scales of the good and evil we did, let everything be taken into account, if that is possible, and let the first judge be our conscience. Perhaps we should say once again, though for a different reason, that we are nobody. At that time a certain man, loved and respected by some of us, I will say his name to spare you the trouble of guessing, Miguel de Unamuno, then rector at the University of Salamanca, no mere fourteen- or fifteen-year-old stripling like us but a venerable gentleman in his seventies, the author of such highly acclaimed books as *Del sentimiento trágico de la vida, La agonía del cristianismo, En torno al casticismo, La dignidad humana*, and many others, a guiding spirit from the first days of war, pledged his support to the ruling Junta of Burgos, exclaiming, Let us save western civilization, I am here at your disposal O sons of Spain. These sons of Spain were the insurgent troops and the Moors from Morocco, and he made a personal donation of five thousand pesetas to what was even then called the Nationalist Spanish Army. Since I cannot remember the prices of those days, I cannot say how many bullets one could buy with five thousand pesetas. Unamuno urged President Azaña to commit suicide, and a few weeks later he made further statements that were no less vehement, My greatest admiration, my deepest respect goes to those Spanish women who held the communist rabble at bay and long prevented it from seizing control of Spain. In a transport of ecstasy he called them holy women. We Portuguese have also had our share of holy women, two examples will suffice, Marília, the shining heroine of *Conspiracy*, and the innocent saint of *The May Revolution*. If the Spanish women have Unamuno to thank for their sainthood, let our Portuguese women give thanks to Senhor Tomé Vieira and Senhor Lopes Ribeiro, one day I should like to descend into hell and count for myself the holy women there. But about Miguel de Unamuno, whom we admired, no one speaks now, he is like an embarrassing wound one tries to conceal, and only his words, almost his last, spoken in reply to General Milan d'Astray, the one who shouted in that same city of Salamanca, Long live death, have been preserved for posterity. Doctor Reis will never learn what those words are, but life is too short for a man to learn everything, and so is his. Because those words were spoken, some of us reconsidered our decision. It was good that Unamuno lived long enough to see his mistake, although only to see it, because he did little to correct it, having little time left, and perhaps too he wished to preserve the tranquillity of his final days. And therefore all I ask is that you wait for our last word, or the next to last, if on that day our minds are still clear and yours is too. I am finished. Some of those present vigorously applaud this hope of salvation, but others protest, indignant at the malicious distortion of Unamuno's Nationalist doctrine, because it was only out of senility, with one foot in the grave, or pique or capriciousness, that Unamuno dared question the magnificent battle cry of the great patriot General Milan d'Astray, who only had wisdom to impart, none to receive. Ricardo Reis does not know what Unamuno will say to the General, he is too shy to ask, or afraid to penetrate the veil of the future, *How much better to pass in silence, without anticipation*, this is what he once wrote, this is what he tries to achieve each day. The old soldiers leave, discussing as they go the words of Unamuno, judging those words as they themselves would like to be judged, for everyone knows that the accused, in his eyes, is always absolved.

Ricardo Reis reads the news he has already read, the call by Unamuno, the rector of Salamanca, Let us save western civilization, I am here at your disposal O sons of Spain, and the five thousand pesetas paid out of his own pocket for Franco's army, and the exhorting of Azaña to commit suicide, but he hasn't got to the holy women yet, not that we need to wait to know how he will express it. Only the other day we heard a simple Portuguese film producer say that on this side of the Pyrenees all women are saints. Ricardo Reis slowly turns the pages, distracts himself with the latest news, items that might as easily have come from there as from here, from this decade or any other, past, present, and future, weddings and baptisms for example, departures and arrivals. The problem is that we cannot choose the news we want to read, like John D. Rockefeller. He runs his eye down the classified advertisements, Apartment to let, he already has one. But wait, here is the steamer *The Highland Brigade* due to leave Lisbon for Pernambuco, Rio de Janeiro, Santos, what news will she bring, persistent messenger, from Vigo. And it appears that all Galicia has united behind General Franco, he is after all a native son of that region. The reader, restless, turns the page and once again encounters the shield of Achilles, which he has not seen for a long time. It is the same display of pictures and captions, a prodigious mandala, a kaleidoscopic universe in which all movement, suspended, offers itself to our contemplation. At last it is possible to count the wrinkles on the face of God, more commonly known by the name of Freire the Engraver, here is his portrait with the implacable monocle, here the necktie he uses to strangle us, even though the physician says we are dying from some disease or bullet wound. Freire's wares are illustrated below, testifying to the infinite wisdom of their creator, who has lived an unblemished and honorable life and received three gold medals, the ultimate distinction conferred by the Deity, who does not however advertise in the *Diário de Notícias*. At one time, Ricardo Reis saw this advertisement as a labyrinth, now he sees it as a circle from which there is no escape or exit, like an endless desert without paths. He adds a small goatee to the portrait of Freire the Engraver and doubles the monocle into spectacles, but not even this makes Freire look like the Don Miguel de Unamuno who also became lost in a labyrinth, from which he managed to emerge, if we give credence to the Portuguese gentleman who stood up to address the assembly, only on the eve of his death, leaving us in doubt as to whether Unamuno held to those almost-last words or instead relapsed into his initial complacency if not complicity, concealing his rage, suppressing his defiance. The yes and no of Unamuno disturbs Ricardo Reis, he is divided between this present, which is common to both their lives, the two linked by news items in the press, and the obscure prophecy of the soldier-orator who, knowing the future, did not reveal everything. A shame Ricardo Reis did not have the courage to ask the man what Don Miguel said to the general, but then he realizes that he kept silent because it had been clearly hinted that he would not be in this world on the day of that repentance, You never learn what those words are, but life is too short for a man to learn everything, and so is yours. Ricardo Reis begins to see the direction the wheel of destiny is turning. Milan d'Astray, who was in Buenos Aires, passed through Rio de Janeiro on his way to Spain, the paths of men do not vary much, and now comes sailing across the Atlantic, glowing with excitement and eager for battle. Within the next few days he will disembark at Lisbon, the ship is the *Almanzora*, then proceed to Seville and from there to Tetuán, where he will replace Franco. Milan d'Astray approaches Salamanca and Miguel de Unamuno, he will shout, Long live death, and then the curtain falls. The Portuguese soldier-orator again asks leave to speak, his lips move, the black sun of the future shines, but the words are inaudible, we cannot even guess what he is saying.

Ricardo Reis is anxious to discuss these matters with Fernando Pessoa, but Fernando Pessoa does not appear. Time drags like a sluggish wave, it is a sphere of molten glass on whose surface myriad glints catch one's eye and engage one's attention, while inside glows the crimson, disquieting core. Days and nights succeed each other in oppressive heat that both descends from the sky and rises from the earth. It is late afternoon before the two old men appear on the Alto de Santa Catarina, they cannot take the burning sun which surrounds the sparse shadows of the palm trees, the glare on the river is too much for their tired eyes, the shimmering air leaves them gasping for breath. Lisbon opens her spigots but there is not a drop of running water, her inhabitants have become caged birds with open beaks and drooping wings. As the city sinks into torpor, the rumor circulates that the Spanish Civil War is nearing its end, which is probable if we bear in mind that the troops of Queipo de Llano are already at the gates of Badajoz, with the divisions of the Civil Guard, which is their Foreign Legion, eager for combat. Woe to him who opposes these soldiers, so great is their desire to kill. Don Miguel sets off from home for the university, taking advantage of the fringe of shade that skirts the buildings along the route. The sun bakes the stones of Salamanca, but the worthy ancient can feel a military breeze in his face, in his contented soul he returns the greetings of his countrymen, the salutes he receives from the soldiers at headquarters or in the street, every one of them the reincarnation of El Cid Campeador, who in his day also said, Let us save western civilization. Ricardo Reis, leaving his apartment early one morning before the sun became too hot, also took advantage of the fringes of shade while waiting for a taxi to appear and take him, panting, up the Calçada da Estrela as far as Prazeres. The visitor does not need to ask the way, he has not forgotten the location or the number, four thousand three hundred and seventy-one, not the number of a door, so there is no point in knocking or inquiring, Is anyone home. If the presence of the living is not in itself enough to dislodge the secrets of the dead, these words serve no purpose. Ricardo Reis reached the railing, placed his hand on the warm stone, the sun, though still not high, has been hitting this spot since dawn. From a nearby path comes the sound of a brush sweeping, it is a widow cutting across at the far end of the road, her face hidden behind a crepe veil. There is no other sign of life. Ricardo Reis descends as far as the bend, where he pauses to look at the river, the mouth of the sea, a most appropriate word, because it is here that the sea comes to quench its unassuageable thirst, sucking lips pressed to the land. Such an image, such a metaphor would be out of place in the austere structure of an ode, but it occurs to us in the early morning, when the mind submits to feeling.

Ricardo Reis does not turn around. He knows that Fernando Pessoa is standing beside him, this time invisible, perhaps forbidden to show himself in the flesh within the precincts of the graveyard, otherwise the place would be too crowded, the streets congested with the dead, the thought makes one want to smile. The voice of Fernando Pessoa asks, What brings you here at this early hour, my dear Reis, is the view from the Alto de Santa Catarina, where Adamastor stands, not enough for you. Ricardo Reis replies without replying, From here we can watch a Spanish general sailing to join the Civil War, are you aware that civil war has broken out in Spain. Go on. They tell me that this general, whose name is Milan d'Astray, is destined to meet Miguel de Unamuno one day, and he will exclaim, Long live death, to which there will be a reply. Go on. I would like to know the reply given by Don Miguel. How can I tell you before he gives it. It might interest you to know that the rector of Salamanca has sided with the army, which intends to overthrow the government and the regime. That is of no interest to me whatsoever. I once thought that loss of freedom might be natural and right in flourishing societies, now I do not know what to think, I was counting on you, you have let me down. The most I can do is to offer a hypothesis. What hypothesis. That your rector of Salamanca will reply by saying that there are circumstances in which to remain silent is to lie, I hear a morbid cry, Long live death, a barbarous and repugnant paradox, General Milan d'Astray is crippled, no insult intended, Cervantes was also crippled, unfortunately today in Spain there are far too many cripples, it pains me to think that General Milan d'Astray might try to start a popular psychology, a cripple who does not possess the spiritual wealth of a Cervantes usually takes consolation in the harm he can cause others. You think he will give this reply. Out of an infinite number of hypotheses, this is one. It does jibe with what the Portuguese soldier said. It is important when things jibe and make sense. What sense can there be in Marcenda's left hand. You still think of her, then. From time to time. You needn't look so far, we are all crippled.

Ricardo Reis is alone. On the lower branches of the elm trees the cicadas begin to chirr, mute but inventing their own voice. A great black vessel enters the straits, only to disappear into the shimmering reflection of the water. The panorama seems unreal.

Ricardo Reis now has another voice in his apartment. He owns a small radio, the cheapest on the market, the popular Pilot model with an ivory-colored Bakelite case, chosen because it occupies little space and can easily be transported from the bedroom to the study, the two rooms where the somnambulist who lives here spends most of his time. Had he decided to buy one before the pleasure of living in new quarters wore off, he would now possess a superheterodyne receiver with twelve vacuum tubes and enough power to rouse the neighborhood and draw a crowd beneath his window. Eager to enjoy the music and listen to the broadcasts, all the housewives in the district would be there, including the two old men, friendly and polite once more because of this latest novelty. But Ricardo Reis only wants to keep up with the news, discreetly, in privacy, the radio lowered to an intimate whisper. He does not explain to himself or try to analyze the restless feeling that brings him to the set, he does not wonder about the hidden message in that dim eye, the dying Cyclops that is the light of the minuscule dial, its expression showing neither joy nor fear nor pity. And he cannot say whether it is the victories of the revolutionary army in Spain that delight him or the resounding defeats of the forces that support the government. Some will argue that the two are the same, but they aren't, no sir, the human soul is more complicated than that. To be pleased that my enemy is beset doesn't mean that I applaud the besetter. Ricardo Reis does not investigate his inner conflict, he leaves his uneasiness alone, like one who, lacking the courage to skin a rabbit, asks another to do the job for him while he stands watching, annoyed at his own squeamishness. Standing close enough to breathe in the warmth released by the skinned flesh, a subtly pleasant smell, he conceives in his heart, or wherever such things are conceived, a loathing for the man capable of the great cruelty of skinning. How can he and I possibly belong to the same human race. Perhaps this is why we hate the hangman and refuse to eat the flesh of the scapegoat.

Lydia was delighted when she saw the radio, How pretty, how nice to be able to hear music at any hour of the day or night. An exaggeration on her part, because that time is a long way off. She is a simple soul able to rejoice at the smallest thing, unless this is a pretext to conceal her distress that Ricardo Reis has become so slovenly in his ways, no longer caring about his appearance, no longer looking after himself. She told him that the dukes of Alba and Medinaceli had left the hotel, to the great disappointment of Salvador, who cherishes a real affection for his clients, especially if they are titled, though in this case they are not, because the idea of calling Don Lorenzo and Don Alonso dukes was nothing but a joke of Ricardo Reis, which it is time to drop. He is not surprised. Now that the day of victory is approaching, they live their final moments of exile in sweet luxury, which explains why the hotels in Estoril are now frequented by what the gossip columns refer to as a select Spanish colony, with plenty of dukes and counts there on vacation. Don Lorenzo and Don Alfonso followed the scent of the aristocracy, and in their old age they will be able to tell their grandchildren, In the days when I was exiled with the Duke of Alba. For the benefit of these Spaniards the Portuguese Radio Club recently introduced a Spanish broadcaster, a woman with a voice like a soubrette in an operetta. She reads the news of the Nationalist advances in the graceful language of Cervantes. May God and the Portuguese Radio Club pardon us this sarcasm, it is provoked by an urge to weep rather than any desire to smile, which is exactly how Lydia feels, who tries valiantly to be merry and lighthearted though weighed by her anxiety for Ricardo Reis in addition to the terrible news from Spain, terrible from her point of view, which as we have seen coincides with that of her brother Daniel. Upon hearing, on the wireless, that Badajoz has been bombarded, she begins to cry like a Mary Magdalene, strange behavior for her, considering that she has never been to Badajoz and has neither family nor possessions there that might have suffered in the bombing. Why are you crying, Lydia, Ricardo Reis asks her, but she has no reply, perhaps it was something Daniel told her, but who told him, what was his source of information. The war in Spain must be much discussed aboard the *Afonso de Albuquerque*, as the sailors scrub the decks and polish the brass, they pass on the latest news among themselves, nor is all the news what the newspapers and radio would have us believe. Aboard the *Afonso de Albuquerque* there is not much confidence in the reassurances of General Mola, who belongs to the quadrille of the matador Franco and has promised that before the month is out we shall hear him address us over Radio Madrid. That other general, Queipo de Llano, says that for Madrid it is the beginning of the end, the revolution is barely three weeks old and almost over. Rubbish, replies the sailor Daniel. But Ricardo Reis, awkwardly trying to console Lydia and dry her tears, and still hoping to win her over to his way of thinking, repeats the news he has read and heard, There you are weeping for Badajoz, don't you realize that the Communists cut an ear off one hundred and ten landowners and then defiled their womenfolk, in other words, raped the poor creatures. How do you know. I read it in the newspapers and also read, in an article written by Tomé Vieira, a journalist and the author of several books, that the Bolsheviks gouged out the eyes of an elderly priest, then poured gasoline on him and set him on fire. I don't believe that. It's in the newspapers, black on white. My brother says one shouldn't always believe what the newspapers say. I'm not in a position to go to Spain to see for myself, I have to believe that they are telling the truth, newspapers don't lie, that would be the greatest crime imaginable. Doctor, you are a learned man while I can scarcely read or write, but I've learned one thing in life, there are lots of truths and they often say different things, we won't know who is lying until the fighting starts. And what if it is true that they gouged out a priest's eyes and poured gasoline on him and burned him alive. Then it's a horrible truth, but my brother says that if the church were on the side of the poor and helped them on this earth, then the poor would be the first to give their lives for the church. And what if they cut the ears off the landowners and raped their wives. That would be another horrible truth, but my brother says that while the poor are suffering on this earth, the rich are already enjoying paradise without going to heaven. You always answer with your brother's words. And you, Doctor, always speak with the words of the newspapers. True enough.

Now there have been disturbances in Funchal and in other places on the island, with crowds looting public offices and dairy farms, and people have been killed or wounded. The situation must be serious, because two warships have been sent out, along with a fleet of airplanes and squads of hunters with machine guns, a military force capable of waging a civil war Portuguese-style. Ricardo Reis does not fully grasp the reason for the uprising, which need not surprise either us or him, because he has only the newspapers to rely on for information. He turns on his ivory-colored Pilot radio. Perhaps the words we hear are more believable than the words we read, the only drawback is that we cannot see the announcer's face, because a look of hesitation, a sudden twitch of the mouth will betray a lie at once, let us hope that someday human inventiveness will make it possible for us, sitting in our own homes, to see the face of the announcer, then at last we will be able to tell the difference between a lie and the truth, and the era of justice will truly begin, and let us say, Amen. The arrow on the dial points to the Portuguese Radio Club, and while the tubes are heating up, Ricardo Reis rests his weary forehead on the radio case. From inside comes a warm odor that makes him feel a little giddy, a distracting sensation, then he notices that the volume knob is switched off. He turns it, at first hears only the deep hum of the carrier wave, then a pause, a sudden burst of music, the song *Cara al sol con la camisa nueva*, the anthem of the Falange for the pleasure and comfort of the select Spanish colony in the hotels of Estoril and at the Bragança. At this very moment in the casino they are having a dress rehearsal for the Night of Silver, to be presented by Erico Braga, and in the hotel lounge the guests glance suspiciously at the green-tinted mirror. The Radio Club announcer then reads a telegram sent by veteran Portuguese legionnaires who served in the fifth division of the Spanish Foreign Legion, they greet their former comrades who are taking part in the siege of Badajoz, a shiver goes up our spine as we listen to those military sentiments, the Christian fervor, the fraternity of arms, the memory of past triumphs, the hope in a bright future for the two Iberian fatherlands united in one Nationalist cause. After listening to the final news bulletin, that three thousand soldiers from Morocco have landed in Algiers, Ricardo Reis switches off the Pilot and stretches out on the bed, desperate at finding himself so alone. He is not thinking about Marcenda, it is Lydia who occupies his thoughts, probably because she is closer at hand, one might say, although there is no telephone in this apartment, and even if there were one, he could hardly call the hotel and say, Good evening, Senhor Salvador, this is Doctor Ricardo Reis speaking, do you remember me, we haven't spoken to each other in ages, I say, those were extremely happy weeks I spent in your hotel, no, no, I don't need a room, I simply wanted to speak to Lydia, could you ask her to come around to my apartment, excellent, how very kind of you to let her off for a couple of hours, I am feeling very lonely, no, it isn't for that, all I need is a little company. He gets up from the bed, gathers together the pages of the newspaper lying all over the floor and on the bedspread, and runs his eye down the list of entertainments, but nothing stirs his interest. For a moment he wishes he were blind, deaf, and dumb, thrice the cripple Fernando Pessoa says we all are, then among the news items from Spain he notices a photograph that had escaped him previously, army tanks bearing the Sacred Heart of Jesus. If this is the coat of arms they are using, then there can be no doubt that this will be a war waged without mercy. He remembers that Lydia is pregnant, with a baby boy, as she constantly tells him, and this baby boy will grow up and go to the wars that are now in the making. One war leads to another, let us do some calculations, the baby comes into the world in March of next year, if the average age when youths go to war is twenty-three or twenty-four, what war will we have in nineteen sixty-one, and where, and why, and over what wasteland. With the eyes of imagination Ricardo Reis sees the boy riddled with bullets, dark and pale like his father but only his mother's son, for his father will not acknowledge him.

Badajoz has surrendered. Spurred by the rousing telegram from the veteran Portuguese legionnaires, the Spanish Foreign Legion achieved miraculous victories, whether at a distance or in hand-to-hand combat, and singled out for special honor were the brave Portuguese legionnaires of the new generation who were anxious to prove themselves worthy of their predecessors, one should add that it always helps to feel that one's native land is not far away. Badajoz has surrendered. Reduced to ruins by continuous bombardment, swords broken, scythes blunted, clubs and hatchets smashed, the city has surrendered. General Mola declared, The hour has come to settle accounts, and the bull ring opened its gates to receive the militiamen taken captive, then closed them, the fiesta is under way, machine guns shout *olé, olé, olé*, the noise is deafening in the bull ring of Badajoz, and the minotaurs dressed in cheap cotton fall on top of one another, mingling their blood in mutual transfusion. When not a single monster is left standing, the matadors will liquidate with their pistols those who were simply wounded, and if any escape this mercy, it is only to be buried alive. All that Ricardo Reis knew about this event was what he read in the Portuguese newspapers, but one newspaper accompanied its report with a photograph of the bull ring in which bodies could be seen scattered here and there, a wagon looked completely out of place, was it meant for deliveries or removals, for bulls or minotaurs. Ricardo Reis learned the rest from Lydia, who had been told by her brother, who had been told by who knows whom, perhaps it was a message from the future when all will finally be resolved. No longer crying, Lydia tells him, Two thousand lost their lives, her lips are trembling, her cheeks flushed. Ricardo Reis tries to console her, takes her by the arm, but she pulls away, not out of any rancor but simply because today she cannot bear it. Later, in the kitchen, as she is washing the dirty dishes that have accumulated, she begins to cry again, and for the first time she asks herself why she comes to this apartment. Is she the doctor's maid, his cleaner, she is certainly not his lover, because that word implies equality, no matter whether male or female, and they are not equal.

Then she does not know if she is crying for the dead of Badajoz or for her own death, which is the death of feeling that she is nobody. Sitting in his study, Ricardo Reis has no idea what is going on. To take his mind off the two thousand dead, a truly incredible number, if Lydia was telling the truth, he reopened *The God of the Labyrinth*, to continue where he had left off, but could get no meaning from the words. He realized that he had forgotten the narrative, so he went back once more to the beginning, The body, discovered by the first chess player, occupied with its outstretched arms the squares of the King and Queen's pawns as well as the next two squares in the direction of the enemy camp. Reaching this point, Ricardo Reis again lost the thread, seeing the chessboard as a desert and the sprawled corpse as a young man who was no longer a young man, then he saw a circle inscribed in that huge square, an arena strewn with bodies crucified on their native soil, and Sacred Hearts of Jesus went from one to the other making sure that there were no survivors. When Lydia walked into the study, done with her chores, Ricardo Reis was sitting with the book closed in his lap, he appeared to be sleeping and looked, caught unawares like this, almost old. She stared at him as if he were a stranger, then left without making a sound. She begins to think, I won't come back here, but she cannot be certain.

Now that General Milan d'Astray has finally arrived, another proclamation is issued from Tetuán, war without mercy, war without truce, war unto death against the Marxist vermin while observing humanitarian principles, As one can gather from the words spoken by General Franco, I have not yet occupied Madrid because I do not wish to sacrifice innocent citizens. Now here is a considerate fellow, someone who would never order the massacre of innocents as Herod did, no, he will wait until they grow up rather than have such a burden on his conscience and overcrowd heaven with angels. It is inconceivable that these fair winds from Spain should not produce similar events in Portugal. The bids have been made, the cards placed on the table and dealt, the time has come to know who is for us and who is against us, let us make the enemy show his face, betray himself by his own duplicity, and let us count as ours all who out of cowardice or greed or fear of losing the little they have seek refuge in the shade of our flag. Therefore the national unions have decided to stage a rally opposing Communism, and as soon as this news is announced, the furor that accompanies all great moments in history grips the entire community. Petitions are signed by patriotic associations, women, either individually or in various committees, demand representation, and in order to put their members into the right frame of mind, some unions hold special meetings, the union of shop assistants, for example, or master bakers, or hotel workers, and in the photographs those present can be seen saluting with stiff raised arms, each rehearsing his role as he awaits the opening ceremony. During these meetings, the manifesto of the national unions is read out and applauded, it is an impassioned declaration of their political allegiance and their confidence in the nation's destiny, as becomes clear from the following excerpts taken at random, There can be no doubt but that the national-corporative workers are Portuguese through and through and staunch Roman Catholics, The national unions call upon Salazar for drastic remedies to great evils, The national unions acknowledge private enterprise and the individual's right to acquire property as the only foundation for every social, economic, and political organization, and for social justice. Since they are struggling for the same cause and fighting the same enemy, members of the Spanish Falange speak to the entire nation on the Portuguese Radio Club, applauding Portugal for wholeheartedly joining this crusade, which actually is historically inaccurate, because everyone knows that we Portuguese have been fighting this crusade for years. But that is typical of the Spaniards, they are always ready to take over, and have to be constantly watched.

Ricardo Reis was never at a political rally in his life, an omission that must be attributed to the peculiarities of his temperament, to his upbringing, to his love of the classics, and also to a certain personal shyness, which should not surprise anyone familiar with his verse. But this national outcry, the civil war in neighboring Spain, perhaps too the unusual venue as demonstrators begin to assemble here in the bull ring of Campo Pequeno, ignite in him a tiny flame of curiosity. What will it be like watching thousands of people gathered together to listen to speeches. What phrases will they applaud and why, how much sincerity will there be on the part of those who speak and those who listen, what will the expressions be on their faces, what gestures will be used. For one who is by nature so incurious, this is an interesting change. Ricardo Reis set out early in order to be sure to get a seat, taking a taxi to arrive more quickly. The night is warm as August draws to a close. Special trams go by, packed to overflowing, the passengers chat amiably, while a few on foot, more inflamed with Nationalist zeal, cry out, Long live the New State. There are union flags, which in the absence of any breeze the standard bearers wave vigorously to display their colors and emblems, here is a heraldic corporative still contaminated with republican traditions, there a guild, to use the word for an artisan association in an earlier age. Entering the arena, Ricardo Reis is swept along by this great torrent of humanity and finds himself among bank employees all wearing a blue armband inscribed with a crucifix and the initials SNB. It is indeed true that the virtue of patriotism pardons all sins and reconciles all contradictions, including this one, because the bankers have taken as their emblem the Cross of Christ, who in His time drove the merchants and money changers, the first branches of this tree, the first flowers of this fruit, from the temple. Just as well for them that Christ was not like the wolf in the fable, because the wolf slaughtered the gentle lambs instead of waiting for them to turn into obstinate sheep. Before, it was all much simpler, now we spend our time asking ourselves if the waters were muddy at their source or became polluted en route.

The arena is practically full, but Ricardo Reis has succeeded in finding a good spot on a bench in the sun, not that it matters today, for all is shadow and darkness. The good thing about his seat is that it is close enough to the platform to see the speakers' faces yet not so close as to prevent him from having a good view of the whole arena. Flags and union banners continue to file in, the latter are all national but many of the flags are not, and understandably, because we do not need to exaggerate the sublime symbol of the Fatherland in order to see that we are among Portuguese and, let it be said without boasting, among the best. The tiers are full, the only room left is in the center, where the banners can be seen to best advantage, which explains why there are so many down there. Acquaintances greet each other, the assembled acclaim the New State, and they are numerous, they stretch forth their arms in a frenzy, jumping up every time a new banner is carried in, saluting in Roman style. Forgive this constant repetition on their part and ours, *O tempora, O mores*, Viriathus and Sertorius fought so hard to expel the imperial occupiers from their country, but despite the struggle of those two heroes Rome returns in the image of her descendants, clearly the easiest domination of all is to buy men, who sometimes offer themselves so cheaply, in exchange for a strip of cloth to wear on their arms, or for the right to adopt the crooked crucifix as their emblem. A brass band plays popular tunes to help pass the time while people wait. At last the officials take their places on the platform and the crowd goes wild with excitement, the air shakes with patriotic cries, Portugal Portugal Portugal, Salazar Salazar Salazar. Salazar is not present, he appears only at his convenience, but Portugal is here, since it is everywhere. To the right of the platform, to the chagrin of the local residents, seats which had remained empty were now taken by Fascist delegates from Italy, dressed in their black shirts and decorations, and to the left now stood the Nazi delegates from Germany, with their brown shirts and armbands bearing the swastika. They all saluted the crowd with outstretched arms, and the crowd responded, rather less disciplined but eager to learn. At this point members of the Spanish Falange made their entrance, dressed in their familiar blue shirts, their uniforms in three different colors but united by a single ideal. To a man, the crowd is on its feet, its cheers filling the air in that universal language known as roaring, and Babel is unified at last by gestures. The Germans speak no Portuguese or Castilian or Italian, the Spaniards speak no German or Italian or Portuguese, the Italians speak no Castilian or Portuguese or German, the Portuguese, however, speak Castilian extremely well, *Usted* if addressing someone, *quanto vale* if buying something, *gracias* if thanking someone, but when souls are in harmony one mighty shout is good enough in all languages, Death to Bolshevism. Silence is restored with some effort, the band finishes its military march with three drumbeats, and now the first speaker of the evening is introduced, Gilberto Arroteia, a shipyard worker from the Navy Arsenal, how they persuaded him remains a secret between himself and temptation. Then a second speech by Luís Pinto Coelho, who represents Portuguese youth, and one begins to see what this is all about, because with words that could hardly be more explicit he calls for the creation of a Nationalist militia. The third speaker is Fernando Homem Cristo, the fourth Abel Mesquita, both from the national unions of Setúbal, the fifth is António Castro Fernandes, who one day will be a government minister, and the sixth Ricardo Durão, whose strong convictions are in keeping with his rank of major. In a few weeks' time he will repeat his speech in Évora, once again in a bull ring, We are gathered here, united by the same patriotic ideal, to declare and show the government of our nation that we are loyally pledged to carry on the traditions and achievements of our Lusitanian ancestors who gave new worlds to the world and spread faith and empire, let us also declare to a fanfare of horns and trumpets that we have gathered here as one man around Salazar, this genius who has dedicated his life to the service of the Fatherland. Finally, seventh in order but first in terms of political influence, Captain Jorge Botelho Moniz from the Portuguese Radio Club reads a motion urging the government to create a civic legion that will dedicate itself entirely to the service of the Fatherland, just as Salazar has, for it is only right that we should follow his example as far as our weak ability permits. This would seem an opportune moment to cite the parable of the seven twigs which are easily broken when separate but when tied together form an unbreakable fasces. Upon hearing the word legion, the crowd rises to its feet once more, always to a man. To say legion is to say uniform, to say uniform is to say shirt, all that remains to be decided is the color, but this is not a matter we can settle here. In any case, rather than be accused of behaving like monkeys we will not choose black or brown or blue, white gets dirty very quickly, yellow is the color of despair, as for red, God forbid, and purple evokes Christ on the road to Calvary, the only color left is green, so the gallant young men of the Portuguese Youth Movement agree that green is fine and dream of nothing else as they wait to be given their uniforms. The rally is drawing to a close, the unions have done their duty.

As one expects of the Portuguese, the crowd leaves the arena in an orderly fashion, some people still cheering but on a subdued note. The more meticulous of the standard bearers roll up their flags and slip them into protective sheaths. The main floodlights in the bull ring have been turned off and there is just enough light for the demonstrators to find their way out. Outside, special trams are filling up, there are also trucks for those who have to travel some distance, and lines waiting to board both. Ricardo Reis, though he was out in the open all through the rally, feels the need for fresh air and declines the taxis, which are snapped up at once by others. He sets out on foot to cross the entire city, walks where there is no sign of the patriotic crusade, these trams belong to other lines, the taxis doze in the squares. From Campo Pequeno to the Alto de Santa Catarina it is almost five kilometers, quite a distance for this doctor who is usually so sedentary in his ways. He arrived home with sore feet, exhausted. As he opened a window to clear the stuffiness in the room, he realized that during the long walk home he had not thought once about what he had seen and heard in the arena. He could not remember a single idea, reflection, comment, it was almost as if he had been carried on a cloud, or transformed into a cloud hovering in midair. Now he wanted to think, to turn it all over in his mind, to reach conclusions, but he tried in vain, all he could see were those black, brown, and blue shirts defending western civilization, the Greeks and Romans. What speech would Don Miguel de Unamuno have made if invited. Perhaps he would have appeared between Durão and Moniz, would have shown himself to the multitude, Here I stand before you, sons of Portugal, nation of suicides who do not cry out, Long live death, I have nothing to say to you, for I myself am old and weak and need someone to protect me. Ricardo Reis contemplates the deep night, anyone with the power of seeing signs and omens would say that something is brewing. It is very late when Ricardo Reis closes the window, and in the end all he can think is, No more political rallies for me. Starting to brush his jacket and trousers, he found himself inhaling the smell of onion, how strange, he could have sworn he had been nowhere near Victor.

The following days bring a spate of news, as if the rally at Campo Pequeno has triggered events throughout the world. A group of North American financiers informed General Franco that they were prepared to back the Spanish Nationalist Revolution, the idea must have come from the influential John D. Rockefeller, because it would be a mistake to keep him completely in the dark, *The New York Times* reported the military coup in Spain, taking every precaution not to injure the old man's weak heart, but there are some risks that cannot be avoided. In the dioceses near the Black Forest, the German bishops announced that the Catholic Church and the Reich will fight shoulder to shoulder against the common foe. In order not to fall behind in this show of strength, Mussolini has warned the world that he is capable of mobilizing eight million men at a moment's notice, many of them still glowing from their victory over that other enemy of western civilization, Ethiopia. But to return to our paternal nest. In addition to the growing number of volunteers joining the Youth Movement, thousands have also enrolled in the Portuguese Legion, as it will come to be known, and the Undersecretary of the Corporations has drafted a statement in which he praises the national unions in the most eloquent terms, their patriotic initiative of holding a political rally, a crucible where Nationalist hearts are forged, now nothing stands in the way of building the New State. It has also been announced that the President of the Council is visiting military installations, touring the munitions factory at Braço de Prata, and inspecting the armaments depot of Beirolas, any subsequent visits, tours, or inspections will be duly reported.

From the newspaper Ricardo Reis learns that the *Afonso de Albuquerque* has sailed to Alicante to pick up refugees. He feels sadness in his heart because of his tie to the fortunes of this ship, though Lydia did not tell him that her sailor brother left for sea on a humanitarian mission. Lydia, for that matter, has not appeared lately, the dirty clothes are piling up, the dust is gathering on the furniture, and things are gradually losing their outline, as if tired of existing, which may also be the effect of eyes tired of seeing. Ricardo Reis has never felt so lonely. He sleeps nearly all day, on top of his unmade bed or on the sofa in the study. He even fell asleep on the toilet, but only once, because he woke then with a terrible fright, dreaming that he had died on the toilet, his trousers down, a corpse with no self-respect. He wrote a long letter to Marcenda, page upon page, mining a whole archaeology of remembrance beginning with that first evening in the hotel, the words flow without interruption from memory to memory, but when he comes to the present, Ricardo Reis cannot find anything to say, to ask for, to offer. So he collected the pages, tapped them straight, flattened out some corners that had been folded over, then tore up the letter methodically, page by page, until it was reduced to pieces so small, not a single word was readable. He did not throw the pieces into the wastebasket, but waited until the early hours of the morning, when everyone was asleep, and went and threw his sad carnival shower of confetti over the park railing. The dawn breeze carried them over the rooftops, and an even stronger wind will pick them up and carry them far away, but not as far as Coimbra. Two days later he copied his poem onto a sheet of paper, Already *impatient for the summer*, knowing that this truth was now a lie, because he felt no impatience, only an infinite weariness. He addressed the envelope to Marcenda Sampaio, poste restante, Coimbra, if she does not claim it in six months, the letter will be destroyed. And that conscientious and prying employee we mentioned earlier, if he takes the letter to Doctor Sampaio's office, no harm will come of it. Upon arriving home, having exercised his paternal prerogative and opened the letter, the father will say to his daughter, You appear to have an unknown admirer, and Marcenda will read the poem, smiling to herself. It does not even occur to her that it is from Ricardo Reis, because he never told her he was a poet, though there are certain similarities in the handwriting.

'm not coming back, Lydia has said, yet here she is knocking at the door. The key to the apartment is in her pocket, but she does not use it, she has her pride, she said she would not come back, it would look bad now if she used the key as if this were her own home, which it never was, and today even less so, if it is possible for something to be less than never. Ricardo Reis opens the door, concealing his surprise. Since Lydia appears to hesitate as to which room she should go to, he moves to the study, she can follow if she wishes. Her eyes are red and swollen, perhaps she has finally decided, after a great struggle with the joy of anticipated motherhood, to have an abortion, because the expression on her face doesn't seem to have been caused by the fall of Irun or the siege of San Sebastian. She says, You must excuse me, Doctor, I wasn't able to come. But immediately, in the same breath, she corrects herself, Not because of this, I just thought you didn't need me anymore. She corrects herself again, I was feeling tired of this life, and having said this, she stands there waiting. For the first time she looked straight at Ricardo Reis, and thought, Perhaps he is ill. I missed you, he said, then fell silent, he had nothing more to say. Lydia took two steps, she will start with the bedroom, make his bed, then go to the kitchen and wash the dishes, then soak his clothes in the washtub, but this is not the reason she came, although she may do all these chores later. Ricardo Reis asks her, Why don't you sit down, then says, Tell me what's wrong, and Lydia begins to sob. Is it because of the child, he asks, and she shakes her head, even manages a glance of rebuke amid her tears, before blurting out, It's because of my brother. Ricardo Reis remembers that the *Afonso de Albuquerque* has returned from Alicante, a port still under the control of the Spanish government, he puts two and two together and finds they make four. Has your brother deserted and stayed behind in Spain. No, he came back with the ship. So then. There's going to be a disaster, a disaster. Look, tell me what this is all about. The sailors, she stopped to dry her tears and blow her nose, are about to mutiny and sail out to sea. Who told you this. Daniel, he told me to keep it a secret but I had to talk to someone I can trust, I came here, Doctor, I have no one else to turn to, my mother has no idea. Ricardo Reis is surprised to find that he is devoid of feeling, perhaps this is fate, we know what will happen, know it is inevitable, yet we remain silent, onlookers only, watching the spectacle of the world even as we leave it. Are you sure, he asked. She nodded, tearful, waiting for the right questions, those to which a simple yes or no can be given, but such questioning requires an act of courage beyond human powers. For the want of anything better let us make do with, for example, What are their plans, surely they don't believe that their going out to sea will bring down the government. Their idea is to make for Angra do Heroísmo, free the political prisoners, take possession of the island, and then wait for riots to break out here. And if nothing happens. If there are no riots, they will go to Spain and join forces with the government. They're mad, they won't even get beyond the straits. That's what my brother said, but they refuse to listen. When is this to take place. He didn't tell me, but it will be within the next few days. And the ships, which ships are involved. The *Afonso de Albuquerque*, the *Dão*, the *Bartolomeu Dias*. They're mad, Ricardo Reis repeats, but he is no longer thinking about the conspiracy which has been revealed with such innocence, what he is recalling is the day of his arrival in Lisbon, the torpedo boats in the dock, their flags drenched like soggy rags, their lifeless hulks painted a deathly gray, The *Dão* is that one nearest you, the porter had told him, and now the *Dão* was about to sail out to sea in defiance. Ricardo Reis took a deep breath, as if he himself were on the prow of the ship, the salt wind in his face, the biting spray. He repeated, They're mad. Can there be a note of hope in his voice, surely not, an absurd illusion on our part, for he cherishes no hope. But everything may turn out all right in the end, who knows, they may even abandon their plan, and if they don't, who knows, they may even make it to Angra, we will see what happens, but you must stop crying, tears won't help, the sailors may change their mind. No, Doctor, you don't know them, as sure as my name is Lydia they won't change their mind. Having spoken her name, she suddenly realized that she should not be here, I can't do any cleaning for you today, I must get back to the hotel at once, I only came to unburden myself, I hope no one has noticed I am missing. Can I do anything to help. It's those sailors who need help, with all that way to go before they reach the straits, the one thing I beg of you, on the souls of your dear ones, is to keep this a secret, even though I wasn't able to keep it myself. Don't worry, my lips are sealed. But they parted enough for a kiss of consolation, and Lydia moaned because she felt so unhappy, although one could detect another deep sound in that moan, we humans are like this, feeling many things at the same moment. As Lydia descended the stairs, Ricardo Reis, most unusual for him, went out on the landing. She looked up, he nodded, they both smiled, certain moments in life seem perfect and this was such a moment, like a page on which there was writing but is now blank again.

When Ricardo Reis went out to lunch the next day, he lingered in the park to gaze at the warships before the Terreiro do Paço. He knew little about ships in general, only that dispatch boats were bigger than torpedo boats, but at a distance they all looked exasperatingly alike. He could not tell which was the *Afonso de Albuquerque* and which the *Bartolomeu Dias*, but the *Dão* he knew, because the porter had told him, The *Dão* is the one nearest you. Lydia must have been dreaming, or her brother had frightened her with a joke, this incredible story of conspiracy and ships heading for sea. Three of them are moored along the quay, as calm as can be in the breeze, and the frigates going upriver, and the ferries for Cacilhas ceaselessly plying to and fro, and the seagulls in the cloudless blue sky, and the sun shining brightly on the expectant river.

What Daniel told his sister is true after all, a poet can sense the fear that trembles in these waters. When do they leave, Within the next few days, Lydia replied, and Ricardo Reis's throat tightens and his eyes cloud with tears, this was how Adamastor's great weeping began. He is on the point of leaving when he hears voices call out in excitement, Over there, over there. They belong to the two old men, and other people are asking, Where, what is it, and children playing leapfrog interrupt their game and call out, Look at the balloon, look at the balloon. Ricardo Reis wiped his eyes with the back of his hand and saw rising into the air, on the other side of the river, an enormous airship, it must be the Graf Zeppelin or the Hindenburg, arriving to drop off mail for South America, on the rudder is a swastika in white, red, and black, like a kite launched by children into the sky, a hovering symbol that has lost its original meaning, a threat rather than a shooting star. The links between men and symbols are curious, we need only think of St. Francis of Assisi joined by blood to the cross of Christ, and the cross of Christ on the armbands of the bank employees at the political rally, it is a miracle that a person does not get lost in this maze of associations. The Hindenburg, its engines roaring, flew over the river in the direction of the castle, then disappeared behind some houses, and the roar gradually died away. The airship is about to drop the mail at Portela de Sacavém, perhaps *The Highland Brigade* will then transport the letters, for in the world there are many recurring paths. The old men return to their bench, the children go back to their leapfrog, the currents of air grow still again, and Ricardo Reis is no wiser. The ships sit in the accumulating heat of the afternoon, their prows facing out to sea, the sailors must be having their lunch, today as every day, unless today is their last day. In the restaurant, Ricardo Reis filled his glass with wine, then the glass of his invisible guest, and as he raised his glass to take the first sip, he made a gesture as if offering a toast. Since we cannot look into his thoughts to see whom or what he was toasting, let us follow the example of the waiters in this establishment, who pay no attention, because this customer may be a little odd but by no means is he the oddest.

The afternoon was most agreeable. Ricardo Reis went down to the Chiado, to the Rua Nova do Almada, to observe the ships at close quarters. On the quay, and as he was crossing the Terreiro do Paço, he recalled that in all these months he had not been to the Café Martinho da Arcada. Fernando Pessoa, on the last occasion, had felt that it would be unwise to challenge the memory of those familiar walls, and somehow they had never gone back, neither of them giving it another thought. For Ricardo Reis there is some excuse, with so many years abroad the habit of going there, if ever a habit, has been broken. Nor will he go there today. Seen from the middle of the square, the ships afloat on that luminous water look like toy boats displayed in a window, on mirrors to give the effect of a fleet in harbor. But when one draws closer, one sees very little, only the sailors going back and forth on deck. At this distance they seem unreal, if they are talking we cannot hear them, and what they are thinking remains a secret. Ricardo Reis was lost in reverie, having forgotten why he came here, he was simply gazing, nothing more, when suddenly he heard a voice beside him, So you've come to see the ships, Doctor. He recognized that voice, it belonged to Victor. His first reaction was puzzlement, where was the smell, then it became clear, Victor was downwind of him. Ricardo Reis felt his heart beat faster, did Victor suspect, had the sailors' plan to mutiny been discovered. The ships and the river, he replied, but could also have mentioned the frigates and the seagulls, also that he was about to take the ferry to Cacilhas just for the pleasure of the crossing, of watching the dolphins leap, but he merely repeated, The ships and the river, and withdrew brusquely, telling himself he had acted foolishly, he should have kept up a natural conversation, if Victor knows there is something afoot, he must surely have found it suspicious to see the doctor there. Then it occurred to Ricardo Reis that he should warn Lydia, was obliged to do so. But he immediately changed his mind, What could I tell her, that I saw Victor in the Terreiro do Paço, it might have been a coincidence, even the police enjoy looking at the river, and Victor could have been off-duty, simply yielding to the seafaring impulse that is common to all Portuguese, and spotting the doctor there, it seemed only natural to greet him, for old times' sake. Ricardo Reis passed the entrance of the Hotel Bragança, went up the Rua do Alecrim, where engraved on stone steps were the words *clínica de enfermedades de los ojos y quirúrgicas, A. Mascaró, 1870,* there is nothing that tells us whether this Mascaró graduated from a medical faculty or was a simple practitioner, in those days the rules regarding diplomas were less strict, even today they are not that strict, we need only recall that Ricardo Reis treated heart patients without any special qualifications. He followed the itinerary of the statues, Eça de Queirós, Chiado, D'Artagnan, poor Adamastor viewed from behind. Pretending that he was admiring the statues, he walked around each slowly, three times, feeling that he was playing cops and robbers, but he soon calmed down, Victor was not following him.

The afternoon passed and darkness fell. Lisbon is a tranquil city with a wide river of legendary fame. Ricardo Reis did not go out to dinner, he scrambled two eggs, folded them into a bread roll, accompanying this meager fare with a glass of wine, and even this he found difficult to swallow. On edge and restless, he went down to the park after eleven o'clock to take another look at the ships. All he could see were the mooring lights, and now he could not even tell the difference between the dispatch boats and the torpedo boats. He was the only soul on the Alto de Santa Catarina, one could no longer count Adamastor, now completely petrified, the screaming throat forever silent, the face terrifying to behold. Ricardo Reis went home, the ships won't leave in the night, because of the risk of running aground. Half-dressed, he lay on his bed, slept, woke up, and went back to sleep, calmed by the great silence throughout the apartment as the first light of day filtered in between the slats of the shutters. When he woke up, nothing had happened, and now that another day had dawned it seemed impossible that anything could happen. He felt ashamed of himself, appalled that he had removed only his shoes and jacket and tie. I'll have a bath, he decided, and was bending down to look for his slippers under the bed when he heard the first cannonade. But perhaps he was mistaken, perhaps a piece of furniture had fallen in the apartment downstairs, perhaps the landlady had fainted with a thud, but another explosion rang out, the windowpanes shook, the ships are firing on the city. He opened the window, on the street, people were in a panic, a woman shouted, God help us, it's a revolution, and ran for dear life toward the park. Ricardo Reis pulled on his shoes, slipped on his jacket, just as well that he had not taken off his clothes, almost as if he had known what would happen. The neighbors were already on the stairs, wrapped in their dressing gowns. When they saw the doctor appear, and a doctor can be relied upon to know everything, they asked in great distress, Are there people hurt, Doctor. His leaving in such haste must mean that someone has called him out to deal with an emergency. Covering their bare necks, they trail after him, standing at the entrance to the building where out of modesty they are partially concealed. When Ricardo Reis arrived at the park, a crowd had already gathered. The residents of this neighborhood are privileged, because there is no better vantagepoint in Lisbon for watching vessels enter and leave. The warships were not firing on the city, the fortress of Almada was firing on the warships. On one of them. Ricardo Reis asked, Which ship is that. Fortunate for him, he asked someone who knew, It's the *Afonso de Albuquerque*. So it was the ship on which Lydia's brother was serving, the sailor Daniel, whom he had never met. He tried to picture his face, but could see only the face of Lydia. At this very moment she must be looking out of a window at the Hotel Bragança, or she has gone into the street in her maid's uniform, she is running to the Cais do Sodré, and now stands at the quay, her hands pressed to her bosom, perhaps weeping, perhaps with dry eyes and flushed cheeks, suddenly letting out a scream because the *Afonso de Albuquerque* has been hit by a shell, then another. Someone on the Alto de Santa Catarina is clapping his hands, at this moment the two old men appear, their lungs bursting, how did they manage to get here so quickly, living as they do at the bottom of the hill, but they would rather die than miss this, and that is certainly possible, considering the effort they have made. It all seems like a dream. Drifting slowly, the *Afonso de Albuquerque* has probably been struck in some vital organ, perhaps the boiler room, the rudder. The fortress of Almada continues to fire, and the *Afonso de Albuquerque* appears to answer, but we are not sure. From this side of the city new booms can be heard, louder, less frequent, That's the fortress of the Alto do Duque, someone remarks, they are lost now, they'll never get away. And at that very moment another ship emerges, a torpedo boat, the *Dão*, almost certainly the *Dão*, trying to shield herself with the smoke of her own stacks and skirting the southern bank in order to escape the guns of the fortress of Almada, but if she gets past Almada she will not escape the Alto do Duque. Shells explode near the shore, this is to get the range, the next volley will strike the ship, and yes, there is a direct hit. A white flag is already being unfurled on the *Dão*, but the firing continues, the ship begins to list, then white sheets, shrouds, funeral shrouds, the end is near, the *Bartolomeu Dias* will not even have time to leave her berth.

It is nine o'clock. One hundred minutes have passed since the hostilities began, the dawn mist has dispersed and the sun shines from a clear sky. They must be searching now for the men who jumped into the sea. From this belvedere there is nothing more to be seen. As the veterans explain what happened to some latecomers, Ricardo Reis sits down on a bench. The old men join him, eager to start up a conversation, but the doctor says nothing, he sits with his head lowered, as if he were the one who had tried to sail out to sea only to be caught in the net. While the adults talk, their excitement subsiding, the children start to play leapfrog and the little girls sing, *I went into Celeste's garden, what did you go there to do, I went there to look for a rose*. More appropriate would be the ballad from Nazaré, *Don't go to sea Tonho, you might drown Tonho, ah Tonho, poor Tonho, what an unfortunate fellow you are*. Lydia's brother is not Tonho, but when it comes to misfortune there is little difference. The old men, indignant, turn away when Ricardo Reis gets to his feet. He finds some comfort when he hears a woman say, out of pity, Poor souls, she is referring to the sailors but Ricardo Reis feels those words as if someone were caressing him, placing a hand on his forehead or gently stroking his hair. In his apartment he throws himself on the unmade bed, covers his eyes with his arm, and weeps freely, weeps foolish tears, because this was not his revolution, *Wise is the man who contents himself with the spectacle of the world*, I must repeat that phrase a thousand times, what should all this matter to one who no longer cares who wins and who loses. Ricardo Reis gets up and puts on his tie, he is about to go out, but passing his hand over his face, he feels his stubble, he need not look in the mirror to know that there are white hairs glistening there among the black, the harbinger of old age. The dice have been thrown, the card played has been covered with the ace of trumps, no matter how fast you run you cannot save your father from the gallows, these are popular sayings to help ordinary men bear the blows of fate. Ricardo Reis, an ordinary man, sets about shaving and washing himself, while he is shaving he doesn't think, he concentrates on the razor scraping at his skin, one of these days he must sharpen the blade. It was half-past eleven when he left his apartment for the Hotel Bragança, and why not, no one should be surprised to see a former guest who stayed for almost three months, who was so dutifully served by one of the chambermaids, a chambermaid whose brother took part in the mutiny, she herself had told him, Yes, Doctor, I have a brother at sea, he is serving on the *Afonso de Albuquerque*, no one should be surprised that Ricardo Reis has come to make inquiries, to see if he can help, poor girl, how she must have suffered, some people are born unlucky.

The buzzer sounds much hoarser, or has his memory started to deceive him. The figurine of the page mounted on the baluster raises its extinguished globe, even in France there were such pages, but he will never find out where this page came from, there is not time to know everything. At the top of the stairs Pimenta appears, about to descend, thinking a client has arrived with luggage, then he stops, not yet recognizing who is coming up. He could have forgotten, so many faces enter and leave the life of a hotel porter, and we must take the poor lighting into account as well. But now the new arrival is so close that even though he keeps his head lowered, there is not a shadow of doubt. Well upon my word, if it isn't Doctor Reis, how are you, Doctor. Good day Pimenta, that chambermaid, what is she called again, Lydia, is she here. Ah, no, Doctor, she went out and hasn't returned, I believe her brother was involved in the mutiny. Pimenta has barely finished speaking when Salvador appears on the landing, pretending to be surprised, Why Doctor, how delighted I am to see you back. Pimenta tells him what he already knows, The doctor would like to speak to Lydia. Ah, Lydia isn't here, but if I could be of any assistance. She had spoken to me about a brother who was serving in the navy, I only came to see if I could offer my services as a doctor. I understand, Doctor Reis, but Lydia went out as soon as the shooting began and she hasn't returned. Salvador always smiles when he is giving information, he makes a good manager, and let us repeat once more, the last time, that he has cause for complaint against this former guest, who slept with one of the chambermaids and perhaps still does, and who now turns up, playing the innocent, if he thinks he is deceiving the manager, he is much mistaken. Do you know where she might have gone, Ricardo Reis asked. She must be around somewhere, she could have gone to the Naval Ministry, or to her mother's house, or to the police station, because the police are always involved in such matters, but do not trouble yourself, Doctor, I will tell her that Doctor Reis was here, and she is sure to go looking for you. Salvador gave another smile, like one who has set a trap and can already see his prey caught by the leg, but Ricardo Reis answered, Yes, do tell her to come and see me, here is my home address, and he wrote the futile directions on a sheet of paper. Annoyed at this response, Salvador stopped smiling, but Ricardo Reis never learned what he was about to say, because two Spaniards came down from the second floor, engaged in heated discussion. One of them asked, *Señor Salvador los ha llevado el diablo a los marineros*. Yes, Don Camilo, the devil has taken them. Good, the hour has come to say *Arriba España, Viva Portugal, Arriba,* exclaimed Don Camilo, and Pimenta added on behalf of the Fatherland, *Viva*. As Ricardo Reis went downstairs, the buzzer sounded, there had once been a bell here, but the guests complained, they said it was like the bell at the gates of a cemetery.

Lydia did not come that afternoon. Ricardo Reis went out to buy the late edition of a newspaper. He scanned the headlines on the front page, then turned to the double center page. At the bottom, Twelve Sailors Killed, and their names and ages followed, Daniel Martins, twenty-three years of age. Ricardo Reis stopped in the middle of the street, holding the newspaper wide open, submerged in silence. The city has come to a standstill, or walks on tiptoe, its forefinger pressed to sealed lips, suddenly there was a deafening noise, the horn of an automobile, a quarrel between two lottery-ticket vendors, a child crying because his mother had cuffed his ear, Any more of that and I'll give you a good hiding. Lydia was not waiting for him, nor was there any indication that she had called. It is almost night. The newspaper reports that the arrested men were taken before the district attorney, then to Mitra, and that the bodies of the dead, some of whom still have to be identified, are in the morgue. Lydia must be searching for her brother, or else she is at her mother's house, both women weeping over this great and irreparable calamity.

A knock at the door. Ricardo Reis ran to open it, his open arms ready to embrace the tearful Lydia, but it was Fernando Pessoa, Ah, it's you. Were you expecting someone else. If you know what has happened, you must realize that yes, I am, Lydia, I believe I told you once, had a brother in the Navy. Is he dead, Yes, he is dead. They were in the bedroom, Fernando Pessoa seated at the foot of the bed, Ricardo Reis in a chair, the room now in total darkness. Half an hour passed in this way, and they heard a clock chiming on the floor above. How strange, Ricardo Reis thought to himself, I don't remember ever having heard that clock before, or perhaps I heard it once and then put it out of my mind. Fernando Pessoa sat with his hands on one knee, his fingers clasped, his head lowered, without stirring he said, I came to tell you that we will not see each other again. Why not. My time is up, do you remember my telling you that I had only a few months left. Yes, I remember. Well, that is the reason, those months have come to an end. Ricardo Reis tightened the knot in his tie, got to his feet, put on his jacket. He went to the bedside table, took *The God of the Labyrinth* and put it under his arm. Let's go then, he said, Where are you going, With you. You should stay here and wait for Lydia. I know I should. To console her after the loss of her brother. I can do nothing for her. And the book, what do you want that for. Despite the time granted me, I never managed to finish it, You won't have time, I will have all the time I could possibly want. You are deceiving yourself, reading is the first faculty one loses, remember. Ricardo Reis opened the book, saw meaningless marks, black scribbles, a page of blotches. The faculty has already left me, he said, but no matter, I'll take the book with me just the same. But why. I relieve the world of one enigma. As they left the apartment, Fernando

Pessoa told him, You forgot your hat. You know better than I do that hats aren't worn where we're going. On the sidewalk opposite the park, they watched the pale lights flicker on the river, the ominous shadows of the mountains. Let's go then, said Fernando Pessoa. Let's go, agreed Ricardo Reis. Adamastor did not turn around to look, perhaps afraid that if he did, he might let out finally his mighty howl. Here, where the sea ends and the earth awaits.

THE GOSPEL
ACCORDING TO
JESUS CHRIST

FOR PILAR

FORASMUCH AS MANY HAVE TAKEN IN HAND TO SET FORTH IN ORDER
a declaration of those things which are most surely believed among
us, even as they delivered them unto us, which from the beginning
were eyewitnesses, and ministers of the word; it seemed good to
me also, having had perfect understanding of all things from the
very first, to write unto thee in order, most excellent Theophilus,
that thou mightest know the certainty of those things, wherein thou
hast been instructed.

Luke 1.1–4

Quod scripsi, scripsi.
What I have written, I have written.

Pontius Pilate

THE SUN APPEARS IN ONE OF THE UPPER CORNERS OF THE rectangle, on the left of anyone looking at the picture. Representing the sun is a man's head that sends out rays of brilliant light and sinuous flames, like a wavering compass in search of the right direction, and this head has a tearful face, contorted by spasms of pain that refuse to abate. The gaping mouth sends up a cry we shall never hear, for none of these things is real, what we are contemplating is mere paper and ink, and nothing more. Beneath the sun we see a naked man tied to a tree trunk with a cloth around his loins to cover those parts we call private, and his feet are resting on a piece of wood set crosswise, to give him support and to prevent his feet from slipping, they are held by two nails driven deep into the wood. Judging from the anguished expression on the man's face and from his eyes, which are raised to heaven, this must be the Good Thief. His ringlets are another reassuring sign, for it is well known that this is how angels and archangels wear their hair, and so it would appear that the repentant criminal is already ascending to the world of heavenly beings. Impossible to say whether the trunk is still a tree that has been arbitrarily turned into an instrument of torture while continuing to draw nourishment from the soil through its roots, inasmuch as the lower part of the picture is covered by a man with a long beard. Richly attired in loose, flowing robes, he is looking upward but not toward heaven. This solemn posture and sad countenance must belong to Joseph of Arimathaea, because the only other person who comes to mind, Simon of Cyrene, after being forced to help the condemned man carry his cross, as was the practice when these executions took place, went about his own affairs, thinking more of a business transaction that called for an urgent decision than of the sufferings of a miserable wretch about to be crucified. Joseph of Arimathaea is that affluent and good-hearted man who donated a grave for the burial of the greatest criminal of all, but this act of generosity will be to no avail when the time comes to consider his beatification, let alone canonization. All he has on his head is the turban he always wears outdoors, unlike the woman in the foreground of the picture, whose hair hangs all the way down her back as she leans forward, enhanced by the supreme glory of a halo, in her case one edged with the finest embroidery. The kneeling woman must be Mary, because, as we know, all the women gathered here have that name, with one exception, she who is also called Magdalene. Anyone viewing this picture who knows the facts of life will swear immediately that this is the woman called Magdalene, for only someone with her disreputable past would have dared appear at such a solemn occasion wearing a low-cut dress with a close-fitting bodice to emphasize her ample bosom, which inevitably draws the lewd stares of passing men and puts their souls at grave risk of being dragged to perdition. Yet the expression on her face is one of contrition, and her wilting body conveys nothing other than her sorrowing soul, which we cannot ignore, even if it is hidden by tempting flesh, for this woman could be completely naked, had the artist so chosen to portray her, and still she would deserve our respect and veneration. Mary Magdalene, if that is her name, is holding to her lips the hand of another woman, who has collapsed to the ground as if bereft of strength or mortally wounded. Her name is also Mary, second in order of appearance but undoubtedly the most important Mary of all, if the central position she occupies in the lower part of the picture has any significance. Apart from her grieving expression and limp hands, nothing can be seen of her body, covered as it is by the copious folds of her mantle and by a tunic tied at the waist with a coarsely woven cord. She is older than the other Mary, which is reason enough, although not the only reason, why her halo should be more elaborate, at least that is what one would conclude in the absence of more precise information about the privileges of rank and seniority observed at that time. Considering, however, the enormous influence of this iconography, only an inhabitant of another planet, where no such drama has ever been enacted, could fail to know that this anguished woman is the widow of a carpenter named Joseph and the mother of numerous sons and daughters, although only one of her children was decreed by fate, or whoever governs fate, to achieve a little renown during his life and a great deal more after his death. Reclining on her left side, Mary, the mother of Jesus, rests her forearm on the hip of another woman, also kneeling and also named Mary, who might well be the real Mary Magdalene although we can neither see nor imagine the neckline of her tunic. Like the first woman in this trinity, she lets her long tresses hang loose down her back, but to all appearances they are fair, unless it is only by chance that the pen strokes are more delicate here, leaving empty spaces between the locks and thus allowing the engraver to lighten the tone. We are not trying to prove that Mary Magdalene was in fact blond, but simply point to the popular belief that women with blond hair, whether it be natural or dyed, are the most effective instruments of sin. Mary Magdalene, who, as everyone knows, was as wicked a woman as ever lived, must have been blond if we accept the opinion held, for better or worse, by half of mankind. It is not, however, because this third Mary has skin and hair fairer than the first that we suggest, despite the damning evidence of the first's exposed bosom, that the third is the Magdalene. What confirms her identity is that this third Mary, as she distractedly supports the limp arm of the mother of Jesus, is looking upward, and her enraptured gaze ascends with such power that it appears to elevate her entire being, it is a light that outshines the halo already encircling her head, a light that overpowers every thought and emotion. Only a woman who has loved as much as we believe Mary Magdalene loved could possibly have such an expression, it is she and no other, and thus we rule out the woman standing beside her. This is the fourth Mary, her hands half raised in a gesture of piety and her expression vague, she is accompanied on this side of the engraving by a youth barely adolescent, his knee bent languidly while with an affected and theatrical right hand he presents the four women playing out the poignant drama in the foreground. This is John, who looks so youthful, his hair in ringlets and his lips trembling. Like Joseph of Arimathaea, he also blocks some of the picture, his body concealing the foot of the tree on the other side, where no birds nest. All we see at the top is a second naked man hoisted into the air and bound and nailed to the wood like the first thief, but this one has smooth hair and his eyes are lowered, perhaps still capable of seeing the ground be- low. His thin face arouses our compassion, unlike the third thief on the other side, who even in the final throes of torment defiantly shows his face, which was not always so pale, for thieving gave him a good living. Thin and smooth haired, the second man bows to the earth that will devour him, this pathetic creature condemned to both death and hell must be the Bad Thief, an honest man when all is said and done, who, free of divine and human laws, did not pretend to believe that sudden repentance suffices to redeem a whole life of evil. Above him, also weeping and wailing like the sun in front, the moon can be seen in the guise of a woman with the most incongruous ring in one ear, an unprecedented liberty no artist or poet is likely to repeat. Both sun and moon illuminate the earth in equal measure, but the ambience of light is circular and shadowless, causing everything on the distant horizon to stand out clearly, turrets and walls, a drawbridge across a moat whose water glistens, Gothic arches, and, on the crest of the farthest hill, the motionless sails of a windmill. Somewhat closer, in this deceptive perspective, four horsemen in armor and helmets, bearing lances, proudly parade their horses with admirable dexterity, but they appear to have come to the end of their display and are making farewell gestures to an invisible audience. The same impression of closing festivities is given by that foot soldier who is on the point of going off, carrying something in his right hand that could be a cloth, perhaps even a mantle or tunic, while two more soldiers look annoyed, frustrated, as if they had lost at gambling, although from afar it is difficult to tell what is in their minute faces. Hovering over these common soldiers and the walled city are four angels, two of them portrayed full length. They weep and mourn, with the exception of the angel who solemnly holds a goblet to the crucified man's right side in order to collect the last drop of blood from a lance wound. In this place known as Golgotha, many have met the same cruel fate and many others will follow them, but this naked man, nailed by hands and feet to a cross, the son of Joseph and Mary, named Jesus, is the only one whom posterity will remember and honor by inscribing his initials in capitals. So this is he whom Joseph of Arimathaea and Mary Magdalene are gazing upon, this is he who causes the sun and moon to weep and who only a moment ago praised the Good Thief and despised the Bad Thief, failing to understand that there is no difference between them, or, if there is a difference, it lies in something else, for good and evil do not exist in themselves, each being merely the absence of the other. Shining above his head with a thousand rays brighter than those of the sun and moon put together is a placard in Roman letters proclaiming him king of the Jews, surrounded by a wounding crown of thorns like that worn, without their even knowing and with no visible sign of blood, by all who are not allowed to be sovereigns of their own bodies. Jesus, unlike the two thieves, has nowhere to rest his feet, the entire weight of his body would be supported by his hands nailed to the wood had he not life enough left in him to hold himself erect over his bent legs, but that life is nearing its end as the blood continues to flow from the abovementioned wound. Between the two wedges that keep the cross upright and that have also been driven into the dark ground, making a gaping wound there as irremediable as any human grave, we see a skull, also a shinbone and a shoulder blade, but what concerns us is the skull, for this is what Golgotha means, skull. No one knows who put these human remains here or for what purpose, perhaps it was simply a sly reminder to these poor wretches about what awaits them before they turn at last to earth, dust, and nothingness. But there are some who claim that this is Adam's skull, risen from the deep murk of ancient geological strata and, because it can not now return there, eternally condemned to behold its only possible paradise which is forever lost. Farther back, in the same field where the horsemen execute one last maneuver, a man is walking away but looking back in this direction. In his left hand he carries a bucket, and in his right a staff. At the tip of the staff there ought to be a sponge, not easy to see from here, and the bucket, one can safely bet, contains water with vinegar. One day, and forever after, this man will be much maligned, accused of having given Jesus vinegar out of spite and contempt when he asked for water, but the truth is that he offered him vinegar and water because at that time it was one of the best ways of quenching thirst. The man walks away, does not wait for the end, he did all he could to relieve the mortal thirst of the three condemned men, making no distinction between Jesus and the thieves, because these are things of this earth, which will persist on this earth, and from them will be written the only possible history.

Night is far from over. Hanging from a nail near the door, an oil lamp is burning, but its flickering flame, like a small, luminous almond, barely impinges on the darkness, which fills the house from top to bottom and penetrates the farthest corners, where the shadows are so dense that they appear to form a solid mass. Joseph awoke with a fright, as if someone had roughly shaken him by the shoulder, but he must have been dreaming, because he lives alone in this house with his wife, who has not so much as stirred and is fast asleep. Not only is it unusual for him to wake in the middle of the night, but he rarely opens his eyes before daybreak, when the gray, cold morning light begins to filter through the chink in the door. How often he has thought of repairing the door, what could be easier for a carpenter than to cover the chink with a piece of wood left over from some job, but he is now so accustomed to seeing that vertical strip of light when he opens his eyes in the morning that he has reached the absurd conclusion that without it he would be trapped forever in the shadows of sleep, in the darkness of his own body and the darkness of the world. The chink in the door is as much a part of the house as the walls and ceiling, as the oven and earthen floor. In a whisper, to avoid disturbing his wife, who was still asleep, he recited words of thanksgiving, words he said each morning upon returning from the mysterious land of dreams, Thanks be to You, Almighty God, King of the Universe, who has mercifully restored my soul to life. Perhaps because he had not fully regained the power of all five senses, five unless at that time people were not yet aware there were five or, conversely, had more and were about to lose those that would serve little purpose nowadays, Joseph watched his body from a distance while it slowly was occupied by a soul making its gradual return, like trickling waters as they wend their way in rivulets and streams before penetrating the earth to feed sap into stems and leaves. Looking at Mary as she lay beside him, Joseph began to realize just how laborious this return to wakefulness could be, and a disturbing thought came to him, that this wife of his, fast asleep, was really a body without a soul, for no soul is present in a body while it sleeps, otherwise there would be no sense in our thanking God each morning for having restored our souls as we awaken. Then a voice within him asked, What thing or person inside us dreams what we dream, and then he wondered, Are dreams perhaps the soul's memories of the body, and this seemed a reasonable explanation. Mary stirred, could her soul have been near at hand, already here in the house, but she did not awaken, no doubt in the midst of some troubled dream, and after heaving a deep sigh like a broken sob she drew closer to her husband, with a sensuousness she would never have dared indulge while awake. Joseph pulled the thick, rough blanket over his shoulders and snuggled up close to Mary. He could feel her warmth, perfumed like a linen chest filled with dried herbs, gradually penetrate the fibers of his tunic and merge with the heat of his own body. Then slowly he closed his eyes, stopped thinking, and, oblivious to his soul, sank back into a deep sleep.

When he woke again, the cock was crowing. A dim, grayish light seeped through the chink in the door. Having patiently waited for the shadows of night to disperse, time was preparing the way for yet another day to reach the world. Because we no longer live in that fabulous age when the sun, to whom we owe so much, was so generous that it halted its journey over Gibeon in order to give Joshua ample time to overcome the five kings besieging the city. Joseph sat up on his mat, drew back the sheet, and at that moment the cock crowed a second time, reminding him that there was another prayer of thanksgiving to be said. Praise be to You, O Lord, our God, King of the Universe, who gave the cock the intelligence to distinguish between night and day, prayed Joseph, and the cock crowed for a third time. Usually, at the first sign of daybreak all the cocks in the neighborhood would crow to one another, but today they remained silent, as if their night had not yet ended or was just beginning. Joseph looked at his wife's face, puzzled by her deep slumber, since normally the slightest noise awakened her, as if she were a bird. Some mysterious power appeared to be hovering over Mary, pressing her down without completely immobilizing her, for even in the shadows her body could be seen to tremble gently, like water rippling in the breeze. Could she be ill, he wondered, but he was distracted from this worrying thought by a sudden urge to urinate, and this, too, was unusual. He rarely felt the need to relieve himself at this early hour or with such urgency. Slipping quietly from under the sheet to avoid waking his wife, for it is written that a man should do everything possible to maintain his self-respect, he cautiously opened the creaking door and went out into the yard. At that hour of the morning everything was gray as ash. Joseph headed for the low shed where he tethered his donkey, and there he relieved himself, listening with dreamy satisfaction to the explosive sound of his urine as it spurted onto the hay scattered on the ground. The donkey turned its head, two huge eyes shining in the dark, then gave its furry ears a vigorous shake before sticking its nose back into the manger, foraging for leftovers with thick, sensuous lips. Joseph fetched the large pitcher used for washing, tipped it sideways, and let the water pour over his hands, then, drying them on his tunic, he praised God who in His infinite wisdom had endowed mankind with the essential orifices and vessels to live, for if any one of them should fail to close or open as required, the result would be death. Looking up at the sky, Joseph was overwhelmed. The sun is slow to appear, in the sky there is not even a hint of dawn's crimson, no shade of rose or cherry, nothing except clouds to be seen from where he stands, one vast roof of low clouds like tiny flattened balls of wool, all identical and the same shade of violet, which deepens and glows on the side where the sun breaks through, then across the sky is increasingly dark until it merges with what remains of the night on the other side. Joseph had never seen such a sky, although old men often spoke of portents in the skies that attested to the power of God, rainbows that covered half the celestial vault, towering ladders that connected heaven and earth, providential showers of manna, but never of this mysterious color, which might just as easily signify the beginning of the world as the end, this roof floating above the earth, made up of thousands of tiny clouds that almost touch one another and reach in all directions like the stones of a wasteland. Terror-stricken, he thought the world was ending and he was the only witness of God's final judgment, the only one. Silence reigns in heaven and on earth, no sounds can be heard from the nearby houses, not so much as a human voice, a child crying, a prayer or curse, a gust of wind, the bleat of a goat or the bark of a dog. Why are the cocks not crowing, he muttered to himself, and repeated the question anxiously, as if the cocks, crowing might be the last hope of salvation. Then the sky began to change. Pink tinges and streaks gradually, almost imperceptibly crept into the violet on the belly of the clouds, until finally it turned red, then was gone, and without warning the sky exploded into light, many shafts of gold that pierced clouds no longer small but now formidable, enormous barges that hoisted blazing sails and plied a sky that had at last been liberated. Joseph's fear subsided, his eyes widened in astonishment and wonder, and with good reason, for he alone was witnessing this spectacle. In a loud voice he praised the Lord of all creation for the eternal majesty of the heavens, whose ineffable splendors leave men struggling with simple words of gratitude, Thanks be to You, O Lord, for this and for that and for that. As he spoke, the tumult of life, whether summoned by his voice or rushing through a door that had carelessly been left open, invaded the space previously occupied by silence, leaving it scarcely any room, a patch here and there, such as those tiny marshes that the murmuring forests engulf and hide from view. The sun rose and spread its light, a vision of unbearable beauty, two enormous hands sending into flight a shimmering bird of paradise that opened its great tail with a thousand iridescent eyes, causing a nameless bird nearby to burst into song. A gust of wind hit Joseph in the face, caught his beard and tunic, eddied around him like a tiny whirlwind moving across a desert, unless he was imagining things and this was nothing more than the blood rushing to his head, a shiver going up his spine like a tongue of fire and stirring a quite different urge.

Moving as if inside a swirling column of air, Joseph went into the house and shut the door behind him. He paused for a moment, waiting for his eyes to become accustomed to the dark. The lamp cast scarcely any light. Wide awake, Mary lay on her back, listening, staring into space, as if waiting. Joseph quietly approached and slowly drew back the sheet. She averted her eyes, began to lift the hem of her tunic, and no sooner had she pulled it to her navel than he was on top of her, his own tunic hitched to his waist. Mary's legs now were open, perhaps they had opened by themselves as she dreamed and she did not close them out of this sudden lassitude, or else from the premonition of a married woman who knows her duty. God, who is omnipresent, was there but, pure spirit that He is, was unable to see how Joseph's flesh touched Mary's, how his flesh penetrated her flesh as had been ordained, and perhaps He was not even there when the holy seed of Joseph poured into the holy womb of Mary, both holy, being the fountain and chalice of life. For in truth, there are things God Himself does not understand, even though He created them. Out in the yard, God could hear neither the gasp that escaped Joseph's lips as he came nor the low moan Mary was unable to suppress. Joseph rested on his wife's body no more than a minute, and perhaps less. Pulling down her tunic and drawing up the sheet, she covered her face with her arm. Joseph stood in the middle of the room, raised his hands, and, looking up at the ceiling, gave the most heartfelt thanksgiving of all, which is reserved for men, I thank You, Almighty God, King of the Universe, for not having made me a woman. By then, God must have already abandoned the yard, for the walls did not shake or cave in, nor did the ground part. All that could be heard was Mary saying, in that submissive voice one expects from women, Thanks be to You, O Lord, for having made me according to Your will. Now, there is no difference between these words and those spoken to the angel Gabriel, for clearly anyone who could say, Behold the handmaiden of the Lord, do with me as You will, might just as easily have said, instead, this prayer. Then the wife of the carpenter Joseph got up from her mat, rolled it up together with that of her husband, and folded the sheet they shared in common.

Joseph and Mary lived in a village called Nazareth, a place of little importance and with few inhabitants, in the region of Galilee. Their house was no different from the others, a lopsided cube made of bricks and clay and as poor as poor could be. No striking examples of imaginative architecture to be found here. To save on material, the house had been built into a hillside, which formed the rear wall and allowed easy access to the flat roof, which also served as a terrace. Joseph, as we know, was a carpenter by trade and fairly capable, although he had neither the skill nor the talent for jobs that required fine workmanship. This criticism should not be taken too seriously, for one needs time to gain experience and acquire skills, and we must not forget that Joseph is barely in his twenties and lives in a place with few resources and even fewer opportunities. Nor should a man be measured simply on the basis of his professional ability. For all his youth, this Joseph is one of the most honest and pious men of Nazareth, assiduous in attending the synagogue and prompt in carrying out his duties, and while he may not be endowed with any special powers of eloquence, he can argue and make astute observations, especially when given a chance to use some apt image or metaphor related to his work, carpentry. He does not possess, however, what one might call a creative imagination, and during his brief life will never come up with a memorable parable to be handed down to posterity, let alone one of those brilliant conceits so clearly expressed that there is nothing more to say yet so obscure and ambiguous that they intrigue scholars for years to come.

As for Mary's talents, these are even less apparent, but no more than we might expect of a sixteen-year-old girl who, although married, is still a baby, as it were, for even in those days people used such expressions. Notwithstanding her frail appearance, she works as hard as all the other women, carding, spinning, and weaving cloth, baking the family bread each morning, fetching water from the well and then carrying it up the steep slope, a large pitcher balanced on her head and another on her hip. In the late afternoon she sets off through the byways and fields of the Lord, gathering wood and cutting stubble and filling an extra basket with cow's dung and the thistles and briers that thrive on the upper slopes of Nazareth, the best thing God could ever have devised for lighting a fire or braiding a crown. It would have been easier to load everything onto a donkey's back, but Joseph needs the beast to carry his lumber. Mary goes barefoot to the well, goes barefoot into the fields, in clothes that are forever getting soiled and torn and that constantly need washing and mending, because new clothes are reserved for her husband, women like Mary making do with very little. When she attends the synagogue, she enters by the side door, as the law requires of women, and even if she finds thirty other women there, or all the women of Nazareth, or even the entire female population of Galilee, they must wait until at least ten men arrive for the service, in which the women will participate only passively. Unlike Joseph her husband, Mary is neither upright nor pious, but she is not to blame for this, the blame lies with the language she speaks if not with the men who invented it, because that language has no feminine form for the words upright and pious.

Now one fine day, four weeks after that unforgettable morning when the clouds in the sky turned a mysterious violet, Joseph happened to be at home. The sun was about to set and he was sitting on the floor, eating his food with his fingers, as was then the custom, while Mary stood waiting for him to finish before having her own supper. Neither spoke, for he had nothing to say and she was unable to express what was on her mind. Suddenly a beggar appeared at the gate outside, a rare occurrence in this village, where people were so poor, a fact unlikely to have escaped the begging fraternity, which had a nose for places where there were pickings, and that was certainly not the case here. Nevertheless Mary ladled into a bowl a good portion of the lentils with chopped onions and mashed chickpeas set aside for her own supper, and took it out to the beggar, who sat on the ground. She did not need her husband's spoken permission, he merely nodded, for as everyone knows those were times when words were few and a simple thumbs down or up was enough to condemn a man to death or save him, as in the arenas of ancient Rome. The sunset, although quite different, was spectacular, too, with its myriad wisps of cloud scattered through the sky, rose-colored, mother-of-pearl, salmon-pink, cherry, adjectives used here on earth so that we may understand one another, for none of these colors, as far as we know, have names in heaven. The beggar must have gone without food for three days to have scraped and licked his bowl clean so quickly, and back he comes to return the bowl and express his gratitude. Mary, opening the door, finds him standing there, but somehow he looks broader and taller than before. So it must be true that there is a great difference between going hungry and just having eaten, for this man's face and eyes are glowing, his tattered clothes flap in a strange wind, blurring her vision so that his rags take on the appearance of rich raiment, a sight that must be seen to be believed. Mary put out her hands to receive the earthenware bowl, which, through some extraordinary optical illusion, perhaps due to the light of the sky, was transformed into a vessel of the purest gold. And, as the bowl passed from his hands into hers, the beggar said in resonant tones, because even the poor man's voice had changed, May the Lord bless you, good woman, and give you all the children your husband desires, and may He also protect you from my sad fate, for, alas, I have nowhere to rest my head in this wretched world. Mary held the bowl in cupped hands, one chalice held by another, as if waiting for the beggar to fill it, which is what he did. Without warning he bent down and gathered a handful of earth and, raising his arm, allowed it to trickle through his fingers while reciting in a low voice, Earth to earth, ashes to ashes, dust to dust, nothing begins without coming to an end, every beginning comes from an ending. Mary was puzzled and asked him, What does that mean, but the beggar simply replied, Good woman, you have a child in your womb and that is man's only destiny, to begin and end, to end and begin. How do you know I'm with child. Even before the belly swells, a child can be seen shining through its mother's eyes. If that is true, then my husband would already have seen his child in my eyes. Perhaps he does not look at you when you look at him. Who are you who knows so much without hearing it from my own lips. I am an angel, but tell no one.

Then his shining robe turned back to rags, he shriveled as if licked by fire, and this wondrous transformation took place just in time, thanks be to God, for no sooner had the beggar quietly disappeared than Joseph emerged in the doorway, his suspicions aroused by whispering voices and

Mary's absence. What else did the beggar want, he asked, and Mary, at a loss for words, could only repeat, From earth to earth, from ashes to ashes, from dust to dust, nothing begins without coming to an end, nothing ends without having a beginning. Was that what he said. Yes, and he also said that a father's child shines through its mother's eyes. Look at me. I am looking. I can see a light in your eyes, said Joseph, and Mary told him, It must be your child. As the evening sky changed from blue to the somber shades of night, the bowl began to glow with a radiance that changed Mary's face, and her eyes seemed to belong to a much older woman. Are you pregnant, Joseph finally asked her. Yes, I am, replied Mary. Why didn't you tell me sooner. I meant to tell you today, I was waiting for you to finish eating. And then the beggar turned up. That's right. What else did he have to say, for he certainly took his time. That the Lord should give me all the children you wished for. What do you have in that bowl to make it shine so. Nothing but earth. Soil is black, clay green, and sand white, of these three sand alone shines in the day, but it is night. Forgive me, I am only a woman and cannot explain these things. You say he took some earth from the ground and dropped it into the bowl, at the same time uttering the words, Earth to earth. Yes, those very words.

Joseph went to open the gate, looked right and left. No sign of him, he's vanished, he told her, and feeling reassured, Mary returned to the house, for the beggar, if he really was an angel, could only be seen if he wished. She set the bowl down on the stone slab of the hearth, took a live coal from the fire and lit the oil lamp, blowing until she raised a tiny flame. Puzzled, Joseph came inside, tried to hide his suspicions, moved with the solemnity of a patriarch, which looked odd in someone so young. Furtively he examined the bowl filled with luminous earth, his expression ironic and skeptical, but if he was trying to assert superiority, he was wasting his time, for Mary's eyes were lowered and her thoughts elsewhere. Using a small stick, Joseph poked at the earth, fascinated as he watched it darken when disturbed, only to regain its brilliance, light sparkling in all directions over the dull surface. There's a mystery here I can't fathom, either the beggar brought this earth with him and you thought he gathered it here, or there is some magic at work, for who ever saw shining earth in Nazareth. Mary remained silent. She was eating what was left of her lentils with bread dipped in oil. As she broke bread, she observed the holy law by giving thanks in the humble tone befitting a woman, Praise be to You, Adonai, Lord God and King of the Universe, who brings forth bread from the earth. She continued eating in silence while Joseph mused at length, as if interpreting a verse from the Torah in the synagogue or a phrase from the prophets, the words Mary had spoken, words he himself spoke when breaking bread, and he tried to imagine what grain might grow out of luminous earth, what bread it would produce, and what light we would carry within us if we ate such bread. Are you sure the beggar took it from the ground, he asked Mary a second time, and Mary answered, Yes, I'm sure. Perhaps it was shining all the time. No, it wasn't shining on the ground. This should have allayed the fears of any husband, but Joseph believed, like all men at that time and in that place, that the truly wise man is on his guard against the wiles and deceptions of women. To converse little with them and pay them even less heed must be the motto of a prudent husband mindful of the advice of Rabbi Josephat ben Yochanan, for at the hour of death each man must give account of any idle conversations he has held with his wife. Joseph asked himself whether this conversation with Mary was necessary, and having decided that it was, given the unusual nature of what had happened, he swore to himself that he would never forget the holy words of the rabbi, his namesake, for Josephat is the same as Joseph, rather than suffer remorse at the hour of death, which, God willing, will be peaceful. Then he asked himself whether he should tell the elders of the synagogue about this curious affair of the mysterious beggar and the luminous earth, and decided he should, to ease his conscience and keep the peace in his own home.

Mary finished eating. She took the bowls outside to wash them, but not the bowl used by the beggar. There are now two lights in the house, that of the oil lamp struggling valiantly against the darkness of night, and the aura from the bowl, flickering yet constant, like a sun that is slow in appearing. Seated on the floor, Mary waits for her husband to resume the conversation, but Joseph has nothing more to say to her, he is mentally rehearsing the speech he will make tomorrow before the council of elders. How frustrating it is, not to know precisely what transpired between his wife and the beggar, not to know what else they might have said to each other, but he decides to question her no further. He might as well believe the story she has now told him twice, because if she is lying, he will never know, while she will know and almost certainly be laughing at him, her mantle covering her face, just as Eve laughed at Adam, but behind his back, for in those days people did not wear mantles. One thought led to another, and Joseph soon convinced himself that the beggar had been sent by Satan. The great tempter, aware that times had changed and that people were now more cautious, was offering not one of nature's fruits but the promise of a different, luminous soil, counting once more on the credulity and weakness of women. Joseph's mind is in turmoil, but he is pleased with himself and the conclusion he has reached. Unaware of her husband's tortuous thoughts about Satan's intrigue, Mary is troubled by a strange feeling of emptiness now that she has told him of her pregnancy. Not an inner emptiness, to be sure, for she knows perfectly well that her womb, and in the strict sense of the word, is full, but an outer emptiness, as if the world has receded and become remote. She recalls, but as if evoking another life, that after supper and before unrolling the mats for the night she always had some task in hand to fill the hours, but now she feels no inclination whatever to rise from where she sits gazing at the light that glows back at her over the rim of the bowl, gazing and awaiting the birth of her child. If truth be told, her thoughts are not that clear, for thought, when all is said and done, as others and we ourselves have observed before, is like a great ball of thread coiled around itself, loose in places, taut in others, inside our head. It is impossible to know its full extent, one would have to unwind and then measure it, but however hard one tries or pretends to try, this cannot be done without assistance. One day, someone will come and tell us where to cut the cord that ties man to his navel and thought to its origin.

The following morning, after a restless night in which he was constantly disturbed by the same nightmare, where he saw himself falling time and time again inside an enormous upturned bowl as if under a starry sky, Joseph went to the synagogue to seek the advice of the elders. His story was extraordinary, though more extraordinary than he knew because, as we know, he had not been told the whole story. Were it not for the high esteem in which he was held by the old men of Nazareth, he would have had to go home with his tail between his legs and the reproachful words of Ecclesiasticus in his ears, To trust a man hastily shows a shallow mind. And he, poor fellow, would not have had the presence of mind to reply with words from the same Ecclesiasticus, regarding the dream that had haunted him all night, What you see in a dream is but a reflection, a face in a mirror. When he finished telling his story, the elders looked at one another and then at Joseph, and the oldest man there, translating the silent mistrust of the council into a direct question, asked, Is this the truth you have spoken, whereupon the carpenter replied, The truth, the whole truth, as God is my witness. The elders then debated among themselves while Joseph waited at a discreet distance, until finally they summoned him and said that they would send three envoys to question Mary herself about this mysterious event in order to discover the identity of the beggar whom no one else had seen, by learning what he looked like, the exact words he used, and if anyone could remember seeing him beg for alms in Nazareth or provide any information about the stranger. Joseph was pleased because, although he would never admit it, he did not want to confront his wife alone. Her habit in recent days of keeping her eyes lowered was beginning to disconcert him. There was modesty in it, but also, unmistakably, something provocative, as in the look of a woman who knows more than she is prepared to disclose or wants others to notice. Verily I say unto you, the treachery of women knows no limits, especially when they feign innocence.

And so the envoys depart, Joseph leading the way, and they are Abiathar, Dothan, and Zacchaeus, names recorded here to forestall any suspicion of historical inaccuracy in the minds of those who have acquired their version of the story from other sources, a version perhaps more in accordance with tradition but not necessarily more factual. The names having been revealed and the existence of the men who used them established, there can be no remaining doubts. The unusual sight of three elders moving in solemn procession through the streets, their robes and beards caught by the breeze, soon drew the local urchins, who gathered around them and began aping their walk as children will, jeering and shouting and chasing after the envoys all the way from the synagogue to the house of Joseph, who was much put out by this boisterous parade. Attracted by the noise, women began to appear in the doorways of the neighboring houses and, sensing something amiss, they sent their children to find out what such a delegation was doing at Mary's door. To no avail, because only the elders were allowed to enter. The door was firmly closed behind them, and no woman of Nazareth, however inquisitive, learned or knows to this day what took place in the house of Joseph, the carpenter. Forced to invent something to satisfy the hunger of their curiosity, they accused the beggar, whom they had never set eyes on, of being a common thief. A great injustice, because the angel, if angel is what he was, did not steal the food he ate, and even delivered a holy prophecy in exchange. While the two senior elders interrogated Mary, the third, the youngest, Zacchaeus, went around the immediate vicinity gathering any details people could remember about a beggar who answered the description given by the carpenter's wife, but none of the neighbors could help, No, sir, no beggar passed this way yesterday, and if he did, he didn't knock at my door, it must have been a thief passing through, who when he found someone at home pretended to be a beggar and then left in a hurry, the oldest trick in the book.

Zacchaeus arrived back at Joseph's house with nothing to report about the beggar just as Mary was repeating for the fourth time the facts we already know. She stood as if guilty of a crime, the bowl set on the ground, and inside it, constant as a throbbing heart, the strange earth. Joseph sat on one side, and the elders sat in front like a tribunal of judges. Dothan, the second of the three, said, It's not that we don't believe your story, but you're the only person who spoke to this man, if he was a man, all your husband knows is that he heard his voice, and now Zacchaeus here tells me that none of your neighbors saw him. As God is my witness, I swear I am telling the truth. The truth, perhaps, but is it the whole truth. I shall drink the water of the Lord and He will prove my innocence. The trial of bitter water is for women suspected of infidelity, but you couldn't have been unfaithful to your husband because he didn't give you enough time. Falsehood is said to be the same as infidelity. That's another kind of infidelity. My words are as true as the rest of me. Then Abiathar, the oldest of the three, told her, We shall question you no further, the Lord will reward you sevenfold for the truth you have spoken or punish you sevenfold if you have deceived us. He fell silent, then turned to Zacchaeus and Dothan and asked them, What shall we do with this bright earth, which prudence demands should not remain here, for it might be one of Satan's tricks. Dothan said, Let this earth return whence it came, let it return to its former darkness. Zacchaeus said, We know not who the beggar is, or why he chose to be seen by Mary alone, or the meaning of the earth that shines in the bowl. Dothan proposed, Let us take it into the desert and scatter it there, far from the eyes of men, that the wind may disperse it and the rain erase it. Zacchaeus said, If this earth is some divine gift, then it must not be removed, if on the other hand it forebodes evil, then let those to whom it was given bear the consequences. Abiathar asked, What do you suggest then, and Zacchaeus replied, That the bowl be buried here and covered up so that there is no contact with the natural earth, for a gift from God, even when buried, is never lost, whereas the power of evil is much diminished if hidden from sight. Abiathar asked, What do you say, Dothan, to which the latter replied, I agree with Zacchaeus, let us do as he says. Abiathar told Mary, Withdraw so that we may proceed. Where shall I go, she asked him, whereupon Joseph, agitated, said, If we are to bury the bowl, let it be somewhere away from the house, for I will never rest with a light buried underneath me. Abiathar reassured him, That can be done, then he told Mary, You remain here. The men went out into the yard, Zacchaeus carrying the bowl. The sound of a spade could soon be heard digging as Joseph briskly set to work, and a few minutes later Mary recognized the voice of Abiathar, You can stop now, the hole is deep enough. Mary peered through the chink in the door, watched her husband cover the bowl with a curved potsherd then lower it into the hole as deep as his arm was long. He rose, grabbed his spade, filled the hole, and stamped the ground down firmly with his feet.

The men remained in the yard, conversing among themselves and gazing at the patch of fresh earth, as if they had just buried a treasure and were trying to memorize the spot. But this was not the topic of conversation, because suddenly Zacchaeus could be heard saying aloud, in a tone of playful reproach, Now then, Joseph, what kind of carpenter are you, when you can't even make a bed for your pregnant wife. The others laughed, and Joseph joined them rather than lose face by showing his annoyance. Mary saw them walk to the gate, and now, seated on the stone slab of the hearth, she was looking around the room, wondering where they could put a bed if Joseph decided to make one. She tried not to think about the earthenware bowl or the luminous earth or whether the beggar was really an angel or only some practical joker. If a woman is promised a bed for her house, she must start thinking about the best place to put it.

BETWEEN THE MONTHS OF TAMMUZ AND AB, WHEN GRAPES were gathered in the vineyards and the figs began ripening amid the dark green vine leaves, certain events took place. Some were normal and commonplace, such as a man and woman coming together in the flesh, and after a while she tells him, I am carrying your child, others quite extraordinary, such as an annunciation entrusted to a passing beggar whose only crime seems to have been that peculiar phenomenon of the bright earth, which is now safe from prying eyes thanks to Joseph's mistrust and the prudence of the elders. The dog days are fast approaching, the fields are bare, nothing but stubble and parched soil. During the oppressive hours of the day Nazareth is a village submerged in silence and solitude. Only when night descends and the stars appear can one sense the presence of a landscape or hear the music of the heavenly planets as they glide past one another. After supper Joseph sat out in the yard, to the right of the door, to get some air. How he loved to feel the fresh evening breeze on his face and beard. Mary joined him, squatting on the ground like her husband but on the other side of the door, and there they remained in silence, listening to the sounds coming from the neighboring houses, the bustle of domestic life, which they, too, would experience once they had children. May God send us a boy, Joseph had prayed throughout the day, and Mary, too, kept thinking, Let it be a boy, dear God, but she had other reasons for wanting a boy. Her belly was slow in growing bigger, weeks and months would pass before her condition became visible, and since, out of modesty and discretion, she saw little of her neighbors, there would be general surprise when she turned into a balloon overnight. Perhaps the real reason for her secretiveness was her fear that someone might connect her pregnancy with the appearance of the mysterious beggar. Such thoughts may strike us as absurd, but in moments of weariness when her mind began to stray, Mary could not help wondering how all this had come about and who was the real father of this child she carried in her womb. As everyone knows, when women are pregnant, they are given to strange cravings and flights of fancy, some of them worse than those of Mary, which we shall not betray lest we tarnish the reputation of this mother-to-be.

Time passed, the weeks dragged, the month of Elul hot as a furnace, with the scorching winds from the southern deserts stifling the atmosphere, a season when dates and figs turn to trickling honey, and the month of Tishri bringing the first rains of autumn to moisten the soil in time for tilling and sowing, and the following month of Heshvan, when olives are gathered and the days finally turn cool. Unable to make anything grand, Joseph decided to make a simple bed where Mary might at last find rest for her swollen and cumbersome body. Heavy rains fell during the last days of Kislev and throughout most of Tebet, forcing him to interrupt his work in the yard. He took advantage of the dry spells to assemble the larger pieces of wood, but usually he had to work indoors in poor light, and there he planed and polished the unfinished frame, covering the floor all around him with shavings and sawdust, which Mary would sweep up later and dispose of in the yard.

In the month of Shebat the almond trees blossomed. In the month of Adar, the feast of Purim had already been celebrated when Roman soldiers appeared in Nazareth, a familiar sight throughout Galilee. Detachments went from village to city and from city to village, while others were dispatched into the country in Herod's kingdom, to inform the people that by order of Caesar Augustus every family domiciled in the provinces governed by the consul Publius Sulpicius Quirinus must participate in a census, which like all the others would bring the records up to date on those who had not yet paid their taxes to Rome. Without exception, every family had to register in their place of birth. Most of the people who gathered in the square to hear the proclamation did not mind the imperial edict, for as natives of Nazareth, settled for generations, they intended to register there. But some families had come from other parts of the kingdom, from Gaulinitis or Samaria, from Judaea, Peraea, or Idumaea, from here and there, from far and wide, and these began making preparations for the long journey, complaining bitterly about the perversity and greed of Rome and asking what would become of their crops, since it was almost time to harvest the flax and barley. And those who had large families, with babes in arms and elderly parents and grandparents, unless they had transportation of their own, wondered from whom they could borrow donkeys, or hire them at a reasonable price, and if there was a long and arduous journey ahead, ample supplies of food would be required, and water bags if they had to cross the desert, and mats and mantles for sleeping, and cooking utensils, and extra clothing, because the cold wet season was not yet over and they might have to spend nights out in the open.

Joseph learned about the edict only after the soldiers left to carry their glad tidings elsewhere. His next-door neighbor, Ananias, suddenly appeared in a great fluster to tell him what had happened. Fortunately for Ananias, he could register in Nazareth, nor would he be celebrating Passover in Jerusalem this year, because of the harvest, so he was spared both journeys. Ananias came to warn his neighbor, but warned him with such a smug expression, as if bearing good news. Alas, even the best of men can be two-faced, and we do not know this Ananias well enough to decide whether his is a momentary lapse from grace or if he has fallen under the influence of one of Satan's wicked angels with spare time on its hands. Joseph, hammering away at a plank of wood, at first did not hear Ananias calling him from the gate. Mary, whose ears were keener, heard a voice call, Joseph, but it was her husband who was being summoned, and who was she to tug at his sleeve and ask, Are you deaf, can't you hear someone calling you from the gate. Ananias called out even louder, the hammering stopped, and Joseph went to see what his neighbor wanted. Ananias was invited in and, after the customary greetings, inquired in the voice of one who seeks reassurance, Where are you from, Joseph, and, surprised, Joseph told him, I'm from Bethlehem of Judaea. Isn't that near Jerusalem. Yes, quite near. And are you going there to celebrate the Passover, asked Ananias, and Joseph replied, No, I've decided not to go this year, because my wife is expecting our child any day now. Oh, is that so. But why do you ask. Whereupon Ananias raised his arms to heaven and wailed mournfully, Poor Joseph, the trouble that awaits you, the aggravation, all this work to be done here and you're expected to put down your tools and travel all that way, so help me God, who sees and assists all things. Without asking the reason for this sudden outburst, Joseph echoed his neighbor's pious sentiment, May God help me as well, to which Ananias, without lowering his voice, replied, Yes, with God all things are possible, He knows and sees all things, both in heaven and on earth, praise be to Him, but, forgive the irreverence, I'm not sure He can do much to help you this time, because you're in the hands of Caesar. What are you trying to tell me. Only that soldiers have been here to proclaim that before the month of Nisan ends, all the families of Israel must go and register in their place of birth, which in your case, dear Joseph, means quite a journey.

Before Joseph had time to react, Shua, the wife of Ananias, appeared, and going straight to Mary, who was standing in the doorway, she began commiserating in the same mournful voice, Poor child, and so delicate, what is to become of you, about to give birth any day now and forced to make the journey to who knows where. To Bethlehem of Judaea, Shua's husband informed her. Good heavens, all that way, Shua exclaimed, and in all sincerity, for once on a pilgrimage to Jerusalem she had gone to nearby Bethlehem to pray at Rachel's tomb. Mary waited for her husband to speak first. Joseph, furious that this news should come to Mary not quietly and with measured words from his own lips but blurted tactlessly by hysterical neighbors, said in a solemn voice, It's true that God doesn't always choose to wield the powers exercised by Caesar, but God has powers denied Caesar. He paused, as if to savor the profundity of what he had just said, before announcing, We shall celebrate the Passover here in Nazareth and then go to Bethlehem, and God willing shall be back in time for Mary to give birth at home, unless He decides that the child be born in the land of our ancestors. It might even be born on the road, murmured Shua, but Joseph overheard her and was quick to remind her, Many a child of Israel has been born on the road, and our child will be just one more. Ananias and his wife could only agree with the wisdom of these words. They had come to sympathize with their hapless neighbors, and to enjoy their own solicitude, only to find themselves rebuffed. But then Mary invited Shua inside to ask her advice about some wool she had to card, and Joseph, wishing to make amends for his harsh words, said to Ananias, Good neighbor, could I ask you to look after my house while I'm away, for we shall be gone for at least a month, counting the time the journey takes, then the seven days of seclusion, and more if by some misfortune the child should be a girl. Ananias promised his neighbor that he would look after the property as if it were his own, and suddenly it occurred to him to ask Joseph, Would you honor me by celebrating the Passover with my family and friends since neither you nor your wife has any relatives here in Nazareth, not after the death of Mary's parents, who were so old when she was born that people still ask themselves how Joachim could possibly have given Anne a daughter. Come now, Ananias, said Joseph, rebuking him playfully, have you forgotten how Abraham muttered into his beard in disbelief when the Lord told him He would give him offspring, and if Almighty God allowed a hundred-year-old man and a wife of ninety to conceive a child, why should my in-laws, Joachim and Anne, who were not as old as Abraham and Sarah, not do the same. Those were other times, Ananias replied, when God was ever present and manifest not just in His works. Well versed in matters of doctrine, Joseph retorted, God is time itself, neighbor Ananias, for God time is indivisible. Ananias was left speechless, for this was not the moment to bring up the old argument about the powers, whether consubstantial or delegated, of God and Caesar. Joseph, despite his demonstration of practical theology, had not forgotten Ananias's sudden invitation to celebrate the Passover with him and his family. He did not wish, however, to accept too quickly, because as everyone knows it is a sign of good breeding to receive favors without being too effusive, otherwise the granter will think we were simply waiting to be asked. So Joseph bided his time before finally thanking Ananias for his thoughtfulness. The women reemerged from the house, Shua saying to Mary, You're an expert at carding, my girl, and Mary blushed on hearing herself praised in front of Joseph.

One pleasant memory Mary would cherish of this auspicious Passover was not having to help with the cooking or serve the men at table. The other women agreed she should be spared these chores in her condition. Don't tire yourself out, they warned her, or you'll do yourself some mischief, and they should know, because most of them were mothers with young children. All she had to do was attend to her husband, who was sitting on the floor with the other men. Bending over with some difficulty, she filled his glass and replenished his plate with unleavened bread, stewed lamb, bitter herbs, and biscuits made of ground dried locusts, a delicacy much appreciated by Ananias, for these biscuits were a family tradition. Several guests declined, doing their best to conceal their disgust and painfully aware that they were unworthy of the edifying example of those prophets in the desert who, making a virtue of necessity, ate locusts as if they were manna. As supper drew to an end, poor Mary sat apart, sweat running down her face, her great belly resting on her haunches, and she scarcely listened to the laughter, banter, stories, and continual reading from the Scriptures, feeling she might depart this world at any moment, her life hanging by the thread of one last, pure, unspoken thought. All she knew was that she was thinking without knowing what she was thinking or why she was thinking. She awoke with a start. In her dream she had seen the beggar's face loom from a great darkness, then his huge body in rags. The angel, if indeed he was an angel, had crept into her sleep unannounced, when he was furthest from her thoughts, and gazed at her intently. She sensed curiosity, but perhaps she was mistaken, he came and went so quickly, and Mary's heart now fluttered like that of a little bird. Difficult to say whether she had been

startled or someone had whispered something embarrassing in her ear. The men and boys still sat on the floor
while the women, hot and harried, rushed back and forth
offering them more helpings, but the men were full now,
and their conversation became more animated as the wine
began to take effect.

Without anyone's noticing, Mary got to her feet. Night
had fallen. There was no moon in the clear sky, only the
twinkling stars, which sent out a kind of echo, a muffled,
barely audible hum which Joseph's wife could feel on her
skin and in her bones, impossible to explain, like a furtive
voluptuous shiver that lingers. She crossed the yard and
looked out. She could see no one. The gate was closed,
but there was a vibration in the air, as if someone had just
run or flown past, leaving only a fleeting sign that would
leave others baffled.

THREE DAYS LATER, AFTER PROMISING HIS CUSTOMERS THAT their jobs would be completed on his return and after making his farewells in the synagogue and entrusting the care of his house and the worldly possessions therein to his neighbor, Ananias, Joseph the carpenter set out with his wife from Nazareth and headed for Bethlehem, where they would register as Rome decreed. If the news had not yet reached heaven, because of some delay in communication or a problem with simultaneous translation, the Lord God must have been surprised to see the landscape of Israel so altered, with hordes of people traveling in all directions, when normally during the first few days after Passover people moved centrifugally, as it were, beginning their return journey from that earthly sun known as Jerusalem. Force of habit, however fallible, and divine perspicacity, the latter absolute, will undoubtedly assist Him to recognize, even from on high, that these are pilgrims slowly making their way back to their towns and villages, but what about this bewildering maze, as those obeying the profane order of Caesar travel at random across more familiar routes. Unless Caesar Augustus is unwittingly complying with the will of God, if it is true that in His divine wisdom He has ordained that Joseph and Mary should go to Bethlehem at this time. Our speculation, arbitrary and irrelevant as it may appear at first, should not be dismissed lightly, for it helps us disprove those commentators who would have us picture Joseph and Mary crossing the inhospitable desert all alone, without so much as a friendly face in sight, trusting solely in God's mercy and the protection of His angels. For no sooner does the couple reach the outskirts of Nazareth than it becomes clear that they will not be on their own. Joseph and Mary meet two large families, a veritable clan of some twenty members, including adults, grandparents, and small children. It is true that these are not all traveling to Bethlehem, one of the families is only going half the distance and will stay in a village near Ramah, the other will head south as far as Beersheba, but even if they should separate before reaching Bethlehem, because there is always the possibility that some will travel faster, the couple will join other travelers on the road, and meet those going in the opposite direction, on their way to register in Nazareth. The men walk ahead in one group, accompanied by all the boys who have reached thirteen, while the women, girls, and grandmothers of every age straggle behind, accompanied by the boys under thirteen. When they set off, the men in solemn chorus recited prayers suited to the occasion, while the women merely mumbled the words, for it is pointless raising your voice if no one is likely to listen, even though they ask for nothing and are grateful for everything.

Among the women only Mary is in an advanced state of pregnancy, and such is the strain on her that, had providence not endowed donkeys with infinite patience and stamina to match, she would long since have given up and begged the others to abandon her at the roadside to await her hour, which we know is near, but who can say when or where, for this is not a race given to making bets or predictions about when or where Joseph's son will be born, and what a sensible religion to have prohibited gambling. Until that hour comes and for as long as this anxious waiting lasts, the pregnant woman will rely less on the distracted attentions of Joseph, who is lost in conversation with the other men, than on the reliable support of the donkey, who must be wondering, if beasts of burden are sensitive to such things, why the whip has not been much in use and why it is allowed to go at its own easy pace, the pace of its species. The women often lag behind, forcing the men, who are far ahead of them, to call a halt until the women get closer but not too close. The men prefer to give the impression that they have only paused for a rest because, although it is true that everyone may use the road, where cocks crow hens must not squawk, at most they may cackle when they lay an egg, for such are the laws of nature that govern the world in which we live. And so Mary journeys on, swaying with the gentle rhythm of her mount, a queen among women, for she alone is permitted to ride, while the other donkeys carry pack loads. To make things easier, she takes the three infants in the party onto her lap in turn, giving their mothers some relief and at the same time preparing herself for motherhood.

On the first day, they soon tired and covered only a short distance. Their legs were unaccustomed to walking for hours on end, we must not forget the number of old people and small children making this journey. The former, after a long life, have spent all their energy and can no longer pretend otherwise, the latter have not yet learned how to conserve their growing strength and wear themselves out after a brief spurt of wild activity, as if life were coming to an end and had to be enjoyed to the full while it lasted. On reaching a large village called Isreel, they stopped at the local caravansary, which they found in a state of chaos and uproar because of the heavy traffic. To tell the truth, there was more uproar than chaos here, because as one's eyes and ears adjusted, some order emerged from that multitude of people and animals within four walls, like a disturbed anthill trying to find its bearings and regroup. Despite the overcrowding, the three families had the good fortune to find shelter under an archway, where the men could huddle together on one side and the women on the other as darkness fell and all in the caravansary, people and animals, settled down for the night. But first the women had to prepare food and fill the water skins at the well, and the men had to unload the donkeys and water them after the camels finished drinking. For in two great gulps a camel can empty a trough, which must be refilled again and again to slake its thirst. After watering and feeding the donkeys, the travelers finally sat down to eat, the men first, of course. How often we need to remind ourselves that Eve was created after Adam and taken from his rib. Will we ever learn that certain things can be understood only if we take the trouble to trace them to their origins.

The men had eaten and were back in their own corner, the women were finishing off the leftovers, when Simeon, one of the most senior of the elders, who lived in Bethlehem but was obliged to register in Ramah, took advantage of the authority conferred by age and the wisdom believed to come thereof by asking Joseph what he would do if Mary, although Simeon did not mention her by name, should still be waiting to give birth when the last day of the census passed. The question was clearly academic, if such a word is apt for the time and place, insofar as only the census officials, skilled in the finer points of Roman law, would know how to deal with a pregnant woman who turned up for registration and said, We've come to register, no one having any idea whether she carried a boy or a girl, not to mention the possibility of twins. Exemplary Jew as he was, the carpenter would never have dreamt of pointing out with simple Western logic that it was not up to those who obeyed laws to defend the defects in them, and if Rome was incapable of foreseeing certain difficulties, then she was ill served by her legislators and her interpreters of Holy Scripture. Faced with this thorny problem, then, Joseph thought long and hard, searching in his mind for a subtle argument that would convince those gathered around the bonfire of his skill in debate. After much reflection, the carpenter raised his eyes from the flickering flames and told them, If by the last day of the census my child has not yet been born, this will be a sign from God that He does not wish the Romans to know of the child's existence. Simeon replied, Such presumption, to claim to know what God does or does not wish. Joseph asked, Does God not see my ways and count all my steps. These words, which we can find in the Book of Job, implied, within the context of this discussion, that before all present or absent Joseph was protesting his humility and submission to the Lord, a sentiment wholly opposed to the diabolic presumption of which Simeon accused him when Joseph had tried to probe the inscrutable will of God. This is how the elder must have interpreted his answer, for he fell silent, waiting for Joseph to continue. The days of each man's birth and death, said Joseph, have been put under seal and guarded by angels ever since the world began, and only the Lord can break those seals, first the one and then the other, although often together, with His right and left hand, and there are times when He is so slow in breaking the seal of death that He seems almost to have forgotten the existence of certain living souls. Joseph paused for breath, then, smiling mischievously, told Simeon, Let us hope this conversation does not remind the Lord of your existence. Those present laughed into their beards, for the carpenter was not showing the respect due to an old man. Simeon, tugging nervously at his sleeve, made no attempt to hide his anger as he told Joseph, Perhaps the Lord was hasty in breaking the seal of your birth and you were born before your time, if this is how you treat your elders, who have seen more of life than you have and gained more wisdom. Whereupon Joseph replied, Listen, Simeon, you asked me what I would do if my child was not born by the last day of the census, and I couldn't answer, I'm not familiar with Roman law, and I suspect neither are you. No, I am not. Then I said. I know what you said, you don't need to repeat it. It was you who started it, accusing me of presuming to know God's will, so forgive me if I hurt your pride, but you were the first to cause offense, and as my elder and better you ought to set an example. There was a murmur of approval around the fire. The carpenter Joseph had clearly won the argument, and the others waited to see how Simeon would respond. Lacking in spirit and imagination, he peevishly said, All you had to do was answer my question respectfully, and Joseph replied, Had I given you the answer you wanted, the foolishness of your question would have been evident to all, therefore you must admit, however much it rankles, that I showed the greater respect by providing you with an opportunity to debate a thing we'd all like to know, namely, whether the Lord would ever choose to conceal His people from the eyes of the enemy. Now you speak about God's people as if they were your unborn child. Don't put words in my mouth, Simeon, words I haven't spoken and will never speak, listen instead to what should be understood in one sense and not in another. Simeon made no attempt to reply to this, he got to his feet and took himself off to a corner along with the other men of his household, who felt obliged to accompany him because of ties of blood and kinship, although they were disappointed in the patriarch's poor showing in this verbal exchange.

The silence that followed the murmurings and whisperings of travelers settling down for the night was broken now and then by muffled conversations in the caravansary, by a shrill cry, the panting and snorting of animals, and the occasional awful bellow of a camel in heat. Then the party from Nazareth, all discord forgotten, could be heard muttering in unison the last and longest of the prayers of thanksgiving offered to the Lord at the end of the day, Praise be to You, O God, King of the Universe, who shuts our eyes without robbing them of light. Grant, O Lord, that we may sleep in peace and awaken tomorrow to a happy and tranquil life, help us to obey Your commandments. Lead us not into temptation and deliver us from evil. Lead us along the path of virtue and protect us from bad dreams, wicked thoughts, and mortal sickness. Spare us visions of death. Within minutes, the more just if not the more weary members of the party were fast asleep, some of them snoring unspiritually. And soon the others joined them, most with nothing more than their tunics to cover them, for only the elderly and the very young, both delicate in their own way, enjoyed the warmth and protection of a coarse blanket or threadbare mantle. Deprived of wood, the fire began to die, only a few weak flames continuing to flicker. Under the archway, the party from Nazareth slept soundly. Everyone except Mary. Unable to stretch out because of her belly, which could have been harboring a giant, she lay against some saddlebags in an effort to rest her aching back. Like the others, she had listened to Joseph arguing with old Simeon, and rejoiced in her husband's victory, as befits any wife no matter how harmless or unimportant the conflict. But she could no longer remember what the argument was about, her recollection of it already submerged in the throbbing of her body, which came and went like the tide of the sea, which she had never seen but had heard others describe, the restless ebb and flow as her child stirred in her womb. The strangest sensation, as if that living creature inside her were trying to hoist her onto its shoulders. Only Mary lay with her eyes open, shining in the shadows, still shining after the last flame had died away. No cause for wonder, for this happens to all mothers, and the wife of the carpenter Joseph was no exception, after the angel appeared to her disguised as a beggar.

Even in the caravansary there were cocks to greet the morning, but the travelers, merchants, drovers, and cameleers had to make an early start and begin preparing, before dawn, for the next leg of their journey. They loaded the animals with baggage and merchandise and made even more noise than on the previous evening. Once they have departed, the caravansary will settle down to a few hours of peace and quiet, like a brown lizard stretched out in the sun. The only remaining guests are those who have decided to rest all day, but by evening another group of travelers will start arriving, some more bedraggled than others but all of them weary, not that this has any effect on their vocal cords, because the moment they arrive, they start shouting their heads off as if possessed by a thousand demons. Back on the road, the party from Nazareth has grown bigger, ten people have joined them, so anyone who imagines this place to be deserted is much mistaken, especially when the feast of Passover and the census coincide.

No one needed to tell Joseph to make his peace with old Simeon, not because he was in the wrong but because he had been taught to respect his elders, especially those who were paying the price for long life by losing both their brains and their influence over a younger generation. So Joseph went up to him and said, I've come to apologize for my insolence last night, I didn't mean to be disrespectful but you know what human nature is, one word leads to another, tempers are lost, and caution is thrown to the winds. Without raising his eyes, Simeon heard him out in silence, then finally spoke, You are forgiven. Hoping his friendly overture would win more from the stubborn old man, Joseph remained at his side for a fair stretch of the road. But Simeon, eyes fixed on the dust at his feet, continued to ignore him, until Joseph in exasperation decided to give up. At that very moment, seemingly roused from his thoughts, the old man placed a hand on Joseph's shoulder and said, Wait. Surprised, Joseph turned, and Simeon stopped and repeated, Wait. The others walked on, leaving the two men standing in the middle of the road, a no-man's-land between the group of men ahead and the group of women behind, which was gradually approaching. Above the women's heads, Mary could be seen swaying with the rhythm of the donkey.

They had left the valley of Isreel. Skirting great rocks, the road curved awkwardly up the first slope before penetrating the mountains of Samaria to the east, then along arid ridges before descending on the other side to the Jordan, where the burning plain stretched southward and the desert of Judaea fired and scorched the ancient scars of a land promised to the chosen few but forever uncertain to whom it should surrender. Wait, said Simeon, and the carpenter obeyed, suddenly uneasy. The women were drawing nearer. Then the old man clutched Joseph by the sleeve, and he confided, When I lay down to rest last night I had a vision. A vision. Yes, a vision, but no ordinary vision, for I could see the hidden meaning of words you yourself spoke, that if your child was still not born by the last day of the census, it would be because the Lord did not wish the Romans to learn of its existence and add its name to their list. Yes, that is what I said, but what did you see. I didn't see anything but suddenly felt that it would be better if the Romans did not learn of your child's existence, that no one should be told of it, and that if the child must be born into this world, at least let it live without torment or glory, like those men up there in front and those women bringing up the rear, let it be as anonymous as the rest of us until the hour of death and forever after. Humble carpenter as I am from Nazareth, what fate could my child possibly hope for other than the one you have just described. Alas, you are not the only one to dispose of your child's life. True, everything is in the hands of the Lord and He knows best. And so say I. But tell me about my child, what have you discovered. Nothing beyond the words you yourself uttered and which took on for me another meaning, as if on seeing an egg I could sense the chick inside. God wills what He creates and has created what He willed, my child is in His hands and there is nothing I can do. That is indeed true, but these are days when God still shares the child with its mother. But should it turn out to be a son, it will belong to me and to God. Or to God alone. All of us belong to God. Not quite all of us, some are divided between God and Satan. How can one tell. If the law had not silenced women forever, perhaps they could reveal what we need to know, for it was woman who invented the first sin from which all the rest came. What do we need to know. Which part of woman's nature is demonic and which divine and what kind of humanity they have. I don't understand, I thought you were referring to my child. No, I was not referring to your child, I was talking about women, who generate beings such as ourselves and who may be responsible, perhaps unknowingly, for this duality in our nature, which is base and yet so noble, virtuous and yet so wicked, tranquil and yet so troubled, meek and yet so rebellious.

Joseph looked back. Mary was advancing on her donkey, a young boy in front of her and astride the saddle like a grown-up, and for a second Joseph thought he was seeing his own son and seeing Mary for the first time, at the head of this group of women. Simeon's strange words still filled his ears, but he found it hard to believe that any woman could wield so much power, especially this unassuming wife of his, who had never shown any sign of being different from other women. Turning to look at the road ahead, he suddenly remembered the episode of the beggar and the luminous earth. He began to tremble, his hair stood on end, he got goose flesh, and when he turned back to take another look at Mary, he saw, saw clearly, a tall stranger walking by her side, so tall that the man was head and shoulders above the women, this had to be the beggar whom he had missed seeing last time. Joseph looked again, and there he was, a sinister presence among those women that defied explanation. Joseph was about to ask Simeon to look, to make sure he was not imagining things, but the old man had moved on, having spoken his mind, and was now rejoining his companions to resume his position as head of his clan, a role he cannot hope to play much longer. Deprived of a witness, the carpenter looked again in his wife's direction. This time the beggar was gone.

HEADING SOUTH, THEY CROSSED THE WHOLE OF SAMARIA at great speed, with one eye on the road and the other nervously scanning their surroundings. They expected some act of hostility, of hatred, from the people living in these parts, descendants of the ancient Assyrians, renowned for their wicked deeds and heretical beliefs, who settled here during the reign of Shalmaneser, king of Nineveh, after the expulsion and dispersion of the twelve tribes. More pagan than Jewish, these people barely acknowledge the five books of Moses as sacred law, and they dare to suggest that the place chosen by God for His temple was not Jerusalem but Mount Gerizim, which lies within their domain. The expedition from Galilee traveled at a brisk pace but could not avoid spending two nights in the open in this enemy territory, with guards and patrols for fear of ambush. The treachery of the villains knew no bounds, and they were capable of refusing water even to someone of pure Hebrew stock who might be dying of thirst. Such was the anxiety of the travelers during this stretch of the journey that, contrary to custom, the men divided into two groups, one in front of the women and children and one behind, to protect them from taunts and insults, or worse. The inhabitants of Samaria, however, must have been going through a peaceful phase, because apart from resentful looks and snide remarks the party from Galilee met with no aggression, no gang of robbers descended from the nearby hills and attacked them with stones.

Shortly before reaching Ramah, those who believed with greatest fervor or who possessed a keener sense of smell swore they were inhaling the sanctified odor of Jerusalem. Here old Simeon and his companions went their separate way, for, as we mentioned earlier, they had to register in a village in this region. Giving profuse thanks to God there in the middle of the road, the travelers made their farewells. The married women filled Mary's head with a thousand and one pieces of advice, the fruits of their experience. Then they parted, some descending into the valley, where they would soon rest after four days on foot, the others making for Ramah, where they would seek shelter in a caravansary, for it would soon be dusk. At Jerusalem, the group that set out from Nazareth will also separate, most of them heading for Beersheba, which they should reach in two days, while the carpenter and his wife will go to nearby Bethlehem. Amid the confusion of embraces and farewells, Joseph called Simeon aside and, with all humility, asked him if he could remember anything more about his vision. I've already told you, it wasn't a vision. Whatever it was, I must know the destiny that awaits my child. If you don't even know your own destiny as you stand here before me asking questions, how can you expect to know the destiny of an unborn child. The eyes of the soul see further, and since yours have been opened by the Lord to certain manifestations reserved for the chosen, I thought you might have seen something where I see only darkness. You may never live to learn your son's destiny, you may, who knows, meet your own fate very shortly, but no more questions, please, stop all this probing and live for the present. And with these words Simeon placed his right hand on Joseph's head, murmured a blessing no one could hear, and rejoined his relatives and friends, who were waiting for him. In single file they made their way down a winding path to the valley, where Simeon's village nestled at the foot of the opposite slope, the houses almost merging with the boulders that stuck out of the ground like bones. Much later, Joseph would learn that the old man died before he could register.

After spending two nights under the stars, exposed to the cold on the barren plain, with no camp fire, for that might betray their presence, the expedition from Nazareth decided to take refuge once more under the archways of a caravansary. The women helped Mary dismount from the donkey, reassuring her, Come, it'll soon be over, and the poor girl whispered back, I know, I can't have long to wait now, and what clearer proof than that great swollen belly. They made her as comfortable as possible in a quiet corner and set about preparing supper, for it was growing late and the travelers planned to eat together. That night there was no conversation, no prayers or stories around the fire, as if the proximity of Jerusalem demanded respectful silence, each man searching his heart and asking, Who is this person who resembles me yet whom I fail to recognize. This is not what they actually said, for people do not start talking to themselves like that, nor was this even in their conscious thoughts, but there can be no doubt that as we sit staring into the flames of a camp fire, our silence can be expressed only with words like these, which say everything. From where he sat, Joseph could see Mary in profile against the light of the fire. Its reddish reflection softly lit one side of her face, tracing her features in chiaroscuro, and he began to realize, with surprise, that Mary was an attractive woman, if one could say this of a person with such a childlike expression. Of course her body was swollen now, yet he could see the agile, graceful figure she would soon regain once their child was born. Without warning, as if his flesh was rebelling after all these months of enforced chastity, a wave of desire surged through his blood and left him dizzy. Mary called out in pain, but he did not go to her assistance. As if someone had doused him with cold water, the sudden memory of the man who two days ago had walked beside his wife dampened Joseph's ardor. The image of that beggar had been haunting both of them ever since Mary discovered she was pregnant, for Joseph did not doubt that the stranger had been in her thoughts throughout the nine months. He could not bring himself to ask his wife what kind of man he was or where he went when he suddenly left. The last thing he wanted was to hear her say in bewilderment, A man, what man. And were Joseph to insist, no doubt Mary would ask the other women to testify, Did any of you see a man in our group, and they would deny seeing him and shake their heads at any such suggestion, and one of them might even answer in jest, Any man who hangs around women all the time is after only one thing. But Joseph would not believe Mary's surprise and that she had not seen the beggar, whether it was man or ghost. I saw him with my own eyes as he walked beside you, he would insist, but Mary, not faltering, would say, As is written in holy law, a wife must obey her husband, so if you insist you saw a beggar walking beside me, I will not contradict you, but believe me I didn't see him. It was the same beggar. But how can you tell, if you didn't see him the first time he appeared. It could only have been him. Much more likely to have been some traveler who was walking so slowly that we all overtook him, first the men, then the women, and he was probably alongside our group when you chanced to look back. Ah, so you admit he was there. Not at all, I'm simply trying as a dutiful wife to find some explanation that will satisfy you. Drowsy, Joseph watches Mary through half-closed eyes in the hope that he will find the truth in her face, but her face is now cast in shadow like the waning moon, her profile a vague outline in the light of the dying embers. Joseph nods, overcome by the effort of trying to understand, taking with him, as he falls asleep, the absurd idea that the beggar might be the image of his own son emerging from the future to tell him, This is what I'll look like one day, but you won't live to see it. Joseph slept with a resigned smile on his lips, a sad smile. He thought he heard Mary saying, God forbid that this beggar has nowhere to rest his head. For verily I say unto you that many things in this world could be known before it is too late, if husbands and wives would only confide in each other as husbands and wives.

Early next morning, most of the travelers who had spent the night in the caravansary left for Jerusalem, but those on foot stayed together, so that Joseph, without losing sight of his countrymen who were heading for Beersheba, accompanied his wife this time, walking alongside her as he had seen the beggar walk, or whatever he was. Joseph is convinced now that God bestowed a favor by allowing him to see his own son even before he is born, a son not wrapped in swaddling clothes, a tiny, unformed creature, smelly and bawling, but a fully grown man, taller than his father and most of the males of his race. Joseph is pleased to be taking his son's place, he is at once father and child, and this feeling is so strong that his real child, the unborn infant inside his mother's womb and heading for Jerusalem, suddenly becomes unimportant.

Jerusalem, Jerusalem, the pilgrims call out devoutly as the city comes into sight, rising before them like an apparition on the crest of the hill beyond the valley, a truly celestial city, the center of the universe. Sparkling in all directions under the midday sun, it is a crystal crown which will turn to purest gold at sunset and ivory in moonlight. Jerusalem, O Jerusalem. The Temple appears at that very moment, as if set there by God, and the sudden breeze that caresses the faces, hair, and clothes of the travelers could be a divine gesture, for, looking carefully at the clouds in the sky, we see a huge hand withdrawing, its fingers soiled with clay, its palm marked with the lines of life and death of every man and creature in this world, but the time has also come for us to trace the lines of life and death of God Himself. Trembling with emotion, the travelers raise their arms to heaven and raise their voices in thanksgiving, no longer in chorus, but each one lost in ecstasy, the more sober of them scarcely moving but looking up and praying with great fervor, as if they were being allowed to speak to God on equal terms. The road leads downward, and when the travelers descend into the valley and climb the next slope, which takes them to the city gates, the Temple will tower higher and higher, also the dreaded Antonia fortress, where even at this distance one can make out the shadowy forms of the Roman soldiers who stand watch on the terraces, and see the gleam of their weapons. The group from Nazareth must say good-bye here, for Mary is exhausted and would never survive the bumpy ride downhill at this fast pace, which accelerates to a headlong rush once the city walls loom into view.

And so Joseph and Mary find themselves alone on the road, she trying to recover her strength, he impatient at the delay, now that they are so close to their destination. The sun beats down on the silent travelers. A muffled cry escapes Mary's lips. Worried, Joseph asks her, Is the pain getting worse, and she can barely say, Yes. Then an expression of disbelief creeps into her face, as though she has encountered something beyond her understanding. She certainly felt the pain in her body, but it seemed to belong to someone else. To whom, then. To the child inside her. How can she feel pain that belongs to another, and yet it could be hers, like an echo that by some strange trick of acoustics is louder than the sound that produced it. Joseph

416

cautiously asks, Is the pain still bad, and Mary does not know how to answer. She would be lying if she said no, yet yes is not true either, so she decides to say nothing, the pain is there, she can feel it, but it is so remote that she has the impression she is watching her child suffer in her womb without being able to go to its assistance. No order has been given, Joseph has not used his whip, yet the donkey begins the steep slope leading to Jerusalem, as if looking forward to a full manger and a long rest. It does not know that there is still some way to go before reaching Bethlehem, and that, once there, things will not be so easy. Julius Caesar, for example, proclaims, Veni, vidi, vici, at the height of his glory, only to be assassinated by his own son, whose sole excuse was that he was adopted. Conflicts between fathers and sons, the inheritance of guilt, the disinheritance of kith and kin, and the sacrifice of innocents go far back in time and promise to continue in the future.

As they entered the city gates, Mary could no longer hold back her cries, now as heartrending as if a lance had pierced her. But only Joseph could hear them, such was the noise coming from the crowd, somewhat less from the animals, although between them they created a din reminiscent of a marketplace. Joseph decided, You're in no condition to go any farther, let's find an inn nearby, tomorrow I'll go on to Bethlehem alone and explain that you're giving birth, you can always register later if it's really necessary, because I know nothing about Roman law, and who can tell, perhaps only the head of the family needs to register, especially in our situation. Mary reassured him, The pain has gone, and she was telling the truth, the stabbing that caused her to cry out had become a mild throbbing, uncomfortable but bearable, rather like wearing a hairshirt. Joseph was relieved. To search for lodging in Jerusalem, with its maze of narrow streets, was a daunting task, especially now, his wife in the throes of childbirth and he as terrified as the next man at the thought of the responsibility, although he would never admit it. He thought to himself that once they reached Bethlehem, which was not much bigger than Nazareth, things would be easier, because people are friendlier in smaller communities. It doesn't matter whether Mary is no longer in pain or simply putting a brave face on things, they are on their way and will soon be in Bethlehem. The donkey receives a slap on its hindquarters, which is not so much a spur to go faster amid all this traffic and indescribable confusion as an affectionate gesture expressing Joseph's relief. Merchants cram the narrow streets, people of every race and tongue jostle one another, but the streets clear almost miraculously whenever a patrol of Roman soldiers or a procession of camels appears, the crowds disperse like the parting waters of the Red Sea. At a steady pace, the couple from Nazareth and their donkey gradually emerge from the seething bazaar full of ignorant, insensitive people, to whom there would be no point saying, See that man over there, that's Joseph, and the woman who looks as if she is about to give birth any minute is Mary, they're on their way to register in Bethlehem. If our kind attempt to identify them goes unnoticed, it is simply because we live in a world where Josephs and Marys of every age and condition abound and can be found at every turn. This is not the only couple called Joseph and Mary expecting a baby, who knows, perhaps two infants of the same sex, preferably male, will be born at the same hour and only a road or a field of corn between them. The destinies that await these infants, however, will be different, even if we name both of them Yeshua, which is the same as Jesus. And lest we are accused of anticipating events by naming an unborn child, the fault lies with the carpenter, who some time ago made up his mind that this is the name he will give his first son.

Leaving by the southern gate, the travelers take the road to Bethlehem, glad that they will soon reach their destination and be able at long last to rest from their tiring journey. Mary's troubles, of course, are not over, for she, and she alone, still has to endure the trial of childbirth, and who knows where or when. According to Holy Scripture, Bethlehem is the location of David's house, the line from which Joseph claims descent, but with the passing of time his relatives have all died, or the carpenter has lost all contact, an unpromising situation which leads us to believe, even before we get there, that the couple will have a problem finding a place. Arriving in Bethlehem, Joseph cannot knock on the first door he comes to and say, I'd like my child to be born here, and expect to be greeted with a welcoming smile from the mistress of the house, Come in, come in, Master Joseph, the water is boiling, the mat laid out on the floor, the swaddling clothes are ready, make yourself at home. Things might have been so in a golden age, when the wolf, rather than eat the lamb, would feed on wild herbs. But this is the age of iron, cruel and unfeeling. The time for miracles has either passed or not come yet, besides, miracles, genuine miracles, whatever people say, are not such a good idea, if it means destroying the very order of things in order to improve them. Joseph is not eager to confront the problems that await him, but he considers how much worse it would be if his child was born by the roadside, and so he forces the donkey, poor beast, to go faster. Only the donkey knows how weary it feels, all God cares about are humans, and not all humans, because some of them live like donkeys or worse, and God makes no effort to help them. One of his fellow travelers told Joseph that there was a caravansary in Bethlehem, a stroke of luck that seems to be the answer to his problem. But even a humble carpenter would find it embarrassing to see his pregnant wife exposed to the morbid curiosity and wagging tongues of drovers and cameleers, and some of those fellows are as brutish as the beasts they handle, and their behavior is much more contemptible, for as men they possess the divine gift of speech, which animals are denied. Joseph finally decides to seek the advice and guidance of the elders of the synagogue, and wonders why he did not think of this sooner. Somewhat relieved, he is about to ask Mary if the pain is still there, but changes his mind and says nothing, we mustn't forget that this whole process, from the moment of impregnation to the moment of birth, is unclean, that vile female organ, vortex and abyss, the seat of all the world's evil, an inner labyrinth of blood, discharges, gushing water, revolting afterbirth, dear God, how can You permit Your beloved children to be born in such impurity. How much better for You and us had You created them from transparent light, yesterday, today, and tomorrow, the beginning, middle, and end alike for everyone, without discrimination between aristocrats and commoners, kings and carpenters. So Joseph asks only, and with seeming indifference, as if preoccupied with more important matters, How do you feel. The question is timely, for Mary now notices something different about the pain she is experiencing, about the pain, rather, that now is experiencing her.

They had been walking for more than an hour, and Bethlehem could not be far. To their surprise, they found the road from Jerusalem deserted, with Bethlehem so close to the city one might expect to see continuous movement of people and animals. At the point where the road forked, one road to Beersheba, the other to Bethlehem, the world appeared to contract and fold over on itself. If you were to visualize the world as a person, it would be like watching a man cover his eyes with his mantle and listen to the travelers' footsteps, just as we listen to the song of birds among the branches, and that indeed is how we must appear to the birds hidden in the trees.

To the right stands the tomb of Rachel, the bride for whom Jacob waited fourteen years. After seven years' service, he was wedded to Leah and had to wait another seven years before being allowed to marry his beloved, who would die in Bethlehem giving birth to a son that Jacob named Benjamin, which means son of my right hand, but Rachel, as she lay dying, rightly called him Benoni, which means child of my sorrow, God forbid that this should be an omen. Houses now begin to appear, mud-colored like those of Nazareth, but here in Bethlehem the color of mud is paler, a mixture of yellow and gray. Mary is near collapse, her body slumping farther forward over the saddlebags with each passing moment. Joseph has come to her aid, and she puts one arm around his shoulder to steady herself. What a pity there is no one here to witness this touching scene, which is all too rare. And so they enter Bethlehem.

Despite Mary's condition, Joseph inquired if there was a caravansary nearby, thinking they might rest until the following morning. Mary was in great pain but still showed no sign of being ready to give birth. But when, on the other side of the village, they reached the caravansary, which was squalid and rowdy, part bazaar and part stable, there was not a quiet corner to be found, even though it was still early and most of the drovers and cameleers would only start arriving later. The couple turned back. Joseph left Mary beneath the shade of a fig tree in a tiny square and went off to consult the elders. There was no one in the synagogue apart from a caretaker, who called out to an urchin playing nearby and told him to accompany the stranger to one of the elders, who might be able to help. Fortune, who protects the innocent whenever she remembers them, decreed that in this latest quest Joseph should pass through the square where he had left his wife, and just in time to save her from the deadly shade of the fig tree, which was slowly killing her, an unforgivable mistake, as fig trees abound in this land and they both should have known better. So, like condemned souls, they set off once more in search of the elder, but he had left for the countryside and was not expected home for some time.

On hearing this, the carpenter summoned his courage and called out, Is there anyone here who for the love of Almighty God will offer shelter to my dear wife, who is about to give birth. All he asked was a quiet corner, they had brought their own mats. And could anyone tell him where to find a midwife in the village who could assist with the birth. Poor Joseph blushed to hear himself blurt out these private worries and concerns. The female slave standing in the doorway went back inside to report to her mistress, and reappeared after a while to tell them that they could not stay there and must look for shelter elsewhere. Since there was little chance of finding a place in the village, her mistress suggested they take refuge in one of the many caves in the nearby slopes. And what about a midwife, asked Joseph, whereupon the slave replied that if her mistress agreed and he wished, she herself could help, for she had been in service all her life and had assisted at many a birth. These are cruel times indeed, when a pregnant woman comes knocking at our door and we deny her shelter in a corner of the yard and send her off to give birth in a cave, like the bears and wolves. Something pricked our conscience, however, and, getting up from where we were sitting, we went to the door to see for ourselves this husband and wife who so desperately needed a roof over their heads. The sadness in that poor girl's face was enough to arouse our maternal instinct, so we patiently explained why we could not possibly take them in, the house was already crowded with sons and daughters, grandchildren, in-laws. As you can see, there simply isn't any room here, but our slave will take you to a cave we use as a stable. There are no animals there at present, and you should be able to make yourselves comfortable. The young couple were most grateful for our generous offer, and we withdrew, feeling we had done our best and that our conscience was clear.

With all this coming and going, walking and resting, inquiring and pleading, the deep blue sky has lost its color and the sun will soon disappear behind that mountain. The slave, Salome, for that is her name, leads the way. She carries some hot coals to make a fire, an earthenware pot to heat water, and salt to rub down the newborn infant as a precaution against infection. And since Mary has brought cloths and Joseph has a knife in his pack to cut the umbilical cord, unless Salome prefers to use her teeth, everything is ready for the birth. A stable, when all is said and done, is as good as a house, and anyone who has slept in a manger knows that it is almost as good as a cradle. And the donkey is not likely to notice any difference, for straw is the same in heaven as on earth. They reached the cave when the hovering twilight was still shedding gold on the hills. If their progress was slow, it was not because of the distance but because now that Mary had a place to rest, she could at last abandon herself to her suffering. She pleaded with them to slow down, for whenever the donkey lost its footing on a stone, she suffered agonizing pain. The waning light outside did not penetrate the darkness of the cave, but with a handful of straw, the live coals, much puffing and blowing, and some dry kindling, the slave soon had a fire blazing as bright as any dawn. Then she lit the oil lamp that was suspended from a rock jutting from the wall, and after helping Mary lie down, she went to fetch water from the nearby wells of Solomon. On returning, she found Joseph distracted with worry, but we must not be too hard on him, for a man is not expected to be able to cope in such a crisis, at most he can hold his wife's hand and hope that everything will be all right. Mary, however, is alone. The world would crumble if a Jewish man in those days attempted any such comforting gesture. The female slave came in, whispered a few words of encouragement, then knelt between Mary's legs, for a woman's legs should be kept apart whenever something goes in or comes out. Salome has lost count of the number of children she has helped bring into the world, and poor Mary's suffering is no different from that of any other woman, for as God warned Eve after she sinned, I will greatly multiply your suffering and your conception, in sorrow you will bring forth children, and after centuries of sorrow and suffering God is not yet appeased and the agony goes on. Joseph is no longer present, not even at the entrance to the cave, he has fled rather than listen to Mary's cries, but the cries follow him, as if the very earth were screaming. The noise is such that three shepherds who were passing with their flocks approached Joseph and asked, What's going on, the earth seems to be screaming, and he told them, My wife is giving birth in that cave. They asked, You're a stranger to these parts, aren't you. Yes, we've come from Nazareth, in Galilee, to register, and no sooner did we arrive than my wife started feeling worse and now she's in labor. The fading light made it difficult to see the faces of the four men, and soon their features would completely disappear, but their voices could still be heard. Have you any food, one of the shepherds said. A little, replied Joseph, and the same voice told him, Once the child is born, let me know, and I'll bring you some sheep's milk, and then a second voice said, And I'll give you cheese. Then a long silence, and the third shepherd spoke. In a voice that seemed to come from the bowels of the earth he said, I'll bring you bread.

The son of Joseph and Mary was born, like any other child, covered with his mother's blood, dripping with mucus, and suffering in silence. He cried because they made him cry, and he will cry for this one and only reason. Wrapped in swaddling clothes, he lies in the manger with the donkey standing nearby but unlikely to bite him because the animal is tethered and cannot move far. Salome is outside burying the afterbirth when Joseph approaches. She waits until he has gone into the cave, lingering there to inhale the cool night and feeling as exhausted as if she herself had just given birth, but this is something she can only imagine, never having had children of her own.

Three men come down the slope. They are the shepherds. They enter the cave together. Mary is reclining, and her eyes are closed. Seated on a stone, Joseph rests his arm on the edge of the manger and appears to be watching over his son. The first shepherd steps forward and says, Here's the milk from my sheep, which I drew with my own hands. Opening her eyes, Mary smiles. The second shepherd steps forward and says in his turn, I myself churned the milk that made this cheese. Mary nods and smiles again. Then the third shepherd, whose massive frame seems to fill the cave, steps forward and, without so much as glancing at the newborn infant's parents, says, I kneaded this bread with my own hands and baked it in the fire that burns beneath the earth. No sooner had he spoken than Mary recognized him.

Since the world began, for every person who is born another dies. The person now close to death is King Herod, who in addition to all imaginable evils suffers from a horrible itch, which has almost driven him insane. He feels as if hundreds of thousands of ants are gnawing incessantly at his body with their tiny savage jaws. Having tried, to no avail, all the balsams known to man, remedies from Egypt and India, the royal physicians scratched their heads, or, to be more precise, were in grave danger of losing their heads, as they frantically tried ablutions and household potions, mixing with water or oil any and all herbs and powders reputed to do some good, however contrary their effect. The king, foaming at the mouth like a mad dog, beside himself with pain and fury, threatens to have them all crucified unless they can relieve his afflictions, which go beyond the unbearable burning in his skin and the convulsions that leave him exhausted and writhing on the floor, his eyes bulging from their sockets as the ants continue to multiply and gnaw beneath his robes. Worst of all is the gangrene that has set in during the last few days, and this mysterious affliction has started tongues wagging in the palace, as worms begin to ravage the genital organs of the royal person and truly devour him alive. Herod's screams echo through the halls and corridors of the palace, the eunuchs attending him are kept awake day and night, the slaves of lower rank flee in terror when they hear him approach. Dragging his body, which stinks of rot despite the perfumes sprinkled lavishly over his robes and rubbed into his dyed hair, Herod is being kept alive only by his own wrath. Carried around in a litter, accompanied by doctors and armed guards, he scours the palace from one end to another in search of traitors, whom he imagines to be lurking everywhere, an obsession he has had for some time. Without any warning he will suddenly point a finger, perhaps at the chief eunuch, accusing him of wielding too much influence, or at some stubborn Pharisee who has criticized those who disobey the law when they should be the first to respect it, there is no need to name names, and that finger was also pointed at his sons Alexander and Aristobulus, who were imprisoned and hastily sentenced to death by a tribunal of nobles convened for the purpose, what choice did the poor king have when in his delirium he saw those wicked sons advancing upon him with bared swords, when in the most terrifying nightmare of all he beheld in a mirror his own severed head. He has escaped that terrible end and can now quietly contemplate the corpses of those who a moment before were heirs to the throne, his own sons found guilty of conspiracy, misconduct, and arrogance and strangled to death.

From the murk of his troubled mind comes another nightmare to disturb the sporadic moments of sleep into which he falls from sheer exhaustion. The prophet Micah comes to haunt him, that prophet who lived at the time of Isaiah and witnessed the terrible wars that the Assyrians waged in Samaria and Judaea. Micah appears before him, denouncing the rich and powerful as befits a prophet, es-

pecially in this accursed age. Covered with the dust of battle and wearing a bloodstained tunic, Micah storms into
his dream in a deafening blast from some other world. With
hands of lightning he pushes open enormous bronze gates
and gives solemn warning, The Lord will come down from
His holy temple and tread upon the high places of the earth.
Then he threatens, Woe to them that devise iniquity and
work evil upon their beds, when the morning is light they
practice it because it is in the power of their hand. And he
denounces those who covet fields and take them by violence, and who take houses, oppressing a man and his house,
even a man and his heritage. After repeating these words
night after night, Micah, as if responding to a signal, van-
ishes into thin air. What causes Herod to wake up in a cold
sweat is not so much the terror of those prophetic cries as
the agonizing thought that this nightly visitor withdraws
just as he is about to reveal something more. The prophet
raises his hand and parts his lips, only to disappear, leaving
the king filled with foreboding. Now, as everyone knows,
Herod is not likely to be intimidated by threats when he
does not feel the slightest remorse for all the deaths he
ordered. For this is the man who had the brother of Mariamne, whom he loved more than any other woman, burned
alive, the man who ordered her grandfather strangled and
finally Mariamne herself, when he accused her of adultery.
It is true that he later suffered a bit of madness and called
for Mariamne as if she were still alive, but he recovered
from it and discovered that his mother-in-law was hatch-
ing a plot, and not for the first time, to remove him from
power. Instantly this viper was dispatched to the pantheon
of the family into which Herod had married, with unfortunate consequences for all concerned, because the king's
three sons became heirs to the throne, Alexander and Aristobulus, whose sad end we have already mentioned, and
Antipater, who soon will meet a similar fate. But we must
not forget, since there is more to life than tragedy and mis-

fortune, that Herod had no fewer than ten comely wives to pamper him and arouse his lust, although by now they could do little for him and he even less for them. Therefore the nightly apparition of an irate prophet intent on haunting the powerful king of Judaea and Samaria, Peraea and Idumaea, Galilee and Gaulanitis, Trachanitis, Auranitis, and Batanaea, would make little impression were it not for that sudden interruption of the dream that leaves him in suspense, awaiting some new threat, but what threat, and how and when.

Meanwhile, in Bethlehem, on the doorstep of Herod's palace, as it were, Joseph and his family continued to live in the cave. They did not expect to stay there long, so there was little point in looking for a house, especially at a time when accommodations were scarce and the profitable practice of renting rooms had not yet been invented. On the eighth day Joseph took his firstborn to the synagogue to be circumcised. Using a knife made of flint, with admirable skill the priest cut the wailing child's foreskin, and the fate of that foreskin is in itself worthy of a novel, from the moment it was cut, a loop of pale skin with scarcely any bleeding, to its glorious sanctification during the papacy of Paschal I, who reigned in the ninth century of Christianity. Anyone wishing to see that foreskin today need only visit the parish church of Calcata near Viterbo in Italy, where it is preserved in a reliquary for the spiritual benefit of the faithful and the amusement of curious atheists. Joseph announced that his son should be called Jesus, and this was the name inscribed in God's register after it was added to the civil register of Caesar. Far from being resigned to this outrage inflicted on his person without any appreciable spiritual benefit in return, the infant howled all the way back to the cave, where its mother, needless to say, was anxiously waiting, this being her first child. Poor little thing, poor little thing, she said soothingly, and opening her tunic, she began to nurse the child, first on the left breast, perhaps because that was closer to her heart. Jesus, although still unaware of his name, for no more than a babe in arms, gave a deep sigh of contentment the moment he felt the gentle pressure of Mary's breast against his cheek and the moist warmth of her skin on his. As the sweet taste of his mother's milk filled his mouth, the pain and indignity of the circumcision became remote, dissipated into a formless pleasure that surfaced and went on surfacing, as if arrested at the threshold and not allowed to define itself completely. On growing up, he will forget these first sensations and find it difficult to believe he ever experienced them, which happens to all of us, wherever we may have been born and whatever our destiny. But Joseph, if we had the courage to ask him about this, and God forbid that we should commit any such indiscretion, would tell us that a father's cares are more to the point, since he now faces the problem of feeding an extra mouth, an expression no less true or apt simply because a child is fed at its mother's breast. Indeed, Joseph has reason to be worried. How are they to live until they return to Nazareth. Mary is weak and in no condition to make the long journey, and besides, she must wait until she is no longer unclean and remain in the blood of her purification for the thirty-three days following her child's circumcision. The little money they brought from Nazareth has nearly all been spent, and Joseph cannot work as a carpenter here without tools or the means to buy wood. Life at that time was hard for the poor and God could not be expected to provide for everyone. From within the cave came a sudden whimper, which soon stopped, a sign that Mary had changed the little Jesus to her right breast, but that short frustration was enough to renew the pain where the child was circumcised. Having sucked to his satisfaction, Jesus will fall asleep in his mother's arms and barely open his eyes when she settles him gently in the manger as if entrusting him to an affectionate and faithful nurse. Joseph, seated at the entrance to the cave, is still trying to decide what to do. He knows that there is no work for him here in Bethlehem, not even as an apprentice, for when he made inquiries, the answer was always the same. If I need any help I'll send for you, empty promises that do not fill a man's belly, although this race has been living off promises since it came into being.

Time and time again one has seen, even in people not particularly given to reflection, that the best way of finding a solution is to let one's thoughts drift until the right moment comes to pounce, like a tiger taking its prey by surprise. And so the false promises of the master carpenters of Bethlehem led Joseph to think about God's true promises, then about the Temple of Jerusalem, still under construction, where there must be demand for laborers, not only bricklayers and stonemasons but also carpenters even if only to square joists and plane boards, basic tasks that are well within Joseph's capabilities. The only drawback, assuming they give him a job, is the time it takes to reach the site, a good hour and a half's walk at a brisk pace, because it is uphill all the way and there is no patron saint of hill climbers to extend a helping hand, unless Joseph rides there, but that would mean finding a safe place to leave his donkey. This may be God's chosen land, but there are still plenty of rogues around if we are to believe the dire warnings of the prophet Micah. Joseph was pondering this when Mary emerged from the cave after feeding her child and settling him down to sleep. How is Jesus, his father asked, conscious of how foolish the question sounded but unable to suppress his pride as the father of a son who already had a name. The child is fine, replied Mary, for whom the name was of no importance. She would have been just as happy to call him my child for the rest of her life, were it not for the fact that she would bear more children, and to refer to them all simply as my child would create as much confusion as in the Tower of

Babel. Joseph said, allowing the words to come out as if he was thinking aloud, which is one way of not showing too much confidence, I must earn a living while we are here, yet there is no suitable work in Bethlehem. Mary said nothing, nor was she expected to speak, she was only there to listen, and her husband had already made an enormous concession by taking her into his confidence. Joseph looked at the sun, trying to decide whether there was enough time for him to go and come back. He went into the cave to fetch his mantle and pack and, on reappearing, told Mary, I'm off, trusting in God to find work for this honest artisan in His tabernacle should He deem him worthy of such an honor. Joseph threw his mantle over his left shoulder, adjusted his pack, and went off without another word.

Truly all is not gloom. Although work on the Temple was making good progress, laborers were still being hired, especially if they accepted low wages. Joseph had no difficulty passing the simple test given by the head carpenter, which should make us reflect whether our earlier disparaging comments about Joseph's professional skills might not have been unjustified. This latest recruit for the Temple site went off giving profuse thanks to God. Along the way he stopped some travelers and asked them to join him in praising the Lord, and they cheerfully obliged, for these people see one man's joy as something to be shared by all. We refer, of course, to people of humble condition. When Joseph reached the spot where Rachel is buried, a thought occurred to him which came from the heart rather than the head, namely, that this woman eager to have another child might die, if you will pardon the expression, at his hands, and before she could even get to know him. Without so much as a word or a glance, one body separates itself from another, as indifferent as the fruit that drops from a tree. Then an even sadder thought came to him, namely, that children die because their fathers beget them and their mothers bring them into the world, and he took pity on his own son, who was condemned to die although innocent. As he stood, filled with confusion and anguish, before the tomb of Jacob's beloved wife, carpenter Joseph's shoulders drooped and his head sank, and his entire body broke out in a cold sweat, and now there was no one passing on the road to whom he could turn for help. For the first time in his life he doubted whether the world had any meaning, and said in a loud voice, like one who has lost all hope, This is where I will die. Perhaps these words, in other circumstances and if spoken with the courage and conviction of those who commit suicide, words devoid of sorrow and weeping, would suffice to open the door by which we depart the land of the living. But most men are inconstant and can be distracted by a cloud on high, by a spider weaving its web, a dog chasing a butterfly, a hen scratching the soil and clucking to its chicks, or something as commonplace as a sudden itch on one's face, which one scratches, wondering, Now what was I thinking about. For this reason Rachel's tomb instantly reverted to a small, windowless whitewashed building, a building like a discarded die forgotten because not needed for the game under way. On the stone at the entrance there are marks left by the sweaty and grimy hands of pilgrims, who have been coming here since ancient times, and the tomb is surrounded by olive trees, which were perhaps already old when Jacob chose this spot for the poor mother's last resting place and felled as many trees as were necessary to clear the ground. When all is said and done, we can confidently say that destiny exists and each man's destiny is in the hands of others. Then Joseph moved on, but not before saying a prayer suited to the time and place. He said, Praise be to You, O Lord our God and God of our forefathers, God of Abraham, God of Isaac, God of Jacob, great, almighty, and wondrous God, praise be to You.

Returning to the cave, he went to look at his little son,

asleep in the manger, before telling his wife that he had found work. He thought to himself, He'll die, he must die, and his heart grieved, but then he reflected that by the natural order of things he himself would die first and that his departure from the land of the living would bestow on his son a limited eternity, a contradiction in terms, an eternity that allows one to go on for a little longer when those whom we know and love no longer exist.

Joseph had been careful not to mention to the head carpenter that he would be staying only a few weeks, five at the most, enough time to take his son to the Temple to complete Mary's purification, and to pack their belongings. He said nothing rather than be turned away, which shows that the carpenter from Nazareth was not familiar with working conditions in his own country, no doubt because he thought of himself, and rightly, as his own master and took little interest in the rest of the working community, which then consisted almost entirely of casual labor. He kept careful count of the remaining days, twenty-four, twenty-three, twenty-two, and to avoid making mistakes he improvised a calendar on one of the cave walls, nineteen, drawing lines that he then erased one at a time, sixteen, watched by an admiring Mary, fourteen, thirteen, who thanked the Lord for having given her, nine, eight, seven, six, such a clever husband, who could turn his hand to anything. Joseph told her, We'll leave after we go to the Temple, for it's time I got back to my work in Nazareth, where I have customers waiting, and she tactfully suggested, rather than appear to be criticizing him, But surely we cannot leave without first thanking the woman who owns the cave and the slave who helped deliver our child and who still calls every day to see how he's coming along. Joseph made no reply. He'd never admit to having overlooked such an act of common courtesy, although he had intended to load the donkey beforehand, tie it up during the ceremony, then set off for Nazareth without wasting any time on thanks and farewells. Mary was right, it would have been ill-mannered to go away without so much as a word of gratitude, but if truth, poor thing, were to be known, Joseph was somewhat lacking in manners. To be reminded of this omission caused him to sulk and become irritable with his wife, behavior which usually served to ease his conscience and silence remorse. So they would stay on for two or three days, make their farewells as was only fit and proper, and leave the inhabitants of Bethlehem with a favorable impression of this devout family from Galilee, courteous and dutiful, notably different when one considers the low opinion the inhabitants of Jerusalem and its environs generally have of people from Galilee.

The memorable day finally arrived when the child Jesus was carried to the Temple in the arms of his mother, who rode the patient donkey that had accompanied and assisted this family since the beginning. Joseph led the donkey by the halter, he was in a hurry to get there, anxious not to lose a whole day's work, even though their departure was imminent. The next day they were on the road as dawn dispersed the last vestiges of night. Rachel's tomb was already some distance behind. When they passed it, the façade had taken on the fiery hue of a pomegranate, so unlike its appearance at night, when it became opaque, or in the light of the moon, when it looked deathly pale. After a while the infant Jesus woke up, and had scarcely opened his eyes when his mother wrapped him for the journey, and he cried to be fed in that plaintive voice, the only voice he has so far. One day, like the rest of us, he will learn to speak with other voices, which will enable him to express other forms of hunger and experience other tears.

On the steep slopes not far from Jerusalem the family merged with the pilgrims and vendors who were flocking to the city, all intent on being the first to arrive but cautiously slowing down and curbing their excitement when they came face to face with the Roman soldiers who were moving through the crowd in pairs, or with a detachment of Herod's mercenary troops, who recruited every imaginable race, many Jews, as one might expect, but also Indumaeans, Galatians, Thracians, Germans, Gauls, and even Babylonians, who are unrivaled as archers. A carpenter who handles only peaceful weapons such as the plane, adze, mallet, or hammer, Joseph becomes filled with such fear and revulsion when he runs into these louts that he can no longer behave naturally or disguise his true feelings. He keeps his eyes lowered, and it is Mary, who has been shut away in the cave for weeks with no one to talk to apart from the female slave, it is Mary who takes a good look around, her dainty little chin held high with understandable pride, for she is holding her firstborn, a mere woman yet capable of giving children to God and her husband. She looks so radiant and happy that some Gauls, fierce, fair, with large whiskers, their weapons at the ready, smile as the family passes, their cruel hearts softened by the sight of the young mother with her first child. Smiling at this renewal of the world, they bare rotten teeth, but it's the thought that counts.

There is the Temple. Viewed at close quarters, the building gives one vertigo, a mountain of stones upon stones which no earthly power seems capable of dressing, lifting, laying, and fitting, yet there they are, joined together by their own weight, without mortar, as if the entire world were a set of building blocks. The uppermost cornices, seen from below, appear to graze the sky, like another but quite different Tower of Babel, which even God will be unable to save because it is doomed to the same destruction, confusion, and bloodshed. Voices will ask, Why, a thousand times, believing there must be an answer, but eventually they will die away, because it is better to be silent. Joseph goes off to tether the donkey in the caravansary set aside for the animals. During Passover and other religious feasts the place gets so crowded that there is not enough room for a camel to shake the flies from its tail, but it is easier now that the last day of the census has passed and travelers have returned to their homes. In the Court of the Gentiles, however, which is bordered by colonnades on all four sides, with the temple precinct in the center, there is a large crowd, money changers, bird catchers, merchants trading lambs and kids, pilgrims gathered here for one reason or another, and numerous foreigners curious to visit the famous Temple built by King Herod. But the court is so spacious that anyone on the far side looks no bigger than an insect, as though Herod's architects, seeing through God's eyes, wanted to show the insignificance of men in the presence of the Almighty, especially if they happen to be Gentiles. As for the Jews, unless they have come for a leisurely stroll, their goal is the middle of the court, the center of their world, the navel of navels, the Holy of Holies. That is where the carpenter and his wife are heading, that is where Jesus is carried after his father purchases two turtledoves from the steward of the Temple, if such a title is appropriate for one who benefits from the monopoly on these religious transactions. The poor birds are ignorant of the fate that awaits them, though the smell of flesh and singed feathers lingering in the air does not deceive anyone, to say nothing of the much stronger stench of blood and excrement as oxen, dragged away to be sacrificed, foul themselves in terror. Joseph cradles the doves in the palms of his callused hands, and the poor birds, in their innocence, peck with satisfaction at his fingers, which he curves to form a cage. It is as if they were trying to tell him, We are happy with our new master. But Joseph's skin is far too rough to feel or decipher the affectionate nibbling of the two doves.

They enter by the Wooden Gate, one of thirteen entrances to the Temple. It has an inscription in Greek and Latin carved into the stonework, which reads as follows,

It is forbidden for any Gentile to cross this threshold and the balustrade surrounding the Temple, trespassers will be put to death. Joseph and Mary enter, carrying Jesus between them, and in due course will make a safe exit, but the doves, as we know, must be killed according to the law before Mary's purification can be acknowledged and ratified. Any ironic or irreverent disciple of Voltaire will find it difficult to resist making the obvious remark that, things being what they are, purity can be maintained only so long as there are innocent creatures to sacrifice in this world, whether turtledoves, lambs, or others. Joseph and Mary climb the fourteen steps to the platform of the Temple. Here is the Court of the Women, on the left the storehouse for the oil and wine used in the liturgy, on the right the Chamber of the Nazirites, priests who do not belong to the tribe of Levi and who are forbidden to cut their hair, drink wine, or go near a corpse. On the opposite side, to the left and right, respectively, of the door facing this one, are the chamber where the lepers who believe themselves cured wait for the priests to come and examine them, and the storehouse where the wood is kept and inspected daily, because rotten and worm-eaten wood must not be thrown on the altar fire. Mary has not much farther to go, she still has to climb the fifteen semicircular steps leading to the Nicanor Gate, also known as the Gate Beautiful, but there she will stop, because women are not permitted to enter the Court of the Israelites, which lies beyond this gate. At the entrance, the Levites receive those who have come to offer sacrifice, but the atmosphere is less pious, unless piety at that time had another meaning. It is not just the smoke rising from the burning fat or the smell of fresh blood and incense but also the shouting of the men, the howling, bleating, and lowing of the animals waiting to be slaughtered, and the last raucous squawk of a bird once able to sing. Mary tells the Levite in attendance that she has come for purification, and Joseph hands over the doves. For one brief moment Mary places her hands over the birds, her only gesture before the Levite and her husband turn away and disappear through the gate. She will not stir until Joseph returns, she simply steps aside so as not to obstruct the passage, and waits, holding her son in her arms.

Within the Court of the Israelites there is a furnace and a slaughterhouse. On two sizable stone slabs, larger animals such as oxen and calves are killed, also sheep, ewes, and male and female goats. There are tall pillars alongside the tables, where the carcasses are suspended from hooks set into the stonework, and here one can watch the frenzied activity as the butchers wield their knives, cleavers, axes, and handsaws, the air filled with fumes rising from the wood and the singed hides, and with the smell of blood and sweat. Anyone witnessing this scene would have to be a saint to understand how God can approve of such appalling carnage if He is, as He claims, the father of all men and beasts. Joseph has to wait outside the balustrade that separates the Court of the Israelites from that of the priests, but from where he stands he has a good view of the high altar, four times higher than the tallest man, and of the Temple proper beyond, for the arrangement is like one of those Chinese boxes with each chamber leading into another. We see the building from afar and think to ourselves, Ah, the Temple, then we enter the Court of the Gentiles and once more think, Ah, the Temple, and now the carpenter Joseph, leaning on the balustrade, looks up and says, Ah, the Temple, and he is right, there is the wide front, with its four columns set into the wall, the capitals festooned with laurel leaves in the Greek style, and the great gaping entrance, which has no door, but to enter that Temple of Temples inhabited by God would be to defy all prohibitions, to pass through the holy place called Hereal, and finally come into Debir, which is the last chamber of all, the Holy of Holies, an awesome stone chamber as empty as the universe, windowless and dark as the tomb, where the light of day has never and will never penetrate, until the hour of its destruction, when all the stones are reduced to rubble. The more remote He is, the more holy he becomes, while Joseph is merely the father of a Jewish child among many. He is about to witness the sacrifice of two innocent doves, that is, the father not the son, for the son, who is just as innocent, is in his mother's arms, perhaps thinking, if such a thing is possible at his age, that this is how the world must always be.

By the altar, which is made of massive slabs of stone untouched by tools since hewn from the quarry and set up in this vast edifice, a barefooted priest wearing a linen tunic waits for the Levite to hand over the turtledoves. He takes the first one, carries it to a corner of the altar, and with a single blow knocks the head from its body. The blood spurts everywhere. The priest sprinkles blood over the lower part of the altar and then places the decapitated bird on a dish to drain the rest of the blood. At the end of the day he will retrieve the dead bird, for it now belongs to him. The other turtledove has the honor of being wholly sacrificed, which means it will be incinerated. The priest ascends the ramp leading to the top of the altar, where the sacred fire burns. On the righthand edge of the altar he beheads the bird, sprinkles its blood over the plinth adorned on each corner with sheeps' horns, then plucks out the entrails. No one pays any attention to what is happening, for this is a death of no consequence. Craning his neck, Joseph tries to identify, amid all the smoke and smells, the smoke and smell of his own sacrifice, when the priest, having poured salt over the bird's head and carcass, tosses the pieces into the fire. Joseph cannot be sure. Crackling in the billowing flames fueled by fat, the limp, disemboweled carcass of the little dove would not even fill a cavity of one of God's teeth. At the foot of the ramp three priests are waiting. A calf topples to the ground, felled by a cleaver, my God, my God, how fragile You have made us and how vulnerable to death. Joseph has nothing more to accomplish here, he must withdraw, collect his wife and child, and return home. Mary is pure once more, not in the strict sense of the word, because purity is something to which most human beings, and above all women, can scarcely hope to aspire. With time and a period of seclusion, her fluxes and humors have settled down, everything has returned to normal, the only difference being that there are now two doves fewer in the world and one more child, who caused their death. The family leaves the Temple by the same gate they entered, Joseph goes to fetch the donkey, and Mary, stepping on a large stone, climbs onto the animal's back while Joseph holds the child. This is not the first time, but perhaps the memory of that turtledove having its entrails plucked out causes him now to linger before handing Jesus back to his mother, as if convinced that no arms can protect his son better than his own. He accompanies his wife and child to the city gate before returning to the Temple site. He will also be here tomorrow to finish his week's work, and then, God willing, they'll be off to Nazareth with all haste.

That same night, the prophet Micah revealed what he had hitherto withheld. As King Herod, by now resigned to his tortured dreams, waited for the apparition to disappear after the usual ranting and raving, which no longer had much effect, the prophet's formidable shape suddenly grew bigger, and he uttered words he had never spoken before, It is from you, Bethlehem, so insignificant among the families of Judah, that the future ruler of Israel has come. And at that moment the king awoke. Like the deepest chord of a harp, the prophet's words continued to resound through the room. Herod lay with his eyes open, trying to fathom the meaning of this revelation, if there was indeed any meaning, and was so absorbed that he scarcely felt the ants gnawing under his skin or the worms tunneling in his entrails. The prophecy was familiar to every Jew and revealed nothing Herod did not already know. Besides, he was never one to waste his time worrying about the sayings of the prophets. What bothered him was a vague disquiet, a sense of agonizing strangeness, as if the prophet's utterance had another meaning and that somewhere in those syllables and sounds lay an imminent and fearsome threat. He tried to rid himself of this obsession and go back to sleep, but his body resisted, aching to the marrow. Thinking offered some measure of relief. Staring up at the beams on the ceiling, where the decoration appeared to vibrate in the light of aromatic torches shielded by fire screens, King Herod searched for an answer but could find none. He then summoned the chief eunuch from among those guarding his bedside and ordered him to fetch at once from the Temple a priest bearing the Book of Micah.

This coming and going from palace to Temple and from Temple to palace went on for almost an hour. Read, ordered Herod when the priest entered the king's bedchamber, and the priest began, The word of the Lord as spoken to Micah of Maresheth in the days of Jotham, Ahaz, and Hezekiah, kings of Judah. He continued reading until Herod told him, Read further on, and the priest, puzzled and uncertain as to why he had been summoned, jumped to another passage, Woe to those who plot evil and lay plans for wicked deeds as they lie abed, but here he stopped, horrified at this involuntary impudence, became tongue-tied, and, hoping Herod might forget what had just been said, he went on, In the end it will come to pass that the Lord's great mansion will rise above the hills. Further on, snarled Herod, impatient to get to the passage that interested him, and the priest finally came to it, But it is from you, Bethlehem, so insignificant among the families of Judah, that the future ruler of Israel will come. Herod raised his hand, Repeat that passage, he insisted, and the priest obeyed. Once more, he ordered him, and the priest read it a third time. That's enough, said the king after a prolonged silence, You may withdraw. All was now clear. The book announced a future birth, nothing else, while the ghost of Micah had come to warn him that this birth had already taken place. Your words, like those of all prophets, could not have been clearer, even when we interpret them badly. Herod thought and thought again, his expression more and more grim and menacing. He then summoned the commander of the guards and gave him an order to be carried out forthwith. When the commander returned to report, Mission fulfilled, Herod gave another command to be carried out at daybreak, now only hours away. So we shall soon know what has been ordered, unlike the priest, who was brutally assassinated by soldiers before he reached the Temple. There is reason to believe that this was the first of the two orders, so close are the likely cause and the logical effect. As for the Book of Micah, it disappeared, and imagine what a loss that would have been had there been only one copy.

A CARPENTER AMONG CARPENTERS, JOSEPH HAD FINISHED
eating his lunch, and he and his companions still had some
free time before the overseer gave the signal to get back to
work. Joseph could sit for a while, stretch out and take a
nap or indulge in pleasant thoughts, imagine himself on
the open road, wandering the countryside amid the hills of
Samaria or, better still, looking down from a great height
on the village of Nazareth, which he sorely missed. His
soul rejoiced as he told himself that this long separation
would soon be over and he would be on his way with only
the morning star in the sky, singing praises to the Lord
who protects our homes and guides our footsteps. Startled, he opened his eyes, afraid that he had dozed off and
missed the overseer's signal, but he had only been daydreaming, his companions were still there, some chatting,
others taking a nap, and the jovial mood of the overseer
suggested that he might give his workers the rest of the
day off. The sun is overhead, sharp gusts of wind drive
the smoke from the sacrificial fires in the opposite direction. In this ravine, which looks onto the site where a hip-

podrome is under construction, not even the gabbling of the vendors in the Temple can be heard. The machine of time appears to have come to a halt, as if it too were awaiting a signal from the mighty overseer of universal space and time. Joseph suddenly became uneasy, after feeling so happy only a moment ago. He looked around him and saw the same familiar building site, to which he had grown accustomed in recent weeks, slabs of stone and wooden planks, a thick layer of white dust everywhere, and sawdust that never seemed to dry. He tried to find some explanation for this unexpected gloom, it was probably the natural reaction of a man who had to leave his work unfinished, even if this particular job was not his responsibility and he had every reason for leaving. Rising to his feet, Joseph tried to calculate how much time was left. The overseer did not even turn to glance in his direction, so Joseph decided to take one last look at the section of the building on which he had worked, to bid farewell, as it were, to the timbers he had planed and the joists he had fitted, if they could possibly be identified, for where is the bee that can claim, This honey was made by me.

After taking a good look around, Joseph was heading back to the site when he paused for a moment to admire the city on the opposite slope, built up in stages, with stones baked to the color of bread. The overseer must have given the signal by now, but Joseph was in no hurry, he gazed at the city, waiting for who knows what. The minutes passed and nothing happened. Joseph muttered to himself, Well, I might as well get back to work, when he heard voices on the path below the spot where he was standing, and, leaning over the stone wall, he saw three soldiers. They must have been walking along the path and decided to stop for a break, two of them were resting on their lances and listening to the third man, who looked older and was probably their officer, although it was not easy to tell the difference unless you were familiar with the

445

various uniforms and knew the significance of the many insignia, stripes, and braids denoting rank. The words, which Joseph could barely make out, sounded like a question, something like, And when will that be, and one of the younger men answered in a clear voice, At the beginning of the third hour, when everyone is indoors. Whereupon the other soldier asked, How many of us are being dispatched, only to be told, I don't know yet but enough men to surround the village. Has an order been given to kill all of them. No, not all of them, only those under the age of three. It's difficult to tell a two-year-old from a four-year-old. And how many will that make, the second soldier wanted to know. According to the census, the officer told them, there must be around twenty-five. Joseph's eyes widened as if they could grasp this conversation better than his ears could, and he trembled from head to foot, because it was clear that these soldiers were talking about killing people. People, what people, he asked himself, bewildered and distressed, No, no, not people, or rather, people, but children. Children under the age of three, the officer in charge said, or perhaps it was one of the junior soldiers, but where, where could this be. Joseph could not very well lean over the wall and ask, Is there a war going on. He felt his legs shaking. He could hear one of the men say gravely, though with relief, How fortunate for us and our children that we don't live in Bethlehem. Does anyone know why they've chosen to kill the children of Bethlehem, one of the soldiers asked. No, the commander didn't say and I'll wager he doesn't know himself, the order came from the king, and that's all we need to know. Tracing a line on the ground with his lance, as if dividing and parceling out destiny, the other soldier said, Wretched are we who not only practice the evil that is ours by nature but must also serve as an instrument of evil for those who abuse their power. But these words went unheard by Joseph, who had stolen away from his vantage point, cautiously at first and then

446

in a mad rush, like a frightened goat, scattering pebbles in all directions as he ran. Unfortunately, without Joseph's testimony we have reason to doubt the authenticity of this soldier's philosophical remark, both in form and content, given the obvious contradiction between the aptness of the sentiment and the humble station of the person who expressed it.

Delirious, bumping into everything, overturning fruit stalls and bird cages, even a money changer's table, and oblivious to the cries of fury from the vendors in the Temple, Joseph is concerned only that his child's life is in danger. He cannot imagine why anyone would want to do such a thing, he is desperate, he chose to father a child and now someone wants to take it from him, one desire is as valid as another, to do and undo, to tie and untie, to create and destroy. Suddenly he stops, realizing the risk he is running if he continues in this reckless flight, the Temple guards might appear and arrest him, he is surprised they have not already been alerted by the uproar. Dissembling as best he can, like a louse taking refuge in the seams of a garment, he disappears into the crowd and instantly becomes anonymous, the only difference being that he walks a little faster than others, but this is hardly noticed amid the labyrinth of people. He knows he must not run until he reaches the city gate, but he is distressed at the thought that the soldiers may already be on their way, ominously armed with lance, dagger, and unprovoked hatred. If they are traveling on horseback, he will never catch up with them, and by the time he gets there, his son will be dead, poor child, sweet little Jesus. At this moment of deepest anguish a foolish thought occurs to him, he remembers his wages, the week's wages he stands to lose, and such is the power of these vile material things that, without exactly coming to a halt, he slows down just long enough to ponder whether he can rescue both his money and his child's life. Quick as it surfaced, this unworthy thought disappears, leaving no sense of shame, that feeling which often, but not often enough, proves our most reliable guardian angel.

Joseph finally puts the city behind him. There are no soldiers on the road for as far as the eye can reach, no crowds gathered as one might expect them to for a military parade, but the most reassuring sight of all is that of children playing innocent games, with none of the wild enthusiasm they display when flags, drums, and horns go marching by. If any soldiers had passed this way, there would be no boys in sight, they would have followed the detachment at least to the first bend in the road, as is the time-honored custom, and perhaps one child, his heart set on becoming a soldier someday, accompanied them on their mission and so learned the fate that awaited him, namely, to kill or be killed. Now Joseph can run as fast as he likes, he takes advantage of the slope, is hampered only by his tunic, which he hitches up over his knees. As in a dream, he has the agonizing sensation that his legs cannot keep up with the rest of his body, with his heart, head, and eyes, and his hands, eager to offer protection, are so painfully slow in their movement. Some people stop on the road and shake their heads disapprovingly at this undignified performance, for these people are known for their composure and noble bearing. The explanation for Joseph's extraordinary behavior in their eyes is not that he is running to save his child's life but that he is Galilean, one of a lot with no real breeding, as has often been observed. He has already passed Rachel's tomb, and that good woman could never have suspected that she would have so much cause to weep for her children, to cover the nearby hills with her cries and lamentations, to claw at her face, tear out her hair, and then beat her bare skull.

Before he comes to the first houses on the outskirts of Bethlehem, Joseph leaves the main road and goes cross-country, I am taking a shortcut, he would reply if we were to question this sudden change of direction, a route that might be shorter but is certainly much less comfortable. Taking care not to encounter any laborers at work in the fields, and hiding behind boulders whenever he sees a shepherd, Joseph makes for the cave where his wife is not expecting him at this hour and his son, fast asleep, is not expecting him at all. Halfway up the slope of the last hill, from where he can already see the dark chasm of the grotto, Joseph is assailed by a terrible thought, suppose his wife has gone to the village, taking the child with her, nothing more natural, knowing what women are, than for her to take advantage of being on her own to make a farewell visit to Salome and several families with whom she has become acquainted in recent weeks, leaving Joseph to thank the owners of the cave with all due formality. He sees himself running through the streets and knocking on every door, Is my wife here. It would be foolish to inquire anxiously. Better, Is my son here, in case some woman, carrying a child in her arms, for example, should ask, on seeing him distressed, Is something wrong. No, nothing, he would reply, Nothing at all, it's just that we have to set off at first light and we still haven't packed. The village, seen from here, with its identical roof terraces, reminds Joseph of the building site, stones scattered everywhere until the workers assemble them, one on top of another, to erect a watchtower, an obelisk to commemorate some victory, or a wall for lamentations. A dog barks in the distance, others bark in response, but the warm evening silence continues to hover over the village like a blessing about to lose its effect, like a wisp of a cloud on the point of vanishing.

This pause was short-lived. In one last spurt the carpenter reached the entrance to the cave and called out, Mary, are you there. She called in reply, and Joseph realized that his legs were weak, probably from all the running, but also from the sheer relief of knowing his child was safe. Inside the cave Mary was chopping vegetables for the evening meal, the child asleep in the manger. Joseph collapsed on the ground but was soon back on his feet, We must leave, we must get out of this place. Mary looked at him in dismay, Are we leaving, she asked, Yes, this very minute, But you said, Be quiet and start packing while I harness the donkey. Aren't we going to eat first. No, we'll eat something on the way. But it will soon be dark and we might get lost, whereupon Joseph lost his temper, Be quiet, woman, I've already told you we're leaving, so do as I say. Tears sprang to Mary's eyes, this was the first time her husband had ever raised his voice to her. Without another word she began gathering their scant possessions. Be quick, be quick, he kept repeating as he saddled the donkey and tightened the straps and crammed whatever came to hand into the baskets, while Mary looked on dumbfounded at this husband she barely recognized. They were ready to leave, the only thing left to be done now was put out the fire with earth. Joseph signaled to his wife to wait until he took a look outside.

The ashen shadows of twilight merged heaven and earth. The sun had not yet set, but the heavy mist, while too high to obscure the surrounding fields, kept the sunlight from them. Joseph listened carefully, took a few steps, his hair on end. A scream came from the village, so shrill that it scarcely sounded human, its echo resounding from hill to hill, and it was followed by more screams and wailing, which could be heard everywhere. These were not weeping angels lamenting human misfortune, these were the voices of men and women maddened by grief beneath an empty sky. Slowly, afraid of being heard, Joseph stepped back to the cave, and collided with Mary, who had disregarded his warning. She was trembling. What are those screams, she asked, but he pushed her back inside without replying and hastily began throwing earth on the fire. What are those screams, Mary asked a second time, invisible in the darkness, and Joseph eventually answered, People are being put to death. He paused and then added in a whisper, Children, by order of Herod, his voice breaking into a dry sob, That's why I said we should leave. There was a muffled sound of clothing and hay being disturbed, Mary was lifting her child from the manger and pressing him to her bosom, Sweet little Jesus, who would want to harm you, her words drowned in tears. Be quiet, said Joseph, don't make a sound, perhaps the soldiers won't find this place, they've been ordered to kill all the children in Bethlehem under the age of three. How did you find out. I overheard it in the Temple and that's why I ran back. What do we do now. We're on the outskirts of the village, the soldiers aren't likely to look inside these caves, they've been ordered to carry out a house-to-house search, so let's hope no one reports us and we're spared. He took another cautious look outside, the screaming had stopped, nothing could be heard now except a wailing chorus, which gradually subsided. The massacre of the innocents had ended.

The sky was still overcast. The advancing darkness and the mist overhead had erased Bethlehem from the sight of those inhabiting heaven. Joseph warned Mary, Don't move from here, I'm going out to the road to see if the soldiers have gone. Be careful, said Mary, forgetting that her husband was in no danger, only children under the age of three, unless someone else had gone out to the road with the intention of betraying him, telling the soldiers, This is Joseph, the carpenter, whose child is not yet three, a boy called Jesus, who could be the child mentioned in the prophecy, for our children cannot be destined for glory now that they are dead.

Inside the cave one could touch the darkness. Mary, who had always feared the dark, was used to having a light in the house, from either the fire or an oil lamp, or both, and the feeling, all the stronger now that she was hiding here in the earth, that fingers of darkness would reach out and touch her lips, filled her with terror. She did not want to disobey her husband or expose her child to danger by leaving the cave, but she was becoming more terrified by the minute. Soon the fear would overpower her fragile defenses of common sense, it was no good telling herself, If there was nothing in the cave before we put out the fire then why should there be anything now, although this thought gave her just enough courage to grope her way to the manger, where she settled her child, and then, carefully creeping around until she found the spot where the fire had been, she poked the ashes with a piece of firewood until a few embers appeared that had not yet completely died. Her fear vanished at once as, remembering the luminous earth, she watched this tremulous glow with crisscrossing flashes like a torch that darts over the ridge of a mountain. The image of the beggar came to her, only to be pushed aside by the urgent need to create more light in that terrifying cave. Fumbling, Mary went to the manger to fetch a handful of straw. Guided by the faint glow on the ground, she was back in an instant and soon had the oil lamp set up in a corner, where it could cast a pale but reassuring light on the nearby walls without attracting the attention of anyone outside. Mary went to her child, who continued to sleep, indifferent to fears, cares, and violent deaths. Taking him in her arms, she went and sat near the lamp and waited.

Time passed. Her child woke without fully opening his eyes, and when Mary saw he was about to cry, she opened her tunic and brought the child's avid mouth to her breast. Jesus was still feeding at his mother's breast when she heard footsteps. Her heart almost stopped beating. Could it be soldiers. But these were the footsteps of one person, and soldiers on a search normally went in pairs at least so that one could aid the other in the event of an attack. It must be Joseph, she thought, and feared he would scold her for having lit the lamp. The steps came closer, Joseph was entering the cave, but suddenly a shiver went up Mary's spine, those were not Joseph's firm, heavy steps, perhaps it was some itinerant laborer seeking shelter for the night, as had happened twice before, although Mary had not been afraid on those occasions, because it never occurred to her that anyone, however heartless and cruel, would harm a woman with a child in her arms. She thought of the infants slaughtered in Bethlehem, some perhaps in their mothers' arms, just as Jesus lies in hers, innocent babes still sucking the milk of life as swords pierced their tender flesh, but then those assassins were soldiers, not vagrants. No, it was not Joseph, and it was not a soldier looking for an exploit he would not have to share, and it was not a laborer without work or shelter. It was the man, again in the guise of a shepherd, who had appeared to her as a beggar, claiming to be an angel, not revealing, however, whether he came from heaven or hell. At first Mary thought it could not possibly be he, but she now realized it could be no one else.

The angel said, Peace be with you, wife of Joseph, and peace be with your child, how fortunate for both of you to have found shelter in this cave, otherwise one of you would now be broken and dead and the other broken though still alive. Mary told him, I heard cries for help. The angel said, One day those cries will be raised to heaven in your name, and even before then you will hear thousands of cries beside you. Mary told him, My husband went to the road to see if the soldiers have left, he must not find you here when he comes back. The angel said, Don't worry, I'll be gone before he returns, I only came to tell you that you will not see me again for some time, that all that was decreed in heaven has come to pass, that these deaths were as inevitable as Joseph's crime. Mary asked, What crime, my husband has committed no crime, he is an honest man. The angel told her, An honest man who committed a crime, you have no idea how many honest men have committed crimes, their crimes are countless, and contrary to popular belief these are the only crimes that cannot be forgiven. Mary asked, What crime did my husband commit. The angel replied, Should I tell you, surely you don't want to share his guilt. Mary said, I swear I am innocent. The angel told her, Swear if you will, but any oath taken before me is a puff of wind that knows not where it's going. Mary pleaded, What crime have we committed. The angel replied, Herod's cruelty unsheathed those swords, but your selfishness and cowardice were the cords that bound the victims' hands and feet. Mary asked, What could I have done. The angel told her, You could not have done anything, for you found out too late, but the carpenter could have done something, he could have warned the villagers that the soldiers were coming to kill their children when there was still time for parents to gather them up and escape, to hide in the wilderness, for example, or flee to Egypt and wait for Herod's death, which is fast approaching. Mary said, Joseph didn't think. The angel retorted, No, he didn't think, but that hardly excuses him. Mary tearfully implored, Angel that you are, forgive him. The angel replied, I am not an angel who grants pardons. Mary pleaded, Forgive him. The angel was unswayed, I've already told you, there's no forgiveness for this crime, Herod will be forgiven sooner than your husband, for it is easier to forgive a villain than a deserter. Mary asked, What are we to do. The angel told her, You will live and suffer like everyone else. Mary asked, And what about my son. The angel said, A father's guilt falls on the heads of his children, and the shadow of Joseph's guilt already darkens his son's brow. Mary sighed, Wretched are we. Indeed, said the angel, and there is nothing to be done. Mary lowered her head, pressed her child closer to her bosom, as if protecting him from the promised evil, and when she turned around, the angel had vanished. But this time there was no sound of footsteps. He must have flown away, Mary thought to herself. She got up and went to the entrance of the cave to see if there was any trace of the angel's flight through the sky or any sign of Joseph nearby.

The mist had cleared, the first stars glittered like metal, and wailing voices could still be heard from the village. Then a thought as presumptuous as spiritual pride itself blotted out the angel's dark warning and caused Mary's head to spin. Suppose her son's salvation was a sign from God, for surely the child's escape from a cruel death must mean something when so many others who perished could do nothing but wait for the opportunity to ask God himself, Why did you kill us, and be satisfied with whatever reply He might choose to give. Mary's delirium soon passed, and the thought occurred to her that she too could be holding a dead child like all those other mothers in Bethlehem, and she shed a flood of tears for the welfare and salvation of her soul. She was still weeping when Joseph returned. She heard him coming but did not stir, did not care if he rebuked her, she was crying now with the other women, all of them seated in a circle with their children on their laps awaiting resurrection. Joseph saw that she wept, understood, and said nothing.

Inside the cave, he did not appear to notice the burning oil lamp. A fine layer of ash now covered the embers, but in the center there was still a faint flicker of flame struggling to survive. As he began unloading the donkey, Joseph reassured Mary, We're no longer in danger, the soldiers have gone, we might as well spend the night here. We'll leave before dawn, avoid the main road, and take a short-cut, and where there are no roads we'll find a way somehow. Mary murmured, All those dead children, which provoked Joseph into asking brusquely, How do you know, have you counted them, and Mary continued, I even knew some of those children. You ought to be thanking God for having spared your own son. I will. And stop staring at me as if I'd committed some crime. I wasn't staring at you. Don't answer in that accusing tone of voice. Very well, I won't say another word. Good. Joseph tethered the donkey to the manger, where there was still some hay. The donkey cannot complain, it has had lots of fodder and plenty of fresh air, but it is not hungry, it is preparing itself for the arduous journey back with a full load. Mary put her child down and said, I'll get the fire going. What for. To prepare some supper. I don't want a fire in here to attract the attention of some passerby, let's eat whatever there is that doesn't need to be cooked. And so they ate.

The light from the lamp made the cave's four inhabitants look like ghosts, the donkey motionless as a statue, not eating though its nose was buried in the straw, the child dozing, the man and woman satisfying their hunger with a few dry figs. Mary laid out the mats on the sandy ground, threw a cover over them, and, as usual, waited for her husband to go to bed. First Joseph went to take another look at the night sky, all was peaceful in heaven and on earth, and no more cries or lamentations could be heard in the village. Rachel only had strength enough left to sigh and whimper inside the houses where doors and souls were tightly closed. Stretched out on his mat, Joseph felt exhausted after all his worry and panic, and he could not even say that his wild chase had saved his son's life. The soldiers had strictly carried out their orders, Kill the children of Bethlehem, without taking any further initiative, such as searching all the caves in the vicinity to ferret out families in hiding or families making their homes there. Normally Joseph did not mind that Mary came to bed only after he had fallen asleep, but on this occasion he could not bear to think of her watching him, in her sorrow, as he lay sleeping. He told her, I do not want you waiting up, come to bed. Mary made no protest. After making sure, as usual, that the donkey was securely tethered, she lay down with a sigh on her mat, closed her eyes, and waited for sleep to come.

In the middle of the night, Joseph had a dream. He was riding down a road leading into a village, when the first houses came into view. He wore a military uniform and was armed with sword, lance, and dagger, a soldier among soldiers. The commanding officer asked him, Where do you think you're going, carpenter, to which Joseph replied, proud of being so well prepared for the mission entrusted to him, I'm off to Bethlehem to kill my son, and as he said those words, he woke with a fearsome growl, his body twitching and writhing with fear. Mary asked him in alarm, What's wrong, what happened, as Joseph kept repeating, No, no, no. Suddenly he broke into bitter sobs. Mary got up, fetched the lamp, and held it near his face, Are you ill, she asked. Covering his face with his hands, he shouted, Take that lamp away at once, woman, and still sobbing, he went to the manger to see if his child was safe. He is fine, Master Joseph, do not worry, in fact the child gives no trouble, good-natured, quiet, all he wants is to be fed and to sleep, and here he rests as peaceful as can be, oblivious to the dreadful death he has miraculously escaped, just think, to be put to death by the father who gave him life, for though death is the fate that awaits all of us, there are many ways of dying. Afraid that the dream might come back, Joseph did not lie down again. Wrapped in his mantle, he sat at the entrance to the cave, beneath an overhanging rock that formed a natural porch, and the moon above cast a black shadow over the opening, a shadow the faint glow of the oil lamp within could not dispel. Had Herod himself been carried past by his slaves, escorted by legions of barbarians thirsting for blood, he would have told them calmly, Don't bother searching this place, continue on, there is nothing here but stone and shadow, what we want is the tender flesh of newborn babes. The very thought of his dream made Joseph shiver. He wondered what it could possibly mean, for, as the heavens could testify, he had raced like a madman down that slope, a Via Dolorosa if ever there was one, he had scaled rocks and walls in his haste to rescue his child, like a good father, yet in the dream he saw himself as a fiend intent on murder. How wise the proverb that reminds us that there is no constancy in dreams. This must be the work of Satan, he decided, making a gesture to drive out evil spirits.

The piercing trill of an unseen bird filled the air, or perhaps it was a shepherd whistling, but surely not at this hour, when the flocks are asleep and only the dogs are keeping watch. Yet the night, calm and remote from all living creatures, showed that supreme indifference which we associate with the universe, or that other absolute indifference, the indifference of emptiness, which will remain, if there is such a thing as emptiness, when all has been fulfilled. The night ignored the meaning and rational order that appear to govern the world in those moments when we can still believe the world was made to harbor us and our insanity. The terrifying dream grew unreal and absurd, was dispelled by the night, the shining moon, and the presence of his child asleep in the manger. Joseph was awake and as much in command of himself and his thoughts as any man could be, his thoughts were now charitable and peaceful, yet just as capable of monstrosity, for example his gratitude to God that his beloved child had been spared by the soldiers who had butchered so many innocents. The night that descends over carpenter Joseph descends also over the mothers of the children of Bethlehem, forgetting their fathers, and even Mary for a moment, since they do not figure here for some strange reason. The hours passed quietly, and at first light Joseph got up, went to load the donkey, and, taking advantage of the last moonlight before the sky turned clear, the whole family, Jesus, Mary, and Joseph, were soon on their way back to Galilee.

Stealing from her master's house, where two infants had been killed, the slave Salome rushed to the cave that morning, convinced that the same sad fate had befallen the child she helped bring into the world. She found the place deserted, nothing remained except footprints and the donkey's hoofprints. Dying embers beneath the ashes, but no bloodstains. Gone, she said, little Jesus has escaped this first death.

Eight months had passed since that happy day when Joseph arrived in Nazareth with his family safe and sound despite many dangers, the donkey less so, for it was limping slightly on its right hoof, when the news came that King Herod had died in Jericho, in one of his palaces where he took refuge to escape the rigors of the Jerusalem winter, which spares neither the weak nor the infirm. There were also rumors that the kingdom, now robbed of its mighty monarch, would be divided among three of his sons who had survived the feuding and destruction, namely, Herod Philip, who would govern the territories lying east of Galilee, Herod Antipas, who would inherit Galilee and Peraea, and Archelaus, who would rule Judaea, Samaria, and Idumaea. One day a passing muleteer with a flair for narrating tales both real and fictitious will give the people of Nazareth a graphic description of Herod's funeral, which he will swear he witnessed. The body, placed in a magnificent sarcophagus made of the purest gold and inlaid with precious stones, was transported on a gilded carriage draped with purple cloth and drawn by two white oxen. The body was also covered with a purple cloth, all that could be seen was a human shape with a crown resting where the head was. Behind followed musicians playing flutes and the professional mourners, who could not avoid the overpowering stink, and as I stood there at the roadside even I felt queasy, then came the king's guards on horseback, then foot soldiers armed with lances, swords, and daggers as if marching to war, an endless procession wending its awesome way like a serpent with no head or tail in sight. In horror I watched those soldiers marching behind a corpse but also to their own death, to that death which sooner or later knocks on every door. Time to leave, promptly comes the order to kings and vassals alike, making no distinction between the rotting body at the head of the procession and those in the rear choking on the dust of an entire army, they are still alive but heading for a place where they will remain forever. Clearly this muleteer would be more at home as an Aristotelian scholar strolling beneath the Corinthian capitals of some academy rather than prodding donkeys along the roads of Israel, sleeping in smelly caravansaries, and narrating tales to rustics such as these of Nazareth.

Among the crowd in the square in front of the synagogue was Joseph, who happened to be passing and had stopped to listen. He did not pay much attention to the descriptive details of the funeral procession, and lost interest when the poet began to strike an elegiac note, for grim experience had made the carpenter wise about that particular chord on the harp. One had only to look at him, his composure when he concealed his youth by becoming solemn and thoughtful, the bitterness that marked him with lines deeper than scars. But what is really disturbing about Joseph's face are the eyes, which are dull and expressionless except for a tiny flicker caused by insomnia. It is true that Joseph gets little sleep. Sleep is the enemy he confronts each night, as if fighting for his very life, and it is a battle he invariably loses, for even when he seems to be winning and falls asleep from sheer exhaustion, he no sooner closes his eyes than he sees a detachment of soldiers appearing on the road, with Joseph himself riding in their midst, sometimes brandishing a sword above his head, and it is just at that moment, when terror overwhelms him, that the leader of the expedition asks, Where do you think you're going, carpenter. And the poor man, who would rather not say, resists with all his might, but the malignant spirits in the dream are too strong for him, and they prise open his mouth with hands of steel, reducing him to tears and despair as he confesses, I'm on my way to Bethlehem to kill my son. We won't ask Joseph if he remembers how many oxen pulled the carriage bearing Herod's corpse or whether they were white or dappled. As he heads for home, all he can think of are the closing phrases of the muleteer's tale, when the man described the multitude accompanying the procession, slaves, soldiers, royal guards, professional mourners, musicians, governors, princes, future kings, and all the rest of us, whoever we might be, doing nothing else in life but searching for the place where we will stay forever. If only it were so, mused Joseph, with the bitterness of one who has given up all hope. If only it were so, he repeated to himself, thinking of all those who never left their place of birth yet death went there to find them, which only proves that fate is the only real certainty. It is so easy, dear God, we need only wait for everything in life to be fulfilled to say, It was fate. Herod was fated to die in Jericho and be borne on a carriage to the fortress of Herodium, but death exempted the infants of Bethlehem from having to travel anywhere. And Joseph's journey, which in the beginning seemed part of some divine plan to save those holy innocents, turned out to be futile. The carpenter listened and said nothing, he ran off to rescue his own child, leaving the others to their fate. So now we know why Joseph cannot sleep, and when he does, it is only to awaken to a reality that will not allow him to forget his dream, even when awake he dreams the same dream night after night, and when asleep, though trying desperately to avoid it, he knows he will encounter that dream again, for it hovers on the threshold between sleep and waking and he must pass it when he enters and when he leaves. This confusion is best defined as remorse. Yet human experience and the practice of communication have shown throughout the ages that definitions are an illusion, like having a speech defect and trying to say love but unable to get the word out, or, better, having a tongue in one's head but unable to feel love.

Mary is pregnant again. No angel disguised as a beggar came knocking at the door this time to announce the child's arrival, no sudden gust of wind swept the heights of Nazareth, no luminous earth was discovered in the ground. Mary told Joseph in the simplest words, I'm with child. She did not say to him, for example, Look into my eyes and see how our second child is shining there, nor did he reply this time, Don't think I hadn't noticed, I was waiting for you to tell me. He just listened, remained silent, and eventually said, Is that so, and carried on planing a piece of wood with apparent indifference, but, then, we know that his thoughts are elsewhere. Mary also knows, since that night of torment when her husband blurted out the secret he had kept to himself, and she was not altogether surprised, she had been expecting something like this after the angel told her in the cave, You will have a thousand cries all around you. A good wife would have said to her husband, Don't fret, what's done is done, and besides, your first duty was to rescue your own child. But Mary has changed and is no longer what one would normally refer to as a good wife, perhaps because she heard the angel utter those grave words that excluded no one, I am not an angel who grants pardons. Had she been allowed to discuss these deep matters with Joseph, who was so well versed in Holy Scripture, he might have pondered the nature of this angel who appeared from nowhere to announce that he did not grant pardons, a statement which seems superfluous, since everyone knows that the power to pardon belongs to God alone. For an angel to say that he does not grant pardons is either meaningless or much too meaningful. An angel of judgment, perhaps, might exclaim, You expect me to forgive you, what a silly idea, I did not come to forgive, I came only to punish. But angels, by definition, leaving aside those cherubim with flaming swords who were posted by the Lord to guard the path to the tree of life lest our first parents or we, their descendants, try to return to steal the fruits, angels, as we were saying, are not vigilantes entrusted with the corrupt albeit socially necessary enforcement of repression. Angels exist to make our lives easier, they protect us when we are about to fall down a well, help us cross the bridge over the precipice, pull us to safety just as we are about to be crushed by a runaway chariot or a car without brakes. An angel worthy of the name could have spared Joseph all this torment simply by appearing in a dream to the fathers of the children of Bethlehem to warn them, Gather your wife and child and flee to Egypt and stay there until I tell you to return, for Herod means to slaughter your child. In this way the children could have all been saved, Jesus hidden in the cave with his parents and the others on their way to Egypt, where they would remain until the same angel returned to tell the fathers, Arise, gather your wife and child and return to Israel, for he who tried to kill your children is dead. Thus the children would return to the places where they came from and where eventually they would meet their deaths at the appointed hour, because angels, however powerful, have their limitations, just like God. After much thought, Joseph might have reached the conclusion that the angel who appeared in the cave was an infernal creature, an agent of Satan disguised this time as a shepherd, and further proof of the weakness and gullibility of women, who can be led astray by a fallen angel. If Mary could speak, if she were less secretive and revealed the details of that strange annunciation, things would be different, Joseph would use other arguments to support his theory, most important, the fact that this so-called angel did not proclaim, I am an angel of the Lord, or, I come in the name of the Lord. He simply said, I am an angel, before adding cautiously, Keep this to yourself, as if afraid for anyone else to know. Some may argue that such details contribute nothing new to our understanding of what is an all-too-familiar story, but as far as this narrator is concerned, it is crucial to know, when interpreting past and future events, whether the angel came from heaven or from hell. Between angels of light and angels of darkness there are differences not just of form but also of essence, substance, and content, and while it is true that whoever created the former also created the latter, He subsequently attempted to correct His mistake.

Mary, like Joseph, but for different reasons, often looks distracted, her expression becomes blank, her hands drop in the middle of some task, her gestures are suddenly interrupted, she stares into the distance, not so surprising for a woman in her condition, were it not for the various thoughts that occupy her mind and that can be summed up in the following question, Why did the angel announce the birth of Jesus yet say nothing of this second child. Mary looks at her firstborn crawling on all fours as children do at that age, she studies him and tries to perceive a special trait, some mark or sign, a star on his forehead, a sixth finger on his hand, but she sees a child like any other, who slobbers, gets dirty, and cries, the only difference being that he is her son. His hair is black like that of his parents, his irises are already losing that whitish tinge inaccurately called milky and assuming their natural, inherited color, a dark brown which gradually turns a somber green if one can so describe a color, but these features are hardly unique, important only when the child belongs to us, or, as in this case, to Mary. Within weeks he will be making his first attempts to stand up and walk, he will fall on his hands countless times, stay there staring, lifting his head with some difficulty as he hears his mother say, Come here, come here, my child. And he will begin to feel the urge to speak, sounds will form in his throat, at first he will not know what to do with them, he will get them mixed up with sounds he already knows and makes, such as gurgling and crying, until he begins to realize that they must be articulated in a different and more deliberate way, and he will move his lips as his father and mother do, until he succeeds in pronouncing his first word, perhaps da or dada or daddy, or perhaps even mummy, in any case after that little Jesus will not have to poke the forefinger of his right hand into the palm of his left hand if his mother and her neighbors ask him for the hundredth time, Where does the hen lay her egg. This is just another of those indignities to which a human being is subjected, trained like a lapdog to respond to certain sounds, a tone of voice, a whistle, or the crack of a whip. Now Jesus is able to answer that the hen can lay her egg wherever she wishes so long as she does not lay it in the palm of his hand. Mary looks at her little son, sighs, downhearted that the angel is not likely to return. You will not see me again for a while, he told her, but if he were to appear now, she would not be as intimidated as before, she would ply the angel with questions until he gave her an answer. Already a mother and expecting her second child, Mary is no innocent lamb, she has learned, to her cost, what suffering, danger, and worry mean, with all that experience on her side she can easily tip the scales to her advantage. It would not be enough for the angel to reply, May the Lord never allow you to see your child as you see me now, with nowhere to lay my head. First, the angel would have to identify this Lord in

466

whose name he claimed to speak, secondly, convince her that he told the truth when he said he had no place to lay his head, which seemed unlikely for an angel unless he meant it only in his role as beggar, thirdly, what future did those dark, threatening words augur for her son, and finally, what was the mystery surrounding that luminous earth buried near the door, where a strange plant had grown after their return from Bethlehem, nothing but stalk and leaves, which they had given up pruning after trying to pull it up by the roots, only to have it reappear with even greater vigor. Two of the elders of the synagogue, Zacchaeus and Dothan, came to inspect the phenomenon, and although they knew little about botany, they were in agreement that the seed must have been in the mysterious soil and then sprouted at the right moment, for as Zacchaeus observed, Such is the law of the Lord of life. Once she became accustomed to this stubborn plant, Mary decided it added a festive touch at the entrance to the house, while Joseph, still suspicious, moved his carpenter's bench to another part of the yard rather than have to look at the thing. He cut it back with an ax and saw, poured boiling water over it, even scattered burning coals around the stalk, but superstition prevented him from taking a spade and digging up the bowl of luminous earth that had been the cause of so much trouble. This was how matters stood when their second child, whom they named James, was born.

Over the next few years there were not many changes in the family, apart from the arrival of more children, including two daughters, while the parents lost the last vestiges of youth. In the case of Mary that was not surprising, for we know how childbearing, and she had borne many children, gradually saps whatever freshness and beauty a woman possesses, causing her face and body to age and wither, suffice it to say that after James came Lisa, after Lisa came Joseph, after Joseph came Judas, after Judas came

Simon, then Lydia, then Justus, then Samuel, and if any more followed, they perished without trace. Children are the pride and joy of their parents, as the saying goes, and Mary did her utmost to appear contented, but after carrying for months on end all those fruits that greedily consumed her strength, she often felt impatient, resentful, but in those days it would never have occurred to her to blame Joseph, let alone Almighty God who governs the life and death of His creatures and assures us that the very hairs of our heads are counted. Joseph had little understanding of the begetting of children, apart from the practical rudiments, which reduce all enigmas to one simple fact, namely, that if a man and woman come together, he will likely impregnate her, and after nine months, or on rare occasions after seven, a child is born. Released into the female womb, the male seed, minute and invisible, transmits the new being chosen by God to continue populating the world He has created. Sometimes, however, this fails to happen, and the fact that the transmission of seed into womb is not always sufficient to create a child is further evidence of the impenetrability of God's design. Allowing the seed to spill onto the ground, as did the unfortunate Onan, whom the Lord punished with death for refusing in this way to give his brother's widow children, rules out any possibility of the woman's becoming pregnant. On the other hand, time and time again, as someone once said, the pitcher goes to the fountain until there is no more water and it comes back empty. For it was clearly God who put Isaac into the little seed that Abraham was still able to produce, and God who poured it into Sarah's womb, because she was past conceiving children. Looking at things from a theogenetic angle, as it were, we may conclude without offending logic, which must preside over everything in this and every other world, that it was God Himself who spurred Joseph to keep having intercourse with Mary, so that they might have lots of children, helping Him assuage the remorse that plagued Him ever since He permitted, or willed, without considering the consequences, the massacre of those innocent children of Bethlehem. But the strangest thing of all, and which goes to show that the ways of the Lord are not only inscrutable but also disconcerting, is that Joseph truly believed he was acting of his own accord and obeying God's will, as he made strenuous efforts to beget more and more children, to compensate for all those killed by Herod's soldiers, so that the numbers would tally in the next census. God's remorse and Joseph's were one and the same, and, if people in those days were already familiar with the expression God never sleeps, we now know that the reason He never sleeps is that He made a mistake which no man would be forgiven. With every child begotten by Joseph, God raised His head a little higher, but He will never raise it fully, because twenty-seven infants were massacred in Bethlehem, and Joseph did not live long enough to impregnate one woman with that many children, and Mary, worn out in body and soul, could never have withstood that many pregnancies. The carpenter's house and yard, though full of children, might as well have been empty.

On reaching the age of five, Joseph's son started going to school. Each morning his mother took him to the synagogue and left him in the charge of the steward who taught beginners, and it was there in the synagogue-and-classroom that Jesus and the other little boys of Nazareth under the age of ten observed the wise man's precept, The child must be instructed in the Torah just as the ox is bred in the corral. The lesson ended at the sixth hour, which we now refer to as midday. Mary would be waiting for her child, and the poor woman was not allowed to ask him what he was learning, even this simple right was denied her, for as the wise man's maxim categorically states, Better that the law go up in flames than it be entrusted to women. Besides, if by any chance little Jesus had already been taught the true status of women in this world, including mothers, he might have given her the wrong answer, the kind of answer that reduces one to insignificance. Take Herod, for example, with all his wealth and power, yet if we were to see him now, we would not even be able to say, He is dead and rotting, because he is nothing but mold, dust, bones, and filthy rags. When Jesus arrived home, his father asked him, What did you learn today, and Jesus, having been blessed with an excellent memory, repeated word for word and without a moment's hesitation the lessons of the day. First the children were taught the letters of the alphabet, then the most important words, and finally whole sentences and passages from the Torah, which Joseph accompanied, beating out the rhythm with his right hand and slowly nodding his head. Standing aside, Mary looked on and learned things she was forbidden to ask, a clever stratagem on the part of women and practiced to perfection throughout the ages. Listening, they soon learn everything, even the difference between falsehood and truth, which is the height of wisdom. But what Mary did not understand, or understand completely, was the mysterious bond between her husband and Jesus, although even a stranger would have noticed the look of wistful tenderness on Joseph's face when he spoke to his firstborn, as if he was thinking to himself, This beloved son of mine is my sorrow. All Mary knew was that Joseph's nightmares, like a scourge on his soul, refused to go away, and were now so frequent that they became as much a habit as sleeping on the right side or waking up with thirst in the middle of the night. Mary, as a good and dutiful wife, still worried about her husband, but for her the most important thing of all was to see her son alive and well, a sign that Joseph's crime had not been too serious, otherwise the Lord would have punished him without mercy, as was His wont. Take Job, broken and leprous, yet he had always been an honest, upright, and God-fearing man. Job's misfortune was that he became involuntarily the cause of a dispute between Satan and God Himself, each clinging tenaciously to his own idea and prerogative. And yet they are surprised when a man despairs and cries out, Perish the day I was born and the night in which I was conceived, let that day turn to darkness and be erased from the calendar and that night become sterile and void of all happiness. It is true that God compensated Job by repaying him twice as much as He had taken, but what of all those other men, in whose name no book was ever written, men deprived of everything and given nothing in return, to whom everything was promised and nothing fulfilled.

But in this carpenter's house life was peaceful, and however frugal their existence, there was always bread on the table and enough food to keep body and soul together. As for possessions, the only thing Joseph had in common with Job was the number of sons. Job had seven sons and three daughters, while Joseph had seven sons and two daughters, giving the carpenter the merit of having put one woman less into the world. However, before God doubled his possessions, Job already owned seven thousand sheep, three thousand camels, five hundred yokes of oxen, and five hundred donkeys, not to mention slaves, of which he had many, whereas Joseph has only his donkey and nothing else. And there's no denying that it is one thing to feed two mouths, then a third, even if only indirectly during the first year, and quite another to find yourself saddled with a houseful of children who need more and more food when they start growing. Since Joseph's earnings were not enough to allow him to hire an apprentice, it was only natural that he make his children work. Besides, this was his fatherly duty, for as the Talmud says, Just as a man must feed his children, he must also teach them to work, otherwise he turns his sons into good-for-nothings. And recalling the precept of the rabbis that the artisan must never think himself inferior to the greatest scholar, we can imagine how proudly Joseph began instructing his older sons one after another as they came of age, first Jesus, then James, then Joseph, then Judas, in the secret skills of the carpenter's trade, ever mindful of the ancient proverb, A child's service is little, yet he is no little fool that despises it. When Joseph returned to work after the midday meal, his sons lent him a hand, a good example of domestic economy and a way to establish a whole dynasty of carpenters for future generations, if God in His wisdom had not decreed otherwise.

As if the humiliation inflicted on the Hebrew race for more than seventy years was not enough to satisfy the shameless arrogance of the empire, Rome decided, using the division of the former kingdom of Herod as a pretext, to update the previous census. This time, however, the men would not have to register in their places of origin, and thus they were spared the damaging effect on agriculture and commerce and all the other upheavals we witnessed Joseph and his family enduring earlier. The new decree ruled that the censors go from village to village, town to town, and city to city and summon all the men, whatever their status, to the main square or other suitable open-air site, where their names, occupations, and taxable wealth would be entered into the public record under the surveillance of guards. Now, it must be said that such procedures are not viewed with favor in this part of the world, which is nothing new, for Holy Scripture narrates the unfortunate decision of King David when he ordered Joab, the leader of his army, Go through all the tribes of Israel from Dan to Beersheba and carry out a census of the people, and since a royal command was never questioned, Joab silenced his doubts, gathered together his army, and set off to do the king's bidding. Nine months and twenty days later Joab returned to Jerusalem with the results of the census, which had been carefully tabulated and verified. There were eight hundred thousand armed soldiers in Israel and five hundred thousand in Judah. Now, we all know that God does not like anyone usurping His authority, especially when it comes to His chosen people, whom He will never allow to be ruled by any other lord or master, least of all by Rome, who bows to false gods and men, first because false gods do not really exist and secondly because of the sheer vanity of that pagan cult. But let us forget Rome for a moment and return to King David, whose heart sank the moment the leader of his army began reading the report, but it was too late, and he confessed, I have committed a grave sin, but I beg you, Lord, forgive your humble servant's folly. And next morning, a prophet named Gad, who was in a manner of speaking the king's soothsayer and his intermediary with Almighty God, came to David as he was rising and told him, The good Lord wishes to know whether you prefer three years of famine on earth, three months of persecution at the hands of your enemies, or three days of plague throughout the land. David did not inquire how many people would have to die in each case, he reckoned that in three days, even with plague, fewer would die than in three years of war or famine. So he prayed, God willing, let there be plague. And God sent a plague, and seventy thousand people died, not counting the women and children, who had not been registered. The Lord finally agreed to lift the plague in exchange for an altar, but the dead were dead, either God had forgotten them or it was not convenient to have them resurrected, since we can safely assume that innumerable inheritances and divisions of property were already being debated and contested, because there is no reason why God's

chosen people should disclaim worldly goods that rightfully belong to them, whether acquired by the sweat of
their brow, in litigation, or as the spoils of war. The outcome is what matters.

But before passing judgment on human and divine actions, we must also bear in mind that God, who lost no
time in making David pay dearly for his mistake, now appears to be unaware of the humiliation being inflicted by
Rome on His chosen children, and, more perplexing still,
He seems indifferent to this blatant lack of respect for His
name and authority. When such a thing happens, that is to
say, when it becomes clear that God is showing no sign of
coming soon, man has no choice but to take His place, to
leave home and restore order in this poor old world of
ours, which belongs to God. The censors, as we said earlier, were strutting around with all the arrogance of those
in power, backed by a military escort, in other words the
soldiers were there to protect them from insults and assault
when people started to rebel in Galilee and Judaea. Testing
their strength, some protest, quietly at first, then gradually
they become more aggressive and defiant, an artisan bangs
on the censor's table and swears they will never get a name
out of him, a merchant takes refuge in his tent with his
entire family and threatens to smash everything and tear
off all his clothes, a farmer sets fire to his harvest and brings
a basket of ashes, saying, This is the money Israel will pay
to those who offend her. Such troublemakers were arrested immediately, thrown into prison, flogged and humiliated, and since human resistance has its limits, frail
creatures that we are, their courage soon failed them, the
artisan shamelessly revealed his most intimate secrets, the
merchant was prepared to sacrifice several daughters in addition to paying his taxes, the farmer covered himself in
ashes and offered himself as a slave. The few who still resisted were put to death, while others, who had long ago
learned that the only good invader is a dead one, took up

arms and fled into the mountains. The arms in question were stones, slings, sticks, clubs and cudgels, a few bows and arrows, hardly enough to wage a war, and the odd sword or lance captured in brief skirmishes but unlikely to do the rebels much good, accustomed as they were, since David's reign, to the primitive weapons of placid shepherds rather than to those of trained warriors. But whether a man is Jewish or not, he takes more readily to war than to peace, especially if he finds a leader who shares his convictions. The insurrection against the Romans began when Joseph's firstborn was eleven years old, and it was led by a man called Judas, who hailed from Galilee and was therefore known as Judas the Galilean or Judas of Galilee. This simple method of naming people was common at the time, as we can see from names such as Joseph of Arimathaea, Simon of Cyrene or the Cyrenian, Mary Magdalene or Mary from Magdala. And if Joseph's son had lived and prospered, he would have been called Jesus of Nazareth or the Nazarene or perhaps something even simpler. But this is mere conjecture, we must never forget that fate is a casket like no other, open and closed at the same time. We can look inside and see all that has happened, the past transformed into fulfilled destiny, but we have no way of seeing into the future, apart from an occasional presentiment or intuition, as we find in this gospel, which could not have been written were it not for those signs and prodigies forecasting a destiny perhaps greater than life itself. But to return to what we were saying, Judas the Galilean had rebellion in his blood. His father, old Hezekiah, had participated in the popular revolts waged against Herod's presumed heirs after his death and before Rome could acknowledge the division of the kingdom and the authority of the new tetrarchs. This is beyond our understanding, for, while we are all made of the same all-too-human substance, the same flesh, bones, blood, skin and laughter, tears and sweat, some of us become cowards and others heroes, some are aggressive and others passive. The same substance used to make a Joseph also made a Judas, and while the latter passed on to his sons the thirst for battle he had inherited from his own father, giving up a peaceful existence in order to defend God's rights, the carpenter Joseph remained at home with his nine young children and their mother, confined to his workbench in order to eke out a living and provide food for his family. For no one can tell who will triumph tomorrow, some say God, others say nobody, one hypothesis is as good as the other, because to speak of yesterday, today, and tomorrow is simply to give different names to the same illusion.

But the men of the village of Nazareth, most of them youths, who went to join the guerrilla force of Judas the Galilean, all disappeared without warning, without a trace, their families sworn to secrecy, and this silence was so strictly observed that no one would have dreamt of asking, Where's Nathanael, I haven't seen him for days, if Nathanael failed to appear at the synagogue or among the reapers in the fields, there was simply one man missing and the others carried on as if Nathanael had never existed, well, not quite, for some saw him entering the village under cover of darkness and leaving again before dawn. Although the only proof of his arrival and departure was the smile on the face of his wife. A smile can be most revealing, a woman may be standing motionless, staring into space, at the horizon, or simply at the wall in front of her, then suddenly she smiles, a pensive smile, like an image coming to the surface and playing on restless water, one would have to be blind to think that Nathanael's wife spent the night without her husband. But human nature is so perverse that some women who were never without their husband at their side began sighing as they imagined those encounters, and they hovered around Nathanael's wife like bees around a flower heavy with pollen. Mary's situation was different, with nine children to care for and a husband who spent his nights tossing and turning in anguish, often waking up the little ones and scaring them out of their wits. After a time they grew used to it, more or less, but the eldest boy, whose own dreams were disturbed by some mysterious presence, was forever waking up. In the beginning he would ask his mother, What's wrong with Father, and she would brush the question aside, reassuring him, It's only a nightmare. She could not very well tell her son, Your father dreamt he was marching with Herod's soldiers along the road to Bethlehem. Which Herod. The father of the present king. Was that why he was groaning and shouting. Yes, that's right. I can't see how being the soldier of a king who's dead can give one nightmares. Your father was never one of Herod's soldiers, he's been a carpenter all his life. Then why does he have nightmares. People don't choose their dreams, dreams choose people, not that I've ever heard that said, but it must be so. And what about all that groaning, Mother. It's because your father dreams he's on his way to kill you. Obviously Mary could never have brought herself to say such things, revealing the cause of her husband's nightmare to Jesus, who like Abraham's son Isaac was cast in the role of the victim who escaped, yet is inexorably condemned.

One day, when he was helping his father make a door, Jesus summoned his courage and questioned him. After a long pause and without raising his eyes, Joseph told him, My son, you are aware of your duties and obligations, perform them and you will be worthy in the eyes of God, but examine your conscience and ask yourself if there are not other duties and obligations waiting to be performed. Is this what you dream, Father. No, the fear that I might have neglected some duty, or worse, that is the cause of my dreams. What do you mean by worse. I didn't think, and the dream itself, the dream is the thought that wasn't thought when it should have been, and now it haunts me night after night and I can't forget it. And what should you have thought. Not even you have the right to ask me that question, and I have no answer to give you. They were working in the shade in the yard, for it was summer and the sun was blazing. Jesus' brothers played nearby, except for the youngest, who was indoors being fed at his mother's breast. James had also been helping, but he soon got tired and bored, little wonder, for the year between them made all the difference, Jesus will soon be old enough for more advanced religious study, he has finished his elementary schooling. In addition to his study of the Torah, the written law, he is already being initiated in the oral law, which is much more difficult and complicated. This explains why at such an early age he was able to conduct a serious conversation with his father, using words properly and debating with reflection and logic. Jesus is almost twelve, on reaching manhood he will perhaps resume this interrupted conversation, if Joseph can find the courage to confide in his son and confess his guilt, that courage which failed Abraham when he was confronted by Isaac, but for the moment Joseph is content to acknowledge and praise the power of God. There can be no doubt that God's upright handwriting bears no resemblance to the crooked lines of men. Just think of Abraham, to whom the angel appeared and said at the last minute, Lay not your hand upon the child, and think of Joseph, who failed to seize the opportunity to save the children of Bethlehem when God sent an officer and three loquacious soldiers instead of an angel to warn him. If Jesus continues as well as he has started, one day he will get around to asking why God saved Isaac and did nothing to protect those poor children, who were as innocent as Abraham's son yet were shown no mercy before the throne of the Lord. And then Jesus will be able to say to Joseph, Father, you mustn't take all the blame, and deep down, who knows, he might dare to ask, When, O Lord, will You come before mankind to acknowledge Your own mistakes.

While the carpenter Joseph and his son Jesus debated these important matters in private, the war against the Romans went on. It had been going on for more than two years, and now and then news of casualties reached Nazareth. Ephraim was killed, then Abiezer, then Naphtali, then Eleazar, but no one knew for certain where their bodies lay, between two stones on a mountain, or at the bottom of a ravine, or swept downstream by the current, or beneath the futile shade of a tree. Unable to hold a funeral for those who had died, the villagers of Nazareth eased their conscience by insisting, We neither caused nor witnessed this bloodshed. News also arrived of great victories. The Romans had been driven out of the nearby city of Sepphoris, also from vast regions of Judaea and Galilee where the enemy dared not venture now, and even in Joseph's own village no Roman soldiers had been sighted for more than a year. Who knows, perhaps this is what prompted the carpenter's neighbor, the inquisitive and obliging Ananias, whom we have not mentioned for some time, to turn up in the yard one day and whisper in Joseph's ear, Follow me outside, and no wonder, because these houses are so tiny that it is impossible to have any privacy, everyone is crammed into one room day and night, whatever the circumstances or occasion, so that when the Day of Judgment finally comes, the Lord God should have no difficulty recognizing his own. So the request did not surprise Joseph, not even when Ananias added furtively, Let us go into the desert. Now, the desert is not simply that barren place, that vast expanse of sand or sea of burning dunes we generally picture when we read or hear the word. Desert, as understood here, can also be found in the green land of Galilee, for it means uncultivated fields, where there are no signs of human habitation or labor. Such places cease to be desert when humans arrive on the scene. But since there are only two men walking across this scrubland and Nazareth is still in sight as they head for three great boulders crowning the summit of the hill, there is no suggestion of the place's being populated, and when the men have gone, the desert will be desert again.

Ananias sits on the ground with Joseph at his side. There is the same age difference between them as there has always been, but, while time passes for everyone, the results can vary. Ananias did not look his years when we first met him, but now seems much older, though the years have also left their mark on Joseph. Ananias hesitates, the decisive manner with which he entered the carpenter's house changed once they were on the road, and Joseph has to coax him to speak without appearing to pry. We've come a long way, he remarked, giving Ananias his cue. This isn't something I could have discussed in your house or mine, explained Ananias, but now, in this remote place, they can converse freely without fear of being overheard. You once asked me to look after your house in your absence, Ananias reminded him. Yes, replied Joseph, and I deeply appreciated your help. Then Ananias continued, Now the time has come for me to ask you to look after my house while I'm gone. Are you taking your wife. No, I'm going alone. But surely if Shua is staying behind, there's no need. She'll be staying with relatives who live in a fishing village. Do you mean to tell me you're divorcing your wife. No, if I didn't divorce her when I found that she couldn't give me a son, why should I divorce her now, it's just that I will be away for a while and I'd prefer Shua to be with relatives. Will you be gone long. I don't know, much depends on how long the war lasts. What does the war have to do with your absence, asked Joseph in surprise. I'm going off to look for Judas the Galilean. What do you want from him. To ask him if he'll allow me to join his army. I don't believe it, a peace-loving man like you, Ananias, getting involved in the war against the Romans, have you forgotten what happened to Ephraim and Abiezer. And also to Naphtali and Eleazar. Precisely, so listen to the voice of reason. No, you listen to me, Joseph, and to the voice that comes from my lips, I've now reached the age at which my father died, and he achieved much more in life than this son of his who couldn't even beget children, I'm not as learned as you or likely to become an elder in the synagogue, all I have to look forward to is death, and I'm tied to a woman I don't even love. Then why not divorce her. Divorcing Shua is no problem, the problem is how to divorce myself, and that's impossible. But how much fighting can you do at your age. Don't worry, I'll go into battle as determined as if I were about to get a woman pregnant. I never heard that expression before. Nor I, it came into my head this very minute. Very well, Ananias, you can rely on me to look after your house until you return. Should I not return and news reaches you that I've been killed, promise me you'll send for Shua so that she can claim my possessions. You have my promise. Let's return now that my mind is at peace. At peace, when you've decided to go to war, I really don't understand you. Ah, Joseph, Joseph, for how many centuries will we have to go on studying the Talmud before we begin to understand the simplest things. Why did we have to come all this way. I wanted to speak to you in the presence of witnesses. The only witnesses we need are Almighty God and this sky that covers us wherever we may be. And what about these stones. These stones are deaf and dumb and cannot bear witness. That may be so, but if you and I were to give a false account of our conversation, these stones would accuse us and go on accusing us until they turned to dust and we to nothingness. Shall we go back. Yes, let's go.

As they went, Ananias turned around several times to look at the stones, until finally they disappeared behind a hillock, then Joseph asked him, Does Shua know. Yes, she knows. And what did she have to say. At first not a word, then she told me I should have abandoned her years ago and left her to her fate. Poor Shua. Once she's with relatives, she'll forget me, and if I die in battle, she'll forget me forever, forgetting is all too easy, that is life. They entered the village, and when they arrived at the carpenter's house, which was the first of two houses on one side, Jesus, who was playing in the road with James and Judas, told them his mother was with the neighbor next door. As the two men turned away, the voice of Judas could be heard announcing solemnly, I am Judas the Galilean, whereupon Ananias looked around and said with a smile to Joseph, Take a look, there goes my leader, but before the carpenter had time to reply, the voice of Jesus could be heard saying, Then you don't belong here. Joseph felt a sword pierce his heart, as if those words were addressed to him, as if the game being played by his son was meant to convey another truth. Then he thought of the three boulders and tried, without knowing why, to imagine what life would be like if henceforth he were obliged to speak every word and perform every action in their presence, and suddenly, remembering God, he was stricken with fear. In Ananias's house they found Mary consoling a distressed Shua, who dried her tears the moment the men arrived, not because she had stopped weeping but because women know from bitter experience when to hide their tears. Hence the well-known saying, They're either laughing or weeping, but it simply is not true, because they weep quietly to themselves. But there was nothing quiet about Shua's grief, and when Ananias departed, she sobbed her heart out. One week later Shua's relatives came to fetch her. Mary accompanied her to the edge of the village, where they embraced and said good-bye. Shua was no longer weeping, but her eyes would never be dry again. Nothing can ease her sorrow or extinguish the flame that burns her tears before they surface and roll down her cheeks.

THE MONTHS PASSED, AND NEWS OF THE WAR CONTINUED
to arrive, sometimes good, sometimes bad, but while the
good news never went beyond vague allusions to victories
that always turned out to be modest, the bad news spoke
of much bloodshed and heavy losses for the rebel army of
Judas the Galilean. One day news came that Eldad had been
killed when the Romans made a surprise attack on a guerrilla ambush, there were many casualties, but Eldad was
the only one from Nazareth to lose his life. Another day
someone said he had heard from a friend, who had been
told by someone else, that Varus, the Roman governor of
Syria, was on his way with two legions to put an end once
and for all to this intolerable insurrection that had been
dragging on for three years. The statement, Varus is on
his way, and the lack of any precise details spread panic
among the people. They expected the dreaded insignia of
war, which bore the initials SPQR, the Senate and People
of Rome, to appear at any moment, heralding the arrival
of a punitive force. Under this symbol and that flag, men
go forth to kill one another, and the same can be said of

those other well-known initials, INRI, Jesus of Nazareth, King of the Jews, but we must not anticipate events, for the dire consequences of Jesus' death will emerge only in the fullness of time. Everywhere there is talk of imminent battle, those with more faith in God predict that before the year is out, the Romans will be expelled from the Holy Land of Israel, but others, less confident, sadly shake their heads and foresee nothing but doom and destruction. And so it turned out.

Following the news that Varus's legions were advancing, nothing happened for several weeks, which allowed the rebels to intensify their attacks on the dispersed troops they were fighting, but the tactics behind this Roman passivity soon became clear, when the scouts of Judas the Galilean reported that one of the legions was heading south in a circular movement, skirting the bank of the river Jordan, then turning right at Jericho to repeat the maneuver northward, like a net cast into the water and retrieved by an experienced hand, or a lasso thrown to capture everything around. And the other legion, carrying out a similar maneuver, was now heading south. A strategy that could be described as a pincer movement, but it was more like two walls closing in simultaneously, knocking down those unable to escape, and finally crushing them. Throughout Judaea and Galilee, the legions' advance was marked with crosses, to which Judas's men had been nailed by their wrists and feet, their bones broken with hammers to hasten their death. The soldiers looted the villages and searched every house. No evidence was needed for them to arrest suspects and execute them. These unfortunates, if you will pardon the irony, had the good fortune to be crucified near their homes, so relatives could remove their bodies once they were dead. And what a sad spectacle it was, as mothers, widows, young brides, and weeping orphans watched the bruised corpses being gently lowered from the crosses, for there is nothing more pitiful for the living than the sight of an abandoned body. The crucified man was then carried to his grave to await the day of resurrection. But there were also men wounded in combat, in the mountains or in some other lonely spot, who, though still alive, were left by the soldiers in the most absolute of all deserts, that of solitary death, and there they remained, slowly burnt by the sun, exposed to birds of prey, and after a time stripped of flesh and bone, reduced to repugnant remains without shape or form. Those questioning if not skeptical souls, who resist the facile acceptance of gospels such as these, will ask how it was possible for the Romans to crucify such a large number of Jews in vast arid regions devoid of trees, apart from the rare stunted bush on which you could barely crucify a scarecrow. But they are forgetting that the Roman army has all the professional skills and organization of a modern army. A steady supply of wooden crosses has been maintained throughout the campaign, as witnessed by all these donkeys and mules following the troops and laden with posts and crossbars, which can be assembled on the spot, and then it is simply a question of nailing the condemned man's extended arms to the crossbar, hoisting the post upright, forcing him to draw in his legs sideways, and securing his two feet, one on top of the other, with a single long nail. Any executioner attached to the legion will tell you that this operation may sound complicated, but it is in fact much more difficult to describe than to carry out.

The pessimists who predicted disaster were right. From north to south and from south to north, men, women, and children flee before the advancing legions, some because they might be accused of having collaborated with the rebels, others simply in terror, for, as we know, they are in danger of being arrested and put to death without a trial. One of these fugitives interrupted his retreat for a few moments to knock on Joseph's door with a message from Joseph's neighbor, Ananias, who had been severely wounded back in Sepphoris. Ananias wanted Joseph to know, The war is lost and there is no hope of escape, send for my wife and tell her to claim my possessions. Is that all he said, asked Joseph. Nothing more, replied the messenger. Why couldn't you have brought him here with you, when you knew you had to pass this way. In his condition he would have been a hindrance, and I had to put my family's safety first. First, perhaps, but surely not to the exclusion of everyone else. What are you trying to say, you yourself are surrounded by children, and if you remain here, that can only be because you are in no danger. There's no time to lose, be on your way and may God go with you, for without Him there is always danger. You sound like a man without faith, for you should know the Lord is everywhere. Indeed, but He often ignores us, and don't speak to me about faith after abandoning my neighbor to his fate. Well, then, why not go and rescue him yourself. That's exactly what I intend to do. This conversation took place in the middle of the afternoon. It was a fine, sunny day, with a few white clouds drifting across the sky like unmanned barges. Joseph went to untie the donkey, called his wife, and told her without further explanation, I'm off to Sepphoris to look for our neighbor, Ananias, who's been badly wounded and cannot make the journey on his own. Mary simply nodded in reply, but Jesus clung to his father and pleaded, Take me with you. Joseph looked at his son, placed his right hand on the boy's head, and told him, You stay here, I'll be back soon, if I make good time, I should be back before dawn, and he could be right, for the distance between Nazareth and Sepphoris cannot be much more than five miles, about the same distance as from Jerusalem to Bethlehem, additional proof that the world is full of coincidences. Joseph did not mount the donkey, he wanted the animal to be fresh for the return journey, firm and steady on its feet and prepared to carry a sick man gently, or, to be precise, a wounded soldier, which is not quite the same thing.

At the foot of the hill where, almost a year before, Ananias had told him of his decision to join the rebel army of Judas the Galilean, the carpenter looked up at the three enormous boulders on the summit, which reminded him of segments of a fruit. Perched on high, they appeared to be waiting for a reply from heaven and earth to the questions posed by all the creatures of this world, even though the creatures cannot voice them, What am I, Why am I here, What other world awaits me, this one being what it is. Were Ananias to ask such questions, we could tell him that at least the boulders remain unscathed by the wind, rain, and heat, and some twenty centuries hence they will probably still be here, and twenty centuries after that, while the world changes all around them. To the first two questions, however, there is no answer.

Throngs of fugitives were to be seen on the road, with the same look of terror on their faces as on that of the messenger sent by Ananias. They looked at Joseph in amazement, and one man, taking him by the arm, inquired, Where are you going, and the carpenter replied, To Sepphoris, to rescue a friend. If you know what's good for you, you'll do no such thing. Why not. The Romans are approaching, and there is no hope of defending the city. I must go, my neighbor is like a brother and there is no one else to fetch him. Heed my advice, and with that the wise counselor went on his way, leaving Joseph standing in the middle of the road, lost in thought, wondering whether his life was worth saving and whether he despised himself. After giving the matter thought, he decided he felt quite indifferent, like someone confronting a void that is neither near nor far, and where there is nowhere to rest one's eyes, for who can focus on emptiness. Then it occurred to him that as a father he had a duty to protect his children, that he ought to return home rather than chasing after a neighbor, and Ananias was no longer even that, for he had deserted his home and sent his wife away. But Joseph's children were safe, the Romans, engaged as they were in pursuing rebels, would do them no harm. Finally reaching a conclusion, Joseph heard himself say aloud, as if he were wrestling with his thoughts, And I am not a rebel either. Without further ado he gave his animal a slap on its haunch, exclaimed, Go, donkey, and continued on.

It was late evening when he arrived at Sepphoris. The long shadows of houses and trees that could be made out at first gradually disappeared into the horizon like dark, cascading water. There were few people on the streets of the city, no women or children, only weary men laying down their awkward weapons as they stretched out, panting for breath, and it was difficult to tell whether they were exhausted from combat or from flight. Joseph asked one of them, Are the Romans approaching. The man closed his eyes, slowly reopened them, and said, They'll arrive by tomorrow, and then, averting his gaze, he told Joseph, Get away from here, take your donkey and leave this place. But I'm searching for a friend who's been wounded, Joseph explained. If you counted all who have been wounded as your friends, you'd be the wealthiest man in the world. Where are the wounded. Here, there, everywhere. But is there some place in the city where they're being nursed. Yes, behind those houses you'll find a garrison where many wounded have been given shelter, perhaps you'll find your friend there, but hurry, for more corpses are being carried out than men brought in alive. Joseph knew the place well, he had been here often, both for work, which was plentiful in a city as rich and prosperous as Sepphoris, and for certain minor religious feasts that did not justify the long and arduous journey to Jerusalem. Finding the storehouse was easy enough, all one had to do was to follow the terrible stench of blood and pus that hung in the air, almost like a game of hide and seek, Hot, cold, hot, cold, it hurts, it doesn't, but now the pain was becoming unbearable. Joseph tethered the donkey to a long pole he found nearby and entered the storehouse, which had been converted into a dormitory. Between the mats on the floor were tiny lamps which provided hardly any light, twinkling stars against a black sky, which helped to guide one's faltering steps. Joseph walked slowly between the rows of wounded men in search of Ananias. There were other strong odors in the air, the smell of oil and wine used to heal wounds, the smell of sweat, excrement, and urine, for some of these unfortunate men were unable to move, and could not help evacuating then and there. He isn't here, Joseph thought to himself as he reached the end of the row. He retraced his steps, walking more slowly this time and looking carefully. Alas, they were all alike, with their long beards, hollow cheeks, sunken eyes, and unwashed bodies covered with sweat. Some of the wounded followed him with anxious expressions, hoping that this able-bodied man had come for them, but the momentary glimmer in their eyes soon disappeared and their long vigil, for who knows what or whom, continued. Joseph came to a halt before an elderly man with white beard and hair. It is he, he thought. Yet Ananias's appearance had changed since Joseph walked past the first time, his beard and hair, white as snow before, now looked dirty, and his eyebrows, still black, looked unnatural. The old man's eyes were closed, and he breathed heavily. In a low voice Joseph called, Ananias, then, moving closer, he repeated the name louder. Little by little, as if he were emerging from the depths of the earth, the old man's eyelids began to move, and when the eyes were fully open, there was no longer any doubt, this was Ananias, the neighbor who had abandoned his home and wife to go and fight the Romans, and here he lies with frightful abdominal wounds and stinking of rotting flesh. At first Ananias does not recognize Joseph, the poor light in this makeshift infirmary does not help, and his eyesight is poorer anyway, but he recognizes him when the carpenter repeats his name in another tone of voice, which almost holds affection. The old man's eyes fill with tears, and he says over and over, It's you, it's you, what are you doing here, what have you come here for, and he tries to raise himself on one elbow and stretch out his arm, but cannot find the strength, his body sags, his whole face twisted with pain. I came for you, said the carpenter, my donkey is tethered outside, and we can be back in Nazareth in no time at all. You shouldn't have come here, the Romans are expected any minute, I can't leave this place, I'm done for, and with trembling hands he opened his tunic. Beneath the rags soaked with wine and oil were two gaping wounds which gave off such a nauseating smell that Joseph held his breath and looked away. The old man covered himself, his arms falling to his sides, as if the effort had been too much for him, Now you know why I can't leave this place, if you tried to move me, my guts would spill out. You'll be all right with a bandage tight around your belly and if we go slowly, insisted Joseph, unconvincingly, because it was obvious that even if he could get the old man onto the donkey's back, they would never make it to Nazareth. Ananias's eyes were shut again, and without opening them he told Joseph, You must go back, I'm warning you, the Romans will be here soon. Don't worry, they won't attack at night. Go home, go home, muttered Ananias, and in reply Joseph said, Try to get some sleep.

He watched over him all night long. Struggling to keep awake, he found himself wondering why he had come to this place, since there had never really been any deep friendship between Ananias and him. There was a considerable difference in their ages, and besides, he had always had certain reservations about Ananias and his wife, who could be nosy and meddlesome even while doing one a favor, and who always gave the impression of expecting to be paid back in kind. But he is my neighbor, Joseph thought, and could think of no better answer to silence his misgivings, he's my fellow creature, a man close to death, with his eyes already shut, as if to savor every minute of his dying, I can't abandon him now. He was sitting in the narrow space between the mat on which Ananias lay and that of a young boy who couldn't have been much older than his son Jesus, the poor lad was moaning quietly and muttering to himself, his lips cracked with fever. Joseph held his hand to comfort him, and Ananias's hand began fumbling as if reaching for a weapon to defend himself, and there the three of them remained, Joseph alive and well between two who were dying, one life between two deaths. Meanwhile the tranquil night sky sent stars and planets into orbit, and a shining white moon came floating through space from the other end of the world, shedding innocence over the whole of Galilee. It was only much later that Joseph emerged from the torpor into which he had reluctantly fallen. He awoke with a sense of relief, because this time he had not dreamed of the road to Bethlehem. Opening his eyes, he saw that Ananias, whose eyes were also open, was dead. At the last moment he had been unable to endure the vision of death, and his hand gripped Joseph's so tightly that Joseph felt his bones were being crushed. To ease the painful grip, he released his other hand, which was clasping the boy's, and noticed that the boy's fever had subsided. Joseph looked out through the open door, there was daylight, a sky in hues of sepia. Human forms stirred in the storehouse, those who could get up unaided went outside to watch the sunrise. They might well have asked one another or even the sky itself, What will this new dawn bring. One day we shall learn not to ask useless questions, but until that day comes, let us take this opportunity to ask ourselves, What will this new dawn bring. Joseph thought to himself, I may as well go, I can do nothing more here, but there was a questioning note in these words that prompted him to think, I could take his body to Nazareth, and the idea seemed so obvious that he almost convinced himself this was why he had come, to find Ananias alive and carry him back dead. The boy asked for water. Joseph held an earthenware bowl to his lips, How do you feel, he asked him. Better. At least the fever seems to have passed. Let me see if I can stand up, said the boy. Be careful, said Joseph, trying to restrain him, then another idea occurred to him. All he could do for Ananias was bury him in Nazareth, but the boy's life could still be saved if Joseph delivered him from this death house, so that one human being could be substituted, in a manner of speaking, for another. He no longer felt compassion for Ananias, whose body now was an empty shell, his soul more remote each time Joseph looked at him. The boy appeared to sense that something good was about to happen to him, and his eyes shone, but before he could ask any questions, Joseph had already gone to bring the donkey. Blessed is the Lord who puts such splendid ideas into the heads of mankind. But the donkey was gone. All that remained was a bit of rope tied to the pole. The thief had wasted no time trying to untie the knot, using a sharp knife, he had simply cut through it.

This latest misfortune drained the strength from Joseph's body. Like one of those felled calves he had watched being sacrificed in the Temple, he dropped to his knees, covered his face with his hands, and shed all the tears that had been welling for the last thirteen years while he waited for the day he would be able to forgive himself or face the final condemnation. God does not forgive the sins He makes us commit. Joseph did not return to the storehouse, for he realized that his actions had become forever meaningless, that the world itself was meaningless. The sun was rising, but why, O Lord, were there thousands of tiny clouds scattered throughout the sky like stones in the desert. Anyone watching Joseph there, as he wiped his tears with the sleeve of his tunic, would have thought he was mourning the death of a relative found with the other wounded men in the storehouse, when the truth was that Joseph had just shed the last of his natural tears, the tears of life's sorrow.

After wandering through the city for more than an hour, hoping that he might still find the stolen animal, he was about to give up and return to Nazareth when he was arrested by Roman soldiers, who had taken Sepphoris. They asked him his name, I am Joseph, son of Eli, and then where he lived, In Nazareth, and where he was going, Back to Nazareth, and what brought him to Sepphoris, Someone told me a neighbor of mine was here, and who was this neighbor, Ananias, and had he found him, Yes, and where had he found him, In a storehouse with others, and what others might they be, Wounded men, and in which part of the city, Over in that direction. They took him to a square where a group of men were assembled, twelve or fifteen sitting on the ground, some of them wounded, and the soldiers ordered him, Join the others. Realizing that the men sitting there were rebels, he protested, I am a carpenter and a man of peace, and one of the rebels spoke up and said, We don't know this man, but the officer in charge of the prisoners refused to listen and, giving Joseph one mighty push, sent him flying to the ground, where he ended up among the others. The only place you're going is to your death, the officer told him. The double shock of this misfortune and the fate awaiting him left Joseph stunned. But once he regained his composure, he felt a great tranquillity, convinced that it was all a nightmare which would soon pass and that there was no point tormenting himself over these threats, for they would vanish the moment he opened his eyes. Then he remembered that when he dreamed of the road to Bethlehem, he was also convinced he would wake up, and he began to tremble as the cruel certainty of his fate finally dawned on him, I'm going to die, to die even though I'm innocent. He felt a hand on his shoulder, the hand of the prisoner beside him, When the commanding officer comes, we'll explain you're not one of us, and he'll order your release. And what about the rest of you. The Romans have crucified every rebel they've captured so far, and they're not likely to treat us any better. God will save you. Surely you're forgetting that God saves souls rather than bodies. The soldiers arrived with more prisoners, in twos and threes, and then a large group of about twenty. The inhabitants of Sepphoris had gathered in the square, and there were even women and children in the crowd. A restless murmur could be heard, but no one dared move without the permission of the Roman soldiers, who were still looking for anyone who might have helped the rebels. After a while another man was dragged into the square, and the soldiers who had captured him announced, That's all for now, whereupon the officer in charge shouted, On your feet, you lot. The prisoners guessed that the commanding officer of the cohort was approaching, and the man sitting beside Joseph told him, Prepare yourself, what he meant was, Prepare yourself for release, as if one needed to prepare oneself for freedom, but if someone came, it was not the commanding officer, nor did anyone learn who it was, because the officer in charge suddenly gave an order in Latin to the soldiers. Needless to say, everything said so far by the Romans has been in Latin, because it would be unthinkable for the descendants of the she-wolf to speak in barbarian tongues, they have interpreters for that purpose, but since the conversation here was between the soldiers themselves, no translation was required. Obeying their superior's orders, the soldiers quickly rounded up the prisoners, Forward march, and the procession of condemned men made its way out of the city, with the crowd trailing behind. Forced to march with the other prisoners, Joseph had nowhere to turn for mercy. He raised his arms to heaven and called out, Save me, I'm not one of them, help me, I'm innocent, at which point a soldier prodded him from behind with the butt of a lance, almost knocking him to the ground. In despair, Joseph felt hatred for Ananias, the one who had got him into this predicament, but the feeling soon passed, giving way to emptiness. He thought to himself, There is nowhere else to go, but he was wrong, and he would soon be there. Strange as it may seem, the certainty of death calmed him. He looked around at his companions in misfortune, who seemed quite composed, some, naturally, were downcast, but others defiantly held their heads high. Most were Pharisees. Then, for the first time, Joseph remembered his children, and for one fleeting moment even his wife, but all those faces and names were too much for his tired brain. In need of sleep and food, he felt weak, could not concentrate, the only image that remained was that of Jesus, his firstborn and his final punishment. He recalled their conversation about his dream and remembered telling Jesus, It just isn't possible for you to ask me all the questions, or for me to give you all the answers, but now the time for answering questions was over.

On a stretch of high ground overlooking the city forty thick posts strong enough to take a man's weight had been erected in rows of eight. At the foot of each post lay a crossbar long enough to allow a man to spread his arms. At the sight of these instruments of torture, some of the prisoners tried to escape, but the soldiers, baring their swords, drove them back. One rebel attempted to impale himself on a sword, but to no avail, he was dragged off at once to be crucified. Then the laborious task began of nailing the wrists of each condemned man to a crossbar before hoisting him up on the upright posts. The screams and moans could be heard throughout the countryside, and the people of Sepphoris wept before this sad spectacle, which they were obliged to watch as a warning. One by one, the crosses went up, a man hanging from each, his legs drawn in as we saw before, who knows for what reason, perhaps an order from Rome intended to make the job easier and save on materials, because one does not need to know much about crucifixions to see that a cross made to the measurements of the average man would require more work and be heavier to carry and more awkward to handle, not to mention the serious disadvantage to the victim, since the closer his feet to the ground, the easier it is to lower his body afterward, without having to use a ladder, thus allowing him to pass directly, as it were, from the arms of the cross into the arms of his family, if he has any, or of the appointed gravedigger, who will not just leave him lying there. It so happened that Joseph was the last to be crucified, and this meant he had to look on as his thirty-nine unknown companions were tortured one by one and put to death. When his turn finally came, he was resigned to his fate and no longer protested his innocence, thus missed his last opportunity to save himself, when the soldier doing the hammering said to the officer in charge, This is the man who said he was innocent. The officer paused for a moment, giving Joseph just enough time to cry out, I'm innocent, but instead Joseph chose to remain silent. The officer looked up and probably decided that the symmetry would be destroyed if the last cross was not raised, and that forty made a nice round figure, so he gave the signal, the nails were driven in, Joseph let out a scream and went on screaming, then they hoisted him up, his weight held by the nails that pierced his wrists, and there were more cries of pain as a long nail was driven through his feet. Dear God, this is the man You created, blessed be Your holy name, since it is forbidden to curse You. Suddenly, as if someone had given another signal, panic gripped the inhabitants of Sepphoris, not because of the crucifixions they had just witnessed but at the sight of flames spreading rapidly through the city, fire destroying the houses and public buildings and even the trees in the inner courtyards. Indifferent to the blaze set by their comrades, four soldiers from the cohort moved between the rows of dying men, methodically breaking their shinbones with iron rods. Sepphoris was burning wherever one looked, as the crucified men expired one after another. The carpenter named Joseph, son of Eli, was a young man in his prime, having just turned thirty-three.

WHEN THIS WAR ENDS, AND IT WILL NOT BE LONG NOW, for as we can see it is already almost over, there will be a final reckoning of those who lost their lives, so many here, so many there, some near, some farther away, and if it is true that with the passage of time the number of those killed in ambushes or open warfare loses all importance and is forgotten, those crucified, who number around two thousand, according to the most reliable statistics, will long be remembered by the people of Judaea and Galilee, even after more wars have broken out and more blood has been spilled. Two thousand crucified is a lot, but it seems even more if we imagine them set out a mile apart along a highway or encircling, for example, the country that one day will be known as Portugal, which has a perimeter more or less that length. Between the river Jordan and the sea, widows and orphans weep, an ancient custom, that is why they are widows and orphans, so that they may weep, and when the boys grow up and go to fight a new war, there will be more widows and orphans to take their place, and even if customs change, if black becomes the color of mourning instead of white, or if women wear black mantillas instead of tearing their hair out, tears of sincere grief will never change.

So far Mary is not weeping, but in her soul she has a presentiment, for her husband has not returned, and in Nazareth it is rumored that Sepphoris was burned and men were crucified. Accompanied by her eldest son, she retraces the route taken by Joseph yesterday. Very likely, at one point or other, her feet will touch the footprints left by her husband's sandals, for this is not the rainy season and there is nothing but the gentlest breeze to disturb the soil. Joseph's footprints are like the prints of a prehistoric animal that inhabited these parts in some bygone age, for we say, Only yesterday, and we might as well say, A thousand years ago, because time is not a rope one can measure from knot to knot, time is a pitched and undulating surface which only memory can make accessible. A group of villagers from Nazareth accompany Mary and Jesus, some moved by compassion, others simply curious, and there are distant relatives of Ananias, but they will return home as uncertain as they left, for since they have not found a body, he may still be alive. It never occurred to them to search the debris of the storehouse, where they might have recognized his body among the charred remains. These Nazarenes had gone half the way, when they met a detachment of soldiers that had been sent to search their village, so some turned back, worried about what might happen to their property, for one can never predict what soldiers will do when they knock on a door and find no one at home. The officer in charge asked why these villagers were on their way to Sepphoris, and they replied, We wanted to see the fire, an explanation which the officer accepted, because fires have had an irresistible attraction for mankind since the world began, there are even those who say that fire is a kind of inner call, an instinctive memory of the original fire, as if ashes somehow preserve what was burned, thus explaining, by this theory, the look of fascination in our faces as we watch a camp fire or the flickering of a candle in a dark room. If we humans were as foolhardy or daring as butterflies, moths, and other winged insects, and threw ourselves, all together, into the flames, then who knows, perhaps the blaze would be so fierce and the light so strong that God would open His eyes and be roused from His torpor, too late, of course, to recognize us, but in time to see the impending void after we went up in smoke.

Although she had left behind a house full of children with no one to look after them, Mary refused to turn back, and she was easy in her mind, because it is not every day that soldiers invade a village and start slaughtering young children. Besides, these Romans were not only willing but even eager to see the children grow up, provided they remained servile and paid their taxes on time. Mother and son are walking along the road by themselves, because Ananias's relatives, some half dozen of them, are so busy chatting that they have fallen behind. Mary and Jesus have only words of anguish to exchange and so prefer to remain silent rather than distress each other. A strange silence hangs everywhere, no birds are singing, the wind has died down, there is nothing but the sound of footsteps, and even that withdraws, like a polite intruder who has entered an empty house by mistake. Sepphoris comes into sight suddenly as they turn a bend in the road. Several houses are still burning, thin columns of smoke rise here and there, walls are blackened, trees scorched from top to bottom, the foliage intact but the color of rust. And there on our right, the rows of crosses.

Mary started running, but they were still some distance away and she had to slow down and catch her breath. As a result of giving birth to all those children without letup, her heart is weaker. Jesus, a respectful son, would like to accompany his mother, remaining at her side, now and later, so that they can share the same joys and sorrows, but she walks so slowly, dragging her feet, At this rate, Mother, we'll never get there. She makes a gesture as if to say, You go ahead and I'll catch up. Leaving the road, Jesus sprints across the field to save time, Father, Father, he calls, hoping that his father will not be there, fearing that he will find him. He reaches the first row, some of the crucified men are still hanging from the crosses, others have already been taken down and lie waiting on the ground. Few have relatives to gather around them, for most of these rebels came from afar, part of a mixed contingent which made its last united assault and is now finally dispersed, each man left to confront alone the ineffable solitude of death. Jesus does not see his father, his heart would rejoice but his reason tells him, Wait, we haven't got to the end of the row. But in fact the end is right here. Stretched out on the ground is the father he has been seeking, there is little blood, only the open wounds on the wrists and feet, You could be sleeping, Father, but no, you are not asleep, how could you possibly sleep with your legs twisted in that position, how charitable of them to remove you from the cross, but there are so many bodies here that the good souls who removed you had no time to straighten your broken bones. The boy named Jesus kneels beside his dead father and weeps, he cannot bring himself to touch the corpse, but then grief overcomes his fear and he embraces the motionless body. Father, Father, he sobs aloud, and another cry accompanies his, What have they done to you, Joseph, it is the voice of Mary, who has arrived at last, exhausted and sobbing her heart out, for when she saw her son come to a halt in the distance, she knew what to expect. Mary's tears overflow when she sees the pitiful state of her husband's legs. We do not know what happens to life's sorrows after death, especially those last moments of suffering, it is possible that everything ends with death, but we cannot be certain that the memory of suffering does not linger at least for several hours in this body we describe as dead, nor can we rule out the possibility that matter uses putrefaction as a last resort to rid itself of the suffering. With a tenderness she would never have permitted herself to show while her husband was alive, Mary pulled down Joseph's tunic after trying to straighten the broken legs that gave him the grotesque appearance of a puppet coming apart. Jesus helped his mother pull the tunic down over the thin shinbones, perhaps the most vulnerable part of the human body and a painful reminder of our fragile state. The feet hung sideways, and flies, drawn by the smell of blood, kept swarming around the wounds inflicted by the nail. Joseph's sandals had fallen to the ground beside the thick trunk of which he was the last fruit. Worn and covered with dust, they would have lain there forgotten if Jesus had not recovered them without thinking. As if obeying an order, and unnoticed by Mary, he tucked the sandals under his belt, a gesture of perfect symbolism, Joseph's firstborn claiming his inheritance, for certain things begin as simply as this, and even today people say, In my father's shoes I become a man.

From a discreet distance Roman soldiers kept a lookout, ready to intervene in the event of disorderly behavior among those mourning and tending to the bodies. But these people showed no sign of making trouble, they were doing nothing but praying as they went from body to body, and this took more than two hours. Rending their garments, they recited the prayer for the dead over each corpse, relatives on the left, others on the right, their voices breaking the evening silence as they chanted, Lord, what is man that You are mindful of him, and the son of man that You should visit him, man is but a puff of wind, his days pass like a shadow, he lives and fails to see death and saves his soul by escaping to the tomb, man born of woman is given little time and much disquiet, he blossoms like a flower and like a flower perishes, what is man that You are mindful of him, and the son of man that You should visit him. And yet, after acknowledging man's utter insignificance in the eyes of God, in tones so deep that they seemed to come from within rather than from the voices themselves, the chorus soared in exaltation to proclaim before Almighty God our unsuspected worth, Do not forget, O Lord, that You made man a little lower than the angels and have crowned him with glory and honor. When the mourners reached Joseph, whom they did not know and who was the last of the forty, they passed on quickly, but the carpenter had taken with him to the other world everything he needed. Their haste was justified, because the law does not allow the crucified to remain unburied until the following day, and the sun was already going down. Jesus, given his youth, did not have to rend his garments, he was exempt from this ceremony of mourning, but his strong, clear voice could be heard above all the others when he intoned, Blessed be the Lord, our God, King of the Universe, who created you with justice, kept you alive with justice, nourished you with justice, who with justice allowed you to know this world, and with justice will resurrect you, blessed be the Lord, who resurrects the dead. Stretched out on the ground, Joseph, if he can still feel the pain of the nails, may perhaps also hear these words, and he must know what part God's justice played in his life, now that he can no longer expect anything more from either the one or the other. The mourners, finished praying, now had to bury their dead, but there were so many dead, and with night fast approaching it was impossible to find a fitting place for all of them, that is to say a real tomb covered with a stone, and as for wrapping the bodies in mortuary cloth or even a simple shroud, there was no hope of that. So they decided to dig a long trench to hold them, which was not the first time nor would it be the last that men were buried where they lay. Jesus too was given a spade, and he set about digging vigorously beside the grown-ups.

Destiny in its wisdom decreed that Joseph be buried in a grave dug by his own son, thus fulfilling the prophecy, The son of man will bury man, while he himself remains unburied. However enigmatic these words seem at first, they merely state the obvious, for the last man, by virtue of being last, will have no one to bury him. But this will not be true of the boy who has just buried his father, the world will not end with him, and we shall be here for thousands and thousands of years in a constant succession of births and deaths, and if man has always been the implacable foe and executioner of man, all the more reason for him to go on being the gravedigger of man.

The sun has now disappeared behind the mountain. Enormous dark clouds over the valley of Jordan move slowly westward, as if pulled by this fading light that tinges their upper edges crimson. It has suddenly become cooler, and rain seems likely tonight although unusual for this time of the year. The soldiers have withdrawn, taking advantage of the waning light to return to their encampment some distance away, where their comrades-in-arms have probably arrived after carrying out a similar search in Nazareth. This is how a modern war should be fought, with the utmost coordination, not in the haphazard fashion of Judas the Galilean's rebel force, and the outcome is there for all to see, thirty-nine of his men crucified, the fortieth an innocent man who came with the best of intentions and met a miserable death. The people of Sepphoris will look among the ruins of their burnt-out city for somewhere to spend the night, and at daybreak each family will salvage what possessions they can from their former homes, then go off to make a new life for themselves elsewhere, because not only has Sepphoris been razed to the ground but Rome will make sure the city is not rebuilt for some time. Mary and Jesus are two shadows in the midst of a dark forest consisting of nothing but trunks. The mother draws her son to her bosom, two frightened souls searching as one for courage, and the dead beneath the ground, it seems, wish to detain the living. Jesus suggested to his mother, Let's spend the night in the city, but Mary told him, We cannot, your brothers and sisters are all alone and they must be famished. They could scarcely see where they were treading. After much stumbling, they finally reached the road, which in the dark stretched out like a parched riverbed. No sooner did they leave Sepphoris than it started raining, heavy drops to begin with, making a gentle sound as they hit the thick dust on the ground. The rain became more insistent, oppressive, the dust soon turned to mud, and Mary and her son had to remove their sandals to avoid losing them. They walk in silence, the mother covering her son's head with her mantle, they have nothing to say to each other, perhaps they are even thinking vaguely that Joseph is not dead after all, that when they get home, they will find him tending to the children as best he can, and he will ask his wife, What on earth possessed you to go out without asking my permission, but the tears have welled up again in Mary's eyes, not only because of her grief but also because of this infinite weariness, this continuous, persistent rain, the grim darkness, all much too sad and black for any hope that Joseph is still alive.

One day someone will tell the widow about the miracle witnessed at the gates of Sepphoris, when the tree trunks used to crucify the prisoners took root again and sprouted new leaves, and miracle is the right word, first because the Romans were in the habit of taking the crosses with them when they left, and secondly because trunks that have been chopped top and bottom have no sap left or shoots capable of transforming a thick, bloodstained post into a living tree. The credulous attributed this wonder to the blood of the martyrs, the skeptics said it was the rain, but no one had ever heard of blood or rain reviving trees once they were made into crosses and abandoned on a mountain slope or the plain of a desert. That it had been willed by God was something no one dared suggest, not only because His will, whatever that may be, is inscrutable, but also because no one could think of any good reason why the crucified of Sepphoris should be the beneficiaries of this peculiar manifestation of divine grace, which was really more in keeping with the style of pagan gods. These trees here will survive a long time, and the day will come when this episode will be forgotten, and since mankind seeks an explanation for everything, whether it be true or false, tales and legends will be invented, containing facts to begin with, then moving gradually away from the facts, until they become pure fantasy. Then eventually the trees will die of old age or be cut down to make way for a road, a school, a house, a shopping center, or a military base, the excavators will unearth the skeletons buried for two thousand years, and the anthropologists will appear on the scene, and an expert in anatomy will examine the remains and announce to a shocked world that there is conclusive evidence that men were crucified in those days with their legs bent at the knee. And people will be unable to refute these scientific findings though they find them aesthetically deplorable.

When Mary and Jesus arrived home drenched to the skin, covered with mud, and shivering with cold, they found the children in better spirits than one might have expected, thanks to the resourcefulness of James and Lisa, who were older than the others. They remembered to light the fire when the night turned cold, and sat huddled against one another around it and tried to forget the pangs of hunger. Hearing someone knocking outside, James went to open the door. The rain poured in as their mother and brother crossed the threshold, it seemed to flood the house. The children stared, and knew their father would not be coming back when Jesus closed the door, but they said nothing until James finally asked, Where is Father. The ground slowly absorbed the water that dripped from wet clothes, and all that broke the silence was the damp wood crackling in the hearth. The children stared at their mother. James repeated the question, Where is Father. Mary opened her mouth to speak, but the word, like a hangman's noose, choked her, forcing Jesus to intervene, Father is dead, he told them, and without knowing why, perhaps as proof that Joseph was dead, he took the wet sandals from his belt and showed them, I brought these back. The older children were already close to tears, but the sight of those forlorn sandals was too much for all of them, and the widow and her nine children were soon crying their hearts out. Not knowing which of them to comfort, she sank to her knees, exhausted, and her children gathered around her, like a cluster of grapes that did not need to be trampled to release the colorless wine of tears. Only Jesus remained standing, clasping the sandals to his bosom, musing that one day he would wear them, or this minute if he could summon the courage. One by one the children stole away from their mother, the older children tactfully leaving her to grieve, the younger ones following their example. Unable to share their mother's sorrow, they simply wept, in this respect young children are like the very old, who cry for nothing, cry even when they no longer feel or because they are incapable of feeling.

Mary knelt in the middle of the room, as if awaiting a decision or sentence. She became aware of her wet clothes, got to her feet, shivering, opened a chest, and took out an old, patched tunic that had belonged to her husband. Handing it to Jesus, she told him, Remove that wet tunic, put this on, and go sit by the fire. Then she called her two daughters, Lisa and Lydia, and made them hold up a mat to form a screen while she too changed, before starting to prepare supper with the few provisions left in the house. Jesus, in his father's tunic, sat by the fire. The tunic was too long for him at the hem and sleeves, in other circumstances his brothers would have laughed at him for looking like a scarecrow, but this was not the time for jesting, not only because they were in mourning but also because of the air of superiority that emanated from the boy, who suddenly appeared to have grown in stature, and this impression became even stronger when, slowly and deliberately, he took his father's wet sandals and held them in front of the fire. James went and sat beside Jesus and asked him in a low voice, What happened to Father. They crucified him with the other rebels, Jesus whispered. But why. Who knows, there were forty men there, and Father was one of them. Perhaps he too was a rebel. Who are you talking about. Father, of course. Impossible, he was always here at home, working at his bench. And what about the donkey, did you find it. Nowhere to be seen, alive or dead. Supper was ready, and they all sat around the common bowl and ate what little food there was. By the time they finished eating, the younger children were nodding off to sleep, their spirits still troubled but their bodies in need of rest. The boys' mats were laid out along the wall at the far end of the room. Mary told the two girls, You will sleep here with me, one on either side to avoid any jealousy. Cold air came through the gap in the door, but the house stayed warm, there was still heat coming from the fire. Huddling up against one another, the children gradually fell asleep despite their sighs. Holding back her tears, Mary waited for them to sleep, for she wished to grieve alone, her eyes were wide open as she contemplated a future without a husband and with nine mouths to feed. But unexpectedly the sorrow left her soul, and her body succumbed to fatigue, and then they were all asleep.

In the middle of the night Mary was awakened by the sound of moaning. She thought she dreamed it, but she had not been dreaming, she heard it a second time, louder. Taking care not to disturb her daughters, she sat up and looked around her, but the light from the oil lamp did not reach the far end of the room. Which of them could it be, she wondered, but knew in her heart it was Jesus who moaned. She got up quietly, went to fetch the lamp from its nail on the door, and raising it above her head, she examined the children one by one. Jesus tossed and turned, muttering to himself as if having a nightmare, he must be dreaming about his father, a mere boy and yet he has already witnessed so much suffering, death, blood, and torture. Mary thought to rouse him, to stop this agony, but changed her mind, she did not want to know what her son was dreaming, and then she noticed he was wearing his father's sandals. She found this strange, it worried her, how foolish, quite uncalled for and so disrespectful, wearing his father's sandals on the very day of the poor man's death. Not knowing what to think, she returned to her mat. Perhaps because of those sandals, and the tunic, her son was reliving his father's fatal adventure from the day Joseph left home, and thus the boy had passed into the world of men, to which he already belonged by the law of God, he was now heir to Joseph's few possessions, a much-mended tunic and a pair of worn sandals, and his dreams, Jesus retracing his father's last steps on earth. It did not occur to Mary that her son might be dreaming about something else.

Day broke with a clear sky. It was warm and bright, and there was no sign of further rain. Mary set out early with all her sons of school age, accompanied by Jesus, who as we mentioned earlier has already finished his studies. At the synagogue she informed the elders of Joseph's death and the probable circumstances that led to his crucifixion, cautiously adding that as many of the burial rites as possible were observed, despite the haste and improvisation with which everything had to be done. Finding herself alone with Jesus as they headed home, she thought to ask him why he had decided to wear his father's sandals, but something dissuaded her at the last moment. He might be at a loss to explain, might feel embarrassed. And unlike the child who gets up in the middle of the night to steal food and is caught in the act, he could not very well make the excuse that he was feeling hungry, unless he meant a kind of hunger unknown to us. Another idea occurred to Mary. Now that her son was the head of the household, it was only right that as his mother and dependent she should show him respect, consideration, take an interest in the dream that disturbed his sleep, Were you dreaming about your father, she asked, but Jesus pretended not to hear, he turned his face away, but his mother, undeterred, repeated the question, Were you dreaming. She was taken aback when her son replied, Yes, then almost immediately said, No, his expression clouding over as if he was seeing his dead father once more. They walked on in silence. When they got home, Mary set about carding wool, thinking to herself that she should make the most of her skills and take on extra work to support her family. Meanwhile Jesus, after looking up at the sky to see if the good weather would hold, fetched his father's workbench from the shed, checked the jobs that still had to be finished, and examined the various tools. Mary was pleased to see her son taking his new responsibilities so seriously. When the younger boys returned from the synagogue and they all sat down to eat, only the most careful observer would have guessed that this family had just lost a husband and father. Jesus's dark, twitching eyebrows betrayed anxiety, but the others, including Mary, seemed tranquil and composed, for it is written, Make bitter weeping and make passionate wailing, and let your mourning be according to his desert for one day or two, lest evil be spoken of you, and so be comforted of your sorrow, for it is also written, Give not your heart unto sorrow, put it away remembering the last end, forget it not, for there is no returning again, him you shall not profit, and will only hurt yourself. There will be a time to laugh and rejoice, as surely as one day follows another, one season another, and the best lesson of all comes from the Book of Ecclesiastes, where it is written, There is nothing better for man in this world than that he should eat, drink, and be merry even as he labors. For to the man who is virtuous in His eyes God gives wisdom and knowledge and joy. That same afternoon, Jesus and James went onto the terrace to repair the roof, which had been leaking throughout the night, and in case anyone is wondering why this minor domestic problem was not mentioned earlier, let me remind him that the death of a human being takes precedence over all else.

Night returned, and another day would soon dawn. The family supped as best they could, then settled down on their mats to sleep. Mary woke with a start in the early hours, no, it was not she who was dreaming but Jesus. It was heartbreaking to hear his moans, which awakened the older children, but it would have taken much more to rouse the little ones, who were enjoying the deep sleep of the innocent. Mary found her son tossing and turning on his mat, his arms raised as if fending off a sword or lance, but he gradually quieted down, either because his attackers had withdrawn or because his life was ebbing away. Jesus opened his eyes and wept in his mother's arms like a little child, even grown men become children again when they are frightened or upset, they do not like to admit it, poor things, but there is nothing like a good cry to relieve one's sorrow. What's wrong, my son, what troubles you, Mary asked in distress, and Jesus could not or would not answer, there was nothing childlike about those pursed lips. Tell me what you were dreaming about, insisted Mary, and trying to encourage him to speak, she asked, Did you see your father. The boy shook his head, released his arms, and fell back on his mat. Try to get some sleep, he told her, and then turning to his brothers, It's nothing, go back to sleep, I'll be all right. Mary rejoined her daughters but lay awake until morning, expecting Jesus' dream to return at any moment. She wondered what this dream could be that caused him so much anguish, but nothing more happened. It did not occur to her that her son might also be lying awake, to keep from dreaming again. What a strange coincidence, she thought, that Jesus, who had always slept peacefully, should start having nightmares immediately after his father's death, God forbid that it should be the same dream, she prayed inwardly. If her common sense assured her that dreams were neither bequeathed nor inherited, she was much deceived, because fathers do not need to confide their dreams to their sons for them to have the same dream at the same hour.

Day finally dawned, and the morning light streamed through the chink in the door. On opening her eyes, Mary saw that Jesus was no longer lying on his mat, Where can he have gone, she asked herself. She got up and went to look outside. He was sitting on a bed of straw in the shed, his head buried in his arms. Chilled by the cool morning air and the sight of her son's solitude, she went up to him, Are you ill, she asked. The boy raised his eyes, No, I'm not ill. Then what's ailing you. It's these dreams I keep having. Dreams, you say. No, the same dream for the last two nights. Did you dream of your father on the cross. No, I already told you, I dream about my father but don't see him. You told me you weren't dreaming about him. That's because I don't see him, but he is in my dreams. And what is this dream that never stops tormenting you. Jesus did not reply immediately, he looked at his mother helplessly, and Mary felt as if a finger had touched her heart, here was her son looking like a little boy, with the wan expression of one who had not slept, but the first signs of a beard, which invited affectionate teasing, this was her firstborn, on whom she would rely for the rest of her life. Tell me everything, she pleaded, and Jesus finally spoke, I dream that I'm in a village that isn't Nazareth and that you are with me, but it's not you, because the woman who's my mother in the dream looks very different, and there are other boys my age, difficult to say how many, with women who could be their mothers, someone has assembled us in a square and we're waiting for soldiers who are coming to kill us, we can hear them on the road, they're nearer, but we can't see them, and I'm still not frightened, I know it's only a dream, then suddenly I feel sure Father is coming with the soldiers, I turn to you for protection, though you may not really be my mother, but you're no longer there, all the mothers have gone, leaving only us children, no longer boys but tiny babies, I'm lying on the ground and start to cry, and all the others are crying too, but I'm the only one whose father is accompanying the soldiers, we look at the opening into the square where we know they will enter, but there's no sign of them, we wait but nothing happens, though their footsteps are getting closer, they're here, no, not yet, then I see myself as I am now, trapped inside the infant, I struggle to get out, it's as if my hands and feet are tied, I call to you, but you're not there, I call to my father, who's coming to kill me, and that's when I woke up, both last night and the night before. As he spoke, Mary shuddered with horror, lowered her eyes in anguish, her greatest fear had been confirmed, somehow, inexplicably, Jesus had dreamed his father's dream, although it was slightly different. She heard her son ask, What was the dream father used to have every night. It was just a nightmare like any other. But what was it about. I don't know, your father never told me. Come now, Mother, don't hide the truth from your own son. It's best forgotten, not good for you to know. How do you know what's good or bad for me. Show some respect for your mother. Of course I respect you, but why hide things that concern me. Don't make me say any more. One day I asked Father why he was haunted by that dream, and he told me that I had no right to ask and that he had nothing to tell me. Well, then, why not accept your father's words. I did accept them while he was alive, but now I am a man, I've inherited his tunic, a pair of sandals, and a dream, and with these I can go out into the world, but I must know more about the dream. Perhaps it won't come back. Staring into his mother's eyes, Jesus told her, I will not insist on knowing so long as the dream does not come back, but if it does, swear to me you'll tell me everything. I swear it, replied Mary, yielding to her son's insistence and authority. From her full heart a silent plea went up to God, a prayer without words, which might have sounded as follows, O Lord, send this dream to haunt my nights until the day I die, but I beseech You, spare my son, spare my son. Jesus warned her, Don't forget your promise. I won't forget, Mary assured him, repeating to herself, Spare my son, O Lord, spare my son.

But he was not spared. Night came, a black cock crowed at dawn, the dream returned, the head of the first horse appeared around the corner. Mary heard her son moan but did not go to comfort him. Shaking with fear and covered with sweat, Jesus knew that his mother was lying there awake and listening. What will she tell me, he wondered, while Mary for her part thought, What will I say to him, and she tried desperately to think how not to tell him everything. In the morning she was readying her sons for the synagogue when Jesus said, I'll come with you, then we can talk in the desert. Mary was so nervous, she kept dropping things as she tried to prepare some food, but the wine of affliction has been poured and now must be drunk. Once the younger children were taken to school, Mary and Jesus left the village, and in the desert they sat beneath an olive tree where no one except God, should He chance to be around, could possibly overhear their conversation. For stones, as we know, cannot speak, even if we strike them one against the other, and as for the earth below, that is where all words turn to silence. Jesus said, Now you must keep your promise, and Mary told him outright, Your father dreamt he was a soldier marching with other soldiers on their way to kill you. To kill me. Yes, to kill you. But that's my dream. I know, she told him, with a sigh of relief, It is easier than I imagined, she thought before saying aloud, Now that you know, let's go home, dreams are like clouds, they come and go, you only inherited this dream because you were so fond of your father, he didn't want to kill you, nor could he ever have done such a thing, even if the Lord Himself ordered him to do so, an angel would have stayed his hand, as happened to Abraham when he was about to sacrifice his son Isaac. Don't speak of things you know nothing of, said Jesus bluntly, and Mary realized that the bitter wine would have to be drunk to the dregs. What I do know, my son, is that the Lord's will must be done, whatever that will may be, and if He ordains one thing now and something quite different later, there's nothing we can do. As she finished speaking, Mary folded her hands in her lap and sat waiting. Jesus asked her, Will you answer all my questions. Of course, she said. When did Father start having this dream. Many years ago. How many years. From the day you were born. Did he have the dream every night. Yes, I believe he did, after a while he didn't bother calling me, people get used to nightmares. Tell me, Mother, was I born in Bethlehem of Judaea. That's right. What happened when I was born that my father should dream he was going to kill me. It didn't happen when you were born. But you just said so. The dream started some weeks later. Later than what. Herod ordered that all infants under the age of three should be slaughtered, why, I wish I knew. Did Father know. If he did, he never told me. So how did Herod's soldiers miss me. We were living in a cave on the outskirts of the village. You mean the soldiers didn't kill me because they couldn't find me. Yes. Was Father a soldier. Never. What did he do, then. He worked on the site of the Temple. I don't understand. I'm trying to answer your questions. But if the soldiers didn't find me because we lived outside the

516

village, and if Father wasn't a soldier and therefore not guilty, and if he had no idea why Herod wanted the infants killed. That's right, your father couldn't understand why Herod ordered the deaths of those children. Then. There's nothing more to tell, and unless you have more questions to ask, I've told you all I know. You're hiding something from me. Perhaps it's that you are blind.

Jesus said nothing more, felt his authority evaporate like moisture in the soil, and sensed the presence of an unworthy thought in his mind, still wavering but monstrous from the moment of its birth. He saw a flock of sheep crossing the slopes of the opposite hill, and both the shepherd and the sheep were the color of earth, like earth moving over earth. Surprise crept into Mary's tense face, that tall shepherd, that manner of walking, so many years later and just at this moment, was it an omen, but then she stared hard and felt less certain, for now the shepherd looked like any other shepherd from Nazareth as he led his tiny flock to pasture, the animals as halting as their owner. The thought that came to Jesus, that struggled to be spoken, until finally he blurted it, was, Father knew those children were going to be slaughtered. It was not a question, so there was no need for Mary to answer. How did he know, and this time it was a question. Your father was working on the Temple site in Jerusalem when he overheard some soldiers discussing what they'd been ordered to do. And then. He ran to save you. And then. He decided there was no need for us to flee so long as we didn't leave the cave. And then. That was all, the soldiers carried out their orders and left. And then. Then we returned to Nazareth. And when did the dream start. The first time was in the cave. Beside himself with grief, Jesus covered his face and cried out, Father murdered the children of Bethlehem. What are you saying, my son, they were murdered by Herod's soldiers. No, Father was to blame, Joseph son of Eli was to blame, because he knew those children were to be killed and did nothing to warn their parents. Once these words were spoken, all hope of consolation was lost forever. Jesus threw himself to the ground and wept. Those children were innocent, innocent, he said bitterly, incredible that a simple boy of thirteen should react so strongly when one thinks how selfish children can be at that age and how indifferent most people are to the misfortunes of others. But people are not all alike, there are exceptions for better and for worse, and this is clearly one of the best, a young boy weeping his heart out because his father did wrong so many years ago, but he could also be weeping on his own account if, as it would appear, he loved this father who was guilty. Mary put out her hand to comfort him, but Jesus drew away, Don't touch me, I am wounded. Jesus, my son. Don't call me your son, you are also guilty. Such are the hasty judgments of adolescence, because Mary was as innocent as the slaughtered infants, it is the men, as every woman knows, who make the decisions, my husband came and said, We're leaving, then changed his mind and without going into details told me, We're not leaving after all, and I even had to ask him, What is that screaming I hear outside. Mary made no attempt to defend herself. It would have been easy to prove her innocence, but she thought of her crucified husband, he too had been killed though innocent, and she realized to her shame and sorrow that she loved him even more now than when he was alive, so she said nothing, for one person's guilt can be assumed by another. She simply said, Let's go home, we have nothing more to discuss here, and her son replied, You go, leave me by myself. There were no tracks of shepherd or sheep to be seen, the desert was truly deserted, and even the few scattered houses on the slope below looked like slabs of stone at an abandoned building site, gradually sinking into the ground. When Mary disappeared from sight into the gray depths of the valley, Jesus fell to his knees and called out, his entire body burning as if he were sweating blood,

Father, Father, why have You forsaken me, because that was how the poor boy felt, forsaken, lost in the infinite solitude of another wilderness, without father, mother, brothers, or sisters, and already following a path of death. Concealed by his sheep, the shepherd sat watching him from afar.

Two days later, Jesus left home. During this time he said very little. Unable to sleep, he spent the nights awake. He could picture the awful massacre, the soldiers entering the houses and searching for cradles, their swords striking, stabbing the tender little bodies, mothers in despair, fathers roaring like chained bulls, and he also had a vision of himself inside a cave he had never seen before. At such moments, as if great waves were slowly engulfing him, he wished he were dead or at least no longer alive. One question that he had not asked his mother bothered him, How many children lost their lives. In his mind's eye they were piled high on top of one another, like beheaded lambs thrown into a heap and about to be cremated in a huge bonfire, and when reduced to ashes, they would go up to heaven in smoke. But since he had not asked this when his mother made her revelation, he felt he could not go to her now and say, By the way, Mother, I forgot to ask you the other day how many of those infants in Bethlehem passed on to a better life, to which she would reply, Ah, my son, try to put it out of your mind, there could not have been more than thirty, and if they died, it was the will of the Lord, for He could have prevented the massacre had He so desired. But Jesus could not stop wondering, How many. He would look at his brothers and ask himself, How many. How many bodies, he wanted to know, did it take to tip the scales against his own salvation. On the morning of the second day, he said to his mother, I can find no rest or peace of mind in this house, you stay here with my brothers, for I am going away. Mary raised her hands to heaven, horrified and close to tears, What are you saying, my eldest son, ready to abandon your widowed mother, whoever heard of such a thing, what is the world coming to, how can you think of leaving your home and family, what will become of us without you. James is only one year younger than me, he'll take my place and provide for all of you, as I did after your husband died. My husband was your father. I don't want to talk about him, I have nothing more to say, give me your blessing for the journey, but with or without it I am off. And where are you going, my son. I'm not sure, perhaps Jerusalem, perhaps Bethlehem, to see the land where I was born. But no one knows you there. Probably just as well, but tell me, Mother, what do you think would happen if anyone recognized me. Hush, your brothers might hear you. One day they too will have to know the truth. But have you thought of the risk, traveling at a time like this, with Roman soldiers on all the roads searching for the rebels of Judas the Galilean. The Romans are no worse than the soldiers who served under the late Herod, and they're not likely to kill me with their swords or nail me to a cross, after all, I've done nothing wrong, I'm innocent. So was your father and look what happened to him. Your husband may have been wrongfully crucified, but his life was not innocent. Jesus, my son, the devil's taken possession of your tongue. How do you know it isn't God. Don't take the name of the Lord in vain. Who can tell when the name of God is taken in vain, neither you nor I, God alone can tell, and I doubt whether we'll ever understand His reasons. My son, where on earth did you pick up such ideas at your age. Who knows, perhaps men are born carrying the truth inside them, but do not speak it because they're not completely sure it is the truth. You've decided, then, to leave us. Yes. Will you come back. I don't know. If that dream is troubling you, by all means go to Bethlehem, and go to the Temple in Jerusalem and consult the teachers, they will advise you and put your mind at rest, then you can come back to your mother and brothers, who need you. I can't promise to return. But how will you survive, your poor father didn't live long enough to teach you everything he knew. Don't worry, I'll work in the fields or tend sheep or persuade some fishermen to take me out to sea with them. Wouldn't you prefer to be a shepherd. Why. I don't know, a feeling, that's all. We'll see what turns up, and now, Mother, I must be on my way. But you can't go like this, let me get you some food for the journey, we haven't much money, but take some, and take your father's pack, which fortunately he left behind. I'll take the food but not the pack. Your father didn't have leprosy. I cannot. One day you'll weep for your father and be sorry you didn't take it. I've already wept for him. You'll weep even more, and you won't be asking then what sins he committed. Jesus made no attempt to reply to these words. The older children, unaware of the conversation between him and their mother, gathered around Jesus and asked, Are you really going away, and James said, I wish I were going with you, for the boy dreamed of adventure, travel, of doing something challenging and different. You must stay here, Jesus told him, someone has to look after our widowed mother, the word widowed slipped out involuntarily and he bit his lip to suppress it, but what he couldn't suppress were his tears, because the vivid memory of his father suddenly caught him like a ray of dazzling light.

After the family had eaten together, Jesus departed. He bade his brothers farewell one by one, embraced his tearful mother, and told her, without knowing why, One way or another I shall always come back, and adjusting his pack on his shoulder, he crossed the yard and opened the gate to the street. There he stopped, as if reflecting. How often we find ourselves on the point of crossing a threshold or making a decision, when further consideration causes us to change our mind and turn back. Mary's face lit up with jubilant surprise, but her joy was short-lived. Jesus lay down his pack, stood mulling over something, then turned back, passed between his brothers without looking at them, and went into the house. When he reappeared a few moments later, he had his father's sandals in his hand. Silently, his eyes lowered as if modesty or some hidden shame prevented him from looking anyone in the eye, he put the sandals into the pack, and without another word or gesture walked off. Mary ran to the gate and her children followed, the older ones indifferent, it seemed, no one waved good-bye, because Jesus didn't look back even once. A neighbor who was passing and saw Jesus leave asked, Where's your son off to, Mary, and Mary replied, He's found work in Jerusalem and he'll be staying there for a while, a barefaced lie as we know, but this matter of telling the truth or lying is complicated, better to make no hasty moral judgments, because if one waits long enough, the truth becomes a lie and a lie becomes the truth.

That night, as everyone in the house lay asleep except for Mary, who could not help wondering how and where her son was at that hour, whether he was safe in a caravansary, or huddled under a tree, or between the rocks of some dark ravine, or, God forbid, taken prisoner by the Romans. She heard the outside gate creak, and her heart leaped, It's Jesus coming back, she thought, momentarily overcome with joy and confusion. What should I do, she was reluctant to open the gate, to appear triumphant, to greet him with words such as, It didn't take you long to come back after giving your mother a sleepless night. That would be humiliating, better to say nothing, pretend to be asleep, let him creep in quietly, and if he lies down on his mat without even saying I'm back, tomorrow I'll pretend to be surprised that the prodigal son has returned. However brief his absence, her happiness is great, for absence too is a kind of death, the difference being that with absence there is still hope. But he's so slow in coming to the door, who knows, perhaps he changed his mind again, Mary cannot bear the suspense any longer, she will peer through the chink in the door without being seen and run back to her mat should her son decide to enter, and if he shows signs of leaving again, she'll be able to stop him. Tiptoeing on bare feet, she went to the door and looked out. The moon was bright, and the yard shone like water. A tall, dark figure, moving slowly, came toward the door, and the moment Mary saw him, she put her hands to her mouth to keep from screaming. It was not her son, it was the beggar, covered with rags as when she first saw him, but now, perhaps because of the moonlight, those rags were suddenly like sumptuous robes that stirred in the breeze. Terrified, she locked the door, What can he want from me, she muttered with trembling lips. The man who had claimed to be an angel moved to one side, was now right at the door, yet made no attempt to enter, Mary could hear him breathing, and then she heard the sound of something ripped open, as if the earth was being split to reveal an enormous abyss. The massive shadow of the angel appeared again, for a brief moment it blocked the entire countryside from her sight, and then, without so much as a glance at the house, he walked to the gate, taking with him, uprooted, the mysterious tree that had sprouted outside the door some thirteen years before, on the very spot where the bowl was buried. Between the opening and closing of the gate, the angel changed back into a beggar and disappeared behind the wall, this time in total silence, dragging the leafy branches with him as though the tree were a plumed serpent. Mary opened the door cautiously and looked out. The world was bright beneath a remote sky. Near the wall of the house was a hole where the plant had been pulled out, and from there to the gate a trail of soil sparkled like the Milky Way, if that term existed in those days. She thought about her son but without heartache now, surely no harm could come to him under such a beautiful sky, serene and unfathomable, and this moon like manna made from light, nourishing the earth's roots and springs. Her soul at peace, she crossed the yard and, fearlessly treading the stars on the ground, went to open the gate. She looked outside, saw that the trail ended a short distance away, as if the iridescence of the leaves had been extinguished or as if, another flight of fancy on the part of this woman who can no longer make the excuse that she is pregnant, the beggar had reverted to his angel form and finally made use of his wings to mark this special occasion. Mary pondered these strange events, and they seemed to her as simple and natural as her own hands in the moonlight. She returned to the house, took the oil lamp from its hook on the wall, and went to take a closer look at the deep hole where the plant had been. At the bottom of it lay the empty bowl. She reached in and lifted it out, the same plain bowl she remembered but with little earth left inside and no longer shining, an ordinary household utensil restored to its proper function. From now on it will be used to serve milk, water, or wine, according to one's taste and means, and how true the saying which reminds us that everyone has his hour and everything its time.

Jesus found shelter on the first night of his travels. It was dusk when he came to a tiny hamlet just outside the city of Jenin, and fate, which had predicted so much ill fortune since the day he was born, relented on this occasion. The owners of the house where, with little hope, he sought shelter turned out to be hospitable people who could never have forgiven themselves if they left a boy of his age out in the open all night, especially at a time like this, with so much fighting and violence everywhere, men being crucified and innocent children hacked to death for no reason. Although Jesus told his kind hosts that he hailed from Nazareth and was on his way to Jerusalem, he did not repeat the shameful lie he had heard his mother tell when she said he left to do a job. He told them he was on his way to consult the teachers of the Temple about a point of holy law that greatly concerned his family. The head of the household expressed his surprise that such an important mission should be entrusted to a mere boy, however advanced in his religious studies. Jesus explained that he was entrusted with this matter as the eldest son, but made no mention of his father. He ate with the family, then settled down under the lean-to in the yard, which was the best they could offer a passing traveler. In the middle of the night the dream returned to haunt him, although this time his father and the soldiers did not get quite so close and the horse's nose did not appear around the corner. Do not imagine, however, that the dream was any less terrifying, put yourself in Jesus' place, suppose you dreamed that the father who gave you life was pursuing you with drawn sword. Those asleep inside were completely unaware of the drama taking place in the yard, for Jesus had learned to hide his fear even while he slept. When the fear became unbearable, he would instinctively cover his mouth with a hand to muffle the cry of anguish throbbing in his head. In the morning, he joined the family for breakfast, then thanked them for their hospitality with such courtesy and eloquence that the whole family felt they were momentarily sharing in the ineffable peace of the Lord, humble Samaritans though they were. Jesus said good-bye and departed, his host's parting words ringing in his ears, Blessed be You, O Lord our God, King of the Universe, who guides our footsteps, words he repeated to himself, praising that same Lord, God, and King, provider of all our needs, as can clearly be seen from everyday experience, in accordance with that most just rule of direct proportion, which says that more should be given to those who have more.

The rest of the journey to Jerusalem was not so easy. In the first place, there are Samaritans and there are Samaritans, which means that even in those days one swallow was not enough to make a summer, it took two, two swallows, that is, not two summers, provided there was a fertile male and female and they had offspring. No more doors opened when Jesus knocked, so our traveler had to find somewhere to sleep outdoors, once under a fig tree of the large spreading variety that resemble a dirndl skirt, on another occasion by joining a caravan which, fortunately for Jesus, had to pitch tent in the open countryside because the nearby caravansary was full. We say fortunately because before this, while crossing some uninhabited mountain, the poor boy was attacked by two cowardly thieves, who took the little money he possessed, which meant that Jesus had no hope of finding lodgings at any of the inns, where everything had to be paid for. Anyone witnessing that episode would have looked with pity on the lad, abandoned to his fate by those heartless rogues, who went off laughing at his plight. He lay there in a lamentable state, with nothing but the sky overhead and the surrounding mountains, the infinite universe stripped of moral significance and peopled with stars, thieves, and executioners. One might argue that a boy of thirteen could not have had sufficient knowledge of science and philosophy, or even sufficient experience of life, for such thoughts, and that this boy in particular, notwithstanding his religious studies in the synagogue and his natural talent for debate, was not capable of the words and deeds attributed to him. There is no lack of carpenters' sons in these parts, or of sons whose fathers were crucified, but even if another man's son had been chosen, we are confident that whoever he was, he would have given us just as much food for thought as young Jesus. First because it is well known that every man is a world unto himself, by the path either of transcendence or immanence, and secondly because this land has always been different from any other, one need only consider how many people, both rich and poor, have traveled here to preach and prophesy, from Isaiah to Malachi, nobles, priests, shepherds, men from every conceivable walk of life, which teaches us to be cautious about jumping to conclusions, the humble origins of a carpenter's son do not give us the right to dismiss him. This boy who is on his way to Jerusalem at an age when most children do not venture outside the front door may not be a genius or luminary, but he deserves our respect. His soul, as he himself confessed, has been deeply wounded, and since the wound is unlikely to heal quickly, given his reflective nature, he has gone out into the world, perhaps to combine his scars into one definitive sorrow. It may seem inappropriate to put the complex theories of modern thinkers into the head of a Palestinian who lived so many years before Freud, Jung, Groddeck, and Lacan, but if you will pardon our presumption, it is not all that foolish, when one considers that the scriptures from which the Jews derive their spiritual nourishment consistently teach that a man, no matter the age in which he lives, is the equal in intellect of all other men. Adam and Eve are the only exceptions, not just because they were the first man and woman but because they had no childhood. And while biology and psychology may be invoked to prove that the human mind as we know it today can be traced back to Cro-Magnon man, that argument is of no interest here, inasmuch as Cro-Magnon man is not even mentioned in the Book of Genesis, which is all Jesus knew about the beginning of the world.

Distracted by these reflections, which are not entirely

irrelevant to the gospel we have been telling, we forgot, to our shame, to accompany Joseph's son on the last leg of his journey to Jerusalem, where he is just now arriving, penniless but safe. Although his feet are badly blistered after the long trip, he is as steadfast as when he left home three days ago. He has been here before, so his excitement is no greater than one might expect from a devout man whose God is about to manifest himself. From this mountain known as Gethsemane, or the Mount of Olives, one can get a view of Jerusalem's magnificent architecture, of the city's Temple, the towers, palaces, and houses, which give the impression of being within reach, but this impression depends on the degree of mystical fervor, which can lead the faithful to confuse the limitations of the body with the infinite power of the universal spirit. The evening is drawing to a close, and the sun is setting over the distant sea. Jesus begins his descent into the valley, wondering where he will spend the night, whether inside or outside the city walls. On other occasions, when he accompanied his parents at Passover, the family spent the night outside the walls, in a tent thoughtfully provided by the civic and military authorities to receive pilgrims, all of them segregated, needless to say, the men with the men, the women with the women, and the children divided according to sex. When Jesus reached the city walls, the night air had already turned chilly. He arrived just as the gates were being closed, but the watchmen allowed him to enter, and as those great wooden crossbars slammed into position, Jesus may have begun to feel remorse for some past sin, imagining himself caught in a trap, its iron teeth about to snap shut, a web imprisoning a fly. At the age of thirteen, however, he cannot have sins that numerous or serious, he is not at an age yet to be killing or stealing or bearing false witness, to be coveting his neighbor's wife or house or fields, his neighbor's male or female slave or ass or ox or any other thing that belongs to his neighbor, therefore this boy walks pure and undefiled, though he may have lost his innocence, for no one can witness death without being affected.

The roads become deserted at this hour as families gather for supper, and on them there are only beggars and vagabonds, who will also retreat into their dens and hideaways, because any minute now Roman soldiers will be scouring the streets in search of malefactors that venture even into the capital of Herod Antipas's kingdom to commit every manner of crime and iniquity despite the severe sentences that await them if they are caught, as we saw in Sepphoris. At the end of the road a night patrol with torches blazing marches past amid the clang of swords and shields and to the rhythm of feet clad in military sandals. Hiding in a dark corner, the boy waited for the soldiers to disappear, then went to look for a place to sleep. He found one among the many building sites around the Temple, a gap between two great stone slabs, with another slab on top to form a roof. There he munched what remained of his hard, moldy bread, along with some dry figs he found at the bottom of his pack. He was thirsty but resigned himself to going without water. Stretching out on his mat, he covered himself with the little mantle he carried as part of his baggage and, curling up to protect himself from the cold, which penetrated from both sides of his precarious refuge, he managed to fall asleep. Being in Jerusalem did not prevent him from dreaming, but perhaps because he was close to God's holy presence, his dream was merely a repetition of familiar scenes that merged with the arrival of the patrol he encountered earlier. He awoke as the sun was rising. Wrapped in his mantle, he dragged himself out of that hole cold as a tomb and saw the houses of Jerusalem before him, low-lying houses made of stone, their walls painted pale crimson by the morning light. Then, with great solemnity, coming as it did from the lips of one who after all is still a boy, he offered up a prayer of thanksgiving, Thanks be to You, O Lord our God, King of the Uni verse, who through the power of Your mercy restored my soul. There are certain moments in life that should be arrested and protected from time, and not simply be transmitted in a gospel or a painting or, as in this modern age, a photograph, film, or video. How much more interesting it would be if the person who lived those moments could remain forever visible to his descendants, so that those of us alive today could go to Jerusalem and see with our own eyes young Jesus, son of Joseph, all wrapped up in his little threadbare mantle, beholding the houses of Jerusalem and giving thanks to the Lord who mercifully restored his soul. Since his life is just beginning at the age of thirteen, one can assume there are brighter and darker hours in store for him, moments of greater joy and despair, pleasure and grief, but this is the moment we ourselves would choose, while the city slumbers, the sun is at a standstill, the light intangible, and a young boy wrapped in a mantle looks wide-eyed at the houses, a pack at his feet and the entire world, near and far, waiting in suspense. Alas, he has moved, the instant is gone, time has carried us into the realm of memory, it was like this, no, it was not, and everything becomes what we choose to invent.

Now Jesus walks through the narrow, crowded streets, it is still too early to go to the Temple, the teachers, as in all ages and places, only start appearing later. Jesus is no longer cold, but his stomach is rumbling, those two remaining figs served only to whet his appetite, Joseph's son is famished. Now he could do with the money those rogues stole from him, for city life is quite unlike that leisurely existence in the country, where one goes around whistling and looking for what may have been left behind by God-fearing laborers who carry out His commandments to the letter, When you are harvesting your fields and leave a sheaf behind, do not turn back to retrieve it, When you pick olives, do not go back to collect those still hanging on the branches, When you gather grapes from your vineyard, do not go rummaging for any you over-looked, leave them to be gathered by the stranger, orphan, or widow, and always remember that you were once a slave in the land of Egypt. Now, because it is a large city, and despite God's decree that His earthly dwelling be built here, these humanitarian precepts are not observed in Jerusalem, so that for anyone arriving without thirty or even three pieces of silver in his pocket the only recourse is to beg and almost certainly be refused, or to steal and run the risk of being flogged, imprisoned, or worse. But this youth is incapable of stealing and much too shy to beg. His mouth waters as he stares at the stacks of loaves, the pyramids of fruits, the cooked meats and vegetables set out on stalls up and down the streets, and the sight of all that food after three days of fasting, if we don't count the Samaritan's hospitality, almost makes him faint. It is true that he is heading for the Temple, but notwithstanding the claims of those mystics who believe in fasting, his mind would be in better condition to receive the word of the Lord if his body were fed. Fortunately, a Pharisee who happened to be passing noticed the boy's weak condition and took pity on him. Posterity will unjustly give the Pharisees the worst possible reputation, but at heart they were decent people, as this encounter clearly shows, Where are you from, asked the Pharisee, and Jesus replied, I'm from Nazareth of Galilee. Are you hungry, the man asked, and the boy lowered his eyes, there was no need to say anything, hunger was written on his face. Have you no family. Yes, but I'm traveling on my own. Did you run away. No, and it is true, he did not run away. We must not forget that his mother and brothers bade him an affectionate farewell at the gate, and the fact that he did not turn back even once does not mean he fled. The words we use are like that, to say yes or no is the most straightforward answer possible and in principle the most convincing, yet the world demands that we start indecisively, Well no, not really, I didn't exactly run away, at which point we have to hear the story all over again, but do not worry, this is unnecessary, first because the Pharisee, who reappears in our gospel, does not need to hear it and, secondly because we know the story better than anyone else. Just think how little the main characters of this gospel know about one another, Jesus does not know everything about his mother and father, Mary does not know everything about her husband and son, and Joseph, who is dead, knows nothing about anything. Whereas we know everything that has been done, spoken, and thought, whether by them or by others, although we have to act as if we too are in the dark, in that sense we are like the Pharisee who asked, Are you hungry, when Jesus' pinched, wan face spoke for itself, No need to ask, just give me something to eat. And that is exactly what the compassionate man did, he bought two loaves still hot from the oven and a bowl of milk, and without a word handed them to Jesus. As the bowl passed between them, it so happened that a little milk spilled on their hands, whereupon they both made the same gesture, which surely comes from the depths of time, each lifted his wet hand to his lips to suck the milk, like kissing bread when it has fallen to the floor. What a pity these two will never meet again after they have sealed such an admirable and symbolic pact. The Pharisee went about his affairs, but not before taking two coins from his pocket and saying, Take this money and return home, the world is much too big for someone like you. The carpenter's son stood there clutching the bowl and the bread, no longer hungry, or perhaps still hungry but not feeling anything. He watched the Pharisee walk away, and only then did he say, Thank you, but in such a low voice that the Pharisee could not possibly have heard him, and if the man expected to be thanked, then he must have thought to himself, What an ungrateful boy. In the middle of the road, Jesus suddenly regained his appetite. He lost no time in eating his bread and drinking his milk, then gave the empty bowl to the vendor, who told him, The bowl is paid for, keep it. Is it the custom in Jerusalem to buy the bowl with the milk. No, but that's what the Pharisee wanted, though you can never tell what's on a Pharisee's mind. So I can keep it. I already told you, it's paid for. Jesus wrapped the bowl in his mantle and tucked it into his pack while thinking that he would have to handle it carefully. These earthenware bowls are fragile and easily broken, they are only made of a little clay on which fortune has precariously bestowed a shape, and the same could be said of mankind. His body nourished and his spirits revived, Jesus set off in the direction of the Temple.

A LARGE CROWD HAD ALREADY GATHERED ON THE CON-
course facing the steep stairway that led up to the entrance.
Ranged along the walls on either side were the tents of the
peddlers and traders selling animals for sacrifice, and here
and there were money changers at their stalls, groups of
people engaged in conversation, gesticulating merchants,
Roman soldiers on foot and on horseback, keeping a watchful eye, slave-borne litters, camels and donkeys laden with
baggage, and frenzied shouting everywhere, interrupted
by the feeble bleats of lambs and goats, some carried in
people's arms or on their backs like tired children, others
dragged by a rope around their neck, but all destined
to perish by sword or fire. Jesus passed the bathhouse
used for purification, climbed the steps, and without stopping crossed the Court of the Gentiles. He entered the Court
of the Women through the door between the Chamber of
the Holy Oils and the Chamber of the Nazirites, and there
he found what he was looking for, the assembly of elders
and scribes who traditionally gathered to discuss holy law,
answer questions, and dispense advice. They stood in

groups, and the boy joined the smallest of these just as a man was raising his hand to ask a question. The scribe invited him to speak, and the man asked, Can you tell me if we should accept, word for word, the commandments given by the Lord to Moses on Mount Sinai, when He promised peace on earth and told us no one would disturb our sleep, when He promised that He would banish dangerous animals from our midst, that the sword would not pass through our land, and that if our enemies pursued us, they would fall under our sword, for as the Lord Himself said, Five of you will pursue a hundred men, a hundred of you ten thousand, and your enemies will fall under your sword. The scribe eyed the man suspiciously and, thinking he might be a rebel in disguise sent by Judas the Galilean to stir up trouble with wicked insinuations about the Temple's passive resistance to Roman rule, he replied brusquely, Those words were spoken by the Lord when our forefathers were in the desert, having fled the Egyptians. The man raised his hand a second time and asked another question, Are we to understand, then, that the Lord's words on Mount Sinai were meaningful only so long as our forefathers did not enter the promised land. If that is how you interpret them, you are not a good Israelite, the words of the Lord must prevail in every age, past, present, and future, for they were in His mind before He uttered them and remained there after He spoke. But it was you yourself who said what you forbid me to think. And what do you think. That the Lord allows that our swords should not be raised against this military force which oppresses us, that a hundred of our men lack the courage to face five of theirs, that ten thousand Jews cower before a hundred Romans. Let me remind you that you are in the Temple of the Lord and not on some battlefield. The Lord is the God of legions. True, but do not forget that God imposed His condition. What condition. The Lord said, So long as you observe my laws and keep my commandments. But

536

what are these laws and commandments we have ignored, that we should accept Roman rule as just and necessary punishment for our sins. The Lord must know. Yes, the Lord must know, and how often man sins without knowing, but would you care to explain why the Lord should make use of the Roman army to punish us instead of confronting His chosen people and punishing us Himself. The Lord knows His intentions and chooses His means. So you're trying to tell me that the Lord wants the Romans to govern Israel. Yes. Well, if that is so, then the rebels fighting the Romans are opposing the Lord and His holy will. You jump to the wrong conclusion. And you, scribe, contradict yourself. God's will may be not-to-will, and that not-to-will may be His will. So the will of man is genuine yet of no importance in the eyes of God. That's right. So man is free. Yes, free so that he might be punished. A murmur went up among the bystanders, some stared at the person who had asked the questions, based on the texts yet politically inopportune, and they looked at him accusingly, as if he were the one who should answer for the sins of all Israel, while the skeptical were reassured by the victory of the scribe, who acknowledged their praise and applause with a complacent smile. The scribe looked around him confidently and asked if there were other questions, like a gladiator who, having dispatched a weak opponent, seeks a more worthy opponent in order to gain greater glory. Another hand went up, and a different question was raised, The Lord spoke to Moses and told him, The stranger in your midst shall be treated as one of your own and you will love him as you love yourselves, for you were strangers in the land of Egypt. But before the man could finish speaking, the scribe, still flushed from his victory, interrupted in a sarcastic voice, I hope you are not about to ask me why we do not treat the Romans as our compatriots since they, too, are foreigners. No, what I want to ask is whether the Romans would treat us as their compatriots if both sides spent less time arguing about the differences between their laws and gods. So you too have come here to anger the Lord with blasphemous interpretations of His holy word, said the scribe. On the contrary, all I ask is whether you truly believe that we are obeying the holy word of the Lord when strangers are strangers not so much to the land in which we live as to the religion we profess. To which strangers do you refer. To some in our own day and age, to many in the past, and probably many more in the years to come. I've no time to waste on enigmas and parables, make yourself clear. When we arrived from Egypt, there were other nations living in the land we now call Israel, whom we had to fight, and in those days we were the strangers, and the Lord commanded us to exterminate the people who opposed His will. The land was promised to us but had to be conquered, we did not buy it, nor was it offered to us. And now we find ourselves living under foreign rule, we have lost the land we made our own. Israel lives forever in the spirit of the Lord, so that wherever His people may be, whether united or dispersed, there the land of Israel will be. In other words, wherever we Jews find ourselves, others will always be the stranger. Certainly, in the eyes of the Lord. But the stranger who lives among us, according to the word of the Lord, must be our compatriot and we must love him as we love ourselves, for we were once strangers in Egypt. That is what the Lord said. In that case, the stranger we are expected to love must also be those who, living among us, are not so powerful that they can rule us, as at present with the Romans. Yes, I agree. Then tell me, do you believe that if one day we become powerful, the Lord will permit us to oppress the stranger He commanded us to love. All Israel can do is obey the will of the Lord, and since the children of Israel are His chosen people, the Lord wills only what is good for them. Even if it means not loving those we should. Yes, if so willed. Willed by whom, the Lord or

Israel. By both, for they are one and the same. Thou shalt not violate the stranger's rights, says the Lord. When that stranger has rights and we acknowledge them, replied the scribe. Once again, those present murmured their approval, and the scribe's eyes gleamed like those of a champion wrestler, discus thrower, gladiator, or charioteer.

Jesus raised his hand. No one present found it strange that a boy his age should come forward to question a scribe or doctor of the Temple, the young have been plagued by doubts ever since the time of Cain and Abel, they tend to ask questions to which adults respond with a condescending smile and a pat on the shoulder, When you grow up, young man, you'll stop worrying about such matters, while the more understanding will say, When I was your age, I thought the same. Some moved away, and others were preparing to do so, which vexed the scribe, who did not want to see his attentive audience leave, but Jesus' question caused many to turn back and listen, What I want to discuss is guilt. You mean your own guilt. No, guilt in general, but also the guilt a man may feel without having sinned himself. Explain yourself more clearly. The Lord said that parents will not die for their children or children for their parents and that each man will be judged for his own crime. This was a precept for those ancient times when an entire family, however innocent, paid for the crime of any one of its members. But if the word of the Lord is forever, there is no end to guilt, and as you yourself just said, saying man is free so that he might be punished, then one is right to believe that the father's guilt, even after his punishment, does not cease but is passed on to his children, just as all of us who are alive today have inherited the guilt of Adam and Eve, our first parents. I am amazed that a boy of your age and humble circumstances should know so much about the scriptures and be able to debate these matters with such ease. I only know what I was taught. Where are you from. From Nazareth of Galilee. I thought as much from your manner of speaking. Please answer my question. We may assume that the gravest sin of Adam and Eve, when they disobeyed the Lord, was not eating the fruit of the tree of the knowledge of good and evil but, rather, its consequence, because their sin prevented the Lord from carrying out the plan He had in mind when He created first man and then woman. Whereupon the second man who asked a question challenged the scribe with another gem of sophistry, which the carpenter's son would never have had the courage to voice in public, Do you mean to say that every human act, such as that of the disobedience in Eden, can interfere with God's will, which is like an island in the ocean assailed on all sides by the turbulent waves of human will. Not exactly, the scribe replied cautiously, the will of the Lord is not content only to prevail over all things, His will makes everything what it is. But you yourself said that it is because of Adam's disobedience that we do not know the plan God conceived for him. That is what our reason tells us, but the will of God, the creator and ruler of the universe, embraces all possible wills, His own as well as that of every man born into this world. If this is so, intervened Jesus with sudden insight, then each man is a part of God. Probably, but even if all men were united as one, that combined part would be but a grain of sand in the infinite desert that is God. Sitting on the ground surrounded by men who watch him with mixed feelings of awe and fear, as if they are in the presence of a magician who has unwittingly conjured up powers greater than his own, the scribe looks less complacent. With drooping shoulders and doleful expression, his hands resting on his knees, his entire body seems to ask that he be left alone with his anguish. People in the group started rising to their feet, some made their way to the Court of the Israelites, some to join other groups still engaged in discussion. Jesus said, You didn't answer my question. The scribe stared at him like someone coming out of a trance, then after a long, tense silence replied, Guilt is a wolf that eats her cub after devouring its father. The wolf of which you speak has already devoured my father. Then it will soon be your turn. And what about you, were you ever devoured. Not only devoured but also spewed up.

Jesus rose to his feet and left. Heading for the gate through which he had entered, he paused and looked back. The column of smoke coming from the sacrificial fires climbed into the heavens, where it dispersed and vanished, as if sucked in by God's mighty lungs. It was mid-morning, more and more people were arriving, while inside the Temple sat a man broken by a sense of emptiness, waiting to regain his composure so that he could reply calmly to one who came wanting to know if the pillar of salt that Lot's wife turned into was rock salt or sea salt, or if Noah got drunk on white wine or red wine. Outside the Temple, Jesus asked the way to Bethlehem, his second destination. He lost his way twice amid the confusion of streets and people before he found the gate through which he had passed while inside his mother's womb thirteen years earlier, almost ready to enter the world. But this was not in Jesus' mind, because the obvious, as we all know, clips the wings of the restless bird of imagination, if any reader of this gospel were to look at a photograph of his pregnant mother when she was carrying him, for example, could he possibly imagine himself inside that womb. Jesus descends in the direction of Bethlehem, now he can reflect on the scribe's answers not just to his own question but also to the questions raised by others. What worries him is the feeling that all those questions were really one question, and that the reply given to each answered all, especially the last reply, which summed up the rest, the insatiable hunger of the wolf of guilt that is forever gnawing, devouring, and spewing up. Thanks to the fickleness of memory we often do not know, or know but try to forget, what caused our guilt, or, speaking metaphorically like the scribe, the lair of the wolf that pursues us. But Jesus knows, and that is where he is going. He has no idea what he'll do when he gets there, but this is better than announcing, I am here, and waiting for someone to ask, What do you want, punishment, pardon, or oblivion.

Like his father and mother before him, he stopped at Rachel's tomb to pray. Then, feeling his heart beat faster and faster, he resumed his journey. The first houses of Bethlehem were within sight, this is the main road into the village, taken by his homicidal father and the soldiers in his dream night after night. In daylight it doesn't seem a place of horror, even the tranquil white clouds drifting across the sky are benevolent gestures from God, and the very earth slumbers beneath the sun, as if bidding us, Let's leave things as they are, there's nothing to be gained by digging up the past, and before a woman with a child in her arms appears at a window asking, Who are you looking for, turn back, erase your footprints, and pray that the endless motion of the hourglass of time will quickly obliterate with its dust all memory of those events. Too late. There is a moment when a fly about to brush past the web still has time to escape, but once it touches the web and finds its wing caught, then the slightest movement suffices to trap and paralyze it completely, forever, however indifferent the spider to its new victim. For Jesus, that moment has passed. In the middle of a square with a spreading fig tree stands a tiny square building, and one does not have to look twice to see it is a tomb. Jesus approached, walked around it slowly, paused to read the faded inscription on one side, and this was enough, he had found what he was looking for. A woman crossed the square, leading a five-year-old child by the hand. She stopped, looked inquisitively at the stranger, and asked him, Where do you come from, and to justify her question added, You're not from these parts. No, I'm from Nazareth in Galilee. Have you relatives here. No, I was visiting Jerusalem, and it seemed a good opportunity to take a look at Bethlehem. Are you passing through. Yes, I'll return to Jerusalem later this afternoon, when it gets cooler. Lifting the child onto her left arm, the woman told him, May the Lord go with you, then turned to leave, but Jesus detained her, asking, Whose tomb is this. The woman pressed the child to her bosom, as if to protect it from some threat, and replied, Twenty-five little boys, who died years ago, are buried here. How many. Twenty-five. I mean how many years ago. Oh, about fourteen. So many. I think that's right, they would be your age if they were alive today. Yes, but what about the little boys. One of them was my brother. You have a brother buried here. Yes. And this child in your arms, is he your son. He's my firstborn. Why did they kill only the little boys. No one knows, I was only seven at the time. But you must have heard your parents and the other grown-ups talking about it. There was no need, I myself saw some of the children being killed. Your brother as well. Yes, my brother. And who killed them. The king's soldiers came searching for little boys up to the age of three, and they killed all of them. Yet you don't know why. No one knows to this day. And after Herod died, did anyone go to the Temple to ask the priests to investigate. I really don't know. If the soldiers had been Romans, one might understand it, but to have our own king ordering his people slaughtered, mere babes, seems very strange, unless there was some reason. The will of kings is beyond our understanding, may the Lord go with you and protect you. It's a long time since I was three. At the hour of death men go back to being children, replied the woman before departing.

Once alone, Jesus knelt beside the boulder covering the entrance to the tomb, took the last piece of stale bread from his pack, rubbed it into crumbs between his palms, and sprinkled the crumbs all along the entrance, as if making an offering to the invisible mouths of the innocents buried there. As he finished, another woman appeared from around the corner, but this woman was very old and bent and walked with the aid of a stick. No longer able to see clearly, she had caught only a fuzzy glimpse of what the boy did. She stopped, watched him carefully, saw him get to his feet and bow his head as if praying for the repose of the souls of those unfortunate infants, and although it is customary, we will refrain from adding the word eternal to souls, for our imagination failed us on the one and only occasion we tried to picture eternal rest. Jesus ended his prayer and looked around him, blank walls, closed doors, nothing except the old woman standing there, dressed in a slave's tunic and leaning on her stick, the living image of that third part of the sphinx's famous enigma about the animal that walks on four feet in the morning, two at midday, and three in the evening, It is man, replied astute Oedipus, who forgot that some do not even get as far as midday, and that in Bethlehem alone twenty-five infants were cut down. The old woman drew closer, hobbling at a snail's pace, and now she stands before Jesus, twists her neck to get a better view of him, and asks, Are you looking for someone. The boy did not answer immediately, in fact he was not looking for anyone, those he sought are all dead, buried here, and are not even what you could call someone, mere infants still in diapers and with pacifiers in their mouths, whimpering, their noses running, yet death struck and turned them into an enormous presence that cannot be contained in any ossuary or reliquary, these are bodies that come out of their graves each night, if there is any justice, to show their wounds, the holes that, opened at sword point, allowed life to escape, No, replied Jesus, I am not. The old woman did not go, she seemed to be waiting for him to continue, so Jesus confided, I was born in this village, in a cave, and was curious to see the place. She stepped back unsteadily and strained her eyes to get a better look, her voice trembling as she asked him, What is your name, where do you come from, who are your parents. No one needs to answer a slave, but the elderly, however low their station, deserve our respect, we must never forget that they have little time left for asking questions, it would be cruel in the extreme to ignore them, after all we might possess the very answer they have been waiting for. My name is Jesus and I come from Nazareth of Galilee, the boy told her, and he seems to have been saying nothing else since he left home. The old woman stepped forward again, And your parents, what are their names. My father's name was Joseph, my mother is Mary. How old are you. I'm almost fourteen. The woman looked around her, as if seeking a place to sit, but a square in Bethlehem of Judaea is not the same as a garden in São Paulo de Alcântara, with its park benches and pleasant view of the castle, here we have to sit on the dusty ground, at best on a doorstep or, if there's a tomb, on the stone by the entrance put there for the respite of the living who come to mourn their loved ones, and perhaps also for those ghosts who leave their rest to shed any remaining tears, as does Rachel, in the tomb nearby, where it is written, Here lies Rachel who weeps for her children and seeks no consolation, for one does not need to be as shrewd as Oedipus to see that this place befits the circumstances, and Rachel's weeping the cause of her grief. The old woman lowered herself onto the stone with effort, and the boy went to help her, but too late, for halfhearted gestures are never made in time. I know you, the old woman told him. You must be mistaken, said Jesus, I've never been here before and I never saw you in Nazareth. The first hands to touch you were not your mother's but mine. How is that, old woman. My name is Salome, and I was the midwife who delivered you. Acting on impulse, which only goes to prove the sincerity of gestures made spontaneously, Jesus fell to his knees at the old woman's feet, wanting both to know everything and to show his gratitude for bringing him out of a limbo without memory into a world that would mean nothing without memory. My mother never mentioned you, said Jesus. There was no need, your parents appeared on my master's doorstep, and I was asked to help, since I had some experience as a midwife. Was that when the innocents were massacred. That's right, you were fortunate they didn't find you. Because we lived in a cave. It was either that or because you'd already left, I never found out, for when I went to see what had happened to you, the cave was empty. Do you remember my father. Yes, I remember him well, at that time he was in his prime, a fine figure of a man, and honest. He's dead. Poor man, he didn't live long, but if you're his heir, what are you doing here, for I assume your mother is still alive. I came to see the place where I was born, also to learn more about the children who were slaughtered here. God alone knows why they had to die, the angel of death, disguised as Herod's soldiers, descended into Bethlehem and slew them. So you believe it was God's will. I'm only an old slave, but all my life I've heard people say that everything that happens in this world can happen only by the will of God. So it is written. God may decide to take me any day now, that I can understand, but these were innocent little children. Your death will be decided by God in His own good time, but it was a man who ordered that the children be killed. The hand of God, then, can do precious little if it cannot come between the sword and little children. You mustn't offend the Lord, good woman. An ignorant old woman like me isn't likely to cause any offense. Today in the Temple I heard it said that every human action, however insignificant, interferes with the will of God, and that man is free only in order to be punished. My punishment doesn't come from being free, it comes from being a slave, the old woman told him. Jesus fell silent. He hardly heard Salome's words, because it suddenly dawned on him that man is a mere toy in the hands of God and forever subject to His will, whether he imagines himself to be obeying or disobeying Him.

The sun was going down, and the fig tree's evil shadow lengthened and came closer. Jesus spoke to the old woman. Salome raised her head with effort, What do you want, she asked. Take me to the cave where I was born, or at least tell me how to get there, if it's too far for you to walk. I'm not very steady on my feet, but you won't find it unless I show you. Is it far from here. No, but there are many caves and they all look alike. Let's go, then. As you wish, she said. Anyone who happened to be watching that day, when Salome and the unknown boy passed by, must have asked himself where those two could have met. But no one ever knew, because the old slave revealed nothing to the day she died, and Jesus never again returned to the land of his birth. Next morning Salome went to the cave where she had left the boy. No sign of him. She was re-lieved, because even if he had still been there, they would have had nothing more to say to each other.

MUCH HAS BEEN SAID ABOUT LIFE'S COINCIDENCES BUT little or nothing about the everyday encounters that guide the course of life, although one could argue that an encounter, strictly speaking, is a coincidence, which obviously does not mean that all coincidences have to be encounters. Throughout this gospel there have been many coincidences, and if we look carefully at the life of Jesus, especially after he left home, we can see that there has been no lack of encounters either. Leaving aside his unfortunate adventure with the thieves, since it is too early to tell what the consequence of that might be in the future, Jesus' first journey on his own has resulted in many meetings, such as the providential appearance of the Pharisee, thanks to whom the boy not only satisfied his hunger but, by eating in haste, reached the Temple in time to listen to the questions and answers that prepared the ground, as it were, for his question about guilt, the question that brought him all the way from Nazareth. When critics discuss the rules of effective narration, they insist that important encounters, in fiction as in life, be interspersed with others of no importance, so that the hero of the story does not find himself transformed into an exceptional being to whom nothing ordinary ever happens. They argue that this narrative approach best serves the ever desirable effect of verisimilitude, for if the episode imagined and described is not, and is not likely to become or supplant, factual reality, there must at least be some similitude, not as in the present narrative, where the reader's credence has clearly been put to the test, Jesus having taken himself to Bethlehem only to come face-to-face as soon as he arrives, with Salome, who assisted at his birth, as if that other encounter, with the woman carrying a child in her arms, whom we deliberately planted there to fill in the story, had not been license enough. The most incredible part of our story, however, is yet to come, after the slave Salome accompanies Jesus to the cave and leaves him there at his request, Leave me alone between these dark walls, that I may hear my first cry in the deep silence, if echoes can last that long. These were the words the woman thought she heard, and so they are recorded here, at the risk of once more offending verisimilitude, but, then, we can always blame the unreliable testimony of a senile old woman. Unsteady on her feet, Salome hobbled off, moving cautiously, one step at a time and leaning heavily on her staff, which she gripped with both hands. It would have been a nice gesture on the boy's part to help this poor, suffering creature return home, but such is youth, selfish and thoughtless, and there is nothing to suggest that Jesus was different from other boys his age.

He sat on a stone, and on a stone beside him was an oil lamp casting its dim light on the cave's rough walls, the dark heap of coals where once there was a fire, and his limp hands and pensive face. This is where I was born, he thought, I once slept in that manger, my father and mother once sat on this very stone I am sitting on now, this is where we took refuge as Herod's soldiers searched the village and slaughtered infants. But hard as I try, I will never hear the cry of life I gave at birth, or the cries of those dying children and the parents who watched them die, there is nothing but silence in this cave where a beginning and an end came together. As I learned in the Temple, parents pay for the sins they have committed, and their children for the sins they may one day commit, but if life is a sentence and death a punishment, there was never a more innocent town than Bethlehem, infants who died in perfect innocence, parents who had done no wrong, nor was there ever a more guilty man than my father, who remained silent when he should have spoken, and now I, whose life was saved so that I could learn of the crime that saved my life, and even if I commit no other offense, this will suffice to kill me. Amid the shadows of the cave Jesus got to his feet, as if to flee, but after a few faltering steps his legs gave way, and he put his hands to his eyes to catch his tears, poor boy, writhing in the dust, tormented by a crime he never committed, condemned to remorse for the rest of his life. This flood of bitter tears will leave its mark in Jesus' eyes forever, a dull glimmer of sadness and despair, always as if he has just stopped crying. Time passed, the sun outside began to set, the earth's shadows grew, the prelude to the great shadow that descends at dusk. The darkness penetrated the cave, where shadows were already threatening to extinguish the lamp's tiny flame, the oil is clearly running out, this is what it will be like when the sun finally disappears, when men say to one another, We are losing our sight, unaware that their eyes are no longer of any use to them.

Jesus is now asleep, yielding to the merciful exhaustion of recent days, his father's horrible death, the inherited nightmare, his resigned mother, and then the journey to Jerusalem, the daunting vision of the Temple, the discouraging words uttered by the scribe, the descent to Bethlehem, the fateful encounter with Salome, who appeared from the depths of time to reveal the circumstances of his birth, therefore it is not surprising that his weary body should have overcome his spirit, he appears to be resting now, but his spirit stirs, in his dream it rouses his body so that they may go together to Bethlehem and there, in the middle of the square, confess their heinous crime. Through the physical instrument of voice his spirit declares, I am he who brought death to your children, judge me, condemn this body I bring before you, abuse and torture it, for only by mortifying the flesh can we hope to gain absolution and the rewards of the spirit. In his dream Jesus sees the mothers of Bethlehem bearing tiny bodies, only one of the infants is alive, and its mother is the woman who spoke to Jesus with a child in her arms, it is she who replies, Unless you can restore their lives, be silent, for who needs words in the presence of death. In self-abasement his soul shrinks into itself like a tunic folded three times, surrendering his defenseless body to the mercy of the mothers of Bethlehem, but his body is spared, because just as the woman with the child is about to tell him, You're not to blame, you may go, a flash of lightning fills the cave and wakes him with a start. Where am I, was his first thought. Struggling to his feet from the dusty ground, tears in his eyes, he saw a giant of a man towering over him with head aflame, then he realized his mistake, the man held a torch in his right hand, the fire almost touched the ceiling of the cave. But the head was so huge, it could have been the head of Goliath, there was nothing hostile about the face, however, with its gratified expression of one who has been searching and found what he wanted. Jesus got to his feet and backed against a wall of the cave, to get a better look at the giant, who was not that big after all, perhaps a span taller than the tallest man of Nazareth. Such optical illusions, without which there can be no prodigies or miracles, were discovered ages ago, and the only reason Goliath did not become a basketball player is that he was born before his time. And who are you, the man asked. Resting his torch on a jutting rock, he stood the two sticks he was carrying against the wall, one with great knots smoothed by constant use, the other still covered with bark and recently cut from a tree. Then, seating himself on the largest stone, he began pulling the vast mantle he wore down over his shoulders. I am Jesus of Nazareth, the boy replied. What are you doing here if you're from Nazareth. Although I'm from Nazareth, I was born in this cave, and I came to see the place where I was born. Where you were born, my lad, was in your mother's belly, and you'll never be able to crawl back in there. Unaccustomed to such language, Jesus blushed at the man's words and could think of nothing to say. Did you run away from home, the man asked. As if searching in his heart to see if his departure could be described as running away, the boy hesitated before answering, Yes. Did you quarrel with your parents. My father's dead. Oh, was all the man said, but Jesus had the strange feeling that the man already knew this, and everything, and all that had been said and all that remained to be said. You didn't answer my question, the man insisted, What question, Did you quarrel with your parents, It's not your business. Don't be rude to me, boy, unless you want a good thrashing, not even God will hear your cries for help in this place. God is eye, ear, and tongue, He sees and hears everything, and it's only because He chooses not to that He doesn't speak everything. What does a boy your age know about God. What I learned in the synagogue. You never heard anyone in the synagogue say that God is eye, ear, and tongue. I myself decided that if this were not so, then God would not be God. And why do you think God has an eye and an ear and not two eyes and two ears like the rest of us. So that one eye cannot deceive the other, or one ear the other, and as for the tongue, there is no problem, because we only have one tongue. The tongue of man is also two-sided, serving both truth and falsehood. God cannot lie. Who's to prevent Him. God Himself, otherwise He'd deny Himself. Have you ever seen Him, Seen who, Seen God, Some have seen Him and announced His coming. The man stared at the boy in silence, as if looking for some familiar trait, then said, True, some believed they've seen Him. He paused, then continued with a mischievous smile, You still haven't answered my question. What question. Did you quarrel with your parents. I left home because I wanted to see the world. You've mastered the art of lying, my boy, but I know who you are, you were born to a simple carpenter named Joseph and a wool carder named Mary. How do you know. I found out one day and have remembered ever since. I don't understand. I'm a shepherd and have spent nearly all my life breeding and caring for my sheep and goats, and I happened to be in these parts when the soldiers came to slaughter the children of Bethlehem, so as you can see, I've known you since the day you were born. Jesus looked at the man nervously and asked, What is your name. My sheep don't know me by a name. But I am not one of your sheep. Who knows. Tell me what you're called. If you insist on giving me a name, call me Pastor, that will be enough to summon me if you ever need me. Will you take me with you to help with the flock. I was waiting for you to ask. Well then. Yes, you may join the flock. The man stood, lifted his torch, and went outside. Jesus followed.

It was darkest night, and the moon had still not risen. Gathered near the entrance to the cave, sheep and goats waited in silence, except for the faint jingling of bells from time to time. Patiently they awaited the outcome of the conversation between the shepherd and his latest helpmate. The man raised the torch, revealing the black heads of the goats and the white snouts of the sheep, some sheep scrawny with sparse hair, others plump with woolly coats, and he told him, This is my flock, take care not to lose even one of these animals. Jesus and the shepherd sat at the entrance to the cave beneath the flickering light of the torch and ate cheese and stale bread from their packs. Then the shepherd went inside and returned with the new stick, the one still covered with bark. He lit a fire and, deftly turning the wood in the flames, slowly scorched the bark until it peeled off in long strips, and then he smoothed down the knots. Allowing the stick to cool, he plunged it back into the fire, but turned it briskly this time so the wood would not burn, darkening and strengthening the surface until it took on the appearance of seasoned wood. Handing the stick to Jesus when it was ready, he said, Here's your shepherd's crook, strong and straight and as good as a third arm. Jesus, although his hands were hardly delicate, dropped the stick with a howl. How could the shepherd hold anything so hot, he asked himself. When the moon finally appeared, they went into the cave to get some sleep. A few sheep and goats followed and lay down beside them. At first light, the shepherd shook Jesus, Time to get up, the flock has to be fed, from now on you'll take them out to pasture, as important a job as you're ever likely to be entrusted with. Walking as fast as their tiny steps allowed, the flock moved on, the shepherd in front, his helpmate at the rear. The cool, transparent dawn seemed to be in no hurry for the sun, envious of that splendor heralding a world reborn. Hours later, an old woman, going slowly with the aid of a stick, emerged from the houses of Bethlehem and entered the cave. She was not surprised that Jesus was no longer there, besides they would have had nothing more to say to each other. Amid the eternal shadows inside the cave a tiny flame continued to shine, because the shepherd had filled the lamp with oil.

Four years from now, Jesus will meet God. This unexpected revelation, which is probably premature according to the rules of effective narration referred to above, is intended simply to prepare the reader for some everyday scenes from pastoral life which will add little of substance to the main thread of our story, thus excusing anyone who might be tempted to jump ahead. Nevertheless, four years is four years, especially at an age when there are so many physical and mental changes in a youth, when his body grows so fast, the first signs of a beard, a swarthy complexion becoming even darker, the voice turning as deep and harsh as a stone rolling down a mountain slope, and that faraway look, as if he is daydreaming, always reprehensible but especially when one has a duty to be vigilant, like sentinels in barracks, castles, and encampments or, lest we stray from our story, like this shepherd boy who has been warned to keep a watchful eye on his master's goats and sheep. Although we do not really know who that master is. Tending sheep at this time and in these parts is work for a servant or slave, who under pain of punishment must give a regular account of milk, cheese, and wool, not to mention the number of animals, which should always be on the increase so that neighbors can see that the eyes of the Lord are looking down with favor on the pious owner of such abundant possessions, and if the owner wishes to conform to the rules of this world, he must have greater trust in the Lord than in the genetic strength of the mating rams of his flock. Yet how strange that Pastor, as he asked to be called, does not seem to have any master over him, for during the next four years no one will come to the desert to collect the wool, milk, or cheese, nor will Pastor ever leave the flock to give account of his duties. All would be well if Pastor were the owner of these goats and sheep. Though it is hard to believe that any owner would allow such an incredible amount of wool to be lost, shearing his sheep only to prevent them from suffocating from the heat, or would use the milk, if at all, only to make the day's supply of cheese, then barter the rest for figs, dates, and bread, or, mystery of mysteries, would never sell lambs and kids from his flock, not even during Passover, when they are much in demand and fetch such high prices. Little wonder, therefore, that the flock continues to grow bigger, as if obeying, with the persistence and enthusiasm of those who feel their life span is guaranteed, that famous mandate given by the Lord, who may have lacked confidence in the efficacy of sweet natural instinct, Go forth and multiply. In this unusual and wayward flock the animals tend to die of old age, but Pastor himself serenely lends a hand by killing those who can no longer keep up with the others because of disease or age. Jesus, the first time this occurred after he started working for Pastor, protested at such cruelty, but the shepherd said, Either I kill them as I've always done, or I leave them to die alone in this wilderness, or I hold up the flock, wait for the old and sick to die, and risk letting the healthy animals starve to death for lack of pasture. So tell me what you would do if you were in my shoes and had power of life and death over your flock. Jesus did not know what to say and changed the subject by asking, Since you don't sell the wool, have more milk and cheese than we need in order to live, and never take the lambs and kids to market, why do you allow this flock to become bigger and bigger, one of these days your goats and sheep will cover every hill in sight and there will be no land left for pasture. Pastor told him, The flock was here and somebody had to look after the animals and protect them from thieves, and that person happened to be me. What do you mean by here. Here, there, everywhere. Are you asking me to believe that this flock has always been here. More or less. Did you buy the first sheep and goat, No, Who then. I simply found them, I don't know if anyone bought them, there was already a flock when I came here. Were they given to you. No one gave them to me, I found them, and they found me. So you are the owner. No, I'm not the owner, nothing in this world belongs to me. For everything belongs to the Lord, as you know, True, How long have you been a shepherd. I was a shepherd before you were born, How many years, Difficult to say, perhaps if we multiplied your age by fifty. Only the patriarchs before the great flood lived that long, and no one nowadays can hope to reach their age. No need to tell me. Yet if you insist you've lived that long, don't expect me to believe you're human. I don't. Now, if Jesus, who was as skilled in the art of interrogation as any disciple of Socrates, had asked, What are you, then, if you are not a man, Pastor would most probably have answered, An angel, but don't tell anyone. This often happens, we refrain from asking a question because we are unprepared or simply too afraid to hear the answer. And when finally we summon the courage to ask, no answer is forthcoming, just as Jesus one day will refuse to answer when asked, What is truth. A question that remains unanswered to this day.

Jesus knows without having to ask that his mysterious companion, whatever he may be, is not an angel of the Lord, because the angels of the Lord forever sing His glory, while men praise Him only out of obligation and on prescribed occasions, although it is worth pointing out that angels have greater reason for singing Glory since they live in intimacy, as it were, with the Lord in His heavenly kingdom. What surprised Jesus from the beginning was that when they left the cave at first light, Pastor, unlike him, did not praise the Lord with all the usual blessings, such as having restored man's soul and having endowed the cock with intelligence, and when obliged to step behind a rock to relieve himself, Pastor did not thank the Lord for the providential orifices and vessels that help the human body function and without which we would be in a sorry state. Pastor looked at heaven and earth as one does on getting out of bed, he muttered something about the fine day ahead, and putting two fingers to his lips, gave a shrill whistle which brought the entire flock to its feet as one. And that was all. Jesus thought he might have forgotten, always possible when one's mind is on other things, such as how to teach this boy, accustomed to the easy life of a carpenter, the rudiments of tending sheep and goats. Now, as we know, in a normal situation among ordinary people, Jesus would not have had to wait long to discover the extent of his master's piety, since Jews in those days gave thanks to the Lord some thirty times a day and on the slightest pretext, as indeed we have often seen in this gospel. But the day passed, and Pastor showed no sign of offering prayers of thanksgiving, dusk fell, and they settled down to sleep out in the open, and not even the majesty of God's sky above touched the shepherd's heart or brought so much as a word of praise or gratitude to his lips, after all, it could have been raining and it was not, a clear sign that the Lord was watching over His creatures. Next morning, after they had eaten and his master was preparing to inspect the flock to make sure that they were all there and that some restless goat had not decided to wander off, Jesus announced in a firm voice, I am leaving. Pastor stopped, looked at him without any change of expression, and said, Have a good journey, but you don't need to tell me, you're not my slave and there is no legal contract between us, you can leave whenever you like. But don't you want to know why I'm leaving. I'm not all that curious. Well, I'll tell you just the same, I'm leaving because I do not want to work with a man who doesn't perform his obligations to the Lord. What obligations. The simplest obligations, such as offering up prayers of thanksgiving. Pastor said nothing, his eyes half smiling, then finally he spoke, I'm not a Jew and therefore have no such obligations to perform. Deeply shocked, Jesus backed away. That the land of Israel was swarming with foreigners and worshipers of false gods he knew all too well, but this was the first time he had actually slept beside such a person and shared his bread and milk. As if holding a sword and shield before him, he exclaimed, The Lord alone is God. Pastor's smile faded and his mouth became twisted and grim, Certainly if God exists, He must be only one, but it would be better if He were two, then there would be a god for the wolf and one for the sheep, a god for the victim and one for the assassin, a god for the condemned man and one for the executioner. God is one, whole, and indivisible, exclaimed Jesus, almost weeping with pious indignation, whereupon Pastor retorted, I don't know how God can live, but he got no further, because Jesus, with all the authority of a teacher in the synagogue, interrupted him, God does not live, God exists. These fine distinctions escape me, but I'll tell you this, I wouldn't like to be a god who guides the dagger in the hand of the assassin while he offers the throat that is about to be cut. You offend God with these irreverent thoughts. You overestimate my importance. Remember, God never sleeps, and one day He will punish you. Just as well He doesn't sleep, so He can avoid the nightmares of remorse. Why speak to me of the nightmares of remorse. Because we're discussing your god. And which god do you serve. Like my sheep, I have no god. But sheep, at least, produce lambs for the altars of the Lord. And I can assure you that their mothers would howl like wolves if they knew. Jesus turned pale and could think of no reply.

All was silent as the flock gathered around them attentively. The sun had already risen, its light casting a crimson glow on the fleecy coats of the sheep and the horns of the rams. Jesus said, I'm off, but didn't move. Pastor waited, leaning on his crook, as composed as if he had all the time in the world. At last Jesus took a few steps, opening a path through the sheep, then suddenly stopped and asked, What do you know about remorse and nightmares. That you are your father's heir. These words were too much for Jesus, his legs buckled, and the pack slipped from his shoulder, and either by chance or necessity his father's sandals fell out, and he could hear the Pharisee's bowl shatter into pieces. Jesus began weeping like a lost child, but Pastor made no attempt to comfort him, he merely said from where he was standing, Do not forget that I've known about you since the day you were born, and now you had better decide whether you're going or staying. First tell me who you are. The time has not yet come for you to know. And when will I know. If you stay, you'll regret not having left, and if you leave, you'll regret not having stayed. But if I leave, I will never know who you are. You're wrong, your hour will come, and when it does, I will be there to tell you, and that's enough conversation for now, the flock can't stand here all day waiting for you to make up your mind. Jesus gathered up the broken pieces of the bowl, looking at them as if he couldn't bear to part with them, but for no good reason, yesterday at this hour he had not yet met the Pharisee, besides, what had happened was only to be expected, earthenware breaks so easily. He scattered the pieces on the ground like sowing seeds, and Pastor said, You will have another bowl, but the next won't break while you are alive. Jesus didn't hear him, he held Joseph's sandals in his hand and was trying to decide if he should wear them. Not so long ago they would have been much too big for him, but time, as we know, can be deceptive, Jesus felt as if he had been carrying his father's sandals in his pack for ages, he would have been very surprised to find they were still too big for him. He slipped them on and, without knowing why, packed his own. Pastor said, Once feet have grown, they don't shrink again, and you will have no sons to inherit your tunic, mantle, and sandals, but Jesus did not discard them, their weight helped keep the almost empty pack on his shoulders. There was no need to give Pastor the answer he wanted, Jesus took his place behind the flock, his heart divided between a vague sense of terror, as if his soul were in peril, and another, even vaguer sense of somber fascination. I must find out who you are, murmured Jesus, choking on the dust raised by the flock as he chased after a sheep that lagged behind, and this, he believed, was the reason he had decided to stay with the mysterious shepherd.

That was the first day. No more was said about matters of faith and blasphemy, about life, death, and inheritance, but Jesus, who had started to watch Pastor, his every attitude and gesture, noticed that each time the shepherd offered up prayers of thanksgiving to the Lord, he got down and placed the palms of his hands on the ground, lowering his head and shutting his eyes, without uttering a word. One day, when he was still a little boy, Jesus had heard some elderly travelers who were passing through Nazareth relate that deep in the earth were vast caverns where one could find cities, fields, rivers, forests, and deserts just like those on the surface of the world, and that this underworld, a perfect image and likeness of the one we live in, was created by the devil after God threw him down from the heavens as punishment for his rebellion. Since God had initially befriended the devil and looked on him with favor, causing the angels to comment that there had never been so close a friendship in the universe, the devil witnessed the birth of Adam and Eve. Having learned how it was done, he repeated the process in his underworld and created a man and woman for himself, with the one difference that, unlike God, he forbade them nothing, which explains why there has never been such a thing as original sin in the devil's world. One of the old men even dared suggest, And because there was no original sin, there was no other kind of sin either. After the men were sent on their way with the help of some persuasive stones thrown by outraged Nazirites, who soon realized what these irreverent old fools were getting at with their remarks, there was a sudden tremor, nothing serious, a mere sign of confirmation coming from the bowels of the earth, which made young Jesus think, capable as he was, even as a boy, of linking cause and effect. And now, watching Pastor kneel before him with his head lowered and palms resting lightly on the ground to feel every grain of sand, every pebble and rootlet and blade sprouting on the surface, Jesus was reminded of that story. Perhaps this man inhabited the hidden world created by the devil in the image and likeness of the visible world. What is he doing here, Jesus asked himself, but he didn't dare probe any further. When Pastor eventually got to his feet, Jesus asked him, What are you doing. I want to be sure the earth is still beneath me. Surely you can tell with your feet. My feet perceive nothing, only my hands can tell me, when you adore your God, you don't raise your feet to Him, you raise your hands, even though you could raise other parts of your body, for example what is between your legs, unless you happen to be a eunuch. Overcome with shame and horror, Jesus turned beet red. Do not offend the God you do not know, he told Pastor severely when he had recovered, but Pastor asked, Who created your body. It was God, of course. Just as it is now, Yes, And did the devil play any part in creating your body. None whatsoever, man's body is God's creation. So all the parts of your body are equally worthy in the eyes of God, Obviously, So God isn't likely to disown what you have between your legs, for example. No, I suppose not, but then the Lord created Adam, yet expelled him from Paradise even though he was His creation. Just give me a straight answer, boy, and stop talking like a teacher in the synagogue. You're trying to make me give the answers you want, but I can tell you, if you wish, all the cases in which man is forbidden by the Lord, under pain of death, to expose his own or another's nakedness, which proves that certain parts of the body are in themselves sinful. No more sinful than the mouth when it utters falsehood and slander, that same mouth with which you praise your Lord before uttering falsehood and after spreading slander. That's enough, I don't want to hear another word. You must hear me out, if only to answer my question. What question. Can God disown what you have between your legs as something not of His making, just answer yes or no. No, He can't, Why not, Because the Lord cannot undo what He has willed. Slowly nodding his head, Pastor said, In other words, your God is the only warden of a prison where the only prisoner is your God. The final echo of these momentous words was still ringing in Jesus' ears when Pastor went on to say in an almost natural voice, You must choose a sheep. What, asked Jesus in bewilderment. I said choose a sheep, unless you prefer a goat. Whatever for. Because you'll need it, unless you really are a eunuch. When Pastor's meaning sank in, the boy was stunned, but worst of all was the surge of vile sensuality once he had suppressed his embarrassment and revulsion. Covering his face with both hands, he said in a hoarse voice, This is the word of the Lord, The man who copulates with an animal will be punished with death and the animal slaughtered, and the Lord also said, Cursed is the man who sins with an animal of any species. Did your Lord say all that. Yes, and now leave me alone, abominable creature, for you are not of God but belong to the devil. Pastor listened impassively, waiting for Jesus' curse to have its full effect, whatever that might be, an apparition, leprosy, the sudden destruction of body and soul. But nothing happened. Wind came playing between the stones, raising a cloud of dust that swept across the wilderness, then nothing, silence, the universe quietly watching men and animals, perhaps waiting to see what meaning they can find, recognize, or construe in those words, it consumes itself in this vigil, the primordial fire is already reduced to ashes, but the response is slow in coming. Then Pastor raised his arms and called out to his flock in a commanding voice, Listen, my sheep, hear what this learned boy has come to teach us, God has forbidden anyone to copulate with you, so fear not, but as for shearing you, neglecting you, slaughtering you, and eating you, all these things are permitted, because for this you were created by God's law and are sustained by His providence. He gave three long whistles and, waving his crook over his head, he cried, Be off, be off with you, whereupon the flock began moving toward the spot where the column of smoke disappeared. Jesus stood watching until the tall figure of Pastor all but vanished from sight and the resigned rumps of the animals merged with the color of the earth. I'm not going with him, Jesus said, but he went. He adjusted the pack on his back, tightened the straps of the sandals that had belonged to his father, and followed the flock at a distance. He caught up with them at nightfall and, emerging from the shadows into the light of the campfire, announced, I'm here.

TOMORROW IS ANOTHER DAY IS A WELL-KNOWN SAYING AND to the point, yet not as simple as it may seem to one who is satisfied with the approximate meaning of words, whether taken separately or together, because everything depends on how a thing is said, which varies according to the mood of the person speaking. When the words are expressed by one whose life is going badly and who hopes for better times, they are not the same as when one utters them as a threat, promising vengeance at some future date. The most extreme case would be one who sighs, Tomorrow is another day, because he is a pessimist by nature and given to expecting the worst. It would not be entirely plausible for Jesus to go around saying this at his age, whatever his meaning or tone of voice, but for us, yes, because like God we know everything about what has been and what is to come, so we can say, mutter, or whisper these words as we watch Jesus go about his tasks as a shepherd boy, crossing the hills of Judah, or, later, descending into the valley of Jordan. And not just because we are writing about Jesus but because every human being is constantly confronted with good and bad, one thing coming after another, day following day. Since this gospel was never meant to dismiss what others have written about Jesus or to contradict their accounts, and since Jesus is clearly the hero of our story, it would be easy for us to go up to him and predict his future, tell him what a wonderful life lies ahead, the miracles he will perform to provide food and restore health, even one to conquer death, but that would hardly be wise, because young Jesus, notwithstanding his aptitude for religious studies and his knowledge of patriarchs and prophets, enjoys the healthy skepticism one associates with youth, so he would send us away with scorn. Yes, he will change his mind when he meets God, but it is much too soon for that great encounter, and before then Jesus will have to go up and down many a mountain slope, milk many a goat and sheep, help make cheese, and barter wares in the villages. He will also kill animals that are diseased or have outlived their usefulness, and he will mourn their loss. But fret not, all you sensitive souls, he will never engage in the horrid vice suggested by Pastor, of coupling with a goat or sheep or both to relieve and satisfy the corrupt flesh that houses his pure soul. This is neither the time nor the place, however, to ponder how often the soul, in order to be able to boast of a clean body, has burdened itself with sadness, envy, and impurity.

Although their initial exchanges on ethical and theological matters remained unresolved, Pastor and Jesus got along well enough with each other, the shepherd patiently teaching him how to tend the flock, the boy listening intently, as if it were a matter of life and death. Jesus learned how to send his crook whirling through the air to land on the rump of an animal that in a moment of distraction or daring had strayed from the flock, but his apprenticeship was painful, because one day, while he was still struggling to master the technique, he threw the crook too low and accidentally hit the tender neck of a newborn kid, with such force that he killed the poor thing outright. Such accidents can happen to anyone, even an experienced and skillful shepherd, but Jesus, who was already burdened with so many sorrows, stiffened with horror as he lifted the little kid, still warm, into his arms. There was nothing to be done. Even the mother goat, after sniffing her child for a moment, moved away and resumed grazing, pawing at tufts of grass, which she pulled at with quick movements of her head, recalling the familiar refrain, A bleating goat doesn't chew much grass, which is another way of saying, You can't cry and eat at the same time. Pastor came to see what happened, Bad luck, no need for you to feel guilty. But I killed the poor little animal, Jesus said mournfully. So you did, but if he'd been an ugly, smelly old billy goat you wouldn't have felt much pity, put him on the ground and let me deal with this while you go attend to that ewe over there that looks as if she's about to give birth. What will you do with the kid. Skin it, of course, unless you expect me to work a miracle and bring it back to life. I swear I'll never touch that meat. Eating the animal we kill is our only way of showing respect, what is wrong is to eat what others have been forced to kill. I refuse to eat it. Please yourself, there will be all the more for me. Pastor drew a knife from his belt, looked at Jesus, and said, This is something else you'll have to learn sooner or later, to study the entrails of the animals created to serve and feed us. Jesus looked away and turned to go, but Pastor, knife in hand, went on to say, Slaves exist to serve us, perhaps we should open them up to see if they carry slaves inside, or open up a monarch to see if he has another monarch in his belly, I'll bet if we met the devil and he allowed us to open him up, we might be surprised to find God jumping out. Pastor still liked to provoke Jesus with these outrageous remarks. Jesus had gradually learned that the best way to deal with this was ignore it and say nothing. For Pastor might have gone even further, suggesting that on opening up God one might find the devil inside. Jesus went off in search of the ewe about to give birth, here at least there were no surprises awaiting him, a lamb like any other would appear, in the image and likeness of its mother, who in turn was identical to her sisters, for the one thing we can expect from these creatures is a smooth continuity of the species. The sheep had already given birth. The newborn lamb, lying on the ground, seemed to be all legs as its mother tried to help it to its feet, gently nudging with her nose, but the poor, dazed creature could only cock its head, as if trying to find the best angle to take in this strange new world. Jesus helped hold it steady on its feet, his hands sticky with the afterbirth, but he did not mind, one gets used to such things when one is in constant contact with animals, and this lamb arrived at the right moment, so pretty with its curly coat and its pink little mouth already searching avidly for milk from those teats, which it is seeing for the first time and could never have imagined from inside its mother's womb. No one has any grounds for complaining about God, when we discover so many useful things from the moment we are born.

Within sight, Pastor stretches the kid's pelt on a wooden frame in the form of a star, the skinned carcass already in his pack, wrapped in cloth. He will salt it later, when the flock settles down for the night, except for the piece Pastor intends to have for his supper, since Jesus is adamant he will not touch the meat of an animal he killed. These scruples on the part of Jesus place him in conflict with the religion he observes and the traditions he respects, including the slaughter of all those other innocent animals sacrificed daily on the altars of the Lord, especially in Jerusalem, where the victims are counted in hecatombs. Given the time and place, Jesus' attitude does seems odd, but perhaps it is really a question of vulnerability, for we must not forget Joseph's tragic death and Jesus' recent discovery of the appalling massacre that took place in Bethlehem almost fifteen years ago, enough to disturb any young mind, not to mention those terrifying nightmares, which we have not mentioned lately, although they still trouble him and refuse to go away. When he can no longer bear the thought that Joseph is coming to kill him, his cries wake the flock in the middle of the night, and Pastor gives him a gentle shake, What's this, what's going on. Delivered from his nightmare, Jesus falls into the shepherd's arms, as if Pastor were his unfortunate father. Soon after joining Pastor, Jesus had confided in him that he had nightmares, though not giving the reason, but Pastor said, Save your breath, I know everything, even what you're hiding from me. This was about the time Jesus rebuked Pastor for his lack of faith and his wickedness, particularly, if you'll forgive my laboring the point, in sexual matters. But Jesus realized that he had no one else in the world, besides the family he had abandoned and forgotten, but not the mother who gave him life, although he often wished she hadn't, and, after his mother, only his sister Lisa, which he couldn't explain, but then memory is like that, it has its own reasons. So gradually Jesus began to enjoy Pastor's company, and it is easy to imagine his relief at not having to live alone with his remorse, at having someone at his side who understood, who would not pretend to forgive what could not be forgiven, someone who would treat him with both kindness and severity in accordance with his innocence and his guilt. We felt this needed explaining, so that the reader would find it easier to understand and accept why Jesus, so different in character and outlook from his ill-bred master, decided to stay with him until the prophesied encounter with God, which promises to be momentous, because God is not likely to appear to a simple mortal without good reason.

But before that, the circumstances and coincidences which we have discussed at length dictate that Jesus meet his mother and some of his brothers in Jerusalem during

Passover, which he thought he would be celebrating for the first time without his family. That Jesus wanted to celebrate Passover in Jerusalem might have angered Pastor, for they were in the hills and the flock needed all their attention. Besides, Pastor was not a Jew and had no other god to honor, so he could well have refused Jesus permission, telling him, Oh no, you don't, you'll stay right here, I'm the one who gives the orders, and there's work to be done. Yet none of this happened, Pastor simply asked, Will you be coming back, but from the tone of his voice he seemed certain that Jesus would return, and indeed, the boy replied without a moment's hesitation, although he was surprised that the words came out so quickly, Yes, I'll be back. Then pick yourself a clean lamb, Jesus, and take it to be sacrificed, since you Jews attach so much importance to such practices. Pastor was putting him to the test, to see if the boy could lead to its death a lamb from the flock they had worked so hard to maintain and protect. No one warned Jesus, no tiny, invisible angel whispered in his ear, Be careful, it's a trap, don't trust him, this man is capable of anything. His gentle nature provided him with a good answer, or perhaps it was the memory of the dead kid and the newborn lamb. I want no lamb from this flock, he said. Why not. I cannot lead to its death an animal that I myself raised. Please yourself, but I hope you realize that you'll have to get a lamb from some other flock. I suppose so, since lambs don't fall from heaven. When are you thinking of leaving, Early tomorrow morning, And you'll be coming back, Yes, I'll be back. They said no more on the subject, although it was difficult to see how Jesus would find enough money to buy a paschal lamb when he could barely scrape together a living. One may presume that, not given to vices that cost money, he still had the few coins given him by the Pharisee almost a year ago, but they didn't amount to much, and, as we said, at this time of the year the prices of livestock in general and of lambs especially rise out of all proportion, so that one really has to put one's trust in God. Despite all the misfortunes that have befallen him, one is tempted to say that a lucky star guides this boy, but it would be feebleminded of this or any other evangelist to believe that celestial bodies so remote from our planet could have any appreciable influence on a human life, however much the devout Magi may have invoked, studied, and compared the stars. For, if what we are told is true, they must have traveled here some years ago, only to see what they saw and to go away again. What we are simply trying to say in this long-winded passage is that our Jesus must somehow find a way to present himself worthily in the Temple with a little lamb, thus fulfilling what is expected of him. For he has proved himself a good Jew even in difficult situations, such as those tense exchanges with Pastor.

About this time the flock was enjoying the rich pastures of the valley of Aijalon, situated between the cities of Gezer and Emmaus. In Emmaus, Jesus tried to earn enough money to buy the much-needed lamb, but he soon saw that after a year of tending sheep and goats he no longer had the aptitude for any other kind of work, not even for carpentry, in which, from lack of practice, he had made no progress. So he took the road that leads up from Emmaus to Jerusalem, wondering what he should do, he had no money to buy the lamb, stealing was out of the question, and it would be more miracle than luck if he found a stray lamb on the road. There are plenty of lambs in sight, some with ropes around their necks following their owners, others fortunate enough to be carried in loving arms. Imagining themselves on an outing, these innocent creatures are excited and nervous, they are curious about everything, and because they cannot ask questions, they use their eyes in the hope of making sense of a world made of words. Jesus sat on a stone by the roadside to think of a solution to this material problem that prevented him from carrying out his spiritual duty, if only another Pharisee, or even the same one, who probably gives alms daily, were suddenly to appear and ask him, Are you in need of a lamb, just as the man had previously asked him, Are you hungry. On that first occasion Jesus did not have to beg in order to receive, but now, with little hope of being given anything, he will have to beg. He already has his hand out, a gesture so eloquent that it dispenses with all explanations, and so expressive that we nearly always avert our eyes rather than be confronted with an unsightly wound or distressing obscenity. A few coins were dropped into Jesus' palm by less distracted travelers, but so few that at this rate the road from Emmaus will never bring him to the gates of Jerusalem. When he adds up what money he already has and what he just collected, there isn't enough to buy even half a lamb, and the Lord, as everyone knows, does not accept an animal on His altars unless it is perfect and whole, He refuses those that are blind, crippled, mutilated, diseased, or contaminated. You can imagine the scandal in the Temple if we were to present ourselves at the sacrificial altar with the hindquarters only, or, if by any misfortune the testicles have been crushed, broken, or cut, that too would exclude it. No one asks this boy why he needs money, but wait, an elderly man with a long white beard now approaches Jesus while his family pauses in the middle of the road, respectfully waiting for the patriarch to rejoin them. Jesus thought he would receive another coin, but he was mistaken. The old man asked, Who are you, and the boy stood up to answer, I am Jesus of Nazareth. Have you no family. Yes, I have. Then why are you not with them. I came to work as a shepherd in Judaea, a deceitful way of telling the truth, or putting the truth at the service of a lie. The old man looked at him quizzically and asked, Why are you begging for alms if you have a trade. I earn my keep but cannot save enough money to buy a lamb for Passover. So that is why you beg. Yes, whereupon the patriarch ordered one of the men in his group, Give this boy a lamb, we can buy another when we get to the Temple. There were six lambs tied to the same rope, the man untied the last of them and handed it to the old man, who told Jesus, Here's your lamb so that you too may offer sacrifice to the Lord this Passover, and without waiting to be thanked, he returned to his family, who received him with smiles and admiration. Before Jesus could thank the old man, he was gone, then suddenly the road was mysteriously empty, between one bend and the next there was only Jesus and the lamb, who had finally found each other on the road from Emmaus thanks to the generosity of an elderly Jew. Jesus clutched the end of the cord, the animal looked up at his new master and started to bleat me-e-e-e in that nervous, tremulous way of young lambs before they are sacrificed to placate the gods. This bleating, which Jesus had heard thousands of times since becoming a shepherd's helpmate, touched his heart, and he felt as if his limbs were dissolving with pity. Here he was, with power as never before over the life of another creature, this immaculate white lamb that had no will and no desire, its trusting little face looking up at him anxiously, its pink tongue showing each time it bleated, and pink flesh beneath its soft hairs, and pink inside its ears, and pink nails on its feet, just as humans have, but nails that would never harden and be called hooves. Jesus stroked the lamb's head, it responded by stretching its neck and rubbing its moist nose against the palm of his hand, sending a shiver up his spine. The spell broke as suddenly as it had begun. At the end of the road, from the direction of Emmaus, other pilgrims appeared in a swarm of fluttering tunics, of packs and staffs, with more lambs and prayers of thanksgiving to the Lord. Jesus lifted his lamb into his arms and started walking.

He had not been back to Jerusalem since that distant day he came out of necessity to discover the burden of sorrow and remorse in life, whether shared like an inheritance or kept entirely to oneself like death. The crowd filling the streets resembled a muddy brown river about to flood the concourse before the steps of the Temple. Holding the lamb in his arms, Jesus watched the people file past, some coming, some going, some carrying animals to be sacrificed, some returning without them, looking joyful and exclaiming, Alleluia, Hosanna, Amen, or saying none of these things, feeling it was inappropriate to walk around shouting Hallelujah or Hip hip hurrah, because there is really not much difference between the two expressions, we use them enthusiastically until with the passage of time and by dint of repetition we finally ask ourselves, What does it mean, only to find there is no answer. The endless column of smoke spiraling above the Temple indicated for miles around that all who had come to offer sacrifices were direct and legitimate descendants of Abel, that son of Adam and Eve who in his day offered to the Lord the firstborn of his flock and their fat, which were favorably received, while his brother Cain, who had nothing to offer but the simple fruits of nature, saw that the Lord for some reason did not so much as look at him. If this was Cain's motive for killing Abel, then we can put our minds at rest, the worshipers here are not likely to kill one another, they all offer the same sacrifice, and how the fat spits and the carcasses sizzle as God in the sublime heavens inhales the odors of all this carnage with satisfaction. Jesus pressed his lamb to his breast, unable to fathom why God could not be appeased with a cup of milk poured over His altar, that sap of life which passes from one being to another, or with a handful of wheat, the basic substance of immortal bread. Soon he will have to part with the old man's generous gift, his for such a short time, the poor little lamb will not live to see the sun set this day, it is time to mount the stairs of the Temple, to deliver it to the knife and sacrificial fire, as if it were no longer worthy of existence or being punished by the eternal guardian of myths and fables for having drunk from the waters of life. Then Jesus decided, in defiance of the law of the synagogue and the word of God, that this lamb would not die, that what he had received to deliver to the altar would continue to live and that he would leave Jerusalem a greater sinner than when he arrived. As if his previous offenses were not enough, he was now committing this one too, but the day will come when he has to pay for all his sins, because God never forgets. The fear of punishment made him hesitate for a moment, but suddenly, in his mind's eye, he saw a horrifying vision, a vast sea of blood, the blood of the countless lambs and other animals sacrificed since the creation of mankind, for that is why men have been put on this earth, to adore and to offer sacrifice. And he saw the steps of the Temple awash with red, as blood came streaming down them, and he saw himself standing in a pool of blood and raising the lifeless body of his beheaded lamb to heaven. Deep in thought, Jesus stood inside a sphere of silence, but then the sphere shattered, and once more he was plunged into the clamor of invocations and blessings, pleas, cries, chants, and the pitiful bleating of lambs, until all was silenced in an instant by three low blasts from the shofar, the long, spiral horn of a ram made into a trumpet. Covering the lamb with his pack, Jesus ran from the concourse and disappeared into a labyrinth of narrow alleyways without worrying where he might end up. When he finally stopped for breath, he was on the outskirts, having left the city by the northern gate, known as that of Ramah, the same gate by which he had entered when he arrived from Nazareth. He sat beneath an olive tree by the side of the road and took the lamb out of his pack, no one would have found it strange to see him sitting there, they would simply have thought, He has traveled a long way and is recovering his strength before taking his lamb to the Temple, how endearing, we do not know whether the person thinking this means the lamb or

Jesus. We find both of them endearing, but if we had to make a choice, the prize would almost certainly go to the lamb, on the condition that it does not grow any bigger. Jesus lies on his back, holding the end of the cord to prevent the lamb from escaping, an unnecessary precaution, the poor animal has no strength, not only because of its tender age but also because of all the excitement, the constant motion back and forth, not to mention the meager food it was given this morning, for it is considered neither fitting nor decent for anyone, lamb or martyr, to die with a full belly.

Stretched out on the ground, Jesus gradually recovers and starts breathing normally again. Between the branches of the olive tree, as it sways gently in the wind, he can see the sky, the sun's rays filtering through gaps in the foliage and playing on his face, it must be about the sixth hour, the sun directly overhead shortens the shadows, and who would ever think that night will come to extinguish this dazzling light. Some people pass on the road, more follow behind, and when Jesus looks again at that group, he receives such a shock that his first impulse is to flee, but how can he, for coming toward him is his own mother accompanied by some of his brothers, the older sons, James, Joseph, and Judas, and Lisa too, but she is a girl and should be mentioned separately rather than listed according to age, which would place her between James and Joseph. They still have not seen him. Jesus goes into the road to meet them, once more carrying his lamb in his arms, but one suspects this is only to make sure his arms are full. First to notice him is James, who waves before turning to their mother in great excitement, and now Mary is looking, they start walking faster, and Jesus too feels obliged to hasten toward them, though he cannot run with the lamb in his arms. We are taking so long over this that the reader might get the impression we do not want them to meet, but this is not so, maternal, fraternal, and filial love should give them wings, yet there are reservations and certain constraints, we know how they separated, we do not know the effect of all those months apart without news of each other. If one keeps walking, one eventually arrives, and there they are, face-to-face, Jesus says, Your blessing, Mother, and his mother says, May the Lord bless you, my son. They embraced, then it was his brothers' turn, then Lisa's, followed by an awkward silence, all of them at a loss for words, Mary was not going to say to her son, Such a surprise, what on earth are you doing here, nor Jesus to his mother, I never expected to find you here, what brings you to the city, the lamb in his arms and the one they have brought speak for themselves, this is the Passover of the Lord, the difference being that one lamb is going to die and the other has been saved. We waited and waited to hear from you, Mary said at length, bursting into tears. Her eldest son stands before her, so tall, so grown-up, with the beginnings of a beard and the weather-beaten complexion of one who has spent his days in the open, exposed to the sun, wind, and dust of the desert. Don't cry, Mother, I have work. I'm a shepherd now. A shepherd. Yes, a shepherd. But I was hoping you'd follow your father and take up the trade he taught you. Well, as things turned out, I became a shepherd, and that's what I am. When are you coming home. I don't know, one day, I suppose. At least accompany your mother and brothers to the Temple. Mother, I'm not going to the Temple. Why not, you have your lamb there. This lamb isn't going to the Temple either. Is there something wrong with it. No, nothing, but he will die a natural death when his time comes. My son, I don't understand. You don't have to understand, if I save this lamb, it's so that someone may save me. Then why not come with your family. I was leaving. Where to, Back to the flock where I belong, Where did you leave it, At present it's in the valley of Aijalon, Where is this valley of Aijalon, On the other side, What

577

other side, On the other side of Bethlehem. Mary stepped back and turned quite pale, how she has aged although barely thirty, Why do you mention Bethlehem, she asked. That's where I met the shepherd who is my master. Who is this man, and before Jesus had time to reply, she said to the others, You go on ahead and wait for me at the entrance. Then taking Jesus by the hand, she led him to the side of the road, Who is this man, she asked a second time. I don't know, Jesus answered. Doesn't he have a name. If he has, he's never told me, I call him Pastor and that's all. What does he look like, He's big, And where did you meet him, In the cave where I was born, Who took you there, A slave named Salome, who told me she helped deliver me, And this man, What about him, What did he say to you, Nothing you don't already know. Mary slumped to the ground, as if a heavy hand were pushing her, That man is a demon. How do you know, did he tell you so. No, the first time I saw him, he told me he was an angel and asked me not to say a word to anyone. When did you see him. The day your father learned I was pregnant, he appeared at our door disguised as a beggar and told me he was an angel. Did you ever see him again. On the road when your father and I traveled to Bethlehem for the census, then in the cave where you were born, and the night after you left home, he walked into the yard, I thought it was you, and peering through the gap in the door, I saw him uproot the plant in the yard, you remember that bush which grew at the very spot where the bowl of bright earth was buried. What bowl, what earth. You were never told, but the beggar gave it to me before he went away, when he returned the bowl after he had finished eating, there was luminous earth inside. For earth to shine, he must have been an angel. At first I believed so, but the devil too has magical powers. Jesus sat beside his mother and left the lamb to roam at will. Yes, I've learned that when they are both in agreement, it's almost impossible to tell the difference between an angel of the Lord and an angel of Satan, he told her. Stay with us, don't go back to that man, do this for your mother's sake. No, I promised to return, and I will keep my word. People make promises to the devil only in order to deceive him. This man, who I'm certain is no man but an angel or demon, has been haunting me since the day I was born, and I want to know why. Jesus, my son, come to the Temple with your mother and brothers, by taking this lamb to the altar you'll fulfill your obligation and the lamb its destiny, and there you can ask the Lord to deliver you from the powers of Satan and all evil thoughts. This lamb will die only when his time comes. But this is its day for dying. Mother, the lambs you gave birth to must die, but you should not make them die before their time. Lambs are not people, and even less so when those people are sons. When the Lord ordered Abraham to kill his son Isaac, no distinction was made then. My son, I'm a simple woman, I have no answer to give you, but I beseech you, give up these evil thoughts. Mother, thoughts are but passing shadows, neither good nor bad in themselves, actions alone count. Praised be the Lord who blessed this poor, ignorant woman with such a wise son, yet I cannot believe this is the wisdom of God. One can learn also from the devil. And I fear you are in his power. If his power saved this lamb, then something has been gained in the world today. Mary made no attempt to reply. They saw James approaching from the city gate. Mary got to her feet, I find my son only to lose him again, she said, to which Jesus replied, If you haven't already lost him, you will not lose him now. He put his hand into his pack and took out the money he had been given as alms, This is all I have. You've worked all those months for so little. I work to earn my keep. You must be very fond of that master of yours to be satisfied with so little. The Lord is my shepherd. Don't offend God, living with a demon. Who knows, Mother, who knows, he could be an angel serving another God who reigns in another heaven. The Lord said, I am the Lord and you will worship no other god. Amen, responded Jesus. He gathered the lamb into his arms and said, I see James approaching, farewell, Mother, and Mary said, One would think you had more affection for that lamb than for your own family. Right now I do, said Jesus. Choking with grief and anger, Mary turned away and ran to meet her other son. She did not look back.

Outside the city walls, Jesus took a different route across the fields before beginning the long descent into the valley of Aijalon. He stopped at a village and bought food with the money his mother had refused, some bread and figs, milk for himself and the lamb, sheep's milk, and if there was any difference, it wasn't noticeable, it's possible, at least in this case, that one mother is as good as another. Anyone surprised that Jesus spends money on a lamb that by rights should now be dead will be told that the boy once owned two lambs, one was sacrificed and lives on in the glory of the Lord, while this other lamb was rejected because it had a torn ear, Take a look, But there's nothing wrong with its ear, they might say, to which Jesus would reply, Well, then, I'll tear it myself, and lifting the lamb to his back, he went on his way. He caught sight of the flock as the evening light began to wane and the sky became overcast with dark, low clouds. The tension in the air spoke of thunderstorms, and indeed lightning rent the sky just as Jesus saw the flock. But there was no rain, it was one of those dry thunderstorms, all the more frightening because they make you feel so vulnerable, without the shield of rain and wind, as it were, to protect you in the naked battle between a thundering heaven that tears itself apart and an earth that trembles and cowers beneath the blows. A hundred paces from Jesus, another blinding flash split an olive tree, which immediately caught fire and blazed like a torch. A loud burst of thunder shuddered across the sky as if ripping it open from end to end, and the impact knocked Jesus to the ground and left him senseless. Two more bolts struck, here, there, like two decisive words, then little by little the peals of thunder grew remote and finally became a gentle murmur, an intimate dialogue between heaven and earth. The lamb, having survived the storm unharmed and no longer afraid, came up to Jesus and put its mouth to his lips, there was no sniffing, one touch was all that was needed. Jesus opened his eyes, saw the lamb, then the livid sky like a black hand blocking whatever light remained. The olive tree still burned. His bones ached when he tried to move, but at least he was in one piece, if that can be said of a body so fragile that it takes only a clap of thunder to knock it to the ground. He sat up with some effort and reassured himself, more by touch than by sight, that he was neither burned nor paralyzed, none of his bones were broken, and apart from a loud buzzing in his head as insistent as the drone of a trumpet, he was all right. He drew the lamb to him and said, Don't be afraid, He only wanted to show you that you would have been dead by now if that was His will, and to show me that it was not I who saved your life but He. One last rumble of thunder slowly tore the air like a sigh, while below, the white patch of the flock seemed a beckoning oasis.

Struggling to overcome his weakness, Jesus descended the slope. The lamb, kept on its cord simply as a precaution, trotted at his side like a little dog. Behind them, the olive tree continued to burn, and the light it cast in the twilight allowed Jesus to see the tall figure of Pastor rise before him like a ghost, wrapped in a mantle that seemed endless and holding a crook that looked as though it might touch the clouds were he to raise it. Pastor said, I was expecting that thunderstorm. I'm the one who should have expected it, replied Jesus. Where did you get the lamb. I didn't have enough money to buy one for Passover, so I stood by the roadside and begged, then an old man came and gave me this lamb. Why didn't you offer it in sacrifice. I couldn't, I just couldn't bring myself to do it. Pastor smiled, Now I begin to understand, He waited for you, let you come to the flock safely, in order to show His might before my eyes. Jesus did not reply, he had more or less said the same thing to the lamb, but having just arrived, he had no desire to get into a discussion about God's motives and acts. So what will you do with your lamb. Nothing, I brought it here so that it could join the flock. The white lambs all look alike, tomorrow you won't even recognize it among the others. My lamb knows me. The day will come when it forgets you, besides the lamb will soon grow tired of always having to come and look for you, better to brand it or cut off a piece of its ear. Poor little beast. What's the difference, after all they branded you when they cut your foreskin so that people would know to whom you belong. It's not the same thing. It shouldn't be, but it is. As they were speaking, Pastor gathered up wood and was now busily trying to light a fire with a flint. Jesus told him, It would be easier to go and fetch a branch from the burning olive tree, whereupon Pastor replied, One should always leave heavenly fire to burn out by itself. The trunk of the olive tree was now one great ember glowing in the darkness, the wind made sparks fly from it and sent incandescent strips of bark and burning twigs into the air, where they soon went out. The sky remained heavy and strangely oppressive. Pastor and Jesus ate together as usual, which led Pastor to remark ironically, This year you're not partaking of the paschal lamb. Jesus listened and said nothing, but deep inside he felt uneasy, from now on he would face the awkward contradiction between eating lambs and refusing to kill them. So what's to be done, asked Pastor, is the lamb to be branded or not. I couldn't do it, said Jesus. Give it to me, then, and I'll do it. With a firm, quick flick of the knife Pastor removed the tip of one of its ears, then holding it up, he asked, What shall I do with this, bury it or throw it away. Without thinking, Jesus replied, Let me have it, and dropped it into the fire. That's exactly how they disposed of your foreskin, said Pastor. Blood dripped from the lamb's ear in a slow trickle that would soon stop. The smoke from the flames gave off the intoxicating smell of charred young flesh. And so at the end of a long day, in which much time had been wasted on childish and presumptuous gestures of defiance, the Lord finally received His due, perhaps because of those intimidating blasts of thunder and lightning, which surely made enough of an impression to persuade these stubborn shepherds to show obedience. The earth quickly swallowed the last drop of the lamb's blood, for it would have been a great shame to lose the most precious drop of all from this much-disputed sacrifice.

Transformed by time into an ordinary sheep, distinguishable from the others only by the missing tip of one ear, this same animal came to lose itself three years later in the wild country bordering the desert south of Jericho. In so large a flock, one sheep more or less may not seem to make much difference, but we must not forget that this flock is like no other, even its shepherds have little in common with shepherds we have heard about or seen, so we should not be surprised if Pastor, looking from a hilltop, noticed that an animal was missing without having to count them. He called Jesus and told him, Your sheep is missing from the flock, go and look for it, and since Jesus himself did not ask Pastor, How do you know the sheep is mine, we will also refrain from asking Jesus. What matters now is to see where Jesus, who is unfamiliar with this region where few have ventured, will go on the broad horizon. Since they came from the fertile land of Jericho, where they had decided not to stay, preferring to wander at their leisure rather than be trapped among people, a person or sheep intent on getting lost was much more likely to choose a place where the effort of searching for food would not interfere with his precious solitude. By this logic, it was clear that Jesus' sheep had deliberately lagged behind the others and even now was probably grazing on the fertile banks of the Jordan, within sight of Jericho for greater safety. Logic, however, is not everything in this life. Often what you expect, as the most feasible outcome of a sequence of events or else foreseeable for some other reason, comes about in the most unlikely way. If this is so, then our Jesus should seek his lost sheep not in those rich pastures back there but in the scorched and arid desert before him. No one need argue that a sheep would not stray off to die of hunger and thirst, first because no one knows what goes on inside a sheep's head, and secondly because you must keep in mind what we just said about the uncertain nature of the foreseeable. And so we find Jesus already making his way into the desert. Pastor showed no surprise at his decision, he said nothing, only gave a slow and solemn nod of the head, which, oddly, looked also like a gesture of farewell.

The desert in this region is not one of those vast tracks of sand with which we are all familiar, here it is more a great sea of parched, rugged dunes straddling one another and creating an inextricable labyrinth of valleys. A few plants barely survive at the foot of these slopes, plants consisting of only thorns and thistles, which a goat might be able to chew but will tear the sensitive mouth of a sheep at the slightest contact. This desert is far more intimidating than one formed by smooth sands and constantly shifting dunes, here every hill announces the threat lurking on the next hill, and when we arrive there in fear and trembling, at once we feel the same threat at our back. In this desert our cries will raise no echo, all we will hear in reply are the hills themselves calling out, or the voice of the mysterious force hidden there. Jesus, carrying nothing but his crook and pack, entered the desert. He had not gone far, had barely crossed the threshold of this world, when he became aware that his father's old sandals were coming apart under his feet. They had been often patched, but Jesus' mending skills could no longer save what had walked so many roads and pressed so much sweat into the dust. As if obeying a commandment, the last of the fibers disintegrated, the patches came undone, the laces broke in several places, and soon Jesus was practically barefoot. The boy Jesus, as we have grown used to calling him, although being Jewish and eighteen years of age, he is more adult than adolescent, suddenly remembered the sandals he had been carrying all this time in his pack, and he foolishly thought they might still fit. Pastor was right when he warned him, when feet grow, they will not shrink again, and Jesus could scarcely believe that once he could slip his feet into these tiny sandals. He confronted the desert in his bare feet, like Adam expelled from Eden, and like Adam he hesitated before taking his first painful step across the tortured earth that beckoned him. But then, without asking himself why he did it, perhaps in memory of Adam, he dropped his pack and crook, and lifting his tunic by the hem pulled it over his head to stand as naked as Adam himself. Pastor cannot see him here, no inquisitive lamb has followed him, only birds venturing beyond this frontier can catch a glimpse of him from the sky, as can the insects from the ground, the ants, the occasional centipede, a scorpion that in panic lifts its tail with its poisonous sting. These tiny creatures cannot remember ever having seen a naked man before and have no idea what he is trying to prove. If they were to ask Jesus, Why did you take off your clothes, perhaps he would tell them, One must walk into the desert naked, a reply beyond the understanding of insects of the genus Hemiptera, Myriapoda, or Arachnida. We ask ourselves, Naked, with all those thorns to graze bare skin and catch in pubic hair, naked, with all those sharp thistles and that rough sand, naked under that

scorching sun which can make a man dizzy and blind, naked, to find that lost sheep we branded with our own mark.
The desert opens to receive Jesus, then closes behind him,
as if cutting off any path of retreat. Silence echoes in his
ears like the noise from one of those dead, empty shells
which, washed ashore, absorb the vast sound of the waves
until some passerby brings it slowly to his ear, listens, and
says, The sea. Jesus's feet are bleeding, the sun pushes aside
the clouds and stabs him, thorns prick his legs like clawing
nails, thistles scratch him. Sheep, where are you, he calls,
and the hills pass on his words, Where are you, where are
you. This would be a perfect echo, but the prolonged, faraway sound of the shell imposes itself, murmuring God,
Go-o-od, Go-o-od. Then, as if the hills were suddenly swept
away, Jesus emerged from the maze of valleys into a flat
and sandy arena, his sheep right in the center. He ran to it
as fast as he could on his blistered feet, but a voice restrained him, Wait.

Slowly billowing upward like a column of smoke, a
cloud twice as tall as any man appeared before him. The
voice came from this cloud. Who speaks, Jesus asked in
terror, already knowing the reply. The voice said, I am
the Lord, and Jesus understood why he had felt the need
to remove his clothes at the edge of the desert. You brought
me here, what do You want with me. For the moment
nothing, but the day will come when I will want everything. What is everything. Your life. You are the Lord,
You always take from us the life You gave us. There is no
other way, I cannot allow the world to become over-
crowded. Why do You want my life. You will know when
the time comes, therefore prepare your body and your soul,
because the destiny that awaits you is one of great good
fortune. My Lord, I do not understand what You mean or
what You want with me. I will give you power and glory.
What power, what glory. You will learn when I summon
you again. And when will that be. Do not be impatient,

live your life as best you can. My Lord, I stand here before You, You have brought me here naked, I beg You, give me today what You would give me tomorrow. It is not a gift. You said you would give. An exchange, nothing more than an exchange. My life in exchange for what. For power. And for glory, You said, but until I know more about this power, until You tell me what it is, over whom and in whose eyes, Your promise comes too soon. You will find Me again when you are ready, but My signs will accompany you henceforth. Lord, tell me. Be quiet, ask no more questions, the hour will come, not a second sooner or later, and then you will know what I want of you. To hear You, Lord, is to obey, but I have one more question. Stop asking Me questions. Please, Lord, I must. Very well then, speak. Can I save my sheep. So that's what's bothering you. Yes, that's all, may I. No. Why not. Because you must offer it in sacrifice to Me to seal our covenant. You mean this sheep. Yes. Let me choose another from the flock, I'll be right back. You heard Me, I want this one. But Lord, can't you see, its ear has been clipped. You are mistaken, take a good look, the ear is perfect. It isn't possible. I am the Lord, and with the Lord all things are possible. But this is my sheep. Again you are mistaken, the lamb was Mine and you took it from Me, now you will recompense Me with the sheep. Your will be done, for You rule the universe, and I am Your servant. Then offer this sheep in sacrifice, or there will be no covenant. Take pity on me, Lord, I stand here naked and have neither cleaver nor knife, said Jesus, hoping he might still be able to save the sheep's life, but God said, I would not be God if I were unable to solve this problem, here. No sooner had He finished speaking than a brand-new cleaver lay at Jesus' feet. Now quickly, said God, for I have work to do and cannot stay here chatting all day long. Grasping the cleaver by the handle, Jesus went to the sheep. It raised its head and hardly recognized him, never having seen him naked before, and as everyone knows, these animals do not have a strong sense of smell. Do you weep, God asked. The cleaver went up, took aim, and came down as swiftly as an executioner's ax or the guillotine, which has not yet been invented. The sheep did not even whimper. All one could hear was, Ah, as God gave a deep sigh of satisfaction. Jesus asked Him, May I go now. You may, and don't forget, from now on you are tied to Me in flesh and blood. How should I take my leave of You. It doesn't matter, for Me there is no front or back, but it's customary to back away from Me, bowing as you go. Tell me, Lord. What a tiresome fellow you are, what's bothering you now. The shepherd who owns the flock, What shepherd, My master, What about him, Is he an angel or a demon, He's someone I know. But tell me, is he an angel or a demon. I've already told you, for God there is no front or back, good-bye for now. The column of smoke was gone, and the sheep too, all that remained were drops of blood, and they were trying to hide in the soil.

When Jesus returned, Pastor stared at him and asked, Where's the sheep, and he explained, I met God. I didn't ask you if you met God, I asked you if you found the sheep. I offered it in sacrifice. Whatever for. Because God was there and I had no choice. With the tip of his crook Pastor drew a line on the ground, a furrow deep as a pit, insurmountable as a wall of fire, then told him, You've learned nothing, begone with you.

Hᴏᴡ ᴄᴀɴ I ɢᴏ ᴀɴʏᴡʜᴇʀᴇ ᴡɪᴛʜ ᴍʏ ꜰᴇᴇᴛ ɪɴ ᴛʜɪs ᴄᴏɴᴅɪ- tion, thought Jesus as he watched Pastor move to the other side of the flock. God, who had so efficiently disposed of the sheep, had not favored poor Jesus with any divine spittle from that cloud to anoint and heal the cuts on his feet, whose oozing blood glistened on the stones. And Pastor is not going to help him, he has withdrawn, expecting his command to be obeyed, he has no intention of watching Jesus prepare to leave, let alone of bidding him farewell. On hands and knees Jesus crawled to the shelter where they stored the tools for handling the sheep, the receptacles for the milk, the cheese presses, and the sheepskins and goatskins they cured before trading them for what they needed, a tunic, a mantle, provisions of every kind. Jesus thought no one would object if he used the skins to make himself a pair of shoes. The thongs he fashioned from strips of goatskin, which were less hairy and therefore more pliable, but on adjusting the shoes, he was uncertain whether the hair should be on the inside or the outside, he ended up using it as padding because of the wretched state of his feet. It would be uncomfortable if the hairs stuck to the sores, but he would be traveling along the banks of the Jordan and needed only put his shod feet into the water for the congealed blood to dissolve. The weight of those clumsy boots, for that is what they look like, when they are soaked in water, will keep the hair from adhering to the scabs without disturbing those protective crusts that are gradually forming. The color of the blood that seeped from the sores showed, a pleasant surprise, that they were not yet infected. On the slow journey northward Jesus stopped twice and sat on the riverbank to plunge his feet into the cool water, which was as good as medicine. It grieved him to be sent away in this manner, after having met God, an event unprecedented in the fullest sense of the word, for to the best of his knowledge there was not a single man in all Israel who could boast of having seen God and lived. It is true that Jesus did not exactly see Him, but if a cloud appears in the desert in the form of a pillar of smoke and says, I am the Lord, and then holds a conversation that is not only logical and sensible but so compelling that it can only be divine, then to have even the slightest doubt is unpardonable. The answer He gave when questioned about Pastor proved that He was indeed the Lord, His tone of contempt as well as of a certain intimacy, and His refusal to say whether Pastor was an angel or a demon. But the most interesting thing was that Pastor's words, unfeeling and seemingly irrelevant, actually confirmed the supernatural character of the encounter, I didn't ask you if you met God, as if to say, That much I knew already, as if the news was no surprise. But Pastor clearly blamed him for the sheep's death, those final words, You've learned nothing, begone with you, could have no other meaning, and the way he moved to the other side of the flock, his back to Jesus, until he disappeared from sight. On one of the occasions when Jesus allowed his mind to ponder what the Lord might want from him when they met again, Pastor's words suddenly came back to him as loudly and sharply as if the shepherd were standing right beside him, You've learned nothing, and at that moment the feeling of loss and solitude was so great as he sat by himself on the bank of the Jordan, watching his feet in the transparent river, a fine thread of blood suspended in the water, from a heel, that suddenly the blood and the heel no longer belonged to him, it was his father who had come there, limping on pierced feet, to find relief in the cool water of the river, and he repeated what Pastor had said, You must start all over again, for you've learned nothing. As if lifting a long, heavy iron chain from the ground, Jesus recalled his life so far, link by link, the mysterious annunciation of his conception, the earth that shone, his birth in the cave, the massacred innocents of Bethlehem, his father's crucifixion, the nightmare he had inherited, the flight from home, the debate in the Temple, the revelation of Salome, the appearance of the shepherd, his experiences with the flock, the rescued lamb, the desert, the dead sheep, God. And as if this last word was too much for his mind to encompass, he concentrated on one question, Why should a lamb rescued from death eventually die as a sheep, an absurd question if ever there was one, it might make more sense if rephrased as follows, No salvation lasts, and damnation is final. And the last link in the chain is sitting now on the bank of the Jordan, listening to the mournful song of a woman who cannot be seen from here, she is hidden among the rushes, perhaps washing clothes, perhaps bathing, while Jesus tries to understand how all these things are connected, the living lamb that became a dead sheep, his feet bleeding his father's blood, and the woman singing, naked, lying on her back in the water, firm breasts above the surface, dark pubic hair ruffled by the breeze, for though it is true that Jesus never saw a naked woman before, if a man can predict, just by encountering a simple column of smoke, what it will be like to be with God when the time comes, then why should he not be able to visualize a naked woman in every detail, assuming she is naked, merely by listening to the song she sings, even though the words are not addressed to him. Joseph is no longer here, he has returned to the common grave in Sepphoris, while Pastor, not so much as the tip of his shepherd's crook is to be seen, and God, if He is everywhere, as people say, perhaps He is now in that current, in the very water where the woman is bathing. Jesus's body received a signal, the place between his legs began to swell, as with all humans and animals, the blood rushing there, causing his sores to dry up at once. Lord, this body has such strength, yet Jesus made no attempt to go in search of the woman, and his hands resisted the violent temptation of the flesh, You are no one until you love yourself, you will not reach God until you love your body. No one knows who spoke these words, God could not have spoken them, for they are not beads from His rosary, Pastor could well have uttered them, except he is far away, so perhaps they were the words of the song the woman sang. Jesus thought, How I wish I could go there and ask her to explain, but the singing had stopped, perhaps swept away by the current, or possibly the woman simply stepped from the water to dry herself and dress, thus silencing her body. Jesus put on his wet shoes and rose to his feet, dripping water everywhere like a sponge. The woman will have a good laugh if she passes this way and sees him wearing this grotesque footwear, but she will stop laughing when her eyes take in the shape beneath his tunic and stare at length into those eyes saddened by sorrows past and present, but looking troubled now for quite a different reason. With few or no words she will remove her clothes again and offer to do what one might expect in such cases, she will take off his shoes with the utmost care and tend those sores, kissing each of his feet and then covering them with her own damp hair, as if protecting an egg or cocoon. No sign of anyone coming down the road,

Jesus looks around him, sighs, looks for a spot to conceal himself, heads there, but comes to a sudden halt, remembering in time that the Lord punished Onan with death for spilling his seed on the ground. Now, Jesus could have provided a more sophisticated interpretation of this old episode, as was his wont, and not been deterred by the Lord's inflexibility, for two reasons, the first being that he had no sister-in-law by whom he was legally bound to provide an heir for a deceased brother, the second and perhaps more compelling reason being that the Lord, according to what He told him in the desert, had definite plans for his future which were yet to be revealed, therefore it would be neither practical nor logical to forget the promise made and risk losing everything, just because an uncontrolled hand strayed where it should not have, for the Lord knows our corporal needs, which are not confined to food and drink, there are other forms of abstention just as hard to endure. These and similar reflections should have encouraged Jesus to follow his natural inclinations and find a quiet spot to satisfy his urge, but instead they distracted him and confused him so much that he soon lost the desire to yield to wicked temptation. Resigned to his own virtue, Jesus lifted the pack to his shoulder, took up his staff, and went on his way.

On the first day of his journey along the banks of the Jordan, Jesus, accustomed to a lonely existence after four years of solitude, kept clear of inhabited places. But as he approached the Lake of Gennesaret, it became increasingly difficult to avoid passing through villages, especially since they were surrounded by cultivated fields that barred his way, moreover his rough appearance aroused the suspicions of the laborers. So Jesus decided to enter the world of men, and was pleasantly surprised by what he found there, all that really bothered him was the noise, which he had forgotten. In the first village he came to, a group of rowdy urchins roared with laughter at the sight of his sandal boots, no great problem, Jesus had enough money to buy new ones, remember that he has not touched any of the money he has been carrying with him since he was given two coins by the Pharisee, to live four years with few needs and no expenses has proved the greatest fortune one could have wished from the Lord. Now after buying the sandals he is left with two coins of little value, but poverty does not worry him, soon he will arrive at his destination, Nazareth, the home where he is certain to return, for on the day he left, and he feels as if he has been away forever, he said, One way or another I shall always come back. Following the thousand bends in the road along the Jordan, he travels at an easy pace, his feet are really in no condition for such a journey, but something else is slowing him down, something deep within, a vague premonition which might be expressed, The sooner I get there, the sooner I must leave. As he proceeds northward along the shore of the lake, he is already on the latitude of Nazareth, should he decide to make straight for home, all he need do is turn toward the setting sun, but he lingers by the waters of the lake, blue, wide, tranquil. He loves sitting on the shore watching the fishermen cast their nets, as a little boy he often came here with his parents, but he never stopped to watch the labors of these men who smell of fish as if they themselves lived in the sea.

As he went, Jesus earned enough to eat by doing what jobs he knew, which were none, or could do, which were few, pulling a boat ashore or pushing it into the water, helping to drag in a full net, and the fishermen, seeing how hungry he looked, would offer him a couple of fish in payment. At first Jesus felt shy and would go off to cook and eat them on his own, but after several days the fishermen invited him to join them. On the third and last day Jesus went out on the lake with two brothers, Simon and Andrew, both older than he, already in their thirties. When they were out on the open water, Jesus, who knew nothing about fishing, laughing at his own awkwardness, tried at the insistence of his new friends to cast the net with that broad gesture which seen from a distance resembles a blessing or a challenge, but he had no success, and once almost fell into the water. Simon and Andrew roared with laughter, well aware that Jesus only knew how to handle goats and sheep, and Simon said, Life would be much easier for us if this flock could be gathered and led, to which Jesus replied, At least they don't go astray or get lost, they are all here in the lake, escaping the net or falling into it day after day. The catch was disappointing, the bottom of the boat almost empty, and Andrew said, Brother, let's turn back, we're not likely to catch more fish today. Simon agreed, You're right, brother, let's go. He slipped the oars into the oarlocks and was about to start rowing to the shore when Jesus suggested, not out of any inspiration or special insight but simply from inexplicable good spirits, that they try three more times, Who knows, perhaps this watery flock, led by its shepherd, has moved to our side. Simon laughed, That's another good thing about sheep, they're visible, and turning to Andrew, told him, Cast the net over there, nothing ventured, nothing gained, whereupon Andrew cast the net and it came back full. The fishermen gasped in amazement, and their amazement turned to awe when the net was cast a second and third time and came back full both times. From water that earlier seemed devoid of fish suddenly there came pouring forth, like a fountain, fish such as never were seen before, gleaming torrents of gills, scales, and fins that left one dazed. Simon and Andrew asked Jesus how he knew that the fish would gather there, and Jesus told them he didn't know, it was impulse when he said to try again. The two brothers had no reason to doubt him, pure chance can work such miracles, but Jesus trembled inside and in the silence of his soul asked, Who did this. Simon said, Give us a hand to sort them, and we should explain now that it was not from the Sea of Galilee that the ecumenical proverb originated which says, Everything that falls into the net is fish. Here different criteria prevail, the net may have caught fish, but the law, as elsewhere, is quite unambiguous, Behold what you may eat of the various aquatic species, you may eat anything in the waters, seas, and rivers that has fins and scales, but that which has neither fins nor scales, whether they be creatures that breed or that live in the water, you will shun and abhor them for all time, you will refrain from eating the flesh of everything in the water that has neither fins nor scales, and treat them as abomination. And so the despised fish with smooth skins, those that cannot be served at the table of the people of the Lord, were returned to the sea, many of them so accustomed to this by now that they no longer worried when caught in the nets, for they knew they would soon be back in the water and out of danger. With their fish mentality, they believed themselves the recipients of some special favor from the Creator, perhaps even of a special love, so that in time they came to consider themselves superior to other fish, for those in the boats must have committed grievous sins beneath the dark water for God to let them perish so mercilessly.

When the three finally reached the shore, taking every precaution not to sink, for the waters of the lake came up to the edge of the boat as if about to swallow it, the people there were dumbfounded. They could not understand how this happened, the other fishermen had returned with empty boats, but by tacit and mutual agreement the three lucky men said nothing of what had brought about their prodigious catch. Simon and Andrew did not want to see their reputations as fishermen diminished in public, while Jesus had no desire to find himself in demand as a lookout for other crews, which, it must be said, would have been only just and fair, if we could abolish once and for all the favoritism that has caused so much harm in this world. Which thought led Jesus to announce that same night that, after four years of constant trial and tribulation which could have been sent only by Satan, he would depart tomorrow for Nazareth, where his family were expecting him. This decision saddened Simon and Andrew, who regretted losing the best lookout ever celebrated in the annals of Gennesaret. And two other fishermen felt regret, these were James and John, the sons of Zebedee, two simple lads whom people used to ask in jest, Who is the father of the sons of Zebedee, throwing both of them into mortified confusion, though they knew the answer, they were obviously his sons. They regretted Jesus' departure not only because it meant no more prodigious catches but because, being younger, and John was even younger than Jesus, they had hoped to form a crew that could compete with the older men. Their simplicity had nothing to do with being stupid or retarded, they simply went through life with their thoughts elsewhere, so that they were always caught by surprise when someone asked them who was the father of the sons of Zebedee, and were always puzzled by the merriment that broke out when they replied, Zebedee, of course. John tried to dissuade Jesus, he went up to him and said, Stay with us, our boat is bigger than Simon's and we can catch more fish, to which Jesus, wise and compassionate, replied, The measure of the Lord is not that of men but the measure of His justice. John went off, crestfallen, and the evening passed without any further approaches from interested parties. Next day, Jesus bade farewell to the first friends he ever made, and with his pack replenished he turned his back on the Lake of Gennesaret where, unless he was mistaken, God had given him a sign, and set out for the mountains that led to Nazareth.

Fate decreed, however, that as he passed through the town of Magdala, a troublesome sore on his foot should open, and it looked as if it would never stop bleeding. Fate also decreed that this misfortune should occur at the very edge of Magdala, directly in front of a house that stood apart, away from the other houses, as if ostracized. When the blood showed no sign of stopping, Jesus called, Anyone home, and a woman appeared in the doorway as if expecting to be called, from the lack of surprise on her face we might assume she is accustomed to people walking into the house without knocking, but on careful reflection we know this is not the case, for the woman is a prostitute, and the respect she owes her profession requires that she close her front door when she receives a client. Jesus, who was sitting on the ground and pressing the open sore, looked up as the woman approached, Help me, he said, and taking hold of her outstretched hand, he struggled to his feet and made a few faltering steps. You're in no state to be walking, she told him, come inside and let me bathe your foot. Jesus did not say yes or no, the woman's perfume was so powerful that the pain vanished as if by magic, and with one arm around her shoulders and another arm, which obviously could not be his, around his waist, he felt turmoil surge through his body, or more precisely through his senses, because it was in his senses, or at least in one of them, which is neither sight nor smell nor taste nor touch, though all of these play some part, that he felt it most, God help him. The woman helped him into the yard, closed the gate, and made him sit. Wait here, she said. She went inside and returned with an earthenware basin and a white cloth. Filling the basin with water, she wet the cloth, knelt at Jesus' feet, rested the injured foot in the palm of her left hand, and washed it gently, removing the dirt and softening the broken scab, which oozed blood and disgusting yellow pus. The woman told him, It will take more than water to heal this, but Jesus said, All I ask is that you bandage my foot so I can reach Nazareth. He was on the point of saying, My mother will treat it, but stopped himself in time, he did not wish to give the impression of being a mama's boy who has only to stub his toe on a stone and he is crying to be comforted and nursed, It's nothing, child, look, it's better already. It's a long way from here to Nazareth, the woman told him, but if that's what you want, let me rub in a little ointment. She went back into the house and seemed to take longer this time. Jesus looks around him in surprise, for he has never seen such a clean and tidy yard. He suspects the woman is a prostitute, not because he is particularly good at guessing people's professions at first glance, besides, not that long ago he himself would have been identified as a shepherd by the smell of goat, yet now everyone would say, He's a fisherman, for he lost one smell only to replace it with another. The woman reeks of perfume, but Jesus, who may be innocent, has learned certain facts of life by watching the mating of goats and rams, he also has enough common sense to know that just because a woman uses perfume, it does not necessarily mean she is a whore. A whore should smell of the men she lies with, just as the goatherd smells of goat and the fisherman of fish, but who knows, perhaps these women perfume themselves heavily because they want to conceal, disguise, or even forget the odor of a man's body. The woman reappeared with a small jar, and she was smiling, as if someone in the house had told her something amusing. Jesus saw her approach, but unless his eyes deceived him, she walked very slowly, the way it is often in dreams, her tunic flowing and revealing the curves of her body as she walked, her hips swaying, her black hair loose over her shoulders and tossing like corn silk in the wind. Her tunic was unmistakably a whore's, her body a dancer's, her laughter a whore's. Deeply troubled, Jesus searched his memory for some apt maxims by his famous namesake, Jesus the son of Sirach, and his memory obliged, whispering discreetly in his ear, Stay away from loose women lest you fall into their snares, Have nothing to do with female dancers lest you succumb to their charms, and finally, Do not fall into the hands of prostitutes lest you lose your soul and all your possessions, and Jesus' soul may well be in danger now that he has reached manhood, but as for his possessions, they are in no danger, for, as we know, he possesses nothing. So he will be quite safe when the moment comes to fix a price and the woman inquires, How much money do you have.

Jesus was prepared and showed no surprise when the woman asked him his name as she rubbed ointment into the sores on his foot, which rested on her lap. I am Jesus, he replied, without adding, of Nazareth, for he had said so earlier, just as the woman who lived here was clearly from Magdala, and when he asked her name, she replied only, Mary. Having carefully examined and dressed his injured foot, Mary Magdalene tied the bandage with a firm knot, That should do, she said. How can I thank you, asked Jesus, and for the first time his eyes met hers, eyes black and bright as coals, also like water running over water, veiled with a sensuality that Jesus found irresistible. The woman did not answer at once, she looked at him as if weighing him, the boy obviously had no money, at length she said, Remember me, that is all I ask, and Jesus assured her, I will never forget your kindness, and then, summoning his courage, Nor will I forget you. Why do you say that, she asked, smiling. Because you are beautiful. You should have seen me in my youth. You are beautiful as you are. Her smile faded, Do you know what I am, what I do, how I earn my living. I do. You only had to look at me, and you knew everything. I know nothing. Not even that I'm a prostitute. That I know. I sleep with men for money. Yes. Then, as I said, you know everything about me. That is all I know. The woman sat down beside him, gently stroked his hand, touched his mouth with the tips of her fingers, If you really want to thank me, spend the day here with me. I cannot, Why, I have no money to pay you, That's no surprise. Please do not mock me. You may not believe me, but I'd sooner mock a man with a full purse. It's not only a question of money. What is it, then. Jesus fell silent and turned his face away. She made no attempt to help him, she could have asked, Are you a virgin, but said nothing and waited. The silence was so great, only their hearts could be heard beating, his louder and faster, hers restless and agitated. Jesus said, Your hair reminds me of a flock of goats descending the mountain slopes of Gilead. The woman smiled but said nothing. Then Jesus said, Your eyes are like the pools of Heshbon by the Gate of Bath-Rabim. The woman smiled again but still said nothing. Then Jesus slowly turned to look at her and said, I have never been with a woman. Mary held his hands, This is how everyone has to begin, men who have never known a woman, women who have never known a man, until the day comes for the one who knows to teach the one who does not. Do you wish to teach me. So that you may thank me a second time. In this way, I will never stop thanking you. And I will never stop teaching you. Mary got to her feet, went to lock the gate, but only after hanging a sign outside, to tell any clients who might come looking for her that she had closed her window because it was now the hour to sing, Awake, north wind, and come, you south, blow upon my garden, that the spices thereof may flow out, let my beloved come into his garden and eat his pleasant fruits. Then together, Jesus' hand once more on the shoulder of Mary, this whore from Magdala who dressed his sores and is about to receive him in her bed, they went inside, into the welcome shade of a clean, fresh room. Her bed was no primitive mat on the floor with a coarse sheet on top, the sort Jesus remembered from his parents' house, this was a real bed, as once described elsewhere, I have adorned my bed with covers and embroidered sheets of Egyptian linen, I have perfumed my couch with myrrh, aloes, and cinnamon. Leading Jesus to the hearth, with its floor of brick, Mary Magdalene insisted

601

on removing his tunic and washing him herself, stroking his body with her fingertips and kissing him softly on the chest and thighs, first one side, then the other. The delicate touch of hands and lips made Jesus shiver, the nails grazing his skin gave him gooseflesh, Don't be frightened, she whispered. She dried him and led him to the bed, Lie down, I'll be with you in a moment. She drew a curtain, there was the sound of splashing water, a pause, perfume filled the air, and Mary reappeared, completely naked. Jesus too was naked, lying as she had left him, he thought, This must be right, for to cover the body she had uncovered would give offense. Mary lingered at the side of the bed, gazed on him with an expression both passionate and tender, and told him, You are so handsome, but to be perfect you must close your eyes. Jesus hesitantly closed them, opened them again, and in that moment he understood the true meaning of King Solomon's words, Your thighs are like jewels, your navel is like a round goblet filled with scented wine, your belly is like a heap of wheat set about with lilies, your breasts are like two fawns that are the twins of a gazelle, and he understood them even better when Mary lay down beside him and took his hands in hers, and drew them to her, and guided them slowly over her body, her hair, face, neck, shoulders, her breasts, which he gently squeezed, her belly, navel, her lower hair, where he lingered, twining and untwining it with his fingers, then the curve of her smooth thighs, and as she moved his hands, she repeated in a whisper, Come, discover my body, come discover my body. Jesus breathed so fast, for one moment he thought he would faint when her hands, the left hand on his forehead, the right hand on his ankles, began caressing him, slowly coming together, meeting in the middle, then starting all over again. You've learned nothing, begone with you, Pastor had told him, and who knows, perhaps he meant to say that Jesus had not learned to cherish life. Now Mary Magdalene instructed him, Discover my body, and she said it again, but in a different way, changing one word, Discover your body, and there it was, tense, taut, roused, and she, naked and magnificent, was above him and saying, There is nothing to fear, do not move, leave this to me. Then he felt part of him, this organ, disappearing inside her, a ring of fire around it, coming and going, a shudder passed through him, like a wriggling fish slipping free with a shout, surely impossible, fish do not shout, no, it was he, Jesus, crying out as Mary slumped over his body with a moan and absorbed his cry with her lips, with a hungry kiss that sent a second, unending shudder through him.

For the rest of that day no one came to knock on Mary Magdalene's door. For the rest of that day she instructed the youth from Nazareth who came to ask her if she could relieve his pain and heal the sores which, unbeknownst to her, began with that other encounter, when Jesus met God in the desert. God had told him, Henceforth you are tied to me in flesh and blood, and the devil, if that is who he was, had spurned him, You've learned nothing, begone with you, and Mary Magdalene, the perspiration running down her breasts, her loose hair seeming to give off smoke, her lips swollen, her eyes dark pools, said, You won't stay with me because of what I taught you, but sleep here tonight. And Jesus, on top of her, replied, What you taught me is no prison but freedom. They slept together, and not only that night. When they woke, it was morning, and after their bodies sought and found each other once more, Mary examined Jesus' foot, It looks much better, but you should wait before journeying home, walking will only make it worse, not to mention all that dust. I cannot stay any longer, you yourself said my foot is much better. Of course you can stay, it's a question of wanting to, and as for the gate in the yard, that will remain locked for as long as we please. What about your life here. My life now is you. But why. Let me answer in the words of King

Solomon, My beloved put in his hand by the hole of the door and my heart trembled. But how can I be your beloved if you don't know me, I am simply someone who came to ask your help, on whom you took pity for his misfortune and ignorance. That is why I love you, because I helped and instructed you, but you will never love me, having neither helped nor instructed me. But you are not in pain. You will find my wound if you look carefully. What wound might that be. This open door through which others have entered, but not my beloved. You said I am your beloved. That is why the door closed behind you as you entered. There is nothing I can teach you, only what I learned from you. Teach me, so that I may know what it is like to learn from you. We cannot live together. You mean you cannot live with a whore. Yes. While you live with me, I will not be a whore, I stopped being one the moment you came into this house, and it is up to you whether or not I continue living as one. You ask too much. Nothing that you cannot give me for one or two days, or for as long as it takes your foot to heal, so that my wound may open once more. It took me eighteen years to get here. A few days more won't make much difference, you're still young. So are you. Older than you, younger than your mother. Do you know my mother, No, Then why did you mention her, Because I'm too young to have a son your age, How stupid of me. No, you're not stupid, only innocent, But I'm no longer innocent, Just because you've been with a woman, No, I lost my innocence before you. Tell me about yourself, but not just yet, for the moment all I want is to feel your left hand under my head and your right hand embracing me.

Jesus stayed in Mary Magdalene's house a week, sufficient time for new skin to form beneath the scabs. The gate remained locked. Several men, driven by lust or wounded pride, knocked impatiently at it, ignoring the sign that told them to keep away. They were curious to see this fellow who took so long, one joker called over the wall, Either he isn't up to it or he has no idea what to do, open the gate, Mary, and I'll show him how it's done. Mary Magdalene went out into the yard to curse him, Whoever you are, boaster, your days of male prowess are over, so be off with you. Damned whore. That's just where you're wrong, for you won't find a woman anywhere more blessed than me. Whether it was because of this incident or because fate so decreed, no one else came knocking at the gate, most likely any man living in Magdala or passing through who heard of Mary's curse wanted to avoid the risk of being made impotent, for it is generally believed that an experienced prostitute can not only inflame a man but also kill his pride and desire forever. And so Mary and Jesus were left in peace for eight days, during which time the lessons given and received became one discourse of gestures, discoveries, surprises, murmurings, inventions, like the pieces of a mosaic that are nothing if taken one by one yet become everything when assembled and put into their proper places. Several times she asked her beloved to talk about himself, but he would change the subject and break into verses such as, I am come into my garden, my sister, my spouse, I have gathered my myrrh with my spice, I have eaten my honeycomb with my honey, I have drunk my wine with my milk, which he recited with passion before partaking of the poetic act itself, verily, verily, I say unto you, dear Jesus, this is no way to hold a conversation. But one day he told her about his father who was a carpenter and his mother who carded wool, about his brothers and sisters, and how he had started to learn his father's trade before going off to be a shepherd for four years, but now he was returning home. He also mentioned the few days he spent on the lake with some fishermen without mastering their skills. Then one evening, when they were eating out in the yard, Jesus took Mary Magdalene into his confidence, and from time to time they looked up at the rapid flight of swallows passing overhead with strident cries. The two, to judge from their silence, have nothing more to say to each other, the man has confessed all to the woman, but she asks, as if disappointed, Is that all, and nodding, he says, Yes, that's all.

The silence deepened, the circling swallows went elsewhere, and Jesus said, My father was crucified four years ago in Sepphoris, his name was Joseph. And you are his eldest son. Yes, I'm the eldest. Then I don't understand, surely you should be looking after your family. We quarreled, but don't ask me any more. No more about your family, then, but what about your time as a shepherd, tell me about that. There's nothing to tell, every day the same thing, goats, sheep, kids, lambs, and milk, lots of milk, milk everywhere. Did you enjoy being a shepherd. Yes, I did. Then why did you leave. I became restless, began to miss my family, felt homesick. Homesick, what is that. Sadness at being so far away. You're lying, Why do you think I'm lying, Because I see not sadness but fear and guilt in your eyes. Jesus did not reply, he got up, walked around the yard, then stopped in front of Mary, One day, if we should meet again, I'll tell you the rest if you promise not to tell anyone. Why not tell me now. I'll tell you when we meet again. You hope that by then I will have given up prostitution, you still don't trust me, you think I might sell your secrets for money or pass them on to the first man who turns up, for amusement or in exchange for a night of love more glorious than those you and I have shared. No, that's not the reason for my silence. Well, I promise you that Mary Magdalene, prostitute or not, will be at your side whenever you need her. Who am I to deserve this. Don't you know who you are.

That night the nightmare returned. It had been more bearable of late, a vague anguish that only occasionally disturbed his sleep, but this night, perhaps because it was the last night Jesus was to sleep in Mary's bed, perhaps because he had mentioned Sepphoris and the men crucified there, the nightmare began to uncoil in twists and turns like a huge snake awakening from hibernation, and to raise its hideous head. Jesus woke with a start, crying out in terror, his body covered with cold sweat. What's wrong, Mary asked in alarm. I was dreaming, only dreaming, he said evasively. Tell me, and those simple words were said with so much love and tenderness that Jesus could not hold back his tears, and after much weeping he revealed what he had hoped to withhold, I dream over and over that my father is coming to kill me. But your father is dead and you are still alive. In my dream I'm still a child back in Bethlehem of Judaea, and my father is coming to kill me. Why in Bethlehem. That's where I was born. Perhaps you think your father didn't want you to be born, and that is why you have this dream. You don't know what happened. No, I don't. Children in Bethlehem died because of my father. Did he kill them. He killed them because he made no attempt to save them, although his was not the hand that drew the sword. And in your dream, are you one of those children. I have died a thousand deaths. Poor man, poor Jesus. That is why I left home. I begin to understand, You think you understand, What more is there to know, What I cannot reveal yet, You mean what you will tell me when we meet again, That's right. Resting his hand on Mary's shoulder, his cheek on her breast, Jesus fell asleep. She stayed awake throughout the night, her heart aching, for it would soon be morning and time to separate. But her soul was at peace, she knew that this man in her arms was the one for whom she had been waiting all her life, the one who belonged to her and to whom she belonged, his body pure, hers defiled, but their world is just beginning. They have been together eight days, but only tonight was their union confirmed, and eight days is nothing compared to a whole future, for this Jesus who has come into my life is so young, and here am I, Mary

Magdalene, in bed with a man, as so often in the past, but this time deep in love and ageless.

They spent the morning preparing for the journey. One would have thought young Jesus was traveling to the end of the world, while in fact he had no more than twenty miles to cover, a distance any healthy man could walk between noon and dusk, notwithstanding the rough road from Magdala to Nazareth, with its steep slopes and rocky terrain. Take care, Mary warned him, you may run into rebel forces still fighting the Romans. After all this time, asked Jesus. You haven't lived here, this is Galilee. But I'm a native of Galilee, they're not likely to do me any harm. You can't be Galilean if you were born in Bethlehem of Judaea. My parents conceived me in Nazareth, and to be honest, I wasn't even born in Bethlehem, I was born in a cave in the earth, and now I feel reborn here in Magdala. Mothered by a whore. You're no whore in my eyes, said Jesus strongly. Alas, that is the life I've led. These words were followed by a long silence, Mary waiting for Jesus to speak, Jesus trying to still his uneasiness. Finally he asked her, Do you intend to remove the sign you hung on the gate to keep men from entering. Mary looked at him with a serious expression, then smiled mischievously, I could not possibly have two men in the house at the same time. What are you saying. Simply that you are leaving but will still be here. She paused, then added, The sign on the gate remains there. People will think you're with a man. And they'll be right, I'll be with you. Are you telling me no man will ever pass through that gate again. Yes, because this woman they call Mary Magdalene stopped being a prostitute the moment you walked into her house. But how will you live. Only the lilies in the fields thrive without working or spinning. Jesus took her hands and said, Nazareth isn't far from Magdala, one day I will return. If you come looking for me, you'll find me here. My desire is to find you all my life. You will find me even after death.

You mean I will die before you. I'm older than you, so most likely I will die first, but if you die before me, I will go on living so that you may find me. And if you die first. Then blessed be the woman who brought you into the world during my lifetime. After this conversation, Mary served Jesus food, and he did not have to tell her, Sit with me, for since their first day together behind locked doors this man and this woman have divided and multiplied between them feelings, gestures, spaces, and sensations without paying much attention to the rules and laws. They certainly would not know what to say if we were to ask them how they would behave outside the privacy of these four walls, where they have been free for some days to forge a world in the simple image and likeness of a man and a woman. A world that is more hers than his, let it be said, but since they are both so confident about meeting again, we need only have the patience to wait for the time when, side by side, they will confront the outside world, where people are already asking themselves anxiously, What's going on in there, and they don't mean the usual antics in the bedroom. After they had eaten, Mary helped Jesus into his sandals and told him, You must leave if you're to reach Nazareth before nightfall. Farewell, said Jesus, and taking up his pack and staff, he went out into the yard. The sky was covered with clouds as if lined with unwashed wool, the Lord must not be finding it easy today to keep an eye on His sheep from on high. Jesus and Mary Magdalene embraced a long time before exchanging a farewell kiss, which did not take long at all, and little wonder, for kissing was not the custom then.

THE SUN HAD JUST SET WHEN JESUS ARRIVED IN NAZARETH, four long years, give or take a week, from the day he left, a mere child driven by desperation to go out into the world in search of someone who might help him understand the unbearable truth about his birth. Four years, however long, may not be enough to heal one's sorrow, but they should bring some relief. He had asked questions in the Temple, traveled mountain paths with the devil's flock, met God, and slept with Mary Magdalene. Reaching Nazareth, he no longer gives the appearance of suffering, except for those tears in his eyes, but that could also be a delayed reaction to the smoke from the sacrifices, or sudden joy in his soul upon looking down at the town from a high pasture, or the fear of a man alone in the desert who has heard a voice say, I am the Lord, or, most likely, for most recent, yearning for the woman he left only a few hours ago, I have comforted myself with raisins, I have strengthened myself with apples, for I am swooning with love.

Jesus might recite these sweet words to his mother and brothers, but he pauses on the threshold to ask himself,

My mother and brothers, not that he does not know who they are, the question is, do they know who he is now, he who asked questions in the Temple, who watched the horizon, who met God, who has experienced carnal love and discovered his manhood. Before this same door once stood a beggar who claimed to be an angel, who if he really was an angel could have burst into the house with a great commotion of ruffled wings, yet he preferred to knock and to beg for alms like any pauper. The door is only latched. Jesus does not need to call out as he did in Magdala, he can walk calmly into his own home, the sores on his feet are completely healed, but then sores that bleed and fester are the quickest healed. There was no need to knock, but he did. He had heard voices over the wall, recognized the voice of his mother coming from farther away, yet could not summon the courage simply to push the door open and announce, I'm here, like one who knows his arrival is welcome and wishes to give a pleasant surprise. The door was opened by a little girl about eight or nine years old, who did not recognize the visitor, the voice of blood and kinship did not come to his assistance by telling her, This is your brother Jesus, don't you remember him. Instead he said, despite the four years that had passed since they last saw each other and despite the fading light, You must be Lydia, and she answered, Yes, amazed that a complete stranger should know her name, but the spell was broken when he said, I'm your brother Jesus, may I come in. In the yard under the lean-to adjoining the house he could see shadowy figures, probably his brothers, now they were looking in the direction of the door, and two of them, the oldest, James and Joseph, approached. They had not heard Jesus' words, but didn't need to go to the trouble of identifying the visitor, for Lydia was already calling out excitedly, It's Jesus, it's our brother, whereupon the shadows stirred and Mary appeared in the doorway, accompanied by Lisa, the other daughter, almost as tall now as her

mother, and both of them called out with one voice, My
son, My brother, and the next moment they were all embracing in joyful reunion in the middle of the yard, always
a happy event, but especially when it is the eldest son returning. Jesus greeted his mother, then each of his brothers, and was greeted warmly by all of them, Brother Jesus,
how good to see you again, Brother Jesus, we thought
you had forgotten us, but no one said, Brother Jesus, you
don't look any richer. They went inside and sat down to
the meal his mother had been preparing when he knocked
at the door. One could almost say to Jesus, coming as he
does from where he does, having indulged his sinful flesh
and kept bad company, one could almost say with the brutal frankness of simple people who suddenly see their share
of food diminish, When it's time to eat, the devil always
brings an extra mouth to feed. No one present dared put
this thought into words, and it would have been wrong if
he had, an extra mouth makes little difference when there
are already nine to feed. Besides, the new arrival has more
right to be here than any of them. During supper, the
younger children wanted to know about his adventures,
while the three older children and Mary observed that there
had been no change in his occupation since their meeting
in Jerusalem, for the smell of fish has long since disappeared, and the wind swept away the sensuous perfume of
Mary Magdalene, and don't forget all the sweat and dust
acquired on the road, unless one were to take a close sniff
at Jesus' tunic, but if his own family did not take such a
liberty, why should we. Jesus told them how he had tended
one of the largest flocks ever seen, how he had recently
been on a lake helping fishermen bring in the most extraordinary catch of fish, and that he had also experienced
the most wonderful adventure any man could imagine or
hope for, but he would tell them about it some other time
and then only some of them. The younger children pleaded,
Tell us, please tell us, and Judas, the middle brother, asked

him in all innocence, Did you make a lot of money while you were away, to which Jesus replied, Not so much as three coins, or two, or even one, nothing, and seeing disbelief on their faces, he emptied his pack without further ado. And truly, he had little to show for his labors, his only belongings a metal knife that was worn and bent, a bit of string, a chunk of bread as hard as a rock, two pairs of sandals reduced to tatters, the remnants of an old tunic. This belonged to your father, said Mary, stroking the tunic, then the larger pair of sandals, she told him, These too were his. The others lowered their heads in memory of their dead father.

Jesus was putting everything back into his pack when he felt a large, heavy knot in the hem of the tunic. The blood rushed to his face, it could only be money, money that he had denied possessing and that must have been put there by Mary Magdalene, and therefore earned not in the sweat of one's brow as dignity demands but with sinful groans and sweat of another kind. His mother and brothers looked at the knot, then all looked at him. Uncertain whether to try to conceal the proof of his deception or bluff his way out without really explaining, Jesus chose the more difficult way. He untied the knot and revealed the treasure, twenty coins the likes of which had never been seen in this house, and said, I had no idea this money was here. Their silent rebuke passed through the air like a hot desert wind, how shameful, the eldest son and caught telling such a lie. Jesus searched his heart but could not be angry with Mary Magdalene, he felt nothing but gratitude for her generosity, this touching act of giving him money she knew he would have been ashamed to accept openly, for it is one thing to say, Your left hand is under my head and your right hand embraces me, and another not to remember that other hands have embraced her. Now it is Jesus who looks at his family, defying them to doubt his word, I had no idea this money was here, which is true but not quite the whole truth, daring them to ask him the question to which there is no answer, If you didn't know you had this money, how do you account for its being here now. He cannot tell them, A prostitute with whom I spent the last eight days put the coins here, money she received from the men she slept with before I came. Scattered on the soiled, threadbare tunic of the man who was crucified four years ago and whose remains were shamefully thrown into a common grave, the twenty coins shine like the luminous earth that one night struck terror in this same household, but no elders will come from the synagogue this time to say, The coins must be buried, just as no one here will ask, Where do they come from, lest the reply oblige us to give them up against our will. Jesus gathers the money into the palms of his hands and says once more, I didn't know I had these coins, as if giving his family one last chance, and then, glancing at his mother, says, It is not the devil's money. His brothers shuddered in horror, but Mary replied without showing any anger, Nor did it come from God. Jesus playfully tossed the coins into the air, once, twice, and said as naturally as if he were announcing he would return to his carpenter's bench the next day, Mother, we'll discuss God in the morning. Then turning to his brothers James and Joseph, he added, I also have something to say to you, and this was no condescending gesture, for both brothers are now of age according to their religion and therefore entitled to be taken into his confidence. But James felt that given the importance of the occasion, something ought to be said beforehand about the justification for the promised conversation, since no brother, however senior, can expect to appear unannounced and say, We must have a talk about God. So with a bland smile he said to Jesus, If, as you say, you traveled hill and dale four years as a shepherd, there couldn't have been much time to attend the synagogue and acquire so much knowledge that no sooner do you return home than you want to talk to us about the Lord. Jesus sensed the barb beneath these words and replied, Ah, James, how little you understand God if you think we have to go in search of Him when He has decided to come to us. Am I right in thinking you refer to yourself. Save your questions until tomorrow, when I will tell you all I have to say. James muttered to himself, no doubt making some sour comment about people who think they know everything. Mary, turning to Jesus with a weary expression on her face, said, You can tell us tomorrow, or the day after tomorrow, or whenever you like, but for now tell us what you intend to do with this money, for we are in great difficulty. Don't you want to know where it came from. You said you didn't know. That's the truth, but I've been thinking and can guess how it got there. If the money doesn't taint your hands, then it won't taint ours. Is that all you have to say about this money. Yes. Then let us spend it, as is only right, on the family. There was a general murmur of approval, even James seemed satisfied with this decision, and Mary said, If you don't mind, we'll put some of the money aside for your sister's dowry. You didn't say anything about Lisa getting married. Yes, in the spring. Tell me how much you need. That depends on what those coins are worth. Jesus smiled and said, I'm afraid I don't know what they are worth, only their value. He laughed, amused by his own words, and the family looked at him in bewilderment. Only Lisa lowered her eyes, she is fifteen, still innocent, but has all the mysterious intuition of adolescence. Among those present, she is the most troubled about the money. Jesus gave a coin to his mother, You can change it tomorrow, then we'll know what it's worth. Someone is sure to ask me where it came from, thinking that whoever posesses such a coin must have others hidden away. Simply tell them that your son Jesus has returned, and that there is no greater fortune than the return of a prodigal son.

That night Jesus dreamed of his father. He had settled down to sleep in the lean-to rather than with all the others inside. He could not bear the idea of sleeping in the same room with ten people, each trying unsuccessfully to get a little privacy, they are no longer like a flock of little lambs but growing fast, all legs and arms and far from comfortable in such cramped quarters. Before falling asleep, he thought about Mary Magdalene and everything they had done together, which stirred him to such a pitch that he had to get up twice and walk in the yard to cool his blood, but when sleep finally came, he slept as peacefully as a small child, it was as if his body were floating slowly downstream while he watched branches and clouds pass overhead, and a silent bird flying back and forth. No sooner did the dream begin than he felt a slight jolt, as if he had brushed against another. He thought it was Mary Magdalene and smiled, and smiling turned his head in her direction, but the body drifting past, carried by the same current beneath the sky and branches and the fluttering silent bird, was that of his father. The usual cry of terror formed in his throat but stopped there, this was not his usual dream, he was not an infant in a public square in Bethlehem awaiting death with other children, there was no sound of footsteps, no neighing of horses or clanking and scraping of weapons, there was only the gentle murmur of water and the two bodies forming a raft as father and son were carried along by the river. All the fear went out of Jesus. Overcome with a feeling of exultation, he called out, Father, in his dream, Father, he repeated, awakening, but now with tears in his eyes, realizing he was alone. He tried to revive his dream, to repeat it, to feel again the brushing jolt and find his father beside him, so that they might float together on these waters to the end of time. He did not succeed that night, but the first dream never returned, from now on he will experience elation instead of fear, companionship instead of solitude, promised life instead of imminent death. Now let the wise men of Holy Scripture explain, if they can, the meaning of Jesus' dream, the significance of this river, the overhanging branches, the drifting clouds, and the silent bird, which made it possible for father and son to be united even though the guilt of the one cannot be pardoned or the sorrow of the other relieved.

The following day Jesus offered to help James with some carpentry, but it soon became clear that good intentions were no substitute for the skills he lacked and had never fully acquired even by the time Joseph died. To meet their father's customers' needs, James had become a reliable carpenter, and even young Joseph, who was not yet fourteen, already knew enough to have been able to teach his eldest brother had such disrespect for seniority been allowed within the strict family hierarchy. James laughed at Jesus' clumsiness and told him, Whoever turned you into a shepherd led you astray, words of lighthearted irony that no one would have suspected of concealing any deeper meaning, but Jesus rose abruptly from the workbench, and Mary rebuked her second son, Speak not of perdition, lest you summon Satan and bring evil into our home. Taken aback, James protested, But I summoned no one, Mother, all I said was, We know what you said, interrupted Jesus, Mother and I heard what you said, it was Mother who linked the word shepherd with perdition, not you, and you don't know why, but she does. I warned you, Mary said. You warned me when the evil had already been done, if it was evil, for when I look at myself, I cannot see it, said Jesus, whereupon Mary told him, There are none so blind as those who will not see. These words annoyed Jesus, and he said reproachfully, Be quiet, Mother, if your son's eyes saw evil, they saw it after you, but these same eyes you call blind have also seen things you've never seen or are likely to see. Her son's authority and stern tone, and the strange thing he said, made Mary yield, but her reply conveyed a final warning, Forgive me, I didn't mean to offend you, may the Lord always protect the light in your eyes and soul. James looked at his mother, then at his brother, saw there was a disagreement but could not imagine what had caused it, clearly something from the past, because his brother had not been back long enough to start an argument. Jesus made for the house, but at the door he turned and said to his mother, Send the children out to play, I must talk to you in private along with James and Joseph. The others left, and the house, which had been so crowded a moment ago, suddenly seemed empty. Four now sat on the floor, Mary between James and Joseph, with Jesus facing them. A long silence followed, as if by common consent they were giving the children time to go far enough away. Finally Jesus spoke, pronouncing his words carefully, I have seen God. The first reaction on the faces of his mother and brothers was awe, followed by disbelief, and between the one and the other there was a hint of cynical mistrust in James's expression, of wonder in that of Joseph, of resigned bitterness in that of Mary. All three remained silent, and Jesus said a second time, I have seen God. If a moment of silence, as the saying goes, marks the passage of an angel, here angels are still passing. Jesus has said all there is to say, his family is at a loss for words, and soon they will rise to their feet and go about their affairs, wondering if this was all a dream. Yet silence, given enough time, has the power to make people speak. Unable to control himself any longer, James asked a question, the most innocent question of all, pure of rhetoric, Are you sure. Jesus did not reply, simply looked at James, perhaps as God had looked at him from within the cloud, and for the third time said, I have seen God. Mary, who had no questions to ask, said, You must have imagined it. Jesus replied, Mother, God spoke to me. James, having recovered his composure, decided this must be some kind of madness, a brother of his speaking to God, how ridiculous, Well, who knows, perhaps it was God who put the money in your pack, he said, smiling ironically. Jesus reddened but spoke coldly, Everything comes to us from the Lord, He is forever finding paths to reach us, and although this money may not have come from Him, it certainly came through Him. And what did the Lord say to you, where did you see Him, and were you asleep or keeping watch. I was in the desert looking for a stray sheep when He called out to me. Are you allowed to tell us what He said. That one day He will ask for my life. All lives belong to the Lord. That's what I told Him. And what did He say. That in exchange for the life I must give Him, I will have power and glory. You will have power and glory after you die, asked Mary, unable to believe her ears. Yes, Mother. What power and glory can be given to someone after death. I don't know. Were you dreaming. I was awake and looking for my sheep in the desert. And when is the Lord going to ask you for your life. I don't know, but He told me we would meet again when I was ready. James looked at his brother in dismay, The sun in the desert affected your brain, you've been suffering from sunstroke, but Mary suddenly asked, And what about the sheep, what happened to the sheep. The Lord ordered me to sacrifice it to seal our covenant. These words provoked James, You're offending the Lord, the Lord made a covenant with His people and He's not likely to make one with an ordinary man like you, the son of a carpenter, a shepherd, and who knows what else. Mary appeared to be following some thread of thought carefully, as if it might break, but by persevering she found the question she had to ask, What sheep was that. The lamb I had with me when we met in Jerusalem at the Gate of Ramah, in the end what I tried to keep from the Lord the Lord took from me. And God, what did God look like when you saw Him. A cloud. Open or closed, asked James. A column of smoke. You're mad, brother. If I am mad, God made me mad. You're in Satan's power, said Mary, shouting more than speaking. It wasn't Satan I met in the desert, it was the Lord, and if it's true that I'm in Satan's power, then the Lord has so ordained. You've been in the clutches of Satan since the day you were born. You ought to know. Yes, I know all right, you chose to live with the devil for four long years rather than with God. And after spending four years with the devil, I met God. You're telling the most awful lies. I'm the son you brought into the world, either believe me or renounce me. I believe you, but not what you say. Jesus got to his feet, raised his eyes to heaven, and said, When the Lord's promise is fulfilled, you will have to believe what people say of me. He went to get his pack and staff and put on his sandals. Dividing the money in two parts, arranging the coins side by side on the ground, he said, This is Lisa's dowry when she marries, and added, The rest will be returned where it came from, and perhaps also be used as a dowry. He turned to the door, was about to leave without saying good-bye, when Mary remarked, I noticed you no longer carry a bowl in your pack. I had one, but it broke. There are four bowls over there, choose one and take it with you. Jesus hesitated, preferring to leave empty-handed, but he went to the hearth where the four bowls were stacked one on top of the other. Choose one, Mary said again. Jesus looked and chose, I'll take this one, which has seen better days. You picked the right one for you, said Mary. Why do you say that. It's the color of the black earth, it neither disintegrates nor breaks. Jesus put the bowl into his pack, tapped his staff on the ground, Tell me once more that you don't believe me. We don't believe you, said his mother, and now less than ever, because you chose the devil's symbol. What symbol are you talking about. That bowl. At that very moment Pastor's words came to Jesus from the depths of memory, You will have another bowl, but the next won't break while you are alive. A rope seemed to have been extended its full length, ending in a circle and tied with a knot. Jesus was leaving home for the second time, but this time he did not say, One way or another I shall always come back. As he turned his back on Nazareth and began descending the first mountain slope, an even sadder thought crossed his mind, What if Mary Magdalene did not believe him either.

This man who carries God's promise with him has nowhere to go except the house of a prostitute. He cannot return to his flock, Begone with you, were Pastor's last words to him, nor can he return home, We don't believe you, his family told him, and his steps begin to falter, he is afraid to proceed, to arrive. It is as if he were back in the desert, Who am I, but the mountains and valleys do not answer, nor the heavens, which ought to know everything. If he goes back now and repeats the question, his mother will say, You're my son, but I don't believe you, so the time has come for Jesus to sit on this stone that has been reserved for him since the world began, to sit and shed tears of misery and loneliness. Who knows, perhaps the Lord will appear to him once more, even if only in the form of smoke, all He has to say is, Come, there's no need for all this weeping and wailing, what's the matter with you, we all have our bad moments, and there's one important thing I should have mentioned earlier, everything is relative in life, and every misfortune becomes bearable when compared with something worse, so dry your tears and behave like a man, you've already made your peace with your father, what more do you want, and as for this friction with your mother, I'll deal with that when the time comes, what didn't please Me much was that business with Mary Magdalene, a common whore, but then you're still young and might as well enjoy life while you can, the one thing doesn't rule out the other, there's a time for eating and a time for fasting, a time for sinning and a time for repenting, a time for living and a time for dying. Jesus wiped his tears on the back of his hand, blew his nose, who knows where, and yes, there is no point spending the whole day here, the desert is what it is, it surrounds us, in some ways protects us, but when it comes to giving, it gives us nothing, it simply looks on, and when the sun suddenly clouds over, so that we find ourselves thinking, The sky mirrors our sorrow, we are being foolish, because the sky is quite impartial and neither rejoices in our happiness nor is cast down by our grief.

People are heading in this direction on their way to Nazareth, and Jesus, a grown man with a beard, does not wish to be seen crying like a child. From time to time a few travelers pass one another on the road, some going up, others coming down, they greet one another effusively, but only after they are certain of their mutual goodwill, for the bandits in these parts are of two types. There are those who assault travelers, like the heartless rogues who robbed Jesus some five years ago when the poor boy was on his way to Jerusalem to find solace. Then there are the rebels, who certainly do not make a habit of traveling the main roads, but they sometimes appear in disguise to spy on the movements of Roman troops before setting up the next ambush, or without any disguise they'll stop wealthy travelers collaborating with the Romans and strip them of their silver, gold, and other valuables, and even well-armed bodyguards are powerless to spare the travelers this outrage. It was natural for the eighteen-year-old Jesus to sigh for adventure as he gazed on those lofty mountains with the ravines and caves where the followers of Judas the Galilean continued to take refuge. He wondered what he would do if a band of rebels appeared from nowhere and invited him to join them, exchanging the amenities of peace for the glory of battle, for it is written that one day the Lord will bring forth a Messiah, who will deliver His people once and for all from oppression and give them strength against future enemies. A gust of mad hope and pride blows like a sign from the Spirit on Jesus' forehead, and for one spellbinding moment this carpenter's son sees himself as captain, leader, and supreme commander, with raised sword, his very presence striking awe and terror in the Roman legions, who throw themselves over precipices like pigs possessed by demons, so much for Senatus Populusque Romanus. Then Jesus remembered that he was promised power and glory, but only after his death, so he might as well enjoy life, and if he must go to war, let it be on one condition, that occasionally he will be allowed to leave the lines and spend a few days with Mary Magdalene, unless they allow one female companion for each soldier, anything more would lead to promiscuity and Mary has already said she has given that up. Let us hope so, for Jesus feels his strength redouble at the thought of the woman who cured his painful wound, which she replaced with the intolerable wound of desire. But here is the problem, how is he to face the locked gate with the sign unless he is absolutely certain he will find on the other side the woman he believes he left behind, who waits for him and him alone, in body and soul, because Mary Magdalene will not accept one without the other.

The day is drawing to a close, the houses of Magdala can be seen in the distance huddled together like a flock. Mary's house, the sheep that wandered off, cannot be seen from here, amid the great boulders that line the road bend after bend. Jesus remembers the sheep he had to kill in order to seal in blood the covenant demanded by the Lord, and his soul, now free of battles and victories, warms at the thought of searching once more for his sheep, not to kill it or lead it back to the flock but so that together they can climb to fresh pastures, which are still to be found if we look carefully enough in this vast and much traveled world, if we look even closer into those impenetrable gorges, sheep that we are. Jesus stopped in front of the door and discreetly confirmed that it was locked. The sign still hangs there, Mary Magdalene is not receiving anyone. Jesus need only call out, It's me, to hear her joyfully sing,

This is the voice of my beloved, behold him who has come leaping over mountains and jumping over hills, there he waits on the other side of this wall, behind this door, and it is true, but Jesus would rather knock on the door, once, twice, without uttering a word, waiting for someone to open. Who's there, what do you want, someone asked from within. Jesus disguised his voice, pretending to be an eager client with money to spend, using words such as, Open up, flower, you won't regret it, I'll pay and service you well, and if the voice was false, his words were true enough when he said, I'm Jesus of Nazareth. Mary Magdalene did not open, the voice did not quite match the words, besides she thought it unlikely that Jesus could be back so soon, when he had said, One day I'll come, Nazareth isn't far from Magdala, after all. People often say such things to please the listener, and one day might mean three months but never tomorrow. Mary Magdalene opens the door, throws herself into Jesus' arms, cannot believe her good fortune. In her excitement she foolishly imagines that he has come back because the sore on his foot reopened, so she leads him inside, sits him down, and fetches the lamp, Your foot, show me your foot, but Jesus tells her, My foot has healed, can't you see. She could have replied, No, I can't, which was true, for her eyes were filled with tears. She had to put her lips to the sole of his foot, which was covered with dust, untie carefully the thongs attaching the sandal to his ankle, and stroke with her fingertips the new skin which had formed, in order to verify that the ointment had done its work, though perhaps love too had played some part in the cure.

During supper she asked no questions, only wanted to know if he had had a good journey or encountered any unpleasantness on the road, small talk and nothing more. When they finished eating, there was a long silence, for it was not her turn to speak. Jesus regarded her, as if from a high rock he were weighing his strength against the sea, not because he feared man-eating fish or dangerous reefs beneath the smooth surface, he was simply putting his courage to the test. He has known this woman for a week, sufficient time to tell whether she will receive him with open arms, yet he is afraid to reveal, now that the moment has come, what has just been rejected by those of his own flesh and blood, who should have been with him also in spirit. Jesus hesitates, tries to find words, but all that comes out is a phrase to gain time, Weren't you surprised to see me back so soon. I began waiting for you the moment you left and did not count the hours between your leaving and returning, nor should I have counted them had you stayed away for ten years. Jesus smiled, he should have known there was no point being evasive with this woman. They sat on the ground, facing each other, a lamp in the middle and the leftovers from their supper. He took a piece of bread, broke it in two, and giving a piece to her, said, Let this be the bread of truth, let us eat it so that we may believe and never doubt, whatever is said and learned here. So be it, said Mary Magdalene. He ate his bread, waited for her to finish hers, and said, for the fourth time, I have seen God. Her expression did not change, she only fidgeted, her hands crossed on her lap, and asked, Was this what you said you would tell me when we met again. Yes, as well as all the other things that have happened to me since I left home four years ago, I feel they are all linked, although I cannot explain how or why. I am your lips and ears, replied Mary Magdalene, whatever you say, you will be saying it to yourself, for I am inside you. Now Jesus can begin to speak, for they have both partaken of the bread of truth, and there are few such moments in life. Night turned to dawn, the flame in the lamp died twice, and Jesus' entire history as we know it was related there, even including certain details we didn't consider worthwhile mentioning and countless thoughts that escaped us, not because he tried to conceal them but simply because this evangelist cannot be everywhere at once. As Jesus began telling in a weary voice what happened after he returned home, grief caused him to waver, just as dark foreboding had made him pause before knocking at the door. Breaking her silence for the first time, Mary Magdalene asked him in a voice of one who already knows the answer, Your mother didn't believe you. That's right, said Jesus. And so you came back to your other home. Yes. If only I could lie to you and tell you that I don't believe you. Why. So that you would do again what you've just done, leave as you left your home, and I, not believing you, would not have to follow you. That doesn't answer my question. True, it is not an answer, well then, if I did not believe you, I would not have to share the dreadful fate that awaits you. How do you know a dreadful fate awaits me. I know nothing about God, except that His pleasure is as terrifying as His displeasure. Whatever put that strange idea into your head. You have to be a woman to know what it means to live with God's contempt, and now you'll have to be more than a man to live and die as one of His chosen. Are· you trying to frighten me. Let me tell you my dream, one night a little boy appeared to me and told me God was horrible, and with those words he disappeared, I have no idea who that child was, where he came from, or who he belonged to. It's only a dream. You of all people speaking of a dream that way. And then what happened. Then I turned to prostitution. But you've given that up. Not in the dream, not even after I met you. Tell me again what the child said. God is horrible. Jesus saw the desert, the dead sheep, the blood on the sand, heard the column of smoke sighing with satisfaction, and said, Yes, that could be, but it's one thing to hear it in a dream and another to experience it in real life. God forbid that you should ever experience it. Each of us has to fulfill his destiny. And you've been given the first solemn warning about yours. Studded with stars, the heavenly dome turns slowly over

Magdala and the wide world. Somewhere in the infinite that He occupies, God advances and withdraws the pawns of the other games He plays, but it is too soon to worry about this one, all He need do for the present is allow things to take their natural course, apart from the occasional adjustment with the tip of His little finger to make sure some stray thought or action does not interfere with the harmony of destinies. Hence His lack of interest in the rest of the conversation between Jesus and Mary Magdalene. And now what will you do, she asks him. You said you would follow me wherever I go. I will be with you wherever you are. What is the difference. None at all, but you can stay here as long as you like, if you don't mind living in what was once a house of sin. Jesus paused, reflected at length, and finally said, I will find work in Magdala, and we can live together as husband and wife. You promise too much, I'm quite content just to sit here at your feet.

Jesus found no work, and met with what he might have expected, jeers, ridicule, insults, which was not surprising, for here was a mere youth living with the notorious Mary Magdalene, It won't be long before we see him sitting at the front door waiting his turn like all her other clients. He tolerated their jibes for several weeks, but finally he said to Mary, I must get away from this place. But where can we go. Somewhere by the sea. They left before dawn, and the people of Magdala came too late to salvage anything from the flames.

Months later, on a cold and rainy winter night, an angel entered the house of Mary of Nazareth without disturbing anyone. Mary herself only noticed the visitor because the angel spoke to her as follows, Know, Mary, that the Lord mixed His seed with that of Joseph on the morning you conceived for the first time, and it was the Lord's seed rather than that of your husband, however legitimate, that sired your son Jesus. Much surprised, Mary asked the angel, So Jesus is my son and also the son of the Lord. Woman, what are you saying, show some respect for precedence, the way you should put it is the son of the Lord and also of me. Of the Lord and also of you. No, of the Lord and of you. You confuse me, just answer my question, is Jesus our son. You mean to say the Lord's son, because you only served to bear the child. So the Lord didn't choose me. Don't be absurd, the Lord was merely passing, as anyone watching would have seen from the color of the sky, when His eye caught you and Joseph, a fine, healthy couple, and then, if you can still remember how God's will was made manifest, He ordained that Jesus be born nine months later. Is there any proof that it was the Lord's seed that sired my firstborn. Well, it's a delicate matter, what you're demanding is nothing less than a paternity test, which in these mixed unions, no matter how many analyses, tests, and genetic comparisons one carries out, can never give conclusive results. There I was thinking the Lord had chosen me for His bride that morning, and now you tell me it was pure chance and He could just as easily have chosen someone else, well, let me tell you, I wish you hadn't descended to Nazareth to leave me in this state of uncertainty, besides, surely any son of the Lord, even with me as the mother, would have stood out at birth and, growing up, would have had the same bearing, appearance, and manner of speaking as the Lord himself, and though people say a mother's love is blind, my son Jesus looks ordinary enough to me. Your first mistake, Mary, is to think I came here only to discuss some sexual episode in the Lord's past, and your second mistake is to think that the beauty and speech of mankind resemble those of the Lord, when I can vouch, as someone close to Him, that the Lord's way of doing things is invariably the opposite of what humans imagine, and strictly between us, I'm convinced the Lord couldn't operate in any other fashion, and the word most frequently on His lips is not yes but no. But surely it's the devil who's the spirit of denial. No, my child, the devil only denies himself, and until you learn to tell the difference, you'll never know to whom you belong. I belong to the Lord. So you belong to the Lord, do you, well your third and biggest mistake is not to have believed your son. You mean Jesus. Yes, Jesus, for no other man saw God or is ever likely to see Him. Tell me, angel of the Lord, is it really true that my son Jesus saw God. Yes, like a child finding his first nest he came running to show you, and you, suspicious, mistrusting, told him that it couldn't be true, that if there was any nest, it was empty, if there were any eggs, they were hollow, and if there were no eggs, a snake devoured them. Forgive me for having doubted. Now I cannot be sure whether you are talking to me or to your son. To him, to you, to both, what can I do to make amends for the harm done. Listen to your maternal heart. Then I should go and find him, tell him that I believe him, ask him to forgive me and come home, where the Lord will summon him when the time comes. I honestly don't know whether you will reach him in time, there is no one more sensitive than an adolescent, you risk being insulted and having the door slammed in your face. If that happens, the demon who bewitched and led him astray is to blame, and I cannot understand how the Lord, as a father, could have permitted such liberties and given the rascal so much freedom. To which demon are you referring. To the shepherd my son accompanied for four years and whose flock he tended for no good reason. Oh, that shepherd. Do you know him. We went to school together. And does the Lord let such a demon thrive and prosper. The harmony of the universe requires it, but the Lord will always have the last word, only we don't know when He will say it, but you'll see, one of these days we'll wake up and find there is no evil in the world, now if you'll excuse me I must be off, if you have any more questions to ask, this is your opportunity. Only one. Fine, go ahead. Why does the Lord want my son. Your son, in a manner of speaking. In the eyes of the world Jesus is my son. Why does the Lord want him, you ask, well there's an interesting question, but unfortunately I cannot answer it, at the moment that's between the two of them, and I don't believe Jesus knows any more than he has already told you. He told me he will have power and glory after death. Yes, I'm aware of that. But what must he do in life to merit this reward the Lord has promised. Come now, you're being stupid, surely you don't believe that such a word exists in the eyes of the Lord or that what you presumptuously refer to as merit has any value or meaning, it's incredible what you people get into your heads when you're nothing but complete slaves of God's absolute will. I'll say no more, for I am truly the servant of the Lord and would have Him do with me as He will, but tell me one thing, after all these months where am I to find my son. It is your duty to go in search of him just as he went in search of his lost sheep. In order to kill it. Don't worry, he won't kill you, but you will certainly kill him by not being present at the hour of his death. How do you know I won't die first. I am sufficiently close to the seat of power to know, and now I must bid you farewell, you've asked all the questions you wanted, except the one question you should have asked, but that's something which no longer concerns me. Explain. Explain it to yourself. And with these words the angel disappeared, and Mary opened her eyes.

The children were all fast asleep, the boys together in two groups of three, James, Joseph, and Judas, the three older boys, in one corner, in the other their younger brothers, Simon, Justus, and Samuel, and lying beside Mary were Lisa on one side, Lydia on the other. Troubled by the angel's words, Mary noticed with alarm and dismay that Lisa was practically naked, her tunic in disarray and pulled up over her breasts as she lay asleep with a smile on her face, the perspiration glistening on her forehead and upper lip, which appeared to be red from kissing. Had Mary not been certain that only one angel had entered, Lisa's appearance would have been enough to convince her that one of those incubuses who violate women in their sleep had secretly been having his way with the poor girl while her mother was engaged in conversation. This probably happens all the time without our knowing, these angels go around in pairs at their leisure, and while one diverts attention by telling fairy tales, the other carries out the wickedness, which strictly speaking is not all that wicked, and probably they will reverse their roles next time, so that the salutary meaning of the duality of flesh and spirit will not be lost on either the dreamer or the person being dreamed about. Mary covered her daughter, pulled the tunic down before waking her and asking in a whisper, What were you dreaming. Taken by surprise, the girl had no time to invent a lie, she confessed that she dreamed of an angel who said nothing but looked at her with as gentle and sweet an expression as one could hope to find in paradise. Did he touch you, asked Mary, and Lisa replied, Mother, no one touches with their eyes. Not altogether convinced, Mary said in an even lower whisper, I too dreamed of an angel. And did your angel speak or was he also silent, Lisa asked in all innocence. He told me your brother Jesus was telling the truth when he said he saw God. Oh, Mother, how wrong we were not to believe Jesus, who is so good and patient, no one could have blamed him had he taken back the money for my dowry. Now we must try to put things right. But we don't know where to find him, he has sent no news, oh, if only we had asked the angel, after all, angels know everything. Of course, but the angel didn't offer to help, he just said it was our duty to look for your brother. Mother, if brother Jesus was truly with the Lord, then our life is going to be different from now on. Different, perhaps, but for the worse. Why. If we don't believe Jesus or his word, how can you expect others to believe, we can't very well go through the streets and squares of Nazareth proclaiming Jesus has seen the Lord, Jesus has seen the Lord, unless we want people chasing us with stones. But if the Lord himself chose Jesus, then surely He will protect us, his family. Don't be too certain, we weren't around when Jesus was chosen, and as far as the Lord is concerned, there are neither fathers nor sons, remember Abraham, remember Isaac. Oh, Mother, how terrible. It would be wise, my child, to keep this matter to ourselves and say as little as possible. Then what will we do. Tomorrow I'll send James and Joseph to look for Jesus. But where, Galilee is so big, and so is Samaria, if he went there, and Judaea and Idumaea are at the end of the world. Your brother has probably gone to sea, remember what he told us when he came, that he had been helping some fishermen. Isn't it more likely that he returned to the flock. Those days are over. How do you know. Try to get some sleep, it's getting late. Who knows, we might dream of our angels again. Perhaps. Whether Lisa's angel, having given its companion the slip, visited her dream once more, no one ever discovered, but the angel who brought Mary tidings was unable to return, because her eyes remained open as she lay in the darkness, yet what she knew was more than enough, and what she suspected filled her with fear.

At daybreak the mats were rolled up, and Mary summoned all her children before her. She explained that she had been thinking seriously about their recent treatment of Jesus, Starting with myself, as his mother, I think we should have been kinder and more understanding, and I've come to the conclusion that it's only right that we go look for him and ask him to come home, for we believe in him and, God willing, will one day believe what he told us. This was what Mary told them, unaware that she was repeating the words used by Joseph, who had also been present during that dramatic moment of family rejection. Who knows, perhaps Jesus would still be here today if that quiet murmur, although we did not point it out at the time, for it was but a murmur, had been on everyone's lips. Mary said nothing about the angel and the angel's words, she just reminded her children of the respect they owed their oldest brother. James dared not question his mother's change of heart, but he continued to doubt his brother's sanity, unless Jesus had fallen under the spell of some dangerous charlatan. He asked, knowing her reply, And who is to go look for our brother Jesus. You must go, as the second oldest, and Joseph will accompany you, together you will travel more safely. Where should we begin. By the Sea of

Galilee, I'm sure you'll find him there. When do we leave. Jesus left months ago, so there's no time to lose. But the rains have started, Mother, and this is no time to be traveling. My son, the circumstances create the need, and the need, when it is great enough, creates the circumstances. Mary's children looked at her in surprise, unaccustomed to such deep maxims from their mother's lips and still too young to know that keeping company with angels can produce these and even more impressive results. Take Lisa, for example, who at this very moment is slowly nodding her head in a daze, the others suspecting nothing.

When the family meeting was over, James and Joseph took a good look at the sky to see if there was any chance of a dry day for their departure despite the recent bad weather. The sky must have noticed, for right over the Sea of Galilee it turned a watery blue which promised an afternoon without rain. Having discreetly made their farewells indoors, since Mary felt the neighbors should know as little as possible, the two brothers finally set out on their journey, not along the road to Magdala, for there was no reason to think Jesus had gone in that direction, but by another route, which would soon bring them to the new city of Tiberias. They went barefoot, with all the mud on the roads they could hardly wear sandals, so they kept them safely in their packs until the weather improved. James had two reasons for choosing the road to Tiberias. First because he was curious, coming from the provinces, to see the palaces and temples he had heard so much about, and secondly because he had been told that the city was situated about halfway up this side of the river. Since they would have to earn a living while searching, James hoped to find work on a building site there, despite what the devout Jews of Nazareth said about the place's being unhealthy because of the polluted air and sulphurous waters nearby. The brothers did not reach Tiberias that day, because the promising signs in the sky came to nothing, within an hour of their departure it started raining again. They were fortunate to come upon a cave big enough to shelter them before the floodwater could sweep them away. They slept in safety, but no longer trusted in the weather.

In Tiberias the only work they found at a building site was unskilled, carting stones, but after a few days they had earned enough to satisfy their modest needs, not that King Herod Antipas was generous to his workers. They inquired if anyone had seen a certain Jesus of Nazareth, perhaps only passing through, He's our brother, looks more or less like us, but we're not sure whether or not he's traveling alone. No one had seen him working there, so James and Joseph went around to all the boat houses. Clearly, if their brother had decided to rejoin the fishermen, he would not have wasted time slaving at a building site under some harsh foreman when the lake was right there. But no one had seen him. Now that the brothers had a little money, the next thing to consider was whether the search along the riverbank, village by village, crew by crew, boat by boat, should be carried out to the north or to the south. James finally decided they should travel south, that road was flatter, the northern road was much more uneven. The weather became stable, the cold bearable, the rain had passed, anyone with more experience of nature's cycle than these two youths had would have recognized, just by sniffing the air and feeling the soil, the first signs of spring. This mission to find their brother was turning into an agreeable country outing, a pleasant holiday by the lake, and James and Joseph were almost in danger of forgetting why they had come, when unexpectedly they met some fishermen who gave them news of Jesus, expressed in the strangest manner. One of the fishermen told them, Yes, we know him, and when you find him, tell him we wait for his return as eagerly as if we were waiting for our daily bread. The brothers were astounded, they could scarcely believe these men were talking about Jesus, perhaps the fishermen had mistaken him for some other Jesus, Judging from your description, he's the same Jesus, but whether he came from Nazareth we cannot say, for he never mentioned it. And why do you wait for his return as eagerly as if waiting for your daily bread, James asked. Because whenever he was in the boat, the fish swam straight into our nets. But our brother knows nothing about fishing, so he can't be the same Jesus. We never said he knows anything about fishing, but he only has to say, Cast your nets on this side, and no sooner are the nets lowered than they come up full. Then why is he no longer with you. Because he moved on after a few days, saying he must help other fishermen, which is true, because he joined us on three occasions, always promising to return. And where is he now. We don't know, last time he left, he was heading south, but he may have gone north without our noticing, he comes and goes at will. James said to Joseph, Let's go south, at least we know our brother is somewhere on this side of the water. This seemed sensible, though they would miss Jesus if he happened to be out on the lake, on one of those miraculous fishing trips. We tend to overlook such details, but fate is not what we imagine, a thing determined according to some principle or other, note how certain encounters, such as the one we have just described, can occur only if the persons concerned happen to be in the same place at the same time, which is not always easy. If we pause for a moment to look up at a cloud in the sky, to listen to the song of a bird, to count the entrances and exits of an anthill, or are so preoccupied that we neither look nor listen nor count but continue on our way, we may miss the perfect opportunity. Believe me, brother Joseph, fate is the most difficult thing of all in this world, as you'll learn when you're my age. Forewarned, the two brothers kept a watchful eye, stopped often to see if any boat was late in returning, several times they even retraced their steps in the hope of taking Jesus by surprise in some unlikely place, till finally they reached the end of the lake. Crossing to the other side of the river Jordan, they asked the first fishermen they met if they knew anything about Jesus. Yes, of course the men had heard about his wondrous deeds, but no one had seen him. James and Joseph went back and headed north again, more observant this time, like fishermen dragging their nets in the hope of catching the king of fish. Whenever they spent the night by the road, they kept watch in turn, lest Jesus take advantage of the moonlight to steal from one place to another. Making inquiries as they went, they reached Tiberias, where they did not have to look for work, they still had some money left thanks to the generosity of the fishermen, who supplied them with fish, prompting Joseph to ask on one occasion, James, has it occurred to you that this fish we are eating might have been caught by our brother, and James replied, That won't improve the taste, unkind words coming from a brother but understandable when one considers James's frustration, God help him, as he wearily went on searching for a needle in a haystack.

They found Jesus an hour, that is to say, by our time, after leaving Tiberias. The first to spot him was Joseph, who has keen eyes and can see things from quite a distance, That's him, over there, he cried. In fact there are two persons coming in this direction, and one is a woman. No, says James, it can't be him. A young boy rarely contradicts an older brother, but Joseph is so overjoyed that he dispenses with the usual rules and conventions, I'm telling you, it's him, But I see a woman there, Yes, a woman with a man, and the man is Jesus. Along the riverbank and across a stretch of flat land between two hills that sloped practically to the water's edge, Jesus and Mary Magdalene could be seen approaching. James stopped and waited, and ordered Joseph to stay with him. The boy reluctantly obeyed, eager as he was to run to his long-lost brother, to embrace him and throw his arms around his neck. James, however, was disturbed by the presence of the woman at Jesus' side. Who is she, he asked himself, refusing to believe that his brother already had carnal knowledge of a woman, the very idea created an enormous gulf between James and his older brother, as if Jesus, who boasted of having seen God, was now in a completely different realm, simply by having carnal knowledge of a woman. One reflection leads to another, though we often do not notice the connection between them, it is like crossing a river by a covered bridge, we walk without looking where we are going, passing over a river we did not know existed, and James too began to think it was not right to remain standing there, as if he were the eldest in the family and Jesus should come to him. No sooner did James stir than Joseph ran to Jesus with open arms and cries of joy, startling into flight a flock of birds that, concealed among the tall reeds, had been foraging in the marsh by the river. James walked faster, to prevent Joseph from delivering any messages that were his responsibility, and coming face-to-face with Jesus, he said to him, Thanks be to the Lord that we found you, brother, and Jesus replied, I am delighted to see both of you in such good health. Mary Magdalene, meanwhile, had lingered behind. Jesus asked, What brings you to these parts, and James suggested, Let's go over there, where no one can hear us. We can talk here, said Jesus, and if you're referring to the woman accompanying me, then let me assure you that whatever you have to say and that I may wish to hear can be said in her presence. The deep silence which followed was that of the sea and the mountains put together, not the silence of four human beings confronting one another and summoning their courage. Jesus seemed older, and his skin was tanned, but his feverish look had gone, and the expression behind his heavy, dark beard was composed, serene, despite the tension of this unexpected encounter. Who is that woman, asked James. Her name is Mary, and she is with me, said Jesus. Is she your wife.

Well, yes and no. I don't understand. That doesn't surprise me. I must talk to you. Go ahead. I've brought a message from Mother. I'm listening. I'd prefer to tell you in private. You heard what I said. Mary Magdalene stepped forward, I can stay out of the way until you've finished your conversation. No, said Jesus, you share all my thoughts, therefore you should know what my mother thinks of me, so I don't have to repeat it to you later. James flushed and made as if to turn away, giving Mary Magdalene a black look that betrayed mixed feelings of hatred and desire. Joseph stretched out his hands to keep them apart, all that he could do. James eventually calmed down, then remembered what he had to say, Mother sent us to find you and accompany you back home, for we believe you, and with God's help perhaps one day we'll believe what you told us. Is that all. Those were Mother's words. So, not willing to believe what I told you, you wait for the Lord to help you change your mind. Whether we believe or not depends on the Lord. You are mistaken, the Lord gave us legs that we might walk, and we walked, I've never heard of any man who waited for the Lord to say, Start walking, and it's the same with our mind, God gave us a mind to use according to our will and desire. I won't argue with you. Just as well, for you wouldn't win. What should I tell Mother. Tell her the message comes too late, that Joseph spoke those same words in time, but she paid no attention, and even should an angel of the Lord appear and convince her that everything I said was true, I have no intention of returning home. You're committing the sin of pride. A tree weeps when cut down, a dog howls when beaten, but a man matures when offended. She's your mother, and we are your brothers. Who are my mother and brothers, my mother and brothers are they who believe me when I speak, they are the fishermen who know that when I join them, they will catch more fish than ever, my mother and brothers are they who do not have to wait for the hour of my death to take pity on my life. Have you no other message for Mother. That is all, but you will hear others speak of me, said Jesus, then turning to Mary Magdalene, Let us go, Mary, the boats are ready to leave, the fish are gathering, time to reap this harvest. As they walked away, James called out, Jesus, should I mention this woman to Mother. Tell her she is with me and her name is Mary, and the name echoed between the hills and over the lake. Crouching on the ground, young Joseph wept bitter tears.

W<small>HEN</small> J<small>ESUS</small> <small>GOES</small> <small>TO</small> <small>FISH</small> <small>WITH</small> <small>THE</small> <small>FISHERMEN</small>, M<small>ARY</small> Magdalene waits for him, usually seated on a rock at the water's edge, or on a nearby hill if there is one, from where she can easily follow the route they sail. Fishing is no longer a slow operation, for there have never been so many fish in this lake, it's like putting one's hand in a bucket filled with fish, but not for everyone, because if Jesus happens to go elsewhere, then the bucket reverts to being almost empty, and hands and arms soon tire of casting net after net to find only an occasional fish or two trapped in the mesh. In despair, the entire fishing community on the western side of the Sea of Galilee goes to ask Jesus, to implore Jesus, to demand that Jesus help them, and in some places they even receive him with festivities and floral tributes, as if it were Palm Sunday. But the bread of humanity being what it is, a mixture of envy and malice with a little charity here and there, the yeast of fear fermenting evil while suppressing good, one group of fishermen began quarreling with another, one village with another, they all wanted Jesus, and let the others provide for themselves as best they can. Whenever they started fighting, Jesus withdrew to the desert, returning only when the troublemakers repented and asked forgiveness for their rough behavior while protesting their love and devotion. But what we will never know is why the fishermen on the eastern side never sent delegates to discuss the drafting of a fair treaty that would benefit all parties, not including the large number of Gentiles of different races and persuasions who are to be found in this region. The fishermen on the other bank could also have sent a fleet with nets and pikes, under cover of darkness, to kidnap Jesus, reducing those on the western side to a meager existence just when they had grown accustomed to plenty.

But let us go back to the day James and Joseph came to ask Jesus to give up this existence and return home despite his newfound prosperity since he took up fishing. By now the two brothers, James in a rage, Joseph in tears, are quickly making their way back to Nazareth, where their mother continues to wonder whether the two sons who left will bring a third, but she is doubtful. Their homeward route from the spot on the shore where they met Jesus obliged them to pass through Magdala. James scarcely knew the town and Joseph not at all, the place didn't appear to have anything of interest to detain them there, so after a brief rest the brothers resumed their journey. As they passed the last of the houses before the wilderness began, they saw on their left the bare walls of a house that had been gutted by fire. The gate to the yard had been forced open but only partially destroyed, and it looked as if the fire had started inside. The passerby hopes that some treasure may be left among the ashes, and if there is no danger of a beam falling on his head, he cannot resist exploring further. Treading carefully, he pokes at the debris with one foot, looking for something shiny, a gold coin, an indestructible diamond, an emerald necklace. James and Joseph entered only out of curiosity, they are not so naive as to imagine that rapacious neighbors have not been here already to loot the place, although the house is so small that any prized possessions almost certainly have been removed by the owners. The roof of the oven had caved in, the brick floor was broken, and there were loose tiles underfoot. There's nothing here, said James, let's go, but Joseph asked, What's that. It was a bedstead, but the legs had been burned and the whole frame badly damaged, a phantom throne with bits of charred drapery hanging in tatters. It's a bed, said James, people like great lords and wealthy merchants actually sleep on such things. This doesn't strike me as a rich person's house, argued Joseph. Appearances can be deceptive, James wisely reminded him. As they left, Joseph noticed a cane hanging outside the gate, the sort used for gathering figs, no doubt it had originally been much longer. What is this doing here, he asked, and without waiting for a reply, either from himself or from his brother, he removed the useless cane and took it with him, a souvenir of a fire, of a house destroyed, of people unknown. No one had seen them enter, no one saw them leave, they are only two brothers going home in soiled tunics and with bad news, one brother frustrated by the memory of Mary Magdalene, the other thinking of the fun he will have playing with the broken cane.

Mary Magdalene, sitting on a rock and waiting for Jesus to return from fishing, thinks about Mary of Nazareth. Until today she simply thought of her as Jesus' mother, now she knows, after questioning him, that his mother is also named Mary, a coincidence of no great consequence when one considers the vast number of Marys on this earth and the many more to come if the fashion persists, but we are inclined to believe that there is nevertheless a sense of solidarity between those who share the same name, Joseph for example may think of himself no longer as the son of Joseph but more as his brother, and this could be God's problem, no one else bears His name. These reflections may seem farfetched for someone like Mary Magdalene, but we are confident that she is perfectly capable of such ideas once her thoughts about the man she loves lead her to think of his mother. Mary Magdalene has never had a son of her own to love, but at long last she has learned what it means to love a man, having practiced the thousand and one deceptions of false love. She loves Jesus as a woman loves a man, but also wants to love him as a mother loves a son, perhaps because she is not much younger than his real mother, who sent a message asking her son to come home, only to be refused. Mary Magdalene wonders how Mary of Nazareth will feel when she receives his answer, but that is not the same as imagining how she herself would suffer were she to lose him, for she would be losing her man rather than her son. O Lord, punish me with both sorrows if necessary, murmured Mary Magdalene as she sat waiting for Jesus to return. And as the boat drew nearer and was pulled ashore, as the baskets laden with glistening fish were hauled in, as Jesus, his feet in the water, helped the fishermen and laughed like a child at play, Mary Magdalene saw herself in the role of Mary of Nazareth and, getting up, she went down to the water's edge and waded in to greet Jesus. Kissing him on the shoulder, she whispered, My son. No one heard Jesus say, Mother, for as we know, words that come from the heart are never spoken, they get caught in the throat and can only be read in one's eyes. Mary and Jesus were rewarded with a basket of fish, and as usual they retired to the house where they would spend the night, for they had no home of their own, going from boat to boat and from mat to mat. In the beginning Jesus often said to Mary, This is no life for you, let's find a house of our own where I can join you whenever possible, but Mary insisted, I don't want to wait behind, I prefer to be with you. One day he asked her if she had any relatives who might offer her shelter, and she told him that her brother Lazarus and sister Martha lived in the village of Bethany in Judaea, although she herself left home when she turned to prostitution, and to spare them embarrassment she moved farther and farther away, until she ended up in Magdala. So your name should really be Mary of Bethany if that's where you were born, said Jesus. Yes, I was born in Bethany, but you found me in Magdala, so I think of myself as being from Magdala. People don't refer to me as Jesus of Bethlehem although I was born there, and I don't think of myself as being from Nazareth, because people there don't want me and I certainly don't want them, perhaps I should say like you, I'm from Magdala, and for the same reason. Don't forget we destroyed our house. But not the memory, replied Jesus. No more was said about Mary's returning to Bethany, this stretch of shore is their whole world, and wherever Jesus may go, she will go with him.

How true, the saying which reminds us that there is so much sorrow in this world, misfortunes grow like weeds beneath our feet. Such a saying could only have been invented by mortals, accustomed as they are to life's ups and downs, obstacles, setbacks, and constant struggle. The only people likely to question it are those who sail the seas, for they know that even greater woe lies beneath their feet, indeed, unfathomable chasms. The misfortunes of seafarers, the winds and gales sent from heaven, cause waves to swell, storms to break, sails to rip, and fragile vessels to founder. And these fishermen and sailors truly perish between heaven and earth, a heaven hands cannot reach, an earth feet never touch. The Sea of Galilee is nearly always tranquil and smooth, like any lake, until the watery furies are unleashed, and then it is every man for himself, although sadly some drown. But let us return to Jesus of Nazareth and his recent worries, which only goes to show that the human heart is never content, and that doing one's duty does not bring peace of mind, though those who are easily satisfied would have us believe otherwise. One could say that thanks to the endless comings and goings of Jesus up and down the river Jordan, there is no longer any hardship, not even an occasional shortage, on the western shore, and not only fishermen have benefited, because the abundance of fish has brought down prices and provided people with more to eat. It is true that some attempts were made to keep prices high by the well-known corporate method of throwing part of the catch back into the sea, but Jesus threatened to go elsewhere if those responsible for this abuse did not apologize and change their ways. So everyone is happy, except Jesus. He is tired of the constant back and forth, the embarking and disembarking, the same routine day in and day out, and since the power of making fish appear clearly comes from the Lord, why should he be condemned to this monotony until the Lord is ready to summon him as promised. Jesus does not doubt that the Lord is with him, for the fish never fail to come when he calls them, which has led him to speculate whether the Lord might not be willing to concede him other powers, on the clear understanding that he put them to good use. For as we have seen, Jesus, who has achieved so much already with nothing but intuition to guide him, should have no difficulty meeting that condition. There was one way to find out, as easy as saying, Oh, and that was to try. If it worked, God approved, and if it didn't, God was showing His displeasure. The first problem was that of choice. Unable to consult the Lord directly, Jesus would have to risk choosing a power, one that would provoke the least objection, it could not be too obvious, yet not so subtle as to go unnoticed by those who would benefit, or by the world, for that would diminish the glory of God, which must be considered above all things. But Jesus could not make up his mind, he was afraid God might ridicule him, humiliate him as He had done in the desert, even now he shuddered at the thought of the embarrassment he would have suffered if the nets had come back empty when he first suggested, Cast your nets on this side. These matters worried him so much that one night he dreamed someone was whispering in his ear, Don't be afraid, remember God needs you, but when he woke up, he could not help wondering who had spoken, an angel, one of the many who go around delivering messages from the Lord, or was it a demon, one of the many who do Satan's bidding. Mary Magdalene was fast asleep beside him, so it could not have been her.

This was how things stood when Jesus set out one day, which seemed no different from any other, to perform the usual miracle. The clouds were low in the sky and there were signs of rain, but it takes more than rain to keep fishermen at home, they are used to every kind of weather. On this particular day the boat belonged to Simon and his brother Andrew, who had witnessed the first miracle, and it was accompanied by the boat of James and John, the sons of Zebedee, because one can never tell if a miracle will always have the same effect, a boat nearby may get some of the fish gathering there. The strong wind carries them swiftly out, and after lowering the sails the fishermen in both boats prepare their nets and wait for Jesus to tell them where they should cast them. At this point the situation starts getting difficult, a storm suddenly comes without warning from the overcast sky, it grows so fierce that the waves swell and rise, driven by the frenzied gale, and those two fragile nutshells are buffeted wildly as the elements unleash their wrath. The plight of the defenseless fishermen brought shouts and lamentations from the people watching on the shore. Wives, mothers, sisters, children, and the occasional good-hearted mother-in-law were gathered there, making such a din with their weeping and wailing that it must have been heard in heaven, Oh, my poor husband, Oh, my beloved son, Oh, my dear brother, Oh, my poor son-in-law, A curse on you, miserable sea, Holy Mother of the Afflicted, help us, Protectress of the

Voyager, come to our aid, but all the children could do was to weep. Mary Magdalene was there too, murmuring, Jesus, Jesus, but she did not pray for him, she knew the Lord was saving him for another occasion, not likely to let him perish in a mere storm at sea, where the only consequence was a few drowned men. She kept on repeating, Jesus, Jesus, as if the very sound of his name could rescue the fishermen, who certainly appeared close to meeting their fate. In the midst of the storm, Jesus watched the despair and destruction all around him, the waves sweeping over the boats and flooding them, the masts breaking, the sails flying through the air, the rain becoming a flood capable of sinking one of the emperor's own ships. Jesus watched and thought, It is not right that these men should die while I live, the Lord will rebuke me, saying, You could have saved those who were with you, yet you made no attempt to save them, as if your father's crime were not enough. To be reminded of that was so painful, Jesus jumped to his feet, and standing as firmly as if on solid ground, he commanded the wind, Be quiet, and told the sea, Be calm, and no sooner had he spoken than the sea and the wind abated, the clouds in the sky dispersed, and the sun appeared in all its glory, ever a wondrous sight in the eyes of us poor mortals. Impossible to describe the rejoicing in the boats, the kissing and embracing, the tears of joy ashore, those on the far bank were puzzled that the storm died down so quickly, those here, as if restored to life, could think of nothing but their lucky escape, and if some spontaneously exclaimed, Miracle, miracle, they seemed unaware that someone had to be responsible for it. A sudden silence fell over the water, the other boats surrounded that of Simon and Andrew, and all the fishermen looked at Jesus, too astonished to speak, for above the roar of the storm they had heard him call out, Be quiet, Be calm, and there he was, Jesus, the man who could summon fish from the sea, and now he had forbidden the sea to deliver men to the fish. Eyes lowered, Jesus sat on the oarsman's bench, his face showing both triumph and disaster, as if on reaching a mountain peak he was now beginning the sad and inevitable descent. Forming a circle, the men waited for him to speak. It was not enough to have tamed the wind and pacified the water, he had to explain how a simple Galilean, an obscure carpenter's son, could have achieved such a miracle, when God himself had abandoned them to death's cold embrace. Jesus rose to his feet and told them, What you have just witnessed was not my doing, the voice that quelled the storm was not mine but that of the Lord speaking through me, as through the prophets, I am only the mouth of the Lord. Simon, who was in the boat with him, said, Just as the Lord sent the storm, He could also have sent it away, but it was your word that saved our lives. Believe me, it was God's doing, not mine. Whereupon John, the younger son of Zebedee, spoke, proving that he was not at all simpleminded, It may have been God's doing, for in Him resides all power, but He acted through you, so clearly it is God's will that we should know you. But you already know me. Only that you came from who knows where and mysteriously filled our boats with fish. I am Jesus of Nazareth, the son of a carpenter who was crucified by the Romans, for a time I was a shepherd for a flock of sheep and goats, and now here I am with you, and perhaps I will go on being a fisherman until the hour of my death. Andrew, the brother of Simon, said, We will stay with you, because any man with your power is condemned to loneliness heavier than any millstone around one's neck. Jesus said, Stay with me if that is what your heart asks, and if the Lord, as John says, wishes that you should know me, but tell no one what has passed here, for the time has not yet come for Him to reveal my fate. Then James, the older son of Zebedee, who like his brother was no simpleton, said, Don't imagine people won't talk, just look at the crowd there on the shore, see how they're waiting to praise you, some so impatient that they're already pushing out their boats to come and join us, and even if we succeed in reining their enthusiasm and persuading them to keep our secret, how can you be sure that God will not continue to manifest Himself through you, however much you dislike the idea. The living image of sorrow, Jesus hung his head and said, We are all in the hands of the Lord. You more than the rest of us, replied Simon, for He has chosen you, but we shall follow you. To the end, said John. Until you have no further need of us, said Andrew. For as long as possible, said James. The boats were fast approaching, with much waving of arms and chanting of prayers and praise and thanks to the Lord. Resigned, Jesus told the others, Let's go, the wine is poured and we must drink it. He did not seek out Mary Magdalene, he knew she was waiting for him as always, it would take more than a miracle to stop her vigil, and the thought of her waiting for him filled his heart with gratitude and peace. Disembarking, he fell into her arms, and showed no surprise when she whispered in his ear, her cheek pressed against his wet beard, You will lose the war but win every battle. Arm in arm and accompanied by friends, they greeted the cheering spectators, who hailed Jesus as if he were a victorious general. Arm in arm, Jesus and Mary climbed the steep path to Capernaum, the village that overlooked the lake, where Simon and Andrew lived and where they had been offered hospitality.

James was right when he warned Jesus that the episode of the storm would be on everyone's lips. Within a few days people for miles around were discussing nothing else. Although, strange to relate, no one seems to have been aware of the storm in Tiberias, even though the lake there is not that wide, as we already mentioned, and from a height one can see from shore to shore on a clear day. When someone arrived with the news that a stranger accompanying the fishermen of Capernaum had quelled the storm just by speaking to it, he was asked to his amazement, What storm. But there was no lack of witnesses to testify that there had indeed been a storm, and there were those who had been involved directly or indirectly, among them some muleteers from Safed and Cana who chanced to be there in the course of their work. It was they who spread the news elsewhere, each man embroidering the story according to his fancy, but the news did not reach everyone, and we know what happens to such tales, they lose credibility after a while, by the time the news reached Nazareth, the tellers were no longer sure if there had been a genuine miracle or simply the lucky coincidence of a word's being tossed to the wind and a gale's growing tired of blowing. A mother's heart, however, is never deceived, and Mary had only to hear the dying echo of this prodigy that people were already questioning to know that her absent son was responsible. She grieved that the loss of her maternal authority had led her to conceal from Jesus the angel's revelation, confident that a message couched in a few words would bring home the son who had left with his own heart grieving. And now that Lisa was married and living in Cana, Mary no longer had anyone in whom to confide her bitterness. She could not turn to James, who had come back in a rage after the meeting with his brother. He spared Mary no details, and gave a withering account of the woman with Jesus, She's old enough to be his mother, and from the look of her there's nothing she doesn't know about life, to put it mildly. Not that James himself knows that much about life, here in this remote village. So Mary unburdened herself to Joseph, the son who in name and appearance reminded her most of her husband, but he gave her little comfort, Mother, we are paying for our mistake, after seeing Jesus, I fear he'll never come home, people say he calmed a storm, and the fishermen themselves told us that he fills their boats with fish as if by magic. Then the angel was right. What angel, asked Joseph, and Mary told him everything that had happened, from the beggar who put glowing earth into the bowl to the appearance of the angel in her dream. They did not hold this conversation inside, for with such a large family it is almost impossible to have any privacy. When these people wish to disclose secrets, they go into the desert, where one might even meet God. Joseph and Mary were still deep in conversation when Joseph, looking over his mother's shoulder, saw a flock of sheep and goats with their shepherd pass over the distant hills. The flock did not appear to be very big or the shepherd very tall, so he watched without saying a word. And when his mother sighed, I will never see Jesus again, he replied pensively, Who knows.

Joseph was right. About a year later, Lisa sent a message to their mother, inviting her on behalf of her in-laws to come to Cana for the wedding of her husband's younger sister, and Mary was asked to bring as many of the children as she wished, they would all be most welcome. Despite this generous invitation Mary was reluctant to be a burden, for there is nothing more tiresome than a widow with a horde of children, so she decided to take her current favorite, Joseph, and Lydia, who like all other girls her age adored parties and celebrations. Cana is not far from Nazareth, little more than an hour away if calculated by our time, and with gentle autumn already here, this promised to be an agreeable outing, even without a wedding to look forward to. They left at sunrise, in order to arrive in Cana in time for Mary to assist in the final preparations for the festivities, for such labor is in direct proportion to the pleasure of the guests. Lisa ran out to meet her mother, brother, and sister, embracing them affectionately. She asked about their health, they asked if she was well and happy, but there was much work to be done, so they moved on quickly. Lisa and Mary went to the bridegroom's house, where the feast was traditionally held, to share the cooking with the other women of the family, and Joseph and Lydia remained in the yard with the children, the boys playing with the boys, the girls dancing with the girls, until it was time for the ceremony to begin. Then off they ran, boys and girls together, behind the men accompanying the bridegroom, friends carrying the customary torches although it was a bright, sunny morning, which shows that a little extra light, even from a torch, is not to be despised. Smiling neighbors came out to greet them, but saved their blessings for when the procession would return bringing the bride. Joseph and Lydia missed the rest of this, but then they have already seen a wedding in their own family, the bridegroom knocking at the door and asking to see the bride, the bride appearing surrounded by her friends, who carry little oil lamps, which are more suited to women than great flaming torches, and then the bridegroom lifts the bride's veil and shouts with joy on finding such a treasure there, as if he has not seen her thousands of times already during the last twelve months of courtship, and not gone to bed with her as often as he pleased. Joseph and Lydia missed all this, because Joseph, who happened to look down the street, saw two men and a woman in the distance. Recognizing Jesus and the woman with him, he felt a strange sensation for the second time, and called to his sister, Look, it's Jesus, and they ran to meet him, but then Joseph stopped, remembering his mother and the coldness with which his brother had received them by the lake, not so much James and him, it is true, as the message they had delivered. So Joseph, thinking to himself that he would eventually have to explain his behavior to Jesus, turned back. Before disappearing around the corner, he took another look and felt envy when he saw his brother gather Lydia into his arms like a feather in flight and smother her with kisses, while the woman and the other man looked on approvingly. Eyes filled with tears of frustration, Joseph ran, came to the house, crossed the yard, jumping to avoid the linen cloths and food set out on the ground and low tables, and called, Mother, Mother. Our own distinctive voices are our saving grace, otherwise mothers everywhere would be looking up only to see someone else's son. One look, and Mary understood when Joseph said to her, Jesus is coming this way. The color drained from her face, then she blushed, smiled, turned serious and pale once more, and these conflicting emotions brought her hand to her breast, as if her heart were no longer beating and she had backed into a wall. Who is with him, she asked, for she was certain someone was with him. A man and a woman, and Lydia, who's still with them, replied Joseph. Is that the woman you saw before. Yes, Mother, but I don't know the man. Lisa joined them, curious, unaware that there was something amiss, What's the matter, Mother. Your brother has arrived for the wedding. You mean Jesus is here in Cana. Yes, Joseph has just seen him. Lisa could not keep from smiling as she murmured to herself, My brother, and that quiet smile of hers betrayed the deepest satisfaction. Let's go and meet him, she said. You go, I'll stay here, her mother answered defensively, and turning to Joseph, she told him, Go with your sister. But Joseph felt resentful that Lydia had been the first to be embraced by Jesus, and Lisa did not have the courage to go on her own, so there they stood, like three criminals awaiting sentence and unsure of the judge's mercy, if the words judge and mercy mean anything here.

Jesus appeared in the doorway, carrying Lydia in his arms, and Mary Magdalene followed behind, but the first to enter was Andrew, the other man in the group and related to the bridegroom, as soon became apparent when he said to those who came smiling to welcome him, No, Simon couldn't come. And while many present were happily absorbed in this family reunion, others eyed one another over a chasm, asking themselves who would be first to set foot on that fragile, narrow bridge, which despite everything still joined the one side to the other. We shall not say, as a poet once said, that children are the greatest joy in this world, but it is thanks to them that adults sometimes succeed in taking difficult steps without losing face, even if they discover afterward that they have not gone very far. Lydia slipped from Jesus' arms and ran to her mother, and as in a puppet show one move led to another move, and another, Jesus went up to his mother and brother, greeted them in the sober, matter-of-fact tone of one who has seen them every day, then moved on, leaving them dumbfounded. Mary Magdalene followed him, and as she passed Mary of Nazareth, the two women, one upright, the other fallen, glanced at each other, not with hostility or contempt but with mutual recognition, which only those familiar with the labyrinthine ways of the feminine heart can understand. The procession was drawing near, shouts and applause could be heard, the tremulous vibration of tambourines, the scattered notes of gentle harps, the rhythm of dancing, the shrill sound of voices as everyone tried to speak at once. Then the guests poured into the yard, the bride and groom were almost swept in amid cheering and clapping as they went before parents and parents-in-law to receive their blessings. Mary was also there, waiting to give her blessing, just as she had blessed her daughter Lisa, then as now without her husband or eldest son at her side to take his rightful place as head of the family. As they sat down to eat, Jesus was offered a special seat, Andrew having quietly informed his relatives that this was the man who filled empty nets with fish and calmed storms, but Jesus refused the honor, choosing to sit with the guests farthest away from the bridal party. Mary Magdalene served Jesus, and no one questioned her presence there. Lisa too went to him several times, to make sure he was all right, and Jesus treated both women in exactly the same way. Watching this from afar, his mother's eyes met those of Mary Magdalene. Mary beckoned her to a quiet corner of the yard and without further ado told her, Take care of my son, for an angel warned me that great tribulations await him, and I can do nothing for him. You may count on me to protect and defend him with my life if necessary. What is your name. I'm known as Mary Magdalene, and I lived as a prostitute until I met your son. Mary said nothing but began to see things more clearly, certain details came back to her, the coins, the guarded statements made by Jesus when she asked where the money came from, James's indignant account of his meeting with Jesus, his remarks about the woman who was with his brother. Now she knew everything, and turning to Mary Magdalene, said, You will always have my blessing and gratitude for all the good you have done my son Jesus. Mary Magdalene leaned over and kissed Mary's shoulder as a mark of respect, but Mary threw her arms around her and held her tight, and there they remained for some moments, embracing each other in silence before returning to the kitchen, where there was work waiting to be done.

The festivities continued, one dish after another was brought in from the kitchen, wine flowed from the pitchers, guests began singing and dancing, when suddenly the steward came and whispered in the ear of the parents of the bride and groom, The wine is running out. They could not have been more dismayed had they been told the roof was falling in, What will we do now, how can we face our guests and tell them there's no more wine, by tomorrow everyone in Cana will know of our shame. My poor daughter, groaned the bride's mother, people will mock her, saying that even the wine ran dry on her wedding day, what have we done to deserve this, and what a bad start to married life. At the tables the guests were draining their goblets, many looking around for someone to serve them more wine, when Mary, who has now entrusted her maternal duties to another woman, decided to put Jesus' miraculous powers to the test before withdrawing into the silence of her own home, ready to depart this world, her mission on earth completed. She looked around for Mary Magdalene, saw her slowly nod her assent, so wasting no time, she went up to Jesus and said, There is no wine. Jesus turned to face his mother, looked at her as if she had spoken from a distance, and asked, Woman, what have I to do with you, shattering words that shocked and amazed those who overheard them, for no son treats in this manner the mother who brought him into the world. In time these words will be rephrased and interpreted in different ways to make them sound less brutal, some have even tried to change their meaning completely, insisting that what Jesus really said was, Why bother me with this, or, What has this to do with me, or, Who asked you to interfere, or, Why should we get involved, woman, or, Why can't you leave this to me, or, Tell me what you want and I'll see what can be done, or even, You can rely on me to do my best to please you. Mary did not flinch, she withstood Jesus' look of disdain and ended her challenge by saying to the servants, which put her son in an awkward position, Whatever he says, do it. As his mother went off, Jesus watched without saying a word or trying to stop her, aware that the Lord had used her, just as He had used the storm and the plight of the fishermen. Jesus raised his goblet, which still held some wine, and pointing to six stone jars of water used for purification, told the servants, Fill these with water, whereupon they filled them to the brim, and each jar held two to three measures. Bring them here, he told them, and they obeyed. Then into each jar Jesus poured a few drops of the wine in his goblet, and ordered the servants, Take them to the steward. Without knowing where the jars came from, the steward sampled the water, which the small quantity of wine had barely colored, and summoned the groom and told him, Every man serves good wine at the beginning, but when the guests have drunk their fill, serves that which is poorer, yet you have kept the best wine until now. The bridegroom, who had never before seen wine served in such jars and who knew, moreover, that the wine had run out, tasted it for himself and confirmed that it was wine by commenting, with an expression of false modesty, on the excellent quality of this vintage. Had it not been for the servants, who spread the news next day, this would have been a buried miracle, for the steward, ignorant of the transmutation, would have remained ignorant, while the groom would have been only too happy to take the credit, and no one expected Jesus to go around saying, I worked such and such a miracle, and Mary Magdalene, who was involved in the plan from the first, was unlikely to start boasting, He worked a miracle, and his mother even less so, because this was something between Mary and her son, the rest of it was a bonus in every sense of the word, as any guest who had his goblet refilled will testify.

Mary of Nazareth and her son conversed no more. Without saying good-bye to anyone, Jesus and Mary Magdalene left that same afternoon and set off for Tiberias. Joseph and Lydia, keeping out of sight, followed them to the outskirts of the village, where they stood watching until the couple disappeared around the bend in the road.

THEN THE LONG WAIT BEGAN. THE SIGNS BY WHICH THE Lord had manifested Himself in the person of Jesus were so far little more than magic tricks, clever, fascinating, with a few quick words of abracadabra, not unlike those performed with rather more style by Oriental fakirs, such as tossing a rope into midair and climbing it without any visible sign of support, no hooks, no hand of a mysterious genie. To work these wonders, Jesus had only to will them, and if anyone had asked him why, he would have had no answer other than that he could hardly ignore the misery of fishermen with empty nets, the danger of that raging storm, or the mortifying lack of wine at that marriage feast, for truly the hour has not yet arrived for the Lord to speak through his lips. Villagers dwelling on this side of Galilee said that a man from Nazareth was going around exercising powers that could only come from God, and that he did not deny it, but in the absence of any reason or explanation for his appearance among them, they might as well take advantage of this sudden abundance and ask no questions. Simon and Andrew were not of this opinion, nor were the sons of Zebedee, but they were his friends and feared for his life. Each morning when he woke up, Jesus asked in silence, Perhaps today, and sometimes he even asked the question aloud, so that Mary Magdalene would hear him, but she said nothing, just lay there sighing, then put her arms around him and kissed him on the forehead and eyes while he breathed in the sweet, warm odor of her breasts. There were days when he went back to sleep, and days when he forgot the question and took refuge in Mary Magdalene's body, as if entering a cocoon from which he could be reborn in some other form. Later he would go down to the lake and to the waiting fishermen, many of whom would never understand him, they kept asking him why he didn't get himself a boat and fish independently, keeping the entire catch for himself. Sometimes, when they were out at sea and resting between catches, still necessary even though the fishing had become as easy as yawning, Jesus would have a sudden premonition, and his heart trembled, but instead of turning to heaven, where, as we know, God resides, his eyes settled with yearning on the lake's calm surface, on that smooth water that shone like the clearest skin, as if he waited with desire and fear to see rising from the depths not fish but the voice that was slow in coming. The day's fishing over, the boat returned laden, and Jesus, with lowered head, once more walked along the shore, Mary Magdalene behind him. And so the weeks and months passed, and the years, the only visible change taking place in Tiberias, where more buildings went up as the city prospered, otherwise things went on as usual in this land that seems to die with every winter and be reborn with every spring, a false observation and a deception on the part of the senses, for spring would be nothing without the sleep of winter.

Jesus was now twenty-five years old, and suddenly the entire universe awakened, there were signs, one after another, as if someone were anxiously trying to make up for lost time. True, the first sign was not exactly a miracle, after all there was nothing that remarkable about Simon's mother's falling ill with a fever and Jesus' going to her bedside and placing his hand on her forehead, something we have all instinctively done at one time or other, without expecting to cure the patient by this simple, natural gesture. But the fever subsided beneath his hand, as poisoned water is absorbed by the soil, and the old woman rose immediately and said, somewhat irrelevantly, Whoever befriends me befriends my son-in-law, then went about her household chores as if nothing had happened. This first sign was a private matter and took place indoors, but the second brought Jesus into open conflict with the written and observed law, though it was perhaps understandable, given human nature and the fact that Jesus was living in sin with Mary Magdalene. Seeing an adulteress about to be stoned to death in accordance with the law of Moses, Jesus intervened and said, Stop, he that is without sin among you, let him cast the first stone at her, as if to say, Were I not living with a prostitute and tainted by her in deed and thought, I might join you in carrying out this punishment. He was taking a big risk, because some of the more callous among the men could have turned a deaf ear to his rebuke and thrown stones, being themselves exempt from the law they were applying, which was meant only for women. What appears to have escaped Jesus, perhaps from lack of experience, is that if we wait for the arrival of sanctimonious judges who believe they alone have the right to condemn and punish, crime is likely to increase dramatically and wickedness to thrive, adulteresses will be on the loose, one minute with this man, the next with another, and adultery brings after it the thousand vices that persuaded the Lord to send down fire and brimstone on the cities of Sodom and Gomorrah, reducing them to ashes. But the evil that was born with the world, and from which the world has learned everything it knows, dear brethren, is like that famous phoenix that no one has ever seen and that even while appearing to perish in the flames is reborn from an egg hatched in its own ashes. Good is delicate, fragile, while Evil need only blow the hot breath of sin into the face of purity for it to be forevermore disfigured, for the stalk of the lily to break and the orange blossom to wither. Jesus told the adulteress, Go and sin no more, but in his heart he had serious doubts.

Another notable event took place on the opposite side of the lake, where Jesus decided he ought to go now and then, lest it be said that all his attention was given to the western shore. So he summoned James and John and suggested, Let's explore the other side, where the Gadarenes live, to see what fortune brings, and on the way back we can fish, so that we have something to show for our journey. The sons of Zebedee warmed to this idea, and after setting their boat on course, began to row, hoping that farther ahead there would be a breeze to help them on their way. And their prayer was answered, their satisfaction, however, soon turned to alarm when a storm came up that promised to be even more violent than the one they had experienced years ago, but Jesus chided the water and the sky, Now then, what's going on here, as if scolding a child, and the water calmed immediately, and the wind went back to blowing at the right speed and in the right direction. All three disembarked, Jesus walking first, James and John following him. They had never been to this region before and were surprised by everything they saw there, but the strangest sight of all on the road was the sudden appearance of a man, if one can use that word to describe the filthy creature with matted beard and wild hair. The stench he gave off was like that of a tomb, and little wonder, for as they soon learned, that was where the man took refuge whenever he managed to break the chains with which he was restrained. It is well known that a madman's strength is twice as great when he flies into a rage, yet he cannot be held with double the number of chains, this had been tried many times but to no avail, because the man was not simply a madman, the unclean spirit that possessed and ruled him made a mockery of all attempts to chain him. Day and night the possessed man went bounding over the mountains, fleeing from himself and his own shadow, and he hid among the tombs and often in them, from where he had to be dragged, to the horror of anyone who happened to be passing. This was how Jesus first saw him, the guards in pursuit, waving their arms at Jesus to get out of harm's way, but Jesus had come in search of adventure and was not going to miss this for anything. John and James, though terrified by the madman, did not abandon their friend, and so they were the first to hear words no one would ever expect to hear, words that undermined the Lord and His laws, as we are about to discover. The fierce man advances with outstretched claws and bared fangs from which hang the remains of rotten flesh, Jesus' hair stands on end with fright, but suddenly the possessed creature throws himself on the ground two paces away and cries out, What do you want of me, Jesus, son of the Almighty, I beseech you in the name of God to stop tormenting me. Now, this was the first time in public, not in private dreams which prudence and skepticism compel us to doubt, that a voice was raised, and a diabolical voice if ever there was one, proclaiming that Jesus of Nazareth was the son of God, something he himself was unaware of until this moment, for during his conversation with God in the desert the question of paternity never came up. I will need you later, was all the Lord said, and even that was suspect, considering that his heavenly father had appeared before him in the guise of a cloud and column of smoke. The possessed man writhed at his feet, and a voice within Jesus finally revealed what had hitherto been concealed, and at that moment, like one who sees himself reflected in another, he felt that he too was possessed and at the mercy of powers which would lead him who knows where, but no doubt ultimately to the grave of graves. He asked the spirit, What is your name, and the spirit answered, Legion, for we are many. In commanding tones, Jesus said, Leave this man, unclean spirit. And no sooner had he spoken than a chorus of infernal voices went up, some reedy and shrill, others deep and hoarse, some as gentle as a woman's, others as harsh as the sound of a saw cutting through stone, some mocking and taunting, others pleading with the humility of paupers, some arrogant, others whining, some prattling like children learning their first words, others crying out like ghosts in distress, but all begging Jesus to allow them to remain, one word from him could drive them from this man's body, For pity's sake, the evil spirits begged, do not expel us. And Jesus asked them, Tell me, then, where do you want to go. Now as it happened, a large herd of pigs was grazing on the slopes of the mountain nearby, and the spirits implored Jesus, Allow us to enter the pigs. Jesus thought for a moment and decided it was the perfect solution, the pigs had to belong to Gentiles, since pork is unclean and forbidden to Jews, it never occurred to him that by eating the pigs the Gentiles would also eat the demons inside them and become possessed, and he failed to foresee the unfortunate events that would follow from this, but the fact is that not even the son of God, who is still not used to such elevated kinship, can see as on a chessboard all the consequences of one move or one decision. In great excitement the evil spirits made bets, awaiting Jesus' reply, and when he said, Yes, giving them permission to pass into the pigs, they cheered in triumph and inhabited the animals instantly. The pigs, either because of the shock of it or because they hated being possessed by demons, went wild and threw themselves over the cliff, all two thousand of them, and into the lake, where they drowned. The wrath of the swineherds tending these innocent animals was indescribable. One minute the poor things had been grazing at their leisure, grubbing in what soft soil they could find for roots and worms, and pawing at the sparse tufts of grass on the parched surface, the next minute they were down below in the water, a pitiful sight, some already lifeless and floating, others almost unconscious but making one last valiant effort to keep their ears above water, for as everyone knows pigs cannot close their eardrums, and once too much water gets in, the creatures drown. Enraged, the swineherds began throwing stones at Jesus and his companions, and were now coming after them, to demand compensation, so much per head multiplied by two thousand, a sum easy enough to calculate, not so easy to pay. Fishermen earn little money, they lead a meager existence, and Jesus could not even claim to be a fisherman. But the Nazarene decided to face the irate swineherds, to explain to them that there is no greater evil in this world than the devil, and that compared with Satan two thousand pigs is nothing, besides, we all suffer losses in this life, material or otherwise, So be patient, brethren, Jesus was prepared to urge them. But the last thing James and John wanted was a heated exchange with the swineherds, any show of friendship or goodwill was unlikely to appease the wrath of those rough characters intent on revenge. Reluctantly Jesus yielded to James and John's arguments, which grew more persuasive as the stones fell closer. They ran down the slope to the water's edge, jumped into their boat, and rowing at top speed, were soon out of danger. Swineherds, as a rule, do little fishing, and if the ones in pursuit had boats, they were nowhere in sight. Some pigs were lost, a soul was saved, the winner is God, said James. Jesus looked at him, his thoughts elsewhere, on something the two brothers watching him wished to hear about and discuss, the strange revelation by the demons that Jesus was the son of God, but Jesus turned to the bank from which they had escaped, gazed at the water, the pigs floating and rolling with the waves, two thousand innocent animals, and he felt an uneasiness rising within him, searching for an outlet, until he could no longer contain himself and exclaimed, The demons, where are the demons, and then he sent up a roar of laughter to heaven, Listen, Lord, either You chose poorly this son who must carry out Your plans, according to what those demons said, or there is something missing in Your powers, for otherwise You would be able to defeat the devil. What are you saying, asked John, appalled by this unthinkable challenge. I'm saying that the demons who possessed the man are now free, for demons as we know don't die, my friends, not even God can kill them, and for all the good I did there I might as well have struck the lake with a sword. On the shore a great crowd was descending, some jumped into the water to retrieve the pigs floating within reach, while others jumped into their boats and set off to gather any they could find.

That night, in the home of Simon and Andrew, which was near the synagogue, the five friends gathered in secret to discuss the extraordinary revelation by the demons that Jesus was the son of God. Greatly puzzled by what had happened, they agreed not to talk until after dusk, and the moment had now come to speak their minds. Jesus began by saying, One cannot trust the father of falsehood, clearly referring to the devil. Andrew said, Truth and falsehood pass through the same lips and leave no mark, the devil does not cease to be the devil just because he may have spoken the truth. Simon said, We knew you were no ordinary man, first there were the fish you helped us catch, then the storm that almost killed us, then the water you turned to wine, then the adulteress you saved from being stoned to death, and now these demons you exorcised. Jesus said, I am not the only one who has driven demons from people. That's true, said James, but you're the first they have addressed as the son of the Almighty. It didn't do much good, either, for in the end it was not they but I who was humiliated. That's not the point, interrupted John, I was there and heard everything, why didn't you tell us you were the son of God. But I'm not sure I am the son of God. How can the devil know if you don't. A good question, but they alone can answer it. Who do you mean by they. I mean God, whose son the devil claims I am, and the devil, who could only have been told by God. A silence fell, as if everyone was giving the powers invoked time to declare themselves, until finally Simon asked, What is there between you and God. Jesus sighed, That's the question I was afraid you would ask. Who would ever believe the son of God would choose to be a fisherman. I've already explained, I'm not even sure I am the son of God. Well, who are you then. Jesus covered his face with his hands, wondered how to begin the confession they wanted from him, his life suddenly seemed to be the life of someone else, perhaps that was it, if the demons spoke the truth, then everything which had happened to him took on a different meaning, and some of those events were only now becoming clear in the light of this. He lowered his hands, looked at his friends one by one with a pleading expression, as if asking them for trust to a greater degree than any man had a right to ask another, then after a long pause he told them, I have seen God. No one said a word, they waited. Lowering his eyes, he continued, I met Him in the desert, and He told me that when the hour came, He would give me power and glory in exchange for my life, but He never said I was His son. More silence. And how did God appear to you, asked James. Like a cloud, a column of smoke. You're sure it wasn't fire. No, not fire but smoke, and He said nothing else, only that He would return at the right moment. What moment is that. I really don't know, perhaps He meant the moment when I must sacrifice my life. And what about this power and glory, when will these be granted. Who knows. Again silence. The heat inside was stifling, yet they were all shivering. Then Simon asked slowly, Are you the Messiah whom we should call the son of God because you have come to deliver God's people from bondage. I, the Messiah. No more incredible than your being the son of the Lord, said Andrew nervously. James said, Messiah or son of God, what I cannot understand is how the devil came to know it, when even the Lord did not confide in you. John said pensively, I wonder what the secret relationship is between the devil and God. Terrified of learning that truth, they eyed each other uneasily, and Simon asked Jesus, What are you going to do, and Jesus replied, The only thing I can do, wait for my hour to come.

And it is fast approaching, but until then Jesus will have two more opportunities to demonstrate his miraculous powers, although it might be better for us to draw a veil over the second, because it was a blunder on his part and resulted in the death of a fig tree as innocent of evil as those pigs the demons sent hurtling into the lake. The first of these two miracles, however, fully deserved to be brought to the attention of the priests of Jerusalem, that it might later be engraved in gold letters over the Temple door, for such a thing had never been witnessed before and indeed was never witnessed thereafter. Historians disagree as to why so many different races should have gathered in that place, whose exact location, let it be said in passing, has also been the subject of debate. Some historians claim the gathering was nothing more than a traditional pilgrimage, the origins of which are obscure, others say the crowd assembled there because of a rumor, later disproved, that an envoy had arrived from Rome to announce a reduction in taxes, there are also some historians who, not offering any hypotheses themselves, argue that only the simpleminded could believe in a tax reduction that would benefit taxpayers, and as for the pilgrimage of obscure origins, it could easily be verified if those who liked to spin such fantasies took the trouble to do a little research. What is beyond dispute is that some four to five thousand people came together there, not counting women and children, and that it turned out that they had nothing to eat. How such careful people, used to traveling and never without a well-stocked pack even on the shortest journey, could have suddenly found themselves without so much as a crust of bread or scrap of meat is something no one has ever been able to explain. But facts are facts, and the facts say that there were twelve to fifteen thousand, this time including women and children, who had gone without food for hours and would soon return to their homes and risk dropping from sheer weakness on route, unless fortunate enough to be rescued by a charitable passerby. The children, who are always the first to complain in any crisis, grew impatient, some of them whimpering, Mother, I'm hungry, and the situation was quickly becoming intolerable. Jesus walked among the multitude with Mary Magdalene, accompanied by Simon, Andrew, James, and John, who since the episode of the pigs and its aftermath went everywhere with Jesus, but unlike the rest of the crowd they had brought some bread and fish and so had come provided. To have set about eating in the presence of all these people, however, would not only have shown complete selfishness but also have put them at some risk, for necessity knows no law, and the most effective form of justice, as Cain taught us, is that which we ourselves grab with both hands. Jesus did not imagine for a moment that he could be of any help to this vast assembly in need of food, but James and John said to him, If you were able to drive demons from a man's body, surely you can give these people the food they need. And how am I to do this if we have no food other than the few provisions we brought for ourselves. As the son of God you must be able to do something. Jesus looked at Mary Magdalene, who told him, There is no turning back now, and her face was filled with compassion, although Jesus did not know if it was meant for him or for the famished multitude. He took the six loaves they had brought with them, broke each loaf in half, and gave them to his companions, then he did the same with the six fish, keeping a loaf and a fish for himself. Then he said, follow me and do as I do. And we know what he did, but will never know how he managed it. Going from person to person, he divided and distributed bread and fish, and each person received a whole loaf and a whole fish. Mary Magdalene and the four friends of Jesus did the same, and they passed through the crowd as a beneficent wind blows over the field of a farm and raises the drooping cornstalks one by one, to the sound of rustling leaves, which were mouths chewing and thanking. It is the Messiah, said some. He's a magician, insisted others, but it never dawned on anyone in the crowd to ask, Could this be the son of God. And to all of them Jesus said, Let those who have ears listen, for unless you divide, you will never multiply.

It was only right for Jesus to teach this rule when he had the opportunity. But he was wrong to apply it to the letter when it was inopportune, as in the case of the fig tree mentioned earlier. He was walking along a country lane when he began to feel hungry, and spotting a green fig tree in the distance, he went to see if it had any fruit on it. But coming closer, he found nothing but leaves, because it was too early for figs. Whereupon Jesus said to the tree, No more fruit will grow on your branches, and at that very moment the fig tree dried up. Mary Magdalene, who was with him, said, You must give to those in need but ask nothing of those with nothing to give. Filled with remorse, Jesus tried to revive the fig tree, but it was quite dead.

A MISTY MORNING. THE FISHERMAN RISES FROM HIS MAT, looks at the whiteness through a chink in the door, and says to his wife, I'm not taking the boat out today, in this kind of mist even the fish lose their way. All the other fishermen, from one shore to another, echo his sentiment, using more or less the same words, they are puzzled by the rare phenomenon of mist at this time of year. Only one man, who is not a fisherman by profession although he lives and works with fishermen, goes to his front door and sees that this is the day he has been waiting for. Looking up at the dull sky, he says, I'm going fishing. At his shoulder, Mary Magdalene asks, Must you, and Jesus replied, I've waited a long time for this day to come. Won't you eat something. Eyes are fasting when they open in the morning, but he embraced her and said, At last I will learn who I am and what is expected of me, then with surprising confidence, for he could not even see his own feet in the mist, he descended the slope to the water's edge, climbed into one of the boats moored there, and began rowing out toward the invisible space in the middle of the lake. The noise of the oars scraping against the sides of the boat and the bubbling and rippling of water around the wood blades carried over the surface, it kept awake those fishermen whose wives had told them, If you can't go out fishing, at least try to get some sleep. Restless and uneasy, the villagers stared at the impenetrable mist in the direction of the lake and waited for the noise of the oars to stop, so they could return to their homes and secure their doors with keys, crossbars, and padlocks, while knowing that if he in the mist is who they think he is and he decides to blow this way, a puff of air from him would knock them down. The mist allows Jesus to pass, but his eyes can see no farther than the tip of the oars and the stern, with its simple plank that serves as a bench. The rest is a blank wall, at first dim and gray, then, as the boat approaches its destination, a diffused light turns the mist white and lustrous, it quivers as if searching for a sound in the silence. The boat, moving into a circle of light, comes to a halt, it has reached the center of the lake. God is sitting at the stern, on the bench.

Unlike the first time, He does not appear as a cloud or column of smoke, which in this weather would be lost in the mist. This time He is a big man, elderly, a great flowing beard over His chest, head uncovered, hair hanging loose, a broad and powerful face, fleshy lips which barely move when He begins to speak. He is dressed like a wealthy Jew, in a long magenta tunic under a blue cape with sleeves and gold braiding, the thick sandals on His feet are those of one who walks a great deal, whose habits are anything but sedentary. When He is gone, we will ask ourselves, What was His hair like, unable to remember whether it was white, black, or brown, judging by His age it must have been white, but there are some whose hair takes a long time to turn white, and He might be one of them. Jesus raised the oars and rested them inside the boat, as if preparing for a lengthy conversation, and simply said, Here

I am. Slowly and methodically, God arranged the folds of the cape over His knees and added, Well, here we are. The voice suggested a smile, though His lips hardly moved, only the long hairs of His mustache and beard quivered like the vibration of a bell. Jesus said, I've come to find out who I am and what I must do henceforth to fulfill my part of the covenant. God said, These are two questions, let us take them one at a time, where would you like to start. With the first, said Jesus, and asked again, Who am I. Don't you know. Well, I thought I knew, I thought I was my father's son. Which father do you mean. My father, the carpenter Joseph, son of Eli, or was it Jacob, for I'm no longer certain. You mean the carpenter Joseph whom they crucified. I didn't know there was any other. A tragic mistake on the part of the Romans, that poor father died innocent, having committed no crime. You said that father, so there is another. I'm proud of you, I can see you're an intelligent lad and perceptive. There was no need for intelligence, I was told by the devil. Are you in league with the devil. No, I'm not in league with the devil, it was the devil who sought me out. And what did you hear from his lips. That I am Your son. Nodding His head slowly in agreement, God told him, Yes, you are my son. But how can a man be the son of God. If you're the son of God, you are not a man. But I am a man, I breathe, I eat, I sleep, and I love like a man, therefore I am a man and will die as a man. In your case I wouldn't be too sure. What do you mean. That's the second question, but we have time, how did you answer the devil when he said you were my son. I didn't answer, I simply waited for the day when I would meet You, then I drove Satan out of the possessed man he was tormenting, the man called himself Legion and said he was many. Where are they now. I have no idea. You said you exorcised those demons. Surely You know better than I that when demons are driven out of a body, nobody knows where they go. And what makes you think I'm familiar with the devil's affairs. Being God, You must know everything. Up to a point, only up to a point. What point is that. The point where it becomes interesting to pretend I do not know. At least You must know how I came to be Your son and for what reason. I can see you are somewhat more confident, not to say impatient, than when I first met you. I was a mere boy then and rather shy, but I'm grown now. And you're not afraid. No. You will be, fear always comes, even to a son of God. You mean you have others. What others. Sons, of course. No, I only needed one. And how did I come to be Your son. Didn't your mother tell you. Does my mother know. I sent an angel to explain things to her, I thought she told you. And when was this angel with my mother. Let Me see, unless I'm mistaken it was after you left home for the second time and before you miraculously changed the water into wine at Cana. So, Mother knew and never said a word, when I told her I saw You in the desert, she didn't believe me, but she must have realized I was telling the truth after the angel's appearance, yet she did not confide in me. You know what women are like, after all you live with one, they have their little sensitivities and scruples. What sensitivities and scruples. Well, let Me explain, I mixed My seed with that of your father before you were conceived, it was the easiest way and the least conspicuous. If the seeds were mixed, how can You be sure I am Your son. I agree that it's usually unwise to be certain about anything, but I'm certain, there is some advantage in being God. And why did You want a son. I didn't have a son in heaven, so I had to arrange for one on earth, which is not all that original, even in religions with gods and goddesses, who can easily give one another children, we have seen some of them descend to earth, probably for a change of scenery, and at the same time they benefit mankind with the creation of heroes and other wonders. And this son who I am, why did You want him. Not, needless to say, for a change of scenery. Why, then. Because I needed someone to help Me here on earth. But surely, being God, You don't need help. That is the second question.

In the silence that followed, one could hear off in the mist, although from which direction one could not tell, the noise of a man swimming this way. To judge from the puffing and panting, he was no great swimmer and close to exhaustion. Jesus thought he saw God smiling and felt sure He was deliberately giving the swimmer time to reach the circle of clear air around the boat. The swimmer surfaced unexpectedly on the starboard side, Jesus was looking on the port side, it was a dark, ill-defined shape which at first he mistook for a pig, its ears sticking out of the water, but after it took a few more strokes he saw it was a man or a creature with human form. God turned His head to the swimmer, not out of idle curiosity but with real interest, as if encouraging him to make one last effort, and this turn of the head, perhaps because it came from God, had an immediate effect, the final strokes were rapid and regular, as if the swimmer had not covered all that distance from the shore. His hands clutched the edge of the boat, although his head was still half in the water, they were huge, powerful hands with strong nails, hands belonging to a body that had to be tall, sturdy, and advanced in years, like God's. The boat swayed, the swimmer's head emerged from the water, then his torso, splashing water everywhere, then his legs, a leviathan rising from the depths, and it turned out to be Pastor, reappearing after all these years. I've come to join you, he said, settling himself on the side of the boat, equidistant between Jesus and God, and yet oddly enough this time the boat did not tip to his side, as if Pastor had no weight or he was levitating and not really sitting, I've come to join you, he repeated, and hope I'm in time to take part in the conversation. We've been talking but still haven't got to the heart of the matter, replied God, and turning to Jesus, He told him, This is the devil whom we have just been discussing. Jesus looked from one to the other and saw that without God's beard they could have passed for twins, although the devil was younger and less wrinkled. Jesus said, I know very well who he is, I lived with him for four years when he was known as Pastor, and God replied, You had to live with someone, it couldn't be with Me, and you didn't wish to be with your family, so that left only the devil. Did he come looking for me or did You send him. Neither one nor the other, let's say we agreed that this was the best solution. So that's why, when he spoke through the possessed man from Gadara, he called me Your son. Precisely. Which means that both of you kept me in the dark. As happens to all humans. But You said I was not human. And that is true, but you have been what might technically be called incarnated. And now what do you two want of me. I'm the one who wants something, not he. But both of you are here, I noticed that Pastor's appearance came as no surprise, You must have been expecting him. Not exactly, although in principle one should always expect the devil. But if the matter You and I have to resolve affects only us, what is he doing here and why don't You send him away. One can dismiss the rabble in the devil's service if they become troublesome in word or deed, but not Satan himself. Then he's here because this conversation concerns him too. My son, never forget what I'm about to tell you, everything that concerns God also concerns the devil. Pastor, whom we shall sometimes refer to as such rather than constantly invoke the Enemy by name, overheard all this without appearing to listen or care, as if in contradiction of God's momentous statement. It soon became clear, however, that his inattentiveness was a sham, because when Jesus said, Let's now turn to the second question, Pastor immediately pricked up his ears.

God took a deep breath, looked at the mist around Him, and murmured in the hushed tone of one who has just made a curious discovery, This is not unlike being in the desert. He turned His eyes toward Jesus, paused awhile, then began speaking, as if resigning himself to the inevitable, Dissatisfaction, My son, was put into the hearts of men by the God who created them, I'm referring to Myself, of course, but this dissatisfaction, one of the qualities which make man in My image and likeness, I nursed in My own heart, and rather than diminish with time it has grown stronger, more pressing and insistent. God stopped for a moment to consider this preamble before going on to say, For the last four thousand and four years I have been the God of the Jews, a quarrelsome and difficult race by nature, but on the whole I have got along fairly well with them, they now take Me seriously and are likely to go on doing so for the foreseeable future. So, You are satisfied, said Jesus. I am and I am not, or rather, I would be were it not for this restless heart of Mine, which is forever telling Me, Well now, a fine destiny you've arranged after four thousand years of trial and tribulation that no amount of sacrifice on altars will ever be able to repay, for You continue to be the god of a tiny population that occupies a minute part of this world You created with everything that's on it, so tell Me, My son, if I should be satisfied with this depressing situation. Never having created a world, I'm in no position to judge, replied Jesus. True, you cannot judge, but you could help. Help in what way. To spread My word, to help Me become the god of more people. I don't understand. If you play your part, that is to say, the part I have reserved for you in My plan, I have every confidence that within the next six centuries or so, despite all the struggles and obstacles ahead of us, I will pass from being God of the Jews to being God of those whom we will call Catholics, from the Greek. And what is this part You have reserved for me in Your plan. That of martyr, My son, that of victim, which is the best role of all for propagating any faith and stirring up fervor. God made the words martyr and victim seem like milk and honey on His tongue, but Jesus felt a sudden chill in his limbs, as if the mist had closed over him, while the devil regarded him with an enigmatic expression which combined scientific curiosity with grudging compassion.

You promised me power and glory, stammered Jesus, shivering with cold. And I intend to keep that promise, but remember our agreement, you will have them after your death. What good will it do me to have power and glory when I'm dead. Well, you won't be dead in the absolute sense of the word, for as My son you'll be with Me, or in Me, I still haven't decided. You haven't decided how I will not be dead. That's right, for example you'll be venerated in churches and on altars to such an extent that people will even forget that I came first as God, but no matter, abundance can be shared, what is in short supply should not be. Jesus looked at Pastor, saw him smile, and understood, Now I see why the devil is here, if Your authority extends to more people in more places, his power also spreads, for his territory will be the same as Yours. You're quite right, my son, and I'm delighted to see how quick you are, for most people overlook the fact that the demons of one religion are powerless to act in another, just as any god, confronting another, can neither vanquish him nor be vanquished by him. And my death, what will that be like. A martyr's death should be painful and, if possible, ignominious, that the believers may be moved to greater devotion. Come to the point and tell me what kind of death I can expect. A painful and ignominious death on a cross. Like my father. You're forgetting that I'm your father. Were I free to make a choice, I'd choose him despite his moment of shame. But you have been chosen and therefore have no say. I want to end our covenant, to have nothing more to do with You, I want to live like any other man. Empty words, My son, don't you see that you're in My power and that all these documents we call covenants, agreements, pacts, or contracts, in which I figure, could be reduced to a single clause, wasting less paper and ink, a clause that bluntly says, Everything in the law of God is necessary, even the exceptions, and since you, My son, are an exception, you are as necessary as the law and I who made it. But with the power You have, wouldn't it be simpler and more honest for You to go out and conquer those other countries and races Yourself. Alas, I cannot, it is forbidden by the binding agreement between the gods ever to interfere directly, can you imagine Me in a public square, surrounded by Gentiles and pagans, trying to persuade them that their god is false while I am their real God, this is not something one god does to another, besides, no god likes another god to come and do in his house what the latter forbids in his own. So You make use of men instead. Yes, My son, man is a piece of wood that can be used for anything, from the moment he is born to the moment he dies, he's always ready to obey, send him and he goes, tell him to stop and he stops, tell him to withdraw and he withdraws, whether in peace or in war, man generally speaking is the best thing that ever happened to the gods. And the wood from which I'm made, since I'm a man, what use will it be put to, since I'm Your son. You will be the spoon I dip into humanity and bring out filled with people who believe in the new god I intend to become. Filled with people You will eat. There's no need for Me to eat those who eat themselves.

Jesus lowered his oars back into the water and said, Farewell, I'm going home, and you can both go back the way you came, you by swimming and You by disappearing as mysteriously as You appeared. Neither God nor the devil stirred, so Jesus added ironically, Then you prefer to go by boat, better still, I'll row you ashore myself so that everyone can see how alike God and the devil are and how well they get on together. Jesus turned the boat to face the direction from which he had come, and rowing vigorously, he entered the mist, which was so thick that he could no longer see God or the devil's face. Jesus felt alive, happy, and unusually strong. The prow of the boat rose with each stroke of the oars like the head of a horse in a race, and he rowed harder, they must be almost there, he wonders how people will react when he tells them, The one with the beard is God, the other is the devil. Glancing over his shoulder at the shore ahead, Jesus could make out a light, and he announced, We're here, and continued rowing, expecting any second to feel the bottom of the boat glide softly over thick mud, and the playful grazing of tiny loose pebbles, but the prow of the boat was pointing instead to the middle of the lake, and as for the light, it was now the same magic circle of light, the bright snare which Jesus thought he had escaped. His head fell, he crossed his arms over his knees in exhaustion, one wrist resting on the other, as if waiting to be bound, he even forgot to pull in the oars, convinced that any further action was futile. But he would not be the first to speak, he would not acknowledge defeat in a loud voice and ask to be forgiven for having defied God's will and also indirectly the devil's interests, the devil being the beneficiary of the consequences of His plan. The silence was short-lived. Sitting there on the bench, God arranged the folds of His tunic and the hood of His cape, then with mock solemnity, like a judge about to pass sentence, said, Let us start again, going back to where I revealed that you are in My power, for until you submit humbly to this truth you waste your time and Mine. Let us start again, agreed Jesus, but be warned, I refuse to work any more miracles, and without miracles Your plan will come to nothing, a mere sprinkle from heaven which cannot satisfy any real thirst. You would be right if it lay within your power not to work miracles. Don't I have that power. What an idea, I work miracles both great and small, naturally in your presence, so that you may reap the benefits on my behalf, but you are superstitious, believing the miracle worker must stand at the patient's bedside for the thing to take place, yet if I so wished, a man dying alone, with no one at his side, without a doctor, nurse, or beloved relative within sight or hearing, if I so wished, I tell you, that man would be saved and go on living as if nothing had happened to him. Then why not do it. Because he would imagine he'd been cured by his own merit and start boasting, I am too good to die, and with all the presumption there already is in this world I've created, I have no intention of encouraging such nonsense. So all my miracles are Yours. All you have worked and will work, and even if you persist in opposing My will, and go out into the world and deny you are the son of God, I will cause so many miracles to occur wherever you pass that you will be obliged to accept the gratitude of those thanking you and thereby thanking Me. Then there is no way out. None whatever, and don't play the lamb taken to be sacrificed, who struggles and bleats pitifully, for your fate is sealed, the sword awaits. Am I that lamb. You are the lamb of God, My son, which God himself will carry to the altar we are preparing here.

Jesus looked to Pastor, not so much for help as for a signal, Pastor's understanding of the world must be different, he is not a man or ever has been, or a god, a glance or raised eyebrow might suggest a reply that would allow Jesus to extricate himself, at least momentarily, from this difficult situation. But all he reads in Pastor's eyes are the words the shepherd spoke to him when he banished him from the herd, You've learned nothing, begone with you. Now Jesus realizes that to disobey God once is not enough, that having refused to offer Him his sacrificial lamb, he must also refuse Him His own lamb, one cannot say yes to God and then say no, as if yes and no were one's left and right hands and the only good work the kind done with both. Because notwithstanding His manifestations of power, the universe and stars, lightning and thunder, voices and flames on mountaintops, God did not force you to slaughter the sheep, it was out of ambition that you killed the animal, and its blood could not be absorbed by all the sand in the desert, see how it has even reached us, that thread of crimson which will follow us wherever we go, you and God and me. Jesus said to God, I will tell men I am Your son, the only son God has, but I do not think that even in this land of Yours it will be enough to enlarge Your kingdom as much as You wish. At last you speak like a true son, you've given up those tiresome acts of rebellion which were beginning to anger Me, you've come around to My way of thinking, therefore know that whatever their race, color, creed, or philosophy, one thing is common to all men, only one, such that none of them, wise or ignorant, young or old, rich or poor, would dare to say, This has nothing to do with me. And what might that be, asked Jesus with interest. All men, replied God, as if imparting wisdom, whoever and wherever they may be and whatever they may do, are sinners, for sin is as inseparable from man as man from sin, man is like a coin, turn it over and what you see is sin. You haven't answered my question. Here is My answer, the only word no man can say does not apply to him is repentance, because all have succumbed to temptation, entertained an evil thought, broken a rule, committed some crime, serious or minor, spurned a soul in need, neglected a duty, offended religion and its ministers, or turned away from God, to all such men you need only say, Repent, repent, repent. But why sacrifice Your own son's life for so little, surely all You have to do is send a prophet. The time when people listened to prophets has passed, nowadays one must administer stronger medicine, shock treatment, to touch men's hearts and stir their feelings. Such as a son of God hanging from a cross. Yes, why not. And what else am I supposed to say to these people, besides urging them to repent, if they grow tired of hearing Your message and turn a deaf ear. Yes, I agree, it may not be enough to ask them to repent, you may have to use your imagination, and don't make any excuses, look at the cunning way you avoided sacrificing your lamb. That was easy enough, the animal had nothing to repent. A subtle reply but meaningless, although meaninglessness too has its charm, people should be left perplexed, afraid that they don't understand and that it is their fault. So I'm to make up stories. Yes, stories, parables, moral tales, even if it means distorting holy law a little, don't let that bother you, the timid always admire it when liberties are taken, I myself was impressed by the way you saved that adulteress from death, and remember, it was I who put that punishment into the commandments I gave. It's a bad sign when You start allowing men to tamper with Your commandments. Only when it suits Me and is useful, you must not forget what I told you about the law and its exceptions, for whatever I will becomes instantly necessary. You said I must die on the cross. That is my will. Jesus looked askance at Pastor, who seemed to be preoccupied, as if contemplating a moment in the future, unable to believe his eyes. Jesus dropped his arms and said, Then do with me as You will.

God was about to rejoice, to rise to His feet and embrace His beloved son, when Jesus stopped Him with a gesture and said, On one condition. You know perfectly well you cannot set conditions, God replied angrily. Then let's call it a plea rather than a condition, the simple plea of a man sentenced to death. Tell me. You are God and therefore can speak only the truth when asked a question, and being God, You know the past, the present, what lies between them, and what the future will bring. That is so, I am time, truth, and life. Then tell me, in the name of all You claim to be, what will the future bring after my death, what will it contain that it would not had I refused to sacrifice myself to Your dissatisfaction and desire to reign far and wide. As if trapped by His own words, God made a halfhearted attempt to shrug this off, Now then, son, the future is infinite and would take a long time to summarize. How long have we been out here in the middle of the lake, surrounded by mist, asked Jesus, a day, a month, a year, well then, let's stay another year, month, or day, allow the devil to leave if he wants to, for in any case his share is guaranteed, and if the benefits are proportional, as seems just, the more God prospers, the more the devil prospers. I'm staying, said Pastor, and these were the first words he spoke since revealing his identity. I'm staying, he said a second time, and added, I myself can see things in the future, but I'm not always certain if what I see there is true or false, in other words I can see my lies for what they are, that is, my truths, but I don't know to what extent the truths of others are their lies. This tortuous statement might have been clearer had Pastor said something more about the future he saw, but he abruptly fell silent, as if he had already said too much. Jesus, who kept his eyes on God, said with wistful irony, Why pretend not to know what You know, You realized I would ask this question, and You know very well You will tell me what I want to hear, so postpone no longer my time of dying. You began dying the moment you were born. True, but now I die all the sooner. God looked at Jesus with an expression which in a person we would describe as respectful, His whole manner became human, and although the one thing did not appear to have anything to do with the other, the mist came nearer the boat, surrounded it like a wall to keep from the world God's words about the consequences of the sacrifice of Jesus, who He claims is His son, with Mary, but whose real father is Joseph, if we go by the unwritten law that tells us to believe only in what we see, although as everyone knows, we mortals do not always see things in the same way, and this has undoubtedly helped preserve the relative sanity of the species.

God said, There will be a church, a religious society

founded by you or in your name, which comes to the same thing, and this church will spread throughout the world and be called Catholic, because universal, although sadly this will not prevent discord and misunderstanding among those who see you, rather than Me, as their spiritual leader, which will last no more than several thousand years, for I was here before you and will continue to be here after you cease to be what you are and what you will be. Speak more clearly, said Jesus. It's impossible, said God, human words are like shadows, and shadows cannot explain light, and between shadow and light stands the opaque body from which words are born. I asked You about the future. It's the future I speak about. What I want to know is how the men who come after me will live. Are you referring to your followers. Yes, will they be happier. Not in the true sense of the word, but they will have the hope of achieving happiness up in heaven, where I reign for all eternity and where they hope to live eternally with Me. Is that all. Surely it is no small thing to live with God. Small, great, or everything, we will only know at the day of final judgment, when You judge men according to the good or evil they have done, until then You reside alone in heaven. My angels and archangels keep Me company. But You have no human beings there. True, and you must be crucified in order that they come to Me. I want to know more, said Jesus, trying hard to shut out the mental image of himself hanging from a cross, covered with blood, dead, How will people come to believe in me and follow me, surely what I say to them or what those who come after me say to them in my name will not be enough, take the Gentiles and Romans, for example, who worship other gods, You don't expect me to believe they will give them up just like that to worship me. Not to worship you but to worship Me. But did You not say that You and me amounts to the same thing, let us not play with words, however, just answer my question. Whoever has faith will come to us. Just

685

like that, as easily as You've just said. The other gods will resist. And You will fight them, of course. Don't be absurd, war occurs only on earth, heaven is eternal and peaceful, and men will fulfill their destiny wherever they may be. You mean men will die for You and for me. Men have always died for gods, even for false and lying gods. Can gods lie. They can. And You are the one and only true god among them. Yes, the one and only true god. Yet You are unable to prevent men from dying for You when they should have been born to live for You on earth rather than in heaven, where You have none of life's joys to offer them. Those joys too are false, for they come from original sin, ask your friend Pastor, he'll explain what happened. If there are any secrets You and the devil do not share, I hope one of them is what I learned from him, even though he says I learned nothing. There was silence, God and the devil faced each other for the first time, both giving the impression of being about to speak, but they didn't. Jesus said, I'm waiting. For what, asked God, as if distracted. For You to tell me how much death and suffering Your victory over other gods will cause, how much death and suffering will be needed in the battles men fight in Your name and mine. You insist on knowing. I do.

Very well then, the church I mentioned will be established, but its foundation, in order to be truly solid, will be dug in flesh, its walls made from the cement of renunciation, tears, agony, anguish, every conceivable form of death. At long last You speak so I can understand, go on. Let's start with someone you know and love, the fisherman Simon, whom you will call Peter, like you, he will be crucified, but upside down, Andrew too will be crucified, on a cross in the shape of an X, the son of Zebedee known as James will be beheaded. What about John, and Mary Magdalene. They will die of natural causes when their time comes, but you will make other friends, disciples, and apostles who will not escape torture, such as Philip, who will be tied to a cross and stoned to death, Bartholomew, who will be skinned alive, Thomas, who will be speared to death, Matthew, the details of whose death I no longer remember, another Simon, who will be sawed in half, Judas, who will be beaten to death, James stoned, Matthias beheaded with an ax, also Judas Iscariot hanged from a fig tree by his own hand. Are all these men to die because of You, asked Jesus. If you phrase the question that way, the answer is yes, they will die for My sake. And then what. Then, My son, as I've already told you, there follows an endless tale of iron and blood, of fire and ashes, an infinite sea of sorrow and tears. Tell me, I want to know everything. God sighed, and in the monotonous tone of one who chooses to suppress compassion He began a litany, in alphabetical order so as not to hurt any feelings about precedence and importance, Adalbert of Prague put to death with a seven-pronged pikestaff, Adrian hammered to death over an anvil, Afra of Augsburg burned at the stake, Agapitus of Praeneste burned at the stake hanging by his feet, Agnes of Rome disemboweled, Agricola of Bologna crucified and impaled on nails, Agueda of Sicily stabbed six times, Alphege of Canterbury beaten to death with the shinbone of an ox, Anastasia of Sirmium burned at the stake and her breasts cut off, Anastasius of Salona strung up on the gallows and decapitated, Ansanus of Siena his entrails ripped out, Antonius of Pamiers drawn and quartered, Antony of Rivoli stoned and burned alive, Apollinaris of Ravenna clubbed to death, Apollonia of Alexandria burned at the stake after her teeth had been knocked out, Augusta of Treviso decapitated and burned at the stake, Aurea of Ostia drowned with a millstone around her neck, Aurea of Syria bled to death by being forced onto a chair covered with nails, Auta shot with arrows, Babylas of Antioch decapitated, Barbara of Nicomedia likewise, Barnabas of Cyprus stoned and burned at the stake, Beatrice of Rome strangled, Benignus of Dijon speared to death, Blaise of Sebaste thrown onto iron spikes, Blandina of Lyons gored by a savage bull, Callistus put to death with a millstone around his neck, Cassian of Imola stabbed with a dagger by his disciples, Castulus buried alive, Catherine of Alexandria decapitated, Cecilia of Rome beheaded, Christina of Bolsena tortured repeatedly with millstones tongs, arrows, and snakes, Clarus of Nastes decapitated, Clarus of Vienne likewise, Clement drowned with an anchor around his neck, Crispin and Crispinian of Soissons both decapitated, Cucuphas of Barcelona disemboweled, Cyprian of Carthage beheaded, young Cyricus of Tarsus killed by a judge who knocked his head against the stairs of the tribunal, and on reaching the end of the letter C, God said, And so on, it's all much the same, with a few variations and an occasional refinement which would take forever to explain, so let's leave it at that. No, continue, said Jesus, so reluctantly God continued, abbreviating wherever possible, Donatus of Arezzo decapitated, Eliphius of Rampillon scalped, Emerita burned alive, Emilian of Trevi decapitated, Emmeramus of Regensburg tied to a ladder and put to death, Engratia of Saragossa decapitated, Erasmus of Gaeta also called Elmo stretched on a windlass, Escubiculus beheaded, Eskil of Sweden stoned to death, Eulalia of Merida decapitated, Euphemia of Chalcedon put to the sword, Eutropius of Saintes beheaded with an ax, Fabian stabbed and spiked, Faith of Agen beheaded, Felicitas and seven sons beheaded with a sword, Felix and his brother Adauctus likewise, Ferreolus of Besançon decapitated, Fidelis of Sigmaringen beaten to death with a spiked club, Firminus of Pamplona beheaded, Flavia Domitilla likewise, Fortunas of Evora probably met the same fate, Fructoasus of Tarragon burned at the stake, Gaudentius of France decapitated, Gelasius likewise with iron spikes, Gengolf of Burgundy assassinated by his wife's lover, Gerard Sagreda of Budapest speared to death, Gerean of Cologne decapitated, the twins Gervase and Protase likewise,

Godleva and Ghistelles strangled, Gratus of Aosta decapitated, Hermenegild clubbed to death, Hero stabbed with a sword, Hippolytus dragged to his death by a horse, Ignatius of Azevedo murdered by the Calvinists, who are not Catholics, Januarius of Naples decapitated after being thrown to wild beasts and then into a furnace, Joan of Arc burned at the stake, John de Britto beheaded, John Fisher decapitated, John of Nepomuk drowned in the river Vltava, John of Prado stabbed in the head, Julia of Corsica whose breasts were cut off before she was crucified, Juliana of Nicomedia decapitated, Justa and Ruffina of Seville the former killed on the wheel and the latter strangled, Justina of Antioch thrown into a caldron of boiling tar and then beheaded, Justus and Pastor, not our Pastor but the one from Alcalá de Henares, decapitated, Kilian of Würzburg decapitated, Lawrence burned on a gridiron, Léger of Autun decapitated after his eyes and tongue were torn out, Leocadia of Toledo thrown to her death from a high cliff, Livinus of Ghent decapitated after his tongue was torn out, Longinus decapitated, Lucy of Syracuse beheaded after having her eyes plucked out, Ludmila of Prague strangled, Maginus of Tarragon decapitated with a serrated scythe, Mamas of Cappodocia disemboweled, Manuel, Sabel, and Ismael, Manuel put to death with an iron nail embedded in each nipple and an iron rod driven through his head from ear to ear and all three beheaded, Margaret of Antioch killed with a firebrand and an iron comb, Maria Goretti strangled, Marius of Persia put to the sword and his hands amputated, Martina of Rome decapitated, the martyrs of Morocco, Berard of Carbio, Peter of Gimignano, Otto, Adjuto, and Accursio, beheaded, those of Japan, all twenty-six crucified, speared, and burned alive, Maurice of Agaune put to the sword, Meinrad of Einsiedeln clubbed to death, Menas of Alexandria also put to the sword, Mercurius of Cappadocia decapitated, Nicasius of Rheims likewise, Odilia of Huy shot with arrows, Paneras beheaded,

Pantaleon of Nicomedia likewise, Paphnutius crucified, Patroclus of Troyes and Soest likewise, Paul of Tarsus, to whom you will owe your first church, likewise, Pelagius drawn and quartered, Perpetua and her slave Felicity of Carthage both gored by a raging bull, Peter of Rates killed with a sword, Peter of Verona his head slashed with a cutlass and a dagger driven into his chest, Philomena shot with arrows and anchored, Piaton of Tournai scalped, Polycarp stabbed and burned alive, Prisca of Rome devoured by lions, Processus and Martinian probably met the same fate, Quintinus nails driven into his head and other parts of his body, Quirinus of Rouen scalped, Quiteria of Coimbra decapitated by her own father, Reine of Alise put to the sword, Renaud of Dortmund bludgeoned to death with a mason's mallet, Restituta of Naples burned at the stake, Roland put to the sword, Romanus of Antioch strangled to death after his tongue was torn out, have you had enough, God asked Jesus, who retorted, That's something You should ask Yourself, go on. So God continued, Sabinian of Sens beheaded, Sabinus of Assis stoned to death, Saturninus of Toulouse dragged to his death by a bull, Sebastian pierced by arrows, Secundus of Asti decapitated, Servatius of Tongres and Maastricht killed by a blow to the head with a wooden clog, Severus of Barcelona killed by having nails embedded in his head, Sidwell of Exeter decapitated, Sigismund king of Burgundy thrown into a well, Sixtus decapitated, Stephen stoned to death, Symphorian of Autun decapitated, Taresius stoned to death, Thecla of Iconium mutilated and burned alive, Theodore burned at the stake, Thomas Becket of Canterbury a sword driven into his skull, Thomas More beheaded, Thyrsus sawed in half, Tiburtius beheaded, Timothy of Ephesus stoned to death, Torquatus and the twenty-seven killed by General Muça at the gates of Guimarães, Tropez of Pisa decapitated, Urbanus, Valeria of Limoges, and Valerian and Venantius of Camerino met the same fate, Victor decapitated, Victor of Marseilles beheaded, Victoria of Rome put to death after having her tongue pulled out, Vincent of Saragossa tortured to death with millstone, grid, and spikes, Virgilius of Trent beaten to death with a wooden clog, Vitalis of Ravenna put to the sword, Wilgefortis or Livrade or Eutropia the bearded virgin crucified, and so on and so forth, all of them meeting similar fates.

That's not good enough, said Jesus, to what others do You refer. Do you really have to know. I do. I refer to those who will escape martyrdom and die from natural causes after having suffered the torments of the world, the flesh, and the devil, and who in order to overcome them will have to mortify their bodies with fasting and prayer, there is even the amusing case of a certain John Schorn, who will spend so much time on his knees praying that he ends up with corns on his knees of all places, and some will say, this will interest you, he has trapped the devil inside a boot, ha ha ha. Me in a boot, said Pastor scornfully, these are old-wives' tales, any boot capable of holding me would have to be as vast as the world, besides, I'd like to see who would be capable of putting the boot on and taking it off afterward. Perhaps only with fasting and prayer, suggested Jesus, whereupon God replied, They will also mortify their flesh with pain and blood and grime and innumerable penances, hair shirts and flagellation, there will be some who never wash and others who throw themselves onto brambles and roll in the snow to suppress carnal desires that are the work of Satan, who sends these temptations to lure souls from the straight and narrow path that leads to heaven, sends visions of naked women, terrifying monsters, abominable creatures, because lust and fear are weapons the demon uses to torment wretched mankind. Is this true, Jesus asked Pastor, who replied, More or less, I simply took what God didn't want, the flesh with all its joys and sorrows, youth and senility, bloom and decay, but it isn't true that fear is one of my weapons, I don't recall having invented sin and punishment or the terror they inspire. Be quiet, God snapped, sin and the devil are one and the same thing. What thing is that, asked Jesus. My absence. How do your explain Your absence, is it because You withdraw or because mankind abandons You. I never withdraw, never. Yet You allow men to abandon You. Those who abandon Me come looking for Me. And when they do not find You, I suppose You blame the devil. No, he's not to blame, I'm to blame, because I cannot reach out to those who seek Me, words uttered by God with an unexpected, poignant melancholy, as if He had suddenly found a limitation to His power. Jesus said, Go on.

There are others, God continued slowly, who go into the wilderness, where they lead solitary lives in caves and grottoes, with nothing but animals for company, and others who choose a monastic existence, and others who climb to the top of high pillars and sit there year in year out, and others, His voice fell and died away, God was now contemplating an endless procession of people, thousands upon thousands of men and women throughout the world entering convents and monasteries, some buildings rustic, many palatial, There they will remain to serve you and Me from morning until night, with vigils and prayers, all with the same mission and the same destiny, to worship us and die with our names on their lips, they will call themselves Benedictines, Cistercians, Carthusians, Augustinians, Gilbertines, Trinitarians, Franciscans, Dominicans, Capuchins, Carmelites, Jesuits, and there will be so many of them that I should dearly like to be able to exclaim, My God, why so many. At this point the devil said to Jesus, Note from what He has told us that there are two ways of parting with one's life, through martyrdom and by renunciation, it isn't enough for all these people to wait until their time comes, they must run to meet their deaths, be crucified, disemboweled, beheaded, burned at the stake, stoned, drowned, drawn and quartered, skinned alive, speared, gored, buried alive, sawed in two, shot with arrows, mutilated, tortured, or to die in their cells, chapter houses, and cloisters, doing penance and mortifying the flesh God gave them, without which flesh they would have nowhere to put their souls, these punishments were not invented by the devil who is talking to you. Is that all, Jesus asked God. No, there are the wars and massacres. No need to tell me of massacres, I almost perished in one, and thinking it over, what a pity I didn't, for then I would have been spared the crucifixion awaiting me. It was I who led your other father to the place where he overheard the soldiers' conversation and therefore I who saved your life. You saved my life only in order to ordain my death at Your pleasure and convenience, as if killing me twice. The end justifies the means, My son. From what You have told me so far I can believe it, renunciation, cloisters, suffering, death, and now wars and massacres, what wars are they. One war after another and unending, especially those waged against you and Me in the name of a god who has yet to appear. How can there possibly be a god who has yet to appear, any true god can only have existed forever and ever. I know it's difficult to understand or explain, but what I'm telling you will come to pass, a god will rise up against us and our followers, entire nations, no, there are no words to describe the massacres then, the bloodshed and slaughter, imagine my altar in Jerusalem multiplied a thousandfold, replace the sacrificial animals with men, even then you will have no idea what those crusades were like. Crusades, what are they, and why do You refer to them in the past if they have yet to take place. Remember, I am time, for Me all that will happen has happened already, all that has happened goes on happening every day. Tell me more about the crusades. Well, My son, this region where we now find ourselves, including Jerusalem, and other territories to the north and west, will be conquered by the followers of the god I mentioned, who has been slow in coming, the followers on our side will do everything possible to expel them from the places you have traveled and I constantly frequent. You haven't done much to rid this land of the Romans. Don't distract me, I'm talking about the future. Go on, then. Furthermore, you were born, you lived, and you died here. I'm not dead yet. That's irrelevant, because as I've just explained to you, for Me what will happen and what has happened are the same thing, and please stop interrupting, otherwise I'll say no more. All right, I'll be quiet. Now then, future generations will refer to this area as the holy places, because you were born, lived, and died here, so it didn't seem fitting that the cradle of the religion you represent should fall into the hands of infidels, this justified the coming of great armies from the west, who for almost two hundred years fought to conquer and preserve for Christendom the cave where you were born and the hill where you will die, to mention only the most important landmarks. Are these armies the crusades. That's right. And did they conquer what they wanted. No, but they slaughtered many people. What about the crusaders themselves. They lost just as many lives, if not more. And all this bloodshed in our name. They will go into battle crying, God wills it. And no doubt die crying, God willed it. Such a nice way to end one's life. The sacrifice isn't worth it. To save one's soul, My son, the body must be sacrificed. And you, Pastor, what do you say about these amazing events that lie ahead. No one in his right mind can possibly suggest that the devil was, is, or ever will be responsible for so much bloodshed and death, unless some villain brings up that wicked slander accusing me of having conceived the god who will oppose this one here. No, you are not to blame, and should anyone blame you, you need only reply that if the devil is false, he could not have created a true god. Who, then, will create this hostile god, asked Pastor. Jesus was at a loss for an answer, and God, who had been silent, remained silent, but a voice came down from the mist and said, Perhaps this God and the one to come are the same god. Jesus, God, and the devil pretended not to hear, but could not help looking at one another in alarm, mutual fear is like that, it readily unites enemies.

Time passed, the mist did not speak again, and Jesus asked, now with the voice of one who expects an affirmative reply, Nothing more. God hesitated, then in a tired voice said, There is still the Inquisition, but if you don't mind, we'll discuss that some other time. What is the Inquisition. The Inquisition is another long story. Tell me. It's best you don't know, you will only feel remorse today for what belongs to tomorrow. And You won't. God, being God, feels no remorse. Well, since I'm already bearing this burden of having to die for You, I can also endure the remorse that ought to be Yours. I wanted to protect you. You've done nothing else from the day I was born. Like most children, you're ungrateful. Let's stop all this posturing, tell me about the Inquisition. Also known as the Tribunal of the Holy Office, the Inquisition is a necessary evil, we will use this cruel instrument to combat the disease that persistently attacks the body of your church in the form of wicked heresies and their harmful consequences along with a number of physical and moral perversions, which, lumped together without regard for order of importance, will include Lutherans and Calvinists, Molinists and Judaizers, sodomites and sorcerers, some of these plagues belong to the future, others can be found in every age. And if the Inquisition is a necessary evil, as You say, how will it proceed to eliminate these heresies. The Inquisition is a police force, a tribunal, and will therefore pursue, judge, and sentence its enemies as would any police force. Sentence them to what. Prison, exile, the stake. Did You say the stake. Yes, in days to come, thousands upon thousands of men and women will be burned at the stake. You mentioned some of them earlier. They will be burned alive because they believe in you, others because they doubt you. Isn't it permitted to doubt me. No. Yet we're allowed to doubt that the Jupiter of the Romans is god. I am the one and only Lord God, and you are My son. You say thousands will die. Hundreds of thousands of men and women, and on earth there will be much sighing and weeping and cries of anguish, the smoke from charred corpses will blot out the sun, human flesh will sizzle over live coals, the stench will be nauseating. And all this is my fault. You are not to blame, your cause demands it. Father, take from me this cup. My power and your glory demand that you drink it to the last drop. I don't want the glory. But I want the power. The mist began to lift, and around the boat water could be seen, smooth, somber water undisturbed by a ripple of wind or the tremor of a passing fin. Then the devil interrupted, One has to be God to countenance so much blood.

The mist advanced again, something else was about to happen, some revelation, some new sorrow or new remorse. But it was Pastor who spoke, I have a proposal to make, he said, addressing God, and God, taken aback, replied, A proposal from you, and what proposal might that be. His tone, cynical and forbidding, would have reduced most to silence, but the devil was an old acquaintance. Pastor searched for the right words before explaining, I've been listening to all that has been said here in this boat, and although I myself have caught glimpses of the light and darkness ahead, I never realized that the light came from burning stakes and the darkness from great piles of bodies. Does this trouble you. It shouldn't trouble me, for I am the devil, and the devil profits from death even more than You do, it goes without saying that hell is more crowded than heaven. Then why do you complain. I'm not complaining, I'm making a proposal. Go ahead, but be quick, I cannot loiter here for all eternity. No one knows better than You that the devil too has a heart. Yes, but you make poor use of it. Today I use it by acknowledging Your power and wishing that it spread to the ends of the earth without the need of so much death, and since You insist that whatever thwarts and denies You comes from the evil I represent and govern in this world, I propose that You receive me into Your heavenly kingdom, my past offenses redeemed by those I will not commit in future, that You accept my obedience as in those happy days when I was one of Your chosen angels, Lucifer You called me, bearer of light, before my ambition to become Your equal consumed my soul and made me rebel against You. And would you care to tell Me why I should pardon you and receive you into My kingdom. Because if You grant me that same pardon You will one day promise left and right, then evil will cease, Your son will not have to die, and Your kingdom will extend beyond the land of the Hebrews to embrace the whole globe, good will prevail everywhere, and I shall stand among the lowliest of the angels who have remained faithful, more faithful than all of them now that I have repented, and I shall sing Your praises, everything will end as if it had never been, everything will become what it should always have been. I always knew you had a talent for leading souls astray, but I never heard you speak with such conviction and eloquence, you almost won me over. So You won't accept or pardon me. No, I neither accept nor pardon you, I much prefer you as you are, and were it possible, I'd have you be even worse. But why. Because the good I represent cannot exist without the evil you represent, if you were to end, so would I, unless the devil is the devil, God cannot be God. Is that Your final word. My first and last, first because that was the first time I said it, last because I have no intention of repeating it. Pastor shrugged and said to Jesus, Never let it be said the devil didn't tempt God, and getting to his feet, he was about to pass one leg over the side of the boat, but stopped and said, In your pack there is something that belongs to me. Jesus could not remember having taken the pack with him into the boat, but in fact there it was, rolled up at his feet, What thing, he asked, and on opening the pack he found nothing inside but the old black bowl he had brought from Nazareth. That's it, that's it, said the devil, picking up the bowl with both hands, One day this will be yours again, but you won't know you have it. He tucked the bowl inside his coarse shepherd's tunic and lowered himself into the water. Without looking at God, he said, as if addressing an invisible audience, Farewell forever, since that is what He has ordained. Jesus followed with his eyes as Pastor gradually swam off into the mist, from a distance he looked once more like a pig with pointed ears, and he was panting furiously, but anyone with a keen ear would have had no difficulty hearing the note of fear in it, fear not of drowning, what an idea, because the devil, as we have just learned, has no end, but of having to live forever. Pastor had disappeared behind the broken fringe of mist when God's voice suddenly rang out in farewell, I will send a man named John to help, but you will have to prove to him that you are who you are. Jesus looked around, but God was no longer there. Just then the mist lifted and vanished, leaving the lake clear and smooth from mountain to mountain, there was no sign of the devil in the water, no sign of God in the air.

On the shore from which he had come, Jesus could see a large crowd and, in the background, numerous tents, evidently an encampment for people who did not live there and who, having nowhere to sleep, had settled themselves as best they could. Curious, he lowered the oars into the water and rowed in that direction. Looking over his shoulder, he saw boats being pushed into the water, and taking a closer look, he saw Simon and Andrew, James and John in them, with others he did not know. Rowing hard, they were soon within speaking distance. Simon called out, Where have you been, obviously this was not what he wanted to know, but he had to begin somewhere, Here on the lake, replied Jesus, an answer as inane as the question, not a good start in this new chapter in the life of the son of God, Mary, and Joseph. Then Simon was clambering into Jesus' boat, and the incomprehensible and impossible was revealed, Do you know how long you've been out here in the mist, while we tried to launch our boats only to be pushed back by strong winds, asked Simon. All day, replied Jesus, then added, All day and night, seeing the intensity in Simon's face. Forty days, shouted Simon, then lowering his voice, You've been on the lake forty days, and all that time the mist never lifted, as if it were hiding something from us, what were you doing out here, we haven't caught a single fish in these waters for forty days. Jesus passed one of the oars to Simon, and both rowed and conversed in harmony, shoulder to shoulder, moving at a pace ideal for exchanging confidences, and Jesus said before any of the other boats could get closer, I've been with God, and I know what the future holds for me, how long I will live and the life that awaits me after this life. What is He like, I mean, what does God look like. God does not appear in only one form, He may be a cloud, a pillar of smoke, even a wealthy Jew, but once you hear His voice, you know Him. What did He say to you. He told me I am His son. Then the devil was right, during that business with the pigs. The devil too was here in the boat and heard everything, he seems to know as much about me as God does, sometimes I think he knows even more than God. And where, Where what, Where were they, The devil was on one side of the boat, between where you are now and the bench at the stern, which is where God sat. What did God say to you. That I am His son and will be crucified. If you're going to the mountains to fight on the rebel side, we'll come with you. You will come with me, but not to the mountains, we will not conquer Caesar with arms but make God triumph with words. With words alone. Also by giving a good example, and giving our lives if necessary. Are these your father's words. Henceforth all my words are His, and those who believe in Him must believe in me, for it is impossible to believe in the father without believing in the son, since the new path the father has chosen for Himself can begin only with me, His son. When you say we will come with you, who do you mean. First of all you, then Andrew your brother, the sons of Zebedee, James and John, which reminds me that God said He would send a man named John to assist me, but that cannot be the same John. We don't need anyone else, this isn't one of Herod's ceremonial processions. Others will come, perhaps some are already there waiting for God's sign, a sign He will manifest through me, that they may believe and follow. What will you tell the people. That they must repent of their sins and prepare themselves for God's new era, which is about to dawn, an era in which His flaming sword will humble those who have rejected and vilified His holy word. But you must tell them you're the son of God. I'll say that my father called me his son and I carried that word in my heart since the day I was born, but God Himself has now come to claim me as His son, one father does not make one forget the other, but the father giving orders today is God, so we must obey Him. Leave this to me, said Simon, dropping his oar and moving to the prow, and he called out in a loud voice, Hosanna, the son of God approaches, he who has spent forty days on the water speaking with his father and now returns to us so that we may repent and prepare ourselves. Don't mention that the devil was also there, Jesus quickly warned him, afraid of the difficulty he would have explaining this if it became public knowledge. Simon gave another cry, louder, causing great excitement among the crowd gathered on the shore, then he hurried back to his seat and told Jesus, I'll row, you stand on the prow, but say nothing, not a single word, until we reach the shore. And so they arrived, Jesus standing on the prow of the boat in his worn tunic and with his empty pack over his shoulder, arms half raised as if wanting to greet someone or bestow a blessing but too shy, not confident enough. Among those waiting, three men were so impatient that they waded in up to their waists. Reaching the boat at last, they began pushing each other, one of them trying with his free hand to touch Jesus' tunic, not because he believed what Simon had said but because he was pulled by the mystery of this man who had been on the lake forty days, like searching for God in the desert, and who now returned from that mountain of cold mist, where he might or might not have seen God. Needless to say, in all the nearby villages people were speaking of nothing else, and the people gathered on the shore had come to see the meteorological phenomenon for themselves. When they heard there was a man lost in the mist, they muttered, Poor fellow.

The boat glided to its destination as if borne on the wings of angels. Simon helped Jesus step ashore, and in annoyance shook off the three men who had jumped into the water, Leave them alone, said Jesus, one day they will hear of my death and regret not having been there to bear my body, so let them accompany me while I'm still alive. Jesus climbed a rise and asked his companions, Where is Mary, and no sooner had he asked than he saw her. It was as if the very sound of her name had released her from a void, one moment she was nowhere to be seen, the next she was there, I'm here, Jesus. Come stand beside me, you too, Simon and Andrew, and James and John, sons of Zebedee, for you all believe me, you believed me when I was unable to tell you I was the son of God, the son summoned by God the father, spending forty days with Him on the lake before returning to tell you that the hour of the Lord has come and that you must repent before the devil gathers the rotting ears of corn fallen from the harvest God holds in His lap, for you are those rotting ears of corn if by sinning you fell from God's loving embrace. A murmur went through the crowd, passed over their heads like ripples on water, many of those present had heard of the miracles performed by this man, some had seen them with their own eyes or even been the beneficiaries of them, I ate that bread and fish, said one, I drank that wine, said another, I was the neighbor of that adulteress, said a third, but however wonderful these wonders were, they were eclipsed by the sublime moment when Jesus was proclaimed the son of God and therefore God Himself, a revelation as remote from those other miracles as the sky is from the earth, and to the best of our knowledge the distance between them has not been measured to this day. A voice came from the crowd, Prove that you're the son of God, and I will follow you. You would follow me forever if your heart were not locked inside your breast, you ask for the proof your senses can grasp, very well, I'll give you proof that will satisfy them but be denied by your mind until, torn between mind and senses, you'll have no choice but to come to me through your heart. Whatever that means, for I haven't understood a word, scoffed the man. What is your name, asked Jesus. Thomas. Come here, Thomas, come with me to the water's edge and watch me make birds of mud, see how easy it is, I mold the body and wings, the head and beak, set these tiny pebbles for the eyes, adjust the long feathers of the tail, balance the legs and claws, and once that is done, I make eleven more, look here, one, two, three, four, five, six, seven, eight, nine, ten, eleven, twelve birds, all of mud, just think, we could even give them names, this is Simon, this one James, this Andrew, this John, and this one, if you don't mind, will be called Thomas, as for the others we will wait until their names appear, names often get delayed along the way and arrive later, and now watch, I throw the net over my little birds to prevent them from escaping, for they will fly away if we're not careful. Are you trying to tell me that if

702

this net is lifted, the birds will fly away, Thomas asked. Yes, if the net is lifted, the birds will fly away. Is this the proof you think will convince me. Yes and no. What do you mean, yes and no. The best proof would be for you not to lift the net, believing the birds will escape if you lift it. But birds made of mud cannot possibly fly. Adam, our first father, was made of mud, and you are one of his descendants. It was God who gave Adam life. Doubt no more, Thomas, and lift the net, for I am the son of God. Well, if you say so, here goes, but I promise you these birds won't fly, and without further ado Thomas lifted the net, and the birds, freed, took flight. Twittering with excitement, they circled twice above the astonished crowd before disappearing into the sky. Jesus said, Look, Thomas, your bird has gone, to which Thomas replied, No, Lord, I'm the bird, kneeling here at your feet.

Some of the men in the crowd surged forward, and several women behind them did the same. They drew near and gave their names, I am Philip, and Jesus saw stones and a cross, I am Bartholomew, and Jesus saw a flayed torso, I am Matthew, and Jesus saw a corpse among barbarians, I am Simon, and Jesus saw the saw that would cut Simon's body, I am James son of Alphaeus, and Jesus saw him being stoned to death, I am Judas Thaddeus, and Jesus saw a club raised over the man's head, I am Judas Iscariot, and Jesus took pity on him, seeing him hang himself from a fig tree. Then Jesus called the others and said, Now that we are all here, the hour has come. And turning to Simon brother of Andrew, he told him, Because we have another Simon with us, you will be known as Peter. Turning their backs to the lake, the men started walking, followed by the women, most of whose names we never learned, not that it matters, for most of them are called Mary, and the rest will answer to that name, a man need only shout, Woman, or Mary, and they will look up and come to do his bidding.

JESUS AND HIS DISCIPLES TRAVELED FROM VILLAGE TO VIL-
lage, and God spoke through Jesus, and here is what He
said, Time has run full circle, and the kingdom of God is
at hand, repent and have faith in this good news. The local
inhabitants, hearing this, saw no difference between time's
running full circle and time's coming to an end, and so
believed the end of the world, which is where time is finally measured, must be fast approaching. They thanked
God for having mercifully sent them advance notice of their
fate through someone who claimed to be His son, a claim
that might even be true, seeing as he worked miracles
wherever he went, provided those seeking his help showed
genuine faith and conviction, as in the case of the leper
who pleaded, If you wish, you can make me clean, and
Jesus, taking pity on the poor wretch covered with festering sores, laid his hand on him and said, It is my wish that
you be clean, and no sooner were those words spoken than
the sores healed, the body was restored to health, and the
leper from whom everyone had fled in horror was now
free of all blemish. Another remarkable cure was that of

the paralytic. Such an enormous crowd had gathered around the door that the sick man had to be hoisted up, bed and all, then lowered through an opening in the roof of the house where Jesus was staying, which probably belonged to Simon, also known as Peter. Moved by the crowd's deep faith, Jesus told the sick man, My son, your sins are forgiven, but it happened that some distrustful scribes, eager to find cause for complaint and always ready to quote holy law, were present, and when they heard what Jesus said, they lost no time in protesting, How dare you say such things, this is blasphemy, only God can forgive, whereupon Jesus asked, Is it easier to say to one sick of the palsy, Your sins are forgiven, than to say, Arise, take up your bed, and walk, and without waiting for an answer, he continued, That you may know that the son of man has power on earth to forgive sins, I say unto you, and he turned to the paralytic, Arise, take up your bed, and go your way, and with these words the man miraculously got to his feet, his strength restored, and taking up the bed, he lifted it onto his shoulders and walked off, praising God.

Obviously we do not all go in search of miracles. In time we become used to our little aches and pains and learn to live with them, not thinking of importuning the divine powers. Sins, however, are quite a different matter, they get under our skin and torment us, sins, unlike a crippled leg, a paralyzed arm, or the ravages of leprosy, fester inside, and God knew what He was talking about when He told Jesus that every man has at least one sin, if not more, to repent. Now since this world is about to end and the kingdom of God is at hand, rather than enter it with our bodies restored by miraculous means we should pay attention to our souls, purify them by repentance, heal them by forgiveness. For if the paralytic from Capernaum spent most of his life on a bed, it was because he sinned, sickness as we all know is the result of sin, therefore we may safely conclude that the essential requirement for good health, not to mention immortality, can only be the utmost purity, a complete absence of sin, either through blessed ignorance or strenuous repudiation, both in thought and deed. Let no one think, however, that our Jesus journeyed through these lands squandering his power to heal and his authority to pardon sins, granted him by the Lord Himself. Though obviously he would have preferred, personally, to become a universal panacea than announce, for God, the end of time and urge men to repent. And in order that sinners not lose too much time wrestling with the difficult decision of confessing, I have sinned, the Lord put certain terrifying threats into Jesus' mouth, as follows, Verily I say unto you that some of you who are present here will not die before seeing the kingdom of God arrive in all its majesty. Imagine the devastating effect such words must have had on those who flocked from all directions to follow Jesus, hoping he would lead them straight to the new paradise the Lord would establish on earth, which would be different from Eden, enjoyed after atonement for Adam's sin by prayer, mortification, and repentance. Since most of these trusting souls were from the working class, artisans and road diggers, fishermen and women of lowly condition, Jesus ventured one day, when God allowed him a little more freedom, to improvise a speech that left its audience spellbound, tears of joy flowing at the prospect of salvation, Blessed are you poor, Jesus told them, for yours is the kingdom of heaven, blessed are you that hunger, for you will be filled, blessed are you that weep, for you will laugh, but then God became aware of what was happening, and although it was too late to retract what Jesus had said, He forced him to speak other words, which turned the tears of joy into grim foreboding, Blessed are you when men hate you, and separate you from their company, and reproach you, and cast out your name as evil, for the son of man's sake. When Jesus finished speaking, it was as if his soul had fallen to his feet, for in that instant all the torments and deaths God had foretold on the lake marched before him. Numb with fear, the crowd watched Jesus sink to his knees, prostrate himself, and pray in silence. No one there could have imagined that he was asking their forgiveness, he, the son of God, who was able to forgive the sins of others. That night, in the privacy of the tent he shared with Mary Magdalene, Jesus said, I am the shepherd who with the same crook leads to sacrifice both the innocent and the wicked, the saved and the lost, those born and those yet to be born, who will deliver me from this guilt, for I now see myself as I once saw my father, he had to answer for twenty lives while I must answer for twenty thousand. Mary Magdalene wept with Jesus and tried to console him, It wasn't your doing, she sobbed. That makes it all the worse, he insisted. And as if she had known all along what we have only come to understand little by little, she said, It is God who draws the paths of fate and decides who must walk them, He chose you to open a path among paths on His behalf, but you will not walk that path or build a temple, others will build it upon your blood and body, you may as well accept the fate He has chosen for you, your every gesture has been determined, the words you will utter wait for you in the places you will visit, there you will find the crippled to whom you will restore limbs, the blind to whom you will give sight, the deaf to whom you will give hearing, the dumb to whom you will give speech, the dead whom you will resurrect. But I have no power over death. You haven't tried. I did try, but the fig tree did not revive. You must wish what God wills, but He cannot deny you what you wish. That He should take from me this burden, that is all I ask. You ask the impossible, Jesus, for the one thing God cannot do is not love Himself. How do you know. Women see things differently, perhaps because our bodies are different, yes, that must be the explanation.

One day, because the earth is too big for the strength of one man, even in a place as small as Palestine, Jesus decided to send his disciples, in pairs, to announce throughout the cities, towns, and villages the coming of God's kingdom, and to teach and preach as he did everywhere they went. And so, finding himself alone with Mary Magdalene, for the other women had gone off with the men according to their tastes and preferences, it occurred to him that since they were traveling to Bethany, which is near Jerusalem, they might as well kill two birds with one stone, if you will pardon the expression, and visit Mary's brother and sister. It was time they made their peace and for the two brothers-in-law to get to know each other. Reunited, they could make the journey together to Jerusalem, for Jesus had arranged a meeting with all his disciples in Bethany in three months' time. There is little to tell about the works of the twelve apostles in the lands of Israel, first because notwithstanding a few details about their lives and the circumstances of their deaths we have not been called upon to narrate their story, secondly because they had not been given any mandate other than to repeat, albeit each in his own way, the precepts of their master, which means they taught just as he did, performing cures as best they could. A pity Jesus forbade them to follow the path of the Gentiles or to enter any city of the Samaritans, this surprising intolerance in one so well educated deprived them of the chance to reduce their future task, because given God's intention of extending the domain of His influence, sooner or later His message would not only reach the Samaritans but, above all, the Gentiles, both here and elsewhere. Jesus instructed his disciples to heal the sick and raise the dead, make lepers clean and drive out demons, but apart from one or two vague references there is no clear evidence that any such miracles were performed, which goes to show that God does not trust just anyone, however strongly recommended. Once they are reunited with

Jesus, the twelve disciples will undoubtedly have something to tell him about the results of their sermons on repentance, but probably little to report about healings, apart from the expelling of some fairly innocuous demons, who do not require much persuasion to pass from one soul to another. But the disciples will certainly tell Jesus how they themselves were often expelled, or given a hostile reception on roads where there were no Gentiles or in cities not populated by Samaritans, their only recourse being to shake the dust from their feet on leaving, as if the fault were that of the dust, which is trodden by everyone without ever complaining. But Jesus told them this was what they must do in such situations, as testimony against those who refused to listen, most regrettable, for this is the word of God Himself that is being rejected. Jesus told them, Don't worry about what to say, inspiration will come to you when you need it. But perhaps it doesn't work like that, after all, soundness of doctrine should come before personal delivery.

The perfume of freshly gathered roses hung in the air, the roads were clean and pleasant, as if angels were walking ahead and sprinkling dew as they went, then brushing the roads with laurel and myrtle. Jesus and Mary Magdalene avoided the caravansaries and the other travelers on the road, not wanting to be recognized, not that Jesus was shirking his duty, never easy under God's watchful eye, but it seemed that the Almighty had decided to grant him a breather, because no lepers came on the road to beg a cure, or possessed souls needing exorcism, and the villages they passed through were quietly rejoicing in the peace of the Lord, as if they had already made progress along the path of repentance. The couple slept wherever they happened to be, seeking no comfort other than each other's lap, sometimes with only the sky for a roof, God's enormous eye, black but speckled with lights, lingering reflections of eyes raised to heaven by generation after generation, interrogating the silence and listening to the only answer silence ever gives. Later, when she is alone in the world, Mary Magdalene will try to recall those days and nights, but she will find it increasingly difficult to preserve her memories of sorrow and bitterness, as if trying in vain to protect an island of love from a tempestuous sea and its monsters. The hour is drawing near, but looking at heaven and earth, one sees no visible sign yet of its approach, just as a bird flies across an open sky without noticing the swift falcon drop like a stone, its claws ready. Jesus and Mary Magdalene, singing as they walk along, make an impression on other travelers, who think to themselves, Such a happy pair, and for the moment nothing could be truer. And thus they reached Jericho, and from there, because of the intense heat and lack of shade, they took two whole days to go up to Bethany. Mary Magdalene wondered how her brother and sister would receive her after all this time, especially since she left home to live as a prostitute, They may think I'm dead, she said, they may even want me dead. Jesus tried to dissuade her from dwelling on such thoughts, Time heals everything, he said, forgetting that the wound inflicted by his own family is still raw and bleeding. They entered Bethany, Mary half covering her face for fear one of the villagers might recognize her. Jesus gently rebuked her, Why are you hiding, your past is now behind you and exists no more. I'm not the person I was, it is true, but I am still bound to who I was by shame. You are now only who you are, and you are with me. Thanks be to God, but the day will come when He takes you from me. Dropping her mantle, Mary showed her face, but no one said, Look, there is Lazarus's sister, the one who went off to live as a prostitute.

This is the house, she said, but could not bring herself to knock or to announce her arrival. Jesus gave the unlocked gate a gentle push and called out, Anyone home, and a woman's voice answered, Who's there, and with those words she appeared in the doorway. This was Martha, the twin sister of Mary Magdalene, but now bearing little resemblance to her, for age had left its mark on Martha, or it could have been the hard life she had led, or purely a matter of temperament and outlook. The first thing she noticed were Jesus' eyes and expression, as if a dark cloud had lifted all at once, leaving his face luminous, but then she saw her sister and became wary, her frown showing displeasure, Who is this man with her, she must have thought, or perhaps, How can he be with her if he is what he seems, but pressed to explain herself, Martha would have been unable to say what he seemed to be. This is probably why, instead of asking her sister, How are you, or, What are you doing here, all she could say was, Who is this man you've brought with you. Jesus smiled, and his smile went straight to Martha's heart like an arrow and there it remained, making it ache with satisfaction, My name is Jesus of Nazareth, he told her, and I'm with your sister, the same words, mutatis mutandis, the Romans would say, as those he used when he took leave of his brother James by the lake, telling him, Her name is Mary Magdalene and she's with me. Pushing the door wide open, Martha said, Come in, make yourself at home, but it was not clear which of them she meant. Once inside the yard, Mary Magdalene took her sister by the arm and told her, I belong here as much as you do, and I belong to this man, who does not belong to you, I've been frank with both of you, so do not flaunt your virtue or condemn my wickedness, I come in peace and in peace I wish to be. Martha said, I will receive you as my sister, and I long for the day when I can welcome you with love, but it's too soon, and she was about to continue when a thought stopped her, she was not sure whether this man standing beside her sister knew about the life her sister had led and might still be leading, and she began to blush, hating the two of them and herself, until Jesus finally spoke so that Martha could learn what she needed to know, for it is not that difficult to tell what people are thinking, and he told her, God judges all of us and does so differently each day, according to what we are each day, now if God were to judge you at this moment, Martha, don't imagine you'd be any different in His eyes from Mary. Explain that more clearly, for I don't understand. There is no more to be said, but keep my words in your heart and repeat them to yourself whenever you look at your sister. Is she no longer. You mean am I no longer a whore, asked Mary Magdalene bluntly, despising her sister's delicacy. Martha flinched, raised her hands to her face, No, I don't want to know, Jesus' words are enough, and unable to restrain herself, she burst into tears. Mary went to her and embraced her, cradling her in her arms, while Martha kept saying between sobs, What a life, what a life, but one could not be certain whether she meant her own life or her sister's. Where is Lazarus, asked Mary. In the synagogue. How is he these days. He still suffers from those bouts of choking, but otherwise his health is not bad. She felt like adding resentfully that Mary was slow in showing concern, for during all those years of guilty absence, this prodigal sister, prodigal with both her time and her body, had not kept in touch with her family, had not once inquired after their brother, whose health had always been precarious. But turning to Jesus, who was observing the hostility between them, Martha told him, Our brother copies out books in the synagogue, it is as much as he can do in his poor state of health, and her tone was of one incapable of understanding how anyone could live without being engaged in some worthwhile task from morning till night. What ails Lazarus, asked Jesus. He chokes, as if his heart were about to stop beating, then he turns so pale, you'd think he was going to pass away. Martha paused before adding, He's younger than we are, she spoke without thinking, perhaps suddenly struck by Jesus' youth, and once again she felt perturbed, felt pangs of jealousy, which brought words to her lips that sounded strange coming from Martha when Mary Magdalene, whose duty and privilege it was to say them, was standing there, You're tired, Martha said to Jesus, Sit down and let me wash your feet. Afterward, when Mary found herself alone with Jesus, she remarked half jokingly, It would seem that we two sisters were born to love you, and Jesus replied, Martha is sad that she has had so little pleasure in life. She's resentful, thinking there is no justice in heaven when a fallen woman gets the prize and a virtuous woman like her goes unrewarded. God will reward her in other ways. Perhaps, but God, having made the world, has no right to deprive women of any of the fruits of His creation. Such as carnal knowledge of men. Of course, just as you came to know woman, and what more could you wish for, being as you are, the son of God. He who lies with you is not the son of God but the son of Joseph. Frankly, ever since you came into my life, I never felt I was lying with the son of a god. You mean of God. If only you weren't.

Martha entrusted a neighbor's little boy with a message for Lazarus, informing him that Mary had returned home, but she did so only after much hesitation, for she was anxious that no one know that their disreputable sister was back in the village, because tongues would start wagging again after all this time. How would she face people on the street the next day, and worse still, how would she find the courage to walk out with her sister. It would be difficult to ignore her neighbors and friends, and she dreaded having to say to them, This is my sister Mary, do you remember her, she's come home, only to receive knowing looks and sly comments, Of course we remember, who doesn't remember Mary, let us hope these prosaic details do not offend our readers, because the story of God is not all divine. Martha was trying to suppress these uncharitable thoughts when Lazarus arrived, and embracing Mary, he said simply, Welcome home, sister, putting aside the sorrow of all those years of separation and silent anxiety. Martha, feeling it was up to her to put a brave face on things, pointed to Jesus and told her brother, This is Jesus, our brother-in-law. The two men exchanged a friendly nod, then sat down to have a chat, while the women prepared a meal together as they had done so many times in the past. Now after they had eaten, Lazarus and Jesus went into the yard to enjoy the cool night air while the sisters remained inside to resolve the important question of how to arrange the sleeping mats, since they were now four instead of two. Jesus, gazing at length at the first stars to appear in the sky, which was still light, finally asked Lazarus, Do you suffer much pain, and Lazarus replied with surprising composure, Yes, I suffer all right. Your suffering will be over, said Jesus. No doubt, when I'm dead. No, I mean very soon. I didn't know you were a physician. Brother, if I were a physician, I wouldn't be able to cure you. Nor can you even if you're not. You are cured, Jesus murmured softly, taking him by the hand. And Lazarus felt the sickness drain from his body like murky water absorbed by the sun. His breathing became easier, his pulse stronger, and he asked nervously, puzzled by what was happening, What's going on, his voice hoarse with alarm, Who are you. A physician I am not, smiled Jesus. In the name of God, tell me who you are. Do not take the name of God in vain. But what am I to make of this. Call Mary, she'll tell you. There was no need to call anyone. Drawn by the sudden raising of voices, Martha and Mary appeared in the doorway, afraid the two men might be quarreling, but they saw at once they were mistaken, a blue light suffused the entire yard, from the sky, and a shaken Lazarus was pointing at Jesus, Who is this man, he asked, for he had only to touch me and say, You are cured, and the sickness left. Martha went to comfort her brother, how could he be cured when he was trembling from head to foot, but Lazarus pushed her away, saying, Mary, you brought him here, tell us who he is. Without stirring from the doorway, Mary Magdalene said, He is Jesus of Nazareth, the son of God. Now even though this region has been favored with prophetic revelations and apocalyptic signs since time immemorial, it would have been perfectly natural for Lazarus and Martha to express utter disbelief, it is one thing for you to acknowledge that you have been cured by miraculous means, and quite another to be told that the man who touched your hand is none other than the son of God himself. Faith and love, however, can achieve much, some even claim they do not have to go together to achieve what they achieve, as it happened Martha threw herself weeping into Jesus' arms, then, alarmed by her daring, she slumped to the ground, where she remained, her face completely transformed as she muttered to herself, And I washed your feet. Lazarus did not move, out of fear, and we might even suggest that if this sudden revelation did not kill him, it was because his sister's timely act of love had given him a new heart. Smiling, Jesus went to embrace him and said, Don't be surprised to find that the son of God is a son of man, frankly, God had no one else to choose, just as men choose their women and women their men. These final words were intended for Mary Magdalene, but Jesus forgot that they would only aggravate Martha's distress and desperate loneliness, this is the difference between God and His son, God does it on purpose, His son out of carelessness, which is all too human. Never mind, today there is rejoicing in this household, and Martha can go back to her sighing tomorrow, but she has one consolation she can be sure of, no one will dare gossip about her sister's past in the streets, squares, and marketplaces of Bethany once they learn, and Martha herself will make sure they are told, that the man with her cured Lazarus of his sickness without the use of potions or infusions of herbs. They were sitting at home enjoying one another's company when Lazarus remarked, There have been

rumors about a man from Galilee going around performing miracles, but it has never been suggested that he is the
son of God. Some news travels faster than others, said Jesus. Are you that man. You have said it. Then Jesus told
his story from the beginning, but not quite everything, he
did not mention Pastor, and he said nothing about God
except that He had appeared to him to announce, You are
My son. Without those rumors of miracles, now turned
into fact by the evidence of this latest miracle, and without
the power of faith and love, it would have been difficult
indeed for Jesus to convince Lazarus and Martha that the
man who would shortly be sharing a mat with their sister
was made of divine spirit. For it was with flesh and blood
that Jesus embraced this woman who had embraced so many
men without fear of God. And let us forgive Martha the
spiritual pride that led her to mutter, under the sheet pulled
over her head so she would not see or hear, I deserve him
more than she does.

Next day the news spread like wildfire, people everywhere in Bethany praised and thanked the Lord, and even
those dry souls who were doubtful to begin with, thinking
the earth too small to hold such wonders, were forced to
change their minds when confronted with a miraculously
cured Lazarus, of whom it should never be said that he
began selling good health to others, for he was so good-
hearted that he would sooner have given it all away. Now
people gathered around the door, curious to see with their
own eyes this miracle-worker, whom they might even be
allowed to touch, a last, definitive proof. The sick and infirm also came in droves, some on foot, others carried in
litters or on the backs of relatives, until the narrow street
where Lazarus and his sister lived was completely filled.
When Jesus became aware of the situation, he sent word
that he would address the crowd in the main square of the
village, where they should go and he would join them
shortly. But any man who holds a bird securely in his hand

716

is not going to be foolish enough to let it escape. So understandably no one moved from his vantage point, and Jesus was obliged to show his face, leaving the house like anyone else, without fanfare, pomp, or ceremony, and without any tremors in heaven or on earth. Here I am, he said, trying to speak naturally, but his words were sufficient to make the inhabitants of an entire village fall to their knees and beg for mercy, Save us, cried some, Cure me, implored others. Jesus cured one man who, being mute, was unable to plead, but he sent the others away because they did not have enough faith. He told them to come back another day, but first they must repent of their sins, because as we know the kingdom of God is at hand and time is about to end. Are you the son of God, they asked, and Jesus answered enigmatically, If I were not, God would strike you dumb rather than permit such a question.

He began his stay in Bethany with these remarkable deeds, while waiting to be reunited with his disciples, who still journeyed through distant lands. Needless to say, people soon arrived from surrounding towns and villages when they heard that the man who worked miracles in the north was now in Bethany. There was no need for Jesus to leave Lazarus's house, because everyone flocked there as though to a place of pilgrimage, but he did not receive them, ordering them instead to gather on a hill outside the village, where he would preach repentance and heal the sick. The excitement and news quickly reached Jerusalem, which made the crowds even larger, until Jesus began asking himself if he should remain there at the risk of provoking riots, which are all too common when crowds get out of control. Humble folk were the first to come from Jerusalem in search of healing, but it was not long before people from every social class began arriving, including a number of Pharisees and scribes who could not believe that anyone in his right mind would have the courage, one might even say the suicidal courage, openly to declare himself the son of

God. They returned to Jerusalem irritated and puzzled, because Jesus never gave a straight answer when questioned. If pressed about his parentage, he said he was the son of man, and if he happened to say father when referring to God, it was clear he meant God as everyone's father and not just his own. There remained the troublesome question of these healing powers he exercised without recourse to trickery or magic. All he needed were a few simple words, Walk, Arise, Speak, See, Be clean, the leper's skin suddenly glowed like dew in the morning light when Jesus touched it with his fingertips, mutes and stammerers became inebriated with words, paralytics jumped out of bed and danced with joy, the blind could not believe their eyes could see again, the lame ran to their heart's content, then playfully pretended to be lame once more, so they could start running all over again. Repent, Jesus told them, Repent, and that was all he asked of them. But the high priests of the Temple, who knew better than anyone of the upheavals provoked in their time by prophets and soothsayers, decided that there should be no more religious, social, and political disturbances, and that from now on they should pay close attention to everything the Galilean did and said, and if it became necessary, to uproot and eliminate the evil, because, in the words of the high priest, This man does not deceive me, the son of man is the son of God. Jesus had not gone to sow in Jerusalem, but here in Bethany he was forging and honing the scythe with which he would be cut down.

Then the disciples began to arrive in Bethany, in pairs, two today, two tomorrow, or even four if they chanced to meet en route. Apart from a few minor details, they all had the same story to tell, about a man who came out of the desert and prophesied in the traditional manner, as if moving boulders with his voice and whole mountains with his arms, he spoke of the punishment in store for people and of the imminent arrival of the Messiah. The disciples never actually saw him, because he was constantly on the move, going from place to place, so their information was secondhand, they would have sought this prophet out, but their three months were nearly up and they didn't wish to miss their meeting. Jesus asked them if they knew the prophet's name, and they told him it was John. So he's here already, said Jesus. His friends did not know what he meant, except for Mary Magdalene, but then she knew everything. Jesus wanted to go look for John, who almost certainly was looking for him, but of the twelve apostles, Thomas and Judas Iscariot still had not arrived, and since they might have more information, their delay was all the more frustrating. The wait for them, however, proved to be justified, because the two latecomers had not only seen John but spoken to him. The others emerged from their tents, pitched outside Bethany, to hear what Thomas and Judas Iscariot had to tell, they sat in a circle in the yard of Lazarus's house, with Martha and Mary and the other women in attendance. Judas Iscariot and Thomas spoke in turn, explaining how John had been in the wilderness when he received the word of God, and went to the banks of the Jordan to baptize and preach penance for the remission of sins, but as the multitudes flocked to him to be baptized, he rebuked them with loud cries that frightened everyone out of their wits, O generation of vipers, who has warned you to flee from the wrath to come, bring forth therefore fruits meet for repentance, and think not to say within yourselves, We have Abraham for our father, for I say unto you that God is able from these stones to raise up children unto Abraham, leaving you despised, and now the ax is put to the root of the trees, therefore every tree that brings not forth good fruit is hewn down and cast into the fire. Terror-stricken, the multitudes asked him, What must we do, and John replied, Let the man who has two tunics share them with him who has none, and the man who has provisions do the same, and to the collectors of taxes John said, Make no demands other than those established by law, and do not think the law is just because you call it the law, and to the soldiers who asked him, And what about us, what must we do, he replied, Use violence against no one, do not sentence anyone falsely, and content yourselves with your wages. Here Thomas, who had begun, fell silent, and Judas Iscariot took over. They asked John if he was the Messiah, and he told them, I baptize you with water unto repentance, but he who comes after me is mightier than I, whose shoes I am not worthy to bear, he will baptize you with the Holy Ghost and with fire, his fan is in his hand, and he will thoroughly purge his floor and gather his wheat into the granary, but the chaff he will burn with unquenchable fire. Judas Iscariot said nothing more, and everyone waited for Jesus to speak, but Jesus, with one finger tracing enigmatic lines on the ground, appeared to be waiting. Then Peter said, So you are the Messiah whose coming John prophesies, and Jesus replied, still scribbling in the dust, You have said it, not I, God only told me I was His son, he paused for a moment, then ended by saying, I will go look for John. We'll go with you, said the son of Zebedee who was also John, but Jesus slowly shook his head, I'll take only Thomas and Judas, because they've seen him, and turning to Judas, he asked, What does he look like. He's taller than you, said Judas, and heavier, he has a long beard as if made of bristles, and he wears nothing except a garment of camel's hair and a leather girdle around his waist, people say that in the wilderness he feeds on locusts and wild honey. He sounds more like the Messiah than I do, Jesus said, rising from the circle.

The three of them set out early the next morning, and knowing that John never stayed more than a few days in the same place and that they would most probably find him baptizing on the banks of the Jordan, they went down from Bethany to a place called Bethabara at the edge of the Dead Sea, intending to travel upriver as far as the Sea of

Galilee, and even farther north to the headwaters if necessary. But their journey was shorter than they imagined, for it was in Bethabara itself that they found John, alone, as if he was expecting them. They caught their first glimpse of the man from afar, a tiny figure seated on the riverbank, surrounded by somber crags resembling skulls and ravines that looked like open scars. To the right, beneath the sun and the white sky, was the sinister Dead Sea, its awesome surface agleam like molten copper. When they came within throwing distance, Jesus asked his companions, Is it he. Shading their eyes with their hands, the disciples took a careful look and replied, Either it is he or his twin. Wait here until I return, and come no closer, said Jesus, and without another word he began making his descent to the river. Thomas and Judas sat on the parched ground and watched Jesus walk away, appearing and disappearing as the land rose and fell, then when he reached the bank, they saw him approaching John, who had not stirred all this time. Let's hope we're not mistaken, said Thomas. We should have gone closer, said Judas Iscariot. But Jesus was certain the moment he saw him and had asked only for the sake of asking. Down below, John rose to his feet and looked at Jesus as he walked toward him. What will they have to say to each other, wondered Judas Iscariot. Perhaps Jesus will tell us, perhaps he won't, said Thomas. Now the two men in the distance were face-to-face and conversing excitedly, judging from the gestures they made with their staffs, and after a while they went to the water's edge, where they disappeared from view behind the jutting embankment, but Judas and Thomas knew what was happening there, because they too had been baptized by John. They had waded into the river until the water came up to their waists. John will scoop up water in his cupped hands, raise it to heaven, then let it fall on Jesus' head, reciting, I baptize you with this water, may it nourish your fire. When this is accomplished, John and Jesus will emerge from the river, retrieve their staffs, and bid each other farewell with an embrace, and John will start walking along the river in a northerly direction, while Jesus returns to us. Thomas and Judas Iscariot stand waiting for him, and he indeed appears, he passes in silence and leads the way to Bethany. Feeling somewhat slighted, his disciples walk behind him, their curiosity unsatisfied, until Thomas, unable to contain himself any longer and ignoring Judas's gesture, asked, Aren't you going to tell us what John said. In good time, replied Jesus. Did he tell you, at least, that you're the Messiah. In good time, said Jesus again, and his disciples wondered if he was telling them, by this repetition, that it was not yet time for the Messiah to appear.

Only Mary Magdalene learned what happened that day. Little was said, Jesus confided, no sooner did we meet than John wanted to know if I was he who has come or if we had to await another. And what did you tell him. I told him the blind regain their sight and the lame walk, the lepers are made clean and the deaf hear, and the poor have the gospel preached to them. And what did he say. The Messiah won't need to do much, so long as he does what is expected of him. Is that what he said. Yes, those were his very words. And what is expected of the Messiah. That's what I asked him, And what answer did he give you, He told me to find out for myself, And then what did he say. Nothing else, he took me to the river, baptized me, and walked away. What words did he use to baptize you. I baptize you with water, and may it nourish your fire. After this conversation with Mary Magdalene, Jesus did not speak for a week. He left Lazarus's house and went to join his disciples just outside Bethany, where he put up a tent away from the others and spent the entire day alone. Not even Mary Magdalene was allowed to enter the tent, and Jesus left it only at night to go into the mountains. Sometimes his disciples secretly followed him, on the pretext that they wanted to protect him from wild beasts, though there were no wild beasts in those parts. They found that he would choose a comfortable spot and sit there staring, not at the sky but straight ahead, as if waiting for someone to appear from the ominous shadow of a ravine or from around the slope of a hill. There was moonlight, so anyone who appeared would have been visible from afar, but no one appeared. At first light Jesus returned to the camp. He ate very little of the food John and Judas Iscariot brought him in turn, and he made no attempt to respond to their greetings. On one occasion he even dismissed Peter brusquely when Peter asked if all was well and if he had any orders to give. Peter was not completely mistaken, he had only spoken too soon, because after eight days Jesus emerged from the tent in broad daylight, rejoined his disciples, ate with them, and when he had finished, he told them, Tomorrow we go up to Jerusalem, to the Temple, there you will do as I do, because the time has come for the son of God to know what use is being made of his father's house, and for the Messiah to begin to do what is expected of him. The disciples wanted to know more, but apart from telling them, You won't have to wait much longer to find out, Jesus would say nothing. The disciples were not accustomed to being spoken to in this way or to seeing his face so severe, he was no longer the gentle, tranquil Jesus they knew, who went wherever God wished without a murmur of complaint. This change had been brought about by circumstances unknown, whatever had led him to separate himself from his disciples and to wander over hill and dale as if possessed by the demons of night, in search of who knows what. Peter, the oldest one there, thought it unfair that Jesus should order them to go up to Jerusalem just like that, as if they were servants and fit only to fetch and carry, to go back and forth with no explanation. So he protested, We recognize your authority and are prepared to obey you in word and deed, both as the son of God and as a man, but is it right that you treat us like irresponsible children or doddery old men, refusing to confide in us, giving orders without asking our opinion or allowing us to make our own decisions. Forgive me, all of you, said Jesus, for I myself do not know what calls me to Jerusalem, all I was told was that I must go, nothing more, you do not have to accompany me. Who told you you must go to Jerusalem. A voice in my head, it tells me what I must and must not do. You're much changed since your meeting with John. Yes, it made me realize that it isn't enough to bring peace, one must also carry a sword. If the kingdom of God is at hand, why carry a sword, asked Andrew. Because God has not revealed by what means His kingdom will come, we've tried peace, now let us try the sword, and God will choose, but I repeat, you do not have to accompany me. You know we will follow you wherever you go, John told him, and Jesus replied, Don't swear it, those of you who go with me will learn.

The next morning, Jesus went to Lazarus's house to say good-bye and also reassure Lazarus and Martha that he was again living with his disciples after his mysterious retreat into the wilderness. Martha told him that her brother had left for the synagogue. So Jesus and his disciples set off on the road to Jerusalem, Mary Magdalene and the other women accompanying them as far as the last houses of Bethany, where they stopped and waved, content to wave although the men did not look back even once. The sky is cloudy and threatens rain, perhaps this is why there are so few people on the road, those with no urgent business in Jerusalem have decided to stay at home and wait for a sign from the heavens. The thirteen men walk, and thick gray clouds rumble above the mountains, as if sky and earth were finally about to come together, the mold and the molded, male and female, concave and convex. They reached the city gates and found, though the road had been deserted, the usual crowd gathered there, and they resigned themselves to a long wait before reaching the Temple. But things turned out differently. The appearance of thirteen men, nearly all of them barefoot, with great staffs, flowing beards, and heavy, dark capes over tunics that had seen better days, caused the startled crowd to fall back and ask among themselves, Where can these men have come from, and who's the one in front. No one knew the answer until a man who had come down from Galilee said, He's Jesus of Nazareth, who claims to be the son of God and performs miracles. Where are they going, asked others, and since the only way of finding out was to follow them, many walked behind them, so that by the time they reached the entrance to the Temple, they were no longer thirteen but a thousand, and the people waited to see what would happen. Jesus walked on the side where the money changers were and said to his disciples, Here is what we have come to do, and with these words he began overturning the tables, berating those who were buying and selling, causing such an uproar that his words would not have been heard but for the fact that his natural voice rang out in stentorian tones, It is written that my house shall be called a house of prayer, but you have made it a den of thieves, and he continued to overturn the tables, scattering coins everywhere, which brought great joy to the horde that rushed to gather this manna. The disciples followed Jesus' example, and the tables of the dove sellers were also thrown to the ground, and the birds, released, flew over the Temple, circling wildly around the distant smoke from the altar, where they will not be burned now, for their savior has come. The Temple guards rushed to the scene, armed with batons to punish, capture, or expel the rioters, only to find themselves up against thirteen formidable Galileans with staffs in hand, who swept aside all who dared approach. Come, come, the lot of you, and feel God's might, they taunted, falling on the guards, destroying everything in sight, and putting a torch to the tents. Soon a second column of smoke was spiraling into the air, and a voice cried out, Call the Roman soldiers, but no one paid attention, for happen what might, the Romans were forbidden by law to enter the Temple. More guards rushed to the scene, this time with swords and lances, they were joined by a few money changers and dove sellers determined not to leave the protection of their property to strangers, so little by little the guards gained the upper hand, and if this struggle was as pleasing to God as the crusades to come, He did not appear to be doing much to help His side. This was the situation when the high priest appeared at the top of the steps accompanied by all the other priests, elders, and scribes who could be summoned in haste, and in a voice powerful enough to match that of Jesus he declared, Let him go this time, but if he shows his face here again, we will cut him down and discard him, as we do to tares that threaten to choke the wheat at harvesttime. Andrew said to Jesus, who had fought at his side, You weren't joking when you said you would bring the sword instead of peace, but staffs are useless as swords, to which Jesus replied, It all depends who is wielding the staff. What do we do now, asked Andrew. Let's return to Bethany, answered Jesus, it's not swords we need but determination. They withdrew in orderly fashion, their staffs pointed at the jeering crowd, who taunted them but went no further, and soon the disciples were safely out of Jerusalem and beating a hasty retreat, all of them exhausted, some even wounded.

When they reached Bethany, they noticed that that the people who appeared in their doorways looked at them with pity, but the disciples thought this only natural, given the lamentable state in which they had returned from battle. They learned the real reason for the gloom on everyone's face when they came to the street where Lazarus lived and sensed a tragedy had occurred. Jesus ran ahead of the others, entered the yard, the people gathered there stepped aside with mournful sighs to let him pass, and from within

came the sound of weeping and lamentation, Oh my beloved brother, Martha could be heard sobbing, Oh my beloved brother, wailed the voice of Mary. Stretched out on
the ground, on a pallet, Lazarus seemed to be sleeping, but
he was not sleeping, he was dead. Nearly all his life he had
suffered from a weak heart, then was cured, as everyone
in Bethany could testify, and now was as composed as if
carved from marble, as serene as if he had already passed
into eternity, soon the first signs of putrefaction will appear, causing those around the corpse to feel even greater
pain. Jesus, as if the strength had suddenly gone from his
legs, fell to his knees, groaning and weeping, How did this
happen, how did this happen, words that never fail to spring
to our lips when we are confronted by something irremediable. We ask how it happened, a desperate, futile attempt
to postpone the awful moment when we must accept the
truth, we ask how it happened, as if we could replace death
with life, exchange what is with what should be. From the
depths of her grief Martha said to Jesus, Had you been
here, my brother would not have died, but I know that
everything you ask of God He will grant you, He granted
you sight for the blind, healing for the lepers, speech for
the mute, and all the other wonders that reside in your will
and await your word. Jesus told her, Your brother will be
raised from the dead, and Martha replied, I know he will
rise to life on the day of resurrection. Jesus stood, an infinite strength took possession of him, in that moment he
knew he could do anything, banish death from this body,
restore it to life, give it speech, movement, laughter, even
tears, but not of sorrow, and truly say, I am the resurrection and the life, he who believes in me, though he were
dead, yet shall he live, and he asked Martha, Do you believe this, and she said, Yes, I believe you are the son of
God who has come into this world. This being so, and
with everything necessary in place, the power and the will
to use that power, all Jesus has to do is stretch out his arms

to that body abandoned by its soul, and say, Lazarus, arise, and Lazarus will rise from the dead, because it is the will of God, but at the very last moment Mary Magdalene placed a hand on Jesus' shoulder and said, No one has committed so much sin in his life that he deserves to die twice, and dropping his arms, Jesus went outside to weep.

LIKE AN ICY GUST OF WIND, THE DEATH OF LAZARUS EXTINguished the zeal John had kindled in Jesus' heart, a zeal in which serving God and serving the people had become one and the same thing. After the first few days of mourning, when the duties and habits of everyday life were gradually resumed, Peter and Andrew went to speak to Jesus. They questioned him about his plans, asked whether they should go preach once more in the towns or instead return to Jerusalem for a fresh assault, the disciples were beginning to feel restless, eager to be doing something, We didn't part with our possessions, our work, and our families, they complained, just to sit around all day. Jesus looked at them as if in a blur and listened as if having difficulty recognizing their voices amid a chorus of discordant cries. After a long silence he told them they must be patient, must wait a little more, he still had some thinking to do, could sense that something was about to happen which would decide their fate once and for all. And he assured them he would soon join them in the camp, which puzzled Peter and Andrew, for why should the two sisters remain alone when the men still had not decided what to do, You don't need to come back for our sake, said Peter, who had no way of knowing that Jesus was torn between two duties, the first toward the men and women who had abandoned everything to follow him, the second here in this house, toward the sisters, duties similar yet opposed, like a face and a mirror. The ghost of Lazarus was present and refused to go away, he was in the harsh words spoken by Martha, who could not forgive Mary for having prevented their brother from being restored to life, nor could she forgive Jesus for not using his God-given power. Lazarus was present too in Mary's tears, for by delivering her brother from a second death she would have to live forever with the remorse of having failed to deliver him from his first. Like an enormous presence filling every space, Lazarus was also in Jesus' troubled soul, in which horses pulled in four directions, or four ropes coiled around winches were slowly tearing him apart, and the hands of God and the devil were amusing themselves, divinely and diabolically, with the remains.

The afflicted and diseased, hoping to be healed, came to the door of the house that had once belonged to Lazarus. Sometimes Martha would appear and drive them away, as if to say, There was no salvation for my brother, why should there be for you, but they would keep returning until they succeeded in reaching Jesus, who healed them and sent them away without once saying, Repent. To be healed is like being reborn without having died, for the newborn have no sins and therefore no need to repent. But these acts of physical rebirth, if I may call them that, although most merciful, left a sour feeling in Jesus' heart, for they were only a postponement of the inevitable, he who today leaves healthy and content will be back tomorrow with new woes that have no remedy. Jesus became so melancholy that one day Martha said, Don't you die on me, for that would be like losing Lazarus all over again, and Mary Magdalene, beneath the sheet they shared, whimpered like a wounded animal hiding in the dark, You need me now more than ever, but I cannot reach you if you lock yourself behind a door beyond human strength. Jesus answered Martha, saying, My death will embrace all the deaths of Lazarus, who will go on dying without ever being restored to life, and to Mary he said, Even if you cannot enter, do not abandon me, even if you cannot see me, stretch out your hand, otherwise I will forget life or it will forget me. A few days later he went to join his disciples, and Mary Magdalene went with him. I'll look at your shadow if you don't wish me to look at you, she told him, and he replied, I wish to be wherever my shadow is if that is where your eyes are. Loving each other, they exchanged these amorous phrases not only because they were beautiful and true, but because shadows were closing in, and it was time for the two to prepare themselves for the darkness of final absence.

News reached the camp that John the Baptist had been taken prisoner. Nothing was known except that he had been arrested and Herod himself ordered his imprisonment. Jesus and his followers were inclined to think that Herod had been provoked by John's prophecies about the coming of the Messiah, which he repeated everywhere between baptisms, He who comes after me will baptize you with fire, and between imprecations, O generation of vipers, who has warned you to flee from the wrath to come. Jesus told his disciples that they must be prepared for every manner of persecution, because rumors had been rife for some time that they were preaching the same message, it was only to be expected that Herod would put two and two together and pursue the carpenter's son, who claimed to be the son of God, and his followers, for this was the second and more powerful head of the dragon threatening to topple him from his throne. Bad news may not be preferable to no news, but it was received with equanimity by men who had been waiting and hoping for everything but lately had had to make do with nothing. They asked one another, and Jesus too, what they should now do, stand together and resist Herod's wickedness, scatter throughout the towns, or retreat into the wilderness, where they could eat wild honey and locusts, as John the Baptist had done before he left to herald the glory of Jesus and, by the looks of it, to meet a miserable end. Yet there was no sign of Herod's troops arriving in Bethany to slaughter more innocents, thus Jesus and his disciples were considering carefully the various alternatives when another report arrived, informing them that John had been beheaded and that his punishment had nothing to do with the coming of the Messiah or the kingdom of God, he had incurred Herod's wrath by speaking out against adultery, of which the king himself was guilty, having married Herodias, his niece and sister-in-law, while her husband still lived. The news of John's death brought tears to the eyes of men and women alike, and the entire camp mourned, but no one believed that he had been killed for the reason given. Judas Iscariot, whom, you may remember, John baptized, was beside himself with rage, he said that Herod's decision must have had a more serious motive, How can this be, he asked the company gathered there, including the women, John proclaims the Messiah is coming to redeem people, and they kill him for condemning an adulterous marriage between uncle and niece, when adultery has been common practice in that family since the time of the first Herod. How can this be, he railed, when God Himself ordered John to proclaim the coming of the Messiah, it must have been God, because nothing can happen without His willing it, so perhaps those of you who know God better than I can explain to me why He should allow His plan to go awry like this on earth, and before you tell me that God knows even if we don't, let me tell you that I insist on knowing what God knows.

A shiver passed through everyone listening, who feared the wrath of God would descend on this insolent fellow, and on themselves for not punishing such blasphemy at once. But since He was not present to deal with Judas, the challenge could only be taken up by Jesus, closest to the Supreme Being whose wisdom was called into question. Had this been another religion and the circumstances different, perhaps things would have gone no further than Jesus' enigmatic smile, which, however faint and fleeting, showed many things, surprise, benevolence, and curiosity, though the surprise was short-lived, the benevolence condescending, and the curiosity somewhat ironic. The smile, leaving, left behind a deathly pallor, a face that suddenly looked cadaverous, as if it had just beheld the image of its own fate. In a voice without expression Jesus finally said, Let the women withdraw, and Mary Magdalene was the first to rise to her feet. Then, after the silence had slowly formed walls and a ceiling to enclose them in the deepest cave on earth, Jesus said, Let John ask God why He allowed a man prophesying such good tidings to die for so paltry a reason. Judas Iscariot was about to speak, but Jesus raised his hand to silence him and said, I now see I must tell you what I learned from God, unless He Himself prevents me. Voices grew louder as the disciples began talking nervously among themselves, afraid of what they were about to hear. Judas alone maintained the attitude of defiance with which he had begun all this. Jesus told them, I know my future and yours, and that of generations to come, I know God's intention and design, and we will speak of these matters, for they concern all of us. Peter asked, Must we know what God has revealed to you, would it not be better to keep it to yourself. If He wished, God could silence me this instant. Then surely He doesn't care whether you remain silent or speak, it's all the same, and if He has spoken through you, He will continue to speak through you, even when you think you oppose His will,

as at present. Do you know, Peter, that I am to be crucified. Yes, you told me. But I didn't tell you that you too,
with Andrew and Philip here, will be crucified, and that
Bartholomew will be skinned alive, and that Matthew will
be butchered by barbarians, and that they will behead James
the son of Zebedee, and that another James, the son of
Alphaeus, will be stoned to death, and Thomas will be
killed with a lance, and Judas Thaddaeus will have his skull
crushed, and Simon will be sawed in half, these things you
didn't know, but I am telling all of you now. This was
received in silence, there is no further reason to fear the
future, once revealed, as if Jesus had finally told them, You
will die, and they replied in chorus, So what, we know
already. But John and Judas Iscariot have not heard what
will happen to them, so they ask, What about us, and Jesus
said, You, John, will live to a ripe old age and die of natural causes, as for you, Judas, keep away from fig trees,
because it won't be long before you hang yourself from
one. So we will die because of you, a voice asked, but no
one ever identified the person who spoke. Because of God,
answered Jesus. What does God want, asked John. He wants
a larger congregation than the one He has at present, He
wants the entire world for Himself. But if God is Lord of
the universe, how can the world belong to anyone but Him,
not just since yesterday or starting tomorrow but from the
beginning of time, asked Thomas. That I cannot tell you,
replied Jesus. But if you've kept all these things in your
heart for so long, why tell us now. Because Lazarus, whom
I healed, died, and John the Baptist, who prophesied my
coming, was killed, and now death has joined us. All creatures have to die, said Peter, and men like all the rest. Many
will die in future because of God and His will. If willed by
God, then it must be for some holy cause. They will die
because they were born neither before nor after. Will they
receive eternal life, asked Matthew. Yes, but the condition
should be less horrible. If the son of God has said what he

has said, he has denied himself, said Peter. You're mistaken, only the son of God is permitted to say these things, and what is blasphemy on your lips is the word of God on mine, replied Jesus. You speak as if we had to choose between you and God, said Peter. You will always have to choose between God and God, and like you and all other men, I am in the middle. So what do you want us to do. Help my death protect the lives of future generations. But you cannot oppose God's will. No, but I can at least try. You are safe because you are the son of God, but we will lose our souls. No, for if you obey me, you will still be obeying God. The edge of a red moon could be seen on the horizon of the distant wilderness. Speak, said Andrew, but Jesus waited until the entire moon, an enormous blood-red disk, had risen from the earth, and only then did he speak, telling them, The son of God must die on the cross so that the will of the father may be done, but if we replace him with an ordinary man, God will no longer be able to sacrifice His son. Do you wish one of us to take your place, asked Peter. No, I myself will take the son's place. For the love of God, explain yourself. An ordinary man, who has proclaimed himself king of the Jews to incite the people to depose Herod from his throne and expel the Romans from the land, and all I ask is that one of you go immediately to the Temple and say that I am this man, and if justice is swift, perhaps God's justice will not have time to stay man's, just as it did not stay the ax of the executioner who beheaded John. Everyone was struck dumb, but not for long, soon there was an outcry of indignation, protest, disbelief. If you are the son of God, then you must die as the son of God, a voice exclaimed, Having eaten your bread, how can I now denounce you, wailed another, Surely he who is destined to be king of the universe cannot wish to be king of the Jews, said one man, Death to anyone who dares stir from here to denounce you, threatened another. At that moment the voice of Judas Iscariot rang out above the din, I'll go. They seized him, were already drawing daggers from their tunics, when Jesus said, Leave him alone and do him no harm. He then rose and embraced Judas, kissing him on both cheeks, Go, my hour is yours. Without a word, Judas Iscariot threw the hem of his cape over one shoulder and vanished into the black night.

The Temple guards, accompanied by Herod's soldiers, came to arrest Jesus at first light. After surrounding the camp by stealth, a small detachment armed with swords and lances quickly advanced, and the soldier in command called out, Where is this man who claims to be king of the Jews. He called a second time, Let the man who claims to be king of the Jews come forward, whereupon Jesus emerged from his tent with a tearful Mary Magdalene and told them, I am king of the Jews. A soldier went up to him and tied his hands, whispering in his ear, Although now my prisoner, if you become my king, remember that I acted under orders from another, and should you ask me to arrest him, I'll obey you as I'm now obeying him. Jesus told him, A king does not arrest another king, a god does not kill another god, and that is why ordinary men were created, so that arrests and killings could be left to them. A rope was also tied around his feet to prevent him from running away, and Jesus said to himself, Too late, I have already fled. Then Mary Magdalene let out a cry as if her heart were breaking, and Jesus said, You will weep for me, and all you women will weep when such an hour be-falls your men or you yourselves, but know that for every tear you shed a thousand would have been shed in times to come had I not died thus. And turning to the soldier in command, he asked of him, Release these men with me, for I am king of the Jews, not they, and without further delay he stepped into the midst of the soldiers. The sun was up and hovering over the roofs of Bethany when the multitude, with Jesus in front, between two soldiers holding the ends of the rope tied around his wrists, began climbing the road to Jerusalem. Behind walked the disciples and their womenfolk, the men fuming, the women sobbing, but their anger and tears were of no avail. What are we to do, they asked themselves under their breath, should we throw ourselves on the soldiers and try to free Jesus, perhaps losing our lives in the struggle, or should we disperse before an order is also given for our arrest. On the horns of this dilemma, they did nothing, and continued following at a distance behind the retinue of soldiers. After a while they saw that the procession had come to a halt, and wondered if the order had been revoked, if now the ropes around Jesus' hands and feet would be untied, but one would have to be naïve to think any such thing. Another knot, however, has come untied, that of Judas Iscariot's life, there on a fig tree by the side of the road where Jesus will pass. Dangling from a branch is the disciple who carried out his master's last wish. The soldier leading the retinue ordered two soldiers to cut the cord and lower the body, He's still warm, observed one of them. Perhaps Judas Iscariot was sitting in the tree with the noose already around his neck, patiently waiting for Jesus to appear in the distance before letting go of the branch, finally at peace with himself now that he had done his duty. Jesus drew near, and the soldiers made no attempt to restrain him. He stood, staring at Judas's face twisted by sudden death. He's still warm, the soldier said a second time, and it occurred to Jesus that he could do for Judas what he had not done for Lazarus, bring him back to life, so that on some other day and in some other place the man might have his own death, remote and obscure, instead of being the haunting symbol of betrayal. But, as we know, only the son of God has the power to bring people back to life, not this king of the Jews who walks here, his spirit broken and his hands and feet bound. The soldier in command told his men, Leave the body there to be buried by the people of Bethany, if the vultures don't eat it first, but check to see whether he is carrying anything of value. The soldiers searched but found nothing, Not a single coin, one of the soldiers said, and little wonder, for the disciple in charge of the community's funds is Matthew, who knows his job, having served as a tax collector in the days when he was called Levi. Didn't they pay him for his betrayal, asked Jesus, and Matthew, who overheard, replied, They wanted to, but he said he was in the habit of settling his accounts, and that's it, he has settled them. The procession continued, but some of the disciples lingered behind to stare in pity at the body, until John said, Let's leave it here, he was not one of us, but the other Judas, also called Thaddaeus, hastened to correct him, Whether we like it or not, he will always be one of us, we may not know what to do with him, but he will go on being one of us. Let's move on, said Peter, this is no place for us, here at the feet of Judas Iscariot. You're right, said Thomas, our place should be at Jesus' side, but that place is empty.

At last they entered Jerusalem, and Jesus was taken before the council of elders, high priests, and scribes. Delighted to see him there, the high priest said, I gave you fair warning, but you refused to listen, your pride won't save you now and your lies will damn you. What lies, asked Jesus. First, that you are king of the Jews. But I am king of the Jews. And second, that you are the son of God. Who told you that I claim to be the son of God. Everyone says so. Pay no heed to them, I am king of the Jews. So you admit you're not the son of God. How often do I have to tell you, I am king of the Jews. Be careful what you say, a statement like that is enough to have you sentenced. I stand by what I've said. Very well, you will appear before the Roman prefect, who is keen to meet the man who wishes to depose him and wrest these territories from Caesar's power. The soldiers escorted Jesus to Pilate's residence. The news had already spread that the man who claimed to be king of the Jews, the one who thrashed the money changers and set fire to their stalls, had been arrested, and people rushed to see what a king looked like when led through the streets for all to see, his hands tied like those of a common thief. And, as always happens, since not everyone is alike in this world, there were some who took pity on Jesus and some who did not, some said, Set the fellow free, he's mad, while some believed that punishing a crime serves as a warning to others, and there were as many of the latter as of the former. The disciples, mingling with the crowd, were distraught. You could easily recognize the women with them because of their tears, but one woman did not weep, she was Mary Magdalene, who grieved in silence.

The distance between the house of the high priest and the prefect's palace was not great, but Jesus thought he would never get there, not because of the hissing and jeering from the crowd, who thus expressed its disappointment with this sad figure of a king, but because he was anxious to keep his appointment with death, lest God look this way and say, What's going on, are you backing out of our agreement. At the palace gates, soldiers from Rome took charge of the prisoner, while Herod's soldiers and the Temple guards remained outside to await the verdict. Apart from a few priests no one was allowed to accompany Jesus into the palace. Seated on his throne, the prefect Pilate, for that was his name, inspected the man being led in, who looked like a beggar, with a heavy beard and bare feet, his tunic soiled with stains both old and new, the new from ripe fruit the gods created for eating rather than for showing hatred and leaving marks of shame. Standing before Pilate, the prisoner waited, his head erect, his eyes fixed on some point between himself and the prefect. Pilate knew only two kinds of culprit, the kind who lowered their eyes and the kind who stared in defiance, the first he despised, the second made him nervous, in either case he lost no time in passing sentence. But this man standing here seemed oblivious of his surroundings, and so self-assured that he might well have been a royal personage, in fact and in law, the victim of a lamentable misunderstanding who would soon have his crown, scepter, and mantle restored. Pilate finally decided the prisoner belonged in the second category, so he began the interrogation without delay, What is your name. I am Jesus son of Joseph and was born in Bethlehem of Judaea, but having lived in Nazareth of Galilee, I am known as Jesus of Nazareth. Who was your father. I just told you, his name was Joseph. What was his trade. Carpenter. Then would you care to explain how a carpenter named Joseph came to father a king. If a king can beget carpenters, why should a carpenter not beget a king. Hearing this, one of the priests intervened, Don't forget, Pilate, this man also claims to be the son of God. That isn't true, I am only the son of man, said Jesus, but the priest continued, Don't let him deceive you, Pilate, in our religion the son of man and of God are one and the same. Pilate waved his hand indifferently, If he had proclaimed himself the son of Jupiter, though he would not be the first, then this case would be of some interest, but whether he is or is not the son of your god is a matter of no importance. Then sentence him for claiming to be king of the Jews, and we'll leave satisfied. It remains to be seen if that will satisfy me, Pilate said sharply. Jesus waited patiently for this dialogue to end and the interrogation to resume. Who do you say you are, the prefect asked Jesus. I am who I am, king of the Jews. And as king of the Jews what do you hope to gain. All that a king can expect. For example. To govern and protect his people. Protect them from what. From whatever threatens them. And from whom. From whoever opposes them. If I understand you rightly, you would defend them against Rome. That is so. And in order to protect them, would you attack the Romans. There is no other way. And expel the Romans from these lands. One thing follows from another. Then you are the enemy of Caesar. I am king of the Jews. Confess you are the enemy of Caesar. I am king of the Jews and will say no more. The high priest raised his hands to heaven in triumph, You see, Pilate, he confesses, and you cannot spare the life of one who publicly declares his hatred of you and Caesar. Sighing with exasperation, Pilate rebuked the priest, Be quiet, then turning to Jesus, asked him, Have you anything more to say. Nothing, said Jesus. Then I have no choice but to sentence you. Do as you must. How do you wish to die. I have already decided, How then, On the cross, Very well, you'll be crucified. Jesus' eyes sought and finally met those of Pilate, Can I ask a favor, he said. So long as it doesn't interfere with the sentence I've just passed. Would you have them put an inscription above my head which says who and what I am, for all to see. Nothing else. Nothing else. Pilate beckoned a secretary, who brought writing materials, and in his own hand Pilate wrote, Jesus of Nazareth, king of the Jews. Roused from his complacency, the high priest suddenly realized what was happening and protested, You mustn't write king of the Jews but Jesus of Nazareth who claimed to be king of the Jews. Annoyed with himself, Pilate regretted not having dismissed the prisoner with a warning, for even the most vigilant of judges could see that this fellow was no threat to anyone let alone to Caesar, and turning to the high priest, he told him dryly, Stop interfering, I have written what I have written. He signaled to the soldiers to remove the condemned man and requested water to wash his hands, as was his custom after passing sentence.

They led Jesus away and took him to a hill known as Golgotha. Despite his strong constitution, his legs soon weakened under the weight of the cross, and the centurion in charge ordered a man who had stopped to watch to relieve the prisoner of his burden. The crowd continued to jeer and shout insults, but now and then someone would utter words of compassion. As for the disciples, they walked in a daze. A woman stopped Peter and challenged him, You also were with Jesus of Galilee, but he denied it, I don't know what you're talking about, and tried to hide in the crowd, only to meet the same woman a second time, and once more she asked him, Were you not with Jesus, and again Peter denied it with an oath, I do not know the man. And since three is a number favored by God, Peter was challenged a third time, and for the third time he swore, saying, I do not know the man. The women went to Golgotha with Jesus, a few on either side, but Mary Magdalene, who stays closest of all, is not allowed to reach him, the soldiers push her away, just as they will make everyone keep their distance from the three crosses that have been put up, two already occupied by convicted men who howl with pain, the third now ready for occupation, standing tall and erect like a column that supports the sky. Ordering Jesus to lie down, the soldiers extend his arms on the crossbar. As they hammer in the first nail, piercing the flesh of his wrist between two bones, a sudden dizziness sends him back in time, he feels the pain as his father felt it before him, sees himself as he saw him on the cross at Sepphoris. Then they drove a nail through his other wrist, and he experienced that first tearing of flesh as the soldiers began to hoist the crossbar to the top of the cross, his entire weight suspended from fragile bones, and it was almost a relief when they pushed his legs upward and hammered another nail through his heels, now there is nothing more to be done but wait for death.

Jesus is dying slowly, life ebbing from him, ebbing, when suddenly the heavens overhead open wide and God appears in the same attire he wore in the boat, and His words resound throughout the earth, This is My beloved son, in whom I am well pleased. Jesus realized then that he had been tricked, as the lamb led to sacrifice is tricked, and that his life had been planned for death from the very beginning. Remembering the river of blood and suffering that would flow from his side and flood the globe, he called out to the open sky, where God could be seen smiling, Men, forgive Him, for He knows not what He has done. Then he began expiring in the midst of a dream. He found himself back in Nazareth and saw his father shrugging his shoulders and smiling as he told him, Just as I cannot ask you all the questions, neither can you give me all the answers. There was still some life in him when he felt a sponge soaked in water and vinegar moisten his lips, and looking down, he saw a man walking away with a bucket, a staff over his shoulder. But what Jesus did not see, on the ground, was the black bowl into which his blood was dripping.

BLINDNESS

For Pilar
For my daughter Violante

IN MEMORIAM
Giovanni Pontiero

If you can see, look.
If you can look, observe.

FROM THE *Book of Exhortations*

The amber light came on. Two of the cars ahead accelerated before the red light appeared. At the pedestrian crossing the sign of a green man lit up. The people who were waiting began to cross the road, stepping on the white stripes painted on the black surface of the asphalt, there is nothing less like a zebra, however, that is what it is called. The motorists kept an impatient foot on the clutch, leaving their cars at the ready, advancing, retreating like nervous horses that can sense the whiplash about to be inflicted. The pedestrians have just finished crossing but the sign allowing the cars to go will be delayed for some seconds, some people maintain that this delay, while apparently so insignificant, has only to be multiplied by the thousands of traffic lights that exist in the city and by the successive changes of their three colours to produce one of the most serious causes of traffic jams or bottlenecks, to use the more current term.

The green light came on at last, the cars moved off briskly, but then it became clear that not all of them were equally quick off the mark. The car at the head of the middle lane has stopped, there must be some mechanical fault, a loose accelerator pedal, a gear lever that has stuck, problem with the suspension, jammed brakes, breakdown in the electric circuit, unless he has simply run out of gas, it would not be the first time such a thing has happened. The next group of pedestrians to gather at the crossing see the driver of the stationary car wave his arms behind the windshield, while the cars behind him frantically sound their horns. Some drivers have already got out of their cars, prepared to push the stranded vehicle to a spot where it will not hold up the traffic, they beat furiously on the closed windows, the man inside turns his head in their direction, first to one side then the other, he is clearly shouting something, to judge by the movements of his mouth he appears to be repeating some words, not one word but three, as turns out to be the case when someone finally manages to open the door, I am blind.

Who would have believed it. Seen merely at a glance, the man's eyes seem healthy, the iris looks bright, luminous, the sclera white, as compact as porcelain. The eyes wide open, the wrinkled skin of the face, his eyebrows suddenly screwed up, all this, as anyone can see, signifies that he is distraught with anguish. With a rapid movement, what was in sight has disappeared behind the man's clenched fists, as if he were still trying to retain inside his mind the final image captured, a round red light at the traffic lights. I am blind, I am blind, he repeated in despair as they helped him to get out of the car, and the tears welling up made those eyes which he claimed were dead, shine even more. These things happen, it will pass you'll see, sometimes it's nerves, said a woman. The lights had already changed again, some inquisitive passersby had gathered around the group, and the drivers further back who did not know what was going on, protested at what they thought was some common accident, a smashed headlight, a dented fender, nothing to justify this upheaval, Call the police, they shouted and get that old wreck out of the way. The blind man pleaded, Please, will someone take me home. The woman who had suggested a case of nerves was of the opinion that an ambulance should be summoned to transport the poor man to the hospital, but the blind man refused to hear of it, quite unnecessary, all he wanted was that someone might accompany him to the entrance of the building where he lived. It's close by and you could do me no greater favour. And what about the car, asked someone. Another voice replied, The key is in the ignition, drive the car on to the pavement. No need, intervened a third voice, I'll take charge of the car and accompany this man home. There were murmurs of approval. The blind man felt himself being taken by the arm, Come, come with me, the same voice was saying to him. They eased him into the front passenger seat, and secured the safety belt. I can't see, I can't see, he murmured, still weeping. Tell me where you live, the man asked him. Through the car windows voracious faces spied, avid for some news. The blind man raised his hands to his eyes and gestured, Nothing, it's as if I were caught in a mist or had fallen into a milky sea. But blindness isn't like that, said the other fellow, they say that blindness is black, Well I see everything white, That little woman was probably right, it could be a matter of nerves, nerves are the very devil, No need to talk to me about it, it's a disaster, yes a disaster, Tell me where you live please, and at the same time the engine started up. Faltering, as if his lack of sight had weakened his memory, the blind man gave his address, then he said, I have no words to thank you, and the other replied, Now then, don't give it another thought, today it's your turn, tomorrow it will be mine, we never know what might lie in store for us, You're right, who would have thought, when I left the house this morning, that something as dreadful as this was about to happen. He was puzzled that they should still be at a standstill, Why aren't we moving, he asked, The light is on red, replied the other. From now on he would no longer know when the light was red.

As the blind man had said, his home was nearby. But the pavements were crammed with vehicles, they could not find a space to park and were obliged to look for a spot in one of the side streets. There, because of the narrowness of the pavement, the door on the passenger's side would have been little more than a hand's-breadth from the wall, so in order to avoid the discomfort of dragging himself from one seat to the other with the brake and steering wheel in the way, the blind man had to get out before the car was parked. Abandoned in the middle of the road, feeling the ground shifting under his feet, he tried to suppress the sense of panic that welled up inside him. He waved his hands in front of his face, nervously, as if he were swimming in what he had described as a milky sea, but his mouth was already opening to let out a cry for help when at the last minute he felt the other's hand gently touch him on the arm, Calm down, I've got you. They proceeded very slowly, afraid of falling, the blind man dragged his feet, but this caused him to stumble on the uneven pavement, Be patient, we're almost there, the other murmured, and a little further ahead, he asked, Is there anyone at home to look after you, and the blind man replied, I don't know, my wife won't be back from work yet, today it so happened that I left earlier only to have this hit me. You'll see, it isn't anything serious, I've never heard of anyone suddenly going blind, And to think I used to boast that I didn't even need glasses, Well it just goes to show. They had arrived at the entrance to the building, two women from the neighbourhood looked on inquisitively at the sight of their neighbour being led by the arm but neither of them thought of asking, Have you got something in your eye, it never occurred to them nor would he have been able to reply, Yes, a milky sea. Once inside the building, the blind man said, Many thanks, I'm sorry for all the trouble I've caused you, I can manage on my own now, No need to apologise, I'll come up with you, I wouldn't be easy in my mind if I were to leave you here. They got into the narrow elevator with some difficulty, What floor do you live on, On the third, you cannot imagine how grateful I am, Don't thank me, today it's you, Yes, you're right, tomorrow it might be you. The elevator came to a halt, they stepped out on to the landing, Would you like me to help you open the door, Thanks, that's something I think I can do for myself. He took from his pocket a small bunch of keys, felt them one by one along the serrated edge, and said, It must be this one, and feeling for the keyhole with the fingertips of his left hand, he tried to open the door. It isn't this one, Let me have a look, I'll help you. The door opened at the third attempt. Then the blind man called inside, Are you there, no one replied, and he remarked, Just as I was saying, she still hasn't come back. Stretching out his hands, he groped his way along the corridor, then he came back cautiously, turning his head in the direction where he calculated the other fellow would be, How can I thank you, he said, It was the least I could do, said the good Samaritan, no need to thank me, and added, Do you want me to help you to get settled and keep you company until your wife arrives. This zeal suddenly struck the blind man as being suspect, obviously he would not invite a complete stranger to come in who, after all, might well be plotting at that very moment how to overcome, tie up and gag the poor defenceless blind man, and then lay hands on anything of value. There's no need, please don't bother, he said, I'm fine, and as he slowly began closing the door, he repeated, There's no need, there's no need.

Hearing the sound of the elevator descending he gave a sigh of relief. With a mechanical gesture, forgetting the state in which he found himself, he drew back the lid of the peep-hole and looked outside. It was as if there were a white wall on the other side. He could feel the contact of the metallic frame on his eyebrow, his eyelashes brushed against the tiny lens, but he could not see out, an impenetrable whiteness covered everything. He knew he was in his own home, he recognised the smell, the atmosphere, the silence, he could make out the items of furniture and objects simply by touching them, lightly running his fingers over them, but at the same time it was as if all of this were already dissolving into a kind of strange dimension, without direction or reference points, with neither north nor south, below nor above. Like most people, he had often played as a child at pretending to be blind, and, after keeping his eyes closed for five minutes, he had reached the conclusion that blindness, undoubtedly a terrible affliction, might still be relatively bearable if the unfortunate victim had retained sufficient memory, not just of the colours, but also of forms and planes, surfaces and shapes, assuming of course, that this one was not born blind. He had even reached the point of thinking that the darkness in which the blind live was nothing other than the simple absence of light, that what we call blindness was something that simply covered the appearance of beings and things, leaving them intact behind their black veil. Now, on the contrary, here he was, plunged into a whiteness so luminous, so total, that it swallowed up rather than absorbed, not just the colours, but the very things and beings, thus making them twice as invisible.

As he moved in the direction of the sitting-room, despite the caution with which he advanced, running a hesitant hand along the wall and not anticipating any obstacles, he sent a vase of flowers crashing to the floor. He had forgotten about any such vase, or perhaps his wife had put it there when she left for work with the intention of later finding some more suitable place. He bent down to appraise the damage. The water had spread over the polished floor. He tried to gather up the flowers, never thinking of the broken glass, a long sharp splinter pricked his finger and, at the pain, childish tears of helplessness sprang to his eyes, blind with whiteness in the middle of his flat, which was turning dark as evening fell. Still clutching the flowers and feeling the blood running down, he twisted round to get the handkerchief from his pocket and wrapped it round his finger as best he could. Then, fumbling, stumbling, skirting the furniture, treading warily so as not to trip on the rugs, he reached the sofa where he and his wife watched television. He sat down, rested the flowers on his lap, and, with the utmost care, unrolled the handkerchief. The blood, sticky to the touch, worried him, he thought it must be because he could not see it, his blood had turned into a viscous substance without colour, into something rather alien which nevertheless belonged to him, but like a self-inflicted threat directed at himself. Very slowly, gently probing with his good hand, he tried to locate the splinter of glass, as sharp as a tiny dagger, and, by bringing the nails of his thumb and forefinger together, he managed to extract all of it. He wrapped the handkerchief round the injured finger once more, this time tightly to stop the bleeding, and, weak and exhausted, he leaned back on the sofa. A minute later, because of one of those all too common abdications of the body, that chooses to give up in certain moments of anguish or despair, when, if it were guided by logic alone, all its nerves should be alert and tense, a kind of weariness crept over him, more drowsiness than real fatigue, but just as heavy. He dreamt at once that he was pretending to be blind, he dreamt that he was forever closing and opening his eyes, and that, on each occasion, as if he were returning from a journey, he found waiting for him, firm and unaltered, all the forms and colours of the world as he knew it. Beneath this reassuring certainty, he perceived nevertheless, the dull nagging of uncertainty, perhaps it was a deceptive dream, a dream from which he would have to emerge sooner or later, without knowing at this moment what reality awaited him. Then, if such a word has any meaning when applied to a weariness that lasted for only a few seconds, and already in that semi-vigilant state that prepares one for awakening, he seriously considered that it was unwise to remain in this state of indecision, shall I wake up, shall I not wake up, shall I wake up, shall I not wake up, there always comes a moment when one has no option but to take a risk, What am I doing here with these flowers on my lap and my eyes closed as if I were afraid of opening them, What are you doing there, sleeping with those flowers on your lap, his wife was asking him.

She did not wait for a reply. Pointedly, she set about gathering up the fragments of the vase and drying the floor, muttering all the while with an irritation she made no attempt to disguise, You might have cleaned up this mess yourself, instead of settling down to sleep as if it were no concern of yours. He said nothing, protecting his eyes behind tightly closed lids, suddenly agitated by a thought, And if I were to open my eyes and see, he asked himself, gripped by anxious hope. The woman drew near, noticed the bloodstained handkerchief, her vexation gone in an instant, Poor man, how did this happen, she asked compassionately as she undid the improvised bandage. Then he wanted with all his strength to see his wife kneeling at his feet, right there, where he knew she was, and then, certain that he would not see her, he opened his eyes, So you've wakened up at last, my sleepyhead, she said smiling. There was silence, and he said, I'm blind, I can't see. The woman lost her patience, Stop playing silly games, there are certain things we must not joke about, How I wish it were a joke, the truth is that I really am blind, I can't see anything, Please, don't frighten me, look at me, here,

I'm here, the light is on, I know you're there, I can hear you, touch you, I can imagine you've switched on the light, but I am blind. She began to weep, clung to him, It isn't true, tell me that it isn't true. The flowers had slipped onto the floor, onto the bloodstained handkerchief, the blood had started to trickle again from the injured finger, and he, as if wanting to say with other words, That's the least of my worries, murmured, I see everything white, and he gave a sad smile. The woman sat down beside him, embraced him tightly, kissed him gently on the forehead, on the face, softly on the eyes, You'll see that this will pass, you haven't been ill, no one goes blind from one minute to the next, Perhaps, Tell me how it happened, what did you feel, when, where, no, not yet, wait, the first thing we must do is to consult an eye specialist, can you think of one, I'm afraid not, neither of us wears glasses, And if I were to take you to the hospital, There isn't likely to be any emergency service for eyes that cannot see, You're right, better that we should go straight to a doctor, I'll look in the telephone directory and locate a doctor who practises nearby. She got up, still questioning him, Do you notice any difference, None, he replied, Pay attention, I'm going to switch off the light and you can tell me, now, Nothing, What do you mean nothing, Nothing, I always see the same white, it's as if there were no night.

He could hear his wife rapidly leaf through the pages of the telephone directory, sniffling to hold back her tears, sighing, and finally saying, This one will do, let's hope he can see us. She dialled a number, asked if that was the surgery, if the doctor was there, if she could speak to him, No, no the doctor doesn't know me, the matter is extremely urgent, yes, please, I understand, then I'll explain the situation to you, but I beg of you to pass on what I have to say to the doctor, the fact is that my husband has suddenly gone blind, yes, yes, all of a sudden, no, no he is not one of the doctor's patients, my husband does not wear glasses and never has, yes, he has excellent eyesight, just like me, I also see perfectly well, ah, many thanks, I'll wait, I'll wait, yes, doctor, all of a sudden, he says he sees everything white, I have no idea what happened, I haven't had time to ask him, I've just arrived home to find him in this state, would you like me to ask him, ah, I'm so grateful to you doctor, we'll come right away, right away. The blind man rose to his feet, Wait, his wife said, first let me attend to this finger, she disappeared for several moments, came back with a bottle of peroxide, another of iodine, cotton wool, a box of bandages. As she dressed the wound, she asked him, Where did you leave the car, and suddenly confronted him, But in your condition you couldn't have driven the car, or you were already at home when it happened, No, it was on the street when I was stationary at a red light, some person brought me home, the car was left in the next street, Fine, let's go down, wait at the door while I go to find it, where did you put the keys, I don't know, he never gave them back to me, Who's he, The man who brought me home, it was a man, He must have left them somewhere, I'll have a look round, It's pointless searching, he didn't enter the flat, But the keys have to be somewhere, Most likely he forgot, inadvertently took them with him, This was all we needed, Use your keys, then we'll sort it out, Right, let's go, take my hand. The blind man said, If I have to stay like this, I'd rather be dead, Please, don't talk nonsense, things are bad enough, I'm the one who's blind, not you, you cannot imagine what it's like, The doctor will come up with some remedy, you'll see, I shall see.

They left. Below, in the lobby, his wife switched on the light and whispered in his ear. Wait for me here, if any neighbours should appear speak to them naturally, say you're waiting for me, no one looking at you would ever suspect that you cannot see and besides we don't have to tell people all our business, Yes, but don't be long. His wife went rushing off. No neighbour entered or left. The blind man knew from experience that the stairway would only be lit so long as he could hear the mechanism of the automatic switch, therefore he went on pressing the button whenever there was silence. The light, this light, had been transformed into noise for him. He could not understand why his wife was taking so long to return, the street was nearby, some eighty or a hundred metres, If we delay any longer, the doctor will be gone, he thought to himself. He could not avoid a mechanical gesture, raising his left wrist and lowering his eyes to look at his watch. He pursed his lips as if in sudden pain, and felt deeply grateful that there were no neighbours around at that moment, for there and then, were anyone to have spoken to him, he would have burst into tears. A car stopped in the street, At last, he thought, but then realised that it was not the sound of his car engine, This is a diesel engine, it must be a taxi, he said, pressing once more on the button for the light. His wife came back, flustered and upset, that good Samaritan of yours, that good soul, has taken our car, It isn't possible, you can't have looked properly, Of course I looked properly, there's nothing wrong with my eyesight, these last words came out inadvertently, You told me the car was in the next street, she corrected herself, and it isn't, unless they've left it in some other street, No, no, I'm certain it was left in this street, Well then it has disappeared, In that case, what about the keys, He took advantage of your confusion and distress and robbed us, And to think I didn't want him in the flat for fear he might steal something yet if he had kept me company until you arrived home, he could not have stolen our car, Let's go, we have a taxi waiting, I swear to you that I'd give a year of my life to see this rogue go blind as well. Don't speak so loud, And that they rob him of everything he possesses, He might turn up, Ah, so you think he'll knock on the door tomorrow and say he took the car in a moment of distraction, that he is sorry and inquire if you're feeling better.

They remained silent until they reached the doctor's surgery. She tried not to think about the stolen car, squeezed her husband's hand affectionately, while he, his head lowered so that the driver would not see his eyes through the rear-view mirror, could not stop asking himself how it was possible that such a terrible tragedy should have befallen him, Why me. He could hear the noise of the traffic, the odd loud voice whenever the taxi stopped, it often happens, we are still asleep and external sounds are already penetrating the veil of unconsciousness in which we are still wrapped up, as in a white sheet. As in a white sheet. He shook his head, sighing, his wife gently stroked his cheek, her way of saying, Keep calm, I'm here, and he leaned his head on her shoulder, indifferent to what the driver might think, If you were in my situation and unable to drive any more, he thought childishly, and oblivious of the absurdity of that remark, he congratulated himself amidst his despair that he was still capable of formulating a rational thought. On leaving the taxi, discreetly assisted by his wife, he seemed calm, but on entering the surgery where he was about to learn his fate, he asked his wife in a tremulous whisper, What will I be like when I get out of this place, and he shook his head as if he had given up all hope.

His wife informed the receptionist, I'm the person who rang half an hour ago because of my husband, and the receptionist showed them into a small room where other patients were waiting. There was an old man with a black patch over one eye, a young lad who looked cross-eyed, accompanied by a woman who must be his mother, a girl with dark glasses, two other people without any apparent distinguishing features, but no one who was blind, blind people do not consult an ophthalmologist. The woman guided her husband to an empty chair, and since all the other chairs were occupied, she remained standing beside him, We'll have to wait, she whispered in his ear. He realised why, he had heard the voices of those who were in the waiting-room, now he was assailed by another worry, thinking that the longer the doctor took to examine him, the worse his blindness would become to the point of being incurable. He fidgeted in his chair, restless, he was about to confide his worries to his wife, but just then the door opened and the receptionist said, Will you both come this way, and turning to the other patients, Doctor's orders, this man is an urgent case. The mother of the cross-eyed boy protested that her right was her right, and that she was first and had been waiting for more than an hour. The other patients supported her in a low voice, but not one of them, nor the woman herself, thought it wise to carry on complaining, in case the doctor should take offence and repay their impertinence by making them wait even longer, as has occurred. The old man with the patch over one eye was magnanimous, Let the poor man go ahead, he's in a much worse state than we are. The blind man did not hear him, they were already

going into the doctor's consulting room, and the wife was saying, Many thanks for being so kind, doctor, it's just that my husband, and that said, she paused, because frankly she did not
know what had really happened, she only knew that her husband was blind and that their car had been stolen. The doctor
said, Please, be seated, and he himself went to help the patient
into the chair, and then, touching him on the hand, he spoke to
him directly, Now then, tell me what is wrong. The blind man
explained that he was in his car, waiting for the red light to
change when suddenly he could no longer see, that several
people had rushed to his assistance, that an elderly woman,
judging from her voice, had said that it was probably a case of
nerves, and then a man had accompanied him home because he
could not manage on his own, I see everything white, doctor.
He said nothing about the stolen car.

The doctor asked him, Has anything like this ever happened
to you before, or something similar, No, doctor, I don't even use
glasses. And you say it came on all of a sudden, Yes, doctor, Like
a light going out, More like a light going on, During the last few
days have you felt any difference in your eyesight, No, doctor, Is
there, or has there ever been any case of blindness in your family, Among the relatives I've known or have heard discussed, no
one, Do you suffer from diabetes, No, doctor, From syphilis,
No, doctor. From hypertension of the arteries or the brain cells,
I'm not sure about the brain cells, but none of these other
things, we have regular medical check-ups at work. Have you
taken a sharp knock on the head, today or yesterday, No, doctor,
How old are you, Thirty-eight, Fine, let's take a look at these
eyes. The blind man opened them wide, as if to facilitate the examination, but the doctor took him by the arm and installed
him behind a scanner which anyone with imagination might
see as a new version of the confessional, eyes replacing words,
and the confessor looking directly into the sinner's soul, Rest
your chin here, he advised him, keep your eyes open, and don't
move. The woman drew close to her husband, put her hand on
his shoulder, and said, This will be sorted out, you'll see. The
doctor raised and lowered the binocular system at his side,

turned finely adjusted knobs, and began his examination. He could find nothing in the cornea, nothing in the sclera, nothing in the iris, nothing in the retina, nothing in the lens of the eye, nothing in the luteous macula, nothing in the optic nerve, nothing elsewhere. He pushed the apparatus aside, rubbed his eyes, then carried out a second examination from the start, without speaking, and when he had finished there was a puzzled expression on his face, I cannot find any lesion, your eyes are perfect. The woman joined her hands in a gesture of happiness and exclaimed, Didn't I tell you, didn't I tell you, this can be resolved. Ignoring her, the blind man asked, May I remove my chin, doctor, Of course, forgive me, If my eyes are perfect as you say, why am I blind, For the moment I cannot say, we shall have to carry out more detailed tests, analyses, an ecography, an encephalogram, Do you think it has anything to do with the brain, It's a possibility, but I doubt it. Yet you say you can find nothing wrong with my eyes, That's right, How strange, What I'm trying to say is that if, in fact, you are blind, your blindness at this moment defies explanation, Do you doubt that I am blind, Not at all, the problem is the unusual nature of your case, personally, in all my years in practice, I've never come across anything like it, and I daresay no such case has ever been known in the entire history of ophthalmology, Do you think there is a cure, In principle, since I cannot find lesions of any kind or any congenital malformations, my reply should be in the affirmative, But apparently it is not in the affirmative, Only out of caution, only because I do not want to build up hopes that may turn out to be unjustified, I understand, That's the situation, And is there any treatment I should follow, some remedy or other, For the moment I prefer not to prescribe anything, for it would be like prescribing in the dark. There's an apt expression, observed the blind man. The doctor pretended not to hear, got off the revolving stool on which he had been seated to carry out the examination, and, standing up, he wrote out on his prescription pad the tests and analyses he judged to be necessary. He handed the sheet of paper to the wife, Take this and come back with your husband once you have the results, meanwhile if there should be any change in his condition, telephone me, How much do we owe you, doctor, Pay in reception. He accompanied them to the door, murmured words of reassurance, Let's wait and see, let's wait and see, you mustn't despair, and once they had gone he went into the small bathroom adjoining the consulting room and stared at length into the mirror, What can this be, he murmured. Then he returned to the consulting room, called out to the receptionist, Send in the next patient.

That night the blind man dreamt that he was blind.

On offering to help the blind man, the man who then stole his car, had not, at that precise moment, had any evil intention, quite the contrary, what he did was nothing more than to obey those feelings of generosity and altruism which, as everyone knows, are the two best traits of human nature and to be found in much more hardened criminals than this one, a simple car-thief without any hope of advancing in his profession, exploited by the real owners of this enterprise, for it is they who take advantage of the needs of the poor. When all is said and done, there is not all that much difference between helping a blind man only to rob him afterwards and looking after some tottering and stammering old person with one eye on the inheritance. It was only when he got close to the blind man's home that the idea came to him quite naturally, precisely, one might say, as if he had decided to buy a lottery ticket on catching sight of a ticket-vendor, he had no hunch, he bought the ticket to see what might come of it, resigned in advance to whatever capricious fortune might bring, something or nothing, others would say that he acted according to a conditioned reflex of his personality. The sceptics, who are many and stubborn, claim that, when it comes to human nature, if it is true that the opportunity does not always make the thief, it is also true that it helps a lot. As for us, we should like to think that if the blind man had accepted the second offer of this false Samaritan, at that final moment generosity might still have prevailed, we refer to his offer to keep the blind man company until his wife should arrive, who knows whether the moral responsibility, resulting from the trust thus bestowed, might not have inhibited the criminal temptation and caused the victory of those shining and noble sentiments which it is always possible to find even in the most depraved souls. To finish on a plebeian note, as the old proverb never tires of teaching us, while trying to cross himself the blind man only succeeded in breaking his own nose.

The moral conscience that so many thoughtless people have offended against and many more have rejected, is something that exists and has always existed, it was not an invention of the philosophers of the Quaternary, when the soul was little more than a muddled proposition. With the passing of time, as well as the social evolution and genetic exchange, we ended up putting our conscience in the colour of blood and in the salt of tears, and, as if that were not enough, we made our eyes into a kind of mirror turned inwards, with the result that they often show without reserve what we are verbally trying to deny. Add to this general observation, the particular circumstance that in simple spirits, the remorse caused by committing some evil act often becomes confused with ancestral fears of every kind, and the result will be that the punishment of the prevaricator ends up being, without mercy or pity, twice what he deserved. In this case it is, therefore, impossible to unravel what proportion of fear and what proportion of the afflicted conscience began to harass the thief the moment he started up the engine of the car and drove off. No doubt he could never feel tranquil sitting in the place of someone who was holding this same steering wheel when he suddenly turned blind, who looked through this windshield and suddenly could no longer see, it does not take much imagination for such thoughts to rouse the foul and insidious monster of fear, there it is already raising its head. But it was also remorse, the aggrieved expression of one's conscience, as already stated, or, if we prefer to describe it in suggestive terms, a conscience with teeth to bite, that was about to put before his eyes the forlorn image of the blind man as he was closing the door, There's no need, there's no need, the poor fellow had said, and from then on he would not be capable of taking a step without assistance.

The thief concentrated twice as hard on the traffic to prevent such terrifying thoughts from fully occupying his mind, he knew full well that he could not permit himself the smallest error, the tiniest distraction. There were always police around and it would only need one of them to stop him, May I see your identity card and driving licence, back to prison, what a hard life. He was most careful to obey the traffic lights, under no circumstances to go when the light was red, to respect the amber light, to wait patiently for the green light to come on. At a certain point, he realised that he had started to look at the lights in a way that was becoming obsessive. He then started to regulate the speed of the car to ensure that he always had a green light before him, even if, in order to ensure this, he had to increase the speed or, on the contrary, to reduce it to the extent of irritating the drivers behind him. In the end, disoriented as he was, tense beyond endurance, he drove the car into a minor road where he knew there were no traffic lights, and parked almost without looking, he was such a good driver. He felt as if his nerves were about to explode, these were the very words that crossed his mind. My nerves are about to explode. It was stifling inside the car. He lowered the windows on either side, but the air outside, if it was moving, did nothing to freshen the atmosphere inside. What am I going to do, he asked himself. The shed where he had to take the car was far away, in a village outside the city, and in his present frame of mind, he would never get there. Either the police will arrest me or, worse still, I'll have an accident, he muttered. It then occurred to him that it would be best to get out of the car for a bit and try to clear his thoughts, Perhaps the fresh air will blow the cobwebs away, just because that poor wretch turned blind is no reason why the same should happen to me, this is not some cold one catches, I'll take a turn round the block and it will pass. He got out and did not bother to lock the car, he would be back in a minute, and walked off. He had gone no more than thirty paces when he went blind.

In the surgery, the last patient to be seen was the good-natured old man, the one who had spoken so kindly about the poor man who had suddenly turned blind. He was there just to arrange a date for an operation on a cataract that had appeared in his one remaining eye, the black patch was covering a void, and had nothing to do with the matter in hand, These are ailments that come with old age, the doctor had said some time ago, when it matures we shall remove it, then you won't recognise the place you've been living in. When the old man with the black eyepatch left and the nurse said there were no more patients in the waiting-room, the doctor took out the file of the man who had turned up blind, he read it once, twice, reflected for several minutes and finally rang a colleague with whom he held the following conversation: I must tell you, today I dealt with the strangest case, a man who totally lost his sight from one instant to the next, the examination revealed no perceptible lesion or signs of any malformation from birth, he says he sees everything white, a kind of thick, milky whiteness that clings to his eyes, I'm trying to explain as best I can how he described it, yes, of course it's subjective, no, the man is relatively young, thirty-eight years old, have you ever heard of such a case, or read about it, or heard it mentioned, I thought as much, for the moment I cannot think of any solution, to gain time I've recommended some tests, yes, we could examine him together one of these days, after dinner I shall check some books, take another look at the bibliography, perhaps I'll find some clue, yes, I'm familiar with agnosia, it could be psychic blindness, but then it would be the first case with these characteristics, because there is no doubt that the man is really blind, and as we know, agnosia is the inability to recognise familiar objects, because it also occurred to me that this might be a case of amaurosis, but remember what I started to tell you, this blindness is white, precisely the opposite of amaurosis which is total darkness unless there is some form of white amaurosis, a white darkness, as it were, yes, I know, something unheard of, agreed, I'll call him tomorrow, explain that we should like to examine him together. Having ended his conversation, the doctor leaned back in his chair, remained there for a few minutes, then rose to his feet, removed his white coat with slow, weary movements. He went to the bathroom to wash his hands, but this time he did not ask the mirror, metaphysically, What can this be, he had recovered his scientific outlook, the fact that agnosia and amaurosis are identified and defined with great precision in books and in practice, did not preclude the appearance of variations, mutations, if the word is appropriate, and that day seemed to have arrived. There are a thousand reasons why the brain should close up, just this, and nothing else, like a late visitor arriving to find his own door shut. The ophthalmologist was a man with a taste for literature and a flair for coming up with the right quotation.

That evening, after dinner, he told his wife, A strange case turned up at the surgery today, it might be a variant of psychic blindness or amaurosis, but there appears to be no evidence of any such symptoms ever having been established, What are these illnesses, amaurosis and that other thing, his wife asked him. The doctor gave an explanation within the grasp of a layman and capable of satisfying her curiosity, then he went to the bookcase where he kept his medical books, some dating back to his university years, others more recent and some just published which he still had not had time to study. He checked the indexes and methodically began reading everything he could find about agnosia and amaurosis, with the uncomfortable impression of being an intruder in a field beyond his competence, the mysterious terrain of neurosurgery, about which he only had the vaguest notion. Late that night, he laid aside the books he had been studying, rubbed his weary eyes and leaned back in his chair. At that moment the alternative presented itself as clear as could be. If it were a case of agnosia, the patient would now be seeing what he had always seen, that is to say, there would have been no diminution of his visual powers, his brain would simply have been incapable of recognising a chair wherever there happened to be a chair, in other words, he would continue to react correctly to the luminous stimuli leading to the optic nerve, but, to use simple terms within the grasp of the layman, he would have lost the capacity to know what he knew and, moreover, to express it. As for amaurosis, here there was no doubt. For this to be effectively the case, the patient would have to see everything black, if you'll excuse the use of the verb to see, when this was a case of total darkness. The blind man had categorically stated that he could see, if you'll excuse that verb again, a thick, uniform white colour as if he had plunged with open eyes into a milky sea. A white amaurosis, apart from being etymologically a contradiction, would also be a neurological impossibility, since the brain, which would be unable to perceive the images, forms and colours of reality, would likewise be incapable, in a manner of speaking, of being covered in white, a continuous white, like a white painting without tonalities, the colours, forms and images that reality itself might present to someone with normal vision, however difficult it may be to speak, with any accuracy, of normal vision. With the clear conscience of having fetched up in a dead end, the doctor shook his head despondently and looked around him. His wife had already gone off to bed, he vaguely remembered her coming up to him for a moment and kissing him on the head, I'm off to bed, she must have told him, the flat was now silent, books scattered on the table, What's this, he thought to himself, and suddenly he felt afraid, as if he himself were about to turn blind any minute now and he already knew it. He held his breath and waited. Nothing happened. It happened a minute later as he was gathering up the books to return them to the bookshelf. First he perceived that he could no longer see his hands, then he knew he was blind.

The ailment of the girl with dark glasses was not serious, she was suffering from a mild form of conjunctivitis which the drops prescribed by the doctor would clear up in no time, You know what to do, for the next few days you should remove your glasses only when you sleep, he had told her. He had been cracking the same joke for years, we might even assume that it had been handed down from one generation of ophthalmologists to another, but it never failed, the doctor was smiling as he spoke, the patient smiled as she listened, and on this occasion it was worthwhile, because the girl had nice teeth and knew how to show them. Out of natural misanthropy or because of too many disappointments in life, any ordinary sceptic, familiar with the details of this woman's life, would insinuate that the prettiness of her smile was no more than a trick of the trade, a wicked and gratuitous assertion, because she had the same smile even as a toddler, a word no longer much in use, when her future was a closed book and the curiosity of opening it had not yet been born. To put it simply, this woman could be classed as a prostitute, but the complexity in the web of social relationships, whether by day or night, vertical or horizontal, of the period here described cautions us to avoid a tendency to make hasty and definitive judgments, a mania which, owing to our exaggerated self-confidence, we shall perhaps never be rid of. Although it may be evident just how much cloud there is in Juno, it is not entirely licit, to insist on confusing with a Greek goddess what is no more than an ordinary concentration of drops of water hovering in the atmosphere. Without any doubt, this woman goes to bed with men in exchange for money, a fact that might allow us to classify her without further consideration as a prostitute, but, since it is also true that she goes with a man only when she feels like it and with whom she wants to, we cannot dismiss the possibility that such a factual difference, must as a precaution determine her exclusion from the club as a whole. She has, like ordinary people, a profession, and, also like ordinary people, she takes advantage of any free time to indulge her body and satisfy needs, both individual and general. Were we not trying to reduce her to some primary definition, we should finally say of her, in the broad sense, that she lives as she pleases and moreover gets all the pleasure she can from life.

It was already dark when she left the surgery. She did not remove her glasses, the street lighting disturbed her, especially the illuminated ads. She went into a chemist to buy the drops the doctor had prescribed, decided to pay no attention when the man who served her commented how unfair it was that certain eyes should be covered by dark glasses, an observation that besides being impertinent in itself, and coming from a pharmacist's assistant if you please, went against her belief that dark glasses gave her an air of alluring mystery, capable of arousing the interest of men who were passing, to which she might reciprocate, were it not for the fact that today she had someone waiting for her, an encounter she had every reason to expect would lead to something good, as much in terms of material as in terms of other satisfactions. The man she was about to meet was an old acquaintance, he did not mind when she warned him she could not remove her glasses, an order, moreover, the doctor had not as yet given, and the man even found it amusing, something different. On leaving the pharmacy the girl hailed a taxi, gave the name of a hotel. Reclining on the seat, she was already savouring, if the term is appropriate, the various and multiple sensations of sensuous pleasure, from that first, knowing contact of lips, from that first intimate caress, to the successive explosions of an orgasm that would leave her exhausted and happy, as if she were about to be crucified, heaven protect us, in a dazzling and vertiginous firework. So we have every reason to conclude that the girl with dark glasses, if her partner has known how to fulfill his obligation, in terms of perfect timing and technique, always pays in advance and twice as much as she later charges. Lost in these thoughts, no doubt because she had just paid for a consultation, she asked herself whether it would not be a good idea to raise, starting from today, what, with cheerful euphemism, she was wont to describe as her just level of compensation.

She ordered the taxi-driver to stop one block before her destination, mingled with the people who were following in the same direction, as if allowing herself to be carried along by them, anonymous and without any outward sign of guilt or shame. She entered the hotel with a natural air, crossed the vestibule in the direction of the bar. She had arrived a few minutes early, therefore she had to wait, the hour of their meeting had been arranged with precision. She asked for a soft drink, which she drank at her leisure, without looking at anyone for she did not wish to be mistaken for a common whore in pursuit of men. A little later, like a tourist going up to her room to rest after having spent the afternoon in the museums, she headed for the elevator. Virtue, should there be anyone who still ignores the fact, always finds pitfalls on the extremely difficult path of perfection, but sin and vice are so favoured by fortune that no sooner did she get there than the elevator door opened. Two guests got out, an elderly couple, she stepped inside, pressed the button for the third floor, three hundred and twelve was the number awaiting her, it is here, she discreetly knocked on the door, ten minutes later she was naked, fifteen minutes later she was moaning, eighteen minutes later she was whispering words of love that she no longer needed to feign, after twenty minutes she began to lose her head, after twenty-one minutes she felt that her body was being lacerated with pleasure, after twenty-two minutes she called out, Now, now, and when she regained consciousness she said, exhausted and happy, I can still see everything white.

A policeman took the car-thief home. It would never have occurred to the circumspect and compassionate agent of authority that he was leading a hardened delinquent by the arm, not to prevent him from escaping, as might have happened on another occasion, but simply so that the poor man should not stumble and fall. In recompense, we can easily imagine the fright it gave the thief's wife, when, on opening the door, she came face to face with a policeman in uniform who had in tow, or so it seemed, a forlorn prisoner, to whom, judging from his miserable expression, something more awful must have happened than simply to find himself under arrest. The woman's first thought was that her husband had been caught in the act of stealing and the policeman had come to search the house, this idea, on the other hand, and however paradoxical it may seem, was somewhat reassuring, considering that her husband only stole cars, goods which on account of their size cannot be hidden under the bed. She was not left in doubt for long, the policeman informed her, This man is blind, look after him, and the woman who should have been relieved because the officer, after all, had simply accompanied her husband to his home, perceived the seriousness of the disaster that was to blight their lives when her husband, weeping his heart out, fell into her arms and told her what we already know.

The girl with the dark glasses was also accompanied to her

parents' house by a policeman, but the piquancy of the circumstances in which blindness had manifested itself in her case, a
naked woman screaming in a hotel and alarming the other
guests, while the man who was with her tried to escape, pulling
on his trousers in haste, somehow mitigated the obvious drama
of the situation. Overcome with embarrassment, a feeling entirely compatible, for all the mutterings of hypocritical prudes
and the would-be virtuous, with the mercenary rituals of love
to which she dedicated herself, after the piercing shrieks she let
out on realising that her loss of vision was not some new and
unforeseen consequence of pleasure, the blind girl hardly dared
to weep and lament her fate when unceremoniously, without
giving her time to dress properly, and almost by force, she was
evicted from the hotel. In a tone of voice that would have been
sarcastic had it not been simply ill-mannered, the policeman
wanted to know, after asking her where she lived, if she had the
money for the taxi, in these cases, the State doesn't pay, he
warned her, a procedure which, let us note in passing, is not
without a certain logic, insofar as these women belong to that
considerable number who pay no taxes on their immoral earnings. She gave an affirmative nod, but, being blind, just imagine,
she thought the policeman might not have noticed her gesture
and she murmured, Yes, I have the money, and then under her
breath, added, If only I didn't, words that might strike us as
being odd, but which, if we consider the circumvolutions of the
human mind, where no short or direct routes exist, these same
words end up by being absolutely clear, what she meant to say
was that she had been punished because of her disreputable
conduct, for her immorality, and this was the outcome. She had
told her mother she would not be home for dinner, and in the
end she was home early, even before her father.

The ophthalmologist's situation was different, not only because he happened to be at home when he was struck by blindness, but because, being a doctor, he was not going to surrender
helplessly to despair, like those who only take note of their body
when it hurts them. Even in the anguish of a situation like this,
with a night of anxiety ahead of him, he was still capable of

remembering what Homer wrote in the *Iliad,* the greatest poem about death and suffering ever written, A doctor is worth several men, words we should not accept as a straightforward expression of quantity, but above all, of quality, as we shall soon see. He summoned the courage to go to bed without disturbing his wife, not even when, muttering and half asleep, she stirred in the bed and snuggled up to him. He lay awake for hours on end, the little sleep he managed to snatch was from pure exhaustion. He hoped the night would never end rather than have to announce, he whose profession was to cure ailments in the eyes of others, I'm blind, but, at the same time, he was anxiously waiting for the light of day, and these are the exact words that came into his mind, The light of day, knowing that he would not see it. In fact, a blind ophthalmologist is not much good to anyone, but it was up to him to inform the health authorities, to warn them of this situation which might turn into a national catastrophe, nothing more nor less, of a form of blindness hitherto unknown, with every appearance of being highly contagious, and which, to all appearances, manifested itself without the previous existence of earlier pathological symptoms of an inflammatory, infectious or degenerative nature, as he was able to verify in the blind man who had come to consult him in his surgery, or as had been confirmed in his own case, a touch of myopia, a slight astigmatism, all so mild that he had decided, in the meantime, not to use corrective lenses. Eyes that had stopped seeing, eyes that were totally blind, yet meanwhile were in perfect condition, without any lesions, recent or old, acquired or innate. He recalled the detailed examination he had carried out on the blind man, how the various parts of the eye accessible to the ophthalmoscope appeared to be perfectly healthy, without any trace of morbid changes, a most rare situation in a man who claimed to be thirty-eight years old, and even in anyone younger. That man could not be blind, he thought, momentarily forgetting that he himself was blind, it's extraordinary how selfless some people can be, and this is not something new, let us remember what Homer said, although in apparently different words.

He pretended to be asleep when his wife got up. He felt the kiss she placed on the forehead, so gentle, as if she did not wish to rouse him from what she imagined to be a deep sleep, perhaps she thought, Poor man, he came to bed late after sitting up to study the extraordinary case of that poor blind man. Alone, as if he were about to be slowly garrotted by a thick cloud weighing on his chest and entering his nostrils, blinding him inside, the doctor let out a brief moan, and allowed two tears, They're probably white, he thought, to well up in his eyes and run over his temples, on either side of his face, now he could understand the fears of his patients, when they told him, Doctor, I think I'm losing my sight. Small domestic noises reached the bedroom, his wife would appear any minute now to see if he was still sleeping, it was almost time for them to go to the hospital. He got up cautiously, fumbled for his dressing-gown and slipped it on, then he went into the bathroom to pee. He turned to where he knew a mirror was, and this time he did not wonder, What's going on, he did not say, There are a thousand reasons why the human brain should close down, he simply stretched out his hands to touch the glass, he knew that his image was there watching him, his image could see him, he could not see his image. He heard his wife enter the bedroom, Ah, you're up already, and he replied, I am. He felt her by his side, Good morning, my love, they still greeted each other with words of affection after all these years of marriage, and then he said, as if both of them were acting in a play and this was his cue, I doubt whether it will be all that good, there's something wrong with my sight. She only took in the last part of the sentence, Let me take a look, she asked, and examined his eyes attentively, I can't see anything, the sentence was obviously borrowed, it was not in her script, he was the one who should have spoken those words, but he simply said, I can't see, and added, I suppose I must have been infected by the patient I saw yesterday.

With time and intimacy, doctors' wives also end up knowing something about medicine, and this one, so close to her husband in everything, had learned enough to know that blindness does not spread through contagion like an epidemic, blindness isn't something that can be caught just by a blind man looking at someone who is not, blindness is a private matter between a person and the eyes with which he or she was born. In any case, a doctor has an obligation to know what he is saying, that is why he is professionally trained at medical school, and if this doctor here, apart from having declared himself blind, openly admits that he has been infected, who is his wife to doubt him, however much she may know about medicine. It is understandable, therefore, that the poor woman, confronted by this irrefutable evidence, should react like any ordinary spouse, two of them we know already, clinging to her husband and showing natural signs of distress, And what are we going to do now, she asked amid tears, Advise the health authorities, the Ministry, that's the first thing to do, if it should turn out to be an epidemic, measures must be taken, But no one has ever heard of an epidemic of blindness, his wife insisted, anxious to hold on to this last shred of hope, Nor has anyone ever come across a blind man without any apparent reasons for his condition, and at this very moment there are at least two of them. No sooner had he uttered this last word than his expression changed. He pushed his wife away almost violently, he himself drew back, Keep away, don't come near me, I might infect you, and then beating on his forehead with clenched fists, What a fool, what a fool, what an idiot of a doctor, why did I not think of it before, we've spent the entire night together, I should have slept in the study with the door shut, and even so, Please, don't say such things, what has to be will be, come, let me get you some breakfast, Leave me, leave me, No, I won't leave you, shouted his wife, what do you want, to go stumbling around bumping into the furniture, searching for the telephone without eyes to find the numbers you need in the telephone directory, while I calmly observe this spectacle, stuck inside a bell-jar to avoid contamination. She took him firmly by the arm and said, Come along, love.

It was still early when the doctor had, we can imagine with what pleasure, finished the cup of coffee and toast his wife had insisted on preparing for him, much too early to find the people whom he had to inform at their desks. Logic and efficacy demanded that his report about what was happening should be made directly and as soon as possible to someone in authority at the Ministry of Health, but he soon changed his mind when he realised that to present himself simply as a doctor who had some important and urgent information to communicate, was not enough to convince the less exalted civil servant to whom, after much pleading, the telephone operator had agreed to put him through. The man wanted to know more details before passing him on to his immediate superior, and it was clear that a doctor with any sense of responsibility was not going to declare the outbreak of an epidemic of blindness to the first minor functionary who appeared before him, it would cause immediate panic. The functionary at the other end of the line replied, You tell me you're a doctor, if you want me to believe you, then, of course, I believe you, but I have my orders, unless you tell me what you want to discuss I can take this matter no further, It's confidential, Confidential matters are not dealt with over the telephone, you'd better come here in person. I cannot leave the house, Do you mean you're ill, Yes, I'm ill, the blind man said after a pause. In that case you ought to call a doctor, a real doctor, quipped the functionary, and, delighted with his own wit, he hung up.

The man's insolence was like a slap in the face. Only after some minutes had passed, had he regained enough composure to tell his wife how rudely he had been treated. Then, as if he had just discovered something that he should have known a long time ago, he murmured sadly, This is the stuff we're made of, half indifference and half malice. He was about to ask mistrustfully, What now, when he realised that he had been wasting his time, that the only way of getting the information to the right quarters by a safe route would be to speak to the medical director of his own hospital service, doctor to doctor, without any civil servants in the middle, let him assume responsibility for making the bureaucratic system do its work. His wife dialled the number, she knew the hospital number by heart. The doctor identified himself when they replied, then said rapidly, I'm fine, thank you, no doubt the receptionist had inquired, How are you, doctor, that is what we say when we do not wish to play the weakling, we say Fine, even though we may be dying, and this is commonly known as taking one's courage in both hands, a phenomenon that has only been observed in the human species. When the director came to the telephone, Now then, what's all this about, the doctor asked if he was alone, if there was anyone within earshot, no need to worry about the receptionist, she had better things to do than listen in to conversations about ophthalmology, besides she was only interested in gynaecology. The doctor's account was brief but full, with no circumlocutions, no superfluous words, with no redundancies, and expressed with a clinical dryness which, taking into account the situation, caused the director some surprise, But are you really blind, he asked, Totally blind, In any case, it might be a coincidence, there might not really have been, in the strict sense of the word, any contagion whatsoever, Agreed there is no proof of contagion, but this was not just a case of his turning blind and my turning blind, each of us in our own home, without our having seen each other, the man turned up blind at the surgery and I went blind a few hours later, How can we trace this man, I have his name and address on file in the surgery, I'll send someone there immediately, A doctor, Yes, of course, a colleague, Don't you think we ought to inform the Ministry about what is happening, For the moment that would be premature, think of the public alarm news of this kind would provoke, good grief, blindness isn't catching, Death isn't catching either, yet nevertheless we all die, Well, you stay at home while I deal with the matter, then I'll send someone to fetch you, I want to examine you, Don't forget that the fact that I am now blind is because I examined a blind man, You can't be sure of that, At least there is every indication here of cause and effect, Undoubtedly, yet it is still too early to draw any conclusions, two isolated cases have no statistical relevance, Unless, at this point, there are more than two of us, I can understand your state of mind but we must avoid any gloomy speculations that might turn out to be groundless, Many thanks, You'll be hearing from me soon, Goodbye.

Half an hour later, after he had managed, rather awkwardly, to shave, with some assistance from his wife, the telephone rang. It was the director again, but this time his voice sounded different, We have a boy here who has also suddenly gone blind, he sees everything white, his mother tells me he visited your surgery yesterday, Am I correct in thinking that this child has a divergent squint in the left eye, Yes, Then there's no doubt, it's him, I'm starting to get worried, the situation is becoming really serious, What about informing the Ministry, Yes, of course, I'll get on to the hospital management right away. After about three hours, when the doctor and his wife were having their lunch in silence, he toying with the bits of meat she had cut up for him, the telephone rang again. His wife went to answer, came back at once, You'll have to take the call, it's from the Ministry. She helped him to his feet, guided him into the study and handed him the telephone. The conversation was brief. The Ministry wanted to know the identity of the patients who had been at his surgery the previous day, the doctor replied that the clinical files contained all the relevant details, name, age, marital status, profession, home address, and he ended up offering to accompany the person or persons entrusted with rounding them up. At the other end of the line, the tone was curt, That won't be necessary. The telephone was passed on to someone else, a different voice came through, Good afternoon, this is the Minister speaking, on behalf of the Government I wish to thank you for your zeal, I'm certain that thanks to your prompt action we shall be able to limit and control the situation, meanwhile would you please do us the favour of remaining indoors. The closing words were spoken with courteous formality, but left him in no doubt that he was being given an order. The doctor replied, Yes, Minister, but the person at the other end had already put the phone down.

A few minutes later, the telephone rang yet again. It was the medical director, nervous, jumbling his words, I've just been told that the police have been informed of two cases of sudden blindness, Are they policemen, No, a man and a woman, they found him in the street screaming that he was blind, and the woman was in a hotel when she became blind, it seems she was in bed with someone, We need to check if they, too, are patients of mine, do you know their names, No names were mentioned, They have rung me from the Ministry, they're going to the surgery to collect the files, What a complicated business, You're telling me. The doctor replaced the receiver, raised his hands to his eyes and kept them there as if trying to defend his eyes from anything worse happening, then he said faintly, I'm so tired, Try to get some sleep, I'll take you to your bed, his wife said, It's pointless, I wouldn't be able to sleep, besides the day isn't over yet, something could still happen.

It was almost six o'clock when the telephone rang for the last time. The doctor, who was sitting beside it, picked up the receiver, Yes, speaking, he said, listened attentively to what he was being told and merely nodded his head slightly before ringing off, Who was that, his wife asked, The Ministry, an ambulance is coming to fetch me within the next half hour, Is that what you expected to happen, Yes, more or less, Where are they taking you, I don't know, presumably to a hospital, I'll pack a suitcase, sort out some clothes, the usual things, I'm not going on a trip, We don't know what it is. She led him gently into the bedroom, made him sit on the bed, You sit here quietly, I'll deal with everything. He could hear her going back and forth, opening and closing drawers and cupboards, removing clothes and then packing them into the suitcase on the floor, but what he could not see was that in addition to his own clothes, she had packed a number of blouses and skirts, a pair of slacks, a dress, some shoes that could only belong to a woman. It vaguely crossed his mind that he would not need so many clothes, but said nothing for this was not the moment to be worrying about such trivialities. He heard the locks click, then his wife said, Done, we're ready for the ambulance now. She carried the suitcase to the door leading to the stairs, refusing her husband's help when he said, Let me help you, that's something I can do, after all, I'm not an invalid. Then they went to sit on the sofa in the sitting-room and waited. They were holding hands, and he said, Who knows how long we shall be separated, and she replied, Don't let it worry you.

They waited for almost an hour. When the door-bell rang, she got up and went to open the door, but there was no one on the landing. She tried the internal telephone, Very well, he'll be right down, she said. She turned to her husband and told him, They're waiting downstairs, they have strict orders not to come up to the flat, It would appear the Ministry is really alarmed. Let's go. They went down in the elevator, she helped her husband to negotiate the last few steps and to get into the ambulance, then went back to the steps to fetch the suitcase, she lifted it up on her own and pushed it inside. At last she climbed in and sat beside her husband. The driver of the ambulance turned round to protest, I can only take him, those are my orders, I must ask you to get down. The woman calmly replied, You'll have to take me as well, I've just gone blind this very minute.

The suggestion had come from the minister himself. It was, whichever way one looked at it, a fortunate not to say perfect idea, both from the point of view of the merely sanitary aspects of the case and from that of the social implications and their political consequences. Until the causes were established, or, to use the appropriate terms, the etiology of the white evil, as, thanks to the inspiration of an imaginative assessor, this unpleasant-sounding blindness came to be called, until such time as treatment and a cure might be found, and perhaps a vaccine that might prevent the appearance of any cases in the future, all the people who had turned blind, as well as those who had been in physical contact or in any way close to these patients, should be rounded up and isolated so as to avoid any further cases of contagion, which, once confirmed, would multiply more or less according to what is mathematically referred to as a compound ratio. Quod erat demonstrandum, concluded the Minister. According to the ancient practice, inherited from the time of cholera and yellow fever, when ships that were contaminated or suspected of carrying infection had to remain out at sea for forty days, and in words within the grasp of the general public, it was a matter of putting all these people into quarantine, until further notice. These very words, Until further notice, apparently deliberate, but, in fact, enigmatic since he could not think of any others, were pronounced by the Minister, who later clarified his thinking, I meant that this could as easily mean forty days as forty weeks, or forty months, or forty years, the important thing is that they should stay in quarantine. Now we have to decide where we are going to put them, Minister, said the President of the Commission of Logistics and Security set up rapidly for the purpose and responsible for the transportation, isolation and supervision of the patients, What immediate facilities are available, the Minister wanted to know, We have a mental hospital standing empty until we decide what to do with it, several military installations which are no longer being used because of the recent restructuring of the army, a building designed for a trade fair that is nearing completion, and there is even, although no one has been able to explain why, a supermarket about to go into liquidation, In your opinion, which of these buildings would best suit our purpose, The barracks offer the greatest security, Naturally, There is, however, one drawback, the size of the place is likely to make it both difficult and costly to keep an eye on those interned, Yes, I can see that, As for the supermarket, we would probably run up against various legal obstacles, legal matters that would have to be taken into account, And what about the building for the trade fair, That's the one site I think we should ignore, Minister, Why, Industry wouldn't like it, millions have been invested in the project, So that leaves the mental hospital, Yes, Minister, the mental hospital, Well then, let's opt for the mental hospital, Besides, to all appearances, it's the place that offers the best facilities because not only does it have a perimeter wall, it also has the advantage of having two separate wings, one to be used for those who are actually blind, the other for those suspected of having the disease, as well as a central area which will serve, as it were, as a no man's land, through which those who turn blind will pass to join those who are already blind, There might be a problem, What is that, Minister, We shall find ourselves obliged to put staff there to supervise the transfers, and I doubt whether we will be able to count on volunteers, I doubt whether that will be necessary, Minister, Why, Should anyone suspected of infection turn blind, as will naturally happen sooner or later, you may be sure, Minister, that the others who still have their sight, will turn him out at once, You're right, Just as they would not allow in any blind person who suddenly felt like changing places, Good thinking, Thank you, Minister, may I give orders to proceed, Yes, you have carte blanche.

The Commission acted with speed and efficiency. Before nightfall, everyone who was known to be blind had been rounded up, as well as a considerable number of people who were assumed to be affected, at least those whom it had been possible to identify and locate in a rapid search operation carried out above all in the domestic and professional circles of those stricken with loss of vision. The first to be taken to the empty mental hospital were the doctor and his wife. There were soldiers on guard. The main gate was opened just enough to allow them to pass through, and then closed at once. Serving as a handrail, a thick rope stretched from the entrance to the main door of the building, Move a little to the right, there you will find a rope, grab it with your hand and go straight on, straight on until you come to some steps, there are six steps in all, the sergeant warned them. Once inside, the rope divided into two, one strand going to the left, the other to the right, the sergeant shouted, Keep to the right. As she dragged the suitcase along, the woman guided her husband to the ward that was nearest to the entrance. It was a long room, like a ward in an old-fashioned hospital, with two rows of beds that had been painted grey, although the paint had been peeling off for quite some time. The covers, the sheets and the blankets were of the same colour. The woman guided her husband to the far end of the ward, made him sit on one of the beds, and told him, Stay here, I'm going to look around. There were more wards, long and narrow corridors, rooms that must have been the doctors' offices, dingy latrines, a kitchen that still reeked of bad cooking, a vast refectory with zinc-topped tables, three padded cells in which the bottom six feet of the walls had padding and the rest was lined with cork. Behind the building there was an abandoned yard, with neglected trees, their trunks looking as if they had been flayed. There was litter everywhere. The doctor's wife went back inside. In a half-open cupboard she found strait-jackets. When she rejoined her husband, she asked him, Can you imagine where they've brought us, No, she was about to add, To a mental asylum, but he anticipated her, You're not blind, I cannot allow you to stay here, Yes, you're right, I'm not blind, Then I'm going to ask them to take you home, to tell them that you told a lie in order to remain with me, There's no point, they cannot hear you through there, and even if they could, they would pay no attention, But you can see, For the moment, I shall almost certainly turn blind myself one of these days, or any minute now, Please, go home, Don't insist, besides, I'll bet the soldiers would not let me get as far as the stairs, I cannot force you, No, my love, you can't, I'm staying to help you and the others who may come here, but don't tell them I can see, What others, You surely don't think we shall be here on our own, This is madness, What did you expect, we're in a mental asylum.

The other blind people arrived together. One after another, they had been apprehended at home, first of all the man driving the car, then the man who had stolen it, the girl with dark glasses, the boy with the squint whom they traced to the hospital where his mother had taken him. His mother did not come with him, she lacked the ingenuity of the doctor's wife who declared herself blind when there was nothing wrong with her eyesight, she is a simple soul, incapable of lying, even when it is for her own good. They came stumbling into the ward, clutching at the air, here there was no rope to guide them, they would have to learn from painful experience, the boy was weeping, calling out for his mother, and it was the girl with dark glasses who tried to console him, She's coming, she's coming, she told him, and since she was wearing her dark glasses she could just as well have been blind as not, the others moved their eyes from one side to another, and could see nothing, while because the girl was wearing those glasses, and saying, She's coming, she's coming, it was as if she really could see the boy's desperate mother coming in through the door. The doctor's wife leaned over and whispered into her husband's ear, Four more have arrived, a woman, two men and a boy, What do the men look like, asked the doctor in a low voice, She described them, and he told her, The latter I don't know, the other, from your description, might well be the blind man who came to see me at the surgery. The child has a squint and the girl is wearing dark glasses, she seems attractive, Both of them came to the surgery. Because of the din they were making as they searched for a place where they might feel safe, the new arrivals did not hear this conversation, they must have thought that there was no one else like themselves there, and they had not been without their sight long enough for their sense of hearing to have become keener than normal. At last, as if they had reached the conclusion that it was not worth while exchanging certainty for doubt, each of them sat on the first bed they had stumbled upon, so to speak, the two men ending up beside each other, without their knowing. In a low voice, the girl continued to console the boy, Don't cry, you'll see that your mother won't be long. There was silence, then the doctor's wife said so that she could be heard all the way down the ward as far as the door, There are two of us here, how many are you. The unexpected voice startled the new arrivals, but the two men remained silent, and it was the girl who replied, I think there are four of us, myself and this little boy, Who else, why don't the others speak up, asked the doctor's wife, I'm here, murmured a man's voice, as if he could only pronounce the words with difficulty, And so am I, growled in turn another masculine voice with obvious displeasure. The doctor's wife thought to herself, They're behaving as if they were afraid of getting to know each other. She watched them twitching, tense, their necks craned as if they were sniffing at something, yet curiously, their expressions were all the same, threatening and at the same time afraid, but the fear of one was not the fear of the other, and this was no less true of the threats they offered. What could be going on between them, she wondered.

At that moment, a loud, gruff voice was raised, by someone whose tone suggested he was used to giving orders. It came from a loudspeaker fixed above the door by which they had entered. The word Attention was uttered three times, then the voice began, the Government regrets having been forced to exercise with all urgency what it considers to be its rightful duty, to protect the population by all possible means in this present crisis, when something with all the appearance of an epidemic of blindness has broken out, provisionally known as the white sickness, and we are relying on the public spirit and cooperation of all citizens to stem any further contagion, assuming that we are dealing with a contagious disease and that we are not simply witnessing a series of as yet inexplicable coincidences. The decision to gather together in one place all those infected, and, in adjacent but separate quarters all those who have had any kind of contact with them, was not taken without careful consideration. The Government is fully aware of its responsibilities and hopes that those to whom this message is directed will, as the upright citizens they doubtless are, also assume their responsibilities, bearing in mind that the isolation in which they now find themselves will represent, above any personal considerations, an act of solidarity with the rest of the nation's community. That said, we ask everyone to listen attentively to the following instructions, first, the lights will be kept on at all times, any attempt to tamper with the switches will be useless, they don't work, second, leaving the building without authorisation will mean instant death, third, in each ward there is a telephone that can be used only to requisition from outside fresh supplies for purposes of hygiene and cleanliness, fourth, the internees will be responsible for washing their own clothes by hand, fifth, it is recommended that ward representatives should be elected, this is a recommendation rather than an order, the internees must organise themselves as they see fit, provided they comply with the aforesaid rules and those we are about to announce, sixth, three times daily containers with food will be deposited at the main door, on the right and on the left, destined respectively for the patients and those suspected of being contaminated, seventh, all the left-overs must be burnt, and this includes not only any food, but also the containers, plates and cutlery which are all made of combustible material, eighth, the burning should be done in the inner courtyards of the building or in the exercise yard, ninth, the internees are responsible for any damage caused by these fires, tenth, in the event of a fire getting out of control, whether accidentally or on purpose, the firemen will not intervene, eleventh, equally, the internees cannot count on any outside intervention should there be any outbreaks of illnesses, nor in the event of any disorder or aggression, twelfth, in the case of death, whatever the cause, the internees will bury the corpse in the yard without any formalities, thirteenth, contact between the wing of the patients and that of the people suspected of being contagious must be made in the central hall of the building by which they entered, fourteenth, should those suspected of being infected suddenly go blind, they will be transferred immediately to the other wing, fifteenth, this communication will be relayed daily at the same time for the benefit of all new arrivals. The Government and Nation expect every man and woman to do their duty. Good night.

In the silence that followed, the boy's voice could be clearly heard, I want my mummy, but the words were articulated without expression, like some automatic and repeater mechanism that had previously left a phrase suspended and was blurting it out now, at the wrong time. The doctor said, The orders we have just been given leave no room for doubt, we're isolated, probably more isolated than anyone has ever been and without any hope of getting out of this place until a cure is found for this disease, I recognise your voice, said the girl with dark glasses, I'm a doctor, an ophthalmologist, You must be the doctor I consulted yesterday, I recognise your voice, Yes, and who are you, I've been suffering from conjunctivitis and I assume it hasn't cleared up, but now, since I'm completely blind, it's of no importance, And the child who's with you, He's not mine, I have no children, Yesterday I examined a boy with a squint, was that you, the doctor asked, Yes, that was me, the boy's reply came out with the resentful tone of someone who prefers people not to mention his physical defect, and with good reason, for such defects, these as much as any others, are no sooner mentioned than they pass from being barely perceptible to being all too obvious. Is there anyone else here I know, the doctor asked, could the man who came to see me at the surgery yesterday accompanied by his wife be here by any chance, the man who suddenly went blind when out driving his car, That's me, replied the first blind man, Is there anyone else, please speak up, we are obliged to live here together for who knows how long, therefore it is essential that we should get to know each other. The car-thief muttered between his teeth, Yes, yes, he thought this would be sufficient to confirm his presence, but the doctor insisted, The voice is that of someone who is relatively young, you're not the elderly patient with the cataract, No doctor, that's not me, How did you go blind, I was walking along the street, And what else, Nothing else, I was walking along the street and I suddenly went blind. The doctor was about to ask if his blindness was also white, but stopped himself in time, why bother, whatever his reply, no matter whether his blindness was white or black, they would not get out of this place. He stretched out a hesitant hand to his wife and met her hand on the way. She kissed him on the cheek, no one else could see that wrinkled forehead, that tight mouth, those dead eyes, like glass, terrifying because they appeared to see and did not see, My time will come too, she thought, perhaps even at this very instant, not allowing me to finish what I am saying, at any moment, just as happened to them, or perhaps I'll wake up blind, or go blind as I close my eyes to sleep, thinking I've just dozed off.

She looked at the four blind people, they were sitting on their beds, the little luggage they had been able to bring at their feet, the boy with his school satchel, the others with suitcases, small, as if they had packed for the weekend. The girl with dark glasses was conversing in a low voice with the boy, on the row opposite, close to each other, with only an empty bed between them, the first blind man and the car-thief were, without realising it, sitting face to face. The doctor said, We all heard the orders, whatever happens now, one thing we can be sure of, no one will come to our assistance, therefore we ought to start getting organised without delay, because it won't be long before this ward fills up with people, this one and the others, How do you know there are more wards here, asked the girl, We went around the place before deciding on this ward which is closer to the main entrance, explained the doctor's wife, as she squeezed her husband's arm as if warning him to be cautious. The girl said, it would be better, doctor, if you were to take charge of the ward, after all, you are a doctor. What good is a doctor without eyes or medicines, But you have some authority. The doctor's wife smiled, I think you should accept, if the others are in agreement, of course, I don't think it's such a good idea, Why not, For the moment there are only six of us here, but by tomorrow we shall certainly be more, people will start arriving every day, it would be too much to expect that they should be prepared to accept the authority of someone they have not chosen and who, moreover, would have nothing to offer them in exchange for their respect, always assuming they were willing to accept my authority and my rules, Then it's going to be difficult to live here, We'll be very fortunate if it turns out to be only difficult. The girl with dark glasses said, I meant well, but frankly, doctor, you are right, it will be a case of everyone for himself.

Either because he was moved by these words or because he could no longer contain his fury, one of the men got abruptly to his feet, This fellow is to blame for our misfortune, if I had my eyesight now, I'd do him in, he bellowed, while pointing in the direction where he thought the other man to be. He was not all that far off, but his dramatic gesture was comical because his jabbing, accusing finger was pointing at an innocent bedside table. Keep calm, said the doctor, no one's to blame in an epidemic, everyone's a victim, If I hadn't been the decent fellow I am, if I hadn't helped him to find his way home, I'd still have my precious eyes, Who are you, asked the doctor, but the complainant did not reply and now seemed annoyed that he had said anything. Then the other man spoke, He took me home, it's true, but then took advantage of my condition to steal my car, That's a lie, I didn't steal anything, You most certainly did, If anyone nicked your car, it wasn't me, my reward for carrying out a kind action was to lose my sight, besides, where are the witnesses, that's what I'd like to know. This argument won't solve anything, said the doctor's wife, the car is outside, the two of you are in here, better to make your peace, don't forget we are going to have to live here together, You can count me out, said the first blind man, I'm off to another ward, as far away as possible from this crook who was capable of robbing a blind man, he claims that he turned blind because of me, well let him stay blind, at least it shows there is still some justice in this world. He picked up his suitcase and, shuffling his feet so as not to trip and groping with his free hand, he went along the aisle separating the two rows of beds, Where are the other wards, he asked, but did not hear the reply if there was one, because suddenly he found himself beneath an onslaught of arms and legs, the car-thief was carrying out as best he could his threat to take his revenge on this man who had caused all his misfortunes. One minute on top, the next underneath, they rolled about in the confined space, colliding now and then with the legs of the beds, while, terrified once more, the boy with the squint started crying again and calling out for his mother. The doctor's wife took her husband by the arm, she knew that alone she would never be able to persuade them to stop quarrelling, she led him along the passageway to the spot where the enraged opponents were panting for breath as they struggled on the ground. She guided her husband's hands, she herself took charge of the blind man whom she found more manageable, and with much effort, they managed to separate them. You're behaving foolishly, said the doctor angrily, if your idea is to turn this place into a hell, then you're going about it in the right way, but remember we're on our own here, we can expect no outside help, do you hear, He stole my car, whimpered the first blind man who had come off worst in the exchange of blows, Forget it, what does it matter, said the doctor's wife, you were no longer in a condition to drive the car when it disappeared, That's all very well, but it was mine, and this villain took it and left it who knows where, Most likely, said the doctor, the car is to be found at the spot where this man turned blind, You're an astute fellow, doctor, yes sir, no doubt about that, piped up the thief. The first blind man made a gesture as if to escape from the hands holding him, but without really trying, as if aware that not even his sense of outrage, however justified, would bring back his car, nor would the car restore his sight. But the thief threatened, If you think you're going to get away with this, then you're very much mistaken, all right, I stole your car, but you stole my eyesight, so who's the bigger thief, That's enough, the doctor protested, we're all blind here and we're not accusing or pointing the finger at anyone, I'm not interested in other people's misfortunes, the thief replied contemptuously, If you want to go to another ward, said the doctor to the first blind man, my wife will guide you there, she knows her way around better than me, No thanks, I've changed my mind, I prefer to stay in this one. The thief mocked him, The little boy is afraid of being on his own in case a certain bogeyman gets him, That's enough, shouted the doctor, losing his patience, Now listen to me, doctor, snarled the thief, we're all equal here and you don't give me any orders, No one is giving orders, I'm simply asking you to leave this poor fellow in peace, Fine, fine, but watch your step when you're dealing with me, I'm not easy to handle when somebody gets up my nose, otherwise I'm as good a friend as you're likely to meet, but the worst enemy you could possibly have. With aggressive movements and gestures, the thief fumbled for the bed where he had been sitting, pushed his suitcase underneath, then announced, I'm going to get some sleep, as if warning them, You'd better look the other way, I'm going to take my clothes off. The girl with dark glasses said to the boy with the squint, And you'd better get into bed as well, stay on this side and if you need anything during the night, call me, I want to do a wee-wee, the boy said. On hearing him, all of them felt a sudden and urgent desire to urinate, and their thoughts were more or less as follows, Now how are we going to cope with this problem, the first blind man groped under the bed to see if there was a chamber pot, yet at the same time hoping he would not find one for he would be embarrassed if he had to urinate in the presence of other people, not that they could see him, of course, but the noise of someone peeing is indiscreet, unmistakable, men at least can use a strategy denied women, in this they are more fortunate. The thief had sat down on the bed and was now saying, Shit, where do you have to go to piss in this place, Watch your language, there's a child here, protested the girl with dark glasses, Certainly, sweetheart, but unless you can find a lavatory, it won't be long before your little boy has pee running down his legs. The doctor's wife intervened, Perhaps I can locate the toilets, I can remember having smelt them, I'll come with you, said the girl with dark glasses, taking the boy by the hand, I think it best that we should all go, the doctor observed, then we shall know the way whenever we need to go, I know what's on your mind, the car-thief thought to himself without daring to say it aloud, what you don't want is that your little wife should have to take me to pee every time I feel the urge. The implication behind that thought gave him a small erection that surprised him, as if the fact of being blind should have as a consequence, the loss or diminution of sexual desire. Good, he thought, all is not lost, after all, among the dead and the wounded someone will escape, and, drifting away from the conversation, he began to daydream. He didn't get very far, the doctor was already saying, Let's form a line, my wife will lead the way, everyone put their hand on the shoulder of the person in front, then there will be no danger of our getting lost. The first blind man spoke up, I'm not going anywhere with him, obviously referring to the crook who had robbed him.

Whether to look for each other or to avoid each other, they could scarcely move in the narrow aisle, all the more so since the doctor's wife had to proceed as if she were blind. At last, they were all in line, the girl with dark glasses led the boy with the squint by the hand, then the thief in underpants and a vest, the doctor behind him, and last of all, safe for the moment from any physical attack, the first blind man. They advanced very slowly, as if mistrustful of the person guiding them, groping in vain with their free hand, searching for the support of something solid, a wall, a door-frame. Placed behind the girl with dark glasses, the thief, aroused by the perfume she exuded and by the memory of his recent erection, decided to put his hands to better use, the one caressing the nape of her neck beneath her hair, the other, openly and unceremoniously fondling her breast. She wriggled to shake him off, but he was grabbing her firmly. Then the girl gave a backward kick as hard as she could. The heel of her shoe, sharp as a stiletto, pierced the flesh of the thief's bare thigh causing him to give a cry of surprise and pain. What's going on, asked the doctor's wife, looking back, I tripped, the girl with dark glasses replied, I seem to have injured the person behind me. Blood was already seeping out between the thief's fingers who, moaning and cursing, was trying to ascertain the consequences of her aggression, I'm injured, this bitch doesn't look where she's putting her feet, And you don't look where you're putting your hands, the girl replied curtly. The doctor's wife understood what had happened, at first she smiled, but then she saw how nasty the wound looked, blood was trickling down the poor devil's leg, and they had no peroxide, no iodine, no plasters, no bandages, no disinfectant, nothing. The line was now in disarray, the doctor was asking, Where is the wound, Here, Here, where, On my leg, can't you see, this bitch stuck the heel of her shoe in me, I tripped, I couldn't help it, repeated the girl before blurting out in exasperation, The bastard was touching me up, what sort of woman does he think I am. The doctor's wife intervened, This wound should be washed and dressed at once, And where is there any water, asked the thief, In the kitchen, in the kitchen there is water, but we don't all have to go, my husband and I will take him there, you others wait here, we'll be back soon, I want to do weewee, said the boy, Hold it in a bit longer, we'll be right back. The doctor's wife knew that she had to turn once to the right, and once to the left, then follow a narrow corridor that formed a right angle, the kitchen was at the far end. After a few paces she pretended that she was mistaken, stopped, retraced her footsteps, then said, Ah, now I remember, and from there they headed straight for the kitchen, there was no more time to be lost, the wound was bleeding profusely. At first, the water from the tap was dirty, it took some time for it to become clear. It was lukewarm and stale, as if it had been putrefying inside the pipes, but the wounded man received it with a sigh of relief. The wound looked ugly. And now, how are we going to bandage his leg, asked the doctor's wife. Beneath a table there were some filthy rags which must have been used as floor cloths, but it would be most unwise to use them to make a bandage, There doesn't appear to be anything here, she said, while pretending to keep up the search, But I can't be left like this, doctor, the bleeding won't stop, please help me, and forgive me if I was rude to you a short time ago, moaned the thief, We are trying to help you, otherwise we wouldn't be here, said the doctor and then he ordered him, Take off your vest, there's no other option. The wounded man mumbled that he needed his vest, but took it off. The doctor's wife lost no time in improvising a bandage which she wrapped round his thigh, pulled tight and managed to use the shoulder straps and the tail of the vest to tie a rough knot. These were not movements a blind person could easily execute, but she was in no mood to waste time with any more pretence, it was enough to have pretended that she was lost. The thief sensed that there was something unusual here, logically it was the doctor who, although no more than an ophthalmologist, should have bandaged the wound, but the consolation of knowing that something was being done outweighed the doubts, vague as they were, that had momentarily crossed his mind. With him limping along, they went back to rejoin the others, and once there, the doctor's wife spotted immediately that the boy with the squint had not been able to hold out any longer and had wet his trousers. Neither the first blind man nor the girl with glasses had realised what had happened. At the boy's feet spread a puddle of urine, the hem of his trousers still dripping wet. But as if nothing had happened, the doctor's wife said, Let's go and find these lavatories. The blind stretched out their arms, looking for each other, though not the girl with dark glasses who made it quite clear that she had no intention of walking in front of that shameless creature who had touched her up, at last the line was formed, the thief changing places with the first blind man, with the doctor between them. The thief's limp was getting worse and he was dragging his leg. The tight bandage was bothering him and the wound was throbbing so badly that it was as if his heart had changed position and was lying at the bottom of some hole. The girl with dark glasses was once again leading the boy by the hand, but he kept his distance as much as possible, afraid that someone might discover his accident, such as the doctor, who muttered, There's a smell of urine here, and his wife felt she should confirm his impression, Yes, there is a smell, she could not say that it was coming from the lavatories because they were still some distance away, and, being obliged to behave as if she were blind, she could not reveal that the stench was coming from the boy's wet trousers.

They were agreed, both men and women, when they arrived at the lavatories, that the boy should be the first to relieve himself, but the men ended up going in together, without any distinction of urgency or age, the urinal was communal, it would have to be in a place like this, even the toilets. The women remained at the door, they are said to have more resistance, but there's a limit to everything, and the doctor's wife was soon suggesting, Perhaps there are other lavatories, but the girl with dark glasses said, Speaking for myself, I can wait, So can I, said the other woman, then there was a silence, then they began to speak, How did you come to lose your sight, Like everyone else, suddenly I could no longer see, Were you at home, No, So it happened when you left my husband's surgery, More or less, What do you mean by more or less, That it didn't happen right away, Did you feel any pain, No, there was no pain but when I opened my eyes I was blind, With me it was different, What do you mean by different, My eyes weren't closed, I went blind the moment my husband got into the ambulance, Fortunate, For whom, Your husband, this way you can be together, In that case I was also fortunate, You were, Are you married, No, no I'm not, and I don't think there will be any more marriages now, But this blindness is so abnormal, so alien to scientific knowledge that it cannot last forever. And suppose we were to stay like this for the rest of our lives, Us, Everyone, That would be horrible, a world full of blind people, It doesn't bear thinking about.

The boy with the squint was the first to emerge from the lavatory, he didn't even need to have gone in there. He had rolled his trousers halfway up his legs and removed his socks. He said, I'm back, whereupon the girl with dark glasses moved in the direction of the voice, did not succeed the first or second time, but at a third attempt found the boy's vacillating hand. Shortly afterwards, the doctor appeared, then the first blind man, one of them asked, Where are the rest of you, the doctor's wife was already holding her husband's arm, his other arm was touched and grabbed by the girl with dark glasses. For several moments the first blind man had no one to protect him, then someone placed a hand on his shoulder. Are we all here, asked the doctor's wife, The fellow with the injured leg has stayed behind to satisfy another need, her husband replied. Then the girl with dark glasses said, Perhaps there are other toilets, I'm getting desperate, forgive me, Let's go and find out, said the doctor's wife, and they went off hand in hand. Within ten minutes they were back, they had found a consulting room which had its own toilet. The thief had already reappeared, complaining about the cold and the pain in his leg. They re-formed the line in the same order by which they had come and, with less effort than before and without incident, they returned to the ward. Adroitly, without appearing to do so, the doctor's wife helped each of them to reach the bed they had previously occupied. Before entering the ward, as if it were self-evident to everyone, she suggested that the easiest way for each of them to find their place was to count the beds from the entrance, Ours, she said, are the last ones on the right-hand side, beds nineteen and twenty. The first to proceed down the aisle was the thief. Almost naked, he was shivering from head to foot and anxious to alleviate the pain in his leg, reason enough for him to be given priority. He went from bed to bed, fumbling on the floor in search of his suitcase, and when he recognised it, he said aloud, It's here, then added, Fourteen, On which side, asked the doctor's wife, On the left, he replied, once again vaguely surprised, as if she ought to know it without having to ask. The first blind man went next. He knew his bed was next but one to the thief's and on the same side. He was no longer afraid of sleeping near him, his leg was in such a dreadful state, and judging from his groans and sighs, he would find it hard to move. On arriving there, he said, Sixteen, on the left, and lay down fully dressed. Then the girl with dark glasses pleaded in a low voice, Can we stay close to you on the other side, we shall feel safer there. The four of them advanced together and lost no time in getting settled. After a few minutes, the boy with the squint said, I'm hungry, and the girl with dark glasses murmured, Tomorrow, tomorrow we'll find something to eat, now go to sleep. Then she opened her handbag, searched for the tiny bottle she had bought in the chemist's. She removed her glasses, threw back her head and, keeping her eyes wide open, guiding one hand with the other, she applied the eye-drops. Not all of the drops went into her eyes, but conjunctivitis, given such careful treatment, soon clears up.

I must open my eyes, thought the doctor's wife. Through closed eyelids, when she woke up at various times during the night, she had perceived the dim light of the lamps that barely illuminated the ward, but now she seemed to notice a difference, another luminous presence, it could be the effect of the first glimmer of dawn, it could be that milky sea already drowning her eyes. She told herself that she would count up to ten and then open her eyelids, she said it twice, counted twice, failed to open them twice. She could hear her husband breathing deeply in the next bed and someone snoring, I wonder how the wound on that fellow's leg is doing, she asked herself, but knew at that moment that she felt no real compassion, what she wanted was to pretend that she was worried about something else, what she wanted was not to have to open her eyes. She opened them the following instant, just like that, not because of any conscious decision. Through the windows that began halfway up the wall and ended up a mere hand's-breadth from the ceiling, entered the dull, bluish light of dawn. I'm not blind, she murmured, and suddenly panicking, she raised herself on the bed, the girl with dark glasses, who was occupying a bed opposite, might have heard her. She was asleep. On the next bed, the one up against the wall, the boy was also sleeping, She did the same as me, the doctor's wife thought, she gave him the safest place, what fragile walls we'd make, a mere stone in the middle of the road without any hope other than to see the enemy trip over it, enemy, what enemy, no one will attack us here, even if we'd stolen and killed outside, no one is likely to come here to arrest us, that man who stole the car has never been so sure of his freedom, we're so remote from the world that any day now, we shall no longer know who we are, or even remember our names, and besides, what use would names be to us, no dog recognises another dog or knows the others by the names they have been given, a dog is identified by its scent and that is how it identifies others, here we are like another breed of dogs, we know each other's bark or speech, as for the rest, features, colour of eyes or hair, they are of no importance, it is as if they did not exist, I can still see but for how long, The light changed a little, it could not be night coming back, it had to be the sky clouding over, delaying the morning. A groan came from the thief's bed, If the wound has become infected, thought the doctor's wife, we have nothing to treat it with, no remedy, in these conditions the tiniest accident can become a tragedy, perhaps that is what they are waiting for, that we perish here, one after the other, when the beast dies, the poison dies with it. The doctor's wife rose from her bed, leaned over her husband, was about to wake him, but did not have the courage to drag him from his sleep and know that he continued to be blind. Barefoot, one step at a time, she went to the thief's bed. His eyes were open and unmoving. How are you feeling, whispered the doctor's wife. The thief turned his head in the direction of the voice and said, Bad, my leg is very painful, she was about to say to him, Let me see, but held back just in time, such imprudence, it was he who did not remember that there were only blind people there, he acted without thinking, as he would have done several hours ago, there outside, if a doctor had said to him, Let's have a look at this wound, and he raised the blanket. Even in the half-light, anyone capable of seeing would have noticed the mattress soaked in blood, the black hole of the wound with its swollen edges. The bandage had come undone. The doctor's wife carefully lowered the blanket, then with a rapid, delicate gesture, passed her hand over the man's forehead. His skin felt dry and burning hot. The light changed again, the clouds were drifting away. The doctor's wife returned to her bed, but this time did not lie down. She was watching her husband who was murmuring in his sleep, the shadowy forms of the others beneath the grey blankets, the grimy walls, the empty beds waiting to be occupied, and she serenely wished that she, too, could turn blind, penetrate the visible skin of things and pass to their inner side, to their dazzling and irremediable blindness.

Suddenly, from outside the ward, probably from the hallway separating the two wings of the building, came the sound of angry voices, Out, out, Get out, away with you, You cannot stay here, Orders have to be obeyed. The din got louder, then quietened down, a door slammed shut, all that could be heard now was a distressed sobbing, the unmistakable clatter made by someone who had just fallen over. In the ward they were all awake. They turned their heads towards the entrance, they did not need to be able to see to know that these were blind people who were arriving. The doctor's wife got up, how she would have liked to help the new arrivals, to say a kind word, to guide them to their beds, inform them, Take note, this is bed seven on the left-hand side, this is number four on the right, you can't go wrong, yes, there are six of us here, we came yesterday, yes, we were the first, our names, what do names matter, I believe one of the men has stolen a car, then there is the man who was robbed, there's a mysterious girl with dark glasses who puts drops in for her conjunctivitis, how do I know, being blind, that she wears dark glasses, well as it happens, my husband is an ophthalmologist and she went to consult him at his surgery, yes, he's also here, blindness struck all of us, ah, of course, there's also the boy with the squint. She did not move, she simply said to her husband, They're arriving. The doctor got out of bed, his wife helped him into his trousers, it didn't matter, no one could see, just then the blind internees came into the ward, there were five of them, three men and two women. The doctor said, raising his voice, Keep calm, no need to rush, there are six of us here, how many are you, there's room for everyone. They did not know how many they were, true they had come into contact with each other, sometimes even bumped into each other, as they were pushed from the wing on the left to this one, but they did not know how many they were. And they were carrying no luggage. When they woke up in their ward and found they were blind and started bemoaning their fate, the others put them out without a moment's hesitation, without even giving them time to take their leave of any relatives or friends who might be with them. The doctor's wife remarked, It would be best if they could be counted and each person gave their name. Motionless, the blind internees hesitated, but someone had to make a start, two of the men spoke at once, it always happens, both then fell silent, and it was the third man who began, Number one, he paused, it seemed he was about to give his name, but what he said was, I'm a policeman, and the doctor's wife thought to herself, He didn't give his name, he too knows that names are of no importance here. Another man was introducing himself, Number two, and he followed the example of the first man, I'm a taxi-driver. The third man said, Number three, I'm a pharmacist's assistant. Then a woman spoke up, Number four, I'm a hotel maid, and the last one of all, Number five, I work in an office. That's my wife, my wife, where are you, tell me where you are, Here, I'm here, she said bursting into tears and walking unsteadily along the aisle with her eyes wide open, her hands struggling against the milky sea flooding into them. More confident, he advanced towards her, Where are you, where are you, he was now murmuring as if in prayer. One hand found another, the next moment they were embracing, a single body, kisses in search of kisses, at times lost in mid-air for they could not see each other's cheeks, eyes, lips. Sobbing, the doctor's wife clung to her husband, as if she, too, had just been reunited, but what she was saying was, This is terrible, a real disaster. Then the voice of the boy with the squint could be heard asking, Is my mummy here as well. Seated on his bed, the girl with dark glasses murmured, She'll come, don't worry, she'll come.

Here, each person's real home is the place where they sleep, therefore little wonder that the first concern of the new arrivals should be to choose a bed, just as they had done in the other ward, when they still had eyes to see. In the case of the wife of

the first blind man there could be no doubt, her rightful and natural place was beside her husband, in bed seventeen, leaving
number eighteen in the middle, like an empty space separating
her from the girl with dark glasses. Nor is it surprising that they
should try as far as possible to stay close together, there are
many affinities here, some already known, others that are about
to be revealed, for example, it was the pharmacist's assistant
who sold eye-drops to the girl with dark glasses, this was the
taxi-driver who took the first blind man to the doctor, this fellow who has identified himself as being a policeman found the
blind thief weeping like a lost child, and as for the hotel maid,
she was the first person to enter the room when the girl with
dark glasses had a screaming fit. It is nevertheless certain that
not all of these affinities will become explicit and known, either
because of a lack of opportunity, or because no one so much as
imagined that they could possibly exist, or because of a simple
question of sensibility and tact. The hotel maid would never
dream that the woman she saw naked is here, we know that the
pharmacist's assistant served other customers wearing dark
glasses who came to purchase eye-drops, no one would be imprudent enough to denounce to the policeman the presence of
someone who stole a car, the taxi-driver would swear that during the last few days he had no blind man as a passenger. Naturally, the first blind man told his wife in a low voice that one of
the internees is the scoundrel who went off with their car, What
a coincidence, eh, but, since in the meantime, he knew that the
poor devil was badly injured in one leg, he was generous
enough to add, He's been punished enough. And she, because
of her deep distress at being blind and her great joy on regaining her husband, joy and sorrow can go together, not like oil
and water, she no longer remembered what she had said two
days before, that she would give a year of her life if this rogue,
her word, were to go blind. And if there was some last shadow
of resentment still troubling her spirit, it certainly blew over
when the wounded man moaned pitifully, Doctor, please help
me. Allowing himself to be guided by his wife, the doctor gently probed the edges of his wound, he could do nothing more,

nor was there any point in trying to bathe it, the infection might have been caused by the deep penetration of a shoe heel that had been in contact with the surface of the streets and the floors here in the building, or equally by pathogenic agents in all probability to be found in the contaminated almost stagnant water, coming from antiquated pipes in appalling condition. The girl with dark glasses who had got up on hearing his moan, began approaching slowly, counting the beds. She leaned forward, stretched out her hand, which brushed against the face of the doctor's wife, and then, having reached, who knows how, the wounded man's hand, which was burning hot, she said sadly, Please, forgive me, it was entirely my fault, there was no need for me to do what I did, Forget it, replied the man, these things happen in life, I shouldn't have done what I did either.

Almost covering these last words, the harsh voice from the loudspeaker came booming out, Attention, attention, your food has been left at the entrance as well as supplies for your hygiene and cleanliness, the blind should go first to collect their food, those in the wing for the contaminated will be informed when it's their turn, attention, attention, your food has been left at the entrance, the blind should make their way there first, the blind first. Dazed by fever, the wounded man did not grasp all the words, he thought they were being told to leave, that their detention was over, and he made as if to get up, but the doctor's wife held him back, Where are you going, Didn't you hear, he asked, they said the blind should leave, Yes, but only to go and collect our food. The wounded man gave a despondent sigh, and once more could feel the pain piercing through his flesh. The doctor said, Stay here, I'll go, I'm coming with you, said his wife. Just as they were about to leave the ward, a man who had come from the other wing, inquired, Who is this fellow, the reply came from the first blind man, He's a doctor, an eyespecialist, That's a good one, said the taxi-driver, just our luck to end up with the one doctor who can do nothing for us, We're also landed with a taxi-driver who can't take us anywhere, replied the girl with dark glasses sarcastically.

The container with the food was in the hallway. The doctor asked his wife, Guide me to the main door, Why, I'm going to tell them that there is someone here with a serious infection and that we have no medicines, Remember the warning, Yes, but perhaps when confronted with a concrete case, I doubt it, Me, too, but we ought to try. At the top of the steps leading to the forecourt, the daylight dazzled his wife, and not because it was too intense, there were dark clouds passing across the sky, and it looked as if it might rain, In such a short time I've become unused to bright light, she thought. Just at that moment, a soldier shouted from the gate, Stop, turn back, I have orders to shoot, and then, in the same tone of voice, pointing his gun, Sergeant, there are some people here trying to leave, We have no wish to leave, the doctor protested, In my opinion that is not what they want, said the sergeant as he approached, and, looking through the bars of the main gate, he asked, What's going on, A person who has injured his leg has an infected wound, we urgently need antibiotics and other medicines, My orders are crystal-clear, no one is to be allowed to leave, and the only thing we can allow in is food, If the infection should get worse which looks all too certain, it could soon prove fatal, That isn't my affair, Then contact your superiors, Look here, blind man, let me tell you something, either the two of you get back to where you came from, or you'll be shot, Let's go, said the wife, there's nothing to be done, they're not to blame, they're terrified and are only obeying orders, I can't believe that this is happening, it's against all the rules of humanity, You'd better believe it, because the truth couldn't be clearer, Are you two still there, I'm going to count up to three and if they're not out of my sight by then, they can be sure they won't get back, ooone, twooo, threee, that's it, he was as good as his word, and turning to the soldiers, Even if it were my own brother, he did not explain to whom he was referring, whether it was to the man who had come to request medicines or to the other fellow with the infected leg. Inside, the wounded man wanted to know if they were going to supply them with medicines, How do you know

I went to ask for supplies, asked the doctor, I guessed as much, after all, you are a doctor, I'm very sorry, Does that mean there will be no medicines, Yes, So, that's that.

The food had been carefully calculated for five people. There were bottles of milk and biscuits, but whoever had prepared their rations had forgotten to provide any glasses, nor were there any plates, or cutlery, these would probably come with the lunch. The doctor's wife went to give the wounded man something to drink, but he vomited. The taxi-driver complained that he did not like milk, he asked if he could have coffee. Some, after having eaten, went back to bed, the first blind man took his wife to visit the various places, they were the only two to leave the ward. The pharmacist's assistant asked to be allowed to speak to the doctor, he wanted the doctor to tell him if he had formed any opinion about their illness, I don't believe this can strictly be called an illness, the doctor started to explain, and then with much simplification, he summed up what he had researched in his reference books before becoming blind. Several beds further on, the taxi-driver was listening attentively, and when the doctor had finished his report, he shouted down the ward, I'll bet what happened is that the channels that go from the eyes to the brain got congested, Stupid fool, growled the pharmacist's assistant with indignation, Who knows, the doctor could not resist a smile, in truth the eyes are nothing more than lenses, it is the brain that actually does the seeing, just as an image appears on the film, and if the channels did get blocked up, as that man suggested, it's the same as a carburetor, if the fuel can't reach it, the engine does not work and the car won't go, as simple as that, as you can see, the doctor told the pharmacist's assistant, And how much longer, doctor, do you think we're going to be kept here, asked the hotel maid, At least for as long as we are unable to see, And how long will that be, Frankly, I don't think anyone knows, it's either something that will pass or it might go on for ever, How I'd love to know. The maid sighed and after several moments, I'd also like to know what happened to that girl, What girl, asked the pharmacist's assistant, That girl from the hotel, what a shock she gave me, there in the middle of the room, as naked as the day she was born, wearing nothing but a pair of dark glasses, and screaming that she was blind, she's probably the one who infected me. The doctor's wife looked, saw the girl slowly remove her dark glasses, hiding her movements, then put them under her pillow, while asking the boy with the squint, Would you like another biscuit, For the first time since she had arrived there, the doctor's wife felt as if she were behind a microscope and observing the behaviour of a number of human beings who did not even suspect her presence, and this suddenly struck her as being contemptible and obscene. I have no right to look if the others cannot see me, she thought to herself. With a shaky hand, the girl applied a few eye-drops. This would always allow her to say that these were not tears running from her eyes.

Hours later, when the loudspeaker announced that they should come and collect their lunch, the first blind man and the taxi-driver offered to go on this mission for which eyes were not essential, it was enough to be able to touch. The containers were some distance from the door that connected the hallway to the corridors, to find them they had to go down on all fours, sweeping the floor ahead with one arm outstretched, while the other served as a third paw, and if they had no difficulty in returning to the ward, it was because the doctor's wife had come up with the idea, which she was at pains to justify from personal experience, of tearing a blanket into strips, and using these to make an improvised rope, one end of which would remain attached to the outside handle of the door of the ward, while the other end would be tied in turn to the ankle of whoever had to go to fetch their food. The two men went off, the plates and cutlery arrived, but the portions were still only for five, in all likelihood the sergeant in charge of the patrol was unaware that there were six more blind people there, since once outside the entrance, even when paying attention to what might be happening behind the main door, in the shadows of the hallway, it was only by chance that anyone could be seen passing from one wing to another. The taxi-driver offered to go and demand the missing portions of food, and he went alone, he had no wish to be accompanied,

We're not five, there are eleven of us, he shouted at the soldiers, and the same sergeant replied from the other side, Save your breath, there are many more to come yet, he said it in a tone of voice that must have seemed derisive to the taxi-driver, if we take into account the words spoken by the latter when he returned to the ward, It was as if he were making fun of me. They shared out the food, five portions divided by ten, since the wounded man was still refusing to eat, all he asked for was some water, and he begged them to moisten his lips. His skin was burning hot. And since he could not bear the contact and weight of the blanket on the wound for very long, he uncovered his leg from time to time, but the cold air in the ward soon obliged him to cover up again, and this went on for hours. He would moan at regular intervals with what sounded like a stifled gasp, as if the constant and persistent pain had suddenly got worse before he could get it under control.

In the middle of the afternoon, three more blind people arrived, expelled from the other wing. One was an employee from the surgery, whom the doctor's wife recognised at once, and the others, as destiny had decreed, were the man who had been with the girl with dark glasses in the hotel and the ill-mannered policeman who had taken her home. No sooner had they reached their beds and seated themselves, than the employee from the surgery began weeping in despair, the two men said nothing, as if still unable to grasp what had happened to them. Suddenly, from the street, came the cries of people shouting, orders being given in a booming voice, a rebellious uproar. The blind internees all turned their heads in the direction of the door and waited. They could not see, but knew what was about to happen within the next few minutes. The doctor's wife, seated on the bed beside her husband, said in a low voice, It had to be, the promised hell is about to begin. He squeezed her hand and murmured, Don't move, from now on there is nothing you can do. The shouting had died down, now a confusion of sounds was coming from the hallway, these were the blind, driven like sheep, bumping into each other, crammed together in the doorways, some lost their sense of direction and ended up in other wards, but the majority, stumbling along, huddled into groups or dispersed one by one, desperately waving their hands in the air like people drowning, burst into the ward in a whirlwind, as if being pushed from the outside by a bulldozer. A number of them fell and were trampled underfoot. Confined in the narrow aisles, the new arrivals gradually began filling the spaces between the beds, and here, like a ship caught in a storm that has finally managed to reach port, they took possession of their berths, in this case their beds, insisting that there was no room for anyone else, and that latecomers should find themselves a place elsewhere. From the far end, the doctor shouted that there were other wards, but the few who remained without a bed were frightened of getting lost in the labyrinth of rooms, corridors, closed doors, stairways they might only discover at the last minute. Finally they realised they could not stay there and, struggling to find the door by which they had entered, they ventured forth into the unknown. As if searching for one last safe refuge, the five blind internees in the second group had managed to occupy the beds, which, between them and those in the first group, had remained empty. Only the wounded man remained isolated, without protection, on bed fourteen on the left-hand side.

A quarter of an hour later, apart from some weeping and wailing, the discreet sounds of people settling down, calm rather than peace of mind was restored in the ward. All the beds were now occupied. The evening was drawing in, the dim lamps seemed to gain strength. Then they heard the abrupt voice of the loudspeaker. As on the first day, instructions were repeated as to how the wards should be maintained and the rules the internees should obey, The Government regrets having to enforce to the letter what it considers its right and duty, to protect the population with all the means at its disposal during this present crisis, etc., etc. When the voice stopped, an indignant chorus of protests broke out, We're locked up here, We're all going to die in here, This isn't right, Where are the doctors we were promised, this was something new, the authorities had promised doctors, medical assistance, perhaps even a complete cure. The doctor did not say that if they were in need of a doctor he was there at their disposal. He would never say that again. His hands alone are not enough for a doctor, a doctor cures with medicines, drugs, chemical compounds and combinations of this and that, and here there is no trace of any such materials, nor any hope of getting them. He did not even have the sight of his eyes to notice any sickly pallor, to observe any reddening of the peripheric circulation, how often, without any need for closer examination, these external signs proved to be as useful as an entire clinical history, or the colouring of mucus and pigmentation, with every probability of coming up with the right diagnosis, You won't escape this one. Since the nearby beds were all occupied, his wife could no longer keep him informed of what was happening, but he sensed the tense, uneasy atmosphere, bordering on open conflict, that had been created with the arrival of the latest group of internees. The very air in the ward seemed to have become heavier, emitting strong lingering odours, with sudden wafts that were simply nauseating, What will this place be like within a week, he asked himself, and it horrified him to think that in a week's time, they would still be confined here, Assuming there won't be any problems with food supplies, and who can be sure there isn't already a shortage, I doubt, for example, whether those outside have any idea from one minute to the next, how many of us are interned here, the question is how they will solve the matter of hygiene, I'm not referring to how we shall keep ourselves clean, struck blind only a few days ago and without anyone to help us, or whether the showers will work and for how long, I'm referring to the rest, to all the other likely problems, for if the lavatories should get blocked, even one of them, this place would be transformed into a sewer. He rubbed his face with his hands, he could feel the roughness of his beard after three days without shaving, It's preferable like this, I hope they won't have the unfortunate idea of sending us razor blades and scissors. He had everything necessary for shaving in his suitcase, but was conscious of the fact that it would be a mistake to try, And where, where, not here in the ward, among all these people, true my wife could shave me, but it would not be long before the others got wind of it and expressed surprise that there should be someone here capable of offering these services, and there inside, in the showers, such confusion, dear God, how we miss having our sight, to be able to see, to see, even if they were only faint shadows, to stand before the mirror, see a dark diffused patch and be able to say, That's my face, anything that has light does not belong to me.

The complaints subsided little by little, someone from one of the other wards came to ask if there was any food left over and the taxi-driver was quick to reply, Not a crumb, and the pharmacist's assistant to show some good will, mitigated the peremptory refusal, There might be more to come. But nothing would come. Darkness fell. From outside came neither food nor words. Cries could be heard coming from the adjoining ward, then there was silence, if anyone was weeping they did so very quietly, the weeping did not penetrate the walls. The doctor's wife went to see how the injured man was faring, It's me, she said, carefully raising the blanket. His leg presented a terrifying sight, completely swollen from the thigh down, and the wound, a black circle with bloody purplish blotches, had got much larger, as if the flesh had been stretched from inside. It gave off a stench that was both fetid and slightly sweet. How are you feeling, the doctor's wife asked him, Thanks for coming, Tell me how you're feeling, Bad, Are you in pain, Yes and no, What do you mean, It hurts, but it's as if the leg were no longer mine, as if it were separated from my body, I can't explain, it's a strange feeling, as if I were lying here watching my leg hurt me, That's because you're feverish, Probably, Now try to get some sleep. The doctor's wife placed her hand on his forehead, then made to withdraw, but before she could even wish him goodnight, the invalid grabbed her by the arm and drew her towards him obliging her to get close to his face, I know you can see, he said in a low voice. The doctor's wife trembled with surprise and murmured, You're wrong, whatever put such an idea into your head, I see as much as anybody here, Don't try to deceive me, I know very well that you can see, but don't worry, I won't breathe a word to anyone, Sleep, sleep, Don't you trust me, Of course, I do, Don't you trust the word of a thief, I said I trusted you. Then why don't you tell me the truth, We'll talk tomorrow, now go to sleep, Yes, tomorrow, if I get that far, We mustn't think the worst, I do, or perhaps it's the fever thinking for me. The doctor's wife rejoined her husband and whispered in his ear, the wound looks awful, could it be gangrene, It seems unlikely in such a short time, Whatever it is, he's in a bad way, And those of us who are cooped up here, said the doctor in a deliberately loud voice, as if being struck blind were not enough, we might just as well have our hands and feet tied. From bed fourteen, left-hand side, the invalid replied, No one is going to tie me up, doctor.

The hours passed, one by one, the blind internees had fallen asleep. Some had covered their heads with a blanket, as if anxious that a pitch-black darkness, a real one, might extinguish once and for all the dim suns that their eyes had become. The three lamps suspended from the high ceiling, out of arm's reach, cast a dull, yellowish light over the beds, a light incapable of even creating shadows. Forty persons were sleeping or desperately trying to get to sleep, some were sighing and murmuring in their dreams, perhaps in their dream they could see what they were dreaming, perhaps they were saying to themselves, If this is a dream, I don't want to wake up. All their watches had stopped, either they had forgotten to wind them or had decided it was pointless, only that of the doctor's wife was still working. It was after three in the morning. Further along, very slowly, resting on his elbows, the thief raised his body into a sitting position. He had no feeling in his leg, nothing except the pain, the rest had ceased to belong to him. His knee was quite stiff. He rolled his body over on to the side of his healthy leg, which he allowed to hang out of the bed, then with both hands under his thigh, he tried to move his injured leg in the same direction. Like a pack of wolves suddenly roused, the pain went through his entire body, before returning to the dark crater from which it came. Resting on his hands, he gradually dragged his body across the mattress in the direction of the aisle. When he reached the rail at the foot of the bed, he had to rest. He was gasping for breath as if he were suffering from asthma, his head swayed on his shoulders, he could barely keep it upright. After several minutes, his breathing became more regular and he got slowly to his feet, putting his weight on his good leg. He knew that the other one would be no good to him, that he would have to drag it behind him wherever he went. He suddenly felt dizzy, an irrepressible shiver went through his body, the cold and fever made his teeth chatter. Supporting himself on the metal frames of the beds, passing from one to the other as if along a chain, he slowly advanced between the sleeping bodies. He dragged his injured leg like a bag. No one noticed him, no one asked, Where are you going at this hour, had anyone done so, he knew what he would reply, I'm off for a pee, he would say, he didn't want the doctor's wife to call out to him, she was someone he could not deceive or lie to, he would have to tell her what was on his mind, I can't go on rotting away in this hole, I realise that your husband has done everything he could to help me, but when I had to steal a car I wouldn't go and ask someone else to steal it for me, this is much the same, I'm the one who has to go, when they see me in this state they'll recognise at once that I'm in a bad way, put me in an ambulance and take me to a hospital, there must be hospitals just for the blind, one more won't make any difference, they'll treat my wound, cure me, I've heard that's what they do to those condemned to death, if they've got appendicitis they operate first and execute them afterwards, so that they die healthy, as far as I'm concerned, if they want, they can bring me back here, I don't mind. He advanced further, clenching his teeth to suppress any moaning, but he could not resist an anguished sob when, on reaching the end of the row, he lost his balance. He had miscounted the beds, he thought there was one more and came up against a void. Lying on the floor, he did not stir until he was certain that no one had woken up with the din made by his fall. Then he realised that this position was perfect for a blind person, if he were to advance on all fours he would find the way more easily. He dragged himself along until he reached the hallway, there he paused to consider how he should proceed, whether it would be better to call from the door or go up to the gate, taking advantage of the rope that had served as a handrail and almost certainly was still there. He knew full well that if he were to call for help from there, they would immediately order him to go back, but the alternative of having only a swaying rope as his support, after what he had suffered, notwithstanding the solid support of the beds, made him somewhat hesitant. After some minutes, he thought he had found the solution. I'll go on all fours, he thought, keeping under the rope, and from time to time I'll raise my hand to see whether I'm on the right track, this is just like stealing a car, ways and means can always be found. Suddenly, taking him by surprise, his conscience awoke and censured him bitterly for having allowed himself to steal a car from an unfortunate blind man. The fact that I'm in this situation now, he reasoned, isn't because I stole his car, it's because I accompanied him home, that was my big mistake. His conscience was in no mood for casuistic discussions, his reasons were simple and clear, A blind man is sacred, you don't steal from a blind man. Technically speaking, I didn't rob him, he wasn't carrying the car in his pocket, nor did I hold a gun to his head, the accused protested in his defence, Forget the sophisms, muttered his conscience, and get on your way.

The cold dawn air cooled his face. How well one breathes out here, he thought to himself. He had the impression that his leg was much less painful, but this did not surprise him, sometime before, and more than once, the same thing had happened. He was now outside the main door, he would soon be at the steps, That's going to be the most awkward bit, he thought, going down the steps head first. He raised one arm to check that the rope was there, and continued on. Just as he had foreseen, it was not easy to get from one step to the next, especially because of his leg which was no help to him, and the proof was not long in coming, when, in the middle of the steps, one of his hands having slipped, his body lurched to one side and was dragged along by the dead weight of his wretched leg. The pain came back instantly, as if someone were sawing, drilling, and hammering the wound, and even he was at a loss to explain how he prevented himself from crying out. For several long minutes, he remained prostrate, face down on the ground. A rapid gust of wind at ground level, left him shivering. He was wearing nothing but a shirt and his underpants. The wound was pressed against the ground, and he thought, It might get infected, a foolish thought, he was forgetting that he had been dragging his leg along the ground all the way from the ward, Well, it doesn't matter, they'll treat it before it turns infectious, he thought afterwards, to put his mind at rest, and he turned sideways to reach the rope more easily. He did not find it right away. He forgot that he had ended up in a vertical position in relation to the rope when he had rolled down the steps, but instinct told him that he should stay put. Then his reasoning guided him as he moved into a sitting position and then slowly back until his haunches made contact with the first step, and with a triumphant sense of victory he clutched the rough cord in his raised hand. Probably it was this same feeling that led him to discover almost immediately, a way of moving without his wound rubbing on the ground, by turning his back towards the main gate and sitting up and using his arms like crutches, as cripples used to do, he eased his seated body along in tiny stages. Backwards, yes, because in this case as in others, pulling was much easier than pushing. In this way, his leg suffered less, besides which the gentle slope of the forecourt going towards the gate was a great help. As for the rope, he was in no danger of losing it, he was almost touching it with his head. He wondered whether he would have much further to go before reaching the main gate, getting there on foot, better still on two feet was not the same as advancing backwards half a hand's-breadth inch by inch. Forgetting for an instant that he was blind, he turned his head as if to confirm how far he still had to go and found himself confronted by the same impenetrable whiteness. Could it be night, could it be day, he asked himself, well if it were day they would already have spotted me, besides, they had only delivered breakfast and that was many hours ago. He was surprised to discover the speed and accuracy of his reasoning and how logical he could be, he saw himself in a different light, a new man, and were it not for this damn leg he would swear he had never felt so well in his entire life. His lower back came up against the metal plate at the bottom of the main gate. He had arrived. Huddled inside the sentry box to protect himself from the cold, the guard on duty thought he had heard faint noises he could not identify, in any case he did not think they could have come from inside, it must have been a sudden rustling of the trees, a branch the wind had caused to brush against the railings. These were followed by another noise, but this time it was different, a bang, the sound of crashing to be more precise, which could not have been caused by the wind. Nervously the guard came out of his sentry box, his finger on the trigger of his automatic rifle, and looked towards the main gate. He could not see anything. The noise, however, was back, louder, as if someone were scratching their fingernails on a rough surface. The metal plate on the gate, he thought to himself. He was about to head for the field tent where the sergeant was sleeping, but held back at the thought that if he raised a false alarm he would be given an earful, sergeants do not like being disturbed when they are sleeping, even when there is some good reason. He looked back at the main gate and waited in a state of tension. Very slowly, between two vertical iron bars, like a ghost, a white face began to appear. The face of a blind man. Fear made the soldier's blood freeze, and fear drove him to aim his weapon and release a blast of gunfire at close range.

The noise of the blast immediately brought the soldiers, half dressed, from their tents. These were the soldiers from the detachment entrusted with guarding the mental asylum and its inmates. The sergeant was already on the scene, What the hell is going on, A blind man, a blind man, stuttered the soldier, Where, He was there and he pointed at the main gate with the butt of his weapon, I can see nothing there, He was there, I saw him. The soldiers had finished getting into their gear and were waiting in line, their rifles at the ready. Switch on the floodlight, the sergeant ordered. One of the soldiers got up on to the platform of the vehicle. Seconds later the blinding rays lit up the main gate and the front of the building. There's no one there, you fool, said the sergeant, and he was just about to deliver a few more choice insults in the same vein when he saw spreading out from under the gate, in that dazzling glare, a black puddle. You've finished him off, he said. Then, remembering the strict orders they had been given, he yelled, Get back, this is infectious. The soldiers drew back, terrified, but continued to watch the pool of blood that was slowly spreading in the gaps between the small cobblestones in the path. Do you think the man's dead, asked the sergeant, He must be, the shot struck him right in the face, replied the soldier, now pleased with the obvious demonstration of the accuracy of his aim. At that moment, another soldier shouted nervously, Sergeant, sergeant, look over there. Standing at the top of the steps, lit up by the white light coming from the searchlight, a number of blind internees could be seen, more than ten of them, Stay where you are, bellowed the sergeant, if you take another step, I'll blast the lot of you. At the windows of the buildings opposite, several people, woken up by the noise of gunshots, were looking out in terror. Then the sergeant shouted, Four of you come and fetch the body. Because they could neither see nor count, six blind men came forward. I said four, the sergeant bawled hysterically. The blind internees touched each other, then touched again, and two of them stayed behind. Holding on to the rope, the others began moving forward.

We must see if there's a spade or shovel or whatever around, something that can be used to dig, said the doctor. It was morning, with much effort they had brought the corpse into the inner courtyard, placed it on the ground amongst the litter and the dead leaves from the trees. Now they had to bury it. Only the doctor's wife knew the hideous state of the dead man's body, the face and skull blown to smithereens by the gunshots, three holes where bullets had penetrated the neck and the region of the breastbone. She also knew that in the entire building there was nothing that could be used to dig a grave. She had searched the parts of the asylum to which they had been confined and had found nothing apart from an iron bar. It would help but was not enough. And through the closed windows of the corridor that ran the full length of the wing reserved for those suspected of being infected, lower down on this side of the wall, she had seen the terrified faces of the people awaiting their turn, that inevitable moment when they would have to say to the others, I've gone blind, or when, if they were to try to conceal what had happened, some clumsy gesture might betray them, a movement of their head in search of shade, an unjustified stumble into someone sighted. All this the doctor also knew, what he had said was part of the deception they had both concocted, so that now his wife could say, And suppose we were to ask the soldiers to throw a shovel over the wall. A good idea, let's try, and everyone was agreed, only the girl with dark glasses expressed no opinion about this question of finding a spade or shovel, the only sounds coming from her meanwhile were tears and wailing, It was my fault, she sobbed, and it was true, no one could deny it, but it is also true, if this brings her any consolation, that if, before every action, we were to begin by weighing up the consequences, thinking about them in earnest, first the immediate consequences, then the probable, then the possible, then the imaginable ones, we should never move beyond the point where our first thought brought us to a halt. The good and the evil resulting from our words and deeds go on apportioning themselves, one assumes in a reasonably uniform and balanced way, throughout all the days to follow, including those endless days, when we shall not be here to find out, to congratulate ourselves or ask for pardon, indeed there are those who claim that this is the much-talked-of immortality, Possibly, but this man is dead and must be buried. Therefore the doctor and his wife went off to parley, the disconsolate girl with dark glasses said she was coming with them. Pricked by her conscience. No sooner did they appear at the main entrance than a soldier shouted, Halt, and as if afraid that this verbal command, however vigorous, might not be heeded, he fired into the air. Terrified, they retreated into the shadows of the hallway, behind the thick wooden panels of the open door. Then the doctor's wife advanced alone, from where she was standing she could watch the soldier's movements and take refuge in time, if necessary. We have nothing with which to bury the dead man, she said, we need a spade. At the main gate, but on the other side from where the blind man had fallen, another soldier appeared. He was a sergeant, but not the same one as before, What do you want, he shouted, We need a shovel or spade. There is no such thing here, on your way. We must bury the corpse, Don't bother about any burial, leave it there to rot, If we simply leave it lying there, the air will be infected, Then let it be infected and much good may it do you, Air circulates and moves around as much here as there. The relevance of her argument forced the soldier to reflect. He had come to replace the other sergeant, who had gone blind and been taken without delay to the quarters where the sick belonging to the army were interned. Needless to say, the air force and navy also had their own installations, but less extensive or important, the personnel of both forces being less numerous. The woman is right, reflected the sergeant, in a situation like this there is no doubt that one cannot be careful enough. As a safety measure, two soldiers equipped with gas masks, had already poured two large bottles of ammonia over the pool of blood, and the lingering fumes still brought tears to the soldiers' eyes and a stinging sensation to their throats and nostrils. The sergeant finally declared. I'll see what can be done, And what about our food, asked the doctor's wife, taking advantage of this opportunity to remind him, The food still hasn't arrived, In our wing alone there are more than fifty people, we're hungry, what you're sending us simply isn't enough, Supplying food is not the army's responsibility, Someone ought to be dealing with this problem, the Government undertook to feed us, Get back inside, I don't want to see anyone at this door, What about the spade, the doctor's wife insisted, but the sergeant had already gone. It was mid-morning when a voice came over the loudspeaker in the ward, Attention, attention, the internees brightened up, they thought this was an announcement about their food, but no, it was about the spade, Someone should come and fetch it, but not in a group, one person only should come forward, I'll go, for I've already spoken to them, said the doctor's wife. The moment she went through the main entrance door, she saw the spade. From the position and distance to where it had landed, closer to the gate than the steps, it must have been thrown over the fence, I mustn't forget that I'm supposed to be blind, the doctor's wife thought, Where is it, she asked, Go down the stairs and I'll guide you, replied the sergeant, you're doing fine, now keep going in the same direction, like so, like so, stop, turn slightly to the right, no, to the left, less, less than that, now forward, so long as you keep going, you'll come right up against it, shit, I told you not to change direction, cold, cold, you're getting warmer again, warmer still, right, now take a half turn and I'll guide you from there, I don't want you going round and round in circles and ending up at the gate, Don't you worry, she thought, from here I'll make straight for the door, after all, what does it matter, even if you were to suspect that I'm not blind, what do I care, you won't be coming in here to take me away. She slung the spade over her shoulder like a gravedigger on his way to work, and walked in the direction of the door without faltering for a moment, Did you see that, sergeant, exclaimed one of the soldiers, you would think she could see. The blind learn quickly how to find their way around, the sergeant explained confidently.

It was hard work digging a grave. The soil was hard, trampled down, there were tree roots just below the surface. The taxi-driver, the two policemen and the first blind man took it in turns to dig. Confronted by death, what is expected of nature is that rancour should lose its force and poison, it is true that people say that past hatreds die hard, and of this there is ample proof in literature and life, but the feeling here, deep down, as it were, was not hatred and, in no sense old, for how does the theft of a car compare with the life of the man who stole it, and especially given the miserable state of his corpse, for one does not need eyes to know that this face has neither nose nor mouth. They were unable to dig any deeper than about three feet. Had the dead man been fat, his belly would have been sticking out above ground level, but the thief was skinny, a real bag of bones, even skinnier after the fasting of recent days, the grave was big enough for two corpses his size. There were no prayers for the dead. We could have put a cross there, the girl with dark glasses reminded them, she spoke from remorse, but as far as anyone there was aware while alive, the deceased had never given a thought to God or religion, best to say nothing, if any other attitude is justified in the face of death, besides, bear in mind that making a cross is much less easy than it may seem, not to mention the little time it would last with all these blind people around who cannot see where they are treading. They returned to the ward. In the busier places, so long as it is not completely open, like the yard, the blind no longer lose their way, with one arm held out in front and several fingers moving like the antennae of insects, they can find their way everywhere, it is even probable that in the more gifted of the blind there soon develops what is referred to as frontal vision. Take the doctor's wife, for example, it is quite extraordinary how she manages to get around and orient herself through this veritable maze of rooms, nooks and corridors, how she knows precisely where to turn the corner, how she can come to a halt before a door and open it without a moment's hesitation, how she has no need to count the beds before reaching her own. At this moment she is seated on her husband's bed, she is talking to him, as usual in a low voice, one can see these are educated people, and they always have something to say to each other, they are not like the other married couple, the first blind man and his wife, after those first emotional moments on being reunited, they have scarcely spoken, in all probability, their present unhappiness outweighs their past love, with time they will get used to this situation. The one person who is forever complaining of feeling hungry is the boy with the squint, despite the fact that the girl with the dark glasses has practically taken the food from her own mouth to give him. Many hours have passed since he last asked about his mummy, but no doubt he will start to miss her again after having eaten, when his body finds itself released from the brute selfishness that stems from the simple, but pressing need to sustain itself. Whether because of what happened early that morning, or for reasons beyond our ken, the sad truth is that no containers were delivered at breakfast time. It is nearly time for lunch, almost one o'clock on the watch the doctor's wife has just furtively consulted, therefore it is not surprising that the impatience of their gastric juices has driven some of the blind internees, both from this wing and from the other, to go and wait in the hallway for the food to arrive, and this for two excellent reasons, the public one, on the part of some, because in this way they would gain time, the private one, on the part of others, because, as everyone knows, first come first served. In all, there were about ten blind internees listening for the noise of the outer gate when it was opened, for the footsteps of the soldiers who would deliver those blessed containers. In their turn, fearful of suddenly being stricken by blindness if they were to come into close contact with the blind waiting in the hallway, the contaminated internees from the left wing dare not leave, but several of them are peering through a gap in the door, anxiously awaiting their turn. Time passed. Tired of waiting, some of the blind internees had sat down on the ground, later two or three of them returned to their wards. Shortly afterwards, the unmistakable metallic creaking of the gate could be heard. In their excitement, the blind internees, pushing each other, began moving in the direction where, judging from the sounds outside, they imagined the door to be, but suddenly, overcome by a vague sense of disquiet that they would not have time to define or explain, they came to a halt and retreated in confusion, while the footsteps of the soldiers bringing their food and those of the armed escort accompanying them could already be heard quite clearly.

Still suffering from the shock of the tragic episode of the previous night, the soldiers who delivered the containers had agreed that they would not leave them within reach of the doors leading to the wings, as they had more or less done before, they would just dump them in the hallway, and retreat. Let them sort it out for themselves. The dazzle of the strong light from outside and the abrupt transition into the shadows of the hallway prevented them at first from seeing the group of blind internees. But they soon spotted them. Howling in terror, they dropped the containers on the ground and fled like madmen straight out of the door. The two soldiers forming the escort, who were waiting outside, reacted admirably in the face of danger. Mastering, God alone knows how and why, their legitimate fear, they advanced to the threshold of the door and emptied their magazines. The blind internees fell one on top of the other, and, as they fell, their bodies were still being riddled with bullets which was a sheer waste of ammunition, it all happened so incredibly slowly, one body, then another, it seemed they would never stop falling, as you sometimes see in films and on television. If we are still in an age when a soldier has to account for the bullets fired, they will swear on the flag that they acted in legitimate defence, as well as in defence of their unarmed comrades who were on a humanitarian mission and suddenly found themselves threatened and outnumbered by a group of blind internees. In a mad rush they retreated to the gate, covered by the rifles which the soldiers on patrol were pointing unsteadily between the railings as if the blind internees who had survived, were about to make a retaliatory attack. His face drained of colour, one of the soldiers who had fired, said nervously, You won't get me going back in there at any price. From one moment to the next, on this same day, when evening was falling, at the hour of changing guard, he became one more blind man among the other blind men, what saved him was that he belonged to the army, otherwise he would have remained there along with the blind internees, the companions of those whom he had shot dead, and God knows what they might have done to him. The sergeant's only comment was, It would have been better to let them die of hunger, when the beast dies, the poison dies with it. As we know, others had often said and thought the same, happily, some precious remnant of concern for humanity prompted him to add, From now on, we shall leave the containers at the halfway point, let them come and fetch them, we'll keep them under surveillance, and at the slightest suspicious movement, we fire. He headed for the command post, switched on the microphone and, putting the words together as best he could, calling to mind words he remembered hearing on vaguely comparable occasions, he announced, The army regrets having been forced to repress with weapons a seditious movement responsible for creating a situation of imminent risk, for which the army was neither directly nor indirectly to blame, and you are advised that from now on the internees will collect their food outside the building, and will suffer the consequences should there be any attempt to repeat the disruption that took place now and last night. He paused, uncertain how he should finish, he had forgotten his own words, he certainly had them, but could only repeat, We were not to blame, we were not to blame.

Inside the building, the blast of gunfire deafeningly echoing in the confined space of the hallway, had caused the utmost panic. At first it was thought that the soldiers were about to burst into the wards and shoot everything in sight, that the Government had changed its tactics, had opted for the whole-sale liquidation of the internees, some crawled under their beds, others, in sheer terror, did not move, some might have thought it was better so, better no health than too little, if a person has to go, let it be quick. The first to react were the contaminated internees. They had started to flee when the shooting broke out, but then the silence encouraged them to go back, and once again they headed for the door leading into the hallway. They saw the bodies lying in a heap, the blood wending its way sinuously on the tiled floor where it slowly spread, as if it were a living thing, and then the containers with food. Hunger drove them on, there stood that much desired sustenance, true it was intended for the blind, their own food was still on its way, in accordance with the regulations, but who cares about the regulations, no one can see us, the candle that lights the way burns brightest, as the ancients have continuously reminded us throughout the ages, and the ancients know about these things. Their hunger, however, had the strength only to take them three steps forward, reason intervened and warned them that for anybody imprudent enough to advance there was danger lurking in those lifeless bodies, above all, in that blood, who could tell what vapours, what emanations, what poisonous miasmas might not already be oozing forth from the open wounds of the corpses. They're dead, they can't do any harm, someone remarked, the intention was to reassure himself and others, but his words made matters worse, it was true that these blind internees were dead, that they could not move, see, could neither stir nor breathe, but who can say that this white blindness is not some spiritual malaise, and if we assume this to be the case, then the spirits of those blind casualties have never been as free as they are now, released from their bodies, and therefore free to do whatever they like, above all, to do evil, which, as everyone knows, has always been the easiest thing to do. But the containers of food, standing there exposed, immediately attracted their attention, such are the demands of the stomach, they heed nothing even when it is for their own good. From one of the containers leaked a white liquid which was slowly spreading towards the pool of blood, to all appearances it was milk, the colour unmistakable. More courageous, or simply more fatalistic, the distinction is not always easy to make, two of the contaminated internees stepped forward, and they were just about to lay their greedy hands on the first container when a group of blind internees appeared in the doorway leading to the other wing. The imagination can play such tricks, especially in morbid circumstances such as these, that for these two men who had gone on a foray, it was as if the dead had suddenly risen from the ground, as blind as before, no doubt, but much more dangerous, for almost certainly filled by a spirit of revenge. They prudently backed away in silence towards the entrance to their wing, perhaps the blind internees were beginning to take care of the corpses as charity and respect decreed, or, if not, they might leave behind without noticing one of the containers, however small, in fact there were not all that many contaminated internees there, perhaps the best solution would be to ask them, Please, take pity on us, at least leave a small container for us, after what has happened it is most likely that no more food will be delivered today. The blind moved as one would expect of the blind, groping their way, stumbling, dragging their feet, yet as if organised, they knew how to distribute tasks efficiently, some of them splashing about in the sticky blood and milk, began at once to withdraw and transport the corpses to the yard, others dealt with the eight containers, one by one, that had been dumped by the soldiers. Among the blind internees there was a woman who gave the impression of being everywhere at the same time, helping to load, acting as if she were guiding the men, something that was obviously impossible for a blind woman, and, whether by chance or intentionally, more than once she turned her head towards the wing where the contaminated were interned, as if she could see them or sense their presence. In a short time the hallway was empty, with no other traces than the huge bloodstain, and another small one alongside, white, from the milk that had spilled, apart from these only criss-crossing footprints in red or simply wet. Resigned, the contaminated internees closed the door and went in search of crumbs, they were so downhearted that one of them was on the point of saying, and this shows just how desperate they were, If we really have to end up blind, if that is our fate, we might as well move over into the other wing now, there at least we'll have something to eat, Perhaps the soldiers will still bring our rations, someone suggested, Have you ever been in the army, another asked him, No, Just as I thought.

Bearing in mind that the dead belonged to the one as much as the other, the occupants of the first and second wards gathered together in order to decide whether they should eat first and then bury the corpses, or the other way round. No one seemed interested in knowing who had died. Five of them had installed themselves in the second ward, difficult to say if they had already known each other, or if they did not, if they had the time and inclination to introduce themselves to each other and unburden their hearts. The doctor's wife could not remember having seen them when they arrived. The remaining four, yes, these she recognised, they had slept with her, in a manner of speaking, under the same roof, although this was all she knew about one of them, and how could she know more, a man with any self-respect does not go around discussing his private affairs with the first person he meets, such as having been in a hotel room where he made love to a girl with dark glasses, who, in her turn, if we mean her, has no idea that he has been interned here and that she is still so close to the man who was the cause of her seeing everything white. The taxi-driver and the two policemen were the other casualties, three robust fellows who could take care of themselves, whose professions meant, in different ways, looking after others, and in the end there they lie, cruelly mowed down in their prime and waiting for others to decide their fate. They will have to wait until those who survived have finished eating, not because of the usual egoism of the living, but because someone sensibly remembered that to bury nine corpses in that hard soil and with only one spade was a chore that would take until dinner-time at least. And since it would not be admissible that the volunteers endowed with good will should work while the others stuffed their bellies, it was decided to leave the corpses until later. The food arrived in individual portions, therefore easy to share out, that's yours, and yours, until there was no more. But the anxiety of some of the less fair-minded blind internees came to complicate what in normal circumstances would have been so straightforward, and although a serene and impartial judgment cautions us to admit that the excesses that took place had some justification, we need only remember, for example, that no one could know, at the outset, whether there would be enough food for everyone. In fact, it is fairly clear that it is not easy to count blind people or to distribute rations without eyes capable of seeing either the rations or the people. Moreover, some of the inmates from the second ward, with more than reprehensible dishonesty, tried to give the impression that there were more of them than there actually were. As always, this is where the presence of the doctor's wife proved to be useful. A few timely words have always managed to resolve problems that a verbose speech would only make worse. No less ill-intentioned and perverse were those who not only tried, but actually succeeded in receiving double rations. The doctor's wife was aware of this abuse, but thought it wise to say nothing. She could not even bear to think of the consequences that would ensue if it were to be discovered that she was not blind, at the very least she would find herself at the beck and call of everyone, at worst, she might become the slave of some of them. The idea, aired at the outset, that someone should assume responsibility for each ward, might have helped, who knows? to solve these difficulties and others, alas, more serious, on condition however, that the authority of the person in charge, undeniably fragile, undeniably precarious, undeniably called into question at every moment, should be clearly exercised for the benefit of all and as such be acknowledged by the majority. Unless we succeed in this, she thought, we shall end up murdering one another in here. She promised herself that she would discuss these delicate matters with her husband and went on sharing out the rations.

Some out of indolence, others because they had a delicate stomach, had no inclination to go and practise grave-digging just after they had eaten. Because of his profession, the doctor felt more responsible than the others, and when he said without much enthusiasm, Let's go and bury the corpses, there was not a single volunteer. Stretched out on their beds, the blind internees were interested only in being left in peace to digest their food, some fell asleep immediately, hardly surprising, after the frightening experience they had been through, the body, even though poorly nourished, abandoned itself to the slow workings of digestive chemistry. Later, as evening was drawing in, when, because of the progressive waning of natural light, the dim lamps appeared to gain some strength, showing at the same time, weak as they were, the little purpose they served, the doctor, accompanied by his wife, persuaded two men from his ward to accompany them to the compound, even if only to balance out the work that had to be done and separate the corpses that were already stiff, once it had been decided that each ward would bury its own dead. The advantage enjoyed by these blind men was what might be called the illusion of light. In fact, it made no difference to them whether it was day or night, the first light of dawn or the evening twilight, the silent hours of early morning or the bustling din of noon, these blind people were for ever surrounded by a resplendent whiteness, like the sun shining through mist. For the latter, blindness did not mean being plunged into banal darkness, but living inside a luminous halo. When the doctor let slip that they were going to separate the corpses, the first blind man, who was one of those who had agreed to help him, wanted to know how they would be able to recognise them, a logical question on the part of a blind man which left the doctor in some confusion. This time his wife thought it would be unwise to come to his assistance for fear of giving the game away. The doctor got out of the difficulty gracefully by the radical method of coming clean, that is to say, by acknowledging his mistake, People, he said, in the tone of voice of someone amused at his own expense, get so used to having eyes that they think they can use them when they no longer serve for anything, in fact, all we know is that there are four from our ward here, the taxi-driver, the two policemen, and one other who was with us, therefore the solution is to pick up four of these corpses at random, bury them with due respect, and in this way we fulfill our obligation. The first blind man agreed, his companion likewise, and once again, taking it in turn, they began digging graves. These helpers would never come to know, blind as they were, that, without exception, the corpses buried were precisely those of whom they had been speaking, nor need we mention the work done, seemingly at random, by the doctor, his hand guided by that of his wife, she would grab a leg or arm, and all he had to say was, This one. When they had already buried two corpses, there finally emerged from the ward, three men disposed to help, most likely they would have been less willing had someone told them that it was already the dead of night. Psychologically, even when a man is blind, we must acknowledge that there is a considerable difference between digging graves by the light of day and after the sun has gone down. The moment they were back in the ward, sweating, covered in earth, the sickly smell of decomposed flesh still in their nostrils, the voice over the loudspeaker repeated the usual instructions. There was no reference whatsoever to what had happened, no mention of gunfire or casualties shot at point-blank range. Warnings such as, To abandon the building without any authorisation will mean immediate death, or The internees will bury the corpses in the grounds without any formalities, now, thanks to the harsh experience of life, supreme mistress of all disciplines, these warnings took on real meaning, while the announcement that promised containers of food three times a day seemed grotesquely ironic or, worse, contemptuous. When the voice fell silent, the doctor, on his own, because he was getting to know every nook and cranny in the place, went to the door of the other ward to inform the inmates, We have buried our dead, Well, if you've buried some, you can bury the rest, replied a man's voice from within, The agreement was that each ward would bury its own dead, we counted four and buried them, That's fine, tomorrow we'll deal with those from here, said another masculine voice, and then in a different tone of voice, he asked, Has no more food turned up, No, replied the doctor, But the loudspeaker said three times a day, I doubt whether they are likely always to keep their promise, Then we'll have to ration the food that might arrive, said a woman's voice, That seems a good idea, if you like, we can talk about it tomorrow, Agreed, said the woman. The doctor was already on the point of leaving when the voice of the first man to speak could be heard, Who's giving the orders here, He paused, expecting to be given an answer, and it came from the same feminine voice, Unless we organise ourselves in earnest, hunger and fear will take over here, it is shameful that we didn't go with the others to bury the dead, Why don't you go and do the burying since you're so clever and sure of yourself, I cannot go alone but I'm prepared to help, There's no point in arguing, intervened another masculine voice, we'll settle this first thing in the morning. The doctor sighed, life together was going to be difficult. He was already heading back to his ward when he felt a pressing need to relieve himself. At the spot where he found himself, he was not sure that he would be able to find the lavatories, but he decided to take a chance. He was hoping that someone would at least have remembered to leave there the toilet paper which had been delivered with the containers of food. He got lost twice on the way and was in some distress because he was beginning to feel desperate and just when he could hold back no longer, he was finally able to take down his trousers and crouch over the open latrine. The stench choked him. He had the impression of having stepped on some soft pulp, the excrement of someone who had missed the hole of the latrine or who had decided to relieve himself without any consideration for others. He tried to imagine what the place must look like, for him it was all white, luminous, resplendent, he had no way of knowing whether the walls and ground were white and he came to the absurd conclusion that the light and whiteness there were giving off the awful stench. We shall go mad with horror, he thought. Then he tried to clean himself but there was no paper. He ran his hand over the wall behind him, where he expected to find the rolls of toilet paper or nails, where in the absence of anything better, any old scraps of paper had been stuck up. Nothing. He felt unhappy, disconsolate, more unfortunate than he could bear, crushed there, protecting his trousers which were brushing against that disgusting floor, blind, blind, blind, and, unable to control himself, he began to weep quietly. Fumbling, he took a few steps and bumped into the opposite wall. He stretched out one arm, then the other, and finally found a door. He could hear the shuffling footsteps of someone who must also have been looking for the lavatories, and who kept tripping, Where the hell are they? the person was muttering in a neutral voice, as if deep down, he was not all that interested in finding out. He passed close to the toilets without realising there was someone there, but no matter, the situation did not degenerate into indecency, if it could be called that, a man caught in an embarrassing situation, his clothes in disarray, at the last minute, moved by a disconcerting sense of shame, the doctor had pulled up his trousers. Then he lowered them, when he thought he was alone, but not in time, he knew he was dirty, dirtier than he could ever remember having been in his life. There are many ways of becoming an animal, he thought, this is just the first of them. However, he could not really complain, he still had someone who did not mind cleaning him.

Lying on their beds, the blind internees waited for sleep to take pity on their misery. Discreetly, as if there was some danger that others might see this distressing sight, the doctor's wife had helped her husband to clean himself as well as she could. There was now that sorrowful silence one finds in hospitals when the patients are asleep and suffer even as they sleep. Sitting up and alert, the doctor's wife looked at the beds, at the shadowy forms, the fixed pallor of a face, an arm that moved while dreaming. She wondered whether she would ever go blind like them, what inexplicable reasons had saved her from blindness so far. With a weary gesture, she raised her hands to draw back her hair, and thought, We're all going to stink to high heaven. At that moment sighs could be heard, moaning, tiny cries, muffled at first, sounds that seemed to be words, that ought to be words, but whose meaning got lost in the crescendo that transformed them into shouts and grunts and finally heavy, stertorous breathing. Someone protested at the far end of the ward. Pigs, they're like pigs. They were not pigs, only a blind man and a blind woman who probably knew nothing more about each other than this.

An empty belly wakes up early. Some of the blind internees opened their eyes when morning was still some way off, and in their case it was not so much because of hunger, but because their biological clock, or whatever you call it, was no longer working properly, they assumed it was daylight, then thought, I've overslept and soon realised that they were wrong, their fellow-inmates were snoring their heads off, there was no mistaking that. Now as we know from books, and even more so from personal experience, anyone who gets up early by inclination or has been forced to rise early out of necessity finds it intolerable that others should go on sleeping soundly, and with good reason in the case to which we are referring, for there is a marked difference between a blind person who is sleeping and a blind person who has opened his eyes to no purpose. These observations of a psychological nature, whose subtlety has no apparent relevance considering the extraordinary scale of the cataclysm which our narrative is struggling to relate, only serve to explain why all the blind internees were awake so early, some, as was said at the outset, were roused by the churning of their empty stomachs in need of food, others were dragged from their sleep by the nervous impatience of the early risers, who did not hesitate to make more noise than the inevitable and tolerable when people cohabit in barracks and wards. Here there are not only persons of discretion and good manners, but some real vulgarians who relieve themselves each morning by coughing up phlegm and passing wind without regard for anyone who might be present, and if truth be told, they behave just as badly for most of the day, making the atmosphere increasingly heavy, and there is nothing to be done, the only opening is the door, the windows cannot be reached they are so high.

Lying beside her husband, as close as possible given the narrowness of the bed, but also out of choice, how much it had cost them in the middle of the night to maintain some decorum, not to behave like those whom someone had referred to as pigs, the doctor's wife looked at her watch. It was twenty-three minutes past two. She took a closer look, saw that the second hand was not moving. She had forgotten to wind up the wretched watch, or wretched her, wretched me, for not even this simple task had she remembered to carry out after only three days of isolation. Unable to control herself, she burst into convulsive weeping, as if the worst of all disasters had suddenly befallen her. The doctor thought his wife had gone blind, that what he so greatly feared had finally happened, and, beside himself, was on the point of asking, Have you gone blind, when at the last minute he heard her whisper, No, no, it isn't that, it isn't that, and then in a drawn-out whisper, almost inaudible, both their heads under the blanket, How stupid of me, I forgot to wind my watch, and she went on sobbing, inconsolable. Getting up from her bed on the other side of the passageway, the girl with dark glasses moved in the direction of the sobbing with arms outstretched, You're upset, can I get you anything, she asked as she advanced, and touched the two bodies on the bed with her hands. Discretion demanded that she should withdraw immediately, and this certainly was the order that came from her brain, but her hands did not obey, they simply made more subtle contact, gently caressing the thick, warm blanket. Can I get you anything, the girl asked once more, and, by now she had removed her hands, raised them until they became lost in that sterile whiteness, helpless. Still sobbing, the doctor's wife got out of bed, embraced the girl and said, It's nothing, I just suddenly felt sad, If you who are so strong are becoming disheartened, then there really is no salvation for us, complained the girl. Calmer now, the doctor's wife thought, looking straight at her, The signs of conjunctivitis have almost gone, what a pity I cannot tell her, she would be pleased. Yes, in all probability she would be pleased, although any such satisfaction would be absurd, not so much because the girl was blind, but since all the others there were blind as well, what good would it do her to have beautiful bright eyes such as these if there is no one to see them. The doctor's wife said, We all have our moments of weakness, just as well that we are still capable of weeping, tears are often our salvation, there are times when we would die if we did not weep, There is no salvation for us, the girl with dark glasses repeated, Who can tell, this blindness is not like any other, it might disappear as suddenly as it came, It will come too late for those who have died, We all have to die, But not to be killed and I have killed someone, Don't blame yourself, it was a question of circumstances, here we are all guilty and innocent, much worse was the behaviour of the soldiers who are here to protect us, and even they can invoke the greatest of all excuses, fear, What if the wretched fellow did fondle me, he would be alive right now, and my body would be no different from what it is now, Think no more about it, rest, try to sleep. She accompanied the girl to her bed, Come now, get into bed, You're very kind, said the girl, then lowering her voice, I don't know what to do, it's almost time for my period and I haven't brought any sanitary napkins, Don't worry, I have some. The hands of the girl with dark glasses searched for somewhere to hold on to, but it was the doctor's wife who gently held them in her own hands, Rest, rest. The girl closed her eyes, remained like that for a minute, she might have fallen asleep were it not for the quarrel that suddenly erupted, someone had gone to the lavatory and on his return found his bed occupied, no harm was meant, the other fellow had got up for the same reason, they had passed each other on the way, and obviously it did not occur to either of them to say, Take care not to get into the wrong bed when you come back. Standing there, the doctor's wife watched the two blind men who were arguing, she noticed they made no gestures, that they barely moved their bodies, having quickly learned that only their voice and hearing now served any purpose, true, they had their arms, that they could fight, grapple, come to blows, as the saying goes, but a bed swapped by mistake was not worth so much fuss, if only all life's deceptions were like this one, and all they had to do was to come to some agreement, Number two is mine, yours is number three, let that be understood once and for all, Were it not for the fact that we're blind this mix-up would never have happened, You're right, our problem is that we're blind. The doctor's wife said to her husband, The whole world is right here.

Not quite all of it. The food, for example, was there on the outside and taking ages to arrive. From both wards, some men had gone to station themselves in the hallway, waiting for orders to come over the loudspeaker. They kept shuffling their feet, nervous and impatient. They knew that they would have to go out to the forecourt to fetch the containers which the soldiers, fulfilling their promise, would leave in the area between the main gate and the steps, and they feared that there might be some ploy or snare, How do we know that they won't start firing, After what they've done already, they're capable of anything, They are not to be trusted, You won't get me going out there, Nor me, Someone has to go if we want to eat, I don't know if it isn't better to die being shot than to die of hunger, I'm going, Me too, We don't all have to go, The soldiers might not like it, Or get worried and think we're trying to escape, that's probably why they shot the man with the injured leg, We've got to make up our minds, We can't be too careful, remember what happened yesterday, nine casualties no more no less, The soldiers were afraid of us, And I'm afraid of them, What I'd like to know is if they too go blind, Who's they, The soldiers, In my opinion they ought to be the first. They were all in agreement, yet without asking themselves why, and there was no one there to give them the one good reason, Because then they would not be able to aim their rifles. The time passed and passed, and the loudspeaker remained silent. Have you already tried to bury your dead, a blind man from the first ward asked for the want of something to say, Not yet, They're beginning to smell and infect everything around, Well let them infect everything and stink to high heaven, as far as I'm concerned, I've no intention of doing anything until I've eaten, as someone once said, first you eat then you wash the pan, That isn't the custom, your maxim is wrong, generally it is after burying their dead that the mourners eat and drink, With me it's the other way round. After a few minutes one of these blind men said, There's one thing that bothers me, What's that, How are we going to distribute the food, As we did before, we know how many we are, the rations are counted, everyone receives his share, it's the simplest and fairest way, But it didn't work, some internees were left without any food, And there were also those who got double rations, The distribution was badly organised, It will always be badly organised unless people show some respect and discipline, If only we had someone here who could see just a little, Well, he'd try coming up with some ruse in order to make sure he got the lion's share, As the saying goes, in the country of the blind, the one-eyed man is king, Forget about sayings, But this is not the same, Here not even the cross-eyed would be saved, As I see it, the best solution would be to share the food out in equal parts throughout the wards, then each internee can be self-sufficient, Who spoke, It was me, Who's me, Me, which ward are you from, From ward two, Who would have believed such cunning, since ward two has fewer patients such an arrangement would be to their advantage and they would get more to eat than us, since our ward is full, I was only trying to be helpful, the proverb also says that if the one who does the sharing out fails to get the better part, he's either a fool or a dullard, Shit, that's quite enough of proverbs, these sayings get on my nerves, What we should do is to take all the food to the refectory, each ward elects three of its inmates to do the sharing out, so that with six people counting there would be little danger of abuse and deception, And how are we to know that they are telling the truth when the others say how many there are in their ward, We're dealing with honest people, Is that a proverb too, No, that's me saying it, My dear fellow, I don't know about honest but we're certainly hungry.

As if it had been waiting all this time for the code word, some cue, an open sesame, the voice finally came over the loudspeaker, Attention, attention, the internees may come and collect their food, but be careful, if anyone gets too close to the gate they will receive a preliminary warning, and unless they turn back immediately, the second warning will be a bullet. The blind internees advanced slowly, some, more confident, towards the right where they thought they would find the door, the others, less sure of their ability to get their bearings, preferred to slide along the wall, in this way there was no possibility of mistaking the way, when they reached the corner all they had to do was to follow the wall at a right angle and there they would find the door. The hectoring voice over the loudspeaker impatiently repeated the summons. The change of tone, unmistakable even for those who had no reason to be suspicious, terrified the blind internees. One of them declared, I'm not budging from here, what they want to do is to catch us outside and then kill us all, I'm not moving either, said another, Nor me, chipped in a third. They were frozen to the spot, undecided, some wanted to go, but fear was getting the better of all of them. The voice came again, Unless within the next three minutes someone appears to collect the containers, we shall take them away. This threat failed to overcome their fear, only pushed it into the innermost caverns of their mind, like hunted animals that await an opportunity to attack. Each one trying to hide behind the other, the blind internees moved fearfully out on to the landing at the top of the steps. They could not see that the containers were not alongside the guide rope where they expected to find them, for they were not to know that the soldiers, out of fear of being contaminated, had refused to go anywhere near the rope which the blind internees were holding on to. The food containers were stacked up together, more or less at the spot where the doctor's wife had collected the spade. Come forward, come forward, ordered the sergeant. In some confusion, the blind internees tried to get into a line so as to advance in orderly fashion, but the sergeant bellowed at them, You won't find the containers there, let go of the rope, let go of it, move over to the right, *your* right, *your* right, fools, you don't need eyes to know which side you have your right hand. The warning was given just in time, some of the blind internees who were punctilious in these matters, had interpreted the order literally, if it was on the right, logically that would mean on the right of the person speaking, therefore they were trying to pass under the rope to go in search of the containers which were God knows where. In different circumstances, this grotesque spectacle would have caused the most restrained spectator to burst into howls of laughter, it was too funny for words, some of the blind internees advancing on all fours, their faces practically touching the ground as if they were pigs, one arm outstretched in mid-air, while others, perhaps afraid that the white space, without a roof to protect them, would swallow them up, clung desperately to the rope and listened attentively, expecting to hear at any minute that first exclamation of triumph once the containers were discovered. The soldiers would have liked to aim their weapons and, without compunction, shoot down those imbeciles moving before their eyes like lame crabs, waving their unsteady pincers in search of their missing leg. They knew what had been said in the barracks that morning by the regimental commander, that the problem of these blind internees could be resolved only by physically wiping out the lot of them, those already there and those still to come, without any phoney humanitarian considerations, his very words, just as one amputates a gangrenous limb in order to save the rest of the body, The rabies of a dead dog, he said, to illustrate the point, is cured by nature. For some of the soldiers, less sensitive to the beauties of figurative language, it was difficult to understand what a dog with rabies had to do with the blind, but the word of a regimental commander, once again figuratively speaking, is worth its weight in gold, no man rises to so high a rank in the army without being right in everything he thinks, says and does. A blind man had finally bumped into the containers and called out as he got hold of them, They're here, they're here, if this man were to recover his eyesight one day, he would certainly not announce the wonderful news with greater joy.

Within seconds, the others had pounced on the containers, a confusion of arms and legs, each man pulling a container towards his side and claiming priority, I'll carry it, no, I will. Those who were still holding on to the rope began to feel nervous, they now had something else to fear, that they might be excluded on account of their idleness or cowardice, when the food was shared out, Ah, you men refused to get down on the ground with your arse in the air and risk the danger of being shot, so nothing to eat for you, remember the proverb, nothing ventured nothing gained. Persuaded by these sententious words, one of the blind men let go of the rope and went, with arms outstretched, in the direction of the uproar, They're not going to leave me out, but suddenly the voices fell silent and there was only the noise of people crawling on the ground, muffled interjections, a dispersed and confused mass of sounds coming from everywhere and nowhere. He paused, undecided, tried to go back to the security of the rope, but he had lost his sense of direction, there are no stars in his white sky, and what could now be heard was the sergeant's voice as it ordered those arguing over the containers to get back to the steps, for what he was saying could have been meant only for them, to arrive where you want to be, everything depends on where you are. There were no longer any blind internees holding on to the rope, all they had to do was to return the way they had come, and now they were waiting at the top of the steps for the others to arrive. The blind man who had lost his way did not dare to move from where he was. In a state of anguish, he let out a loud cry, Please, help me, unaware that the soldiers had their rifles trained on him as they waited for him to tread on that invisible line dividing life from death. Are you going to stay there all day, you blind bat, asked the sergeant, in a somewhat nervous voice, the truth being that he did not share the opinion of his commander, Who can guarantee that the same fate won't come knocking at the door tomorrow, as for the soldiers it is well known that they need only to be given an order and they kill, to be given another order and they die, You will shoot only when I say so, the sergeant shouted. These words made the blind man realise that his life was in danger. He fell to his knees and beseeched them, Please help me, tell me where I have to go, Keep on walking, blind man, keep on walking this way, a soldier called from beyond in a tone of false camaraderie, the blind man got up, took three paces, then suddenly came to another halt, the tense of the verb aroused his suspicion, keep on walking this way is not the same as keep going, keep on walking this way tells you that this way, this very way, in this direction, you will arrive where you are being summoned, only to come up against the bullet that will replace one form of blindness with another. This initiative, which we might well describe as criminal, was taken by a soldier of disreputable character, whom the sergeant immediately rebuked with two sharp commands given successively, Halt, Half turn, followed by a severe call to order directed at this disobedient fellow, who to all appearances belonged to that class of people who are not to be trusted with a rifle. Encouraged by the sergeant's kind intervention, the blind internees who had reached the top of the steps suddenly made a tremendous racket which served as a magnetic pole for the blind man who had lost his way. Now more sure of himself, he advanced in a straight line, Keep on shouting, keep on shouting, he beseeched them, while the other blind internees applauded as if they were watching someone complete a long, dynamic but exhausting sprint. He was given a rapturous welcome, the least they could do, in the face of adversity, whether proven or foreseeable, you know who your friends are.

This camaraderie did not last long. Taking advantage of the uproar, some of the blind internees had sneaked off with a number of containers, as many as they could carry, a patently disloyal way of forestalling any hypothetical injustices in the distribution. Those of good faith, who are always to be found no matter what people may say, protested with indignation, that they couldn't live like this, If we cannot trust each other, where are we going to end up? some asked rhetorically, although with full justification, What these rogues are asking for is a good hiding, threatened others, they had not asked for any such thing, but everyone understood what those words meant, an inaccurate expression that can be tolerated only because it is so very apt. Already gathered in the hallway, the blind internees came to an agreement, this being the most practical way of resolving the first part of the difficult situation in which they found themselves, that they would distribute the remaining containers equally between the two wards, fortunately an even number, and set up a committee, also on an equal basis, to carry out an investigation with a view to recovering the missing, that is to say, stolen containers. They wasted some time in debate, as was becoming their habit, the before and the after, that is to say, whether they should eat first and then investigate, or the other way round, the prevailing opinion being that, taking into account all the hours of enforced fasting they had spent, it would be more convenient to start by satisfying their stomachs and then proceeding with their inquiries, And don't forget that you have to bury your dead, said someone from the first ward, We haven't killed them yet and you want us to bury them, replied one witty fellow, amusing himself with this play on words. Everyone laughed. However they were soon to discover that the culprits were not to be found in the wards. At the doors of both wards, waiting for their food to arrive, the blind internees claimed to have heard passing along the corridors people who seemed to be in a great hurry, but no one had entered the wards, much less carrying containers of food, that they could swear to. Someone remembered that the safest way of identifying these fellows would be if they were all to return to their respective beds, obviously those that remained unoccupied must belong to the thieves, so all they had to do was to wait until they returned from wherever they had been hiding and licking their chops and then pounce on them, so that they might learn to respect the sacred principle of collective property. To proceed with this plan, however opportune and in keeping with a deep-seated sense of justice, had one serious disadvantage insofar as it would mean postponing, no one could foresee for how long, that much desired breakfast, already gone cold. Let's eat first, suggested one of the blind men, and the majority agreed that it was better that they should eat first. Alas, only the little that had remained after that infamous theft. At this hour, in some hiding place amongst these old and dilapidated buildings, the thieves must be gorging themselves on double and triple rations that unexpectedly seemed to have improved, consisting of coffee with milk, cold in fact, biscuits and bread with margarine, while decent folk had to content themselves with two or three times less, and not even that. Outside the loudspeaker could be heard summoning the contagious to fetch their food rations, the sound also reached some of the internees in the first wing, as they were sadly chewing on water biscuits. One of the blind men, undoubtedly influenced by the unwholesome atmosphere left by the theft of food, had an idea, If we were to wait in the hallway, they would get the fright of their lives just to see us there, they might even drop the odd container, but the doctor said he did not think this would be right, it would be an injustice to punish those without blame. When they had all finished eating, the doctor's wife and the girl with dark glasses carried the cardboard containers into the yard, the empty flasks of milk and coffee, the paper cups, in a word, everything that could not be eaten. We must burn the rubbish, the doctor's wife then suggested, and get rid of these horrible flies.

Seated on their respective beds, the blind internees settled down to wait for the pack of thieves to return, Thieving dogs, that's what they are, commented a rough voice, unaware that he was responding to a reminiscence of someone who is not to blame for not knowing how to say things in any other manner. But the scoundrels did not appear, they must have suspected something, suspicions no doubt raised by some astute fellow amongst them like the one here who suggested giving them a good hiding. The minutes went by, several of the blind men had stretched out, some were already asleep. For this, my friends, is what it means to eat and sleep. All things considered, things could be worse. So long as they go on supplying us with food, for we cannot live without it, this is like being in a hotel. By contrast, what a torment it would be for a blind man out there in the city, yes, a real torment. Stumbling through the streets, everyone fleeing at the very sight of him, his family in a panic, terrified of approaching him, a mother's love, a child's love, a myth, they would probably treat me just as I am treated in this place, lock me up in a room and, if I was very lucky, leave a plate outside the door. Looking at the situation objectively, without preconceptions or resentments which always cloud our reasoning, it had to be acknowledged that the authorities had shown great vision when they decided to unite the blind with the blind, each with his own, which is a wise rule for those who have to live together, like lepers, and there can be no doubt that the doctor there at the far end of the ward is right when he says that we must organise ourselves, the question, in fact, is one of organisation, first the food, then the organisation, both are indispensable for life, to choose a number of reliable men and women and put them in charge, to establish approved rules for our co-existence here in the ward, simple things, like sweeping the floor, tidying up and washing, we've nothing to complain about there, they have even provided us with soap and detergent, making sure our beds are always made, the important thing is not to lose our self-respect, to avoid any conflict with the soldiers who are only doing their duty by keeping us under guard, we do not want any more casualties, asking around if there is anyone willing to entertain us in the evening with stories, fables, anecdotes, whatever, just think how fortunate we would be if someone knew the Bible by heart, we could repeat everything since the creation of the world, the important thing is that we should listen to one another, pity we haven't a radio, music has always been a great distraction, and we could follow the news bulletins, for example, if a cure were to be discovered for our illness, how we should rejoice.

Then the inevitable happened. They heard shots being fired in the street, They're coming to kill us, someone shouted, Calm down, said the doctor, we must be logical, if they wanted to kill us, they would come here to shoot us, not outside. The doctor was right, it was the sergeant who had given the order to shoot in the air, not some soldier who had suddenly been struck blind when his finger was on the trigger, clearly there was no other way of controlling and intimidating the new internees as they stumbled from the vans, the Ministry of Health had informed the Ministry of Defence, We're despatching four van-loads, And how many does that make, About two hundred internees, Where are all these people going to be accommodated, the wards reserved for the blind internees are the three in the wing on the right, according to the information we've been given, the total capacity is one hundred and twenty, and there are already some sixty to seventy internees inside, minus a dozen or so whom we were obliged to kill, There is one solution, open up all the wards, That would mean the contaminated coming into direct contact with those who are blind, In all probability, sooner or later, the former will also go blind, besides, the situation being as it is, I suppose we'll all be contaminated, there cannot be a single person who has not been within sight of a blind man, If a blind man cannot see, I ask myself, how can he transmit this disease through his sight, General, this must be the most logical illness in the world, the eye that is blind transmits the blindness to the eye that sees, what could be simpler, We have a colonel here who believes the solution would be to shoot the blind as soon as they appear, Corpses instead of blind men would scarcely improve the situation, To be blind is not the same as being dead, Yes, but to be dead is to be blind, So there are going to be about two hundred of them, Yes, And what shall we do with the taxi-drivers, Put them inside as well. That same day, in the late afternoon, the Ministry of Defence contacted the Ministry of Health, Would you like to hear the latest news, that colonel we mentioned earlier has gone blind, It'll be interesting to see what he thinks of that bright idea of his now, He already thought, he shot himself in the head, Now that's what I call a consistent attitude, The army is always ready to set an example.

The gate had been opened wide. In keeping with barracks routine, the sergeant ordered that a column should be formed five deep, but the blind internees were unable to get the numbers right, sometimes they were more than five, at other times less, and they all ended up by crowding around the entrance, like the civilians they were, without any sense of order, they did not even remember to send the women and children ahead, as in other shipwrecks. It has to be said before we forget, that not all of the gunshots had been fired in the air, one of the van-drivers had refused to go with the blind internees, he protested that he could see perfectly well, the outcome, three seconds later, was to prove the point made by the Ministry of Health when it decreed that to be dead is to be blind. The sergeant gave the aforementioned orders, Keep going, there's a stairway with six steps, when you get there, go slowly up the steps, if anyone trips, who knows what will happen, the only recommendation overlooked was that they should follow the rope, but clearly if they had used it they would have taken forever to enter, Listen, cautioned the sergeant, his mind at rest because all of them were already inside the gate, there are three wards on the right and three on the left, each ward has forty beds, families should stay together, avoid crowding, wait at the entrance and ask those who are already interned for assistance, everything is going to be all right, settle in and keep calm, keep calm, your food will be delivered later.

It would not be right to imagine that these blind people, in such great numbers, proceed like lambs to the slaughter, bleating as is their wont, somewhat crowded, it is true, yet that is how they had always existed, cheek by jowl, mingling breaths and smells, There are some here who cannot stop crying, others who are shouting in fear or rage, others who are cursing, some-one uttered a terrible, futile threat, If I get my hands on you, presumably he was referring to the soldiers, I'll gouge your eyes out. Inevitably, the first internees to reach the stairway had to probe with one foot, the height and depth of the steps, the pres-sure of those coming from behind knocked two or three of those in front to the ground, fortunately nothing more serious occurred, nothing except a few grazed shins, the sergeant's ad-vice had proved to be a blessing. A number of the new arrivals had already entered the hallway, but two hundred persons can-not be expected to sort themselves out all that easily, moreover blind and without a guide, this painful situation being made even worse by the fact that we are in an old building and badly designed at that, it is not enough for a sergeant who knows only about military affairs to say, there are three wards on each side, you have to know what it's like inside, doorways so narrow that they look more like bottlenecks, corridors as crazy as the other inmates of the asylum, opening for no clear reason and closing who knows where, and no one is ever likely to find out. Instinctively, the vanguard of blind internees had divided into two columns, moving on both sides along the walls in search of a door they might enter, a safe method, undoubtedly, assuming there are no items of furniture blocking the way. Sooner or later, with know-how and patience, the new inmates will settle in, but not before the latest battle has been won between the first lines of the column on the left and the contaminated confined to that side. It was only to be expected. There was an agreement, there was even a regulation drawn up by the Ministry of Health, that this wing would be reserved for the contaminated, and if it was true that it could be foreseen that in all likelihood, every one of them would end up blind, it was also true, in terms of pure logic, that until they became blind there was no guarantee that they were fated to blindness. There is then a person sitting peacefully at home, confident that at least in his case all will turn out well, when suddenly he sees coming directly towards him a howling mob of the people he most fears. At first, the contaminated thought this was a group of inmates like themselves, only more numerous, but the deception was short-lived, these people were blind all right, You can't come in here, this wing is ours, it isn't for the blind, you belong to the wing on the other side, shouted those on guard at the door. Some of the blind internees tried to do a turnaround and find another entrance, they didn't care if they went left or right, but the mass of those who continued to flock in from outside, jostled them relentlessly. The contaminated defended the door with punches and kicks, the blind retaliated as best they could, they could not see their adversaries, but knew where the blows were coming from. Two hundred people could not get into the hallway, or anything like that number, so it was not long before the door leading to the courtyard, despite being fairly wide, was completely blocked, as if obstructed by a plug, they could go neither backwards nor forwards, those who were inside, crushed

and flattened, tried to protect themselves by kicking and elbow-
ing their neighbours, who were suffocating, cries could be
heard, blind children were sobbing, blind mothers were fainting, while the vast crowd that had been unable to enter pushed
even harder, terrified by the bellowing of the soldiers, who
could not understand why those idiots had not gone through.
There was one terrible moment of violent backsurge as people
struggled to extricate themselves from the confusion, from the
imminent danger of being crushed, let us put ourselves in the
place of the soldiers, suddenly they see a considerable number
of those who had entered come hurtling out, they immediately
thought the worst, that the new arrivals were about to turn
back, let us remember the precedents, there might well have
been a massacre. Fortunately, the sergeant was once more equal
to the crisis, he himself fired into the air, simply to attract attention, and shouted over the loudspeaker, Calm down, those
on the steps should draw back a little, clear the way, stop pushing and try to help each other. That was asking too much, the
struggle inside continued, but the hallway gradually emptied
thanks to a much greater number of blind internees moving to
the door of the right wing, there they were received by blind inmates who were happy to direct them to the third ward, so far
free, or to the beds in the second ward which were still unoccupied. For one moment it looked as if the battle would be resolved in favour of the contaminated, not because they were
stronger and had more sight, but because the blind internees,
having perceived that the entrance on the other side was less en-
cumbered, broke off all contacts, as the sergeant would say in
his discussions about strategy and basic military tactics. However, the triumph of the defenders was of short duration. From
the door of the right wing came voices announcing that there
was no more room, that all the wards were full, there were even
some blind internees still being pushed into the hallway, precisely
at that moment when, once the human stopper up until then
blocking the main entrance dispersed, once the considerable
number of blind internees who were outside, were able to advance and take shelter under the roof where, safe from the

threats of the soldiers, they would live. The result of these two displacements, practically simultaneous, was to rekindle the struggle at the entrance of the wing on the left-hand side, once again blows were exchanged, once more there were shouts, and, as if this were not enough, in their confusion some of the bewildered blind internees, who had found and forced open the hallway door leading directly into the inner courtyard, cried out that there were corpses out there. Imagine their horror. They withdrew as best they could, There are corpses out there, they repeated, as if they would be the next to die, and, within a second, the hallway was once more the raging whirlpool it had been at its worst, then, in a sudden and desperate impulse, the human mass swerved towards the wing on the left, carrying all before it, the resistance of the contaminated broken, many of them no longer merely contaminated, others, running like madmen, were still trying to escape their black destiny. They ran in vain. One after the other they were stricken with blindness, their eyes suddenly drowned in that hideous white tide inundating the corridors, the wards, the entire space. Out there in the hallway, in the yard, the blind internees, helpless, some badly bruised from the blows, others from being trampled, dragged themselves along, most of them were elderly, many women and children, beings with few or no defences, and it was nothing short of a miracle that there were not more corpses in need of burial. Scattered on the ground, apart from some shoes that had lost their feet, lie bags, suitcases, baskets, each individual's bit of wealth, lost for ever, anyone coming across these objects will insist that what he is carrying is his.

An old man with a black patch over one eye, came in from the yard. He, too, had either lost his luggage or had not brought any. He had been the first to stumble over the corpses, but he did not cry out. He remained beside them and waited for peace and silence to be restored. He waited for an hour. Now it is his turn to seek shelter. Slowly, with his arms outstretched, he searched for the way. He found the door of the first ward on the right-hand side, heard voices coming from within, then asked, Any chance of a bed here.

The arrival of so many blind people appeared to have brought at least one advantage, or, rather, two advantages, the first of these being of a psychological nature, as it were, for there is a vast difference between waiting for new inmates to turn up at any minute, and realising that the building is completely full at last, that from now on it will be possible to establish and maintain stable and lasting relations with one's neighbours, without the disturbances there have been up until now, because of the constant interruptions and interventions by the new arrivals which obliged us to be for ever reconstituting the channels of communication. The second advantage, of a practical, direct and substantial nature, was that the authorities outside, both civilian and military, had understood that it was one thing to provide food for two or three dozen people, more or less tolerant, more or less prepared, because of their small number, to resign themselves to occasional mistakes or delays in the delivery of food, and quite another to be faced with the sudden and complex responsibility of feeding two hundred and forty human beings of every type, background and temperament. Two hundred and forty, take note, and that is just a manner of speaking, for there are at least twenty blind internees who have not managed to find a bed and are sleeping on the floor. In any case, it has to be recognised that thirty persons being fed on rations meant for ten is not the same as sharing out to two hundred and sixty, food intended for two hundred and forty. The difference is almost imperceptible. Now then, it was the conscious assumption of this increased responsibility, and perhaps, a hypothesis not to be disregarded, the fear that further disturbances might break out, that determined a change of procedure on the part of the authorities, in the sense of giving orders that the food should be delivered on time and in the right quantity. Obviously, after the struggle, in every respect lamentable, that we had to witness, accommodating so many blind internees was not going to be easy or free of conflict, we need only remember those poor contaminated creatures who before could still see and now see nothing, of the separated couples and their lost children, of the discomfort of those who had been trampled and knocked down, some of them twice or three times, of those who are going around in search of their cherished possessions without finding them, one would have to be completely insensitive to forget, as if it were nothing, the misfortunes of these poor people. However, it cannot be denied that the announcement that lunch was about to be delivered was like a consoling balm for everyone. And if it is undeniable that, given the lack of adequate organisation for this operation or of any authority capable of imposing the necessary discipline, the collection of such large quantities of food and its distribution to feed so many mouths led to further misunderstandings, we must concede that the atmosphere changed considerably for the better, when throughout that ancient asylum there was nothing to be heard except the noise of two hundred and sixty mouths masticating. Who is going to clean up this mess afterwards is a question so far unanswered, only in the late afternoon will the voice on the loudspeaker repeat the rules of orderly conduct that must be observed for the good of all, and then it will become clear with what degree of respect the new arrivals treat these rules. It is no small thing that the inmates of the second ward in the right wing have decided, at long last, to bury their dead, at least we shall be rid of that particular stench, the smell of the living, however fetid, will be easier to get used to.

As for the first ward, perhaps because it was the oldest and therefore most established in the process and pursuit of adaptation to the state of blindness, a quarter of an hour after its inmates had finished eating, there was not so much as a scrap of dirty paper on the floor, a forgotten plate or dripping receptacle. Everything had been gathered up, the smaller objects placed inside the larger ones, the dirtiest of them placed inside those that were less dirty, as any rationalised regulation of hygiene would demand, as attentive to the greatest efficiency possible in gathering up leftovers and litter, as to the economy of effort needed to carry out this task. The state of mind which perforce will have to determine social conduct of this nature cannot be improvised nor does it come about spontaneously. In the case under scrutiny, the pedagogical approach of the blind woman at the far end of the ward seems to have had a decisive influence, that woman married to the ophthalmologist, who has never tired of telling us, If we cannot live entirely like human beings, at least let us do everything in our power not to live entirely like animals, words she repeated so often that the rest of the ward ended up by transforming her advice into a maxim, a dictum, into a doctrine, a rule of life, words which deep down were so simple and elementary, probably it was just that state of mind, propitious to any understanding of needs and circumstances, that contributed, even if only in a minor way to the warm welcome the old man with the black eyepatch found there when he peered through the door and asked those inside, Any chance of a bed here. By a happy coincidence, clearly indicative of future consequences, there was a bed, the only one, and it is anyone's guess how it survived, as it were, the invasion, in that bed the car-thief had suffered unspeakable pain, perhaps that is why it had retained an aura of suffering that kept people at a distance. These are the workings of destiny, arcane mysteries, and this coincidence was not the first, far from it, we need only observe that all the eye-patients who happened to be in the surgery when the first blind man appeared there have ended up in this ward, and even then it was thought that the situation would go no further, In a low voice, as always, so that no one would suspect the secret of her presence there, the doctor's wife whispered into her husband's ear, Perhaps he was also one of your patients, he is an elderly man, bald, with white hair, and he has a black patch over one eye, I remember you telling me about him, Which eye, The left, It must be him. The doctor advanced to the passageway and said, slightly raising his voice, I'd like to touch the person who has just joined us, I would ask him to make his way in this direction and I shall make my way towards him. They bumped into each other midway, fingers touching fingers, like two ants that recognise each other from the manoeuvring of their antennae, but this won't be the case here, the doctor asked his permission, ran his hands over the old man's face, and quickly found the patch. There is no doubt, here is the one person who was missing here, the patient with the black patch, he exclaimed, What do you mean, who are you, asked the old man, I am, or rather I was your ophthalmologist, do you remember, we were agreeing on a date for your cataract operation, How did you recognise me, Above all, by your voice, the voice is the sight of the person who cannot see, Yes, the voice, I'm also beginning to recognise yours, who would have thought it, doctor, now there's no need for an operation, If there is a cure for this, we will both need it, I remember you telling me, doctor, that after my operation I would no longer recognise the world in which I was living, we now know how right you were, When did you turn blind, Last night, And they've brought you here already, The panic out there is such that it won't be long before they start killing people off the moment they know they have gone blind, Here they have already eliminated ten, said a man's voice, I found them, the old man with the black eyepatch simply said, They were from the other ward, we buried our dead at once, added the same voice, as if concluding a report. The girl with dark glasses had approached, Do you remember me, I was wearing dark glasses, I remember you well, despite my cataract, I remember that you were very pretty, the girl smiled, Thank you, she said, and went back to her place. From there, she called out, The little boy is here too, I want my mummy, the boy's voice could be heard saying, as if worn out from some remote and useless weeping. And I was the first to go blind, said the first blind man, and I'm here with my wife, And I'm the girl from the surgery, said the girl from the surgery. The doctor's wife said, It only remains for me to introduce myself, and she said who she was. Then the old man, as if to repay the welcome, announced, I have a radio, A radio, exclaimed the girl with dark glasses as she clapped her hands, music, how nice, Yes, but it's a small radio, with batteries, and batteries do not last forever, the old man reminded her, Don't tell me we shall be cooped up here forever, said the first blind man, Forever, no, forever is always far too long a time, We'll be able to listen to the news, the doctor observed, And a little music, insisted the girl with dark glasses, Not everyone likes the same music, but we're all certainly interested in knowing what things are like outside, it would be better to save the radio for that, I agree, said the old man with the black eyepatch. He took the tiny radio from his jacket pocket and switched it on. He began searching for the different stations, but his hand was still too unsteady to tune into one wavelength, and to begin with all that could be heard were intermittent noises, fragments of music and words, at last his hand grew steadier, the music became recognisable, Leave it there for a bit, pleaded the girl with dark glasses, the words got clearer, That isn't the news, said the doctor's wife, and then, as if an idea had suddenly struck her, What time is it, she asked, but she knew that no one there could tell her. The tuning knob continued to extract noises from the tiny box, then it settled down, it was a song, a song of no significance, but the blind internees slowly began gathering round, without pushing, they stopped the moment they felt a presence before them and there they remained, listening, their eyes wide open tuned in the direction of the voice that was singing, some were crying, as probably only the blind can cry, the tears simply flowing as from a fountain. The song came to an end, the announcer said, At the third stroke it will be four o'clock. One of the blind women asked, laughing, Four in the afternoon or four in the morning, and it was as if her laughter hurt her. Furtively, the doctor's wife adjusted her watch and wound it up, it was four in the afternoon, although, to tell the truth, a watch is unconcerned, it goes from one to twelve, the rest are just ideas in the human mind. What's that faint sound, asked the girl with dark glasses, it sounded like, It was me, I heard them say on the radio that it was four o'clock and I wound up my watch, it was one of those automatic movements we so often make, anticipated the doctor's wife. Then she thought that it had not been worth putting herself at risk like that, all she had to do was to glance at the wrist-watches of the blind who had arrived that day, one of them must have a watch in working order. The old man with the black eyepatch had one, as she noticed just that moment, and the time on his watch was correct. Then the doctor asked, Tell us what the situation is like out there. The old man with the black eyepatch said, Of course, but I'd better sit, I'm dead on my feet. Three or four to a bed, keeping each other company on this occasion, the blind internees settled down as best they could, they fell silent, and then the old man with the black eyepatch told them what he knew, what he had seen with his own eyes when he could still see, what he had overheard during the few days that elapsed between the start of the epidemic and his own blindness.

In the first twenty-four hours, he said, if the rumour going round was true, there were hundreds of cases, all alike, all showing the same symptoms, all instantaneous, the disconcerting absence of lesions, the resplendent whiteness of their field of vision, no pain either before or after. On the second day there was talk of some reduction in the number of new cases, it went from hundreds to dozens and this led the Government to announce at once that it was reasonable to suppose that the situation would soon be under control. From this point onwards, apart from a few inevitable comments, the story of the old man with the black eyepatch will no longer be followed to the letter, being replaced by a reorganised version of his discourse, re-evaluated in the light of a correct and more appropriate vocabulary. The reason for this previously unforeseen change is the rather formal controlled language, used by the narrator, which almost disqualifies him as a complementary reporter, however important he may be, because without him we would have no way of knowing what happened in the outside world, as a complementary reporter, as we were saying, of these extraordinary events, when as we know the description of any facts can only gain with the rigour and suitability of the terms used. Returning to the matter in hand, the Government therefore ruled out the originally formulated hypothesis that the country was being swept by an epidemic without precedent, provoked by some morbid as yet unidentified agent that took effect instantaneously and was marked by a complete absence of any previous signs of incubation or latency. Instead, they said, that in accordance with the latest scientific opinion and the consequent and updated administrative interpretation, they were dealing with an accidental and unfortunate temporary concurrence of circumstances, also as yet unverified, in whose pathogenic development it was possible, the Government's communiqué emphasised, starting from the analysis of the available data, to detect the proximity of a clear curve of resolution and signs that it was on the wane. A television commentator came up with an apt metaphor when he compared the epidemic, or whatever it might be, to an arrow shot into the air, which upon reaching its highest point, pauses for a moment as if suspended, and then begins to trace its obligatory descending curve, which, God willing, and with this invocation the commentator returned to the triviality of human discourse and to the so-called epidemic, gravity tending to increase the speed of it, until this terrible nightmare tormenting us finally disappears, these were words that appeared constantly in the media, and always concluded by formulating the pious wish that the unfortunate people who had become blind might soon recover their sight, promising them meanwhile, the solidarity of society as a whole, both official and private. In some remote past, similar arguments and metaphors had been translated by the intrepid optimism of the common people into sayings such as, Nothing lasts forever, be it good or bad, the excellent maxims of one who has had time to learn from the ups and downs of life and fortune, and which, transported into the land of the blind, should be read as follows, Yesterday we could see, today we can't, tomorrow we shall see again, with a slight interrogatory note on the third and final line of the phrase, as if prudence, at the last moment, had decided, just in case, to add a touch of a doubt to the hopeful conclusion.

Sadly, the futility of such hopes soon became manifest, the Government's expectations and the predictions of the scientific community simply sank without trace. Blindness was spreading, not like a sudden tide flooding everything and carrying all before it, but like an insidious infiltration of a thousand and one turbulent rivulets which, having slowly drenched the earth, suddenly submerge it completely. Faced with this social catastrophe, already on the point of taking the bit between their teeth, the authorities hastily organised medical conferences, especially those bringing together ophthalmologists and neurologists. Because of the time it would inevitably take to organise, a congress that some had called for was never convened, but in compensation there were colloquia, seminars, round-table discussions, some open to the public, others held behind closed doors. The overall effect of the patent futility of the debates and the occurrence of certain cases of sudden blindness during the sessions, with the speaker calling out, I'm blind, I'm blind, prompted almost all the newspapers, the radio and television, to lose interest in such initiatives, apart from the discreet and, in every sense, laudable behaviour of certain organs of communication which, living off sensational stories of every kind, off the fortunes and misfortunes of others, were not prepared to miss an opportunity to report live, with all the drama the situation warranted, the sudden blindness, for example, of a professor of ophthalmology.

The proof of the progressive deterioration of morale in general was provided by the Government itself, its strategy changing twice within the space of some six days. To begin with, the Government was confident that it was possible to circumscribe the disease by confining the blind and the contaminated within specific areas, such as the asylum in which we find ourselves. Then the inexorable rise in the number of cases of blindness led some influential members of the Government, fearful that the official initiative would not suffice for the task in hand, and that it might result in heavy political costs, to defend the idea that it was up to families to keep their blind indoors, never allowing them to go out on the street, so as not to worsen the already difficult traffic situation or to offend the sensibility of persons who still had their eyesight and who, indifferent to more or less reassuring opinions, believed that the white disease was spreading by visual contact, like the evil eye. Indeed, it was not appropriate to expect any other reaction from someone who, preoccupied with his thoughts, be they sad, indifferent, or happy, if such thoughts still exist, suddenly saw the change in expression of a person heading in his direction, his face revealing all the signs of total horror, and then that inevitable cry, I'm blind, I'm blind. No one's nerves could withstand it. The worst thing is that whole families, especially the smaller ones, rapidly became families of blind people, leaving no one who could guide and look after them, nor protect sighted neighbours from them, and it was clear that these blind people, however caring a father, mother or child they might be, could not take care of each other, otherwise they would meet the same fate as the blind people in the painting, walking together, falling together and dying together.

Faced with this situation, the Government had no alternative but to go rapidly into reverse gear, broadening the criteria it had established about the places and spaces that could be requisitioned, resulting in the immediate and improvised utilisation of abandoned factories, disused churches, sports pavilions and empty warehouses. For the last two days there has been talk of setting up army tents, added the old man with the black eyepatch. At the beginning, the very beginning, several charitable organisations were still offering volunteers to assist the blind, to make their beds, clean out the lavatories, wash their clothes, prepare their food, the minimum of care without which life soon becomes unbearable, even for those who can see. These dear people went blind immediately but at least the generosity of their gesture would go down in history. Did any of them come here, asked the old man with the black eyepatch, No, replied the doctor's wife, no one has come, Perhaps it was a rumour, And what about the city and the traffic, asked the first blind man, remembering his own car and that of the taxi-driver who had driven him to the surgery and had helped him to dig the grave, Traffic is in a state of chaos, replied the old man with the black eyepatch, and gave details of specific cases and accidents. When, for the first time, a bus-driver was suddenly struck by blindness as he was driving his vehicle on a public road, despite the casualties and injuries resulting from the disaster, people did not pay much attention for the same reason, that is to say, out of force of habit, and the director of public relations of the transport company felt able to declare, without further ado, that the disaster had been caused by human error, regrettable no doubt, but, all things considered, as unforeseeable as a heart attack in the case of someone who had never suffered from a heart complaint. Our employees, explained the director, as well as the mechanical and electrical parts of our buses, are periodically subjected to rigorous checks, as can be seen, showing a direct and clear relation of cause and effect, in the extremely low percentage of accidents in which, generally speaking, our company's vehicles have been involved. This laboured explanation appeared in the newspapers, but people had more on their minds than worrying about a simple bus accident, after all, it would have been no worse if its brakes had failed. Moreover, two days later, this was precisely the cause of another accident, but the world being what it is, where the truth often has to masquerade as falsehood to achieve its ends, the rumour went round that the driver had gone blind. There was no way of convincing the public of what had in fact happened, and the outcome was soon evident, from one moment to the next people stopped using buses, they said they would rather go blind themselves than die because others had gone blind. A third accident, soon afterwards and for the same reason, involving a vehicle that was carrying no passengers, gave rise to comment such as the following, couched in a knowingly popular tone, That could have been me. Nor could they imagine, those who spoke like this, how right they were. When two pilots both went blind at once a commercial plane crashed and burst into flames the moment it hit the ground, killing all the passengers and crew, notwithstanding that in this case, the mechanical and electrical equipment were in perfect working order, as the black box, the only survivor, would later reveal. A tragedy of these dimensions was not the same as an ordinary bus accident, the result being that those who still had any illusions soon lost them, from then on engine noises were no longer heard and no wheel, large or small, fast or slow, was ever to turn again. Those people who were previously in the habit of complaining about the ever-increasing traffic problems, pedestrians who, at first sight, appeared not to know where they were going because the cars, stationary or moving, were constantly impeding their progress, drivers who having gone round the block countless times before finally finding a place to park their car, became pedestrians and started protesting for the same reasons, after having first voiced their own complaints, all of them must now be content, except for the obvious fact that, since there was no one left who dared to drive a vehicle, not even to get from A to B, the cars, trucks, motor-bikes, even the bicycles, were scattered chaotically throughout the entire city, abandoned wherever fear had gained the upper hand over any sense of propriety, as evidenced by the grotesque sight of a tow-away vehicle with a car suspended from the front axle, probably the first man to turn blind had been the truck-driver. The situation was bad for everyone, but for those stricken with blindness it was catastrophic, since, according to the current expression, they could not see where they were putting their feet. It was pitiful to watch them bumping into the abandoned cars, one after the other, bruising their shins, some fell, pleading, Is there anyone who can help me to my feet, but there were also those who, naturally brutish or made so by despair, cursed and fought off any helping hand that came to their assistance, Leave me alone, your turn will come soon enough, then the compassionate person would take fright and make a quick escape, disappear into that dense white mist, suddenly conscious of the risk to which their kindness had exposed them, perhaps to go blind only a few steps further on.

That's how things are out there, the old man with the black eyepatch concluded his account, and I don't know everything, I can only speak of what I was able to see with my own eyes, here he broke off, paused and corrected himself, Not with my eyes, because I only had one, now not even that, well, I still have it but it's no use to me, I've never asked you why you didn't have a glass eye instead of wearing that patch, And why should I have wanted to, tell me that, asked the old man with the black eyepatch, It's normal because it looks better, besides it's much more hygienic, it can be removed, washed and replaced like dentures, Yes sir, but tell me what it would be like today if all those who now find themselves blind had lost, I say physically lost, both their eyes, what good would it do them now to be walking around with two glass eyes, You're right, no good at all, With all of us ending up blind, as appears to be happening, who's interested in aesthetics, and as for hygiene, tell me, doctor, what kind of hygiene could you hope for in this place, Perhaps only in a world of the blind will things be what they truly are, said the doctor, And what about people, asked the girl with dark glasses, People, too, no one will be there to see them, An idea has just occurred to me, said the old man with the black eyepatch, let's play a game to pass the time, How can we play a game if we cannot see what we are playing, asked the wife of the first blind man, Well, not a game exactly, each of us must say what we saw at the moment we went blind, That could be embarrassing, someone pointed out, Those who do not wish to take part in the game can remain silent, the important thing is that no one should try to invent anything, Give us an example, said the doctor, Certainly, replied the old man with the black eyepatch, I went blind when I was looking at my blind eye, What do you mean, It's very simple, I felt as if the inside of the empty orbit were inflamed and I removed the patch to satisfy my curiosity and just at that moment I went blind, It sounds like an allegory, said an unknown voice, the eye that refuses to acknowledge its own absence, As for me, said the doctor, I was at home consulting some reference books on ophthalmology, precisely because of what is happening, the last thing I saw were my hands resting on a book, My final image was different, said the doctor's wife, the inside of an ambulance as I was helping my husband to get in, I've already explained to the doctor what happened to me, said the first blind man, I had stopped at the lights, the signal was red, there were people crossing the street from one side to the other, at that very moment I turned blind, then that fellow who died the other day took me home, obviously I couldn't see his face, As for me, said the wife of the first blind man, the last thing I can remember seeing was my handkerchief, I was sitting at home and crying my heart out, I raised the handkerchief to my eyes and went blind that very moment, In my case, said the girl from the surgery, I had just gotten into the elevator, I stretched out my hand to press the button and suddenly stopped seeing, you can imagine my distress, trapped in there and all alone, I didn't know whether I would go up or down, and I couldn't find the button to open the door, My situation, said the pharmacist's assistant, was simpler, I heard that people were going blind, then I began to wonder what it would be like if I too were to go blind, I closed my eyes to try it and when I opened them I was blind, Sounds like another allegory, interrupted the unknown voice, if you want to be blind, then blind you will be. They remained silent. The other blind internees had gone back to their beds, no easy task, for while it is true that they knew their respective numbers, only by starting to count from one end of the ward, from one upwards or from twenty downwards, could they be certain of arriving where they wanted to be. When the murmur of their counting, as monotonous as a litany, died away, the girl with dark glasses related what had happened to her, I was in a hotel room with a man lying on top of me, at that point she fell silent, she felt too ashamed to say what she was doing there, that she had seen everything white, but the old man with the black eyepatch asked, And you saw everything white, Yes, she replied, Perhaps your blindness is different from ours, said the old man with the black eyepatch. The only person still to speak was the chambermaid, I was making a bed, a certain person had gone blind there, I held up the white sheet up before me and spread it out, tucked it in at the sides as one does, and as I was smoothing it out with both hands, suddenly I could no longer see, I remember how I was smoothing the sheet out, very slowly, it was the bottom sheet, she added, as if this had some special significance. Has everyone told their story about the last time they could see, asked the old man with the black eyepatch, I'll tell you mine, if there's no one else, said the unknown voice, If there is, he can speak after you, so fire away, The last thing I saw was a painting, A painting, repeated the old man with the black eyepatch, and where was this painting, I had gone to the museum, it was a picture of a cornfield with crows and cypress trees and a sun that gave the impression of having been made up of the fragments of other suns, Sounds like a Dutch painter, I think it was, but there was a drowning dog in it, already half submerged, poor creature, In that case it must be by a Spanish painter, before him no one had ever painted a dog in that situation, after him no other painter had the courage to try. Probably, and there was a cart laden with hay, drawn by horses and crossing a stream, Was there a house on the left, Yes, Then it was by an English painter, Could be, but I don't think so, because there was a woman as well with a child in her arms, Mothers and children are all too common in paintings, True, I've noticed, What I don't understand is how in one painting there should be so many pictures and by such different painters, And there were some men eating, There have been so many lunches, afternoon snacks and suppers in the history of art, that this detail in itself is not enough to tell us who was eating, There were thirteen men altogether, Ah, then it's easy, go on, There was also a naked woman with fair hair, inside a conch that was floating on the sea, and masses of flowers around her, Obviously Italian, And there was a battle, As in those paintings depicting banquets and mothers with children in their arms, these details are not enough to reveal who painted the picture, There were corpses and wounded men, It's only natural, sooner or later, all children die, and soldiers too, And a horse stricken with terror, With its eyes about to pop out of their sockets, Exactly, Horses are like that, and what other pictures were there in your painting, Alas, I never managed to find out, I went blind just as I was looking at the horse. Fear can cause blindness, said the girl with dark glasses, Never a truer word, that could not be truer, we were already blind the moment we turned blind, fear struck us blind, fear will keep us blind, Who is speaking, asked the doctor, A blind man, replied a voice, just a blind man, for that is all we have here. Then the old man with the black eye-patch asked, How many blind persons are needed to make a blindness, No one could provide the answer. The girl with dark glasses asked him to switch on the radio, there might be some news. They gave the news later, meanwhile they listened to a little music. At a certain point some blind internees appeared in the doorway of the ward, one of them said, What a pity no one thought of bringing a guitar. The news was not very encouraging, a rumour was going round that the formation of a government of unity and national salvation was imminent.

When, at the beginning, the blind internees in this ward could still be counted on ten fingers, when an exchange of two or three words was enough to convert strangers into companions in misfortune, and with another three or four words they could forgive each other all their faults, some of them really quite serious, and if a complete pardon was not forthcoming, it was simply a question of being patient and waiting for a few days, then it became all too clear how many absurd afflictions the poor wretches had to suffer, each time their bodies demanded to be urgently relieved or as we say, to satisfy their needs. Despite this, and although knowing that perfect manners are somewhat rare and that even the most discreet and modest natures have their weak points, it has to be conceded that the first blind people to be brought here under quarantine, were capable, more or less conscientiously, of bearing with dignity the cross imposed by the eminently scatological nature of the human species. Now, with all the beds occupied, all two hundred and forty, not counting the blind inmates who have to sleep on the floor, no imagination, however fertile and creative in making comparisons, images and metaphors, could aptly describe the filth here. It is not just the state to which the lavatories were soon reduced, fetid caverns such as the gutters in hell full of condemned souls must be, but also the lack of respect shown by some of the inmates or the sudden urgency of

others that turned the corridors and other passageways into latrines, at first only occasionally but now as a matter of habit.
The careless or impatient thought, It doesn't matter, no one can
see me, and they went no further. When it became impossible
in any sense, to reach the lavatories, the blind internees began
using the yard as a place to relieve themselves and clear their
bowels. Those who were delicate by nature or upbringing spent
the whole day restraining themselves, they put up with it as best
they could until nightfall, they presumed it would be night
when most people were asleep in the wards, then off they
would go, clutching their stomachs or squeezing their legs together, in search of a foot or two of clean ground, if there was
any amidst that endless carpet of trampled excrement, and, to
make matters worse, in danger of getting lost in the infinite
space of the yard, where there were no guiding signs other than
the few trees whose trunks had managed to survive the mania
for exploration of the former inmates, and also the slight
mounds, now almost flattened, that barely covered the dead.
Once a day, always in the late afternoon, like an alarm clock set
to go off at the same hour, the voice over the loudspeaker
would repeat the familiar instructions and prohibitions, insist
on the advantages of making regular use of cleansing products,
remind the inmates that there was a telephone in each ward in
order to request the necessary supplies whenever they ran out,
but what was really needed there was a powerful jet from a hose
to wash away all that shit, then an army of plumbers to repair
the cisterns and get them working again, then water, lots of
water, to wash the waste down the pipes where it belongs, then,
we beseech you, eyes, a pair of eyes, a hand capable of leading
and guiding us, a voice that will say to me, This way. These
blind internees, unless we come to their assistance, will soon
turn into animals, worse still, into blind animals. This was not
spoken by the unknown voice that talked of the paintings and
images of this world, the person saying it, though in other
words, late at night, is the doctor's wife lying beside her husband,
their heads under the same blanket, A solution has to be found
for this awful mess, I can't stand it and I can't go on pretending

that I can't see, Think of the consequences, they will almost certainly try to turn you into their slave, a general dogsbody, you will be at the beck and call of everyone, they will expect you to feed them, wash them, put them to bed and get them up in the morning and have you take them from here to there, blow their noses and dry their tears, they will call out for you when you are asleep, insult you if you keep them waiting, How can you of all people expect me to go on looking at these miseries, to have them permanently before my eyes, and not lift a finger to help, You're already doing more than enough, What use am I, when my main concern is that no one should find out that I can see, Some will hate you for seeing, don't think that blindness has made us better people, It hasn't made us any worse, We're on our way though, just look at what happens when it's time to share out the food, Precisely, someone who can see could supervise the distribution of food to all those who are here, share it out with impartiality, with common sense, there would be no more complaints, these constant arguments that are driving me mad would cease, you have no idea what it is like to watch two blind people fighting, Fighting has always been, more or less, a form of blindness, This is different, Do what you think best, but don't forget what we are here, blind, simply blind, blind people with no fine speeches or commiserations, the charitable, picturesque world of the little blind orphans is finished, we are now in the harsh, cruel, implacable kingdom of the blind, If only you could see what I am obliged to see, you would want to be blind, I believe you, but there's no need, because I'm already blind, Forgive me, my love, if you only knew, I know, I know, I've spent my life looking into people's eyes, it is the only part of the body where a soul might still exist and if those eyes are lost, Tomorrow I'm going to tell them I can see, Let's hope you won't live to regret it, Tomorrow I'll tell them, she paused then added, Unless by then I, too, have finally entered their world.

But it was not to be just yet. When she woke up next morning, very early as usual, her eyes could see as clearly as before. All the blind internees in the ward were asleep. She wondered how she should tell them, whether she should gather them all

together and announce the news, perhaps it might be preferable
to do it in a discreet manner, without ostentation, to say, for example, as if not wishing to treat the matter too seriously, Just
imagine, who would have thought that I would keep my sight
amongst so many who have turned blind, or whether, perhaps
more wisely, pretend that she really had been blind and had suddenly regained her sight, it might even be a way of giving the
others some hope. If she can see again, they would say to each
other, perhaps we will, too, on the other hand, they might tell
her, If that's the case, then get out, be off with you, whereupon
she would reply that she could not leave the place without her
husband, and since the army would not release any blind person
from quarantine, there was nothing for it but to allow her to
stay. Some of the blind internees were stirring in their beds and,
as every morning, they were relieving themselves of wind, but
this did not make the atmosphere any more nauseating, satura-
tion point must already have been reached. It was not just the
fetid smell that came from the lavatories in gusts that made you
want to throw up, it was also the accumulated body odour of
two hundred and fifty people, whose bodies were steeped in
their own sweat, who were neither able nor knew how to wash
themselves, who wore clothes that got filthier by the day, who
slept in beds where they had frequently defecated. What use
would soaps, bleach, detergents be, abandoned somewhere
around the place, if many of the showers were blocked or had
become detached from the pipes, if the drains overflowed with
the dirty water that spread outside the wash-rooms, soaking the
floorboards in the corridors, infiltrating the cracks in the flagstones. What madness is this to think of interfering, the doctor's
wife began to reflect, even if they were not to demand that I
should be at their service, and nothing is less certain, I myself
would not be able to stand it without setting about washing and
cleaning for as long as I had the strength, this is not a job for one
person. Her courage which before had seemed so resolute,
began to crumble, to gradually desert her when confronted
with the abject reality that invaded her nostrils and offended her
eyes, now that the moment had come to pass from words to

actions. I'm a coward, she murmured in exasperation, it would have been better to be blind than go around like some faint-hearted missionary. Three blind internees had got up, one of them was the pharmacist's assistant, they were about to take up their positions in the hallway to collect the allocation of food intended for the first ward. It could not be claimed, given their lack of eyesight, that the distribution was made by eye, one container more, one container less, on the contrary, it was pitiful to see how they got muddled over the counting and had to start all over again, someone with a more suspicious nature wanted to know exactly what the others were carrying, arguments always broke out in the end, the odd shove, a slap for the blind women, as was inevitable. In the ward everyone was now awake, ready to receive their ration, with experience they had devised a fairly easy system of distribution, they began by carrying all the food to the far end of the ward, where the doctor and his wife had their beds as well as the girl with dark glasses and the boy who was calling for his mummy, and that is where the inmates went to fetch their food, two at a time, starting from the beds nearest the entrance, number one on the right, number one on the left, number two on the right, number two on the left, and so on and so forth, without any ill-tempered exchanges or jostling, it took longer, it is true, but keeping the peace made the waiting worthwhile. The first, that is to say, those who had the food right there within arm's reach, were the last to serve themselves, except for the boy with the squint, of course, who always finished eating before the girl with dark glasses received her portion, so that part of what should have been hers invariably finished up in the boy's stomach. All the blind internees had their heads turned towards the door, hoping to hear the footsteps of their fellow-inmates, the faltering, unmistakable sound of someone carrying something, but this was not the noise that could suddenly be heard but rather that of people running swiftly, were such a feat possible for people who could not see where they were putting their feet. Yet how else could you describe it when they appeared panting for breath at the door. What could have happened out there to send them running in here, and there were the three of them trying to get through the door at the same time to give the unexpected news, They wouldn't allow us to bring the food, said one of them, and the other two repeated his words, They wouldn't allow us, Who, the soldiers, asked some voice or other, No, the blind internees, What blind internees, we're all blind here, We don't know who they are, said the pharmacist's assistant, but I think they must belong to the group that all arrived together, the last group to arrive, And what's this about not allowing you to bring the food, asked the doctor, so far there has never been any problem, They say all that's over, from now on anyone who wants to eat will have to pay. Protests came from all sides of the ward, It cannot be, They've taken away our food, The thieves, A disgrace, the blind against the blind, I never thought I'd live to see anything like this, Let's go and complain to the sergeant. Someone more resolute proposed that they should all go together to demand what was rightfully theirs, It won't be easy, said the pharmacist's assistant, there are lots of them, I had the clear impression they form a large group, and the worst is that they are armed, What do you mean by armed, At the very least they have cudgels, this arm of mine still hurts from the blow I received, said one of the others, Let's try and settle this peacefully, said the doctor, I'll go with you to speak to these people, there must be some misunderstanding, Of course, doctor, you have my support, said the pharmacist's assistant, but from the way they're behaving, I very much doubt that you will be able to persuade them, Be that as it may, we have to go there, we cannot leave things like this, I'm coming with you, said the doctor's wife. The tiny group left the ward except for the one who was complaining about his arm, he felt that he had done his duty and stayed behind to relate to the others his hazardous adventure, their food rations two paces away, and a human wall to defend them, With cudgels, he insisted.

Advancing together, like a platoon, they forced their way through the blind inmates from the other wards. When they reached the hallway, the doctor's wife realised at once that no diplomatic conversation would be possible, and probably never likely to be. In the middle of the hallway, surrounding the containers of food, a circle of blind inmates armed with sticks and metal rods from the beds, pointing outwards like bayonets or lances, confronted the desperation of the blind inmates who were surrounding them and making awkward attempts to force their way through the line of defence, some with the hope of finding an opening, a gap someone had been careless enough not to close properly, they warded off the blows with raised arms, others crawled along on all fours until they bumped into the legs of their adversaries who repelled them with a blow to their backs or a vigorous kick. Hitting out blindly, as the saying goes. These scenes were accompanied by indignant protests, furious cries, We demand our food, We have a right to eat, Rogues, This is outrageous, Incredible though it may seem, there was one ingenuous or distracted soul who said, Call the police, perhaps there were some policemen amongst them, blindness, as everyone knows, has no regard for professions or occupations, but a policeman struck blind is not the same as a blind policeman, and as for the two we knew, they are dead and, after a great deal of effort, buried. Driven by the foolish hope that some authority would restore to the mental asylum its former tranquillity, impose justice, bring back some peace of mind, a blind woman made her way as best she could to the main entrance and called out for all to hear, Help us, these rogues are trying to steal our food. The soldiers pretended not to hear, the orders the sergeant had received from a captain who had passed through on an official visit could not have been clearer, If they end up killing each other, so much the better, there will be fewer of them. The blind woman ranted and raved as mad women did in bygone days, she herself almost demented, but from sheer desperation. In the end, realising that her pleas were futile, she fell silent, went back inside to sob her heart out and, oblivious of where she was going, she received a blow on the head that sent her to the floor. The doctor's wife wanted to run and help her up, but there was such confusion that she could not move as much as two paces. The blind internees who had come to demand their food were already beginning to withdraw in disarray, their sense of direction completely lost, they tripped over one another, fell, got up, fell again, some did not even make any attempt, gave up, remained lying prostrate on the ground, exhausted, miserable, racked with pain, their faces pressed against the tiled floor. Then the doctor's wife, terrified, saw one of the blind hoodlums take a gun from his pocket and raise it brusquely into the air. The blast caused a large piece of stucco to come crashing down from the ceiling on to their unprotected heads, increasing the panic. The hoodlum shouted, Be quiet everyone and keep your mouths shut, if anyone dares to raise their voice, I'll shoot straight out, no matter who gets hit, then there will be no more complaints. The blind internees did not move. The fellow with the gun continued, Let it be known and there is no turning back, that from today onwards we shall take charge of the food, you've all been warned, and let no one take it into their head to go out there to look for it, we shall put guards at the entrance, and anyone who tries to go against these orders will suffer the consequences, the food will now be sold, anyone who wants to eat must pay. How are we to pay, asked the doctor's wife, I said no one was to speak, bellowed the armed hoodlum, waving his weapon before him. Someone has to speak, we must know how we're to proceed, where are we going to fetch the food, do we all go together, or one at a time, This woman is up to something, commented one of the group, if you were to shoot her, there would be one mouth less to feed, If I could see her, she'd already have a bullet in her belly. Then addressing everyone, Go back to your wards immediately, this very minute, once we've carried the food inside, we'll decide what is to be done, And what about payment, rejoined the doctor's wife, how much shall we be expected to pay for a coffee with milk and a biscuit, She's really asking for it, that one, said the same voice, Leave her to me, said the other fellow, and changing tone, Each ward will nominate two people to be in charge of collecting people's valuables, all their valuables of whatever kind, money, jewels, rings, bracelets, earrings, watches, everything they possess, and they will take the lot to the third ward on the left, where we are accommodated, and if you want some friendly advice, don't get any ideas about trying to cheat us, we know that there are those amongst you who will hide some of your valuables, but I warn you to think again, unless we feel that you have handed in enough, you will simply not get any food and be left to chew your banknotes and munch on your diamonds. A blind man from the second ward on the right asked, And what are we to do, do we hand over everything at once, or do we pay according to what we eat, It would seem I haven't explained things clearly enough, said the fellow with the gun, laughing, first you pay, then you eat and, as for the rest, to pay according to what you've eaten would make keeping accounts extremely complicated, best to hand over everything at one go and then we shall see how much food you deserve, but let me warn you again, don't try to conceal anything for it will cost you dear, and lest anyone accuses us of not proceeding honestly, note that after handing over whatever you possess we shall carry out an inspection, woe betide you if we find so much as a penny, and now I want everybody out of here as quickly as possible. He raised his arm and fired another shot. Some more stucco crashed to the ground. And as for you, said the hoodlum with the gun, I won't forget your voice, Nor I your face, replied the doctor's wife.

No one appeared to notice the absurdity of a blind woman saying that she won't forget a face she could not see. The blind internees had already withdrawn as quickly as they could, in search of the doors, and those from the first ward were soon informing their fellow-inmates of the situation, From what we've heard, I don't believe that for the moment we can do anything other than obey, said the doctor, there must be quite a number of them, and worst of all, they have weapons. We can arm ourselves too, said the pharmacist's assistant, Yes, some sticks cut from the trees if there are any branches left within arm's reach, some metal rods removed from our beds that we shall scarcely have the strength to wield, while they have at least one firearm at their disposal, I refuse to hand over my belongings to these sons of a blind bitch, someone remarked, Nor I, joined in another, That's it, either we all hand over everything, or nobody gives anything, said the doctor, We have no alternative, said his wife, besides, the régime in here, must be the same as the one they imposed outside, anyone who doesn't want to pay can suit himself, that's his privilege, but he'll get nothing to eat and he cannot expect to be fed at the expense of the rest of us, We shall all give up what we've got and hand over everything, said the doctor, And what about those who have nothing to give, asked the pharmacist's assistant, They will eat whatever the others decide to give them, as the saying rightly goes, from each according to his abilities, to each according to his needs. There was a pause, and the old man with the black eyepatch asked, Well then, who are we going to ask to be in charge, I suggest the doctor, said the girl with the dark glasses. It was not necessary to proceed to a vote, the entire ward was in agreement. There have to be two of us, the doctor reminded them, is anyone willing to offer, he asked, I'm willing, if no one else comes forward, said the first blind man, Very well, let us start collecting, we need a sack, a bag, a small suitcase, any of these things will do, I can get rid of this, said the doctor's wife, and began at once to empty a bag in which she had gathered cosmetics and other odds and ends at a time when she could never have imagined the conditions in which she was now obliged to live. Amongst the bottles, boxes and tubes from another world, there was a pair of long, finely pointed scissors. She could not remember having put them there, but there they were. The doctor's wife raised her head. The blind internees were waiting, her husband had gone up to the bed of the first blind man, he was talking to him, the girl with the dark glasses was saying to the boy with the squint that the food would be arriving soon, on the floor, tucked behind the bedside table, was a bloodstained sanitary napkin, as if the girl with dark glasses were anxious, with maidenly and pointless modesty, to hide it from the eyes of those who could not see. The doctor's wife looked at the scissors, she tried to think why she should be staring at them in this way, in what way, like this, but she could think of no reason, frankly what reason could she hope to find in a simple pair of long scissors, lying in her open hands, with its two nickel-plated blades, the tips sharp and gleaming, Do you have it there, her husband asked her, Yes, here it is, she replied, and held out the arm holding the empty bag while she put the other arm behind her back to conceal the scissors, What's the matter, asked the doctor, Nothing, replied his wife, who could just as easily have answered, Nothing you can see, my voice must have sounded strange, that's all, nothing else. Accompanied by the first blind man, the doctor moved towards her, took the bag in his hesitant hands and said, Start getting your things ready, we're about to begin collecting. His wife unclasped her watch, did the same for her husband, removed her earrings, a tiny ring set with rubies, the gold chain she wore round her neck, her wedding ring, that of her husband, both of them easy to remove, Our fingers have got thinner, she thought, she began putting everything into the bag, then the money they had brought from home, a fair amount of notes varying in value, some coins, That's everything, she said, Are you sure, said the doctor, take a careful look, That's everything we have of any value. The girl with dark glasses had already gathered together her belongings, they were not so very different, she had two bracelets instead of one, but no wedding ring. The doctor's wife waited until her husband and the first blind man had turned their backs and for the girl with dark glasses to bend down to the boy with the squint, Think of me as your mummy, she was saying, I'll pay for us both, and then she withdrew to the wall at the far end. There, as all along the other walls, there were large nails sticking out that must have been used by the mad to hang treasures and other baubles. She chose the highest nail she could reach, and hung the scissors there. Then she sat down on her bed. Slowly, her husband and the first blind man were heading in the direction of the door, they would stop to collect possessions on both sides from those who had something to offer, some protested that they were being robbed shamefully, and that was the honest truth, others divested themselves of their possessions with a kind of indifference, as if thinking that, all things considered, there is nothing in this world that belongs to us in an absolute sense, another all too transparent truth. When they reached the door of the ward, having finished their collection, the doctor asked, Have we handed over everything, a number of resigned voices answered yes, some chose to say nothing and in the fullness of time we shall know whether this was in order to avoid telling a lie. The doctor's wife looked up at the scissors. She was surprised to find them so far up, hanging from one of the nails, as if she herself had not put them there, then she reflected that it had been an excellent idea to bring them, now she could trim her husband's beard, make him look more presentable, since, as we know, living in these conditions, it is impossible for a man to shave as normal. When she looked again in the direction of the door, the two men had already disappeared into the shadows of the corridor and were making their way to the third ward on the left, where they had been instructed to go and pay for their food. Today's food, tomorrow's as well, and perhaps for the rest of the week, And then, the question had no answer, everything we possessed will have gone in payment.

Surprisingly enough, the corridors were not congested as usual, because normally as the internees left their wards they inevitably tripped, collided and fell, those assaulted swore, hurled obscenities, their assailants retaliated with further insults, but no one paid any attention, a person has to give vent to his feelings somehow, especially if he is blind. Ahead there was the sound of footsteps and voices, they must be the emissaries from the other wards who were complying with the same orders, What a situation we're in, doctor, said the first blind man, as if our blindness were not enough, we've fallen into the clutches of blind thieves, that seems to be my fate, first there was the car-thief, now this rabble who are stealing our food at gunpoint, That's the difference, they're armed, But cartridges don't last for ever, Nothing lasts for ever, but in this case it might be preferable if it did, Why, If the cartridges were to run out, then that would mean that someone had used them up, and we already have too many corpses, We're in an impossible situation, It has been impossible ever since we came into this place, yet we go on putting up with it, You're an optimist, doctor, No, I'm not an optimist, but I cannot imagine anything worse than our present existence, Well, I'm not entirely convinced that there are limits to misfortune and evil, You may be right, said the doctor, and then, as if he were talking to himself, Something has to happen here, a conclusion that contains a certain contradiction, either there is something worse than this, after all, or, from now on, things are going to get better, although all the indications suggest otherwise. Having steadily made their way and having turned several corners, they were approaching the third ward. Neither the doctor nor the first blind man had ever ventured here, but the construction of the two wings, logically enough, had strictly adhered to a symmetrical pattern, anyone familiar with the wing on the right would have no difficulty in getting their bearings in the wing on the left, and vice-versa, you had only to turn to the left on the one side while on the other you had to turn right. They could hear voices, they must be of those ahead of them, We'll have to wait, said the doctor in a low voice, Why, Those inside will want to know precisely what these inmates are carrying, for them it is not all that important, since they have already eaten they're in no hurry, It must be almost time for lunch, Even if they could see, it would do this group no good to know it, they no longer even have watches. A quarter of an hour later, give or take a minute, the barter was over. Two men passed in front of the doctor and the first blind man, from their conversation it was apparent that they were carrying food, Careful, don't drop anything, said one of them, and the other was muttering, What I don't know is whether there will be enough for everyone. We'll have to tighten our belts. Sliding his hand along the wall, with the first blind man right behind him, the doctor advanced until his hands came into contact with the door jamb, We're from the first ward on the right, he shouted. He made as if to take a step forward, but his leg came up against an obstacle. He realised it was a bed standing crosswise, placed there to serve as a trading counter, They're organised, he thought to himself, this has not suddenly been improvised, he heard voices, footsteps, How many of them are there, his wife had mentioned ten, but it was not inconceivable that there might be many more, certainly not all of them were there when they went to get the food. The fellow with the gun was their leader, it was his jeering voice that was saying, Now, let's see what riches the first ward on the right has brought us, and then, in a much lower tone, addressing someone who must have been standing nearby, Take note. The doctor remained puzzled, what could this mean, the fellow had said, Take note, so there must be someone here who can write, someone who is not blind, so that makes two, We must be careful, he thought, tomorrow this rascal might be standing right next to us and we wouldn't even know it, this thought of the doctor's was scarcely any different from what the first blind man was thinking, With a gun and a spy, we're sunk, we shall never be able to raise our heads again. The blind man inside, the leader of the thieves, had already opened the bag, with practised hands he was lifting out, stroking and identifying the objects and money, clearly he could make out by touch what was gold and what was not, by touch he could also tell the value of the notes and coins, easy when one is experienced, it was only after some minutes that the doctor began to hear the unmistakable sound of punching paper, which he immediately identified, there nearby was someone writing in the braille alphabet, also known as anaglyptography, the sound could be heard, at once quiet and clear, of the pointer as it punched the thick paper and hit the metallic plate underneath. So there was a normal blind person amongst these blind delinquents, a blind person just like all those people who were once referred to as being blind, the poor fellow had obviously been roped in with all the rest, but this was not the moment to pry and start asking, are you one of the recent blind men or have you been blind for some years, tell us how you came to lose your sight. They were certainly lucky, not only had they won a clerk in the raffle, they could also use him as a guide, a blind person with experience as a blind person is something else, he's worth his weight in gold. The inventory went on, now and then the thug with the gun consulted the accountant, What do you think of this, and he would interrupt his bookkeeping to give an opinion, A cheap imitation, he would say, in which case the fellow with the gun would comment, If there is a lot of this, they won't get any food, or Good stuff, and then the commentary would be, There's nothing like dealing with honest people. In the end, three containers of food were lifted on to the bed, Take this, said the armed leader. The doctor counted them, Three are not enough, we used to receive four when the food was only for us, at that same moment he felt the cold barrel of the gun against his neck, for a blind man his aim was not bad, I'll have a container removed every time you complain, now beat it, take these and thank the Lord that you've still got something to eat. The doctor murmured, Very well, grabbed two of the containers while the first blind man took charge of the third one and, much slower now, because they were laden, they retraced the route that had brought them to the ward. When they arrived in the hallway, where there did not appear to be anyone around, the doctor said, I'll never again have such an opportunity, What do you mean, asked the first blind man, He put his gun to my neck, I could have grabbed it from him, That would be risky, Not as risky as it seems, I knew where the gun was resting, he had no way of knowing where my hands were, even so, at that moment I'm convinced that he was the blinder of the two of us, what a pity I didn't think of it, or did think of it but lacked the courage, And then what, asked the first blind man, What do you mean, Let's assume you had managed to grab his weapon, I don't believe you would have been capable of using it, If I were certain it would resolve the situation, yes I would, But you're not certain, No, in fact I'm not, Then better that they should keep their arms, at least so long as they do not use them against us. To threaten someone with a gun is the same as attacking them, If you had taken his gun, the real war would have started, and in all likelihood we would never have got out of that place alive, You're right, said the doctor, I'll pretend I had thought all that through, You mustn't forget, doctor, what you told me a little while ago, What did I say, That something has to happen, It has happened and I didn't make the most of it, It has to be something else, not that.

When they entered the ward and had to present the meagre amount of food they had brought to put on the table, some thought they were to blame for not having protested and demanded more, that's why they had been nominated as the representatives of the group. Then the doctor explained what had happened, he told them about the blind clerk, about the insulting behaviour of the blind man with the gun, also about the gun itself. The malcontents lowered their voices, ended up by agreeing that undoubtedly the ward's interests were in the right hands. The food was finally distributed, there were those who could not resist reminding the impatient that little is better than nothing, besides, by now it must be almost time for lunch, The worst thing would be if we got to be like that famous horse that died when it had already got out of the habit of eating, someone remarked. The others gave a wan smile and one said, It wouldn't be so bad if it's true that when the horse dies, it doesn't know it's going to die.

The old man with the black eyepatch had understood that the portable radio, as much for the fragility of its structure as for the information known about the length of its useful life, was to be excluded from the list of valuables they had to hand over in payment for their food, in consideration of the fact that the usefulness of the set depended in the first place on whether there were or were not batteries inside and, in the second place, on how long they would last. Judging by the rather husky voices still coming from the tiny box, it was obvious that little more could be expected of it. Therefore the old man with the black eyepatch decided not to have any more general broadcasts, additionally because the blind internees in the third ward on the left might turn up and take a different view, not owing to the material value of the set, which is virtually negligible in the short term, as we have seen, but owing to its immediate utility, which is undoubtedly considerable, not to mention the feasible hypothesis that where there is at least one gun there might also be batteries. So the old man with the black eyepatch said that, from now on, he would listen to the news under the blanket, with his head completely covered, and that if there were any interesting news-item, he would alert the others at once. The girl with dark glasses asked him to allow her to listen to a little music from time to time, So as not to forget, she argued, but he was inflexible, insisted that the important thing was to know what was going on outside, anyone who wanted music could listen to it in their own head, after all our memory ought to be put to some good use. The old man with the black eyepatch was right, the music on the radio was already as grating as only a painful memory can be, so for this reason he kept the volume as low as possible, waiting for the news to come on. Then he turned the sound up a little and listened attentively so as not to lose a single syllable. Then he summarised the news-items in his own words, and transmitted them to his immediate neighbours. And so from bed to bed, the news slowly circulated round the ward, increasingly distorted as it was passed on from one inmate to the next, in this way diminishing or exaggerating the details, according to the personal optimism or pessimism of those relaying the information. Until that moment when the words dried up and the old man with the black eyepatch found he had nothing more to say. And it was not because the radio had broken down or the batteries were used up, experience of life and lives has convincingly shown that no one can govern time, it was unlikely that this tiny set would last long, but finally someone fell silent before it went dead. Throughout this first day spent in the clutches of those blind thugs, the old man with the black eyepatch had been listening to the radio and passing on the news, rejecting the patent falseness of the optimistic prophecies being officially communicated and now, well into the night, with his head out of the blanket at last, he was listening carefully to the wheeze into which the waning power of the radio had transformed the announcer's voice, when suddenly he heard him call out, I'm blind, then the noise of something striking the microphone, a hasty sequence of confused sounds, exclamations, then sudden silence. The only radio station he had been able to get on the set had gone silent. For some time to come, the old man with the black eyepatch kept his ear to the box that was now inert, as if waiting for the announcer's voice to return and for the news to continue. However, he sensed, or rather knew, that it would return no more. The white sickness had not only blinded the announcer. Like a line of gunpowder, it had quickly and successively reached all those who happened to be in the studio. Then the old man with the black eyepatch dropped the radio on the floor. The blind thugs, if they were to come sniffing out hidden jewels, would find justification, had such a thought crossed their mind, for the omission of portable radios from their list of valuables. The old man with the black eyepatch pulled the blanket up over his head so that he could weep freely.

Little by little, under the murky yellowish light of the dim lamps, the ward descended into a deep slumber, bodies comforted by the three meals consumed that day, as had rarely happened before. If things continue like this, we'll end up once more reaching the conclusion that even in the worst misfortunes it is possible to find enough good to be able to bear the aforesaid misfortunes with patience, which, applied to the present situation, means that contrary to the first disquieting predictions, the concentration of food supplies into a single entity for apportioning and distribution, had its positive aspects, after all, however much certain idealists might protest that they would have preferred to go on struggling for life by their own means, even if their stubbornness meant going hungry. Unconcerned about tomorrow, forgetful that he who pays in advance always ends up being badly served, the majority of the blind internees, in all the wards, slept soundly. The others, tired of searching in vain for an honourable way out of the vexations suffered, also fell asleep one by one, dreaming of better days than these, days of greater freedom if not of greater abundance. In the first ward on the right, only the doctor's wife was still awake. Lying on her bed, she was thinking about what her husband had told her, when for a moment he suspected that amongst the blind thieves there was someone who could see, someone whom they might use as a spy. It was curious that they had not touched on the subject again, as if it had not occurred to the doctor, accustomed as he was to the fact, that his own wife could still see. It crossed her mind, but she said nothing, she had no desire to utter the obvious words, What he is unable to do after all, I can do. What is that, the doctor would ask, pretending not to understand. Now, with her eyes fixed on the scissors hanging on the wall, the doctor's wife was asking herself, What use is my eyesight, It had exposed her to greater horror than she could ever have imagined, it had convinced her that she would rather be blind, nothing else. Moving cautiously, she sat up in bed. Opposite her, the girl with the dark glasses and the boy with the squint were asleep. She noticed that the two beds were very close together, the girl had pushed hers over, almost certainly to be closer to the boy should he need to be comforted or have someone to dry his tears in the absence of his mother. Why did I not think of it before, I could have pushed our beds together and we could have slept together, without this constant worry that he might fall out of bed. She looked at her husband, who was fast asleep, in a deep sleep from sheer exhaustion. She had not got round to telling him that she had brought the scissors, that one of these days she would have to trim his beard, a task that even a blind man is capable of carrying out so long as he does not bring the blades too close to his skin. She has found a good excuse for not mentioning the scissors, Afterwards all the men here would be pestering me and I'd find myself doing nothing except trimming beards. She swung her body outwards, rested her feet on the floor and searched for her shoes. As she was about to slip them on, she held back, stared at them closely, then shook her head and, without making a noise, put them back. She passed along the aisle between the beds and slowly made her way towards the door of the ward. Her bare feet came into contact with the slimy excrement on the floor, but she knew that out there in the corridors it would be much worse. She kept looking from one side to the other, to see if any of the blind internees were awake, although whether several of them might be keeping vigil, or the entire ward, was of no importance so long as she did not make a noise, and even if she did, we know how pressing our bodily needs can be, they do not choose their hour, in a word, what she did not want was that her husband should wake up and sense her absence in time to ask her, Where are you going, which is probably the question husbands most frequently put to their wives, the other being Where have you been, One of the blind women was sitting up in bed, her shoulders resting against the low head-rest, her empty gaze fixed on the wall opposite, but she could not see it. The doctor's wife paused for a moment, as if not sure whether to touch that invisible thread that hovered in the air, as if the slightest contact would irrevocably destroy it. The blind woman raised her arm, she must have perceived some gentle vibration in the atmosphere, then she let it drop, no longer interested, it was enough not to be able to sleep because of her neighbours' snoring. The doctor's wife continued walking in ever greater haste as she approached the door. Before heading for the hallway, she looked along the corridor that led to the other wards on this side, further ahead, to the lavatories, and ultimately to the kitchen and refectory. There were blind inmates lying up against the walls, those who on arrival had been unsuccessful in finding a bed, either because in the assault they had lagged behind, or because they lacked the strength to contest a bed and win their battle. Ten metres away, a blind man was lying on top of a blind woman, the man caught between her legs, they were being as discreet as they could, they were the discreet kind, but you would not have needed very sharp hearing to know what they were up to, especially when first one and then the other could no longer repress their sighs and groans, some inarticulate word, which are the signs that all that is about to end. The doctor's wife stopped in her tracks to watch them, not out of envy, she had her husband and the satisfaction he gave her, but because of an impression of another order, for which she could find no name, perhaps a feeling of sympathy, as if she were thinking of saying to them, Don't mind my being here, I also know what this means, continue, perhaps a feeling of compassion, Even if this instant of supreme pleasure should last you a lifetime, you will never become united as one. The blind man and the blind woman were now resting, apart, the one lying beside the other, but they were still holding hands, they were young, perhaps even lovers who had gone to the cinema and turned blind there, or perhaps some miraculous coincidence brought them together in this place, and, this being the case, how did they recognise each other, good heavens, by their voices, of course, it is not only the voice of blood that needs no eyes, love, which people say is blind, also has a voice of its own. In all probability, though, they were taken at the same time, in which case those clasped hands are not something recent, they have been clasped since the beginning.

The doctor's wife sighed, raised her hands to her eyes, she had to because she could barely see, but she was not alarmed, she knew they were only tears. Then she continued on her way. On reaching the hallway, she went up to the door leading to the courtyard. She looked outside. Behind the gate there was a light which outlined the black silhouette of a soldier. On the other side of the street, the buildings were all in darkness. She went out on to the top of the steps. There was no danger. Even if the soldier were to become aware of her shadow, he would only shoot if she, having descended the stairs, were to get nearer, after being warned, from that other invisible line which represented for him the frontier of his safety. Accustomed now to the constant noises in the ward, the doctor's wife found the silence strange, a silence that seemed to occupy the space of an absence, as if humanity, the whole of humanity, had disappeared, leaving only a light and a soldier keeping watch over it. She sat on the ground, her back resting against the door jamb, in the same position in which she had seen the blind woman in the ward, and stared ahead like her. The night was cold, the wind blew along the front of the building, it seemed impossible that there should still be wind in this world, that the night should be black, she wasn't thinking of herself, she was thinking of the blind for whom the day was endless. Above the light, another silhouette appeared, it was probably the guard's relief, Nothing to report, the soldier would be saying before going off to his tent to get some sleep, neither of them had any idea what was happening behind that door, probably the noise of the shots had not even been heard out here, an ordinary gun does not make much noise. A pair of scissors even less, thought the doctor's wife. She did not waste time asking herself where such a thought had come from, she was only surprised at its slowness, at how the first word had been so slow in appearing, the slowness of those to follow, and how she found that the thought was already there before, somewhere or other, and only the words were missing, like a body searching in the bed for the hollow that had been prepared for it by the mere idea of lying down. The soldier approached the gate, although he is standing against the light, it is clear that he is looking in this direction, he must have noticed the motionless shadow, although, for the moment, there is not enough light to see that it is only a woman seated on the ground, her arms cradling her legs and her chin resting on her knees, the soldier points the beam of a torch at her, now there can be no doubt, it is a woman who is about to get up with a movement as slow as her previous thought had been, but the soldier is not to know this, all he knows is that he is afraid of that figure of a woman who seems to be taking ages to get to her feet, in a flash he asks himself whether he should raise the alarm, the next moment he decides against it, after all, it is only a woman and she is some way away, in any case, as a precaution he points his weapon in her direction, but this means putting the torch aside and, with that movement, the luminous beam shone directly into his eyes, like a sudden burning, an impression of being dazzled remained in his retina. When he recovered his vision, the woman had disappeared, now this guard will be unable to say to the person who comes to relieve him, Nothing to report.

The doctor's wife is already in the left wing, in the corridor that will take her to the third ward. Here too there are blind inmates sleeping on the floor, more of them than in the right wing. She walks noiselessly, slowly, she can feel the slime on the ground sticking to her feet. She looks inside the first two wards, and sees what she expected to see, bodies lying under blankets, there is a blind man who is also unable to sleep and says so in a desperate voice, she can hear the staccato snoring of almost everyone else. As for the smell that all this gives off, it does not surprise her, there is no other smell in the entire building, it is the smell of her own body, of the clothes she is wearing. On turning the corner into the corridor giving access to the third ward, she came to a halt. There is a man at the door, another guard. He has a stick in his hand, he is wielding it in slow motion, to one side then the next, as if blocking the passage of anyone who might try to approach. Here there are no blind inmates sleeping on the ground and the corridor is clear. The blind man at the door continues his uniform toing-and-froing, he seems never to tire, but it is not so, after several minutes he takes his staff in the other hand and starts all over again. The doctor's wife advanced keeping close to the wall on the other side, taking care not to rub against it. The curve made by the stick does not even reach halfway across the wide corridor, one is tempted to say that this guard is on duty with an unloaded weapon. The doctor's wife is now directly opposite the blind man, she can see the ward behind him. Not all the beds are occupied. How many are there, she wondered. She advanced a little further, almost to the point where his stick could reach, and there she came to a halt, the blind man had turned his head to the side where she was standing, as if he had sensed something unusual, a sigh, a tremor in the air. He was a tall man, with large hands. First he stretched out before him the hand holding the stick and with rapid gestures swept the emptiness before him, then took a short step, for one second, the doctor's wife feared that he might be able to see her, that he was only looking for the best place to attack her, Those eyes are not blind, she thought with alarm. Yes, of course they were blind, as blind as those of all the inmates living under this roof, between these walls, all of them, all of them except her. In a low voice, almost in a whisper, the man asked, Who's there, he did not shout like a real guard, Who goes there, friend or foe, the appropriate reply would be, Friend, whereupon he would say, Pass, but keep your distance, however, things did not turn out this way, he merely shook his head as if he were saying to himself, What nonsense, how could anyone be there, at this hour everyone is asleep. Fumbling with his free hand, he retreated back towards the door, and, calmed by his own words, he let his arms hang. He felt sleepy, he had been waiting for ages for one of his comrades to come and relieve him, but for this to happen it was necessary that the other, on hearing the inner voice of duty, should wake up by himself, for there were no alarm clocks around nor any means of using them. Cautiously, the doctor's wife reached the other side of the door and looked inside. The ward was not full. She made a rapid calculation, decided there must be some nineteen or twenty occupants. At the far end, she saw a number of food containers piled up, others were lying on the empty beds. As was only to be expected, they don't distribute all the food they receive, she thought. The blind man seemed to be getting worried again, but made no attempt to investigate. The minutes passed. The sound of someone coughing loudly, obviously a heavy smoker, could be heard coming from inside. The blind man turned his head apprehensively, at last he would get some sleep. None of those lying in bed got up. Then the blind man, slowly, as if afraid that they might surprise him in the act of abandoning his post or infringing at one go all the rules guards are obliged to observe, sat down on the edge of the bed blocking the entrance. For a few moments, he nodded, then he succumbed to the river of sleep, and in all certainty as he went under he must have thought, It doesn't matter, no one can see me. The doctor's wife counted once more those who were asleep inside, Including him there are twenty of them, at least she had gathered some real information, her nocturnal excursion had not been in vain, But was this my only reason for coming here, she asked herself, and she preferred not to pursue the answer. The blind man was sleeping, his head resting against the doorjamb, his stick had slipped silently to the floor, there was a defenceless blind man and with no columns to bring crashing down around him. The doctor's wife consciously wanted to think that this man had stolen the food, had stolen what rightfully belonged to others, that he took food from the mouths of children, but despite these thoughts, she did not feel any contempt, not even the slightest irritation, nothing other than a strange compassion for that drooping body before her, the head lolling backwards, the long neck covered in swollen veins. For the first time since she had left the ward she felt a cold shiver run through her, it was as if the flagstones were turning her feet to ice, as if they were being scorched. Let's hope it isn't fever, she thought. It couldn't be, more likely some infinite weariness, a longing to curl up inside herself, her eyes, especially her eyes, turned inwards, more, more, more, until they could reach and observe inside her own brain, there where the difference between seeing and not seeing is invisible to the naked eye. Slowly, ever more slowly, dragging her body, she retraced her footsteps to the place where she belonged, she passed by blind internees who seemed like sleepwalkers, as she must have seemed to them, she did not even have to pretend that she was blind. The blind lovers were no longer holding hands, they were asleep and lying huddled beside each other, she in the curve made by his body to keep warm, and taking a closer look, they were holding hands, after all, his arm over her body, their fingers clasped. There inside the ward, the blind woman who had been unable to sleep was still sitting up in bed, waiting until she became so tired that her body would finally overcome the obstinate resistance of her mind. All the others appeared to be sleeping, some with their heads covered, as if they were still searching for some impossible darkness. On the bedside table of the girl with dark glasses stood the bottle of eye-drops. Her eyes were already better, but she was not to know.

If, because of a sudden illumination that might quell his suspicions, the blind man entrusted with keeping an account of the ill-gotten gains of the miscreants had decided to come over to this side with his writing board, his thick paper and puncher, he would now almost certainly be occupied in drafting the instructive and lamentable chronicle of the inadequate diet and the many other privations of these new fellow-inmates who have been well and truly fleeced. He would begin by saying that from where he had come, the usurpers had not only expelled the respectable blind inmates from the ward in order to take possession of the entire space, but, furthermore, had forbidden the inmates of the other two wards on the left-hand side any access or use of the respective sanitary installations, as they are called. He would remark that the immediate outcome of this infamous tyranny was that all those poor people would flock to the lavatories on this side, with consequences easy to imagine for anyone who still remembers the earlier state of the place. He would point out that it is impossible to walk through the inner courtyard without tripping over blind inmates getting rid of their diarrhoea or in contortions from ineffectual straining that had promised much and in the end resolved nothing, and, being an observant soul, he would not fail, deliberately, to register the patent contradiction between the small amount the inmates consumed and the vast quantity they excreted, perhaps thus showing that the famous relationship between cause and effect, so often cited, is not, at least from a quantitative point of view, always to be trusted. He would also say that while at this hour the ward of this thieving rabble must be crammed with containers of food, here it will not be long before the poor wretches are reduced to gathering up crumbs from the filthy floors. Nor would the blind accountant forget to condemn, in his dual role as participant in the process and its chronicler, the criminal conduct of these blind oppressors, who prefer to allow the food to go bad rather than give it to those who are in such great need, for while it is true that some of this foodstuff can last for weeks without going off, the rest, especially the cooked food, unless eaten immediately, soon turns sour or becomes covered in mould, and is therefore no longer fit for human consumption, if this sorry lot can still be thought of as human beings. Changing the subject but not the theme, the chronicler would write, with much sorrow in his heart, that the illnesses here are not solely those of the digestive tract, whether from lack of food or because of poor digestion of what was eaten, most of the people arriving here, though blind, were not only healthy, but some to all appearances were positively bursting with health, now they are like the others, unable to raise themselves from their miserable beds, stricken by influenza that spread who knows how. And not a single aspirin is there to be found anywhere in these five wards to lower their temperatures and relieve the pain of their headaches, what little was left was soon gone, after one had rummaged even through the lining of the women's handbags. Out of discretion, the chronicler would abandon any idea of making a detailed report of all the other ills that are afflicting most of the nearly three hundred inmates being kept in this inhumane quarantine, but he could not fail to mention at least two cases of fairly advanced cancer, for the authorities had no humanitarian scruples when rounding up the blind and confining them here, they even stated that the law once made is the same for everyone and that democracy is incompatible with preferential treatment. As cruel fate would have it, amongst all these inmates there is only one doctor, and an ophthalmologist at that, the last thing we needed. Arriving at this point, the blind accountant, tired of describing so much misery and sorrow, would let his metal punch fall to the table, he would search with a trembling hand for the piece of stale bread he had put to one side while he fulfilled his obligations as chronicler of the end of time, but he would not find it, because another blind man, whose sense of smell had become very keen out of dire necessity, had filched it. Then, renouncing his fraternal gesture, the altruistic impulse that had brought him rushing to this side, the blind accountant would decide that the best course of action, if he was still in time, was to return to the third ward on the left, there, at least, however much the injustices of those hoodlums stirred up in him feelings of honest indignation, he would not go hungry.

This is really the crux of the matter. Each time those sent to fetch the food return to their ward with the meagre rations they have been given there is an outburst of angry protest. There is always someone who proposes collective action, a mass demonstration, using the forceful argument about the cumulative strength of their numbers, confirmed time and time again and sublimated in the dialectic affirmation that determined wills, in general merely capable of being added one to the other, are also very capable in certain circumstances of multiplying among themselves ad infinitum. However, it was not long before the inmates calmed down, it was enough that someone more prudent, with the simple and objective intention of pondering the advantages and risks of the action proposed, should remind the enthusiasts of the fatal effects handguns tend to have, Those who went ahead, they would say, would know what awaits them there, and as for those behind, best not to think of what might happen in the likely event that we should take fright at the first shot, more of us would be crushed to death than shot down. As an intermediate decision, it was decided in one of the wards, and word of this decision was passed on to the others, that, for the collection of food, they would not send the usual emissaries who had been subjected to derision but a sizable group, some ten or twelve persons to be more precise, who would try to express as one voice, the general discontent. Volunteers were asked to come forward, but, perhaps because of the aforementioned warnings of the more cautious, few came forward for this mission in any of the wards. Fortunately, this patent show of moral weakness ceased to have any importance, and even to be a cause for shame, when, proving prudence to be the correct response, the outcome of the expedition organised by the ward that had thought up the idea became known. The eight courageous souls who had been so bold were immediately chased away with cudgels, and while it is true that only one bullet was fired, it is also true that it was not aimed as high as the first shots, the proof being that the protesters claimed they had heard it whistle right past their heads. Whether there had been any intent to kill we shall perhaps discover later, for the present we shall give the marksman the benefit of the doubt, that is to say, either that the shot was no more than a warning, although a more serious one, or the leader of these rogues underestimated the height of the demonstrators whom he imagined to be shorter, or, a disconcerting thought, his mistake was to imagine them taller than they really were, in which case an intent to kill would inevitably have to be considered. Leaving aside these trifling questions for the moment and turning to issues of general concern, which are those that matter, it was truly providential, even if merely a coincidence, that the protesters should have declared themselves the representatives of such and such a ward. In this way, only that ward had to fast for three days as a punishment, and fortunately for them, for they could have had their provisions cut off for ever, as is only just when someone dares to bite the hand that feeds him. So, during these three days, there was no other solution for those from the rebellious ward than to go from door to door and beg a crust of bread, for pity's sake, if possible with a bit of meat or cheese, they did not die of hunger, to be sure, but they had to take an earful, With ideas like that, what do you expect, If we had listened to you, where would we be now, but worst of all was to be told, Be patient, be patient, there are no crueller words, better to be insulted. And when the three days of punishment were over and it was thought that a new day was about to dawn, it became clear that the punishment of that unhappy ward where the forty rebellious inmates were quartered, was not yet over after all, for the rations which up until now had barely been enough for twenty, were now reduced to the point where they would not satisfy the hunger of ten. You can imagine, therefore, their outrage and indignation, and also, let it hurt whom it may, facts are facts, the fear of the remaining wards, who already saw themselves being besieged by the needy, their reactions divided between the classic duties of human solidarity and the observance of the ancient and no less time-honoured precept that charity begins at home.

Things were at this stage when an order came from the hoodlums that more money and valuables should be handed over inasmuch as they considered that the food supplies had exceeded the value of the initial payment, which moreover, according to them, had generously been calculated to be on the high side. The wards replied in despair that not so much as a coin was left in their pockets, that all the valuables collected had been scrupulously handed in, and that, a truly shameful argument, no decision could be altogether equitable if it were to ignore the difference in value of the various contributions, that is to say, in simple language, it was not fair that the upright man should pay for the sinner, and therefore that they should not cut off the provisions from someone, who in all probability, still had a balance to their credit. Obviously, none of the wards knew the value of what had been handed over by the others, but each ward thought it had every right to go on eating when the rest had already used up their credit. Fortunately, thanks to the fact that these latent conflicts were nipped in the bud, the hoodlums were adamant, their order had to be obeyed by everyone, if there had been any differences in the evaluation these were known only to the blind accountant. In the wards the exchanges were heated and bitter, sometimes becoming violent. Some suspected that certain selfish and dishonest inmates had withheld some of their valuables when the collection took place, and therefore had been given food at the expense of those who had given away everything to benefit the community. Others alleged, adopting what up until that moment had been a collective argument, that what they had handed over, should in itself be enough for them to go on being fed for many days to come, instead of being forced to feed parasites. The threat made by the blind thugs at the outset, that they would carry out an inspection of the wards and punish those who had disobeyed their orders, ended up by being carried out inside each of the wards, the honest at loggerheads with the dishonest, and even the malicious. No great fortunes were discovered, but some watches and rings came to light, mostly belonging to men rather than women. As for the punishments exacted by internal justice, these were nothing more than a few random slaps, a few half-hearted and badly aimed punches, most of the exchanges were verbal insults, some accusing expression culled from the rhetoric of the past, for example, You'd steal from your own mother, just imagine, as if a similar ignominy, and others of even greater consideration would only be committed the day that everyone went blind, and, having lost the light of their eyes, even lost the guiding spirit of respect. The blind thugs received the payment with threats of harsh reprisals, which fortunately they did not carry out, the assumption being that they had forgotten, when the truth is that they already had another idea, as would soon be revealed. If they were to carry out their threats and further injustices, they would aggravate the situation, perhaps with immediate dramatic consequences, insofar as two of the wards, in order to conceal their crime of holding back valuables, presented themselves in the name of others, burdening the innocent wards with transgressions they had not committed, one of them so honest, in fact, that it had handed over everything on the first day. Fortunately, in order to spare himself more work, the blind accountant had decided to keep note of the various contributions that had just been made on a single and separate sheet of paper, and this was to everyone's advantage, both the innocent and the guilty, for the fiscal irregularity would almost certainly have caught his attention if he had entered them against the respective accounts.

After a week, the blind hoodlums sent a message saying that they wanted women. Just like that, Bring us women. This unexpected demand, although not altogether unusual, caused an outcry as one might have expected, the bewildered emissaries who had come with the order returned at once to communicate that the wards, the three on the right and the two on the left, not excepting the blind men and women who were sleeping on the floor, had decided unanimously to ignore this degrading imposition, arguing that human dignity, in this instance feminine, could not be debased to this extent, and that if the third ward on the left-hand side had no women, the responsibility, if any, could not be laid at their door. The reply was curt and intransigent, Unless you bring us women, you don't eat. Humiliated, the emissaries returned to the wards with this order, Either you go there or they will give us nothing to eat. The women on their own, those without any partner, or at least any fixed partner, protested at once, they were not prepared to pay for the food for other women's menfolk with what they had between their legs, one of them was even so bold as to say, forgetting the respect she owed her own sex, I'll go there if I want to, but whatever I may earn is for me, and if I so please, I'll move in with them, then I'll have a bed and my keep assured. These were the unequivocal words she uttered, but she did not put them into action, she remembered in time the horrors she would experience if she had to cope on her own with the erotic frenzy of twenty desperate men whose urgency gave the impression they were blinded by lust. However, this declaration made so lightly in the second ward on the right-hand side, did not fall on stony ground, one of the emissaries, with a particular sense of occasion, supported her by proposing that women volunteers should come forward for this service, taking into account that what one does on one's own initiative is generally less arduous than if one has to do something under duress. Only one last scruple, one last reminder of the need for caution, prevented him from ending his appeal by quoting the well-known proverb, When the spirit is willing, your feet are light. Even so, no sooner had he stopped speaking than the protests erupted, anger broke out on all sides, without pity or compassion, the men were morally defeated, they were accused of being yobs, pimps, parasites, vampires, exploiters, panderers, according to the culture, social background and personal disposition of the women who were rightly indignant. Some of them declared their remorse at having given in, out of sheer generosity and compassion, to the sexual overtures of their companions in misfortune who were now showing their ingratitude by trying to push them into the worst of fates. The men tried to justify themselves, that it was not quite like that, that they should not dramatise, what the hell, by talking things over, people can come to some understanding, it was only because custom demands that volunteers should be asked to come forward in difficult and dangerous situations, as this one undoubtedly is, We are all at risk of dying of hunger, both you and us. Some of the women calmed down by this reasoning, but one of the others, suddenly inspired, threw another log on the fire when she asked ironically, And what would you do if these rascals instead of asking for women had asked for men, what would you do then, speak up so that everyone can hear. The women were jubilant, Tell us, tell us, they chorused, delighted at having backed the men up against the wall, caught in the snares of their own reasoning from which there was no escape, now they wanted to see how far that much lauded masculine logic would go, There are no pansies here, one man dared to protest, And no whores either, retorted the woman who had asked the provocative question, and even if there were, they might not be prepared to prostitute themselves for you. Put out, the men shrugged their shoulders, aware that there was only one answer capable of satisfying these vindictive women. If they were to ask for men, we would go, but not one of them had the courage to utter these brief, explicit and uninhibited words, and they were so dismayed that they forgot that there was no great harm in saying this, since those sons of bitches were not interested in relieving themselves with men but with women.

Now what did not occur to any of the men appeared to have occurred to the women, there could be no other explanation for the silence that gradually descended on the ward where these confrontations took place, as if they had understood that for them, victory in a verbal battle of wits was no different from the defeat that would inevitably follow, perhaps in the other wards the debate had been much the same, since we know that human reason and unreason are the same everywhere. Here, the person who passed the final judgment was a woman already in her fifties who had her old mother with her and no other means of providing her with food, I'll go, she said, without knowing that these words echoed those spoken by the doctor's wife in the first ward on the right-hand side, I'll go, there are few women in this ward, perhaps for that reason the protests were fewer or less vehement, there was the girl with dark glasses, there was the wife of the first blind man, there was the girl from the surgery, there was the chambermaid, there was one woman nobody knew anything about, there was the woman who could not sleep, but she was so unhappy and wretched that it would be best to leave her in peace, for there was no reason why only the men should benefit from the women's solidarity. The first blind man had begun by declaring that his wife would not be subjected to the shame of giving her body to strangers in exchange for whatever, she had no desire to do so nor would he permit it, for dignity has no price, that when someone starts making small concessions, in the end life loses all meaning. The doctor then asked him what meaning he saw in the situation in which all of them there found themselves, starving, covered in filth up to their ears, ridden with lice, eaten by bedbugs, bitten by fleas, I, too, would prefer my wife not to go, but what I want serves no purpose, she has said she is prepared to go, that was her decision, I know that my manly pride, this thing we call male pride, if after so many humiliations we still preserve something worthy of that name, I know that it will suffer, it already is, I cannot avoid it, but it is probably the only solution, if we want to live, Each person proceeds according to whatever morals they have, that's how I see it and I have no intention of changing my ideas, the first blind man retorted aggressively. Then the girl with dark glasses said, The others don't know how many women are here, therefore you can keep yours for your exclusive use, we shall feed both you and her, I'd be interested to see how you feel then about your dignity, how the bread we bring you will taste, That's not the point, the first blind man started to reply, the point is, but his words tailed off, were left hanging in the air, in reality he did not know what the point was, everything he had said earlier had been no more than certain vague opinions, nothing more than opinions belonging to another world, not to this one, what he ought to do, no doubt about it, was to raise his hands to heaven thanking fortune that his shame might remain, as it were, at home, rather than bear the vexation of knowing that he was being kept alive by the wives of others. By the doctor's wife, to be absolutely precise, because as for the rest, apart from the girl with dark glasses, unmarried and free, about whose dissipated life-style we have more than enough information, if they had husbands they were not to be seen. The silence that followed the interrupted phrase seemed to be waiting for someone to clarify the situation once and for all, for this reason it was not long before the person who had to speak spoke up, this was the wife of the first blind man, who said without so much as a tremor in her voice, I'm no different from the others, I'll do whatever they do, You'll do as I say, interrupted her husband, Stop giving orders, they won't do much good here, you're as blind as I am, It's indecent, It's up to you not to be indecent, from now on you don't eat, this was her cruel reply, unexpected in someone who until today had been so docile and respectful towards her husband. There was a short burst of laughter, it came from the hotel maid, Ah, eat, eat, what is he to do, poor fellow, suddenly her laughter turned to weeping, her words changed, What are we to do, she said, it was almost a question, an almost resigned question to which there was no answer, like a despondent shaking of the head, so much so that the girl from the surgery did nothing but repeat, What are we to do. The doctor's wife looked up at the scissors hanging on the wall, from the expression in her eyes you would say she was asking herself the same question, unless what she was looking for was an answer to the question she threw back at them, What do you want from me.

However, to everything its proper season, just because you rise early does not mean that you will die sooner. The blind inmates in the third ward on the left-hand side are well organised, they had already decided that they would begin with those closest, with the women from the wards in their wing. The application of this method of rotation, a more than apt expression, has all the advantages and no drawbacks, in the first place, because it will allow them to know, at any given moment, what has been done and what remains to be done, like looking at a clock and saying of the day that is passing, I've lived from here to here, I've so much or so little left, in the second place, because when the round of the wards has been completed, the return to the beginning will bring with it an undeniable air of renovation, especially for those with a very short sensory memory. So let the women in the wards in the right wing enjoy themselves, I can cope with the misfortunes of my neighbours, words that none of the women spoke but which they all thought, in truth, the human being to lack that second skin we call egoism has not yet been born, it lasts much longer than the other one, that bleeds so readily. It also has to be said that these women are enjoying themselves on two counts, such are the mysteries of the human soul, for the inescapable impending threat of the humiliation to which they are to be subjected, aroused and exacerbated in each ward sensual appetites that increasing familiarity had jaded, it was as if the men were desperately putting their mark on the women before they were taken off, it was as if the women wanted to fill their memory with sensations experienced voluntarily in order to be able better to defend themselves from the aggression of those sensations which, if they could, they would reject. It is inevitable that we should ask, taking as an example the first ward on the right-hand side, how the question of the difference between the number of men and women was resolved, even discounting the impotent of the males in the group, as in the case of the old man with the black eyepatch as well as others, unidentified, both old and young, who for one reason or another, neither said nor did anything worth bringing into our narrative. As has already been mentioned, there are seven women in this ward, including the blind woman who suffers from insomnia and whom nobody knows, and the so-called normal couples, are no more than two, which would leave an unbalanced number of men, because the boy with the squint does not yet count. Perhaps in the other wards there are more women than men, but an unwritten law, that soon gained acceptance here and subsequently became statutory decrees that all matters have to be resolved in the wards in which they have surfaced in accordance with the precepts of the ancients, whose wisdom we shall never tire of praising, if you would be well served, serve yourself. Therefore the women from the first ward on the right-hand side will give relief to the men who live under the same roof, with the exception of the doctor's wife, who, for some reason or other, no one dared to solicit either with words or an extended hand. Already the wife of the first blind man, after having made the first move with that abrupt reply she had given her husband, did, albeit discreetly, what the other women had done, as she herself had announced. There are, however, certain resistances against which neither reason nor sentiment can do anything, such as is the case of the girl with dark glasses, whom the pharmacist's assistant, however many arguments he offered, however many pleas he made, was unable to win over, thus paying for his lack of respect at the outset. This same girl, there's no understanding women, who is the prettiest of all the women here, the one with the shapeliest figure, the most attractive, the one whom all the men craved when the word about her exceptional looks got around, finally got into bed one night of her own free will with the old man with the black eyepatch, who received her like summer rain and satisfied her as best he could, pretty well given his age, thus proving once more, that appearances are deceptive, that it is not from someone's face and the litheness of their body that we can judge their strength of heart. Everyone in the ward thought that it was nothing more than an act of charity that the girl with dark glasses should have offered herself to the old man with the black eyepatch, but there were men there, sensitive and dreamers, who having already enjoyed her favours, began to allow their thoughts to wander, to think there could be no greater prize in this world than for a man to find himself stretched out on his bed, all alone, thinking the impossible, only to realise that a woman is gently lifting the covers and slipping under them, slowly rubbing her body against his body, and then lying still, waiting for the heat of their blood to calm the sudden tremor of their startled skin. And all this for no good reason, just because she wanted to. These are fortunes that do not go to waste, sometimes a man has to be old and wear a black eyepatch covering an eye-socket that is definitively blind. And then there are certain things that are best left unexplained, it's best just to say what happened, not to probe people's inner thoughts and feelings, as on that occasion when the doctor's wife had got out of bed to go and cover up the boy with the squint whose blanket had slipped off. She did not go back to bed at once. Leaning against the wall at the far end of the ward, in the narrow space between the two rows of beds, she was looking in desperation at the door at the other end, that door through which they had entered on a day that seemed so remote and that now led nowhere. She was standing there when she saw her husband get up, and, staring straight ahead as if he were sleepwalking, make his way to the bed of the girl with dark glasses. She made no attempt to stop him. Standing motionless, she saw him lift the covers and then lie down, whereupon the girl woke up and received him without protest, she saw how those two mouths searched until they found each other, and then the inevitable happened, the pleasure of the one, the pleasure of the other, the pleasure of both of them, the muffled cries, she said, Oh, doctor, and these words could have sounded so ridiculous but did not, he said, Forgive me, I don't know what came over me, in fact, we were right, how could we, who hardly see, know what even he does not know, Lying on the narrow bed, they could not have imagined that they were being watched, the doctor certainly could not, he was suddenly worried, would his wife be asleep, he asked himself, or was she wandering the corridors as she did every night, he made to go back to his own bed, but a voice said, Don't get up, and a hand rested on his chest with the lightness of a bird, he was about to speak, perhaps about to repeat that he did not know what had got into him, but the voice said, If you say nothing it will be easier for me to understand. The girl with dark glasses began to weep, What an unhappy lot we are, she murmured, and then, I wanted it too, I wanted it too, you are not to blame, Be quiet the doctor's wife said gently, let's all keep quiet, there are times when words serve no purpose, if only I, too, could weep, say everything with tears, not have to speak in order to be understood. She sat on the edge of the bed, stretched her arm over the two bodies, as if gathering them in the same embrace, and, bending over the girl with dark glasses, she whispered in her ear, I can see. The girl remained still, serene, simply puzzled that she should feel no surprise, it was as if she had known from the very first day but had not wanted to say so aloud since this was a secret that did not belong to her. She turned her head ever so slightly and responded by whispering into the ear of the doctor's wife, I knew, at least, I'm not entirely sure, but I think I knew, It's a secret, you mustn't tell a soul, don't worry, I trust you, And so you should, I'd rather die than betray you, You must call me "tu," Oh, no, I couldn't, I simply couldn't do it. They went on whispering to each other, first one, then the other, touching each other's hair, the lobe of the ear, with their lips, it was an insignificant dialogue, it was a profoundly serious dialogue, if this contradiction can be reconciled, a brief conspiratorial conversation that appeared to ignore the man lying between the two of them, but involved him in a logic outside the world of commonplace ideas and realities. Then the doctor's wife said to her husband, Lie there for a little longer, if you wish, No, I'm going back to our bed, Then I'll help you. She sat up to give him greater freedom of movement, contemplated for an instant the two blind heads resting side by side on the soiled pillow, their faces dirty, their hair tangled, only their eyes shining to no purpose. He got up slowly, looking for support, then remained motionless at the side of the bed, undecided, as if he had suddenly lost all notion of the place where he found himself, then she, as she had always done, took him by one arm, but the gesture now had another meaning, never had he so badly needed someone to guide him as at this moment, although he would never know to what extent, only the two women really knew, when the doctor's wife stroked the girl's cheek with her other hand and the girl impulsively took it and raised it to her lips. The doctor thought he could hear sobbing, an almost inaudible sound that could have come only from tears trickling slowly down to the corners of the mouth where they disappear to recommence the eternal cycle of inexplicable human joys and sorrows. The girl with dark glasses was about to remain alone, she was the one who ought to be consoled, for this reason the doctor's wife was slow to remove her hand.

Next day, at dinner-time, if a few miserable pieces of stale bread and mouldy meat deserved such a name, there appeared in the doorway of the ward three blind men from the other side. How many women have you got in here, one of them asked, Six, replied the doctor's wife, with the good intention of leaving out the blind woman who suffered from insomnia, but she corrected her in a subdued voice, There are seven of us. The blind thugs laughed, Too bad, said one of them, you'll just have to work all the harder tonight, and another suggested, Perhaps we'd better go and look for reinforcements in the next ward, It isn't worth it, said the third blind man who knew his sums, it works out at three men for each woman, they can stand it. This brought another burst of laughter, and the fellow who had asked how many women there were, gave the order, When you've finished, come over to us, and added, That's if you want to eat tomorrow and suckle your menfolk. They said these words in all the wards, and still laughed at the joke with as much gusto as on the day they had invented it. They doubled up with laughter, stamped their feet, beat their thick cudgels on the ground, until one of them suddenly cautioned, Listen here, if any of you has got the curse, we don't want you, we'll leave it until the next time, No one's got the curse, the doctor's wife calmly informed him, Then prepare yourselves and don't be long, we're waiting for you. They turned and disappeared. The ward remained in silence. A minute later, the wife of the first blind man said, I cannot eat any more, she had precious little in her hand, and she could not bear to eat it. Nor me, said the blind woman who suffered from insomnia, Nor me, said the woman whom nobody seems to know, I've already finished, said the hotel maid, Me too, said the girl from the surgery, I'll throw up in the face of the first man who comes near me, said the girl with dark glasses. They were all on their feet, shaking and resolute. Then the doctor's wife said, I'll go in front. The first blind man covered his head with the blanket as if this might serve some purpose, since he was already blind, the doctor drew his wife towards him and, without saying anything, gave her a quick kiss on the forehead, what more could he do, it wouldn't make much difference to the other men, they had neither the rights nor the obligations of a husband as far as any of these women were concerned, therefore no one could come up to them and say, A consenting cuckold is a cuckold twice over. The girl with dark glasses got in behind the doctor's wife, then came the hotel maid, the girl from the surgery, the wife of the first blind man, the woman no one knows and, finally, the blind woman suffering from insomnia, a grotesque line-up of foul-smelling women, their clothes filthy and in tatters, it seems impossible that the animal drive for sex should be so powerful, to the point of blinding a man's sense of smell, the most delicate of the senses, there are even some theologians who affirm, although not in these exact words, that the worst thing about trying to live a reasonable life in hell is getting used to the dreadful stench down there. Slowly, guided by the doctor's wife, each of them with her hand on the shoulder of the one in front, the women started walking. They were all barefoot because they did not want to lose their shoes amidst the trials and tribulations they were about to endure. When they arrived in the hallway of the main entrance, the doctor's wife headed for the outer door, no doubt anxious to know if the world still existed. When she felt the fresh air, the hotel maid remembered, frightened, We can't go out, the soldiers are out there, and the blind woman suffering from insomnia said, All the better for us, in less than a minute we'd be dead, that is how we ought to be, all dead, You mean us, asked the girl from the surgery, No, all of us, all the women in here, at least then we'd have the best of reasons for being blind. She had never had so much to say for herself since she'd been brought here. The doctor's wife said, Let's go, only those who have to die will die, death doesn't give any warning when it singles you out. They passed through the door that gave access to the left wing, they made their way down the long corridors, the women from the first two wards could, if they had wished, tell them what awaited them, but they were curled up in their beds like animals that had been given a good thrashing, the men did not dare to touch them, nor did they make any attempt to get close, because the women immediately started screaming.

In the last corridor, at the far end, the doctor's wife saw a blind man who was keeping a lookout, as usual. He must have heard their shuffling footsteps, and informed the others, They're coming, they're coming. From within came cries, whinnying, guffaws of laughter. Four blind men lost no time in removing the bed that was blocking the entrance, Quickly, girls, come in, come in, we're all here like studs in heat, you're going to get your bellies filled, said one of them. The blind thugs surrounded them, tried to fondle them, but fell back in disarray, when their leader, the one who had the gun, shouted, The first choice is mine as you well know. The eyes of all those men anxiously sought out the women, some extended avid hands, if in passing they happened to touch one of them they finally knew where to look. In the middle of the aisle, between the beds, the women stood like soldiers on parade waiting to be inspected. The leader of the blind hoodlums, gun in hand, came up to them, as agile and frisky as if he were able to see them. He placed his free hand on the woman suffering from insomnia, who was first in line, fondled her back and front, her hips, her breasts, between her legs. The blind woman began to scream and he pushed her away, You're a worthless whore. He passed on to the next one, who happened to be the woman that no one knew, now he was fondling her with both hands, having put his gun into his trouser pocket, I say, this one isn't at all bad, and then he moved on to the wife of the first blind man, then the employee from the surgery, then the hotel maid, and exclaimed,

Listen, men, these fillies are pretty good. The blind hoodlums whinnied, stamped their feet on the ground, Let's get on with it, it's getting late, some yelled, Take it easy, said the thug with the gun, let me first take a look at the others. He fondled the girl with dark glasses and gave a whistle, Now then, here's a stroke of luck, no filly quite like this one has turned up before. Excited, as he went on fondling the girl, he passed on to the doctor's wife, gave another whistle, This one is on the mature side, but could turn out to be quite a woman. He drew the two women towards him, and almost drooled as he said, I'll keep these two, when I've finished with them, I'll pass them on to the rest of you. He dragged them to the end of the ward, where the containers of food, packets, tins had been piled up, enough supplies to feed a regiment. The women, all of them, were already screaming their heads off, blows, slaps, orders could be heard, Shut up, you whores, these bitches are all the same, they always have to start yelling, Give it to her good and hard and she'll soon be quiet, Just wait until it's my turn and you'll see how they'll be asking for more, Hurry up there, I can't wait another minute. The blind woman suffering from insomnia wailed in desperation beneath an enormous fellow, the other four were surrounded by men with their trousers down who were jostling each other like hyenas around a carcass. The doctor's wife found herself beside the bed where she had been taken, she was standing, her trembling hands gripping the railings of the bed, she watched how the blind leader with the gun tugged and tore the skirt of the girl with dark glasses, how he took down his trousers and, guiding himself with his fingers, pointed his member at the girl's sex, how he pushed and forced, she could hear the grunts, the obscenities, the girl with dark glasses said nothing, she only opened her mouth to vomit, her head to one side, her eyes turned towards the other woman, he did not even notice what was happening, the smell of vomit is only noticed when the atmosphere and all the rest does not smell the same, at last the man shuddered from head to foot, gave three violent jolts as if he were riveting three girders, panted like a suffocating pig, he had finished. The girl with dark glasses wept in silence. The blind man with the gun withdrew his penis, still dripping and said in a hesitant voice, as he stretched out his arm to the doctor's wife, Don't get jealous, I'll be dealing with you next, and then raising his voice, I say, boys, you can come and get this one, but treat her nicely for I may need her again. Half a dozen blind men advanced unsteadily along the passageway, grabbed the girl with dark glasses and almost dragged her away. I'm first, I'm first, said all of them. The blind man with the gun had sat down on the bed, his flaccid penis was resting on the edge of the mattress, his trousers rolled down round his ankles. Kneel down here between my legs, he said. The doctor's wife got on to her knees. Suck me, he said, No, she replied, Either you suck me, or I'll give you a good thrashing, and you won't get any food, he told her, Aren't you afraid I might bite off your penis, she asked him, You can try, I have my hands on your neck, I'd strangle you first if you tried to draw blood, he replied menacingly. Then he said, I seem to recognise your voice, And I recognise your face, You're blind and cannot see me, No, I cannot see you, Then why do you say that you recognise my face, Because that voice can have only one face, Suck me, and forget the chitchat, No, Either you suck me, or your ward won't see another crumb of bread, go back there and tell them that if they have nothing to eat it's because you refused to suck me, and then come back to tell me what happened. The doctor's wife leaned forward, with the tips of two fingers on her right hand she held and raised the man's sticky penis, her left hand resting on the floor, touched his trousers, groped, felt the cold metallic hardness of the gun, I can kill him, she thought. She could not. With his trousers round his ankles, it was impossible to reach the pocket where he had put his weapon. I cannot kill him now, she thought. She moved her head forward, opened her mouth, closed it, closed her eyes in order not to see and began sucking.

Day was breaking when the blind hoodlums allowed the women to go. The blind woman suffering from insomnia had to be carried away in the arms of her companions, who could scarcely drag themselves along. For hours they had passed from one man to another, from humiliation to humiliation, from outrage to outrage, exposed to everything that can be done to a woman while leaving her still alive. As you know, payment is in kind, tell those pathetic men of yours that they have to come and fetch the grub, the blind man with the gun said mockingly as they left. And he added derisively, See you again, girls, so prepare yourselves for the next session. The other blind hoodlums repeated more or less in chorus, See you again, some called them fillies, others whores, but their waning libido was obvious from the lack of conviction in their voices. Deaf, blind, silent, tottering on their feet, with barely enough will-power not to let go of the hand of the woman in front, the hand, not the shoulder, as when they had come, certainly not one of them would have known what to reply if they had been asked, Why are you holding hands as you go, it simply came about, there are gestures for which we cannot always find an easy explanation, sometimes not even a difficult one can be found. As they crossed the hallway, the doctor's wife looked outside, the soldiers were there as well as a truck that was almost certainly being used to distribute the food to those in quarantine. Just at that moment, the blind woman suffering from insomnia lost the power of her legs, literally, as if they had been cut off with a single blow, her heart also gave up, it did not even finish the rhythmic contraction it had started, at last we know why this blind woman could not sleep, now she will sleep, let us not wake her. She's dead, said the doctor's wife, and her voice was expressionless, if it were possible for such a voice, as dead as the word it had spoken, to have come from a living mouth. She raised the suddenly dislocated body, the legs covered in blood, her abdomen bruised, her poor breasts uncovered, brutally scarred, teeth marks on her shoulder where she had been bitten. This is the image of my body, she thought, the image of the body of all the women here, between these outrages and our sorrows there is only one difference, we, for the present, are still alive. Where shall we take her, asked the girl with dark glasses, For the moment to the ward, later we shall bury her, said the doctor's wife.

The men were waiting at the door, only the first blind man was missing, he had covered his head with his blanket once more when he realised the women were coming back, and the boy with the squint, who was asleep. Without hesitation, without having to count the beds, the doctor's wife laid the blind woman who suffered from insomnia on the bed she had occupied. She was unconcerned that the others might find it strange, after all, everyone there knew that she was the blind woman who was most familiar with every nook and cranny in the place. She's dead, she repeated, What happened, asked the doctor, but his wife made no attempt to answer him, his question might be simply what it appeared to mean, How did she die, but it could also imply What did they do to you in there, now, neither for the one nor for the other of these questions could there be an answer, she simply died, from what scarcely matters, it is foolish for anyone to ask what someone died from, in time the cause will be forgotten, only two words remain, She died, and we are no longer the same women as when we left here, the words they would have spoken we can no longer speak, and as for the others, the unnameable exists, that is its name, nothing else. Go and fetch the food, said the doctor's wife. Chance, fate, fortune, destiny, or whatever is the precise term for that which has so many names, is made of pure irony, how else could we understand why it was precisely the husbands of two of the women who were chosen to represent the ward and collect their food, when no one could imagine that the price would be what had just been paid. It could have been other men, unmarried, free, with no conjugal honour to defend, but then it had to be these two, who certainly will not now wish to bear the shame of extending a hand to beg from these degenerate rogues who have violated their wives. The first blind man said it, with all the emphasis of a firm decision, Whoever wishes can go, but I'm not going, I'll go, said the doctor, I'll go with you, said the old man with the black eyepatch. There won't be much food, but I warn you it's quite a weight, I still have the strength to carry the bread I eat, What always weighs more is the bread of the others, I have no right to complain, the weight carried by the others will buy me my food. Let us try to imagine, not the dialogue for that is over and done with, but the men who took part in it, they are there, face to face, as if they could see each other, which in this case is impossible, it is enough that the memory of each of them should bring out from the dazzling whiteness of the world the mouth that is articulating the words, and then, like a slow irradiation coming from this centre, the rest of the faces will start to appear, one an old man, the other not so old, and anyone who can still see in this way cannot really be called blind. When they moved off to go and collect the wages of shame, as the first blind man protested with rhetorical indignation, the doctor's wife said to the other women, Stay here, I'll be right back. She knew what she wanted, she did not know if she would find it. She needed a bucket or something that would serve the purpose, she wanted to fill it with water, even if fetid, even if polluted, she wanted to wash the corpse of the woman who had suffered from insomnia, to wipe away her own blood and the sperm of others, to deliver her purified to the earth, if it still makes sense to speak of the purity of the body in this asylum where we are living, for purity of the soul, as we know, is beyond everyone's reach.

Blind men lay stretched out on the long tables in the refectory. From a dripping tap over a sink full of garbage, trickled a thread of water. The doctor's wife looked around her in search of a bucket or basin but could see nothing that might serve her purpose. One of the blind men was disturbed by this presence and asked, Who's there, She did not reply, she knew that she would not be welcome, that no one would say, You need water, then take it, and if it's to wash the corpse of a dead woman, take all the water you want. Scattered on the floor were plastic bags, those used for the food, some of them large. She thought they must be torn, then reflected that by using two or three, one inside the other, not much water would be lost. She acted quickly, the blind men were already getting down from the tables and asking, Who's there, even more alarmed when they heard the sound of running water, they headed in that direction, the doctor's wife got out of the way and pushed a table across their path so that they could not come near, she then retrieved her bag, the water was running slowly, in desperation she forced the tap, then, as if it had been released from some prison, the water spurted out, splashed all over the place and soaked her from head to foot. The blind men took fright and drew back, they thought a pipe must have burst, and they had all the more reason to think so when the flood reached their feet, they were not to know that it had been spilled by the stranger who had entered, as it happened the woman had realised that she would not be able to carry so much weight. She tied a knot in the bag, threw it over her shoulder, and, as best she could, fled.

When the doctor and the old man with the black eyepatch entered the ward with the food, they did not see, could not see, seven naked women and the corpse of the woman who suffered from insomnia stretched out on her bed, cleaner than she had ever been in all her life, while another woman was washing her companions, one by one, and then herself.

On the fourth day, the thugs reappeared. They had come to exact payment from the women in the second ward, but they paused for a moment at the door of the first ward to ask if the women there had yet recovered from the sexual orgy of the other night, A great night, yes sir, exclaimed one of them licking his chops and another confirmed, Those seven were worth fourteen, it's true that one of them was no great shakes, but in the middle of all that uproar who noticed, their men are lucky sods, if they're man enough for them. It would be better if they weren't, then they'd be more eager. From the far end of the ward, the doctor's wife said, There are no longer seven of us, Has one of you vamoosed, someone in the group asked, laughing, She didn't vamoose, she died, Oh, hell, then you lot will have to work all the harder next time, It wasn't much of a loss, she was no great shakes, said the doctor's wife. Disconcerted, the messengers did not know how to respond, what they had just heard struck them as indecent, some of them even came round to thinking that when all is said and done all women are bitches, such a lack of respect, to refer to a woman like that, just because her tits weren't in the right place and she had no arse to speak of. The doctor's wife was looking at them, as they hovered there in the doorway, undecided, moving their bodies like mechanical dolls. She recognised them, she had been raped by all three of them. At last, one of them tapped his stick on the ground, Let's go, he said. Their tapping and their warning cries, Keep back, keep back, it's us, died away as they made their way along the corridor, then there was silence, vague sounds, the women from the second ward were receiving the order to present themselves after dinner. Once more the tapping of sticks could be heard, Keep back, keep back, the shadows of the three blind men passed through the doorway and they were gone.

The doctor's wife who had been telling the boy with the squint a story, raised her arm and, without a sound, took the scissors from the nail. She said to the boy, Later I'll tell you the rest of the story. No one in the ward had asked her why she had spoken with such disdain of the blind woman who had suffered from insomnia. After a while, she removed her shoes and went to reassure her husband, I won't be long, I'm coming straight back. She headed for the door. There she paused and remained waiting. Ten minutes later the women from the second ward appeared in the corridor. There were fifteen of them. Some were crying. They were not in line, but in groups, tied to each other with strips of cloth that had clearly been torn from their bedclothes. When they had passed, the doctor's wife followed them. Not one of them perceived that they had company. They knew what awaited them, the news of the abuses they would suffer was no secret, nor were these abuses anything really new, for in all certainty this is how the world began. What terrified them was not so much the rape, but the orgy, the shame, the anticipation of the terrible night ahead, fifteen women sprawled on the beds and on the floor, the men going from one to the other, snorting like pigs, The worst thing of all is that I might feel some pleasure, one of the women thought to herself. When they entered the corridor giving access to the ward they were heading for, the blind man on the lookout alerted the others, I can hear them, they'll be here any minute. The bed being used as a gate was quickly removed, one by one the women entered, Wow, so many of them, exclaimed the blind accountant, as he counted them enthusiastically, Eleven, twelve, thirteen, fourteen, fifteen, fifteen, there are fifteen of them. He went after the last one, put his eager hands up her skirt, This one is game, she's mine, he was saying. They had finished sizing up the women and making a preliminary assessment of their physical attributes. In fact, if all of them were condemned to endure the same fate, there was no point in wasting time and cooling their desire as they made their choice according to height and the measurement of busts and hips. They were soon taking them off to bed, already stripping them by force, and it was not long before the usual weeping and pleas for mercy could be heard, but the replies when they came, were always the same, If you want to eat, open your legs. And they opened their legs, some were ordered to use their mouth like the one who was crouched down between the knees of the leader of these ruffians and this one was saying nothing. The doctor's wife entered the ward, slipped slowly between the beds, but she need not even have taken these precautions, no one would have heard her had she been wearing clogs, and if, in the middle of the fracas, some blind man were to touch her and become aware that it was a woman, the worst that could happen to her would be having to join the others, not that anyone would notice, in a situation like this it is not easy to tell the difference between fifteen and sixteen.

The leader of these hoodlums still had his bed at the far end of the ward where the containers of food were stacked. The beds near his had been removed, the fellow liked to move at will without having to keep bumping into his neighbours. Killing him was going to be simple. As she slowly advanced along the narrow aisle, the doctor's wife studied the movements of the man she was about to kill, how he threw his head back as he took his pleasure, as if he were offering her his neck. Slowly, the doctor's wife approached, circled the bed and positioned herself behind him. The blind woman went on doing what was expected of her. The doctor's wife slowly raised the scissors, the blades slightly apart so that they might penetrate like two daggers. Just then, at the last minute, the blind man seemed to be aware of someone's presence, but his orgasm had transported him from the world of normal sensations, had deprived him of any reflexes, You won't have time to come, the doctor's wife reflected as she brought her arm down with tremendous force.

The scissors dug deep into the blind man's throat, turning on themselves they struggled with the cartilage and the membraneous tissues, then furiously went deeper until they came up against the cervical vertebrae. His cry was barely audible, it might have been the grunting of an animal about to ejaculate, as was happening to some of the other men, and perhaps it was, and at the same time as a spurt of blood splashed on to her face, the blind woman received the discharge of semen in her mouth. It was her cry that startled the blind men, they were more than used to hearing cries, but this was quite unlike the others. The blind woman was screaming, where had this blood come from, probably, without knowing how, she had done what it had crossed her mind to do and bitten off his penis. The blind men left the women, approached groping their way, What's going on, what's all this screaming, they asked, but the blind woman now had a hand over her mouth, someone had whispered in her ear, Be quiet, and then gently pulled her back, Say nothing, it was a woman's voice, and this calmed her, if that is possible in such distressing circumstances. The blind accountant arrived ahead of the others, he was the first to touch the body which had toppled across the bed, the first to run his hands over it, He's dead, he exclaimed almost immediately. The head was hanging down on the other side of the bed, the blood was still spurting out, They've killed him, he said. The blind men stopped in their tracks, they could not believe their ears, How could they have killed him, who killed him, They've made an enormous slit in his throat, it must have been that whore who was with him, we've got to get her. The blind men stirred once more, more slowly this time, as if they were afraid of coming up against the blade that had killed their leader. They could not see that the blind accountant was hastily rummaging through the dead man's pockets, that he was removing his gun and a small plastic bag with about ten cartridges. Everyone was suddenly distracted by an outcry from the women, already on their feet, in panic, anxious to get away from that place, but some had lost any notion of where the ward door was located, they went in the wrong direction and ran into the blind men who thought the women were about to attack them, whereupon the confusion of bodies reached new heights of delirium. At the far end of the ward, the doctor's wife quietly awaited the right moment to make her escape. She had a firm grip on the blind woman, in her other hand she held the scissors ready to land the first blow if any man should come near her. For the moment, the free space was in her favour, but she knew that she could not linger there. A number of women had finally found the door, others were struggling to free themselves from the hands holding them back, there was even the odd one still trying to throttle the enemy and deliver another corpse. The blind accountant called out with authority to his men, Keep calm, don't lose your nerve, we'll get to the bottom of this matter, and anxious to make his order all the more convincing he fired a shot into the air. The outcome was exactly the opposite of what he expected. Surprised to discover that the gun was already in other hands and that they were about to have a new leader, the blind hoodlums stopped struggling with the women, gave up trying to dominate them, one of the men having given up the struggle altogether because he had been strangled. It was at this point that the doctor's wife decided to move. Striking blows left and right, she opened a path. Now it was the blind thugs who were calling out, who were being knocked over and climbing all over each other, anyone there with eyes to see, would perceive that, compared with this, the previous upheaval had been a joke. The doctor's wife had no desire to kill, all she wanted was to get out as quickly as possible and, above all, not to leave a single blind woman behind. This one probably won't survive, she thought as she dug the scissors into a man's chest. Another shot was heard, Let's go, let's go, said the doctor's wife, pushing any blind women whom she encountered ahead of her. She helped them to their feet, repeated, Quickly, quickly, and now it was the blind accountant who was shouting from the far end of the ward, Grab them, don't let them escape, but it was too late, the women were already out in the corridor, they fled, stumbling as they went, half dressed, holding on to their rags as best they could. Standing still at the entrance to the ward, the doctor's wife called out in a rage, Remember what I said the other day, that I'd never forget his face, and from now on think about what I am telling you, for I won't forget your faces either, You'll pay dearly for this outrage, threatened the blind accountant, you and your companions and those so-called men of yours, You neither know who I am nor where I've come from, You're from the first ward on the other side, volunteered one of the men who had gone to summon the women, and the blind accountant added, Your voice is unmistakable, you need only utter one word in my presence and you're dead, The other fellow said the same thing and now he's a corpse, But I'm not a blind man like him or you, when you lot turned blind, I already knew everything about this world, You know nothing about my blindness. You're not blind, you can't fool me, Perhaps I'm the blindest of all, I've already killed and I'll kill again if I have to, You'll die first of hunger, from today onwards there will be no more food, even if you were all to come offering on a tray the three holes you were born with. For each day that we're deprived of food because of you, one of the men here will die the moment he steps outside this door, You won't get away with this, Oh, yes we will, from now on we shall be collecting the food, and you can eat what you've hoarded there, Bitch, Bitches are neither men nor women, they're bitches, and you know now what they're worth. Enraged, the blind accountant fired in the direction of the door. The bullet whizzed past the heads of the blind men without hitting anyone and lodged itself in the corridor wall. You didn't get me, said the doctor's wife, and take care, if your ammunition runs out, there are others here who would like to be leader too.

She moved away, took a few steps, still firm, then advanced along the wall of the corridor, almost fainting, suddenly her legs gave way, and she fell to the ground. Her eyes clouded over, I'm going blind, she thought, but then realised it would not be just yet, these were only tears blurring her vision, tears such as she had never shed in all her life, I've killed a man, she said in a low voice, I wanted to kill him and I have. She turned her head in the direction of the ward door, if the blind men were to come now, she would be unable to defend herself. The corridor was deserted. The woman had disappeared, the blind men, still startled by the gunfire and even more by the corpses of their own men, did not dare come out. Little by little she regained her strength. Her tears continued to flow, slower and more serene, as if confronted by something irremediable. She struggled to her feet. She had blood on her hands and clothes, and suddenly her exhausted body told her that she was old, Old and a murderess, she thought, but she knew that if it were necessary, she would kill again, And when is it necessary to kill, she asked herself as she headed in the direction of the hallway, and she herself answered the question, When what is still alive is already dead. She shook her head and thought, And what does that mean, words, nothing but words. She walked on alone. She approached the door leading to the forecourt. Between the railings of the gate she could just make out the shadow of a soldier who was keeping guard. There are still people out there, people who can see. The sound of footsteps behind her caused her to tremble, It's them, she thought and turned round rapidly with her scissors at the ready. It was her husband. As they went past, the women from the second ward had been shouting out what had happened on the other side, that a woman had stabbed and killed the leader of the thugs, that there had been shooting, the doctor did not ask them to identify the woman, it could only be his wife, she had told the boy with the squint that she would tell him the rest of the story later, and what would have become of her now, probably dead as well, I'm here, she said, and went up to him and embraced him, not noticing that she was smearing him with blood, or noticing but unconcerned, for until now they had shared everything. What happened, the doctor asked, they said a man was killed, Yes, I killed him, Why, Someone had to do it, and there was no one else, And now, Now we're free, they know what awaits them if they ever try to abuse us again, There's likely to be a battle, a war, The blind are always at war, always have been at war, Will you kill again, If I have to, I shall never be free from this blindness, And what about the food, We shall fetch it, I doubt whether they'll dare to come here, at least for the next few days they'll be afraid the same might happen to them, that a pair of scissors will slit their throat, We failed to put up resistance as we should have done when they first came making demands, Of course, we were afraid and fear isn't always a wise counsellor, let's get back, for our greater safety we ought to barricade the door of the wards by putting beds on top of beds, as they do, if some of us have to sleep on the floor, too bad, better that than to die of hunger.

In the days that followed, they asked themselves if that was not what was about to happen to them. At first they were not surprised, from the outset they had become used to it, there had always been delays in the delivery of food, the blind thugs were right when they said the soldiers were sometimes late, but then they perverted this reasoning when, in a playful tone of voice, they affirmed that for this reason they had no choice but to impose rationing, these are the painful obligations of those who have to govern. On the third day when there was no longer as much as a rind or crumb, the doctor's wife with some companions, went out into the forecourt and asked, Hey, why the delay, whatever happened to our food, we haven't eaten for the last two days. Another sergeant, not the one from the time before, came up to the railing to declare that the army was not responsible, that no one there was trying to take the bread from their mouths, that military honour would never allow it, if there was no food it was because there was no food, and all of you stay where you are, the first one to advance knows the fate that waits for him, the orders have not changed. This warning was enough to send them back inside, and they conferred amongst themselves, And now what do we do if they won't bring us any food, They might bring some tomorrow, Or the day after tomorrow, Or when we no longer have the strength to move, We ought to go out, We wouldn't even get as far as the gate, If only we had our sight, If we had our sight we wouldn't have landed in this hell, I wonder what life is like out there, Perhaps those bastards might give us something to eat if we went there to ask, after all if there's a shortage for us, they must be running short too, That's why they're unlikely to give us anything they've got, And before their food runs out we will have died of starvation, What are we to do then, They were seated on the floor, under the yellowish light of the only lamp in the hallway, more or less in a circle, the doctor and the doctor's wife, the old man with the black eyepatch, amongst the other men and women, one or two from each ward, from the wing on the left as well as from the one on the right, and then, this world of the blind being what it is, there occurred what always occurs, one of the men said, All I know is that we would never have found ourselves in this situation if their leader hadn't been killed, what did it matter if the women had to go there twice a month to give these men what nature gave them to give, I ask myself. Some found this amusing, some forced a smile, those inclined to protest were deterred by an empty stomach, and the same man insisted, What I'd like to know is who did the stabbing, The women who were there at the time swear it was none of them, What we ought to do is to take the law into our own hands and bring the culprit to justice, If we knew who was responsible, we'd say this is the person you're looking for, now give us the food, If we knew who was responsible. The doctor's wife lowered her head and thought, He's right, if anyone here should die of hunger it will be my fault, but then, giving voice to the rage she could feel welling up inside her contradicting any acceptance of responsibility, But let these men be the first to die so that my guilt may pay for their guilt. Then she thought, raising her eyes, And if I were now to tell them that it was I who killed him, they would hand me over, knowing that they would be delivering me to certain death. Whether it was the effect of hunger or because the thought suddenly seduced her like some abyss, her head spun as if she were in a daze, her body moved despite herself, her mouth opened to speak, but just at that moment someone grabbed and squeezed her arm, she looked, it was the old man with the black eyepatch, who said, Anyone who gave himself up, I'd kill him with my own hands, Why, people in the circle asked, Because if shame still has any meaning in this hell where we're expected to live and which we've turned into the hell of hells, it is thanks to that person who had the courage to go and kill the hyena in its lair, Agreed, but shame won't fill our plates, Whoever you may be, you're right in what you say, there have always been those who have filled their bellies because they had no sense of shame, but we, who have nothing, apart from this last shred of undeserved dignity, let us at least show that we are still capable of fighting for what is rightfully ours, What are you trying to say, That having started off by sending in the women and eaten at their expense like low-life pimps, the time has now come for sending in the men, if there are any, Explain yourself, but first tell us where you are from, I'm from the first ward on the right-hand side, Go on then, It's very simple, let's go and collect the food with our own hands, Those men are armed, As far as we know, they have only one gun and the ammunition will run out sooner or later, They have enough to make sure that some of us will die, Others have died for less, I'm not prepared to lose my life so that the rest can enjoy themselves. Would you also be prepared to starve, if someone should lose his life so that you might have food, the old man with the black eyepatch asked sarcastically, and the other man gave no reply.

In the entrance of the door leading to the wards in the right-hand wing, appeared a woman who had been listening out of sight. She was the one who had received the spurt of blood in her face, the one into whose mouth the dead man had ejaculated, the one in whose ear the doctor's wife had whispered, Be quiet, and now the doctor's wife is thinking, From here where I'm sitting in the midst of others, I cannot tell you to be quiet, don't give me away, but no doubt you recognise my voice, it's impossible that you could have forgotten it, my hand covered your mouth, your body against mine, and I said, Be quiet, and the moment has come to know whom I really saved, to know who you are, that is why I am about to speak, that is why I am about to say in a loud, clear voice so that you might accuse me, if this is your destiny and mine, I am now saying, Not only the men will go, but also the women, we shall return to that place where they humiliated us so that none of that humiliation may remain, so that we might rid ourselves of it in the same way that we spat out what they ejaculated into our mouths. She uttered these words and waited, until the woman replied, Wherever you go, I shall go, that was what she said. The old man with the black eyepatch smiled, it seemed a happy smile, and perhaps it was, this is not the moment to ask him, it is much more interesting to observe the expression of surprise on the faces of the other blind men, as if something had passed over their heads, a bird, a cloud, a first hesitant glimmer of light. The doctor took his wife's hand, then asked, Are there still people here intent on discovering who killed that fellow, or are we agreed that the hand that stabbed him was the hand of all of us, or to be more precise, the hand of each one of us. No one replied. The doctor's wife said, Let's give them a little longer, if, by tomorrow, the soldiers have not brought our food, then we advance. They got up, went their separate ways, some to the right, others to the left, imprudently they had not reflected that some blind man from the ward of the thugs might have been listening, fortunately the devil is not always behind the door, a saying that could not have been more appropriate. Somewhat less appropriate was the blast that came from the loudspeaker, recently it had spoken on certain days, on others not at all, but always at the same time, as had been promised, clearly there was a timer in the transmitter which at the precise moment started up the recorded tape, the reason why it should have broken down from time to time we are never likely to know, these are matters for the outside world, it is in any case serious enough, insofar as it muddled up the calendar, the so-called counting of the days, which some blind men, natural obsessives, or lovers of order, which is a moderate form of obsession, had tried scrupulously to follow by making little knots in a piece of string, this was done by those who did not trust their memory, as if they were writing a diary. Now it was the time that was out of phase, the mechanism must have broken down, a twisted relay, some loose soldering, let's hope the recording will not keep going back for ever to the beginning, that was all we needed as well as being blind and mad. Along the corridors, through the wards, like some final and futile warning, boomed an authoritarian voice, the Government regrets having been forced to exercise with all urgency what it considers to be its rightful duty, to protect the population by all possible means in this present crisis, when something with all the appearance of an epidemic of blindness has broken out, provisionally known as the white sickness, and we are relying on the civic spirit and cooperation of all citizens to stem any further contagious, assuming that we are dealing with a contagious disease and that we are not simply witnessing a series of as yet inexplicable coincidences. The decision to gather together in one place all those infected, and, in adjacent but separate quarters all those who have had any kind of contact with them, was not taken without careful consideration. The Government is fully aware of its responsibilities and hopes that those to whom this message is directed will, as the upright citizens they doubtless are, also assume their responsibilities, bearing in mind that the isolation in which they now find themselves will represent, above any personal considerations, an act of solidarity with the rest of the nation's community. That said, we ask everyone to listen attentively to the following instructions, first, the lights will be kept on at all times, any attempt to tamper with the switches will be useless, they don't work, second, leaving the building without authorisation will mean instant death, third, in each ward there is a telephone that can be used only to requisition from outside fresh supplies for purposes of hygiene and cleanliness, fourth, the internees will be responsible for washing their own clothes by hand, fifth, it is recommended that ward representatives should be elected, this is a recommendation rather than an order, the internees must organise themselves as they see fit, provided they comply with the aforesaid rules and those we are about to announce, sixth, three times daily containers with food will be deposited at the main door, on the right and on the left, destined respectively for the patients and those suspected of being contaminated, seventh, all the left-overs must be burnt, and this includes not only any food, but also the containers, plates and cutlery which are all made of combustible material, eighth, the burning should be done in the inner courtyards of the building or in the exercise yard, ninth, the internees are responsible for any damage caused by these fires, tenth, in the event of a fire getting out of control, whether accidentally or on purpose, the firemen will not intervene, eleventh, equally, the internees cannot count on any outside intervention should there be any outbreaks of illnesses, nor in the event of any disorder or aggression, twelfth, in the case of death, whatever the cause, the internees will bury the corpse in the yard without any formalities, thirteenth, contact between the wing of the patients and that of the people suspected of being contagious must be made in the central hall of the building by which they entered, fourteenth, should those suspected of being infected suddenly go blind, they will be transferred immediately to the other wing, fifteenth, this communication will be relayed daily at the same time for the benefit of all new arrivals. The Government, but at that very moment the lights went out and the loudspeaker fell silent. Unconcerned, a blind man tied a knot in the piece of string he was holding in his hands, then he tried to count them, the knots, the days, but he gave up, there were knots overlapping, blind knots in a manner of speaking. The doctor's wife said to her husband, The lights have gone out, Some lamp that had fused, and little wonder when they have been switched on for all this time, They've all gone out, the problem must have been outside, Now you're as blind as the rest of us, I'll wait until the sun comes up. She went out of the ward, crossed the hallway, looked outside. This part of the city was in darkness, the army's searchlight was not working, it must have been connected to the general network, and now, to all appearances, the power was off.

The following day, some earlier, others later, because the sun does not rise at the same time for all those who are blind, it often depends on the keenness of hearing of each of them, men and women from the various wards began gathering on the outer steps of the building with the exception, needless to say, of the ward occupied by the hoodlums, who at this hour must be having their breakfast. They were waiting for the thud of the gate being opened, the loud screeching of hinges that needed to be greased, the sounds that announced the arrival of their food, then the voice of the sergeant on duty, Don't move from where you are, let no one approach, the dragging of soldiers' feet, the dull sound of the containers being dumped on the ground, the hasty retreat, once more the creaking of the gate, and finally the authorisation, Now you can come out. They waited until it was almost midday and midday became the afternoon. No one, not even the doctor's wife, wanted to ask about the food. So long as they did not ask the question they would not hear the dreaded no, and so long as it was not spoken they would go on hoping to hear words like these, It's coming, it's coming, be patient, put up with your hunger for just a little longer. Some, however much they wanted, could not stand it any longer, they fainted there and then as if they had suddenly fallen asleep, fortunately the doctor's wife was there to come to the rescue, it was incredible how this woman managed to notice everything that was happening, she must be endowed with a sixth sense, some sort of a vision without eyes, thanks to which those miserable wretches did not remain there to broil in the sun, they were carried indoors at once, and with time, water and gentle slaps on the face, all of them eventually came round. But there was no point in counting on the latter for the war, they would not even be able to grab a she-cat by the tail, an old-fashioned expression which never explained for what extraordinary reason a she-cat should be easier to deal with than a tom-cat. Finally the old man with the black eyepatch said, The food hasn't come, the food won't come, let's go and get our food. They got up, God knows how, and went to assemble in the ward furthest away from the stronghold of the hoodlums, rather than have any repetition of the imprudence of the other day. From there they sent spies to the other wing, blind inmates who lived there and were more familiar with the surroundings, At the first suspicious movement, come and warn us. The doctor's wife went with them and came back with some disheartening information, They have barricaded the entrance with four beds stacked one on top of the other, How did you know there were four, someone asked, That wasn't difficult, I felt them, Did no one realise you were there, I don't think so, What are we going to do, Let's go, the old man with the black eyepatch suggested once more, let's stick to what was decided, it's either that or we're condemned to a slow death. Some will die sooner if we go there, said the first blind man, Anyone who is going to die is already dead and does not know it, That we're going to die is something we know from the moment we are born, That's why, in some ways, it's as if we were born dead, That's enough of your foolish talk, said the girl with the dark glasses, I cannot go there alone, but if we are now going to go back on what was agreed, then I'm simply going to lie on my bed and allow myself to die, Only those whose days are numbered will die, no one else, said the doctor, and raising his voice, he asked, Those who are determined to go, raise their hand, this is what happens to those who do not think twice before opening their mouth to speak, what was the point in asking them to raise their hands if there was no one there to count them, or so it was generally believed, and then say, Thirteen, in which case a new discussion would almost certainly start up to establish what, in the light of logic, would be more correct, whether to ask for another volunteer to avoid that unlucky number, or to avoid it by default, drawing lots to decide who should drop out. Some had raised their hand with little conviction, with a gesture that betrayed hesitation and doubt, whether because aware of the danger to which they were about to expose themselves, or because they realised the absurdity of the order. The doctor laughed, How ridiculous, to ask you to put up your hands, let's proceed in another manner, let those who cannot or do not wish to go withdraw, the rest stay behind to agree upon the action to be taken. There were stirrings, footsteps, murmurs, sighs, little by little, the weak and nervous dropped out, the doctor's idea had been as excellent as it was generous, in this way it will be less easy to know who had remained and who was no longer there. The doctor's wife counted those who had remained, they were seventeen, counting herself and her husband. From the first ward on the right hand side, there was the old man with the black eyepatch, the pharmacist's assistant, the girl with dark glasses, and all the volunteers from the other wards were men with the exception of that woman who had said, Wherever you go, I shall go, she is here too. They lined up along the passageway, the doctor counted them, Seventeen, we're seventeen, That's not very many, remarked the pharmacist's assistant, we'll never manage. The front line of attack, if I may use a rather military term, will have to be a narrow one, said the old man with the black eyepatch, we have to be able to fit through a door, I'm convinced it would only complicate matters if there were more of us, They'd shoot the lot of us, agreed another, and everyone seemed pleased that in the end they were few.

Their arms we are already familiar with, bars taken from the beds, which might serve just as well as a crowbar or a lance, according to whether the sappers or assault troops were going into battle. The old man with the black eyepatch, who had clearly learned something about tactics in his youth, suggested that everyone should stay together, facing in the same direction, since this was the only way to avoid attacking each other, and that they should advance in absolute silence, so that the attack might benefit from the element of surprise, Let's take off our shoes, he suggested. Then it's going to be difficult for each of us to find our own shoes, someone said, and another commented, Any shoes left over will truly be dead men's shoes, with the difference that in this case, at least, there will always be someone to step into them, What is all this talk about dead men's shoes, It's a saying, to wait for dead men's shoes means to wait for nothing at all, Why, Because the shoes the dead were buried in were made of cardboard, they served their purpose, souls have no feet, as far as we know, And there's another point, interrupted the old man with the black eyepatch, when we get there, six of us, the six who are feeling bravest, will shove the beds inside as hard as they can, so that all of us may enter, In that case, we'll have to lay down our arms, I don't think that will be necessary, they might even help, if used upright. He paused, then said, with a sombre note in his voice, Above all, we must not split up, if we do we're as good as dead, And what about the women, said the girl with dark glasses, don't forget the women, Are you going as well, asked the old man with the black eyepatch, I'd rather you didn't, And why not, I'd like to know, You're very young, In this place, age is of no account, nor sex, therefore don't forget the women,

No, I won't forget, the voice in which the old man with the black eyepatch spoke these words appeared to come from another dialogue, those that follow were already in their place, On the contrary, if only one of you women could see what we cannot see, take us along the right path, with the tip of our metal bars at the throats of these ruffians, as accurately as that other woman did, That would be asking too much, we can't easily repeat what we've done once already, besides, who's to say that she didn't die there and then, there has been no news of her, the doctor's wife reminded them, Women are born again in one another, the respectable are reborn as whores, whores are reborn as respectable women, said the girl with dark glasses. This was followed by a long silence, for the women everything had been said, the men would have to find the words, and they knew already that they would be incapable of doing so.

They filed out, the six braver ones in front as had been agreed, amongst them was the doctor and the pharmacist's assistant, then came the others, each armed with a metal rod from his bed, a brigade of squalid, ragged lancers, as they crossed the hallway one of them dropped his weapon, which made a deafening sound on the tiled floor like a blast of gunfire, if the hoodlums were to hear the noise and get wind of what we're up to, then we're lost. Without telling anyone, not even her husband, the doctor's wife ran ahead, looked along the corridor, then very slowly, keeping close to the wall, she gradually drew nearer to the entrance of the ward, there she listened attentively, the voices within did not sound alarmed. She brought back this information without delay and the advance recommenced. Apart from the slowness and the silence with which the army moved, the occupants of the two wards that were located before the stronghold of the hoodlums, aware of what was about to happen, gathered at the doors so as not to miss the imminent clamour of battle, and some of those more on edge, excited by the smell of gunpowder about to be lit, decided at the last minute to accompany the group, a few went back to arm themselves, they were no longer seventeen, they had at least doubled in number, the reinforcements would certainly displease the old man with the black eyepatch, but he was never to know that he was commanding two regiments instead of one. Through the few windows that looked on to the inner courtyard entered the last glimmer of light, grey, moribund, as it rapidly faded, already slipping away into the deep black well of the night ahead. Apart from the inconsolable sadness caused by the blindness from which they inexplicably continued to suffer, the blind internees, this at least was in their favour, were spared any fits of depression produced by these and other similar atmospheric changes, proven to be the cause of innumerable acts of despair in the remote past when people had eyes to see. When they reached the door of that cursed ward, it was already so dark that the doctor's wife failed to notice that there were not four but eight beds forming a barrier, doubled in number in the meantime like the assailants, however with more serious immediate consequences for the latter, as will soon be confirmed. The voice of the old man with the black eyepatch let out a cry, it was the order, he did not remember the usual expression, Charge, or perhaps he did, but it would have struck him as ridiculous to treat with such military consideration, a barrier of filthy beds, full of fleas and bugs, their mattresses rotted from sweat and urine, the blankets like rags, no longer grey, but all the colours that disgust might wear, this the doctor's wife already knew, not that she could see it now, since she had not even noticed the reinforced barricade. The blind inmates advanced like archangels surrounded by their own splendour, they thudded into the obstacle with their weapons upright as they had been instructed, but the beds did not move, no doubt the strength of this brave vanguard was not much greater than that of the weaklings who came behind and by now could scarcely hold their lances, like someone who carried a cross on his back and now has to wait to be raised up on it. The silence had disappeared, those outside were shouting, those inside started shouting, probably no one has noticed to this day how absolutely terrible are the cries of the blind, they appear to be shouting for no good reason, we want to tell them to be quiet and then end up shouting ourselves, all that's wanting is for us to be blind too, but that day will come. This then was the situation, some shouting as they attacked, others shouting as they defended themselves, while those on the outside, desperate at not having been able to move the beds, flung down their weapons willy-nilly and, all of them at once, at least those who managed to squeeze into the space in the doorway, and those who couldn't fit in pressed behind those in front, they started pushing and pushing and it looked as if they might succeed, the beds had even moved a little, when suddenly, without prior warning or threat, three shots rang out, it was the blind accountant aiming low. Two of the assailants fell, wounded, the others quickly retreated in disarray, they tripped on the metal rods and fell, as if demented the walls of the corridor multiplied their shouts, shouting was coming from the other wards too. It was now almost pitch-black, it was impossible to know who had been hit by the bullets, obviously one could ask from afar, Who are you, but it did not seem appropriate, the wounded must be treated with respect and consideration, we must approach them gently, place our hand on their forehead, unless that is where the bullet unfortunately happened to strike, then we must ask them in a low voice how they are feeling, assure them it is not serious, the stretcher-bearers are already on the way, and finally give them some water, but only if they are not wounded in the stomach, as is expressly recommended in the first-aid handbook. What shall we do now, asked the doctor's wife, there are two casualties lying there on the ground. No one asked her how she knew there were two of them, after all, there had been three shots, without reckoning with the effect of the ricochets, if there had been any. We must go and look for them, said the doctor, The risk is great, observed the old man with the black eyepatch despondently, who had seen that his assault tactics had resulted in disaster, if they suspect there are people here they'll start firing again, he paused and added sighing, But we must go there, speaking for myself, I'm ready, I'm going too, said the doctor's wife, there will be less danger if we crawl, the important thing is to find them quickly, before those inside there have time to react, I'm going too, said the woman who had declared the other day, Wherever you go, I go, of the many that were there no one thought to say that it was very easy to check who was wounded, correction, wounded or dead, for the moment no one yet knows, it was enough that they should all start saying, I'm going, I'm not going, those who remained silent were the latter.

And so the four volunteers began crawling, the two women in the middle, a man on either side as it happened, they were not acting out of male courtesy or some gentlemanly instinct so that the women should be protected, the truth is that everything will depend on the angle of the shot, if the blind accountant should fire again. After all, perhaps nothing will happen, the old man with the black eyepatch had come up with an idea before they went, possibly better than the earlier ones, that these companions here should start to talk at the top of their voices, even to shout, besides they had every reason to do so, so that they might drown the inevitable noise of their comings and goings, and also whatever might happen in the meantime, God knows what. In a few minutes, the rescuers reached their destination, they knew it before even coming into contact with the bodies, the blood over which they were crawling was like a messenger come to tell them, I was life, behind me there is nothing, My God, thought the doctor's wife, all this blood, and it was true, a thick pool, their hands and clothing stuck to the ground as if the floorboards and floor tiles were covered in glue. The doctor's wife raised herself on her elbows and continued to advance, the others had done the same. Stretching out their arms, they finally reached the corpses. Their companions back there continued to make as much noise as they could, and now sounded like professional mourners in a trance. The hands of the doctor's wife and of the old man with the black eyepatch grabbed the ankles of one of the casualties, in their turn the doctor and the other woman had grabbed an arm and leg of the other wounded man, now they were trying to drag them away out of the firing line. It was not easy, to achieve this they had to raise themselves up a little, to go on all fours, it was the only way of putting to good use the little strength they still possessed. The shot rang out, but this time did not hit anyone. The overwhelming terror did not make them flee, on the contrary, it helped them to summon that last ounce of energy that was needed. An instant later they were already out of danger, they got as close as they could to the wall on the side where the ward door was situated, only a stray bullet could possibly reach them, but it was doubtful that the blind accountant was skilled in ballistics, even elementary ones such as these. They tried to lift the bodies but gave up. Because of their weight they could only drag them, and with them, half congealed, trailed the blood already spilled as if spread by a roller, and the remaining blood, still fresh, that continued to flow from the wounds. Who are they, asked those who were waiting, How are we to know if we cannot see, said the old man with the black eyepatch, We can't stay here, said someone, if they decide to launch an attack we'll have more than two casualties, remarked another, Or corpses, said the doctor, at least I cannot feel their pulse. Like an army in retreat, they carried the corpses along the corridor, on reaching the hallway they came to a halt, and one would have said they had decided to camp there, but the truth of the matter was different, what had happened was that they were drained of all energy, I'm staying right here, I can't go any further. It is time to acknowledge that it must seem surprising that the blind hoodlums, previously so overbearing and aggressive, revelling in their own easy cruelty, now only defend themselves, raise barricades and fire from inside there at will, as if they were afraid to go out and fight in open territory, face to face, eye to eye. Like everything else in this life, this too, has its explanation, which is that after the tragic death of their first leader, all spirit of discipline or sense of obedience had gone in the ward, the serious error on the part of the blind accountant was to have thought that it was enough to take possession of the gun in order to usurp power, but the result was exactly the opposite, each time he fires, the shot backfires, in other words, with each shot fired, he loses a little more authority, so let's see what happens when he runs out of ammunition. Just as the habit does not make the monk, the sceptre does not make the king, this is a fact we should never forget, and if it is true that the royal sceptre is now held by the blind accountant, one is tempted to say that the king, although dead, although buried in his own ward, and badly, barely three feet under the ground, continues to be remembered, at least he makes his powerful presence felt by the stench. Meanwhile, the moon appeared. Through the door of the hallway that looks out on to the outer yard enters a diffused light that gradually becomes brighter, the bodies that are on the ground, two of them dead, the others still alive, slowly begin gaining volume, shape, characteristics, features, all the weight of a horror without a name, then the doctor's wife understood that there was no sense, if there ever had been any, in going on pretending to be blind, it is clear that here no one can be saved, blindness is also this, to live in a world where all hope is gone. She could tell in the meantime who was dead, this is the pharmacist's assistant, this is the fellow who said the blind hoodlums would shoot at random, they were both right after a fashion, and don't bother asking me how I know who they are, the answer is simple, I can see. Some of those who were present already knew as much and had remained silent, others had been suspicious for some time and now saw their suspicions confirmed, the surprise of the others was unexpected, and yet, on reflection, perhaps we should not be surprised, at another time the revelation would have caused much consternation, uncontrolled excitement, how fortunate for you, how did you manage to escape this universal disaster, what is the name of the drops you put in your eyes, give me your doctor's address, help me to get out of this prison, by now it came to the same thing, in death, blindness is the same for all. What they could not do was to remain there, defenceless, even the metal bars from their beds had been left behind, their fists would serve for nothing. Guided by the doctor's wife, they dragged the corpses out on to the forecourt, and there they left them in the moonlight, under the planet's milky whiteness, white on the outside, black at last on the inside. Let's return to the wards, said the old man with the black eyepatch, we'll see later on what can be organised. This is what he said, and they were mad words that no one heeded. They did not divide up according to where they had come from, they met up and recognised each other on the way, some heading for the wing on the left, others for the wing on the right, the doctor's wife had been accompanied this far by that woman who had said, Wherever you go, I go, this was not the idea she now carried in her head, quite the contrary, but she did not want to discuss it, vows are not always fulfilled, sometimes out of weakness, at other times because of some superior force with which we had not reckoned.

An hour passed, the moon came up, hunger and terror hold sleep at bay, in the wards everyone is awake. But these are not the only reasons. Whether because of the excitement of the recent battle, even though so disastrously lost, or because of something indefinable in the air, the blind internees are restless. No one dares go out into the corridors, but the interior of each ward is like a beehive inhabited by drones, buzzing insects, as everyone knows, little given to order and method, there is no evidence that they have ever done anything in their lives or preoccupied themselves in the slightest with the future, even though in the case of the blind, unhappy creatures, it would be unjust to accuse them of being exploiters and parasites, exploiters of what crumb, parasites of what refreshment, one has to be careful with comparisons, in case they should turn out to be frivolous. However, there is no rule without an exception, and this was not lacking here, in the person of a woman who entered the ward, the second one on the right-hand side, and at once began rummaging through her rags until she found a tiny object which she pressed in the palm of her hand, as if anxious to conceal it from the prying eyes of others, old habits die hard, even when that moment comes when we thought they were lost for ever. Here, where it ought to have been one for all and all for one, we witnessed how the strong cruelly took the bread from the mouths of the weak, and now this woman, remembering that she had brought a cigarette lighter in her hand-luggage, unless she had lost it in all the upheaval, searched for it anxiously and is now furtively hiding it, as if her survival depended on it, she does not think that perhaps one of these companions in misfortune might have one last cigarette on them, and cannot smoke it because they do not have that tiny essential flame. Nor would there be time now to ask for a light. The woman has gone out without saying a word, no farewell, no goodbye, she makes her way along the deserted corridor, passes right by the door of the first ward, no one inside there noticed her pass, she crosses the hallway, the descending moon traced and painted a vat of milk on the floor tiles, now the woman is in the other wing, once more a corridor, her destination lies at the far end, in a straight line, she cannot go wrong. Besides, she can hear voices summoning her, figuratively speaking, what she can hear is the rumpus being made by the hoodlums in the last ward, they are celebrating their victory, eating and drinking to their heart's content, ignore the deliberate exaggeration, let us not forget that everything is relative in life, they eat and drink simply what is to hand, and long may it last, how the others would love to partake of the feast, but they cannot, between them and the plate there is a barricade of eight beds and a loaded gun. The woman is on her knees at the entrance to the ward, right up against the beds, she slowly pulls the covers off, then gets to her feet, she does the same with the bed on top, then with the third one, her arm cannot reach the fourth, no matter, the fuses are ready, now it is only a question of setting them alight. She can still remember how to regulate the lighter in order to produce a long flame, she got it, a tiny dagger of light, as bright as the sharp point of a pair of scissors. She starts with the bed on top, the flame laboriously licks the filthy bed-clothes, then it finally catches fire, now the bed in the middle, now the bed below, the woman caught the smell of her own singed hair, she must be careful, she is the one who has to set the pyre alight, not the one who must die, she can hear the cries of the hoodlums within, at that moment it suddenly occurred to her, Suppose they have water and manage to put out the flames, in desperation she got under the first bed, ran the lighter along the mattress, here, there, then suddenly the flames multiplied, transformed themselves into one great curtain of fire, a spurt of water passed through them, splashed on to the woman, but in vain, her own body was already feeding the bonfire.

What is it like in there, no one can risk entering, but our imagination must serve for something, the fire quickly spreads from bed to bed, as if wanting to set all of them alight at the same time, and it succeeds, the hoodlums wasted indiscriminately and to no avail the little water they still had, now they are trying to reach the windows, unsteadily they climb on to the headrests of the beds which the fire has still not reached, but suddenly the fire is there, they slip, fall, with the intensity of the heat the window-panes begin to crack, to shatter, the fresh air comes whistling in and fans the flames, ah, yes, they are not forgotten, the cries of rage and fear, the howls of pain and agony, there they have been mentioned, note, in any case, that they will gradually die away, the woman with the cigarette lighter, for example, has been silent for some time.

By this time the other blind inmates are fleeing in terror towards the smoke-filled corridors, Fire, fire, they are shouting, and here we may observe in the flesh how badly planned and organised these human communities in orphanages, hospitals and mental asylums have been, note how each bed, in itself, with its framework of pointed metal bars, can be transformed into a lethal trap, look at the terrible consequences of having only one door to wards occupied by forty people, not counting those asleep on the floor, if the fire gets there first and blocks their exit, no one will escape. Fortunately, as human history has shown, it is not unusual for good to come of evil, less is said about the evil that can come out of good, such are the contradictions of this world of ours, some warrant more consideration than others, in this instance the good was precisely the fact that the wards have only one door, thanks to this factor, the fire that burnt the hoodlums tarried there for quite a while, if the confusion does not get any worse, perhaps we will not have to lament the loss of other lives. Obviously, many of these blind inmates are being trampled under foot, pushed, jostled, this is the effect of panic, a natural effect, you could say that animal nature is like this, plant life would behave in exactly the same way, too, if it did not have all those roots to hold it in the ground, and how nice it would be to see the trees of the forest fleeing the flames. The protection afforded by the inner part of the yard was fully exploited by the blind inmates who had the idea of opening the existing windows in the corridors looking on to it. They jumped, stumbled, fell, they weep and cry out, but for now they are safe, let us hope that once the fire causes the roof to cave in and launches a whirlwind of flames and burning embers into the sky and the wind, it will forget to spread to the tree tops. In the other wing the panic is much the same, a blind man only has to smell smoke to imagine at once that the flames are right by him, which does not happen to be true, soon the corridor was crammed with people, unless someone imposes some order here, the situation will be disastrous. At a certain point, someone remembers that the doctor's wife still has her eyesight, where is she, people ask, she can tell us what is happening, where we should go, where is she, I'm here, I've only just managed to get out of the ward, the boy with the squint was to blame because no one knew where he had got to, now he's here with me and I'm holding him firmly by the hand, they would have to pull off my arm before I'd let go of him, with my other hand I'm holding my husband's hand, and then comes the girl with dark glasses, and then the old man with the black eyepatch, where there is the one there is the other, and then the first blind man, and then his wife, all together, as compressed as a pinecone, which, I very much hope, will not open even in this heat. Meanwhile, a number of blind inmates from here had followed the example of those in the other wing, they jumped into the inner yard, they cannot see that the greater part of the building on the other side is already one great bonfire, but they can feel on their faces and hands the blast of heat coming from there, for the moment the roof is still holding up, the leaves on the trees are slowly curling. Then someone shouted, What are we doing here, why don't we get out, the reply, coming from amidst this sea of heads, needed only four words, The soldiers are there, but the old man with the black eyepatch said, Better to be shot than burnt to death, it sounded like the voice of experience, therefore perhaps he was not really the person speaking, perhaps through his mouth the woman with the cigarette lighter had spoken, she who had not had the good fortune to be struck by the last bullet fired by the blind accountant. Then the doctor's wife said, Let me pass, I'll speak to the soldiers, they cannot leave us to die like this, soldiers too have feelings. Thanks to the hope that the soldiers might indeed have feelings, a narrow gap opened up, through which the doctor's wife advanced with considerable effort, taking her group with her. The smoke clouded her vision, soon she would be as blind as the others. It was almost impossible to enter the hallway. The doors opening on to the yard had been broken down, the blind inmates who had taken refuge there quickly realised the place was unsafe, they wanted to get out, pushed with all their might, but those on the other side resisted, held out as best they could, for the moment their greater fear was that the soldiers might suddenly appear, but as their strength gave out and the fire spread nearer, the old man with the black eyepatch was proved to be right, it would be preferable to die by a bullet. There was not long to wait, the doctor's wife had finally managed to get out on to the porch, she was practically half naked and with both her hands occupied she could scarcely fight off those who wanted to join her small group as it advanced, to catch, in a manner of speaking, the moving train, the soldiers would be goggle-eyed when they saw her appear before them with her breasts half exposed. It was no longer the moonlight that was illuminating the wide empty space that extended as far as the gate, but the harsh glare of the blaze. The doctor's wife shouted, Please, for your own peace of mind, let us out, do not shoot. No reply came from over there. The searchlight was still extinguished, nothing could be seen to move. Nervously, the doctor's wife went down two steps, What's going on, asked her husband, but she did not reply, could not believe her eyes. She descended the remaining steps, walked in the direction of the gate, still dragging behind her the boy with the squint, her husband and company, there was no doubt about it, the soldiers had gone, or been taken away, they too stricken by blindness, everyone finally blind.

Then, to simplify matters, everything happened at once, the doctor's wife announced in a loud voice that they were free, the roof of the right wing collapsed with a terrifying crash, sending out flames on all sides, the blind inmates rushed into the yard, shouting at the top of their voices, some did not make it, they remained inside, crushed against the walls, others were trampled under foot and transformed into a formless, bloody mass, the fire that has suddenly spread will soon reduce all of this to ashes. The gate is wide open, the madmen escape.

Say to a blind man, you're free, open the door that was separating him from the world, Go, you are free, we tell him once more, and he does not go, he has remained motionless there in the middle of the road, he and the others, they are terrified, they do not know where to go, the fact is that there is no comparison between living in a rational labyrinth, which is, by definition, a mental asylum and venturing forth, without a guiding hand or a dog-leash, into the demented labyrinth of the city, where memory will serve no purpose, for it will merely be able to recall the images of places but not the paths whereby we might get there. Standing in front of the building which is already ablaze from end to end, the blind inmates can feel the living waves of heat from the fire on their faces, they receive them as something which in a way protects them, just as the walls did before, prison and refuge at once. They stay together, pressed up against each other, like a flock, no one there wants to be the lost sheep, for they know that no shepherd will come looking for them. The fire gradually begins to die down, the moon casts its light once more, the blind inmates begin to feel uneasy, they cannot remain there, For all eternity, as one of them said. Someone asked if it was day or night, the reason for this incongruous curiosity soon became apparent, Who knows, they might bring us some food, perhaps there has been some confusion, some delay, it has happened before, But the soldiers are no longer here. That doesn't mean a thing, they might have gone away because they're no longer needed, I don't understand, For example, because there is no longer any danger of infection, Or because a cure has been found for our illness, That would be good, it really would, What are we going to do, I'm staying here until daybreak, And how will you know it is daybreak, By the sun, by the heat of the sun, And what if the sky is overcast, There is only a limited number of hours and then it must be day at some point. Exhausted, many of the blind had sat down on the ground, others, weaker still, simply collapsed into a heap, some had fainted, it is possible that the cool night air will restore consciousness, but we can be certain that when it is time to break camp, some of these unfortunates will not get up, they have resisted until now, they are like that marathon runner who dropped dead three metres from the finish line, when all is said and done, what is clear is that all lives end before their time. Also seated or stretched out on the ground were those blind inmates who are still awaiting the soldiers, or others instead of them, the Red Cross is one hypothesis, they might bring them food and the other basic comforts, for these people disenchantment will come a little later, that is the only difference. And if anyone here believed that a cure had been discovered for our blindness, this does not appear to have made him any more contented.

For other reasons, the doctor's wife thought that it would be better to wait until night was over, as she told her group, The most urgent thing right now is to find some food and in the dark this would not be easy. Have you any idea where we are, her husband asked, More or less, Far from home, Quite a distance. The others also wanted to know how far they were from their homes, they told her their addresses, and the doctor's wife did her best to explain, the boy with the squint cannot remember, and little wonder, he has not asked for his mother for quite some time. If they were to go from house to house, from the one that is closest to the one furthest away, the first house will be that of the girl with dark glasses, the second one that of the old man with the black eyepatch, then that of the doctor's wife, and finally the house of the first blind man. They will undoubtedly follow this itinerary because the girl with dark glasses has already asked that she should be taken to her home as soon as possible, I can't imagine what state my parents will be in, she said, this sincere preoccupation shows how groundless are the preconceived ideas of those who deny the possibility of the existence of deep feelings, including filial ones, in the, alas, abundant cases of irregular conduct, especially in matters of public morality. The night turned cool, there is not much left for the fire to burn, the heat still coming from the embers is not enough to warm the blind inmates, numb with cold, who find themselves farthest away from the asylum gate, as is the case of the doctor's wife and her group. They are seated in a huddle, the three women and the boy in the middle, the three men around them, anyone seeing them there would say that they had been born like that, it is true that they give the impression of being but one body, one breath and one hunger. One after the other, they eventually fell asleep, a light sleep from which they were roused several times because blind inmates, emerging from their own torpor, got up and stumbled drowsily over this human obstacle, one of them actually stayed behind, there was no difference between sleeping there or in some other place. When day dawned, only a few thin columns of smoke rose from the embers, but not even these lasted for long, for it soon began to rain, a fine drizzle, a mere mist, it is true, but nevertheless persistent, to begin with it did not even touch the scorched earth, but transformed itself at once into vapour, but, as it continued to fall, as everybody knows, a soft water eats away hard stone, let someone else make it rhyme. It is not only the eyes of some of these inmates that are blind, their understanding is also clouded, for there can be no other explanation for the tortuous reasoning that led them to conclude that the much desired food would not arrive in this rain. There was no way of convincing them that the premise was wrong and that, therefore, the conclusion, too, had to be wrong, they simply would not be told that it was still too early for breakfast, in despair, they threw themselves to the ground in floods of tears. It won't come, it's raining, it won't come, they repeated, if that lamentable ruin were still fit for even the most primitive habitation, it would go back to being the madhouse it once was.

The blind man who, after tripping, had stayed behind that night, could not get to his feet. Curled up, as if anxious to protect the last of the heat in his belly, he did not stir despite the rain, which had started to get heavier. He's dead, said the doctor's wife, and the rest of us had better get away from here while we still have some strength. They struggled to their feet, tottering and dizzy, holding on to each other, then they got into line, in front the woman with eyes that can see, then those who though they have eyes cannot see, the girl with dark glasses, the old man with the black eyepatch, the boy with the squint, the wife of the first blind man, her husband, and the doctor last of all. The route they have taken leads to the city centre, but this is not the intention of the doctor's wife, what she wants is to find a place as soon as possible where she can leave those following behind in safety and then go in search of food on her own. The streets are deserted, either because it is still early, or because of the rain that is becoming increasingly heavy. There is litter everywhere, some shops have their doors open, but most of them are closed, with no sign of life inside, nor any light. The doctor's wife thought that it would be a good idea to leave her companions in one of these shops, taking care to make a mental note of the name of the street and the number on the door just in case she should lose them on the way back. She paused, said to the girl with dark glasses, Wait for me here, don't move, she went to peer through the glass-panelled door of a pharmacy, thought she could see the shadowy forms of people lying on the ground, she tapped on the glass, one of the shadows stirred, she knocked again, other human forms slowly began moving, one person got up turning his head in the direction where the noise had come from, They are all blind, the doctor's wife thought, but she could not fathom how they came to be here, perhaps they were members of the pharmacist's family, but if this was the case, why were they not in their own home, with greater comfort than a hard floor, unless they were guarding the premises, against whom, and for what purpose, this merchandise being what it is, can cure and kill equally well. She moved away, a little further ahead she looked inside another shop, saw more people lying down, women, men, children, some appeared to be preparing to leave, one of them came right up to the door, put his arm outside and said, It's raining, Is it raining much, was the question from inside, Yes, we'll have to wait until it eases off, the man, it was a man, was two paces from the doctor's wife, he had not noticed her presence, and was therefore startled when he heard her say, Good-day, he had lost the habit of saying Good-day, not only because the days of the blind, strictly speaking are never likely to be good, but also because no one could be entirely sure whether it was afternoon or night, and if now, in apparent contradiction to what has just been explained, these people are waking up more or less at the same time as morning, that is because some of them only went blind a few days ago and still have not entirely lost their sense of the succession of days and nights, of sleep and wakefulness. The man said, It's raining, and then asked, Who are you, I'm not from here, Are you out searching for food, Yes, we haven't eaten for four days, And how do you know it is four days, That's what I reckon, Are you alone, I'm with my husband and some companions, How many of them are there, Seven altogether, If you're thinking of staying here with us, forget it, there are far too many of us already, We're only passing through, Where have you come from, We've been interned ever since this epidemic of blindness began, Ah, yes, the quarantine, it didn't do any good, Why do you say that, They allowed you to leave, There was a fire and, at that moment, we realised that the soldiers who were guarding us had disappeared, And you left, Yes, Your soldiers must have been amongst the last to go blind, everyone is blind, the whole city, the entire country, if anyone can still see, they say nothing, keep it to themselves, Why don't you live in your own house, Because I no longer know where it is, You don't know where it is, And what about you, do you know where your house is, Me, the doctor's wife was about to reply that that was precisely where she was heading with her husband and companions, all they needed was a quick bite to eat to recover their strength, but at that very moment she saw the situation quite clearly, somebody who was blind and had left their home would only manage to find it again by some miracle, it was not the same as before, when blind people could always count on the assistance of some passerby, whether to cross the street, or to get back on to the right path in the case of having inadvertently strayed from the usual route, All I know is that it is far from here, she said, But you'll never be able to get there, No, Now there you have it, it's the same with me, it's the same with everyone, those of you who have been in quarantine have a lot to learn, you don't know how easy it is to find yourself without a home, I don't understand, Those who go around in groups as we do, as most people do, when we have to look for food, we are obliged to go together, it's the only way of not losing each other, and since we all go, since no one stays behind to guard the house, assuming that we ever manage to find it again, the likelihood is that it will already be occupied by another group also unable to find their house, we're a kind of merry-go-round, at the outset there was some conflict, but we soon became aware that we, the blind, in a manner of speaking, have practically nothing we may call our own, except for what we are wearing, The solution would be to live in a shop selling food, at least so long as supplies lasted there would be no need to go out, Anyone who did that, the least that might happen to them would be never to have another moment's peace, I say the least, because I've heard of the case of some who tried, shut themselves away, bolted the door, but what they could not do was get rid of the smell of food, those who wanted to eat gathered outside, and since those inside refused to open the doors, the shop was set alight, it was a blessed remedy, I didn't see it myself, others told me, in any case it was a blessed remedy, and as far as I know no one else dared to do the same, And do people no longer live in houses and flats, Yes, they do, but it comes to the same thing, countless people must have passed through my house, who knows if I'll ever find it again, besides, in this situation, it's much more practical to sleep in the shops at ground level, in warehouses, it saves us having to go up and down stairs,

It's stopped raining, said the doctor's wife, It's stopped raining, repeated the man to those inside. On hearing these words, those who were still stretched out got to their feet, gathered up their belongings, haversacks, hand-luggage, bags made out of cloth and plastic, as if they were setting off on an expedition, and it was true, they were off in pursuit of food, one by one they began emerging from the shop, the doctor's wife noticed that they were well wrapped up even if the colours of their clothing scarcely harmonised, their trousers either so short that they exposed their shins, or so long that the bottoms had to be turned up, but the cold would not get to this lot, some of the men wore a raincoat or an overcoat, two of the women wore long fur coats, not an umbrella to be seen, probably because they are so awkward to carry, and the spokes are always in danger of poking someone's eye out. The group, some fifteen people, moved off. Along the road, other groups appeared, as well as people on their own, up against the walls men were satisfying the urgent need felt each morning by their bladder, the women preferred the privacy of abandoned cars. Softened by the rain, the excrement, here and there, was spread all over the pavement.

The doctor's wife went back to her group, huddled together out of instinct under the awning of a cake-shop that gave off a smell of soured cream and other rancid products. Let's go, she said, I've found a refuge, and she led them to the shop the others had just left. The stock in the shop was intact, there was nothing amongst the merchandise that could be eaten or worn, there were fridges, washing-machines for both clothes and dishes, ordinary stoves as well as microwave ovens, food mixers, juicers, vacuum cleaners, the thousand and one electro-domestic inventions destined to make life easier. The atmosphere was charged with unpleasant odours, making the invariable whiteness of the objects absurd. Rest here, said the doctor's wife, I'm going to look for some food, I have no idea where I'll find it, nearby, far away, I cannot say, wait patiently, there are groups out there, if anyone tries to come in, tell them the place is occupied, that ought to be enough to send them away, that's the custom now, I'm coming with you, said her husband, No, it's best I should go alone, we must find out how people are surviving now, from what I've heard everyone must have gone blind, In that case, quipped the old man with the black eyepatch, it's just as if we were still in the mental asylum, There's no comparison, we can move about freely, and there must be a solution to the food problem, we won't die of hunger, I must also try to get some clothes, we're reduced to rags, she herself was in the greatest need, practically naked from the waist upwards. She kissed her husband, at that moment she felt something akin to a pain in her heart. Please, whatever happens, even if someone should try to come in, do not leave this place, and if you should be turned out, although I don't believe this will happen, but just to warn you of all the possibilities, stay together near the door until I arrive. She looked at them, her eyes filled with tears, there they were, as dependent on her as little children on their mother. If I should let them down—she thought. It did not occur to her that all around her the people were blind yet managed to live, she herself would also have to turn blind in order to understand that people get used to anything, especially if they have ceased to be people, and even if they have not quite reached that point, take the boy with the squint there, for example, who no longer even asks for his mother. She went out to the street, looked and made a mental note of the door number, the name of the shop, now she had to check out the name of the street on that corner, she had no idea where this search for food might take her, or what food, it might be only three doors away or three hundred, she could not afford to get lost, there would be no one from whom to ask the way, those who could see before were blind, and she, who could see, would not know where she was. The sun had broken through, it shone on the pools of water that had formed amidst the litter and it was easier to see the weeds that were sprouting up between the paving stones. There were more people outside. How do they find their way around, the doctor's wife asked herself. They did not find their way around, they kept very close to the buildings with their arms stretched out before them, they were constantly bumping into each other like ants on the trail, but when this happened no one protested, nor did they have to say anything, one of the families moved away from the wall, advanced along the wall opposite in the other direction, and thus they proceeded and carried on until the next encounter. Now and then they stopped, sniffed in the doorways of the shops in the hope of catching the smell of food, whatever it might be, then continued on their way, they turned a corner, disappeared from sight, soon another group turned up, they did not seem to have found what they were looking for. The doctor's wife could move with greater speed, she did not waste any time entering the shops to find out if there were any edible goods, but it soon became clear that it would not be easy to stock up in any quantity, the few grocers' shops she found seemed to have been devoured from inside and were like empty shells.

She had already travelled far from where she had left her husband and companions, crossing and re-crossing streets, avenues, squares, when she found herself in front of a supermarket. Inside it was no different, empty shelves, overturned displays, in the middle wandered the blind, most of them on all fours, sweeping up the filth on the floor with their hands, hoping to find something they might be able to use, a can of preserves that had withstood the pounding of those who had desperately tried to open it, some packet or other, whatever the contents, a potato, even if trampled, a crust of bread, even if as hard as stone. The doctor's wife thought, Despite everything, there must be something, the place is vast. A blind man got to his feet and complained that a bit of glass had got lodged in his knee, the blood was already trickling down one leg. The blind persons in the group gathered round him, What happened, what's the matter, and he told them, A glass splinter in my knee, Which one, The left one, one of the blind women crouched down. Take care, there might be other pieces of glass around, she probed and fumbled to distinguish one leg from the other, Here it is, she said, and it's still pricking in the flesh, one of the blind men started laughing, Well if it's pricking, make the most of it, and the others, both men and women, joined in the laughter. Bringing her thumb and forefinger together, a natural gesture that requires no training, the blind woman removed the piece of glass, then bandaged the knee with a rag she found in the bag over her shoulder, finally she cracked her own little joke to the amusement of all, Nothing to be done, no more pricking, everyone laughed, and the wounded man retorted, Whenever you feel the urge, we can have a go and find out what pricks most, there certainly are no married men and women in this group, since no one appeared to be shocked, they must all be people with lax morals who enter into casual relationships, unless the latter happen to be indeed husband and wife, hence the liberties they take with each other, but they really do not give that impression, and no married couple would say these things in public. The doctor's wife looked around her, whatever was still usable was being disputed amidst punches that nearly always missed and much jostling that made no distinction between friend and foe, and it sometimes happened that the object provoking the struggle escaped from their hands and ended up on the ground, waiting for someone to trip over it, Hell, I'll never get out of here, she thought, using an expression that formed no part of her usual vocabulary, once more showing that the force and nature of circumstances have considerable influence over language, remember that soldier who said shit when ordered to surrender, thereby absolving future expletives from the crime of bad manners in less dangerous situations. Hell, I'll never get out of here, she thought again, and just as she was preparing to leave, another thought came to her like a happy inspiration, In an establishment like this there must be a storeroom, not necessarily a large deposit, for that would be located elsewhere, probably some distance away, but back-up supplies of certain products in constant demand. Excited at the idea, she began looking for a closed door that might lead her to the cave of treasures, but they were all open, and there inside, she found the same devastation, the same blind people rummaging through the same litter. Finally, in a dark corridor, where the light of day scarcely penetrated, she saw what looked like a cargo lift. The metal doors were closed and at the side there was another door, smooth, of the kind that slide on a track, The basement, she thought, the blind people who got this far found their path impeded, they must have realised there was an elevator, but it didn't occur to anyone that it was also normal for there to be a staircase in the event of there being a power cut, for example, as was now the case. She pushed the sliding door and received, almost simultaneously, two overwhelming impressions, first, that of the total darkness she would have to penetrate in order to reach the basement, and then the unmistakable smell of food, even when stored in jars and containers we call sealed, the fact is that hunger has always had a keen sense of smell, the kind that penetrates through all barriers, just as dogs do. She quickly turned back to rescue from the litter the plastic bags she would need to transport the food, at the same time asking herself, Without light, how am I to know what to take, she shrugged her shoulders, what a stupid thing to worry about, her concern now, given the state of weakness in which she found herself, ought to be whether she would have the strength to carry the bags once they were full, retrace her steps back from where she had come, at that moment, she was gripped by the most awful fear, that of not being able to return to the spot where her husband was waiting for her, she knew the name of the street, this she had not forgotten, but she had taken so many turnings, despair paralysed her, then slowly, as if her arrested brain had finally started to move, she saw herself bent over a map of the city, searching with the tip of her finger for the shortest route, as if she had two sets of eyes, one set watching her consult the map, another perusing the map and working out the route. The corridor remained deserted, a stroke of luck, given her nervous state because of the discovery she had made, she had forgotten to close the door. She now closed it carefully behind her only to find herself plunged into total darkness, as sightless as those blind people out there, the only difference was in the colour, if black and white can, strictly speaking, be thought of as colours. Keeping close to the wall, she began to descend the stairs, if this place should turn out not to be a secret, after all, and someone were to rise from the depths, they would have to proceed as she had seen on the street, one of them would have to abandon the safety of having somewhere to lean against, brushing against the vague presence of the other, perhaps for an instant foolishly fearing that the wall did not continue on the other side, I'm going mad, she thought, and with good reason, making this descent into a dark pit, without light or any hope of seeing any, how far would it be, these underground stores are usually never very deep, first flight of steps, Now I know what it means to be blind, second flight of steps, I'm going to scream, I'm going to scream, third set of steps, the darkness is like a thick paste that sticks to her face, her eyes transformed into balls of pitch, What is this before me, and then another thought, even more terrifying, And how shall I find the stairs again, a sudden unsteadiness obliged her to crouch down in order to avoid simply falling over, almost fainting, she stammered, It's clean, she was referring to the floor, it seemed remarkable to her, a clean floor. Little by little she recovered her senses, she felt dull pains in her stomach, not that this was anything new, but at this moment it was as if there were no other living organ in her body, there had to be others, but they gave no sign of being there, her heart, yes, her heart was pounding like a great drum, for ever working blindly in the dark, from the first of all darknesses, the womb in which it was formed, to the last where it would cease. She was still clutching the plastic bags, she had not let go of them, now all she had to do was to fill them, calmly, a storeroom is not a place for ghosts and dragons, here there is nothing but darkness, and darkness neither bites nor offends, as for the stairway I'm bound to find it, even if it means walking all the way round this awful place. Her mind made up, she was about to get to her feet, but then remembered she was as blind as all the others, better to do as they did, to advance on all fours until she came across something, shelves laden with food, whatever it might be, so long as it can be eaten as it is, without having to be cooked or specially prepared, since there is no time for fancy cooking.

Her fear crept surreptitiously back, she had scarcely gone a few metres, perhaps she was mistaken, perhaps right there before her, invisible, a dragon was waiting for her with its mouth open. Or a ghost with outstretched hand, to carry her off to the dreadful world of the dead who never cease to die, because someone always comes to resuscitate them. Then, prosaically, with an infinite, resigned sadness, it occurred to her that the place where she found herself was not a store for food, but a garage, she actually thought she could smell the gasoline, the mind suffers delusions when it succumbs to the monsters it has itself created. Then her hand touched something, not the ghost's viscous fingers, not the fiery tongue and fangs of the dragon, what she felt was the contact of cold metal, a smooth vertical surface, she guessed, without knowing what it was called, that this was the upright of a set of shelves, She calculated there must be others just like this, standing parallel to this one, as was the custom, it was now a question of finding out where the food products were, not here, for this smell is unmistakable, it is the smell of detergent. Without giving another thought to the difficulties she would have in finding the stairs, she began investigating the shelves, groping, sniffing, shaking. There were cardboard containers, glass and plastic bottles, jars of all sizes, tins that were probably preserves, various cartons, packets, bags, tubes. She filled one of the bags at random, Could all this be for eating, she thought to herself with some disquiet. The doctor's wife passed on to the next set of shelves, and the unexpected happened, her blind hand that could not see where it was going, came up against and knocked over some tiny boxes. The noise they made on hitting the floor almost made her heart stop beating, Matches, she thought. Trembling with excitement, she stooped down, ran her hand over the ground, found what she was looking for, this is a smell one never confuses with any other, and the noise of the little match-sticks when we shake the box, the sliding of the lid, the roughness of the sand-paper on the outside, which is where the phosphorus is, the scraping of the match-head, finally the sparking of the tiny flame, the surrounding space a diffuse sphere as luminous as a star glimmering through the mist, dear God, light exists and I have eyes to see, praised be light. From now on, the harvest would be easy. She began with the boxes of matches, and almost filled a bag. No need to take all of them, the voice of common sense told her, then the flickering flames of the matches lit up the shelves, over here, then over there, soon the bags were full, the first had to be emptied because it contained nothing useful, the others already held enough riches to buy the city, nor need we be surprised at this difference of values, we need only recall that there was once a king who wanted to exchange his kingdom for a horse, what would he not give were he dying of hunger and was tempted by these plastic bags full of food. The stairway is there, the way out to the right. But first, the doctor's wife sits on the ground, opens a packet of chorizo sausage, another with slices of black bread, a bottle of water, and, without remorse, starts eating. If she were not to eat now she would not have the strength to carry the provisions where they were needed, she being the provider. When she had finished, she slipped the bags over her arms, three on each side, and with her hands raised before her, she went on striking matches until she reached the stairs, then she climbed them with some effort, she still had not digested her food, which needs time to pass from the stomach to the muscles and nerves, and, in her case, to what had shown the greatest resistance, her head. The door slid noiselessly open, And what if there is someone in the corridor, thought the doctor's wife, what shall I do. There was no one, but she started asking herself again, What shall I do. When she reached the exit, she could turn round and shout inside, There is food at the end of the corridor, stairs lead to the store in the cellar, make the most of it, I have left the door open. She could have done it, but decided not to. Using her shoulder, she closed the door, she told herself that it was better to say nothing, just imagine what would happen, the blind inmates running all over the place like madmen, a repetition of what happened in the mental asylum when fire broke out, they would roll down the stairs, be trampled and crushed by those coming behind, who would also stumble and fall, it is not the same thing to put one's foot on a firm step as to put it on a slippery body. And when the food is finished, I shall be able to come back for more, she thought. She now gripped the bags with her hands, took a deep breath, and proceeded along the corridor. They would not be able to see her, but there was the smell of what she had eaten, The sausage, what a fool I was, it would be like a living trail. She gritted her teeth, clutched the bags with all her strength, I must run, she said. She remembered the blind man whose knee had been cut by a splinter of glass, If the same thing happens to me, if I don't look out and step on broken glass, we may have forgotten that this woman is wearing no shoes, she still has not had time to go to a shoeshop like blind people in the city, who despite being unfortunates without sight, can at least choose footwear by touch. She had to run, and she did. At first, she had tried to slip through the groups of blind people, trying not to touch them, but this obliged her to go slowly, to stop several times in order to ascertain the way, enough to give off the smell of food, for auras are not only per-fumed and ethereal ones, in no time a blind man was shouting, Who's eating sausage around here, no sooner were those words spoken than the doctor's wife threw caution to the wind and broke into reckless flight, colliding, jostling, knocking people over, with a devil-may-care attitude that was wholly reprehen-sible, for this is not the way to treat blind people who have more than enough reasons to be unhappy.

When she reached the street, it was raining buckets, All the better, she thought, panting for breath, her legs shaking, in this rain the smell will be less noticeable. Someone had grabbed the last rag that had barely covered her from the waist up, she was now going around with her breasts exposed and glistening, a re-fined expression, with the water from heaven, this was not lib-erty leading the people, the bags, fortunately full, are too heavy for her to carry them aloft like a flag. This is somewhat incon-venient, since these tantalising odours are travelling at a height that brings dogs on the scent, of course without masters to look after them and feed them, there is virtually a pack of them following the doctor's wife, let's hope none of these hounds remembers to take a bite to test the resistance of the plastic. In a downpour like this, which is almost becoming a deluge, you would expect people to be taking shelter, waiting for the weather to improve. But this is not the case, there are blind people everywhere gaping up at the heavens, slaking their thirst, storing up water in every nook and cranny of their bodies, and others, who are somewhat more far-sighted, and above all sensible, hold up buckets, bowls and pans, and raise them to the generous sky, clearly God provides the cloud according to the thirst. The possibility had not occurred to the doctor's wife that not so much as a drop of the precious liquid was coming from the taps in the houses, this is the drawback of civilisation, we are so used to the convenience of piped water brought into our homes, and forget that for this to happen there have to be people to open and close distribution valves, water towers and pumps that require electrical energy, computers to regulate the deficits and administer the reserves, and all of these operations require the use of one's eyes. Eyes are also needed to see this picture, a woman laden with plastic bags, going along a rain-drenched street, amidst rotting litter and human and animal excrement, cars and trucks abandoned any old way, blocking the main thoroughfare, some of the vehicles with their tyres already surrounded by grass, and the blind, the blind, open-mouthed and staring up at the white sky, it seems incredible that rain should fall from such a sky. The doctor's wife reads the street signs as she goes along, she remembers some of them, others not at all, and there comes a moment when she realises that she has lost her way. There is no doubt, she is lost. She took a turning, then another, she no longer remembers the streets or their names, then in her distress, she sat down on the filthy ground, thick with black mud, and, drained of any strength, of all strength, she burst into tears. The dogs gathered round her, sniffed at the bags, but without much conviction, as if their hour for eating had passed, one of them licks her face, perhaps it had been used to drying tears ever since it was a puppy. The woman strokes its head, runs her hand down its drenched back, and she weeps the rest of her tears embracing the dog. When she finally raised her eyes, the god of crossroads be praised a thousand times, she saw a great map before her, of the kind that town councils set up throughout city centres, especially for the benefit and reassurance of visitors, who are just as anxious to say where they have been as to know precisely where they are. Now that everyone is blind, you might be tempted to think that the money has been ill-spent, but it is a question of being patient, of letting time take its course, we should have learnt this once and for all, that destiny has to make many turnings before arriving anywhere, destiny alone knows what it has cost to bring this map here in order to let this woman know where she is. She was not as far away as she thought, she had simply made a detour in the other direction, all you have to do is to follow this street until you come to the square, there you count two streets to the left, then you take the first street on the right, that is the one you are look-ing for, the number you have not forgotten. The dogs gradually left her, something distracted them on the way, or they are fa-miliar with the district and are reluctant to stray too far, only the dog that has dried her tears accompanied the person who had wept them, probably this encounter of the woman and the map, so well prepared by destiny, included the dog as well. The fact is that they entered the shop together, the dog of tears was not surprised to see people lying on the ground, so still that they might have been dead, the dog was used to this, sometimes they let him sleep amongst them, and when it was time to get up, they were nearly always alive. Wake up, if you're asleep, I've brought food, said the doctor's wife, but first she had closed the door, in case anyone passing in the street should hear her. The boy with the squint was the first to raise his head, weakness pre-vented him from doing any more, the others took a little longer, they were dreaming they were stones, and we all know how deeply stones sleep, a simple stroll in the countryside shows it to be so, there they lie sleeping, half buried, awaiting who knows what awakening. The word food, however, has magic powers, especially when hunger is pressing, even the dog of tears, who knows no language, began wagging its tail, this instinctive move-ment reminded it that it still had not done what is expected of wet dogs, to shake themselves vigorously, splashing everything around, for them it is easy, they wear their pelt as if it were a coat. Holy water of the most efficacious variety, descended

directly from heaven, the splashes helped the stones to transform themselves into persons, while the doctor's wife participated in this process of metamorphosis by opening the plastic
bags one after the other. Not everything smelled of what it
contained, but the aroma of a chunk of stale bread would be as
good, speaking in exalted terms, as the essence of life itself.
They are all awake at last, their hands are shaking, their faces
anxious, it is then that the doctor, as had happened before to the
dog of tears, remembers who he is, Careful, it's not a good idea
to eat too much, it could be harmful, What's doing us harm is
hunger, said the first blind man, Take heed of what the doctor is
saying, his wife rebuked him, and her husband fell silent, thinking with faint resentment, He doesn't even know anything
about eyes, unjust words these, especially if we take into account that the doctor is no less blind than the others, the proof
being that he was unaware that his wife was naked from the
waist up, it was she who asked him for his jacket to cover herself, the other blind inmates looked in her direction, but it was
much too late, if only they had looked before.

As they were eating, the woman told them of her adventures,
of everything that had happened to her and everything that she
had done, without mentioning that she had left the door to the
storeroom closed, she was not entirely sure of the humanitarian
motives she had given to herself, to compensate she told them
about the blind man who got a piece of glass stuck in his knee,
they all laughed heartily, well, not all of them, the old man with
the black eyepatch only reacted with a weary smile, and the boy
with the squint had ears only for the noise he made as he
chewed his food. The dog of tears received his share, which he
quickly repaid by barking furiously when anyone outside shook
the door hard. Whoever it was, they did not persist, there was
talk of mad dogs going around, not knowing where I'm putting
my feet makes me quite mad enough. Calm was restored, and it
was then, when everyone's initial hunger had been assuaged,
that the doctor's wife related the conversation she had had with
the man who had come out of this same shop to see if it was
raining. Then she concluded, If what he told me is true, we can-

not be certain of finding our homes as we left them, we don't even know whether we shall be able to get into them, I'm speaking of those who forgot to take the keys when they left, or lost them, we, for example, do not have them, they disappeared in the fire, it would be impossible to find them now amongst the ashes, she uttered that word and it was as if she were seeing the flames devouring her scissors, first burning the congealed blood that remained on them, then licking at the edges the sharp points, blunting them, and gradually making them dull, pliable, soft, formless, no one would believe that this instrument could have perforated someone's throat, once the fire has done its work it will be impossible in this unified mass of molten metal, to distinguish which are the scissors and which the keys, I've got the keys, said the doctor, and awkwardly introducing three fingers into a small pocket near the waistband of his tattered trousers, he brought out a tiny ring with three keys, How do you happen to have them when I had put them in my handbag which got left behind, I removed them, I was afraid they might get lost, I felt they were safer if they were always with me, and it was also a way of convincing myself that one day we would go back home, It's a relief to have the keys, but we might find the house with the door smashed in, They may not even have tried. For some moments, they had forgotten the others, but now it was important to know, from all of them, what had happened to their keys, the first to speak was the girl with dark glasses, My parents remained at home when the ambulance came to fetch me, I don't know what became of them afterwards, then the old man with the black eyepatch spoke up, I was at home when I went blind, they knocked at the door, the owner of the house came to tell me there were some male nurses looking for me, it wasn't the moment to be thinking about keys, that left only the wife of the first blind man, but she said, I cannot say, I've forgotten, she knew and remembered, but what she did not wish to confess is that when she suddenly saw that she was blind, an absurd expression, but so deeply rooted in the language that we've been unable to avoid it, she had run from the house screaming, calling out to her neighbours, those who were still in the building thought twice about going to her assistance, and she, who had shown herself so steadfast and capable when her husband had been struck by this misfortune, now went to pieces, abandoning her home with the door wide open, it did not even occur to her to ask that they should allow her to turn back, just for a minute, the time to close the door and say I'll be right back. No one asked the boy with the squint about the key to his house, since he cannot even remember where he lives. Then the doctor's wife gently touched the hand of the girl with dark glasses, Let's start with your house which is nearest, but first we must find some clothes and shoes, we can't go around like this, unwashed and in rags. She started to get up, but noticed that the boy with the squint, consoled by now and his hunger satisfied, had gone back to sleep. She said, let's rest then, let's sleep a little, then later we can go and see what awaits us. She took off her drenched skirt, then, to find some warmth, she snuggled up to her husband, and the first blind man and his wife did the same. Is that you, he had asked, she remembered their home and it pained her, she did not say, Console me, but it was as if she had thought it, what we do not know is what feeling could have led the girl with dark glasses to put her arm round the shoulder of the old man with the black eyepatch, but there is no doubt that she did so, and there they remained, she sleeping, but not him. The dog went to lie down at the door, blocking the entrance, he is a gruff, ill-tempered animal when he does not have to dry someone's tears.

They dressed and put their shoes on, what they still had not solved was some way of washing themselves, but they already looked quite different from the other blind people, the colours of their clothes, notwithstanding the relative scarcity of the range on offer, for, as people often say, the fruit is hand-picked, go well with each other, that is the advantage of having someone on the spot to advise us, You wear this, it goes better with those trousers, the stripes don't clash with the spots, details like that, to the men, of course, these matters do not make a blind bit of difference, but both the girl with dark glasses and the wife of the first blind man insisted on knowing what colours and styles they were wearing, so that, with the help of their imaginations they have some idea of how they look. As for footwear, everyone agreed that comfort should come before beauty, no fancy lacing and high heels, no calf or patent leather, given the state of the roads such refinements would be absurd, what they want here are rubber boots, completely waterproof and coming halfway up the leg, easy to slip into and out of, there is nothing better for walking through mud. Unfortunately, boots of this kind could not be found for everyone, there were no boots to fit the boy with the squint, for example, the larger sizes were like boats on him, so he had to settle for a pair of sports shoes with no clearly defined purpose, What a coincidence, his mother would say, wherever she might be, when someone told her what had happened, those are exactly the shoes my son would have chosen had he been able to see. The old man with the black eyepatch, whose feet were on the large side, solved the problem by wearing basketball shoes, specially made for players six foot tall and with extremities to match. It is true that he looks somewhat comical, as if he were wearing white slippers, but he will look ridiculous only for a while, within ten minutes the shoes will be filthy, just like everything else in life, let time take its course and it will find a solution.

It has stopped raining, there are no blind people standing about gaping. They go around not knowing what to do, they wander through the streets, but never for very long, walking or standing still is all the same to them, they have no other objective than the search for food, the music has stopped, never has there been so much silence in the world, the cinemas and theatres are only frequented by the homeless who have given up searching, some theatres, the larger ones, had been used to keep the blind in quarantine when the Government, or the few survivors, still believed that the white sickness could be remedied with devices and certain strategies that had been so ineffectual in the past against yellow fever and other infectious plagues, but this came to an end, not even a fire was needed here. As for the museums, it is truly heart-breaking, all those people, and I do mean people, all those paintings, all those sculptures, without a single visitor standing before them. What are the blind in this city waiting for, who knows, they might be awaiting a cure if they still believed in it, but they lost that hope when it became public knowledge that the epidemic of blindness had spared no one, that not a single person had been left with the eyesight to look through the lens of a microscope, that the laboratories had been abandoned, where there was no other solution for the bacteria but to feed on each other if they hoped to survive. In the beginning, many of the blind, accompanied by relatives who so far had maintained some sense of family solidarity, still rushed to the hospitals, but there they found only blind doctors feeling the pulse of patients they could not see, listening to them back and front, this was all they could do, since they still had their hearing. Then, feeling the pangs of hunger, those patients who could still walk began to flee the hospitals, they ended up dying unprotected on the streets, their families, if they still had them, could be anywhere, and then, so that they might be buried, it was not enough for someone to trip over them accidentally, their corpses had to start to smell, and even then, only if they had died in some main thoroughfare. Little wonder that there are so many dogs, some of them already resemble hyenas, the spots on their pelt are like those of putrefaction, they run around with their hind quarters drawn in, as if afraid that the dead and devoured might come back to life in order to make them pay for the shame of biting those who could not defend themselves. What's the world like these days, the old man with the black eyepatch had asked, and the doctor's wife replied, There's no difference between inside and outside, between here and there, between the many and the few, between what we're living through and what we shall have to live through, And the people, how are they coping, asked the girl with dark glasses, They go around like ghosts, this must be what it means to be a ghost, being certain that life exists, because your four senses say so, and yet unable to see it, Are there lots of cars out there, asked the first blind man, who was unable to forget that his had been stolen, It's like a cemetery. Neither the doctor nor the wife of the first blind man asked any questions, what was the point, when the replies were such as these. As for the little boy with the squint, he has the satisfaction of wearing the shoes he had always dreamt of having and he is not even saddened by the fact that he cannot see them. This is probably the reason why he does not look like a ghost. And the dog of tears, who trails after the doctor's wife, would scarcely deserve to be called a hyena, he does not follow the scent of dead meat, he accompanies a pair of eyes that he knows are alive and well.

The home of the girl with dark glasses is not far away, but after being starved for a week, it is only now that the members of this group begin to recover their strength, that is why they walk so slowly, in order to rest they have no option but to sit on the ground, it had not been worthwhile taking so much trouble to choose colours and styles, when in such a short time their clothes are filthy. The street where the girl with dark glasses lives is not only short but narrow which explains why there are no cars to be seen here, they could pass in one direction only, but there was no place to park, it was prohibited. That there were also no people was not surprising, in streets like these there are many moments throughout the day when there is not a living soul to be seen, What's the number of your house, asked the doctor's wife, number seven, I live on the second floor in the flat on the left. One of the windows was open, at any other time that would be a sign that there was almost certainly someone at home, now everything was uncertain. The doctor's wife said, No need for all of us to go up, we two shall go on our own, the rest of you wait below. She realised the front door leading on to the street had been forced, the mortice lock was clearly twisted, a long splinter of wood had almost come away from the doorpost. The doctor's wife mentioned none of this. She let the girl go ahead since she knew the way, she did not mind the shadows into which the stairway was plunged. In her nervous haste, the girl with dark glasses stumbled twice, but laughed it off, Just imagine, stairs that I used to be able to go up and down with my eyes closed, clichés are like that, they are insensitive to the thousand subtleties of meaning, this one, for example, does not know the difference between closing one's eyes and being blind. On the landing of the second floor, the door they were looking for was closed. The girl with dark glasses ran her hand over the moulding until she found the bell, There's no light, the doctor's wife reminded her, and the girl received these four words that only repeated what everyone knew like a message bringing bad news. She knocked at the door, once, twice, three times, the third time loudly, using her fists and calling out, Mummy, daddy, and no one came to open, these terms of endearment did not affect the reality, no one came to say to her, Dearest daughter, you've come at last, we had given up hope of ever seeing you again, come in, come in, and let this lady who is your friend come in too, the house is a little untidy, pay no attention, the door remained closed. There is no one here, said the girl with dark glasses, and burst into tears leaning against the door, her head on her crossed forearms, as if with her whole body she were desperately imploring pity, if we did not have enough experience of how complicated the human spirit can be we would be surprised that she should be so fond of her parents as to indulge in these demonstrations of sorrow, a girl so free in her behaviour, but not far away is someone who has already affirmed that there does not exist nor ever has existed any contradiction between the one and the other. The doctor's wife tried to console her, but had little to say, it is well known that it is practically impossible for people to remain for a long time in their houses, We could ask the neighbours, she suggested, if there are any, Yes, let's go and ask, said the girl with dark glasses, but there was no hope in her voice. They began by knocking on the door on the other side of the landing, where once again no one replied. On the floor above the two doors were open. The flats had been ransacked, the wardrobes were empty, in the cupboards where food had been stored there was nothing to be found. There were signs that someone had been here recently, no doubt a group of vagrants, as they were all more or less by now, wandering from house to house, from absence to absence.

They went down to the first floor, the doctor's wife rapped on the nearest door, there was an expectant silence, then a gruff voice asked suspiciously, Who's there, the girl with dark glasses stepped forward, It's me, your upstairs neighbour, I'm looking for my parents, do you know where I can find them, what happened to them, she asked. They could hear shuffling footsteps, the door opened and a gaunt old woman appeared, nothing but skin and bone, emaciated, her long white hair dishevelled. A nauseating smell of mustiness and an indefinable putrefaction caused the two women to step back. The old woman opened her eyes wide, they were almost white, I know nothing about your parents, they came to fetch them the day after they took you away, at that time I could still see, Is there anyone else in the building, Now and then I can hear people climbing up or going down the stairs, but they are from outside and only come here to sleep, And what about my parents, I've already told you I know nothing about them, And what about your husband, your son and daughter-in-law, They took them away too, But left you behind, why, Because I was hiding, Where, Just imagine, in your flat, How did you manage to get in, Through the back and up the fire escape, I smashed a window-pane and opened the door from inside, the key was in the lock, And how have you managed since then to live all alone in your flat, asked the doctor's wife, Who else is here, asked the startled old woman turning her head, She's a friend of mine, she's with my group, the girl with dark glasses reassured her, And it's not just a question of being alone, what about food, how have you managed to get food during all this time, insisted the doctor's wife, The fact is that I'm no fool and I'm perfectly capable of looking after myself, If you'd rather not say, don't, I'm simply curious, Then I'll tell you, the first thing I did was to go round all the flats and gather up any food I could find, whatever might go bad I ate at once, the rest I kept, Do you still have some left, asked the girl with dark glasses, No, it's finished, replied the old woman with a sudden expression of mistrust in her sightless eyes, a way of speaking that is always used in similar situations, but it has no basis in fact, because the eyes, the eyes strictly speaking, have no expression, not even when they have been plucked out, they are two round objects that remain inert, it is the eyelids, the eyelashes and the eyebrows, that have to take on board the different visual eloquences and rhetorics, notwithstanding that this is normally attributed to the eyes, So what are you living on now, asked the doctor's wife, Death stalks the streets, but in the back gardens life goes on, the old woman said mysteriously, What do you mean, The back gardens have cabbages, rabbits, hens, they also have flowers, but they're not for eating, And how do you cope, It depends, sometimes I pick some cabbages, at other times I kill a rabbit or chicken, And eat them raw, At first I used to light a fire, then I got used to raw meat, and the stalks of the cabbages are sweet, don't you worry yourselves, my mother's daughter will not die of hunger. She stepped back two paces, almost disappeared into the darkness of the house, only her white eyes shone, and she said from within, If you want to go into your flat, go ahead, I won't stop you. The girl with dark glasses was about to say no, many thanks, it isn't worth it, to what purpose, if my parents aren't there, but suddenly she felt the desire to see her room, to see my room, how foolish, if I'm blind, at least to touch the walls, the bedcover, the pillow where I used to rest my crazy head, over the furniture, perhaps on the chest of drawers there might still be the flowers in the vase she remembered, unless the old woman had thrown them on the floor, annoyed that they could not be eaten. She said, Well, if you don't mind, I'll accept your offer, it's very kind of you, Come in, come in, but don't expect to find any food, what I have is barely enough for me, besides it would be no good to you unless you like raw meat, Don't worry, we have food, Ah, so you have food, in that case you can repay the favour and leave me some, We'll give you some food, don't worry, said the doctor's wife. They had already walked down the corridor, the stench had become unbearable. In the kitchen, dimly lit by the waning light outside, there were rabbit skins on the floor, chicken feathers, bones, and on the table, in a dirty plate covered in dried blood, unrecognisable pieces of meat, as if they had been chewed over and over again, And the rabbits and hens, what do they eat, asked the doctor's wife, Cabbages, weeds, any scraps left over, said the old woman, Don't tell us the hens and rabbits eat meat, The rabbits don't yet, but the hens love it, animals are like people, they get used to everything in the end. The old woman moved steadily, without tottering, she moved a chair out of the way as if she could see, then pointed to the door that led on to the emergency stairs, Through here, be careful not to slip, the handrail is not very secure. And what about the door, asked the girl with dark glasses, You only have to push the door, I have the key, it's somewhere around, It's mine, the girl was about to say, but at that same instant reflected that this key would be no good to her if her parents, or someone acting on their behalf, had taken away the others, the ones for the front door, she could not ask this neighbour to allow her to pass every time she wanted to come in or go out. She felt her heart contract slightly, probably because she was about to enter her own home and discover that her parents were not there, or for whatever reason.

The kitchen was clean and tidy, the dust on the furniture was not excessive, another advantage of this rainy weather, as well as having made the cabbages and greens grow, in fact, the back gardens, seen from above, had struck the doctor's wife as being jungles in miniature, Could the rabbits be running around freely, she asked herself, most unlikely, they would still be housed in the rabbit-hutches waiting for that blind hand to bring them cabbage leaves then grab them by the ears and pull them out kicking, while the other hand prepares the blind blow that will break the vertebrae near the skull. The memory of the girl with dark glasses had guided her into the flat, just as the old woman on the floor below neither tripped nor faltered, her parents' bed was unmade, they must have come to detain them in the early hours of morning, she sat down there and wept, the doctor's wife came to sit beside her, and told her, Don't cry, what else could she say, what meaning do tears have when the world has lost all meaning, In the girl's room on the chest of drawers stood the glass vase with the withered flowers, the water had evaporated, it was there that her blind hands directed themselves, her fingers brushed against the dead petals, how fragile life is when it is abandoned. The doctor's wife opened the window, she looked down into the street, there they all were, seated on the ground, patiently waiting, the dog of tears was the only creature to raise his head, alerted by his keen hearing. The sky, once more overcast, began to darken, night was approaching. She thought that today they would not need to go and search for some refuge where they might sleep, they would stay here. The old woman is not going to be at all pleased if everyone starts tramping through her house, she murmured. Just at that moment, the girl with dark glasses touched her on the shoulder, saying, The keys were in the lock, they did not take them. The problem, if there was one, was therefore resolved, they would not have to put up with the ill-humour of the old woman on the first floor, I'm going down to call them, it will soon be night, how good, at least today we shall be able to sleep in a proper home with a roof over our heads, said the doctor's wife, You and your husband can sleep in my parents' bed, We'll see about that later, I'm the one who gives the orders here, I'm in my own home, You're right, just as you wish, the doctor's wife embraced the girl, then went down to look for the others. Climbing the stairs, chattering with excitement, now and then tripping on the stairs despite having been told by their guide, There are ten steps to each flight, it was as if they had come on a visit. The dog of tears followed them quietly, as if this were an everyday occurrence. From the landing, the girl with dark glasses looked down, it is the custom when someone is coming up, whether it be to find out who it is, if the person is a stranger, or to greet someone with words of welcome if they are friends, in this case no eyes were needed to know who was arriving. Come in, come in, make yourselves comfortable. The old woman on the first floor had come to her door to pry, she thought this lot was one of those mobs who turned up to sleep, in this she was not wrong, she asked, Who's there, and the girl with dark glasses replied from above, It's my group, the old woman was puzzled, how had she been able to reach the landing, then it dawned on her and she was annoyed with herself for having forgotten to retrieve the keys from the front door, it was as if she were losing her proprietorial rights over this building in which she had been the sole occupant for many months. She could find no better way of compensating for her sudden frustration than to say, opening the door, Remember you said you'd give me some food, don't go forgetting your promise. And since neither the doctor's wife nor the girl with dark glasses, the one busy guiding those who were arriving, the other in receiving them, made any reply, she shouted hysterically, Did you hear me, a mistake on her part, because the dog of tears, who at that precise moment was passing her, leapt at her and started barking furiously, the entire stairway echoed with the uproar, it was perfect, the old woman shrieked in terror and rushed back into her flat, slamming the door behind her, Who is that witch, asked the old man with the black eyepatch, these are things we say when we do not know how to take a good look at ourselves, had he lived as she had lived, we should like to see how long his civilised ways would last.

There was no food apart from what they had brought in the bags, they had to be sparing with it down to the very last drop, and, as for lighting, they had been most fortunate to find two candles in the kitchen cupboard, kept there to be used whenever there happened to be a power cut and which the doctor's wife lit for her own benefit, the others did not need them, they already had a light inside their heads, so strong it had blinded them. Though meagre rations were all this little group had, yet it ended up as a family feast, one of those rare feasts where what belongs to one, belongs to everybody. Before seating themselves at the table, the girl with dark glasses and the doctor's wife went down to the floor below, they went to fulfill their promise, were it not more exact to say that they went to satisfy a demand, payment with food for their passage through that customs house. The old woman received them, whining and surly, that cursed dog that only by some miracle did not devour her, You must have a lot of food to be able to feed such a beast, she insinuated, as if expecting, by means of this accusing observation, to arouse in the two emissaries what we call remorse, what they were really saying to each other, it would be inhumane to leave a poor old woman to die of starvation while a dumb animal gorges itself on scraps. The two women did not turn back to get more food, what they were carrying was already a generous ration, if we take into account the difficult circumstances of life at present, and this strangely enough, was how the old lady on the floor below appraised the situation, when all is said and done, less mean-hearted than she seemed, and she went back inside to find the keys for the back door, saying to the girl with dark glasses, Take it, this key is yours, and, as if this were not enough, she was still muttering as she closed her door, Many thanks. Amazed, the two women returned upstairs, so the old witch had feelings after all, She was not a bad person, living all that time alone must have unhinged her, commented the girl with dark glasses without appearing to think what she was saying. The doctor's wife did not reply, she decided to keep any conversation for later, and once all the others were in bed, some of them asleep, and the two women were sitting in the kitchen like mother and daughter trying to gather strength for the other chores to be done around the house, the doctor's wife asked, And you, what are you going to do now, Nothing, I'll wait here until my parents return, Alone and blind, I've got used to being blind, And what about solitude, I'll have to accept it, the old woman below also lives alone, You don't want to become like her, feeding on cabbages and raw meat, while they last, in these buildings around here there appears to be no one else living, you would be two women hating each other for fear that the food might come to an end, each stalk you gathered would be like taking it from the other's mouth, you didn't see that poor woman, you only caught the stench coming from her flat, I can assure you that not even where we were living before were things so repugnant, Sooner or later, we shall all be like her, and then it will all be over, there will be no more life, Meanwhile, we're still alive, Listen, you know much more than I do, compared with you I'm simply an ignorant girl, but in my opinion we're already dead, we're blind because we're dead, or if you would prefer me to put it another way, we're dead because we're blind, it comes to the same thing, I can still see, Lucky for you, lucky for your husband, for me, for the others, but you don't know how long you will go on seeing, should you become blind you will be like the rest of us, we'll all end up like the neighbour below, Today is today, tomorrow will bring what tomorrow brings, today is my responsibility, not tomorrow if I should turn blind, What do you mean by responsibility, The responsibility of having my eyesight when others have lost theirs, You cannot hope to guide or provide food for all the blind people in this world, I ought to, But you cannot, I shall do whatever I can to help, Of course you will, had it not been for you I might not be alive today, And I don't want you to die now, I must stay, it's my duty, I want my parents to find me if they should return, If they should return, you yourself said it, and we have no way of knowing whether they will still be your parents,

I don't understand, You said that the neighbour below was a good person at heart, Poor woman, Your poor parents, poor you, when you meet up, blind in eyes and blind in feelings, because the feelings with which we have lived and which allowed us to live as we were, depended on our having the eyes we were born with, without eyes feelings become something different, we do not know how, we do not know what, you say we're dead because we're blind, there you have it, Do you love your husband, Yes, as I love myself, but should I turn blind, if after turning blind I should no longer be the person I was, how would I then be able to go on loving him, and with what love, Before, when we could still see, there were also blind people, Few in comparison, the feelings in use were those of someone who could see, therefore blind people felt with the feelings of others, not as the blind people they were, now, certainly, what is emerging are the real feelings of the blind, and we're still only at the beginning, for the moment we still live on the memory of what we felt, you don't need eyes to know what life has become today, if anyone were to tell me that one day I should kill, I'd take it as an insult, and yet I've killed, What then would you have me do, Come with me, come to our house, And what about the others, The same goes for them, but it's you I most care about, Why, I ask myself that question, perhaps because you have become almost like a sister, perhaps because my husband slept with you, Forgive me, It's not a crime that calls for pardon, We would suck your blood and be like parasites, There were plenty of them when we could see, and as for blood, it has to serve some purpose besides sustaining the body that carries it, and now let's try to get some sleep for tomorrow is another day.

Another day, or the same one. When he woke up, the boy with the squint wanted to go to the lavatory, he had diarrhoea, something that had disagreed with him in his weak condition, but it soon became obvious that it was impossible to go in there, the old woman on the floor below had clearly taken advantage of all the lavatories in the building until they could no longer be used, only by some extraordinary stroke of luck none of the seven, before going to bed last night, had needed to satisfy the urge to relieve their bowels, otherwise they would already know just how disgusting those lavatories were. Now they all felt the need to relieve themselves, especially the poor boy who could not hold it in any longer, in fact, however reluctant we might be to admit it, these distasteful realities of life also have to be considered, when the bowels function normally, anyone can have ideas, debate, for example, whether there exists a direct relationship between the eyes and feelings, or whether the sense of responsibility is the natural consequence of clear vision, but when we are in great distress and plagued by pain and anguish that is when the animal side of our nature becomes most apparent. The garden, exclaimed the doctor's wife, and she was right, were it not so early, we would find the neighbour from the flat below already there, it's time we stopped calling her the old woman, as we have disrespectfully done so far, she would already be there, as we were saying, crouched down, surrounded by hens, because the person who might ask the question almost certainly does not know what hens are like. Clutching his belly, protected by the doctor's wife, the boy with the squint went down the stairs in agony, worse still, by the time he reached the last steps, his sphincter had given up trying to resist the internal pressure, so you can imagine the consequences. Meanwhile, the other five were making their way as best they could down the emergency stairs, a most suitable name, if they have any inhibitions left since the time they lived in quarantine, this was the moment to lose them. Scattered throughout the back garden, groaning with the effort, suffering whatever remained of futile shame, they did what had to be done, even the doctor's wife who wept as she looked at them, she wept for all of them, which they seemed no longer to be able to do, her own husband, the first blind man and his wife, the girl with dark glasses, the old man with the black eyepatch, the boy, she saw them squatting on the weeds, between the knotty cabbage stalks, with the hens watching, the dog of tears had also come down to make one more. They cleaned themselves as best they could, superficially and in haste, with some handfuls of grass or broken bits of brick, wherever the arm could reach, in some cases the attempt to tidy up only made matters worse. They went back up the emergency stairs in silence, the neighbour on the first floor did not appear to ask them who they were, where they had come from, where they were going, she must still be sleeping off her supper, and when they got into the flat, first they did not know what to say, then the girl with dark glasses pointed out that they could not remain in that state, it is true that there was no water with which to wash themselves, pity there was no torrential rain like that of yesterday, they would go out once more into the garden, but now naked and without shame, they would receive on their head and shoulders the generous water from the sky above, they would feel it running down their back and chest, down their legs, they could gather it in their hands, clean at last and in this cup offer it to someone to quench their thirst, no matter who, perhaps their lips would gently touch their skin before finding the water, and desperately thirsty as they were, they would eagerly gather the last drops from that shell, thus arousing, who knows, another thirst. What leads the girl with dark glasses astray, as we have seen on other occasions, is her imagination, what would she have to remember in a situation like this, tragic, grotesque, desperate as it was. Despite everything, she is not without some sense of the practical, the proof being that she went to open the wardrobe in her room, then that of her parents, where she gathered up sheets and towels, Let's clean ourselves up with these, she said, it's better than nothing, and there is no doubt that it was a good idea, when they sat down to eat they felt quite different.

It was at the table that the doctor's wife told them what was on her mind. The time has come to decide what we want to do, I'm convinced the entire population is blind, at least that is my impression from observing the behaviour of the people I have seen so far, there is no water, there is no electricity, there are no supplies of any kind, this must be what chaos is, this is what is really meant by chaos. There must be a government, said the first blind man, I'm not so sure, but if there is, it will be a government of the blind trying to rule the blind, that is to say, nothingness trying to organise nothingness, Then there is no future, said the old man with the black eyepatch, I cannot say whether there will be a future, what matters for the moment is to see how we can live in the present, Without a future, the present serves no purpose, it's as if it did not exist, Perhaps humanity will manage to live without eyes, but then it will cease to be humanity, the result is obvious, which of us think of ourselves as being as human as we believed ourselves to be before, I, for example, killed a man, You killed a man, asked the first blind man in alarm, Yes, the one who gave orders on the other side, I stabbed him in the throat with a pair of scissors, You killed him to avenge us, only a woman could avenge the women, said the girl with dark glasses, and revenge, being just, is something human, if the victim has no rights over the wrong-doer then there can be no justice, Nor humanity, added the wife of the first blind man, Let's get back to the matter we were discussing, said the doctor's wife, if we stay together we might manage to survive, if we separate we shall be swallowed up by the masses and destroyed, You mentioned that there are organised groups of blind people, observed the doctor, this means that new ways of living are being invented and there is no reason why we should finish up by being destroyed, as you predict, I don't know to what extent they are really organised, I only see them going around in search of food and somewhere to sleep, nothing more, We're going back to being primitive hordes, said the old man with the black eyepatch, with the difference that we are not a few thousand men and women in an immense, unspoiled nature, but thousands of millions in an uprooted, exhausted world, And blind, added the doctor's wife, When it starts to become difficult to find water and food, these groups will almost certainly disband, each person will think they have a better chance of surviving on their own, they will not have to share anything with others, whatever they can grab belongs to them and to no one else, The groups going around must have leaders, someone who gives orders and organises things, the first blind man reminded them, Perhaps, but in this case those who give the orders are just as blind as those who receive them, You're not blind, said the girl with dark glasses, that's why you were the obvious person to give orders and organise the rest of us, I don't give orders, I organise things as best I can, I am simply the eyes that the rest of you no longer possess, A kind of natural leader, a king with eyes in the land of the blind, said the old man with the black eyepatch, If this is so, then allow yourselves to be guided by my eyes so long as they last, therefore what I propose is that instead of dispersing, her in her house, you in yours, let us continue to live together, We can stay here, said the girl with dark glasses, Our house is bigger, Assuming it has not been occupied, the wife of the first blind man pointed out, When we get there we'll find out, and if it should be occupied we can come back here, or go and take a look at your house, or yours, she added, addressing the old man with the black eyepatch, and he replied, I have no home of my own, I lived alone in a room, Have you no family, asked the girl with dark glasses, No family whatsoever, Not even a wife, children, brothers and sisters, No one, Unless my parents turn up, I shall be alone just like you. I'll stay with you, said the boy with the squint, but did not add, Unless my mother turns up, he did not lay down this condition, strange behaviour, or perhaps not so strange, the young quickly adapt, they have their whole life before them. What do you think, asked the doctor's wife, I'm going with you, said the girl with dark glasses, all I ask is that you should bring me here once a week just in case my parents should happen to return, Will you leave the keys with the neighbour below, There's no alternative, she cannot take more than she has taken already, She might destroy things, Now that I've been here, perhaps not, We're coming with you too, said the first blind man, although we should like, as soon as possible, to pass by our home and find out what has happened, Of course, No point in passing by my house, I've already told you it was just a room. But you'll come with us, Yes, on one condition, at first sight it must seem scandalous for someone to lay down conditions when he is being done a favour, but some old people are like that, they make up in pride for the little time remaining to them, What condition is that, asked the doctor, When I start becoming an impossible burden, you must tell me, and if, out of friendship or pity, you should decide to say nothing, I hope I'll still have enough judgment to do the necessary, And what might that be, I'd like to know, asked the girl with dark glasses, Withdraw, take myself off, disappear, as elephants used to do, I've heard it said that recently things have been different, none of these animals reach old age, You're not exactly an elephant, Nor am I exactly a man, Especially if you start giving childish replies, retorted the girl with dark glasses, and the conversation went no further.

The plastic bags are now much lighter than when they were brought here, not surprisingly, the neighbour on the first floor also ate from them, she ate twice, first last night, and today they left her some more food when they asked her to take the keys and look after them until the rightful owners turned up, a question of keeping the old girl sweet, because as for her character we have learned more than enough, and the dog of tears also had to be fed, only a heart of stone would have been capable of feigning indifference before those pleading eyes, and while we are on the subject, where has the dog disappeared to, he is not in the flat, he did not go out the door, he can only be in the back garden, the doctor's wife went off to take a good look, and this was, in fact, where he was, the dog of tears was devouring a hen, the attack had been so quick that there was not even time to raise the alarm, but if the old woman on the first floor had eyes and kept a count on her hens, who can tell, out of anger, what fate might befall the keys, Between the awareness of having committed a crime and the perception that the human being whom he was protecting was going away, the dog of tears hesitated only for an instant, then began at once to scratch the soft earth, and before the old woman on the first floor appeared on the landing of the fire escape to sniff out the sounds that were coming into her flat, the hen's carcass was buried, the crime covered up, remorse reserved for some other occasion. The dog of tears sidled upstairs, brushed like a breath of air past the skirts of the old woman, who had no idea of the danger she had just faced, and went to settle beside the doctor's wife, where he announced to the heavens the feat he had just achieved. The old woman on the first floor, hearing him bark so ferociously, feared, but as we know all too late, for the safety of her larder, and, craning her neck upwards, called, This dog must be kept under control before he kills one of my hens, Don't worry, replied the doctor's wife, the dog isn't hungry, he has already eaten, and we're leaving right away, Right away, repeated the old woman, and there was a break in her voice as if of pain, as if she wanted to be understood in a quite different way, for example, You're going to leave me here all alone, but she did not utter another word, only that Right away which asked for no reply, the hard of heart also have their sorrows, this woman's heart was such that later she refused to open her door to bid farewell to these ingrates to whom she had given free access to her house. She heard them go downstairs, they were talking amongst themselves, saying, Watch you don't stumble, Put your hand on my shoulder, Hold on to the bannister, the usual words, but now much more common in this world of blind people, what did surprise her was to hear one of the women say, It's so dark in this place that I can't see a thing, that this woman's blindness should not be white was already surprising in itself, but that she could not see because it was so dark, what could this mean, She wanted to think, tried hard, but her weak head did not help, soon she was saying to herself, I must have misheard, whatever it was. In the street, the doctor's wife remembered what she had said, she must watch what she was saying, she could move like someone who has eyes, But my words must be those of a blind person, she thought.

Assembled on the pavement, she arranged her companions in two rows of three, in the first one she placed her husband and the girl with dark glasses, with the boy with the squint in the middle, in the second row the old man with the black eyepatch and the first blind man, one on either side of the other woman. She wanted to keep all of them close to her, not in the usual fragile Indian file, which can be broken at any moment, they only needed to encounter a more numerous or more aggressive group, and it would be like a steamer at sea cutting in two a sailboat that happened to cross its path, we know the consequences of such accidents, shipwrecks, disasters, people drowned, futile cries for help in that vast expanse of water, the steamer already sailing on ahead, not even aware of the collision, this is what would happen to this group, a blind person here, another there, lost in the disordered currents of the other blind people, like the waves of the sea that never stop and do not know where they are going, and the doctor's wife, too, not knowing to whose assistance she should hasten first, placing her hand on her husband's arm, perhaps on that of the boy with the squint, but losing the girl with dark glasses, the other two, the old man with the black eyepatch, far away, heading for the elephants' graveyard. What she is doing now is to pass around herself and all the others a cord made from strips of cloth knotted together while the rest were asleep, Don't hold on to me, she said, but hold on to the rope with all your strength, do not let go under any circumstances, whatever may happen. They were careful not to walk too closely to avoid tripping each other, but they needed to feel the proximity of their neighbours, a direct contact if possible, only one of them did not have to worry himself with these new questions of overland tactics, this was the boy with the squint who walked in the middle, protected on all sides. None of our blind friends thought to ask how the other groups navigate, if they too are advancing tied to each other by this or other processes, but the reply should be easy from what we have been able to observe, groups in general, except in the case of a more cohesive group for good reasons unknown to us, gradually gain and lose adherents throughout the day, there is always one blind man who strays and is lost, another who was caught by the force of gravity and tags along, he might be accepted, he might be expelled, depending on what he is carrying with him. The old woman on the first floor slowly opened the window, she does not want anyone to know that she has this sentimental weakness, but no noise can be heard coming from the street, they have already gone, they have left this place where almost no one ever passes, the old woman ought to be pleased, in this way she will not have to share her hens and rabbits with the others, she should be pleased but is not, in her blind eyes appear two tears, for the first time she asked herself if she had some good reason for wanting to go on living. She could find no reply, replies do not always come when needed, and it often happens that the only possible reply is to wait for them.

Along the route they were taking they would pass two blocks away from the house where the old man with the black eye-patch had his bachelor room, but they had already decided that they would travel on, there was no food to be found there, clothing they do not need, books they cannot read. The streets are full of blind people out searching for food. They go in and out of shops, enter empty-handed and nearly always come out empty-handed, then they debate among themselves the need or advantage of leaving this district and going to forage elsewhere in the city, the big problem is that, things being as they are, without running water, the gas cylinders empty, as well as the danger of lighting fires inside the houses, no cooking can be done, assuming that we would know where to look for the salt, the oil and seasoning, were we to try and prepare a few dishes with some hint of the flavours from the past, if there were some greens, simply having them boiled would leave us satis-fied, the same being true of meat, apart from the usual rabbits and hens, dogs and cats could be cooked if they could be caught, but since experience is truly the mistress of life, even these animals, previously domesticated, learned to mistrust ca-resses, they now hunt in packs and in packs they defend them-selves from being hunted down, and since, thanks be to God, they still have eyes, they are better equipped to avoid danger, and to attack if necessary. All these circumstances and reasons have led us to conclude that the best food for humans is what is preserved in cans and jars, not only because it is often already cooked, ready to be eaten, but also because it is so much easier to transport and handy for immediate use. It is true that on all these cans, jars and different packets in which these products are sold there is a date beyond which it could be risky to consume them and even dangerous in certain cases, but popular wisdom was quick to put into circulation a saying to which in a sense there is no answer, symmetrical with another saying no longer much used, what the eyes do not see the heart does not grieve over, people would now often say, eyes that do not see have a cast-iron stomach, which explains why they eat so much rubbish. Heading the group, the doctor's wife makes a mental calculation of the food she still has in reserve, there will be enough, if that, for one meal, without counting the dog, but let him sort himself out with the means at his disposal, the same means that served him so well to grab the hen by the neck and cut off its voice and life. She will have at home, as you may remember, and provided that no one has broken in, a reasonable quantity of preserves, enough for a couple, but there are seven persons here who have to be fed, her reserves will not last long, even if she were to enforce strict rationing. Tomorrow, or within the next few days, she will have to return to the underground storeroom of the supermarket, she will have to decide whether to go alone or to ask her husband to accompany her, or the first blind man who is younger and more agile, the choice is between the possibility of carrying a larger quantity of food and acting speedily, without forgetting the conditions of the retreat. The rubbish on the streets, which appears to be twice as much since yesterday, the human excrement, that from before semi-liquified by the torrential downpour of rain, mushy or runny, the excrement being evacuated at this very minute by these men and women as we pass, fills the air with the most awful stench, like a dense mist through which it is only possible to advance with enormous effort. In a square surrounded by trees, with a statue in the middle, a pack of dogs is devouring a man's corpse. He must have died a short while ago, his limbs are not rigid, as can be seen when the dogs shake them to tear from the bone the flesh caught between their teeth. A crow hops around in search of an opening to get close to the feast. The doctor's wife averted her eyes, but it was too late, the vomit rising from her entrails was irresistible, twice, three times, as if her own still-living body were being shaken by other dogs, the pack of absolute despair, this is as far as I go, I want to die here. Her husband asked, What's the matter, the others bound together by the cord, drew closer, suddenly alarmed, What happened, Did the food upset you, Something that was off, I don't feel a thing, Nor me, All the better for them, all they could hear was the uproar from the dogs, the sudden and unexpected cawing of a crow, in the upheaval one of the dogs had bitten its wing in passing, quite unintentionally, then the doctor's wife said, I couldn't stop myself, forgive me, but some of the dogs here are eating another dog. Are they eating our dog, asked the boy with the squint, No, our dog as you call him, is alive, and prowling around them but he keeps his distance. After eating that hen, he can't be very hungry, said the first blind man. Are you feeling better, asked the doctor, Yes, let's be on our way, The dog isn't ours, it simply latched on to us, it will probably stay behind now with these other dogs, it may have stayed with them before, but it has refound its friends, I want to do a poo, Here, I've got stomachache, it hurts, complained the boy. He relieved himself on the spot as best he could, the doctor's wife vomited once more, but for other reasons. Then they crossed the vast square and when they reached the shade of the trees, the doctor's wife looked back. More dogs had appeared and they were already contesting what remained of the corpse. The dog of tears arrived with its snout touching the ground as if it were following some trail, a question of habit, for this time a simple glance was enough to find the woman he was looking for.

The march continued, the house of the old man with the black eyepatch was already some way behind them, now they are making their way along a broad avenue with tall imposing buildings on either side. The cars here are expensive, capacious and comfortable, which explains why so many blind people are to be seen sleeping in them, and from all appearances, an enormous limousine has actually been transformed into a permanent home, probably because it was much easier to return to a car than to a house, the occupants of this one must do what was done back there in quarantine to find their bed, groping their way along and counting the cars from the corner, twenty-seven, right-hand side, I'm back home. The building at whose door the limousine is parked is a bank. The car had brought the chairman of the board to the weekly plenary meeting, the first to be held since the epidemic of white sickness had been declared, and there had been no time to park it in the underground garage until the meeting was over. The driver went blind just as the chairman was about to enter the building by the main entrance as usual, he let out a cry, we are referring to the driver, but he, meaning the chairman, did not hear it. Moreover, attendance at the plenary board meeting would not be as complete as its designation suggested, for during the last few days some of the directors had gone blind. The chairman did not get round to opening the session, the agenda of which had provided for a discussion of measures to be taken in the event that all the directors and their deputies went blind, and he was not even able to enter the board-room for when the elevator was taking him up to the fifteenth floor, between the ninth and the tenth floors to be exact, the electric power was cut off, never to be restored. And since disasters never come singly, at that same moment the electricians went blind who were responsible for maintaining the internal power supply and consequently that also of the generator, an old model, not automatic, that had long been awaiting replacement, this resulted, as we said before, in the elevator coming to a halt between the ninth and tenth floors. The chairman saw the attendant who was accompanying him go blind, he himself lost his sight an hour later, and since the power did not come back and the cases of blindness inside the bank multiplied that day, in all probability the two are still there, dead, needless to say, shut up in a coffin of steel, and therefore happily safe from voracious dogs.

There being no witnesses, and if there were there is no evidence that they were summoned to the post-mortems to tell us what happened, it is understandable that someone should ask how it was possible to know that these things happened so and not in some other manner, the reply to be given is that all stories are like those about the creation of the universe, no one was there, no one witnessed anything, yet everyone knows what happened. The doctor's wife had asked, What will have happened to the banks, not that she was much concerned, despite having entrusted her savings to one of them, she raised the question out of simple curiosity, simply because she thought of it, nothing more, nor did she expect anyone to make a reply such as, for example, In the beginning, God created heaven and earth, the earth was without form and empty, and darkness was upon the face of the deep, and the spirit of God moved upon the face of the waters, instead of this what really happened was that the old man with the black eyepatch said as they were proceeding down the avenue, As far as I could judge when I still had an eye to see, at first, it was pandemonium, the people, afraid of ending up blind and unprovided for, raced to the banks to withdraw their money, feeling that they ought to safeguard their future, and this is understandable, if someone knows they will no longer be able to work, the only remedy, for as long as they might last, is to have recourse to the savings made in times of prosperity when long-term provisions were made, assuming in fact that the people were prudent enough to build up their savings little by little, the outcome of this precipitous run on the banks was that within twenty-four hours some of the main banks were facing ruin, the Government intervened to plead for calm and to appeal to the civic conscience of citizens, ending the proclamation with the solemn declaration that it would assume all the responsibilities and duties resulting from this public calamity they were facing, but this calming measure did not succeed in alleviating the crisis, not only because people continued to go blind but also because those who could still see were interested only in saving their precious money, in the end, it was inevitable, the banks, bankrupt or otherwise, closed their doors and sought police protection, it did them no good, between the noisy crowds that gathered in front of the banks there were also policemen in plain clothes who demanded what they had saved with so much effort, and some, in order to demonstrate at will, had even advised their command that they were blind and were therefore dismissed, and the others, still in uniform and on active service, their weapons trained on the dissatisfied masses, suddenly lost sight of their target, the latter, if they had money in the bank, lost all hope and, as if that were not enough, they were accused of having entered into a pact with the established authority, but there was worse to come when the banks found themselves attacked by furious hordes of whom some were blind and others not, but all of them desperate, here it was no longer a question of calmly handing in a cheque to be cashed at the counter and saying to the teller, I wish to withdraw my savings, but to lay hands on everything possible, on the cash in the till, whatever had been left in some drawer or other, in some safe-deposit box carelessly left open, in some old-fashioned money-bag as used by the grandparents of an older generation, you cannot imagine what it was like, the vast and sumptuous halls of the head office, the smaller branch offices in various districts witnessed truly terrifying scenes, nor should we forget the automatic tills, forced open and stripped of the very last note, on the screen of some of them appeared an enigmatic message of thanks for having chosen this bank. Machines are really very stupid, it might be more precise to say that these machines had betrayed their owners, in a word, the whole banking system collapsed, blown over like a house of cards, and not because the possession of money had ceased to be appreciated, the proof being that anyone who has it does not want to let go of it, the latter allege that no one can foresee what will happen tomorrow, this no doubt also being in the thoughts of the blind people who installed themselves in the vaults of the banks, where the strong-boxes are kept, waiting for some miracle to open wide those heavy metal doors that separate them from this wealth, they leave the place only to go in search of food and water or to satisfy the body's other needs, and then return to their post, they have passwords and hand signs so that no stranger may penetrate their stronghold, needless to say they live in total darkness, not that it matters, in this particular blindness everything is white. The old man with the black eyepatch related these tremendous happenings about banks and finance as they slowly crossed the city, with the odd stop so that the boy with the squint might pacify the unbearable turmoil in his intestines, and, despite the persuasive tone he gave to this impassioned description, it is logical to suspect that there was some exaggeration in his account, the story about the blind people who live in the bank vaults, for example, how could he have known if he does not know the password or the hand signal, in any case it was enough to give us some idea.

The light was fading when they finally arrived in the street where the doctor and his wife live. It is no different from the others, there is squalor everywhere, groups of blind people wandering aimlessly about, and, for the first time, but it was mere chance that they had not encountered them before, two huge rats, even the cats avoid them as they go on the prowl, for they are almost as big as they are and in all certainty much more ferocious. The dog of tears looked at both the rats and the cats with the indifference of someone who lives in another sphere of emotions, this we might say, were it not for the fact that the dog continues to be the dog that he is, an animal of the human type. At the sight of familiar places, the doctor's wife did not make the usual melancholy reflection, that consists in saying, How time passes, only the other day we were happy here, what shocked her was the disappointment, she had unwittingly believed that, being hers, she would find the street clean, swept, tidy, that her neighbours would be blind in their eyes, but not in their understanding, How stupid of me, she said aloud, Why, what is wrong, asked her husband, Nothing, daydreams, How time passes, what will the flat be like, he wondered, We'll soon find out. They did not have much strength, and so climbed the stairs very slowly, pausing for breath on each landing, It's on the fifth floor, the doctor's wife had said. They went up as best they could, each under his or her own steam, the dog of tears now in front, now behind, as if it had been born to guide a flock, under orders not to lose a single sheep. There were open doors, voices within, the usual foul odour wafting out, twice blind people appeared on the threshold and looked with vacant eyes, Who's there, they asked, the doctor's wife recognised one of the voices, the other voice was not that of someone who lived in the building. We used to live here, was all she said. A flicker of recognition also showed on her neighbour's face, but she did not ask, Are you the doctor's wife, perhaps she might say once back inside, The people from the fifth floor are back. On reaching the last flight of stairs, even before setting foot on the landing, the doctor's wife was already announcing, The door is locked. There were signs of an attempt at a forced entry but the door had withstood the assault. The doctor put his hand into the inside pocket of his new jacket and brought out the keys. He held them in mid-air, waiting, but his wife gently guided his hand towards the keyhole.

Leaving aside the household dust that takes advantage of a family's absence to leave a subtle film on the surface of the furniture, it may be stated in this connection that these are the only occasions the dust has to rest, without being disturbed by a duster or vacuum cleaner, without children running back and forth unleashing an atmospheric whirlwind as they pass, the flat was clean, any untidiness was only what might be expected when one leaves in a hurry. Even so, while on that day they were expecting a summons from the Ministry and the hospital, the doctor's wife with the kind of foresight that leads sensible people to settle their affairs while alive, so that after their death, the tiresome need for a frantic putting of things in order does not arise, washed the dishes, made the bed, tidied the bathroom, the result was not exactly perfect, but truly it would have been cruel to ask any more of her with those trembling hands and tear-filled eyes. It was nevertheless a kind of paradise that the seven pilgrims had reached and this impression was so overwhelming, with no great disrespect for the strict meaning of the term, we could call it transcendental, that they stopped in their tracks in the entrance as if paralysed by the unexpected smell in the flat and it was simply that of a flat in need of a good airing, at any other time we would have rushed to open all the windows, To air the place, we would say, today the best thing to do would be to have them sealed up so that the putrefaction outside would be unable to come in. The wife of the first blind man said, We're going to dirty the whole place, and she was right, if they were to come in with these shoes covered in mud and excrement, paradise would in a flash become hell, the latter being the second place, according to the competent authorities where the putrid, fetid, nauseating, pestilential stench is the worst thing condemned souls have to bear, not the burning tongs, the cauldrons of boiling pitch and other artefacts of the foundry and the kitchen. From time immemorial it has been the custom of housewives to say, Come in, come in, really, it doesn't matter, I can clean up any dirt later, but this one, like her guests, knows where they have come from, she knows that in the world she lives in what is dirty will get dirtier still, therefore she asks them if they would be so kind as to remove their shoes on the landing, it is true that their feet are not clean either, but there is no comparison, the towels and sheets of the girl with dark glasses had some effect, they've got rid of most of the muck. So they went in without their shoes, the doctor's wife searched for and found a large plastic bag into which she put all the shoes intent upon giving them a good scrub, she had no idea when or how, then she carried them out on to the balcony, the air outside would not get any worse on this account. The sky began to darken, there were heavy clouds, If only it would rain, she thought. With a clear idea of what had to be done, she returned to her companions. They were in the sitting-room, silent, on their feet, for, despite their exhaustion, they had not dared to find themselves a chair, only the doctor vaguely ran his hands over the furniture leaving marks on the surface, the first dusting was under way, some of this dust is already stuck to his fingertips. The doctor's wife said, Take your clothes off, we can't remain in this state, our clothes are almost as dirty as our shoes, Take off our clothes, asked the first blind man, here, in front of each other, I don't think it's right, If you wish, I can put each of you in a different part of the flat, the doctor's wife replied ironically, then there will be no need to feel embarrassed, I'll take off my clothes right here, said the wife of the first blind man, only you can see me, and even were that not the case, I haven't forgotten that you have seen me worse than being naked, it's my husband who has the poor memory, I can't see what possible interest there can be in recalling disagreeable matters long since forgotten, muttered the first blind man, If you were a woman and had been where we have been, you would change your tune, said the girl with dark glasses, starting to undress the boy with the squint. The doctor and the old man with the black eyepatch were already naked from the waist up, now they were removing their trousers, the old man with the black eyepatch said to the doctor who was at his side, Let me lean on you while I get out of these trousers. They looked so ridiculous the poor fellows as they jumped about, it almost made you want to weep. The doctor lost his balance, dragged the old man with the black eyepatch with him as he fell, fortunately they both found the situation amusing, and it was pitiful to watch them, their bodies covered with every kind of filth imaginable, their private parts all besmeared, white hairs, black hairs, this was what the respectability of old age and a worthy profession had come to. The doctor's wife went to help them get to their feet, shortly there would be darkness all around and no one will have any cause to feel embarrassed, Are there any candles in the house, she wondered, the answer was that she recalled having seen two ancient lamps, an old oil lamp, with three nozzles, and an old paraffin lamp of the kind with a glass funnel, for the present, the oil lamp will be good enough, I have oil, a wick can be improvised, tomorrow I'll go in search of some paraffin in one of those stores, it will be much easier to find than a can of food, Especially if I don't look for it in the grocer's, she thought, surprising herself that she was still capable of joking even in this situation. The girl with the dark glasses was slowly undressing, in a way that gave the impression that there would always be something more no matter how many clothes she removed, one last article of clothing to cover her nakedness, she cannot explain this sudden modesty, but had the doctor's wife been closer, she would have seen the girl blushing, even though her face was so dirty, let those who can, try to understand women, one of them suddenly assailed by shame after having gone around sleeping with men she scarcely knew, the other perfectly capable of whispering in her ear perfectly calmly, Don't be embarrassed, he cannot see you, she would be referring to her own husband, of course, for we must not forget how the shameless girl tempted him into bed, well, as everyone knows, with women it is always a case of buyer beware. Perhaps, in the meantime, the reason is something else, there are two other naked men here, and one of them has slept with her.

The doctor's wife gathered up the clothes lying scattered on the floor, trousers, shirts, a jacket, petticoats and blouses, some soiled underwear, the latter would take at least a month's soaking before she got them clean again, she bundled them up into an armload, Stay here, she told them, I'm coming straight back, She took the clothes out on to the balcony, as she had done with the shoes, there she in turn undressed, looking at the black city under the heavy sky. Not so much as a pale light in the windows, nor a waning reflection on the house fronts, what was there was not a city, it was a great mass of pitch which, on cooling, had hardened in the shape of buildings, rooftops, chimneys, all dead, all faded. The dog of tears appeared on the balcony, it was restless, but now there were no tears to lick up, the despair was all inside her, eyes were dry. The doctor's wife felt cold, she remembered the others, standing naked in the middle of the room, waiting for who knows what. She entered. They had turned into simple, sexless forms, vague shapes, shadows losing themselves in the half-light, But this does not affect them, she thought, they fade into the surrounding light, and it is the light which does not allow them to see. I'm going to put a light on, she said, At the moment I'm almost as blind as the rest of you, Has the electricity come back on, asked the boy with the squint, No, I'm going to light an oil lamp, What's that, the boy asked again, I'll show you later. She rummaged for a box of matches in one of the plastic bags, went to the kitchen, she knew where she had stored the oil, she did not need much, she tore a strip from a dish towel in order to make wicks, then returned to the room where the lamp stood, it was going to be useful for the first time since it was manufactured, at first this did not appear to be its destiny, but none of us, lamps, dogs or humans, knows at the outset, why we have come into this world. One after the other, over the nozzles of the lamp, three tiny almonds of light lit up, from time to time they flicker until they give the impression that the upper part of the flames is lost in mid-air, then they settle down again as if they were becoming dense, solid, tiny pebbles of light. The doctor's wife said, Now that I can see, I'm going to get clean clothes, But we're dirty, the girl with the dark glasses said. Both she and the wife of the first blind man were covering their breasts and their sex with their hands, This is not for my sake, the doctor's wife thought, but because the light of the lamp is looking at them. Then she said, It is better to have clean clothes on a dirty body, than to have dirty clothes on a clean body. She took the lamp and went to search in the drawers of the chest, in the wardrobe, after a few minutes she returned, she brought pyjamas, dressing-gowns, skirts, blouses, dresses, trousers, underwear, everything neces- sary for dressing seven people decently, it is true that the people were not all the same size, but in their gauntness they were like so many twins. The doctor's wife helped them to dress, the boy with the squint finished up with a pair of the doctor's trousers, the kind you wear to the beach or in the countryside, and which turn us all into children. Now we can sit down, sighed the wife of the first blind man, Please guide us, we do not know where to put ourselves.

The room is like all sitting-rooms, it has a low table in the middle, all around there are sofas that can accommodate every- one, on this one here sit the doctor and his wife along with the old man with the black eyepatch, on the other the first blind man and his wife. They are exhausted. The boy fell asleep at once, with his head on the lap of the girl with dark glasses, hav- ing forgotten all about the lamp. An hour passed, this was akin to happiness, under the softest of lights their grimy faces looked washed, the eyes of those who were not asleep shone, the first blind man reached out for his wife's hand and pressed it, from this gesture we can see how a rested body can contribute to the harmony of the mind. Then the doctor's wife said, Shortly we'll have something to eat, but first we should decide how we are going to live here, don't worry, I am not about to repeat the speech that came over the loudspeaker, there's enough room to accommodate everyone, we have two bedrooms that can be used by the couples, the others can sleep in this room, each on his own sofa, tomorrow I must go in search of some food, our supplies are running out, it would be helpful if one of you were to come with me to help me carry the food, but also so that you can start to learn the way home, to recognise the street corners, one of these days I might fall ill, or go blind, I am always waiting for it to happen, in which case I'll have to learn from you, on another matter, there will be a bucket on the balcony for our physical needs, I know that it is not pleasant to go out there, what with all the rain we've had and the cold, but it is, in any case, better than having the house smelling to high heaven, let us not forget that that was our life during the time when we were interned, we went down all the steps of indignity, all of them, until we reached total degradation, the same might happen here albeit in a different way, there we still had the excuse that the degradation belonged to someone else, not now, now we are all equal regarding good and evil, please, don't ask me what good and what evil are, we knew what it was each time we had to act when blindness was an exception, what is right and what is wrong are simply different ways of understanding our relationships with the others, not that which we have with ourselves, one should not trust the latter, forgive this moralising speech, you do not know, you cannot know, what it means to have eyes in a world in which everyone else is blind, I am not a queen, no, I am simply the one who was born to see this horror, you can feel it, I both feel and see it, and that's enough of this dissertation, Let's go and eat. No one asked any questions, the doctor simply said, If I ever regain my sight, I shall look carefully at the eyes of others, as if I were looking into their souls, Their souls, asked the old man with the eyepatch, Or their minds, the name does not matter, it was then that, surprisingly, if we consider that we are dealing with a person without much education, the girl with the dark glasses said, Inside us there is something that has no name, that something is what we are.

The doctor's wife had already put on the table some of the little food that was left over, then she helped them to sit down and said, Chew slowly, that helps to deceive your stomach. The dog of tears did not come to beg for food, it was used to fasting, moreover it must have thought that, after the banquet that morning, it had no right to take even a little food from the mouth of the woman who had wept, the others appeared not to interest him. In the middle of the table, the lamp with three flames was waiting for the doctor's wife to give the promised explanation, it finally happened after they had eaten, Give me your hands, she said to the boy with the squint, then guided his fingers slowly, saying, This is the base, round as you can see, and this the column that sustains the upper part with the oil container, here, watch you don't burn yourself, these are the nozzles, one, two, three, from these emerge twisted strips of material that suck up the oil from inside, a match is put to them and they start burning until the oil is finished, they give off a weak light but it's good enough to see each other, I can't see, One day you will see and on that day I'll give you the lamp as a present. What colour is it, Have you ever seen anything made of brass, I don't know, I don't remember, what is brass, Brass is yellow, Ah. The boy with the squint pondered for a moment, Now he is going to ask for his mother, thought the doctor's wife, but she was wrong, the boy simply said that he wanted water, that he was very thirsty, You will have to wait till tomorrow, we have no water in the house, at this very moment she remembered that there was water, some five litres or more of precious water, the whole contents of the toilet cistern, it could not be worse than what they had been drinking during the quarantine. Blind in the darkness, she went to the bathroom, feeling her way along, she raised the lid of the cistern, she really could not see if there was water, there was, her fingers told her, she searched for a glass, plunged it in with great care and filled it, civilisation had returned to the primitive sources of slime. When she entered

the room everyone remained seated where they were. The lamp
lit up their faces which turned towards her, it was as if she had
said, I am back, as you can see, take advantage, remember this
light won't last for ever. The doctor's wife brought the glass to
the boy with the squint's lips and said, Here is your water, drink
slowly, slowly, and savour it, a glass of water is a marvellous
thing, she was not talking to him, she was not talking to anyone, simply communicating to the world what a marvellous
thing a glass of water is. Where did you get it, is it rain water,
asked the husband, No, it's from the cistern. Didn't we have a
large bottle of water when we left this place, he asked again, the
wife said, Of course, why didn't I think of it, a half-full bottle
and another that had not even been started, what luck, don't
drink, don't drink anymore, she said to the boy, we are all going
to drink fresh water, I'll put our best glasses on the table and we
are going to drink fresh water. This time she took the lamp and
went to the kitchen, she returned with the bottle, the light
shone through it, it made the treasure inside sparkle. She put it
on the table, went to fetch the glasses, the best they had, of
finest crystal, then, slowly, as if she were performing a rite, she
filled them. At last, she said, Let's drink. The blind hands groped
and found the glasses, they raised them trembling. Let's drink,
the doctor's wife said again. In the middle of the table, the lamp
was like a sun surrounded by shining stars. When they had put
the glasses back on the table, the girl with the dark glasses
and the old man with the eyepatch were crying.

It was a restless night. Vague in the beginning, and imprecise,
the dreams went from sleeper to sleeper, they lingered here,
they lingered there, they brought with them new memories,
new secrets, new desires, that is why the sleepers sighed and
murmured, This dream is not mine, they said, but the dream
replied, You do not yet know your dreams, in this way the girl
with the dark glasses came to find out who the old man with
the black eyepatch was, lying there asleep two paces away, in
this way he thought he knew who she was, he merely thought
he did, it is not enough for dreams to be reciprocal in order to
be the same. As dawn broke it began to rain. The wind beating

fiercely against the windows sounded like the cracking of a thousand whiplashes. The doctor's wife woke up, opened her eyes and murmured, Listen to that rain, then she closed them again, in the room it was still black night, now she could sleep. She barely managed a minute, she woke abruptly with the idea that she had something to do, but without yet understanding what it might be, the rain was saying to her, Get up, what did the rain want, Slowly, so as not to disturb her husband, she left the bedroom, crossed the sitting-room, paused for an instant to make sure they were all sleeping on the sofas, then she proceeded along the corridor as far as the kitchen, it was over this part of the building that the rain fell with the greatest force, driven by the wind. With the sleeve of her dressing-gown she cleaned the steamed-up glass panel of the door and looked outside. The entire sky was one great cloud, the rain poured down in torrents. Piled up on the balcony-floor were the dirty clothes they had taken off, there was the plastic bag with the shoes waiting to be washed. Wash. The last veil of sleep was suddenly torn, this was what she had to do. She opened the door, took one step, immediately the rain drenched her from head to foot, as if she were beneath a waterfall. I must take advantage of this water, she thought. She went back into the kitchen and, making as little noise as possible, began gathering together bowls, pots and pans, anything in which she could collect some of the rain that was falling from heaven in sheets, harried about by the wind, sweeping over the roofs of the city like a large and noisy broom. She took them outside, arranged them along the balcony up against the railing, now there would be water to wash the dirty clothes and filthy shoes, Don't let it stop, she murmured as she searched in the kitchen for soap and detergents, scrubbing brushes, anything that might be used to clean a little, at least a little, of this unbearable filth of the soul. Of the body, she said, as if to correct this metaphysical thought, then she added, It's all the same. Then, as if this had to be the inevitable conclusion, the harmonious conciliation between what she had said and what she thought, she quickly took off her drenched dressing-gown, and, now, receiving on her body, sometimes a caress, sometimes the whiplash of the rain, she began to wash the clothes and herself at the same time. The sound of water that surrounded her prevented her from noticing right away that she was no longer alone. At the door to the balcony stood the girl with dark glasses and the wife of the first blind man, we cannot tell what presentiments, what intuition, what inner voices might have roused them, nor do we know how they found their way here, there is no point searching for explanations for the moment, conjectures are free. Help me, said the doctor's wife when she saw them, How, since we cannot see, asked the wife of the first blind man. Take off your clothes, the less we have to dry afterwards, the better, But we can't see, the wife of the first blind man repeated, It does not matter, said the girl with the dark glasses,We shall do what we can, And I shall finish off later, said the doctor's wife, I shall clean whatever is still dirty, and now to work, let's go, we are the only woman in the world with two eyes and six hands. Perhaps in the building opposite, behind those closed windows some blind people, men, women, roused by the noise of the constant beating of the rain, with their head pressed against the cold window-panes covering with their breath on the glass the dullness of the night, remember the time when, like now, they last saw rain falling from the sky. They cannot imagine that there are moreover three naked women out there, as naked as when they came into the world, they seem to be mad, they must be mad, people in their right mind do not start washing on a balcony exposed to the view of the neighbourhood, even less looking like that, what does it matter that we are all blind, these are things one must not do, my God, how the rain is pouring down on them, how it trickles between their breasts, how it lingers and disappears into the darkness of the pubis, how it finally drenches and flows over the thighs, perhaps we have judged them wrongly, or perhaps we are unable to see this the most beautiful and glorious thing that has happened in the history of the city, a sheet of foam flows from the floor of the balcony, if only I could go with it, falling interminably, clean, purified, naked. Only God sees us, said the wife of the first blind man, who, despite disappointments and setbacks, clings to the belief that God is not blind, to which the doctor's wife replies, Not even he, the sky is clouded over, Only I can see you, Am I ugly, asked the girl with the dark glasses, You are skinny and dirty, you will never be ugly, And I, asked the wife of the first blind man, You are dirty and skinny like her, not as pretty, but more than I, You are beautiful, said the girl with the dark glasses, How do you know, since you have never seen me, I have dreamt of you twice, When, The second time was last night, You were dreaming about the house because you felt safe and calm, it's only natural after all we've been through, in your dream I was the home, and in order to see me you needed a face, so you invented it, I too see you as beautiful, and I never dreamt of you, said the wife of the first blind man, Which only goes to show that blindness is the good fortune of the ugly, You are not ugly, No, as a matter of fact I am not, but at my age, How old are you, asked the girl with the dark glasses, Getting on for fifty, Like my mother, And her, Her, what, Is she still beautiful, She was more beautiful once, that's what happens to all of us, we were all more beautiful once, You were never more beautiful, said the wife of the first blind man. Words are like that, they deceive, they pile up, it seems they do not know where to go, and, suddenly, because of two or three or four that suddenly come out, simple in themselves, a personal pronoun, an adverb, a verb, an adjective, we have the excitement of seeing them coming irresistibly to the surface through the skin and the eyes and upsetting the composure of our feelings, sometimes the nerves that cannot bear it any longer, they put up with a great deal, they put up with everything, it was as if they were wearing armour, we might say. The doctor's wife has nerves of steel, and yet the doctor's wife is reduced to tears because of a personal pronoun, an adverb, a verb, an adjective, mere grammatical categories, mere labels, just like the two women, the others, indefinite pronouns, they too are crying, they embrace the woman of the whole sentence, three graces beneath the falling rain. These are moments that cannot last for ever, these women have been here for more than an hour, it is time they felt cold, I'm cold, said the girl with the dark glasses. We cannot do anything more with the clothes, the shoes are spick and span, now it is time for these women to wash themselves, they soak their hair and wash each other's backs and they laugh as only little girls laugh when they play blind man's buff in the garden before becoming blind. Day broke, the first rays of sun peered over the shoulder of the world before hiding once more behind the clouds. It continues to rain but with less force. The washerwomen went back to the kitchen, they dried themselves and rubbed themselves with the towels the doctor's wife had gone to fetch from the bathroom cupboard, their skins smell strongly of detergent, but such is life, if you haven't got a dog to hunt with use a cat, the soap disappeared in a twinkling of the eye, even though this house seems to have everything or is it just that they know how to make the best use of what they have got, at last, they covered themselves, paradise was out there, the dressing-gown of the doctor's wife is soaking wet, but she put on a flowered dress that she had not worn for years and which made her the prettiest of the three.

When they entered the sitting-room, the doctor's wife saw that the old man with the black eyepatch was sitting up on the sofa where he had slept. He held his head between his hands, his fingers plunged into the thatch of white hair which still grew from his forehead to the back of his neck, and he was calm, tense, as if he wanted to hold on to his thoughts, or, on the contrary, to stop them altogether. He heard them come in, he knew where they came from, and what they had been doing, that they had been naked, and if he knew all this it was not because he had suddenly regained his sight and, like the other old men, crept up to spy on not one Susanna in her bath, but on three, he was blind, he stayed blind, he had only got to the kitchen door from where he heard what they were saying on the balcony, the laughter, the noise of the rain and the beating of the water, he breathed in the smell of the soap, then he returned to the sofa, thinking that there was still life in this world, to ask whether there was still any part of it left for him. The doctor's wife said, The women have already washed, Now it is the men's turn, and the old man with the black eyepatch asked, Is it still raining, Yes, it is raining and there is water in the basins on the balcony, Then I prefer to wash in the bathroom, in the tub, he pronounced the word as if he were showing his birth certificate, as if he were explaining, I am of the generation in which people did not speak of baths but of tubs, and added, If you don't mind, of course, I do not want to dirty the house, I promise that I shall not spill any water on the floor, at least, I shall do my best, In that case I shall bring you some water into the bathroom, I'll help, I can manage on my own, I have to be of some use, I am not an invalid, Come, then. On the balcony, the doctor's wife pulled an almost full basin of water inside. Take a hold here, she said to the old man with the black eyepatch, guiding his hands, Now, they lifted the basin at one go. Just as well that you came to help me, I could not have managed alone, Do you know the saying, What saying, Old people cannot do much but their work is not to be despised, That's not the way it goes, All right, instead of old people, it should be children, and instead of despise, it should be disdain, but if sayings are to retain any meaning and to continue to be used they have to adapt to the times. You are a philosopher, What an idea, I am just an old man. They emptied the basin into the bath, then the doctor's wife opened a drawer, she remembered that she still had one new bar of soap. She put it into the hand of the old man with the black eyepatch, You are going to smell nice, better than us, use it all, do not worry, there may not be any food, but there is bound to be soap in these supermarkets, Thank you, Watch you don't slip, if you want I'll call my husband to help you, Thanks, I prefer to wash by myself, As you like, and here, wait, give me your hand, there's a razor and a brush, if you want to shave off that beard, Thanks. The doctor's wife left. The old man with the eyepatch took off the pyjamas which had been allotted to him in the distribution of clothes, then, carefully, he got into the bath. The water was cold and there was little of it, less than a foot, how different is this sad puddle from receiving it in buckets from heaven as the three women had. He knelt on the bottom of the bath, took a deep breath, with both hands together he suddenly splashed water against his chest which almost took his breath away. He rapidly splashed water all over himself so as not to have time to shiver, then, step by step, systematically, he started to soap himself, to rub heavily starting from the shoulders, arms, chest and stomach, his groin, his penis, between his legs, I am worse than an animal, he thought, then the thin thighs down to the layer of grime that covered his feet. He made lather so that the cleaning process should be extended, he said, I have to wash my hair and moved his hands back to untie the eye-patch, You too need a bath, he loosened it and dropped it into the water, now he felt warm, he wet and soaped his hair, he was a man of foam, white in the middle of an immense white blind-ness where nobody could find him, if that was what he thought, he was deceiving himself, at that moment he felt hands touch-ing his back, gathering the foam from his arms, and from his chest and spreading it over his back, slowly, as if, being unable to see what they were doing, they had to pay closer attention to the job. He wanted to ask, Who are you, but he couldn't speak, now he was shivering, not from the cold, the hands continued to wash him gently, the woman did not say, I am the doctor's wife, I am the wife of the first blind man, I am the girl with dark glasses, the hands finished their task, withdrew, in the silence one could hear the gentle noise of the bathroom door closing, the old man with the eyepatch was alone, kneeling in the bath as if imploring a favour from heaven, trembling, trembling, Who could it have been, he asked himself, his reason told him that it could only have been the doctor's wife, she is the one who can see, she is the one who has protected us, cared for us and fed us, it would not be surprising that she should have given me this discreet attention, it is what his reason told him, but he did not believe in reason. He continued to shiver, he did not know whether it was from excitement or from cold. He found the eyepatch at the bottom of the bath, rubbed it hard, wrung it dry and put it back, with it he felt less naked. When he entered the sitting-room, dry, perfumed, the doctor's wife said, We al-ready have one man who is clean and shaven, and then, in the tone of voice of someone who has just remembered something that should have been done and was not, You had no one to wash your back, what a pity. The old man with the black eye-patch did not reply, he merely thought that he had been right not to believe in reason.

They gave what little food there was to the boy with the squint, the others would have to wait for fresh supplies. In the larder there were some jars of preserves, some dried fruit, sugar, some left-over biscuits, some dry toast, but they would use these reserves and others added to them only in case of extreme necessity, the food from day to day would have to be earned, just in case by some misfortune the expedition returned empty-handed, meanwhile two biscuits per person with a spoonful of jam, There is strawberry and peach, which do you prefer, three walnut halves, a glass of water, a luxury while it lasts. The wife of the first blind man said that she too wanted to look for food, three would not go amiss, even being blind, two of them could help to carry the food and besides, were it possible, bearing in mind that they were not that far away, she would like to go and see what state her home was in, if it had been occupied, if the people were known to her, for example neighbours from the building whose family had grown because some relatives from the provinces had arrived with the idea of saving themselves from the epidemic of blindness that had attacked their village, the city always enjoys better resources. Therefore the three of them left, dressed in what dry clothes they could find in the house, the others, those that have been washed, have to wait for better weather. The sky remained overcast but there was no threat of rain. Swept along by the water, especially in the steeper streets, the rubbish had piled up in small heaps leaving wide stretches of pavement clean. If only the rain would last, in this situation sunshine would be the worst that could happen to us, said the doctor's wife, we've got enough filth and bad smells already, We notice it more because we are washed, said the wife of the first blind man and her husband agreed, although he suspected that the cold bath had given him a cold. There were crowds of blind people in the streets, they took advantage of the break in the weather to search for food and to satisfy there and then their need to defecate which they still had

despite the little food and drink they took in. Dogs sniffed everywhere, they scrabbled in the rubbish, the odd one carried a
drowned rat in its mouth, a very rare occurrence that could
only be explained by the extraordinary abundance of the recent
downpours, the flood caught him in the wrong place, being a
good swimmer was of no use to him. The dog of tears did not
mix with his former companions in the pack and the hunt, his
choice is made, but he does not wait to be fed, he is already
chewing heaven knows what, these mountains of rubbish hide
unimaginable treasures, it is all a matter of searching, scratching and finding. The blind man and his wife will also have to
search and scratch in their memory when the occasion arises,
now they had memorised the four corners, not of the house
where they live, which has many more, but of their street, the
four street corners which will serve them as cardinal points, the
blind are not interested where east and west lie, or north or
south, all they want is that their groping hands tell them that
they are on the right road, formerly, when they were still few,
they used to carry white sticks, the sound of the continuous
taps on the ground and the walls was a sort of code which allowed them to identify and recognise their route, but today,
since everybody is blind, a white stick, in the middle of the general clamour, is less than helpful, quite apart from the fact that,
immersed in his own whiteness, the blind man may come to
doubt whether he is actually carrying anything in his hand.
Dogs, as everyone knows, have, in addition to what we call instinct, other means of orientation, it is certain that because of
their shortsightedness they do not rely much on their sight,
however, since their nose is well ahead of their eyes, they always
get to where they want, in this case, just to be sure, the dog of
tears lifted its leg to the four corners of the wind, the breeze
will take on the task of guiding it home if it were to get lost one
day. As they went along the doctor's wife looked up and down
the streets in search of food shops where she could build up
their much reduced larder. The looting had not been complete
because in old-fashioned groceries there were still some beans
or some chick peas in the storerooms, they are dried pulses

which take a long time to cook, one thing is water, another thing is fuel, therefore they are not much appreciated these days. The doctor's wife was not particularly keen on the tendency of proverbs to preach, nevertheless something of this ancient lore must have remained in her memory, the proof being that she filled two of the bags they had brought with beans and chick peas, Keep what is of no use at the moment, and later you will find what you need, one of her grandmothers had told her, the water in which you soak them will also serve to cook them, and whatever remains from the cooking will cease to be water, but will have become broth. It is not only in nature that from time to time not everything is lost and something is gained.

Why they were loaded with bags of beans and peas and anything else they happened to pick up when they were still some distance away from the street where the first blind man and his wife lived, for that is where they are going, is a question that could only occur to someone who has never in his life suffered shortages. Take it home, even if it's a stone, that same grandmother had said, but she forgot to add, Even if you have to go around the earth, this was the feat they were now embarked upon, they were going home by the longest route. Where are we, the first blind man asked, he addressed the doctor's wife, that is what she had eyes for, and he said, This is where I went blind, on this corner with the traffic lights, Right here, on this corner, Precisely on this spot. I do not want to remember what happened, trapped in the car without being able to see, people shouting outside, and me shouting desperately that I was blind, until that man turned up and took me home, Poor man, the wife of the first blind man said, he will never steal a car again, We are so afraid of the idea of having to die, said the doctor's wife, that we always try to find excuses for the dead, as if we were asking beforehand to be excused when it is our turn, All this still seems like a dream, the wife of the first blind man said, it is as if I were dreaming that I am blind, When I was at home, waiting for you, I also thought so, said her husband. They had left the square where it had happened, now they climbed some narrow labyrinthine streets, the doctor's wife hardly knows these places but the first blind man does not get lost, he knows the way, she says the names of the streets and he says, Let's turn to the left, Let's turn to the right, finally he says, This is our street, the building is on the left-hand side, roughly in the middle, What is the number, asked the doctor's wife, he can't remember, Now then, it's not that I cannot remember, it's gone from my head, he said, that was a bad omen, if we do not even know where we live, if the dream has replaced our memory, where will that road take us, All right, this time it is not serious, it was lucky that the first blind man's wife had the idea of coming on the excursion, there we already have her saying the house number, this helped her to avoid having to have recourse to the first blind man, who was priding himself on the fact that he can recognise the door by the magic of touch, as if he were carrying a magic wand, one touch, metal, one touch, wood, with three or four more he would arrive at the full pattern, I'm sure it is this one. They entered, the doctor's wife first, What floor is it, she asked, The third, answered the first blind man, his memory was not as bad as had appeared, some things we forget, that's life, others we remember, for example, to remember when, already blind, he had entered this door, On what floor do you live, asked the man who had not yet stolen the car, Third, he replied, the difference being that this time they are not going up in the elevator, they walk up the invisible staircase which is at once dark and luminous, how people who are not blind miss electric light, or sunlight, or the light of a candle, now the doctor's wife has got used to the semi-darkness, halfway up they run into two blind women from the upper floors coming down, perhaps from the third, nobody asked, it is true the neighbours are not, in fact, the same.

The door was closed. What are we going to do, asked the doctor's wife, Leave it to me, said the first blind man. They knocked once, twice, three times. There's nobody in, one of them said at exactly the moment when the door opened, the delay was not surprising, a blind person at the back of the flat cannot come running to answer the door. Who is it, what do you want, asked the man who opened the door, he had a serious look on his face, he was polite, he must be someone we can talk to. The first blind man said, I used to live in this flat, Ah, the other replied, Is there anybody with you, My wife, and also a friend of ours, How can I be sure that this was your flat, That's easy, the wife of the first blind man said, I can tell you everything there is inside. The other man paused a few seconds, then he said, Come in. The doctor's wife went in last, here nobody needed a guide. The blind man said, I am alone, my family went to look for food, perhaps I should have said the women, but I do not think it would be proper, he paused and then added, Yet you may think that I should know, What do you mean, asked the doctor's wife, The women I referred to are my wife and my two daughters, and I should know when it is proper to use the expression "women." I am a writer, we are supposed to know such things. The first blind man felt flattered, imagine, a writer living in my flat, then a doubt rose in him, was it good manners to ask him his name, he might even have heard of his name, it was even possible that he had read him, he was still hesitating between curiosity and discretion, when his wife put the question directly, What is your name, Blind people do not need a name, I am my voice, nothing else matters, But you wrote books and those books carry your name, said the doctor's wife, Now nobody can read them, it is as if they did not exist. The first blind man felt that the conversation was moving too far from the topic which he was most interested in, And how do you come to be in my flat, he asked, Like many others who no longer live where they used to live, I found my house occupied by people who did not want to listen to reason, one might say that we were kicked down the stairs, Is your house far away, No, Did you try to get it back, asked the doctor's wife, it is now quite common for people to move from house to house, I have already tried twice, And are they still there, Yes. And what are you going to do now that you know that this is our flat, the first blind man wanted to know, are you going to throw us out as they did to you, No, I have neither the age nor the strength for that, and even if I did, I do not believe that I would be capable of such a speedy procedure, a writer manages to acquire in life the patience he needs to write. You will leave us the flat, though, Yes, if we cannot find another solution, I cannot see what other solution could be found. The doctor's wife had already guessed what the writer's reply would be, You and your wife, like the friend who is with you, live in a flat, I imagine, Yes, in her flat in fact, Is it far away, Not really, Then, if you'll permit me, I have a proposal to make, Go on, That we carry on as we are, at this moment we both have a place where we can live, I shall continue to keep a watchful eye on what is happening to mine, if one day I find it free, I shall move in immediately, you will do the same, Come here at regular intervals and when you find it empty, move in, I am not sure I like the idea, I didn't expect you to like it but I doubt whether you would prefer the only remaining alternative, What is that, For you to recover this flat which is yours, But, in that case, Precisely, in that case we shall have to find somewhere else to live, No, don't even think about it, intervened the wife of the first blind man, Let's leave things as they are, and see what happens, It occurred to me that there is another solution, said the writer, And what might that be, asked the first blind man, We shall live here as your guests, the flat is big enough for all of us, No, said the wife of the first blind man, We shall carry on as before, living with our friend, there is no need to ask if you agree, she added, addressing the doctor's wife, And there is no need for me to reply, I am obliged to all of you, said the writer, all this time I have been waiting for someone to reclaim the flat, To accept what one has is the most natural thing when one is blind, said the doctor's wife, How have you managed since the outbreak of the epidemic, We came out of internment only three days ago, Ah, you were in quarantine, Yes, Was it hard, Worse than that, How horrible, You are a writer, you have, as you said a moment ago, an obligation to know words, therefore you know that adjectives are of no use to us, if a person kills another, for example, it would be better to state this fact openly, directly, and to trust that the horror of the act, in itself, is so shocking that there is no need for us to say it was horrible, Do you mean that we have more words than we need, I mean that we have too few feelings, Or that we have them but have ceased to use the words they express, And so we lose them, I'd like you to tell me how you lived during quarantine, Why, I am a writer, You would have to have been there, A writer is just like anyone else, he cannot know everything, nor can he experience everything, he must ask and imagine, One day I may tell you what it was like, then you can write a book, Yes, I am writing it, How, if you are blind, The blind too can write, You mean that you had time to learn the braille alphabet, I do not know braille, How can you write, then, asked the first blind man, Let me show you. He got up from his chair, left the room and after a minute returned, he was holding a sheet of paper in his hand and a ball-point pen, this is the last complete page I have written, We cannot see it, said the wife of the first blind man, Nor I, said the writer, Then how can you write, asked the doctor's wife, looking at the sheet of paper where in the half-light of the room she could make out tightly compressed lines, occasionally superimposed, By touch, the writer answered smiling, it is easy, you place the sheet over a soft surface, for example some sheets of paper, then it's just a question of writing, But if you cannot see anything, said the first blind man, A ball-point pen is an excellent tool for blind writers, it does not permit them to read what they have written, but it tells them where they have written, they only have to follow with their fingers the impression left by the last written line, then you write as far as the edge of the paper, and calculating the distance to the next line is very easy, I notice that some lines overlap, said the doctor's wife, gently taking the sheet out of his hand, How do you know, I can see, You can see, have you recovered your sight, how, when, the writer asked excitedly, I suppose I am the only person who has never lost it, And why, what is the explanation for this, I have no explanation, there may not be one, That means that you saw everything that has happened, I saw what I saw, I had no option, How many people were in the quarantine, Nearly three hundred, From when, From the beginning, we only came out three days ago, as I said, I believe that I was the first person to go blind, said the first blind man, That must have been horrible, That word again, said the doctor's wife, Forgive me, suddenly everything I have been writing about since we turned blind, my family and I, strikes me as being ridiculous, About what, About what we suffered, about our life, Everyone has to speak of what they know, and what they do not know they should ask, That's why I ask you, And I will answer, I don't know when, some day. The doctor's wife brushed the writer's hand with the paper. Would you mind showing me where you work and what you are writing, Not at all, come with me, Can we come too, asked the wife of the first blind man, The flat is yours, said the writer, I am only passing through. In the bedroom there was a tiny table with an unlit lamp. The dim light entering through the window, allowed one to see to the left some blank sheets, others on the right-hand side had been written on, in the middle there was one half writ-ten. There were two new ball-point pens next to the lamp. Here it is, said the writer. The doctor's wife asked, May I? without waiting for a reply she picked up the written pages, there must have been about twenty, she passed her eye over the tiny hand-writing, over the lines which went up and down, over the words inscribed on the whiteness of the page, recorded in blindness, I am only passing through, the writer had said, and these were the signs he had left in passing. The doctor's wife placed her hand on his shoulder, and with both hands he reached out for it and raised it slowly to his lips, Don't lose yourself, don't let yourself be lost, he said, and these were unexpected, enigmatic words that did not seem to fit the occasion.

When they returned home, carrying enough food for three days, the doctor's wife, interrupted by the excited interjections from the first blind man and his wife, told what had happened. And that night, as was only right, she read to all of them a few pages from a book she had gone to fetch from the study. The boy with the squint was not interested in the story, and after a little while he fell asleep with his head on the lap of the girl with the dark glasses and his feet resting on the legs of the old man with the eyepatch.

Two days later the doctor said, I'd like to know what has happened to the surgery, at this stage we are no use for anything, neither it nor I, but perhaps one day people will recover their sight, the instruments must still be there waiting, We can go whenever you want, said his wife, Right now, And we could take advantage of this walk to pass by my home, if you don't mind, said the girl with the dark glasses, Not that I believe that my parents have returned, it's only to ease my conscience, We can go to your house too, said the doctor's wife. Nobody else wanted to join this reconnoitre of homes, not the first blind man and his wife, for they already knew what they could count on, the old man with the black eyepatch also knew, but not for the same reasons, and the boy with the squint because he still could not remember the name of the street where he had lived. The weather was bright, it seemed that the rain had stopped and the sun, though pale, could already be felt on their skin, I don't know how we can continue to live if the heat gets any worse, said the doctor, all this rubbish rotting all over the place, the dead animals, perhaps even people, there must be dead people inside the houses, the worst thing is that we are not organised, there should be an organisation in each building, in each street, in each district, A government, said the wife, An organisation, the human body is also an organised system, it lives as long as it keeps organised, and death is only the effect of a disorganisation, And how can a society of blind people organise itself in order to survive, By organising itself, to organise oneself is, in a way, to begin to have eyes, Perhaps you're right, but the experience of this blindness has brought us only death and misery, my eyes, just like your surgery, were useless, Thanks to your eyes we are still alive, said the girl with the dark glasses, We would also be alive if I were blind as well, the world is full of blind people, I think we are all going to die, it's just a matter of time, Dying has always been a matter of time, said the doctor, But to die just because you're blind, there can be no worse way of dying, We die of illnesses, accidents, chance events, And now we shall also die of blindness, I mean, we shall die of blindness and cancer, of blindness and tuberculosis, of blindness and AIDS, of blindness and heart attacks, illnesses may differ from one person to another but what is really killing us now is blindness, We are not immortal, we cannot escape death, but at least we should not be blind, said the doctor's wife, How, if this blindness is concrete and real, said the doctor, I am not sure, said the wife, Nor I, said the girl with the dark glasses.

They did not have to force the door, it opened normally, the key was on the doctor's key ring which had remained in the house when they had been taken off for quarantine. This is the waiting-room, said the doctor's wife, The room I was in, said the girl with the dark glasses, the dream continues, but I don't know what dream it is, whether it is the dream of dreaming which I experienced that day when I dreamt that I was going blind, or the dream of always having been blind and coming, still dreaming, to the surgery in order to be cured of an inflammation of the eyes in which there was no danger of becoming blind, The quarantine was no dream, said the doctor's wife, Certainly not, nor was it a dream that we were raped, Nor that I stabbed a man, Take me to my office, I can get there on my own but you take me, said the doctor. The door was open. The doctor's wife said, The place has been turned upside down, papers on the floor, the drawers of the file cabinet have been taken, It must have been the people from the Ministry, not to waste time looking, Probably, And the instruments, At first sight, they seem to be in good order, That, at least, is something, said the doctor, he advanced alone with his arms outstretched, he touched the box with the lenses, his oph-thalmoscope, the desk, then, addressing the girl with the dark glasses, he said, I know what you are trying to say, when you say that you are living a dream. He sat down at the desk, placed his hands on the dusty top, then with a sad, ironic smile, as if he were talking to someone sitting opposite him, he said, No, my dear doctor, I am very sorry, but your condition has no known cure, if you want me to give you one last piece of advice, cling to the old saying, they were right when they said that patience is good for the eyes. Don't make us suffer, said the woman, For-give me, both of you, we are in the place where miracles used to be performed, now I don't even have the evidence of my magic powers, they have taken it all away, The only miracle we can perform is to go on living, said the woman, to preserve the fragility of life from day to day, as if it were blind and did not know where to go, and perhaps it is like that, perhaps it really does not know, it placed itself in our hands, after giving us in-telligence, and this is what we have made of it, You speak as if you too were blind, said the girl with the dark glasses, In a way I am, I am blind with your blindness, perhaps I might be able to see better if there were more of us who could see, I am afraid you are like the witness in search of a court to which he has been summoned by who knows who, in order to make a state-ment about who knows what, said the doctor, Time is coming to an end, putrescence is spreading, diseases find the doors open, water is running out, food has become poison, that would be my first statement, said the doctor's wife, And the second, asked the girl with dark glasses, Let's open our eyes, We can't, we are blind, said the doctor, It is a great truth that says that the worst blind person was the one who did not want to see, But I do want to see, said the girl with dark glasses, That won't be the reason you will see, the only difference would be that you would no longer be the worst blind person, and now, let's go, there is nothing more to be seen here, the doctor said.

On their way to the home of the girl with dark glasses, they crossed a large square with groups of blind people who were listening to speeches from other blind people, at first sight, neither one nor the other group seemed blind, the speakers turned their heads excitedly towards their listeners, the listeners turned their heads attentively to the speakers. They were proclaiming the end of the world, redemption through penitence, the visions of the seventh day, the advent of the angel, cosmic collisions, the death of the sun, the tribal spirit, the sap of the mandrake, tiger ointment, the virtue of the sign, the discipline of the wind, the perfume of the moon, the revindication of darkness, the power of exorcism, the sign of the heel, the crucifixion of the rose, the purity of the lymph, the blood of the black cat, the sleep of the shadow, the rising of the seas, the logic of anthropophagy, painless castration, divine tattoos, voluntary blindness, convex thoughts, or concave, or horizontal or vertical, or sloping, or concentrated, or dispersed, or fleeting, the weakening of the vocal cords, the death of the word, Here nobody is speaking of organisation, said the doctor's wife, Perhaps organisation is in another square, he replied. They continued on their way. A bit further on, the doctor's wife said, There are more dead in the road than usual, Our resistance is reaching its end, time is running out, the water is running out, disease is on the increase, food is becoming poison, you said so before, the doctor reminded her, Who knows whether my parents are not among these dead, said the girl with dark glasses, and here, I am passing by without seeing them, It's a time-honoured custom to pass by the dead without seeing them, said the doctor's wife.

The street where the girl with dark glasses lived, seemed even more deserted than usual. At the door to the building there was the body of a woman. Dead, half devoured by stray animals, luckily the dog of tears had not wanted to come today, it would have been necessary to keep him from digging his teeth into this corpse. It is the neighbour from the first floor, said the doctor's wife, Who, where, asked her husband, Right here, the first-floor neighbour, you can smell her, Poor woman, said the girl with dark glasses, why did she have to go out into the street, she never went out, Perhaps she felt that her death was near, perhaps she could not stand the idea of staying alone in the flat to rot, said the doctor. And now we can't go in, I don't have the keys, Perhaps your parents have returned and are inside waiting for you, said the doctor, I don't believe it, You are right not to believe it, said the doctor's wife, here are the keys. In the palm of the dead woman's half-open hand resting on the ground there was a set of keys, shining, sparkling. Perhaps they are hers, said the girl with dark glasses, I don't think so, she had no reason to bring her keys to where she was thinking of dying, But being blind, I would not be able to see them, if she thought of bringing them down so that I would be able to get into the flat, We don't know what she was thinking of when she decided to take the keys, perhaps she thought that you would regain your eyesight, perhaps she suspected that there was something unnatural, too easy, about the way we moved around when we were here, perhaps she heard me say that the stair was dark, that I could barely see, or perhaps it was none of that, delirium, dementia, as if, having lost her mind, she had got it into her head to give you the keys, the only thing we know is that her life ended when she set foot outside the door. The doctor's wife picked up the keys, handed them to the girl with dark glasses and then asked, And now, what do we do, are we going to leave her here, We cannot bury her in the street, we have no tools to lift the stones, said the doctor, There is the garden in the back, In that case we'll have to take her up to the second floor and then down by the emergency stairs, That's the only way, Do we have enough strength for this task, asked the girl with dark glasses, The question is not whether we have enough strength, the question is whether we can allow ourselves to leave this woman here, Certainly not, said the doctor, Then the strength must be found. They did manage, but it was hard work dragging the body upstairs, not because of what it weighed, little enough, and less still since the cats and dogs had been at it, but because the body was rigid, stiff, they had trouble turning the corners of the narrow staircase, during the short climb they had to rest four times. Neither the noise, nor the voices, nor the smell of putrefaction brought any other of the inhabitants of the building on to the landings, Just as I thought, my parents are not here, said the girl with dark glasses. When they finally got to the door they were exhausted and they still had to cross to the back of the building and go down the emergency stairs, but there with the help of the saints, they get down the stairs, the burden is lighter, the bends easier to manoeuvre because the stairs were out in the open, one only had to be careful not to let the poor creature's body slip from one's hands, a tumble would leave it beyond repair, not to mention the pain which, after death, is worse.

The garden was like an unexplored jungle, the recent rains had caused the grass and the weeds carried on the wind to grow in abundance, there would be no lack of fresh food for the rabbits which jumped about, and chickens manage even in hard times. They were sitting on the ground, panting, the effort had exhausted them, by their side the corpse rested like them, guarded by the doctor's wife who chased off the hens and rabbits, the rabbits only curious, their noses twitching, the chickens with their beaks like bayonets, ready for anything. The doctor's wife said, Before leaving, she remembered to open the doors of the rabbit hutches, she did not want the rabbits to die of hunger, The difficult thing isn't living with other people, it's understanding them, said the doctor. The girl with dark glasses cleaned her dirty hands on a clump of grass that she had pulled up, it was her own fault, she had grasped the corpse where she should not have, that's what happens when you're blind. The doctor said, What we need is a spade or a shovel, here one can see that the true eternal return is that of words, which now return, spoken for the same reasons, first for the man who stole the car, now for the old woman who returned the keys, once buried nobody will know the difference, unless somebody remembers them. The doctor's wife had gone up to the flat of the girl with dark glasses in order to find a clean sheet, she had to choose the least dirty of them, when she came down the hens were at it, the rabbits were merely chewing the fresh grass. Having covered and wrapped the body, the wife went in search of a spade or shovel. She found both in a garden shed along with other tools. I'll deal with this, she said, the ground is damp, it is easy to dig, you take a rest. She chose a spot where there were no roots of the type that have to be cut with an axe, and don't imagine that this is an easy job, roots have their own little ways, they know how to take advantage of the softness of the soil in order to avoid the blow and weaken the deadly effect of the guillotine. Neither the doctor's wife nor her husband nor the girl with dark glasses, the former because she was digging, the latter two because their eyes were of no use to them, noticed the appearance of blind people on the surrounding balconies, not many, not on all of them, they must have been attracted by the noise of the digging, even in soft soil there is noise, not forgetting that there is always some hidden stone that responds loudly to the blow. There were men and women who appeared as fluid as ghosts, they could have been ghosts attending a burial out of curiosity, merely to recall how it had been when they were buried. The doctor's wife finally saw them when she had finished digging the grave, she straightened her aching back and raised her arm to her forehead to wipe away the sweat. Then, carried away by an irresistible impulse, without thinking, she called out to those blind people and to all the blind of this world, She will rise again, note that she did not say She will live again, the matter was not quite that important, although the dictionary is there to confirm, reassure or suggest that we are dealing with complete and absolute synonyms. The blind people took fright and went back inside their flats, they could not understand why such words had been said, besides they could not have been prepared for such a revelation, it was clear that they did not go to the square where the magic utterances were made, in respect of which all that was needed to complete the picture was the addition of the head of the praying mantis and the suicide of the scorpion. The doctor said, Why did you say she will rise again, to whom were you talking, To a few blind people who appeared on the balconies, I was startled and I must have frightened them, And why those words rather than any others, I don't know, they came into my head and I said them, The next we know you'll be preaching in the square we passed along the way, Yes, a sermon about the rabbit's tooth and the hen's beak, come and help me now, over here, that's right, take her by the feet, I'll raise her from this end, careful, don't slip into the grave, that's it, just so, lower her slowly, more, more, I made the grave a little deeper because of the hens, once they start scratching, you never know where they'll finish up, that's it. She used the shovel to fill the grave, stamped the earth firmly down, made the little mound that always remains of the earth that is returned to the earth, as if she had never done anything else in her life. Finally, she picked a branch from a rosebush growing in the corner of the yard and planted it at the head of the grave. Will she rise again, asked the girl with the dark glasses, Not her, no, replied the doctor's wife, those who are still alive have a greater need to rise again by themselves and they don't, We are already half dead, said the doctor, We are still half alive too, answered his wife. She put the shovel and the spade back in the shed, took a good look around the yard to check that everything was in order, What order, she asked herself and provided her own answer, The order that wants the dead where they should be among the dead, and the living among the living, while the hens and rabbits feed some and feed off others, I'd like to leave a small sign for my parents, said the girl with dark glasses, just to let them know that I am alive, I don't want to destroy your hopes, said the doctor, but first they would have to find the house and that is most unlikely. Just remember that we wouldn't have got there without someone to guide us, You're right, and I don't even know if they are still alive, but unless I leave them some sign, anything, I shall feel as if I had abandoned them. What's it to be then, asked the doctor's wife, Something they might recognise by touch, said the girl with the dark glasses, the sad thing is that I no longer have anything on me from the old days. The doctor's wife looked at her, she was sitting on the first step of the emergency stairs, with her hands limp on her knees, her lovely face anguished, her hair spread over her shoulders, I know what sign you can leave them, she said. She went rapidly up the stairs, back into the house and returned with a pair of scissors and a piece of string,

What are you thinking of, asked the girl with dark glasses, worried when she heard the snipping of the scissors cutting off her hair, If your parents were to return, they would find hanging from the door handle a lock of hair, who else could it possibly belong to but their daughter, asked the doctor's wife, You make me want to weep, said the girl with the dark glasses, and she had no sooner said it, than she lowered her head over the folded arms on her knees and gave in to her sorrows, her sadness, to the emotions aroused by the suggestion made by the doctor's wife, then she noticed, without knowing by what emotional route she had arrived there, that she was also crying for the old woman on the first floor, the eater of raw meat, the horrible witch, who with her dead hand had restored to her the keys to the flat. And then the doctor's wife said, What times we live in, we find the order of things inverted, a symbol that nearly always signified death has become a sign of life, There are hands capable of these and greater wonders, said the doctor, Necessity is a powerful weapon, my dear, said the woman, and now that's enough of philosophy and witchcraft, let's hold hands and get on with life. It was the girl with dark glasses herself who tied the lock of hair to the door handle, Do you think my parents will notice it, she asked, The door handle is like the outstretched hand of a house, said the doctor's wife, and with this commonplace expression, as one might say, they concluded the visit.

That night once again they had a reading, there was no other way of distracting themselves, what a pity, the doctor was not, for example, an amateur violinist, what sweet serenades might otherwise be heard on this fifth floor, their envious neighbours would say, Either they are doing very well or else they are completely irresponsible and think they can escape misery by laughing at the misery of others. Now there is no music other than that of words, and these, especially those in books, are discreet, and even if curiosity should bring someone from the building to listen at the door, they would hear only a solitary murmur, that long thread of sound that can last into infinity, because the books of this world, all together, are, as they say the universe is, infinite. When the reading ended, late that night, the old man with the eyepatch said, That's what we have come to, listening to someone reading, I'm not complaining, I could stay here for ever, said the girl with dark glasses, I am not complaining either, I only mean that this is all we are good for, listening to someone reading us the story of a human mankind that existed before us, let's be glad of our good fortune at still having a pair of seeing eyes with us here, the last pair left, if they are extinguished one day, I don't even want to think about it, then the thread which links us to that human mankind would be broken, it will be as if we were to separate from each other in space, for ever, all equally blind, As long as I can, the girl with dark glasses said, I'll keep on hoping, hoping to find my parents, hoping the boy's mother will turn up, You forgot to speak of the hope we all have, What's that, Regaining our sight, It's mad to cling to such hopes, Well, I can tell you, without such hopes I would already have given up, Give me an example, Being able to see again, We've already had that one, give me another, I won't, Why, You wouldn't be interested, And how do you know that I wouldn't, what do you think you know about me that you can by yourself decide what interests me and what doesn't, Don't get angry, I didn't mean to hurt you, Men are all the same, they think because they came out of the belly of a woman they know all there is to know about women, I know very little about women, and about you I know nothing, as for men, in my opinion, by modern criteria I am now an old man and one-eyed as well as being blind, Have you nothing else to say against yourself, A lot more, you can't imagine how the list of self-recriminations grows with advancing age, I am young and have my fair share already, You haven't done anything really bad yet, How do you know, if you've never lived with me, You're right, I have never lived with you, Why do you repeat my words in that tone of voice, What tone of voice, That one, All I said was that I have never lived with you, Come on, come on, don't pretend that you don't understand, Don't insist, I beg you, I do insist, I want to know, Let's return to hopes, All right, The other example of hope which I refused to give was this, What, The last self-accusation on my list, Please, explain yourself, I never understand riddles, The monstrous wish of never regaining our sight, Why, So that we can go on living as we are, Do you mean all together, or just you and me, Don't make me answer, If you were only a man you could avoid answering, like all others, but you yourself said that you are an old man, and old men, if longevity has any sense at all, should not avert their face from the truth, answer me, With you, And why do you want to live with me, Do you want me to tell in front of everybody, We have done the dirtiest, ugliest, most repulsive things together, what you can tell me cannot possibly be worse, All right, if you insist, let it be, because the man I still am loves the woman you are, Was it so very difficult to make a declaration of love, At my age, people fear ridicule, You were not ridiculous, Let's forget it, please, I have no intention of forgetting it or of letting you forget it either, It's nonsense, you forced it out of me and now, And now it's my turn, Don't say anything you may regret later, remember the black list, If I'm sincere today, what does it matter if I regret it tomorrow, Please stop, You want to live with me and I want to live with you, You are mad, We'll start living together here, like a couple, and we shall continue living together if we have to separate from our friends, two blind people must be able to see more than one, It's madness, you don't love me, What's this about loving, I never loved anyone, I just went to bed with men. So you agree with me then, Not really, You spoke of sincerity, tell me then if it's true that you really love me, I love you enough to want to be with you, and that is the first time I've ever said that to anyone, You would not have said it to me either if you had met me somewhere before, an elderly man, half bald with white hair, with a patch over one eye and a cataract in the other, The woman I was then wouldn't have said it, I agree, the person who said it was the woman I am today, Let's see then what the woman you will be tomorrow will have to say, Are you testing me, What an idea, who am I to put you to the test, it's life that decides these things, It's already made one decision.

They had this conversation facing each other, blind eyes staring into blind eyes, their faces flushed and impassioned and when, because one of them had said it and because both of them wanted it, they agreed that life had decided that they should live together, the girl with dark glasses held out her hands, simply to give them, not in order to know where she was going, she touched the hands of the old man with the eyepatch, who gently pulled her towards him, and so they remained sitting side by side, it was not the first time, obviously, but now the words of engagement had been spoken. None of the others said anything, nobody congratulated them, nobody expressed wishes of eternal happiness, to tell the truth these are not the times for festivities and hopes, and when the decisions are so serious as these seem to have been, it is not even surprising that someone might think that one would have to be blind to behave in this way, silence is the best applause. What the doctor's wife did, however, was to put some sofa cushions out in the hallway, enough to make a comfortable bed, then she led the boy with the squint there and told him, From today you will sleep here. As to what happened in the living-room, there is every reason to believe that on that first night it finally became clear whose was the mysterious hand that washed the back of the old man with the black eyepatch on that morning when there was such an abundance of water, all of it purifying.

The next day, while still in bed, the doctor's wife said to her husband, We have little food left, we'll have to go out again, I thought that today I would go back to the underground food store at the supermarket, the one I went to on the first day, if nobody else has found it, we can get supplies for a week or two, I'm coming with you and we'll ask one or two of the others to come along as well, I'd rather go with you alone, it's easier, and there is less danger of getting lost, How long will you be able to carry the burden of six helpless people, I'll manage as long as I can, but you are quite right, I'm beginning to get exhausted, sometimes I even wish I were blind as well, to be the same as the others, to have no more obligations than they have, We've got used to depending on you, If you weren't there, it would be like being struck with a second blindness, thanks to your eyes we are a little less blind, I'll carry on as long as I can, I can't promise you more than that, One day, when we realise that we can no longer do anything good and useful we ought to have the courage simply to leave this world, as he said, Who said that, The fortunate man we met yesterday, I am sure that he wouldn't say that today, there is nothing like real hope to change one's opinions, He has that all right, long may it last, In your voice there is a tone which makes me think you are upset, Upset, why, As if something had been taken away from you, Are you referring to what happened to the girl when we were at that terrible place, Yes, Remember, it was she who wanted to have sex with me, Memory is deceiving you, you wanted her, Are you sure, I was not blind, Well, I would have sworn that, You would only perjure yourself, Strange how memory can deceive us, In this case it is easy to see, something that is offered to us is more ours than something we had to conquer, But she didn't ever approach me again, and I never approached her, If you wanted to, you could find each other's memories, that's what memory is for, You are jealous, No, I'm not jealous, I was not even jealous on that occasion, I felt sorry for her and for you, and also for myself because I could not help you, How are we fixed for water, Badly. After the extremely frugal breakfast, lightened by some discrete, smiling hints at the events of the previous night, the words appropriately veiled out of consideration for the presence of a minor, an odd precaution if we remember the terrible scenes that he witnessed during the quarantine, the doctor's wife and her husband set off, accompanied this time only by the dog of tears, who did not want to stay at home.

The state of the streets got worse with every passing hour. The rubbish seemed to increase during the hours of darkness, it was as if from the outside, from some unknown country where there was still a normal life, they were coming in the night to empty their trash cans, if we were not in the land of the blind we would see through the middle of this white darkness phantom carts and trucks loaded with refuse, debris, rubble, chemical waste, ashes, burnt oil, bones, bottles, offal, flat batteries, plastic bags, mountains of paper, what they don't bring is leftover food, not even bits of fruit peel with which we might be able to allay our hunger, while waiting for those better days that are always just around the corner. It is still early in the morning but the heat is already oppressive. The stench rises from the enormous refuse pile like a cloud of toxic gas, It won't be long before we have outbreaks of epidemics, said the doctor again, nobody will escape, we have no defences left, If it's not raining, it's blowing gales, said the woman, Not even that, the rain would at least quench our thirst, and the wind would blow away some of this stench. The dog of tears sniffs around restlessly, stops to investigate a particular heap of rubbish, perhaps there was a rare delicacy hidden underneath which it can no longer find, if it were alone it would not move an inch from this spot, but the woman who wept has already walked on, and it is his duty to follow her, one never knows when one might have to dry more tears. Walking is difficult, in some streets, especially the steep ones, the heavy rainwater, transformed into torrents, had thrown cars against other cars or against buildings, knocking down doors, smashing shop windows, the ground is covered with thick pieces of broken glass. Wedged in between two cars the body of a man is rotting away. The doctor's wife averts her eyes. The dog of tears moves closer, but death frightens it, it still takes two steps forward, suddenly its fur stands on end, a piercing howl escapes from its throat, the trouble with this dog is that it has grown too close to human beings, it will suffer as they do. They crossed a square where groups of blind people entertained themselves by listening to speeches from other blind people, at first sight neither group seemed to be blind, the speakers turned their heads excitedly towards the listeners and the listeners turned their heads attentively to the speakers. They were extolling the virtues of the fundamental principles of the great organised systems, private property, a free currency market, the market economy, the stock exchange, taxation, interest, expropriation and appropriation, production, distribution, consumption, supply and demand, poverty and wealth, communication, repression and delinquency, lotteries, prisons, the penal code, the civil code, the highway code, dictionaries, the telephone directory, networks of prostitution, armaments factories, the armed forces, cemeteries, the police, smuggling, drugs, permitted illegal traffic, pharmaceutical research, gambling, the price of priests and funerals, justice, borrowing, political parties, elections, parliaments, governments, convex, concave, horizontal, vertical, slanted, concentrated, diffuse, fleeting thoughts, the fraying of the vocal cords, the death of the word. Here they are talking about organisation, said the doctor's wife to her husband, I noticed, he answered, and said no more. They continued walking, the doctor's wife went to consult a street plan on a street corner, like an old roadside cross pointing the way. We are very close to the supermarket, around here she had broken down and wept the day that she had got lost, grotesquely weighed down by the plastic bags which luckily were full to the brim, in her confusion and anguish she had to depend on a dog to console her, the same dog who is here snarling at the packs of other dogs who are coming too close, as if it were telling them, You don't fool me, keep away from here. A street to the left, another to the right and there is the entrance to the supermarket. Only the door, that's it, there is the door, there is the whole building, but what cannot be seen are people going in and coming out, that ant-heap of people which we find at all hours in these shops that live on the comings and goings of vast crowds. The doctor's wife feared the worst and said to her husband, We have arrived too late, there won't be a crumb left in there, Why do you say that, I don't see anybody going in or coming out, Perhaps they have not yet discovered the basement storeroom, That's what I am hoping for. They were standing on the pavement opposite the supermarket when they spoke these words. Beside them, as if they were waiting for the traffic lights to turn green, there were three blind people. The doctor's wife did not notice the expression on their faces, which was of puzzled surprise, a kind of confused fear, she did not see that one of them opened his mouth to speak and then closed it again, she did not notice the sudden shrug of shoulders, You'll find out, we assume the blind man was thinking. As they were crossing the middle of the road, the doctor's wife and her husband were unable to hear the comment of the second blind person, Why did she say that she did not see, that she did not see anybody going in or coming out, and the third blind person answered, It's just a manner of speaking, a moment ago, when I stumbled you told me to watch where I was putting my feet, it's the same thing, we still haven't lost the habit of seeing, Oh God, how many times have I heard that before, exclaimed the first blind man.

The daylight illuminated the whole of the wide hall of the supermarket. Almost all the shelves were overturned, there was nothing but refuse, broken glass, empty wrappers, It is strange, said the doctor's wife, even if there is no food here, I don't understand why there is nobody around. The doctor said, You are right, it does not seem normal. The dog of tears whimpered softly. Its hair was standing on end again. The doctor's wife said to her husband, There is a bad smell in here, There's a bad smell everywhere, said the husband, It's not that, it's another smell, of rotting, There must be a dead body somewhere, I don't see anything, In which case you must be imagining it. The dog began to whine. What's the matter with the dog, asked the doctor, He's nervous, What are we going to do, Let's see, if there is a corpse we just give it a wide berth, at this stage the dead no longer frighten us, For me it's easier, I can't see them. They crossed the hall of the supermarket until they reached the door which opened on to the corridor leading to the basement store. The dog of tears followed them, but it stopped from time to time, howled to them, then duty obliged it to continue. When the doctor's wife opened the door, the stench grew stronger, It smells terrible, said her husband, You stay here, I'll be right back. She went down the corridor, it became darker with every step and the dog of tears followed her as if it were being dragged along. Filled with the stench of putrefaction, the air seemed thick. Halfway down, the woman vomited, What can have happened here, she thought between retchings and then she murmured these same words over and over again until she got to the metal door which went down into the basement. Confused by her nausea, she had not noticed before that there was a tenuous shimmer of light down there. Now she knew what it was. Small flames flickered around the edges of the two doors, that of the staircase and that of the goods lift. A new attack of vomiting gripped her stomach, it was so violent that it attracted the attention of the dog. The dog of tears gave a very long howl, it let out a wail that seemed never-ending, a lament which resounded through the corridor like the last voice of the dead down in the basement. The doctor heard the vomiting, the convulsions, the coughing, he ran as well as he could, he stumbled and fell, he got up and fell again, at last he held his wife in his arms, What happened, he asked, with a trembling voice she replied, Get me out of here, please, get me out of here, for the first time since the onset of blindness, it was the doctor who guided his wife, he guided her without knowing where, anywhere away from those doors, those flames that he could not see. When they had got out of the corridor, her nerves suddenly went to pieces, her sobbing became convulsive, there is no drying tears like these, only time and exhaustion can stop them, therefore the dog did not approach, it just looked for a hand to lick. What happened, the doctor asked again, what did you see, They are dead, she managed to say between sobs, Who is dead, They are, and she could not go on. Calm yourself, tell me when you can. A few minutes later she said, They are dead, Did you see anything, did you open the door, asked her husband, No, I only saw will-o'-the-wisps around the doors, they clung there and danced around and did not let go, I think it must have been phosphorised hydrogen as a result of the decomposition of the bodies, What could have happened, They must have found the basement, rushed down the stairs looking for food, I remember how easy it was to slip and fall on those steps, and if one fell, they would all fall, they probably never reached where they wanted to go, or if they did they could not return because of the obstruction on the staircase, But you said that the door was closed, Most likely other blind people closed it, converting the basement into an enormous tomb and I am to blame for what happened, when I came running out of there with my bags, they must have suspected that it was food and went in search of it, In a way, everything we eat has been stolen from the mouths of others and if we rob them of too much we are responsible for their death, one way or another we are all murderers, A small consolation, I don't want you to start burdening yourself with imaginary guilt, when you already have a hard enough time shouldering the responsibility for six real and useless mouths, How could I live without your useless mouth, You would live in order to support the other five who are there, The question is, for how long. It won't be for much longer, when everything is finished we shall have to roam the fields in search of food, we'll pick all the fruit from the trees, we'll kill all the animals we can lay our hands on, if in the meantime dogs and cats do not start devouring us. The dog of tears did not react, this matter did not concern it, its recent transformation into a dog of tears had not been in vain.

The doctor's wife could hardly drag herself along. The shock had robbed her of all her strength. When they left the super-market, she fainting, he blind, neither would be able to say who was assisting the other. Perhaps the intensity of the light had made her dizzy, she thought that she was losing her eyesight, but she was not afraid, it was only a fainting fit. She did not fall, nor even lose consciousness. She needed to lie down, close her eyes, breathe steadily, if she could just rest for a few minutes she was sure that she would regain her strength, she had to, her plastic bags were still empty. She did not want to lie down on the filth in the street, or return to the supermarket, not even dead. She looked around. On the other side of the street, a bit further on, was a church. There would be people inside, as everywhere, but it would be a good place to rest, at least it al-ways had been. She said to her husband, I need to recover my strength, take me over there, There, where, I'm sorry, bear with me, and I'll tell you, What is it, A church, if I could only lie down for a while, I'd feel like new, Let's go. Six steps led up to the church, six steps, which the doctor's wife climbed with great difficulty, especially since she also had to guide her husband. The doors were wide open, which was a great help, a revolving door, even of the simplest type, would on this occasion have been a difficult obstacle to overcome. The dog of tears hesitated on the threshold. Despite the freedom of movement enjoyed by dogs in recent months, all of them had genetically programmed into their brains the prohibition which once, long ago, fell on the species, that on entering churches, probably because of that other genetic code which obliges them to mark their territory wherever they go. The good and faithful services rendered by the forebears of this dog of tears, when they licked the festering sores of saints before they were recognised and approved as such, nevertheless acts of compassion of the most selfless kind, because, as we well know, not just any beggar can become a saint, no matter how many wounds he may have on his body, and in his soul too where the tongues of dogs cannot reach. The dog now had the courage to enter the sacred space, the door was open, there was no doorkeeper, and the strongest reason of all, the woman who had wept had already gone in, I do not know how she manages to drag herself along, she murmurs but a single word to her husband, Hold me, the church is full, it is almost impossible to find even a foot of floor unoccupied, one might literally say that there is no stone upon which to rest one's head, again the dog of tears proved its usefulness, with two growls and a couple of charges, all without malice, it opened up a space where the doctor's wife let herself fall, giving in to the faint, at last fully closing her eyes. Her husband took her pulse, it is firm and regular, only a little faint, then he tried to lift her up, she's not in a good position, it is important to get the blood back into the brain quickly, to increase the cerebral irrigation, the best thing would be to sit her up, put her head between her knees and trust to nature and the force of gravity. At last, after some failed attempts, he managed to lift her up. A few minutes later, the doctor's wife gave a deep sigh, moved almost imperceptibly, and started to regain consciousness. Don't get up just yet, her husband told her, keep your head down for a while longer, but she felt fine, there was no sign of vertigo, her eyes could already distinguish the tiles on the floor which the dog of tears had left reasonably clean thanks to his energetic scrabbling before lying down himself. She raised her head to the slender pillars, to the high vaults, to confirm the security and stability of her blood circulation, then she said, I am feeling fine, but at that very moment she thought she had gone mad or that the lifting of the vertigo had given her hallucinations, it could not be true what her eyes revealed, that man nailed to the cross with a white bandage covering his eyes, and next to him a woman, her heart pierced by seven swords and her eyes also covered with a white bandage, and it was not only that man and that woman who were in that condition, all the images in the church had their eyes covered, statues with a white cloth tied around the head, paintings with a thick brushstroke of white paint, and there was a woman teaching her daughter how to read and both had their eyes covered, and a man with an open book on which a little child was sitting, and both had their eyes covered, and another man, his body spiked with arrows, and he had his eyes covered, and a woman with a lit lamp, and she had her eyes covered, and a man with wounds on his hands and feet and his chest, and he had his eyes covered, and another man with a lion, and both had their eyes covered, and another man with a lamb, and both had their eyes covered, and another man with an eagle, and both had their eyes covered, and another man with a spear standing over a fallen man with horns and cloven feet, and both had their eyes covered, and another man carrying a set of scales, and he had his eyes covered, and an old bald man holding a white lily, and he had his eyes covered, and another old man leaning on an unsheathed sword, and he had his eyes covered, and a woman with a dove, and both had their eyes covered, and a man with two ravens, and all three had their eyes covered, there was only one woman who did not have her eyes covered, because she carried her gouged-out eyes on a silver tray. The doctor's wife said to her husband, You won't believe me if I tell you what I have in front of my eyes, all the images in this church have their eyes covered, How strange, I wonder why, How should I know, perhaps it was the work of someone whose faith was badly shaken when he realised that he would be blind like the others, maybe it was even the local priest, perhaps he thought that when the blind people could no longer see the images, the images should not be able to see the blind either, Images don't see, You're wrong, images see with the eyes of those who see them, only that now blindness is the lot of everyone, You can still see, I'll see less and less all the time, even though I may not lose my eyesight I shall become more and more blind because I shall have no one to see me, If the priest covered the eyes of the images, That's just my idea, It's the only hypothesis that makes any sense, it's the only one that can lend some dignity to our suffering, I imagine that man coming in here from the world of the blind, where he would have to return only to go blind himself, I imagine the closed doors, the deserted church, the silence, I imagine the statues, the paintings, I see him going from one to the other, climbing up to the altars and tying the bandages with a double knot so that they do not come undone and slip off, applying two coats of paint to the pictures in order to make the white night into which they are plunged still thicker, that priest must have committed the worst sacrilege of all times and all religions, the fairest and most radically human, coming here to declare that, ultimately, God does not deserve to see. The doctor's wife did not have a chance to reply, somebody beside her spoke first, What sort of talk is that, who are you, Blind like you, she said, But I heard you say that you could see, That's just a manner of speaking which is hard to give up, how many more times will I say it, And what's this about the images having their eyes covered, It's true, And how do you know when you are blind, You would know too if you did what I did, go and touch them with your hands, the hands are the eyes of the blind, And why did you do it, I thought that in order to have got to where we are someone else must have been blind, And that story about the parish priest covering the eyes of the images, I knew him very well, he would be incapable of doing such a thing, You never know beforehand what people are capable of, you have to wait, give it time, it's time that rules, time is our gambling partner on the other side of the table and it holds all the cards of the deck in its hand, we have to guess the winning cards of life, our lives, Speaking of gambling in a church is a sin, Get up, use your hands if you doubt my words, Do you swear it is true that the images have their eyes covered, What do you want me to swear on, Swear on your eyes, I swear twice on the eyes, on yours and mine. Is it true, It's true. The conversation was overheard by the blind people in their immediate vicinity, and it goes without saying that there was no need to wait for the confirmation by oath before the news started to circulate, to pass from mouth to mouth, in a murmur which shortly changed its tone, first incredulous, then alarmed, again incredulous, it was unfortunate that there were several superstitious and imaginative people in the congregation, the idea that the sacred images were blind, that their compassionate or pitying eyes only stared out at their own blindness, became all of a sudden unbearable, it was tantamount to having told them that they were surrounded by the living dead, one scream was enough, then another and another, then fear made all the people rise up, panic drove them to the doors, here the inevitable repeated itself, since panic is much faster than the legs which carry it, the feet of the fugitive trip up in their flight, even more so when one is blind, and there he lies on the ground, panic tells him, Get up, run, they are going to kill you, if only he could get up, but others have already run and fallen too, you have to be strong-minded not to burst out laughing at this grotesque entanglement of bodies looking for arms to free themselves and for feet to get away. Those six steps outside will be like a precipice, but finally, the fall will not be very serious, the habit of falling hardens the body, reaching the ground is, in itself, a relief, I'm staying where I am is the first thought, and sometimes the last, in fatal cases. What does not change either is that some take advantage of the misfortune of others, as is well known, since the beginning of the world, the heirs and the heirs of the heirs. The desperate flight of these people made them leave their belongings behind, and when necessity conquers fear, they come back for them, then the difficult problem will be to settle in a satisfactory manner what is mine and what is yours, we shall see that some of the little food we had has vanished, probably this was a cynical ruse on the part of the woman who said that the images had their eyes covered, the depths some people will stoop to, they invent such tall tales merely to rob poor people of the few crumbs remaining to them. Now, the fault was the dog's, seeing the square empty it went foraging around, it rewarded itself for its efforts, as was only fair and natural, and it showed, in a manner of speaking, the entrance to the mine which meant that the doctor's wife and her husband left the church without remorse over the theft, with their bags half full. If they can use half of what they grabbed they can be content, regarding the other half they will say, I don't know how people can eat this, even when misfortune is common to all, there are always some who have a worse time than others.

The report of these events, each one of its kind, left the other members of the group aghast and confused, it has to be noted that the doctor's wife, perhaps because words failed her, did not even manage to convey to them the feelings of utter horror she experienced at the basement door, that rectangle of pale flickering lights at the top of the staircase which led to the other world. The description of the bandaged eyes of the images left a strong enough impression on their imaginations, though in quite different ways, the first blind man and his wife, for example, were rather uneasy, for them it was mainly an unpardonable lack of respect. The fact that all human beings were blind was a calamity for which they were not responsible, these are misfortunes nobody can avoid, and for that reason alone covering the eyes of the holy images struck them as an unpardonable offence, and if the parish priest had done it, even worse. The reaction of the old man with the black eyepatch was quite different, I can imagine the shock you must have had, I imagine a museum in which all the sculptures have their eyes covered, not because the sculptor did not want to carve the stone until he reached the eyes, but covered, as you say, with bandages, as if a single blindness were not enough, it's strange that a patch like mine does not create the same effect, sometimes it even gives people a romantic air, and he laughed at what he had said and at himself. As to the girl with the dark glasses, she said that she only hoped she would not have to see this cursed gallery in her dreams, she had enough nightmares already. They ate the rancid food at their disposal, it was the best they had, the doctor's wife said that it was becoming ever more difficult to find food, perhaps they should leave the city and go to live in the country, there at least the food they gathered would be healthier, And there must be goats and cows on the loose, we can milk them, we'll have milk, and there is water from the wells, we can cook what we want, the question is to find a good site, then everybody gave his opinion, some more enthusiastic than others, but for all of them it was obvious that the decision was pressing and urgent, the boy with the squint expressed his approval without any reservations, possibly because he retained pleasant memories from his holidays. After they had eaten, they stretched out to sleep, they always did, even during the quarantine, when experience taught them that a body in repose can put up with a lot of hunger. That evening they did not eat, only the boy with the squint got something to assuage his complaints and to allay his hunger, the others sat down to hear the reading, at least their minds would not be able to complain of lack of nourishment, the trouble is that the weakness of the body sometimes leads to a lack of attention of the mind, and it was not for lack of intellectual interest, no, what happened was that the brain slipped into a half sleep, like an animal settling down for hibernation, goodbye world, therefore it was not uncommon that the listeners gently lowered their eyelids, forced themselves to follow with the eyes of the soul the vicissitudes of the plot until a more energetic passage shook them from their torpor, it was not simply the noise of the book snapping shut, the doctor's wife had these subtle touches, she did not want to let on that she knew that the dreamer was drifting off to sleep.

The first blind man appeared to have entered into this soft state, but this was not the case. True, his eyes were closed, and he paid only scant attention to the reading, but the idea that they would all go to live in the country kept him from falling asleep, it seemed to him a serious error to go so far from his home, however kind the writer was, it would be useful to keep an eye on it, turn up from time to time. The first blind man was therefore wide awake, if any other proof were needed it would be the dazzling whiteness before his eyes, which probably only sleep would darken, but one could not even be sure of that, since nobody can be asleep and awake at the same time. The first blind man thought that he had finally cleared up this doubt when suddenly the inside of his eyelids turned dark, I've fallen asleep, he thought, but no, he had not fallen asleep, he continued hearing the voice of the doctor's wife, the boy with the squint coughed, then a great fear entered his soul, he thought he had passed from one blindness to another, that having lived in the blindness of light, he would now pass into a blindness of darkness, the fear made him tremble, What's the matter, his wife asked, and he replied stupidly, without opening his eyes, I am blind, as if that were news, she tenderly held him in her arms, Don't worry, we're all blind, there's nothing we can do about it, I saw everything dark, I thought I had gone to sleep, but I hadn't, I am awake, That's what you should do, sleep, don't think about it. He was annoyed by this advice, here was a man in great distress, and his wife could say nothing other than that he should sleep. He was irritated and, about to utter a harsh reply, he opened his eyes and saw. He saw and shouted, I can see. His first shout was still one of incredulity, but with the second and the third and many more the evidence grew stronger, I can see, I can see, he madly embraced his wife, then he ran to the doctor's wife and embraced her too, it was the first time he had seen her, but he knew who she was, and the doctor, and the girl with dark glasses and the old man with the black eyepatch, there was no mistaking him, and the boy with the squint, his wife came behind him, she did not want to let him go, and he interrupted his embraces to embrace her again, then he turned to the doctor, I can see, I can see, doctor, he addressed him by his title, something they had not done for a long time, and the doctor asked, Can you see clearly, as before, are there no traces of whiteness, Nothing at all, I even think that I can see better than before, and that's no small thing, I've never worn glasses. Then the doctor said what all of them were thinking without daring to say it, It is possible that we have come to the end of this blindness, it is possible that we will all recover our eyesight, hearing those words, the doctor's wife began to cry, she should have been happy yet she was crying, what strange reactions people have, of course she was happy, my God, it is easy to understand, she cried because all her mental resistance had suddenly drained away, she was like a new-born baby and this cry was her first and still-unconscious sound. The dog of tears went up to her, it always knows when it is needed, that's why the doctor's wife clung to him, it is not that she no longer loved her husband, it is not that she did not wish them all well, but at that moment her feeling of loneliness was so intense, so unbearable, that it seemed to her that it could be overcome only by the strange thirst with which the dog drank her tears.

The general joy turned into nervousness, And now, what are we going to do, asked the girl with dark glasses, after all that has happened I won't be able to sleep, Nobody will, I believe we should stay here, said the old man with the black eyepatch, he broke off as if he still had some doubts, then he concluded, Waiting. They waited. The three flames of the lamp lit up the circle of faces. At first, they had talked animatedly, they wanted to know exactly what had happened, if the change had taken place only in the eyes or whether he had also felt something in his brain, then, little by little, their words grew despondent, at a certain moment it occurred to the first blind man to say to his wife that they would be going home the next day, But I am still blind, she replied, It doesn't matter, I'll guide you, only those present who heard it with their own ears could grasp how such simple words could contain such different feelings as protection, pride and authority. The second person to regain his eyesight, already late into the night, when the lamp, running out of oil, was flickering, was the girl with dark glasses. She had kept her eyes open as if sight had to enter through them rather than be rekindled from within, suddenly she said, I think I can see, it was best to be prudent, not all cases are the same, it even used to be said there is no such thing as blindness, only blind people, when the experience of time has taught us nothing other than that there are no blind people, but only blindness. Here we already

have three who can see, one more and they would form a majority, but even though in the happiness of seeing again we
might ignore the others, their lives will be very much easier, not
the agony it was until today, look at the state of that woman,
she is like a rope that has broken, like a spring that could no
longer support the pressure it was constantly subjected to. Perhaps it was for this reason that the girl with dark glasses embraced her first, and the dog of tears did not know whose tears
it should attend to first, both of them wept so much. Her second embrace was for the old man with the black eyepatch, now
we shall know what words are really worth, the other day we
were so moved by the dialogue which led to the splendid commitment by these two to live together, but the situation has
changed, the girl with dark glasses has before her an old man
whom she can now see in the flesh, the emotional idealisations,
the false harmonies on the desert island are over, wrinkles are
wrinkles, baldness is baldness, there is no difference between a
black eyepatch and a blind eye, that is what, in other words, he is
going to say to her. Look at me, I am the man you said you were
going to live with, and she replied, I know you, you're the man I
am living with, in the end these are words that are worth even
more than those that wanted to surface, and this embrace as
much as the words. The third one to regain his sight the next day
at dawn was the doctor, now there could no longer be any
doubt, it was only a question of time before the others would recover theirs. Leaving aside the natural and foreseeable expansive
comments of which there has already been sufficient mention
above, there is now no need for repetition, even concerning the
chief characters of this narrative, the doctor asked the question
which hung in the air, What is happening out there, the reply
came from the very building in which they lived, on the floor
below someone came out on the landing shouting, I can see, I
can see, it looks like the sun will rise over a city in celebration.

   The next morning's meal turned into a banquet. What was
on the table, besides being very little, would repel any normal
appetite, as happens at all moments of elation, the strength of
feelings took the place of hunger and their happiness was the

best nourishment, nobody complained, even those who were still blind laughed as if the eyes which could already see were theirs. When they had finished, the girl with dark glasses had an idea, What if I now went to the door of my own flat with a piece of paper saying that I'm here, my parents would know where to find me if they return, Let me come with you, I want to know what is happening out there, said the old man with the black eyepatch, And we will go out too, said he who had been the first blind man to his wife, Perhaps the writer can already see and is thinking about returning to his own place, on the way I shall try to find something to eat. I'll do the same, said the girl with dark glasses. Minutes later, alone now, the doctor sat down beside his wife, the boy with the squint was dozing in a corner of the sofa, the dog of tears, stretched out with his muzzle on its forepaws, opened and closed its eyes from time to time to show that it was still watchful, through the open window, despite the fact that they were so high up, the noise of excited voices could be heard, the streets must be full of people, the crowd shouting just three words, I can see, said those who had already recovered their eyesight and those who were just starting to see, I can see, I can see, the story in which people said, I am blind, truly appears to belong to another world. The boy with the squint murmured, he must be in the middle of a dream, perhaps he saw his mother and was asking her, Can you see me, can you see me, The doctor's wife asked, And the others, and the doctor answered, He will probably be cured by the time he wakes, it will be the same with the others, most likely they are already regaining their sight at this very moment, our man with the black eyepatch is in for a shock, Why, Because of the cataract, after all the time since I last examined him it must have deteriorated, Is he going to stay blind, No, when life gets back to normal, and everything is working again, I shall operate, it is a matter of weeks, Why did we become blind, I don't know, perhaps one day we'll find out, Do you want me to tell you what I think, Yes, do, I don't think we did go blind, I think we are blind, Blind but seeing, Blind people who can see, but do not see.

The doctor's wife got up and went to the window. She looked down at the street full of refuse, at the shouting, singing people. Then she lifted her head up to the sky and saw everything white, It is my turn, she thought. Fear made her quickly lower her eyes. The city was still there.

PUBLISHERS' NOTE

The translator died before completing his revision
of this translation. The Publishers acknowledge the
help of Margaret Jull Costa in fulfilling this task.